PR
LEE TO

"Lee Tobin McClain dazzles with unforgettable characters, fabulous small-town settings and a big dose of heart."

—Susan Mallery, New York Times bestselling author

"Lee Tobin McClain's books make my heart sing."

—Debbie Macomber, New York Times bestselling author

"[A] magnetic second chance romance... McClain pits her charming, authentic characters against the realistic problems of everyday life, making for a story that is deeply emotional but never soapy...Readers won't want to put this down."

—Publishers Weekly, STARRED REVIEW of *The Forever Farmhouse*

SECOND CHANCE SPRINGTIME

A SMALL-TOWN CHRISTIAN ROMANCE

HOME TO ORCHARD SPRINGS
BOOK 2

LEE TOBIN MCCLAIN

1

It was a Monday morning in early March, and Courtney Chase had *way* too much to do before her four home daycare kiddos arrived.

Over the weekend, she had moved into the apartment above what would soon be Abbott Farm's produce stand. There were still tons of boxes to unpack. She'd stayed up late last night to clear space in her front room, making it safe for the little ones.

The farm would be wonderful for the kids she cared for, but she had to show their mothers that the place was as suitable as her big suburban home had been. She needed their enthusiastic word-of-mouth advertising to help her gain more clients.

An hour and a half until the kids arrived. She brushed back her out-of-control hair and looked ruefully at her ripped jeans and ancient, hot pink t-shirt. The first order of business, after letting the dog out, was a shower and more presentable clothes. Then she'd work on unpacking.

She hurried downstairs with Bubbles, her goldendoodle, running behind her. Once outside, Bubbles bounded ahead, pausing to sniff at all the new-to-her farm scents. Normally shy and skittish, she seemed thrilled with their new home and the opportunity to run off leash.

Then, to Courtney's dismay, a late-model SUV appeared, bumping along the rutted road that led to her home. Bubbles ran back toward the entryway, barking.

Why were her clients here already? She checked the time on her phone. No, they weren't due for more than an hour. There was no message asking if they could come early.

So much for her plans to make herself and her home presentable.

Still, as four kids and two moms spilled out from the vehicle, Courtney couldn't help smiling. She loved the little ones she cared for. Loved kids in general and had always wanted to have a big family of her own. Maybe someday...

She knelt and held out her arms, and the kids crashed into her, knocking her over. "This place is *cool*!" said five-year-old Gavin, the leader of the little group.

"It *is* cool!" Courtney smiled and greeted each child, then stood to face the mothers, now picking their way across the muddy path in ridiculously inappropriate footwear. Lexie and Sheila were lifelong Pennsylvania residents. Even though their own homes had neat walkways leading from car to house to road, they should know that March here was rainy, and farms got muddy.

"You're early, ladies, and I'm still getting set up. But isn't this fabulous?" She gestured around at the fields, the barn, the covered bridge in the distance. "We're going to have so much fun today!"

Lexie Silverton looked around with a slight curl of the lip. "If you like this kind of thing," she said. Then she grimaced down at her white designer sneakers, now marred with dirt. “I’m going to need to go home and change my shoes before we head out shopping,” she told her sister Sheila.

“Me too,” Sheila said. She wore heeled boots that kept sinking into the wet ground. “Sorry we’re early, Courtney. We wanted to get a head start on our shopping, because we’re going a bunch of places. We should have let you know.”

Courtney smiled at Sheila. “It’s fine, if you don’t mind that half the toys are still boxed up. And that I look like a mess.”

“You look fine,” Sheila said. “I have to admit, though, I liked your old place better. I mean, I understand why you moved, but my goodness, your ex is a doctor. I’d have thought you’d find yourself a little house of your own, at least.”

“It’s complicated,” Courtney said. She’d known Lexie and Sheila since they’d all played at the country club swimming pool, but they hadn’t been close friends even back then. She hadn’t confided the details of her marriage, divorce, and money woes to them. How she’d used her family money to help her ex pay off medical school, how he’d talked her into pooling their resources to buy their house...how he'd cleaned out their accounts before announcing he wanted a divorce.

Once the sale of their home went through, she'd have a small nest egg. Until then, she was getting a crash course in making ends meet.

The kids ran around, throwing a ball for Bubbles and exploring the grassy area beside the driveway. Gavin discovered the perfect-for-climbing apple tree and hoisted himself up.

"Careful, honey." Courtney walked closer to the child. "No higher."

"This isn't going to work," Lexie said behind her.

Courtney helped Gavin jump down and then turned back to see Lexie and Sheila exchanging meaningful glances. "What's not going to work?" she asked them.

"Driving all the way out here, and the mud..." Lexie trailed off, frowning.

All the way out here? They were ten minutes outside of Orchard Springs, though admittedly, it felt like a different world. Which was what she'd wanted.

"And your house is, well, it's a shed!" Sheila's brow wrinkled as she looked at Courtney's new home. "Is it safe for the kids?"

Courtney's stomach churned, but she tried to stay upbeat. She'd figured she might have to sell her clients on the new location. "It *was* a shed," she corrected. "Pop Abbott is having it renovated. It's going to get better and better. And yes, it's safe. I made sure of that first thing."

"But is it going to work for the kids?" Sheila asked. "What happens on rainy days?"

"Plenty of indoor space," she said, gesturing to the empty first floor area. "And I have permission to use the barn for play, too."

Lexie was shaking her head. "I feel for you. This is such a comedown from your old home. But it's not at all what I have in mind for my Gavin."

Sweat trickled down Courtney's back. She needed this job, these customers. She knew that part of her appeal as a home daycare provider had been her big home in the same neighborhood as Sheila and Lexie, but she'd thought that her degree in child development and her love of kids were more important. "There are so many opportunities for enrichment," she said, trying not to sound as desperate as she felt. "We're going to plant a garden. And there's lots of room to explore."

"I'm sorry, but I can't have my three come home filthy every day," Sheila said, her nose wrinkling. "It's too much to deal with, especially with Brett being so picky about the house."

"Come on, kids," Lexie said. "You won't be here today, after all."

"I wanna stay!" Gavin bellowed.

Not surprisingly, the other three followed his lead, whining and crying that they wanted to stay with Miss Courtney. Little Sierra even threw herself down on the ground for a tantrum. Right in a muddy spot, of course.

Lexie grabbed towels from the back of the SUV and started wiping Gavin's feet, ignoring his fuss. "You'll have to stay with Grandma," she told the kids. "We'll stop at Toy-Mart on the way home. Each of you may have one new toy if you don't make a fuss."

They quieted instantly, of course. They were kids.

"Over here," Sheila said to her three. "Everybody wipe off on a towel before you get in."

Courtney felt like crying herself as she watched the kids climb into the SUV. Their moms could be difficult, but she adored the little ones. She turned away to conceal her emotion.

And froze.

Who was that walking down the dirt road toward them, slim and tanned as a male model?

Was she seeing things? It couldn't be...

Lexie opened the driver's-side window. "Is that David, the golf caddy? You're back together with him?"

"No, no, I'm not with him," Courtney said distractedly. "I haven't even seen him in years." That was so Lexie, to define a person by the part-time job they'd held in high school.

For Lexie, high school had been the pinnacle. She'd been a cheerleader and on the homecoming court. The status levels of high school could never change in her mind, not when any alteration might displace her from the top of the heap.

High school had been fine for Courtney, but it hadn't been the best time of her life. And that was doubly true for David, from what she'd heard. He'd gone far, far beyond his foster-kid golf-caddy days.

She couldn't take her eyes off him. He was even better looking than he'd been at eighteen.

"I never did trust that guy," Lexie said. "Now I'm sure we made the right decision." She started the vehicle.

David continued walking toward them, looking mildly curious.

And then it dawned on Courtney, why he didn't seem to recognize her. *He* looked the same as he'd looked when they'd known each other before, only better.

She, though, had gained weight after her miscarriage. A fair amount of it. That was one of the reasons her husband had cited for leaving her, the jerk.

She was learning to accept her changed body, but to have David not even recognize her... ouch.

The SUV left in a spray of gravel, not

slowing down as it passed David a little too closely.

Courtney couldn't move, not even to comfort Bubbles, now cowering behind her, barking.

She had thought the day couldn't get any worse, but she'd been wrong.

2

As the SUV drove off, spitting gravel, David approached the woman who was staring at him in an odd, intense way.

He forced aside his tight, visceral attraction. It was ridiculous. He'd moved back to Pop's place to start a farm stand and make a success of it while he figured out where to go next in his overturned life. Not to go wild over a random woman standing in front of a shed.

He looked more closely. No, not random. She looked a little familiar...

"David." The woman walked toward him

slowly, hips swaying in faded jeans, a slight blush on her face.

That voice. That husky, sultry voice.

And then, with a shock, he recognized her. "Courtney?"

Could it be her, the woman who'd never left his heart, despite all his efforts to forget her? Her face was fuller, her hair longer, and that body… He swallowed hard. She'd been pretty before, but now, she was as lush and curvy as the strategically draped woman in a painting he and his buddies had giggled over on an art museum field trip.

They stood staring at each other. Behind Courtney, a fluffy dog cowered. The March breeze bent the branches of the apple tree behind her.

Courtney recovered first. "What are you doing here?"

Her faintly accusatory tone brought him out of his stunned silence. "I'm here to meet with the person living in the old shed," he said, nodding at the refurbished structure behind her. "To talk about the farm stand."

"I was to meet the person planning the farm stand startup sometime in the next couple of days. But that's not you." She tilted her head to one side. "Is it?"

He drew in a breath and let it out slowly, nodding. "It is. And… you're not telling me that you're the person living here, are you?" That would make no sense. Courtney's family was one of the wealthiest in town.

"Yes, I am. So…" She trailed off, then spoke again. "Who did you talk to about this meeting?"

"Jenn. My foster sister."

"Me, too."

David glanced back toward Pop's farmhouse and shook his head. This situation had the feel of a very misguided setup. His foster sister Jenn, now living with her new husband right next door to Pop, had fallen in love, and she wanted everyone to be as happy as she was.

Plus, she kept saying that she was worried about David.

They all worried about each other, all four foster kids who'd lived with Ma and Pop Abbott during their teen years. The Flock, they called themselves. They'd all grown up and moved on, but they'd stayed close. Jenn had relocated back here in the winter, when

Pop had been having some problems. Now David had joined her to help with the farm stand that was part of their rehabilitation of Abbott Farm.

The dog who'd been hiding behind Courtney peeked out and barked once. David took a step closer and the dog leaped backward.

"Your dog doesn't like strangers," he guessed.

"She doesn't like men."

"What's her name?"

"Her name is Bubbles, and no, I didn't name her that. The frat boys who were her former owners did. They thought it was funny."

David patted the side of his leg, but the dog refused to come closer. Better not to focus on her, then.

How was he supposed to make small talk with *Courtney*? "So, I heard you did get married," he blurted out.

"I'm not married anymore," she said flatly. "He left."

"Idiot." He spoke automatically, and then felt his face heat. No need to reveal to her that he still found her attractive, that he couldn't understand how any man could let her go. He rushed on. "Why wouldn't you go back to your folks instead of..." He glanced at the building behind her.

"Instead of living above a rebuilt shed?" she asked.

She'd read his mind, so he nodded.

Two vertical lines appeared between her eyebrows. "Mom moved away," she said. "My dad..." She trailed off.

David had a sense of unreality that he was standing here talking to Courtney Chase. He'd dreamed of her so often that he half-wondered if he were dreaming now. "Your dad passed away?"

"No," she said. "He's, uh, actually, he's in prison."

A slo-mo movie started up in his mind, of the well-dressed, always-on-the-phone businessman he'd caddied for at the country club. *He* was in prison?

She answered the question he didn't ask. "Tax evasion, fraud, you name it. We lost everything. Mom's living with her sister down in South Carolina, pretending it never happened. She didn't invite me along, and I wouldn't have gone, anyway."

It was a lot to process. "Wow, so that's why... *are* you the person supposed to help with the farm stand on evenings and weekends?"

She nodded slowly. "I am. But I might need to make a change."

David's heart curled in on itself. *Because of me.* She'd never thought him good enough for anything but a summer fling. Now, although their circumstances had reversed, she probably still thought he was low-class.

He inhaled the earthy, fertile fragrance of spring, watched the dog flop down a safe distance away. "Understandable. It won't work on my end, either." There was no way he could work closely with this woman he'd once loved with all his teenaged heart.

Her eyebrows shot up. "No, wait, that's not what I meant."

He shifted his feet. He wanted to escape the uncomfortable feelings Courtney aroused in him, wanted to go demand that Jenn tell him why she'd set him up.

But the good manners Ma and Pop had drilled into him wouldn't let him just march off. He sighed. "What *did* you mean, then?"

3

Courtney lifted her chin. She couldn't let a second job slip away from her today. "I still need to work the farm stand. More than just evenings and weekends, if that's possible. I was hoping to grow my in-home daycare into a bigger business, but my two main clients just quit." She gestured toward the road the moms and kids had left on.

"I'm sorry to hear it." He frowned. "But we haven't discussed hiring for more than the part-time role at this point."

"We?" she asked, stalling for time.

"The Flock," he explained. "Me, Jenn, Stone, and Allie. Pop's put us in charge of this whole farm rehabilitation, and we're making decisions as a group."

"I see." With how close the four foster teens had been, Courtney would have guessed they all hated her for ending her summer romance with David to marry a medical student. She wouldn't have blamed them.

But she and Jenn had gotten reacquainted over the winter, attending a Bible study together. Jenn was the reason Courtney had found this place to live when she'd moved out of the house she'd shared with her husband.

Maybe, with Jenn's help, she could get the group on her side.

She couldn't count on that, though. She looked back toward her new home. "I'm not asking for a long-term role here. I'm just in a tough spot. If you can't hire me for more hours, I need to look for a full-time job."

"Let's talk about it," he said.

She read in his eyes that he was doubting her capacity to do any work at all for him. "We can sit out here," she said, gesturing toward the bench that ran along the front of the building. "I'm still unpacking, inside."

His eyes softened a little. "I'll help you while we talk. I've moved a lot. Just give me a job. Want me to unpack your kitchen?"

"You'd do that?" After how she'd treated him, and given that he'd become a super-successful entrepreneur, his offer surprised her. Not to mention the way she'd changed. She'd noticed that men who used to jump to do her bidding when she was slender seemed to look right through the chubbier version of herself.

Maybe that was why David was being nice. Maybe he saw her as a fat charity case.

"Come on," he said, reading her doubt and responding to it. "I talk better when I'm doing something, anyway."

She was in no position to turn down help. She hooked Bubbles to the railing on her long line and led the way to her upstairs apartment.

In the kitchen, Courtney realized just how *big* David was. At least six feet tall, broad shouldered and muscular. And he radiated heat, she noticed, as she edged past him to get to her towering stacks of boxes.

She sucked in a breath. "It's going to be nice when I get unpacked," she said, trying to sound as if she was accustomed to being in a small space with a large, gorgeous man. "Jenn's husband Eddie did a terrific job of renovating the apartment."

It was the perfect situation for Courtney. Her ex had moved a couple of towns over, to where the hospital was, so there was little risk of running into him in Orchard Springs. But between her family's comedown and her divorce, a lot of gossip floated around town. Living out here would help her avoid it.

David turned in a slow circle, looking thoughtful. "I assume Eddie got the building permits for the farm stand?" He studied her stacks of boxes and lifted one down easily, his muscles flexing.

Wow. She opened the box, hiding her warm face. "Um, building permits, yes. The licensing to sell food and that sort of thing still has to be done."

He took another box from the top of the stack and set it down beside the first one. "You have a lot of stuff."

"Right?" She looked around and heaved out a sigh. "I put more than half of what I own in storage, but I probably still brought too much for such a small apartment."

"Why did your clients quit on you?" David opened a box and started unwrapping dishes.

"They said it was too muddy and far from town."

He frowned, setting dishes in the cupboard, raising an eyebrow until she okayed their placement. "It's a mile out of town. And every place is muddy this time of year."

"Yeah. They also thought this place, or what they saw of it from outside, wasn't nice enough for their children."

"Well... it's pretty basic," he said diplomatically, looking around. "But the farm itself is great for kids."

"That's what I thought." She opened a box of pots and pans and started stacking them in the cupboard beside the stove. "Tell me about your plans for the farm stand."

He leaned back against the counter with an easy smile. "I'm still getting up to speed, but I'll tell you what I know. You probably heard from Jenn that it's part of the whole renovation of the farm into a tourist attraction. We're doing the farm stand first so we can start making some money and getting some publicity this spring while we work on the bigger jobs."

"That's smart." She tried to fit the last couple of pots into the cupboard, to no avail, then restacked them in a big box. More stuff for the storage unit.

"Jenn told me the person living here—you—had some expertise."

She nodded. "Nothing professional, but my mom was a nut about fresh foods. We spent a lot of time scouring the countryside to get the best produce." She didn't add that her mother had only started dragging Courtney along when she'd gained a little weight, trying to interest her in the same light vegetable diet she ate herself.

Courtney did love vegetables. But she also loved everything else. The stress of her father's criminal trial, her divorce, and the related financial challenges... all of it meant the weight she'd gained after miscarrying had never come off. And it might not.

Her doctor said she was perfectly healthy, and she felt good. But now that she'd run into a handsome—wow, so handsome—blast from the past... David awakened all her insecurities.

Still, she had to support herself. "Do you think... is there any role you'd hire me for full time? I'll do anything. I'm strong. I'm a hard worker, and I'm not proud."

He raised an eyebrow.

She could tell what he was thinking. "I've changed, David," she said. "I'm not a country club flower anymore. I know how to work."

He tilted his head to one side, studying her. Scrutinizing her, really, not like an old friend, but like a successful businessman considering a personnel decision.

"Let's go downstairs and look the place over," he said, "and we'll think about it."

That meant this was a sort of job interview. And Courtney *had* to impress him, if she were to have any chance of expanding her part-time gig into a full-time one.

4

They walked downstairs into the main part of the building, soon to be a produce stand. David tried to focus on the space, but he couldn't help looking at Courtney and remembering how she used to be. She'd worn jeans when she was a teenager too, but they were designer-label jeans, the kind his foster sisters had envied. Not anymore.

She still had brunette hair that curled down her back, still had big, stunning eyes, still had full, kissable lips.

He couldn't believe that she was living here and was trying to talk him into expanding her job. He was definitely blaming

Jenn for this. He intended to scold his foster sister the moment he saw her.

Courtney's fluffy dog walked over to him slowly and sniffed his hand. But when he reached farther to pet her, she leapt away and cowered.

"Sorry," Courtney said. "Like I said, she's scared of men. She's a rescue."

"Got it."

"So I'm happy to do nights and weekends as agreed, but I would love to have some daytime work as well."

He looked around, thinking. The Flock had told him they needed someone to do nights and weekends and that their tenant was peppy and charming. They were right: that described Courtney.

Now, though, she needed more. And he remembered poverty enough to be sympathetic.

But that claim that she was a hard worker? She'd only become poor recently. He doubted she'd learned so quickly how to work hard.

They walked around the bottom floor of the structure. The smell of sawdust, plus the new beams and boards on one side of the building, revealed that it had been recently repaired. In front were two garage doors that could be raised to make the place more of an open-air shop.

"Eddie made sure that the structure is sound. But it's not quite finished."

"Looks like it needs shelving built and a coat of paint." David crossed his arms and looked around, envisioning the produce stand hopping and bustling.

"Exactly," she said. "I'm good at painting. I painted our whole house."

She couldn't mean the house where she'd grown up, so she must be describing the marital home. "Why did you paint it instead of having someone do it?" He was trying to figure out her lifestyle.

She shrugged. "I like to keep busy, and my ex worked long hours. The point is, I can help you with the painting or take it entirely off your hands."

It didn't really make sense to David to engage Courtney for that kind of work when there were trained painters he could hire. He felt reluctant to shut her down completely, though. "Why not just do childcare like you were doing?"

"The moms who dumped me today will gossip. Plus, I have to admit that they're right. This isn't the best situation for in-home childcare. It would be better if I had a fenced-in area, like at my old place." She blew out a sigh. "I could get a daycare job, but..."

David had been friends with a couple of daycare workers. "Pay is low in that type of job, isn't it?"

"It can be. Especially if you're not the business owner. And beyond living expenses, I need to build up some kind of reserve since I'm on my own."

David understood that. He remembered saving like mad to build up an emergency fund as soon as he'd moved away from Abbott Farm. He hadn't wanted to spend his paychecks and rely on credit cards for emergencies, like some of his friends had done.

Now, even though money wasn't an issue, he tended to save more than spend.

Courtney spoke again. "Anyway. I'd like to get full-time hours, at least. Maybe additional part-time work as well. If you don't need me full-time here, I could work the produce stand on the side as planned while I work full time somewhere else."

He was impressed that she wanted to work more than full time, given her background. "I mean, if you're desperate, I can float you a loan. Or make it a gift, for old times."

She stiffened and shook her head. "No, I don't want that. I want to work for it. And I can help you succeed. I know I can."

He couldn't keep the doubt off his face. He did want to succeed, but he wasn't sure how a former country clubber who'd fallen on hard times could help that happen.

She must have read his expression. "Tell me the issues you have with hiring me," she said, challenging him.

He lifted an eyebrow. "What can you do for me that a hired handyman couldn't?"

She smiled, and it made him remember that she'd always loved a good argument. "What's your idea of a farm stand?" she asked.

"The freshest veggies you can get anywhere," he said.

"Right, in summer and early fall. But

what else? What do farm stands do in the other seasons?"

"Well, the Flock wants to set up a number of enterprises."

"No," she said. "I mean your part—the farm stand. You want to do better than your brother and sisters, right? To support Pop Abbott?"

He grinned a little. She knew him all too well, knew how competitive he was. "I do," he said.

"And yet you've never started this type of business."

"I'll have to get up to speed on the industry."

"I'm guessing income needs to come in sooner rather than later for your Pop, doesn't it?"

"It does." He thought of the older man who had been so influential during his teenage years, who had taken him in and helped him become a man instead of a half-delinquent boy. He owed the man everything.

"How well do you know your potential customers?" Courtney asked.

He shrugged, lifted his hands. "People

from Orchard Springs and surrounding towns. Primarily women, but some men. I mean, doesn't everyone like vegetables?"

"Come on," she said. "I'm going to show you something."

HALF AN HOUR LATER, David followed Courtney into a large building that housed the Keystone Farmers Market.

The place was big, almost warehouse-like, but with a warm wooden interior and large windows facing the fields and distant ridges. Big displays of apples, carrots, and Brussels sprouts lined two walls, while the third held craft and kitchen items and what looked like a wine bar. It wasn't crowded on this cold morning. Several groups of women, plus a few individual shoppers, walked around without hurry, scouting out the offerings. There was a little cluster of tables in the middle of the sales floor where a few people were drinking hot beverages or eating pastries.

"Let's wander around," Courtney said, "and then we can sit at the tables and compare notes."

"Sounds good." David scanned the place with an entrepreneur's eye. He appreciated the colorful displays—they were definitely a draw. Interesting, too, were the painted slogans on the walls with homey messages like "Live, Laugh, Love" and "Today is a good day." They were targeting a particular type of audience, and he was interested to consider who would like that vibe.

Normally, he would have done a lot more research before starting up a new business. But he'd been stuck running his previous startup until finalizing the sale of it just last week. Complicating everything had been the fact that the buyer was overseas. Two trips to Singapore in the past month had kept him busy.

Plus, honestly, he'd figured that starting a farm stand would be a breeze. This was just something he could do to help Pop while figuring out his next move.

Courtney, though, was taking it seriously, and her attitude was contagious.

When he glanced over in her direction, he saw that a couple of ladies had stopped to speak with her. She listened, then spoke back to them. Not everyone would have noticed her little flinch, or the way her shoulders hunched afterward, but David was accustomed to reading body language.

Without a second thought, he strode over and held out a hand to the women. "I'm David Gonzalez," he said, before looking at Courtney. "How's it going?" he asked her.

"Fine," she said with an odd little tilt of her head.

"I remember you," one of the women said. "I'm Sheila. You used to work at the country club, didn't you?"

Both Sheila and the other woman watched him closely, in between glancing at Courtney and one another.

"I did," he said. "I caddied there during high school, but I'm not sure I remember you."

"Oh, I wasn't much of a golfer," Sheila said. "Too busy sunbathing."

David didn't remember these particular women, but he remembered the type.

Courtney introduced the other woman as Lexie, Sheila's sister.

"So, you're shopping here?" Lexie asked brightly. "Together?"

David didn't believe in secrecy when

starting up a business. The more word of mouth they could get, the better. "We're exploring possibilities for a similar business at Abbott Farm," he said.

"That makes sense," Lexie said. "You people like working outdoors."

David looked at her blankly.

"Landscaping and harvesting and such," she clarified.

Was this woman really categorizing him as a migrant farmworker? *That* hadn't happened to him in quite a while.

"Oh, Lexie, that's funny," Courtney said. "David is an international businessman. He's started multiple companies. We're lucky to have him in town to work on this project, even briefly, as busy as he is."

The woman who had spoken blushed, and then looked him up and down with new interest. "Oh, I didn't mean..."

David waited a beat to see how she would frame her remark, but she just trailed off.

He wasn't going to start a fight. She was a potential customer. "Hey, not a problem," he said, smiling at her. "I've started some businesses, but I have a lot to learn about agritourism."

"It was nice to see you again," Courtney said, giving David a let's-get-out-of-here look. "Looks like you already found a place for the kids."

"We dumped them on our mom," Sheila said. "I'm sorry we had to pull them out of your daycare. It's great you landed on your feet so quickly." She looked at David, then at Courtney, then at David again.

So these were the women who'd dumped Courtney as a daycare provider just this morning. David had had enough of their innuendos. "Come on," he said to Courtney, nodding toward the tables. "I'll buy you a soda, and we can talk through what we found out here."

"Sounds good." They walked together to the counter, selected sodas, and sat down at a small table.

A few more customers had come in by now. Sheila and Lexie drifted to the other side of the building, talking rapidly.

"So," Courtney said, "that was awkward. 'You people like working outdoors?' Come on."

David shook his head. "Nothing I haven't heard before, but it's been a while. Things are different in the city, but I guess rural areas tend to cling to some older beliefs."

"Everyone here isn't backward," she said. "But those two are. And they're also our customers."

"I see that," he said. "Let's watch them shop."

So they did, observing Lexie and Sheila and the other shoppers as they tasted samples and picked up bottles of wine, chatting with one another.

"They're not in a hurry," he observed. "No kids or jobs to get back to."

"Nope. Some are moms, like Lexie and Sheila are, but they use a lot of childcare."

"Which puts them in a higher spending bracket." David continued to watch.

"I like a lot of what they do here. Wouldn't mind emulating some of it. Not wine, though. None of the Flock are fans, plus Pop wouldn't allow it."

"I'm just as glad. We don't have to be identical to this market—we can do something different. See anything else you'd like to feature at our stand?"

He kind of liked that she was calling it *our* stand. "The knickknacks and wall hangings seem to be popular," he said. Then, noting that Sheila and Lexie had strolled closer to them, he added, "Mind if I do a little customer survey?"

"Go for it," she said.

He beckoned the two women over. "What's missing here that you'd like to see at a farmers market?" he asked.

"Candles, soaps, lotions," Sheila said.

"Or probiotics," Lexie said. "The pickled stuff. Sauerkraut and kimchi."

"Thanks, ladies," David said, making a note on his phone. "We plan to open around Easter, with produce from other local farms, until Abbott Farm is fully up and running. But we may include other offerings, so we appreciate your input. Hope you'll come by."

"Of course, we will," Sheila said warmly.

"With that personal invitation, we *definitely* will," Lexie added, scanning him from head to toe.

"That was uncomfortable," David said after the two had drifted off. "You said she's married, right?"

"She is," Courtney said. She opened her

mouth as if to say more about Lexie, then seemed to change her mind. "Anything else you'd like to see today?"

"Let's talk to the business owner. Maybe we can collaborate." He was surprised to find himself getting excited about the project.

"Sure," she said. "He's over there by the vegetables. But first..." She touched his arm.

Every cell in his body snapped to attention.

"Will you hire me full-time for a few weeks? Remember, I'll clean and paint, and I'll also be your consultant about what upscale women in rural Pennsylvania want in a farm stand. Where else can you find that combination of skills?"

David tried to keep his ambivalence from showing on his face. Courtney still drew him, and he didn't need that stress when he knew nothing could come of it. But he did want to succeed, and Courtney would help with that. "Okay," he said. "Let's try it for a week or two."

"Three weeks," she bargained. "And a raise from what I was going to get as the night and weekend person."

"How much are you asking for?"

"I'll leave that to you if you'll give me three weeks," she said, with a faint smile.

He respected her bargaining savvy. She was right to think that, coming from an international business environment, he'd be more generous than most employers here.

"Three weeks, then," he said, holding out a hand.

But when they clasped for a handshake, and he felt her soft skin, he didn't want to let go.

And that right there was the problem.

5

On Tuesday, Courtney set out to show David that she was the perfect person to do this job, at least for now.

Her determination to convince him was even stronger after she'd spent yesterday evening scouring online listings for childcare jobs. There weren't many. The most promising ones were in more populated areas an hour or more away.

It would be so much better if she could make this farm stand situation work while she tried to figure out what to do and where to go next in her life.

Eddie had brought over paint and supplies, so she spread drop cloths and taped off trim. It was a mild-enough day that she opened one of the garage doors that fronted the farm stand. Bubbles ran in and out, delighted with the freedom but never straying far from Courtney.

She opened the first paint can, hesitated, then poured some into a roller tray. David had said she could help with painting, but they hadn't agreed on a plan. At the same time, she wanted to show him she could work independently and that she wouldn't have to ask questions every five minutes.

Would he be happy or angry that she was getting started without him?

Half an hour later, when she'd finished painting around the trim on one wall, he came in.

She sucked in a breath. He wore casual jeans that clung to his narrow hips, and a flannel shirt with sleeves rolled up. His dark hair was a little damp.

He looked way, way too good. Courtney hadn't felt any interest in a man since her marriage had dissolved, and she'd wondered if her heart was closed down for good.

Apparently not.

David looked around the building, his eyebrows lifting. "I see you got started without me."

She opened her mouth to apologize, and then snapped it shut. She needed to project confidence. She took a breath and rolled her roller through the paint. "It's a good day to get a lot done, warm and dry," she said. "I figured you were busy, so I just got started."

He looked around, then back at her. His face broke into a smile. "Thanks for that," he said. "I like a woman with initiative."

Courtney's heart turned over as she looked into his approving eyes. She coughed and turned back to her work. "I'm not sure I'll be able to get the whole interior covered today, but I'll try," she said.

David walked over and inspected the supplies. "Two can work faster than one," he said, and picked up a paintbrush.

"I can get this done, if you have other work to do." She'd seen that he had a leather laptop case with him. "I don't know if you noticed, but there's a small office at the back of the stand. I cleaned it up and brought a card table and chair down last night."

"You *do* take initiative." He gave her another killer smile. "I like that, but I'll do a little painting. I think better when I'm moving."

They worked in silence for a little while. Bubbles ran in, took one look at David, and ran out again, tail between her legs. The next time she peeked in the door, Courtney put down her brush and called to the dog. She put her hand in her pocket, and Bubbles, recognizing a treat, gave a sharp bark.

"That's right, come," she encouraged.

Bubbles hesitated, her fear obviously warring with her desire for the piece of beef jerky in Courtney's hand.

Courtney walked over to the side of the building farthest from David. Moving just a few feet from the door, she coaxed the big doodle inside. She rubbed the dog's curly head before handing her the treat. Bubbles scarfed it down before taking off.

When she saw David watching, she lifted her hands, palms up. "Baby steps," she said. "I'd like to get her less afraid of men, so you're actually helping by being here."

"Glad to do it," he said, as he continued painting around a small side window.

Since he seemed to be in a good mood,

she brought her roller pan over to the wall he was working on and started painting in big swatches. "So, I did a little research on local jobs and came up empty. I just want you to know that I appreciate you giving me the temporary job." She sucked in a breath for courage. "I'd actually be interested in running the farm stand for the summer, if it can work for you."

"You're definitely enthusiastic," he said, his expression noncommittal. "We'll see. You're still looking for other opportunities, though, right? If this doesn't work out?"

"I looked at all the childcare openings online and made some calls, too," she said. "Any job I could get would be a commute. I'd have to be away from the farm longer than Bubbles can be alone."

Hearing her name, the dog trotted over, stopping just a couple of arms' lengths from Courtney and David.

"She's sweet," David said, "but if she's the only factor inhibiting you from making a living... couldn't you find her a good home with someone else?"

Courtney bit her lip, looking at her beloved pup, and shook her head. "Come here, baby," she said, pulling out another piece of jerky. This time, Bubbles came almost to Courtney's outstretched hand. Then David reached for more paint, and the movement startled her. She ran to the other side of the building.

"Was she abused?" he asked.

"Yep. Pretty obvious, isn't it? A group of frat boys got her as a puppy and kept her in a crate most of the time. Let her out when they wanted to use her to attract women, or to entertain themselves trying to get her to drink beer or eat marijuana gummies."

David's jaw dropped.

"Somebody finally reported the situation to a rescue organization," she went on, "and, small towns being what they are, the folks at the rescue knew I'd been looking for a dog. I met her and fell in love."

Bubbles lingered at the open door, and Courtney went over and knelt beside her, rubbing her sturdy sides and feeding her the jerky she still held in her hand. She hugged the dog, and Bubbles responded by licking her face.

Courtney looked over at David. "So anyway," she said, "I know it's not logical to keep her if it means I can't get a job away, but... I can't give her up. And I'm in a spot since realizing this place isn't the best for in-home childcare." She didn't intend to live over a shed for the rest of her life, and hopefully, after the house sale went through, she'd be able to afford a nicer place.

"Bubbles does look pretty attached." David smiled. "Is that what you want to do, going forward? In-home childcare?"

"There's nothing wrong with that," she said, feeling defensive.

He lifted his hands, palms out. "Of course not. I just don't remember that being an interest of yours when we were... younger."

"It wasn't," she said, and started rolling paint again. "In fact..." She paused and glanced over at him. Would he understand the reason why she'd become so obsessed with caring for kids?

He lifted an eyebrow. "You can tell me," he said, smiling. "Don't worry. I've been mentoring at-risk boys for years now. I've heard it all."

"I didn't know you did that," she said, impressed.

"You gotta give back," he said easily. "I

just hope you have more realistic ambitions than they do. A lot of kids have goals like becoming a pop star or playing in the NFL."

She laughed. "No risk of that. Actually, doing in-home childcare is a substitute for what I really want to do."

"Which is..."

"Be a stay-at-home mom with a big family. At least four or five kids."

"Ah." He turned back to his painting, his jaw tightening.

Weird reaction. "What's wrong with that? Everyone's entitled to a fantasy."

"That's not a fantasy," he said. He wasn't looking at her, and his voice was a little tight. "That's a worthy goal."

She stepped back from the wall to check for bare spots. "Yeah, well, I doubt I can do it."

"Why not?"

She gestured toward herself. "I'm fat," she said flatly. "Men like skinny."

His eyebrows shot up almost to his hairline, then he shook his head and chuckled. "You have no idea how beautiful you are, do you?"

Heat rose to her face, a good heat. He *still*

thought she was beautiful? It was hard to believe, and yet his answer had been totally spontaneous.

David walked over to the utility sink and started cleaning his paintbrush. "I need to get on with my office work, research regulations," he said. He grabbed his laptop and walked quickly into the office area.

After another hour of painting, Courtney had the first coat done. She peeked in the office and saw David frowning at his laptop.

"Is there anything else I can do to help?" she asked. "We need to wait for the first coat to dry before going on with the painting."

He was squinting at the screen, looking annoyed. "I'm trying to figure out these regulations on the county website," he said. "They don't make a lot of sense."

She leaned over his shoulder to look at the screen more closely and was surprised to see large text and an unusual font. "Oh wow, what site is that?"

He shoved the computer away, closing it at the same time. "County site. I'll look at it another time. I'm about to lay off work, too."

"Okay," she said. "Then I'll plan to work on the second coat tomorrow."

"That's fine." He seemed eager to leave, but also troubled.

As he walked away, she said, "You know, Eddie Wilson is familiar with local permits and regulations, since he's worked as a handyman around here for a while. He might be able to explain—"

"I can figure it out," David snapped.

"I didn't mean... Okay, whatever." She didn't know what had pushed him into a bad mood, but she wasn't going to waste time worrying about it.

David Gonzalez was super handsome and desirable. She'd seen how Sheila and Lexie had looked at him at the farmers market. He could have his pick of women, and the fact that he'd called her beautiful was no indication that he wanted to date her.

Even if he did have some interest in her, left over from their teen years, it wouldn't last. She'd learned that from her husband. She'd gained a little weight, and poof. He was gone, leaving only his cruel words behind, echoing in her ears.

Courtney knew Jeremy was wrong, that his whole attitude was wrong. She knew that beauty and worth came in all shapes and sizes.

But she also knew that the world was a lot nicer when you fit into societal ideas of beauty.

David did. She didn't. And that was that.

6

When David got back to Pop's house, he debated going up to his bedroom right away. Uncharacteristically, he felt like taking a nap. Felt like escaping from Courtney and all his thoughts about her.

Courtney loved kids and wanted a family. Even if she developed an interest in David, which was questionable, she wouldn't, shouldn't, pursue it. Being a family man wasn't in the picture for him. During their summer romance, the problem had been his lack of money and prospects. Now the tables were turned, but there was still a huge reason he couldn't be what she was looking for.

Instead of going in the front door, he went around to the back of the farmhouse and tapped on the door of the sunporch, which his foster sister Jenn had converted into an office. She used it to work the flower farming business, her contribution to the renewal of Abbott Farm.

"David!" she cried joyfully, even though she'd seen him just this morning. "Come on in."

It was one of the best things about moving back here. David had no good memories from his biological family, but the Flock had become a better one. Jenn was a true sister.

He walked in and gave her a hug. Chester, Pop's elderly bulldog, lumbered to his feet and offered a token woof. He stood, wagging his stubby tail, his whole back end wiggling.

David knelt and gave the bulldog a good ear rub as he looked around. The office, once a cluttered mess, was now a model of organization. There was a desk at one end of the narrow space, an old oak piece David recognized from one of the spare farmhouse bedrooms, now refinished. Low shelves lined the walls, and there were bright rugs on the floor. Windows stretched from the shelves to the ceiling, and the room was awash in sunlight.

"Looks good in here," he said. "Well done, mini Jenny."

"Thanks, I love it. It's perfect for planning out my flower fields. Want to stay and chat or are you just passing through?" Then she tilted her head to one side, studying him. "What's wrong?"

"Nothing much," he said.

"Sit down," she ordered, pointing to the glider that was the only piece of furniture remaining from the old days when the sunporch was Ma's domain. "I'll get you a cup of coffee."

"Pop's coffee?" he whispered. "Thanks, but no thanks."

She laughed. "You don't have to whisper. He's out having lunch with friends. And I got myself a good coffeemaker. Hang on."

She disappeared into the house, and David sat down and let the memories flood him. He'd come to Abbott Farm reluctantly, an angry city kid fresh out of foster families that would take him. Ma and Pop Abbott hadn't paid any attention to his attitude. They'd just given him a room of his own, hearty, delicious meals, and rules.

And love. Lots and lots of love.

That was the story for all of them, really. That was why, when they'd learned that Pop was struggling after Ma's death, they'd strategized and planned ways to help him rescue his deteriorating farm.

Jenn had been the first to come, earlier this winter. She'd pulled Pop out of his slump and assessed the condition of the farm, then gotten their neighbor, handyman Eddie Wilson, to help develop a plan for turning the place into an agritourism site. She was using her own background as a florist and her love of flowers to develop what looked like it was going to be a booming cut-flower business for the farm.

Now, it was David's turn to contribute.

Jenn emerged from the kitchen with two steaming cups of coffee. She handed David one of them, and when he saw the "Best Ma Ever" on the side, he smiled. He'd bought that for Ma right before he'd left at eighteen.

Sitting down on the other end of the glider, Jenn pulled her legs up under her and looked at him steadily. "Now. What's wrong?"

David sighed. "You could always read me," he said. "It's working with Courtney. I don't know if I can do it."

"Uh-oh. Still? Have you spent any time with her yet?"

"Yes. Including this morning, painting with her and that ridiculous dog."

"You don't like Bubbles?"

"Well," he said, "she's cute. But she's afraid of me, and it sounds like Courtney can't leave her by herself for long."

Jenn nodded. "Eddie hasn't been able to pet her yet, either. She's scared of men, I guess."

David seized on the subject of Jenn's new husband. "How's Eddie doing? Is he around?"

"He usually stops in for lunch," she said, her face softening. "Before he does, let's figure out what to do about Courtney. Is it really going to be a problem to work with her? I mean, we promised her that apartment and the part-time job, but I know you two have a history."

There was no hiding anything from Jenn. "It's... a challenge."

"Because you still feel for her or because you're mad at her?"

"Both," he said instantly. He couldn't deny he still found her incredibly attractive, but he also remembered, all too well, the sting of her rejection.

Jenn sipped coffee, watching him over the rim of her cup. "Is there anything we can do? I hate to break our agreement with her, the job and the housing, but you come first. Maybe I could help her find something else."

"No." He appreciated Jenn's being automatically on his side, more than she knew. "Her daycare clients dropped her when she moved out here, and she needs to find a full-time job. She's pushing me to let her work at the market full time. First getting it started, then running it."

Jenn's eyes sparkled. "Is there any chance that you two could—"

"No," he interrupted. "And I don't want to talk about it." He didn't want to open those doors, didn't want to think about what he couldn't have.

"Understood," Jenn said. And then her

face lit up as Eddie came in through the screen door. She jumped to her feet, and they embraced with obvious affection.

David was jealous of what Jenn and Eddie had, he could admit that. But also, he realized suddenly, he feared losing his closeness with Jenn, now that she and Eddie had married.

He'd better get used to it, though. Undoubtedly, the other members of the Flock would find partners and settle down.

David would be a fool to try for a relationship again. It was not for him. He'd had multiple examples, to where even he, a slow learner, got the point. He needed to forget about finding a loving partner and embrace the idea of being Uncle David to his foster siblings' kids.

Eddie knelt beside Chester, petting him as they talked about Jenn's recent delivery of seeds. She'd decided they should plant some vintage vegetables in addition to flowers.

"How's your work going?" David asked Eddie.

"Great. Busy." Eddie stood. "I'm looking forward to hearing your plans for the farm stand. I saw Courtney's been hard at work painting it with the supplies I dropped off."

"Yeah." David didn't want to go into the complications of Courtney again. "Maybe we could meet up sometime. I need to figure out what permits we need and how fast I can get them."

"Anytime," Eddie said. "But you couldn't do better than to have Courtney help you finesse that. She's got a way with people, and growing up in the wealthier neighborhoods, she'll impress the bureaucrats involved. Way more than Pop or I would."

"I'll think about it." He knew Eddie was just trying to help, but he hated the idea of getting Courtney even more involved in the business.

A car door slammed outside, and Pop climbed out of the passenger side of an ancient Chevy. It took him a minute to get himself straightened up and walking.

Pop was smiling, waving to his friend, but there was no denying he was getting up there. Eighty-five if he was a day.

Pop had not only given David a home when no one else would, but he'd also provided a model of how to be a decent man.

Now it was David's turn to help Pop. After all, he was the one who'd built businesses before and knew what was involved.

He owed Pop, and he would man up and do what he needed to do. Including working with Courtney.

But it wasn't going to be easy.

7

Courtney spent Saturday morning in town, stopping at the hardware store and the lumberyard. Errands completed, she strolled toward the bakery where her Bible study group was meeting.

The Bible study was sorely needed. Both for spiritual insight, and for a distraction from thinking about David.

The wind blew back her hair and cooled her face. She breathed in air rich with the fragrance of spring.

She and David had been avoiding each other for the past few days—at least as much as possible—but he acted attracted to her sometimes when they were forced to work together. She'd seen his dimple show at something she said, noticed his eyes lingering on her. She couldn't help it; that made her happy.

And there she was, thinking about him again.

Stop it, she told herself.

She turned her attention to her surroundings. The downtown area was lively, with many Orchard Springs residents enjoying the unseasonably warm day. She stepped around a dog, passed an older couple, and then, on impulse, walked into the only clothing store in downtown Orchard Springs.

She'd shopped here routinely as a child and teen, and even in her early married days. But she hadn't been in since her family's financial situation—and her own—had gone downhill.

She didn't intend to purchase anything, but she figured she might get some style ideas that she could try to replicate from the thrift store.

She was flipping through a rack of retro denim skirts when she heard whispering behind her. She glanced back.

Oh, joy. Sheila and Lexie.

They strolled over.

"How's it going?" Lexie asked.

"Oh, fine," she said, feeling wary. She asked about their kids, which seemed like a safe topic.

"We're still trying to find the right childcare for them," Sheila said.

For an instant, Courtney wondered if she could talk them into coming back to her as a daycare provider. They must be realizing it wasn't so easy to find a situation that worked.

She loved the kids, but did she want to deal with these moms every day?

Not at all.

"So, what are you shopping for?" Lexie asked.

"Oh, just browsing," Courtney said. "I like these denim skirts." She held one up to show the other women.

"Cute," Sheila said. She started looking through a rack of shirts.

Lexie stepped close to Courtney.

"This is the Misses section," she said, her voice artificially sweet.

Courtney didn't know what Lexie's odd tone was about and didn't much care. She moved on from the skirts to the same rack of blouses that Sheila was looking at.

"The bigger sizes are over in the *Women's* section," Lexie said, loudly enough that several other women in the store took notice.

Courtney stared at her. "Did you really just say that out loud?"

Lexie didn't answer. She looked around as if seeking reinforcement, but the shopkeeper crossed her arms and frowned, and a couple of other shoppers looked away. Lexie's face flushed a little.

"Yeah, Lex, that's mean," Sheila said. "Just because she's gained weight..." Sheila cut herself off, and now she looked embarrassed, too.

Courtney crossed her arms over her chest—which suddenly felt very oversized—and stared the two women down. "I always tried to teach your kids manners. I hope you find someone else who can do that, because the two of you certainly can't."

She spun and headed out of the shop, getting a thumbs-up from the saleswoman and even hearing someone applaud behind her.

Her slight sense of triumph ebbed

quickly, though, because what they said was true.

She *did* hover between regular and plus sizes. She *had* gained weight.

So why was she daydreaming about handsome David? Why was she even thinking she'd meet a man who would accept this body?

She stepped around other pedestrians, her vision blurring, her throat tight as she headed toward the bakery where the Bible study was being held.

She had never needed anything so much in her life.

8

David stormed into the produce stand building late Monday afternoon. He wanted to vent to someone. Not just anyone, but Courtney. She was in on this project and would understand.

She knelt in front of a shelving unit, drill in hand. When he came in, she turned to him. "You don't look happy," she said.

"That permit clerk is stonewalling me again." He paced around the room. "I'm going to have to get in touch with his supervisor. Or else grease his palms. I can't tell which would work better."

"Neither." Courtney put down her drill and stood gracefully. "I'll talk to them."

She looked comfortable in her ripped jeans and T-shirt. Comfortable and gorgeous. There was no hiding that figure, even under baggy work clothes.

"Who were you dealing with?" she asked as she pulled her hair tie out and shook down her hair. She stretched her back and neck.

David's mouth went dry, and for a moment, he couldn't think.

"Don't you know his name?"

"Uh, it was a guy named Tommy. Tommy Bretz."

"Ah. I know him." She frowned a minute, thinking. "Have you eaten anything today?"

"Not since breakfast." Jenn had gotten into the habit of fixing eggs or oatmeal for him and Pop, and David had to admit it was a good thing. Otherwise, he'd have probably grabbed a protein bar and been out the door.

"Okay, I have a plan," she said. "You're hungry and cranky, so we'll get dinner first. We'll go to McFadden's Pub. Tommy's mom works there, and he has dinner there a lot. If we run into him, we might be able to pull something off."

David wasn't used to being told what to

do, but he was frustrated and out of ideas. "You think that'll work?"

"They serve really good fish and chips," she said, which wasn't an answer. She headed for the stairs that led to her apartment. "Give me twenty minutes to get cleaned up. And you go put on casual clothes. None of that suit business."

She sounded like she knew what she was talking about. Maybe, like Jenn and Eddie had said, Courtney really would smooth the way for him.

Half an hour later, they were at a bar-restaurant on the far side of Orchard Springs. David didn't remember the place from when he'd lived here before, and Courtney confirmed that it was only five years old.

The parking lot was packed, and when they went inside, they saw why. Irish music blared from speakers, and at least half the tables held pitchers of green beer. Most customers wore green, and the servers had on Kiss Me, I Work At McFadden's T-shirts.

Courtney clapped a hand to her forehead. "I completely forgot. It's St. Patrick's Day. And I didn't even wear green!" She looked down at her pink sweater and gray slacks with dismay.

You look just fine, he wanted to say, but didn't.

A harried-looking waitress told them to "sit anywhere you can find." They scanned the room, and David spotted a table for two against the wall. "Let's grab that," he said, and urged her before him with a hand on the small of her back.

She moved so gracefully. And this close, even amongst the fragrance of fried food and beer, she smelled good. Like roses.

He forced himself to drop his hand and followed her as she wove her way between tightly packed tables, waving greetings to a few people along the way. When they reached the table, David was grateful it was a little bit quiet, being off to the side.

"I must be getting old," he said. "This place is too loud for me."

"Me, too," she said. "But I'm not much for bars as a general rule. McFadden's has good food, though, and a lot of people come here just for that. You'll see."

They studied the menus the waitress handed them. "I know why I don't drink," he said, making conversation but also genuinely curious to know her better. "Why don't you, though?"

"You first," she said, smiling.

He waved a hand. "Family of origin," he said. "My folks weren't what you'd call alcoholics, but they would have done better with some inhibitions that alcohol removed."

"Same with my folks," she said.

They ordered food and soft drinks, and then David went back to the topic of their families. "Hard to believe our parents have anything in common," he said. "Mine were petty criminals who ended up dumping me so they could run from the law." It was a sentence he'd said to only a few people, like the Flock. He was surprised to find himself admitting that truth to Courtney.

"Not so different," she said. "My parents drank martinis at the club, and they drank a lot of them. Dad was doing business deals drunk, and Mom was too far gone to notice. So when Dad got into some shady stuff... well, it probably wouldn't have happened if he hadn't had the lack of inhibitions you mentioned."

"You said your dad's in prison?" It was

hard to picture the snobbish man he'd avoided when caddying at the country club as a prisoner in an orange jumpsuit.

She nodded. "Five more years."

"Do you visit?"

She blew out a breath. "I make myself go once every few months. He doesn't really want to see me, and it's hard for me to see him like that."

That was understandable from Courtney's end. "I'd think he would welcome visitors. Your mom, does she visit him often?"

Courtney shook her head. "She went a couple of times at the beginning. It really threw her into an emotional meltdown. Moving out of state was a good way for her to avoid dealing with him and with what's happened."

He reached across the table and took her hand. "I'm sorry you have to handle that," he said. "It must be rough. And to go from living the country club life to..." He trailed off.

"To an attic over a produce stand?" She looked amused. "It's definitely different, but you know what? It's okay. It's brought me closer to people who are my genuine friends, and it's made me think about what's really important in life. Strengthened my faith."

Watching her talk, he admired her resilient attitude toward what had been a huge family misfortune. He forgot to let go of her hand until their food arrived, big platters of fish and chips and tall glasses of soda.

The aroma made David's mouth water. "This looks fantastic. I'm starving."

"Told you so. You'll be in a much better mood after eating this. You were pretty cranky." She ate a French fry, her eyes still on his. "Dig in. It's fantastic."

He didn't want to look away, but he forced himself to focus on the food, not Courtney's appeal. He dipped a piece of fish in tartar sauce. Crispy on the outside, tender inside, a fresh taste. "Wow," he said when he'd swallowed. "Pardon me while I scarf down this whole plate in the next thirty seconds." He picked up another piece of fish.

"Right there with you." She took a delicate bite of fish and her eyes closed. "Mmmm. Heavenly."

David was transfixed.

After another bite, she met his eyes. "What? Do I have ketchup on my face?"

"No. I'm just glad you enjoy your food."

Her cheeks turned pink and she put her fork down.

"What's wrong?"

She shrugged. "Just, you know, I need to watch what I eat."

His innocent comment must have made her self-conscious. "I like to see people enjoy food. And also, you don't need to watch what you eat. You're perfect."

The color in her face heightened. "I'm anything but perfect," she said. But she did take another bite of fish.

A few minutes later, Courtney looked across the room. "There's Tommy," she said. "Let me go talk to him. I'll see what I can find out."

"Finish your meal," he said.

"I'm done." She stood and made her way across the room.

David finished his plate and what was left on hers, watching her. She obviously had no idea how pretty she was, but the men in the restaurant didn't have the same problem. She fielded numerous comments and greetings. She had a friendly smile for everyone, but she also knew how to dodge away from a drunk guy who tried to grab her hand.

Finally, she reached the bar and slid into a seat next to the middle-aged, balding man who'd given David nothing but problems today. When David had spoken with him, he'd worn a sour expression, but to Courtney, he was all smiles. He listened while she spoke, nodding.

Then he put a hand on her arm, leaning closer, and she edged away.

David had had enough. He walked over to the bar—not slowed by anyone's greeting, like Courtney had been—and pulled a bar stool around so he could speak with both of them.

"*You,*" Tommy said, his sour expression coming back. The smell of alcohol emanated from him.

Courtney glanced at David with a small frown and a "zip it" gesture. "It will be good for the community to get this project off the ground," she said. "I'm sure your mom thinks so, too."

The bartender, a sixty-something woman with long gray hair pulled back in a braid, walked over. She must be Tommy's mother. "What can I get you?" she asked David.

David shook his head, then checked himself and ordered a non-alcoholic beer. Not good to take up bar space without ordering. When she brought the drink over, Courtney spoke up. "Hey Whitney, wouldn't it be great to get a produce stand going out at Abbott Farm?"

"Sure would," the woman said. "I love me some farm-fresh vegetables."

Courtney nodded toward Tommy. "Your son has the chance to fast track us," she said. "Don't you think he should?"

Tommy's eyes narrowed as he looked at David. "Don't like that guy," he said. His voice carried, and several other patrons looked their way.

"But you like me, right?" Courtney asked with a smile.

"Sure do," Tommy said with a slow smile.

"I'm going to be working on the project," she said. "I need the job, so I really hope you can do this for us."

"Working with *him*?" Tommy's lip curled.

"Yes, out at Abbott Farm," she said.

Tommy's mother was polishing glasses

behind the bar. "He's one of the foster kids, honey," she said. "He's footing the bill for all this, from what I heard."

David took a step back, not sure what amazed him more. The speed with which gossip traveled in Orchard Springs, or the way Courtney was using her people skills to get what they both wanted.

"I really would like more fresh produce for sale out our way," Tommy's mother said. "Now, you get the man what he needs to make that happen."

Tommy looked at David and blew out a disgusted breath. "Fine, you can come in tomorrow," he said. "Just drop the attitude, will you?"

"Of course," David said, though he had no idea what the man was talking about. He hadn't displayed any kind of attitude. He'd just been businesslike. But apparently, that wasn't the way to get things done here.

As he and Courtney thanked Tommy again and headed back to their table, Tommy's mother came out from behind the bar and stopped them. "You'd better go with him tomorrow," she said to Courtney. Then she addressed David. "Let her do the negotiating for you with any other permits you need," she said. "She's got the small-town touch. What I hear, you're rubbing people the wrong way with all your rushing."

"I rush?" he asked, amazed. To him, the process had seemed to move at glacial speed.

"Word on the street," she said, winking at him. "You're welcome."

As they left the restaurant, David's thoughts spun. Tommy's mother had made a good point, and her opinion paralleled what Jenn and Eddie had tried to tell him before. Courtney was a real asset. He needed to keep her on the team, no matter how hard it was for him to be around her without making a move.

"You have the full-time job, if you still want it," he said.

"Really? Thank you!" Courtney threw her arms around him.

Although her hug was quick, the soft feeling of her hair and the rose scent of her perfume stayed with him. Wow.

Working with her while keeping his emotional distance wasn't going to be easy.

9

"Come on, you have to do it!"

Courtney looked at Jenn, hunched over a laptop in Courtney's upstairs apartment. "I can't. I'll only get haters."

"No, you won't. Don't you want to achieve your goal?" Jenn typed for another minute and then held up the computer. "Voila! Ready to go."

Courtney blew out a breath. Why had she agreed to set up a dating profile? She read over the description. "Active Christian woman looking for companionship, friends first."

"That's totally bland," she said.

Jenn shrugged. "It's the photos that make it. Believe me, I know. All my friends in LA used online sites for finding dates, and changing their pictures was what made the difference."

"Great." Courtney flopped back against the bed.

Bubbles leaned against her, begging for attention.

"So let's look through your photos," Jenn said. "If they're bad, I'll take better ones. This place is so cute, we'll do a couple shots up here. And some with Bubbles, of course. And then we'll do outdoor ones, so you look all active."

"Ugh. I hate pictures of myself." But Courtney passed her phone over to Jenn, who started scrolling through her photos.

"This is cute," Jenn said. She held up a picture of Courtney in front of a classroom of little ones. "And it shows who you are."

"I don't know... all of those kids had photo clearances, but still."

"Their backs are to you, and we can blur them a little so no one would ever distinguish who they are." She scrolled on. "Why aren't there any better pictures of you? And why do you still have photos of The Loser?"

Courtney knew Jenn was referring to her ex-husband. "I don't know... it seemed petty to delete them."

"Petty is okay sometimes," Jenn said. "Believe me, I got rid of every shot of my California fiancé, and it felt great. And Eddie's glad I don't have those."

Courtney snorted. No one cared whether she had pictures of her ex on her phone, but she should probably take Jenn's advice sometime soon.

"This is pretty," Jenn said, holding up a headshot.

"My high school graduation picture, and no," Courtney said. "I'm not making someone think he's getting a fit eighteen-year-old and then having him get *this.*" She gestured at her body.

"We need to work on your self-esteem," Jenn said. "Which should come from God, but also from what we're doing now. Go ahead, put on something cute and I'll upload that picture of you teaching."

Courtney went reluctantly to her little

closet and flipped through her clothes. She held out a loose, ruffled dress, pink and white.

Jenn shook her head immediately. "Low self-esteem dress," she said. "Try something blue, you look good in blue. And pick something that actually fits you."

Courtney went to her drawers and pulled out a lightweight sweater in royal blue. She held it up to herself.

"Perfect!" Jenn clapped her hands. "Put it on and we'll start posing. Let's do outdoor shots mostly. Guys love outdoorsy girls."

After a few shots in the apartment, they went downstairs with Bubbles following along behind them.

"Let's do a pensive one," Jenn said, giggling. "Maybe you'll find an intellectual in Orchard Springs. After all, you said you liked reading in the interests section."

So Courtney leaned against a split-rail fence and looked off into the distance. Then Jenn posed her beside a tree with a book.

"Now," Jenn said, "pick up that rake, there. We'll have you raking in front of the barn, for all the farmers looking for love."

"Looking for a strong woman to help with the work, more like," Courtney said, but she grabbed the rake and faked raking, then leaned on it and smiled.

"That's perfect!" Jenn studied the photo. "Now, a couple with Bubbles. Have her put her paws on your shoulders so guys can see how big she is. We don't want any wimpy guys who are scared of big dogs."

Courtney laughed and urged Bubbles to jump up, then giggled as the dog licked her face.

"Another cute one," Jenn crowed. "We're gonna have so many great options."

"You're a good photographer," Courtney said. It was true. Jenn's joking around had made her forget her self-consciousness.

"Come on, we'll go upstairs and look at them on the big screen," Jenn said. "We'll make our final choices and add them to your profile."

David's car pulled up, and he climbed out of his vehicle with a couple of hardware-store bags in his hands. "What's going on here?"

"We're taking pictures for Courtney's online dating profile," Jenn said.

David's eyes widened. "You're online dating?"

Courtney felt too uncomfortable to answer. Was it pathetic, looking for love this way?

"She's going to start," Jenn said.

David frowned. "Are you sure that's a good idea, now, when you just got a new job?" He gestured toward the farm stand.

"She's not working twenty-four-seven," Jenn said. "And she has a goal she wants to achieve. This is part of that."

"What's the goal?"

Courtney felt her cheeks heating. "To be a mom. To have a bunch of kids."

David made a disgusted sound in his throat and strode into his office without another word.

"Don't mind him, he's always been moody," Jenn said. "Come on, let's add these to your profile!" She hurried up the stairs, leaving Courtney no choice but to follow along.

When she got there, Jenn was studying the website. "Oh my gosh, you're not going to believe this," she said.

"What?"

"You already have three responses!"

Courtney didn't know whether to laugh or cry.

10

On Friday evening at 6 p.m., David shuffled around the papers on his desk, looking for something else to do. The sun was low, the light slanting through the windows golden. Geese traveling back north honked overhead.

He didn't want to admit that he was staying out here at the farm stand waiting to see Courtney's date, but he was.

The door opened and he feigned being busy, but it was only Jenn.

"What are you doing still here?" she asked. "Even I quit obsessing about work half an hour ago."

"Just finishing up." He countered with a

question of his own. "What are *you* doing here? I thought Courtney had a date."

"Ahhhh." Jenn nodded and grinned. "You're waiting to check the guy out. I'm just here to make sure Courtney chose an outfit that shows off her assets."

Exactly what David *didn't* want. He turned back to his laptop.

Jenn came and looked over his shoulder before he could close the web page he'd been looking at.

"Online Dating: Seven Danger Signs to Look For"? Jenn looked amused. "You're sure you're working?"

"I just want her to be safe," David said defensively.

There was a sound from the upstairs apartment, and then Courtney came down, slowly. "I heard you guys talking down here. I'm so nervous! I haven't dated in forever."

David stared. She wore a blue sweater that fit her like a dream, black pants, and high-heeled boots. She looked amazing.

Way too amazing. "You're wearing *that*?" he asked.

"Oh, stop it," Jenn said. "You know she looks great."

"She does look great. Too great. This guy, whoever it is, is gonna have a hard time not attacking you."

Both women glared at him. "That's a very backward thing to say," Jenn told him. "You don't joke about men attacking women."

He held up his hands, palms out. "Sorry. I didn't mean *attack,* literally. I just meant..." He trailed off, then met Courtney's eyes, wary and nervous. "You look great," he said.

A car pulled up outside, and then a door slammed. "Hello?" came a deep voice.

All three of them went to the window and looked out. The guy was perfectly normal looking, wearing a white dress shirt and dark slacks.

And he was carrying a single rose. How corny could you get?

"Awwww, he brought you a rose," Jenn said. "Go on, go out and say hello!"

Courtney squeezed her eyes shut and bowed her head for an instant. Then she lifted her chin and marched out as if she were meeting at best a tax man, at worst an executioner.

David and Jenn stood at the window, watching the two of them greet each other.

David saw the guy's gaze skim Courtney up and down, subtly, and felt like punching him.

"You're not going out there." Jenn held on to David's arm.

He pulled away. "I'm just gonna find out his last name," he said, and strode out.

He approached the pair and extended a hand to the guy. "Hi," he said. "David Gonzalez." He waited.

The guy looked puzzled. "Michael Cunningham," he said, shaking David's hand. "Do you two… live together?"

Courtney laughed. "No, he's my boss. I live in the upstairs apartment. Alone," she added, frowning at David.

"Oh wow, that's good." Michael let out a nervous laugh. "You never know with online dating. I've met some, um, *interesting* people." He smiled at Courtney. "But you seem great. Should we go?"

"Yes," Courtney said. "This date is feeling a little crowded here."

"Where are you going to be?" David asked.

"None of your business!" Courtney hissed.

"Talia Mercato," Michael said, naming an upscale Italian eatery a couple of towns over.

"Perfect." Courtney took his arm, which seemed excessive, although the gravel driveway *was* a little rough for the kind of boots she was wearing.

Which made her legs look a mile long.

He watched them drive off, his insides churning.

Jenn came up beside him. "If this is how you feel, why don't you ask her out yourself?"

"Reasons," David said. "Want to go to Talia Mercato for dinner?"

"And stalk them?" Jenn asked. She stepped away and stared at him. "That is so rude."

"I'll go by myself if you won't come. I have a bad feeling about that guy."

"Do you really?" Jenn asked. "Or are you just being an overprotective, jealous jerk?"

"I really do," he said.

"I'll go," Jenn said, "if we can just hang outside. I know that area. There's a park and a walking trail right next to the restaurant."

"Fine," he said. "We can wait out there and follow them home. Make sure she gets back okay."

Jenn just shook her head at him. "Come on, I'll make us sandwiches," she said with a long-suffering sigh.

An hour later, David and Jenn were at the park, bundled up against the evening chill, eating sandwiches and drinking coffee from a big Thermos. "You still haven't answered my question," Jenn said. "Why don't you ask Courtney out? You were always crazy about her, and she about you."

David really didn't want to discuss it all with Jenn. "I have my reasons," he said.

"You said that before. What are they?" she asked in her pushy way.

He drew in a deep breath, wondering if he should tell her the truth. He really didn't want it spread around the entire Flock, and to Eddie. But Jenn would keep his situation under wraps if he asked her to.

"I hope we didn't miss them," he said, delaying the decision of whether to tell her. The bench where they sat faced the restaurant, a football-field distance away and half hidden by a couple of evergreen trees. The park's streetlights clicked on as darkness fell.

Jenn checked her watch. "I doubt they'd be done with dinner already," she said. "Unless it's not going well. Having a whole fancy dinner on the first date is risky. What if they hate each other? I always did a first meet at a coffee shop, so I wouldn't be stuck with a jerk for hours."

"Wait. You did online dating?"

"A little. And don't try to change the subject. We were talking about you."

David decided to deliberately misunderstand. "I never tried online dating," he said. "I liked meeting women in a more natural way, in person."

"Right, and you don't have any trouble finding the self-confidence to ask someone out," Jenn said. "*Except* for Courtney, it seems."

They were back to that. Jenn was like a dog who'd gotten hold of a bone and wouldn't let it go. "We're working together," he said. "That makes it creepy for me to ask her out."

"It does not. Half the couples I know met in the workplace." She wiped her hands on a napkin. "You're making excuses. Is it because she's gained weight?"

"What?" David stared at Jenn. "You have to be joking. She's gorgeous. Even prettier than when she was a skinny high school kid."

"Good." Jenn patted his hand. "I figured you weren't one of those guys who's only attracted to bony fashion-model types. Just making sure, because if you *were* down on her because of her weight, I'd have to beat you up."

"Stop scaring me," he said.

The restaurant door opened, and a few people came out. Courtney and Michael weren't among them. But a minute later, it opened again, and this time the two of them appeared. They were silhouetted against the sunset, and Michael had his hand on Courtney's back.

He said something to her, and she shook her head and stepped away from him. They stood talking for a couple of minutes. Then she nodded, and they headed across the parking lot in Jenn and David's direction.

"What do you think they're doing?" Jenn asked.

"Taking a walk," David said, "or sitting

down to watch the sunset from the park. He's going for a romantic setting."

"Sounds like the voice of experience," Jenn teased.

As Courtney and Michael came closer, they glanced at each other and slid down the bench to where they'd be more concealed behind the trees.

The couple stopped at the trailhead of a walking path that led into the woods. "Just a short walk," Michael said, his words clearly audible to David and Jenn.

"No thanks. I don't have the shoes for it. I think I want to go home."

"Oh, come *on,*" Michael said, his voice whiny and irritated.

"Not the way to win her heart," Jenn whispered to David.

"No," Courtney said. "I'd like to go home."

"But we've barely had time to get to know each other. I thought we'd have a couple glasses of wine and talk awhile at dinner, but you don't drink."

"No, I don't. Which was on my profile, I think."

"I didn't see that." He put an arm around

her. "I mostly looked at your pictures, to be honest. You're gorgeous."

She twisted away from him. "Oh, stop." Now *she* sounded irritated.

"What, I can't touch you? After all I paid for that dinner?"

"I thought this was a date, not a financial transaction." Courtney took another step back and slid her hand into her pocket. "Are you taking me home, or should I call for a ride?"

He stood glaring at her, then shifted as if to step forward.

David was on his feet instantly.

Jenn stood too and gripped his arm. "Let her handle it."

"Just so you know," Courtney said in a conversational tone, "I have pepper spray in my pocket."

"Get your own ride." He cursed and stomped off toward his car, leaving Courtney standing at the trailhead.

Jenn rushed forward, David beside her. "Are you okay?"

Courtney looked up at the darkening sky, sighing. "Yes, I'm okay. I knew you guys were there."

"How?"

"Saw your car, so I was looking for you." She glared after her date. "Wow, what a loser."

"I'm going to go have a word with him," David said.

"No!" Both women grabbed him, Courtney on one side and Jenn on the other.

"What? He can't get away with acting like that."

Courtney and Jenn exchanged eye rolls. "Men get away with acting like that all the time," Jenn said.

"Sometimes they even stalk their employees," Courtney added, looking pointedly at David. "What made you think coming along on my date was a good idea? Because I'm guessing it was your idea, and Jenn just joined in to police you."

"Exactly," Jenn said.

"So, what's going on?"

"I didn't think you were being careful enough about meeting a guy from online," he said. "Don't you know the statistics?"

"I do," she said. "It's pretty safe. Plus, I never would have come this far into a secluded area with him if I hadn't realized you two were here."

"And she has pepper spray," Jenn pointed out.

"True," David said, and spread his hands. "The truth is, I care about you and I don't want to see you hurt."

Courtney's mouth had been open, probably to continue arguing, but she closed it abruptly. She studied him for a moment. "Well then, thank you," she said. "I felt safer with you here."

Which made David feel like some kind of superhero, if only for a moment.

11

The morning after her fairly disastrous online date, Courtney stayed in bed a little later than usual. She called Bubbles up onto her bed and lay in the warm blankets, petting the dog and thinking.

She'd known Michael was not for her within ten minutes of starting their dinner together—just not her type. Too braggy, too pushy, in that way that indicated an essential insecurity. His actions when she didn't want to drink or let him touch her just confirmed her bad impression.

That David and Jenn had followed them to the restaurant... It was super annoying.

But she had to admit, when she saw David's car, she'd felt a rush of happiness and reassurance. And when she located the two of them sitting on the bench, barely visible in the twilight, she felt utter relief. She could escape Michael the jerk sooner.

The big question was, why had David followed her? It was a little strange. Creepy, except David wasn't creepy. He was a good guy all around.

Plus, having Jenn there had eroded any thought of David being weird with her or wanting to get into a fight with Michael.

It seemed to show that he cared about her. But every time they got a little closer, he backed away. What was that all about?

Confused, she sat up in bed, leaned back against her pillows, and pulled her computer into her lap, twisting a little sideways so that Bubbles could continue taking up most of the bed.

There were eight new responses to her online dating profile. Huh. Even with all the pictures—pictures that showed her as she was—guys were interested. Maybe she'd been wrong about her looks, about her lack of appeal.

Maybe her ex-husband had been completely wrong about her. That would be nice. She shelved the thought to consider later.

Ignoring the notifications from the dating site, she saw that the church newsletter had arrived. She clicked on it and skimmed through the messages and notices.

When she got to a blurb for the singles group, she read more closely. Apparently, they were having an activity tomorrow afternoon.

She knew the two women who ran the group, vaguely. They were both very peppy and had urged her to join, but she had been too raw from her divorce. Maybe she should give it a try now, though. It had to beat going out on another date like last night.

On the other hand, maybe she should forget about marriage and consider adopting, being a single mom. It wasn't as if she had dozens of models of healthy marriages. Her own parents had basically had a marriage of convenience—when it had become inconvenient, they just weren't together.

Enough. She rubbed her hands over Bubbles' sides, getting the dog excited. "Come on," she said. "We girls have to stick together. And I know you need to go outside."

She pulled on jeans and a sweatshirt, and they went downstairs.

She let Bubbles out and then heard a sound in the building and turned. "David?"

"In here," he called from the office area.

After Bubbles did her business, Courtney walked back toward David's office, the dog following behind her.

David was in his Saturday clothes, too—ancient-looking jeans and a concert T-shirt. Even in that, he looked great. Her heart pounded in reaction to him, but she took a couple of deep breaths and told herself to let it go.

"How are you doing this morning?" he asked, turning away from his computer as if he were glad to do it. "Hope you're not having any bad feelings from your date."

She shrugged. "No bad feelings, but I'm not sure the online thing is for me."

"Yeah. Definitely, that date wasn't any good. I'm sorry about stalking you."

"It's okay," she said. "I was actually pretty glad to see you and Jenn. But please don't do it again."

"As long as you don't do online dating again," he said, raising an eyebrow. Their eyes met and held.

Impatient with herself, Courtney looked away. She wasn't going to get into sharing puppy-dog-eye looks with David when he wasn't going to take anything further. "What are you working on?" she asked, looking over his shoulder.

"Oh, nothing. Just trying to figure this out before our workmen come on Monday to finish off the building."

She noticed the screen looked different, darkened around the edges and with the text that was showing enlarged. She asked him why.

"Dyslexia," he said in a matter-of-fact tone. "Sometimes, with a complicated text, I use this highlighting software that helps me focus."

"Really? I had no idea." She studied him with new respect. He'd built up businesses and made a ton of money, even with a disability that made reading a challenge?

"I'm not exactly proud of it," he said. "It's why I dropped out of college."

"It shouldn't be a reason to drop out of

college," she said. "I know there are programs, offices for students with disabilities, things like that. They should've been willing to help you."

"They probably were," he said. "I was pretty proud back in those days. I'm sure I didn't want the label."

"I get it," she said. "If there's any way I can help, let me know."

He fumbled around his desk and pulled out a thick book. "If you're serious, you can summarize this for me." He handed the book to her. "Not the whole thing, just the section about farm stands. You don't have much to do next week, work-wise, since the workmen will be here, so maybe this kind of project would be a good thing."

"Of course! No problem. Do you want me to write up a summary, or..."

"Nope. Just tell me the highlights."

"You've got it," she said. "Teamwork."

"Teamwork," he echoed.

Their eyes met again, lingered, and there was something speculative in his. But then he shook his head a little and turned away.

There he went again. Flirting and then backing off.

Well, she'd help him out by summarizing the book. She'd see if she could do some more research for him, too.

But as for anything romantic, that seemed to be off the table.

Well, fine. She wasn't going to throw herself at someone who didn't want her. She decided to talk to April and Ashleigh about the church singles group, see if it was too late to attend their activity tomorrow after church.

12

The next day after church, Courtney went home, changed into cute, casual clothes—jeans and a sweater that made her look thinner—and headed back toward church, where the singles group was meeting up.

April and Ashleigh had been full of enthusiasm, telling her about the trip they were planning to visit local covered bridges. It sounded fun, a good way to distract herself from the unobtainable David.

She arrived at the church and greeted the seven or eight people who were already milling around the parking lot. Others were driving up. Good. It looked like there was a decent turnout.

Her goal was to meet—just meet—at least three men. She had to start somewhere.

She was chatting with one nice guy from church—Man Number One—when an all-too-familiar Porsche drove up.

No. This could not be true. David couldn't be joining the group.

But he pulled up, parked, and got out of the car. He headed over toward the little crowd.

Would she never escape the man? Why was he here? He must be looking to date, but to her, he'd made it seem like that wasn't a possibility.

Maybe he just wanted to date anyone *but* her.

April and Ashleigh went over to him, practically jumping up and down with excitement.

"You came!" Ashleigh said, then turned to April. "See? I told you the new guy in town would want to meet people."

"Can you drive?" April asked. "We're car-pooling, and wow, it would be great to ride in a Porsche!"

"Sure," he said. "My car fits five in a pinch, so I can take four."

After a little more discussion of the car situation and the route, and the arrival of a few more latecomers, they milled around those driving. Several of the women came over to David's car, and Ashleigh and April joined them.

Vanessa, a pretty redhead, spoke up. "I call shotgun in the Porsche!"

David looked at Courtney. "Ride with me?"

And squeeze into that small back seat? "No thanks," she said.

So she ended up riding in a car with three guys, thereby meeting her three-man goal right out of the gate. There was one other car, mixed men and women, and then David, who of course had ended up driving four women.

Courtney was baffled that David had come—and annoyed by it. But as they drove along the country roads, she felt the tension seeping out of her. The guys were all laughing about a couple of controversies in the church.

"Anastasia Redding wants to change worship time from ten to ten-thirty," a man named Tom said. "Not that big a deal, but the governing committee has had like six meetings about it already."

"How about the women's group wanting to fire the kid who does video in the services?" Chris, an older guy, said.

"I'm for that," Tom said. "He's always behind, and I never know what comes next in the song."

"Use the hymnal, dude," Chris said. "It's not hard."

They reached the first covered bridge and climbed out. The classic structure was red with a peaked roof, stretched over a rushing stream. Aside from birdsong and the sound of the stream, it was quiet.

At least, it was quiet until the rest of the cars arrived and people poured out, talking and laughing. Everyone started taking photos and walking around to explore the bridge.

Patrick, the guy she had initially met, called everybody to listen up. He was a professor at the local college and seemed to like lecturing.

He explained that the bridge had been

built in 1882. "It has a queen post truss design with vertical plank siding and a covered gable roof," he said.

After a few more details about the bridge's construction, people's eyes were starting to glaze. Courtney decided to ask a simpler question. "How come bridges are covered? Is it just for decoration?"

"No," Patrick said, looking gratified that someone was paying attention to him. "They're covered to protect them from the weather. You'll notice that they're mostly made of wood, and they're mostly in parts of the country that get a fair amount of rain and snowfall. You don't see covered bridges in the west, where it's more arid."

A couple of the guys teased Patrick for acting like a professor on his day off, but Courtney didn't mind him. He was kind of fun with all his facts.

David seemed to be trying to listen, but the women clustering around him kept joking and talking to him. He was laughing along, but he didn't look like he was having a whole lot of fun—not to Courtney's eye. She knew him pretty well.

They drove on to the next site, and now the guys in the car were talking about David.

"Nobody's impressed with my truck anymore," Tom complained. "Not since Mr. Porsche joined the group."

"Right? He totally ruined our opportunities."

"How come you didn't want to ride with him like everybody else?" Patrick asked Courtney. "I heard him ask you."

Courtney shrugged. "I work with him. I don't need to spend my free time with him." There. She sounded totally not in love with him.

"Are you going to give us a lecture about the next bridge?" one of the guys teased Patrick.

He laughed. "I don't know. I seem to lose my audience when I get into the statistics."

The next bridge was in a wooded area with a hillside rising up on the road behind it. It was a weathered white color and shorter than the previous bridge.

"Okay, Prof, tell us your story," one of Courtney's car-mates said. "Come on, everyone, gather around for some more fun facts about covered bridges."

There was general groaning, but everyone did gather around.

"This bridge," Patrick said dramatically, "is said to be haunted."

"Really?" Ashleigh gasped.

"I don't believe in hauntings," someone said.

"According to local legend, there was a young couple who came here swimming against their parents' orders," Patrick explained. "They jumped off the bridge, and one of them drowned. The other's body was never found. So there are arguments about whether one or two ghosts haunt the bridge."

"Oh, how sad!" Ashleigh's normally cheerful smile turned downward.

"You don't really believe that, do you?" Courtney asked him.

"No," he said. "I don't believe in ghosts, and I haven't been able to find any documentation that the couple even came here, let alone jumped off the bridge and died. But it does make a good story."

"Come take a picture with me, David!" It was Vanessa, the red-haired woman who'd called shotgun in David's car. A couple of other singles had asked if they could take her place, and she'd refused.

David looked over at Courtney with a pleading expression.

She ignored him.

That photo got taken, and then several others, including people who wanted a photo with the Porsche—and David and the bridge in it. That meant David had to move the car, but he did it without complaint. He was being a good sport, and it made her like him better.

While people were studying their photos and exploring the bridge, David walked over to Courtney. "Help," he said. "Everyone's fallen in love with my car."

"And with you." She laughed at him. "You got yourself into this."

"I couldn't say no to Ashleigh and April," he said. "They're very convincing."

"They are," she said. "But driving that car... it's a chick magnet."

"Not what I'm looking for," he said. "Plus, it's really not a country car. If I stick around, I'm going to have to get a truck."

"Good idea," she said, keeping her voice noncommittal. She was glad he wasn't bragging and preening with all the flattery, but she didn't want him to know that.

Then her car was ready to go, so she waved and left.

They saw two other bridges. Courtney was feeling better and better, just enjoying her time with the other singles who weren't obsessed with David. It was relaxed and fun, a good way to meet friends if not dates.

At the last bridge, nobody seemed to want to leave.

"Is that it?" someone said.

"Unless you know of another bridge not too far," Ashleigh said.

David and Courtney looked at each other.

"You're all welcome to come to Abbott Farm, to see Sweet Briar Bridge," Courtney said.

"I second that. Pop Abbott won't mind."

"You live there?" Vanessa asked.

"I do. Courtney does as well."

Vanessa's face fell.

"Not together!" Courtney glanced at David. "I rent an apartment in one of the outbuildings. We could grab sandwiches on the way and have a picnic."

Everyone loved the idea. They stopped at a sandwich shop, picked up food, and then went to the bridge and had a picnic on the banks. Everyone raved about how pretty the bridge was, maybe the prettiest they'd seen, surrounded by a grassy lawn perfect for picnicking, flowering trees just starting to bloom, and the red barn in the background. Lots of photos got taken here, too.

Courtney suddenly realized that the bridge might be an asset to the farm, a draw for visitors.

By popular request, she brought out Bubbles, and the dog let a couple of the women pet her, although she still leaped away from the men.

Patrick launched into a description of kissing bridges. Apparently, covered bridges were notorious places where young men would sneak a kiss on the way to or from town. This time, the group listened with more interest.

Courtney glanced over at David, only to find him making his way toward her. Her face heated.

He stood next to her as Patrick continued

his lecture. “Are you thinking what I’m thinking?” he asked in a low voice.

About kissing? “I don’t know, what are you thinking?”

“About marketing possibilities with the bridge,” he said.

Relief mingled with disappointment. “Yes! All our brochures and marketing materials should have the covered bridge on them. Get people to combine a trip to the farm stand with a visit to the covered bridge. People could even bring blankets and have picnics.”

“We could sell sandwiches and snacks in the produce stand. Even picnic baskets.”

“I love that!” Courtney said. “But... maybe we’d better get the basics down first. Jenn said you guys want to start small.”

“Good point, good point. I think we need additional permits if we’re selling prepared food, too.”

“But the bridge can still be a feature.” Courtney sat down on a bench that overlooked the stream.

“We’ll have to ask Pop if there’s a history to it.” David sat beside her. “We can include that in some of our marketing materials. People love nostalgia."

"Patrick might know the bridge's history, too," she said. "Or be able to find out."

David looked annoyed. "Patrick," he said, "seems like a know-it-all."

"Or maybe he's just smart," Courtney said, smiling.

David's male competitiveness was kind of funny. This had been a good trip—both fun for her personally, and useful for their plans for the farm stand.

13

On Monday morning, David trudged through the rain from the farmhouse to the produce stand building. He had to get the workers started on the final renovations: upgrading the plumbing for a bigger sink area, installing lighting, and refinishing a damaged section of the floor. After doing that, he headed back toward the farmhouse, pulling his rain gear closer around him.

He hadn't seen Courtney. Hadn't even looked toward the stairs that led to her apartment. The guys were making an early start, and he'd texted her and told her to sleep in, he would handle it.

He guessed her sleeping in wouldn't last long, once the guys started drilling and banging around.

The rain was cold, the ground soaked. It was dark, as if the sun hadn't even risen.

The shadowy, cold, damp weather matched his mood.

Yesterday, with the singles group, had been a mixed bag. It had been hard to see Courtney laughing and having fun with other men. And yeah, a couple of the women had acted like they liked him, but he knew the truth: they liked his car and the wealth it represented.

He didn't want to attract women with his wealth. He'd been there and done that and it hadn't turned out well.

What he wanted was a family. A good, strong family, not a neglectful one like his own family of origin. Unfortunately, kids weren't in the cards for him, but at least he wanted a wife, a partner.

And not just any partner. He wanted Courtney.

Except Courtney wanted a big family, and that was something he couldn't give her.

He should never have gone yesterday.

Yes, April and Ashleigh had been convincing as they'd talked him into it. But the reason he'd gone, really, was knowing Courtney would be there. That was pathetic and it needed to stop.

He needed to figure out how to live as a single man, not follow Courtney around on her dates and singles activities, watching her look for a mate who could give her the family she wanted.

Rain drummed around him, soaking through his athletic shoes and his so-called water-resistant coat.

Suddenly, a rusty-gold creature flashed by him in the rain.

"Bubbles!" He looked around for Courtney but didn't see her. Heading in the direction the dog had gone, he reached for his phone and called her.

The call failed. He shoved the phone back in his pocket, mentally criticizing the bad reception here, and ran faster after the dog.

She stopped at the bank of the stream.

"Bubbles! Here, girl!" he called.

She looked back, then ran from him,

along the stream bed toward the covered bridge.

He slowed down as he approached the bridge. When he reached the shelter of the grassy area under the bridge, he stopped, squinting into the gloom.

He heard a sound, whining. Bubbles was here. Somehow, she'd gotten herself up behind the rocky area where the bridge's edge met the ground.

"Hey, girl, it's okay," he said, trying to keep his voice soft, kneeling to make himself small. "Come here."

She didn't come, but she didn't run away.

He reached for his phone, moving slowly so as not to startle her. He hit Courtney's number again with the same result: the call failed.

He moved closer to Bubbles, talking softly, moving slowly. She didn't run away, but she cowered back. It looked like she might have hurt her leg on the rocks.

He fumbled in his jacket pocket and there, like a miracle, he found an old package of peanut butter crackers. He pulled them out and unwrapped them, and at the sound of the cellophane, the dog's head lifted.

He moved a little closer and she cowered again, so he stopped. He rustled the wrapper again and then tossed her a cracker.

It didn't land close enough for her to easily reach, and she didn't move toward it. But her alert expression told him she was interested.

He got out another cracker and tossed it directly under her nose. She sniffed it and then snapped it into her mouth and crunched it down.

What was he going to do if he got close to her? She was likely to run away again if he touched her, and he'd be back where he started. Courtney must be out looking for her, frantic.

Slowly, quietly, he unbuckled his belt and slid it off. Then he moved a little closer and tossed the dog another cracker.

She ate it.

Closer, and then another cracker. She ate it and looked at him expectantly.

He broke the remaining two crackers into pieces and moved a little closer as he tossed her each scrap. The last one, he held in his hand and handed it to her, and she ate it from his hand.

As she crunched, he looped his belt through her collar and gripped the makeshift leash. Success!

"Come on, girl, let's go find Mom." He tugged gently, and crinkled the empty cellophane package.

Finally, reluctantly, she went with him.

He walked with her through the rain, talking quietly to her, using his most soothing voice. He could see that she was limping a little, but she didn't seem to be badly hurt. And he was pretty sure she wouldn't tolerate being carried.

He heard Courtney's voice, calling her dog. She sounded panicked.

"I've got her," he yelled. "She's safe!"

Bubbles barked excitedly.

"Bubbles!" Courtney appeared out of the rainy fog. She ran to him and the dog and knelt, ignoring the mud, hugging the wet dog to her. Then she looked up at David. "You found her!"

He knelt down too, then, and Bubbles bounced with excitement. "I think she hurt her leg a little," he said as Courtney hugged him. "We'd better get her inside."

"Thank you, thank you, thank you!" She hugged David again once they were standing.

He felt like a million bucks. He'd done something for Courtney. He wanted to keep doing that, keep helping her, make life easier for her.

Which wasn't what he was supposed to be doing. He was supposed to be figuring out how to live as a single man. Instead, he wanted to help this woman, to make her smile like that, again and again.

He had to tell himself, convince himself: that wasn't going to happen.

She let go and stepped back, her face clouding.

"What's wrong?" he asked.

"I'm worried about this happening again, because of the workmen. That's why she ran away. I guess I'll mostly keep her in the apartment."

"How will she be with the noise?"

Courtney looked down at the dog. "Honestly? She hates it. She keeps pacing and crying."

He knelt and petted the wet dog. She shook herself, further soaking him and Courtney. But she stayed beside him rather than tugging away toward Courtney, and he felt that as a triumph. And he didn't want her suffering with the workers and their noise.

"Tell you what," he heard himself saying. "For the next few days, I think you and Bubbles should move into the farmhouse with me and Pop."

14

Courtney couldn't believe she was moving in with David.

And yet here she was on Tuesday morning, climbing out of her car with a bag full of Bubbles' supplies. To her astonishment, Bubbles saw David and rushed to him.

"She finally likes me," David said, laughing and petting her. "All it took was rescuing her in a rainstorm. He pulled Courtney's suitcases out of the back of her car.

It was another gloomy day, with rain threatening. The workers had started early this morning, hammering and drilling and talking, radio on. The sound of several strangers had put Bubbles on edge. It was good to escape.

They approached the farmhouse. Courtney had visited Jenn here once, before she'd married Eddie and moved next door. She'd also known Pop Abbott for years, just from seeing him around town. But her family didn't move in the same circles as he, his wife, and their flock of foster kids. Ma and Pop hadn't been members of the country club. Weren't the type.

But Pop had been gracious about having her move into the outbuilding, and now he came out onto the big wraparound porch to greet them. "Welcome, welcome, come on in," he said, remarkably spry for being in his eighties. "I've got coffee on. Have a cup?"

"Coffee sounds wonderful," she said gratefully. She hadn't taken the time to make any this morning.

"If you don't like his, I can make you a cup from Jenn's *good* coffeemaker," David said, grinning at Pop. He nodded at the suitcases he was carrying. "I'll take these upstairs."

"Don't listen to him. My coffee's just

fine." Pop poured her a cup from an ancient-looking Mr. Coffee.

Courtney set her bag of supplies on the counter. Bubbles pressed against Courtney's leg, and she rubbed the big dog's head. "We're going to stay here for a few days, girl! You'll like the extra space." At least, she hoped that was true.

When Pop approached to hand her the coffee. Bubbles leapt away and retreated to hide behind the table.

"Sorry she's so skittish." Courtney took the chair Pop indicated, Bubbles cowering behind her. "She's like that with everyone, especially men, at first."

Pop made his way to the refrigerator and pulled out a small slice of cheese. He sat down at the table catty-corner to Courtney, broke off a piece of cheese, and held it out toward Bubbles.

The dog leaned forward and stretched her neck toward it, keeping her feet planted. Her nose was twitching.

Pop moved a little closer, patiently.

Bubbles leaned farther forward. She delicately took the cheese from Pop's hand and then backed away to eat it.

David walked into the kitchen. "I put you in the room at the top of the stairs to the left," he said. "Bathroom's across the hall."

"I really appreciate your taking me in. Bubbles will be so much safer and happier here."

"I guess she will," David said, and nodded toward Pop.

Bubbles stood beside the older man, taking bits of cheese from his hand, a surprising and sweet sight.

"Pop has a way with animals. Kids, too."

They smiled at each other, and Courtney felt a buzz of awareness again. *Watch out,* she told herself, but she couldn't worry too much. No, things weren't perfect with David, but she was feeling better about their relationship. He genuinely seemed to like her. And he'd found Bubbles in that awful rainstorm, which was a hero move if there ever was one.

A bark came from the back of the house. "I forgot about your dog!" Coutney said. "Where is he?"

"In my bedroom." Pop rubbed Bubbles' floppy ears. "Wanted to get her used to the place before she meets him."

"Oh no, will he be upset?" A dogfight hadn't been on Courtney's list of worries about moving in.

"Nothing much upsets Chester. Or me, for that matter. We're both too old to get upset." He turned to David. "Let him out, would you?"

David walked toward the back of the house. A minute later, Pop's big bulldog came racing into the kitchen. He stopped, stiff-legged, when he saw Bubbles, and barked.

Bubbles peeked out from behind Courtney, barking just as much.

"It's okay, girl, it's Chester. He's friendly." At least, Courtney hoped he was friendly around other dogs. She knelt beside Bubbles and held out a hand to Chester, and the bulldog came closer, sniffing.

She scratched his wrinkled head. Bubbles had quieted down but was quivering, so Courtney petted her with her other hand. Slowly, Chester moved toward Bubbles.

"You be nice, boy," Pop ordered.

Courtney eased herself back into her chair. The two dogs sniffed each other. Would they get along, or would Courtney and Bubbles quickly find themselves back out in the rain?

Bubbles' big plume of a tail twitched first, and then Chester's stub seemed to wag his whole back end.

Suddenly, Bubbles bowed, front low, back end high, facing Chester. She let out a challenging little "woof."

Chester barked once, too, and sprang toward her, and they chased each other around the kitchen, then through the living room and dining room and back into the kitchen, where they both flopped down, panting.

"Guess they're friends," David said.

"Old Chester needs a friend." Pop reached down and patted the bulldog's haunch.

Courtney's phone vibrated in her pocket. She checked it and let out a sigh. "It's my mom."

"Take it in the front room or upstairs," Pop said.

Reluctantly, Courtney headed toward the front room and greeted her mother.

"I hadn't heard from you for a while, so I'm checking in," Mom said.

Guilty. She'd missed their usual Sunday

phone call, and then hadn't called yesterday, either, busy with the workers and with Bubbles running away. "How are you?" she asked her mother. "What have you been doing?"

"Oh, did some shopping with my neighbor," Mom said. "And there's a bridge club in the apartment complex. They've asked me to join."

"I'm glad you're settling in," Courtney said, meaning it. "Have you talked to Dad?"

"Not too much, lately," Mom said vaguely. "How are you? Have you been working out? Eating well?"

Courtney restrained a groan. Even if Mom didn't mean to focus on Courtney's weight, she always seemed to land there. "I'm fine, thanks," she said.

"I've been hearing stories about you and that caddy you used to date," Mom said.

"Really? From whom?"

"I still have my sources in Orchard Springs."

Courtney glanced into the kitchen where David and Pop were talking. They didn't need to overhear this part of the conversation. She whistled to Bubbles and headed upstairs.

The bedroom where she found her suitcases was small, but cute, with an iron-framed double bed covered by a handmade quilt. There were gauzy curtains at the windows and a rug on the floor. Bubbles turned herself around a couple of times and then flopped down onto the rug.

"I can see why you like the caddy," Mom was saying. "He was always so attractive."

"His name is David," Courtney said.

"I hear he's done well. *Quite* well."

"That's true." She wondered where her mother was going with this. Mom was always going someplace.

"So..." Mom trailed off, then spoke again. "I don't want you to get hurt, honey. Men are so superficial. And, well... a handsome, successful man like that is probably going to go for a different kind of woman."

Courtney suddenly got the point. After all, it was nothing she hadn't said to herself.

Rich, handsome men like David went for thin, gorgeous women. Not curvy, fluffy country girls like her. She sat down on the bed and pulled a pillow over her middle. "Message received," she said.

After the call ended, Courtney stood and

looked at herself in the wood-framed full-length mirror.

She'd felt kind of cute this morning in her red sweater and jeans, but now, all she could see was the size of her thighs and the roll around her middle.

15

David pulled his car around to the entrance of the Lancaster hospital. He'd brought Pop here early this morning for a routine procedure and had gone to bring around the car while Pop got released.

It was a pretty day. A gusty breeze tossed the heads of the crocuses blooming in the flower bed beside the hospital exit, and the flanking trees were greening up a little.

Just six months ago, David had struggled to relax enough to take a whole day off from work to help a friend. He'd done it, but he'd stressed and brought his laptop and phone and generally been a pain in the neck to be around.

He was glad he was getting some perspective on his workaholism. Glad for the chance to help Pop.

And, selfishly, he was glad to get away from Courtney and her confusing mixed signals. Sometimes he felt a strong connection to her as they laughed together about Pops' jokes or about the budding friendship between Bubbles and Chester. Other times, she simply closed down, responding in monosyllables to his attempts at conversation. What was it with her?

He couldn't get terribly angry, though, when he was pretty sure he was giving off the same type of mixed signals himself.

Pop emerged from the hospital doors in a wheelchair, per hospital regulations. He wasn't being pushed by a hospital staffer, though, but by Pastor Steve.

David got out of the car, walked over, and shook the pastor's hand. "Putting you to work, eh?" he asked.

"Always glad to help this guy. He's been a longtime parishioner and friend." The pastor helped Pop to his feet, and the orderly who'd been following behind took the wheelchair away. "I've seen you in church a couple of times, and heard you went to the singles event. Glad you're getting involved."

"I'm enjoying getting to know everyone. Enjoying your sermons, too." David meant it. "Everything okay with you?" He asked that because the pastor looked haggard, with dark circles under his eyes and pasty skin. Maybe he'd been in here for medical reasons, himself, but David didn't want to ask directly. Medical stuff was private. He knew that better than anyone.

"Pastor Steve is here visiting a good friend who's quite ill," Pop explained.

"I'm sorry to hear it," David said.

"Thank you." The pastor sighed. "She's been in a coma for years now, but lately she's really deteriorating. That's why they moved her from her care home to the hospital. She may be nearing the end of her journey."

"That must be hard to deal with," David said, sensing that this friend was a particularly close one.

Pop put a hand on the pastor's shoulder. "Praying for you both," he said.

"Thank you. Well!" Pastor Steve rubbed

his hands together. "I don't want to hold you men up. You're looking like you could run a marathon," he added to Pop.

"I'm in good shape for the shape I'm in," Pop said.

David admired how stoically Pop took his occasional health issues. He handled them with more grace than David had ever handled his.

As they drove through town, Pop shared Pastor Steve's story. "It was a difference in, well, I don't know how you'd describe it," Pop said. "Steve was squeaky clean, and this woman had a checkered past. The pastor shouldn't have let that get in his way, but he did, and he's regretted it ever since." He looked sideways at David. "You still hung up on Courtney's country club background?"

"No," David said automatically, though he wasn't sure that was true.

"Well, good, because you're a lot more likely to fit in there than she is, now," Pop said.

When they reached the farm, David impulsively pulled over beside the covered bridge. "Do you feel well enough to tell me the history of the bridge?" he asked Pop.

"I'll tell you *my* history with it," Pop said. "I proposed to Kimmy Jean here."

"What?" David stopped and stared at the man. Talk about a good marketing story.

"Sure did. Right in the middle of that bridge." Pop's eyes twinkled. "I wasn't the only one to steal a kiss here, either."

"That's a great memory," David said.

"It is, looking back, but I was a ball of nerves at the time. Didn't think she'd have a country boy like me, since she was a town girl."

"Guess you were wrong," David said, smiling.

"I was. Turned out she didn't think I'd have *her*, because she couldn't have kids."

The words hung in the air as David's smile fell off his face. That was a little too close to home.

Pop didn't seem to notice David's reaction. "She knew I wanted a family, a son to take over the farm, but she'd been told she'd never have children."

"But... you had Ronald," David said, puzzled.

"He was a surprise," Pop said. "A blessing we didn't ever expect. When we didn't have more, we started fostering. Got every bit as much joy out of you kids as we'd have gotten out of a dozen kids of our own." He paused, looking thoughtfully at the bridge. "And I wouldn't trade a day with Kimmy Jean for anything."

David was pretty sure Pop didn't know about his own fertility issues, because almost no one did. But the story seemed pointed directly at him, nonetheless.

Pop clapped a hand on David's shoulder. "You're doing real well with this project. All of the Flock, but especially you, with the farm stand. You work hard, and I know you could be putting your time and energy into something bigger and more profitable. I want you to know that I'm grateful."

The words hit David right in the heart. He'd never gotten affirmation from his family of origin; his parents, when they'd bothered to notice him, had thought him defective because he struggled in school. His workaholism, his scramble for success and money, had a lot to do with proving them wrong.

Pop was handing out the type of compliment David had always longed to hear.

It felt good. Made David feel like less of a loser. Even made him wonder if Courtney might be able to get past his limitations.

16

"I'm hitting the wall," David said to Courtney on Saturday evening, closing his laptop. They'd been working at the kitchen table for three hours straight, developing a marketing strategy for the farm stand and planning their first orders. David felt like his eyes were two burning fireballs.

Courtney looked up, smiled, and stretched, shifting her shoulders from side to side. "Same."

David looked away, trying to tell himself he didn't *really* want to give her a back rub.

It was her last night in the farmhouse. The workmen had finished up yesterday, and the place had aired out and dried today. Tomorrow, they'd move her back into her upstairs apartment.

Having her here had been... nice. They'd shared meals and spent time with Pop and laughed a lot. The house felt fuller, more like it used to feel when Ma was alive and all the Flock was living here. Things would be quieter once Courtney and Bubbles left.

"Should we take a walk, clear out the cobwebs and figure out what's next?" she asked.

"Let's do that. Should we take the dogs?"

Courtney looked down at the floor, where both Chester and Bubbles lay on their sides, sleeping. Chester chose that moment to let out a snore, and Bubbles' feet made running motions, her plume of a tail thumping.

"I think they're sleeping pretty well," Courtney said. "Let's leave them to it."

As they found jackets and hats against the April chill, David psyched himself up. He needed to talk to Courtney. Needed to find out whether there was any chance for them as a couple, despite his limitations. A moonlit spring evening might just be the time to do it.

Or it might be the time to steal a kiss.

They strolled out the driveway and down the lane, walking toward the covered bridge. They discussed timing to start arranging and then stocking shelves, and about the soft launch they planned for just two weeks from now. But they were both tired of the topic, and they soon lapsed into silence.

Ask her now. "So, how's the dating scene going?" he asked her.

She made a face. "You've seen me. I'm home every night."

"Through choice or..."

"I got a call from one of the singles group guys," she said. "We might get together next week."

"You don't sound enthused." He fervently hoped this was true.

She shrugged. "Sometimes I wish I could get what I want without going through the whole dating process. You know?"

It was the perfect opening. "I'm with you there," he said. It was true: he'd dated enough that he'd started to find it boring, and that attitude had probably been apparent to the women he'd gone out with. "Do you ever think about adopting?"

"Instead of trying to find a husband first? I've thought about it." She let out a sigh. "I just really want to have the whole thing, you know. Get married, get pregnant, all of it."

His heart sank. If adoption wasn't an option, then he needed to count himself out as a partner for Courtney.

"What about you?" She glanced over at him, turning the tables. Moonlight shone on her hair. "Do you want kids, a family? Or are you still all about building business empires?"

He forced a laugh. "Like this, you mean?" he asked, waving a hand toward the farm stand.

"This, and all the other stuff you work on. I've seen you on that laptop late at night most nights."

"Yeah, just keeping track of things." He kicked a stone and watched it bounce along the gravel road. "I've had some challenges in the past few years. Changed my perspective on a lot of things."

"What kind of challenges?"

They were approaching the bridge, a

dark hulk against the starry sky. Moonlight sparkled on the stream beneath, and the sound of flowing water eased some of the tension in his shoulders.

Just tell her, he urged himself. "I, uh, I had cancer."

She gasped. "Oh no, David, you're so young! Was it... pretty bad?"

"Bad enough," he said. His stomach tightened. "A rare type of blood cancer."

"Wow." She slowed down beside the bench that overlooked the stream and the bridge. "Do you want to talk about it? How are you doing now?"

At least she hadn't totally freaked out like Christie, one of the two women who'd made him wary of sharing this information. "I'm doing well," he said. "Three years NED. No evidence of disease. Two more years, and I'll be in the clear, or as close as I'll ever be."

"Do you have to go in for scans?"

"Blood tests every six months. I have one in a couple of weeks, and if that's clean, it'll go down to once a year."

She put an arm around him for a quick squeeze, then dropped it and stared across the water. For a moment they just listened to its burbling sound. From the moist ground came the smell of spring, of new growth and rebirth.

David felt lighter, having told her the truth. Her reaction was kind and caring. But she didn't know the whole story. Was she wondering about his health now, even thinking about the fertility implications?

"How did you cope?" she asked. "It must have been tough, being single. Or did you have someone supporting you?"

"You mean a girlfriend? No. I was doing some dating, but that's not an easy way to start a relationship. All of that pretty much fell away."

"Wow, so you had to handle it alone. I'm sorry."

He shook his head. "No. I wasn't alone. I had the Flock. When I got the diagnosis, Jenn flew down. Stone was there for several of my treatments, and Allie came during the summer, when she was out of school."

"I'm so glad you had them."

"They were great. When my treatments got me down, one of them always found a way to visit, and we did video calls most weeks. I couldn't have managed without them, and my faith. The whole ordeal drew me closer to God."

"I'm sure it did," she said, sounding thoughtful. "Wow, I had no idea you were going through all that."

"I swore everyone to secrecy," he said. "In the business world, you have to maintain an illusion that you're Superman, invincible. If people found out I had a cancer diagnosis, they'd be a lot less likely to trust me with their projects and investments."

"I guess that's so." She leaned down, picked up a stick, and started breaking it into pieces. "You said it changed your perspective. What did you mean by that?"

Trust Courtney to see through to the heart of things, to know what was really important. "I used to be driven to succeed, and I still am."

"I'm aware of that," she said in a rueful tone, and he laughed. Courtney had smoothed down local ruffled feathers on several occasions in the past couple of weeks. David was still learning the unspoken etiquette of doing business in a small town.

"I started thinking about other things that mattered more than business success, though," he said. "The way the Flock was there for me mattered way more than my big bank account. I thought about Ma and Pop Abbott, compared them to my biological family... you know, the typical midlife revelation for a workaholic."

She laughed a little. "I guess that's one good outcome from living through something challenging."

David blew out a breath. Should he tell her the rest of it? He felt emotionally drained, both from revealing this huge issue in his past, and from trying not to wrap his arms around her, so kind and compassionate and beautiful in the moonlight. "It's been a process," he said, and didn't want to go further. "Guess what, Pop told me he proposed to Ma here." He pointed at the bridge.

"He *did*?"

"Uh-huh, and they had their first kiss here, too. And apparently, they weren't the only ones."

"It's a real kissing bridge," she said with a sigh. "That's so romantic."

Acting on pure male instinct, he stood and held out a hand. "Want to walk through?"

She looked up at him, her pretty eyes huge, her forehead a little wrinkled. She knew what he was thinking.

"If you'd rather go back, we can." He didn't want to pressure her. "It's up to you." And he shot up a fervent prayer that she would say yes.

17

Courtney looked up at David, his hand outstretched, his eyes dark and intense. It was pretty clear what choice he was offering.

Walk through the bridge, and follow in the footsteps of all the couples whose romances had started here, on this bridge. Or turn around and walk away.

She didn't feel ready. Her stomach was in knots.

But she wanted to be with him, to know him in all kinds of new ways. Wanted to feel those strong arms around her. "Let's go through," she said, meeting his eyes steadily as she stood.

They walked toward the bridge hand in hand. Walked in, and it was like a beautiful world of their own. Moonlight came through the bridge's row of small high windows, making a pattern on the floor. The creaking of the boards beneath them reminded her of how old the structure was, how much it had seen.

When they reached the middle of the bridge, David slowed, then stopped and turned to face her, still holding her hand. With his other hand, he gently stroked the side of her face. "I've wanted to kiss you since I came home," he said, his voice a tone deeper than usual.

"I've... thought about it, too." She looked into his eyes, wanting to memorize this moment, this feeling.

He pulled her closer and wrapped his arms around her.

As his lips brushed over hers. Courtney was swept away. Her heart pounded like the beating of a bird's wings as she inhaled the masculine scent of him. Her breathing quickened.

Then he smiled—she felt it against her lips—and kissed her more deeply.

She felt like she was going to float away, dizzied by the feel of his muscular arms beneath her hands. As his lips teased hers, she clung closer, feeling like she might pass out.

He's good at this. He's done it a lot of times.

He's not going to go for a woman like you.

The negative voices clamored, but she shut them out and slid her arms around him, exploring his strong back. He forked his fingers through her hair, holding her steady while he deepened the kiss.

When he leaned her against the wall of the bridge, his hands sliding down her back, she felt a moment's uneasiness. What was he expecting here? And did he like the way her body felt, or did he find it too soft, too round?

He groaned a little and kissed the side of her neck. "You smell so good," he said. "You're driving me crazy just by being you." He pulled back to look her in the eyes. "Don't worry. I respect you."

His words chased away her fears, and she relaxed into his arms. He was passionate, but his hands didn't roam where they shouldn't. At least for now, he wasn't going to push. He was a gentleman, and she really, really liked that. Really, really liked *him*.

. . .

THE NEXT MORNING passed in a happy blur. Courtney woke up from sweet dreams and wore her prettiest dress to church. She received tons of compliments, plus an invitation for a date from another guy in the singles group, which she happily turned down. The only disappointment was that David wasn't at church. It was the first time he'd missed services since he'd come back to town. He must have had as much trouble sleeping after their kiss as she had.

There were a couple of babies baptized, and Courtney spoke the words of the service with feeling, moved by the tenderness the parents displayed toward their little ones. She loved watching them be carried around the church by the two pastors, one all smiles, one wailing.

Suddenly it hit her like a bolt of lightning: she'd changed.

After her miscarriage, she'd felt bitterly jealous of those who had the good fortune to have healthy babies. Gender reveal posts on social media had been painful; baby showers pure torture.

She'd prayed to heal, and she was amazed to discover that it was happening. Partly because now, she had a ray of hope on her horizon.

David had changed from a relentlessly driven businessman to someone who valued family. That was what she had gotten out of his comments earlier last night. That boded well for the idea that he might want to settle down.

And his wonderful, passionate kiss suggested that he had real feelings for her.

She knew she shouldn't get ahead of herself. One kiss didn't make a relationship.

But they'd been working together closely, even living in the same house for most of the past week. They'd gotten to know each other as adults, way beyond the summer crush they'd shared.

She appreciated that he had told her about his cancer diagnosis. It was just one more thing that suggested he wanted to be real and to be closer.

She'd searched blood cancer online and realized there were lots of different kinds. He'd said his was rare. She was curious and concerned and wanted to ask him more about it.

Back at the farmhouse, she changed into a T-shirt and jeans and packed the clothes and toiletries she had brought over. She planned to clean the apartment above the produce stand before settling back in, knowing that dust from the work downstairs had probably floated up to her apartment. She went down the stairs with Bubbles at her heels.

David came into the kitchen, wearing jeans and a flannel shirt, his hair wet from the shower. Bubbles rushed to greet him.

David rubbed the top of Bubbles' head. "I can help you move out," he said to Courtney without looking at her. His tone was flat.

Was that the way to greet a woman you kissed almost senseless last night? She wanted to read his expression, but he was looking away, busying himself with putting away some dishes from the drainer.

"Look, I think Chester knows Bubbles is leaving," she said. Indeed, the bulldog lay with his big wrinkled head on his paws, watching Bubbles as she paced eagerly, keen to go outside.

David laughed a little but still didn't look at Courtney. "They can visit."

What had changed since last night?

They carried her things out to the car, stepping out of each other's way politely, holding the door for one another. As if they were distant strangers. Then he drove her across the farm to the farm stand.

They carried her things upstairs, the silence between them deafening. When he'd brought up her last suitcase, he stood awkwardly in the middle of her living room. Still not saying anything.

"What's wrong?" she asked finally.

"We need to talk," he said at almost the same moment.

That didn't sound good. "Sure. Want to sit down?" She motioned toward the couch.

"No, I'll be quick," he said.

The pinprick of anxiety inside her grew.

"A relationship between us isn't going to work." He said the words looking out the window, as if there was something fascinating just beyond the rolling hills.

The words didn't compute for a minute, and then they did. "Can I ask why?"

"I just… I just have some issues," he said.

That sounded fake, but she was too hurt to ask him questions.

Instead, her mind raced to put this new information into a familiar framework.

He'd obviously changed his mind about her after kissing her in the moonlight. Maybe the kiss had just been a casual impulse. Maybe, up close and personal, her overweight body had turned him off.

She looked down at her suitcases around her, at Bubbles, sitting alert and looking anxious. She took a deep breath, trying to stay calm. "This feels like a breakup."

"No, just something that can't start up," he said. "I'm going to take off."

"Sure," she said faintly. "You'll forgive me if I don't walk you to the door." She sat down abruptly on the couch.

She listened to his footsteps leaving, his car motor starting up.

She'd been right. Her mother had been right. The mean girls were right.

There would be no wonderful relationship for Courtney, not with David. No babies to baptize. No one to hold her hand.

She slid to the floor and pulled Bubbles close, taking comfort in the love of her dog.

18

David spent the next week working himself mercilessly. He hired two locals and started training them to work part time in the farm stand. He sanded and painted shelves, commissioned signs, brought in their first loads of nonperishable merchandise—honey, crafty stuff, jewelry.

He went back to the farmhouse exhausted every night, fell into bed... and then couldn't sleep.

The problem was Courtney.

Memories of kissing her filled his consciousness, crowding out thoughts of business and success and his future. He'd been overwhelmed with the emotion of it, and it had scared and exhilarated him.

He'd been attracted to women before, of course, sometimes with a strong physical attraction. That had been there with Courtney, so much so that he'd had to work to restrain himself from pushing things too far.

Thank heavens he had.

The real problem had come from his emotional reaction to kissing her. The moment he'd held her in his arms, he hadn't wanted to let her go. Not *ever*. His mind had filled with the thought that he wanted this, every day for the rest of his life. That he wanted to wake up with Courtney and laugh with her, cook meals with her, raise kids with her...

And there was the problem. She wanted to have children. He couldn't provide that. Couldn't provide her most cherished dream, the dream that was central to who she was. Would block it, in fact. If he got into something long term with Courtney, she would never be able to meet the man who was able to father the children she wanted. Courtney was loyal to a fault. She'd never cheat and she'd never initiate a divorce.

She'd just quietly wilt under the weight of her broken dreams.

He couldn't do that to her, so he'd stopped things in their tracks. But that, too, had been painful and difficult. The expression on her face when he'd told her he couldn't get into a relationship with her... it would stick with him, always.

Courtney would move on. Already, she'd gone out on a date with one of the men she'd rode with on the covered bridge outing. Working long hours, he couldn't help but be there when the guy picked her up.

Unlike the last time, though, he hadn't been able to chase after her on the excuse that she was at risk. This guy wasn't some online stranger; he was from the church. They knew each other, knew people in common. She was perfectly safe with him.

Except that he'd seen the way the guy looked at her. It had seemed a little like the way someone looked at an ice cream sundae with double hot fudge. He might be a church friend, but he was a man. He wanted Courtney.

Of course he did. She was an incredibly desirable woman. She would have no trouble at all in finding a good man who would give her the children she dreamed of.

So he worked himself to the bone, focusing on his goal of making the farm stand a huge success.

On Friday afternoon, Courtney came downstairs, Bubbles behind her, and started helping Mrs. Fisher, one of the new workers, spread the "opening soon" banner she was working on. Mrs. Fisher was in her mid-forties, and her kids had recently left the nest. She was salt-of-the-earth, practical, and smart. She'd been a good hire.

Harry, the high school student he'd hired, wasn't quite so polished, but he was strong and eager to earn money. David had put him to work hauling supplies and driving to town to pick up deliveries. Apparently Courtney knew him, too, because she waved to him, called out a hello, and asked after his mom.

David approached, and Harry hurried off to the truck. Good. No slacking off on the job. Mrs. Fisher, too, ducked her head and started filling in the letters she'd sketched out.

Which left him to talk to Courtney. "You

don't have to help," he said. He'd texted her after their pseudo-breakup, telling her they didn't need to work together, that he wanted her to focus on research and to summarize her findings in a series of reports.

"You're killing yourself and you look awful. I was hired to help, I'll work on the banner."

"Would it be all right if I took off early, since Courtney is helping?" Mrs. Fisher asked. "I'm going out to dinner, and I'd love an extra hour to get ready."

It was a precedent he didn't want to set. He opened his mouth to protest, but Courtney spoke before he could. "Isn't it your anniversary tonight?"

"Twenty-five years," Mrs. Fisher said, smiling. "We're actually going away for the weekend."

"Of course," David said gruffly. "Go ahead and take the rest of the afternoon off."

"Thank you!" Mrs. Fisher handed over her materials to Courtney and speed-walked toward her car as if she was afraid he would change his mind.

He was worried that Courtney would start talking about their relationship, or lack thereof, but she stood studying the sign. "It's nice," she said. "Mrs. Fisher is doing a good job, but I think a little color would attract attention. How about if we fill in the words "Farm Market" in green?"

He frowned. "In your reports, you said that neutrals were in style in the latest markets. That's what we were going for."

"True. Mostly neutral is great, but a pop of color would stand out, especially on gray days, which we have a lot of here. If you don't like green lettering, how about a basket of red tomatoes in the corner of the sign?"

"Can you hand-draw it?"

She laughed and shook her head. "No, but Mrs. Fisher can. She was a graphic design major in college. I can fill in the letters, though, and you can put her to work on the artsy touches next week." She picked up a paint can and a brush and looked up at him. "Is that okay?"

"Sure," he said. He brought out more materials and worked beside her, putting together a display table he'd picked up last minute from the unfinished furniture store.

They worked together in a silence that was almost comfortable. At least, *Courtney* seemed comfortable, painting letters and singing along to the country playlist she'd hooked up to a speaker and her phone.

David wasn't nearly so comfortable. Once he'd ascertained that she wasn't going to try to discuss their relationship, perversely, he wanted to. "Did you have a good time on your date last night?"

Her hand went still. She looked over at him, her eyes cool. "Yes, I did. Tom's very nice. Why do you ask?"

"Just making conversation," he said quickly. "Where did you go?" Even as he said it, embarrassment filled him. It wasn't his business and he shouldn't be interested, but something inside him compelled him to keep tabs on her.

"We went to Plain and Simple," she said. "It's an Amish restaurant over by the interstate."

David was relieved. He didn't know the place specifically, but the Amish restaurants he'd been in were brightly lit, family-oriented places. No candlelight and romance possible at one of those.

"And then," she went on, "he'd arranged for us to take a ride in an Amish buggy. It was so cool! For all the years I've lived here, I've never ridden in a buggy."

Okay, David could deal with that. "I'm surprised an Amish family would make that available to outsiders," he said. "Who drove?"

"Oh, Tom did. Apparently, he grew up in an Amish community and knows the lifestyle. He has a really interesting history."

David blew out a sigh. He'd asked for it. Now, he could envision Courtney on a moonlit buggy ride with a "really interesting" guy. No doubt they'd stopped in a covered bridge.

No doubt he'd kissed her.

"You seem to be recovering pretty well from our little breakup," he said.

She studied him again and then spoke. "What else am I going to do, David? Curl up in a ball and cry?"

"No, no—"

"I let myself do that for one night," she said. "You can just ask Bubbles. But I'm stronger than that, and so I moved on." She shrugged and went back to painting.

The high school boy, Harry, pulled into the yard and started unloading supplies.

David went to help him, relieved at having a reason to get away from Courtney, with her strength that apparently let her forget him far better than he could forget her.

She'd acted a little smug about her date, he thought. She was angry, and understandably so. No one liked to be dumped. Not that he and Courtney had been in a real relationship, not a long-term one, but it had still felt like he was dumping her. Still felt like a breakup.

What she didn't understand was that he was doing it for her, for her dreams of a family. She had no idea that he was aching inside, hating the idea of her moving on, longing to hold her again.

While David was putting away the supplies Harry had brought, the young man went over to Courtney and knelt beside her. Was there *any* man who didn't want to be close to her? He started to approach, but she gave him a subtle hand signal and a shake of the head, then continued having an earnest conversation with the boy.

Growling to himself, he went back into the stand and put the rest of the items away. When he came out, Harry was nowhere to be seen, and Courtney had started on the second sign.

"Where's Harry?"

"He went home," she said. "He was pretty tired. I told him you wouldn't mind."

"I *do* mind. I had more for him to do, especially with Mrs. Fisher going home early."

"It's five o'clock," she said. "That's his official quitting time."

David frowned. "He won't get far watching the clock."

Courtney rolled her eyes. "He's a high school kid," she said. "This is a part-time job. Yeah, he can learn from you, become more professional, but it's not going to sink in right away."

"Humph." David went over and continued putting together the display table, turning the Allen wrench with unnecessary force.

"Look," Courtney said. "You need to be nicer to your workers. And you can't expect them to put in extra hours without warning."

"That's what the business world is like," he said.

"That's not business in a farm stand in a small town," she said. "Mrs. Fisher and

Harry have lives. They're not on a career path here. This is a part-time job that was supposed to fit into their lifestyles. That's what you told them, anyway."

David winced. "Were they talking to you about the job? Have I been a jerk of a boss?"

"Yes, you have," she said, sitting back on her knees to look over at him. "In fact, Harry was ready to quit, but I told him I'd talk to you."

David frowned. Harry was basically a good worker, and the best of the four kids he'd interviewed. He didn't want to lose him. "What should I do differently?"

"First, use me more when you need extra work done. I can stand up to you. They can't."

"You don't mind?" he asked. "Because..." He trailed off, not sure how to refer to what had happened between them.

"No, I don't mind," she said. "I mean, yes, you were a jerk to me as well, in a different way. But I have a job to do here and you need to let me do it."

A text came into her phone, and she looked at it.

David immediately went into jealousy

mode. Was it Tom, offering up another moonlit buggy ride?

She texted back, waited for a return text, and texted again. Then she looked over at him. "That was Mrs. Fisher," she said. "She wants to quit, too. Said she talked to her husband about it and they agreed it wasn't worth the stress."

David winced. If one of his workers wanted to quit, he could blame it on them. But if both wanted to quit, the problem was probably him. Which was what Courtney had been saying.

And out here in the country, and in small-town Orchard Springs, there weren't a ton of workers to choose from.

"You're treating them like they're working on the New York Stock Exchange," she said. "Mrs. Fisher says that wasn't what she thought it was going to be, helping to set up a farm stand."

Put like that, it did sound ridiculous. "How do I keep them? I mean… I could give them a raise."

"That's always nice," she said, "but you're already paying them beyond what they could make anywhere else around here."

"I know I am." He'd researched local wages, found them ridiculous, and paid what he thought was fair.

"And yet they still want to quit," she said. "You must be killing them, David."

"I don't know how else to be." Especially when he was trying to keep his mind off kissing the beautiful woman in front of him.

"Just be nice to them," she said. "Maybe order pizza and snacks one day. Tell them when they do a good job. Ask about their families."

"Soft skills," he said, barely restraining himself from rolling his eyes. "Really? That's the answer?"

"Well," she said, "you have to mean it. You can't just fake-ask them one question and then start driving them hard again."

"Soft skills," he said again. "I guess... I'm lacking in them, aren't I?"

"Let's just say you aren't using the right techniques for the culture here," she said. "Plus, you're not used to being the direct supervisor of the worker bees, are you?"

"No," he said. "I've been at the top for a few years, passing down orders for others to execute. But I've been a caddy, for Pete's sake."

"Right, so take yourself back to those days. Think about the customers you liked and those you didn't. Model the nice ones. That's all."

"I'll try. Thanks, I guess."

She smiled. "Just giving you the same kind of tough love you give your workers," she said. "I'm going to finish this sign and then head out." She lifted an eyebrow.

"But you said you'd..." He trailed off. There was no reason the rest of the signage couldn't be done over the weekend, or next week. "That's fine," he said, even as he wondered where she was headed on a Friday night. Probably another date.

She continued painting. "I was testing you," she said. "You passed. Good job." She put the last brushstroke down and wiped her hands. "Let me know if you need any work done this weekend. Otherwise, I'll see you Monday."

"Will do." He watched her head inside, feeling like a fool. His goal had been to get Courtney out of his mind. Instead, she was just filling it more.

19

When Courtney brought Bubbles downstairs the next morning, she was relieved that David's office was empty and he wasn't in the building.

Good. He was a workaholic, and she wouldn't have been at all surprised to find him here on a Saturday morning.

She followed Bubbles outside. The goldendoodle did her business, then romped, ears flying in the breeze.

Courtney was just about to go inside when she saw a car approaching. It stopped, and a woman in a cashmere sweater set and white slacks emerged.

Courtney's heart lurched. "Mom! I wasn't expecting you!"

"It was a last-minute trip. I tried to call, but you don't seem to have reception," she said. "Fortunately, that elderly gentleman told me where to find you."

"Pop Abbott?"

"Yes, the old farmer," she said.

Bubbles had run to Courtney's side and was peering out at Mom as if trying to know whether or not she was friendly. Mom had met Bubbles, but she'd not spent time with the dog.

Courtney waited for an explanation, but one was not forthcoming. Mom surveyed the farm stand. "My goodness, this is... rustic," she said.

"Yes, it is." Courtney tried to adjust her mind to the fact that her mother was suddenly here, in this place where Courtney was creating her new self, or trying to.

"What are you doing, working here so early? Where are you living?"

"I live right upstairs," Courtney said, pointing.

"There?" Mom sounded shocked.

"It's pretty nice, actually," she said.

"Come on in and I'll give you a cup of coffee. You can see the place." *And I can figure out how to survive this visit without wrecking my self-esteem.*

Upstairs, Mom looked around with confusion. "But… it's so small compared to your other house."

"Yep," Courtney said, as she made Mom a cup of coffee. "Creamer?"

"No, thanks." Mom patted her flat stomach. "Watching my figure."

"Right." Courtney brought the black coffee over to her mother and then made herself a cup, defiantly pouring in an extra big dose of creamer.

When she perched on the couch next to her mother, about to probe about why she was in town, Mom spoke first.

"Why are you living here?"

"I get free rent in exchange for working the farm stand," she said. "It may be temporary, or I may stay through the summer. I'm not sure."

"My goodness," Mom said, "you need free rent?"

Courtney restrained an eye roll. Mom might be a little ditzy, but surely she knew

Courtney had been struggling financially, just like she had. "Yes, don't you remember? Jeremy took most of our savings out of our accounts. Left just enough that a judge wouldn't call it fraud. He claimed he needed the money to pay bills we'd accumulated just before the divorce. Which wasn't true, but I didn't want to argue with him."

"Oh, darling, always argue when it comes to money," Mom said. "Would you like to go to lunch at the club?"

"You still belong?" If Mom was curious about Courtney's financial situation, Courtney was also curious about Mom's. Had she really maintained membership in the country club, even though she no longer lived in Orchard Springs?

"I still have connections," Mom corrected. "They're allowing me to come this weekend, as Bitsy Morse's guest."

Which still begged the question of why Mom was even here. It was a can of worms Courtney didn't want to open. "Come look around the farm first," she said.

. . .

An hour later, Courtney and her mother had walked all around the farm. Courtney found herself with a small child's desire to impress the woman who'd raised her. She pointed out all the attractive features: the newly renovated barn, the big vegetable garden being rototilled right now by one of the seasonal employees Jenn and Eddie had hired, the fields marked off for flowers. She talked about the Flock's plan for starting up farm stay visits and wedding photo shoots in addition to the produce stand she and David were working on.

Mom's "hmmm" and "uh-huh" responses showed Courtney that her mother was not all that interested in farm life.

When they walked past the farmhouse, Pop Abbott called out to them from one of the rocking chairs on the wraparound porch. "Come on up and sit a spell," he said, standing to beckon to them.

It would be a relief to have someone else join their uncomfortable tete-a-tete. "Let's take a break with Pop before going to lunch," she urged her mother.

"Okay, I guess." Mom followed Courtney up the steps.

"So you found her," Pop said to Mom. "And I see she's dragged you all around the place. Sit down, and I'll bring out something to drink. Coffee, tea, lemonade?"

"Lemonade, thank you," Courtney said.

"Black coffee for me," Mom said. "Watching my calories."

Was it possible to have PTSD from her teen years of being lectured about weight, diets, and calories? Courtney had been relatively thin back then, but not thin enough to satisfy her mother.

"Here you go," Pop said, coming back out with a tray that held two glasses of lemonade and a steaming mug of coffee. He set their drinks down on the table between their rocking chairs and then took a seat opposite them. "How are you enjoying your visit so far?" he asked Mom.

"Oh, it's lovely to come back, but I'm quite happy living down south. The weather is so much nicer."

Pop nodded. "Every February, I get the urge to pull up stakes and move south. But by April, when it's pretty like this? You can't beat Pennsylvania." He gestured toward the yard in front of them. "Just look at those crocuses coming up, and daffodils about to burst into bloom. And it gets even prettier come May."

"I suppose," Mom said.

Pop's bulldog chose that moment to lumber to his feet. Mom gave a little jump. "Oh! I didn't know there was a dog there. My, he's... big."

Chester approached her, and she retracted her legs, looking alarmed.

"He won't hurt you," Pop said. "Just wants to meet a new friend."

Courtney knew what was really bothering her mother: the twin strands of drool coming from the corners of the bulldog's mouth. "Come here, boy," she said, clapping her hands lightly.

Chester waddled over and plopped down beside Courtney, and she scratched his wrinkled head. "I'm sorry I haven't brought Bubbles to see him in a couple of days," she said to Pop.

"He sure did enjoy having you and Bubbles stay here," Pop said.

Courtney's mother's eyebrows shot almost into her hairline. "You were *staying* here? Doesn't that young man live here too?"

"His name's David, Mom, and yes. Bubbles and I stayed almost a week while the heavy work was being done on the stand." Courtney drained her glass of lemonade.

"Don't you worry," Pop said, his voice soothing as he smiled at her mother. "I chaperoned the young folks. No hanky-panky on my watch."

Mom's eyes widened.

"Where are you ladies headed next?" Pop asked, seeming oblivious to Mom's reaction to his words.

"Lunch at the club," Mom said. She turned to Courtney. "You'll want to change your clothes?"

"Of course, Mom." Courtney would have changed out of her joggers and T-shirt to go anywhere for lunch.

"Let me get you some more lemonade and coffee," Pop said. He stood and walked inside.

"Let's get going," Mom said. "And you shouldn't wear yellow, it washes you out."

"Thanks for that," Courtney said, hearing her tone revert to that of her tween years. Great.

"And those sweats... well, I know you're

trying to conceal the weight you've gained, but wearing loose clothes just emphasizes it."

"I said I was going to change!" Courtney snapped. "You showed up unannounced on Saturday morning, and now you're criticizing my wardrobe choices?"

"You never know who you'll run into," Mom said. "Speaking of which, where is that caddy?"

Courtney closed her eyes for a brief moment, praying for strength. "I don't know where David is. Let's go, okay?" The last thing she wanted was an encounter between her mother and David.

Mom stood.

Courtney went to the screen door. "Hey, Pop, don't bother about the drink refills. We need to get going." The faster they got to lunch, the faster it would be over.

THE CLUB WAS JUST as Courtney remembered. Full of mostly women lunching: some golfers, some groups just here socializing, and some golf widows looking for something interesting to see and do.

Courtney and her mother provided that. Their table was like a receiving line, as women, singly and in groups, and a few men stopped by to say hello.

Courtney was wearing form-fitting black slacks and a preppy sweater at her mother's suggestion. She'd curled her hair and put in earrings, too.

"You look nice," Mom said between visitors. "I'm glad you took my advice. You never know who you'll meet."

"I'm not looking to…" She trailed off, looking more closely at her mother. Mom had redone her lipstick and put on heeled boots before coming in, and she was scanning the room. "Wait a minute. Is there something you're not telling me? About you and Dad?"

Mom twisted her wedding ring around her finger. It interlocked with the huge rock that had been her engagement ring. "I've been thinking, shall we say."

"Thinking about breaking up with Dad?" Courtney bit her lip, concerned. Her parents' marriage had never seemed particularly close. All the same, she didn't want her parents to end their marriage, especially when

Dad was at a low point. "Don't you think you should stand by him?"

"I can't *afford* to stand by him," Mom said impatiently. "Even when he gets out, we'll have nothing. That's not what I signed up for when I married your father."

"Mom! You sound like a gold digger who's hit a dry spell," she said.

"That's... a fairly apt description. But there are other, richer veins of gold all around you. You just have to notice them." She studied a group of men who'd just come in from the golf course with interest.

Courtney glanced over and cringed inwardly. Two older gentlemen and two men closer to Courtney's age were surveying the restaurant. The younger men were the husbands of Sheila and Lexie.

Please, let them not be meeting their wives. "I think those men are married, Mom," she said.

"The older ones, too? Oh, that's Hank Harrington. He *is* married, not that that would stop him. But who's the other older man?"

"I don't know, and we should stop staring." Courtney wanted to sink into the

Italian tile floor. Her mother had obviously made some decisions while she'd been staying with her sister, and to Courtney's mind, they didn't reflect well on her.

"Courtney! It's been so long since we've seen you here!" It was Lexie. Of course. And it looked like Sheila wasn't here to smooth out her sister's behavior.

"Just here with my mom," Courtney said, pasting a fake smile on her face. "Mom, you remember Lexie Silverton, don't you?"

"Oh yes, dear." Mom held out her hand as if Lexie might kiss her ring. "Look at you! You're absolutely lovely. No one would guess you'd had a child."

Lexie preened. "It's not that hard if you work at it," she said. "You look wonderful, too."

"Thank you." Mom hadn't let go of Lexie's hand. "Tell me, who is the older gentleman with your father?"

Courtney kicked her mother under the table. Mom ignored her.

"Mr. Kumar?" Lexie squinted toward the large table where her father, her husband, and Sheila and her husband had settled. The attractive older man was there, too.

"Does he belong to the club?" Mom asked.

"Not yet," Lexie said. "He's visiting from Saudi Arabia, but I think he's considering relocating."

"And what does he do?"

Lexie looked at Mom with curiosity. No doubt Mom's interest in Mr. Kumar would soon be common knowledge. "Something in finance?" Lexie shrugged. "Why? Do you want to meet him?"

"Oh, perhaps some other time," Mom said. "I don't want to interrupt your family time."

"We'll stop over after lunch," Lexie promised, sounding pleased. Getting into the middle of other families' drama was one of her favorite hobbies.

"That would be lovely, dear," Mom said, her voice equally delighted.

Courtney wanted to jump out of her chair, run out the door, and commandeer a golf cart. Anything to take her far, far away from here. "Mom," she said, "you're being a little obvious, aren't you?"

"Sometimes, one has to be," Mom said

airily. "Especially with older men. They need encouragement."

Courtney didn't know what to say to that. When their waiter took their orders, she followed her mother's lead and ordered a grilled chicken salad with dressing on the side.

Should she discuss Mom's behavior with her or let it go? Courtney wasn't usually the one to correct social etiquette. Her mother had done enough of that for both of them.

Now, though, she was feeling enough of an "ick" factor to speak up, whatever the consequences. She prayed for guidance, a matter of a couple of seconds with her eyes closed, then entered the fray. "I don't think you should be meeting men when you're still married to Dad."

Mom shrugged. "I'm just laying some groundwork. Oh, look, there's Kitty Meekerson. My, she's aged." Mom patted her own dyed and coiffed hair.

For the first time, Courtney wondered how her mother had afforded to get her hair done so perfectly. Courtney had resorted to cutting her own hair.

In fact...

Courtney studied her mother more closely. "Did you get a face lift?" she asked bluntly.

Mom smiled. "I did, and I'm glad it took you some time to notice. I hate it when they look unnatural."

"But how did you afford that? You were just talking about being short of money."

"There's such a thing as a payment plan," Mom said, sounding defensive. "And your aunt helped. But obviously, I need to pay it all off as soon as possible. Hence, Mr. Kumar."

Courtney stared. She'd thought she knew her mother, but never in a million years would she have expected this. "You got dolled up and came to Orchard Springs to try to meet someone?"

"Ah, here are our salads." Mom smiled sweetly at the server. "Thank you, dear. These look lovely."

The limp lettuce and dry-looking chicken strips were anything but lovely, but Courtney didn't focus on that. "Why would you come man-hunting in Orchard Springs if you're looking for a sugar daddy? We have farmers here, and men who work at the pretzel factory or run a machine shop. Sure, there are a few wealthier people, like the ones in this room, but they're mostly married. Orchard Springs isn't exactly a haven for single, silver-fox billionaires."

"Ah, but there's where you're wrong," Mom said. "I heard through the grapevine that there are some new enterprises developing in Orchard Springs that are going to draw a better class of people to the region. In fact, I suspect that our Mr. Kumar is an example of that."

Courtney picked up a forkful of salad, and then set down her fork. "So you're moving back to find a man," she said flatly.

"It depends on who I meet while I'm here visiting. I have more than one iron in the fire."

"Sounds like step one would be to divorce my father," Courtney said. "Have you even spoken to him in the past six months?"

Mom nodded. "He calls. We speak on the phone every few weeks, but it's painful. The truth is, with our whole lifestyle swept away, there's just not..." She let out a heavy breath and looked out the floor-to-ceiling windows toward the golf course, blinking rapidly. She cleared her throat. "There's just not much there between us."

Courtney sipped ice water, studying her mother over the rim of her glass. "If you're looking for husband number two on the basis of wealth, aren't you setting yourself up for the exact same thing?" This felt surreal, counseling her mother as she'd counsel one of her girlfriends about to make a bad decision.

"Oh, let's get off this topic. Except... don't look now, but that handsome gentleman is looking our way."

Courtney sighed. "So you're going to go through with meeting Mr. Kumar?"

"Yes," Mom said, "but I'm not talking about him. I'm talking about the dark-haired man who just came in off the golf course. Isn't that David, the former caddy?"

Noooo. Courtney took a subtle glance in the direction her mom had indicated.

Of course, David stood at the bar, chatting with a couple of other golfers. And of course, he spotted them and started over.

20

David scanned the country club dining room as he stood at the bar, chatting idly with the trio he'd golfed with today.

It had been nice to get out on the course. Courtney had been right when she'd called him on his workaholism. He needed to lighten up and relax, and golf was great for that. One of the benefits of caddying here throughout his high school years was that he'd gotten free access to the course during off hours. And caddying with golfers, good and bad, had been a virtual university in the sport. He'd gotten pretty good at it, and he enjoyed it. Not to mention the frequent business deals that took place before, during, or after a golf match.

Like a magnet, his eyes were drawn to Courtney. He was surprised to see her here. He'd thought she'd given up the lifestyle. But maybe that older woman was a friend. Or... yes. It had to be her mother.

Just as he realized that, the older woman smiled and beckoned him over.

"Uh-oh, Gonzalez, you're being summoned," one of his buddies said.

"Who's that, Loretta Chase?" The older member of the group looked in the same direction as David. "Shame what happened to her husband, but she seems to have bounced back."

"Her daughter as well," his buddy Ethan said. "Courtney's a doll. Haven't seen her around much, but I'll keep an eye out now."

"Just don't let your wife catch you."

"Hey, hey, hey, a man can look," Ethan protested.

David put down his glass of soda. "Later," he said to his friends. He straightened his shoulders and walked over.

He was mostly accustomed to environments like this now. In fact, the Orchard

Springs Country Club was significantly smaller and more low-key than the types of places he normally frequented.

But being here, and especially seeing women like Mrs. Chase, cast him right back into his foster-kid, golf-caddy days. Something he really didn't want to relive.

He greeted Mrs. Chase, and then Courtney, who looked worn down. Interesting. He'd detected that she didn't have a good relationship with her mother, and from her expression and demeanor, it had been an accurate guess.

"Sit down, won't you?" Mrs. Chase invited, nudging a chair out from the table.

It would be rude not to join them, and he also was curious. Very curious. Partly about whether Mrs. Chase would insult him, like some of the older members who knew his background tended to do. And partly about what her being here meant for Courtney. She hadn't said anything about expecting her mother for a visit, but then again, he and Courtney weren't exactly on best-friends, confide-everything terms just now.

"So how are you?" Mrs. Chase asked. "I'm impressed that you've done so well."

How did she know he'd done well? "The small-town gossip train may exaggerate things a bit," he said.

"Oh, I think what I've heard is pretty accurate," she said. "Not from this one, though." She patted Courtney's arm. "She's let herself get completely out of touch with the better people in town."

"I think Courtney's been pretty busy," he said. "New apartment, new job. Lots of changes."

Courtney glanced at him but didn't speak.

"Oh, how sweet of you to stand up for her," Mrs. Chase said. She looked speculatively from him to Courtney. Her face broke into a smile, and she gave a little hand-clap. "I've noticed that sometimes men from the Latin countries..." She trailed off as if she was trying to find a tactful way to finish her sentence.

"I was born in Baltimore, but go on," he said, fascinated.

Courtney closed her eyes briefly. Praying for deliverance, maybe?

"I just meant that sometimes Hispanic

men like a different type of figure than is popular here in the US," she said.

David had no idea of what to say. There were so many things wrong with Mrs. Chase's statement. But he didn't want to critique a woman twenty or thirty years his senior.

After the silence had stretched on a little too long, Courtney straightened up and spoke. "I'm sure David doesn't appreciate being lumped together with a whole giant cultural group, if Hispanic is even one group," she said. "That's like saying all white men like tall women, or all Asian men like… I don't know, potatoes!"

David laughed. "Potatoes?"

"Well, it's true," Courtney's mom said, sounding defensive. "I didn't mean to stereotype. I'm *happy* if you like Courtney's style."

"I do like it." He looked at Courtney and was sorry to see the misery in her eyes, sorry he'd laughed. "I need to get going. I'll see you back at the farm." He gave Courtney's shoulder a little squeeze to show his support, but she didn't look up.

"Wonderful to see you," Mrs. Chase said.

"Likewise. Have a good visit." As he

walked away, David was amused that Courtney's mom wanted to match up him and Courtney. He'd welcome the assistance, if he thought it had a chance of working.

He was in the lobby talking to a contractor he'd met earlier that day when Courtney and her mother walked by on the other side of a row of potted palms. "Don't you see, this David could be the solution to all our money problems!" Mrs. Chase was saying.

"Mom, stop." Courtney sounded distressed.

"You need to dress better and wear more makeup. Men are superficial. It's all about how you look."

He heard no answer from Courtney, and the two women headed out the door.

David felt like his world was spinning in an entirely new direction from anything he'd ever expected. Mrs. Chase, who'd only looked down on him in his younger years, now wanted her daughter to improve her looks in order to snare him and gain access to his money.

What neither woman knew was that Courtney didn't need to change her looks at all. She was absolutely perfect as she was, whether wearing a dressy outfit, like now, or old jeans and a T-shirt, like he usually saw her wearing at the farm. And David would willingly give Courtney anything his money could provide, if it would make her life easier.

But none of that mattered, not when he couldn't give her the thing she most desired, a family.

21

"So then," Courtney said to Jenn, as they sat on the bench outside the farm stand, "Mom starts talking about how Hispanic men like a different body type."

Jenn raised an eyebrow. "How did that come up? And what does it even mean?"

"It means they like fat women, which is ridiculous." Courtney let her face drop into her hands. "And I don't know how it came up! Before he came over, she was talking to me about her own odds of finding a billionaire boyfriend to put her back into financial solvency. She was checking out some guy who was with Lexie's family, asking Lexie about him in a not-very-subtle way. Which I'm sure will come back to haunt me."

"Sounds like quite a visit." Jenn patted her arm. "I'm sorry you went through that, but David will understand that it's your mom, not you, with those views."

It was Sunday afternoon, another nice spring day. They were in the final stretch before the farm stand opened next weekend, and Jenn had taken a break from supervising the planting of her flower fields to help with a surprise they were planning for Pop Abbott.

Courtney had tossed and turned for a while last night, reliving those awful moments in the country club. "It would be funny if it weren't so embarrassing," she said.

"Embarrassing because of David?" Jenn asked. When Courtney nodded, she went on. "I still notice a spark when I see you two together," she said. "Is there... anything to report?"

"Other than my mom making a fool of herself and of me? No. Not really." Courtney *could* report that she and David had kissed, but that wasn't news for her to share with David's sister. Let him share it himself, if he wanted to.

Which he almost certainly didn't. Apparently, he wanted to wipe the whole episode out of his memory.

She couldn't tell, though. They'd start to feel connected, working together, and then suddenly he would back off, like he'd remembered he didn't want this, want her, after all.

"Speaking of David..." Jenn trailed off. She was looking down the road.

David was walking toward them, Eddie by his side.

"I need to get David alone and apologize for Mom," Courtney said.

"I can help." Jenn stood and took her husband's hand and drew him into the shed. He went very willingly.

Courtney stood and faced David, sticking her hands into her back pockets. "Hey, look, I'm sorry about my mom. She was being ridiculous with all her comments. I hope she didn't hurt your feelings."

He laughed, shaking his head. "Think

nothing of it. I was surprised, at first, that she was being so friendly. But it's something I've seen before. Money changes people's attitudes. It's funny to me that she likes me now."

His words were perfectly polite, his expression bland. But she felt the distance between them, and whether or not it was a good idea, she wanted to bridge it. "Have you had that happen a lot, people being nice to you because of your money?"

"Yeah. Some."

"Women?"

He nodded. "Goes with the territory. You've probably experienced the same thing."

She shrugged. "With women, we're mostly valued for our looks. When those change, people's attitudes change. Although I will say, my husband was pretty disappointed when all my family money was gone. That, plus my weight gain, kind of destroyed what there was between us."

"Was that all there was between you?"

This was getting into dangerous territory. When she and David had dated years ago—

if you could call their secret relationship dating—she'd ended it in favor of going out with Jeremy, who'd wanted to stick around Orchard Springs, get married, and start a family.

Look how well that had turned out. "I thought we shared the same dreams," she said, "but as it turned out, we didn't. Or his dreams changed."

David straightened. "I hope your luck is better next time," he said, and strode toward his office inside the produce stand.

Courtney looked after him, shaking her head. There it was again. He acted as if he wanted to talk, connect, get close, and then abruptly, he left. Admittedly, this time, the topic had been an awkward one. But he was the one who'd asked for more details about her marriage.

Be careful what you ask for, David, she thought.

And she needed to do the same, because the conversation had made her uncomfortably aware that she was trying for a repeat of the same thing. Trying to find a man who would give her a family, give her the kids she so wanted.

Intellectually, she knew she needed to let go and let God. But her heart didn't quite trust that he'd make it happen, and so here she was in her human fallibility, mucking things up.

What she needed to do, she decided, was to focus on her work and not on David. Not her mother. Not that awkward episode at the country club. She stood and walked into the shed.

They all worked on setting up displays inside the produce stand for a little while. When young Harry arrived, it was time to raise up the signs and put them into place: one on the highway, pointing the way, and the other, bigger one on the outside of the stand.

Once they'd done that, and admired their work, they covered the main sign with a sheet while Jenn went to get Pop.

Jenn and Pop arrived in the golf cart they'd just acquired to help Pop get around. He climbed out and stood, inspecting the building with a wide smile. "Haven't you all done a good job," he said.

"It was David and Courtney who did it,"

Eddie said. "Jenn and I are just here for the glory."

"Well, it's real nice," Pop said. He leaned on Jenn's arm until Eddie brought out a chair for him.

"Are we ready?" Courtney asked.

David was smiling at Pop. "We are," he said.

Then he, Eddie, and Harry whisked the sheet off the sign. "Abbott Farm Market," it said. There was a picture of Ma and Pop Abbott with a flock of chickens and chicks around them, representing the children they'd fostered.

Pop stared at the sign for a long moment, and then he covered his face with his hands.

"Don't you like it?" Courtney asked, worried.

"I think he *really* likes it," Jenn said. She went and stood on one side of Pop, and David knelt on the other side. They both put their arms around the older man whose shoulders shook.

"I *think* this is happy crying," Courtney said to Eddie, who was standing off to the side with her.

"I think so. His family means everything

to him, and this will ensure that the name lives on."

"That makes sense." Pop Abbott had always been dedicated to his wife, his farm, and his foster kids. His home and family.

It was interesting, Courtney thought, that the family in question wasn't a blood one. The Flock was here for him, but they were his foster kids. What an amazing father figure he'd been to them, having this much impact and inspiring this much loyalty even though he and Ma had only parented them during their teen years.

Courtney, her mother, and her father didn't have anywhere near the kind of connection Pop Abbott's family did, even though they shared the same blood.

They brought Pop inside and showed him around, and then at his request, went on with their work while he watched from a chair on the sidelines. It was fun and exciting; their hard work was paying off.

"So, we're really opening next weekend?" Jenn asked. "You're aware it's Easter weekend, right?"

"Right." Courtney and David looked at each other. They'd debated this between themselves over and over. "You explain it," Courtney said.

"We'll do a soft opening on Friday and Saturday. No publicity, just a practice run to make sure we've got our cash systems and our customer service all in good shape. We'll tell a few friends and it'll all be low-key."

Courtney took over the explanation. "We'll be closed on Easter, of course. Throughout the next week, we'll be open but low-key, getting all the kinks out. And then the weekend after Easter will be the big opening, with balloons and bells and whistles."

"Lots of social media marketing," David said, "and we'll have real pictures from the week before, and hopefully a few testimonials."

"Should we invite the Flock?" Jenn asked. "And if so, for which? The soft opening or the main event?"

"Whatever works with Allie's spring break and Stone's…" David trailed off and looked at Jenn. "Stone's schedule, I guess."

"Whenever. Hopefully we can coordinate it so they both come at the same time. I love it when the whole Flock is together." Jenn smiled at David.

"Pop loves it, too," David said. He looked over toward the older man, and his eyes widened. "Pop!"

At the agitation in his tone, they all turned to look at Pop. He was slumped over in the chair, eyes closed.

22

David paced the hospital hallway, berating himself. He should have paid more attention when Pop said he was tired the past couple of days, that he wasn't feeling well. He should have been watching Pop more closely today, instead of being caught up in the final touches of getting the stand ready to open.

Since ambulance service was slow and spotty here, David had driven a half-conscious Pop to the hospital two towns over, Jenn in the back seat with him, someone from 9-1-1 on the phone the whole way. Courtney and Eddie had followed in Eddie's car. Pop had been taken back immediately—

the ER didn't mess with the kind of chest pain Pop was complaining about, especially with an older patient—and Jenn and David, for all intents and purposes Pop's next of kin, had been allowed to stay with him. Once the tests had shown he was stable, they'd transferred him to the Cardiac Care Unit.

Jenn had gone home with Eddie to contact Stone and Allie, and to care for Eddie's daughter Paisley and his mother, along with Bubbles and Chester. That left David and Courtney to stay at the hospital with Pop, who was sleeping in between tests.

Just as Courtney got back from the hospital cafeteria with coffee and a bag containing some kind of snacks, the nurse came out from the CCU. "You're welcome to wait in the cardiac lounge," she said, indicating a quiet, dimly lit room at the end of the hall. "He's stable for now and sleeping, and we should let him get some rest."

"You'll let us know if there are changes?" David asked.

"Of course. I know where you are, and I have your cell phone number if you want to walk around."

"Take mine too, just in case." Courtney

scribbled her number on a scrap of paper and handed it to the nurse.

They went into the lounge, and David chugged coffee and ate a sandwich from the bag Courtney had brought. Several times, he opened up his mouth to share what he was thinking and then closed it again.

They hadn't discussed that weird encounter in the club, beyond Courtney's quick apology. Nor had he mentioned the conversation he'd overheard. It had confirmed that Courtney's mother was a gold digger, but was Courtney?

She'd grown up in luxury, and then had it snatched away. He almost couldn't blame her if she were trying to get it back, but he didn't want to be the victim of that kind of machinations. He'd never gotten that vibe from her before, though.

"Kind of puts things in perspective, doesn't it?" Courtney was nibbling on half a sandwich, unlike David, who'd scarfed a whole one down and started on another.

David nodded. "Yeah. The farm stand is nothing if Pop..." He trailed off. He didn't even want to say the words out loud.

Courtney nodded, understanding. And

certainty washed over David: *this* was what was important. Having someone to share life's ups and downs. Supporting each other in times of trouble. It was what Ma and Pop had had, what Pop missed so intensely in the nine months since Ma had passed on.

They waited in silence for a good hour. Courtney flipped through a magazine and answered a few texts. David leaned his head back and tried to doze—he hadn't slept well last night—and then gave up the effort. He took to pacing in the hall again, until he caught the doctor on duty, who gave a mostly reassuring report.

"He's had a minor heart attack. What we call a non-ST elevation myocardial infarction. It's a partial blockage, not a complete one. He may need an angioplasty or surgery. We'll consult with one of our cardiologists and run some more tests."

"Can I see him now?"

"He's resting, but you can go take a look."

David went toward Pop's room. At the doorway, he took a breath for courage and then went in.

Pop lay in the bed, with oxygen and an IV hooked up. His eyes were closed.

Anyone would look small in a hospital bed, but Pop, normally such a big, tall man, seemed to have shrunk three sizes. His coloring was pale, almost gray, and David had a sudden image of what it would be like to see Pop laid out for burial.

He thought of all the things he hadn't said to Pop, all the things he hadn't done. Oh, sure, he'd thanked Pop for taking him in during his teenage years, multiple times. Especially when Ma was alive, he'd written cards to both of them, expressing in writing what was harder to say out loud.

But there was more to say, more to do. He wanted Pop to experience more joy of the sort he'd had when he'd seen the sign and the new farm stand's progress. He wanted to make a huge success of it, not for his own glory, but to give Pop an awareness that what he'd done, working the farm for all these years, hadn't been in vain.

David had been working hard, but he intended to work harder. He walked over to the bed and put a light hand on Pop's shoulder. "Stay strong, old man," he said in a low voice. "The Flock has your back, and we'll bring Abbott Farm back to thriving. You have my word."

Pop's eyes flickered open. He reached up and touched David's hand, still resting on his shoulder. "I know you'll take care of things," he said. "And Chester. Take care of Chester."

That sounded alarmingly like last wishes and exhortations, and David wasn't having any of that. "We'll take care of Chester and the farm for now, but you've got to come home, strong and well. We all need you. Not just Chester."

"You're a good boy," Pop said, before his eyes closed again.

David took a moment to wipe his eyes and blow his nose before walking briskly out of the room. The nurse wasn't fooled; she put a hand on his arm. "Your father will be okay," she said. "He's a strong man, and we have excellent doctors here at Commonwealth General. Go, get some rest."

"I'll be in the waiting room," he said. "I'll let you know if I leave."

His throat was still tight, so he took a minute to walk around the hospital. He wasn't quite ready to face Courtney.

In the end, though, that wasn't the best

idea. Hospitals didn't hold good memories for him. By the time he went back to the little waiting room, he was working hard to avoid a true flashback.

He came into the waiting room and slumped into a chair.

"What's wrong?" Courtney asked. "Did Pop seem okay?"

"Yeah." David forced himself to sit up straight. "He's resting, and the doc says he's doing well. It's just… he told me to take care of Chester."

She got that, instantly. "Does he think he's not going home?"

"I don't know. We just have to be here for him and do a lot of praying."

"I've been praying." She tilted her head to one side. "You were gone a long time. Did they let you stay in his room all that time?"

"No. Sorry. I walked around a little. Which just took me back to some bad times."

"Someone you love, or your own cancer treatments?"

"My own treatments."

She studied him, eyes steady. "Want to talk about it?"

He didn't. But he had to.

He sucked in a breath and decided to tell her the whole truth. "My cancer treatments had some side effects." *Get it out into the open.* "Unfortunately, I probably won't be able to father children."

Her eyes widened. "Oh, David, I'm so sorry." Her eyes actually filled with tears. "You would be a terrific father. And your kids would be gorgeous."

Her words created an image in his mind: of being in the hospital for the birth to his child. Holding a little dark-haired baby in his arms. Maybe a boy, but a girl would be fine.

To his surprise and dismay, his throat tightened and tears pressed against the back of his eyes, too. He looked away from Courtney's sympathetic face, let his forehead drop into his hand. He subtly wiped away the one tear he'd let fall and then took deep breaths. "Whoa," he said to her, when he'd settled himself. "Wasn't quite aware of how much that diagnosis had affected me, until now."

"I'm sure." She sat for a moment, quiet.

How had his revelation affected *her*, beyond a feeling of sympathy? This revelation had ended two of his previous relationships, and Courtney very much wanted children.

Would she recoil from him in horror, see him as less of a man?

She glanced over at him. "I find hospitals kind of triggering, too, to be honest," she said. "I had a miscarriage with some complications. I was here for several days, recovering from that. It wasn't a happy time."

"I'm sorry." David wasn't quite sure how to deal with that information. He knew miscarriages were major losses, from something that had happened to one of Jenn's friends. "Are you all right now?"

She nodded, forcing a smile. "I'm okay physically. But losing a baby at almost six months was rough."

"Six months! That's... oh man, Courtney, that's awful." He went over and knelt beside her chair. "You must have had all kinds of preparations made." He shook his head, hurting for her. "No wonder you're so intense about having kids."

"Yeah," she said. "Nothing can replace the little girl I lost, but I really do want to have more kids. I obsess about it sometimes."

"That makes sense," he said, an arm awkwardly around her, patting her back.

The room was quiet around them, lit

only by lamps, with soft furniture and wooden tables with magazines and tissue boxes. It was a kind place, where sad and worried people could come to cry or wait for news.

Out in the brightly lit hall, quiet voices and the squeak of rubber-soled shoes denoted medical professionals doing their jobs. An occasional announcement on the intercom drifted in, barely audible.

In here, what he could mostly hear was Courtney sniffling. He got up, grabbed a box of tissues, and brought them to her.

"Thanks," she said, trying to smile, and then blew her nose.

It wasn't elegant, but it was real and understandable.

And it was understandable, too, that she'd want to have more children. And that she'd want them to be biological kids, so she could have the experience of pregnancy with a happier ending.

He wanted that for her, too. He really, really wished he could give it to her. But he couldn't.

And now she knew it.

23

The next morning, David and Jenn walked out of the Cardiac Care Unit together. Jenn had spoken to the cardiologist a little while before. David had missed meeting him by just a few minutes.

"He said he'll be around all morning and will look in on Pop," Jenn told him. "He knows one of the Flock will be around or in the waiting room, and he said he'd check in."

"Stone's flying in?" Stone was the oldest of them, and while he'd had his issues with Pop, he'd taken steps toward reconciliation, and he loved the man.

"Tomorrow," Jenn said. "And Allie texted

that she's going to try to get a flight after school, so she may be in tonight."

They exchanged information about a few farm details. David and Courtney had gone home last night while Jenn and Eddie had taken the night shift. Now, it was time for a changing of the guards.

The hospital's white noise surrounded them, along with the smell of strong cleaning products. It was a sterile environment... sterile and cold. David would be glad to get Pop away from here. Used to being outdoors and controlling his own life, Pop wouldn't heal well in a hospital.

David wanted to prove his worth and his love to Pop, and the way to do that was to make a big success of the farm stand. That would involve working with Courtney. How would that go, now that Courtney knew of his limitations?

"Look," Jenn said, "there's the doctor now, talking to Courtney."

"That's strange." Sure enough, a ginger-haired man in a white coat stood very close to Courtney, talking quietly. His head was inclined toward her, and he reached out and touched her arm lightly.

You're just going to be a supportive friend to her, David told himself. "Guy looks like a close talker," he said to Jenn, proud of how calm his voice sounded.

"I think that's…" Jenn trailed off.

The doctor put an arm around Courtney. She shifted, looking uncomfortable, but didn't step away.

David's adrenaline surged. "I'm gonna go talk to him."

"Wait!" Jenn said, but David ignored her. Because the guy was kind of rubbing Courtney's back now, in a way that was way too familiar for a new acquaintance. David needed to show him that Courtney had friends in the world, looking out for her.

He approached the two of them and stuck out a hand. "David Gonzalez," he said. "Mr. Abbott's son."

"Ah, yes." The doctor dropped his arm from around Courtney and snapped back into professional mode. And he *did* look professional, and spoke that way, too, dropping words David only half understood.

No matter how impressive the guy looked, a man was a man. David saw something extremely unprofessional in the doctor's eyes when they rested on Courtney.

The doctor repeated most of what Jenn had already told David. In addition, he had another important test result back. "We're about ready to schedule him for surgery, either later today or tomorrow." He looked at Courtney. "You'll be here for that?"

"I may be." She glanced from the doctor to David. "I'm sorry. I should have introduced you. David, this is Dr. Jeremy Reese. My, uh, my ex husband."

David's senses reeled.

"Biggest mistake I ever made, letting her go," the doctor said, smiling at Courtney. It was a knowing smile, a smarmy smile. A smile that said he was confident he could get Courtney back if he wanted to.

And it seemed he did want to. From the way he looked at her to the possessive hand he kept putting on her arm, his interest in her was obvious.

The implications crashed into David's consciousness. If this man was Courtney's ex-husband, then he was the father of the child she'd miscarried, the one she'd carried almost to term.

In other words, *he* could father children.

David couldn't.

He blew out a breath and tried to focus on the details around him. The voices of two technicians walking down the hall, laughing. The smell of hospital food as an attendant carried a tray to the CCI unit and went inside. The quiet crying of someone in the waiting room.

David's every instinct told him to put some kind of claim on Courtney. To call her sweetheart, to put a possessive hand on her like the doctor had done, to mention plans they had later. Partly to wipe the confidence off the man's face, and partly to placate his cave man side that kept pounding its chest and yelling "mine."

But if you cared for someone, you cared for their overall well-being, not for your own interests. Maybe it would be in Courtney's best interests to get back together with this undoubtedly fertile, undoubtedly wealthy and successful man.

Oh, David didn't really think it would be a good thing for Courtney. She'd told David her ex didn't like her body, and he seemed to have cleaned her out financially.

And why, if he wanted to get back with her, if he thought divorcing her was a mistake, had he let her go on living in a one-bedroom apartment above a shed? He was a doctor, he could have at least paid some kind of alimony or made a settlement to get her started, couldn't he?

Something was off in this picture, and David didn't know what it was, but he meant to find out. At that point, he'd know whether to try to save Courtney from this cocky doctor, or to nudge her into his arms.

He turned away from the unpleasant sight of Courtney being embraced by her doctor ex, and saw Ronald, Pop's biological son, in earnest conversation with the CCU nurse. A moment later, Ronald walked into the unit.

Uh-oh. Ronald was nothing but trouble.

24

After a very bizarre encounter with her ex, Courtney felt too agitated to go back and sit in the waiting room. David wasn't there, anyway. She checked with a nurse coming out of CCU and was told that David and another man were visiting Pop. Good. She wasn't needed, not immediately, anyway.

She would have liked to go for a walk outside, but the day had turned rainy and cold. So she wandered the hospital corridors, trying to process what had just happened.

Jeremy was working at the hospital here. She'd known that, but she hadn't *known* it. Seeing him in his white coat had evoked powerful memories in her, both of how much she'd cared for him, and of how badly he'd hurt her.

His friendliness had been truly bizarre. The last time she'd seen him, he'd been throwing things into his SUV willy-nilly, moving out of their house. When she'd tried to talk with him about the alarmingly low balances in their joint accounts, he'd refused.

So why had his attitude turned around? Did he really think that their breakup had been a big mistake?

She got on the elevator and hit a random floor button. Only when the elevator door opened did she realize that her choice of floor had been anything but random. She'd come to the maternity unit.

As she stepped off the elevator, the memories washed over her like an ocean wave, so overwhelming that she grabbed the back of a chair beside the elevator and then eased herself down into it.

The floor was busy, just as it had been when she'd had her stay here. Women walking around with big pregnant bellies, nurses in soft-soled shoes talking in encouraging voices. Pictures of babies lining the wall opposite the nurses' station.

She didn't want to intrude on the families here. Most of them were excited and joyous. One woman seemed scared and a nurse was talking earnestly to her.

No doubt one or two families were mired in sadness, as she had been.

In her mind, she nudged at the pain she'd worked so hard to bury. There—*there* was the moment when she'd learned the baby had no heartbeat. Telling Jeremy about it. Going through labor and delivery with her mother present, but not Jeremy. He'd told her he had to be on shift, but the truth, she'd learned later, was that he hadn't been able to handle the experience of watching her give birth to a stillborn baby.

Because it *had* been a baby. A little girl, they'd told her.

Hazy with pain and grief, she'd let her mother manage the details, so she'd never had the chance to hold the baby, name her, let alone have a funeral. Since it had happened a week short of six months, the event was considered a miscarriage, not a birth.

A woman in nurse's scrubs approached

her. "We remember you, sweetie. How are you doing?"

Courtney remembered her too, though not with a lot of clarity. The woman had been kind, and she'd tried to let Courtney make her own choices. "I'm doing well. I always meant to write you a thank-you note. You were lovely to me when I was going through labor and delivery."

The woman patted her shoulder. "It's my job, but I really feel for certain patients. You were one of them. So you're okay?"

"I am." Courtney swallowed hard. "I'm here with a friend whose father is ill. I guess on some level I wanted to revisit the place where... where it all happened."

"Of course you did. Technically, we don't allow visitors who aren't family, but you stay as long as you want to."

As the nurse walked away, the elevator doors opened and Jeremy stepped out. He knelt before her and took her hands. "Someone in the nurses' station called and let me know you were here," he said. He stood and pulled her to her feet, then folded her into a hug. "I'm so sorry, Courtney. For what happened, and for how poorly I handled it."

She inhaled the familiar smell of him and let him hold her, trying to derive comfort from it. Even let a tear drip down onto the shoulder of his white coat. His stethoscope pushed into her chest.

Down the hall, happy voices chimed, then the squall of a newborn.

Courtney's tears overflowed. She sobbed for a long moment in Jeremy's arms, and shockingly, he allowed it. He even got her a tissue from the table and wiped her tears. Then he led her into the elevator. "Let's go down to the lobby," he said. "We can talk without hearing... that."

Dimly, she felt how strange this was. Jeremy, supposedly her hated ex, had his arm around her. Tenderly, slowly, he guided her toward a couch in a deserted corner of the lobby and sat down beside her.

"You went through so much," he was saying. "I'm so, so sorry it happened, and that I wasn't able to be there for you."

They were words she'd really wanted to hear before. Now, they just made her curious. She took a tissue from the table beside them, wiped her face and blew her nose.

"Sorry about that," she said, trying to flash him a smile. Going right back into the pleaser mode that had characterized her role in the marriage.

"You have every right to cry," he said. "I understand that now."

She waited, testing her own feelings. Did his new attitude bring back the love she'd lost for him?

"I was very immature, and what happened was traumatic for me, too. That miscarriage was the ruin of us, but Courtney... we can try again."

That was such a shocking statement that she stared him in the eyes. Was he joking?

He wasn't.

"You were so angry when we divorced," she said slowly. "You emptied our joint accounts. You said hateful things."

He stared down at the carpet in front of them, nodding. "I was wrong. Immature."

"You do know I've been struggling financially?"

"I heard you were living rough," he said.

"But we can put all that in the past. Buy a new home. Start a family."

Jeremy wanted to get back together with her. Was she dreaming?

DAVID STOOD outside Pop's door, hearing the rise and fall of voices in the room as Ronald talked and talked. He was making some kind of case to Pop. David suspected that it had to do with money. That Ronald had come because he was afraid Pop would die and write him out of his will.

Finally, after letting Ronald's lecture go on for another ten minutes, David had had enough. He went inside. Ronald moved to one side, blocking David's view, but it looked like Ronald had been guiding Pop's hand in signing some official-looking document.

David crossed the room in three long strides. "What are you doing?"

"We've had a nice talk. I'll let you rest now, Pop." Ronald whisked the pen from the old man's hand. He stood and gave David an artificial smile. Then he started shuffling through the papers in his hands. "I'll keep the signed copy," he said, "but here. You can see the unsigned one, see what Pop has agreed to in regard to the farm."

He thrust the papers into David's hand, then walked past him toward the door.

David put the papers down. He went to Pop's bed and sat beside him. "You okay?" he asked.

Pop was nodding, barely awake. "Ronald... came," he said. A smile crossed his wrinkled face. "I knew he would come."

David restrained a snort. Ronald hadn't come because he was so caring. He'd come because he wanted something.

"Sorry... sleepy." Pop leaned back against the pillows and closed his eyes.

David sat a moment until Pop's breathing grew regular, then picked up the papers Ronald had handed him and left.

In the waiting room, he tried to scan the legal documents, but they danced and blurred before his eyes. Legalese was bad enough, but when combined with small print and David's dyslexic brain, it was impossible to comprehend.

Where was Courtney? She was the one he needed. She would be able to read the papers and tell him how best to proceed. If not Courtney, then maybe Jenn could come early, or maybe Allie or Stone had arrived.

He searched the area, texted both Courtney and Jenn, and then took the elevator down to the lobby. When he emerged from the elevator, he checked his phone, but there was no response from either woman.

And then he saw why.

On a couch in a corner, Courtney sat talking earnestly to her ex, the good Doctor Reese. David stepped closer and realized they were holding hands.

It felt like a hard kick to the gut. He'd never have believed it, but it sure looked like they were getting back together.

25

Courtney sat listening to Jeremy detail the advantages of their getting back together. Talking about advances in treatments for miscarriages.

It was hard to pay attention, given how fast her thoughts were racing.

Over his shoulder, she watched a mother and child. The little boy was having some kind of tantrum, starting to fuss. The mother was trying to shush him, reason with him.

Poor kid. The hospital was a hard place for little ones, and if someone he cared about was ill, it was no wonder he was acting out.

"It makes all the sense in the world for us to try again," Jeremy was saying when she tuned back in. "And I've changed, but I don't expect you to trust that right away. We can see a counselor, like you wanted to before."

It *did* make sense and seem practical, given how much she wanted to be a stay-at-home mom with a big family. Here was her opportunity to fulfill her dream, being handed to her. Jeremy was saying words she'd dreamed of him saying.

And yet, her heart pulled in another direction: toward David.

David didn't need to change. He was already mature, already kind, already concerned about others. He was a good son to Pop, a good brother to his flock of foster siblings. Successful, but not boastful. Wealthy, but not flashing his money around.

And he cared for her. He'd shown her that in so many ways. Shown her, not just told her, like Jeremy was doing now.

"I've gotten into a new specialty that's very lucrative," Jeremy was saying. "There's really no limit on how much I could make. How much *we* could have. A bigger home, vacations, as many kids as you wanted."

Why wasn't she jumping up and down with delight?

But she knew why she wasn't finding the picture he painted to be an appealing one. It was because the person she'd be doing those wonderful things with was wrong, all wrong.

The little boy behind Jeremy was now screaming.

"Just a minute," he said to her. He stood and walked over to the mother and son.

Wow, maybe he *had* changed, if he was moved to help a struggling mother and child.

He spoke to them briefly and pointed at the exit.

The woman spoke back. The child continued to cry.

Jeremy pointed again and talked intently. The woman started gathering her things.

Jeremy came back and sat beside her again. "Sorry about that. The hospital isn't the place for screaming kids."

Oh. So he hadn't changed.

"Let me tell you about the new specialty I'm adding," he said. "It's bariatrics. The study of obesity. It fits right in with my cardiology."

Courtney stared at him, her heartbeat

seeming to slow although her face felt impossibly hot.

"It's a huge problem in the U.S. There's an industry building up around ways to help, and I want to be a part of that." He took her hands. "I could help you, too. I understand, now, that a lot of women gain weight after miscarrying. There are all kinds of hormonal reasons. It wasn't your fault."

She tried to shake off her sudden feeling of exposure and embarrassment, tried to take in what he was saying. Was it what it sounded like?

"So what I didn't realize before, but I realize now, is that I can help you." He must have read something in her eyes, because he held up a hand, keeping her other hand grasped in his. "If you want. Only if you want. It's totally up to you."

The woman with the child hitched him onto her hip, gathered her purse and diaper bag, and walked out, shooting a glare toward Jeremy. The elevator door pinged. Quiet voices were audible from the information desk.

Jeremy was looking at her with a hopeful expression. "So what do you think? Should we give it a try? At least go on a date to start with? I know it can take time, but I've learned how to woo a woman since—"

"Not a good argument," she interrupted. "I don't want to hear about your wooing of other women."

He held up his hands, palms out. "I needed to sow some wild oats, but that's over with now. I'm ready to be true to you."

"If I fix myself," she said flatly. "If I use your expert help to lose weight."

"Only if you want to. For your own health."

"My health is fine," she said. "And my life is fine. I'm actually much happier now than I was when we were married, and I think it's because of the subtle put-downs I didn't even realize were happening at the time. I'm just starting to realize why I always felt down on myself."

"Hey, now," Jeremy protested. "I may have joked around a little, but I never put you down."

"You may not have intended to," she continued, ignoring him. "Maybe making little comments about what I was wearing or how I looked was just normal to you." She suddenly realized that the put-downs had felt normal to her, too, because she'd grown up with them.

"Give me an example," he challenged. There was an almost indulgent look in his eyes. He didn't think she could come up with one.

"That's easy. You just told me about your specialty in bariatrics and how it could help me lose weight. That's a big, passive-aggressive put-down."

"You weren't listening," he said, a hint of impatience creeping into his voice. "I said it was up to you."

She stood. "It *is* up to me. All of it. And I choose to say, thanks but no thanks. I don't want your help with my weight, and I don't want to get back together."

He reached out and touched her hip. "Not even a date?"

Angry heat rose in her neck. She flicked his hand off her hip. "Not a date, not anything. I'm through with you. But since our house just sold, our lawyers may have some dealings."

His mouth twisted to one side. "They'll deal, all right."

"And if you try to leave me in the poorhouse again," she said, "There are some employees and administrators at this hospital who'd be very interested to hear about it." She spun and walked toward the elevator, not looking back to see his reaction to her words.

She felt strong. She felt independent. And she wanted to see David.

Because suddenly, it had crystalized for her. It wasn't the biological fact of having children that mattered, it was loving them. And that could happen with David, if things ever went that far.

COURTNEY FOUND David in the waiting room, huddled with Jenn over some paperwork.

She refocused on the reason they were in the hospital, then walked over to them. "How's Pop?"

"Doing well." Jenn smiled up at her. "They want to take him in for surgery later today. They're very optimistic. Didn't you think, David?"

For the first time, David's eyes left the document in front of them. He looked up at

Jenn, then glanced at Courtney. "I did think they were optimistic," he said.

There were furrows on his brow that hadn't been there before. Even so, he was the best-looking man she'd ever seen. "Are you okay?" she asked him. "You look like you could use a good meal. Want to go out and grab—"

"Excuse me a minute," he said to Jenn, cutting off Courtney's words. He jerked his head sideways toward the hallway, indicating that she should follow him.

She did, an uneasy feeling creeping over her.

"Look," he said as he faced her. "I need to back off. *We* need to back off, from each other. It would be better if you went on home."

Had she said something wrong? "I just want to be here for you."

He ignored that. "I already asked Jenn if she could find you a ride. She said Eddie's going back and can drive you."

She tried to pull the discussion away from the practicalities and back to the important topic. "You said we need to back off, but we haven't given ourselves a chance to be together. I'm interested in exploring that, though."

"Are you?" he asked cooly. "Well, I'm not."

The words stabbed her, but she pressed on. "Is it because of what you told me before, about the... the results of the cancer? Because we can work around that."

He met her eyes for a brief, vulnerable moment, and then his expression went stone-faced again. "I don't want to discuss that. Look, I just need some distance."

"You don't even want my friendship?" Her voice squeaked on the last word. It was better than outright crying, but only marginally.

"No, I'm fine. I don't need you and your help."

He was so definite. So certain. So cold. She swallowed hard, turned, and rushed toward the elevator, making it inside before she burst into tears.

26

On Thursday, three days after the disastrous time at the hospital with David and Jeremy, Courtney made her way into the Bean Counter Café as if she were reaching a safety buoy after a long, cold swim. Not because of the excellent dark roast coffee, but because two members of her Bible study group were meeting her today.

She'd tried to keep busy, filling Pop's freezer with single-serving meals for when he arrived home from the hospital. His surgery had gone well and he was recovering.

She'd had to hear it through Jenn, because David wasn't speaking to her. Oh, he'd answer if she had a question, or grunt out information needed as they approached the soft opening of the farm stand—tomorrow! —but anything other than business was off limits. He simply ignored her.

She got her coffee and went into the side room that Suzette, the owner, reserved for groups who needed meeting space. Yellow gingham curtains framed the wide windows that lined one wall, letting in morning sunshine. On the walls, paintings of chickens and roosters gave the room a whimsical feel.

Mary, the group leader, was the only person besides Jenn who had been able to meet on short notice. As Courtney approached, Mary smiled and stood, one hand on the big meeting table for balance.

Courtney hugged her gently. Mary had late-stage kidney disease and was so, so thin. And yet she radiated peace.

Courtney really needed some of that peace.

Jenn came in with her own steaming cup of coffee and a plate of cinnamon scones. "Please, eat some of these so I don't eat them all myself," she said.

"They smell great." Courtney forced a smile for her friend. She took a scone and bit off a small corner of it, then set it down on a napkin. She wasn't hungry.

Mary buttered her scone and took a big bite, and Courtney and Jenn smiled at one another. Everyone wanted Mary to gain weight, to get stronger.

"Any new information about Pop?" Courtney asked Jenn.

"He's still recovering well from the surgery. I think they'll send him home tomorrow."

"Wonderful." Mary wiped her hands and smiled at Courtney and Jenn. "When it's an emergency meeting like this, we'd better get right down to business. And remember, what's said in Bible study stays in Bible study. Courtney, what's going on?"

Courtney sucked in a breath. "Thank you both for taking the time to meet. I've really been struggling with something. A couple of things, really."

"Start at the beginning, sweetheart," Mary said.

So she did. She summed up her history with David years ago, and then told them how they'd started working together and enjoying it. How they'd gotten closer, shared more of themselves. Blushing, she admitted that they'd shared a wonderful kiss.

"Ever since then, it's been a push-pull from him. He acts like he cares, and then he pulls away." She glanced at Jenn, then added, "There's a medical issue he told me about in confidence, but it's not a problem for me, and I told him that. But now, suddenly, he's backed off completely. I don't know why, but I'm afraid—" She broke off.

"What are you afraid of, honey?" Mary asked.

"I'm afraid it's my weight," Courtney burst out. "He's never said that. He's been positive about how I look, but what if he was just being kind? I was always curvy, but you might remember that I used to be thinner. Then... well, I had a miscarriage. A very late miscarriage."

"Oh, no!" Jenn reached out and squeezed Courtney's hand. "That must have been so hard."

Courtney swallowed hard. "It was. I kind of spiraled into grief. But the point is, I gained weight afterward, which I've blamed myself for, but apparently, it's common for women to gain weight after a miscarriage."

"I've heard of that," Mary said, nodding. "Why do you think David doesn't like your appearance, given that he's shown you a lot of signs that he's attracted to you?"

She shook her head. "I don't know. It's just, that's what I always come back to. My mom has always been obsessed with appearance and weight, and my ex-husband said my weight was one reason he left me."

Jenn put a hand on Courtney's. "I'm so sorry that happened. Mothers… wow, they can have such an influence on us. And your ex sounds like a jerk."

"He is. And he has a specialty in bariatric medicine now, probably courtesy of me."

Mary reached for her large leather-covered Bible. She pulled it close, as if she found comfort in it. Then she put it down and reached for both of their hands. "Let's ask God to be here with us," she said. "And then we'll find some answers in His word."

After a quick prayer, Mary started flipping through the pages of her Bible. "I've probably highlighted every verse about appearances," she said. "Here's one of my favorites. It's part of Psalm 139:14. 'I praise you because I am fearfully and wonderfully made; your works are wonderful, I know that full well.'" She paused, then read it aloud again, more slowly.

Courtney didn't get the connection, and her confusion must have shown on her face.

"You see, dear, we're all fearfully and wonderfully made by our heavenly father. Whose works are *wonderful.*"

"So that means we're wonderful," Jenn said. "We're made that way."

"Well, sure, but..." Courtney trailed off, not wanting to discount Mary's point.

"What is it, dear?"

"I mean... I can buy that in theory. In fact, I truly believe we're all woven together by God. He thinks we're great, sure. But what about someone who doesn't meet conventional standards of beauty, like me?"

"Or like me?" Mary gave Courtney a strong glance.

Courtney's face heated. "But you *are* wonderful. Everyone can see that."

"And they can see it about you, too, but you have to be open to people's positive opinions. If you're looking for disparagement, you can find it." She flipped backward through her Bible. "Take a look at 1 Samual 16, verse 7. 'The Lord does not look at the things man looks at. Man looks at the outward appearance, but the Lord looks at the heart.'"

"And that's what's important, what we should focus on, I guess," Jenn said. "I believe that. It might be physical attraction that gets people together, but it's what's inside that makes people truly love us. I can see that, just from me and Eddie."

Courtney nodded and tried to take in Mary's wisdom, the Bible's truth. "I see how the heart's the most important thing. I mean, take my mom. She's spent years being concerned about her appearance. And criticizing mine. It would have been better, her life would be richer, if she'd focused that energy on improving her own heart. Communing with God, reading the Bible, going to church. Or even just getting a career or more hobbies. She seems kind of... hollow."

"Exactly," Mary said. "It's easier to see in others than in ourselves, isn't it?"

"It is," Courtney said slowly. "But... man looks at the outward appearance. Well, if I'm going to have the big family I'm looking for, I'd really like to do it with a partner, a husband. But what man is going to marry me, given this?" She gestured at her own body.

Mary and Jenn glanced at each other. "First of all," Jenn said, "you're wrong about yourself. Plenty of men think you're gorgeous, and I happen to know David is one of them. And look at all the hits you got on your dating profile. He's not the only one."

"She's right," Mary said. "Your self-image is way off-kilter, and if that comes from your childhood, you may need to get some counseling about it."

"You could be right," Courtney said. "Because I don't know how to get rid of that voice that says 'don't eat that scone,' and 'wear black, it's thinning,' and 'don't you think you ought to go to the gym?'"

Mary smiled, a little bit sadly. "Our mothers' voices are especially strong," she said. "But if you memorize scripture, you can use it to counter whatever negative thoughts come up. Now, let's take a look at one more verse, from Proverbs 31, verse 30." She waited while they turned to it in their Bibles, then read aloud: "'Charm is deceptive, and beauty is fleeting, but a woman who fears the Lord is to be praised.'"

She placed her hand on the page as if she needed its comfort. "This one's personal to me. I really struggled with losing my looks due to my illness. And just due to age, like everyone else. Beauty is fleeting." As they both rushed in to reassure her, she waved aside their praise. "Thank you, but I see what I see when I look in the mirror. But here's the interesting thing." She looked from Courtney to Jenn and then back again. "My husband has grown more attentive, and more caring, even more passionate," a slight flush stained her cheeks, "as my looks have gone downhill. It's as if he sees what's inside more than what's outside now."

"That's wonderful." Courtney tried to keep a grudging sound out of her voice. It must be nice to have a husband who saw your inner beauty, something Mary had in vast quantities. Courtney aspired to that kind of beauty, the kind that lasted. She was marking pages in her Bible and taking notes, hoping to grow in that regard. "But for those of us who aren't married to such a great guy... well, I guess it's up to chance whether we meet someone like that or not."

She'd thought David might be the type to favor inner beauty, but apparently, he wasn't.

"Ah," Mary said. "It's not up to chance. God has a plan for our lives, for good and not for evil. He wants to give you hope and a future."

"Which was our verse from Jeremiah, a couple of weeks ago," Jenn said. "There's also the one from Proverbs. 'Trust in the Lord with all your heart, and do not rely on your own understanding.' Courtney, he *does* have a plan for you and you have to trust him. Don't lean on what's in your own head. That can be deceitful."

"Like when it tells a gorgeous young woman that she's unattractive," Mary said. "In that case, Courtney, your own understanding is dead wrong."

Courtney felt like she was drinking from a fire hose, taking it all in. "I'm going to memorize as many of these verses as I can. Any other ideas on how to get the bad stuff out of my brain so I can focus on trusting God?"

"Absolutely," Mary said. "Philippians 4,

verses 6 and 7. They've been a roadmap for me through this illness. Maybe they'll help you too."

"Will you read it aloud for us?" Jenn asked, flipping pages and then handing the Bible to Mary.

"Of course," Mary said. "'Do not be anxious about anything, but in everything, by prayer and petition, with thanksgiving, present your requests to God.' That's the formula. And if you read on, you'll see the result you can get: 'And the peace of God, which transcends understanding, will guide your heart and your minds through Christ Jesus.'"

She put her hand flat on the page again, as if absorbing the words into her very skin. "So here's what you do. First, don't be anxious about anything, including meeting some guy to father your children. That's not a good basis for a relationship, anyway, is it?"

"No," Courtney admitted. "It backfired with my husband."

"That's why you broke up with David, way back!" Jenn said, as if a light bulb had gone off over her head. "Jeremy was going to be a doctor, and David wasn't even that keen on college. So Jeremy looked like the better provider and you chose him."

"I did," Courtney said slowly. "I leaned on my own understanding. I got worried that if I wanted a big family, I'd better get going young."

"Anxiety got you nowhere," Jenn said. "Or rather, it got you to the wrong place."

"Exactly," Mary said. "So stop being anxious, and go on to the next step. "'By prayer and petition, with thanksgiving, present your requests to God.'"

"Pray for the perfect man," Jenn said. "I'll pray for that, too."

"As will I," Mary said, and the support warmed Courtney's heart. With these two prayer warriors going to battle for her, success seemed closer. "But remember," Mary went on, "the crucial two words: with thanksgiving. We're not to pray in fear, as if we don't think God's strong enough to do what we need. We're to pray with thanksgiving." She reached for Courtney's hand. "Like this: Father, we thank you for guiding Courtney to the man you've already planned for her to meet. We thank you for everything that's led her to this place, even the things that have been painful." She released Courtney's hand and smiled. "Keep praying like that, and I think you'll feel the peace of God coming over you."

"And a peaceful woman is more attractive than an anxious, worried one," said the ever-practical Jenn.

As they gathered their things, they chatted, and by the time she was in her car, Courtney felt better. Not great, but much better.

She still hurt about David's rejection and Jeremy's implied criticism of her weight. All of it reminding her of her mother's critical attitude.

But she also felt the strength of friendship with these women, and especially, the strength of God.

And she had a plan. She was going to memorize all the verses they'd discussed today and recite them in her head. She was going to pray—with a thankful heart—for the family she so desired.

And she was going to keep reminding herself that God had a plan for her, one that might be different from what her limited human mind could offer.

27

On Easter afternoon, David walked into Pop's kitchen to find the rest of the Flock there, cooking.

They'd all changed into jeans and T-shirts after church, and Allie, who was a bossy little thing, had insisted that the Flock was going to cook Easter dinner together.

David had another agenda: he wanted to refocus on the success of Abbott Farm, and especially the farm stand after its soft opening. And he wanted to un-focus on Courtney.

They'd worked together for the past two days, along with Jenn and Allie and Stone, organizing and evaluating the soft opening, helping customers, hauling supplies, cleaning up messes. It had been incredibly hard for David to see Courtney all day, every day. He couldn't help thinking about her holding hands with her ex-husband. He had to guess that they were back together, or headed in that direction.

The thought of that stabbed his heart. But he felt bad about how he'd treated her, about the look in her eyes when he'd told her to leave the hospital. No matter how hurt he felt, he hated causing her pain.

She hadn't seemed to be suffering the past two days, though, not exactly. She'd mostly seemed okay. Peaceful. Quiet, but that could have been because of the noise that always happened when the Flock was together. Allie and Stone were planning to stay through the hard opening next weekend. Pop's house was crowded, but having three of the Flock there, and Jenn right next door, had been wonderful for all of them.

Courtney had been a little bit on the outside, though Jenn especially had tried to include her. But Courtney didn't seem as upset as he'd expected her to be. She didn't seem nearly as upset as he was. Instead, she had a quiet peace in her eyes that made David want to yell at her.

"Peel these potatoes." Allie handed him a five-pound bag, a vegetable brush, and a peeler. "Don't make a mess."

"I'm not one of your kindergartners," he said mildly. Then he dumped the potatoes into a sink full of water and started scrubbing them. When she came over to inspect his work, he put an arm around her and gave her a little side squeeze. "Glad you're here," he said, meaning it.

"Get used to it," she said. "If I lose my teaching job, I may be back permanently."

"That would be the best." He pulled out a potato and started to peel it.

"It would," Jenn agreed. "You too, Stone. You guys have to get back here permanently."

Stone smiled like he was thinking. He was cooking some vegetable concoction that looked questionable but smelled great. As did the ham baking in the oven.

David liked hearing his foster sisters' laughter, too.

This was what he'd have, going forward. This was his family. Not a wife and kids of his own, but he was luckier than a lot of people, having this home to come back to, having the Flock.

"How's Pop?" he asked when there was a break in the chatter. Pop had been doing well since he'd come home from the hospital, but he hadn't felt up to church today. The last David had seen him, he was resting in the front room.

"Paisley's with him," Jenn said. Paisley was Eddie's daughter, whom Jenn was in the process of adopting. "And Chester, of course. And Eddie too, if he's done chopping firewood."

"And everything's straightened out with Ronald?" he asked. After he'd handed over Ronald's legal papers to Jenn, they'd gone over them together and shared them with Allie and Stone. They were none of them lawyers, but they'd seen what looked like flaws. When David had told them how Ronald had moved Pop's hand over the paper, almost forcing him to sign, Stone and Allie had made discreet inquiries among the hospital staff. An indignant nurse had told them how Ronald had insisted on staying against medical advice, haranguing Pop.

That was enough for the Flock to consult a lawyer, who'd evaluated their case and contacted Ronald. The contract he'd gotten Pop to sign had been nullified.

"He's backed off," Jenn said. "Fortunately."

"For now," Stone said, and they all nodded. "He's determined to ruin our plans for Abbott Farm. Which I'm *not* going to let him do."

"He's nothing if not persistent," Jenn said.

As soon as he finished peeling the potatoes, David dropped them in boiling water, dried his hands, and made his way into the living room. He wanted to check on Pop for himself.

Eddie's daughter Paisley sat cross-legged on the floor beside the couch where Pop was dozing. She had a picture book and appeared to be reading it to Chester. The big bulldog had barely left Pop's side since he came home.

Eddie was reading a magazine in a chair beside the fire. "You guys still okay in there?"

he asked. "I could help, but I figure the Flock needs their time together."

"We've got this." David went back into the kitchen.

There was a lull in the conversation, and David seized the opportunity to talk about the farm stand. He'd analyzed their receipts with the help of a computer model, and he was pretty sure it was going to be successful. He couldn't help bragging a little until Stone called him on it. "We get it, brother," he said. "You're the best businessman of all of us."

That stopped David short. "Am I like that?"

Stone, Allie, and Jenn glanced at each other.

"Yes," Jenn said finally. "Especially when something's bothering you. You go back into being Mr. Competitive-Businessman-Money's-All-That- Matters."

"What happened between you and your old girlfriend?" Allie asked.

Not wanting to answer, he went over and fork-tested the potatoes. Not even close to done.

"You're stalling," Stone said. "What happened?"

David let the fork clatter onto the counter and turned to face them. "I saw her snuggling up with her ex-husband," he said, unable to keep the bitterness out of his voice. "He's a doctor. The cardiologist who worked with Pop, actually."

All eyes were on him now.

"That just stinks," Allie said finally.

"Yeah. Everything happens for a reason, but still." Stone looked up from the cheese he was grating, shaking his head. "Sorry, man."

"Now, just a minute," Jenn said. "Are you sure you saw what you think you saw?"

"Hugging and holding hands, yeah." The words felt dragged out of him.

"You might want to actually ask Courtney. It's hard to imagine her getting back together with that jerk. He treated her terribly."

"You must have misinterpreted the situation." Allie tilted her head to one side, frowning. "I mean, we all saw her working hard the last couple of days. No mention of a boyfriend or a date, and she went upstairs to her apartment when we closed down."

"She's spending today with Mary from

our Bible study and her family, not with her ex," Jenn said.

David leaned back against the counter, facing all of them. "Even if I did misinterpret it, there's no way we can be together."

"Why not?" Allie and Stone said the words at the same time.

David sucked in a breath, let it out slowly. "Because," he said, "she wants a big family, and I'm… not able to provide that. Since the cancer treatments, I'm infertile."

There was shock on all their faces. Jenn came over and hugged him. "I didn't know. I'm so sorry."

Allie came over and joined in their hug, and even Stone clapped him on the shoulder lightly.

The instant sympathy of his brother and sisters soothed an ache deep inside him.

"You know," Allie said, when they all let go of each other, "families aren't only by blood. You guys have been more of a family to me than my blood relatives for most of my life."

"Same," Jenn said, and Stone nodded.

"You have so much to offer a woman,

David," Allie said. "You might not realize it, especially with that little fertility glitch—"

"It's not just a glitch," he said. "It's a big deal." He glanced at Stone for confirmation.

"I get that," Stone said. He was a guy and could understand that fathering kids, biological kids, was important to a man's image of himself. "But Allie's right," Stone continued. "Women love you, and you know how to treat them right. You're not perfect, but none of us are."

"It's your background that makes you insecure." Jenn sounded like a TV psychologist. "The way your parents treated you when you were a child. The dyslexia. But God's bigger than all that, and you're one hundred percent worthy to him."

"And to most women," Allie added. "Especially because you're kind of cute." She punched his arm gently.

"But," Jenn said, "you're going to have to make a case to Courtney, because you've driven her crazy these past few weeks, running hot and cold."

"Flowers and chocolate," Stone advised.

Paisley ran into the kitchen. "Chester needs some biscuits," she said, and then went still when she saw them all standing close together. She took a step backward, eyes curious.

"Come on, honey, let's get him some." Jenn opened the cannister of dog biscuits and held it out to the little girl. "Hug before you leave," she said, and Paisley wrapped her arms around Jenn, then rushed back toward the living room with a handful of treats for the dog.

"Not my blood, but my baby," Jenn said softly. "I'm so happy to be adopting her."

"Which will be finalized soon!" Allie danced over to Jenn and hugged her. "And we need to start planning the celebration!"

As the women went off on that topic, David heated milk and drained the potatoes and thought about what his siblings had said.

It was true what they'd said about blood. That didn't matter as much, as long as you had a family.

And he *did* have a family. They were bustling around him now, talking and laughing. Pop came in to supervise, or pretend to. Eddie helped Paisley set the table, and

Chester roamed the kitchen finding scraps of food they'd dropped.

This was family. And it mattered way more than building new businesses and making money. Mattered even more than making the farm stand a success.

David had some thinking, maybe even some planning, to do.

28

At the end of the official opening day of the farm stand, the Saturday after Easter, Courtney wiped her forehead on her sleeve and twisted and turned her back, flexing her shoulders.

It had been a wild day. Busy in the best kind of way. People who'd visited during the soft-opening stage had returned with family and friends. Curious strangers from nearby towns had seen their social media postings and stopped by.

Even Lexie and Sheila had stopped in with their husbands and kids. Courtney had occupied herself with hugging the little ones. David and Jenn had focused on the two women, showing them various wares, selling them on how wonderful they were. Both Lexie and Sheila had left with bulging shopping bags full of things they probably didn't need.

Most surprising of all, Courtney's mother had shown up, on the arm of a short, portly, well-dressed man Courtney had never seen before. She'd introduced him as George Albrecht, and said they were passing through on their way to visit George's children in Toronto. George looked at her mother fondly and was pleasant to Courtney. Probably most relevant, to Mom at least, he drove a sleek car that made even David whistle in admiration.

Courtney had hugged her mother and whispered a question: "Are you happy?"

"Of course," Mom had said firmly.

Mom had gotten what she wanted. Maybe things would work out. Courtney hoped for the best, for both of them.

Now, their 5:00 closing time had passed and they were still ringing up customers. Allie stood on a wooden crate and let out a loud whistle through her fingers. "Okay, folks, it's closing time. Please take your purchases to the register and Courtney will check you out. We'll be open again on Monday."

They'd debated staying open on Sundays, at least in the afternoon, but for now, they'd agreed that everyone needed a day of rest.

She saw David hauling in crates from their outdoor display, his muscles rippling in his short-sleeved shirt. He glanced in her direction, and she looked away quickly, focusing on the customer in front of her.

David had been confusing her all week. He'd been cold during the soft opening. But something must have changed, because after Easter, he'd spoken to her, brought her coffee, and helped her carry things. He was being attentive now, but why?

Finally, all the customers had driven off. The rest of the Flock—Jenn, Allie, and Stone—were putting things away, cleaning off the counters, counting money.

David came over to where Courtney was picking up a head of lettuce that had ended up on the floor. "Take a walk with me?" he asked.

She looked at him warily. "Why?"

"Need to talk to you," he said. He must

have read the trepidation on her face, because his expression softened. "It's nothing bad, I promise."

"Okay, if you think they can spare us." She snapped her fingers, and Bubbles came running over. She'd take Bubbles along for comfort, in case what he thought wasn't bad was actually painful.

"Do you guys mind if we leave for a few?" David called to his foster siblings.

"Get outta here," Stone said from behind a push broom.

Jenn waved them away. "You two have worked the hardest all along. Take a break. We've got it from here." She gave Courtney a particularly warm smile.

So they walked down the dirt road, away from the farm house and toward the covered bridge. Bubbles trotted beside them, obviously happy to be released from the long leash that had kept her restricted all day.

David didn't leave Courtney waiting. "I'm sorry I said what I did, at the hospital. I was wrong, and I hope you can forgive me."

She glanced over at him, then looked away, out over the fields. "That depends. Why did you go off on me like that?"

He heaved a sigh. “I saw you with your ex in the hospital lobby,” he said. “You were sitting close together. At one point, you were holding hands. I thought you and he were getting back together.”

Her eyes widened. “No way! I’d have to be self-destructive to get back together with Jeremy.”

“That’s what the Flock said. But… he did want to, didn’t he?”

It was Jenn’s turn to sigh. “He did, yeah. He even offered to help me lose weight.”

“What?” David came to a full stop, putting a hand on her arm.

She turned to face him. “Uh-huh. He has a weight-loss specialty now, and he offered to use it to help me. Only if I wanted to.”

David closed his eyes for a brief moment and shook his head. “You’re perfect as you are,” he said. “Did you smack him?”

“I felt like it, but no.” It had taken a lot of thinking and praying, but she’d pretty much gotten over Jeremy’s backhanded offer of togetherness.

They walked on, Bubbles romping beside them. Courtney kicked at a stone and watched it skip ahead on the gravel road. A big magnolia was starting to bloom, and a goldfinch sang from the top of a thistle, twittering and warbling.

She was just wondering if that was it, if David had said all he wanted to say, when he spoke again.

"I know you want a big family. I can't provide you with that, biologically. Is that a deal breaker for you?"

She glanced sideways at him. "What deal would it break?"

He nervous-laughed a little, his dimple showing. "I'm getting ahead of myself. I, well, I'm hoping we can pursue the connection we've been starting to build."

Courtney's heart beat faster, but she tried to stay calm, tried to think. "And by pursue the connection you mean... what? Date? Work together?" They were almost to the covered bridge, and she glanced from it to him. "Kiss?"

"All of that," he said, his steps slowing. "I just want to spend time with you, to get to know you better, understand you, help you. I want to *be* with you." He hesitated. "But, like I said, I have a pretty serious limitation. And knowing what I do about you, knowing about your losing a baby, I don't want to take away your opportunity to have a child, biologically."

Courtney looked ahead at the bridge, then down at the rushing water beneath it, roaring with the waters of spring. She took deep breaths, trying to calm down enough to figure out what she felt.

Her overwhelming sensation was joy—joy at David's sincerity, at his desire to spend time with her. But she had to be careful, think it through.

She'd wanted to have a large family ever since she'd been a lonely only child. And that desire had intensified when she'd lost the baby.

But maybe that desire wasn't of God. Maybe it was her own will talking. She loved kids so much that she thought that had to be part of His plan for her life. But maybe he had another way of making that happen, a way that didn't involve her carrying a baby in her body. Or maybe, with medical advances, there was a way for her to do that even if David couldn't be the biological father.

Bubbles ran over with a stick in her mouth, and David wrestled it from her and threw it far for her to chase. The dog that had once been so terrified of him now idolized him.

Bubbles was a shelter dog, and Courtney loved her way beyond what was reasonable.

For that matter, she loved the kids she'd cared for, Gavin and Sierra and the others who'd stopped in today.

There was no reason she couldn't love foster or adoptive kids just as much.

"Families aren't only about blood relationships," she said slowly. "Look at you and your Flock. You're true brothers and sisters. So… no, it's not a deal breaker."

Relief washed over his face. He tugged her to the bench that faced the stream and the bridge. "The truth is," he said, "I want to marry you."

All the air rushed out of Courtney's lungs. "What?" she squawked.

"I know, I know," he said. "I'm getting ahead of myself again, but I want you to know I'm sincere, and I'm not going to go cold or back off again. So… " He pulled a box out of his pocket and kept talking. "I want to give you the world, Courtney. You deserve it. Foster kids, adoptive kids, a farmhouse of your own, dogs and chickens…"

"Chickens?" she said, just to say something. One word was all she could manage.

"Yes, chickens." He took her hand and squeezed it. "If you want them. You're so kind and caring and resilient and smart. You've had some tough experiences, but they've made you stronger, not bitter. I don't know if you'll ever come to feel the way I do, but if you did, I'd be the luckiest man on earth." He sank to his knees in front of her and handed her the box. "I'm not even going to ask the question, because I don't want to pressure you into answering. I just want you to know that I love you, and I'll always love you."

Tears rose and overflowed as she stared at his earnest and very handsome face. This was everything she hadn't known she wanted.

He took the box from her hand, opened it, and held it up.

She gasped. Inside was the biggest diamond she'd ever seen. Ridiculously big, way too much for a country girl.

But wouldn't Lexie and Sheila—and her mother—be impressed?

"You... it's beautiful but... you didn't need..."

"You deserve it and you're worth it." He slid it onto her finger. "Just try it on. I'll have it sized for when the right time comes to do a real proposal. And I don't want to do that until I've gained your trust and, well, your love."

But when he slid the ring onto her finger, it fit perfectly.

"Walk through the bridge?" he asked.

"Okay..." She felt almost faint, but it was with happiness. "That diamond is way too big," she said as they walked toward the bridge, hand in hand.

"I know. I'll get you a smaller one for everyday." He said it carelessly.

Hmmm. There could be benefits to marrying a millionaire.

"I know it'll take time for you to trust me. I've been a jerk."

"It will take time, for sure." Her heart was singing though.

Inside the bridge, he turned to her. Sunlight slanted down through the windows, catching dust motes that danced in the air. "Do I have a chance?" he asked.

"More than a chance," she said. She leaned forward and kissed him gently.

He pulled her to him and kissed her, so tenderly and thoroughly that she lost track of time.

She'd said she needed time, but she already knew. She'd have her large family, though it would be different from what she'd thought when she'd married Jeremy all those years ago. Not a suburban home in a cookie-cutter neighborhood, but a big old farmhouse with a wraparound porch, like Pop's. On a farm, where kids who needed it could get a fresh start, as David and his siblings had.

She felt the strength of David's arms around her, and the power that came from letting God's will be done. She offered up a wordless prayer of thanks.

EPILOGUE

They were so busy with the farm stand that Courtney regretted agreeing to help Jenn host a Memorial Day picnic at Abbott Farm. But as soon as she dragged herself over to where Jenn and Mary and Mary's husband were arranging tables for the picnic, right beside the flower field blooming with red poppies, she got excited about the event. As guests trickled in, she got even happier.

David had insisted on having the food catered, and it was delicious. They couldn't help talking a little about the future of Abbott Farm, what the next steps would be, but

Stone soon turned the talk in a different direction.

"When are the two of you going to set a date?" he asked David.

Courtney and David exchanged glances. "We're talking about it," Courtney said.

David's foster siblings were immediately excited, talking over each other. Jenn finally prevailed, turning to David. "You know, when you get married, you get to open that letter Ma saved for you," she said.

"I *am* curious." He turned to Courtney. "When Jenn was cleaning out the house, she found letters Mom had saved from each of us, talking about what we wanted from the future. We're not supposed to open them until our wedding day, so..." He raised his eyebrows.

"Soon," she said. She just wanted to savor this feeling of being newly engaged a little longer. She changed the subject. "So, what's everyone doing for the summer?"

Pop, sitting back in one of the loungers they'd brought out, overheard the question. "I plan to stay right here on the farm and watch my kids make it shine again," he said. He looked healthy and happy.

Eddie's mom, in the lounger beside his, agreed. "I'm going to play with my granddaughter while she's still young enough to think that's fun," she said. She smiled fondly at Paisley, who'd just chased Chester and Bubbles toward the food area. All three plopped down.

In the distance, sunlight brightened the sign above the farm stand. "I'm glad we closed early," she admitted.

"Me, too," David said, coming to sit beside her on a picnic bench and taking her hand.

They'd been incredibly busy, but they'd still found time to be together. It was fun to get to know each other again. All Courtney's running around at the farm stand might have made her lose weight, but on the frequent occasions David took her out for dinner, he encouraged her to order dessert, to have another piece of bread with fancy butter. It was worlds different from dining with Jeremy, who'd watched every bite she ate.

A number of the workers they'd hired had shown up at the picnic. Mrs. Fisher had brought her husband, and the high school student, Harry, was sitting with them.

A new worker, the woman they'd hired to start a farm-stay program this summer, seemed a little standoffish, and her eight-year-old daughter was downright rude. Too bad, since they'd be living on the farm for the summer. But Courtney couldn't let herself worry about that, not today.

A wiry older woman with spikey silver hair sat down beside Pop and started talking to him, leaning close. Courtney saw the Flock watching with curiosity and interest. Pop just might have some new experiences in front of him.

The one cloud on their horizon was Ronald. He'd shown up at the farm again a couple of weeks ago, this time acting sweet toward Pop, convincing the older man that he wanted to help and be close. After David and Eddie had taken him aside for a stern talk, he'd left, but with the threat that he'd soon return. So they had to stay ready.

Eddie tapped on his water glass, getting everyone's attention. "Jenn and I have an announcement to make." He looked at Jenn.

"I'm going to have a baby," she said, her eyes excited, cheeks pink.

Courtney's stomach gave a little lurch.

As everyone cheered, David looked at Courtney and squeezed her hand. "This is hard for you," he said.

It was, but she was determined to celebrate her friends' happiness, not be jealous of it. She caught Jenn's eye and blew her a kiss, and Jenn rushed over and gave her a quick hug.

As everyone sank back into their ordinary conversations, David spoke quietly to Courtney. "You know," he said, "we can start our family too. Anytime you like." He kissed her hand.

They'd talked a lot about how to approach that, and were leaning toward doing foster care, at least at first.

"I know," she said, glancing down at the engagement ring she wore all the time now. "Soon."

A few minutes later, a loud exclamation had them both turning to see what was going on. It was Stone. He got up so quickly that he tipped over his chair. "Who invited *her*?" he said, directing his question to Courtney and Jenn, as he gestured toward the other guests. His voice was low and angry.

He didn't wait for an answer, but turned and stormed into the farmhouse.

Courtney looked around the gathering, wondering who Stone had been referring to.

"Let him go," David said. "He'll get over it."

"Do you know what's going on?"

"I have a guess, but..."

"It's Stone's story to tell," Courtney said. She met David's eyes, and suddenly, she knew exactly what she wanted. "Let's get married this summer," she said.

He whooped and stood and pulled her out of her chair, spinning her around in a jig that had everyone laughing.

Courtney was the happiest she'd ever been. But looking at her husband-to-be's face, she knew that even more happiness was in store for them. "I can't wait to start our lives together," she said.

He wrapped her in his arms. "Me, either. How about we get married *before* summer? Like, next week?" He smiled at her with one eyebrow raised. He meant it. And why wait, after all?

Feeling warm and loved and excited, she kissed him. Springtime had turned out to be perfect for falling in love. It might just be the perfect time to get married, too.

TURN THE PAGE TO LEARN MORE ABOUT *A SECRET SUMMER CHILD,* BOOK THREE IN THE *HOME TO ORCHARD SPRINGS* SERIES.

A SECRET SUMMER CHILD

HOME TO ORCHARD SPRINGS

A struggling single mom must share a home with the former bad boy who doesn't know he's the father of her child...

When Elena Meeker moves to Abbott Farm for the summer, she hopes the fresh air, sunshine, and small-town kindness will help her bullied eight-year-old daughter get happy again. Elena's desperate enough that she's considering telling her high school boyfriend, Stone Smith, that he's the father of her child. If he comes to visit the farm where he grew up, she'll try to get to know him again. She'll make nice. That way, she can figure out whether learning the truth about Stone would help or hurt her daughter's fragile psyche.

But Stone does more than visit: he moves into the other side of the bunkhouse where she and her daughter are living. Turns out her summer job of helping Pop Abbott and his flock start a farm-stay program will require coordinating with Stone, who's slated to run the organic farm startup. If they want to help their struggling daughter, they must deal with the feelings that still spark between them... and the differences that tore them apart.

Order A Secret Summer Child today!

Turn the page for a sneak peek of *Wintertime Secrets*, Book One in the *Home to Orchard Springs* series.

WINTERTIME SECRETS
CHAPTER ONE

Home was a light in the window.

And after a long flight from LA, then a three-hour drive through Pennsylvania's farm country—on top of everything that had happened in the past week—Jennifer Ridge needed home.

She climbed from her rental car and stretched, then shivered in her lightweight jacket. Wind swept across the fields, blowing powdery snow onto the porch where she'd spent so many hours as a troubled teen.

She tapped on the farmhouse door. When there was no response, she tried the doorknob, found it unlocked, and stepped inside.

Pop Abbott, still a large, tall man though he was now in his eighties, emerged from the kitchen and hurried toward her. His twelve-year-old bulldog, Chester, stood in the middle of the entryway, barking.

In the dim light, Pop caught his foot on a stack of something. His arms flailed as he tried to catch himself. Then he went down with an "oof," landing heavily on his back.

"Pop!" Jenn rushed forward, dropping her purse and overnight bag and kneeling beside the gray-haired man. "Are you okay?"

"Fine," he rasped, but he clearly wasn't. He looked around as if he'd never seen the entryway of his own farmhouse.

She checked for blood but didn't see any. Chester continued barking until Jenn held out a hand to the burly dog. He sniffed, then licked her fingers in passing as he made his way over to Pop. He snuffled at his owner and then looked at Jenn, as if she would know what to do.

"Where does it hurt?" she asked Pop.

"Who are you?" he asked.

That stung. Had he hit his head? "It's me, Jenn," she said. "Your foster daughter. Mini-Jenny, remember?"

He smiled, his face creasing into a million wrinkles. "Of course I do. How old are you now?"

"I'm twenty-eight." He couldn't be expected to keep track of her age, along with those of all the other kids they'd cared for.

"Ma will be so glad to see you."

A cold hand clutched Jenn's heart. Ma—Kimmie Jean—had been gone for eight months. Was Pop really that confused, when he'd been fine at the funeral? Had he had a stroke, suffered a head injury? He wasn't moving.

The phone call that had gotten her here, from a church friend of Pop's, echoed in her head. *He's not himself. Not recovering from the loss of Kimmie Jean. Staying isolated.*

She thanked the Lord that she'd been able to drop everything and come. Or rather, she'd been the only one, among the foster siblings with whom she'd spent her teen years, who had nothing to drop, having lost her boyfriend, her job, and her so-called best friend, all on the same day.

"Pop, come on. Let's get you up and into a chair." She slid an arm under Pop's shoulders. Lifted, or tried to.

He didn't budge.

"You have to help me here, Pop," she said. "On a count of three. One, two, three."

Pop gamely tried to swing himself up, but he didn't have near the strength he used to have. Clearly, he hadn't been doing crunches at the gym any more than Jenn had. They were a pair.

"Let's try again," she said, but despite two more efforts, it was impossible to get Pop to his feet. His eyes were fluttering shut, and though he insisted he didn't hurt anywhere, she was worried.

"I'm going to have to call 9-1-1," she said.

Pop's eyes shot open, full of indignation. "No! I'm not having news of me falling getting out all over Orchard Springs. People will think I'm old."

Despite her concern, Jenn smiled. "We have to do something," she told him. "You can't lie here all night. Floor's too hard," she added, knocking on the wide oak boards, trying to make a joke.

He waved a hand toward the kitchen. "Call Eddie," he said. "Phone number's on the fridge. He helps me out sometimes."

"Eddie Wilson?" The name made Jenn

flush warm and cold. "Does he still live next door?"

Pop nodded and closed his eyes.

Pulling one of Ma's hand-crocheted afghans from the back of the couch, she tucked it around Pop, then lifted his head to place a throw pillow underneath. Chester promptly lay down beside his master. He would keep watch.

Jenn made her way through the dimly lit hallway to the farmhouse kitchen. No wonder Pop had tripped. She nearly went down herself on a stack of old magazines.

She flipped on the light and recoiled.

Dirty dishes filled every surface. A pan on the stove held crusted *something,* it wasn't clear what. The table was littered with crumbs, and a half-eaten peanut butter sandwich sat on a paper plate in front of Pop's chair.

She leaned forward and looked at it more closely, and her stomach twisted. Gray-green mold spotted the bread.

Oh, she'd definitely have to do a conference call with her foster siblings, and soon. Right now, though, she needed to get someone to help her get Pop into bed, and if it had to be Eddie Wilson...

She swallowed hard, then searched the front of the fridge, littered with children's drawings from years ago mingled in with workers' business cards and a takeout menu from the Chinese restaurant in town.

Then she saw it: a page from one of Ma's flowered notepads with that big, sweeping handwriting. She'd looked at that writing every day for months, reading and rereading the letter he'd sent her.

She shoved that memory out of her mind and pulled the note off the fridge.

"Eddie Wilson. 814-222-9181. Call anytime."

It was late to call, but what else could she do? She pulled out her phone and punched in Eddie's number.

TEN MINUTES after receiving the phone call, Eddie Wilson knelt beside his elderly neighbor. He held a hand to the man's forehead—not feverish—and then put a finger on his wrist. Pulse rate seemed normal.

Pop Abbott's eyes fluttered open and he

smiled. "I'm okay," he said. "Just can't quite get myself up."

"I'll help." He slid an arm behind Pop's shoulders and carefully lifted him to a sitting position, then to his feet. Pop was a big, tall man, and though he'd lost some muscle tone in recent years, he was still plenty heavy.

Jenn steadied him from the other side. "Do you want to sit, Pop? Or lie down?"

While the older man considered the question, Eddie took a sideways glance at Jenn. He hadn't seen her in years, except from a distance at Ma Abbott's funeral.

She was as pretty as he remembered, maybe more so. Slim but with curves, blonde hair past her shoulders, and big brown eyes. Still almost as tiny as she'd been in her teens. No wonder she hadn't been able to get Pop off the ground by herself.

Vivid memories flashed into his mind. Of Jenn beckoning him over to join in some game she and her foster siblings were playing, of her handing him a flower she'd picked—she loved flowers even back then. He remembered her smiles and light touches, almost like she'd had a crush on him, the solitary older boy from next door.

It had been obvious enough that his friends teasingly suggested he ask her out. But she'd been six years his junior, way too young at the time.

Later, he'd put his toe in those waters and discovered he liked them too well. He'd forced himself to pull away.

He'd made promises, promises he hadn't kept. Did she remember that? Did she resent it?

"Think I'll go to bed," Pop said, interrupting Eddie's memories.

"Good idea," Jenn said. Then, nodding toward the back of the house, she added to Eddie, "It's this way. But you probably already know that."

"It's about time one of you came back to help Pop," he grouched, trying to hide his confusing feelings. He put one hand under Pop's elbow, the other arm around his shoulders.

Jenn glared at Eddie across the older man's barrel-shaped chest. "It would have been nice to be told what was going on by some of you so-called friendly neighbors." Her voice was snippy. "Friendly Neighbors" was the slogan of Orchard Springs, painted on the sign at the edge of town. Without exception, the Abbotts' foster kids had made fun of the concept.

Most of them ended up loving it here, but that was because of the kind farm couple who'd helped them through adolescence. Not so much because of the townspeople, who could be judgmental about the new, trendily dressed, mouthy teens Ma and Pop welcomed in from the city.

Eddie hadn't minded the newcomers. As an only child, living on a rural route half a mile out of town, he'd appreciated the company.

He'd appreciated Pop, too. The man had been kinder and gentler than Eddie's strict father.

Eddie and Jenn helped Pop through the cluttered house, sidestepping boxes and pushing aside stacks of books and magazines. Soon they reached the first-floor bedroom, where they eased Pop onto the double bed. He took a breath and, with Eddie's help, swung his feet up. Jenn removed his slippers, and he settled in with a sigh.

Jenn pulled the sheets and comforter over him, tucking him in like she cared. Well, she probably did care, somewhat. She'd come, finally, after all. "Do you need anything?" she asked Pop. "Water, aspirin? It didn't look like you hit your head, but—"

Pop lifted up a minute, looking around the room. "Chester?"

The bulldog who was Pop's constant companion seemed to hear his name. He came through the door, eyed the bed, and then flung himself up to the upholstered bench at the foot of it. He sat and panted for a moment, his tongue hanging out, then jumped the rest of the way up and settled beside Pop's feet.

Pop smiled and lay back against the pillows, then reached out and squeezed Jenn's hand. "Glad you came home, honey," he said. Then he looked at Eddie. "Thank you, neighbor." He gave a big sigh and closed his eyes.

"We'll talk tomorrow," Jenn said, patting his arm. Then she stood and followed Eddie out of the bedroom.

In the kitchen, she turned to him. "Thank you for coming over so late. Sorry I got cranky."

"No problem, but I should get home. To..." He paused. His daughter Paisley was the last person he wanted to tell Jenn about, and besides, she was long asleep. He hoped. "To Mom," he said finally.

One eyebrow lifted. "Is she okay?"

"Yes." He didn't elaborate, and he saw the questions in her eyes. A thirty-four-year-old man still living with his mother... yeah. It was one reason he rarely dated: the skeptical expression that so often crossed women's faces when they heard about his living situation.

Jenn moved across the kitchen, stepping over trash that had overflowed from the tall wastebasket. She looked at the sink full of dishes. "I didn't know conditions had gotten so bad here. What's going on with Pop? Do you think he's sick, or depressed? It's not dementia, is it?"

"I don't know. He seems sharp enough when I talk to him." Eddie helped Pop as much as he could, bringing over groceries and plowing the long driveway, but he hadn't been invited inside in months. Now, he understood why. Pop must have been embarrassed about the condition of the house.

"He needs more than I can give in a few days," Jenn said.

"Looks like it." Eddie eased toward the door. "But I'm sure you've got your life to get back to."

She raised an eyebrow but didn't comment on his assumption. Her expression grew thoughtful. "Someone's going to have to stay for a bit. We'll figure something out."

"We, meaning who?"

"The Flock," she said. "Me, David, Stone, and Allie."

"Not Yolanda?" he asked, before he could stop himself.

Yolanda was Jenn's older biological sister, and she'd come to Ma and Pop's farm to live as a teenager, briefly, a couple of years after Jenn had. But two more different people could scarcely be imagined. Yolanda had wreaked some havoc in the short time she'd lived in Orchard Springs.

Wreaked some havoc in Eddie's life, too, afterwards.

Jenn shook her head, the corners of her mouth turning down. "No. We've lost touch."

She sounded sad, but Eddie wasn't. He was relieved.

Yolanda wouldn't be coming back, and although for Pop's sake, he hoped Jenn would get some of the other foster kids to come and help, he prayed it wouldn't be Jenn who stayed.

No matter how pretty and caring she was, there was a secret she could never, never find out.

ABOUT THE AUTHOR

Lee Tobin McClain is the New York Times bestselling author of more than forty novels. A professor-turned-writer, she finds inspiration in her beautiful and brilliant daughter, her goofy goldendoodle, and her aptly named cat, Trouble.

Connect with Lee and join her newsletter:
www.leetobinmcclain.com

COPYRIGHT PAGE

Lee Tobin McClain: McClain@setonhill.edu
www.leetobinmcclain.com

جھیل کنارہ کنکر

نازیہ کنول نازی

القریش پبلی کیشنز

سرکلر روڈ چوک اردو بازار لاہور

فون: 042-37652546, 37668958

www.alquraish.com email: info@alquraish.com

بہترین کتابیں۔۔۔۔۔۔۔

جدید انداز اور معیار کے ساتھ

باہتمام محمد علی قریشی

باراوّل 2014ء

مطبع .... نیئر اسد پریس لاہور

کمپوزنگ .... القریش گرافکس

قیمت .... -/600روپے

انتساب

لال مسجد کے ان پاکیزہ پھولوں اور کلیوں کے نام.....
جو راہِ خدا میں ظلم کی آندھی کی بھینٹ چڑھ کر
ہمیشہ کے لئے امر ہو گئے۔

پیش لفظ

جب میں نے یہ ناول لکھنا شروع کیا تو ذہن میں کوئی خاص سوچ یا مقصد نہیں تھا۔ بس ادارے نے کہا کہ آپ کا ناول ہونا چاہئے۔ میں نے دو اقساط لکھ کر بھجوا دیں۔ مگر اس وقت مجھے بالکل اندازہ نہیں تھا کہ میں کیا لکھنے والی ہوں۔ مجھے یاد ہے میں اس ناول کی تیسری قسط لکھ رہی تھی جب ایک رات اللہ رب العزت کی پاک ذات کی طرف سے مجھے خواب میں کچھ ایسے مناظر دکھائے گئے کہ جن کو دیکھنے کے بعد میری روح لرز اُٹھی۔ پاکستان کی قابل فخر بیٹی عافیہ صدیقی اور تمام اُمت مسلمہ پر ہونے والے مظالم جو کبھی پردہ سکرین پر نہیں آسکے، میں نے خواب میں خود اپنی آنکھوں سے دیکھے۔ اور بعد میں ایسے ہی بہیمانہ واقعات کی مختلف باوثوق حوالوں اور کتابوں نے تصدیق بھی کر دی۔

اس خواب میں مجھ سے پوچھا گیا کہ اللہ نے مجھے لکھنے کی صلاحیت اور ہنر بخشا مگر میں نے اس صلاحیت اور ہنر سے آج تک جو بھی لکھا، اپنے لئے لکھا۔ اپنی شہرت، پیسوں اور کامیابیوں کے لئے۔ اللہ کے لئے کیا لکھا؟ اپنے قلم سے اللہ کی پاک ذات سے محبت کا کتنا حق ادا کیا؟ اللہ اور اللہ کے پیارے بندوں کے لئے کیا کِیا؟ ایک بے چینی تھی جو میری روح میں بھر دی گئی تھی۔ اس خواب کے بعد ناول کے اختتام تک میں نے کیا لکھا، کیسے لکھا پتہ ہی نہیں چلا۔

''اے مژگاں محبت'' کے بعد ''جھیل کنارہ کنکر'' وہ واحد ناول ہے جس کی تخلیق میری روح کی آسودگی کا باعث بنی اور اس ناول کے لئے جو تعریفی اسناد اور دعائیں مجھے ملیں انہوں نے میرا سر فخر سے بلند کر دیا۔

''جھیل کنارہ کنکر'' کی تخلیق کا باعث صرف ایک خواب تھا۔ اور اس خواب میں، میں عافیہ صدیقی کے ساتھ تھی۔ جتنی گولیاں اس بہادر بیٹی کے وجود میں قطعی بے گناہی کے باوجود اُتریں ان سب گولیوں پر ہمارے حکمرانوں کی بے حسی، بزدلی اور بے شرمی صاف صاف درج تھی۔

مگر پھر بھی مجھے فخر ہے کہ میں اس پاکستان کی بیٹی ہوں جو عافیہ کا پاکستان ہے۔ جو پوری اسلامی دنیا میں واحد ایٹمی طاقت ہے۔ وہ پاکستان کہ جس کی سرزمین خون کی ندیوں کا بہاؤ دیکھ کر بھی، ڈرون حملوں میں اپنے معصوم شہریوں کی ہلاکتیں دیکھ کر بھی، ہماری بزدلی، بے حسی اور بے شرمی کے باوجود، ہماری نااتفاقیوں اور

عیاشیوں کے باوجود، ایک اللہ کے سوا اہل مغرب کی طرف جھکاؤ کے باوجود قائم و دائم ہے اور رہتی دنیا تک قائم و دائم رہے گا۔

میں ایک محبِ وطن بیٹی ہوں۔ پاکستان میرا عشق، میرا جنون ہے۔ میں مر بھی جاؤں تو اس پیارے وطن کی محبت کا حق ادا نہیں کر سکتی۔ مگر ''جھیل کنارہ کنکر'' کی تخلیق وطن عزیز سے محبت کا ایک چھوٹا سا اظہار ضرور رہے گا۔

میں شکر گزار ہوں ماہنامہ آنچل اور جناب طاہر قریشی صاحب کی، جن کی محبت، شفقت اور تعاون سے مجھے آنچل کے پلیٹ فارم پر یہ انقلابی ناول لکھنے کا موقع ملا۔ اور اس کے بعد ان تمام لوگوں کی جن کے سونے جیسے دلوں سے میرے لئے خوشبو جیسی دعائیں نکلیں اور جنہوں نے دل کی گہرائیوں سے میری اس کوشش کو سراہا۔ میں Facebook پر اپنی فرینڈز شینی خان، دانیہ امتیاز، حمیرہ ندیم نفیس، ایس اے شہزادی، مالا بھٹی، کشمالہ خان، سدِ ملک، مشال، فاری، شمیم علی، نازیہ خرم، انائیہ چوہدری، آئمہ نور، ارم گل مہرو، زاہرہ خان، قرۃ العین سمیت دیگر تمام دوستوں کی محبتوں اور دعاؤں کی ہمیشہ شکر گزار رہوں گی۔

دعاؤں میں یاد رکھیے گا۔

نازیہ کنول نازی

اے شمع کوئے جاناں
ہے تیز ہوا مانا
لو اپنی بچا رکھنا رستوں پر نگاہ رکھنا
ایسی ہی کسی شب میں، آئے گا یہاں کوئی
ایک زخم دکھانے کو
ٹوٹا ہوا ایک تارا مٹی سے اٹھانے کو
آنکھوں میں نمی ہوگی چہرے پر دھواں ہوگا
ہاتھوں کی لکیروں میں، گزرے ہوئے سالوں کا
اک ایک نشاں ہوگا
بولے گا نہ کچھ لیکن فریاد کناں ہوگا
اے شمع کوئے جاناں
وہ خاک بسر راہی، وہ سوختہ پروانہ
جب آئے یہاں اس کو، مایوس نہ لوٹانا
ہو تیز ہوا کتنی، لو اپنی بچا رکھنا
رستے پر نگاہ رکھنا، راہی کا پتا رکھنا

سارے گھر میں گمبھیر خاموشی کا راج تھا۔ گاڑی گیراج میں پارک کرنے کے بعد وہ جیسے ہی گھر میں داخل ہوا، اذیت وکوفت کی ایک لہر پورے بدن میں سرائیت کر گئی۔ آج زندگی کو اس سے روٹھے کتنے سال ہو گئے تھے۔ اسے یقین ہی نہ آتا تھا کہ جس کے بغیر وہ چند لمحے بڑی مشکل سے گزارتا تھا اس کے بغیر اس نے اتنے سال زندہ رہ کر گزار کیسے لیے تھے۔ کسی کے بغیر یہ دن کس اذیت و ٹوٹ پھوٹ میں بسر ہوئے یہ الگ کہانی تھی۔

سنی کے کمرے سے ٹی وی چلنے کی آواز آ رہی تھی۔ جس کا مطلب تھا کہ وہ اپنے کمرے میں تھا۔ وہ تھکا تھکا سا لاؤنج میں پڑے صوفے پر ڈھے گیا۔

''صاحب کھانا لگا دوں؟'' حفیظ بابا اس کی موجودگی کی اطلاع پاتے ہی فوری کچن سے نکل آئے تھے۔ میکال نے سر صوفے کی پشت گاہ سے ٹکا کر پلکیں موند لیں۔

''نہیں بابا، بھوک نہیں ہے۔''

''آپ نے صبح بھی کچھ نہیں کھایا تھا صاحب کل رات بھی۔''

''کوئی فرق نہیں پڑتا بابا، ابھی ایک پارٹی میں جا رہا ہوں۔ وہاں کچھ کھا لوں گا۔ آپ فکرمند نہ ہوں۔ سنی کو کھانا کھلا کر سلا دیجیے گا اور خود بھی کھا لیجیے گا۔''

اپنے کمرے کی طرف بڑھتے ہوئے اس نے حفیظ بابا کو ہدایت کی تھی۔ وہ خاموشی سے سر جھکا کر کھڑے رہے۔ ابھی وہ شاور لے کر نکلا تھا کہ سیل بج اٹھا۔

''میکال کے بچے' کہاں ہو تم پارٹی شروع ہو گئی ہے۔''

کال پک کرتے ہی مسز رحیم کی تھکی تھکی سی مگر پر شکوہ آواز سماعتوں سے ٹکرائی تھی۔ وہ شرمندہ ہو گیا۔

''ایم سوری آپا' بس ابھی نکل رہا ہوں صرف پندرہ منٹ دے دیں پلیز۔''

دوسری طرف جانے اس کی التجا سنی گئی تھی کہ نہیں مگر کال کٹ گئی تھی۔ وہ سیل شرٹ کی جیب میں ڈالتا جلدی جلدی بال سنوارنے لگا۔

پچھلے گزرے چند سال نے اسے بہت بدل دیا تھا۔ گورا رنگ سانولے پن میں ڈھل گیا آنکھوں کے نیچے سیاہ حلقے پڑ گئے۔ جسم کی ہڈیاں اُبھر آئی تھیں۔ اب بھلا آئینے کے سامنے آنے اور خود کو سنوارنے کا دل بھی کہاں رہا تھا۔

بال سنوار کر پرفیوم کا چھڑکاؤ کرتے ہی اس نے جوتے پہنے، جلدی سے ٹائی کی ناٹ لگائی اور گاڑی کی چابی اٹھا کر فوراً باہر کی طرف لپک گیا۔ صد شکر کہ سنان کو اس کی آمد کی خبر نہیں ہوئی تھی۔ ورنہ اس وقت اس کا اکیلے گھر سے نکلنا ممکن ہی نہیں تھا۔

خاصی ریش ڈرائیونگ کے ساتھ وہ تقریباً بیس منٹ میں مسز رحیم کے سامنے تھا۔

''تم انتہائی سٹوپڈ اور فضول شخص ہو میکال! اب بہن کے رُتبے میں آ گئی تو کچھ کہہ بھی نہیں سکتی، وگرنہ وہ کان کھینچتی کہ یاد رکھتے۔''

اُسے دیکھتے ہی وہ پھر خفا ہوئی تھیں۔ وہ اس درگت پر محض کان کھجا کر رہ گیا۔

''سوری آپا! آج آفس میں بہت کام تھا۔''

''بس رہنے دو۔ یہ فضول کے بہانے کسی اور کو سنانا۔''

وہ کوئی عذر سننے کو تیار ہی نہیں تھیں۔ میکال بے بسی سے کندھے اُچکا کر رہ گیا۔ تبھی اُس کی نظر غیر ارادی طور پر سامنے اُٹھی تھی اور پھر وہ جیسے وہیں فریز ہو کر رہ گیا۔ ''وہ'' بھی آج کی اس تقریب میں شامل تھی۔ میکال کو لگا جیسے وہ سانس بھی نہیں لے سکے گا۔ مسز رحیم سے اس کی کیفیت چھپی نہیں رہ سکی تھی۔ تبھی ایک نظر سامنے موجود ہانیہ صفدر پر ڈالتے ہوئے وہ مسکرا کر بولیں۔

''ہانیہ آئی ہے۔ بہت اصرار کے بعد سمجھو زبردستی بلوایا ہے اسے یہاں، صرف تمہارے لئے۔ اس تقریب کو ارینج کرنے کا مقصد ہی تم دونوں کو ایک دوسرے کے قریب لانا تھا۔ ساری غلط فہمیاں دور کر لو اپنی۔''

''اب نہیں آپا! اب بہت دیر ہو چکی ہے۔''

جلتی آنکھوں سے اسے باتوں میں مشغول دیکھتے ہوئے اس نے جیسے خود کلامی کی تھی، پھر سر جھٹک کر پیچھے پلٹ آیا۔ دل کے زخم پھر رِسنے لگے تھے۔ خدا خدا کر کے تو اسے صبر آیا تھا اور مسز رحیم جیسے پھر سے اس کا صبر آزمانے پر تُل گئی تھیں۔

وہ پیچھے آ کر ایک خالی نشست پر ٹِک گیا۔ سلگتی، جلتی نگاہیں نافرمان ہو کر اب بھی اسی چہرے کا طواف کر رہی تھیں، جسے دیکھے بغیر اس کی صبح نہیں ہوتی تھی۔ جسے رات میں سونے سے پہلے پیار کیے بغیر اسے قرار نہیں آتا تھا۔ کتنی عجیب

بات تھی کہ جب وہ اس کے پاس تھی تو اسے اردگرد کی دنیا میں کشش محسوس ہوتی تھی۔ اب جبکہ وہ دنیا سے کنارہ کش ہو کر صرف اسی کے ہجر کا روگی ہو گیا تھا تو وہ اس سے چھن گئی تھی۔

وہ کسی بات پر مسکرا رہی تھی اور میکال کو لگا جیسے اس کی مسکراہٹ نے ساری محفل میں رنگ بکھیر دیئے ہوں۔ مسز رحیم اب کھانا سرو کرنے کا آغاز کر رہی تھیں۔ وہ بددل سا وہاں سے اٹھ گیا۔

''میں واپس جا رہا ہوں آپا! میری طبیعت ٹھیک نہیں ہے۔''

''ایسی کی تیسی تمہاری طبیعت کی۔ میرا اتنا خرچہ کروا کر اب تم جا رہے ہو۔ بیٹھے رہو آرام سے۔ کھانے کے بعد میں نے تھوڑا ڈانس وانس کا پروگرام رکھا ہے۔ تم ہانیہ سے.....''

''مجھے ہانیہ سے کوئی بات نہیں کرنی آپا! نہ اب میرا اس کی لائف سے کوئی لینا دینا ہے، بس۔''

بیزاری سے مسز رحیم کی بات کاٹ کر اس نے دبا دبا سا احتجاج کیا تھا۔ جواب میں وہ تپ اُٹھیں۔

''بہت پٹو گے تم میرے ہاتھ سے میکال! بتائے دے رہی ہوں میں تمہیں۔''

وہ مصروف تھیں۔ میکال کو ان کی سخت ناراضگی کا علم نہ ہوتا تو بنا ڈانٹ کی پروا کئے چلا آتا، مگر اسی وقت مسٹر رحیم صاحب نے اسے اپنی طرف بلا لیا تو وہ خفا خفا سا مسز رحیم کو دیکھتا ان کے قریب چلا آیا۔

''تم کہاں جا رہے ہو؟ کھانا لگ گیا ہے۔ آؤ مل کر کھاتے ہیں۔''

''مجھے بھوک نہیں۔''

''لگ جائے گی بھوک بھی۔ تم آؤ تو سہی۔ اور یہ سنی کہاں ہے؟''

''گھر پر ہی ہے۔ مجھے دیر ہو رہی تھی، اس لئے اسے ساتھ نہیں لایا۔''

''چلو...... جیسی تمہاری مرضی۔'' رسانیت سے کہہ کر انہوں نے زبردستی میکال کو اپنے ساتھ بٹھا لیا۔

''ویسے ہانیہ آج بہت اچھی لگ رہی ہے۔ میں اگر ساٹھ کے پیٹے میں نہ ہوتا تو......''

ہونٹ دبا کر وہ ذرا سا مسکرائے تھے۔ میکال انہیں خفگی سے دیکھ کر رہ گیا۔ کھانے کے بعد مشروب کا دور چلا اور پھر ڈانس کا۔ سب ڈانس کے نام پر بس یونہی تھرک رہے تھے۔ اُس نے دیکھا ایک لڑکا ہانیہ کو ڈانس کی آفر کر رہا تھا مگر اس نے انکار کر دیا۔ اس وقت اگر وہ اس لڑکے کی آفر قبول کر لیتی تو جانے وہ کیا کر بیٹھتا۔ وہ ڈانس فلور کے بالکل سامنے بیٹھی تھی۔ وہ کچھ سوچتے ہوئے اٹھا اور اپنے قریب بیٹھی ماڈرن سی لڑکی کو ڈانس کی آفر کر دی، جسے اس لڑکی نے فوراً سے پیشتر قبول کر لیا۔

ہانیہ اپنے ٹیبل پر اکیلی بیٹھی تھی، لہٰذا اس کی نظریں ڈانس فلور پر ہی تھیں۔ میکال جس وقت لڑکی کے ساتھ اس کے مقابل آیا، وہ کٹ کر رہ گئی۔ اس کے ہاتھ لڑکی کی کمر کے گرد تھے مگر اسے وہ ہاتھ اپنی گردن کے گرد، اپنا گلا گھونٹتے ہوئے محسوس ہو رہے تھے۔ اگر اسے معلوم ہوتا کہ میکال وہاں آئے گا تو شاید وہ کسی قیمت پر کبھی وہاں نہ آتی۔

لہولہو ہوتے دل کے ساتھ اس نے نظریں پھر اٹھائی تھیں اور اس بار اس نے جو منظر دیکھا تھا، اس کے بعد کچھ اور دیکھنے کی تاب اس میں نہیں تھی۔ وہ اُٹھی تھی اور کچھ سوچتے ہوئے مسز رحیم کی طرف چلی آئی تھی۔

''مسز رحیم! ایک فیور دیں گی؟'' بنا اُن کی مصروفیت کو خاطر میں لائے وہ انہیں ہاتھ پکڑ کر سائیڈ پر لے آئی تھی۔

''ہاں بولو میری جان!''

''آپ پلیز کچھ دیر تک میکال کو یہیں مصروف رکھیے گا۔ میں گھر جا رہی ہوں اپنے بیٹے سے ملنے۔''

''ٹھیک ہے تم جاؤ۔ میں اسے روک لوں گی۔''

''تھینکس۔'' بوجھل لہجے میں وہ صرف یہی کہہ سکی تھی۔ پیچھے وہ مسکراتی نگاہوں سے اسے جاتے ہوئے دیکھتی رہیں۔
میکال، ہانیہ کے اُٹھتے ہی ڈانس فلور سے اُتر آیا تھا۔
''چلی گئی وہ؟'' مسز رحیم کے قریب آ کر اس نے استفسار کیا تو وہ مسکرا کر بولیں۔
''ہاں۔ مگر تمہارے گھر گئی ہے، اپنے بیٹے سے ملنے۔''
''وہ یقیناً اسے ساتھ لے جائے گی۔''
''نہیں..... کہیں نہیں لے جاسکتی وہ اسے۔ میری ساری محنت پر تو پانی پھیر ہی دیا ہے تم نے۔ اب خدا کا واسطہ ہے تمہیں، فوری گھر جاؤ اور اسے منالو۔ یہ فاصلے اگر ابھی سمیٹے نہ گئے تو عمروں سے لمبی جدائی جھیلنی پڑ جائے گی میکال! بڑا ذاتی تجربہ ہے میرا۔ وہ ایک ہستی جس کے بغیر دنیا خالی خالی سی، بے معنی لگے، اسے انا کی بھینٹ نہیں چڑھانا چاہئے۔ ورنہ ساری عمر کی بے سکونی اور رونا نصیب میں لکھا جاتا ہے۔''
قدرے شکستہ لہجے میں وہ اسے سمجھا رہی تھیں۔ میکال تقریب اور ان کی محبتوں کے لئے ان کا شکریہ ادا کرتا وہاں سے نکل آیا۔

❁......❁......❁

شہر خاموشاں میں اس وقت غروب ہوتے سورج کی نارنجی کرنوں کے ساتھ ہی ایک عجیب سی خاموشی بکھرتی گئی تھی۔ آس پاس سے گزرتے لوگوں کی آمد و رفت کا سلسلہ بھی مانند پڑ گیا تھا۔ ہاتھ میں تازہ پھولوں کے گلدستے کے ساتھ جونہی وہ شہر خاموشاں کی حدود میں داخل ہوا اس کی نگاہ سامنے لگے شیشم کے اس پیڑ کی طرف اٹھی تھی جس کے نیچے ابھی چند ہفتے قبل ایک نئی لحد تیار کی گئی تھی۔
پچھلے چند ہفتوں میں عذیر اس کامنی سی لڑکی کو روزانہ اسی وقت اس لحد کے نزدیک' درخت کے تنے سے ٹیک لگائے اردگرد سے قطعی بے نیاز بیٹھے دیکھتا تھا۔ روز وہ تازہ پھول اور پانی لاتی' قبر پر پہلے پانی اور پھر پھول بکھیرتی پھر خاموشی سے دونوں بازو' گھٹنوں کے گرد لپیٹ کر شیشم کے پیڑ کے تنے کے ساتھ ٹیک لگا کر بیٹھ جاتی۔ ایک طرح سے اس نے اپنے سارے سلسلے مٹی کے اس ڈھیر سے وابستہ کر رکھے تھے۔ عذیر کو اس لمحے بے ساختہ معروف مصنفہ بشریٰ رحمٰن کے وہ چند الفاظ یاد آئے تھے۔ جو انہوں نے کسی کی یاد میں شاید ایسے ہی کسی موقع پر تحریر کیے تھے۔
''شہر خاموشاں میں جانے والے وہاں جا کر اتنے بے پروا کیوں ہو جاتے ہیں جا کر کوئی خیر خیریت کی خبر کیوں نہیں بھیجتے خوابوں میں آتے ہیں تو کھل کر بات کیوں نہیں کرتے سارے سلسلے مٹی کے ایک ڈھیر سے کیوں وابستہ ہو جاتے ہیں۔''
اسے لگتا تھا جیسے اس نے اسے کہیں دیکھا ہے مگر کہاں یہ اسے یاد نہیں آتا تھا۔ شاید اسے علم ہی نہیں تھا کہ عورتوں کا قبرستان میں آنا جانا مناسب نہیں۔ وگرنہ شاید وہ یوں روز پابندی سے وہاں نہ آتی۔
جانے چند ہفتے قبل مٹی کے ڈھیر تلے اترنے والی اس ہستی سے اس کا کیا تعلق تھا؟ وہ کیوں اسے کسی اور ہی دیس کی باسی لگتی تھی۔
روز وہ اس کے بارے میں سوچتا تھا اور روز رات گئے تک خود سے الجھتے ہوئے بے چین رہتا تھا۔

❁......❁......❁

درخت جاں پر عذاب رت تھی نہ برگ جاگے نہ پھول آئے
بہار وادی سے جتنے پنچھی' ادھر کو آئے ملول آئے
وہ ساری خوشیاں جو اس نے چاہیں اٹھا کے جھولی میں اپنی رکھ لیں
ہمارے حصے میں عذر آئے جواز آئے اصول آئے

شام ڈھل رہی تھی۔ آسمان پر سیاہ بادل کسی بھی پل برسنے کو تیار دکھائی دے رہے تھے۔ میکال حسن نے تھکی تھکی سی نظر اٹھا کر آسمان کی طرف دیکھا اور نگاہیں پھر سے عائشہ برہان کے خوب صورت چہرے پر ٹکا دیں۔ جو آسمان کی طرح اپنی آنکھوں کے گہرے بادل لیے کسی گزرے ہوئے طوفان کی مانند خاموش بیٹھی تھی۔

''تو یہ طے ہے کہ ہمیں آج کے بعد نہیں ملنا؟''

گہری سانس بھرتے ہوئے اس نے پوچھا تھا۔ جواب میں عائشہ برہان نے ذرا سا رخ پھیر لیا۔ اس کی آنکھوں میں موٹے موٹے آنسو انمول ہیروں کی مانند دمک رہے تھے۔

''ہوں......!''

''زندگی کا اتنا لمبا سفر میرے بغیر طے کر لو گی؟'' دھیرے سے ہاتھ بڑھا کر اس نے اس کے سرد ہاتھوں کو اپنی گرفت میں لیا تھا۔ جواب میں اس کی سسکاری نکل گئی۔

''پتا نہیں..... یہاں زندگی کا اعتبار کسے ہے میکال' ہو سکتا ہے میں ابھی یہاں سے اٹھ کر جاؤں اور صبح تم تک میرے مرنے کی خبر پہنچ جائے۔''

''نہیں......!'' وہ اس کی طرف دیکھ نہیں رہی تھی میکال تڑپ اٹھا۔

''نہیں عائش' ایسا مت کہو پلیز' میں تمہیں چھوڑ سکتا ہوں ہمیشہ کے لیے کھو نہیں سکتا۔''

اس کا سیل بار بار بج رہا تھا مگر اس میں اتنی سی ہمت بھی نہیں تھی کہ وہ پاکٹ سے سیل نکال کر باہر سڑک پر پھینک دے۔ پچھلے پچیس منٹ میں وہ پچاس لاکھ کا نقصان کر بیٹھا تھا۔ مگر اسے پروا نہیں تھی۔ عائشہ برہان کے لفظ اس کا آخری دیدار' کسی بھی اہم میٹنگ سے بڑھ کر تھا اس کے لیے۔ عائشہ نے بس ایک نظر اٹھا کر اس کی طرف دیکھا تھا اور پھر فوراً سے پیشتر نگاہیں پھیر لی تھیں۔

''تم میری زندگی میں آنے والے پہلے اور آخری شخص ہو میکال۔ نہ تم سے پہلے کوئی نظر میں جچا نہ تمہارے بعد میں کسی سے دل لگا پاؤں گی شاید میں کبھی تمہیں بھلا بھی نہ سکوں کہ یہ میرے اختیار میں نہیں ہے مگر ایک چیز میرے اختیار میں ہے۔''

بوجھل آواز میں بولتے بولتے اچانک اس نے سر اٹھایا تھا۔

''میں تمہیں دفن کر سکتی ہوں یہاں۔''

اپنے دل پر ہاتھ رکھتے ہوئے اس کی آنکھ سے ایک اور موتی ٹوٹ کر گرا تھا۔

''تم وہ شخص ہو میکال جسے زندگی سے پیار کروانا آتا ہے تمہیں دلوں میں گھر کرنا آتا ہے۔ کسی بھی لڑکی کے دل کو اپنے قدموں کی آہٹ پر دھڑکانا آتا ہے تم محبت کی نگری کے وہ مسافر ہو میکال جو خواب دکھاتا ہے اور پھر اپنے اسیروں کو ہمیشہ ہمیشہ کے لیے اپنے تصور میں قید کر لیتا ہے اور میں...... میں وہ بدنصیب لڑکی ہوں جو صرف تمہاری رفاقت کے خواب دیکھ سکتی ہے' مگر تمہیں پا نہیں سکتی۔ اس لیے آج میں یہاں تم سے مل کر ہمیشہ ہمیشہ کے لیے تمہیں اپنی یادوں میں قید کر لینا چاہتی ہوں تم سمجھ لینا کہ ہم کبھی ملے ہی نہیں تھے۔''

''کیا تمہارے لیے یہ سمجھ لینا آسان ہے؟''

''نہیں.....مگر اس کے سوا کوئی حل بھی تو نہیں ہے۔''

''حل نکالا جا سکتا ہے آخر تم مجھے اپنے گھر والوں سے بات کرنے کیوں نہیں دے رہیں؟'' وہ زچ ہوا تھا۔ عائشہ نے اپنے ہاتھ اس کی گرفت سے نکالتے ہوئے آنسو پونچھ لئے۔

''نہیں میکال! اب اس کا کوئی فائدہ نہیں ہے کیونکہ تم میری فیملی کو نہیں جانتے۔ یہ لوگ ایک بار اگر کوئی بات طے کرلیں تو پھر مرتے دم تک اس سے پیچھے نہیں ہٹتے اور میں ان بیٹیوں میں سے نہیں ہوں جو اپنی خواہشات کے لیے اپنے ماں باپ کے سامنے تن کر کھڑی ہو جاتی ہیں۔'' سر جھکائے بہت دھیمے لہجے میں وہ کہہ رہی تھی۔

''میری ماں نے زندگی میں بہت دکھ دیکھے ہیں۔ پاپا کی رحلت کے بعد بہت مشکل سے پال پوس کر بڑا کیا ہے ہمیں۔ میں انہیں مزید کوئی دکھ نہیں دینا چاہتی۔ میں وہ ہرگز نہیں کرنا چاہتی جو میری آپی نے کیا' بہت مشکل سے سنبھالا ہے میری ماں نے خود کو میں دوبارہ انہیں اس اذیت میں نہیں دھکیل سکتی۔''

''اچھی بات ہے مگر میرا کیا قصور ہے۔ کس چیز کی کمی ہے مجھ میں؟ تم اپنی ماں کے عمر بھر کے دکھوں کا مداوا مجھے دکھ سونپ کر کیوں کرنا چاہتی ہو؟''

اس بار میکال کے لہجے میں دکھ کی آمیزش تھی۔

''کیا قصور ہے میرا کہ میں ساری زندگی خوشی کے لیے ترستا رہوں تم میری آئیڈیل ہو عائش پہلی محبت ہو میری' میں یوں آسانی سے تمہیں کھو کر زندہ نہیں رہ سکتا۔ بہت شدت سے چاہا ہے میں نے تمہیں۔ زندگی میں کسی کو تمہارا مقام نہیں دے سکوں گا۔ میری زندگی میں کوئی اور لڑکی کبھی تمہاری جگہ نہیں لے سکے گی۔ سچ میں مر جاؤں گا۔ تمہیں اپنی ماں کی پروا ہے میری نہیں۔''

اس کا لہجہ بھیگ گیا تھا۔ عائشہ کو لگا وہ سانس بھی نہیں لے پائے گی۔

''ایم سوری میکال' رئیلی ویری سوری۔'' اس کی آنکھوں سے بھی لہو ٹپک رہا تھا۔ وہ رخ پھیر گیا۔

''نہیں' تم ایک سنگدل اور منافق لڑکی ہو' میں کبھی تمہیں اس بے وفائی کے لیے معاف نہیں کروں گا۔''

''میکال......!'' بہت شدت سے تڑپ کر اس نے اسے پکارا تھا مگر میکال نے پلٹ کر اس کی طرف نہیں دیکھا تبھی وہ اٹھ کھڑی ہوئی تھی۔

''میں جا رہی ہوں تم سمجھ لینا تمہیں جس عائشہ برہان سے محبت ہوئی تھی وہ مر گئی۔ خدا حافظ......!''

اسے جانے کی جلدی تھی وہ ہارے ہوئے شکستہ جواری کی طرح چپ چاپ بیٹھا رہ گیا۔

شام اپنی تمام تر اداسی کے ساتھ رخصت ہو رہی تھی۔ اسے لگا جیسے وہ اپنی متاع کل لٹا چکا ہو۔ اس میں اتنی سی ہمت بھی نہیں رہی تھی کہ وہ اٹھ کر اسے اس کے گھر تک ڈراپ ہی کر دیتا۔ تاہم اپنی گاڑی کی چابی ضرور اس نے اس کے پرس میں ڈال دی تھی۔

محبت بچھڑ رہی تھی اور وہ جیسے آنکھوں میں ریت بھرے خود اپنی ہی بربادی کا تماشا دیکھ رہا تھا۔

آخری بار ملو
ایسے کہ جلتے ہوئے دل
راکھ ہو جائیں کوئی اور تقاضا نہ کریں
چاکِ وعدہ نہ سلے' زخم تمنا نہ کھلے

اسے میکال حسن اور اس کی عائشہ جی میں کوئی دلچسپی نہیں تھی تبھی فوری اٹھ کھڑی ہوئی تو نہال کو بھی اس کی تقلید کرنی پڑی...... وہ دونوں یونیورسٹی کے بے حد اچھے دوست تھے اور اس وقت جاگنگ کے لیے نکلے تھے۔ نہال اس روز گھر آ کر بھی میکال حسن کے لیے خاصا اپ سیٹ رہا تھا۔

❁......❁......❁

ریاض حسن صاحب ریٹائرڈ کرنل تھے۔ زندگی کا طویل حصہ آرمی جیسی خشک جاب میں بسر کرنے کے باوجود اپنے گھر والوں کے ساتھ ان کا رویہ بے حد نرم، شگفتہ اور دوستانہ تھا۔ قدرت نے انہیں زندگی کے ہر میدان میں آسودگی ہی آسودگی سے نوازا تھا۔ بہترین جاب، محبت کرنے والی بے مثال بیوی اور بے حد سمجھ دار، فرماں بردار بچے......!

وہ اپنے مالک حقیقی کا جتنا بھی شکر ادا کرتے، کم تھا۔

کمال حسن ان کے سب سے بڑے ہونہار بیٹے تھے اور شادی شدہ تھے۔ ریاض صاحب نے آرمی سے ریٹائرمنٹ کے بعد اپنا ذاتی کاروبار شروع کر دیا تھا۔ جس میں کمال ان کے ہم قدم تھا۔ پچھلے دس سال میں ان کی گتے کی فیکٹری ترقی کر کے کہاں سے کہاں پہنچ گئی تھی۔ اسی لیے دو سال قبل ریاض صاحب نے کمال کو اپنی یو کے والی فرم کا چارج سنبھالنے کے لیے وہاں بھیج دیا تھا۔ میکال ان دنوں اپنا ایم بی اے مکمل کر کے نیا نیا بزنس کی طرف آیا تھا۔ وہ بھی ریاض صاحب کی ضد و اصرار پر، ورنہ وہ اپنے بل بوتے پر ہی کچھ کرنا چاہتا تھا۔ میکال سے چھوٹا نہال ابھی یونیورسٹی میں پڑھ رہا تھا۔ جبکہ مائرہ کالج میں تھی۔

میکال کی طبیعت اپنے دونوں بھائیوں سے قدرے مختلف تھی۔ وہ اپنے آپ میں مگن رہنے والا بہت ریزرو نیچر کا مالک تھا۔ کمال کی بیوی عینا ان کی چچا زاد تھی اور بے حد شگفتہ مزاج کی حامل خاتون تھی۔

غیا کے والد فیاض حسن صاحب کا اپنا بزنس تھا اور وہ ساتھ والے پورشن میں ہی قیام پذیر تھے۔ عینا کی ایک چھوٹی بہن سارا اور ایک بڑا بھائی سمیر تھا۔ پچھلے پچیس سالوں سے دونوں گھرانوں کی محبت مثالی تھی۔ صبح کا ناشتا ہوتا یا دوپہر کا لنچ یا پھر رات کا ڈنر دونوں گھرانوں کے افراد ایک ہی میز پر مل جل کر کھانا کھاتے تھے۔ مائرہ اور سارا ایک ہی کالج میں پڑھ رہی تھیں اور دونوں میں گہری دوستی تھی۔ نہال اور سمیر آپس میں بہت کلوز فرینڈ تھے۔ گھر میں ہر وقت دھما چوکڑی کا ماحول رہتا تھا مگر میکال اس ماحول کا حصہ نہیں تھا۔ اس کی گھر میں کسی کے ساتھ بھی فرینڈ شپ نہیں تھی۔ جتنا وقت وہ گھر پر گزارتا تھا اس کی یہی کوشش ہوتی تھی کہ اپنے کمرے میں بند رہے۔ عینا کے ساتھ بھی بس واجبی سی دعا سلام تھی اس کی یہی وجہ تھی کہ ریاض صاحب اسے کمال کی جگہ یو کے بھیجنے پر بضد تھے مگر وہ عائشہ کی وجہ سے ان کی اس ضد کے سامنے اڑ گیا تھا۔

عائشہ اسے اتنی دور بھیجنے کے حق میں نہیں تھی مگر..... اب تو بازی ہی اُلٹ گئی تھی۔ یو کے جانے کا فیصلہ کر کے اپنے بند کمرے میں وہ بہت دیر تک بے آواز روتا رہا تھا۔

❁......❁......❁

عائشہ برہان نے جس وقت قدم گھر کی دہلیز پر رکھے وہاں عجیب سناٹے کا راج تھا۔ یوں لگتا تھا جیسے کسی کی مرگ ہو گئی ہو اور مرگ تو ہو گئی تھی خود اپنے آپ کو مار کر باہر دفن کرنے کے بعد ہی وہ گھر واپس لوٹی تھی۔

لاؤنج خالی پڑا تھا وہ کچھ دیر گم صم سی وہیں بیٹھی خود کو سنبھالنے کی کوشش کرتی رہی پھر صوفے کی پشت گاہ سے سر ٹکا کر

پلکیں موند لیں۔ ایک عجیب سی تھکن جیسے اس کی رگ رگ میں سرائیت کر گئی تھی۔ عین اسی لمحے اسے اپنی ماں کے کمرے سے اپنی بڑی بہن کے چنگھاڑنے کی آواز سنائی دی تھی۔

''آپ ٹھیک نہیں کر رہی ہیں امی۔ وہ لڑکا کسی بھی طور سے عائشہ کے قابل نہیں ہے۔ دیکھنے سے ہی پاگل لگتا ہے۔ کیسی ماں ہیں آپ؟ خاندان سے رشتہ بنائے رکھنے کے لیے اپنی بیٹی کو سولی پر چڑھا دیں گی۔''

اس کا دل چاہا وہ دونوں کانوں پر انگلیاں رکھ لے مگر وہ بے حس بنی بیٹھی رہی۔ بہن کے بعد اب اس کی ماں چیخ رہی تھی۔

''بکواس بند کرو اپنی اور دفع ہو جاؤ یہاں سے، کوئی حق نہیں ہے تمہیں اپنی ماں کے فیصلوں میں ٹانگ اڑانے کا، تم نے جو کرنا تھا اپنی باری پر کر چکی اب میں اسے کسی پاگل سے بیاہوں یا ہوش مند سے یہ میرا اور اس کا معاملہ ہے سمجھیں تم؟''

''ظلم کر رہی ہیں آپ اور وہ بھی اپنی سگی اولاد پر۔ ماں سے بڑھ کر اس روئے زمین پر کوئی رشتہ خوب صورت اور مخلص نہیں، ماں سے زیادہ اولاد کا غمگسار دوسرا کوئی نہیں، ماں تو بن کہے اپنی اولاد کے دل کا حال جان لیتی ہے۔ آپ کیسی ماں ہیں جو آپ کو اس کی آنکھوں میں تیرتے آنسو دکھائی نہیں دے رہے۔''

ایک بار پھر اسے اپنی بہن کی آواز سنائی دی تھی اور اس کے فوراً بعد ہی ماں کی۔

''تم بکواس بند کرو گی یا میں دھکے دے کر نکال دوں تمہیں یہاں سے؟''

''نکال دیں، یہی کر سکتی ہیں آپ، مجھے تو لگتا ہی نہیں کہ آپ ہماری سگی ماں ہیں مجھ پر داؤ نہیں چلا تو چھوٹی بیٹی کو اپنی جھوٹی انا پر قربان کر رہی ہیں۔''

اس کے حق میں کسی قابل وکیل کی مانند بولتی اس کی بہن از حد جرأت کا مظاہرہ کرتے ہوئے کمرے سے نکل آئی تھی۔ عائشہ نے پلکوں سے ٹوٹ کر گال پر پھسلتے آنسو کو مٹھی میں دبا لیا۔ تھوڑی دیر بعد اسے سیڑھیوں پر اپنی بہن کی سینڈل کی ٹک ٹک کی آواز سنائی دی تھی۔ وہ بے جان سی بیٹھی رہی۔ اس کی بہن اب خاموشی سے اس کے پہلو میں صوفے پر آ بیٹھی تھی۔

''یوں چپ کر کے بیٹھے رہنے سے زندگی کے مسائل حل نہیں ہوتے۔ سمجھیں تم؟''

''میرے پاس اس کے سوا دوسرا کوئی حل نہیں ہے آپا۔''

''کیوں حل نہیں ہے صاف انکار نہیں کر سکتیں؟ تم پڑھی لکھی سمجھ دار لڑکی ہو وہ شخص جو کسی بھی طرح سے کسی لڑکی کے قابل نہیں ہے تم اس شخص سے شادی کا تصور بھی کیسے کر سکتی ہو؟ اور پھر میکال...... اس سارے کھیل میں اس کا کیا قصور ہے اسے کس بات کی سزا دے رہی ہو تم؟''

طائشہ کی آنکھوں میں خفگی تھی، غصہ تھا، رنج تھا۔

عائشہ نے آہستہ سے رخ پھیر لیا۔ اس کی آنکھیں اس لمحے جیسے جل رہی تھیں۔

''آج جو میرے ساتھ ہو رہا ہے یہ آپ کا نصیب تھا آپا مگر آپ نے اپنے نصیب سے بغاوت کر کے اپنی پسند کا ہم سفر چن لیا، دو سال پہلے اگر آپ ایسا نہ کرتیں تو آج میں میکال کے لیے کچھ بھی کر سکتی تھی۔ مگر اب نہیں آپا، مجھ میں دو سال پہلے والا تماشا دوبارہ دیکھنے کی ہمت نہیں ہے۔''

''نہیں ہے تو مرو، میرا کیا جاتا ہے۔''

عائشہ کے جواب نے اسے تپا دیا تھا تبھی مزید بحث کیے وہ اٹھ گئی تھی مگر عائشہ سر جھکائے ٹپ ٹپ بہتے آنسوؤں کے

میکال حسن کو یوکے آئے ہوئے دوسرا سال تھا۔ جب اس روز اسکائپ پر مائرہ نے اس سے رابطہ کیا۔

''السلام علیکم! بھائی کیسے ہیں آپ؟ ٹھیک ٹھاک ہیں نا؟ آپ کے لیے ایک گڈ نیوز ہے۔''

ہر روز آن لائن ہوتے ہی وہ یونہی شروع ہو جاتی تھی۔ میکال جو ابھی کیمرا سیٹ کر رہا تھا ایک دم سے چونک اٹھا۔

''گڈ نیوز؟''

''جی ہاں گڈ نیوز' سنیں گے؟''

''ہوں۔''

''مما نے آپ کے لیے لڑکی پسند کر لی ہے اور پتا ہے لڑکی کون ہے...... ہانیہ صفدر۔'' مسکرا کر مطلع کرتے ہوئے اس نے گویا دھماکا کر ڈالا تھا۔ وہ سرتا پیر ہل کر رہ گیا۔

''وہاٹ مگر میری مرضی کے بغیر یہ کیسے ہو سکتا ہے۔ میں ابھی شادی کے حق میں نہیں ہوں۔''

''تو کیا ہوا۔ ہم لوگ تو ہیں نا اور پھر ہانیہ جیسی لڑکی تو چراغ لے کر ڈھونڈنے سے بھی نہیں ملے گی۔ آپ نے تو دیکھا ہی ہوا ہے انہیں۔ کل نہال بھائی کی برتھ ڈے پارٹی میں آئی تھیں۔ اتنی پیاری لگ رہی تھیں کہ بس مت پوچھیں۔ ویسے بھی آپ کو کون سا ان کے ساتھ رہنا ہے۔ وہ تو یہاں رہیں گی ہمارے پاس۔''

مائرہ اپنا راگ الاپ رہی تھی۔ میکال نے تنگ کر لائن ڈسکنکٹ کر دی۔

دو سال ہو گئے تھے مگر آج بھی اس کے دل میں اپنی محبت کا زخم تازہ تھا۔ آج بھی بیدار ہو کر آنکھ کھلتے ہی وہ بے تابی سے موبائل دیکھتا کہ شاید عائشہ کی طرف سے کوئی میسج آیا ہو' دن بھر اس کی یاد چٹکی بن کر کاٹتی رہتی۔ رات میں بستر پر لیٹتا تو وہ چھم سے تصور میں آ موجود ہوتی۔ اس کی ہر یاد اب بھی اس کے دل سے لپٹی تھی۔

''پتا ہے میکال جب ہماری شادی ہو گی نا تو میں روز تمہیں بہت پیار سے لاڈ کر کے جگایا کروں گی۔''

اس روز وہ دونوں قریبی پارک آئے تھے جب عائشہ نے بہت ترنگ میں اس سے کہا تھا میکال اس کی بات پر مسکرایا تھا۔

''اچھا' مثال کے طور پر کیسے جگایا کرو گی؟''

''اوں...... سوچنے دو...... ہاں...... تم سو رہے ہو گے میں کمرے میں آؤں گی تمہیں آواز دوں گی مگر تم آنکھیں نہیں کھولو گے۔ تب میں بیڈ پر تمہارے پہلو میں بیٹھ کر ذرا سا جھکوں گی۔ پھر اپنے لب تمہاری پیشانی پر رکھ دوں گی تم ذرا سا کسمساؤ گے اور میں پیشانی کے بعد تمہاری آنکھوں کو باری باری چوموں گی۔ پھر دونوں گالوں پر پیار کروں گی پھر......!'' وہ شرما بھی رہی تھی اور بتا بھی رہی تھی، میکال کی آنکھیں شرارت سے چمک اٹھیں۔

''ہوں اور تمہیں پتا ہے پھر اس کے بعد میں کیا کروں گا؟''

''نہیں تم بتا دو۔''

''شادی کے بعد بتاؤں گا۔''

عائشہ کا چہرہ سرخ ہو رہا تھا۔ میکال کا دل چاہا اسے خود میں جذب کر لے۔

اسے خبر بھی نہ ہوئی اور اس کی آنکھوں کے گوشے نمی سے بھیگ گئے۔ اسی لمحے اس نے اپنے گھر کا نمبر ڈائل کیا تھا۔

''السّلام علیکم امی!'' کئی بیلز کے بعد اس کی کال مسز حسن نے ریسیو کی تھی۔

''وعلیکم السّلام کیسے ہو بیٹا۔''

''ٹھیک ہوں۔'' چاہنے کے باوجود وہ ان سے اپنے لہجے کی نمی چھپا نہیں سکا تھا۔

''مگر مجھے ٹھیک نہیں لگ رہے ہو کیا تم رو رہے ہو میکال؟''

وہ ماں تھیں اور ماؤں کے دلوں کے ساتھ قدرت نے عجیب سگنل فٹ کیے ہوتے ہیں سمندر پار سے بھی انہیں اپنی اولاد کی آنکھوں میں آنسو دکھائی دے جاتے ہیں۔ میکال نے ان کے سوال پر اپنی آنکھیں رگڑ لیں۔

''نہیں مما' ایسی کوئی بات نہیں' بس کل سے زکام ہوا ہے۔ خیر چھوڑیں آپ اس بات کو' مجھے آپ سے کچھ اور بات کرنی تھی۔''

''جی میری جان کہو۔''

''مما، مائرہ بتا رہی تھی آپ لوگوں نے میرے لیے کوئی لڑکی پسند کی ہے۔''

''ہاں بہت پیاری بچی ہے ہانیہ' تمہارے پاپا کے بہت عزیز دوست کی بیٹی ہے تم جانتے تو ہو نہیں۔ بہت پسند آئی ہے ہمیں' بس میں اور تمہارے پاپا تو رشتہ کر آئے ہیں۔''

''مگر مما آپ لوگوں کو مجھ سے پوچھنا چاہیے تھا۔ میں ابھی شادی نہیں کر سکتا پلیز آپ نہال کی کر دیں۔''

''پاگل ہوئے ہو اس کی ابھی تعلیم مکمل نہیں ہوئی ہے۔''

''تو کیا ہوا جب پاپا نے آپ سے شادی کی تھی تو آپ کی بھی تعلیم مکمل نہیں ہوئی تھی۔''

''عورت اور مرد میں فرق ہوتا ہے بیٹے' ایک لڑکا جو ابھی اپنے پیروں پر کھڑا بھی نہیں ہوا میں اس کے لیے اس بچی کا ہاتھ مانگ لوں جو ہزاروں نہیں لاکھوں میں ایک ہے اور تم کیا سمجھتے ہو اس کے لیے رشتوں کی کمی ہے۔ ہرگز نہیں' بہت لوگ ہیں اس کے لیے جھولی پھیلانے والے مگر تمہارے پاپا کی محبت کی وجہ سے وہ لوگ ہماری عزت کر رہے ہیں۔''

''جو بھی ہو' میں اس شادی کے لیے تیار نہیں ہوں' سوری۔'' اس کا ضبط جواب دے رہا تھا۔ تبھی حتمی لہجہ اختیار کرتے ہوئے اس نے لائن کاٹ دی تھی۔

دوسری طرف مسز حسن سر تھام کر رہ گئی تھیں۔

''کیا ہوا مما؟''

نہال لاؤنج میں مسز حسن کے پاس ہی بیٹھا تھا۔ وہ نفی میں سر ہلاتے ہوئے چپ چاپ سی وہیں بیٹھ گئیں۔

''میکال نے شادی سے انکار کر دیا ہے۔''

''کیوں؟''

''پتا نہیں؟''

''مجھے پتا ہے۔'' گہری سانس بھرتے ہوئے اس نے ہاتھ میں پکڑی کتاب بند کر دی تھی۔ مسز حسن نے چونک کر اس کی طرف دیکھا۔

''کیا پتا ہے؟''

''اس کی زندگی میں ایک لڑکی تھی مما' عائشہ برہان ..... پاپا کے آفس میں ہی کام کرتی تھی میکال بہت چاہتا ہے اسے' مگر بدقسمتی سے اس لڑکی کے گھر والوں نے اس کی شادی کہیں اور کر دی اسی لیے وہ گھر اور ملک چھوڑ کر گیا ہے۔''

''تمہیں کیسے پتا ہے یہ سب؟''

''میکال کے دوست نے بتایا تھا آج کل یو کے میں اسی کے ساتھ ہوتا ہے۔ پل پل کی خبر دیتا رہتا ہے اس کی۔ میکال اپنے ساتھ ٹھیک نہیں کر رہا ہے مما' وہ خود کو تباہ کر رہا ہے۔''

ایک کے بعد ایک یہ کیا انکشاف ہو رہا تھا۔ وہ یہ ساری باتیں سن کر حیران ہو گئی تھیں۔ اسی روز رات میں انہوں نے ریاض حسن صاحب سے بات کی تھی۔

''میری تو کچھ سمجھ میں نہیں آ رہا کہ کیا کروں؟''

''تم فکر مت کرو' ہانیہ بہت پیاری بچی ہے' یقیناً وہ اسے سمیٹ لے گی۔''

''مگر وہ ہانیہ سے شادی پر تیار نہیں ہے۔''

''ہو جائے گا ہم پلاننگ ہی ایسی کریں گے کہ اس کے پاس فرار کا کوئی راستہ ہی کھلا نہ رہے۔''

''مگر......!''

''اگر مگر چھوڑو اللہ بہتر کارساز حقیقی ہے۔ یقیناً وہ سب کچھ بہتر کر دے گا۔'' حسن صاحب تھکے ہوئے تھے لہٰذا لائٹ آف کر کے سو گئے۔ تاہم مسز حسن اس رات ایک پل کے لیے بھی نہیں سو سکی تھیں۔

❁ ..... ❁ ..... ❁

تمہاری یاد کی کرنوں کو اکثر ذہن میں رکھ کر
میں اپنی نیند کھوتا ہوں تو یہ میری محبت ہے
ہوا' احساس' خوشبو' چاندنی کو دیکھ کر اکثر
تیرے دھوکے میں رہتا ہوں تو یہ میری محبت ہے
فلک کے چاند تاروں کے حسیں جھرمٹ میں جان جاں
تیرے چہرے کو تکتا ہوں تو یہ میری محبت ہے
میں اپنی زندگی کے سارے جذبوں کو میری جاناں
تمہارے نام کرتا ہوں تو یہ میری محبت ہے!

''یار آخر تم بتا کیوں نہیں دیتیں کہ تمہیں اس شادی پر کیا اعتراض ہے۔ تم یہ شادی کیوں نہیں کرنا چاہتیں؟'' وہ کوئی تیسری بار اس سے پوچھ رہی تھی۔ ہانیہ صفدر نے پلٹ کر اسے دیکھا۔ بھیگی ہوئی پلکوں اور سرخ چہرے کے ساتھ وہ رخ موڑے کھڑکی کے قریب کھڑی رو رہی تھی۔

''بتا دوں گی تو کیا ہو جائے گا کیا تم یہ شادی رکوا دو گی؟''

''ہاں، رکوا بھی سکتی ہوں' تمہیں پتا ہے تمہارے لیے میں کچھ بھی کر سکتی ہوں مگر تم منہ سے کچھ پھوٹو تو سہی۔''

وہ اس کے لیے پریشان تھی۔ ہانیہ گہری سانس بھرتی کھڑکی سے پلٹ آئی۔

''یہ شادی رکوا دو ہادیہ' جیسے بھی ہو سکتا ہے پلیز.... نہیں تو میں مر جاؤں گی' دیکھ لینا تم ٹھیک ایک ہفتے کے بعد ان

ہاتھوں پر مہندی کی جگہ خون رچے گا۔ ڈولی کی جگہ جنازہ اٹھے گا میرا۔'' گلوگیر لہجے میں وہ شروع ہوئی تو پھر بولتی چلی گئی۔

ہادیہ نے بے ساختہ اپنا سر پیٹ لیا۔

''تم پاگل ہوگئی ہو ہانی' اور کچھ نہیں یار ماں باپ اولاد کا بھلا سوچتے ہیں ہمیشہ۔''

''بھلا..... یہ بھلا سوچا ہے میرے ماں باپ نے میرا۔ ایک شخص جس کے پاس آپ کو دینے کے لیے کچھ بھی نہیں، خالص محبت' خالص جذبات کچھ بھی نہیں اس کے ساتھ میرا رشتہ جوڑ کر بھلا کیا ہے میرے گھر والوں نے؟ ایسا بھلا کرتا ہے کوئی اپنی سگی اولاد کے ساتھ؟ میں کیا لولی لنگڑی ہوں' اندھی ہوں' پچاس سال سے اوپر عمر ہوگئی ہے میری یا پھر بد کردار ہوگئی ہوں۔ کیوں یہ لوگ کسی بوجھ کی طرح گلے سے اتار پھینکنا چاہتے ہیں مجھے' کیوں؟'' وہ دوبارہ آبدیدہ ہوگئی تھی۔

ہادیہ اس بار اسے دیکھ کر رہ گئی۔

''تم غلط سوچ کی شکار ہورہی ہو ہانیہ' میکال بھائی اتنے بھی برے نہیں ہیں کہ کوئی لڑکی ان سے شادی نہ ہونے کے لیے یوں رورو کر آنکھیں سجالے اور پھر آج کل اتنے اچھے لڑکے ملتے کہاں ہیں۔ لڑکیوں کے ماں باپ کی نیندیں اڑی ہوئی ہیں شکر کرو کہ گھر بیٹھے اتنا اچھا بر مل گیا ہے تمہیں ورنہ آج کل حسین سے حسین لڑکیاں صرف ایک نام کے لیے کس کس عذاب کا شکار ہورہی ہیں تم نہیں جانتیں۔''

''میں جاننا بھی نہیں چاہتی' کوئی شوق نہیں ہے مجھے شادی وادی کا اور ایک بٹے ہوئے انسان سے شادی کا تو ہرگز نہیں' میں جس حال میں ہوں خوش ہوں۔''

''آج خوش ہو' ساری عمر خوش نہیں رہ سکوگی' پانچ سال دس سال پندرہ سال کتنا عرصہ جوان رہوگی ایک وقت آئے گا جب تم تنہا چلتے چلتے تھک جاؤ گی اور تب تمہارے اندر یہ خواہش بیدار ہوگی کہ کوئی ہو' جو زندگی کے سفر میں تمہارے ساتھ چلے مگر تب وقت گزر چکا ہوگا۔ پھر کیا کروگی؟''

''خودکشی کرلوں گی مگر میکال حسن جیسے کسی فضول انسان سے شادی نہیں کروں گی۔'' مرغی کی ایک ٹانگ کی طرح وہ اپنی بات سے پیچھے نہیں ہٹی تھی۔

ہادیہ اپنے گال پیٹ کر رہ گئی۔

''کیوں نہیں کروگی اتنا خوب صورت اور اچھا رشتہ ہے۔''

''تمہیں لگتا ہوگا تم کرلو' ویسے بھی مشکل میں دوست ہی دوستوں کے کام آتے ہیں۔ تم نے دیکھا نہیں فلموں کہانیوں میں فرینڈز کیسی کیسی قربانیاں نہیں دیتیں اپنی فرینڈز کے لیے۔ میری تو پھر بھی حقیقی زندگی ہے وہ بھی بے حد مختصر یہاں تو دوسرا جنم بھی نہیں کہ رو دھو کر ایک قطعی ناپسندیدہ شخص کے ساتھ یہ جیون بیتالوں اور اگلے جنم میں مجھے میری پسند کا شخص مل جائے۔'' ہادیہ بیڈ سے اتر کر صوفے پر اس کے پاس آبیٹھی۔

''آپ کی اطلاع کے لیے عرض ہے محترمہ کہ یہاں میری بھی ایک ہی زندگی ہے وہ بھی بے حد مختصر اور دوسری بات، تمہارے علم میں ہے کہ میری نسبت بچپن سے ہی تمہارے عاشق مزاج اسٹوپڈ بھائی کے ساتھ طے ہے۔ نہ ہوتی تو میکال حسن جیسے آئیڈیل شخص کو پانا میری اوّلین ترجیح ہوتی۔''

چٹخارہ لے کر کہتی وہ یہ جان ہی نہ سکی کہ اس کی بات نے ہانیہ کو پھر سے کتنا بے چین کردیا ہے۔ قدرے اضطراب میں لب کاٹتی ہوئی وہ اٹھی تھی اور پھر سے کھڑکی میں جا کر کھڑی ہوگئی۔

''مجھے بھی یہی لگتا تھا کہ وہ آئیڈیل ہے مگر اس کے کردار نے مجھے غلط ثابت کر دیا وہ ایک بٹا ہوا شخص ہے ہادی چار سال کسی لڑکی کو ٹوٹ کر چاہتا رہا ہے اسے اپنی محبت اور دیوانگی کا احساس دلاتا رہا ہے۔ کوئی اتنا عرصہ کسی کے ساتھ چل کر اس کی جگہ کسی اور کو کیسے دے سکتا ہے۔ کیسے بھلا سکتا ہے اسے ایک دم سے؟ کسی اور کے ساتھ کیسے نئی زندگی شروع کر سکتا ہے۔ جبکہ اس کے پاس دوسرے شخص کو دینے کے لیے کچھ بھی نہ ہو۔''

شادی سے انکار کی اصل وجہ سامنے آ گئی تھی۔ ہادیہ چاپ چاپ اسے دیکھتی رہی۔

''میں بہت صاف گو لڑکی ہوں ہادی' بہت ایماندار ہوں' رشتوں کے معاملے میں۔ مجھ سے منافقت برداشت نہیں ہوتی، وہ شخص جو چار سال کسی کی چاہ' کسی کی پسند' کسی کے خوابوں میں رہا ہے وہ میرا کیسے ہو سکتا ہے؟ کیا رہا ہو گا میرے لیے اس شخص کے پاس خالص محبت' خالص چاہ' خالص خواب...... کچھ بھی تو نہیں۔ وہ میرا چہرہ بھی دیکھے گا تو اس چہرے میں تشبیہ اسی کی نظر آئے گی جو اس کی اولین پسند ہے میں برتی ہوئی چیزیں استعمال نہیں کرتی ہادیہ۔ برتا ہوا شخص کیسے قبول کر لوں؟ مجھے کسی کی سیکنڈ چوائس بننے کا کوئی شوق نہیں' بس...... جو میرا ہم سفر بنے' اس کی ہر سانس مجھ سے مخلص ہو' میرے ہوتے ہوئے اس کے دل و دماغ پر کسی دوسری لڑکی کی پرچھائی بھی نہ پڑے۔ وہ صرف میرا ہو ہادی صرف میرا۔ میرے پہلو میں لیٹ کر اس کے دھیان میں پنچھی کسی اور کی یاد کے آسمان کو نہ چھوئیں' بس......!'' ذرا سی جذباتی ہوئی وہ لڑکی اسے بے حد پیاری لگی تھی۔

وہ صوفے سے اٹھ کر اس کے پاس کھڑکی کے قریب آ کھڑی ہوئی۔

''تمہاری سوچ اور پسند تو بہت اچھی ہے میری جان، مگر افسوس...... جیسا نایاب ہیرو تمہیں مطلوب ہے وہ ساٹھ ستر سال پہلے تو کہیں ملتا ہو گا اب ممکن نہیں ہے کیونکہ موجودہ دور میں صرف ایک لڑکی پر دنیا حرام کر لینا فلموں کہانیوں میں تو چلتا ہے حقیقی زندگی میں نہیں۔ یہاں مرد ہو یا عورت زندگی کے سفر میں ہر نئے موڑ پر' نئے ہم سفر کے ساتھ چلنا پسند کرتے ہیں سویٹی۔ ایک ہی محبت کو روگ بنا کر دل سے لگا لینا مرد تو خاص طور اپنی شان کے خلاف سمجھتے ہیں۔''

''تو سمجھتے رہیں یار' میں شادی کے لیے مر تو نہیں رہی۔'' وہ تپی تھی ہادیہ مسکرا کر رہ گئی۔

''ٹھیک ہے' تو چل کر انکل کو یہ بات بتا دو' سب ٹھیک ہو جائے گا۔''

''کاش میں ایسا کر سکتی' کاش وہ اتنے سخت باپ نہ ہوتے' کاش......!''

''جب کچھ بھی اختیار میں نہیں ہے تو فضول میں اپنی جان کیوں ہلکان کر رہی ہو' تین دن ہو گئے تمہیں بھوک ہڑتال کیے کیا یہ اس مسئلے کا حل ہے؟''

''نہیں، مگر یہ اذیت' یہ بے چینی' یہ غصہ میری جان لے لے گا ہادی میں جب جب میکال حسن کے متعلق سوچتی ہوں میری شریانیں پھٹنے لگتی ہیں۔ وہ شخص مجھے وقت سے پہلے مار دے گا دیکھ لینا تم۔'' ہانیہ کے لہجے میں گہرا اضطراب تھا۔ ہادیہ تڑپ کر رہ گئی۔

''پاگل ہو گئی ہو' خبردار جو دوبارہ کبھی ایسی بات منہ سے نکالی تو۔''

''میں سچ کہہ رہی ہوں ہادی دیکھ لینا تم' اگر یہ شادی نہ رکی تو میری سانس میرا دل ضرور رک جائے گا۔''

''نہیں' ایسا کچھ نہیں ہو گا تم میکال حسن سے شادی نہیں کرنا چاہتیں ٹھیک ہے مت کرنا میں وعدہ کرتی ہوں تمہاری شادی اس سے نہیں ہونے دوں گی۔ مگر تم دوبارہ کبھی مرنے کی بات نہیں کرو گی ٹھیک ہے؟''

اس کی بے چینی محبت سے مشروط تھی۔ ہانیہ کی پلکیں بھیگ گئیں۔

''اتنے کم دنوں میں تم کیا کرو گی؟''

''کچھ نہ کچھ تو کروں گی' اپنی کسی سہیلی کو اس کی پہلی بیوی اور اس کے ڈھیر سارے بچوں کی اماں بنا کر عین نکاح کے وقت سامنے لے آؤں گی۔ ابھی کل ہی کسی کہانی میں یہ سب پڑھا تھا میں نے تم بے فکر رہو' سب ٹھیک ہو جائے گا' میں ہوں نا۔''

وہ اس کی صحیح درد آشنا تھی ہانیہ اس کے گلے لگ کر رو پڑی۔

''تھینکس ہادی' تم نہ ہوتیں تو جانے میں کب کی مر چکی ہوتی۔''

''اف پھر مرنے کی بات' اب تم مار کھاؤ گی مجھ سے اور کچھ نہیں۔''

ایک دھموکا اس کی نازک کمر پر رسید کرتے ہوئے وہ بولی تو ہانیہ روتے میں مسکرا دی۔

''اب جلدی سے فریش ہو جاؤ میں کھانا بھجوا رہی ہوں اچھی طرح کھا لینا او کے۔'' اسے خود سے الگ کرتے ہوئے اس نے ہدایات جاری کیں تو وہ اس کا شکریہ ادا کرتی واش روم کی طرف بڑھ گئی۔

❁.......❁.......❁

صفدر منیر باجوہ صاحب حال ہی میں آرمی سے کرنل کے عہدے پر ریٹائر ہوئے تھے۔

ہانیہ ان کی اکلوتی بیٹی تھی۔ اس سے بڑا ان کا صرف ایک بیٹا جاذب تھا۔ جو مڈل کے بعد اعلیٰ تعلیم حاصل کرنے کے لیے ان کی بڑی بہن کے پاس انگلینڈ چلا گیا تھا۔ ہانیہ اس سے پورے سات سال چھوٹی تھی۔ وہ ففتھ میں تھی جب صفدر منیر باجوہ صاحب کی محبوب بیوی ''آسیہ بانو'' کا انتقال ہو گیا۔ یہ سانحہ ان کے لیے اتنا شدید ثابت ہوا کہ عین بیوی کے سوئم والے دن وہ خود بھی ہارٹ اٹیک کا شکار ہو کر اسپتال جا پہنچے۔ مگر قدرت کو ابھی انہیں زندگی کی نعمت سے نوازنا تھا۔ لہٰذا ایک ہفتہ اسپتال میں رہ کر دوبارہ گھر لوٹ آئے۔

ہانیہ اس ایک ہفتے میں رشتہ داروں کی موجودگی کے باوجود ملازمین کے رحم و کرم پر رہی تھی۔ گزرتے وقت کے ساتھ ساتھ صفدر صاحب نے تو خود کو سنبھال لیا۔ مگر بیٹی کے لیے زیادہ حساس ہوتے گئے۔ جاذب اس وقت پندرہ سال کا تھا مگر پھر بھی ہانیہ کے کمرے میں گھسا اسے گلے سے لگائے روتا رہتا تھا۔

صفدر باجوہ صاحب کے مزاج میں حاکمیت اور سختی تھی۔ وہ چاہتے ہوئے بھی اپنے بچوں سے فری نہیں تھے۔ یہی وجہ تھی کہ آسیہ بیگم کی رحلت کے بعد جہاں اس گھر سے خوشیاں روٹھی تھیں وہیں رشتہ داروں نے بھی آنا جانا کم کر دیا۔ جاذب کو واپس چلے جانا تھا ایسے میں آٹھ سال کی ہانیہ کو ملازمین کے رحم و کرم پر چھوڑ کر بے فکر رہنا ان کے لیے ممکن نہیں تھا۔ لہٰذا خاصی سوچ و بچار کے بعد بالآخر انہیں وہ فیصلہ کرنا پڑا۔ جس کے لیے انہوں نے کبھی سوچا بھی نہیں تھا۔ صرف ہانیہ کی زندگی اور مستقبل کے لیے انہیں ذکیہ بیگم کو بیوی بنا کر آسیہ بیگم کی جگہ اس گھر میں لانا پڑا تھا کہ جس کے در و دیوار سے جھلکتی وحشت صاف دکھائی دیتی تھی۔ ذکیہ بیگم کو پہلے شوہر سے طلاق ہو چکی تھی۔ لہٰذا صفدر باجوہ کی زندگی میں آنے کے بعد وہ اگر بہت اچھی چوائس ثابت نہیں ہو سکی تھیں تو اتنی بری بھی نہیں تھیں۔

ہانیہ ''باجوہ ہاؤس'' میں ذکیہ بیگم کی آمد کے بعد منیر صاحب سے مزید دور ہو گئی تھی۔ وہ شخص جو صرف اس کی ماں سے محبت کا دعوے دار تھا۔ اسی شخص کو ماں کی وفات کے بعد کسی اور کے ساتھ مطمئن دیکھ کر روز جانے کتنے آتش فشاں تھے جو اس کے اندر پھٹتے تھے۔ مرد ذات سے بدگمانی کا پہلا بیج یہ شادی ہی ثابت ہوئی تھی۔ جس کے لیے وہ قطعی یہ ماننے کو تیار نہیں تھی کہ یہ شادی صرف اس کے مستقبل اور تحفظ کے لیے کی گئی ہے۔ وہ سوچتی کہ کاش اس کی ماں زندہ ہوتی تو ہرگز باجوہ صاحب کو اس بے وفائی کے لیے معاف نہ کرتی۔ اندر ہی اندر کی گھٹن اور کھولن نے اس کی ذات میں بہت سے

رخنے ڈال دیے تھے۔ وہ پہلے سے زیادہ حساس اور تنہا ہو گئی تھی۔ یہ اس کی حساسیت اور تنہائی کا احساس ہی تھا کہ بہت چھوٹی سی عمر میں اس نے رنگوں سے کھیلنا شروع کر دیا۔ اپنے اندر کے غبار کو وہ مختلف مناظر اور تصاویر کے ذریعے باہر نکالتی تھی۔ وہ میٹرک میں تھی جب اس کی پھوپھو زاد ہادیہ پاکستان دیکھنے کے شوق میں اس کے پاس چلی آئی اور پھر اس کا دل ایسا لگا پاکستان میں کہ جاذب کی خفگی اور ماں کے اعتراض کے باوجود وہ ''باجوہ ہاؤس'' کی ہو کر ہی رہ گئی۔ ہانیہ کے بی اے کے بعد اس نے بھی مزید تعلیم کے لیے اسی کے ساتھ یونیورسٹی میں داخلہ لے لیا۔ دونوں ایک ہی کمرے میں سوتیں اور ہر جگہ اکٹھی رہتیں۔ صحیح معنوں میں ہادیہ کے آجانے سے ہانیہ کی زندگی میں بہت بڑی تبدیلی آئی تھی۔ وہ اب زندگی جینے لگی تھی۔ مارننگ واک' ایوننگ واک' یونیورسٹی کے فکشنز میں دل لگانے لگی تھی۔ ذکیہ بیگم خود کو ان دونوں کے معاملات سے دور ہی رکھتیں۔

ریاض مصطفیٰ صاحب' صفدر منیر باجوہ صاحب کے قریبی دوستوں میں سے تھے۔ انہی کے گھر ایک تقریب میں انہیں اور ان کی بیگم کو ہانیہ پسند آئی تھی اور دونوں ہی اسے اپنے گھر کی بہو بنانے پر تل گئے۔ صفدر صاحب نے میکال کو دیکھا تھا۔ انہیں وہ پسند تھا۔ لہٰذا ریاض صاحب کے سوال پر انہوں نے اپنی رضامندی کا اظہار کر دیا۔

دونوں گھروں میں شادی کی تیاریاں ہو رہی تھیں اور دونوں فریق' جن کی شادی ہو رہی تھی دونوں ہی اس بندھن پر خوش اور راضی نہیں تھے۔

ادھوری باتیں ہی زندگی ہیں
وہ گزری باتیں ہی زندگی ہیں
اگرچہ دل کی اداس اجڑی ہوئی رتوں میں
بکھر گئی ہیں
کئی زمانوں سے ساری باتیں، وہ گزری باتیں
سلگتی شاموں کے جلتے بجھتے الاؤ میں ہی پگھل گئی ہیں
ادھوری باتیں ضروری باتیں
یہ خشک ہوتی ہوئی رگوں کی سیاہ قبروں میں نیم مردہ
ڈسی ہوئی خواہشوں کے ہمراہ، پڑی ہوئی ہیں
یہ آنکھ کی پتلیوں میں تھک کے، بھٹکتی پلکوں پہ سو گئی ہیں
تمام باتیں درست جاناں، تمام خدشے بجا ہیں لیکن
ہر ایک امکانِ زندگی میں......
رگوں میں اور روح کی زمین میں
انہی کی یادیں بھٹک رہی ہیں
انہی کے دم سے لطیف جذبوں، ٹھٹھرتے جذبوں
بجھی تمناؤں میں رمک ہے
ادھوری باتیں ہی زندگی ہیں، وہ گزری باتیں ہی زندگی ہیں
خیال رکھنا......!
ادھوری باتیں بھلا نہ دینا
وہ گزری باتیں بھلا نہ دینا......
خیال رکھنا......!

ٹیوب ویل چل رہا تھا۔
لہلہاتی سرسبز فصلیں، ٹھنڈا ٹھار پانی جذب کرتیں ایکدم سے جوان دکھائی دینے لگی تھیں۔
زائر ملک نے دونوں ہاتھوں کے پیالے میں پانی بھر کر کئی بار منہ پر چھپا کے مارے...... گرمی کا زور انتہا پر تھا۔ وہ ابھی کھڑا ہوا تھا کہ حویلی سے پیغام آ گیا۔

''زائر......او زائر بڑی حویلی میں چوہدرانی صاحبہ یاد کر رہی ہیں تجھے۔''

''خیر ہے......؟'' عقیل مزارع کی اطلاع پر اس نے ہاتھ قمیص کے دامن سے خشک کرتے ہوئے سر اٹھا کر اسے دیکھا۔

''آہو خیر ہی ہے' وہ اصل میں چوہدرانی صاحبہ کی پوتی آ رہی ہے باہر سے' اسی کو لینے ائرپورٹ جانا ہے تجھے۔''

''پوتی...... یہ اتنے سالوں بعد چوہدرانی کی پوتی کہاں سے آ گئی؟'' وہ حیران ہوا تھا۔ جب عقیل مزارعے نے بتایا۔

''یار کہا تو ہے باہر کے ملک سے آ رہی ہے۔ پہلے تو مجھے بھی نہیں پتا تھا' آج ہی حویلی میں سب کو پتا چلا ہے کہ ان کی ایک پوتی بھی ہے۔ آخر ایک ہی تو بیٹا تھا چوہدرانی صاحبہ کا۔''

''ہوں' تم چلو میں آتا ہوں۔''

تازہ شیو والے شفاف چہرے سے پانی کی بوندیں یوں گر رہی تھیں جیسے دمکتے موتی ہوں۔ عقیل مزارع' اس کی تسلی پر اپنے کندھے پر پڑا پٹکا درست کرتے ہوئے واپس پلٹا تھا۔

''ذرا جلدی آ جانا' چوہدرانی صاحبہ بڑی بے صبری سے تیرا انتظار کر رہی ہیں۔''

''ٹھیک ہے' ٹھیک ہے' آ جاتا ہوں' تو جا۔'' اب کے اس کے ماتھے پر ہلکی سی شکن ابھری تھی' جواب میں عقیل مزارع بنا مزید کچھ کہے' آگے بڑھ گیا۔ اس کے جانے کے بعد وہ شیشم کے بڑے سے پیڑ کے تنے سے ٹیک لگا کر بیٹھ گیا۔

''دو پتر اناراں دے......

ساڈا دکھ سن کے روندے پتھر پہاڑاں دے''

اپنی مخصوص ٹون میں' پلکیں موندے' قدرے دھیمی آواز میں وہ گنگنانا شروع ہوا تھا۔ جب کرم داد قریب سے گزرتے ہوئے اس کے پاس آ کھڑا ہوا۔

''اوئے زائر یار' پانچ سال ہو گئے تجھے اس کا جوگ لیے ہوئے' اوئے خدا کا واسطہ ہے یار' اب بھول جا اسے' چھوڑ دے اس کا پیچھا۔''

''چھوڑ دیا' مگر اسے بھلانا میرے بس میں نہیں ہے۔'' کرم داد کی نصیحت پر فوراً سے پیشتر آنکھیں کھولتے ہوئے وہ بولا تھا۔

''کیوں نہیں ہے بس میں' وہ دنیا کی آخری لڑکی تو نہیں تھی اور پھر تجھ میں کس چیز کی کمی ہے' کھڑی کھلوتی لڑکی کو اکھ چک کے دیکھ لے تو سڑ کے سوا ہو جائے' کیوں نئیں سمجھتا تو......''

کرم داد اس کا درد آشنا تھا۔ تبھی ہزار بار پہلے کی ہوئی نصیحت دہراتے ہوئے جذباتی ہوا تھا۔ زائر نے جواب میں پھر سے پلکیں موند لیں۔

''جن کے سنہری خوابوں کو کالی سیاہ تقدیر کے گھور اندھیرے چاٹ جائیں' انہیں کسی بات کی سمجھ نہیں لگتی کرم داد' میری خوشیوں اور سنہری خوابوں کو بھی میری تقدیر کے اندھیروں نے نگل لیا ہے۔''

''چھوڑ یار' مت کر ایسی مایوسی کی باتیں' دنیا کسی ایک شخص پر ختم نہیں ہو جاتی۔''

''میری ہو گئی ہے۔''

''خود کی ہے تُو نے' ورنہ آج کل ایسی محبت کوئی نہیں کرتا۔''

''میں تو کرتا ہوں ناں' خیر چھوڑ' حویلی جا رہا ہوں میں' چل رہے ہو ساتھ؟''

''نہیں' میں ذرا کھیتوں کی طرف جا رہا تھا' پانی کا مسئلہ ہو گیا ہے' تو جا۔''

''چل ٹھیک ہے پھر رب راکھا۔''

''رب راکھا'' کرم داد بھی اس کے ساتھ ہی اٹھ کھڑا ہوا تھا۔

اگلے پندرہ منٹ میں اس کے قدم حویلی کے شاندار بیرونی دروازے کو پار کر رہے تھے۔

''السلام علیکم چوہدرانی صاحبہ۔''

''وعلیکم السلام زائر' کہاں تھے' میں کب سے تمہاری راہ دیکھ رہی ہوں۔''

''خیریت؟''

''ہوں' خیر ہی ہے۔ وہ لندن سے میری پوتی آرہی ہے' اسے لینے کے لیے ابھی فوراً لاہور ائرپورٹ کے لیے نکل جاؤ شاباش۔''

''وہ تو ٹھیک ہے چوہدرانی صاحبہ' لیکن میں انہیں پہچانوں گا کیسے؟''

''ارے...... اس میں کیا مشکل ہے' وہاں جو لڑکی سب سے پیاری ہو سمجھ لینا وہی میری پوتی ہے۔''

اس بار چوہدرانی کے الفاظ پر وہ ذرا سا رخ پھیرتے ہوئے مسکرایا تھا۔

''چوہدرانی صاحبہ شہر کی ساری لڑکیاں ہی خوب صورت اور پیاری ہوتی ہیں' اب سب کی سب تو آپ کی پوتیاں نہیں ہو سکتی ناں۔''

''ہوں' یہ بھی ٹھیک ہے' اچھا ایک کام کر' یہ فون رکھ اپنے پاس' وہ تجھے خود کال کر کے بتادے گی' کہ کہاں ہے' پھر جہاں وہ کہے وہیں چلے جانا' ٹھیک ہے......؟''

''جی ٹھیک ہے؟''

وہ اسی حویلی میں پل بڑھ کر جوان ہوا تھا' تبھی مزید کوئی نقطہ اعتراض اٹھائے چوہدرانی سے گاڑی کی چابی لے کر واپس پلٹ آیا۔ حویلی میں چوہدرانی کو سو بکھیڑے تھے' کچن سے بھانت بھانت کی اشتہا انگیز خوشبوئیں اٹھ رہی تھیں' کونے کونے کو الگ چمکایا جارہا تھا' وہ اپنی ہی دھن میں سرسری سی ایک نگاہ اطراف میں ڈالتے ہوئے گاڑی کی طرف بڑھ آیا۔

''زائر...... جب ہماری شادی ہوگی' تم مجھے بڑی سی گاڑی میں سیر کراؤ گے ناں؟''

''ہاں۔''

کسی کی جگر جگر کرتی ستارے سی روشن نگاہوں میں دیکھتے ہوئے اس نے اقرار کیا تھا۔

''سچی؟'' اس کے اقرار پر وہ بے حد خوش ہوئی تھی۔

''ہوں سچی۔''

''ہائے اللہ' بس پھر تو پکی بات ہے میری شادی تم سے ہی ہوگی۔''

''ان شاء اللہ۔''

اس نے مسکرا کر کہا تھا اور پھر اس مسکراہٹ کا بدلہ لینے کے لیے اس کی تقدیر سالوں اس پر ہنستی رہی تھی۔ بے ساختہ اس لمحے اسے نوجوان شاعر راشد ترین کی ایسی ہی ایک نظم شدت سے یاد آئی تھی۔

بڑے ہی نازوں سے پلنے والی
وفا کے رستے پہ چلنے والی
تمام رشتوں کو توڑ کے تم

ہمیں اکیلا ہی چھوڑ کے تم
کہ غیر لوگوں کا پاس کرکے
ہمارے دل کو اداس کرکے
ہمیں محبت شناس کرکے
کسی سے چاہت جتا رہی ہو
سنا ہے اپنوں سے میں نے جاناں
بڑی حویلی میں جا رہی ہو
وہ ایک لڑکے کی چاہتوں کو
ہماری ساری رفاقتوں کو
جو ایک پل میں بھلا کے تم نے
خطوط سارے جلا کے تم نے
سبھی کو ہم پہ ہنسا کے جاناں
کسی سے الفت نبھا رہی ہو
سنا ہے اپنوں سے میں نے جاناں
بڑی حویلی میں جا رہی ہو
بڑی حویلی کے رہنے والوں کی
زندگانی بھی دیکھ لینا
دلوں پہ کرتے ہیں جبر کیسا
یہ حکمرانی بھی دیکھ لینا
یہ ناز تیرے بجا ہیں لیکن
غیر لوگوں کا کیا بھروسہ
یہ غیر لوگوں کے طنز سارے
کبھی بھی دل پر نہ سہہ سکو گی
بڑے ہی نازوں سے پلنے والی
پہ جشن کیسا منا رہی ہو
سنا ہے لوگوں سے میں نے جاناں
بڑی حویلی میں جا رہی ہو
وہ ایک شاعر کی زندگانی کے
خواب سارے ہی نوچ ڈالے
جو اس نے تیرے لیے بنے تھے
جو اس نے تیرے لیے چُنے تھے
اب اس کی قسمت میں فرقتوں کے

اداس موسم کے رتجگے ہیں
تمہیں تو شاید پتا نہیں ہے
یہ سارے قسمت کے فیصلے ہیں
تمہیں پتا ہے وہ تیرا شاعر
سبھی سے کیسے الجھ گیا ہے
جو اس نے لکھے تھے چاہتوں سے
خطوط سارے جلا رہی ہو
سنا ہے اپنوں سے میں نے جاناں
بڑی حویلی میں جا رہی ہو

گاڑی کے ایکسیلیٹر پر اچانک اس کا دباؤ بڑھا تھا مگر پھر ایکدم سے ہی اس نے اسپیڈ بڑھادی وہ سمجھتا تھا کہ اس کی چچازاد اور بچپن کی منگ سائرہ افضل ہی اس کی زندگی ہے جس کی خوب صورت آنکھوں کے ہر خواب کو اس نے پورا کرنا ہے مگر......اس نے غلط سمجھا تھا' وہ اس کی زندگی نہیں تھی۔

❁......❁......❁

''پاپا میں آپ کو صاف لفظوں میں کہہ چکا ہوں مجھے یہ شادی نہیں کرنی' کسی قیمت پر بھی نہیں۔''

وہ ابھی آدھے گھنٹے قبل ریاض صاحب کے ایمرجنسی بلاوے پر پاکستان آیا تھا اور اب گھر میں شادی کا ماحول دیکھ کر پہلے ٹھٹکا' پھر بڑی بھابی سے اپنے مایوں کا سن کر بدک اٹھا۔ تاہم ریاض صاحب اطمینان سے سگار پیتے رہے تھے جس پر وہ مزید مشتعل ہو اٹھا۔

''میں آپ سے کچھ کہہ رہا ہوں پاپا......''

''سن لیا ہے' تم بھی سن لو' اس شادی سے تمہاری زندگی پر کوئی اثر نہیں پڑنے والا' یہ صرف پیپر میرج ہوگی اور بس......''

''مگر کیوں' ایسی کون سی افتاد پڑ گئی ہے' اس لڑکی پر جو یوں اس کے گھر والے اسے سر سے اتار پھینکنا چاہتے ہیں۔''

''کنٹرول یور سیلف میکال' خبردار اس بچی کے کردار پر کیچڑ مت اچھالنا' یہ میرے دل کی خوشی ہے کہ وہ میرے گھر میری بیٹی بن کر آئے۔''

''اگر یہ آپ کی خوشی ہے تو میرے علاوہ اس گھر میں آپ کا ایک اور بھی کنوارہ بیٹا ہے' یہ فرائض منصبی اسے سونپ دیجیے۔''

اس بار اس کا لہجہ گستاخانہ تھا' مسز حسن کو جلال آ گیا۔

''زبان سنبھال کر بات کرو میکال' اپنے باپ سے بات کر رہے ہو تم' کسی ملازم سے نہیں۔ اور شادی طے ہو چکی ہے کل برأت جانی ہے' اگر تم نے اپنے پاپا کی عزت نہ رکھی تو یاد رکھنا میں تمہیں اپنا دودھ معاف نہیں کروں گی۔''

''یہ صاف بلیک میلنگ ہے مما۔''

''جو بھی سمجھو' ہم بھائی صاحب کی عزت کو رسواء نہیں کر سکتے' ہم نے خود دامن پھیلا کر ان سے ان کی بیٹی کا ہاتھ مانگا ہے' اب کس منہ سے انکار کریں۔''

ان کے لہجے میں کسی قسم کی رعایت کی گنجائش نہیں تھی' میکال غصے اور بے بسی سے لب بھینچتا انہیں دیکھتا رہ گیا۔

❁ ...... ❁ ...... ❁

برات آ گئی تھی۔

ہانیہ کو آخری لمحے تک امید تھی کہ ہادیہ اس کی مدد کرے گی' مگر نکاح کے وقت وہ تو گدھے کے سر سے سینگ کی مانند غائب ہو گئی تھی۔ ہانیہ کو اس سے اس دھوکے بازی کی امید نہیں تھی' نہال جو اس کا یونیورسٹی فیلو تھا' وہ بھی کہیں غائب ہو گیا تھا' وہ خون کے گھونٹ پیتی بار بار پلکیں جھپک کر اپنے آنسو ضبط کرنے کی کوشش کرتی رہی۔

نکاح نامے پر سائن کرتے وقت اس نے پھر سر اٹھا کر سامنے دیکھا' مگر ہادیہ نہیں تھی' اس کا چہرہ ضبط کی شدت سے سرخ ہو گیا تھا۔ دلہا بنے میکال کا موڈ بھی کچھ خاص خوشگوار نہیں تھا' بھیگی بھیگی سی سرد رات برقی قمقموں کا حصہ بنی' دھیرے دھیرے گزر رہی تھی' جب وہ کانچ کی گڑیا سی لڑکی اپنے مکمل سنگھار کے ساتھ' کسی تصویر کی مانند خاموش' اسٹیج پر اس کے برابر میں آ بیٹھی۔

اگلے دو گھنٹوں میں اُول فضول رسموں کے بعد بالآخر رخصتی کا وقت بھی آ گیا۔ میکال صفدر صاحب اور جاذب کے ساتھ دیگر رشتہ داروں سے مل کر واپس پلٹا' تو اس نے جاذب اور ہادیہ کو ہانیہ کے ساتھ کھڑے روتے ہوئے دیکھا' وہ دونوں اسے گاڑی کے قریب لا رہے تھے' وہ وہیں رک گیا۔

اگلے پانچ منٹ میں جب وہ گاڑی کے پاس پہنچ گئی تھی اس نے ذکیہ بیگم کو دیکھا تھا' بھیگی ہوئی پلکوں کے ساتھ وہ ہانیہ کو پیار دینے کے لیے اس کے قریب آئی تھیں' جب اس نے درشتگی سے ان کے بڑھے ہوئے ہاتھ پرے جھٹک دیئے۔

''ڈونٹ ٹچ می' سوتیلی عورت کبھی ماں نہیں بن سکتی' بالآخر یہ ثابت کر دیا آپ نے۔'' اس کے لہجے میں غصے کے ساتھ ساتھ غراہٹ تھی۔ میکال جاذب سے مصافحہ کرتے ہوئے ٹھٹک گیا۔

''آج اگر میری ماں زندہ ہوتیں تو کبھی یوں میری خوشی کی پروا کیے بغیر ایک قطعی ناپسندیدہ شخص کے ساتھ میری زندگی کا سودا نہ کرتیں۔''

وہ اپنے اندر کا غبار نکال رہی تھی۔ جاذب اور ہادیہ کے چہرے کا رنگ اڑ گیا۔ وہ بھی اس جیسا ہی کیس تھی' یقیناً اس کے ساتھ بھی زبردستی کا سودا ہوا تھا' پھر بھی وہ شدید اذیت و ذلت کا شکار لب بھینچ کر سرخ چہرے کے ساتھ گاڑی میں آ بیٹھا۔ اپنی سسرال سے گھر تک وہ لب بھینچے خاموش بیٹھا رہا تھا۔ مگر گھر واپسی کے بعد وہ کہاں نکل گیا کسی کو خبر نہیں ہو سکی تھی۔

❁ ...... ❁ ...... ❁

ضبط گریہ سے سرخ آنکھیں لیے' چپ چاپ بے آواز روتے ہوئے وہ عائشہ برہان کے سامنے بیٹھا تھا۔ اور وہ جو فقط دو ہی سال میں ''رل'' کر رہ گئی تھی' یوں صبح سویرے اسے شکستہ پا دیکھ کر ٹھٹک گئی' اندر کو دھنسی آنکھوں میں گہرا کرب آن ٹھہرا تھا' میکال کو روتے دیکھ کر اسے لگا' جیسے اس کا دل کٹ کر رہ گیا ہو۔

''میکال' کیا ہوا ہے' رات تو فرسٹ نائٹ تھی ناں تمہاری شادی کی......؟''

''ہاں......'' ضبط کے باوجود اس کا لہجہ بے حد بوجھل ہو رہا تھا۔

''پھر...... یہاں کیوں چلے آئے......؟''

''بس یونہی۔''

''پاگل ہوئے ہو' کیا سوچ رہی ہو گی وہ' تمہیں ایسا نہیں کرنا چاہیے تھا۔''

''مجھے ایسا نہیں کرنا چاہیے تھا' اور وہ...... جو ساری کائنات کا مالک ہے' کیا اسے ایسا کرنا چاہیے تھا......؟''

ایکدم سے وہ بے حد جذباتی ہوا تھا۔ عائشہ از حد حیرانی سے اسے دیکھتی رہ گئی۔

''کیوں کرتا ہے وہ ایسے عائش؟ خود ہی دل میں کسی کے لیے محبت ڈال کر' پھر خود ہی دل اجاڑ دیتا ہے، کیوں؟ وہ تو شہ رگ سے بھی زیادہ قریب ہے' ستر ماؤں سے زیادہ بڑھ کر پیار کرنے والا ہے' وہ کیسے دیکھ سکتا ہے مجھے یوں سسکتے ہوئے' کیوں اتنا بے بس کر دیا ہے اس نے مجھے کہ میں چاہتے ہوئے بھی کچھ نہیں کر پا رہا' میں نے جسم نہیں مانگا تھا' اس سے' روح مانگی تھی' محبت مانگی تھی' مگر اس نے جسم دے دیا' محبت نہیں دی' کیوں نہیں دیتا وہ محبت' نہیں دینی تھی تو کیوں ہوا پانی خوراک سے بھی زیادہ ضروری بنایا اس نے اسے' کیوں......؟''

جذب کے عالم میں کہتے ہوئے وہ تڑپ اٹھا تھا۔ عائشہ کی آنکھیں آنسوؤں سے بھر آئیں۔

''گھر جاؤ میکال' یہ وقت ایسی باتوں کا نہیں ہے۔''

''میرا دل نہیں چاہ رہا گھر جانے کو......''

عائشہ کے آنسو پونچھنے پر وہ پھر کرب انگیز لہجے میں بولا تھا۔ جواب میں وہ افسردہ سی اٹھ کھڑی ہوئی۔

''خدا کا واسطہ ہے میکال' یوں اس طرح سے اپنی اور میری زندگی کو مشکل میں مت ڈالو' میں آل ریڈی بہت کٹھن حالات کا سامنا کر رہی ہوں' مجھے اور اذیت مت دو' پلیز۔''

وہ ٹھیک کہہ رہی تھی' اسے اچانک اپنی حماقت کا احساس ہوا تھا۔

''سوری۔'' دائیں ہاتھ سے آنکھیں پونچھتے ہوئے وہ جونہی کھڑا ہوا' عائشہ نے اس کا ہاتھ تھام لیا۔

''میری جان ہے تم میں' یہ یاد رکھنا' اب جاؤ۔''

میکال نے اس کی بات سنی تھی اور بہت آہستگی سے اپنا ہاتھ اس کے ہاتھ سے چھڑاتے ہوئے پھر گاڑی میں آ بیٹھا تھا۔

کوئی میرے دل دا' حال نہ جانے او ربا
رو رو کے سکھ گئے نین نمانے او ربا
کوئی میرے دل دا' حال نہ جانے او ربا

وہ عائشہ برہان کو پیچھے چھوڑ آیا تھا اور اب اس کی گاڑی میں' سلو ڈرائیونگ کے ساتھ' گونجتی راحت فتح علی خان کی آواز' اسے اپنے دل کی ترجمان لگ رہی تھی۔

جیڑے ٹر جاندے پیچھاں مڑ کے نئیں تکدے
ہویا کی قصور ساتھوں' اے وی تے نئیں دسدے
کیتھے جا کے لائے اونھے اپنے ٹھکانے او ربا
کوئی میرے دل دا' حال نہ جانے او ربا
حال نہ جانے او ربا......!!!!

گاڑی کی اچانک بریک کے ساتھ ہی اس کا طلسم بھی ٹوٹا تھا' ریاض حسن صاحب اس کی ذہنی کیفیت سے آگاہ تھے تبھی انہوں نے گھر میں سب کو منع کر دیا تھا کہ وہ اسے کچھ نہ کہیں۔

صبح کی سپیدی خاصی پھیل چکی تھی' وہ بے دلی سے گاڑی پارک کرنے کے بعد تیزی سے سیڑھیاں کراس کرتا اوپر اپنے کمرے میں آیا اور بنا کسی بھی تبدیلی کو اہمیت دیئے وارڈ روب سے اپنے کپڑے لے کر واش روم میں گھس گیا۔

نیچے ناشتے کی میز پر، صفدر صاحب کی فیملی کی طرف سے ناشتا آچکا تھا' مگر وہ مروتاً بھی نیچے نہیں آیا تھا۔ ہانیہ بیدار ہونے کے بعد اپنے متوقع حال پر بنا واویلا کیے' وارڈ روب کی طرف چلی آئی۔

میکال واش روم سے نکلا تو وہ اپنے کپڑے لے کر واش روم میں گھس گئی۔ اگلے پندرہ منٹ کے بعد وہ فریش ہو کر کمرے میں واپس آئی تو میکال بستر پر آڑھا ترچھا لیٹا سونے کی تیاری کر رہا تھا۔ وہ ایک سرسری نگاہ اس پر ڈالتی' اپنے بال سلجھانے لگی۔

❁ ...... ❁ ...... ❁

شہر خاموشاں میں اس روز معمول سے کہیں بڑھ کر سناٹا تھا۔

وہ بے قرار سا اِدھر اُدھر نگاہ دوڑاتا اپنی ماں کی قبر کے قریب آ کھڑا ہوا۔ انتہائی رقت و محبت کے ساتھ فاتحہ پڑھ کر وہ ابھی چہرے پر ہاتھ پھیر رہا تھا جب اس کی بھٹکتی بے قرار نگاہ اس پر پڑی تھی۔

ہر روز کی طرح سیاہ چادر میں لپٹی، وہ سبک روہوا کی مانند' خراماں خراماں چلتی اپنی مطلوبہ قبر تک گئی تھی' پھر اس کے دیکھتے ہی دیکھتے اس نے قبر پر پانی کا چھڑکاؤ کیا' اس کام سے فارغ ہو کر اس نے ہاتھ میں پکڑے شاپر سے تازہ پھولوں کی پتیاں نکال کر اس قبر پر بکھیر دی تھیں' اس نے ذرا سی ترچھی نگاہ کر کے دیکھا' وہ اب قبر کے پہلو میں بیٹھی' بہت محبت اور عجیب یاسیت کے ساتھ اس پر بکھری تازہ گلاب کی پتیوں کو اپنے دائیں ہاتھ سے محسوس کرتی' قبر پر ہاتھ پھیر رہی تھی۔

عذیر سے صبر نہ ہو سکا۔

فاتحہ سے فارغ ہونے کے بعد' وہ بہت سوچتے ہوئے اس قبر کے قریب آیا تھا۔

''ایکسکیوز می۔''

اس کی پکار پر اس لڑکی کی محویت ٹوٹی تھی' وہ یوں چونکی تھی گویا کسی گہرے خواب سے بیدار ہوئی ہو۔

''جی......'' بنا پلٹ کر دیکھے اس نے چادر کو چہرے پر مزید پھیلا لیا تھا۔

''میرا نام عذیر ہے' میں یہاں روز اپنی ماں کی قبر پر فاتحہ پڑھنے کے لیے آتا ہوں' کیا میں جان سکتا ہوں' مٹی کے اس ڈھیر تلے' آپ کا کون سا رشتہ دفن ہے؟''

''میرا رشتہ......؟'' اس کے سوال پر ہلکے سے بڑبڑاتے ہوئے' وہ بے کلی سے کھڑی ہوئی تھی۔

''کوئی رشتہ نہیں۔''

''کوئی رشتہ نہیں تو روز یہاں کیا لینے آتی ہیں' آندھی' طوفان' بارش کی بھی پروا نہیں کرتیں' اس بات کا بھی احساس نہیں کہ عورت کا یوں روز قبرستان میں آنا کسی طور مناسب نہیں۔''

عذیر کو حیرانی کے ساتھ ساتھ غصہ بھی آیا تھا۔ وہ چپ چاپ کھڑی رہی۔

''کون ہو تم؟''

تیوری چڑھاتے ہوئے اب اس نے سوال بدلا تھا۔ مگر لڑکی کے چہرے پر وہی بے نیازی تھی۔

''پتا نہیں۔''

زیر لب بڑبڑا کر ایک نظر سامنے موجود قبر پر ڈالتے ہوئے وہ پلٹ گئی تھی اور عذیر جو آج ہر صورت اسے جان لینا چاہتا تھا' لب بھینچے کھڑا اسے جاتے ہوئے دیکھتا رہا۔

❁ ...... ❁ ...... ❁

پت جھڑ کی دہلیز پر تنہا
بے چہرہ پتوں کی صورت
ہم کو آج لیے پھرتی ہے
تیرے دھیان کی تیز ہَوا

تھکن سے چور بدن کے ساتھ، بنارات کا کھانا کھائے' وہ لان کی طرف بنی سیڑھیوں پر بیٹھی یوں سرد ہوا کے تھپیڑے برداشت کر رہی تھی' جیسے خزاں رت میں درخت سے گرا کوئی پتا' بھاری قدموں کا بوجھ برداشت کرتا ہے۔

دو سال ہو گئے تھے اس نے پلٹ کر زندگی کو نہیں دیکھا تھا' مگر آج' دو سال کے بعد' میکال کے غیر متوقع ایس ایم ایس اور پھر آنسوؤں نے اسے اندر سے کاٹ کر رکھ دیا تھا۔ اس کا دیور آیا تھا' دس سال کینیڈا میں مقیم رہنے کے بعد اسے پاکستان اور اپنے گھر والوں کی یاد آئی تھی' تاہم وہ اسے دیکھ کر ٹھٹک گیا تھا۔

وہ میکال سے مل کر شکستہ دلی کے ساتھ گھر واپس آئی تھی' جب اس کا سامنا' اس سے ہوا تھا۔

''لو آ گئی تمہاری بھاوج' مل لو......'' گھر میں قدم رکھتے ہی اسے اپنی ساس کی فخریہ آواز سنائی دی تھی اور جواب میں جس ہینڈسم سے لڑکے نے پلٹ کر حیرانی سے اسے' دیکھا تھا' وہ اس کا دیور اریج تھا۔ عائشہ اس کی حیرانی کی وجہ جانتی تھی' تبھی اس کا سر جھکتا چلا گیا تھا۔

اسی روز شام میں جب وہ رات کا کھانا تیار کر رہی تھی' وہ اس کے پاس کچن میں آیا تھا۔

''ایکسکیوز می' اگر آپ کو ناگوار نہ گزرے تو کیا میں کچھ دیر یہاں بیٹھ سکتا ہوں؟'' وہ چونکی تھی تاہم اس نے پلٹ کر اسے نہیں دیکھا تھا۔

''جی ہاں۔''

''کیا بنا رہی ہیں......؟'' دونوں بازو سینے پر باندھتے ہوئے وہ قریب آیا تھا۔

''چکن بریانی۔'' عائشہ نے بے حد مختصر جواب پر اکتفا کیا۔ وہ کچھ دیر خاموش کھڑا رہا پھر کچن کی صلیب سے ٹیک لگاتے ہوئے سنجیدگی سے بولا۔

''آپ ایک سمجھ دار' خوب صورت خاتون ہیں' یقیناً پڑھی لکھی بھی ہوں گی کیا میں جان سکتا ہوں اس کے باوجود آپ نے میرے بھائی سے شادی کرنے کا احمقانہ فیصلہ کیوں کیا؟''

عائشہ جانتی تھی وہ یہی سوال کرے گا' تبھی اس کے دل پر جیسے کسی نے چٹکی کاٹی تھی۔

''ہوں' یہ میری امی کا فیصلہ تھا اور میں ان کے فیصلے سے بغاوت نہیں کر سکی؟''

''لیکن کیوں' یہ جانتے ہوئے بھی کہ وہ ایک ایب نارمل شخص ہے' بیوی کے حقوق ادا کرنا تو ایک طرف' وہ اس گھر میں آپ کو آپ کا جائز مقام بھی نہیں دلوا سکتا' اور کچھ بعید نہیں کہ رات میں سوتے ہوئے نقصان بھی پہنچا دے' پھر بھی آپ کے گھر والوں نے یہ فیصلہ کیا' کیوں؟''

عائشہ کو اس کے سوالات سے الجھن ہو رہی تھی مگر پھر بھی وہ اسے جواب دینے پر مجبور تھی۔ کیونکہ اسے اس گھر میں رہنا تھا' اب وہ آٹے کے کنستر سے آٹا نکال رہی تھی۔

''کیونکہ میری بڑی بہن کا رشتہ ان سے طے تھا' اور میرے بھائی کو آپ کے گھر والوں نے باہر کے خواب دکھا رکھے تھے' میری بہن اس رشتے کے لیے راضی نہیں تھی' اس لیے اس نے اپنی مرضی سے شادی کر لی' اس شادی کے بعد میرے گھر والوں کو جہاں برادری سے بے دخل ہونے کا خدشہ لاحق ہوا' وہیں سارے خواب بھی مٹی میں ملتے ہوئے محسوس

ہوئے' اسی لیے انہوں نے میری قربانی دی' تاہم مجھے اس پر کسی سے کوئی گلہ نہیں' کیونکہ یہ میرے نصیب کا لکھا ہے اور انسان نصیب کے لکھے سے کبھی نہیں بھاگ سکتا۔ ایم اے انگلش اور نفسیات کرنے کے باوجود' میں اپنی ماں کے حقوق سے آنکھیں نہیں پھیر سکتی' جس عورت نے مجھے جنم دے کر مجھے پروان چڑھایا' میری پرورش کی' اس کا یہ حق ہے کہ وہ چاہے تو مجھے کسی ایب نارمل شخص سے بیاہ دے یا پھر جان سے مار دے۔''

ضبط کی ہزار کوششوں کے باوجود بات کے اختتام پر اس کا لہجہ بھیگ گیا تھا۔ اریج کی آنکھوں میں مزید حیرانی عود آئی۔

''گڈ...... داد دیتا ہوں آپ کی فرماں برداری کی' مگر کاش آپ کو جنم دینے والی آپ کی ماں آپ کو جان سے مار دیتی' کیونکہ ہر روز کے مرنے سے ایک بار کا مرنا' کہیں بہتر ہوتا ہے۔''

اس بار اس کے لہجے میں ذرا سی تلخی تھی۔ اپنی بات مکمل کرنے کے بعد وہ وہاں ٹھہرا نہیں تھا۔ عائشہ کی آنکھوں میں جھلملاتے آنسوؤں کے دونوں قطرے کسی پکے ہوئے پھل کی طرح ٹوٹ کر اس کے گالوں پر لڑھکتے ہوئے گریبان میں جذب ہو گئے۔

ہوا کی خنکی میں مزید اضافہ ہو گیا تھا مگر وہ بے حس سی وہیں بیٹھی رہی۔ اندر دوزخ جلتے ہوں تو باہر کی خنکی کوئی معنی نہیں رکھتی۔ اس کا بھائی باہر چلا گیا تھا۔ بہن نے خفگی میں دوبارہ کبھی حال بھی پوچھنا گوارہ نہیں کیا' رہ گئی ماں تو وہ مہینے میں ایک آدھ بار چکر لگا کر اس کا حال دریافت کر جایا کرتی تھی۔

روز کھیتوں میں مشقت نے اس کے ہاتھ خاصے کھردرے کر ڈالے تھے۔ پھر بھی نم آنکھوں سے وہ اپنے ہاتھ سامنے پھیلائے جانے ان میں کیا تلاش رہی تھی۔ شاید وہ دن جب اس نے گھر کے بدترین حالات سے مجبور ہو کر پہلی بار قدم گھر سے باہر نکالے تھے اور ریاض حسن صاحب کی کمپنی جوائن کی تھی۔

وہ ایک مشفق اور مہربان انسان تھے۔ پھر ان کی بیٹی مائرہ سے اس کی بہت اچھی فرینڈ شپ تھی ان کا چھوٹا بیٹا نہال بھی اسے تھوڑا بہت جانتا تھا' تبھی اسے ان کی کمپنی میں جاب مل گئی تھی اور اس جاب سے اس نے بہت کچھ سیکھا تھا۔ ان دنوں گھر کے بدترین حالات کے ساتھ ساتھ اس کے دل کی دنیا بھی درہم برہم تھی۔

یونیورسٹی میں جو شخص اس کا ''متاعِ حیات'' تھا' اس شخص کے والدین نے صرف اس لیے اسے قبول نہیں کیا کہ وہ اور اس کی فیملی ان کے اسٹینڈرڈ کی نہیں تھی۔ دوسری وجہ اعتراض اس کا جاب کرنا تھا۔ وہ جاب جو اس کی خوشی نہیں مجبوری تھی۔ اس کی ماں نے زندگی میں بہت دکھ دیکھے تھے' وہ اپنی ذات سے ان دکھوں کا ازالہ کرنا چاہتی تھی' اس کا بھائی بیروزگار تھا بہن کم پڑھی لکھی تھی ایسے میں اچانک والد کی رحلت اور اس کے بعد پے در پے آنے والے مسائل نے اسے اپنی ذات سے یکسر غافل کر دیا تھا۔

''ارمغان کریم'' جو اس کی پہلی محبت اور خواہش تھا' سے دستبرداری آسان نہیں تھی' کیونکہ اس کے بہت سے خوب صورت خواب اس شخص کی رفاقت سے جڑے تھے اور خوابوں کا ٹوٹنا یا ان سے دستبردار ہو جانا کتنا تکلیف دہ ہے یہ وہی جان سکتا ہے جس نے یہ اذیت سہی ہو۔ اس نے ارمغان کو چھوڑ دیا تھا مگر اس کے بارہا اصرار پر بھی وہ جاب نہیں چھوڑی تھی۔ جس سے اس کے گھر کی دال روٹی کا سلسلہ چل رہا تھا۔

وہ اپنی ماں کے لیے جان دے سکتی تھی مگر اس کی ماں اسے محض جان بھی نہیں سکی۔

مہینے کے اختتام پر آفس ٹائم کے بعد وہ مارکیٹ نکل جاتی تھی اور بچت کے سارے پیسوں سے اپنے رشتوں کے لیے ان کی ضرورت کی تمام چھوٹی بڑی چیزیں خود خرید کر لاتی' جنہیں بعض اوقات خاصے احسان کرنے والے انداز میں قبول کیا جاتا۔

شعور سنبھالنے سے لے کر اب تک اسے اپنی ذات کی تنہائی شدت سے محسوس ہوتی تھی۔ وہ جتنی بھی تھک کر گھر آتی' اس کے گھر والوں نے کبھی اس کا احساس نہیں کیا تھا' دل چاہتا تو کھانا کھالیتی' نہیں تو کوئی اسے زبردستی کہہ کر کھلانے والا نہیں تھا۔ اس گھر کے دستور نرالے تھے مگر عائشہ برھان کی حساس طبیعت ان نرالے دستوروں سے کبھی بغاوت نہیں کر سکی تھی۔

سردی کا احساس مزید شدت اختیار کر چکا تھا' تبھی وہ اٹھ کر اندر کمرے میں چلی آئی تھی۔ جہاں اس کا ''نام نہاد'' شوہر ساری دنیا سے بے خبر گہری نیند کے مزے لوٹ رہا تھا۔ وہ تشنہ لب سی بیڈ کے ایک کنارے پر ٹک گئی۔

اسے یاد آ رہا تھا جب وہ زخمی روح کے ساتھ دلہن بنی اس گاؤں نما شہر میں آئی تھی تو ایک عجیب سی گھٹن کا احساس' اس کی جان پر بنا رہا تھا۔ مختلف سوچیں تھیں جو ذہن کا گھیراؤ کیے ہوئے تھیں۔ پتا نہیں کس شخص کے ساتھ اس کا نصیب پھوڑ آگیا ہوگا' پتا نہیں وہ دیکھنے میں کیسا ہوگا؟ شدید تھکن کے ساتھ یہ اذیت ناک خیالات اسے اور بھی نڈھال کر رہے تھے' اپنی ماں کی خوشی کے لیے اس نے قربانی تو دے دی تھی مگر پتا نہیں وہ اس قربانی کی لاج بھی رکھ پائے گی کہ نہیں' یہی خدشہ اسے پریشان کیے ہوئے تھا' جس وقت اسے کمرے میں لے جایا گیا تب تک اس کی الجھن برقرار رہی تھی تاہم جس وقت کوئی کمرے میں داخل ہوا' پھر بنا دروازہ لاک کیے اس کے پاس بیڈ پر بیٹھا اور بنا کسی سلام دعا کے فٹ سے اس کا ہاتھ پکڑ کر جب اس شخص نے اس سے پوچھا۔

''تم میری دلہن ہو ناں......؟'' تب وہ برف ہوگئی۔

فوراً سے پیشتر نظر اٹھا کر اس نے اپنے سامنے بیٹھے اپنے مجازی خدا کو دیکھا تھا' گہری سانولی رنگت پر' باہر کو آتے پیلے دانتوں نے اسے ابکائی پر مجبور کر دیا تھا' بال بہت ہلکے تھے اور دلہا ہونے کے باوجود اس شخص کی گردن پر جو سیاہی تھی' وہ سیاہی اسے اپنی ساری زندگی پر محیط نظر آ رہی تھی۔

اس کا دل چاہا وہ خوب ہنسے یا پھر اپنے نصیب کی سیاہی پر کسی کے گلے لگ کر خوب روئے۔

''اماں کہتی ہیں تم میری دلہن ہو' اماں ٹھیک کہتی ہیں ناں؟''

''ہاں۔'' بہت دیر کے بعد ڈبڈبائی آنکھوں سے اس کی طرف دیکھتے ہوئے اس کے لبوں نے جنبش کی تھی پھر فوراً اٹھ کر لباس تبدیل کر لیا۔ رات بھر شدت سے روتے ہوئے وہ اپنے پہلو میں لیٹے شخص کے خراٹوں سے بیزار رہی تھی۔

اگلے ایک ہفتے کے بعد اس شخص کو اپنے نصیب کا لکھا سمجھ کر وہ کسی بچے کی مانند اسے ٹریٹ کر رہی تھی۔ سب سے پہلا کام جو اس نے اس شخص سے کروایا تھا وہ ٹوتھ برش کا استعمال تھا۔ باتھ لینے میں بھی وہ اس کی مدد کرتی تھی' تبھی وہ کسی حد تک دیکھنے لائق ہو گیا تھا۔

ابھی یہ امتحان جاری تھا کہ اس روز اس کی ساس نے اسے نیا حکم سنا دیا۔

''بہو! ایک ماہ ہو گیا ہے تمہاری شادی کو' ہم نے گھر کے کام کاج کے علاوہ اور کچھ نہیں کہا تم سے' اب تم اس گھر کی بیٹی ہو' زمینوں کے کام کاج میں بھی دلچسپی لو' سب کچھ ملازمین پر چھوڑ کر نہیں بیٹھ سکتے۔''

اس کے پاس سوائے ان کے حکم پر سر جھکانے کے اور کوئی جواب نہیں تھا۔ صبح ناشتہ کیے بغیر وہ گھر سے نکلتی تھی اور شام گئے تھکن سے چُور بدن کے ساتھ گھر واپس لوٹتی تھی۔ گزرے دو سالوں میں کیا کچھ برداشت نہیں کیا تھا اس نے' مگر 'شکوہ' نام کی کوئی چیز کبھی اس کے لبوں پر نہیں آئی تھی۔ تاہم اب اریج کی اس گھر میں آمد نے اسے بہت ڈسٹرب کر کے رکھ دیا تھا۔

❁ ...... ❁ ...... ❁

وہ سو کر اٹھا تھا' ہانیہ کمرے میں نہیں تھی۔

تکیہ بانہوں میں دبا کر کچھ دیر وہ سستی سے پڑا رہا' پھر اٹھ کر فریش ہونے کے بعد نیچے ہال میں چلا آیا۔ جہاں قریب ہی کچن میں سارہ اور مائرہ اسی کے ٹاپک پر بات کر رہی تھیں۔

''میکال بھائی اس شادی پر خوش نہیں ہیں' کل رات بھی گھر سے باہر رہے ہیں۔''

مائرہ کہہ رہی تھی' تبھی سارہ بول اٹھی۔

''میکال بھائی خوش نہیں ہیں تو ہانیہ بھابی کون سی خوش ہیں' ویسے بھی وہ نہال بھائی میں زیادہ انٹرسٹڈ تھیں' صفدر انکل نے زبردستی انہیں اس شادی کے لیے مجبور کیا ہے' بڑی زیادتی ہوئی ہے نہال بھائی اور ہانیہ بھابی کے ساتھ سچی۔''

''تمہیں کیسے پتا کہ نہال بھائی ہانیہ بھابی میں انٹرسٹڈ تھے؟'' مائرہ چونکی تھی اور اس سے زیادہ شاید وہ ٹھٹک گیا تھا۔

''سمیر بھائی سے پتا چلا' کل رات وہ نہال بھائی کے کمرے میں ان سے اسی ٹاپک پر بات کر رہے تھے' ہانیہ بھابی کے کلاس فیلو ہیں ناں نہال بھائی۔''

''اگر ایسی بات تھی تو نہال بھائی کو اسٹینڈ لینا چاہیے تھا۔''

''لیا تھا انہوں نے' انکل اور آنٹی سے بات بھی کی تھی' مگر انہوں نے ان کی بات کو اہمیت نہیں دی' ابھی وہ پڑھ رہے ہیں ناں' اس لیے۔''

دونوں اپنی باتوں میں مگن تھیں اور شاید دونوں کو ہی اس کی آمد کی خبر نہیں تھی' میکال کو لگا جیسے اس کی آنکھوں میں دھواں بھر گیا ہو۔ کیا یہ سب اسی کی زندگی میں ہونا ضروری تھا؟

شام ڈھلے دن بھر کی آوارہ گردی کے بعد' قدرے تھک کر اس نے قدم دوبارہ گھر کی دہلیز پر دھرے تھے۔ گھر میں اب بھی کچھ مہمان ٹھہرے ہوئے تھے۔ کچھ ہی دیر بعد ولیمے کی تقریب تھی' ہانیہ صفدر کو ایک بار پھر دلہن بنا دیا گیا تھا تاہم اس سے کسی نے بھی بات نہیں کی' وہ خود بھی کسی سے بات کرنے کی پوزیشن میں نہیں تھا' تبھی چپ چاپ اپنے کمرے میں چلا آیا۔

ہانیہ نے صرف ایک بار سر اٹھا کر اس کی طرف دیکھا تھا پھر چپ چاپ سر جھکا لیا' سارہ اور مائرہ میکال کی کمرے میں آمد کے بعد فوراً وہاں سے کھسک گئی تھیں۔ میکال کچھ دیر لب بھینچے ہوئے اپنے اندر اٹھتے طوفان کو ضبط کرنے کی کوشش کرتا رہا' پھر کچھ سوچتے ہوئے بیڈ پر اس کے پاس آ بیٹھا۔

''السلام علیکم۔'' ہانیہ اس کے سلام کا جواب دینا نہیں چاہتی تھی پھر بھی اس نے سر اٹھایا تھا۔

''وعلیکم السلام۔'' لٹھ مار جواب پر وہ کچھ دیر لب بھینچے خاموش بیٹھا رہا پھر بولا۔

''آج ہماری شادی کا دوسرا دن ہے' اس لیے میں کچھ باتیں آپ کے گوش گزار کرنا ضروری سمجھتا ہوں۔ اصل میں مس ہانیہ' میں اس شادی کے لیے ایک فیصد بھی تیار نہیں تھا' یوں سمجھیے میرے والدین نے زبردستی مجبور کر کے یہ پھندا میرے گلے میں فٹ کیا ہے' میں عائشہ برہان میں انٹرسٹڈ تھا' عائشہ برہان..... میری پہلی محبت' میرا پہلا خواب' میری پہلی خواہش اور میری زندگی میں آنے والی پہلی آئیڈیل لڑکی ہے' بدقسمتی سے ہماری شادی نہیں ہو سکی مگر پھر بھی میں اس کے ہر پل میں موجود ہوں' اور وہ..... وہ میری ہر سانس میں موجود ہے' میں دھوکے باز' منافق انسان نہیں ہوں اس لیے یہ سب کچھ آپ کو صاف صاف بتا رہا ہوں' میرے پاس آپ کو دینے کے لیے کچھ بھی نہیں ہے نہ کوئی پیار' نہ عہد' نہ مقام' اس گھر میں آپ کسی کی بہو' یا بیٹی بن کر تو رہ سکتی ہیں' بیوی بن کر نہیں' کیونکہ میں اپنا پیار اپنی پہلی محبت پر نچھاور کر چکا ہوں' اب آپ چاہیں تو یہاں اس گھر میں رہ سکتی ہیں' اور اگر چاہیں تو یہاں سے جا سکتی ہیں' مجھے کوئی اعتراض نہیں ہو

گا۔'' اچھی طرح دل کا غبار نکالنے کے بعد وہ اٹھ کھڑا ہوا تھا۔

ہانیہ صفدر کو لگا شاید اب وہ زندگی میں کبھی اپنا سر اوپر نہیں اٹھا سکے گی' اسے یکلخت اپنی گردن پر بے تحاشا بوجھ محسوس ہوا تھا۔ یہ سب باتیں جو اس نے اس سے کہی تھیں وہ یہ سب باتیں پہلے سے جانتی تھی مگر کاش اس وقت اس شخص نے اس سے یہ سب باتیں نہ کہی ہوتیں۔ گلے میں ایک دم سے آنسوؤں کا پھندا لگا تھا۔

میکال کمرے سے نکل گیا' وہ چپ چاپ بیٹھی حنائی ہاتھوں پر آنسوؤں کے انمول موتی گراتی رہی' جانے کیوں اس لمحے اسے پروین شاکر کی وہ نظم شدت سے یاد آرہی تھی۔

میں وہ بدنصیب دلہن ہوں
جسے شادی کی پہلی رات
کوئی گھونگھٹ اٹھا کے یہ کہہ دے
میرا سب کچھ تمہارا ہے
''سوائے دل کے''

کسی کی شخصیت اور عزت نفس کی بھلا اس سے بڑھ کر توہین اور کیا ہونی تھی؟

ولیمہ کی تقریب میں بھی وہ اس سے کھچا کھچا سا رہا تھا۔

''ہانی تم ٹھیک ہوناں؟'' اسے پتھر کے مجسمے کی مانند خاموش بیٹھے دیکھ کر ہادیہ فوراً اس کے پاس آئی تھی۔

''ہوں' مجھے کیا ہونا ہے؟''

''کیا تم ابھی تک مجھ سے ناراض ہو؟''

''نہیں۔''

''تو پھر ٹھیک سے بات کیوں نہیں کر رہیں' میکال بھائی نے کچھ کہا تو نہیں ناں؟''

''نہیں۔''

''فار گاڈ سیک ہانی پلیز' تم اندازہ نہیں کرسکتیں تمہاری وجہ سے میں کتنی پریشان ہوں؟''

''کیوں؟''

''کیا مطلب کیوں' میری دوست ہو تم' اگر تم خوش نہیں ہو تو میں......''

''اتنی بکواس کافی ہے' مزید سننے کی ہمت نہیں ہے مجھ میں' تم لوگوں نے مل جل کر میرے ساتھ جو کیا ہے اس کے لیے میں کبھی تم میں سے کسی کو بھی معاف نہیں کروں گی' مگر...... یہ ہڈی جو زبردستی تم لوگوں نے میرے گلے میں فٹ کی ہے' میں اسے نگل کر دکھاؤں گی' تم لوگوں کو مجھ پر ہنسنے کا مزید موقع نہیں ملے گا۔''

''ہانی...... تم ایسا کیوں سوچ رہی ہو' ہم کیوں ہنسیں گے تم پر' ہم سب نے تو تمہاری خوشی کے لیے......''

''جسٹ شٹ اپ اوکے۔'' لہو رنگ آنکھوں کے ساتھ اس بار وہ غرائی تھی۔ ہادیہ کا چہرہ سرخ پڑ گیا' شدید پریشان ہونے کے ساتھ ساتھ وہ اب خاصی رنجیدہ بھی تھی مگر دلہن بنی ہانیہ کو اس بات سے کوئی فرق نہیں پڑتا تھا اس نے سوچ لیا تھا کہ آگے اب اسے کیا کرنا ہے۔

❁......❁......❁

ائرپورٹ کی عمارت کے باہر ہاتھ باندھے کھڑا وہ گاڑی کے بونٹ سے ٹیک لگائے ہوئے تھا جب ثانیہ کی نگاہ اس پر پڑی اور وہ جیسے وہیں ساکت رہ گئی۔

پورے پانچ سال کے بعد وہ یوں بالکل اچانک کبھی سامنے آ جائے گا' اس کے وہم وگمان میں بھی نہیں تھا۔ دل تھا کہ جیسے دھڑکنا ہی بھول گیا تھا۔ بڑی مشکل سے رخ پھیر کر' کپکپاتی انگلیوں سے اس نے اپنی دادو کا موبائل نمبر پریس کیا تھا جب جواب میں بھاری مردانہ آواز اس کی سماعتوں میں اتری۔

''جی میڈم' اگر آپ لاہور ائرپورٹ پہنچ چکی ہیں تو براہ کرم باہر تشریف لے آیئے' میں آپ کا منتظر کھڑا ہوں۔''

ثانیہ کو اس آواز پر بھی اس کے لہجے کا گمان ہوا تھا۔ وہ نہیں چاہتی تھی کہ وہ اسے دیکھے تبھی جلدی جلدی ٹرالی گھسیٹتی وہ ائرپورٹ کی عمارت سے باہر نکل آئی۔ ایک مرتبہ پھر اس کی انگلیاں وہی نمبر پریس کر رہی تھیں۔

''ہیلو...... میں عمارت سے باہر کھڑی ہوں' رائیٹ سائیڈ پر جو......'' ابھی وہ اسے بتا ہی رہی تھی کہ وہ سیل فون کان سے لگائے اس کے قریب آ کھڑا ہوا۔

''ایکسکیوزمی۔'' وہ پلٹی تھی اور اس بار زمین زائر ملک کے پیروں تلے سے کھسک گئی تھی۔

''دو پتر اناراں دے......

ساڈا دکھ سن سن کے روندے پتھر پہاڑاں دے''

گاؤں کے بابا جوگی کی آواز پورے کرب کے ساتھ اس کی سماعتوں میں ہتھوڑے برسا رہی تھی۔

''ثانیہ......'' جانے کیسے اس کے لب حرکت کر پائے تھے' مگر سامنے کھڑی اس لڑکی نے فوراً سے پیشتر آنکھوں پر گلاسز چڑھا کر' گاڑی کا بیک ڈور کھول لیا۔

''اگر تم دادی ماں کے بھیجے گئے ڈرائیور ہو تو فوراً سے پیشتر سامان گاڑی میں رکھ کر چلو۔''

کوئی شناسائی نہیں تھی اس کے لہجے میں...... وہ بمشکل خود کو سنبھال کر' سامان گاڑی کی ڈگی میں منتقل کرتا' ڈرائیونگ سیٹ پر آ بیٹھا۔

''بچے کہاں ہیں......؟'' اگلے ہی پل گاڑی اسٹارٹ کرتے ہوئے اس نے پوچھا تھا مگر وہ اسے بنا کوئی جواب دیئے اپنے سیل فون پر تیزی سے کچھ ٹائپ کرنے لگی' کچھ ہی دیر میں اس کا سیل بج اٹھا تھا۔

''ہوں اشعر...... جی میں پہنچ گئی ہوں پاکستان...... جی جی میں اپنا خیال رکھوں گی' آپ بھی اپنا اور بچوں کا خیال رکھیے گا...... جی ٹھیک ہے' اللہ حافظ۔''

کال پک کرتے ہی اس نے تیز لہجے میں کسی کو اطلاع دی اور سیل مٹھی میں دبوچ لیا۔

زائر نہیں جانتا تھا' کہ اس نے کس سے بات کی ہے مگر اسے برا ضرور لگا تھا۔ حویلی پہنچنے تک دونوں کے درمیان خاموشی چھائی رہی تھی' وہ یوں دکھائی دے رہی تھی جیسے اسے جانتی ہی نہ ہو۔

لانگ شرٹ کے ساتھ' کھلے پائنچوں والے ٹراوزر میں ملبوس اس وقت وہ دوپٹے اور حیا دونوں سے بے نیاز تھی۔ زائر نے ایک آخری نظر اس پر ڈالنے کے بعد خاصے زوردار جھٹکے سے حویلی کے مین گیٹ کے سامنے گاڑی روک دی۔ جہاں اس وقت گاؤں کے سیدھے سادے لوگوں کا جم غفیر اس ''جل پری'' کا دیدار کرنے کے لیے جمع تھا۔ بڑی ہیل کے سیاہ جوتوں کے ساتھ جیسے ہی وہ گاڑی کا دروازہ کھول کر باہر نکلی' گاؤں کی عورتیں یوں اس پر پل پڑیں جیسے وہ نکاح کی تقریب میں بٹنے والا چھوارا یا ننھے منے بچوں میں برات کے وقت لٹایا جانے والا کوئی دس کا نوٹ ہو۔

خود زائر کے لیے بھی یہ صورت حال خاصی غیر متوقع تھی تبھی اس نے سرعت سے گاڑی سے نکلنے کے بعد' لوگوں کو پیچھے ہٹا کر' ثانیہ کے لیے رستہ بنایا اور پھر بنا اس کے ردعمل کی پروا کیے اس کا مومی ہاتھ تھام کر تیزی سے حویلی کے کھلے ہوئے گیٹ کی طرف بڑھ گیا۔

چوہدرانی صاحبہ بے تابی سے ان دونوں کا انتظار کر رہی تھیں۔ وہ ثانیہ کا ہاتھ ان کے ہاتھ میں دے کر سرعت سے واپس پلٹ آیا۔ برقی قمقموں سے جگمگاتی اس حویلی میں اس وقت شاید اس کی ضرورت بھی نہیں تھی۔ چوہدرانی کو بتا کر اگلے تیں منٹ کے بعد وہ دوسرے گاؤں میں اپنے چھوٹے سے گھر کے دروازے پر کھڑا دستک دے رہا تھا۔ اس کی زوردار دستک کے جواب میں دروازہ کھولنے والی اس کی ماں تھی۔

''السلام علیکم اماں۔''

''وعلیکم السلام' جیتارہ۔'' دروازہ کھلا چھوڑ کر اس کی ماں سائیڈ پر ہو گئی تھی۔

''ماں صدقے جائے اس بار بڑے دن لگا دیئے تُو نے' سب خیر تو تھی ناں؟''

''ہاں اماں خیر ہی تھی' وہ چوہدرانی کی پوتی آئی ہے باہر سے' اسی کو لینے ائرپورٹ جانا تھا' اسی لیے چوہدرانی صاحبہ نے نہیں آنے دیا' تجھے تو پتا ہے وہ کتنا انحصار کرتی ہیں مجھ پر۔''

صحن میں بچھی واحد چارپائی پر بیٹھ کر جوتے اتارنے کے بعد وہ فوراً ہینڈ پمپ کی طرف بڑھ گیا تھا۔ شدید تھکن اور گرمی نے برا حال کر چھوڑا تھا۔ اماں اب اس کی تائید میں سر ہلا رہی تھیں۔

''ہاں یہ بات تو ہے' اللہ کا خاص کرم ہے مجھ پر' ماشاءاللہ سے میرا بیٹا بہت لائق ہے۔''

زائر کے ہاتھ تیزی سے ہینڈ پمپ چلاتے ہوئے ٹھنڈا پانی نکال رہے تھے۔ اس کی بات پر خوش ہوتے ہوئے اماں اب باورچی خانے میں چلی گئی تھیں وہ وہیں ہینڈ پمپ کے قریب بیٹھ کر کپڑوں سمیت نہانے میں مشغول ہو گیا۔ اچھی طرح نہانے کے بعد اس نے اندر کمرے میں جا کر کپڑے تبدیل کر لیے تھے۔

اماں اس کی اس عادت سے بہت خائف تھیں مگر اس کا بچپن سے یہی معمول تھا' کپڑے بدل کر جس وقت وہ باہر چارپائی پر آ کر بیٹھا' اماں اس کے لیے کھانا نکال لائی تھیں' چنے کی دال اور کدو کا سالن بنا تھا۔ اسے یہ سالن پسند نہیں تھا مگر بھوک کے شدید احساس کے زیراثر اس نے سامنے پڑی تندوری روٹی کے نوالے توڑنے شروع کر دیئے تھے' تبھی سیڑھیوں پر کسی کے قدموں کی چاپ ابھری تھی۔

''بوا میں نے سارے کپڑے اتار لیے ہیں مگر وہ زائر کی شرٹ ساتھ والوں کی چھت پر......'' اپنے دھیان میں بولتی وہ آ رہی تھی کہ اچانک سیڑھیوں کے وسط میں ٹھٹک گئی۔ پتھر ہوئے زائر کی نگاہیں اسے ازحد حیرانی سے دیکھ رہی تھیں' جبکہ اس کا ہاتھ ہوا میں ہی معلق رہ گیا تھا۔ کیسا دن چڑھا تھا آج کہ شاک پر شاک لگ رہے تھے۔

اماں اس کی کیفیت بھانپ کر اب اسے بتا رہی تھیں۔

''پچھلے جمعے آئی تھی سائرہ' تیرے ابا جا کر لائے ہیں اسے' موے سسرال والوں نے بالکل ہی بچی کو لاوارث سمجھ لیا' بہت گھمنڈ ہے انہیں اپنی دولت پر' میں نے فیصلہ کر لیا ہے اب سائرہ اس گھر میں دوبارہ نہیں جائے گی۔'' اماں کی آواز نے اس کا طلسم توڑا تھا۔ زائر نے سر جھٹک کر نوالہ دوبارہ کٹوری میں رکھ دیا۔ شدید بھوک کا احساس اچانک ہی ختم ہو گیا تھا۔

''روٹی اٹھا لے اماں' مجھے بھوک نہیں ہے۔''

''زائر......'' اس کے اٹھ کھڑے ہونے پر اماں نے پکارا تھا مگر...... وہ سنی ان سنی کرتا بیرونی دروازہ کھول کر گھر سے باہر نکل گیا' گاؤں کے بابا جوگی کی آواز پورے کرب کے ساتھ اس کی سماعتوں میں ہتھوڑے برسا رہی تھی۔

''دو پتر اناراں دے......

ساڈا دکھ سن سن کے' روندے پتھر پہاڑاں دے''

وہ چار سال کا تھا جب ایک روز اماں اس کی انگلی پکڑ کر اسے سائرہ کے والد ماسٹر افضل صاحب کی کلاس میں شیشم کے اس گھنے پیڑ کے تلے چھوڑ آئی' جہاں گاؤں کے دیگر بچے جمع ہو کر ماسٹر افضل صاحب سے درس لیا کرتے تھے۔

ماسٹر افضل رشتے میں اس کی اماں کے سگے ماموں زاد بھائی تھے۔ ان کی بیوی سائرہ کے بچپن میں ہی ہیضہ کی شکار ہو کر چل بسی تھی۔ یہی وجہ تھی کہ اماں نے اس چھوٹی سی بچی کو اپنے سینے سے لگا لیا تھا۔ وہ سارا دن انہی کے گھر کھیلتی' پھر شام میں ماسٹر صاحب اسے لینے آ جاتے تو ان کے ساتھ اپنے گھر سونے کے لیے چلی جاتی۔

زائر کو وہ شروع سے ہی بہت اچھی لگتی تھی' یہی وجہ تھی کہ دونوں فرصت کے تمام لمحات ایک دوسرے کے ساتھ گزارتے۔ سائرہ کے بڑے ہونے پر اس کی گھریلو ذمہ داریوں نے اس کا زائر کے گھر آنا جانا کم کر دیا تو وہ جیسے تڑپ کر رہ گیا۔ اسے سائرہ کے ساتھ کی عادت ہو چکی تھی لہٰذا اس نے خود ماسٹر صاحب کے گھر جا کر ان کے گھر کے کاموں میں (جو پہلے ماسٹر صاحب خود سرانجام دیا کرتے تھے) سائرہ کی مدد کرنی شروع کر دی۔

ایک دوسرے کے احساس کا یہ جذبہ بڑھتے بڑھتے کب محبت کا روپ دھار گیا انہیں خبر ہی نہ ہو سکی' پتا تو اس روز چلا جب ایک شام زائر نے ماسٹر صاحب کو اماں سے ان دونوں کی شادی کی بات سنی' مارے خوشی کے اس کے پاؤں زمین پر نہیں ٹکتے تھے' سائرہ اس کے لیے کسی نشے سے کم ہرگز نہیں تھی۔ اس روز اس نے پہلی بار گھر سے پیسے چرا کر سائرہ کے لیے رنگ برنگی خوب صورت چوڑیاں خریدی تھیں کیونکہ سائرہ کو چوڑیاں بہت پسند تھیں۔

زائر نے اسے چوڑیاں دیتے ہوئے اپنے اور اس کے درمیان قائم ہونے والے رشتے کا بھی بتا دیا تھا اور حسب توقع وہ بھی خوش ہوئی تھی۔ اب اکثر وہ اسے تنگ کرنے لگا تھا۔ کبھی اس کے ساتھ برتن دھلاتے ہوئے چپکے سے اس کا ہاتھ پکڑ لیتا' تو کبھی ماسٹر صاحب کے ساتھ باتیں کرتے ہوئے نظر بچا کر اس کے پاؤں پر اپنا پاؤں رکھ دیتا' ایک دوبار اس نے غیر اخلاقی حرکت کرنے کی کوشش بھی کی تھی مگر سائرہ نے سختی سے اسے ڈپٹ کر رکھ دیا۔ زندگی بے حد خوب صورت اور خوش گوار بسر ہو رہی تھی کہ اچانک اسے میٹرک کے بعد مزید تعلیم کے لیے شہر کے ہوسٹل میں قیام کرنا پڑا اور پیچھے جیسے اس کی دنیا ہی بدل گئی۔

دو سال کے صبر آزما کڑے انتظار کے بعد وہ شاندار نمبروں سے ایف اے کر کے گاؤں واپس لوٹا تو اس کے خطوط کے جواب گول کرنے والی سائرہ افضل نے اس کے ساتھ شادی سے ہی صاف انکار کر دیا۔

زائر کے شدید دکھ اور اصرار پر اس نے بتایا تھا کہ اس کے زندگی کے لیے چند خواب ہیں جن پر وہ کبھی سمجھوتہ نہیں کر سکتی۔ اسے بہترین گھر' گاڑی اور بہت ساری دولت چاہیے تھی جو گاؤں کے نمبردار کا آوارہ بیٹا اسے مہیا کرنے کو تیار بیٹھا تھا۔

اس نے زائر سے صاف کہہ دیا تھا کہ وہ صرف محبت پر اکتفا کرنے والی لڑکی نہیں ہے۔ نہ ہی اس میں اتنی ہمت اور صبر ہے کہ وہ ساری زندگی چھوٹی' چھوٹی خوشیوں کے لیے ترس کر گزار دے۔ زائر کا مان ٹوٹا تھا' سائرہ کے اجنبی لہجے اور عجیب وغریب فرمائش نے اس کی حسرتوں کا خون کیا تھا مگر پھر بھی اس نے اس سے وعدہ کیا تھا کہ وہ اسے یہ سب چیزیں دے گا بس وہ تھوڑا سا انتظار کر لے مگر سائرہ نے اسے چھوٹ نہیں دی۔

اس نے اُسے یہ کہہ کر اپنی دہلیز سے رخصت کر دیا کہ وہ شہر جائے اور جا کر وہ سب چیزیں جو اس کا خواب ہیں حاصل کرنے کی کوشش کرے تبھی ان دونوں کی شادی ممکن ہو سکے گی بصورت دیگر نمبردار کے بیٹے کی آفر بری نہیں ہے۔

وہ اس کی دہلیز سے پلٹ آیا تھا' بے حد شکستہ اور رنجیدہ۔

ماسٹر افضل اکلوتی بیٹی کی ضد کے سامنے قطعی لاچار ہو کر رہ گئے تھے۔ جبکہ اس کی اپنی ماں سائرہ کو لعن طعن کرتی نہیں

تھکتی تھی۔ زائر کا باپ ان دنوں دوسرے گاؤں میں چوہدریوں کے گھر کا منشی تھا اور حویلی میں ان کی قدر ایسے ہی کی جاتی تھی جیسے وہ حویلی کا ہی کوئی فرد ہو۔

صرف اپنی محبت کو پانے کے لیے وہ ماں سے مزید تعلیم کی ضد کر کے دوبارہ شہر چلا آیا اور یہاں تعلیم کے ساتھ ساتھ راتوں رات امیر بننے کے جنونی خواب نے اسے بگڑے ہوئے لڑکوں کے ٹولے کا حصہ بنا دیا۔

ہر طرح کی غلط کاریوں میں ملوث ان لڑکوں نے اسے راتوں رات امیر بننے کے لیے جس شارٹ کٹ راستے کی ترغیب دی' اس راستے کی پہلی سیڑھی پر ہی اس کا ٹکراؤ ثانیہ عباس سے ہوا تھا اور یہیں سے اس کی زندگی میں ایک نئی دلچسپ کہانی نے جنم لیا تھا۔

❁......❁......❁

ایک دن نام تیرا......
خواب کی طرح آنکھ میں بسایا تھا
آج تک نیند کو ترستے ہیں......!

ڈریسنگ ٹیبل کے سامنے کھڑی وہ اپنی تیاری کو فائنل ٹچ دے رہی تھی جب دروازے پر بیل ہوئی' جلدی جلدی واچ پہنتے ہوئے اس نے موبائل اٹھایا اور کمرے سے نکل آئی۔

ابھی تھوڑی دیر بعد اسے اپنی دوست سعدیہ کے گھر سالگرہ کی تقریب میں جانا تھا۔ سعدیہ کے فون پر فون آرہے تھے' اس نے لاسٹ کال پر ڈرائیور بھجوانے کے لیے کہا تھا اور اب دروازے پر ہونے والی ڈور بیل کی آواز سن کر وہ سرعت سے دروازے کی طرف آئی تھی۔

''کون......'' دروازے کے ہینڈل پر ہاتھ رکھتے ہوئے اس نے سرسری سا پوچھا تھا۔ جب آواز آئی۔

''زائر ملک۔''

''آ گئے تم' پچھلے بیس منٹ سے تیار ہو کر بیٹھی ہوں' اور وہ تمہاری مالکن شہزادی' فون پر فون کیے جا رہی ہے یہ نہیں کہ تمہیں جلدی پہنچنے کی ہدایت کر دے۔''

وہ اسے سعدیہ کا ڈرائیور سمجھ رہی تھی تبھی بنا سوچے سمجھے شروع ہو گئی تھی۔ دوسری طرف اسے دو ہفتوں سے ٹیلی کرتے زائر ملک نے قدرے حیران ہو کر اسے پیچھے دھکیلا اور تیزی سے فلیٹ میں داخل ہو کر دروازہ لاک کر دیا۔

''نہ میری کوئی مالکن ہے' نہ میں کسی کا ملازم ہوں' میرا مقصد اس وقت اس گھر کا صفایا کرنا ہے' شرافت سے بنا چوں چراں کیے سب کچھ نکال کر ٹیبل پر رکھتی جاؤ' نہیں تو اس پسٹل کی ساری گولیاں تمہارے وجود میں اتار دوں گا۔''

قطعی رف حلیے میں ہلکی ہلکی بڑھی ہوئی شیو کے ساتھ اس پر پسٹل تانے کہتا وہ اسے ساکت ہی تو کر گیا تھا۔ ثانیہ عباس کے وہم وگمان میں بھی نہیں تھا کہ وہ یوں لوٹی جا سکتی ہے' اس کے خوب صورت چہرے کا رنگ پل میں سفید پڑ گیا تھا۔ زائر ملک کی ہدایت کے عین مطابق اس نے سب سے پہلے اپنا موبائل فون کپکپاتے ہاتھوں سے میز پر رکھا' پھر دونوں کلائیوں سے گولڈ کے خوب صورت نفیس کڑے اتارے' کانوں میں پہنی گولڈ کی ہلکی پھلکی بالیاں اتار کر میز پر رکھیں' اس کا پرس ابھی صوفے پر پڑا تھا' اس نے وہ بھی اٹھا کر اس کے حوالے کر دیا۔

''اس وقت میرے پاس یہی کچھ ہے۔'' اس کی آواز سے صاف لگ رہا تھا کہ وہ بہت ڈر گئی ہے۔ زائر گہری نگاہوں سے اسے دیکھتا اس کے بیڈروم کی طرف بڑھ گیا تھا' تبھی وہ تڑپ کر پیچھے لپکی تھی۔

''دیکھئے میں سچ کہہ رہی ہوں' میرے پاس جو کچھ بھی تھا میں آپ کے حوالے کر چکی ہوں' مزید اب کچھ بھی نہیں ہے۔''

''شٹ اپ'' اس کے منمنانے پر وہ دھاڑا تھا کیونکہ اس کے پاس اس لڑکی سے متعلق مکمل معلومات تھیں۔ وہ باہر سے آئی تھی اور اپنی ایک ملازمہ کے ساتھ اس شاندار لگژری فلیٹ میں رہتی تھی۔ زائر نے اسے دو ہفتے پہلے ایک ریستوران میں دیکھا تھا اور پھر شادی کی ایک تقریب میں' وہ ہر جگہ بہترین لباس کے ساتھ قیمتی جیولری سے لدی پھندی ہوتی تھی تبھی اپنے دوست کی انویسٹی گیشن پر ففٹی پرسنٹ شیئر کے لیے وہ بلاخوف وخطر اس کے فلیٹ میں گھس آیا تھا۔ خوش قسمتی سے اس وقت اس کی ملازمہ کہیں بھی دکھائی نہیں دے رہی تھی تبھی اس کا حوصلہ بڑھ گیا تھا۔

اپنی محبت کو پانے کے لیے فی الوقت وہ کچھ بھی کر سکتا تھا یہاں تک کہ اس لڑکی کا خون بھی' مگر...... اس کی نوبت نہیں آئی تھی۔

لڑکی اب اس کے سامنے ہاتھ جوڑے کھڑی تھی۔

''دیکھیے میرے لیے دولت کی کوئی وقعت نہیں ہے' پپ...... پلیز اب آپ یہاں سے چلے جائیں۔''

مگر وہ اس کی التجا کو قطعی نظر انداز کیے اب وارڈروب کھول رہا تھا کچھ دیر اِدھر اُدھر ہاتھ مار کر چیک کرنے کے بعد اس کے ہاتھ ایک جیولری کا ڈبا لگا تھا' جسے دیکھنے کے بعد اس کے لبوں پر ہلکی سی مسکان بکھر گئی۔

''سنیں پلیز' اسے رکھ دیں' یہ میری ماما کی نشانی ہے پلیز۔'' وہ تڑپ کر اس کے سامنے آئی تھی' مگر زائر نے اسے پیچھے دھکیل دیا۔

''شٹ اپ۔''

''پلیز میں آپ کے سامنے ہاتھ جوڑتی ہوں' یہ میری مما کی واحد نشانی ہے میرے پاس' اسے واپس کر دیں' پلیز۔''

اب وہ بری طرح رو رہی تھی۔ زائر دروازے کی چوکھٹ پر پہنچ کر رکا تھا' وہ لڑکی اب اس کے پیروں میں گرنے کا سوچ رہی تھی' تبھی اس نے پلٹ کر دیکھا اور پھر جیسے ایکدم سے اس کا ارادہ بدل گیا۔

''ٹھیک ہے یہ لو۔'' پلٹ کر تحمل سے کہتے ہوئے اس نے جیولری بکس اس کی طرف بڑھایا تھا' ثانیہ عباس آنکھوں میں آنسو لیے حیرانی سے اسے دیکھتی رہ گئی۔ کپکپاتے ہاتھوں سے اس نے وہ ڈبا تھاما تھا جب اس نے فوراً سے پیشتر اس کا بازو تھام لیا۔

''تمہیں یہ جیولری چاہیے ناں' ٹھیک ہے رکھ لو' مگر بدلے میں مجھے بھی کچھ چاہیے۔'' اس بار اس کے الفاظ سے زیادہ اپنے جسم پر پھسلتی اس کی نگاہوں نے اسے سہما دیا تھا۔

''نہیں' تم ایسا کچھ نہیں کر سکتے میرے ساتھ۔''

خوف کے ساتھ ساتھ اس نے غصہ دکھانے کی کوشش بھی کی تھی' مگر زائر ملک نے پروا نہیں کی۔

''کیوں؟ میں نامرد ہوں؟'' ثانیہ عباس کے احتجاج کو یکسر نظر انداز کرتے ہوئے اب وہ اسے اپنی طاقت دکھا رہا تھا۔ ثانیہ کی کلائی میں پڑی کانچ کی ساری چوڑیاں ٹوٹ کر قالین پر بکھر چکی تھیں۔ جبکہ اس کا میک اپ سے دمکتا چہرہ اب کھنڈر عمارت کا نقشہ پیش کر رہا تھا۔

وہ ساری عمر ایبروڈ رہی تھی مگر پھر بھی اسے اللہ کی قائم کردہ حدود کا پاس تھا جبکہ دوسری طرف اسلامی مملکت میں پلنے بڑھنے والے اس شخص کے ماں باپ کی سالوں کی اچھی تربیت پر اس کے برے دوستوں کی چند روزہ بری صحبت اپنا اثر دکھا رہی تھی۔

گناہ کبیرہ کی بھینٹ چڑھے اس طوفان کو کسی طور ٹلتے نہ دیکھ کر اس نے اس کے پاؤں پکڑ لیے تھے۔

''مم میری بات سنیں پلیز...... خدا کا واسطہ ہے آپ کو' مجھ پر ترس کھائیں' میں بہت دکھی لڑکی ہوں۔''

''جسٹ شٹ اپ او کے' بہت خطرناک آدمی ہوں میں' میرا دماغ خراب مت کرو۔'' اس کے چہرے پر تھپڑ رسید کرتے ہوئے وہ غرّایا تھا' تبھی وہ سسک اٹھی۔

''میں جانتی ہوں' آپ یہاں صرف سب کچھ لوٹنے آئے ہیں' مگر...... میری عزت کوئی فالتو سامان نہیں ہے' آپ مسلمان ہیں' اللہ کی قائم کردہ حدود کی خلاف ورزی کر کے آپ اس پاک ذات کے غضب سے نہیں بچ سکیں گے۔''

زائر کے دل پر چوٹ پڑی تھی مگر دماغ اتنا ماؤف تھا کہ اس کے لیے اس وقت جیسے خود کو سنبھالنا ممکن ہی نہیں رہا تھا۔

ثانیہ اب اس کے سامنے دوپٹے سے بے نیاز بیٹھی تھی۔

''بکواس بند کرو۔ میں یہاں تمہارے آنسو دیکھنے نہیں آیا۔'' وہ غرّایا تھا۔

ثانیہ نے ہاتھ جوڑ دیئے۔

''آپ میرے لیے کچھ بھی مت کریں' مگر اللہ کے لیے تو کر سکتے ہیں ناں' اسی اللہ کا واسطہ ہے آپ کو' مجھے گنہگار مت کریں' اگر آپ نے میری بربادی کی قسم کھا ہی لی ہے تو پلیز مجھ سے نکاح کر لیں پھر اس کے بعد چاہے فوری طلاق دے دیجیے گا میں گلہ نہیں کروں گی' پلیز۔''

ٹپ ٹپ ٹپ' اس کی آنکھوں سے آنسو یوں گر رہے تھے جیسے ساون کی جھڑی لگی ہو۔ زائر از حد ڈسٹرب ہو کر چلّا اٹھا۔

''بکواس بند کرو اپنی' نہ میں ایسی فضولیات میں پڑنا چاہتا ہوں' نہ تم میرے لیے اتنی اہم ہو کہ میں تم سے ایسا کوئی تعلق جوڑتا پھروں۔''

''مم' میں جانتی ہوں' میں نہیں ہوں' مگر اللہ تو ہے ناں' اس کی رضا کے لیے' اس کے عذاب سے بچنے کے لیے کر لیں' پلیز۔''

اس کے آنسوؤں میں' اس کی التجاؤں میں کچھ ایسا تھا کہ جس نے اسے بے چین کر کے رکھ دیا تھا۔ جانے کیا سوچ کر وہ اٹھا تھا اور اسے بازو سے پکڑ کر گھسیٹتے ہوئے' باہر اس میز تک لے آیا جہاں اس گھر سے برآمد ہونے والا سامان رکھا تھا' وہ سب سامان وہاں سے اٹھا کر اسے اسی طرح بازو سے پکڑ کر کھینچتے ہوئے وہ نیچے اپنی گاڑی تک لایا اور اگلے ہی پل اسے گاڑی میں دھکیل کر' فرنٹ سیٹ پر بیٹھے اپنے دوست کے ساتھ آ بیٹھا۔

''مجھے اس لڑکی سے نکاح کرنا ہے ابھی اور اسی وقت۔''

''وھاٹ' تمہارا دماغ تو خراب نہیں ہو گیا؟ تم یہاں چوری کرنے آئے تھے چوری ہونے نہیں۔''

''جو کہا ہے وہ کرو پلیز۔'' اس بار اس کا لہجہ اتنا روڈ تھا کہ اس کے دوست نے حیرانی سے اس کی طرف چند ثانیے دیکھنے کے بعد گاڑی آگے بڑھا دی تھی۔ اسی دن کے اختتام پر وہ شاندار ہوٹل کے کمرے میں ثانیہ عباس کے سامنے اس کے شوہر کی حیثیت سے بیٹھا تھا۔

''اب کیا ارادہ ہے تمہارا؟'' بنا سلام دعا کے اس کے مقابل بیٹھا وہ پوچھ رہا تھا۔ ثانیہ عباس چہرہ جھکاتے ہوئے رو پڑی۔

''میں جانتی ہوں آپ نے جو بھی کیا ہے محض ضد اور غصے کی وجہ سے کیا ہے' پھر بھی میں آپ کی بہت ممنون ہوں' بے شک میرا رب بہترین محافظ ہے۔''

وہ سج دھج کر دلہن نہیں بنی تھی مگر پھر بھی اس کے چہرے پر بے تحاشہ حسن اور نور بکھرا ہوا تھا۔ زائر نے ہاتھ بڑھا کر

اسے اپنے پہلو میں گرایا اور کمرے کی لائٹ آف کر دی۔
اگلی صبح وہ اس کے بیدار ہونے تک نہا دھو کر فریش ہو چکا تھا۔
ثانیہ کی آنکھ کھلی تو وہ جوگرز پہن رہا تھا۔
''میں جا رہا ہوں، تمہارا سامان اور تمام نقدی وہ سائیڈ ٹیبل کی دراز میں محفوظ ہے۔ نکال لینا۔''
''مطلب؟'' وہ ایکدم سے حیران ہو کر اٹھی تھی۔
''مطلب...... میں تمہارے گھر میں ڈکیتی کے لیے آیا تھا، تاکہ بڑا مال ہاتھ لگنے پر کوئی کاروبار کرسکوں اور اپنی محبت اپنی بچپن کی منگیتر کو حاصل کرسکوں، لیکن اب میں وہ سب یہیں چھوڑ کر جا رہا ہوں، کیونکہ مجھے تمہاری لوٹی ہوئی دولت پر اپنے خوابوں کا تاج محل کھڑا نہیں کرنا۔'' وہ اس سے رخ پھیرے ہوئے بیٹھا تھا۔ ثانیہ کے لبوں پر اداس سی مسکان بکھر گئی۔
''بہت شکریہ، لیکن اب وہ سب میں آپ کو اپنی رضا سے دے رہی ہوں آپ لے جائیں۔''
''ہرگز نہیں۔'' وہ کھڑا ہوا تھا جب اس نے سرعت سے اس کا ہاتھ تھام لیا۔
''میرا طلاق نامہ......؟'' اور یہاں اس نے بے ساختہ پلٹ کر اس کی طرف دیکھا تھا۔
''بھیج دوں گا جلد۔'' سرعت سے کہہ کر وہ رکا نہیں تھا کمرے سے نکل گیا تھا پیچھے ثانیہ عباس دیر تلک گھٹنوں کے گرد بازو لپیٹے بیٹھی اسے سوچتی رہی۔
کیسا رہزن تھا وہ، اور کیسی انوکھی چوری کی تھی اس نے......!
وہ اپنے اپارٹمنٹ میں واپس لوٹ آئی تھی۔

✿ ...... ✿ ...... ✿

شام ڈھل رہی تھی اور درختوں پر بیٹھے پرندے اب اپنے اپنے ٹھکانوں کی تلاش میں، فضا کی وسعتوں میں اڑتے دکھائی دے رہے تھے۔ عصر کے قریب اس کی ملازمہ بھی گاؤں سے واپس لوٹ آئی تھی، اسی روز شام میں اس نے اپنی کلوز فرینڈ ایمن کو بلا کر زائر ملک سے متعلق ساری کہانی اس کے گوش گزار کر دی۔
''گڈ...... یہ تو نیو ٹرینڈ نکل آیا، مطلب اب لوگ گھروں میں گھسیں گے، مگر کوئی مال و دولت لوٹنے کے بجائے سیدھے آپ کی پیشانی سے پسٹل لگائیں گے، اور آپ کو بنا جانے، بنا سمجھے نکاح کر کے اپنی زوجیت میں لے لیں گے، نہ فکر نہ فاقہ، عیش کر کاکا، مطلب ساری ٹینشن ہی ختم ہو گئی۔''
تالی بجاتے ہوئے اس نے صاف اس کا مذاق اڑایا تھا۔ تبھی وہ روہانسی ہو کر پلٹی تھی۔
''تمہیں لگتا ہے میں بکواس کر رہی ہوں؟''
''ہاں۔''
''جسٹ شٹ اپ، میں بکواس نہیں کر رہی، اس شخص کے پاس نکاح نامہ موجود ہے۔''
''یوڈفر گرل، وہ جو کوئی بھی تھا اس نے تمہیں بے وقوف بنایا ہے، فلموں کہانیوں میں بھی ایسا نہیں ہوتا کہ کوئی شخص ڈکیتی کی نیت سے آپ کے گھر میں گھسے اور پھر آپ کے کہنے پر شرافت سے نکاح کر کے اپنا کام نکالتا پھرے، مائینڈ اٹ محترمہ یہاں ایسا انسان کا بچہ کوئی بھی نہیں ہے جو شخص آپ کے آنسوؤں یا خدا رسول کے واسطوں سے اپنی بدنیتی کا ارادہ بدل کر نکاح جیسے جھنجٹ میں پڑتا پھرے، وہ مولوی، وہ گواہ، جو تم نے دیکھے سب بکواس اور ڈرامہ ہوں گے، ایسے

آوارہ لڑکوں کے لیے، ایسے ڈرامے قطعی مشکل نہیں اور تم دیکھ لینا وہ دوبارہ بھی آئے گا، ممکن ہے تین بار طلاق طلاق بھی کہہ دے، مگر یہ سب سوائے دھوکے کے اور کچھ بھی نہیں ہوگا۔"

ایمن کے لہجے میں خفگی بھی تھی اور سفاکی بھی۔ ثانیہ مضطرب سی رو پڑی۔

"میرا دل نہیں مانتا۔"

"مجھے پتا ہے، اس عمر میں لڑکیوں کے دل کسی بھی فریب کو کب مانتے ہیں بھلا' انہیں تو وہی سولہ آنے سچ دکھائی دے رہا ہوتا ہے جو وہ محض خود دیکھنا چاہ رہی ہوتی ہیں' مگر میں اپنی دوست کو کوئی جھوٹا ڈھکوسلہ نہیں دے سکتی، تمہیں چاہیے کہ تم یہ سب آج ہی آنٹی یا گاؤں میں اپنے دادا دادی سے شیئر کرو' میرا خیال ہے تمہارا اب یہاں اس اپارٹمنٹ میں رہنا خطرے سے خالی نہیں' کیونکہ ہو سکتا ہے اس بار وہ اپنے ساتھ اپنے دوستوں کو بھی لائے۔"

ایمن کا خدشہ غلط نہیں تھا' وہ چپ بیٹھی آنسو بہاتی رہی' کتنا تکلیف دہ تھا یہ تصور کہ کسی نے اسے اپنے نام کا "لالی پاپ" دے کر لوٹ لیا ہے۔

ایمن واپس جا چکی تھی مگر وہ اسی پوزیشن میں بیڈ پر دونوں ٹانگوں کے گرد بازو لپیٹے بیٹھی سوچتی رہی۔ ٹپ ٹپ آنکھوں سے آنسو یوں گر رہے تھے' جیسے کسی خاموش جھیل میں جھرنا گرتا ہو۔ وہ کالج لائف میں تھی جب اچانک اس کے بابا کی رحلت ہوگئی۔ ان کی وفات کے بعد اس کی بہادر ماں نے نہ صرف ان کے وسیع کاروبار کو سنبھالا' بلکہ اپنے دونوں بچوں کی پرورش میں بھی کوئی کسر اٹھا نہیں رکھی۔

اپنی ماں سے اکثر پاکستان میں اپنے ددھیالی رشتہ داروں کے متعلق مختلف کہانیاں سننے کو ملتی رہتی تھیں۔ اس کے دادا' دادی اور ایک تایا پاکستان میں مقیم تھے۔ جبکہ اس کے پاپا کو پسند کی شادی کے جرم میں خاندان سے عاق کر دیا گیا تھا۔

اس کے بابا رحلت سے قبل آخری بار اپنے گاؤں گئے تھے' مگر انہیں معافی نہیں ملی' پاکستان سے واپسی کے دو ہفتے بعد ان کی رحلت ہوگئی۔ اس موقع پر اس کی دادی اور تایا ان کے پاس آئے تھے اور بہت روئے تھے۔ بابا کی رحلت کے دو ماہ بعد اس کے دادا بھی غم اور بیماری سے ہار گئے۔ وہ چونکہ ان سے زیادہ اٹیچ نہیں تھی لہٰذا اسے اس بات کا زیادہ افسوس نہیں ہوا۔

کالج لائف کے دوران ہی اس کی اپنے پاپا کے عزیز دوست طارق انکل کے اکلوتے بیٹے اشعر سے دوستی ہوگئی تھی۔ وہ بے حد وجاہت کا حامل ایک ضدی اور غصیلا لڑکا تھا مگر اس کے پیار میں بہت شدت بھی تھی۔ وہ چونکہ اپنے بابا سے بہت اٹیچ تھی لہٰذا ان کی رحلت کے بعد اپنے آپ کو سنبھالنے کے لیے اس نے اشعر کا سہارا لیا اور پھر جیسے اس سہارے کی عادی ہوتی گئی۔

اشعر کے بغیر جیسے اس کی زندگی ہی نامکمل تھی' اس کی شدت اور پسند کو دیکھتے ہوئے اس کی مما نے ان دونوں کا رشتہ طے کر دیا۔ انہی دنوں اشعر کی توجہ اس سے ہٹ کر اپنی ایک دور پرے کی کزن پر مبذول ہوگئی جو نئی نئی لندن آئی تھی۔ وہ اسے ٹائم اور کمپنی دے رہا تھا جو ثانیہ کے لیے کسی طور قابل برداشت نہیں تھا۔

اسی بات کو لے کر دونوں کے بیچ جھگڑے بھی ہوئے مگر...... کوئی حل نہ نکل سکا۔ نتیجتاً ثانیہ نے جذباتیت کا مظاہرہ کرتے ہوئے یہ رشتہ ختم کر دیا اور اشعر کا اپنے گھر میں داخلہ تک ممنوع کر دیا جس پر مشتعل ہو کر اس نے اسے دھمکی دے ڈالی کہ وہ اسے اس حرکت کی سزا ضرور دے گا' مگر اس سے پہلے کہ وہ ایسا کچھ کرتے ہوئے اسے نقصان پہنچاتا وہ اپنی مما سے ضد کر کے پاکستان چلی آئی۔ تاہم اس نے اپنے ددھیال والوں کو اپنے پاکستان میں قیام سے مطلع نہیں

کیا تھا۔

جس نقصان سے ڈر کر وہ لندن سے بھا گی تھی، وہ نقصان پاکستان میں ہو گیا تھا۔ آنسو تھے کہ ٹپ ٹپ بہتے ہی چلے جا رہے تھے اور رات تھی کہ اندھیرے کی بکل مارتے ہوئے سرد سے سرد ترین ہوتی جا رہی تھی۔

❁ ...... ❁ ...... ❁

''زائر پتر......!'' وہ مضطرب سا چارپائی پر پڑا پہلو بدل رہا تھا جب اچانک اس کے سیل فون پر اماں کی کال آ گئی اور اسے نا چاہتے ہوئے بھی اس وقت ان کی کال پک کرنی پڑی۔

''جی اماں۔''

''ماں صدقے جائے کتنے دن سے تُو نے گاؤں کا چکر نہیں لگایا سب ٹھیک تو ہے ناں۔''

''ہاں اماں، سب ٹھیک ہی ہے، جاب ڈھونڈ رہا ہوں، تُو سنا گھر میں سب کیسے ہیں ابا اور سائرہ وغیرہ۔''

''سب ٹھیک ہیں، بس ایک گڑبڑ ہو گئی ہے۔''

''گڑبڑ......کیسی گڑبڑ......'' وہ چونک کر چارپائی پر اٹھ بیٹھا تھا۔ جب اماں نے قدرے خاموشی کے بعد اسے بتایا۔

''وہ......اپنی سائرہ ہے ناں۔''

''ہاں......کیا ہوا اسے؟'' اس کا دل بے ساختہ ہی زور سے دھڑ کا تھا۔

''کچھ نہیں......اس نے نکاح کر لیا ہے، نمبردار کے بیٹے افضل کے ساتھ۔''

''کیا......؟'' اسے لگا جیسے وہ چارپائی سے نیچے گر پڑا ہو۔

''ہاں پتر......مجھ بدنصیب کو نہیں پتا چلا کہ اس کرموں جلی نے کب اور کیسے یہ قدم اٹھایا، تیرے ابا نے تو ایسا دل پر لیا کہ بستر سے ہی لگ گئے، ابھی کل تاپ اترا ہے ان کا......اپنی بیٹی ہوتی تو شاید زندہ زمین میں گاڑ دیتے، مگر پرائے خون پر کیا زور چلتا ہے۔''

اماں اب شاید رو رہی تھیں مگر وہ تو سن ہی نہیں رہا تھا۔ سائیں سائیں کرتی سماعتوں میں سوائے سناٹے کے اور کچھ اترتا محسوس نہیں ہو رہا تھا۔

یہ......کیسے ہو سکتا تھا؟

وہ تو ''اس'' سے محبت کرتی تھی، پھر نمبردار کے بیٹے کے ساتھ نکاح کیسے کر سکتی تھی؟ اس کا دماغ گھوما تھا اور وہ فوراً گاؤں واپس آیا تھا۔ سائرہ اس وقت بڑی مسرور سی تندور پر روٹی لگا رہی تھی جبکہ ماسٹر افضل نڈھال سے صحن میں بچھی چارپائی پر پڑے تھے، اسے بنا دستک دیئے گھر میں داخل ہوتے دیکھ کر سائرہ کے چہرے کا رنگ فق ہوا تھا۔

''زائر......تو......؟''

''ہاں میں......پوچھنے آیا ہوں تجھ سے کہ نمبردار کے بیٹے کے ساتھ تیرے نکاح کی خبر کتنی سچ ہے۔''

''تم کون ہوتے ہو یہ پوچھنے والے؟'' اچانک اس نے بے رخی سے رخ پھیرا تھا۔ زائر کا دل کٹ کر رہ گیا۔

''میں کون ہوتا ہوں، اپنے باپ سے پوچھ، جس نے میری ماں سے ہم دونوں کی شادی کی بات پکی کی تھی۔'' اس کا بازو پکڑ کر جھٹکا دیتے ہوئے وہ چلایا تھا۔ تبھی وہ تپ اٹھی۔

''ہولی بول، یہاں اونچا کوئی نہیں سنتا، رہ گئی بات میرے ابا کی تو اس نے کوئی گناہ نہیں کر دیا تیری اماں سے ہماری شادی کی بات کر کے، جس کا حساب لینے آ گیا ہے تُو یہاں؟ تین مہینے ہو گئے تجھے شہر کی گلیوں کی خاک چھانتے ہوئے، کچھ کمایا، کچھ بنایا، نہیں......بنا بھی نہیں سکتے، تیرے جیسے نکھٹو صرف عاشقی کر سکتے ہیں یا نوکری، تیسرا کوئی کام کرنا ان

کے بس کی بات نہیں، اس لیے بھول جا کہ میں تجھ جیسے کنگلے کے ساتھ اپنی زندگی برباد کروں گی، اکلوتی دھی ہوں اپنے ابا کی، میرے جیسی سوہنی دوسری کڑی نہیں اس پنڈ میں، ایسے ہی نمبردار کا بیٹا فدا نہیں ہو گیا مجھ پر، آیا بڑا بچپن کی منگ حاصل کرنے والا؟ جہاں سے آیا ہے کان لپیٹ کر چلا جا، نہیں تو افضل سے کہہ کر وہ درگت بناؤں گی تمہاری کہ کیا یاد رکھیں گے تمہارے ماں باپ بھی۔"

سخت اشتعال میں آئی وہ خالص دیہاتی لہجے میں بولتے ہوئے اسے پل میں اس کی اوقات یاد دلا گئی تھی۔ زائر کا بس نہ چلتا تھا کہ اس کا گلا گھونٹ دیتا۔ اس وقت اس نے غصے میں اسے ایک زناٹے دار تھپڑ دے مارا تھا مگر پھر سائرہ کے چلا کر شور مچانے پر وہ زیادہ دیر وہاں کھڑا نہیں رہ سکا۔

اس رات اس کا وجود جیسے کسی دوزخ میں گر پڑا تھا، جلتا وجود، جلتی آنکھیں، جلتے آنسو اور پھٹتے اعصاب...... ایک ایک لمحہ عذاب کیسے بن جاتا ہے کوئی اس وقت اس سے پوچھتا۔

زندگی بھر ساتھ چلنے کے وعدے کرنے والے لوگ اچانک کسی ڈگر پر ہاتھ چھڑا کر واپس پلٹ جائیں تو جینا دشوار کیسے ہو جاتا ہے کوئی اس وقت اس سے پوچھتا، کتنے ہی روز تک ان دیکھی آگ کے ساتھ تیز بخار میں جلنے کے بعد بھی جب اسے قرار نہیں آیا تو اس روز وہ بنا کسی کو بتائے شہر چلا آیا۔

تیزی سے ڈھلتی شام کے سرمئی دھندلکوں کے ساتھ اس کے قدم ثانیہ عباس کے لگژری اپارٹمنٹ کی طرف بڑھ رہے تھے اور اگلے تیس منٹ کے بعد وہ اس کے دروازے پر تھا۔ اس وقت وہ جس سکون کی پناہ کے لیے بے آب تڑپ رہا تھا وہ سکون ثانیہ عباس کے علاوہ اسے اور کوئی نہیں دے سکتا تھا۔

وہ اک بے نام سی الفت' وہ اک معصوم سی چاہت
وہ میری ذات کا حصہ' وہ میری زیست کا قصہ
مجھے محسوس ہوتا ہے وہ میرے پاس ہے اب بھی
وہ جب جب یاد آتا ہے نگاہوں میں سماتا ہے
زباں خاموش ہوتی ہے مگر یہ آنکھ روتی ہے
میں خود سے پوچھ لیتا ہوں
جسے میں پیار کرتا ہوں
اسے کیا پیار تھا مجھ سے؟
جواب ''ہاں'' سوچ لیتا ہوں
اسے بھی پیار تھا ''شاید''
اسی ''شاید'' سے وابستہ ہے اب تو ہر خوشی میری
یہی اک لفظ ''شاید'' بن گیا ہے زندگی میری

دروازے پر دستک کی آواز ابھری تھی

ایمن جو کچن میں اس کے لیے چائے بنا رہی تھی' چونک کر پلٹی اور پھر ثانیہ کے اٹھنے سے قبل اس نے ملازمہ کو آواز دے ڈالی۔

''بوا...... ذرا دروازے پر دیکھیں کون ہے؟'' ثانیہ کا دل دستک کی آواز پر زور سے دھڑکا تھا مگر وہ خاموش بیٹھی تھی۔

''بی بی جی! کوئی زائر صاحب آئے ہیں' ثانیہ بی بی کا پوچھ رہے ہیں؟'' تین منٹ کے بعد ملازمہ نے واپس آکر اسے اطلاع دی' وہ تپ اٹھی۔

''دیکھا میں نے کہا تھا ناں وہ آئے گا دوبارہ' لیتی ہوں میں اس کی خبر' آیا بڑا نکاح کرنے والا'' ہاتھ صافی سے خشک کر کے وہ بیرونی دروازے کی طرف آئی تھی۔

''جی فرمائیے۔'' کڑی نگاہوں سے باہر پریشان حال کھڑے زائر ملک پر اک نظر ڈالنے کے بعد اس نے خاصے چبھتے ہوئے لہجے میں کہا تھا' جب وہ بولا

''مجھے ثانیہ عباس سے بات کرنی ہے۔''

''کیوں؟'' اب اس نے دونوں بازو سینے پر باندھ لیے تھے وہ ٹھٹک گیا۔

''کیا مطلب کیوں؟ بیوی ہے وہ میری۔ نکاح ہوا ہے میرا اس کے ساتھ۔''

''اچھا؟ کہاں ہے نکاح نامہ؟'' کسی تھانیدار کی طرح وہ اس کے سامنے تن کر کھڑی تفتیش کر رہی تھی۔ زائر اب حیرانی

ے اسے دیکھ رہا تھا۔

''آپ کون ہوتی ہیں مجھ سے نکاح نامہ مانگنے والی؟''

''ثانیہ عباس کی اکلوتی اور عزیز دوست ہوتی ہوں میں' جو بکواس اور فراڈ نکاح کے نام پر آپ نے اس بے ضرر سی لڑکی کے ساتھ کیا ہے اس کے لیے میں آپ کو چھوڑوں گی نہیں۔''

''جسٹ شٹ اپ...... نہ تو میں نے کوئی بکواس کی ہے نہ کسی کے ساتھ کوئی فراڈ کیا ہے۔ میرا نکاح ہوا ہے ثانیہ کے ساتھ' وہ بھی کورٹ میں۔ آپ جا کر اس سے پوچھ سکتی ہیں' جہاں تک نکاح نامے کا تعلق ہے تو وہ بھی محفوظ ہے میرے پاس' کسی سے ڈرتا نہیں ہوں میں اگر ڈر ہے تو صرف اللہ رب العزت کی پاک ذات کا اور بس۔''

غصے سے اس کے چہرے کی رنگت سرخ پڑ گئی تھی پھر اس سے پہلے کہ ایمن اس سے کچھ کہتی وہ ایک ہاتھ سے اسے سائیڈ پر ہٹاتے ہوئے دندناتا ہوا اپارٹمنٹ کے اندر چلا آیا' جہاں ثانیہ ہونق کھڑی اسے دیکھ رہی تھی۔

''کیا تماشا ہے یہ؟ ہوں...... تمہیں پتا ہے نا ہمارا نکاح ہوا ہے کورٹ میں' پھر کیوں نہیں اپنی دوست کو بتایا؟'' اسے کندھوں سے تھامے وہ درشتگی سے پوچھ رہا تھا مگر وہ خاموشی سے اسے دیکھے گئی۔

''کیا بُرا کیا ہے میں نے تمہارے ساتھ بولو؟ یہ پاکستان ہے یہاں آئے روز گھروں میں ڈکیتیاں ہوتی ہیں اور ان ڈکیتوں میں ہر جگہ صرف سامان ہی نہیں لٹتا' عزتیں بھی لوٹی جاتی ہیں مگر میں نے ایسا نہیں کیا' میں نے وہ کیا جو کبھی نہیں ہوتا' کوئی نہیں کرتا' کیا بگاڑ سکتی ہو تم میرا' بولو......؟'' اس بار اس نے اس کے شانوں کو جھٹکا دیا تھا' تبھی ایمن اس کی طرف لپکی تھی۔

''ثانی کو چھوڑو' نہیں تو میں شور مچا دوں گی۔''

''شٹ اپ!'' اس کی دھمکی پر وہ دھاڑتے ہوئے پلٹا تھا۔

''خبردار اگر میرے اور اس کے درمیان میں آنے کی کوشش کی تو' بیوی ہے یہ میری جو سلوک چاہوں کر سکتا ہوں مگر کروں گا نہیں صرف اس کی عزت کے لیے' اب میں نکاح نامے کے ساتھ ہی آؤں گا پھر دیکھوں گا کیسے روکتی ہو تم مجھے۔'' وہ اشتعال کا شکار تھا ایمن اسے کڑے تیوروں سے گھورتی رہ گئی اور وہ چلا گیا۔

''آیا بڑا نیکو کار کہیں کا' دیکھ لینا ثانی! اب وہ شام کبھی نہیں آئے گی جب یہ فضول شخص حقیقی نکاح نامے کے ساتھ ادھر کا رخ کرے۔ اس کے تو وہم و گمان میں بھی نہیں ہوگا کہ اس کا ٹکراؤ تمہاری جگہ یوں کسی اور کے ساتھ ہو جائے گا۔ بہر حال تمہارا اب یہاں رکنا خطرے سے خالی نہیں ہے' وہ غنڈا موالی شخص کچھ بھی کر سکتا ہے' چلو ابھی میری طرف چلتے ہیں۔'' جلدی جلدی کام نپٹاتے ہوئے ایمن کہہ رہی تھی' وہ سر جھکائے خاموش کھڑی رہی یوں جیسے کچھ بھی نہ کہنا چاہتی ہو۔

❁......❁......❁

رات آدھی سے زیادہ ڈھل چکی تھی جب اچانک ہانیہ کی آنکھ میکال کے موبائل فون کی تیز بپ پر کھل گئی' وہ شاید جاگ رہا تھا تبھی فوراً سے پیشتر کال پک کر کے بیڈ سے اٹھ گیا۔

''ہیلو عائش!'' اس کی بھاری آواز ہانیہ کی سماعتوں میں اتری تھی اور پھر جیسے اس کی آنکھوں سے نیند کی پریاں خود بخود رخصت ہونا شروع ہو گئیں۔ وہ کمرے سے نکل کر ٹیرس کی طرف چلا گیا تھا مگر اس کی آواز ہنوز کمرے میں آ رہی تھی۔

''خوش ہو ناں میری زندگی برباد کر کے' یہی کرنا تھا تو کیوں آئیں میری زندگی میں' کیوں محبت کے خواب دکھائے

مجھے، میں تمہیں نہیں بھول پا رہا عائش! نہیں جی سکتا میں تمہارے بغیر۔'' اس کی آواز رندھی ہوئی تھی۔ ہانیہ عجیب سی جلن محسوس کرتے ہوئے بیڈ پر اٹھ بیٹھی۔ اب وہ کہہ رہا تھا۔

''میں کچھ نہیں جانتا' مجھے میری عائشہ چاہیے' وہ عائشہ جو میری محبت ہے' جو بن کہے میرے اندر کے اضطراب کو بھانپ لیتی ہے۔ جس کے پاس میرے سکون اور خوشیوں کی چابی ہے' وہ شخص تمہارے قابل نہیں ہے عائش! وہ تمہیں مار دے گا۔'' ہانیہ اس کی کہانی سے زیادہ واقف نہیں تھی تبھی چپ چاپ سنتی رہی تقریباً بیس منٹ گزر گئے اور اب وہ کہہ رہا تھا۔

''میرا دل چاہتا ہے میں خودکشی کرلوں مگر دونوں جہان کی بربادی کا خیال ہر بار ارادے کو کمزور کر دیتا ہے' میں تمہیں کبھی معاف نہیں کروں گا عائش! کبھی بھی نہیں۔''

کسی چھوٹے سے بچے کی طرح ہرٹ اس شخص کے لیے جانے کیوں اس کا دل دکھا تھا۔ مگر وہ چاہنے کے باوجود اس شخص کے لیے کچھ بھی نہیں کر پا رہی تھی۔

تقریباً تیس منٹ کے بعد وہ دوبارہ کمرے میں آیا تو وہ زلفیں بکھرائے بیڈ پر بیٹھی تھی۔ میکال صرف ایک لمحے کے لیے اس کے قریب رکا تھا پھر سر جھٹکتے ہوئے واش روم کی طرف بڑھ گیا۔

اگلے پندرہ منٹ کے بعد وہ فریش ہو کر دوبارہ کمرے میں واپس آیا تو ہانیہ اسی پوزیشن میں بیٹھی تھی۔ وہ بنا اس پر نگاہ کیے بیڈ کے کونے پر ٹک گیا۔

''ایکسکیوزمی! اگر آپ کو ناگوار نہ گزرے تو کیا ہم چند منٹ کے لیے بات کر سکتے ہیں؟'' میکال نے اس کی صدا پر خاموشی سے گردن پھیر کر اس کی طرف دیکھا تھا۔

''پلیز......'' اسے اپنی طرف دیکھتے پا کر اس نے التجا کی۔

''بولو۔'' وہ رخ پھیر کر بھاری لہجے میں بولا تھا۔ ہانیہ نے اپنی نظریں اس کے چہرے پر جما دیں۔

''مجھے نہال نے بتایا تھا کہ آپ عائشہ جی سے بہت پیار کرتے ہیں اور شاید وہ بھی' پھر آپ نے ان سے شادی کیوں نہیں کی؟ آپ مرد تھے' با اختیار تھے' چاہتے تو ان کے لیے اسٹینڈ لے سکتے تھے مگر پھر بھی آپ نے انہیں اکیلا چھوڑ دیا' کیوں......؟''

''میں نے اکیلا نہیں چھوڑا اسے وہ خود مجھے اکیلا چھوڑ گئی ہے۔'' وہ رنجیدہ تھا' ہانیہ اسے دیکھ کر رہ گئی۔

''کیوں؟ جو پیار کرتے ہیں وہ اکیلا تو نہیں چھوڑتے۔''

''مجھے نہیں پتا' میرا سر درد سے پھٹ رہا ہے' پلیز سو جاؤ۔'' بے زاری سے کہتے ہوئے وہ بیڈ سے اٹھا تھا' جب ہانیہ نے سرعت سے اس کی کلائی تھام لی۔

''میں آپ کی ہم سفر ہوں میکال! آپ کے دکھ اور سکھ کی ساتھی ہوں' مجھ سے آپ کا یہ درد اور اضطراب برداشت نہیں ہو رہا' مجھے بتائیں میں آپ کے لیے ایسا کیا کروں کہ آپ کو سکون مل جائے۔''

''مجھے نہیں پتا۔'' اجنبیت سے بازو چھڑا کر کہتے ہوئے وہ کیبنٹ کی طرف بڑھ گیا تھا تاکہ سگریٹ اور ماچس تلاش کر سکے' تبھی وہ پھر اس کے قریب آئی تھی۔

''میں پوری کوشش کروں گی کہ عائشہ جی کو آپ کی زندگی میں واپس لے آؤں مگر اس کے لیے آپ کو میری ایک بات ماننی ہو گی۔'' کتنی رسانیت سے وہ کہہ رہی تھی' میکال چونکے بغیر نہ رہ سکا۔

''مانیں گے ناں پلیز......'' میکال رخصتی کے وقت اپنی ذات کے لیے اُس کی ناپسندیدگی نہ جان گیا ہوتا تو شاید اس

کے انداز اور خلوص پر ہرگز حیران نہ ہوتا۔

''کیسی بات؟''

''یہی کہ اپنا خیال رکھیں گے خود کو کوئی نقصان نہیں پہنچائیں گے اور مجھے اپنی بیوی نہیں دوست سمجھیں گے' ٹھیک ہے۔'' وہ اسے بالکل کسی چھوٹے بچے کی طرح ہی ٹریٹ کررہی تھی' وہ سر جھٹک کر بیڈ پر آ گیا۔

''یہ دھواں کبھی کسی درد کو اپنے اندر تحلیل نہیں کرتا میکال! اس لیے اپنا جگر جلانا فضول ہے' آئیں میں آپ کو سلاتی ہوں کیونکہ اس وقت آپ کے لیے نیند بہت ضروری ہے۔''

اس کے سر جھٹکنے پر وہ بھی واپس پلٹی تھی اور پھر آگے بڑھ کر اس نے میکال کے لبوں سے سگریٹ نکالتے ہوئے مسل کر پھینک دی۔ وہ اسے کھری کھری سنانا ہی چاہتا تھا کہ ہانیہ نے اس کے مقابل بیٹھتے ہوئے اپنا ہاتھ اس کے کندھے پر ٹکا دیا۔

''سو جائیے پلیز' سارے دکھ' ساری محرومیاں بھلا کر۔'' عجیب جادوئی انداز میں اس کے بالوں میں انگلیاں چلاتے ہوئے وہ اب سرگوشی کررہی تھی۔ میکال کی سانسیں اس کے وجود سے اٹھتی خوشبو کے نشے میں گم ہونے لگیں۔

وہ خود کو اس کے حصار سے نکالنا چاہتا تھا' اسے یہ باور کرانا چاہتا تھا کہ وہ کمزور نہیں ہے جو اس کے حسن کے جادو کے سامنے ہتھیار پھینک دے مگر وہ کمزور پڑ گیا تھا۔

اگلی صبح ہانیہ کی آنکھ کھلی تو وہ آفس کے لیے تیار ہو رہا تھا۔ وہ فوراً سے پیش تر بیڈ سے اتر آئی۔

''میں تیاری میں آپ کی مدد کروں؟''

''نہیں۔'' کتنے خلوص سے وہ پوچھ رہی تھی مگر وہ اس کی طرف دیکھنے کا روادار بھی نہیں تھا۔

''ٹھیک ہے مگر ناشتہ تو کریں گے ناں آپ؟'' مگر اس بار وہ پھر اس کا سوال نظرانداز کرتے ہوئے پرفیوم کا چھڑکاؤ کرنے لگا۔ عین اسی پل اس کے سیل پر عائشہ برہان کی کال آئی تھی۔

''السلام علیکم!''

''وعلیکم السلام! تم ٹھیک ہو ناں میکال؟'' وہ اس کے لیے متفکر تھی۔ میکال شکستہ سا بیڈ پر ٹک گیا۔

''ہوں' تم کیسی ہو؟''

''میں ٹھیک ہوں رات میری ساس کی طبیعت ٹھیک نہیں تھی۔ اریج انہیں اسپتال لے کر گیا تھا' میں بھی ساتھ تھی۔ اس لیے تمہارے ایس ایم ایس کا جواب نہ دے سکی' تین بجے گھر واپس آئی تو فوری تمہیں کال کی' خدا کا واسطہ ہے میکال! ماضی کو ذہن سے جھٹک دو' اگر تم خوش نہیں رہو گے تو میرے لیے اس قربانی کو نبھانا بہت مشکل ہو جائے گا' مجھے مزید کمزور مت کرو میکال پلیز۔''

''او کے' اگین سوری! ابھی میں آفس جا رہا ہوں' واپسی پر تم سے بات کرتا ہوں۔'' ہانیہ کی موجودگی کے باعث اس نے بنا بحث کیے کال ڈراپ کردی تھی' اگلے ہی پل وہ کمرے سے نکل کر سیڑھیوں سے نیچے آیا تو مسز حسن اسے تیار دیکھ کر ٹھٹک گئیں۔

''میکال! اتنی صبح تیار ہو کر کہاں جا رہے ہو؟''

''اتنی صبح نہیں ہے مما! دن کے دس بج چکے ہیں اور میں آفس جا رہا ہوں۔''

''آفس...... تمہارا دماغ تو خراب نہیں ہو گیا' آج تمہاری شادی کو تیسرا دن ہے' ابھی گھر مہمانوں سے بھرا پڑا ہے' تمہارے سسرال والے دوپہر میں پہنچ رہے ہیں اور تم آفس جا رہے ہو۔'' وہ حیران ہی تو رہ گئی تھیں۔

تبھی وہ ماتھے پر بل ڈالتے ہوئے انتہائی بدتمیزی سے بولا۔

''مما پلیز میں نے ساری دنیا کے دل رکھنے کا ٹھیکا نہیں اٹھایا ہوا ہے جو کچھ آپ لوگ میری زندگی کے ساتھ کر چکے ہیں، کافی ہے۔ اس سے زیادہ کا حق نہیں رکھتے آپ مجھ پر۔'' اس کا لہجہ محض تلخ ہی نہیں حتمی بھی تھا۔

ہانیہ سن سی سیڑھیوں پر کھڑی رہی جبکہ مسز حسن از حد حیرانی کے ساتھ اسے ٹکر ٹکر دیکھتی رہ گئی تھیں۔

''خدا حافظ۔'' ٹائی کی ناٹ ٹھیک کرتا اگلے ہی پل وہ لمبے لمبے ڈگ بھرتا گھر سے نکل گیا تھا۔ مسز حسن پلٹ کر شرمندہ نگاہوں سے ہانیہ کو دیکھ رہی تھیں مگر وہ لبوں پر نرم سی مسکراہٹ پھیلا کر انہیں مطمئن کرتی نہال کے کمرے کی طرف چلی آئی۔

✿......✿......✿

''نہال۔'' تکیہ بانہوں میں دبائے بیڈ پر آڑھا ترچھا لیٹا تھا، جب ہانیہ کی پکار پر اس کی آنکھ کھل گئی۔

''ہوں؟'' تکیے کو اور بھی شدت سے بانہوں میں دباتے ہوئے اس نے ہانیہ کی طرف دیکھا تھا۔

''اٹھ جاؤ، صبح ہوگئی ہے۔''

''پتا ہے مجھے، تمہاری شادی کو تیسرا دن ہے، تمہیں تو اپنے کمرے میں ہونا چاہیے تھا میرے سر پر کیوں سوار ہوگئی ہو صبح صبح۔''

''حال پوچھنے آئی تھی تمہارا، اسٹوپڈ۔''

''کیوں؟'' ہانیہ کے کشن مارنے پر وہ کہنیوں کے بل اٹھ بیٹھا تھا۔

''میرے حال کو کیا ہوا؟''

''سنا ہے خراب ہے، مجھے لگا شاید میری شادی کے صدمے نے تمہارے حواس سلب کر دیئے ہیں اور تم رات رات بھر روتے رہتے ہو۔''

''اچھا، اتنی بڑی خوش فہمی؟'' وہ مسکرایا تھا مگر ہانیہ اس مسکراہٹ میں چھپی اذیت کو دیکھ سکتی تھی تبھی منہ چڑاتے ہوئے اس کے پہلو میں ٹک گئی۔

''خوش فہمی نہیں ہے یہ، چلو اب فریش ہو جاؤ۔ نہیں تو تمہیں پتا ہے میں تمہارے ساتھ کیا کرنے والی ہوں۔''

''ہوں پتا ہے مجھے، پوری جنگلی بلی ہو اور ہمیشہ پنجے جھاڑ کر میرے پیچھے پڑی رہتی ہو۔'' شرارت سے اس کے بال کھینچتا، وہ بیڈ کی پٹی سے ٹیک لگا گیا تھا۔

''کہو، کیسے نزول ہوا صبح صبح؟''

''کچھ نہیں، مجھے تم سے عائشہ جی کے بارے میں بات کرنی تھی۔''

''عائشہ جی کے بارے میں؟ خیریت......؟'' وہ حیران ہوا تھا، ہانیہ نے رخ پھیر لیا۔

''ہوں، خیریت ہی ہے۔''

''کیا جاننا چاہتی ہو عائشہ جی کے بارے میں؟''

''یہی کہ وہ کون ہیں، میکال کے ساتھ ان کی فرینڈ شپ کیسے ہوئی اور سب سے بڑی بات کہ انہوں نے محبت کے باوجود میکال کے ساتھ شادی کیوں نہیں کی؟''

''کیا میکال بھیا نے اس ٹاپک پر تم سے کوئی بات کی ہے؟'' وہ اب پریشان ہو رہا تھا، ہانیہ نے نفی میں سر ہلا دیا۔

''نہیں مگر وہ ان کو لے کر بہت پریشان ہیں۔''

''ہوں، عائشہ جی اصل میں میکال بھیا کی یونیورسٹی فیلو ہیں۔ یونیورسٹی پریڈ سے ہی بھیا انہیں پسند کرتے تھے مگر وہ ان میں انٹرسٹڈ نہیں تھیں کیونکہ وہ کسی ارمغان نامی شخص سے محبت کرتی تھیں اور انہی کے ساتھ شادی کرنا چاہتی تھیں مگر انہی دنوں ان کی بڑی بہن نے گھر سے بھاگ کر پسند کی شادی کرلی شاید اسی لیے عائشہ جی یونیورسٹی چھوڑ گئیں اور ہماری ہی کمپنی میں جاب کرنے لگیں تاکہ اپنی فیملی کو سپورٹ کرسکیں، بھیا کے ساتھ ان کی محبت یہیں پروان چڑھی مگر اس سے پہلے کہ بھیا انہیں باقاعدہ پرپوز کرتے ان کی ماں نے ان کا رشتہ طے کردیا۔ گھر کے ابتر حالات کی وجہ سے ان کی ماں نے اپنی بڑی بیٹی کی نسبت خاندان کے ایک نیم پاگل شخص کے ساتھ طے کر رکھی تھی تاکہ اس شخص کا بھائی عائشہ جی کے بھائی کو باہر سیٹ کروادے مگر ان کی بہن یہ قربانی دینے پر تیار نہ ہوئیں تو ان کی ماں نے یہ ہڈی عائشہ جی کے گلے میں فٹ کردی، بس یہی کہانی ہے عائشہ جی کی۔''

''اس کا مطلب ہے کہ عائشہ جی اپنی ازدواجی زندگی سے خوش نہیں ہیں۔''

''کیسے ہوسکتی ہیں ایک نیم پاگل شخص کے ساتھ کوئی کیسے خوش رہ سکتا ہے۔'' نہال اب اسے دیکھ رہا تھا، ہانیہ اثبات میں سرہلاتی آنے والے دنوں میں اپنے کردار اور قربانی کے بارے میں سوچنے لگی۔

۞......۞......۞

وہ کچن میں برتن دھو رہی تھی جب اریج آفس سے گھر واپس آیا۔

لاؤنج میں ٹی وی فل والیم کے ساتھ چل رہا تھا اور اس کی ساس، اپنی بیٹی کے ساتھ ٹی وی کے سامنے براجمان بڑے انہماک سے کوئی ڈرامہ دیکھ رہی تھیں۔ اریج سب کو سلام کرتا وہیں بیٹھ گیا۔

''ایک کپ چائے مل سکتی ہے اس وقت؟'' اپنی ماں اور بہن کا انہماک دیکھ کر اس نے کچن کی طرف منہ کرتے ہوئے صدا لگائی تھی۔ جواب میں عائشہ دو تین منٹ کے بعد ہی چائے کا کپ لے کر حاضر ہوگئی۔

''شکریہ۔'' وہ اس کا ممنون ہوا تھا مگر جیسے ہی نظر اس کے ہاتھوں پر پڑی، ٹھٹک گیا۔

''یہ......آپ کے ہاتھ پر چوٹ......؟''

''ہاں آج کھیت میں کام کرتے ہوئے اپنی کم عقلی سے ہاتھ کٹوا بیٹھی ہے اپنا، میں نے تو بہتیرا کہا ہے کہ دھیان سے کام کیا کرو مگر میری کوئی بات یہ سنتی کہاں ہے۔''

''کیا مطلب؟ کھیتوں میں کام کرنے کے لیے اتنے ملازم ہیں پھر یہ کیوں گئیں کھیت پر؟'' عائشہ کے بجائے اپنی ماں کے جواب پر وہ شاکڈ ہی تو رہ گیا تھا۔ تبھی وہ چمکتے ہوئے بولی تھیں۔

''تو کیا کریں اسے تاج بنا کر سر پر سجالیں، پورے چار لاکھ روپے لگے ہیں اس کے بھائی کے ویزے پر، مفت میں بیاہ کر نہیں لائے کہ شہزادی بنا کر رکھیں۔''

وہ سر جھکائے مجرم بنی کھڑی تھی۔ اریج نے چائے کا کپ سائیڈ ٹیبل پر پٹخ دیا۔

''ساڑھے چار لاکھ اس کے بھائی کو دیئے تھے اسے نہیں پھر یہ کیوں یہاں غلاموں جیسی زندگی بسر کریں؟''

''تم حد سے بڑھ رہے ہو اریج! میں دیکھ رہی ہوں اس لڑکی کے لیے تمہاری ہمدردیاں کچھ زیادہ ہی بڑھنے لگی ہیں۔''

''یہی سوچ سکتی ہیں آپ، اس کے علاوہ میں آپ سے کوئی امید رکھ بھی نہیں سکتا۔'' انتہائی تلخی سے کہتا وہ صوفے سے اٹھ کر اپنے کمرے کی طرف بڑھ گیا تھا، پیچھے عائشہ کتنی ہی دیر تک مجرموں کی طرح سر جھکائے اپنی ساس کی صلواتیں سنتی رہی تھی۔

اسی رات جب وہ اپنے بیڈ پر پہلو کے بل لیٹی سسکیاں بھر رہی تھیں، اسے اپنے کندھے پر مردانہ ہاتھ کی گرماہٹ

محسوس ہوئی تھی۔ روتے روتے وہ چونک کر پلٹی تو اس کا نیم پاگل شوہر فل آنکھیں کھولے اسے ہی دیکھ رہا تھا۔
''تم رو رہی ہو؟''
''نہیں۔'' اسے دیکھ کر اس کے آنسو اور شدت سے بہنے لگے تھے۔
''جھوٹ، مجھے پتا ہے تمہیں امی نے مارا ہے، میں جب صبح اٹھوں گا ناں تو بہت سارا جھگڑا کروں گا ان کے ساتھ، پھر تم نہیں روؤ گی ناں؟''
''نہیں۔''
''تم بہت اچھی ہو، میں امی کو کہوں گا تو وہ تمہیں نہیں ماریں گی، ٹھیک ہے؟''
کسی چھوٹے سے بچے کی طرح معصوم انداز میں وہ اسے بہلا رہا تھا۔ عائشہ نے اپنے آنسو پونچھ کر سر اثبات میں ہلا دیا۔
''گڈ گرل۔'' وہ اس کی فرماں برداری پر خوش ہوا تھا پھر عائشہ کے دیکھتے ہی دیکھتے وہ اس پر جھکا اور اس کی پیشانی کو چوم لیا۔
''اب سوئیں، آج میں تمہیں ناں اپنے بازو پر سلاؤں گا۔''
جانے وہ آج اس پر اتنا نثار کیوں ہو رہا تھا۔ عائشہ قدرے حیرانی سے اس کی طرف دیکھتی وہیں تکیے پر سر رکھے چپ چاپ پلکیں موند گئی تھی۔

❀ .... ❀ .... ❀

شام گہری ہو رہی تھی اور وہ سڑک کے کنارے سر جھکائے متفکر بیٹھا تھا۔
اس نے ثانیہ عباس کی دوست ایمن سے وعدہ کیا تھا کہ وہ شام میں نکاح نامے کے ساتھ آئے گا مگر...... وہ نہیں جا سکا تھا۔
اس کا نکاح نامہ اس کے دوست عاطف کے پاس تھا اور وہ ملک سے باہر تھا۔ دو ہفتوں کے طویل انتظار کے بعد عاطف کے وطن واپس پلٹنے پر وہ اس کی طرف گیا تھا مگر اسے یہ سن کر شدید جھٹکا لگا جب عاطف نے اس سے کہا۔
''ایک شرط پر نکاح نامہ مل سکتا ہے تمہیں۔''
''کیسی شرط؟'' بنا چائے کے کپ کو ہاتھ لگائے اس نے الجھن بھری نگاہوں سے اس کی طرف دیکھا تھا۔ جب وہ مسکرا دیا۔
''بہت معمولی سی ہے۔ دیکھو ہم نے تمہیں ثانیہ عباس کے گھر ڈکیتی کے لیے بھیجا، اتنی محنت کی، اس کی شب و روز سرگرمیوں پر نظر رکھی مگر ہوا کیا، تم نے مال بھی نہیں ہتھیایا اور ہوشیاری دکھاتے ہوئے لڑکی بھی پٹالی، اب سیدھی سی بات ہے جو لڑکی ہاتھ لگی ہے اس میں ہمارا حصہ بھی ہونا چاہیے نا؟''
''بکواس بند کرو، وہ لڑکی میری عزت ہے اور میں تم میں سے کسی کو بھی اپنی عزت کے ساتھ کھیلنے کی اجازت نہیں دوں گا۔''
''اجازت مانگ کون رہا ہے تم سے، ہم تو اپنا حصہ مانگ رہے ہیں۔'' عاطف کے ساتھ ساتھ اس بار وہاں موجود عاقب نے ہنس کر اس کا مذاق اڑایا تھا تبھی کاشف بول اٹھا۔
''ویسے آپس کی بات ہے تم یہ کیسے ثابت کرو گے کہ وہ لڑکی تمہاری عزت ہے؟''

''کاشف پلیز، میں یہاں اس وقت تم سے الجھنے کے لیے نہیں آیا لہٰذا بہتر ہوگا کہ تم لوگ مجھے پریشان نہ کرو۔'' وہ دہاڑا تھا، جب عاطف بولا۔

''پریشان تو تم ہمیں کر رہے ہو دیکھو ناں، تم صرف اپنی بچپن کی منگیتر سے پیار کرتے ہو، اسی کو پانے کے لیے تم نے ثانیہ عباس کے گھر ڈکیتی کا پروگرام بنایا بعد میں نیت خراب ہونے پر محض گناہ سے بچنے کے لیے تم نے اس سے نکاح کیا، ہم بھی انسان ہیں یار! ہماری بھی نیت خراب ہو سکتی ہے اب ہم تینوں اس سے نکاح تو نہیں کر سکتے مگر حصہ تو ہمارا بھی بنتا ہے ناں۔'' آنکھ مار کر لب دباتے ہوئے وہ زائر کو زہر لگا تھا۔ تبھی شدید غصے میں لپک کر اس کا گریبان پکڑتے ہوئے وہ جل کر بولا تھا۔

''ایسی کی تیسی تمہارے حصے کی، وہ لڑکی میرے نام کا حصہ ہے۔ میں اسے طلاق دے کر چھوڑ سکتا ہوں مگر عزت بنا کر اپنا نام دے کر لوٹ نہیں سکتا، سمجھے تم۔'' کاشف اس کے جلال پر فوراً اٹھ کر قریب آیا تھا۔

''چل چھوڑ یار، ٹھیک ہے دے اسے نکاح نامہ اپنے لیے کوئی اور سہی۔''

وہ زائر کے غصے سے اچھی طرح واقف تھا، تبھی مصالحت کی کوشش کی تھی زائر دو ہفتوں کے بعد نکاح نامے کے ساتھ، ثانیہ عباس کے اپارٹمنٹ کی طرف آیا تو وہاں لگا تالا اس کا منہ چڑا رہا تھا۔

سائرہ افضل کے ساتھ ثانیہ عباس بھی جیسے اس کی دسترس سے دور چلی گئی تھی۔ انہی دنوں اس نے اپنی ماں کی التجا پر حویلی میں ایک ڈرائیور کی حیثیت سے ملازمت اختیار کی تھی بعد ازاں وہ چوہدرانی صاحبہ کا لاڈلا بنتا گیا اور انہوں نے زمینوں اور باغات کے سارے معاملات بھی اس کے سپرد کر دیئے۔

سائرہ کے والد ماسٹر افضل کی وفات ہو گئی تھی اور تبھی بہت عرصے کے بعد اس نے اسے دیکھا تھا۔ وہ بُری طرح رو رہی تھی مگر اس کا حسن گم گشتہ ہو گیا تھا، وہ جو فخر سے کہتی تھی کہ گاؤں میں اس جیسا حسین دوسرا کوئی نہیں، اب وہ حسن جیسے کہیں چھپ کر رہ گیا تھا۔ بڑھے ہوئے وزن کے ساتھ چہرے پر پڑی چھائیوں اور سانولے پن نے اسے کہیں کا نہیں چھوڑا تھا۔

زائر اگلے روز اپنے اندر کے اضطراب سے تنگ آ کر پھر شہر چلا آیا تھا، بارش ہو رہی تھی اور وہ مارکیٹ میں تھا جب اچانک اس کی نگاہ شاپنگ کرتی ثانیہ عباس پر پڑی اور پھر جیسے اس کا دماغ گھوم گیا۔

گاڑی کا فرنٹ ڈور زور سے بند کرتے ہوئے وہ تیزی سے اس کی طرف لپکا تھا اور پھر اس سے پہلے کہ وہ ٹیکسی یا رکشہ کو ہاتھ دے کر روکتی، زائر نے اس کا ہاتھ تھام لیا۔ ثانیہ جیسے کرنٹ کھا کر پلٹی تھی، اسے ایک فیصد بھی امید نہیں تھی کہ وہ دوبارہ اس کی زندگی میں آئے گا مگر وہ آ گیا تھا۔

ازحد سنجیدہ چہرے پر غصے کی ہلکی سی سرخی لیے وہ اسے بنا کچھ کہے خاموشی سے کھینچتے ہوئے گاڑی کی طرف لے آیا تھا۔

✿ .... ✿ .... ✿

اس روز وہ قبرستان نہیں آئی تھی۔

عذیر شہر خاموشاں کی خاموش دنیا میں کافی دیر تک اپنی والدہ کی قبر کے پاس بیٹھا، فاتحہ خوانی کرنے کے بعد اس کا انتظار کرتا رہا تھا مگر وہ نہیں آئی تھی۔

اگلے روز اس کی بے چینی دیکھنے لائق تھی۔

اس روز بہت بارش ہوئی تھی، سڑکوں پر ٹریفک کا نظام درہم برہم ہو کر رہ گیا تھا۔ وہ ابھی جاگا تھا کہ اس کی فیانسی سلمیٰ

کی کال آ گئی۔

”ہیلو......عذیر......!“

”بول رہا ہوں‘ کبھی دعا سلام بھی کر لیا کرو اٹھ کر۔“

”تم پر سلامتی بھیجنے کا کوئی فائدہ نہیں کیونکہ تم ہر وقت ویسے ہی میری دعاؤں کے حصار میں رہتے ہو خیر میں انڈیا جا رہی ہوں‘ تم نے اپنی دادو سے ہماری شادی کی بات کی؟“

”نہیں یار ابھی دادو سے میری بات نہیں ہو سکی ہے‘ سمیر اور نمیر وغیرہ کو بتا دیا ہے‘ میرا خیال ہے وہ دادو سے بات کر لیں گے‘ تم ٹینشن مت لو میرے گھر میں سب میرے فیصلے کا احترام کرتے ہیں۔“

”چلو اچھی بات ہے‘ ویسے میں اگلے کچھ روز میں پاکستان کا چکر لگا رہی ہوں بہت شوق ہے مجھے پاکستان دیکھنے کا۔“

”گڈ‘ میں بھی یو کے آ رہا ہوں۔“

”خیریت؟“

”ہوں‘ خیریت ہی ہے بزنس کے سلسلے میں ایک ضروری میٹنگ اٹینڈ کرنی ہے۔“

”کب تک آؤ گے؟“

”پندرہ بیس دن تو لگ جائیں گے‘ چلو اب مجھے آفس جانا ہے شام میں بات کرتے ہیں۔“

”ٹھیک ہے اپنا خیال رکھنا‘ خدا حافظ۔“

دادو اس کے کمرے میں آ گئی تھیں تبھی اس نے گھبرا کر فوری لائن کاٹ دی‘ سلمٰی اس کی یونیورسٹی فیلو تھی اور اسے پسند کرتی تھی چھ ماہ قبل وہ لوگ یو کے شفٹ ہو گئے تھے مگر ان کا رابطہ برقرار رہا تھا۔ عذیر کی لائف میں چونکہ کوئی لڑکی نہیں تھی لہٰذا اس نے اپنے طور پر اسے انگیجمنٹ رنگ پہنا دی تھی۔ اس روز بہت دنوں کے بعد وہ آفس سے اٹھ کر شہر خاموشاں کی طرف آیا تھا‘ شاید اس امید پر کہ وہ آئے گی مگر اس روز پھر وہ نہیں آئی تھی۔

شاید اس نے اس کے کہے کا مان رکھ لیا تھا مگر عذیر کا دل اس فرماں برداری کو قبول نہیں کر پا رہا تھا۔ وہ اس سے صرف ایک بار ملنا چاہتا تھا اس کے بارے میں کھل کر جاننا چاہتا تھا مگر شاید یہ ابھی اس کی تقدیر کو منظور نہیں تھا۔

اگلے چند روز میں اس کی مصروفیات مزید بڑھ گئی تھیں۔ اس کے قبرستان جانے کا معمول بھی مستقل نہیں رہا تھا۔ مگر پھر بھی وہ لڑکی اس کے حافظے میں محفوظ تھی‘ ایک ہفتے بعد اس روز وہ پھر آفس سے اٹھ کر سیدھا قبرستان کی طرف آیا تھا اور......تبھی وہ اسے دکھائی دے گئی تھی۔

مکمل سیاہ چادر میں خود کو چھپائے‘ عادت کے عین مطابق وہ مطلوبہ قبر کے پاس بیٹھی اس پر ہاتھ پھیر رہی تھی۔

عجیب یاسیت کا ماحول تھا

عذیر اپنی جگہ پر ٹھٹک کر کھڑا اسے دیکھتا رہا۔

اس نے سنا تھا رشتے صرف سانس کی ڈوری سے بندھے ہوتے ہیں‘ جیسے ہی یہ ڈوری ٹوٹتی ہے‘ رشتوں کا احساس اور زندگی میں ان کی اہمیت بھی دم توڑنے لگتی ہے۔ خود وہ بھی اس کا تجربہ کر چکا تھا‘ اس کی زندگی میں اس کی ماں اتنی اہمیت کی حامل تھی کہ اسے لگتا تھا وہ ان کے بغیر سانس بھی نہیں لے سکتا مگر ان کی رحلت کے چار سال بعد بھی وہ نہ صرف سانس لے رہا تھا بلکہ زندگی نے اسے اتنا مصروف کر دیا تھا کہ اب اکثر اسے ان کی روح کے ایصال ثواب کے لیے درود پاک پڑھنے کے لیے بھی ٹائم نہیں ملتا تھا حالانکہ ان کی رحلت کے شروع کے دنوں میں ہر روز ان کے لیے بے شمار نوافل اور درود پاک پڑھنا اس نے اپنا معمول بنا لیا تھا مگر......

اس لڑکی کو دیکھ کر یہ نہیں لگتا تھا کہ رشتے سانس سے بندھے ہوتے ہیں' اُدھر چہرہ منوں مٹی کے ڈھیر تلے دفن ہوا اور ادھر اس شخص کی ذات سے جڑے سارے باب بند۔

مگر وہاں شیشم کے اس پیڑ تلے منوں مٹی کے ڈھیر تلے دفن اس رشتے سے شاید اس کی زندگی کا تعلق ذرا سا بھی کمزور نہیں ہوا تھا کیونکہ وہ اب بھی آندھی طوفان کی پروا کیے بغیر ہر روز وہاں آ رہی تھی بس اس نے اپنا وقت تبدیل کر لیا تھا۔

عذیر کے پاس اس روز زیادہ ٹائم نہیں تھا مگر اس نے لڑکی کا چہرہ ضرور دیکھ لیا تھا بے شک وہ بے تحاشا خوب صورت لڑکی تھی۔

❀ ...... ❀ ...... ❀

دروازے پر دستک کی آواز ابھری تھی

عذیر جو ابھی قبرستان سے واپس لوٹا تھا' اپنا سفری بیگ تیار کرتے ہوئے چونک کر پلٹا۔

''السّلام علیکم!'' اس سے چھوٹا سمیر اس کے پلٹ کر دیکھنے پر دونوں بازو سینے پر باندھے' کچھ ہی فاصلے پر کھڑا دکھائی دیا۔

''وعلیکم السّلام' خیریت؟ آج اتنی جلدی گھر کیسے پلٹ آئے آپ؟''

ہنوز اپنے کام میں مصروف وہ اس سے پوچھ رہا تھا' سمیر دو قدم چل کر بیڈ پر بیٹھ گیا۔

''عمیر کی طبیعت ٹھیک نہیں تھی صبح' اسی لیے سو رہا تھا میں نے سوچا اس کے حصے کی صفائی آج میں کرلوں' کھانا باہر سے منگوالیں گے' اصل میں اس نے بھی پرسوں میرے حصے کے برتن دھوئے تھے جب میں گھر واپسی پر بہت تھکا ہوا تھا۔''

''گڈ! اس کا مطلب ہے آج کل نمیر کے ساتھ اچھے تعلقات چل رہے ہیں تمہارے۔'' بیگ میں شیونگ کا سامان اور موزے رکھتے ہوئے عذیر مسکرایا تھا۔ جواب میں سمیر کے لبوں پر بھی مسکراہٹ بکھر گئی۔

''ہوں' کہہ سکتے ہیں اصل میں جب تک کوئی خاتونِ خانہ اس گھر میں نہیں آ جاتی' تب تک سب سے بنا کر رکھنا مجبوری ہے۔ ویسے سلمٰی بھابی کب تک آ رہی ہیں پاکستان؟''

''پتا نہیں' کافی دنوں سے میرا اس سے رابطہ نہیں ہوا شاید انڈیا چلی گئی ہے وہ' ویسے اگلے کچھ روز میں آنے کا امکان ہے اس کا کیونکہ اسے بھی تم لوگوں سے ملنے اور پاکستان دیکھنے کا بہت شوق ہے۔''

''آہم...... رابطہ بھی نہیں ہے اور پل پل کی خبر بھی ہے' ویسے آج قبرستان نہیں گئے آپ؟''

''گیا تھا بلکہ وہیں سے آ رہا ہوں' ایک گھنٹے بعد فلائٹ ہے میری' تم ذرا عمیر کو کال کرو مجھے ائرپورٹ تک چھوڑ آئے۔''

''ٹھیک ہے' واپسی کب تک ہوگی؟''

''اس بار تاخیر ہو سکتی ہے کیونکہ کام کا لوڈ زیادہ ہے پھر بھی جلدی واپس آنے کی کوشش کروں گا۔ تم دادو' زبیر اور عمیر کا خصوصی خیال رکھنا۔''

''جو حکم جناب! فکر ہی نہ کریں آپ۔''

عذیر اپنی تیاری کو فائنل ٹچ دے رہا تھا اسے بزنس کے سلسلے میں یو کے جانا تھا' سمیر امسکراتے ہوئے کمرے سے نکل گیا۔

❀ ...... ❀ ...... ❀

شام کے سرمئی اندھیروں میں
یوں تیری یاد ساتھ چلتی ہے
جیسے پربت کے سبز پیڑوں پر
برف کے بعد دھوپ پڑتی ہے
جیسے صحرا کی ریت اڑ اڑ کر اجنبی کا طواف کرتی ہے
آہ بھرتا ہوں اشک پیتا ہوں
روز مرتا ہوں روز جیتا ہوں
کتنی معصوم آرزوؤں کو کس طرح لوگ توڑ جاتے ہیں
جیسے دم توڑتے مسافر کو قافلے چھوڑ جاتے ہیں
شام کے سرمئی اندھیروں میں یوں تیری یاد ساتھ چلتی ہے

قبرستان میں اس وقت اُس کے علاوہ اور کوئی نہیں تھا۔

تازہ تیار کی گئی لحد کے قریب درخت کے تنے سے ٹیک لگائے بیٹھی، آپ ہی آپ وہ اپنے یونیورسٹی پیریڈ کے دنوں میں کھو گئی تھی۔

کلاس میں گہرا سناٹا چھایا تھا۔ ڈائس کے اس پار صرف سر جاوید ہمدانی کے بولنے کی آواز وہاں بیٹھے ہر طالب علم کی سماعتوں میں اتر رہی تھی۔

''دہشت گرد کیا ہوتا ہے اسٹوڈنٹس؟''

لیکچر کے دوران اچانک انہوں نے اپنے سامنے بیٹھے طلباء و طالبات پر ایک گہری نظر ڈالتے ہوئے پوچھ لیا تھا' ساری کلاس کو جیسے سانپ سونگھ گیا۔

''آپ کے ذہنوں میں کیا ہے' ایک شخص جو باہر سے بم لے کر آتا ہے اور کسی بھی گھر میں گھس جاتا ہے' کیا وہ دہشت گرد ہے یا اس گھر میں موجود افراد جو اس بم پکڑے ہوئے شخص کو روکنے یا قابو کرنے کی کوشش کرتے ہیں' وہ دہشت گرد ہیں؟''

فاطمہ نہیں جانتی تھی کہ سر ہمدانی اس ٹاپک پر گفتگو کیوں کر رہے ہیں مگر وہ انہیں بہت توجہ سے دیکھ رہی تھی' ان کے سرخ و سفید چہرے پر دبا دبا سا جوش تھا۔

''جو شخص بم لے کر آئے گا' وہی دہشت گرد ہوگا سر!''

''رائٹ! لیکن اگر وہ شخص آپ کے گھر کے سربراہ کو خرید لے' اس کا منہ پیسوں سے بھر کر آپ کی زندگی کا سودا کرے تو دہشت گرد کون ہوگا؟'' حورعین فاطمہ کے جواب پر انہوں نے پھر سوال داغ دیا تھا' وہ سر جھکا گئی۔

''دونوں سر۔''

''رائٹ! اور اگر اسی گھر کے زندہ بچ جانے والے لوگ صرف اس لیے کہ وہ زندہ بچ گئے اپنے سربراہ کا ساتھ دیں' تو دہشت گرد کون ہوگا؟''

''سب گھر والے سر! کیونکہ ظالم کا ساتھ دینے والا بھی ظالم ہوتا ہے۔''

''جی ہاں اور یہی بات آج میں آپ کو سمجھانے کی کوشش کر رہا ہوں' ہم مسلم تو شاید صحیح معنوں میں کبھی بھی نہیں تھے مگر حب الوطن پاکستانی بھی نہ بن سکے۔ ہم نے ہمیشہ ان لوگوں کا ساتھ دیا' جو ظلم کرتے ہیں۔ کس لیے؟ صرف اور

صرف اپنے ذاتی مفاد کے لیے' ذرا سی زمین' چند پُرکشش جابز' ذرا سی سہل زندگی کے لیے وہ زندگی جو پانی کے بلبلے سے زیادہ اہمیت نہیں رکھتی' ہمیں نہیں فرق پڑتا کوئی ہمیں کیا کہہ رہا ہے' ہماری خودداری اور قربانیوں کے باوجود ہمیں ذلیل کر رہا ہے۔ ہمیں اس بات سے بھی فرق نہیں پڑتا کہ اسلام دشمن عناصر' ان لوگوں کے ساتھ کیا کر رہے ہیں جن کے سینوں میں وہ قرآن پاک' وہ مقدس کتاب محفوظ ہے کہ جس کی حفاظت کا ذمہ خود اس عرش بریں کے مالک نے لیا ہے' ہمیں نہیں فرق پڑتا کہ ہمارے ملک کے ساتھ کیا ہو رہا ہے' وہ کیسی سازشیں' وہ کیسا دیمک ہے جو اندر ہی اندر اسے چاٹ رہا ہے' رات کے اندھیروں میں کتنے چہرے ہیں جو پیسوں کے عوض اللہ اور اس کے رسول محمد صلی اللہ علیہ وسلم کے دشمنوں کے سپرد کر دیئے جاتے ہیں ایک اسلام ہے جو ساری دنیا میں پھیلا ہے اور جس کے خلاف ساری شیطانی قوتیں مل کر بھی اپنے گندے اور گھٹیا مقاصد حاصل نہیں کر پا رہیں' ہمیں نہیں فرق پڑتا اس بات سے کہ یہاں حق کا کلمہ بلند کرنے والے' ہر حق پرست کو' ہمارے حکمران جب چاہیں جس وقت چاہیں سمندر پار کالے پانیوں کی نذر کر دیتے ہیں مگر...... ہمیں فرق پڑتا ہے' جب کوئی ہماری پارٹی پر انگلی اٹھائے اگر کوئی پیپلز پارٹی میں ہے تو کوئی مسلم لیگ کا بندہ اٹھ کر پیپلز پارٹی کو غلط کہے۔ اپنا مذہب' اپنی وطنیت' اپنی آزادی ہم سب پر شب خون گوارا کر سکتے ہیں مگر پارٹی پر نہیں...... کیوں......؟ کیونکہ ہم ظلم کا ساتھ دینے والے ظالم ہیں۔ ہماری آنکھوں کے سامنے اگر ہمارے جسم کا کوئی حصہ کٹ رہا ہے تو ہم اس پر احتجاج کرنے کے بجائے' جو حصہ سلامت ہے اس پر مطمئن رہیں گے' پھر کیوں نہ دنیا ہمیں کہے کہ ہم دہشت گرد ہیں' وہ مسلمان جو سیسہ پلائی دیوار کی مثال ہیں' وہ مسلمان جنہیں ایک جسم کی مانند قرار دیا گیا ہے' وہی ظلم پر آواز اٹھانے کی بجائے ذرا سے مفاد کے لیے ظلم کا ساتھ دیں تو کون کہتا ہے کہ وہ ظالم نہیں ہیں' دہشت گرد نہیں ہیں۔''

بھرپور جوش میں بولتے ہوئے سر ہمدانی کا لہجہ اک دم بھرا گیا تھا۔

''کیا انجام ہوگا اس مفاد پرستی کا' اس ظلم اور بے حسی کا؟ کس قیامت پر اپنے اعمال اٹھا کر رکھ دیئے ہیں ہم نے؟ قیامتیں تو یہاں ہر روز بپا ہوتی ہیں' روز ایک نیا ظلم' ایک نیا بم دھماکہ' ایک نیا ڈرون حملہ' قیامت ہی تو بپا کرتا ہے دلوں پر۔ پھر کیوں شعور نہیں آ رہا ہے ہمیں' کیسی نیند ہے یہ غفلت کی' جو ہمارے جسموں کو کچلنے مسلنے پر بھی ٹوٹنے نہیں دے رہی' ہمیں کیوں محمود احمدی نژاد نصیب نہیں ہو رہا' کیوں ہم اپنے دفاع کے لیے بھی بندوق اٹھاتے ہیں تو ساری دنیا میں ذلیل و رسوا کر کے رکھ دیئے جاتے ہیں' صرف اسی لیے کہ ہم نے اپنے نفس جس کے لیے' ہمیں حکم دیا گیا تھا کہ کسی طور جنت سے کم قیمت پر نہ بیچیں' مادی دنیا کی ذرا سی آسائشات کے لیے گروی رکھ چھوڑے ہیں' قصور کس کا ہے؟ تباہی کس کی ہے؟ اپنی دنیا و آخرت کی بربادی کا ذمہ دار کون ہے؟ نفس کا گھوڑا تو بے لگام ہے جس راہ پر ڈالو گے سرپٹ بھاگتا چلا جائے گا مگر راہ کا انتخاب کس نے کرنا ہے؟''

پریڈ کا ٹائم پورا ہو گیا تھا۔ سر ہمدانی بنا کلاس پر الوداعی نظر ڈالے اپنا رجسٹر اٹھا کر بوجھل قدموں سے کلاس چھوڑ گئے تھے۔ حور عین فاطمہ اس روز ایک پل کے لیے بھی ان کے لیکچر کے حصار سے باہر نہیں نکل سکی تھی۔

وہ سوچتی تھی بھلا حالات کے شکنجے میں پھنسے چند غریب ممالک کے مسلمان اپنے سے تین گنا بڑے مکار دشمن کا کیا بگاڑ سکتے ہیں مگر یہ اسے آج یاد آیا تھا کہ طارق بن زیاد نے جب اندلس کو فتح کیا تھا تو اس کی دسترس میں بھی چند مٹھی بھر مسلمان سپاہی ہی تھے۔ محمود غزنوی نے فتوحات کی جو ناقابل فراموش تاریخ رقم کی' ان کا سامنا بھی اپنے سے تین گنا بڑے دشمن کے ساتھ ہی ہوا تھا۔

بھلا جنگیں کبھی ہتھیاروں سے بھی لڑی جاتی ہیں؟

وہ مذہب جو امن و سلامتی اور سکون کا مذہب ہے۔ عالمگیر مذہب ہے' جس کے پیروکار دنیا کے کونے کونے میں

موجود ہیں' اس مذہب کو اگر بدنام کر رہے تھے تو وہ لوگ کون تھے؟ مسلمانوں کے روپ میں' چہروں پر داڑھیاں سجا کر' اسلامی نام اپنا کر' حقیقی اسلام کے متوالوں کی رسوائی کرنے والے وہ بناوٹی چہرے کس کے تھے؟

کس مذہب کے پیروکار تھے وہ؟ کیا تعلیمات تھیں اس مذہب کی' کیا مقاصد تھے؟ وہ سوچتی جاتی تھی اور کڑھتی جاتی تھی۔

پھر ایک روز اس نے سنا کہ پاکستانی حکومت نے سر جاوید ہمدانی کو لاپتا افراد کی لسٹ میں ڈال کر امریکہ کے حوالے کر دیا۔ اس روز وہ دیر تک اپنے اندر اٹھتے دھماکوں کا شور سنتی رہی تھی۔

کون تھے یہ ''لاپتا افراد؟''

کیسے اور کہاں کھپا دیئے جاتے تھے کہ سال گزرنے کے باوجود کبھی ان کا نام ونشان ہی نہیں ملتا تھا۔ کیا کہانی تھی ان لاپتا افراد کے پیچھے؟

بے بس مکینوں کے گھروں میں بجھتے چولہوں اور بااختیار محلوں میں لگتے دولت کے انباروں کے پیچھے تاریخ کی کیسی سسکیاں گھٹی ہوئی پڑی تھیں۔

وہ نہیں جانتی تھی کہ سر جاوید ہمدانی کی طرح ایک روز اسے بھی کالے پانیوں کا سفر طے کرنا پڑے گا۔ پانچ منٹ کی مختصر سی نیند کے بعد اچانک اس کی آنکھ کھل گئی تھی۔ قبرستان میں اس وقت اس سے کچھ ہی فاصلے پر ایک نشئی بیٹھا اسے گھور رہا تھا۔ تبھی وہ گھبرا کر اٹھی تھی اور سرپٹ بھاگتے ہوئے قبرستان سے نکل گئی' شام ڈھل رہی تھی وہ شکستہ قدموں کو گھسیٹتی ایک بار پھر اُس یزداں کی طرف چلی آئی تھی جہاں آج کل زندگی اپنا کٹھن ترین سفر مکمل کر رہی تھی۔

۞......۞......۞

یہ اُس سے دو ہفتے بعد کی بات تھی۔

سردی کی شدت میں ایک دم سے اضافہ ہو گیا تھا۔ اس نے فٹ پاتھ سے اٹھنے کی کوشش کی مگر ہمت جواب دے گئی' پاس ہی کسی مسجد کے اسپیکر سے اذان کی آواز بلند ہو رہی تھی۔ اس کی آنکھوں سے آنسو بہنا شروع ہو گئے۔

''حیّ علی الصلوٰۃ' حیّ علی الصلوٰۃ...... (آؤ نماز کی طرف)۔''

''حیّ علی الفلاح...... حیّ علی الفلاح...... (آؤ کامیابی کی طرف)۔''

''اللہ اکبر' اللہ اکبر...... (اللہ بہت بڑا ہے' اللہ بہت بڑا ہے)''

''لا الہ الا اللہ...... (نہیں کوئی عبادت کے لائق سوائے اللہ کے)''

اللہ کے گھر سے بلاوا آ گیا تھا' مگر آج وہ اس پاک و بے نیاز ذات کے سامنے حاضر ہونے کی پوزیشن میں نہیں تھی۔ زندگی نے بہت بے رحمی سے اس پر اپنی رعایت کے دروازے بند کر دیئے تھے۔ شدید سرد موسم میں بھوک اور نقاہت کے سبب اسے چکر آ رہے تھے۔ اس وقت اس کے لیے اپنی آنکھوں کو کھلے رکھنا بھی بے حد دشوار ہو رہا تھا۔

سونے کے محل میں مخملی بستر پر سونے والی وہ شہزادی' بھیانک حالات کی بھینٹ چڑھ گئی تھی۔

پچھلے ایک ہفتے سے وہ قبرستان بھی نہیں جا سکی تھی اور اسی بات کا اسے قلق تھا۔ رات جیسے جیسے آگے سرکتی جا رہی تھی اس کی پریشانی میں اضافہ ہوتا جا رہا تھا تبھی اس نے آنسوؤں سے بھری آنکھیں اٹھا کر اوپر آسمان کی طرف دیکھا اور پھر جیسے ہمت پکڑتی ہوئی اٹھ کھڑی ہوئی۔ وہ نہیں جانتی تھی کہ اسے کہاں جانا ہے' اس کی منزل کیا ہے مگر اسے یقین تھا اس کا رحمٰن اور رحیم ربّ اسے کبھی بے آسرا نہیں چھوڑے گا۔ وہ اس کے لیے رزق اور محفوظ پناہ گاہ کا انتظام ضرور کرے گا۔

چند قدم چلنے کے بعد کسی سوچ کے تحت وہ اس شان دار عمارت کے بڑے سے آہنی گیٹ کے سامنے رک گئی تھی'

اردگرد ایک سہمی نظر ڈالنے کے بعد اس نے کپکپاتے ہاتھوں سے دروازے پر زوردار دستک دے ڈالی تھی' چند لمحوں کی کوشش کے بعد گیٹ وا ہوگیا تھا۔

''جی فرمائیے۔'' گیٹ کے اس پار سترہ اٹھارہ سالہ لڑکا کھڑا اس کا منہ تک رہا تھا' وہ خاموش کھڑی رہی۔

''ارے آپ کچھ بول کیوں نہیں رہیں' میں سمجھ گیا آپ ضرور سلمٰی بھابی ہوں گی۔ یوکے سے آئی ہیں ناں؟''

بنا اس کے حال پر غور کیے' اپنے ہی مفروضے کے تحت اس نے گویا 'تکا'' لگایا تھا۔ حورعین اس کے قیاس پر چونک کر خالی خالی سی نگاہوں سے اسے دیکھنے لگی۔ جانے وہ کس غلط فہمی کا شکار تھا۔

''آپ کچھ بول کیوں نہیں رہیں' مانا کہ بھیا نے ہماری بڑی خطرناک مثالیں پیش کی ہوں گی مگر اب ہم ایسے بھی ہٹلر نہیں ہیں کہ اتنی دور سے آئی اپنی پیاری بھابی کو دروازے سے ہی باہر لوٹا دیں' آئیں پلیز۔''

حورعین فاطمہ کی سمجھ میں نہیں آرہا تھا کہ وہ اسے اپنی دستک کا کیا جواز پیش کرے اگر اس نے اسے ایسی ویسی لڑکی سمجھ کر چلتا کردیا تو وہ کہاں جائے گی مگر اس کی نوبت ہی نہیں آئی تھی۔

وہ جو کوئی بھی تھا اسے تو اس وقت رحمت کا فرشتہ ہی لگا تھا بھی دل ہی دل میں خدا کا شکر ادا کرتی وہ بنا وضاحت کیے اس کے پیچھے چل پڑی تھی۔

پُرشکوہ عمارت باہر سے جتنی شاندار دکھائی دے رہی تھی اندر سے اس کا حسن اور بھی دیدہ زیب تھا۔ رنگا رنگ پھولوں سے سجا لان' اندر طویل راہداری عبور کرکے' کشادہ حال میں اس وقت اس خوب صورت بنگلے کے مکین اکٹھے بیٹھے چائے پی رہے تھے' نظر کے سامنے ہی فل والیم میں ٹی وی چل رہا تھا۔

وہ دھڑ دھڑ کرتے دل کے ساتھ یونہی سر جھکائے کھڑی رہی' جب وہ لڑکا بولا۔

''بڑی اماں! دیکھیے تو کون آیا ہے؟'' اس کی اطلاع پر وہاں بیٹھے تمام افراد نے اسے چونک کر دیکھا تھا۔

''کون ہے یہ......؟'' آنکھوں پر بڑا سا چشمہ سیٹ کیے خاصی ضعیف عورت نے توجہ سے اس کی طرف دیکھا تھا۔ حورعین کو اپنی سانسیں خشک ہوتی ہوئی محسوس ہوئیں۔

''بوجھیں تو جانیں۔'' اسے ساتھ لانے والا لڑکا شرارت پر آمادہ ہو رہا تھا۔

حورعین فاطمہ کے لیے اپنی ٹانگوں پر مزید کھڑا رہنا دشوار ہوگیا۔ اسے اس وقت اپنے اعصاب چٹختے محسوس ہو رہے تھے۔

''پہیلیاں مت ڈالو عمیر! صاف صاف بتاؤ کسے پوچھے بنا گھر میں گھسا لائے ہو؟'' بڑی ماں کے لہجے میں سختی تھی۔

وہ جی جان سے کانپ گئی' جانے اب اس کی تقدیر کا کیا فیصلہ ہونے والا تھا۔

''توبہ کریں بڑی اماں! آپ مجھے ایسا سمجھتی ہیں یہ تو سلمٰی بھابی ہیں' عذیر بھیا کی ہونے والی بیوی' یوکے سے آئی ہیں' باقی معلومات آپ خود لے لیجیے۔'' وہ ایسا ہی تھا ازحد کھلنڈرا اور بے پروا' گھر میں سب کو اس سے شکایتیں رہتی تھیں۔ اب بھی بڑی ماں اسے خاصی مشکوک نگاہوں سے دیکھنے کے بعد حورعین کی طرف متوجہ ہوئی تھیں۔

''بیٹھو بیٹا۔'' اس کے حلیے کو قدرے مشکوک نگاہوں سے دیکھنے کے بعد انہوں نے خاصی حلاوت سے کہا تھا۔

حورعین دل ہی دل میں انجانے سے خوف کی شکار ہونے کے باوجود ان کی ہدایت پر چپ چاپ بیٹھ گئی۔

''کیسا ہے عذیر! اور تمہارا سامان کہاں ہے؟'' اس کے بیٹھتے ہی ان کے پہلے سوال نے حورعین فاطمہ کی گھبراہٹ میں اضافہ کردیا تھا۔ عزت اور جان کا خوف نہ ہوتا تو وہ کبھی جھوٹ بول کر ان کے اعتماد کو ٹھیس نہ پہنچاتی۔

''جی ٹھیک ہے' سامان ٹیکسی میں ہی رہ گیا' مجھے یاد ہی نہیں رہا؟''

''ارے تم اکیلی آئی ہو پاکستان؟''

ایک اور مشکل سوال؟

وہ اتنے سارے لوگوں کے سامنے خود میں سر اٹھا کر بات کرنے کا حوصلہ بھی نہیں کر پا رہی تھی۔

''جی......''

''دیکھا' بہت لاپروا لڑکا ہے یہ عذیر! ڈر رہا ہوگا کہ کہیں ہم اس کی پسند کو ریجیکٹ نہ کر دیں' سچ پوچھو تو میرا ارادہ بھی یہی تھا اسے چیزوں کی پہچان نہیں ہے' انسانوں کی کہاں سے ہوگی مگر تمہیں دیکھنے کے بعد تو یقین ہی نہیں آ رہا کہ وہ اتنی اچھی لڑکی بھی پسند کر سکتا ہے' زندگی میں پہلی بار کوئی ڈھنگ کا کام کیا ہے اس نے۔''

ان لوگوں کی کہانی کچھ کچھ اس کی سمجھ میں آ رہی تھی' مگر اس کے باوجود اس نے لبوں پر خاموشی کا قفل لگا رکھا تھا۔ کتنا چیپ لگ رہا تھا کسی کے احساسات کے ساتھ کھیلنا مگر تقدیر نے اسے کتنا بے بس کر دیا تھا' اس کی آنکھیں کچھ سوچ کر پھر آنسوؤں سے بھر آئیں۔

''میرا خیال ہے بچی تھک گئی ہے' جاؤ عمیر اسے عذیر کے کمرے میں چھوڑ آؤ۔''

دادی اماں اب نماز کے لیے اٹھ رہی تھیں یا شاید اس کے لیے کچھ کھانے پکانے وہ شکر کا کلمہ پڑھتی فوراً اٹھ کھڑی ہوئی۔

''بھابی! ہمارا انٹروڈیکشن تو لے لیں۔'' عمیر سے بڑا نمیر اچانک چلایا تھا' وہ ٹھٹک گئی۔ تبھی عمیر نے اس کا ہاتھ تھام لیا۔

''بھابی ابھی تھکی ہوئی ہیں' ان کے روم میں آ کے کراؤ انٹروڈیکشن جس نے کروانا ہے۔'' وہ اس کی سائیڈ لے رہا تھا حورعین فاطمہ نے گھبرا کر آہستہ سے اپنا ہاتھ اس کے ہاتھ سے نکال لیا۔

وہ ابھی عذیر نامی شخص کے شان دار کمرے میں بیٹھی تھی جب نمیر کھانے کی ٹرے ہاتھ میں لیے اس کے پیچھے ہی کمرے میں چلا آیا۔

''یہ لیں بھابی! پہلے ہمارے پاکستانی کھانے کو ٹیسٹ کریں پھر ہم آپ کو اپنا انٹروڈیکشن کرواتے ہیں۔'' عمیر کی طرح نمیر کے لہجے میں بھی شگفتگی تھی۔

حورعین کھانے کی ٹرے دیکھ کر اپنا خوف بھول گئی۔

وہ کھانا کھا رہی تھی' جب عمیر نے اسے بتایا۔

''عذیر بھائی نے آپ کو ہم سب کے نام تو بتائے ہوں گے' کام میں بتا دیتا ہوں' یہ جو نمیر ہے ناں بھابی! پورے دو سال بڑا ہے مجھ سے مگر ایک نمبر کا جھوٹا' فلرٹی اور بے ایمان شخص ہے۔ کاہل اور ہڈحرام تو رج کے ہے اکثر اس کے حصے کے کام بھی میں ہی کرتا ہوں اور جو سمیر بھائی ہیں انہیں تو ہر پندرہ منٹ کے بعد کسی بھی لڑکی سے عشق ہو جاتا ہے' گھر کے کام کاج میں سوائے کوکنگ اور صفائی کے دوسرے کسی کام کو ہاتھ نہیں لگاتے' ابھی آئیں گے ناں کلب سے تو ان کے نخرے دیکھیے گا آپ' بس دو ہی کام کے بندے ہیں اس گھر میں' ایک محترم عمیر صاحب یعنی کہ میں اور دوسرا چھٹکو' نام تو اس کا زبیر ہے مگر پیار سے سب چھٹکو کہتے ہیں۔ چار سال پہلے جب ممی کی ڈیتھ ہوئی تو وہ صرف تین سال کا تھا' شاید اسی لیے اس کے اندر ایک خلاء ہے جس نے اتنی چھوٹی سی عمر میں اس کے لبوں پر چپ کا قفل لگا دیا ہے' ابھی وہ ہوم ورک کر رہا ہے صبح آپ اس سے ضرور ملیے گا۔'' عمیر کی زبان کے آگے خندق نہیں تھی' نان اسٹاپ بولتا وہ اسے بے حد اچھا لگا تھا۔ کیا وہ ان لوگوں کو دھوکا دے کر خوش اور مطمئن رہ پائے گی؟

کیا ہوگا اگر عذیر نامی وہ شخص گھر واپس لوٹ آیا تو......؟

سوالات نہیں اژدھے تھے جو تصورات میں اسے نگلنے کو بے چین ہو رہے تھے۔ بھوک کے باوجود اس نے کھانے سے ہاتھ روک دیا۔ اگلے تیس منٹ عمیر اور نمیرا اسے آرام کرنے کی تلقین کرتے کمرے سے نکل گئے۔

اس نے اٹھ کر اٹیچ باتھ سے وضو کیا اور عشاء کی نماز کے لیے کھڑی ہوگئی۔ ابھی تک اس نے کمرے کو سرسری نظر سے دیکھا تھا' نماز سے فارغ ہو کر جس وقت اس نے دعا میں ہاتھ اٹھائے آپ ہی آپ آنسو اس کے گالوں پر بہہ نکلے۔

بے شک اس کے مہربان اور رحیم ربّ نے اس کے رزق اور محفوظ پناہ گاہ کا انتظام کر دیا تھا۔ جائے نماز سے اٹھ کر جس وقت وہ بیڈ کی طرف آئی اس کی آنکھیں پھٹی کی پھٹی رہ گئیں۔ وہاں سائیڈ ٹیبل پر اس شخص کی تصویر دھری تھی جسے اس کے روز قبرستان آنے پر اعتراض تھا۔

پتا نہیں یہ محض اتفاق تھا یا کوئی آزمائش مگر وہ پریشان ضرور ہوگئی تھی۔

اسے اس شخص کے گھر میں نہیں آنا چاہیے تھا۔ بے چینی سی بے چینی تھی۔ جانے وہ کب واپس لوٹ آئے' کیا سمجھے گا وہ اسے' چور یا پھر کسی گینگ میں ملوث عورت......

وہ کیسے اسے اپنی صفائی دے پائے گی' اگر اس نے بے عزت کر کے گھر سے نکال دیا تو وہ کہاں جائے گی؟ اس کے لیے تو اللہ ربّ العزت کی اتنی بڑے کائنات میں کہیں کوئی جائے پناہ ہی نہیں رہی تھی۔

کتنے چبھتے ہوئے سوال تھے اور دھیرے دھیرے سرکتی رات...... اس نے تھک کر سر بیڈ کی پٹی سے ٹکا دیا تھا۔

❀......❀......❀

دو پتر چناراں دے

ساڈا دکھ سن سن کے روندے پتھر پہاڑاں دے

چاندنی رات تھی۔

سردی کی شدت کے باعث اس وقت سارے گاؤں پر جیسے ''ہو'' کا عالم تھا۔ لوگ سرِ شام اپنے اپنے گھروں میں دبک کر سو جاتے تھے مگر اس کی قسمت میں نیند نہیں تھی۔

گاؤں کے بابا جوگی کی آواز رات کے گمبھیر سناٹے میں گونجتی' کسی لوری کی طرح ہی محسوس ہو رہی تھی' وہ مضمحل سا فصلوں کو پانی لگا تا رہا۔

بابا جوگی کی زندگی کی کہانی بھی عجب تھی۔ جوانی میں انہیں کسی لڑکی سے عشق ہوا تھا اور پھر وہ لڑکی کسی اور کے ساتھ بیاہ کر چلی گئی۔ اس کی شادی کے بعد بابا جوگی جو نمبرداروں کا بڑا ہونہار لائق فائق بیٹا تھا' جیسے ساری دنیا سے کنارہ کش ہوگیا۔ عشق کے روگ نے ایسا اس کے دل کو جکڑا کہ پھر بربادی ہی بربادی نصیب کا حصہ بنتی گئی مگر اس نے جوگ نہیں چھوڑا' اس کی آواز میں اب بھی اتنا کرب تھا کہ سننے والے کو اپنا دل کٹتا محسوس ہوتا تھا۔

گزرے وقت کے ساتھ ساتھ جہاں نمبرداری گئی وہیں جوانی کے ایام بھی رخصت ہوگئے۔ تھوڑی بہت زمین جو بچ رہی تھی اس پر بابا جوگی نے کاشت کاری شروع کر دی تھی' اب اس کا بیٹا جوان تھا مگر بیوی جوانی میں ہی داغِ مفارقت دے گئی تھی۔ پچھلے دنوں اس نے بیٹے کی شادی کر دی تھی گھر میں بہو آگئی' اس کے علاوہ اس کے مرحوم بھائی کے تین بیٹے بھی اپنی اپنی فیملیز کے ساتھ اسی کے گھر میں رہتے تھے۔ ایک ہفتہ قبل بابا جوگی اپنی فصلوں میں بیجائی کر رہا تھا جب اچانک ایک کتے نے پیچھے سے آ کر اسے کاٹ لیا۔ بابا نے اسے مار کر بھگا دیا تھا مگر تب تک کتا اپنا کام کر چکا تھا۔ وہ گھر

آیا تو گھر والوں نے دیسی گڑ اس کے زخم پر باندھ دیا۔ اس سے افاقہ نہ ہوا تو اگلے دن نمک اور سرخ مرچ کا نسخہ بنا کر زخم کو لپیٹ دیا جس سے زخم کی حالت بگڑنا شروع ہوگئی' پورا ہفتہ وہ لوگ اسپتال جانے کے بجائے گاؤں کے ستر فیصد کم فہم لوگوں کی مثال اتنے سیریس مسئلے پر اپنے دیسی نسخے آزماتے رہے۔

زائر شہر سے گاؤں واپس آیا اور اسے پتا چلا تو وہ فوراً بھاگ کر ان تک پہنچا اور زبردستی لڑ کر جوگی بابا کو اسپتال لے آیا مگر تاخیر ہو چکی تھی۔ زہر کا اثر جوگی بابا کے جسم میں پھیلنا شروع ہو گیا تھا۔ ڈاکٹر نے اچھی طرح معائنے کے بعد اسے کسی بڑے شہر کے اسپتال لے جانے کی ہدایت کی تھی مگر اس کے گھر والوں نے پھر بے پروائی کا مظاہرہ کیا۔

زائر ابھی تھوڑی دیر پہلے جب بابا جوگی سے ملنے گیا تو گھر والوں نے اسے زنجیروں میں جکڑ کر ایک علیحدہ کمرے میں قید کر رکھا تھا۔ کسی کو اس کے پاس جانے اور بات کرنے کی اجازت نہیں تھی' گھر والوں کے بقول بابا کو دورے پڑنے لگے تھے اور وہ ہر قریب آنے والے کو کاٹنے کی کوشش کرتے۔

زائر کا دل بابا جوگی کے حال پر کٹ کر رہ گیا تھا۔ ان کے گھر والوں کی بے پروائی اور جہالت نے اس ملنگ صفت انسان کو کس مشکل سے دوچار کر دیا تھا۔ وہ بہت دیر تک بابا کے پاس بیٹھا رہنے کے بعد جب اٹھنے لگا تو بابا نے اسے پکارا تھا۔

''اوئے پتر اوئے۔

''جی چاچا۔'' وہ فوراً پلٹا تھا۔ بابا کی آنکھیں سرخ ہو رہی تھیں اور ان کے گوشوں میں نمی چھلک رہی تھی۔

''اج چھڈ کے نہ جا پترا۔ تُو جائیں گا تے میرے گر والے مینوں زہر دا ٹیکا لگا کے ہمیش دی نیند سوا دیون گے۔'' (تم جاؤ گے تو میرے گھر والے مجھے زہر کا ٹیکہ لگا کر ہمیشہ کی نیند سُلا دیں گے)

بابا جوگی کی بات پر وہ شاکڈ ہی تو رہ گیا تھا پھر ان کی حالت کے پیش نظر اس نے سر جھٹک دیا۔

''نہ چاچا! ایسا نہ سوچ تیرے گھر والے تو تجھ سے پیار کرتے ہیں پھر اب تو تیرا علاج بھی چل رہا ہے دیکھنا تُو دنوں میں بھلا چنگا ہو جائے گا۔ تُو فکر نہ کر میں ادھر باہر ہی بیٹھا ہوں۔''

اس نے اپنی طرف سے پوری تسلی دی تھی اور اب گاؤں کی خاموش سرد رات میں پھر بابا کی درد بھری آواز گونج رہی تھی۔ وہ فصلوں کو پانی دینے کے بعد وہیں ڈیرے پر پڑی چارپائی پر دراز ہو گیا۔

اس کے دھیان کے پنچھی اس وقت ثانیہ عباس کے تصور کے گرد منڈلا رہے تھے جو پانچ سال کے بعد اس کی زندگی میں پھر سے لوٹ آئی تھی۔ اسے ہی سوچتے جانے کب اس کی آنکھ لگ گئی' اگلی صبح وہ اٹھا تو سب سے پہلی خبر اسے کل رات بابا جوگی کی ہونے والی وفات کی ملی تھی۔ کل رات واقعی ان کے گھر والوں نے انہیں زہر کا ٹیکا لگا کر ان سے ہمیشہ کے لیے اپنی جان چھڑا لی تھی۔

زائر جیسے ساکت رہ گیا تھا۔

وہ آواز جو درد بن کر گاؤں کی فضا میں گونجتی تھی' جہالت کی بھینٹ چڑھ کر ہمیشہ کے لیے خاموش ہوگئی' کتے کا کاٹا وہ شخص ابدی نیند سو گیا تھا' مگر اس کے لواحقین اب اسے کفن پہنانے' غسل دینے اور اس کی چارپائی کو ہاتھ تک لگانے کو تیار نہیں تھے۔ انہیں ڈر تھا کہ کہیں انہیں جراثیم نہ لگ جائیں۔

تب وہ اٹھا تھا اس نے خود بابا کو غسل دیا' کفن پہنایا اور پھر اپنے دوستوں کو بلا کر جیسے تیسے نماز جنازہ کروا کر اس بدنصیب شخص کو مٹی کے سپرد کر دیا۔

وہاں قبرستان میں مٹی کے اس ڈھیر کے نیچے ایک اور انسان کی زندگی کی کہانی اپنے انجام کو پہنچ گئی تھی۔

کہنے کو محبت ہے لیکن
اب ایسی محبت کیا کرنی
جو نیند چرالے آنکھوں سے
جو خواب دکھا کر پلکوں کو، تعبیر میں کانٹے دے جائے
جو غم کی کالی راتوں سے، ہر آس کا جگنو لے جائے
جو مشکل کر دے جینے کو اور مرنے کو آسان کرے
وہ دل جو پیار کا مندر ہو، اس دل کو ہی ویران کرے
اب ایسی محبت کیا کرنی؟
جو عمر کی نقدی لے جائے اور پھر بھی جھولی خالی ہو
وہ صورت دل کا روگ بنے جو صورت دیکھنے والی ہو
جو قیس بنا دے انساں کو، جو رانجھا اور فرہاد کرے
اب ایسی محبت کیا کرنی جو خوشیوں کو برباد کرے

رات جیسے جیسے سرکتی جا رہی تھی اس کی وحشت میں اضافہ ہوتا جا رہا تھا۔ نیند کی مہربان پری تھی کہ جیسے اس سے روٹھ ہی گئی تھی۔ زندگی کسی پر کیسے تنگ پڑ جاتی ہے بھلا اس سے بہتر کون جان سکتا تھا۔

وہ جانتی تھی کہ اس نے ایک قطعی اجنبی گھر کے دروازے پر دستک دے کر بہت بڑا رسک لیا تھا مگر فی الوقت اس کے پاس اس کے علاوہ دوسرا کوئی راستہ بھی نہیں تھا۔ بہت پہلے ایک بار وہ اس بنگلے میں آئی تھی اپنی کالج فیلو کے ہمراہ مگر یہ قیام پانچ دس منٹ سے زیادہ کا نہیں تھا، اپنی کالج فیلو کو وہاں چھوڑنے کے بعد وہ ڈرائیور کے ساتھ اپنے گھر واپس آ گئی تھی مگر اس بنگلے کی مالکن کے پیار اور اپنائیت نے اسے بہت متاثر کیا تھا۔ رات بھی وہ اسی پیار اور اپنائیت کو یاد کر کے اس گھر کی طرف بڑھ آئی تھی مگر اب وہ مکین وہ بے لوث پیار لٹانے والی مالکن نہیں رہی تھی۔

صبح ہو گئی تھی۔

وہ بے قرار سی بیڈ سے اٹھ کر کھڑکی کی طرف آئی تھی جب اس کی سماعتوں میں عمیر کی آواز پڑی۔

''جی عذیر بھیا! میں ابھی خود سے کال کرنے ہی والا تھا آپ کو......''

اور وہ جس کا دل پہلے ہی قرار نہیں پا رہا تھا ان الفاظ پر جیسے ٹھٹک ہی تو گئی تھی۔ دوسری طرف عذیر عمیر کے الفاظ پر مسکرایا تھا۔

''کیوں خیریت......؟''

''اب خیریت کہاں، ہماری عزیز از جان، پیاری بھابی سلمیٰ یہاں پہنچ چکی ہیں۔'' کتنی کھنک اور خوشی تھی عمیر کے لہجے میں مگر عذیر کے سوال نے اس کی خوشی پر جیسے اوس ڈال دی۔

''بھابی......کون سی بھابی...... سلمیٰ تو یہاں ہے میرے پاس، یہ تو ابھی پاکستان گئی ہی نہیں۔'' اور اس بار شاک لگنے کی باری عمیر کی تھی۔

''کیا مطلب؟ اگر سلمیٰ بھابی آپ کے پاس ہیں تو پھر وہ کون ہیں جنہیں میں سلمیٰ بھابی سمجھ کر آپ کے کمرے میں چھوڑ آیا ہوں؟''

''کوئی حال نہیں تمہارا' نجانے کب سدھرو گے تم؟ اب پتا نہیں کیسے گھسا لیا ہے گھر میں اور جانے میرے کمرے سے کیا کیا کچھ چرالیا ہوگا اس نے' عمیر کے بچے میں واپس آرہا ہوں' تجھے چھوڑوں گا نہیں۔''

اب وہ خفا ہورہا تھا۔ عمیر سوری کرنے کے بعد کال کاٹ کر سیدھا اس کے کمرے کی طرف چلا آیا' جہاں حورعین کھڑکی کے قریب کھڑی رسوائی کے خوف سے کسی خشک پتے کی طرح کانپ رہی تھی۔

❁......❁......❁

کب تک دل کی خیر منائیں' کب تک راہ دکھلاؤ گے
کب تک دو گے چین کی مہلت' کب تک یاد نہ آؤ گے
بیتا دید امید کا موسم' خاک اڑائی آنکھوں نے
کب بھیجو گے درد کا بادل' کب برکھا برساؤ گے
عہد وفا یا ترکِ محبت' جو چاہو سو آپ کرو
اپنے بس کی بات ہی کیا ہے ہم سے کیا منواؤ گے
کس نے وصل کا سورج دیکھا' کس پر ہجر کی رات ڈھلی
گیسوؤں والے کون تھے' کیا تھے ان کو کیا جتلاؤ گے؟
فیض دلوں کے بھاگ میں ہے' گھر بھرنا بھی لٹ جانا بھی
تم اس لطف وکرم پہ پیارے' کتنے دن اتراؤ گے؟

''کون ہیں آپ؟'' دروازہ رسان سے پش کرتے ہوئے عمیر کمرے میں داخل ہوا تھا' حورعین کی آنکھیں آنسوؤں سے بھرآئیں۔

''اسے کہتے ہیں شکل مومناں تے کرتوت کافراں' میں پوچھتا ہوں یہی گھر ملا تھا آپ کو ڈکیتی کرنے کے لیے۔''

''میں ڈکیت نہیں ہوں۔''

بے لچک لہجے میں عمیر کے گستاخانہ الزام پر وہ تڑپ اٹھی تھی۔

''میری طرف دیکھو' میرے ہاتھ خالی ہیں۔ کیا ڈکیت ایسے ہوتے ہیں؟''

''میں کچھ نہیں جانتا' آپ مجھے بتائیں آپ کون ہیں؟''

اس کے آنسوؤں سے نظر چراتا وہ اب رخ پھیرے کھڑا تھا۔ حورعین کی ہمت جواب دے گئی' اسے جو خدشہ لاحق تھا وہ ہوگیا تھا تبھی وہ سر جھکاتے ہوئے بولی تھی۔

''حور......حورعین فاطمہ۔''

''کون حورعین فاطمہ؟'' وہ پوچھ رہا تھا اور اب وہ اسے کیا بتاتی کہ حورعین فاطمہ کون تھی۔

''بہت لمبی کہانی ہے حورعین فاطمہ کی' کہاں سنو گے تم؟''

''مگر میں سننا چاہتا ہوں' یہ جاننا چاہتا ہوں کہ آپ کس مقصد کے تحت جھوٹ بول کر اس گھر میں گھسی ہیں؟'' وہ جذباتی ہورہا تھا۔ حورعین نے آنسو پونچھ لیے۔

''میں جھوٹ نہیں بولتی' میں نے کوئی جھوٹ نہیں بولا۔ تم خود غلط فہمی کا شکار ہوئے تھے اور میرا یہاں آنے کا کوئی مقصد نہیں' سوائے عزت کی چھت کے۔''

''تو پھر آپ کی اطلاع کے لیے عرض ہے کہ یہ گھر ہم نے ابھی بے آسرا لوگوں کے لیے وقف نہیں کیا' آپ کی

بھلائی اسی میں ہے کہ فوراً سے پیش تر آپ یہاں سے چلی جائیں۔''
بے لچک لہجے میں کہتے ہوئے اب وہ نیا حکم جاری کر رہا تھا۔ اس کے آنسو پھر روانی سے بہنے لگے۔
''میں آپ کے آنسوؤں سے متاثر ہونے والا نہیں ہوں، اگر آپ چاہتی ہیں کہ میں سارے گھر والوں کے سامنے آپ کی بے عزتی نہ کروں تو پلیز شرافت سے چلی جائیں۔'' حورعین کی خاموشی نے اسے مزید تپایا تھا' تبھی وہ بولی تھی۔
''چلی جاؤں گی' میں یہاں ہمیشہ رہنے کے ارادے سے نہیں آئی تھی۔ صرف ہانیہ صفدر کا حوالہ مجھے اس بنگلے کی طرف لے آیا تھا۔''
''ہانیہ صفدر...... ہانیہ صفدر کو کیسے جانتی ہیں آپ؟'' اب کے وہ چونکا تھا۔ حورعین نے اپنی نظریں اس کے چہرے پر جمادیں۔
''میری کالج فیلو تھی' چند سال قبل میں اسی کے ساتھ اس گھر میں آئی تھی۔''
''آئی سی' کیا مما سے ملی تھیں آپ؟''
''ہوں' ملی تھی۔ بہت پیار دیا تھا انہوں نے مجھے' اسی لیے تو بے آسرا ہو کر اس در کی طرف چلی آئی۔'' اس بار اس کے لہجے میں آنسوؤں کی آمیزش تھی' عمیر کے چہرے کا تناؤ کچھ کم ہوا۔
''کیا میں جان سکتا ہوں' آپ نے اپنا گھر کیوں چھوڑا؟''
''میں نے نہیں چھوڑا' حالات اور تقدیر کی طرح میرے گھر کی دیواریں بھی مجھ پر تنگ پڑ گئی تھیں۔''
''کیوں؟'' وہ سب جان لینے پر بضد تھا۔ حورعین کا دل درد سے کراہ اٹھا۔ کتنا مشکل تھا گزرے ہوئے دنوں کا سفر کرنا' بیتی ہوئی گھڑیوں کو یاد کرنا مگر...... اسے یہ سفر کرنا تھا۔
گالوں پر پھسلتے آنسوؤں کے ساتھ اسے بیتی ہوئی گھڑیوں کو یاد کرنا تھا۔

❁ ...... ❁ ...... ❁

ثانیہ عباس' حورعین فاطمہ اور ہانیہ صفدر تینوں کالج فیلو تھیں۔
حورعین چھوٹی سی تھی جب اس کی مما کی ڈیتھ ہوگئی۔ اس کے پاپا ایک نیک اور پرہیز گار آدمی تھے' شہر میں ان کے برابر کا دوسرا رئیس آدمی نہیں تھا۔ اس کی مما کی رحلت کے بعد اس کے پاپا نے کچھ اس طرح سے اس کی پرورش کی تھی کہ اسے کبھی زندگی میں ماں کے وجود سے محرومی کا احساس ہی نہیں ہوا' اسے بھولے سے بھی یاد نہیں آتا تھا کہ بچپن میں اس نے کبھی ہل کر پانی بھی پیا ہو' گھر میں نوکروں کی بڑی فوج موجود تھی' اس کی ایک پکار پر ملازم بھاگے آتے تھے۔ بچپن میں ہی اس کا اپنا علیحدہ شان دار کمرا تھا' وہ اسکول لائف میں آئی تو اس کے محبوب باپ نے اسے گاڑی بھی علیحدہ خرید کر دے دی۔
صدقہ' خیرات کرنے میں بھی وہ کسی قسم کے بخل سے کام نہیں لیتے تھے۔ کالج لائف میں ہانیہ صفدر اور ثانیہ عباس کا شمار اس کی بہترین دوستوں میں ہوتا تھا۔ ثانیہ اور ہانیہ کے پاپا اس کے پاپا کے قریبی دوستوں میں سے تھے' اس کے پاپا کی خواہش تھی کہ وہ صحافت کا پیشہ اپنائے' خود اسے بھی ساری دنیا کی معلومات رکھنے میں دل چسپی تھی لہٰذا اپنے پاپا کی خواہش پر کالج لائف سے ہی اس نے صحافت کو جوائن کر لیا تھا۔
کالج میں جب بھی وہ ہانیہ اور ثانیہ کے ساتھ فرصت میں بیٹھتی اس کا موضوع گفتگو ''پاکستان اور اس کی بقاء'' ہوتا تھا۔ ان تینوں نے بہت سے ایسے علاقوں کا وزٹ کیا تھا جہاں بسنے والے لوگ غربت کی نچلی ترین زندگی' انتہائی کسمپرسی کے

ساتھ بسر کرنے پر مجبور تھے۔

صرف اپنے اکاؤنٹس کاغذی نوٹوں سے بڑھانے والے لوگ اقتدار میں آ کر کیسے لوگوں کو ''اجتماعی خودکشی'' پر مجبور کر دیتے تھے' اس نے دیکھا تھا۔ غربت اور جہالت کی چکی میں پستے بہت سے دیہات کا وزٹ کرنے کے بعد اس نے ایک این جی او بنانے کا فیصلہ کیا تھا۔ جس کا مقصد ہر طرح کے ظلم کا شکار لوگوں کو ریلیف دلانا تھا۔

ہر روز کالج سے واپسی پر شام کی چائے اپنے پاپا کے ساتھ پینے کے دوران وہ ان سے اپنے ارادے اور خواب شیئر کرتی اور جواب میں اس کے پاپا اسے مکمل سپورٹ کی یقین دہانی کرواتے' انہیں خوشی تھی کہ ان کی بیٹی نے زندگی کے مختصر سفر کے لیے' بہت سے دوسرے بے راہ رو نوجوانوں کی طرح غلط راستے کا انتخاب کرنے کے بجائے ایک بامقصد اور قابلِ ستائش راہ کا انتخاب کیا تھا۔

انہی دنوں امریکہ میں ''ورلڈ ٹریڈ سینٹر'' کی تباہی کا شور اٹھا اور ساتھ ہی مسلمانوں کی تضحیک و بربادی کا بھی۔

کئی کئی سال اپنا وطن چھوڑ کر' اپنا تن من دھن امریکہ پر قربان کرنے والے پاکستانیوں کے ساتھ ''سپر پاور'' نے جو شرمناک سلوک کیا' اس کے بعد اسے اور اس کے پاپا کو قوی امید تھی کہ اب پاکستانی حکومت اور عوام' ایران کی طرح امریکہ کے نام پر تھوکنا بھی پسند نہیں کریں گے مگر...... اس کی حیرت کی انتہا نہ رہی جب وطن عزیز کے سالار نے ''صرف ایک ورلڈ ٹریڈ سینٹر'' کی خود ساختہ تباہی پر سپر پاور کا غصہ ٹھنڈا کرنے کے لیے خود کو اور ایک ایٹمی پاور کی حامل اسلامی مملکت کو بطور غلام اسی ملک کے سپرد کر دیا۔ جواب میں امریکہ بہادر نے جس درندگی سے عراق اور افغانستان میں لاکھوں بے گناہ مسلمانوں کو بربریت کے ساتھ موت کی نیند سلایا' اس پر خود انسانیت کا سر بھی شرم سے جھک گیا۔

عراق اور افغانستان کی شرمناک تباہی کے بعد وطن عزیز میں دشمن ملک کی دراندازی نے اسے اور اس جیسے دردمند دل رکھنے والے بہت سے دوسرے پاکستانیوں کی راتوں کی نیند اڑا دی تھی۔

طاقت کے نشے میں چُور ایک مست ہاتھی چیونٹیوں کی طرح اُمت مسلمہ کو کچل رہا تھا اور ساری دنیا چپ تھی یوں جیسے مسلمانوں کے جسموں سے بہنے والا خون' خون نہیں پانی ہو۔ انہی دنوں جب کہ ان کا سیکنڈ ائیر بھی مکمل نہ ہوا تھا کہ ثانیہ کے پاپا ایبروڈ شفٹ ہو گئے۔ ثانیہ نے اسے بتایا تھا کہ اس کے ممی پاپا کی لو میرج تھی جس کی وجہ سے وہ اپنے خاندان سے کٹ کر رہ گئے تھے۔ تنہائی اکیلے پن اور اپنوں کی بے رخی نے انہیں دیارِ غیر شفٹ ہونے پر مجبور کیا تھا مگر...... دیارِ غیر بھی انہیں راس نہیں آ سکا تھا اور کچھ ہی عرصہ میں ان کی ڈیتھ ہو گئی۔

اسے یاد تھا ان دنوں اس کے پاپا بہت ملول رہا کرتے تھے مگر وہ پھر بھی ان سے اپنے ناز اٹھوانا نہیں بھولی تھی۔ چھوٹی چھوٹی باتوں پر ناراض ہو کر منہ پھلا لینا اس کی عادت بن چکی تھی مگر اس کے پاپا بنا اکتائے اس کے ناز اٹھاتے' وہ غصے میں گاڑی لے کر نکل جاتی تو پیچھے ان کی جان پر بن جاتی۔ کالج سے فراغت کے بعد اس کے پاپا نے اسے مزید تعلیم کے لیے امریکہ بھجوا دیا۔

وہ امریکہ آنے کے حق میں نہیں تھی نا ہی اس کے پاپا یہ چاہتے تھے مگر یہ ثانیہ عباس تھی جس کے اصرار نے اسے امریکہ آنے اور وہاں امریکیوں کا مسلمانوں کے ساتھ غیر انسانی سلوک دیکھنے پر مجبور کیا' ان دنوں اسے گمان بھی نہیں تھا کہ اس کی زندگی کیا کروٹ لینے والی ہے۔

وہ امریکہ آئی' اس نے یہاں انسانی تفریق اور بے حسی دیکھی' کتے کے پلّے کو بھی پیار کرنے والے اور ان کا خیال رکھنے والے امریکیوں کا' مسلمان اور پاکستانیوں کے ساتھ بدتر رویہ اور سلوک دیکھ کر جہاں وہ شاکڈ اور دکھی ہوئی وہیں دوسرا دھچکا اسے پاکستان میں اپنے محبوب باپ کی دوسری شادی کی خبر سن کر لگا تھا۔ اس کے وہم و گمان میں بھی نہیں تھا

کہ اس پر جان لٹانے والے اس کے پاپا عمر کی اس سیڑھی پر ایسا کوئی قدم اٹھائیں گے' اپنی ماں کے کھونے کے بعد اپنے آئیڈیل باپ پر کسی اور کا قبضہ اسے گوارا ہی نہیں تھا۔ یہی وجہ تھی کہ وہ بیمار پڑ گئی تھی' ذہنی انتشار اور غصے کے سبب اس نے پاکستان اور اپنے گھر سے بھی مکمل لاتعلقی اختیار کرلی۔ اس نے یہ جاننے کی زحمت ہی گوارا نہیں کی کہ اگر اس کے باپ نے ایسا کیا تو کیوں کیا؟

جن دنوں اسے یہ اطلاع دی گئی اس کے امتحانات چل رہے تھے مگر اس خبر نے اسے ذہنی طور پر یوں اپ سیٹ کیا کہ وہ امتحان بھی نہ دے سکی۔

ثانیہ عباس اور اس کے فیانسی اشعر نے ان دنوں اس کی دوستی کا خوب حق نبھایا تھا' ہر روز وہ اسے کہیں نہ کہیں گھمانے لے جاتے تھے۔ انہی دنوں امریکہ میں اس کی پہلی ملاقات سر جاوید ہمدانی کے ساتھ ہوئی تھی' وہ دل کے مریض تھے اور ہمیشہ کہتے تھے۔

''اس دل میں اُمت مسلمہ پر ہونے والی زیادتیوں اور مظالم کا اتنا درد ہے کہ بے چارہ چھلنی ہو کر رہ گیا ہے۔''

وہ ایک وفد کے سلسلے میں وہاں آئے تھے اور تقریباً تین ہفتے امریکہ میں ان کا قیام رہا تھا' جتنے دن وہ امریکہ میں رہے حورعین روز ان سے ملنے جاتی رہی' بے حد رعب دار چہرے والے سر جاوید ہمدانی کی خوب صورت آنکھوں کے گوشے ہمہ وقت نم رہتے تھے۔ انہوں نے حورعین کو بتایا تھا کہ وہ پاکستان میں ہسٹری کے پروفیسر تھے اور ایک پاکستانی اخبار میں کالم لکھتے ہیں' ان کے دل میں مسلمانوں اور خصوصاً اپنے ہم وطن پاکستانیوں کے لیے بہت درد تھا' وہ حبیب خدا محمد صلی اللہ علیہ وسلم اور علامہ اقبال کو اپنا روحانی پیشوا تسلیم کرتے تھے۔ حورعین نے ان کے ہاتھ میں اکثر علامہ اقبال کی اردو اور فارسی کتابوں کا کوئی نہ کوئی نسخہ دیکھا تھا' انہی کی وجہ سے اس نے بھی اقبال کو پڑھنا شروع کیا تھا اور پھر جیسے وہ ان کی شیدائی ہو کر رہ گئی تھی۔

کیسی پیشن گوئیاں تھیں جو اس مردِ حُر نے سالوں پہلے اپنے الفاظ میں اقوام عالم کے سامنے کھول کر رکھ دی تھیں۔ فارسی اور اردو' ہندی کلام میں ان کی ہر غزل' ہر نظم' ہر شعر اپنے اندر گہرے سمندر چھپائے ہوئے تھا۔ وہ سوچتی تھی سالوں پہلے اقبال کو کیسے پتا چل گیا تھا کہ مسلمان اپنی کاہلی' بزدلی اور عاقبت نااندیشی کے سبب ذلت و رسوائی کا شکار ہونے والے ہیں؟ ساری دنیا میں دہشت پھیلانے والے انگریز مکڑی کے جالوں کی طرح مسلم ممالک کے سالاروں کو اپنے جال میں پھنسا کر ان ممالک کے بے قصور' معصوم ایشیائی مسلمانوں پر' اپنی طاقت کا قہر توڑنے والے ہیں؟ سالوں پہلے اقبال کو کیسے خبر ہو گئی تھی کہ اہل مغرب اقوام مشرق کے ساتھ مکاری اور سازشوں کا خونی کھیل کھیلنے والے ہیں۔

ان دنوں وہ ساری ساری رات جاگ کر اقبال کو پڑھتی تھی اور روتی رہتی تھی۔

بعد ازاں سر جاوید ہمدانی پاکستان چلے گئے کچھ ہی عرصہ کے بعد اسے پاکستان میں اپنے پاپا کے شدید علیل ہونے کی خبر ملی تھی تبھی وہ سارے گلے شکوے بھلا کر فوراً پاکستان چلی آئی اور یہاں آ کر جب اس نے اپنے محبوب باپ کی حالت دیکھی تو کلیجہ منہ کو آ گیا' یہ اس کے پہلے والے صحت مند' ہنستے مسکراتے پاپا تو تھے ہی نہیں محض چند ہفتوں کے اندر وہ جیسے ختم ہو کر رہ گئے تھے۔ وہ کتنی دیر ان سے لپٹ کر روتی رہی تھی۔

اس کی سوتیلی ماں کے لہجے میں گو اس کے لیے لگاوٹ اور مٹھاس تھی مگر...... بالا ہی بالا۔ وہ اپنے تمام کام سیدھے کر چکی تھیں' بڑی ہوشیاری سے انہوں نے اس کے پاپا کا جما جمایا کاروبار اپنے بھائیوں کے ہاتھ میں دے دیا تھا۔

اپنے باپ کی زندگی میں ہی وہ جیسے بے بس ہو کر رہ گئی تھی۔ ہر گزرتے دن کے ساتھ ان کی گرتی ہوئی صحت نے

اسے مزید پریشان کر دیا تھا تبھی اس پر اِس حقیقت کا ادراک ہوا کہ اس عورت نے اس کے پاپا کی سادگی اور رحم دلی سے ناجائز فائدہ اٹھا کر اس کے گھر میں ایک ملازمہ کی حیثیت سے کام کرتے ہوئے اس کے پاپا کو بلیک میل کیا اور بعد میں ان کی ساکھ خراب کرنے کی دھمکی دے کر محض ان کی دولت اور جائیداد ہتھیانے کے لیے ان پر نکاح کا دباؤ ڈالا۔

پاکستان میں ان دنوں لبرل حکومت کی طرف سے نئے پاس ہونے والے خواتین کے حقوق کے قانون کا پورا پورا فائدہ اٹھاتے ہوئے بالآخر وہ عورت اس کے باپ کے ساتھ نکاح کرنے میں کامیاب ہوگئی تھی اور اس کے پاپا جنہوں نے اس کی مما کی رحلت کے بعد عورت نام کا باب ہی اپنی زندگی میں ہمیشہ کے لیے بند کر دیا تھا صرف اپنی بیٹی کی نظروں سے نہ گرنے کے لیے اس کی دھمکیوں اور سازش کا شکار ہو کر کسی بے بس پرندے کی طرح محض پھڑ پھڑا کر رہ گئے۔ حورعین کو اپنی کوتاہی اور بدگمانی کا احساس ہوا تو وہ بہت روئی مگر تب تک بساط لپیٹی جا چکی تھی۔ اس کی سوتیلی ماں نے اپنے مقصد میں کامیابی کے لیے پچھلے تین ماہ سے انہیں خوراک میں سلو پوائزن دینا شروع کر رکھا تھا' جس کے نتیجے میں وہ اب اس حالت میں تھے کہ ڈاکٹرز نے بھی جواب دے دیا تھا۔

اپنی وفات سے چند روز قبل انہوں نے اپنے ذاتی وکیل کو بلوا کر اپنی تمام جائیداد اور کاروباری شیئرز کا وارث اپنی بیٹی حورعین فاطمہ کو بنا دیا تھا۔ وصیت کے کاغذات بھی وکیل کے پاس ہی رکھوائے تھے۔

حورعین پر جہاں اپنے محبوب باپ کی اچانک جدائی کا پہاڑ گرا وہیں اس کی جوان سوتیلی ماں بھی وکیل سے وصیت سن کر سناٹے میں آ گئی تھی۔ اس کا کھیل فلاپ ہوگیا' اب تک کی محنت اکارت گئی تھی' تبھی اشتعال میں اس نے حورعین پر گھر کے دروازے بند کر دیئے۔

بعد ازاں وکیل کی مداخلت اور کچھ ہانیہ صفدر کے پاپا کرنل صفدر مصطفیٰ کی کوششوں سے اسے گھر واپس مل گیا مگر سکون نہیں ملا۔

سارا سارا دن وہ اپنے کمرے میں بند اپنے پاپا کو یاد کر کے روتی رہتی یا پھر اداس تتلی کی مانند کبھی لان میں کبھی لاؤنج میں گھنٹوں سوچوں میں گم بیٹھی رہتی' اسی تنہائی اور اکیلے پن سے اکتا کر اس نے پھر سے تعلیم کا سلسلہ شروع کیا اور سر جاوید ہمدانی کی یونیورسٹی میں ایڈمیشن لے لیا۔

جاوید ہمدانی صاحب ہسٹری کے پروفیسر تھے اور اکثر لیکچر کے لیے ان کا موضوع گفتگو ''پاکستان واحد اسلامی ایٹمی پاور اور امریکہ کی اجارہ داری'' ہوا کرتا تھا۔ لیکچر کے دوران اکثر جذباتی ہوتے ہوئے وہ رو پڑتے تھے۔

اقبال کی طرح ان کے اندر بھی اپنی قوم کے لیے بڑا درد تھا۔ وقت کے فرعون کے لیے ان کے ایک ایک لفظ سے نفرت اور بغاوت کی بُو آتی تھی۔ اس روز لیکچر کے دوران انہوں نے اپنی کلاس سے پوچھا تھا۔

''اسٹوڈنٹس......! آپ میں سے کتنے لوگ انٹرنیٹ استعمال کرتے ہیں؟'' ان کا انداز ہمیشہ سے یونہی انوکھا اور چونکا دینے والا ہوتا تھا شاید تبھی ان کے طلبہ اور طالبات ان کے لیکچر کو مس کرنے کا تصور بھی نہیں کرتے تھے۔ اس وقت بھی ان کے سوال کے جواب میں کئی ہاتھ بلند ہوئے تھے۔

''کیوں؟'' بلند ہوئے ہاتھوں پر نگاہ ڈالتے ہوئے انہوں نے بڑے چبھتے ہوئے لہجے میں پوچھا۔

''معلومات کے لیے سر!'' کلاس کے ایک کونے سے پھنسی پھنسی سی آواز ابھری تھی۔

''گڈ! تو اب تک کیا معلومات حاصل ہوئی آپ کو؟'' ان کے چہرے پر تلخ مسکراہٹ بکھری تھی مگر ان کے سوال کا کوئی جواب نہ مل سکا۔

''میں جانتا ہوں وہ کون سی معلومات ہیں' جنہیں جاننے کے لیے آپ رات رات بھر اپنے کمروں میں جاگ کر

کمپیوٹر کے سامنے گھنٹوں اپنا وقت برباد کر کے حاصل کرنا چاہتے ہیں' یہی تو کارنامہ سرانجام دیا ہے ہمارے لبرل جرنیل نے کہ رہی سہی اسلامی معاشرے کی دیوار بھی گرادی۔ دشمن جانتا ہے کہ نوجوان کسی بھی ملک کا سرمایہ ہوتے ہیں اسی لیے تو اس نے آپ لوگوں کی رگ رگ میں انٹرنیٹ' کیبل' فیس بک اور موبائل فون کا نشہ اتار دیا ہے۔ سونے پر سہاگہ اس زہر تک رسائی اتنی آسان کردی کہ کوئی چاہتے ہوئے بھی خود کو تباہ ہونے سے بچا ہی نہیں سکتا۔ آزادی کے نام پر جس بے حیائی کو اس ملک میں فروغ دیا جارہا ہے میں اس کے نتیجے میں ہونے والی تباہی کو ابھی سے محسوس کررہا ہوں۔ بہت دل چسپ حقیقت ہے کہ گناہ میں لذت ہے اور نیکی میں راحت مگر ہمیں راحت نہیں چاہیے ہم لذت کے پیچھے بھاگ رہے ہیں اس لذت کے پیچھے کہ جس کی طلب نے ہمیں راہِ حق سے تو بھٹکایا ہی تھا' خونی رشتوں کی تمیز بھی چھین لی' اللہ ربّ العزت کی قائم کردہ حدود کہ جن کی خلاف ورزی کرتے ہوئے پہلے کبھی ایک لمحے کے لیے تو ہمارا ضمیر ہمیں ملامت کرتا تھا۔ اس معلومات کے چکر نے وہ احساس بھی ختم کردیا۔ اب ماں' بہن' بیٹی ہو ہمیں نہیں پتا چلتا کہ وہ نفس کا گھوڑا بے لگام ہونے پر ہمارے ہاتھوں محفوظ رہ سکیں گی کہ نہیں۔ یہی دشمن کی بڑی کامیابی ہے وہ وقت جو نماز اور قرآن کی تلاوت میں صرف ہونا چاہیے تھا۔ فیس بک اور موبائل پر لمبی لمبی کالوں کی نذر ہو کر برباد ہوتا محسوس ہی نہیں ہورہا ایسا نشہ چڑھتا جارہا ہے گمراہی کا ہم پر کہ ہمیں ملکوں کی تباہی کا کوئی احساس ہی نہیں۔ حکومت ہماری بربادی کے لیے کیسے کیسے لائحہ عمل ترتیب دے رہی ہے یہ جاننے کی بھی فرصت نہیں رہی۔''

حسب معمول وہ جذباتی ہوگئے تھے مگر ان کے طلبہ و طالبات کو دوبارہ ان کی شکل دیکھنا بھی نصیب نہیں ہوئی' اسی ہفتے وہ ایک سوچی سمجھی سازش کے تحت گرفتار ہو کر امریکہ کے حوالے کردیئے گئے تھے۔

ان کے طلبہ اور گھر والے ان کی اچانک گمشدگی پر پریشان تھے مگر چار ماہ تک انہیں ہوا ہی نہیں لگنے دی گئی کہ ان کے ساتھ کیا ہوا ہے؟

بہت دنوں کے بعد میڈیا کے تھرو انہیں اس بات کی خبر ملی تھی کہ جاوید صاحب کو ڈالرز کے عوض کالے پانیوں کی نذر کردیا گیا ہے۔ اس خبر کے منظر عام پر آنے کے بعد حورعین نے ایک مرتبہ پھر تعلیم کو خیر باد کہہ کر صحافت کی دنیا میں اپنے فرائض سرانجام دینے شروع کردیئے' وہ ہر صورت اپنے محبوب استاد کی رہائی چاہتی تھی مگر ایسا نہیں ہوسکا تھا۔

✿ ...... ✿ ...... ✿

ان دنوں وہ افغانستان کے شہر قندھار میں تھی جب اسے یہ خبر ملی کہ پاکستانی حکومت نے مساجد گرانے کے شرمناک اقدام کے بعد اسلام آباد میں موجود لال مسجد پر حملہ کردیا ہے۔ وہ لال مسجد کہ جس سے منسلک جامعہ اور جامعہ فریدیہ کا شمار ملک کے بہترین مدارس میں ہوتا تھا جہاں ہزاروں طلبہ و طالبات زیر تعلیم تھے۔ دس سال کے بچوں' یتیم بچیوں اور غریب طلبہ و طالبات کی بڑی تعداد جہاں زیور تعلیم سے آراستہ ہورہی تھی' اسی لال مسجد پر تاریخ کے بدترین جرنیل نے اپنی ہی افواج کو سرحدوں سے بلا کر دھاوا بول دیا تھا۔

صرف اپنے سامراجی خدا کی خوشنودی اور اطاعت کے لیے اس نے کچھ یوں بساط بچھائی کہ ملک کے عوام بھی ڈگمگا کر رہ گئے صحیح کیا ہے اور غلط کیا؟ کروڑوں پاکستانیوں کی طرح حورعین کے لیے بھی وہی سچ تھا جو مفاد پرست میڈیا دکھا رہا تھا مگر...... وہ عقل کی اندھی نہیں تھی اس کا لاشعور اسے باور کروا رہا تھا کہ سچ وہ نہیں ہے جو کیمرے کی آنکھ دکھا رہی ہے بلکہ سچ وہ ہے جسے مسجد کی دیواروں کے اندر مسمار کیا جارہا ہے' صرف اس جرم میں کہ انہوں نے فرعونیت کے خلاف آواز کیوں اٹھائی؟

اسلامی نظامِ حکومت قائم کرنے کا نعرہ کیوں لگایا؟ وہ مساجد و مدارس کہ جنھوں نے ہمیشہ اسلامی تہذیب و ثقافت کی

حفاظت کی۔انہیں مسمار کرنے پر شور کیوں مچایا؟ لوگ واہ واہ کر رہے تھے۔
اپنے ہی ملک کے معصوم بچوں اور بچیوں پر ٹوٹی قیامت کو سراہ رہے تھے۔ شیطانی قوتوں اور اسلام کے مابین بپا ہونے والی اس انوکھی جنگ کو محض عبدالرشید غازی اور مشرف کی جنگ سمجھ رہے تھے انہیں خبر ہی نہیں تھی کہ وہ کس بدبختی کا شکار ہو رہے ہیں۔

اس وقت سر جاوید ہمدانی کی بیٹی اس درس گاہ میں زیرِ تعلیم تھی، حورعین نے اسے وہاں سے نکل آنے کا مشورہ دیا تھا۔ میڈیا پر بار بار دکھائی جانے والی فوٹیج سے بدگمان (کہ جس میں بچوں اور بچیوں کی یرغمالی کا ڈھنڈورا پیٹا جا رہا تھا۔ وہ چاہتی تھی کہ اس کے محبوب استاد کی بیٹی اس جنگ سے نکل آئے مگر اس بچی کا پیغام سن کر وہ شاکڈ رہ گئی تھی، اس نے کہلوایا تھا۔

''انسان جب سارے گناہوں سے تھک کر بے آسرا ہو جاتا ہے تو اسے اللہ یاد آتا ہے، ساری دنیا سے ٹھوکریں کھا کر، وہ اللہ کے گھر کا رخ کرتا ہے تاکہ اسے سرخروئی اور پناہ مل جائے اور تم کہہ رہی ہو میں یہاں سے بھاگ آؤں؟ بھاگ کر آ جاؤں گی تو کہاں جاؤں گی؟ اللہ کے گھر سے بھاگ آنے والوں کو کہاں ٹھکانا ملتا ہے؟ یہاں آگ لگی ہے، اللہ اور اس کے رسول محمد صلی اللہ علیہ وسلم کے متوالوں اور جاں نثاروں پر انہی کے اسلامی ملک میں قہر ڈھایا جا رہا ہے اور تم کہتی ہو میں یہ میدان چھوڑ کر آ جاؤں، اس بدبودار مٹی سے بنے تن کو لے کر باہر آ بھی گئی تو کتنے دن سنبھال کر رکھوں گی، محشر کے روز جب آقا علیہ السلام اپنی امت کی شفاعت کے لیے اللہ ربّ العزت کا رحم طلب کریں گے تو میں کس منہ سے ان کی شفاعت طلب کروں گی؟ مجھے قیامت صدیوں پر محیط نہیں لگتی حورعین! یزید نے بھی طاقت کے نشے میں یونہی آلِ رسول پر ظلم ڈھایا تھا مگر کیا ہوا، آج تک اس کی نسل اس کے فعل پر پچھتا رہی ہے، یہ بھی پچھتائیں گے۔ ہمیں جنت کے بدلے جان کا سودا مہنگا نہیں ہے تم کہو اپنے میڈیا سے کہ وہ یہاں آ کر ان سرنگوں اور بنکرز کی تصویریں بنائیں جس کا ڈھنڈورا پیٹا جا رہا ہے، ہمیں دکھائیں کہ وہ ہتھیار کہاں ہیں جس کا الزام یہ ہم پر لگا رہے ہیں، میں جانتی ہوں، ہمیں کس جرم کی سزا دی جا رہی ہے اور میں یہ بھی جانتی ہوں کہ ہمارے مرنے کے بعد یہاں ہماری اموات کو جائز قرار دینے کے لیے اسلحہ رکھوا دیا جائے گا مگر تب کوئی اس کا پول کھولنے والا نہیں ہو گا، ہم نے اپنا معاملہ اپنے ربّ کے سپرد کر دیا۔ بے شک وہی انصاف کرنے والا ہے، یہ گولیوں سے چھلنی دیواریں یہ جا بجا بکھرے قرآن پاک کے صفحات، ہمارے جسموں کے اڑتے چیتھڑے یہ گواہی دیں گے کہ یہاں کیسا ''کربلا'' برپا کیا گیا ہے۔ میں تمہیں آخری خط لکھوں گی حورعین! مگر اس سے پہلے یہاں آؤ اور دیکھو یہ ننھی معصوم پریاں، جن کے ہاتھوں میں ڈنڈے دکھا دکھا کر تمہارے میڈیا نے ہمیں رسوا کیا ہے۔ آ کر دیکھو کیسی سہمی بیٹھی ہیں گولیوں کی تڑتڑاہٹ پر، ہوا پانی خوراک گیس سے محرومی بھی انہیں وقت کے یزید کے سامنے نہیں جھکا سکی جو سر صرف اللہ ربّ العزت کے سامنے جھکنا جانتے ہوں وہ پھر کبھی کسی نمرود، کسی فرعون، کسی یزید کے سامنے نہیں جھکتے۔ تم لوگ میڈیا پر صرف مولانا عبدالعزیز کے مسجد سے فرار کی فوٹیج پر گمراہ ہو سکتے ہو مگر وقت کے فرعون کے سامنے اپنی بقاء اور تشخص کے لیے دیوار بن کر کھڑے نہیں ہو سکتے۔ یہ جاننے کی کوشش نہیں کر سکتے کہ ہم نے خود مجبور کر کے عبدالعزیز صاحب کو باہر کیوں بھیجا؟''

سترہ اٹھارہ سالہ اس بچی کے الفاظ نے اسے ساکت کر دیا تھا۔ جنگ ختم ہو چکی تھی حق اور باطل کی جنگ میں بظاہر باطل نے طاقت کے بل پر حق کا گلا گھونٹ دیا تھا مگر درحقیقت لوحِ محفوظ میں بدبختی اور پچھتاوے کا ایک اور باب ہمیشہ کے لیے درج ہو چکا تھا۔

وہ کوئی اسکالر نہیں تھی کہ اللہ اور اس کے پیارے رسول محمد صلی اللہ علیہ وسلم کے دین کی سرخروئی کے لیے کلمہ حق بلند

کرتی اور بھٹکے ہوئے بدنصیب لوگوں کو راہ راست کی طرف لاتی نہ ہی وہ کوئی مشہور و معروف رائٹر تھی کہ اپنے قلم سے اپنے مسلمان ہونے کا حق ادا کرتی اور اپنی تحریروں کے ذریعے لوگوں کو حق اور سچ کی پہچان کرواتی پھر بھی اس کا دل کٹ رہا تھا۔

نظر کے سامنے اس وقت جامعہ حفصہ سے متعلق ڈاکومنٹری فلم چل رہی تھی' یہ سی ڈی اس کی خواہش پر اس کی ایک دوست نے اسے ارسال کی تھی' اسی کے ساتھ اسے ''عینی'' کا آخری خط بھی موصول ہوا تھا جو اس پری نے جامعہ حفصہ میں اپنی شہادت سے قبل اس کے نام تحریر کیا تھا۔ ڈاکومنٹری فلم میں ایک غیر مسلم جامعہ حفصہ اور جامعہ فریدیہ کو اندر سے دکھا رہا تھا۔ بے حد نفاست کے ساتھ وہاں بہترین تعلیم اور طلبہ و طالبات کی ضروریات کی ہر شے موجود تھی' چھوٹی سی کینٹین جہاں نمکو' بسکٹ' جوس اور اسی طرح کی دوسری استعمال کی چیزیں دستیاب تھیں۔ طالبات کے لیے ایک بے حد نفیس چھوٹے سے کمرے میں رنگ برنگی چوڑیاں' ٹاپس' جیولری' پونیاں اور ایسی ہی دیگر اشیاء بھی موجود تھیں۔ عبدالرشید غازی اس غیر مسلم وزیٹر کو پوری عمارت دکھا رہے تھے وہاں کوئی سرنگ' کوئی خفیہ تہہ خانہ یا اسلحہ وغیرہ نہیں تھا جس کا ان پر الزام لگایا جا رہا تھا۔ ایک بڑے سے ہال نما کمرے میں درجنوں طالبات قرآن پاک کھولے اس مقدس کتاب کی تلاوت کر رہی تھیں بالکل چھوٹی چھوٹی معصوم بچیاں......

ایک طرف شفاف حوض میں جامعہ فریدیہ کے معصوم صورت طلبہ نماز عصر کے لیے مل کر وضو کر رہے تھے۔ حورعین کا دل کٹ کر رہ گیا' ایک غیر مسلم اس پاکیزہ درس گاہ کو کلیئر کر رہا تھا اور اس عمارت کے اندر رہنے والے معصوم لوگوں کی سچائی کو دنیا کے سامنے لا رہا تھا جب کہ ایمان والے خود کو مسلمان کہلانے والے' اللہ اور اس کے پیارے رسول محمد صلی اللہ علیہ وسلم کو ماننے والے محض چند ٹکوں کی خاطر ایک ظالم جرنیل کے حکم پر اپنا ایمان اور آخرت داؤ پر لگا کر کھڑے ہو گئے تھے۔ بنا سچائی جانے اپنے ہی ملک کے معصوم باشندوں کا خون بہانے کو تل گئے تھے۔ قیامت بھلا اس سے بڑھ کر کیا ہونی تھی؟ نظر کے سامنے جامعہ حفصہ کی ایک بچی پکار پکار کر کہہ رہی تھی۔

''اے اللہ! ہماری لاشیں تو گریں گی مگر مساجد قائم رہیں گی' ہمارے خون کی ندیاں تو بہیں گی مگر اسلام کی عظمت پر آنچ نہیں آنے دیں گے۔ اے اللہ! تُو جانتا ہے ہمیں دھمکیاں دی جا رہی ہیں' رات دن ڈرایا جاتا ہے ہم یہ کر دیں گے ہم وہ کر دیں گے۔ اے مالک! ہم کچھ نہیں جانتے' ہمیں صرف اتنا پتا ہے کہ ہم اپنی جانوں کے مالک تھے' جان لے کر تیرے رستے میں نکل آئے ہیں۔ اے اللہ! تیرے لیے اگر ہمیں اپنی جان بھی دینی پڑی تو ہم پیچھے نہیں ہٹیں گے' جانیں دے دیں گے۔ یا اللہ! تیرے دین کی سرخروہی چاہیے' حاکم الحکمین تیرے دین کی سرخروئی چاہیے تُو ہماری جانوں کو قبول کر لے' ہمارے بھائیوں کو جزائے خیر عطا کر' مساجد کی عظمت کی خاطر' قرآن کے تقدس کی خاطر' اسلامی نظام کی خاطر جان دینے کے فیصلے ہو چکے ہیں' وصیتیں لکھی جا چکی ہیں' کشتیاں جلائی جا چکی ہیں' واپسی کے تمام راستے مسدود ہو چکے ہیں' اب شریعت ہو گی یا شہادت ہو گی۔ اے اللہ! کبھی ہمیں کہا جاتا ہے کہ یہ بنیاد پرست ہیں' کبھی کہا جا رہا ہے کہ جاہل ہیں' کبھی کہا جاتا ہے دہشت گرد ہیں۔ اے اللہ! ہم نے یہ سارے القابات تیری محبت میں قبول کر لیے۔''

حورعین کی آنکھیں بے دریغ آنسو لٹا رہی تھیں اور اس کا دل جیسے کٹتا جا رہا تھا۔ وہ اگر مان بھی لیتی کہ وہ لوگ غلط تھے تو یہ کیسا طریقہ تھا غلطی کو سدھارنے کا' جو سلوک کوئی غیر مسلم بھی نہ کرتا' وہ سلوک اللہ اور اس کے رسول صلی اللہ علیہ وسلم پر ایمان رکھنے والے ایک بظاہر مسلم حکمران نے کر دیا تھا۔ صرف ایک ورلڈ ٹریڈ سینٹر کی تباہی کا بدلا لینے کے لیے سپر پاور ملک نے تین اسلامی ممالک ادھیڑ کر وہاں کروڑوں لوگوں کو کچل کر مسل کر رکھ دیا تھا جب کہ اس تباہی میں کسی بھی طور سے مسلمان ملوث نہیں تھے پھر بھی ان کی زندگیوں کو تہس نہس کر دیا گیا تھا۔ لاشوں کے ڈھیر لگا دیئے گئے تھے' نفرت

کے سمندر میں ہر پاکستانی کو ڈبو ڈبو کر تباہ و برباد کر دیا گیا تھا اور یہاں جامعہ حفصہ کی تباہی پر سب یوں خاموش تماشائی بنے تھے جیسے یہ ان کا معاملہ ہی نہ ہو' جیسے مرنے والے وہ شہداء ان کے کچھ لگتے ہی نہ ہوں' جیسے قیامت کے روز انہیں نبی کریم صلی اللہ علیہ وسلم کا سامنا ہی نہ کرنا ہو' ان کی شفاعت ہی نہ درکار ہو۔

وہ چلّانا چاہتی تھی' چلّا چلّا کر ہر فرد سے پوچھنا چاہتی تھی' مجھے بتاؤ جامعہ حفصہ میں قرآن پاک کی تعلیم حاصل کرنے والی کتنی دہشت گرد طالبات نے ملکوں کے ملک تباہ کیے' دہشت گردی کی تعلیم پانے والے لال مسجد کے کتنے طلباء نے دنیا کے امن کو نقصان پہنچایا؟ اگر وہ لوگ کسی اور جمہوری ملک کے شہری ہوتے تو کیا یوں ان کی جانوں کے سودے کیے جاتے؟

ان پر یوں دہشت گردی کا لیبل لگا کر' اصل حقائق چھپا کر' انہیں اپنے ہی ملک میں اپنوں کی آنکھوں کے سامنے محض طاقت کے بل بوتے پر' رسوا کر کے شہید کیا جاتا؟

وہ ہاتھ جنھوں نے ان پر گولیاں برسائیں' کیا روزِ محشر انہیں نبی کریم صلی اللہ علیہ وسلم کی شفاعت کی ضرورت نہیں رہی تھی' کیا اس روز کوئی سپر پاور کوئی جرنیل انہیں اللہ کے قہر سے بچا سکتا تھا؟

اس وقت بے ساختہ اس کے دماغ میں یہ شعر گونجا تھا۔

گنہ گاروں کو جب جنت کے دروازے پہ روکیں گے
آواز آئے گی جانے دو' یہ امت ہے محمدؐ کی

کیوں؟ اسلام کے متوالوں کے سینے ہی گولیوں سے چھلنی کیوں؟

ڈاکومنٹری فلم سائیڈ پر رکھنے کے بعد اس نے سر جاوید ہمدانی کی بیٹی قرۃ العین کا آخری خط اٹھایا تھا' جو اس ننھی پری نے جانے کس حال میں لکھا تھا۔

''عزیزی حورعین! شروع اللہ رب العزت کے پاک اور بابرکت نام سے جو بڑا مہربان اور نہایت رحم کرنے والا ہے۔ جس وقت تمہاری نگاہیں یہ خط پڑھ رہی ہوں گی میں اس دنیا میں نہیں ہوں گی کیونکہ وقت کے ناخدا نے اپنے ضمیر کی قیمت ہمارا خون طے کر لی ہے۔ ہم سنا کرتے تھے کہ کشمیر میں بہنیں خون کی مہندی لگاتی ہیں' اپنی خواہشات کو روند دیتی ہیں' تمناؤں کو مار دیتی ہیں مگر ہم نے اس کا عملی مظاہرہ لال مسجد میں دیکھا' لگتا ہی نہیں کہ ہم اس قوم کی بیٹیاں ہیں۔ حورعین! شاید تم آندرے بہرنگ کو جانتی ہو' جو کہ ایک کٹر عیسائی ہے' پیشہ ور قاتل ہے۔ جس نے خود درجنوں مسلمان طلبہ و طالبات کے قتل کا اعتراف کیا' ساری دنیا کے سامنے تسلیم کیا کہ وہ دنیا بھر سے بالعموم اور یورپ سے بالخصوص مسلمانوں کا خاتمہ چاہتا ہے اس کو کسی بھی مرحلے پر ایسی کارروائی کا موقع ملا تو وہ ہرگز ضائع نہیں کرے گا مگر اس کے باوجود اسے قانونی پاگل قرار دے کر سزا سے مستثنیٰ کر دیا گیا' کیوں؟

ساری دنیا کی بھوک اور دولت کی ہوس ہمارے ہی حکمرانوں کو کیوں؟

ساری دنیا میں امن اور انسانیت کا ڈھنڈورا پیٹنے والے یہودیوں نے اب تک عراق' افغانستان اور پاکستان میں لاکھوں مسلمانوں کو موت کی نیند سلا دیا مگر ان کے خلاف تو کسی نے کوئی جنگ کوئی آپریشن نہیں کیا' کیوں؟

جس جنگ سے ہمارا کوئی واسطہ ہی نہیں اسی جنگ کو ہم پر مسلط کر کے یہاں روز سیکڑوں پاکستانیوں کی زندگی کے چراغ بجھائے جاتے ہیں مگر ان کا حساب لینے والا کوئی نہیں۔ تم بتاؤ حورعین! ایسے حالات میں اللہ کے بندوں کے پاس سوائے جہاد کرنے کے اور کون سا راستہ باقی بچا رہتا ہے۔

کوئی مجھے بتائے کہ کیوں ہماری درس گاہوں کو ہمارا مقتل بنا دیا گیا' صرف اس لیے کہ ہم نے اللہ اور اس کے رسول

محمد صلی اللہ علیہ وسلم کی تعلیمات پر عمل پیرا ہونے کی بات کی تھی؟

یہ ہمیں کیوں کہہ رہے ہیں کہ باہر نکل آؤ ورنہ مار دیئے جاؤ گے؟ ہمیں یہاں سے نہیں جانا کہیں بھی نہیں، چاہے خاک میں ہی کیوں نہ مل جانا پڑے۔ ہمیں مرنے کا افسوس نہیں ہے حورعین! صرف اس بات کا دکھ ہے کہ طاقت کے نشے میں چُور ایک بدمست ہاتھی نے ساری قوم کو گمراہ کر کے، ہم حفاظ قرآن پر بم برسائے اور ساری قوم دم سادھے چپ چاپ تماشا دیکھتی رہی، نہ صرف تماشا دیکھتی رہی بلکہ اس بدمست ہاتھی کو شاباش بھی دیتی رہی، آخری دم تک ہمیں یہ گمان رہا کہ یہ ہمارے مسلمان بھائی ہیں اور کوئی مسلمان کسی دوسرے مسلمان کو قتل نہیں کر سکتا مگر ہمیں کیا پتا تھا کہ ملک پاکستان میں اسلام کے نفاذ کا نعرہ لگانا اب ایک جرم بن چکا ہے۔

مجھے بتایا گیا ہے کہ دنیا میں 196 ممالک میں سے 58 مسلم ممالک ہیں۔ چھ ارب کے قریب انسانوں میں سے ڈیڑھ ارب مسلمان ہیں، دنیا کے معدنی ذخائر میں سے 75 فی صد کے مالک مسلمان ہیں۔ دنیا کی بہترین بندرگاہیں، گزرگاہیں، آبی اور زمینی ذخائر، فضائی راستے مسلمانوں کے پاس ہیں۔ سب سے اچھا محل وقوع مسلم ممالک کا ہے۔ تیل کے لباب بھرے کنوئیں اور سونے کی کانیں ان کی ہیں، یہ زرخیز زمینوں، دریاؤں اور نہروں کے مالک ہیں، محنتی کسان ہیں، پسینہ بہانے والے مزدور ہیں، جان کی بازی لگانے والے فوجی ہیں، مذہب اور وطن کی خاطر کٹ کر مرنے والے جاں باز ہیں، اعلیٰ دماغ ہیں، باصلاحیت ہیں۔ ان کا مذہب مکمل ضابطۂ حیات ہے، سب کچھ ہے ان کے پاس۔ ہاں نہیں ہے تو دور اندیش، نڈر اور بہادر قیادت نہیں ہے، کوئی ایسا کپتان نہیں جو عالم اسلام کی ڈولتی ناؤ کو کنارے لگا دے۔ یہ سامراج اور یہودی پالیسی اگر یونہی اس ملک پر قابض رہی تو یہاں عبرت کے نشانوں کے سوا اور کچھ نہیں رہے گا، یہ لوگ کبھی کسی باصلاحیت شخص کو ہمارا رہنما نہیں بننے دیں گے، یہ عالمی طاقتیں ہم پر ایسے ہی ایمان اور ضمیر فروش لوگوں کو قابض رکھیں گی۔ یونہی نایاب ہیروز کو خرید کر اور باغی شہزادوں پر دہشت گردی کا الزام لگا کر انہیں عقوبت خانوں میں ڈالتی رہیں گی۔ میں پوچھتی ہوں حورعین! کیا ہمارے لاشے اجتماعی قبروں میں ڈالنے، برساتی نالوں میں پھینکنے اور مسجد کی دیواروں پر چیتھڑوں کی صورت چپکا دینے سے ہمارا خون چھپ جائے گا؟ نہیں...... قوم کو اس بے حسی کا قرض چکانا پڑے گا، دیکھ لینا۔ فی امان اللہ!''

خط کیا تھا ایک مرثیہ تھا۔ حورعین کو لگا اس کا دماغ سُن اور آنکھیں پتھر ہو گئی ہوں، اس روز وہ ثانیہ عباس کے ساتھ بیٹھی چائے پی رہی تھی جب ثانیہ نے اس سے پوچھا۔

''میں نے سنا ہے تم پرویز مشرف پر کوئی فیچر لکھ رہی ہو؟''

''ہوں۔''

''کیوں؟ میرا مطلب ہے ایک فیچر لکھ کر تم کیا کر لوگی، لوگ چند لمحوں کے لیے پڑھیں گے اور ایک سائیڈ پر ڈال دیں گے، بس۔''

''تو تم کیا چاہتی ہو، میں کیا کروں؟''

''میں کیا چاہتی ہوں؟ میں چاہتی ہوں تم کچھ ایسا کرو جو اس ملک کی تقدیر بدلے، تیسرے درجے کے یہ لوگ بدنام زمانہ جیلوں میں چیخ چیخ کر بے بسی کی موت مرنے کی بجائے اپنے حق کے لیے سر اٹھانا سیکھیں۔''

''نہیں اٹھا سکتے کیونکہ یہاں جو سر اٹھتا ہے وہ یا تو کاٹ دیا جاتا ہے یا رات کی تاریکی میں ڈالروں کے عوض غیروں کے سپرد کر دیا جاتا ہے۔ اس ملک کے دو بڑے مسائل ہیں ثانیہ! ایک جہالت اور ایک بھوک، باقی جتنے بھی مسائل ہیں وہ سب انہی دو مسائل کی کوکھ سے پھوٹ کر پل بڑھ رہے ہیں، تمہیں پتا ہے بش کا کیا کہنا ہے، وہ کہتا ہے کہ پرویز مشرف

نے اس کی ایماء پر اپنا نصاب تبدیل کیا ہے' پاکستانیوں کے دلوں میں امریکہ کے لیے بڑھتی ہوئی نفرت کا ایک حل ان کے خیال میں نصاب کی من پسند تبدیلی ہے لہٰذا انہوں نے میٹرک تک کے نصاب میں مشرف کو کہہ کر اپنی مرضی کی تبدیلیاں کروالی ہیں۔''

''ویری گڈ! اس شخص پر قوم کے بہت سے قرض ہیں حور! اس شخص نے اسلام دشمن قوتوں کو دوست بنایا' پاکستان کی 62 سالہ پالیسی پر یوٹرن لیا جس کی وجہ سے کشمیری مجاہدین دہشت گرد قرار پائے۔ اس نے صرف ایک کال پر افغان پالیسی بدل ڈالی جس کی وجہ سے لاکھوں افغان بھائیوں کو امریکہ سپر پاور نے گاجر مولی کی طرح کاٹ کر رکھ دیا۔ یہ وہ شخص ہے حور! جس نے سرعام اللہ اور اس کے پیارے رسول محمد صلی اللہ علیہ وسلم کے احکامات کی پامالی شروع کی اور اللہ کے گھروں پر فوج کو چڑھا دیا۔ اسی نے محبِ وطن علماء اور طلبہ کا خون بہایا اور دینی مدارس کو ہراساں کیا' جن کے بارے میں خود علامہ اقبالؒ کا فرمان ہے۔

''ان مکتبوں کو اسی حال میں رہنے دو' غریب مسلمانوں کے بچوں کو انہی مدارس میں پڑھنے دو' اگر یہ ملا اور درویش نہ رہے تو جانتے ہو کیا ہوگا؟ جو کچھ ہوگا میں اسے اپنی آنکھوں سے دیکھ آیا ہوں' اگر برصغیر کے مسلمان ان مدرسوں کے اثر سے محروم ہوگئے تو بالکل اسی طرح ہوگا جس طرح اندلس میں مسلمانوں کی آٹھ سو برس کی حکومت کے باوجود آج ''غرناطہ اور قرطبہ کے کھنڈرات'' اور الحمرا کے نشانات کے سوا وہاں اسلام کے پیروکار اور اسلامی تہذیب کا کوئی نقش نہیں ملتا۔ ہندوستان میں بھی آگرہ کے تاج محل اور دہلی کے لال قلعہ کے سوا مسلمانوں کی آٹھ سو سالہ حکومت اور ان کی اسلامی تہذیب کا کوئی نشان نہیں ملے گا اور ہماری بدبختی دیکھو ہم خود ایسے لوگوں کو منتخب کر کے ایوانوں تک لاتے ہیں تاکہ یہ ڈالروں کے عوض ہماری جانوں کا سودا کریں ہم پر ڈرون حملے کروائیں' بدنام زمانہ جیلوں میں ہم پر ذہنی اور جسمانی ٹارچر کروائیں یا اندھے بہرے کنوؤں میں پھنکوا کر بھول جائیں۔''

''صحیح کہتی ہو یار! اس شخص کے صرف ایک فرمان سے سیکڑوں بے گناہ اور عام پاکستانی شہری امریکہ کے حوالے کردیئے گئے' اس کے حکم پر جہادی تنظیموں پر پابندیاں لگ گئیں' راتوں رات درجن بھر فلاحی ورفاہی اداروں کے دفاتر سیل کروا دیئے' صرف اس شخص کی وجہ سے اسلام پسند لوگ دہشت گرد قرار پائے' اسی نے کراچی کو انسانی خون میں ڈبو دیا' عورت کو بے جان آزادی دی' قوم کی بیٹیوں کو میراتھن کے نام پر نیم برہنہ سڑکوں پر دوڑایا' ملک بھر میں شراب نوشی' رقص وسرود' کلب اور بار سجائے' فحاشی اور عریانی کو فروغ دینے کے لیے بل منظور کروائے' آئین پاکستان کا حلیہ اسی نے بگاڑا۔ تمہیں پتا ہے اس شخص نے شاہراہ دستور پر کھڑے ہو کر فضا میں مکا لہرا کر کہا تھا۔

''دیکھ لی طاقت' اسے کہتے ہیں طاقت۔''

صرف اسی شخص کی وجہ سے اس کی لاجسٹک سپورٹ کی وجہ سے امریکی ایجنسیاں ٹڈیوں کی طرح پاکستان پر چھا گئیں' صرف اس شخص کی وجہ سے امریکہ جس مسلمان کی طرف اشارہ کرتا اسے زنجیروں میں جکڑ کر ایف بی آئی (امریکی ایجنسی) کے حوالے کر دیا جاتا اور اس کی نقد قیمت وصول کی جاتی۔ سیکڑوں انمول ہستیوں کا لین دین ٹکوں میں کیا اس شخص نے۔''

''ہوں' اس کا اعتراف تو اس نے خود بھی کیا ہے' نائن الیون کے بعد جس طرح سے اس شخص نے سب کچھ امریکہ کے حوالے کیا' اس کے بعد ملک کے بڑے شہروں سے ہزاروں مذہبی رہنما' علماء' عالم دین' دینی مدارس اور اسلامی فلاحی تنظیموں کو فنڈنگ فراہم کرنے والے گرفتار کر کے محض شک اور شبہ کی بناء پر رات کی تاریکی میں گھروں سے اٹھا کر لاپتا کردیئے گئے' امریکہ کے ہاتھ گروی رکھے گئے پاکستان میں اس شخص نے محب دین اور محب وطن پاکستانیوں کی جیسے

منڈی لگادی تھی، پورے چھ سو مجاہدین کی امریکہ حوالگی پر اسے کروڑوں ڈالر دیئے گئے جس کا اعتراف اس شخص نے اپنی کتاب ''In the Line of Fire'' کے 23 ویں باب Manhunt میں خود کیا ہے۔''

''اچھا میں نے یہ کتاب نہیں پڑھی، کیا لکھا ہے اس باب میں؟''

''اس باب میں لکھا ہے کہ نائن الیون کے فوراً بعد جب القاعدہ کے کئی ارکان افغانستان سے بھاگ کر پاکستان میں آگئے تھے تو ہم نے ان کے ساتھ چوہے بلی کے کئی کھیل کھیلے، مجاہدین کو گرفتار کر کے امریکہ کے حوالے کیا اور اس کے عوض ہم نے کئی ملین ڈالر انعام میں پائے، جنہیں ہم پر یہ الزام لگانے کی عادت ہو چکی ہے کہ ہم دہشت گردی کے خلاف جنگ میں کافی کردار ادا نہیں کر رہے وہ سی آئی اے سے پوچھ لیں کہ حکومت پاکستان کو وہ انعام میں کتنی رقم ادا کر چکی ہے۔''

''ویری سیڈ، ان لوگوں کے پاس طاقت اور اختیار ہے تو یہ ہر قسم کی دہشت گردی اپنا کر بھی حق پر ہیں اور غریب مجاہدین جو ان کی زیادتیوں اور مظالم کا شکار ہیں وہ بے گناہ ان کے ہتھے چڑھ کر بدنام ہو رہے ہیں صرف اس لیے کیونکہ اللہ کے سوا ان کا کوئی پرسان حال نہیں، ہے ناں۔''

''ہوں، بہت ظلم ہوا ہے افغانستان اور عراق میں یار! چھوٹے چھوٹے معصوم بچوں اور عورتوں کو اتنی بے دردی سے مارا ہے امریکہ بہادر نے کہ انسانیت بلبلا اٹھتی ہے، تمہیں پتا ہے فرعون نے سیکڑوں نومولود بچے قتل کروا دیئے تھے' صرف اسی خوف کے پیش نظر کہ ان میں سے کوئی بڑا ہو کر اسے اور اس کی خدائی کو ختم نہ کر دے۔ امریکہ بھی یہی کر رہا ہے، چن چن کے مسلمانوں کو مار رہا ہے کیونکہ فرعون کی طرح اسے بھی اپنی خدائی کا خاتمہ مسلمانوں کے ہاتھوں ہوتا نظر آتا ہے، اسی لیے اس نے اپنی طاقت اور پیسے کے بل پر بعض مسلم حکمرانوں کے ایمان اور ضمیر خرید لیے ہیں مگر یہ سودا بہت گھاٹے کا سودا ہے حورعین! کیونکہ یہ دنیا فانی ہے اور سپر پاور صرف اللہ ربّ العزت کی ذات ہے جو چاہے تو ایک پل میں سب فنا کر کے رکھ دے مگر یہ کھیل ابھی اتنی جلدی ختم ہونے والا نہیں ہے، بہت بڑی ہے دوزخ۔ اب تو بس قیامت کے دن ہی یہ بساط الٹی جائے گی خیر تم نے بتایا نہیں، تم کیا کرنا چاہتی ہو؟''

''تم بتاؤ یار! میں کیا کروں، میرا دل درد سے پھٹ رہا ہے، مجھے رات میں نیند نہیں آتی۔ امت مسلمہ کی چیخیں اور آہیں میرا کلیجہ نوچتی ہیں، مجھے بتاؤ ثانیہ! میں کیا کروں؟ کہاں سے ایک اور اقبالؒ اور قائدؒ لاؤں؟''

ثانیہ دیکھ سکتی تھی کہ اس کا حال بہت ابتر تھا۔ بے حد رف کپڑوں میں اس نے کئی روز سے بال سنوارنے کی زحمت بھی گوارہ نہیں کی تھی تبھی وہ بولی تھی۔

''تم بھی وہی کرو حورعین! جو اقبال نے کیا، مسلمانوں کی سوئی ہوئی غیرت کو جگاؤ، انہیں بتاؤ کہ تاریخ کیا کہتی ہے انہیں بتاؤ حورعین کہ دمشق میں جب ایک نصرانی جرنیل نے ایک مسلمان کو مارا پیٹا تھا تو اس وقت کے امیر معاویہ نے اس نصرانی جرنیل کے ساتھ کیا کیا، عموریہ میں رومی عیسائی سلطنت کے زیر اثر ایک عیسائی نے ایک مسلمان عورت کو تھپڑ مارا تو اس وقت کے عباسی خلیفہ نے اس کے ساتھ کیا کیا، حق پر چلنے کی دعوت دو حورعین! حق اور سچ کی آواز بلند کرو۔''

''مگر کیسے؟ کیا تم نہیں جانتیں کہ مشرف نے حق اور سچ کے متوالوں کے ساتھ کیا کیا؟ کن مسلمانوں کی بات کرتی ہو تم، وہ جن کے دلوں میں ایمان کی شمع روشن تھی، جو نڈر اور دین حق پر چلنے والے تھے جو ہمارا سرمایہ تھے، وہ سب تو ظلم اور دہشت گردی کی بھینٹ چڑھ گئے ثانیہ! ہم نے خود بندوق اٹھا کر دشمن کے ہاتھ میں تھمائی کہ لو اور ہمیں مارو اب کن مسلمانوں کی بات کرتی ہو تم؟ کون اٹھے گا نعرہ حق پر اور جو اٹھے گا وہ کیا کرے گا، جس سلطنت کا سالار اپنا ضمیر اور ایمان بیچ دے وہاں کوئی اقبال کیا کر سکتا ہے؟''

''اقبال کا درد صرف کسی ایک علاقے کے لیے نہیں تھا' تم حوصلہ رکھو حورعین! توحید اور ایمان کی شمع کبھی بجھائی نہیں جاسکتی۔ اسلام کی فطرت ہے اسے جتنا دباؤ گے یہ اتنا ہی ابھرے گا۔ تم ساری دنیا کے لیے امن کا پیغام لے کر اٹھو اور چھا جاؤ۔''

ثانیہ عباس نے اسے حوصلہ دیا اور وہ اپنے ربّ کا نام لے کر اٹھ کھڑی ہوئی تھی۔ حق اور سچ کی صدا بلند کرنے کے لیے اس نے اپنا ایک علیحدہ اخبار بھی نکالا' جس کا مقصد صرف مسلمانوں کے خلاف ہونے والی سازشوں کا پردہ چاک کرنا اور ان کا دفاع کرنا تھا' اس کے ساتھ مسلمانوں کی سوئی ہوئی غیرت جگانا اور مسلم حکمرانوں کو ان کے فرائض منصبی سے بے پروائی پر شرم دلانا تھا مگر......

یہ سلسلہ زیادہ دیر تک نہیں چل سکا تھا' ابھی چھ ماہ بھی نہیں ہوئے تھے کہ ایک روز وہ اپنے ہی ملک میں دشمنوں کے ہتھے چڑھ گئی تھی۔ اس کی سوتیلی ماں نے اس سے کہا تھا۔

''کیا چاہتی ہو تم' اس ملک میں امن نہ رہے' اپنے سے دس گنا بڑے ملک کو آنکھیں دکھا کر ہم یہاں اپنے اوپر کوئی صلیبی جنگ مسلط کرلیں' کیوں نہیں عزت اور سکون سے جیتی ہو تم؟ ایک بار کسی کی نگاہ میں آگئیں تو عبرت بنا دیں گے یہ لوگ تمہاری زندگی کو' تم کیوں اپنے ساتھ ہمیں بھی لے کر ڈوب مرنا چاہتی ہو۔''

مگر اس نے اپنی سوتیلی ماں کی کسی بھی بات کا کوئی جواب نہیں دیا تھا۔ چپ چاپ ناشتا کرنے کے بعد وہ ڈائنگ ٹیبل سے اٹھ گئی تھی تاہم اس کی ماں کا کہا اکارت نہیں گیا تھا' قوم کو غفلت کی نیند سے جگانے کی بہت کڑی قیمت چکانی پڑی تھی اسے۔

✿......✿......✿

موسم سرد ہو رہا تھا۔

گاڑی کی فرنٹ سیٹ پر بیٹھی وہ قریبی درختوں سے ہجرت کرتے پرندوں کو بغور دیکھ رہی تھی جب اچانک ایک پولیس موبائل نے اس کا راستہ روک لیا' اس کے ڈرائیور نے قدرے حیرانی سے اس کی طرف دیکھا تھا' جیسے وہ جاننے کی کوشش کر رہا ہو کہ پولیس موبائل نے اسے کیوں روکا ہے۔

''باہر آؤ۔'' گاڑی رکتے ہی پولیس کی ایک کرخت چہرے والی خاتون حورعین کی سائیڈ پر آئی تھی اور اس نے اپنے ہاتھ میں موجود موٹے سے ڈنڈے سے اس کی طرف کا دروازہ بجایا تھا' وہ حیران و پریشان سی باہر نکل آئی۔

''کیا مسئلہ ہے؟''

''چٹاخ......!'' اس کی آنکھوں کی حیرانی کے جواب میں اس کے چہرے پر زوردار تھپڑ پڑا تھا' وہ ششدر ہی تو رہ گئی۔

''کیا بدتمیزی ہے یہ؟''

''جسٹ شٹ اپ یو بچ۔'' اس بار جس شخص نے اسے تھپڑ مارا تھا' وہ مسلمان نہیں تھا۔ حورعین اپنے ڈرائیور کے سامنے بنا کسی قصور کے ایسی انہونی پر کٹ کر رہ گئی۔ مگر اس سے پہلے کہ وہ مزید کچھ کہتی پولیس والوں نے انتہائی بے رحمی سے اسے کھینچتے ہوئے اپنی موبائل کیب میں دھکیل دیا۔ وہ ابھی چلانا ہی چاہتی تھی کہ اس کے ہونٹوں اور آنکھوں پر پٹی باندھ دی گئی' اگلے ہی پل اس کے دونوں ہاتھ مروڑ کر اس کی پشت پر باندھ دیئے گئے تھے۔ حورعین کے وہم و گمان میں بھی نہیں تھا کہ اس پر اچانک ایسی افتاد ٹوٹ پڑے گی شاید تبھی وہ گھبرا گئی تھی مگر اسے تسلی تھی کہ یقیناً وہ لوگ کسی بہت بڑی غلط فہمی کا شکار ہو کر اس کے ساتھ یہ سب کر رہے ہیں' جیسے ہی انہیں اپنی غلط فہمی کا احساس ہوگا وہ اس سے معذرت

کرتے ہوئے اسے چھوڑ دیں گے اور تب وہ ان لوگوں کے خلاف خوب احتجاج کرے گی۔

مگر......اس کی نوبت نہیں آئی تھی۔

وہ ابھی معاملے کو سمجھنے کی کوشش کر رہی تھی جب اچانک کسی نے اس کا دوپٹا نوچ کر دور پھینک دیا' اس کے ہاتھ بندھے ہوئے تھے مگر پھر بھی اس نے احتجاج کی کوشش کی تھی جواب میں اس پر لاتوں' ٹھڈوں' گھونسوں اور مکوں کی بارش کر دی گئی' اسے سنبھلنے کا موقع بھی نہیں دیا گیا تھا۔ وہ بے ہوش ہونے کے قریب تھی' جب اس نے ان لوگوں کو انگریزی میں اسلام کے خلاف انتہائی واہیات بکواس کرتے ہوئے سنا۔ وہ لوگ مختصر جملوں میں پاکستان اور اسلام کے خلاف بکواس کر رہے تھے۔ حورعین کا دماغ مکمل طور پر اندھیرے میں ڈوبتا گیا۔ جس وقت اسے ہوش آیا' اس کا سارا بدن درد کے شکنجے میں تھا۔ اسے اپنے ساتھ لانے والے انسانیت سے ماورا لوگ اب اسے گاڑی سے گھسیٹتے ہوئے نیچے اتار رہے تھے' اسے اب تک معلوم نہیں ہو سکا تھا کہ وہ کون لوگ ہیں اور اسے کہاں لائے ہیں؟

گاڑی سے اترتے ہوئے وہ ذرا سی لڑکھڑائی تھی جب انہوں نے زور سے اس کے سر پر بندوق کا بٹ دے مارا' حورعین کو اپنا دماغ ایک مرتبہ پھر تاریکی میں ڈوبتا ہوا محسوس ہوا تھا۔ وہ لوگ اسے گھسیٹتے ہوئے کسی عمارت کی طرف لے جا رہے تھے اگلے کچھ ہی لمحوں میں انہوں نے اسے انتہائی بے دردی سے ایک کمرے میں دھکیل دیا تھا۔ حورعین کے اعصاب پھر سے جواب دے گئے۔ رات کا جانے کون سا پہر تھا جب اس کی آنکھ دوبارہ کھلی' وہ جس عمارت میں تھی وہاں ہُو کا عالم تھا۔ مگر وقفے وقفے سے کسی کے چیخنے اور کراہنے کی آوازیں آ رہی تھیں۔ خود حورعین کی آنکھ بھی کسی کے چیخنے پر کھلی تھی۔ کچھ ہی دیر میں اس کی سماعتوں نے ہولناک تشدد کی آوازیں سنی تھیں۔ حورعین کا دل جیسے ساکت رہ گیا جانے کیوں کسی انہونی کا احساس اسے بے چین کر رہا تھا۔

درندگی ہی درندگی کے اس جنگل میں امن اور تہذیب کا ڈھنڈورا پیٹنے والے بے رحم لوگ اپنی طاقت کے بل بوتے پر محکوم ممالک کے بے بس لوگوں پر ایسی ایسی قیامتیں بپا کر رہے تھے کہ انسانیت بلبلا اٹھتی تھی۔ بنا کسی آئین و قانون کے وہاں صرف طاقت ہی کا بول بالا تھا۔ جہاں صرف طاقت کے بل بوتے پر سیاہ کو سفید' رات کو دن' جھوٹ کو سچ اور صحیح کو غلط کہلوایا جاتا تھا۔ حورعین نے دیکھا وہ ایک تاریک حجرے میں لا کر پھینکی گئی تھی۔ اس جگہ کے حدود اربعے سے اندازہ ہو رہا تھا کہ وہ اپنے ملک میں نہیں ہے وہ جگہ بگرام جیل کی تھی جس کے بارے میں کچھ ہی عرصہ قبل اس نے افغانستان میں اپنے قیام کے دوران ریسرچ کی تھی' بدنام زمانہ اس جیل میں کیا کچھ نہیں ہوتا تھا؟

مارے پیاس کے حورعین کے گلے میں جیسے کانٹے اگ آئے تھے' پورے چہرے اور جسم پر تشدد تکلیف کا احساس الگ کراہنے پر مجبور کر رہا تھا۔ وہ نہیں جانتی تھی کہ وہ کہاں ہے مگر اس کا دل ضرور دھڑک دھڑک کر گواہی دے رہا تھا کہ وہ جہاں بھی ہے اس کے ساتھ بہت بُرا ہونے والا ہے۔

❁......❁......❁

چل چھوڑ تمنا جذبوں کی' ہر شے کا سودا ہوتا ہے
ہر چیز بکاؤ ہوتی ہے ہر فرد یہاں پر تاجر ہے
ہر وقت تجارت ہوتی ہے
تم آپ ہی اپنے دام کہو
چپ رہ کے نہیں سرِعام کہو
کیا لو گے اپنی یاری کا؟

کیا لو گے تم دل داری کا؟
غم خوار بنو گے کتنے میں، تم پیار کرو گے کتنے میں؟
سب جذبے میرے نام کرو، ہم نام تم اپنے دام کہو
پر دام چکانے کی خاطر......
ہم اپنا دفتر کھولیں تو ہم اپنی جیب ٹٹولیں تو
بس پیار ملے گا تھوڑا سا، اظہار ملے گا تھوڑا سا
یہ سکّے یہاں کب چلتے ہیں، کیا ادھار ملے گا تھوڑا سا؟
یہ دنیا بے اعتباری کی، ہے غرض یہ ہر بیوپاری کی
چل چھوڑ تمنا جذبوں کی، بس سودے ہی دیکھ آئیں ہم
ہم خالی ہاتھ ہی آئے تھے چل خالی ہاتھ ہی جائیں ہم

بارش گزرتے ہر لمحے کے ساتھ تیز ہو رہی تھی۔ میکال جیکٹ سے پانی کی بوندیں جھاڑتا دروازہ آہستہ سے پش کرتے ہوئے جیسے ہی کمرے میں داخل ہوا، اس کی نظر سیدھی اسٹڈی ٹیبل پر سر رکھے سوئی ہوئی ہانیہ صفدر پر پڑی، وہ شاید کچھ لکھتے لکھتے سو گئی تھی۔ میکال اس سے نظر چراتے ہوئے بیڈ پر آ بیٹھا۔ بھاری بوٹوں کو پیروں سے علیحدہ کر کے وہ اٹھا اور وارڈ روب سے اپنا سوٹ لے کر واش روم میں گھس گیا۔ تقریباً بیس منٹ بعد وہ فریش ہو کر دوبارہ کمرے میں آیا تو ہانیہ قلم ہاتھ میں پکڑے اسی پوزیشن میں سو رہی تھی۔

ڈارک بلیو سوٹ میں ملبوس، سلکی بالوں کو کیچر میں مقید کیے، بنا کسی میک اپ کے بھی اس وقت وہ بے حد خوب صورت دکھائی دے رہی تھی۔ اس کا کندھے پر پڑا اسکلی دوپٹا زمین کو چھو رہا تھا۔ میکال نے قریب آ کر وہ صفحہ اس کی گرفت سے نکال لیا جس پر کچھ دیر پہلے وہ لکھ رہی تھی۔

''میرا خیال ہے ''محبت'' ایک خوب صورت تتلی ہے۔ جس کے ہزاروں رنگ کسی بھی دل کو اپنی طرف متوجہ کر لیتے ہیں مگر...... ہم انسان جب اس تتلی کو مٹھی میں بھرنے کی کوشش کرتے ہیں تو اس کے رنگ جذب کرنے والے کی مٹھی میں ہی رہ جاتے ہیں اور محبت مر جاتی ہے۔''

کتنی خوب صورت بات اس نے کس سلیقے سے لکھی تھی۔ وہ اس کا درد سمجھ سکتا تھا، تبھی صفحہ وہیں میز پر احتیاط سے رکھتے ہوئے وہ کمپیوٹر کے سامنے آ کر بیٹھ گیا۔ باہر بادل کی گرج سے اچانک ہانیہ کی آنکھ کھلی تھی، سلکی بال سمیٹتے ہوئے وہ کرسی سے اٹھی تو میکال کو کمرے میں موجود پا کر ٹھٹک گئی۔

''السّلام علیکم!'' دوپٹا سلیقے سے اوڑھتے ہوئے وہ قریب آئی تھی۔

''وعلیکم السّلام!'' اس کے قریب آ کر بیٹھنے پر بادل نخواستہ اس نے سلام کا جواب دیا تھا۔

''آج صبح ہونے سے پہلے گھر آ گئے خیریت؟'' وہ اس سے فرینک ہونے کے لیے پوچھ رہی تھی مگر میکال نے اس بار اس کے سوال کا جواب نہیں دیا، اس کا چہرہ بے حد سپاٹ تھا۔ ہانیہ کو بے ساختہ شدید ہتک کا احساس ہوا مگر پھر بھی وہ مسکرائی تھی۔

''میکال...... کیا ہم اچھے دوست نہیں بن سکتے؟''

''کیوں...... نہال کی دوستی کم پڑ گئی ہے؟'' تیزی سے کی بورڈ پر انگلیاں چلاتے ہوئے اس نے بھرپور طنز سے پوچھا تھا۔ وہ محسوس ہی نہ کر سکی۔

''نہیں، بے شک وہ میرا بہت اچھا، بہترین دوست ہے اور ہمیشہ رہے گا مگر آپ کی اور بات ہے میکال! آپ میرے شوہر ہیں، میری زندگی کے ساتھی، میں آپ کے ہر دکھ اور سکھ کی ہم سفر ہوں اور میرے خیال میں ہر بیوی کو اپنے شوہر کی بہترین دوست ہونا چاہیے۔''

''مگر میں تمہارے ساتھ زندگی گزارنا نہیں چاہتا۔'' پل میں مشتعل ہوتے ہوئے وہ اپنی جگہ سے اٹھا اور کھڑکی کے قریب چلا آیا جہاں سے ٹھنڈی ہوا کے جھونکے کمرے کی خنکی میں اضافہ کر رہے تھے۔

ہانیہ کو لگا میکال نے اس کے منہ پر زور کا تمانچہ دے مارا ہو، کتنے ہی لمحوں تک وہ چپ رہی تھی پھر میکال کے سگریٹ سلگانے پر وہ اٹھ کر اس کے قریب چلی آئی۔

''آپ کو کیوں لگتا ہے میکال کہ میں آپ کی ذات پر بوجھ ہوں میرا اللہ گواہ ہے میرے لیے یہ گھر، یہ کمرا، یہ بیڈ آپ کی ذات سب عائشہ جی کی امانت ہے۔ میں یہ ہرگز نہیں چاہتی کہ آپ مجھے ان کی جگہ دیں مگر میرے توسط سے اگر آپ ان کو پالیں تو کیا برا ہے؟ میں وعدہ کرتی ہوں آپ سے، میں انہیں آپ کی زندگی میں واپس لاؤں گی لیکن جب تک ایسا نہیں ہوتا تب تک تو آپ کو میرا وجود برداشت کرنا پڑے گا میں وعدہ کرتی ہوں میں آپ سے اپنا کوئی حق طلب نہیں کروں گی ہم اس کمرے میں دو اجنبی لوگوں کی طرح ہی اپنا وقت گزاریں گے مگر اس کمرے کی حدود کے باہر آپ کو میرا بھرم رکھنا ہوگا تاکہ ایک یا دو سال کے بعد جب میں آپ کے گھر والوں کو آپ کی دوسری شادی کے لیے مناؤں تو آپ کے کردار پر کوئی حرف نہ آئے۔''

''تمہیں میرے لیے کسی بھی قسم کی قربانی دے کر مجھ پر احسان کرنے کی ضرورت نہیں ہے، سمجھی؟ دوسری شادی میرا حق ہے اور میں جب چاہوں یہ حق استعمال کر سکتا ہوں، کسی کی مجال نہیں کہ مجھے روکے۔''

اس کے نرم لہجے پر بھی وہ بھڑکا تھا ہانیہ کی آنکھوں میں ایک دم سے نمی آ گئی۔

''بے شک آپ ایسا کر سکتے ہیں مگر جب تک ایسا نہیں ہوتا، تب تک تو ہم اچھے دوستوں کی طرح رہ ہی سکتے ہیں ناں پلیز۔''

سر جھکاتے ہوئے نم لہجے میں کہتی وہ بے حد آزردہ لگ رہی تھی۔ میکال بنا اس پر نگاہ ڈالے بے زاری سے پلٹ گیا۔

اگلے روز بیدار ہونے کے بعد وہ شاور لے کر نکلا تھا، جب اس نے دیکھا کہ نہال اس کے کمرے میں موجود فریج سے ٹھنڈے پانی کی بوتل نکال کر ہانیہ پر انڈیل رہا تھا اور وہ بچاؤ کی کوشش کرتی، اس کے ساتھ الجھ رہی تھی۔ ہنستا، کھلکھلاتا نہال اس کے دونوں ہاتھ قابو کیے اسے منہ چڑا رہا تھا۔ وہ سرخ چہرے کے ساتھ نظر انداز کرتا آئینے کے سامنے جا کھڑا ہوا۔

''میکال...... میں آپ کی مدد کروں؟'' نہال سے بازو چھڑاتے ہوئے وہ فوراً میکال کی طرف لپکی تھی جبکہ وہ بے نیازی سے تقریباً غراتے ہوئے بولا۔

''کوئی ضرورت نہیں ہے۔''

وہ اس کا لہجہ پہچان گئی تھی تبھی نہال کے سامنے مزید بے عزت ہونے سے بچنے کے لیے کمرے سے نکل آئی۔ کچن میں عینا بھابی، مائرہ اور سارہ ناشتا تیار کرنے میں مصروف تھیں وہ بھی ان کا ہاتھ بٹانا ہی چاہتی تھی کہ نہال اس کے سر پر آ کھڑا ہوا۔

''ہانی! مجھے تم سے ضروری بات کرنی ہے میرے ساتھ آؤ پلیز۔'' میکال سیڑھیوں پر تھا جب اس نے نہال کے یہ

الفاظ سنے ہانیہ نے جواب نہیں دیا تھا مگر عینا بھابی ضرور بولی تھیں۔

''نہال! ہانیہ اب میکال کی بیوی اور تمہاری بھابی ہے' تمیز سے بات کیا کرو۔''

''تمیز مائی فٹ...... ہانیہ میری دوست تھی اور دوست رہے گی۔'' کتنا واضح جواب تھا اس کا۔ میکال جو ناشتے کے لیے بیٹھ چکا تھا' بریڈ کا ایک بائیٹ لیتے ہی اٹھ کھڑا ہوا۔

''مجھے آفس کے لیے دیر ہو رہی ہے' چلتا ہوں خدا حافظ۔''

اس کا چہرہ تن گیا تھا' مسز حسن بنا کچھ کہے خاموشی سے اسے دیکھتی رہیں اور وہ تیز تیز قدم اٹھاتا ڈائننگ ہال سے نکل گیا' اس کے سر میں اس وقت شدید درد ہو رہا تھا۔ ڈرائیونگ میں بھی دشواری پیش آ رہی تھی۔ وہ ایک بٹا ہوا شخص تھا۔ اپنی ذات کی تکمیل اور سکون کے لیے اسے ایک مکمل عورت درکار تھی مگر تقدیر نے اسے جس عورت کا ہم سفر کیا' وہ بھی ایک بٹی ہوئی عورت تھی۔

اس کی طرح دو کشتیوں میں سوار.......

ایک فرض اور ایک محبت

اس وقت اس کا بس نہیں چل رہا تھا کہ وہ گاڑی کو کسی درخت میں دے مارتا۔ نہال اس کے جانے کے بعد زبردستی ہانیہ کو کھینچتا ہوا اپنے کمرے میں لے آیا تھا۔

''سچ سچ بتاؤ ہانی! میکال بھیا کا رویہ تمہارے ساتھ کیسا ہے پلیز۔'' ہانیہ دیکھ سکتی تھی کہ وہ اس کے معاملے میں بہت حساس ہے' تبھی لبوں پر مسکراہٹ پھیلاتے ہوئے ہنس کر بولی۔

''بہت اچھا' بے حد کیئرنگ۔''

''جھوٹ۔'' اسے جیسے یقین ہی نہیں آیا تھا۔

''جھوٹ کیوں؟ میرے چہرے پر جھوٹ لکھا نظر آ رہا ہے تمہیں؟'' صرف اپنا بھرم رکھنے کے لیے اس نے چہرے پر مصنوعی غصہ طاری کیا تھا' نہال سر جھٹک کر رہ گیا۔

''وہ اپ سیٹ ہیں نہال! ایک شخص جسے آپ بہت چاہتے ہیں مگر وہ آپ کی دسترس سے دور کسی اور کے حصار میں تکلیف دہ زندگی گزار رہا ہو تو آپ چاہتے ہوئے بھی خود کو نارمل نہیں رکھ سکتے' میرا خیال ہے کہ ہمیں ان کی فیلنگز کو سمجھنا چاہیے انہیں کچھ مزید ٹائم دینا چاہیے۔''

''ہوں۔'' ٹراؤزر کی پاکٹس میں دونوں ہاتھ گھساتے ہوئے نہال نے سر جھکاتے ہوئے ہامی بھری تھی۔ وہ اداسی سے مسکراتے ہوئے اس کے بال بکھیر کر رہ گئی۔

رات میں پھر میکال کی واپسی خاصی لیٹ ہوئی تھی۔ گاڑی پورچ میں کھڑی کرنے کے بعد جس وقت وہ ہال میں آیا' ہانیہ' سارہ اور مائرہ کے ساتھ خوش گپیوں میں مصروف تھی۔ وہ سرسری سی ایک نظر ان تینوں پر ڈالتا اوپر اپنے کمرے کی طرف آ گیا۔ پاؤں کو جوتوں کی قید سے آزاد کرنے کے بعد وہ بیڈ پر لیٹا تھا جب وہ آہستہ سے دروازہ پش کرتے ہوئے کمرے میں چلی آئی۔

''السلام علیکم!'' عادت سے مجبور اس نے سلام کیا تھا مگر حسب توقع میکال نے اسے جواب نہیں دیا۔

''کھانا لاؤں آپ کے لیے؟'' بیڈ کے کنارے پر ٹکتے ہوئے اس نے پوچھا مگر وہ ہنوز خاموش رہا۔ یوں جیسے اس کی شکل بھی نہ دیکھنا چاہتا ہو۔

''آپ نے صبح ناشتا بھی نہیں کیا تھا کچھ تو کھا لیں پلیز۔''

''جسٹ شٹ اپ! او کے۔ تمھیں کیا لگتا ہے میں تمہاری خدمتوں پر بیٹھا ہوں۔'' بلاوجہ وہ اس پر غصہ ہوا تھا' ہانیہ اسے دیکھ کر رہ گئی۔

''میں نے آپ کا کیا نقصان کیا ہے میکال! آپ میرے ساتھ اس طرح سے بات کیوں کرتے ہیں؟''

ضبط کے باوجود بھی اس کی آنکھوں اور لہجے میں نمی آ گئی تھی۔

''میں جانتی ہوں آپ کے ساتھ زیادتی ہوئی ہے مگر اس زیادتی میں میرا کوئی قصور نہیں ہے۔ شادی سے پہلے ہی نہال کی زبانی مجھے آپ کی اور عائشہ جی کی محبت کا پتا تھا' اسی لیے آپ کی طرح میں بھی اس شادی کے حق میں نہیں تھی۔ بہت کوشش کی میں نے کہ میں آپ کی زندگی کا حصہ نہ بنوں مگر کاتب تقدیر کے سامنے ہماری ایک نہیں چلتی۔ پلیز میکال مجھ سے دشمنوں والا رویہ مت رکھیں پلیز......''

میکال حسن کے پیروں پر ہاتھ رکھتے ہوئے اس نے التجا کی تھی' جواب میں میکال نے اس کے ہاتھ اپنے پیروں سے ہٹا دیئے۔

''میرے سر میں بہت درد ہو رہا ہے' پلیز سو جاؤ۔''

''نہیں! میں آپ کا سر دباتی ہوں۔'' آنسو پونچھ کر میکال کے منع کرنے کے باوجود وہ اپنے نرم ہاتھوں سے اس کا سر دبانے لگی تھی۔ میکال کو اس کے ہاتھوں کی نرماہٹ سے عجیب سے سکون کا احساس ہوا' اس کی پلکیں خود بخود بند ہونے لگی تھیں جب وہ بولی۔

''میں عائشہ جی سے مل کر ان سے دوستی کرنا چاہتی ہوں میکال! میں چاہتی ہوں وہ یہاں آئیں آپ سے ملیں' زندگی کو انجوائے کریں۔''

مگر میکال سو چکا تھا' ہانیہ ساری رات بیڈ کی پشت گاہ سے ٹیک لگائے اس کے سرہانے بیٹھی رہی تھی۔

اگلے ایک ہفتے میں اس کی عائشہ برہان سے دعا سلام ہوگئی' پہلی بار جب اس نے اسے بتایا کہ وہ میکال کی بیوی ہے تو وہ ساکت رہ گئی تھی بھلا کوئی بیوی اتنی اعلیٰ ظرف کیسے ہو سکتی تھی کہ اپنے شوہر کی محبوبہ سے دوستی کرے' اسے اپنے گھر آنے کی دعوت دے۔

اس روز مسز حسن کو بتا کر وہ مارکیٹ آئی تھی' مقصد صرف عائشہ سے ملنا تھا' مختصر سی شاپنگ کے بعد وہ دونوں ریستوران میں بیٹھی تھیں' جب اس نے میکال کو کال کی' وہ کسی میٹنگ میں مصروف تھا مگر پھر بھی اس نے اس کی کال پک کر لی تھی۔

''میکال آپ مصروف نہیں ہیں تو مارکیٹ آ سکتے ہیں؟''

''کیوں؟''

''وہ میں آج مارکیٹ آئی تھی۔''

''سوری! مجھے ابھی ایک ضروری میٹنگ اٹینڈ کرنی ہے' میں نہیں آ سکتا۔'' اس کی پوری بات سنے بغیر اس نے صاف انکار کر دیا تھا۔

''لیکن میرے ساتھ عائشہ جی بھی ہیں میں......''

''ٹھیک ہے میں آتا ہوں ابھی' تم جہاں ہو میسج کر دو خدا حافظ۔'' ایک مرتبہ پھر روکھے لہجے میں اس کی بات سنے بغیر اس نے کال کاٹ دی تھی۔ ہانیہ کو لگا جیسے کسی نے اس کا دل چیر کر رکھ دیا ہو' کاش اس کے پاپا نے بھی اس کی مما سے اتنی ہی محبت کی ہوتی جتنی میکال حسن نے عائشہ برہان سے کی تھی۔ آنکھوں میں ہلکی سی نمی کے باوجود وہ مسکرائی تھی۔

''وہ آرہے ہیں پلیز آپ ان سے ٹھیک سے ملیے گا۔ وہ آپ کو لے کر بہت پریشان ہیں۔''
کتنی التجا کے ساتھ وہ اس سے کہہ رہی تھی۔ عائشہ کو یقین نہیں آرہا تھا کیا کوئی بیوی اتنا بڑا دل اور ظرف بھی رکھ سکتی تھی؟

''یہ سب ٹھیک نہیں ہے مسز ہانیہ! آپ کو ایسا نہیں کرنا چاہیے۔''
''ہوں، میں سمجھتی ہوں مجھے ایسا نہیں کرنا چاہیے مگر میں کیا کروں میرے شوہر کی خوشی آپ کی ذات میں ہے...... ایکسکیوز می۔'' اس کے موبائل پر بپ ہوئی تھی۔ کال مسز حسن کی طرف سے تھی، تبھی وہ عائشہ سے معذرت کرتی اٹھ کر سائیڈ پر آگئی۔
''جی مما۔''
''بیٹا آپ کے گھر والے آئے ہیں آپ سے ملنے، آپ فوری گھر آجاؤ۔''
''سوری مما! میں ابھی گھر نہیں آسکتی۔ شام تک آسکوں گی، آپ میری طرف سے انہیں پوچھ لیجیے گا۔'' ازحد رف لہجے میں کہہ کر اس نے فوراً کال کاٹ دی تھی۔
وہ جنگ جو زندگی نے اس پر مسلط کر دی تھی اس جنگ میں آخری سانس تک اسے فائٹ تو کرنی ہی تھی۔

❂......❂......❂

میکال آ گیا تھا۔
عائشہ برہان کو دیکھتے ہی اس شخص کی آنکھوں میں اتنے خوب صورت رنگ اترے تھے کہ وہ حیران رہ گئی تھی۔ وہ شخص جو اس کے سامنے صرف نفرت اور بیزاری کی علامت بنا رہتا تھا۔ اسی میکال حسن کو اس لمحے اس نے محبت کے چشمے میں ڈھلتے دیکھا تھا۔ وہ عائشہ برہان کے سامنے بیٹھی تھی مگر اس شخص نے اس پر ایک نگاہ غلط ڈالنا بھی گوارہ نہیں کیا تھا۔ ٹیبل پر بیٹھتے ہی اس نے عائشہ برہان کا ہاتھ تھاما تھا۔
''کیسی ہو عائش؟''
کیسی بے قراری اور تڑپ تھی اس کے لہجے میں۔ ہانیہ اپنے نظر انداز کیے جانے پر گنگ بیٹھی رہ گئی تھی۔
''ٹھیک ہوں، تم کیسے ہو؟'' عائشہ برہان نے اس کی موجودگی کا لحاظ کرتے ہوئے اپنا ہاتھ اس کی گرفت سے نکال لیا تھا تبھی وہ عائشہ کو جواب دینے کے بجائے اس کی طرف مڑا تھا۔
''تم گھر جاؤ ہانیہ پلیز......'' اسے گمان نہیں تھا کہ وہ اس سے کچھ ایسا بھی کہہ سکتا ہے، تبھی وہ حیرانی سے اسے دیکھتی رہ گئی تھی۔
''تم نے سنا نہیں ہے میں نے کیا کہا ہے، جاؤ یہاں سے۔'' دومنٹ کے بعد ہی اس کی خاموشی پر وہ تپ اٹھا تھا۔ تبھی وہ عائشہ برہان کے سامنے اپنی بے عزتی پر شدید دکھی ہوتی وہاں سے اٹھ آئی تھی۔ اس کے جانے کے بعد عائشہ نے میکال سے کہا تھا۔
''یہ سب کیا ہے میکال؟''
''میری محبت۔'' جواب میں اس نے اس کے دونوں ہاتھ تھام لیے تھے۔
''نہیں، یہ محبت نہیں ہے میں سوچ بھی نہیں سکتی تھی کہ تم جیسا نرم مزاج، خوش گفتار ایک آئیڈیل شخص اپنی بیوی کے ساتھ ایسا جاہلانہ رویہ بھی رکھ سکتا ہے، کیا قصور ہے اس لڑکی کا بولو۔''
''اس کا قصور یہ ہے عائش کہ یہ میری زندگی میں میری مرضی کے خلاف زبردستی آئی اور اس کا دوسرا قصور یہ ہے کہ وہ

ایک منافق لڑکی ہے بے شک وہ میری بیوی ہے مگر محبت نہال سے کرتی ہے' میرے چھوٹے بھائی سے۔''
''نہیں، میں نہیں مانتی۔''
''نہ مانو' تمہارے ماننے یا نہ ماننے سے کیا ہوجائے گا۔'' بے نیازی سے کہتے ہوئے اب وہ اس کے ہاتھ سہلا رہا تھا۔ عائشہ نے چپکے سے اپنے ہاتھ اس کی گرفت سے نکال لیے۔
''بہرحال' حقیقت خواہ کچھ بھی ہو مگر یہ ٹھیک نہیں ہے میکال! میں نہیں چاہتی کہ تمہاری مجھ سے محبت میری جیسی کسی دوسری لڑکی کی آنکھوں میں آنسوؤں کا باعث بنے' کوئی میرے جیسا دوسرا مجھ سے نفرت کرے اور میرے مرنے کی دعائیں مانگے۔''
''کیا بکواس ہے عائش! ایسا کچھ بھی نہیں ہے۔''
''نہیں، تم نہیں جانتے میکال! عورت بڑے سے بڑا دکھ بہادری سے برداشت کرسکتی ہے' بڑے سے بڑا نقصان سہہ سکتی ہے مگر ایک بیوی کی حیثیت سے اپنے شوہر کی تقسیم برداشت نہیں کرسکتی۔ ہانیہ واقعی بہت اچھی لڑکی ہے کچھ تو ایسا ہوگا اس میں جو خدا نے میری جگہ اسے تمہارا ہم سفر بنایا۔''
''مگر عائش......!''
''اگر مگر کو چھوڑ دو میکال! بس اتنا یاد رکھو قدرت کو ہمارا ملاپ منظور نہیں تھا اگر ہوتا تو اس وقت ہانیہ صفدر کی جگہ عائشہ برہان تمہاری بیوی ہوتی۔ میرا دل ٹوٹا اور اجڑا ہے میکال! اس لیے دل ٹوٹنے اور اجڑنے کی تکلیف کیا ہوتی ہے' میں اچھی طرح سے سمجھ سکتی ہوں۔''
میکال حسن کی بات کاٹتے ہوئے وہ ازحد آزردہ لہجے میں بولی تھی' وہ خاموشی سے اسے دیکھے گیا۔
''ہانیہ صفدر کا حق ہے کہ تم اس کا خیال رکھو اور اس سے محبت کرو اگر وہ شکستہ دل ہے تو تم اپنی محبت سے اس کے زخموں پر پھاہے رکھو' اسے زندگی کی طرف لاؤ' جہاں تک میری زندگی کا سوال ہے تو میں اپنی لائف سے مطمئن ہوں' میں نے شاید تمہیں بتایا تھا کہ میرا دیور اریج ایبروڈ سے مستقل پاکستان آ گیا ہے' وہ میرا بہت خیال رکھتا ہے' میں اپنی قربانی پر خاک پڑتے نہیں دیکھ سکتی میکال! اسی لیے آج آخری بار تم سے استدعا کررہی ہوں پلیز مجھ سے فون پر بھی رابطہ مت رکھنا' میں نہیں چاہتی کہ میرے سسرال میں کسی کو مجھ پر انگلی اٹھانے کا موقع ملے۔''
نظریں جھکائے قدرے بدلے ہوئے لہجے میں وہ اس سے استدعا کررہی تھی۔ میکال آزردہ سا اسے دیکھتا رہ گیا' تبھی کوئی ان کی ٹیبل کے قریب آیا تھا۔
''ایکسکیوزمی!'' عائشہ اور میکال نے ایک ساتھ سر اوپر اٹھا دیکھا تھا اور پھر جیسے عائشہ کے چہرے کا رنگ ایک دم سے اڑ گیا۔
''اریج آپ؟'' فوراً سے پیش تر وہ اپنی سیٹ سے کھڑی ہوئی تھی۔
''جی' ایک دوست کے ساتھ ڈنر کا پروگرام تھا' وہ ابھی پہنچا نہیں تبھی آپ پر نظر پڑ گئی تو اس طرف آ گیا۔'' بنا اس سے کوئی وضاحت طلب کیے وہ عام لہجے میں روانی سے اسے بتا رہا تھا۔ عائشہ سے نظریں اٹھانا موت ہوگیا۔
''یہ...... یہ میکال صاحب ہیں' شش...... شادی سے پہلے میں انہی کی کمپنی میں جاب کرتی تھی' اتنے دنوں بعد اچانک مارکیٹ میں ملے تو کھانے کے لیے اصرار کرنے لگے۔ مم...... میں بس ابھی اٹھنے ہی والی تھی۔''
وہ ایک دم سے اتنی گھبرا گئی تھی کہ میکال بھی اسے دیکھتا رہ گیا۔
جانے کیوں اس لمحے اسے عائشہ برہان کی گھبراہٹ اور تعارف پسند نہیں آیا تھا۔ اریج سے مصافحے کے بعد وہ گہری

نگاہوں سے اسے دیکھتا وہاں سے اٹھ آیا تھا جب کہ اریج ایک نظر اسے دیکھنے کے بعد عائشہ برہان کے گھبرائے گھبرائے سے چہرے پر نگاہ ڈالتا اسے اپنے پیچھے آنے کا کہہ کر ہوٹل سے نکل گیا۔

✿......✿......✿

ہانیہ جس وقت گھر واپس آئی کرنل صاحب اور ان کی فیملی اس کے انتظار میں بیٹھی تھی۔ وہ اس وقت کسی سے بھی ملنے کی خواہش مند نہیں تھی تبھی خود کو کمپوز کرتی تھوڑی دیر ان کے پاس بیٹھی رہی پھر خرابی طبیعت کا بہانہ کرتی اپنے کمرے میں چلی آئی۔

ہادیہ اور جاذب کو اس سے ایسے روّیے کی امید نہیں تھی، خود مسز حسن بھی اس کی بے مروتی پر حیران رہ گئی تھیں مگر اسے کسی کی پروا نہیں تھی، جانے کیوں اس لمحے اسے اپنا دل پھٹتا ہوا محسوس ہو رہا تھا۔

کرنل صاحب اور دیگر لوگوں کے جانے کے بعد وہ کمرے سے نکل کر لان میں آ بیٹھی تھی جب نہال چپکے سے لاؤنج سے اٹھ کر لان کی سیڑھیوں پر اس کے پہلو میں آ بیٹھا۔

''ہانیہ! پریشان ہو؟''

''ہاں!'' بناء اس کی طرف دیکھے اس نے خلافِ توقع جواب دیا تھا' وہ گہری سانس بھر کر رہ گیا۔

''کیوں......اب کیا ہوا ہے؟''

''پتا نہیں۔'' وہ بے آواز رو رہی تھی' نہال کا دل جیسے کٹ کر رہ گیا۔

''مگر مجھے پتا ہے تم ضرور میکال بھائی کی وجہ سے پریشان ہو۔''

''میں اس شخص کی وجہ سے پریشان نہیں ہوں نہال!''

فوراً سے پیش تر بہتے آنسوؤں کی پروا کیے بغیر اس نے وضاحت دی تھی۔

''وہ شخص تو میرا آئیڈیل ہے صرف ایک لڑکی کی محبت کو روگ بنا کر اسے اپنی زندگی کا نصب العین بنانے والا میرا یقین کرو مجھے بہت خوشی ہے کہ وہ شخص محبت کے معاملے میں اتنا ایمان دار ہے بقول ہادیہ کے آج سے پچاس سال پہلے والا ہیرو ہے مگر...... پتا نہیں کیوں میں اس کی نفرت سے ہارتی جا رہی ہوں...... پتا نہیں کیوں۔''

اب وہ بچوں کی طرح رو رہی تھی۔ میکال جو گاڑی پارک کرنے کے بعد وہاں سے گزر رہا تھا اسے روتے دیکھ کر وہیں رک گیا۔

''میں اس کی نفرت نہیں سہہ پا رہی نہال! پتا نہیں کیوں۔'' کانپتے لہجے میں آنسوؤں کی آمیزش تھی' وہ ایک پل ٹھہرنے کے بعد اپنے کمرے میں آ گیا تھا جب کہ نہال اب اپنی انگلیوں کی پوروں پر اس کے آنسو چن رہا تھا۔

''پاگل ہو تم اور کچھ نہیں۔''

وہ کچھ اور کہہ بھی نہیں سکتا تھا۔ اس رات بہت دیر تک وہ روتی رہی تھی اور نہال بہت دیر تک اس کے پاس بیٹھا اس کی برین واشنگ کرتا رہا تھا۔ میکال اگلے روز خرابی طبیعت کے باعث دوپہر میں لنچ کے لیے گھر آیا' تو وہ سیڑھیوں پر نہال کے تنگ کرنے کے سبب اندھا دھند بھاگتی اس سے بری طرح ٹکرا گئی۔ اس وقت اگر وہ فوری اسے نہ تھام لیتا تو دونوں کا گر جانا یقینی تھا۔

''کیا مصیبت ہے یہ، کبھی بچپنے سے نکل بھی آیا کرو۔''

نہال کو دیکھ کر ایک دم سے اس کا پارہ چڑھا تھا جب کہ وہ اس کی چوڑی پشت کے پیچھے چھپتے ہوئے منمنائی تھی۔

''سوری میکال......وہ......نہال مجھے ڈرا رہا ہے اس کے ہاتھ میں زندہ چھپکلی ہے۔''

اس کی اطلاع پر میکال نے نہال کی طرف دیکھا تو واقعی اس کے ہاتھ میں زندہ چھپکلی تھی اور وہ مسکرا رہا تھا۔

''شرم آنی چاہیے تمہیں ایسی بچوں جیسی حرکتیں کرتے ہوئے۔'' وہ بگڑا تھا جب کہ وہ بے شرمی سے بولا۔

''اس میں شرم کی کیا بات ہے، صبح ہانیہ نے میرے موزے چھپا دیئے تھے۔ میں پورا ایک گھنٹہ اکیڈمی سے لیٹ ہو گیا' اب میرا حق ہے کہ میں اپنا بدلہ لوں۔''

شکایتی لہجے میں کہتے ہی اس نے چھپکلی ہانیہ کی طرف اچھال دی تھی' جواب میں وہ فلک شگاف چیخ مارتے ہوئے خوب زور سے میکال حسن کے ساتھ لپٹ گئی۔ اس کی ٹانگیں اس لمحے بری طرح کپکپا رہی تھیں۔ میکال جھنجلا کر رہ گیا جب کہ ہانیہ کی چیخوں پر مسز حسن اور عینہ بھابی اپنے کمروں سے بھاگتے ہوئے نکلی تھیں۔

''کیا ہوا ہے؟'' نہال جس کا ہنس ہنس کر برا حال ہو رہا تھا۔ ان دونوں کو دیکھتے ہی زبردستی ہنسی روک گیا۔

''کچھ نہیں مما! حساب کتاب کلیئر ہو رہا تھا' وہ دیکھیے ہانیہ کے پیروں میں چھپکلی۔'' ہانیہ کا یہ سننا تھا کہ وہ اور بھی زور و شور سے چیخیں مارنے لگی جب کہ میکال کی پشت کے گرد اس کی گرفت اور بھی سخت ہو گئی تھی۔ اتنی سخت کہ اسے اس کے ناخن اپنے وجود میں گڑتے محسوس ہو رہے تھے۔

''شرم کرو نہال! کیوں فضول میں تنگ کر رہے ہو اسے دیکھو کتنی بری حالت ہو گئی ہے اس کی۔'' عینہ بھابی نے نہال کو ڈپٹتے ہوئے فوراً ہانیہ کی سائیڈ لی تھی، تبھی وہ ہنستے ہوئے بولا۔

''دیکھ رہا ہوں یہ آپ عورتیں جتنا چھپکلی سے ڈرتی ہیں اتنا آخرت اور قبر سے ڈریں تو قسم سے ساری کی ساری بنا ٹکٹ سیدھی جنت میں جائیں۔''

''بہت بدتمیز ہو گئے ہو تم' بھلا اتنا بھونڈا مذاق بھی کرتا ہے کوئی؟'' ہانیہ اب رو رہی تھی جب کہ میکال نرمی سے اپنا آپ چھڑاتا اوپر کمرے کی طرف بڑھ گیا تھا۔ تبھی مسز حسن نہال پر برہم ہوئی تھیں مگر وہ سنی ان سنی کرتا ہانیہ کے قریب چلا آیا۔

''اے...... کیا ہوا؟'' اسے شدت سے روتے دیکھ کر فوراً اس کے دل کو کچھ ہوا تھا' تبھی نرمی سے اس کے ہاتھ تھامے تو ہانیہ نے آنسوؤں سے بھیگے سرخ چہرے کے ساتھ سر اٹھا کر درشتی سے اس کے ہاتھ پرے جھٹک دیئے۔

''شٹ اپ! خبردار اگر دوبارہ تم نے مجھ سے بات کرنے کی کوشش کی تو......'' اس کی آنکھوں سے غصے کی چنگاریاں نکل رہی تھیں' نہال کی جان پر بن گئی۔

''سوری ہانیہ! مجھ سے غلطی ہو گئی۔ دوبارہ ایسے تنگ نہیں کروں گا' وعدہ! پلیز معاف کر دو پلیز۔''

''جسٹ شٹ اپ۔'' تنک کر کہتی وہ اپنے کمرے کی طرف بڑھ گئی تھی جب اس نے اس کا ہاتھ پکڑ لیا۔

''جان لے لوں گا تمہاری اگر مجھ پر ایسی کوئی پابندی لگائی یا سیریسلی ناراض ہوئی تو۔'' اس کی آنکھوں میں نمی جھلک رہی تھی۔ ہانیہ خفگی سے اس کی طرف دیکھتی سیڑھیوں پر بیٹھ گئی۔

''ایک شرط پر معاف کروں گی اور وہ یہ کہ تم شام میں مجھے میری پسند کا ڈنر کراؤ گے وہ بھی میری پسند کے ریستوران میں۔''

''ٹھیک ہے منظور...... سو بار منظور......'' پہلی بار وہ فوری مان گیا تھا' ہانیہ بے ساختہ ہنس پڑی۔

''پاگل!'' مسز حسین اور عینہ بھابی مطمئن انداز میں ایک دوسرے کی طرف دیکھتیں اپنے اپنے کمروں کی طرف بڑھ گئی تھیں۔

اب تیری یاد سے وحشت نہیں ہوتی مجھ کو
زخم کھلتے ہیں اذیت نہیں ہوتی مجھ کو
اب کوئی آئے چلا جائے میں خوش رہتا ہوں
اب کسی شخص کی عادت نہیں ہوتی مجھ کو
ایسا بدلا ہوں تیرے شہر کا پانی پی کر
جھوٹ بولوں تو ندامت نہیں ہوتی مجھ کو
ہے امانت۔ میں خیانت سو کسی کی خاطر
کوئی مرتا ہے تو حیرت نہیں ہوتی مجھ کو
اتنا مصروف ہوں جینے کی ہوس میں اے دوست!
سانس لینے کی بھی فرصت نہیں ہوئی مجھ کو

موسم میں اچانک تبدیلی آئی تھی۔ آناً فاناً آسمان پر بادل چھائے اور ہلکی ہلکی بوندا باندی شروع ہوگئی۔ ثانیہ پچھلے کئی دنوں سے ایمن کی طرف رہ رہی تھی۔ وہیں اس نے فون کر کے اپنی مما کو زائر ملک والے واقعے قصے کے بارے میں بتا دیا تھا۔ ثانیہ کی دوست ایمن کی طرح اس کی مما نے بھی اس سانحے پر غم و غصے کا اظہار کیا تھا۔ وہ بھی زائر سے ان کے نکاح کو کسی طور سچ ماننے کو تیار نہیں تھیں۔

ایمن کی طرح ان کا بھی یہی خیال تھا کہ زائر نے نکاح کے نام پر اسے بے وقوف بنایا ہے' اسی لیے انہوں نے اسے سختی سے تلقین کی تھی کہ جب تک وہ پاکستان نہیں آجاتیں' وہ اکیلی اپنے اپارٹمنٹ نہیں جائے گی۔

ایمن کو بھی انہوں نے اس کا خیال رکھنے کی ہدایت کی تھی۔ ان کی ہدایت کے پیش نظر ہی وہ ایمن کے ساتھ رہ رہی تھی مگر اس روز ایمن کو ایک ضروری سیمینار اٹینڈ کرنا تھا لہٰذا اپنی چند ضروری چیزوں کے لیے مجبوراً اسے اکیلے ہی مارکیٹ آنا پڑا۔ اس کے وہم و گمان میں بھی نہیں تھا کہ شاپنگ سے واپسی پر وہ زائر ملک کی نظروں کے حصار میں آجائے گی اور وہ شخص بے خوف و خطر اسے یوں ڈنکے کی چوٹ پر ہاتھ پکڑ کر اپنے ساتھ لے جائے گا۔

اس وقت وہ ثانیہ کو مارکیٹ سے سیدھا اس کے اپارٹمنٹ لے آیا تھا۔ رف چہرے اور سرد ہاتھوں کے ساتھ ثانیہ عباس کا دل بہت تیزی سے دھڑک رہا تھا۔ عجیب صورت حال بن گئی تھی وہ فون کر کے ایمن کو زائر کے بارے میں مطلع بھی نہ کر سکی' جانے اب وہ اس کے ساتھ کیا سلوک کرنے والا تھا۔ اپارٹمنٹ پر ملازمہ بھی نہ تھی کہ اسی کا حوصلہ ہوتا۔ وہ بہت کنفیوژ حالت میں اس کے ساتھ اندر آئی تھی' جب وہ بولا۔

''دیکھو میرا یقین کرو میری وجہ سے جو کچھ بھی تمہارے ساتھ ہوا میں اس کے لیے تم سے بہت شرمندہ ہوں مگر میں تمہیں نقصان پہنچانے کا سوچ بھی نہیں سکتا۔ یہ رہا نکاح نامہ دکھا دو اپنی دوست کو اور بھی کسی کو دکھانا چاہتی ہو تو دکھا دو۔ مجھے کسی کا ڈر نہیں ہے' ہاں اس روز میں شام کو نہیں آسکا اس کی وجہ یہ تھی کہ یہ نکاح نامہ میرے دوست کے پاس تھا اور وہ ملک سے باہر تھا۔ تم میری عزت ہو ثانیہ! میں تمہارے ساتھ کوئی فراڈ کرنے کا سوچ بھی نہیں سکتا۔''

اس کا ہاتھ پکڑ کر اپارٹمنٹ کے اندر لاتے ہوئے وہ اس کے مقابل بیٹھ گیا تھا۔ ثانیہ کا سر اٹھا کر اس کی طرف دیکھنا محال ہوگیا۔

''تم بھروسا کرتی ہو ناں مجھ پر' ہے ناں؟'' اب وہ اس کے ہاتھ کو دبا رہا تھا۔ ثانیہ نفی میں سر ہلانا چاہتی تھی مگر جانے کیسے اس کا سر اثبات میں ہل گیا۔

''شکریہ...... بہت بہت شکریہ۔''

وہ مسرور ہوا پھر اگلے ہی پل اس نے اس کے دونوں ہاتھ اپنی گرفت میں لے لیے۔

''میں تم سے جھوٹ نہیں بولوں گا ثانیہ! حقیقت یہی ہے کہ مجھے تمہاری ذات میں کوئی دلچسپی نہیں تھی، صرف ایک لمحے کے لیے نفس بہکا اور پھر تمہاری بات دل پر لگ گئی۔ میرا ارادہ یہی تھا کہ میں نکاح کے بعد تمہیں فوری طلاق دے کر یہ کہانی ختم کر دوں گا مگر میں ایسا نہیں کر سکا۔ پچھلے دو ہفتوں سے میں روز یہاں کا چکر لگا رہا ہوں مگر تم مجھے نہیں ملیں میں کوئی پروفیشنل ڈکیت یا لٹیرا نہیں ہوں ثانیہ! میری کہانی صرف اتنی سی ہے کہ میں نے بچپن سے ہی ایک لڑکی کو چاہا اور اس کے خواب دیکھے صرف اس کی خواہشات کی تکمیل کے لیے غلط راستہ اپنایا مگر پھر بھی وہ مجھے نہیں ملی، اس نے صرف اس لیے مجھے ٹھکرا دیا کہ میرے پاس دولت نہیں تھی۔ میں بہت اداس تھا، مجھے لگا شاید مجھے تمہاری بد دعا لگ گئی ہے، اسی لیے میں ہر صورت تم سے مل کر تم سے معافی مانگنا چاہتا تھا مجھے معاف کر دو ثانیہ! پلیز۔''

شدت سے اس کے ہاتھ دباتے ہوئے وہ معافی مانگ رہا تھا۔ ثانیہ بوکھلا کر رہ گئی۔

''تم کہو گی تو میں تمہیں ابھی طلاق دے کر چلا جاؤں گا اگر ایسا نہیں چاہو گی تو میں وعدہ کرتا ہوں میری وجہ سے کبھی تمہاری آنکھوں میں آنسو نہیں آئیں گے، مجھے معاف کر دو ثانیہ! پلیز۔'' کتنا بے بس لگ رہا تھا وہ اس کے سامنے۔ ثانیہ نے اپنے ہاتھ اس کی گرفت سے نکال لیے۔

''آپ ایسا مت کہیں پلیز، میرے ساتھ جو ہوا شاید وہی تقدیر کا لکھا تھا بہر حال میں نے اپنی مما کو سب بتا دیا ہے، وہ کل پاکستان آ رہی ہیں وہی فیصلہ کریں گی کہ مجھے آپ کے ساتھ زندگی گزارنی چاہیے یا نہیں۔'' اس کے لہجے میں ہلکی سی لرزش تھی، زائر گہری سانس بھر کر رہ گیا۔

باہر شام رات میں تبدیل ہو رہی تھی، ہلکی ہلکی بوندا باندی نے ایک دم سے تیز بارش کا روپ دھار لیا تھا، زائر جانے کے لیے اٹھ کھڑا ہوا۔

''ٹھیک ہے تو پھر میں کل ہی آؤں گا، پر اس بار کہیں مت جانا، مجھے زندگی میں دھوکا پسند نہیں ہے۔''

ثانیہ کا سر ہنوز جھکا ہوا تھا، عین اسی لمحے لائٹ چلی گئی۔

''دروازہ بند کر لو بلکہ ہو سکے تو اپنی فرینڈ کو فون کر کے بلا لو، موسم کے تیور ٹھیک نہیں ہیں۔'' وہ اسے تنبیہ کر رہا تھا، ثانیہ نے گھبرا کر اس کی طرف دیکھا پھر آہستہ سے اس کا ہاتھ تھام لیا۔

''ابھی آپ رک جائیں پلیز، مجھے اندھیرے میں اس موسم سے بہت ڈر لگتا ہے۔'' زائر نے اس کی التجا پر ایک نظر اس کے چہرے کی طرف دیکھا پھر ایک نظر باہر طوفان کی صورت اختیار کرتی بارش کو، اس وقت واقعی اس کا وہاں رکنا ضروری تھا۔

✿ ...... ✿ ...... ✿

ہم خوابوں کے بیوپاری تھے، پر اس میں بڑا نقصان ہوا\
کچھ بخت میں ڈھیروں کالک تھی، کچھ اب کے غضب کا کال پڑا\
ہم راکھ لیے ہیں جھولی میں اور سر پر ساہوکار کھڑا\
جب دھرتی صحرا صحرا تھی، ہم دریا دریا روئے تھے\
جب ہاتھ کی ریکھائیں چپ تھیں اور سر سنگیت میں کھوئے تھے\
تب ہم نے جیون ہستی میں کچھ خواب انوکھے بوئے تھے

کچھ خواب سجل مسکانوں کے، کچھ خواب کبت دیوانوں کے
کچھ لفظ جنہیں معافی نہ ملی، کچھ گیت شکستہ مانوں کے
کچھ مہر وفا کی شمعوں کے، کچھ پر پاگل پروانوں کے
کچھ اپنی گھائل ہستی سے خوش ہو کے لہو چھڑکایا تھا
ماٹی میں ماس کی کھاد بھری اور نس نس کو زخمایا تھا
ہم بھول گئے پچھلی رت میں، کیا کھویا تھا، کیا پایا تھا
ہر بار گگن نے وہم دیا
اب کے برکھا جب آئے گی
ہر بیج سے کونپل پھوٹے گی، ہر کونپل پھول کھلائے گی
سر پر چھایا چھتری ہوگی اور دھوپ گھٹا بن جائے گی
جب فصل کٹی تو کیا دیکھا
کچھ درد کے ٹوٹے گجرے تھے
کچھ زخمی خواب تھے کانٹوں پر، کچھ خاکستر سے گجرے تھے
اور دور افق کے ساغر میں
کچھ ڈوبتے، ڈولتے بجرے تھے
اب گھاٹ نہ گھر، دہلیز نہ در
اب پاس رہا ہے کیا بابا
بس تن کی گٹھڑی باقی تھی، جا یہ بھی تُو لے جا بابا
ہم بستی چھوڑے جاتے ہیں تُو اپنا فرض نبھا بابا

موسم میں ایک دم سے تبدیلی آئی تھی۔ باہر کہیں بادل زور سے گرجا تھا۔ زائر کے ہاتھ پر ثانیہ عباس کے ہاتھ کی گرفت مزید مضبوط ہوگئی تھی۔

زائر اس کے خوف کو محسوس کرتا، اگلے ہی پل اس کے مقابل بیٹھ گیا تھا۔

''کیا تمہیں بھی دوسری بہت سی لڑکیوں کی طرح چمکتی بجلی اور گرجتے بادلوں سے ڈر لگتا ہے؟''

''ہوں۔'' وہ صرف سر ہلا سکتی تھی۔ زائر کی آنکھوں میں ایک دم سے سائرہ افضل کا سراپا لہرا گیا۔ وہ بہت نڈر تھی کسی چیز سے نہیں ڈرتی تھی، چھپکلی، کاکروچ، سانپ، چوہا ہر چیز کے پیچھے بھاگ کر جب تک اسے مار نہیں دیتی تھی اسے چین نہیں آتا تھا۔ اکثر شدید خطرناک موسم میں بنا آندھی طوفان کی پروا کیے وہ بڑی بے فکری سے اوپر چھت پر جا کر کپڑے وغیرہ اتار لاتی تھی۔ رات میں لائٹ نہ ہوتی تو سکون سے دیا جلا کر اپنی کڑھائی وغیرہ کا کام مکمل کرتی رہتی ''ڈر'' جیسا لفظ اس کے لیے قطعی ناآشنا تھا۔ شاید اسی لیے اسے اس سے محبت ہوئی تھی کہ اس میں عام لڑکیوں جیسی کوئی بات ہی نہیں تھی اور شاید اسی لیے اس نے بڑی جی داری سے اسے ٹھکرا کر نمبردار کے بیٹے کے ساتھ نکاح کر لیا تھا۔ کوئی پھانس تھی جو اس کے دل میں چبھی تھی، تبھی وہ آہستہ سے اپنا ہاتھ ثانیہ عباس کی گرفت سے نکالتے ہوئے اٹھ کھڑا ہوا تھا۔

''تم بیٹھو میں لائٹ کا انتظام کرتا ہوں۔'' ثانیہ کی اندھیرے میں جان جاتی تھی مگر پھر بھی اس نے اثبات میں سر ہلا دیا تھا۔ وہ لاؤنج میں صوفے پر بیٹھی رہی جب وہ کچن سے کینڈل جلا کر لے آیا۔

''کیا اندھیرے سے بھی ڈر لگتا ہے؟'' کینڈل ٹیبل پر سیٹ کرتے ہوئے بہت سرسری سے لہجے میں اس نے پوچھا تھا جب وہ بولی۔

''ہوں۔''

''اور مجھ سے؟'' اچانک پلٹ کر اس کی طرف دیکھتے ہوئے اس نے اسے کنفیوژ کر دیا تھا۔ ثانیہ کا دل زور سے دھڑک اٹھا۔

''پتا نہیں۔''

''یہ تو کوئی جواب نہ ہوا پلیز بتاؤ ناں مجھ سے بھی ڈر لگتا ہے کہ نہیں؟'' اب وہ پھر سے اس کے مقابل آ بیٹھا تھا۔ ثانیہ سے نظریں اٹھانا دشوار ہو گیا۔

''نہیں۔''

''کیوں؟'' اس کی ''نہیں'' پر بے ساختہ وہ مسکرایا تھا۔

''پتا نہیں۔''

''یہ تو غلط بات ہے یار! اصولاً تو اس وقت سب سے زیادہ ڈر آپ کو مجھ سے ہی لگنا چاہیے کیونکہ اتنے خراب موسم میں جب کہ تنہائی بھی میسر ہو' کچھ بھی ہو سکتا ہے۔''

اس کے خوب صورت لبوں کے گوشوں میں مسکراہٹ دبی تھی' ثانیہ کا چہرہ سرخ ہو گیا۔

''میں جانتی ہوں آپ ایسا کچھ نہیں کریں گے؟''

''کیوں؟'' اب اس کی خوب صورت نگاہوں میں اشتیاق تھا۔ ثانیہ نے رخ پھیر لیا۔

''کیونکہ میں آپ کی منزل نہیں ہوں۔'' زائر نے اس کے جواب پر بے ساختہ گہری سانس بھری تھی پھر اٹھ کر باہر روڈ کی طرف کھلنے والی کھڑکی میں آ کھڑا ہوا۔

''یہاں منزلوں کی خبر کسے ہے ثانیہ جی! سالوں ساتھ چلنے والے ایک لمحے میں ہاتھ چھڑا کر ایک دم سے راستہ بدل لیتے ہیں یوں کہ پھر پیچھے پلٹ کر انہیں آپ کی طرف دیکھنا بھی یاد نہیں رہتا بہر حال مجھے کردار کے معاملے میں ہلکا مت سمجھئے گا کیونکہ عورت کا وجود میری کمزوری نہیں ہے۔ مجھے ابھی تک سمجھ نہیں آ رہا کہ اس روز مجھے کیا ہو گیا تھا۔ سوائے سائرہ کے آج تک میں نے کسی لڑکی کو غور سے نہیں دیکھا نہ مجھے اس میں کوئی دلچسپی ہے' میں زندگی کی آخری سانس تک صرف سائرہ کا ہو کر رہنا چاہتا تھا مگر اس نے میرے پیار کو اس قابل نہیں سمجھا۔ محبت' عزت اور دولت میں سے اس نے دولت کو چن لیا اور تمہیں پتا ہے ناں دو محبت کرنے والے دلوں کے درمیان جب دولت آ جاتی ہے تو کیا ہوتا ہے؟ تقدیر سالوں تک اس دل کی سرزمین پر صرف آنسو ہی آنسو کاشت کرتی ہے اور صدیوں تک آنسو ہی آنسو کاٹتی رہتی ہے۔'' پل میں اس کی خوب صورت غلافی آنکھوں کے گوشے سرخ ہو گئے تھے۔ ثانیہ دل میں عجیب سی کسک محسوس کرتی خاموش بیٹھی رہی۔

''لیکن اسی دل کی سرزمین سے محبت کی بہار جب دستک دے کر بے مراد لوٹ جاتی ہے تو پھر کوئی لاکھ سر پٹختا رہے محبت اس کے لیے کبھی اپنا در وا نہیں کرتی۔ میرے دل میں بھی اب سائرہ کے لیے کوئی خواہش نہیں ہے' وہ محبت جو اس کی ذات سے وابستہ تھی اب میرے دل میں اس کا مقبرہ ہے اور مقبروں پر صرف یادوں کے دیئے جلائے جاتے ہیں' ان کے ساتھ خوابوں کو پیوستہ نہیں کیا جاتا۔''

جانے وہ اسے کیا باور کرانا چاہتا تھا ثانیہ یک ٹک اس کی طرف دیکھتی رہی۔ عین اسی لمحے موسم نے کروٹ بدلی ہلکی

ہلکی بارش نے شدید طوفان کی صورت اختیار کر لی تھی' کھلی کھڑکی سے تیز ہوا کے جھکڑ اسے اچھا خاصا سہما گئے تھے' اس کی صورت دیکھتے ہوئے زائر نے تیزی سے تمام کھلی ہوئی کھڑکیوں کے پٹ بند کر دیئے۔

''اتنے خراب موسم میں جب کہ ملازمہ بھی ساتھ نہ ہو آپ کو یہاں اکیلے نہیں رہنا چاہیے۔'' وہ رخ پھیرے کھڑا تھا' ثانیہ اس کے ''تم'' اور ''آپ'' میں الجھتی سر جھکا گئی۔

''میں تنہا نہیں رہتی' ملازمہ گاؤں گئی ہوئی ہے اور میں ایمن کی طرف رہتی ہوں۔ ابھی بارکیٹ سے سیدھے وہیں جانا تھا مگر آپ زبردستی یہاں لے آئے۔''

''ایمن کی طرف کیوں رہتی ہیں آپ؟'' اس کی وضاحت پر وہ حیرانی سے پلٹا تھا جب وہ بولی۔

''لاسٹ ٹائم جب آپ یہاں آئے تھے تو وہ بہت ڈر گئی تھی اس کا کہنا ہے کہ آپ نے مجھ سے نکاح کا محض ڈرامہ کیا تھا ورنہ فلموں' ڈراموں میں بھی ایسا نہیں ہوتا کہ کوئی چوری کی نیت سے آپ کے گھر میں گھسے اور پھر نیت خراب ہونے پر آپ کی منت کی لاج رکھتے ہوئے آپ سے نکاح کر لے' اسی لیے وہ نہیں چاہتی کہ آپ دوبارہ میری تذلیل کرنے کے لیے یہاں آئیں اور میں آپ کو یہاں ملوں۔''

ثانیہ کے الفاظ نے اسے بے ساختہ ہنسنے پر مجبور کیا تھا۔ تبھی روشن نگاہیں اس کے خوب صورت سراپا پر جمائے وہ اس کے قریب آیا اور اپنے دونوں ہاتھ اس کے شانوں پر دھر دیئے۔

''کس چیز پر اعتراض ہے اسے میرے شرافت سے نکاح کرنے پر یا بقول اس کے دوبارہ تذلیل پر؟''

''دونوں پر۔'' بنا سر اٹھائے اس نے جواب دیا تھا' زائر پھر ہنس دیا۔

''پگلی ہو تم دونوں اور کچھ نہیں۔'' ایک ہلکی سی چپت اس کے سر پر لگاتے ہوئے اس نے سر جھٹکا تھا تبھی ثانیہ کا صوفے پر دھرا سیل وائبریٹ کرنے لگا اس نے جلدی سے اٹھا کر کال پک کر لی۔

''ہیلو۔''

''کہاں مر گئی ہو' تمہیں پتا ہے میں پچھلے دو گھنٹوں سے پاگلوں کی طرح تمہارے سیل پر کالز کر رہی ہوں' کیوں نہیں اٹھا رہیں تم۔'' اس کی آواز سے اس کی پریشانی کا اندازہ لگایا جا سکتا تھا۔ وہ گہری سانس بھر کر رہ گئی۔

''سوری ایمن! میرا سیل سائلنٹ پر تھا تمہاری کالز کا پتا ہی نہیں چلا۔''

''کیوں؟ تم کیا انڈے سینکنے بیٹھ گئی تھیں جو سیل کو سائلنٹ پر لگا چھوڑا۔''

''نہیں یار! موسم اچانک بہت خراب ہو گیا تھا' میں مارکیٹ سے سیدھی ادھر اپارٹمنٹ میں ہی آ گئی' ابھی تھوڑی دیر میں' میں بس تمہیں کال کرنے ہی والی تھی۔''

''جسٹ شٹ اپ! میری طرف سے بھاڑ میں جاؤ تم۔'' وہ اس سے شدید خفا تھی تبھی چنگھاڑتے ہوئے کال ڈراپ کر گئی تو ثانیہ نے بھی سیل آف کر دیا۔ وہ اپنی اس دوست کے مزاج اور غصے سے بہت اچھی طرح واقف تھی۔ اس وقت اگر زائر وہاں نہ ہوتا تو یقیناً وہ اسے فوری کال بیک کر کے مناتی' پوری وضاحت دیتی مگر اس وقت وہ خود اس سے بچنا چاہتی تھی' تبھی سیل آف کر کے رکھ دیا۔ اس بات سے قطعی بے نیاز کہ ایمن اس کے لیے پوری رات کتنی پریشان رہے گی۔

''کیا کہہ رہی تھی ایمن؟'' اس کے گہری سانس بھرنے پر زائر پوچھے بغیر نہیں رہ سکا تھا۔ ثانیہ نے ایک نظر اسے دیکھ کر رخ پھیر لیا۔

''کچھ نہیں' پریشان ہو رہی تھی میں نے اسے مطلع نہیں کیا تھا ناں کہ میں ادھر آ گئی ہوں اس لیے۔''

''ہوں......پھر؟''

''پھر کچھ نہیں، وہ اس وقت غصے میں ہے میں نے اپنا سیل آف کر دیا۔''

''لیکن میرے خیال میں آپ کو ایسا نہیں کرنا چاہیے تھا بلکہ اسے بتانا چاہیے تھا کہ اس وقت میں آپ کے ساتھ ہوں۔''

''نہیں اگر میں یہ بتا دیتی تو اس نے اپنی اور میری جان ایک کر دینی تھی۔ میرے معاملے میں وہ بہت پوزیسو ہے، صبح مما کے آنے کے بعد میں اس سے بات کروں گی۔''

''چلیں ٹھیک ہے، جو آپ بہتر سمجھیں۔'' گہری سانس بھر کر کہتے ہوئے وہ اس کے پہلو میں ہی صوفے پر ٹک گیا تھا۔

''ایک بات پوچھوں ثانیہ؟'' کچھ لمحوں کی خاموشی کے بعد اس نے پوچھا تھا۔

''جی۔''

''صبح اگر آپ کی مما نے مجھ سے ملنے کے بعد ہمارے نکاح نامے کو ریجیکٹ کر دیا اور مجھے پسند نہ کیا تو کیا آپ مجھ سے کنارہ کشی اختیار کر لیں گی؟''

''ہاں۔'' ایک لمحے کے توقف کے بعد اس نے فوری فیصلہ سنا دیا تھا۔ زائر کے دل کو دھچکا سا لگا۔

''اور اگر میں ایسا نہ چاہوں تو؟''

''آپ ایسا نہ چاہیں تب بھی میں وہی کروں گی جو میری مما کہیں گی۔''

''کیوں؟ کیا میں اتنا برا ہوں؟''

''میں نے کب کہا؟'' اب وہ سر اٹھائے اس کی آنکھوں میں دیکھ رہی تھی۔ زائر نے پلکیں موند کر سر صوفے کی پشت گاہ سے ٹکا دیا۔

''ہم کو حسرت ہی رہی ٹوٹ کے چاہے جاتے
دل میں بس جاتے تو ہرگز نہ بھلائے جاتے
میری دنیا میں کوئی ایک تو ایسا ہوتا
روح کے گھاؤ جسے رو کے دکھائے جاتے
آپ آئے ہیں تو ڈھارس سی بندھی ہے ورنہ
ہم سے یہ ہجر کے صدمے نہ اٹھائے جاتے''

آنکھیں بند کیے بہت جذب کے عالم میں وہ یہ غزل اسے سنا رہا تھا۔ ثانیہ یک ٹک اس کے چہرے کے خوب صورت نقوش کو دیکھتی بے چین سی اٹھ کھڑی ہوئی۔

''میرا خیال ہے آپ نے شام سے کچھ نہیں کھایا ہوگا، میں آپ کے لیے چائے بنا کر لاتی ہوں۔'' جانے کیوں اس لمحے زائر ملک کی قربت اسے کمزور کر رہی تھی تبھی فرار چاہا تو زائر نے پٹ سے آنکھیں کھول دیں۔

''کیوں، اب ڈر نہیں لگے گا؟''

''نہیں۔'' اس کی پلکیں ہولے ہولے لرز رہی تھیں، وہ مسکرایا۔

''ٹھیک ہے جائیے، میری نیک تمنائیں آپ کے ساتھ ہیں۔''

ٹیبل سے کینڈل اٹھا کر اسے تھماتے ہوئے وہ شرارتی ہوا تھا۔ ثانیہ بنا اس کی آنکھوں میں دیکھے خاموشی سے کچن کی

طرف بڑھ گئی۔ کیبنٹ میں کھانے پینے کی مختلف چیزوں کے ساتھ خشک دودھ کے ڈبے بھی رکھے تھے اس نے چولہا جلا کر پانی بوائل کیا پھر کیبنٹ سے بسکٹ نکال کر ٹرے میں کپ ترتیب دینے لگی۔

اگلے دس منٹ میں جس وقت اس نے زائر کے سامنے ٹیبل پر ٹرے رکھی، جانے اس کے منہ میں کیا آیا کہ اٹھ کر اسے چھیڑ بیٹھا۔

''ثانیہ......تمہارے پاؤں میں چھپکلی۔''

اس کا یہ کہنا تھا اور ثانیہ کا چیخ مار کر اس کی طرف لپکنا تھا۔ زائر ہنس رہا تھا جب کہ وہ زرد پتے کی طرح کانپتی اس کے بازو سے لگی تھی۔ اس لمحے ثانیہ عباس کے دل کی تیز دھڑکنوں کو وہ اپنے وجود میں اترتا محسوس کر رہا تھا۔

''پاگل لڑکی ہو تم ثانیہ عباس اور کچھ نہیں۔'' ثانیہ سمجھ گئی تھی کہ اس نے مذاق کیا ہے، شاید تبھی اس کی آنکھیں آنسوؤں سے بھر گئی تھی۔ زائر اس کی آنکھوں میں نمی دیکھ کر شرمندگی محسوس کر رہا تھا مگر اس نے ثانیہ عباس سے کچھ نہیں کہا، چائے پینے کے دوران وہ بہت خاموشی سے اسے دیکھتا رہا تھا۔

بارش کا زور ٹوٹ چکا تھا تاہم تیز ہوا کے جھکڑ اب بھی بند کھڑکیوں کے کواڑوں پر دستک دے رہے تھے۔ ثانیہ چائے پینے کے بعد برتن کچن میں رکھ کر آئی تو وہ اس کا ہاتھ تھامتے ہوئے اٹھ کھڑا ہوا۔

''مجھے نیند آ رہی ہے پلیز سلا دیں۔''

''مم......میں؟'' وہ اس کی عجیب وغریب فرمائش پر حیران ہی تو رہ گئی تھی۔

''جی ہاں آپ۔''

''لل......لیکن میں آپ کو کیسے سلا سکتی ہوں؟''

''ادھر آئیں، میں بتا دیتا ہوں۔'' اس کا ہاتھ تھام کر بیڈ روم کی طرف بڑھتے ہوئے اس نے کہا تھا، وہ ہکا بکا سی اسے دیکھتی رہ گئی۔

''آپ کو نہیں پتا، پچھلے تین ہفتوں سے میں بہت بے سکون ہوں۔'' بیڈ پر لیٹ کر اسے اپنے پہلو میں بٹھاتے ہوئے وہ بہت سنجیدگی سے اسے کہہ رہا تھا۔ ثانیہ کی جان مشکل میں پھنس گئی۔

''میں جانتا ہوں آپ کو میری ذات میں دلچسپی نہیں ہے، ہونی بھی نہیں چاہیے۔ ایک قطعی اجنبی شخص جس کے بارے میں آپ کچھ بھی نہ جانتے ہوں بھلا اس کی ذات سے آپ کو کیا دلچسپی ہو سکتی ہے مگر ہمارے بیچ ایک تعلق تو ہے ناں ثانیہ؟''

اس کے لہجے میں عجیب سی آنچ تھی۔ ثانیہ کا دل اس کی سماعتوں میں دھڑکنے لگا۔ وہ ہرگز نہیں جانتی تھی کہ اس کا کیا ارادہ ہے؟ اگر جانتی ہوتی تو شاید کبھی اس کے قریب نہ بیٹھتی۔ اس کا ایک ہاتھ زائر کی گرفت میں تھا جب کہ دوسرے ہاتھ سے وہ اب اس کے بال سہلا رہی تھی۔ زائر نے دھیرے سے پلکیں موند لیں۔ بہت دنوں کے بعد اسے سکون محسوس ہو رہا تھا اور اب وہ کبھی اس سکون کو کھونے کا رسک نہیں لے سکتا تھا۔

چند لمحے پہلے ثانیہ نے اسے اپنا فیصلہ سنا دیا تھا، صبح سورج کی پھوٹتی کرنوں کے ساتھ کچھ بھی ہو سکتا تھا۔ ثانیہ عباس کی ماں اسے ہمیشہ کے لیے اپنی بیٹی سے دور کر کے پھر سے بے سکون کر سکتی تھی تبھی اپنے اور اس کے رشتے کو مضبوط کرنے کے لیے اس نے اپنے دونوں ہاتھ ثانیہ عباس کے کندھوں پر جماتے ہوئے اسے اپنے اوپر گرا لیا، وہ اس کی گرفت میں ذرا سی کسمسائی تھی مگر زائر نے پروا کیے بغیر حصار مزید مضبوط کر دیا۔

''مجھے غلط مت سمجھنا ثانیہ! مگر اپنے رشتے کو بچانے کے لیے میں کچھ بھی کر سکتا ہوں۔''

''نہیں......آپ نے وعدہ کیا تھا' آپ ایسا کچھ نہیں کریں گے۔''
وہ گھبرائی تھی تبھی اس نے آنکھیں کھول دیں۔
''وہ وعدہ اس وقت کیا تھا' جب مقصد صرف اپنی خواہش کا حصول تھا مگر اب میرا ارادہ بدل گیا ہے اب میں ہمیشہ تمہیں اپنی زندگی میں شامل دیکھنا چاہتا ہوں اور یہ تبھی ممکن ہے جب تمہارے پیروں میں میری محبت کی زنجیر ہو' ایسی زنجیر جس کی وجہ سے تم چاہتے ہوئے بھی مجھ سے الگ نہ رہ سکو۔''
وہ شخص ذہین بھی تھا اور شاطر بھی۔ ثانیہ اس کا ارادہ جان کر دنگ رہ گئی تھی۔
''میں ایسا نہیں کر سکتی' میں نے اپنی مما سے وعدہ کیا ہے میں ان کے اعتبار کو ٹھیس نہیں پہنچا سکتی۔''
''مگر میں تمہارا شوہر ہوں' قانونی اور شرعی شوہر۔ تم میرے حکم سے سرتابی نہیں کر سکتیں۔''
''کر سکتی ہوں کیونکہ یہ رشتہ صرف نفس کی خواہش پر قائم ہوا تھا' دل کی خواہش پر نہیں۔''
اس کی بانہوں میں مچلتے ہوئے اس نے اپنا آپ اس سے چھڑا لیا تھا۔
''مگر اب اس میں دل کی خواہش بھی شامل ہے۔''
پھر سے اس کے آنچل کو تھامتے ہوئے وہ بے خود ہوا تھا۔ ثانیہ سٹپٹا کر رہ گئی' وہ اٹھ کر بھاگنا چاہتی تھی مگر زائر ملک نے اسے اتنا موقع نہیں دیا تھا۔ وہ ٹھان چکا تھا کہ اسے کیا کرنا ہے تبھی ثانیہ کی التجاؤں اور آنسوؤں کا بھی اس پر کوئی اثر نہیں ہوا تھا۔ صبح میں ابھی چند ہی ساعتیں باقی تھیں جب وہ اٹھ کر کمرے سے نکل گیا۔
اگلے پچیس منٹ کے بعد فریش ہو کر وہ دوبارہ کمرے میں آیا تو ثانیہ کے آنسو سسکیوں میں ڈھل چکے تھے۔
''تم ایک بے ہودہ' جنگلی انسان ہو' میں لعنت بھیجتی ہوں تمہاری رفاقت پر' یاد رکھنا' تم میں وہ کبھی نہیں ہونے دوں گی جو تم چاہتے ہو، سنا تم نے۔''
اسے کمرے میں داخل ہوتے دیکھ کر ہی وہ چلائی تھی' زائر شرمندہ سا اس کے مقابل جا بیٹھا۔
''ایم سوری ثانیہ......میں......''
''جسٹ شٹ اپ! میں اس وقت تمہاری صورت بھی نہیں دیکھنا چاہتی۔''
وہ رو رہی تھی' زائر اس کے ابتر حال پر ایک نظر ڈالتا' خاموشی سے کمرے سے نکل آیا۔
اگلے دو گھنٹوں کے بعد وہ ثانیہ کے اپارٹمنٹ میں اس کی ماں اور دوست ایمن کے مقابل بیٹھا انہیں اپنے بارے میں بتا رہا تھا۔
''میں مانتا ہوں میں نے ثانیہ کو پانے کے لیے جو طریقہ اپنایا وہ ٹھیک نہیں تھا مگر حقیقت یہی ہے کہ میں دل سے ان کی عزت کرتا ہوں اور ہمیشہ کرتا رہوں گا۔''
''ہمیں تمہاری عزت سے کوئی لینا دینا نہیں' ثانیہ امیر باپ کی بیٹی ہے۔ پیدا ہونے سے لے کر اب تک محلوں میں رہی ہے' سونے کے چمچ سے کھایا ہے' شاندار گاڑیوں میں گھومی ہے۔ تمہارے پاس کیا ہے اسے دینے کے لیے' ایک ٹوٹی پھوٹی چاردیواری' گھڑے کا ٹھنڈا پانی اور رات کی باسی روٹی؟''
وہ تلوار جو سائرہ افضل نے اس کے دل پر چلائی تھی۔ وہی تلوار ثانیہ کی مما کے ہاتھ میں تھی' زائر کا دل کٹ کر رہ گیا۔
''آپ صحیح کہہ رہی ہیں میرے پاس واقعی وہ دولت نہیں ہے جس کا آپ ذکر کر رہی ہیں مگر زندگی گزارنے کے لیے صرف یہی دولت کافی نہیں ہوتی۔ ایک دولت اور بھی ہوتی ہے' محبت کی دولت، جو بہت کم ماؤں کی بیٹیوں کو نصیب ہوتی ہے مگر جس کے لیے ہر ماں دعا میں ہاتھ اٹھا کر اللہ سے دعا کرتی ہے۔''

”تم اپنی محبت اپنے پاس سنبھال کر رکھو کیونکہ جس محبت پر تم اتنا اترا رہے ہو وہ محبت میری بیٹی چند ٹکوں میں خرید سکتی ہے۔“

”میری محبت نہیں خرید سکتی آپ کی بیٹی! اپنا آپ بیچ دے تب بھی نہیں۔“

ایک لمحے میں وہ مشتعل ہوا تھا۔ ثانیہ کی مما ناگواری سے اسے دیکھ کر رہ گئیں۔

”زیادہ جنگلی پن دکھانے کی ضرورت نہیں ہے، بہتر ہوگا تم میری بیٹی کو طلاق دو اور یہاں سے دفع ہو جاؤ۔“

ایمن ثانیہ کے ساتھ بیٹھی تھی، زائر کی آنکھیں لمحوں میں سرخ ہو گئیں۔

”سوری! میں ایسا نہیں کر سکتا۔“

”تو ٹھیک ہے ہم کورٹ سے رجوع کر لیں گے خلع کے لیے۔“

اب وہ اسے دھمکی دے رہی تھیں، وہ مضطرب سا اٹھ کھڑا ہوا۔

”کر لیں رجوع، میں دیکھتا ہوں دنیا کی کون سی عدالت مجھے آپ کی بیٹی سے الگ کرتی ہے۔“

اپنی بات مکمل کرتے ہی وہ بیرونی دروازے کی طرف بڑھا تھا پھر کچھ یاد آنے پر پلٹا اور ثانیہ عباس کے قریب آ کھڑا ہوا۔

”ایک بات یاد رکھنا ثانیہ! جب میں نفس کا غلام ہوا تھا تو تم نے مجھے خدا یاد دلایا تھا، آج میں بھی وہی کر رہا ہوں اگر میری وجہ سے تم نے کسی معصوم کی جان لی تو یاد رکھنا میں تمہیں تمہارے اس گناہ کے لیے کبھی معاف نہیں کروں گا اور شاید میرا خدا بھی تمہیں معاف نہ کرے۔“

لہجے اور آنکھوں میں ڈھیروں اضطراب لیے اسے خبردار کرنے کے بعد وہ پھر وہاں ٹھہرا نہیں تھا۔

اگلے چند دنوں میں مسز عباس نے عدالت میں خلع کے لیے کیس دائر کروا دیا مگر زائر ملک تو ایسا غائب ہوا کہ پھر پلٹ کر خبر ہی نہیں لی تبھی وہ کیس ختم کر کے ثانیہ کو اپنے ساتھ انگلینڈ لے آئیں، انہی دنوں ثانیہ کی طبیعت خراب رہنا شروع ہو گئی تھی۔

ثانیہ چیک اپ کروانے کے حق میں نہیں تھی، اسے خوف تھا کہ کہیں زائر ملک کی مراد پوری نہ ہو جائے مگر...... کب تک؟

اس روز طبیعت زیادہ خراب ہونے پر بالآخر اسے مسز عباس کے ساتھ ڈاکٹر کے پاس جانا پڑا تھا اور پھر وہی ہوا جس کا اسے ڈر تھا، وہ تین ہفتوں کی حاملہ تھی۔ مسز عباس نے اسے ابارشن کا مشورہ دیا تھا، وہ خود بھی یہی چاہتی تھی مگر پھر زائر کے الفاظ نے اسے روک دیا اگر زائر جیسا آزاد منش، پینڈو شخص اللہ کی قائم کردہ حدود کا خیال رکھ سکتا تھا تو پھر وہ تو اس سے زیادہ پرہیزگار، پڑھی لکھی تھی۔

اشعر علی کو بھی اس کے نکاح اور پھر حاملہ ہونے کا پتا چل چکا تھا تبھی وہ جیسے ٹوٹ پھوٹ کر رہ گیا، اس کا بس نہ چلتا تھا کہ ثانیہ کو شوٹ کر ڈالے۔ کتنی بڑی بے ایمانی کی تھی اس لڑکی نے اس کے ساتھ۔ وہ ہرگز اسے معاف کرنے والا نہیں تھا۔ مسز عباس کو اس کے ارادوں کی خبر ہو گئی تھی تبھی وہ بیٹی کو لے کر ایک رات چپکے سے پاکستان چلی آئیں یوں کہ ان کے سسرال کو بھی کانوں کان خبر نہ ہو سکی۔ ثانیہ ابارشن کے حق میں نہیں تھی جب کہ وہ ہر صورت یہ ابارشن کروانا چاہتی تھیں مگر ایسا نہیں ہو سکا تھا۔

❁......❁......❁

کبھی وہ مجھ سے کہتا تھا کہ میری زندگی تم ہو

تم ہی ہو آرزو میری' میری تو ہر خوشی تم ہو
نہ دیکھوں میں اگر تم کو تو آنکھیں نور ہی کھو دیں
میری آنکھوں میں جانِ جاں چمکتی روشنی تم ہو
مجھے ہر خوف سے ہٹ کر یہ دنیا کو بتانا ہے
کہ اپنے پیار کا بندھن تو صدیوں سے پرانا ہے
ہمیں اک دوسرے کی ذات کی تکمیل کرنی ہے
سمندر کے کنارے پھر ہمیں اک گھر بنانا ہے
وہ گھر جس میں بہاروں' خوشبوؤں' رنگوں کا میلہ ہو
یہاں سے دور سبزے میں وہ گھر اپنا اکیلا ہو
میں ہر صبح تمہاری آنکھ سے دیکھوں حسیں منظر
تمہارے حسن کا جادو میری آنکھوں میں پھیلا ہو
مگر پھر یوں ہوا حالات نے اس کو بدل ڈالا
بھلا کر اس کی سب باتیں ہمارا دل کچل ڈالا
بنائے ساحلوں پر گھر سمندر سے حسین اس کے
مگر وائے مقدر کہ بدل ڈالے مکین اس کے
کسی کا ہاتھ ہاتھوں میں وہ لے کر اب بھی چلتا ہے
مگر جب تنہا ملتا ہے تو بس اتنا ہی کہتا ہے
سنو......
بچھڑ کے تم سے جو دل پر لگا ہے گھاؤ گہرا ہے
ہمارے دل کی وادی میں جہاں تھا راج خوشیوں کا
وہاں اب ''درد'' ٹھہرا ہے

عینا کمال اپنے شوہر کمال حسن کے پاس انگلینڈ واپس جا چکی تھیں۔ میکال کا ارادہ بھی وہیں شفٹ ہونے کا تھا کیونکہ عائشہ اذہان کی کنارہ کشی کے بعد اس کا پاکستان میں دل ہی نہیں لگ رہا تھا۔ مگر اچانک حسن صاحب کی طبیعت ناساز ہوگئی تھی لہٰذا مجبوراً اسے اپنا ارادہ ملتوی کرنا پڑا تھا تاہم وہ بہت اپ سیٹ ہو کر رہ گیا تھا۔

اس روز موسم بہت خوب صورت ہو رہا تھا۔ ہانیہ اور نہال اس وقت ایوننگ واک پر نکلے تھے۔ ہانیہ آج کل نہال سے گاڑی ڈرائیو کرنا سیکھ رہی تھی۔ جاتی گرمیوں اور آتی سردیوں کے ان اداس دنوں میں سرسبز درختوں نے شفاف سڑک پر ڈھیروں زرد پتے بکھیر دیئے تھے۔ انہی پتوں پر قدم قدم نہال حسن کے ساتھ پیدل چلتے ہوئے ہانیہ اس سے کہہ رہی تھی۔

''پتا ہے نہال! دنیا میں محبت سے زیادہ دلچسپ اور عجیب چیز اور کوئی نہیں' جسے یہ مل جاتی ہے اسے خوب صورت بنا دیتی ہے اور جس سے یہ چھن جاتی ہے اسے پتھر بنا کر رکھ دیتی ہے' میں نے دیکھے ہیں محبت کی بستی میں پتھر ہوئے لوگ۔''

لانگ شرٹ اور ٹراؤزر میں ملبوس' دونوں بازو سینے پر باندھے وہ بہت سنجیدہ دکھائی دے رہی تھی۔ نہال نے سڑک

کے وسط میں پڑا پتھر پاؤں کی ٹھوکر سے دور اچھال دیا۔

''مجھے لگتا ہے تم میکال بھیا کے ساتھ شادی پر خوش نہیں ہو' ہے ناں ہانی؟''

''ہوں۔'' پہلی بار اس کے قیاس پر اس نے یوں اعتراف کیا تھا' وہ چونک اٹھا۔

''ہانی......''

''ہاں نہال! میں میکال حسن کے ساتھ زبردستی اس بندھن پر خوش نہیں ہوں۔ ہر روز رات میں ایک ہی بیڈ پر اس کے پہلو میں لیٹی' میں اپنی بے بسی پر تڑپ تڑپ کر روتی ہوں' میرا بس نہیں چلتا کہ میں اپنا چہرہ نوچ لوں' مجھے آئینے میں اپنے چہرے سے زیادہ بھیانک اور کوئی چیز نظر نہیں آتی۔ میں عذاب بن کر ایک ناپسندیدگی کے تاثر کے ساتھ اس کے سر پر سوار نہیں رہنا چاہتی۔ کوئی مجھے ایک بار نظر انداز کرے تو میں اسے دس بار نظر انداز کرتی ہوں مگر میں کیا کروں' پاپا نے تو جیسے کسی ناکردہ گناہ کی طرح میرے وجود کو اپنی زندگی سے نکال پھینکا ہے' میں انہیں کبھی معاف نہیں کروں گی' اس زیادتی کے لیے میں انہیں کبھی معاف نہیں کروں گی۔''

پہلی بار وہ جذباتی دکھائی دے رہی تھی' نہال شاکڈ رہ گیا۔

''ہانی...... یہ کیا کہہ رہی ہو؟''

''پتا نہیں۔'' سنگی بنچ پر بیٹھ کر وہ اب رونے لگی تھی۔ وہ پریشان ہو گیا۔

''ہانی پلیز مجھے بتاؤ کیا ہوا ہے' کیا میکال بھیا نے تم سے کچھ کہا ہے؟''

''نہیں۔''

''تو پھر تم نے یہ سب کیوں کہا' میں مانتا ہوں تمہارے ساتھ زیادتی ہوئی ہے مگر میکال بھیا بھی اس شادی کے لیے خوش نہیں تھے پھر بھی پتا نہیں کیوں مما پاپا نے اسے اپنی انا کا مسئلہ بنالیا' مجھے یہ سب پسند نہیں ہے۔ ماں باپ کے فیصلوں کی اہمیت اپنی جگہ مگر انہیں اپنے بچوں کی زندگیوں کو یوں ضد اور انا کا مسئلہ نہیں بنالینا چاہیے۔''

سر جھٹکتے ہوئے وہ بھی جذباتی ہوا تھا۔ ہانیہ نے آنسو پونچھ لیے۔

''شاید اسے ہی تقدیر کا لکھا کہتے ہیں' خدا ایسے ہی اپنے بندوں کو دکھاتا ہے کہ وہ ہے مگر میں بھی ہار ماننے والوں میں سے نہیں ہوں۔ میں دکھاؤں گی میکال حسن کو کہ ہانیہ صفدر بھی کسی سے کم نہیں ہے۔''

''ہوں' یہ ہوئی ناں بات۔ میں اپنی ہانی کو کسی بھی محاذ پر کبھی شکستہ نہیں دیکھ سکتا۔''

وہ خوش ہوا تھا۔ ہانیہ گہری سانس بھر کر رہ گئی' تبھی وہ بولا تھا۔

''ہادیہ کی کال آئی تھی کل میرے نمبر پر' تمہیں لے کر وہ بہت ڈسٹرب ہے شاید رو بھی رہی تھی' تم اس سے بات کیوں نہیں کرنا چاہتی۔ وہ تمہاری بہترین دوست ہے ہانی! تم میکال بھیا کی زیادتی کا بدلہ اس سے کیوں لے رہی ہو؟''

''پتا نہیں۔'' اس بار نہال کے سوال پر بے زاری جتاتے ہوئے وہ فوراً اٹھ کھڑی ہوئی تھی' نہال بھی ساتھ ہی اٹھ کھڑا ہوا۔

''یہ ٹھیک نہیں ہے ہانیہ! مانا اس نے تمہارے اعتماد کو ٹھیس پہنچائی ہے مگر دوستوں کو یوں چھوٹی چھوٹی خطاؤں پر زندگی سے نکال پھینکنا درست نہیں ہے' وہ بتا رہی تھی کہ انکل اور آنٹی بھی تمہارے سلوک کو لے کر بہت پریشان ہیں اور شاید جاذب بھی' انکل کا ارادہ ہے کہ تمہارے فرض سے سبکدوش ہونے کے بعد وہ اب ہادیہ اور جاذب کی نیا بھی پار لگا دیں مگر صرف تمہاری وجہ سے یہ نیک کام التوا کا شکار ہو رہا ہے۔''

''کیوں' کیا میں نے ان کی خوشیوں پر پابندی لگا رکھی ہے؟''

''نہیں، لیکن جس طرح سے شادی کے بعد تم ایک بار بھی وہاں نہیں گئیں، انہیں لگتا ہے تم شادی پر بھی نہیں جاؤ گی تبھی وہ تمہارا غصہ ٹھنڈا ہونے کا انتظار کر رہے ہیں۔''

''مگر مجھے کوئی غصہ نہیں ہے، یہ میری زندگی ہے اور میرے خیال سے اسے اپنی مرضی اور اختیار سے گزارنے کا حق بھی میرے پاس ہونا چاہیے۔''

''رائٹ......لیکن......''

''پلیز اسٹاپ اٹ نہال! بہتر ہوگا کہ ہم اس ٹاپک پر کوئی بات نہ کریں، میں منافق نہیں ہوں میرا دل اگر ان لوگوں سے ملنے کو نہیں چاہتا تو میں زبردستی وہاں جا کر ان کے ساتھ گھل مل کر نہیں رہ سکتی۔ پتا نہیں یہ لوگ مجھے میرے حال پر چھوڑ کیوں نہیں دیتے۔''

وہ بہت زیادہ قنوطیت اور بے زاری کا شکار ہو رہی تھی۔ نہال گہری سانس بھر کر رہ گیا۔

''ہوں، میں سمجھ سکتا ہوں، دلوں میں فرق آ جائے تو پھر تعلق نبھائے نہیں جاتے، گھسیٹے جاتے ہیں۔''

بہت دھیمے لہجے میں وہ بہت گہری بات کہہ گیا تھا۔ ہانیہ کی آنکھیں پھر بھرّانے لگیں۔

اسے اس وقت اپنی ذات اور سڑک پر بکھرے زرد پتوں میں کوئی فرق محسوس نہیں ہو رہا تھا۔

بہت سے دن اداسیوں کی نذر کرنے کے بعد اس روز پھر اس کی میکال سے مڈ بھیڑ ہو گئی تھی۔ وہ کمپیوٹر کے سامنے بیٹھا تھا، ہانیہ چپکے سے اس کے پہلو میں آ کر بیٹھ گئی۔

''کیا ہو رہا ہے؟'' بہت لگاوٹ سے اس نے پوچھا تھا مگر میکال نے حسب توقع نہ اس کی طرف دیکھا، نہ اس کے سوال کا جواب دیا۔

''میرا اکاؤنٹ بھی بنا دیں فیس بک پر پلیز۔''

اگلے ہی پل شرارت سے کہتے ہوئے اس نے اپنا سر اس کے کندھے پر دھر دیا تھا جب کہ اس کے بازو میکال کے بازو کے گرد لپٹے تھے مگر وہ اب بھی خاموشی سے اپنے کام میں مصروف رہا تھا۔

''اف......! ایک ہزار فرینڈ ہیں آپ کے اکاؤنٹ میں، میں عائشہ جی کو بتاؤں گی۔''

''جسٹ شٹ اپ، او کے۔''

اس بار وہ بھنایا تھا۔ ہانیہ تذلیل کے باوجود ڈھٹائی سے مسکرا دی۔

''اتنا ڈرتے ہیں عائشہ جی سے، ویسے محبت واقعی انسان کو بہت کمزور کر دیتی ہے، ہے ناں؟''

''میرا دماغ مت کھاؤ، جا کر سو جاؤ چپ چاپ۔''

کتنی بے زاری اور نفرت تھی اس شخص کے لہجے میں، ہانیہ کا دل کٹ کر رہ گیا۔ مگر پھر بھی وہ بہت ضبط سے بولی تھی۔

''کیسے سو جاؤں، نیند ہی نہیں آ رہی۔ آپ آ کر سلا دیں پلیز......''

''اتنا فضول ٹائم نہیں ہے میرے پاس۔''

''تو ٹھیک ہے پھر میں بھی یہیں بیٹھی رہوں گی آپ کے پاس، چاہے پوری رات بیت جائے۔''

''تم اپنی حد سے بڑھ رہی ہو ہانیہ صفدر!''

اس بار سلگ کر کمپیوٹر شٹ ڈاؤن کرتے ہوئے وہ اس کے پہلو سے اٹھ گیا تھا۔ ہانیہ کے لبوں پر پھیکی سی مسکان بکھر گئی۔

''اچھا، کیا ہیں میری حدود؟''

اس نے پوچھا تھا مگر میکال حسن جواب دینے کی بجائے بیڈ پر چت لیٹ گیا تھا۔ جانے کیوں اس لمحے اسے روشنی سے وحشت ہو رہی تھی۔ آنکھوں پر بازو رکھ کر اس نے خود کو ہانیہ صفدر سے لاتعلق ظاہر کیا تھا مگر وہ اس بے زاری پر بھی اٹھ کر اپنی جگہ پر جانے کے بجائے اس کے پہلو میں آ بیٹھی تھی۔

''میں نہیں جانتی میکال کہ آپ زندگی میں کبھی مجھ سے محبت کریں گے یا نہیں مگر مجھے اس بات کی بہت خوشی ہے کہ آپ نے عائشہ جی سے محبت کا حق ادا کر دیا۔''

اس بار یاسیت سے کہتے ہوئے اس نے اپنا سر میکال حسن کے کشادہ سینے پر ٹکا دیا تھا۔ اس کی آنکھوں سے نکلنے والے گرم گرم آنسو اسے اپنے اندر جذب ہوتے محسوس ہوئے تھے شاید تبھی وہ بھپر کر اٹھا تھا۔

''عائشہ' عائشہ' عائشہ...... آج کے بعد میرے سامنے اگر بھولے سے بھی تمہاری زبان پر اس کا نام آیا تو میں تمہاری زبان کھینچ لوں گا۔ وہ میری محبت' میری زندگی ہے اور میں نے یہ حق کسی کو نہیں دیا کہ وہ مجھ سے میری محبت کو ڈسکس کرے' تمہاری جو اوقات ہے بہتر ہوگا تم اسی میں رہو ورنہ مجھ سے کسی بھی قسم کی رعایت کی امید مت رکھنا۔''

حقارت سے اسے پرے دھکیلتے ہوئے اس نے جیسے اسے کوڑا مارا تھا۔ اس سے بڑھ کر بھلا اس کی ذات کی توہین اور کیا ہوتی تھی شاید تبھی وہ بلبلا اٹھی۔

''مجھے اپنی اوقات میں رہنا بہت اچھی طرح آ گیا ہے میکال حسن! مگر کاش کہ آپ بھی اپنی اوقات میں رہنا سیکھ لیں' کس بات کا اتنا گھمنڈ ہے آپ کو' بولیں...... میرے سامنے آپ کی کیا اوقات ہے؟''

''جسٹ شٹ اپ؟''

اس بار پھنکارتے ہوئے وہ خود پر سے اپنا اختیار کھو بیٹھا تھا۔ ہانیہ اپنے رخسار پر پڑنے والے اس جاندار تھپڑ سے لڑکھڑا کر رہ گئی تھی۔

''اپنے باپ سے پوچھنا جا کر اپنی اوقات' جنہوں نے راتوں رات زبردستی تمہیں میرے گلے کا ڈھول بنا دیا' پتا نہیں کیا کیا گل کھلائے ہوں گے کہ انہیں یوں میرے پاپا کے پاؤں پکڑنے پڑے' تمہیں تو کوئی نہ کوئی لڑکا چاہیے دل بہلانے کے لیے خواہ وہ شوہر کے روپ میں ہو یا اس کے بھائی کے۔''

ہانیہ پھٹی پھٹی آنکھوں سے اس کی طرف دیکھ رہی تھی اور وہ انتہائی گھٹیا الفاظ میں اپنے اندر کا زہر نکال رہا تھا۔ ہانیہ کو لگا جیسے اس کے جسم کا تعلق روح سے ٹوٹ گیا ہو بھلا کوئی یوں اتنی بے رحمی سے بھی کسی کی ذات کے بخیے ادھیڑ سکتا تھا؟

وہ چلا کر اس کا منہ توڑنا چاہتی تھی مگر اس کے اعضاء جیسے جواب دے گئے تھے۔

رنج' حیرانی' اذیت' غصہ' کیا نہیں تھا اس کی آنکھوں میں۔

ایک لمحے میں وہ خوب صورت آنکھیں جیسے لہو ٹپکانے لگی تھیں۔ جسم دہکتا انگارہ بن گیا تھا' تبھی شدید اشتعال میں وہ آگے بڑھی تھی اور اس نے اس کا گریبان تھام لیا تھا۔

''کیا جانتے ہو تم میرے کردار کے بارے میں' ہاں...... ! کیا سوچ کر اتنا گھٹیا بہتان لگایا ہے تم نے مجھ پر؟ کیا سمجھتے ہو تم کہ میری قسمت اگر تمہارے ساتھ پھوٹ گئی تو تم کوئی بہت اعلیٰ و ارفع چیز ہو' میں لعنت بھیجتی ہوں تم پر اور تمہاری رفاقت پر' وہ بھی ہزار بار۔''

زخمی ناگن کی طرح پھنکار کر کہتی وہ اس پر اس کی اہمیت واضح کر گئی تھی۔

''ہانیہ صفدر اتنی گری پڑی نہیں ہے کہ تم جیسا شخص اٹھ کر اس کے کردار پر انگلی اٹھا سکے اب تک اگر میں تم پر فدا رہی تو یہ میرے کردار کی کمزوری نہیں' محض نرم دلی تھی مجھے لگا شاید تمہیں کسی بہت اپنے کی ضرورت ہے مگر نہیں تم جیسے لوگ اسی

قابل ہوتے ہیں کہ انہیں دھتکار دیا جائے۔ ایک بات ہمیشہ یاد رکھنا میکال حسن! کسی انسان کی اوقات نہیں کہ وہ کسی دوسرے انسان سے محبت کر سکے یہ تو صرف اور صرف اللہ ربّ العزت کا کمال ہے کہ وہ کسی انسان کے دل اور اس کی آنکھوں میں، کسی دوسرے انسان کے لیے محبت ڈال دے، تم بھی ڈرو میکال حسن! اس گھڑی، اس لمحے سے جب تم میرے لیے روؤ اور مجھ پر تمہارے آنسو اثر ہی نہ کریں۔''

لہو ٹپکاتی آنکھوں کے ساتھ اس نے نفرت سے اسے پرے دھکیلا تھا۔ میکال حسن اس کے اس عجیب وغریب روپ پر حیران ہی تو رہ گیا تھا۔

وہ کمرے سے نکل گئی تھی، میکال نڈھال سا بیڈ پر بیٹھا گیا۔ اس نے واقعی اس لڑکی کے کردار کے لیے بہت غلط لفظ استعمال کیے تھے شاید اسے ایسا نہیں کرنا چاہیے تھا۔

رات دھیرے دھیرے آگے سرکتی جارہی تھی مگر وہ سو نہیں پا رہا تھا۔ سر میں ایک دم سے شدید درد کا احساس ہوا تھا، وہ دونوں ہاتھوں میں سر تھام کر بیٹھا رہا۔

❁ .... ❁ .... ❁

میکال حسن کو ہانیہ صفدر کی بددعا لگ گئی تھی۔ گھر میں، آفس میں، پارٹیز میں، وہ ہر جگہ اس کے اعصاب پر سوار ہو کر رہ گئی تھی۔ اپنے کردار کی چوٹ پر جو مشتعل انداز اس نے اپنایا تھا، وہ اس کے ذہن سے نکل ہی نہیں رہا تھا۔ اسے حیرت ہو رہی تھی کہ پچھلے ایک ماہ میں اس نے جتنا ہانیہ صفدر کے بارے میں سوچا تھا اتنا عائشہ اذہان کے بارے میں بھی نہیں سوچ سکا تھا۔

ایک دم سے وہ بہت بے نیاز ہو کر رہ گئی تھی۔ پچھلے ایک ماہ سے وہ انگلینڈ میں تھا مگر اسے جیسے کوئی فرق نہیں پڑ رہا تھا۔ اس کی واپسی پر بھی اس کی بے نیازی برقرار رہی تھی۔

سارہ اور مائرہ ہاسٹل شفٹ ہو گئی تھیں۔ نہال کا ایم بی اے بھی مکمل ہو گیا تھا اور آج کل وہ اور ہانیہ دونوں آفس جارہے تھے۔ میکال کا دل جیسے بزنس سے بھی اچاٹ ہو گیا۔

اس وقت شام ڈھل رہی تھی۔ ریاض حسن صاحب اور مسز حسن شام کی چائے سے لطف اندوز ہو رہے تھے۔ ہانیہ وہاں نہیں تھی مگر نہال وہیں بیٹھا ٹی وی دیکھ رہا تھا۔ تبھی ریاض حسن صاحب نے سرسری سی ایک نگاہ اس پر ڈالتے ہوئے کہا تھا۔

''جانے کیوں مگر مجھے لگتا ہے آسیہ! جیسے ہم نے اپنے بچوں کے ساتھ زیادتی کی ہے، شاید ہمیں میکال کی مرضی کے خلاف ہانیہ بیٹی سے اس کی شادی نہیں کرنی چاہیے تھی۔''

''جی! میرے بھی یہی احساسات ہیں۔ میکال اس شادی سے خوش نہیں ہے اور شاید ہانیہ بھی۔''

''کیا ہانیہ بیٹی نے آپ سے اس بارے میں کوئی بات کی ہے؟''

''نہیں، لیکن میں جانتی ہوں وہ بہت حساس بچی ہے، ماں کی وفات کے بعد اس کی شخصیت جیسے ایک دم سے بدل کر رہ گئی ہے۔ جہاں تک میرا خیال ہے میکال کا رویہ اس کے ساتھ ٹھیک نہیں ہے۔ میں نے اتنے دنوں میں ایک بار بھی اسے دل سے ہنستے مسکراتے نہیں دیکھا، اپنے گھر والوں سے بھی قطع تعلق کر لیا ہے اس نے شاید میکال کی طرح وہ بھی اس شادی سے خوش نہیں ہے۔''

''ہوں شاید ایسا ہی ہے، مگر میری سمجھ میں میکال کا رویہ نہیں آرہا، وہ ایسا کیوں کر رہا ہے؟''

''میں جانتی ہوں وہ ایسا کیوں کر رہا ہے۔''

کپ کے کنارے پر انگلی پھیرتے ہوئے مسز حسن نے کہا تھا۔ جواب میں ریاض حسن صاحب چونک اٹھے۔

''کیا مطلب؟''

''میکال کسی اور لڑکی میں انٹرسٹڈ تھا' شاید وہ لڑکی آپ کے آفس میں ہی کام کرتی تھی' عائشہ اذہان نام تھا اس کا' مجھے اگر یہ بات پہلے معلوم ہو جاتی تو میں کبھی عائشہ کی جگہ ہانیہ کے لیے ضد نہ کرتی۔''

''مگر عائشہ کی شادی تو اڑھائی سال پہلے ہی ہو چکی ہے' اس نے آفس سے ریزائن کر دیا تھا۔''

اس بار چونکنے کی باری مسز حسن کی تھی۔

''یہ آپ کیا کہہ رہے ہیں......؟''

''پاپا ٹھیک کہہ رہے ہیں مما۔''

کب سے خاموش بیٹھے نہال نے ٹی وی آف کرتے ہوئے گفتگو میں حصہ لیا تھا۔

''عائشہ جی کی شادی میکال بھیا کی شادی سے دو سال پہلے ہی ہو گئی تھی۔ وہ بھیا کی یونیورسٹی فیلو تھیں' گھریلو حالات کی وجہ سے جاب کرتی تھیں۔ بھیا ان سے شادی کرنا چاہتے تھے مگر ان کی ماں نے پہلے ہی ان کا رشتہ کہیں اور طے کر دیا' اسی لیے وہ جاب بھی چھوڑ گئیں۔''

''وہاٹ......تم نے یہ سب مجھے پہلے کیوں نہیں بتایا؟''

''بتایا تھا مما! مگر شاید آپ کو یاد نہیں رہا بہرحال آپ سب کچھ جان بھی لیتیں تو کیا کر سکتی تھیں۔ میکال بھائی نے عائشہ کو نہیں چھوڑا' عائشہ نے خود میکال بھیا کو چھوڑا ہے۔''

وہ خود بھی اپ سیٹ تھا' مسز حسن الجھ کر رہ گئیں۔

''ہانیہ میری دوست ہے مما! وہ کیسی لڑکی ہے میں بہت اچھی طرح سے جانتا ہوں' اسی لیے میں بھی اس شادی کے حق میں نہیں تھا اور اب......جس طرح سے میکال بھیا بار بار اسے ٹیز کر رہے ہیں' میں یہ سب برداشت نہیں کر سکتا۔ ہانیہ صفدر کی آنکھوں میں آنسو دیکھنا میرے لیے دنیا کا مشکل ترین کام ہے لہٰذا پلیز آپ میکال بھیا کو سمجھائیں نہیں تو میں ان سے لڑ پڑوں گا۔''

ریموٹ صوفے پر اچھالتے ہوئے اس نے خاصی سنجیدگی کے ساتھ کہا اور اگلے ہی پل بنا کوئی بات سنے اٹھ کر اپنے کمرے کی طرف آ گیا۔ پیچھے ریاض حسن صاحب اور مسز آسیہ حسن دیر تک وہیں بیٹھے اس موضوع کو ڈسکس کرتے رہے تھے۔

❀......❀......❀

اسے کہنا......
بچھڑنے سے محبت تو نہیں مرتی
بچھڑ جانا محبت کی صداقت کی علامت ہے
محبت ایک فطرت ہے......
اور فطرت کب بدلتی ہے......
سو جب ہم دور ہو جائیں، نئے رشتوں میں کھو جائیں
تو یہ مت سوچ لینا تم، محبت مر گئی ہو گی
نہیں ایسا نہیں ہو گا......
میرے بارے میں سن کر جب تمہاری آنکھ بھر آئے
چھلک کر ایک بھی آنسو، پلک پر جو ٹھہر جائے
تو بس اتنا سمجھ لینا......
جو میرے نام سے اب بھی تیرے دل کو عقیدت ہے
تیرے دل میں بچھڑ کر بھی ابھی میری محبت ہے
محبت تو بچھڑ کر بھی سدا آباد رہتی ہے
محبت ہو کسی سے تو ہمیشہ یاد رہتی ہے

چاندنی رات تھی۔ سرد ہواؤں سے بے نیاز کھڑکی میں کھڑی وہ میکال حسن کے بارے میں سوچ رہی تھی، جس سے ترک تعلق کیے آج اسے پورا ڈیڑھ ماہ ہونے کو آیا تھا۔ اس نے اپنا موبائل نمبر بدل لیا تھا گھر سے نکلنا بھی ترک کر چکی تھی۔ اس روز جب اریج اسے ہوٹل سے لایا تھا تو پورے راستے اس کا موڈ بنا رہا تھا۔ گاڑی میں اس نے اس کی طرف دیکھنا تو درکنار بات کرنا بھی گوارا نہیں کیا تھا مگر وہ بے نیاز سی خاموش بیٹھی رہی تھی۔

گھر آ کر تھوڑی دیر کے بعد وہ نارمل ہو گیا تھا تاہم اس روز کے بعد عائشہ اذہان کا اس سے سامنا بہت کم ہوا تھا۔ نہی دنوں اس کا بھائی دبئی میں سیٹ ہو گیا تھا۔ اس کی ساس اپنی بیٹی کی بڑھتی عمر اور زبان سے سخت عاجز تھی، دولت جائیداد کے باوجود کوئی رشتہ نہیں آ رہا تھا۔ تبھی انہوں نے عائشہ سے کہا کہ وہ اپنے بھائی کے لیے اپنی ماں سے رشتے کی بات کرے، عائشہ اپنی نند کو پسند نہیں کرتی تھی کیونکہ اس کی عادتیں اور کردار کھلی کتاب کی مانند اس کے سامنے تھے تاہم ساس کی بات رکھنے کے لیے اس نے اپنی ماں سے بات کر لی تھی اور اس کی حیرت کی انتہا نہ رہی جب اس کی ماں نے ذرا سی سوچ بچار کے بعد یہ رشتہ منظور کر لیا۔

چٹ منگنی، پٹ بیاہ کے مصداق فوری شادی کے دن رکھ دیئے گئے تھے۔ عائشہ اس افراتفری پر بوکھلا کر ہی تو رہ گئی

تھی۔ دونوں طرف سے شادی کی تیاری اس کے کندھوں پر آ پڑی جب کہ اس کی جان پہلے ہی سکون میں نہیں تھی۔

اس وقت بھی جب وہ تھکن سے چُور ساری دنیا سے کٹ کر کھڑی تھی‘ اس کا شوہر کمرے میں آ گیا تھا۔

”آشا۔“ وہ اسے عائشہ کے بجائے آشا ہی پکارتا تھا۔ اس کے خیالوں کا تسلسل ٹوٹ گیا‘ چونک کر پلٹتے ہوئے اس نے ایک نظر اپنے شوہر پر ڈالی تھی۔

”ہوں۔“

”میں نے باہر جانا ہے‘ اماں سے کہو گیٹ کھولے۔“

بچوں کی طرح مچل کر ضد کرتے ہوئے اس نے منہ بسورا تھا۔ وہ گہری سانس بھر کر رہ گئی۔

”نہیں‘ اس ٹائم باہر نہیں جاتے‘ میں وعدہ کرتی ہوں صبح لے جاؤں گی آپ کو۔“

”سنیں، میں نے ابھی جانا ہے‘ اریج بھی گیا ہے‘ میں بھی جاؤں گا۔“

وہ اپنی ضد پر اڑ رہا تھا‘ عائشہ پریشان ہو کر رہ گئی تھی کیونکہ وہ جانتی تھی شام کے بعد اسے اور اس کے شوہر کو گھر سے باہر نکلنے کی اجازت نہیں تھی۔ شادی سے پہلے ایک بار اس کا شوہر آنکھ بچا کر شام کے بعد گھر سے نکل گیا تھا اور قریب ہی روڈ پر حادثے کا شکار ہو گیا‘ تاہم ٹریفک کم ہونے کی وجہ سے اسے زیادہ چوٹیں نہیں آئی تھیں۔ اس روز کے بعد سے اس پر پابندی عائد ہو گئی تھی تبھی وہ اسے ٹال رہی تھی مگر وہ تو جیسے کچھ سننے کو تیار ہی نہیں تھا۔

”جمال میں......“ ابھی وہ اسے سمجھانے کے لیے لفظ ڈھونڈ ہی رہی تھی کہ اس کے شوہر نے غصے سے بگڑتے ہوئے قریبی ٹیبل پر پڑا گلدان اٹھا کر اس کے سر پر دے مارا۔

عائشہ کے لیے یہ حملہ قطعی غیر متوقع تھا‘ تبھی وہ اپنا دفاع نہیں کر سکی تھی‘ گلدان اس کی پیشانی پر لگا تھا اور اگلے ہی لمحے خون کا ایک فوارا ابل پڑا تھا۔ عائشہ تیورا کر گری تھی اور اس کے بعد اسے کوئی ہوش نہیں رہا تھا۔ اریج جو اپنا موبائل فون چارج پر بھول گیا تھا‘ اٹھانے کے لیے واپس آیا تو جمال چیخ رہا تھا وہ گھبرا کر اس کے کمرے کی طرف بھاگا‘ اس کی ماں بھی سیڑھیوں سے بھاگی آئیں‘ تبھی سامنے کا منظر دیکھ کر ان دونوں کے ہاتھوں کے طوطے اڑ گئے۔ سامنے فرش پر پڑی عائشہ اذہان کی پیشانی سے بہنے والے خون نے اس کا چہرہ چھپا دیا تھا‘ بجلی کی سی سرعت سے لپک کر وہ اس کی طرف بڑھا اور بنا کچھ بھی سوچے سمجھے اگلے ہی پل اسے اپنے بازوؤں میں اٹھا کر گاڑی کے قریب لے آیا۔ اس کی ماں باہر تک آئی تھی مگر وہ اس سے قبل ہی گاڑی لے کر نکل چکا تھا۔

❁......❁......❁

عائشہ اذہان کی جس لمحے آنکھ کھلی‘ وہ اسپتال کے سرد کمرے میں تھی۔ اس کے بائیں بازو میں ڈرپ لگی تھی‘ آنکھ کھلتے ہی شدید تکلیف کے احساس نے اسے کراہنے پر مجبور کیا تھا۔ اریج جو ابھی کمرے میں داخل ہوا تھا‘ اس کی آہ پر فوراً لپک کر قریب آیا۔

”کیسی طبیعت ہے اب آپ کی؟“ ڈیڑھ ماہ کے بعد پہلی بار اس نے اسے براہ راست مخاطب کیا تھا۔ وہ اپنا ہاتھ پیشانی تک لے جاتے لے جاتے رک گئی۔

”ٹھیک ہوں۔“

”مگر ٹھیک لگ نہیں رہی ہیں‘ اچھا لڑکا تھا وہ اس روز ہوٹل والا‘ سوٹ کر رہا تھا آپ کے ساتھ پھر بھی پتا نہیں کیوں آپ میرے پاگل بھائی کے پلّے بندھ گئیں۔“

وہ اس پر طنز نہیں کر رہا تھا مگر پھر بھی عائشہ کے دل میں درد کی لہر اٹھی تھی۔

''پتا نہیں لوگ کیسے رشتوں کی مروت میں اپنی پوری زندگی' اپنے خوابوں کا سودا کر لیتے ہیں' کم از کم میں ایسا کبھی نہیں کر سکتا۔'' اب کے رخ پھیرتے ہوئے وہ دل گرفتگی سے بولا تھا۔ عائشہ نے جواب میں چپ چاپ پلکیں موند لیں۔ ڈرپ لگنے کے باعث اسے وہاں شدید ٹھنڈ کا احساس ہو رہا تھا مگر اس نے ارتج سے نہیں کہا۔ عجیب بے حسی سی سوار ہو گئی تھی اس پر، تبھی وہ بولا تھا۔

''یہ ڈرپ مکمل ہو جاتی ہے تو گھر چلتے ہیں' کسی چیز کی ضرورت ہو تو بتا دیجیے گا' لا دوں گا۔''

سرسری سی ایک نظر اس کی ڈرپ کی رفتار پر ڈالتے ہوئے وہ جانے کے لیے اٹھ کھڑا ہوا تھا۔ اگلے پچیس منٹ کے بعد نڈھال سی عائشہ گاڑی میں اس کے ساتھ فرنٹ سیٹ پر بیٹھی تھی۔

''یہ جو اسپتال ہوتے ہیں ناں' زندان ہوتے ہیں لوگوں کے لیے' لوگ شفا لینے آتے ہیں یہاں جانے کہاں کہاں سے دھکے کھا کر' پیسے لٹا کر ان شفاء خانوں تک پہنچتے ہیں مگر یہاں انسانیت کی خدمت سے اکتائے' تعلیم یافتہ لوگ' مسیحائی کے عوض جو سلوک ان کے ساتھ کرتے ہیں' وہ دیکھنے لائق نہیں ہوتا' ڈاکٹرز تو چلو بے حس ہی سہی' نرسز کا گھمنڈ' سنگ دلی اور مریضوں کے ساتھ بے حد بُرا رویہ دیکھ کر' میں ہمیشہ ان شفاخانوں کی طرف آنے سے گھبراتا ہوں۔ خدا کے واسطے اگلی دفعہ خیال کیجیے گا۔ بہت سے لوگوں کو بے موت ان زندانوں میں بے بسی کی موت مرتے دیکھا ہے میں نے۔''

سر جھکائے گاڑی اسٹارٹ کرتے ہوئے اس نے اسے تنبیہ کی تھی' عائشہ اب بھی لبوں پر چپ کا قفل لگائے بیٹھی رہی۔

اگلے چند دنوں میں اس نے ارتج کو بہت ڈسٹرب دیکھا تھا۔ پوری پوری رات جاگ کر سگریٹ پھونکتا رہتا' گھر کا راستہ تو جیسے اسے بھول ہی گیا تھا۔ کئی کئی دن کے بعد گھر آتا بھی تھا تو کسی کے پاس نہیں بیٹھتا تھا۔ عائشہ اذہان کے ساتھ اس گھر میں ہونے والے ظلم بھی اب جیسے اس کی توجہ سمیٹنے میں ناکام رہے تھے۔

اس روز اس کے سامنے اس کی نند نے اس کے چہرے پر بھرپور تمانچہ دے مارا تھا مگر وہ ٹس سے مس نہیں ہوا' اپنا والٹ اٹھا کر بے نیازی سے باہر نکل گیا تھا۔ صبح سے شام تک کولہو کے بیل کی طرح وہ گھریلو کاموں میں جُتی رہتی تھی۔ مگر وہاں اس کا احساس کرنے والا کوئی نہیں تھا۔ جانے اس سے ایسی کیا خطاء سرزد ہوئی تھی کہ اس کے واحد ہمدرد نے بھی اس کے حق سے اپنا ہاتھ کھینچ لیا تھا۔

اس روز بہت بارش ہوئی تھی۔ عائشہ کو پچھلے تین چار روز سے شدید بخار نے بے حال کر رکھا تھا۔ پھر بھی وہ اپنے فرائض مکمل تندہی سے سرانجام دے رہی تھی' تیز بخار کے سبب آنکھیں جیسے جل رہی تھیں جب کہ سر یوں چکرا رہا تھا جیسے ابھی گر پڑے گی۔ رات گئے کچن سے فراغت پا کر وہ اپنے کمرے میں آئی اور بناء کچھ کھائے پیے ہی بستر پر ڈھیر ہو گئی' اسے خبر ہی نہ ہوئی کہ کب اس کا شوہر کمرے سے نکلا اور گھر سے باہر چلا گیا۔ خبر تو اس وقت ہوئی جب اس کی ساس نے انتہائی بے رحمی سے اس کے بال اپنی مٹھی میں جکڑتے ہوئے اسے گہری نیند سے اٹھایا۔

''ہڈ حرام' منحوس' میرا بیٹا وہاں زخمی پڑا ہے اور تو یہاں میٹھی نیند کے مزے لوٹ رہی ہے۔''

تیز چنگھاڑ نے اسے اچھا خاصا بدحواس کر دیا تھا۔ اس کی سمجھ میں ہی نہ آیا کہ ہوا کیا ہے؟ سرد فرش پر گری تو کہنیوں اور دانتوں میں اٹھنے والے شدید درد نے ہوش بحال کیے' وہ ابھی ٹھیک سے سنبھلی بھی نہیں تھی کہ ساس نے پھر اسے دو تھپڑ جڑ دیے۔

''چل نکل یہاں سے منحوس ماری' آئی بڑی شہزادی کہیں کی۔''

اعصاب شکن گالیاں بکتی ہوئی اس کی ساس اسے سیڑھیوں سے نیچے گھسیٹ لائی تھی۔ وہ بلبلا کر ان سے رحم کی درخواست کرتی رہ گئی' باہر موسم اپنے تیور بدل چکا تھا' گرجتے بادلوں کے ساتھ رفتہ رفتہ تیز ہوتی بارش نے جیسے اس کے حواس معطل کر دیئے۔ اس کا شوہر زخمی حالت میں لاؤنج میں دھرے صوفے پر پڑا تھا' وہ لپک کر اس کی طرف بڑھنا چاہتی تھی مگر اس کی ساس اور ان کی مدد کے لیے آئی نند نے اسے بنا کوئی موقع دیئے' دھکے دے کر گھر سے باہر نکال دیا تھا۔ وہ اوندھے منہ گیٹ کے اس پار سیڑھیوں پر جا پڑی تھی' باہر جنوں خیز ہواؤں اور زور پکڑتی بارش نے اسے مزید سہا دیا۔ تبھی اریج کی گاڑی کے ٹائر اس سے کچھ ہی فاصلے پر چرچرائے تھے۔

۞......۞......۞

دانش وراں تو وی نئیں جیہڑے حل ہوندے
ایسے نقطے وی عشق سمجھا' دیندا
لوکی پیراں دے ہتھ' نئی چومن دیندے
عشق کیتاں دے پیرا چما' دیندا

''میکال......'' وہ آفس کے لیے نکل رہا تھا جب مسز حسن کی پکار پر ان کے قریب چلا آیا۔ تھکے تھکے سے اعصاب اور آنکھوں میں دوڑتی رت جگوں کی سرخی اس کے اندر کے حال کا بخوبی پتا دے رہی تھی۔ مسز حسن نے ہاتھوں میں پکڑا ڈائجسٹ سائیڈ پر رکھ دیا۔

''بیٹھو! مجھے کچھ بات کرنی ہے تم سے۔''

''سوری مما! میں اس وقت آفس سے لیٹ ہو رہا ہوں۔''

''آفس امپورٹنٹ نہیں ہے۔'' چہرے پر حد درجہ سنجیدگی طاری کیے وہ خفگی سے بولی تھیں۔ میکال لب بھینچتا ان کے مقابل ٹک گیا۔

''جی فرمائیے۔''

''مجھے ہانیہ کے بارے میں بات کرنی ہے' وہ بہت پیاری اور سلجھی ہوئی بچی ہے' میرا خیال تھا تم اسے خوش رکھو گے مگر ایسا نہیں ہے۔''

میکال کے چہرے کی طرف دیکھتے ہوئے انہوں نے بات کی تمہید باندھی تھی۔ وہ سر جھکائے بیٹھا رہا۔

''مجھے تم سے یہ امید نہیں تھی میکال! مجھے نہیں پتا تھا کہ تم اگر شادی نہیں کرنا چاہتے تو اس کے پیچھے کیا وجہ ہے' پتا لگ بھی جاتا تب بھی شاید میں تمہاری کوئی مدد نہیں کر سکتی تھی کیونکہ تم نے جس لڑکی کو پسند کیا وہ تم سے پہلے بیاہ کر کہیں اور جا چکی تھی' ایسے میں اگر ہانیہ نہ ہوتی تب بھی کسی نہ کسی لڑکی نے تو تمہاری زندگی میں آنا تھا ناں پھر ہانیہ کے ساتھ ایسا تضحیک آمیز سلوک کیوں؟''

وہ پوچھ رہی تھیں مگر میکال اب بھی سر جھکائے خاموش بیٹھا رہا تھا۔

''میں بہت شرمندہ ہوں اس بچی سے' میرے نزدیک اس میں اور مائرہ میں کوئی فرق نہیں ہے' بھابی صاحبہ کی وفات کے بعد اس کی زندگی بہت بدل گئی ہے۔ ترستی ہے وہ خوشیوں کے لیے' وہ اس قابل نہیں ہے کہ اس کے ساتھ یوں تضحیک آمیز سلوک کیا جائے' میں نہیں چاہتی کہ بھائی صاحب کو کسی بات کا پتا چلے' اس لیے درخواست کر رہی ہوں تم سے اس بچی کو ستانا چھوڑ دو' پلیز......'' وہ التجا کر رہی تھیں تبھی ان کی نگاہ میکال کی بھرائی آنکھوں پر پڑی اور وہ جیسے تڑپ اٹھیں۔

''میکال...... میری جان! مجھے بتاؤ' کیا مسئلہ ہے' کیوں کر رہے ہو تم یہ سب؟ میں تمہاری ماں ہوں بیٹے۔''
فوراً اٹھ کر اس کے پہلو میں بیٹھتے ہوئے انہوں نے اس کا چہرہ اپنے ہاتھوں کے پیالے میں لیا تھا' تبھی وہ اٹھ کر نیچے قالین پر بیٹھا اور اپنا سر ان کی گود میں رکھتے ہوئے رو پڑا۔

''ایم سوری مما...... مجھے کچھ سمجھ میں نہیں آ رہا کہ میرے ساتھ کیا ہو رہا ہے' بہت بے چینی ہے میرے اندر' ایک عجیب سا طوفان مجھے اندر سے تہس نہس کرنے کو مچل رہا ہے۔''

اس کی آواز بھرّا گئی تھی کسی ننھے سے معصوم بچے کی مانند وہ ان کی گود میں منہ چھپائے دیر تک روتا رہا اور آسیہ بیگم بے چین و متفکر سی' اس کے بالوں میں محبت سے انگلیاں پھیرتی جانے کیا کیا پڑھ کر اس پر پھونکتی رہیں۔

❁......❁......❁

کہیں دور دشتِ خیال میں
کوئی قافلہ ہے رکا ہوا
کہیں خالی آنکھ کی گود میں
کئی رت جگے ہیں پڑے ہوئے
کہیں عہد ماضی کی راہ پر
کوئی یاد سی کہیں کھو گئی
کہیں خواب زاروں کے درمیاں
مجھے زندگی نے بسر کیا
میرے ماہ و سال کی گود میں' نہ وصال کا کوئی چاند ہے
کوئی آس ہے نہ امید ہے
نہ کسی ستارے کا ساتھ ہے

ٹپ' ٹپ' ٹپ...... گزرے ہر لمحے کے ساتھ حور عین فاطمہ کی آنکھوں سے آنسو ٹوٹ کر بکھر رہے تھے اور عمیر ہمدانی اس کے سامنے دم سادھے' بُت بنا بیٹھا اس کی روداد سن رہا تھا۔ وہ روداد جو روح چھید کر رکھ دیتی تھی۔ گزرے ہوئے وہ لمحے آج بھی نشتر بن کر اس کی روح میں چبھتے تھے۔ آج بہت دنوں کے بعد اس نے اپنی ذات کو ان تکلیف دہ لمحوں کے سپرد کیا تھا۔

بگرام جیل کی یادیں وہاں بیتا ہر لمحہ' آج بھی اس کی رگوں سے لہو نچوڑتا تھا۔ ساری دنیا کے لیے امن اور تہذیب کا نعرہ لگانے والے یہود' مل کر ان عقوبت خانوں میں کیسے انسانیت کی دھجیاں بکھیر رہے تھے' اس نے اپنی آنکھوں سے دیکھا تھا۔

''سپر پاور'' کہلانے والے سورما کو جس ملک کے عوام میں بڑھتی ہوئی نفرت پر تشویش تھی' اسی عوام کے انمول ہیروں کو وہ بدترین بربریت کی بھینٹ چڑھا کر صفحہ ہستی سے مٹا رہا تھا اور اسے اس پر کوئی تشویش نہیں تھی۔ وہ سانس لینے کو رکی تھی' جب عمیر نے بے تابی سے پوچھا۔

''پھر...... پھر کیا ہوا' کیا آپ کو بھی سر جاوید ہمدانی کی طرح امریکہ کے حوالے کر دیا گیا؟''

''ہاں۔'' اس کے سوال پر نرمی سے آنسو پونچھتے ہوئے وہ بیڈ سے اٹھ کھڑی ہوئی تھی' عین اسی لمحے سمیر نے اس

کمرے میں انٹری دی۔

''تو جناب عمیر صاحب یہاں تشریف فرما ہیں اور وہاں کچن میں ڈھیر سارے برتن پڑے میرا منہ چڑا رہے ہیں۔''

صد شکر کہ حورعین نے اپنے آنسو پونچھ لیے تھے پھر بھی اپنے دھیان میں بولتا وہ اس کی طرف دیکھ کر چونکا تھا۔

''ارے' آپ رو رہی ہیں؟''

رات وہ اس سے نہیں ملا تھا مگر نمیر نے اس کی گھر واپسی پر اسے اس کے بارے میں بتا دیا تھا' تبھی کمرے سے نکلتے ہی اس نے ادھر کا رخ کیا تھا۔ حورعین اس کے غیر متوقع سوال پر چونک اٹھی تھی جب کہ عمیر اس اچانک مداخلت پر گہری سانس بھرتے ہوئے اس کے پہلو سے اٹھ کھڑا ہوا تھا۔

''چلیے بھابی! باقی کی کہانی پھر سہی' میں نے کہیں پڑھا تھا لفظ جھوٹے ہو سکتے ہیں مگر لہجے کبھی فریبی نہیں ہوتے۔ جانے کیوں آپ کے آنسوؤں اور لہجے سے مجھے بھی سچ کی خوشبو آ رہی ہے' اس لیے جب تک عذیر بھائی نہیں آ جاتے آپ یہاں قیام کر سکتی ہیں۔''

اپنی بات کہہ کر وہ کمرے میں رکا نہیں تھا جب کہ سمیر حیران رہ گیا۔

''یہ کیا کہہ گیا ہے؟'' عمیر کی بات چونکہ اس کے سر کے اوپر سے گزر گئی تھی تبھی اس نے حورعین سے استفسار کیا تھا' مگر وہ بھی نفی میں سر ہلا گئی۔

''کچھ نہیں' آپ چلیے' میں بھی باہر آتی ہوں۔''

''جی شیور۔'' سمیر اس کے گریز کا برا منائے بغیر شرافت سے باہر نکل گیا تھا۔

اسی روز شام میں عذیر ہمدانی کی واپسی ہوگئی تھی' وہ کچن میں نمیر کی ہیلپ کروا رہی تھی' سمیر حسب معمول کلب گیا تھا جب کہ عمیر ابھی ابھی زبیر کو ٹیوشن سے لانے کے لیے گھر سے نکلا تھا' بڑی ماں کی طبیعت ٹھیک نہیں تھی پھر بھی وہ لاؤنج میں صوفے پر بیٹھی' حورعین کو دعائیں دے رہی تھیں کہ جس نے مہمان ہونے کے باوجود ان کی ذمہ داری سنبھال لی تھی۔ عذیر حسب عادت شور مچاتا ہوا گھر میں داخل ہوا تھا۔

''عمیر...... عمیر......'' حورعین کا دل اس کی پکار پر زور سے دھڑک اٹھا۔ ایک مشکل ٹلی نہیں تھی کہ دوسری آ پڑی تھی۔ نمیر جو اسے پیاز کاٹ کر دے رہا تھا' بنا اس کے ہاتھوں کی لرزش پر غور کیے مسکرا اٹھا۔

''لیں بھابی! آ گئے آپ کے صاحب بہادر' ابھی آپ یہاں نہ ہوتی ناں تو انہوں نے ایک ماہ سے پہلے نہیں آنا تھا۔'' حورعین کے لب اس کی شرارت پر بمشکل پھیلے تھے' وہ اسے وکٹری کا نشان بنا کر دکھاتا کچن سے نکل گیا۔

''السلام علیکم عذیر بھائی۔''

''وعلیکم السلام! عمیر کہاں ہے؟'' دھپ سے بڑی ماں کے پہلو میں صوفے پر گرتے ہوئے انہیں سلام کرنے کے بعد اس نے نظر اٹھا کر نمیر کو دیکھا تھا' حورعین کو لگا جیسے اس کا دل رک جائے گا۔

''وہ تو زبیر کو ٹیوشن سے لینے گیا ہے' خیریت؟''

''اس کے ہوتے خیریت ہو سکتی ہے' ایک نمبر کا بے وقوف' الو کا پٹھا ہے یہ لڑکا۔''

''کیا ہو گیا ہے عذیر! کیوں آتے ہی شروع ہو گئے؟''

بڑی ماں کی تسبیح مکمل ہوگئی تھی تبھی وہ بولیں' تو وہ غصے سے سر جھٹک کر کھڑا ہو گیا۔

''کیا ہوا ہے؟ آپ کو پتا ہے بڑی ماں! اس نے کیا کیا ہے؟'' انگاروں پر لوٹتا وہ شخص اس کا بھانڈا بس پھوڑنے ہی والا تھا تبھی متوقع رسوائی کے خوف سے' آنسوؤں سے بھری آنکھوں کے ساتھ وہ کچن کے دروازے پر آ کھڑی ہوئی۔

''کیا کیا ہے عمیر نے؟'' بڑی ماں کے ساتھ ساتھ نمیر کے کان بھی کھڑے ہو گئے تھے تبھی عذیر کی نگاہ اس پر پڑی تھی۔

''تت......تم......؟'' حورعین کو گمان نہیں تھا کہ وہ اسے یوں فوری پہچان لے گا مگر اس نے اسے پہچان لیا تھا' وہ بنا کوئی جواب دیئے چپ چاپ کھڑی رہی۔

''ایسے کیا دیکھ رہے ہو' تمہیں کیا لگا ہم اسے نہیں رکھیں گے' ارے پہلی بار زندگی میں کوئی ڈھنگ کا فیصلہ کیا ہے تم نے' وگرنہ مجھے تو یہی خدشہ تھا کہ نجانے کیسی لڑکی کو اپنے متھے مار لیا ہے تم نے۔''

اس کی نگاہوں کی تقلید میں حورعین کو دیکھتے ہوئے بڑی ماں شفقت سے مسکرائی تھیں' عذیر حیران سا بالوں میں ہاتھ پھیر کر رہ گیا۔

''مگر......''

''ارے چھوڑو اگر مگر کو' بہت پیاری بچی ہے' ابھی کل آئی ہے اور آج سارا گھر بھی سنبھال لیا' میرا دل تو بہت خوش ہے اتنی بھلی صورت کی بچی تو شاید میں بھی تمہارے لیے نہیں ڈھونڈ سکتی تھی۔''

''ہاں بھیا! بھابی واقعی بہت گریٹ ہیں' میں نے اور بڑی ماں نے فیصلہ کر لیا ہے ہم کل ہی سارے خاندان میں آپ دونوں کی شادی کی خبر عام کر دیں گے۔''

اس کی سنے بغیر بڑی ماں اور نمیر نے فوری اپنی قیمتی رائے پیش کر دی تھی' وہ ہکا بکا سا انہیں دیکھ کر رہ گیا۔

''بڑی ماں! ایسا کچھ نہیں ہے' آپ لوگ واقعی پاگل ہو چکے ہیں۔''

''ہاں' اب تو تم پاگل ہی کہو گے' چپ چاپ تمہاری پسند کو قبول جو کر لیا ہے میں پوچھتی ہوں تم نے ہم سب کی رائے لیے بغیر اس بچی سے نکاح کیا تھا' تب تم پاگل نہیں تھے۔'' بڑی ماں جانے کیا سمجھی بیٹھی تھیں' وہ بوکھلا گیا۔

''نکاح؟''

''اور نہیں تو کیا' تم نے کیا سمجھا تھا' مجھے پتا نہیں چلے گا۔ ارے دادی ہوں تمہاری یہ بال یونہی دھوپ میں سفید نہیں کیے میں نے۔''

''اُف......!'' دادی کی قیاس آرائی پر اس نے اپنے بال مٹھیوں میں جکڑ لیے تھے' نمیر اس کی الجھن پر مسرور ہوتا وہاں سے کھسک گیا۔ عین اسی لمحے عمیر نے قدم لاؤنج میں دھرے تھے۔

''ارے عذیر بھائی! اتنی جلدی آ گئے آپ' ابھی تو ہفتہ بھی پورا نہیں ہوا۔''

نمیر کی طرح اس کے لبوں پر بھی محظوظ کن مسکراہٹ تھی۔ وہ سلگ کر ایک نظر اس پر ڈالتے ہوئے حورعین کے مقابل آ کھڑا ہوا۔

''ذرا میرے کمرے میں تشریف لائیے' بہت ضروری بات کرنی ہے آپ سے۔''

حورعین جانتی تھی وہ اس سے ایسا ہی کہے گا' تبھی بھیگی پلکوں کے ساتھ اس کی طرف دیکھتی وہ سر جھکا گئی۔ اگلے پانچ منٹ کے بعد بڑی ماں کے اشارے پر وہ اس کے کمرے کی طرف بڑھ آئی۔ عمیر کی نگاہوں میں بھی اس کے لیے حوصلہ افزائی تھی۔

''کون ہو تم؟'' کمرے میں اس کے قدم دھرتے ہی وہ جو بے قرار سا کھڑکی میں کھڑا تھا' فوراً پلٹ کر اس کی طرف بڑھا۔ حورعین بس ایک نظر اسے دیکھ کر رہ گئی۔

''میں نے عمیر کو بتایا ہے کہ میں کون ہوں؟''

''مجھے بتانے میں کوئی حرج ہے؟'' پینٹ کی جیبوں میں دونوں ہاتھ پھنسائے وہ بہت کڑی نگاہوں سے اسے گھور رہا

تھا' وہ رخ پھیر گئی۔

''نہیں...... میرا نام حورعین فاطمہ ہے' آپ کی کزن ہانیہ صفدر کی کلاس فیلو رہی ہوں' اسی کے ساتھ چند سال قبل اس گھر میں آئی تھی میں مگر میں نے آپ کے گھر والوں کو کوئی دھوکا نہیں دیا' یہ لوگ خود غلط فہمی کا شکار ہیں۔''

''اچھا اور وہ جو دادو شادی کی بات کر رہی ہیں وہ؟''

''میں نے انہیں ایسا کچھ نہیں کہا' نہ شادی کے لیے نہ نکاح کے لیے۔''

''ٹھیک ہے' مگر میں جاننا چاہوں گا' آپ یہاں کیوں آئیں؟'' اس کی پوزیشن اور انداز میں تبدیلی نہیں آئی تھی' وہ بے چین سی ہتھیلیاں مسلنے لگی۔

''مجھے نہیں پتا تھا کہ یہ آپ کا گھر ہے' میں تو صرف پناہ چاہتی تھی' کہیں بھی کیونکہ میرے اپنے محل میں میری عزت اور جان کو خطرہ لاحق ہو گیا تھا۔''

''کہاں ہے آپ کا محل؟''

''یہیں' اسی شہر میں۔ کچھ ہی فرلانگ کے فاصلے پر۔''

''ہوں اور وہ روز قبرستان میں جو باقاعدگی سے حاضری دیتی ہیں وہ؟''

''وہ میرا پرسنل ہے۔''

''ٹھیک ہے مگر میں بالکل نہیں چاہوں گا کہ میرے گھر والے آپ کی وجہ سے کسی قسم کی غلط فہمی کا شکار ہوں۔ اس لیے بہتر ہے کہ آپ فوری اپنے منہ سے انہیں سب سچ بتا دیں۔''

حورعین کے گریز نے اس کا موڈ خراب کر دیا تھا' اپنے بھائی کی طرح وہ بھی اسے کسی قسم کی رعایت دینے کو تیار نہیں تھا' تبھی اس کی پریشانی بڑھ گئی تھی۔

''بتا دوں گی مگر ابھی چند روز مجھے یہاں رہنے دیں پلیز' ایک ملازمہ کی حیثیت سے ہی سہی۔''

''ٹھیک ہے مگر ایک بات آپ اچھی طرح سے جان لیں' میری دادو ایک سادہ لوح مگر سخت خاتون ہیں اگر ان پر یہ جھوٹ کھل گیا تو وہ آپ کو ایک پل کے لیے بھی یہاں نہیں رہنے دیں گی' میں اچھی طرح سے جانتا ہوں انہیں اور شاید عمیر بھی تبھی اس نے ان سے یہ نکاح والا جھوٹ گھڑا ہوگا۔ لڑکوں والا گھر ہونے کی وجہ سے وہ محلے کی کسی لڑکی کو بھی گھر میں گھسنے نہیں دیتیں' آج تک انہوں نے کسی لڑکی کو ملازمہ نہیں رکھا' میری کسی گرل فرینڈ کو بھی یہاں آنے اور رکنے کی اجازت نہیں ہے جہاں تک سلمیٰ کا تعلق ہے تو وہ انڈین نژاد ہے میں نے اپنے طور پر اسے رنگ پہنائی تھی تاہم میرے گھر والوں نے اسے نہیں دیکھا اگر میرے حوالے سے بنا کسی تعلق کے وہ بھی یہاں آتی تو شاید چند گھنٹوں سے زیادہ نہ رک سکتی' بہر حال یہ ساری تفصیل سنانے کا مقصد یہی ہے کہ دادو کے سامنے بہت احتیاط سے رہنا' باقی میں کوشش کروں گا کہ آپ کو یہاں کسی قسم کی کوئی تکلیف نہ ہو جب تک آپ یہاں رہیں۔''

وہ لگی لپٹی رکھنے والا شخص نہیں تھا۔ حورعین کی نگاہوں میں ممنونیت در آئی۔

''بہت شکریہ' میں آپ کا یہ احسان ہمیشہ یاد رکھوں گی۔''

''ویلکم۔'' اس بار اس کے چہرے پر سرسری سی نظر ڈالنے کے بعد وہ فوری کمرے سے نکل گیا تھا۔ حورعین نے بے ساختہ سر اٹھا کر اوپر کمرے کی چھت کو تکتے ہوئے اللہ کا شکر ادا کیا۔

❁......❁......❁

میں نفرتوں کے جہاں میں رہ کر' جفا کروں گا تو کیا کروں گا
یہ ٹھیک کہتے ہو بے وفا ہوں' وفا کروں گا تو کیا کروں گا
بس ایک تُو ہی تُو رہ گیا ہے جہان سارا تو کھو چکا ہوں
تجھے بھی اپنی انا میں آ کر' خفا کروں گا تو کیا کروں گا
ہزار سجدے تو کر چکا ہوں' قضا تمہاری محبتوں میں
میں اب دکھاوے کا کوئی سجدہ ادا کروں گا تو کیا کروں گا
بغیر پانی کے کوئی مچھلی بھلا کبھی زندہ رہ سکی ہے
میں تجھ کو کھو کر کسی کا ہو کر' بتا کروں گا تو کیا کروں گا

ائر پورٹ سے گاؤں تک اپنے شان دار استقبال پر ثانیہ عباس نے جیسے خود کو سنبھالے رکھا تھا وہ ہی جانتی تھی مگر کب تک......؟ رات کی تاریکی میں تنہائی میسر آتے ہی ضبط کے سارے بندھ جیسے ٹوٹ گئے تھے۔ کیا ضروری تھا کہ پانچ سال کے طویل عرصے کے بعد' وطن واپسی پر وہ شخص یوں غیر متوقع طور پر بالکل اچانک اس کے سامنے آتا؟

کیا ضروری تھا کہ دل میں دبی ہوئی راکھ کو پھر سے ہوا ملتی؟

وہ سونا چاہتی تھی مگر نیندوں کے قافلے تو عرصہ ہوا اس سے روٹھ چکے تھے۔ گزرے پچھلے پانچ سالوں میں ایک دن بھی ایسا نہیں تھا جب وہ شخص اسے یاد نہ آیا ہو۔

گو پچھلے پانچ سالوں میں اس نے زندگی کو بہت سیٹ کر لیا تھا۔ اسے جینے کے ڈھنگ آ گئے تھے' مگر پھر بھی اندر کہیں ایک خلاء تھا جو پُر ہونے کا نام نہیں لے رہا تھا۔ اس کے دونوں بچے اب بڑے ہو گئے تھے' انگلینڈ جیسے ایڈوانس ملک میں پرورش پانے کے باوجود وہ اپنے باپ کو یاد کرتے تھے۔ کیا کیا نہیں ہو گیا تھا گزرے پانچ سالوں میں؟ اس کے کزن اشعر حسین نے بارہا اسے شادی کی پیش کش کی تھی' مگر...... وہ بھلا اب ایسی کسی پوزیشن میں رہی ہی کہاں تھی۔

دل تھا کہ ٹوٹ پھوٹ کر بکھر جانے کو بے تاب ہو رہا تھا۔ سرسراتی ہوا کے سرد جھونکے' جیسے سانسیں لُوٹ لینے کو مچل رہے تھے۔

وہ بیڈ سے اٹھ کر کھڑکی کے قریب آ کھڑی ہوئی۔ آنسو تھے کہ بے دریغ بہتے ہی چلے جا رہے تھے۔ وہ اسے سوچنا نہیں چاہتی تھی مگر وہ اس کی سوچوں میں آنے کے لیے بھلا اس کی مرضی کا پابند ہی کہاں تھا۔ دن رات' سوتے جاگتے' اس کا جب دل چاہتا وہ بے دھڑک اس کی سوچ کے در وا کرتے' اس کے تصورات کی دنیا میں چلا آتا تھا۔ اس وقت بھی ایسا ہی ہوا تھا۔

زائر ملک کی یاد' بہت بے رحمی سے اس کی سوچوں کے تمام در وا کرتی ہوئی اس کے تصور میں چلی آئی تھی۔

❁......❁......❁

زائر ملک ان دنوں شہر میں تھا۔ ثانیہ عباس اپنی ماں کے ہاتھوں بے حد مجبور ہو کر اس روز چیک اپ کے لیے اسپتال آئی تھی۔ اس کی ماں نے اس سے وعدہ کیا تھا کہ وہ اس کا ابارشن نہیں کروائیں گی مگر چیک اپ ضروری ہے تاہم حقیقت میں وہ اس کے ابارشن کے لیے ہی اسے وہاں لائی تھیں۔

زائر کا دوست اتفاق سے اسی اسپتال میں تھا' ان دنوں وہ اپنے ایک دوست کے ساتھ جو روڈ ایکسیڈنٹ میں زخمی ہوا تھا' وہیں رہ رہا تھا۔ اس کا جو دوست وہاں پر اٹینڈینٹ تھا' اس کا خوب خیال رکھ رہا تھا' اس وقت بھی اسے چائے فراہم کرتے ہوئے اسے چھیڑ بیٹھا۔

''لے یار، دیکھ کتنا خیال رکھتا ہوں تیرا پھر بھی تُو مہینوں ادھر کا رخ نہیں کرتا۔'' زائر نے مسکرا کر چائے کا کپ پکڑا تھا۔

''مہربانی، مگر کیا کروں میں اللہ کی مخلوق کو ان اسپتالوں میں بے بسی کی موت مرتے نہیں دیکھ سکتا اسی لیے نہیں آتا۔''

''چھوڑ یار! تُو اس فیلڈ میں آتا تو تجھے پتا چلتا' کیسے لوگ سر میں درد کر دیتے ہیں صبح سے لے کر شام تک۔''

''اس درد کے پیسے بھی دیتے ہیں۔''

''ہوں' پیسہ تو زندگی کے نظام کو چلانے کا سبب ہے' تُو دیکھ ابھی ڈاکٹر ناہید کے پاس ایک عورت آئی ہے اپنی بیٹی کو لے کر اور تجھے پتا ہے وہ کیا چاہتی ہے؟''

''کیا؟''

''ابارشن...... وہ بھی ایسی حالت میں جب کہ اس کی بیٹی کی جان کو خطرہ ہے۔''

''وہاٹ؟''

''ہاں یار! یہاں صبح سے شام تک پتا نہیں کیسے کیسے تماشے ہوتے ہیں' اللہ نے ماں کے قدموں تلے جنت رکھی ہے کیونکہ وہ صرف بچہ پیدا ہی نہیں کرتی بلکہ اپنے بچوں کی بہترین تربیت بھی کرتی ہے انہیں صحیح اور غلط کا فرق سمجھاتی ہے مگر آج کل کچھ مائیں یوں اپنے مقام اور فرض سے غفلت برتتے ہوئے ہیں کہ خدا کی پناہ' اسلامی معاشرے کا چہرہ ہی خراب کر کے رکھ دیا ہے انہوں نے' ذرا سی عیش پسند زندگی کے لیے آخرت کی رسوائی مول لے لی ہے اور انہیں اس پر کوئی پچھتاوا بھی نہیں۔''

اس کا دوست اپنے خیالات اور دکھ کا اظہار کر رہا تھا' زائر کو فوراً ثانیہ عباس کی فکر لاحق ہوگئی' پتا نہیں وہ کہاں تھی اور کیسی تھی؟

ابھی وہ اسی کے بارے میں سوچ رہا تھا جب اچانک اس کی نگاہ وارڈ کے دروازے کے قریب سے گزرتی ثانیہ عباس کی ماں پر جا پڑی۔ صرف ایک ملاقات کے باوجود اس نے فوراً انہیں پہچان لیا تھا۔

''مسز عباس اور یہاں؟'' وہ چونکا ہی نہیں بلکہ حیران رہ گیا تھا۔

''ہوں' یہی تو ہیں وہ خاتون جو اپنی بیٹی کا ابارشن کروانے آئی ہیں۔''

اس کے دوست کی نگاہ بھی اس کی نظروں کی تقلید میں مسز عباس پر جا پڑی تھی' تبھی اس نے اس کی معلومات میں اضافہ کرنا ضروری سمجھا تھا۔ زائر کا دماغ جیسے بھک سے اڑ گیا۔ کسی اسپرنگ کی طرح وہ اپنی جگہ سے اٹھا اور فوراً مردانہ وارڈ سے باہر نکل آیا' ثانیہ سر جھکائے ڈاکٹر ناہید کے کمرے میں بیٹھی تھی تاہم ڈاکٹر ناہید اور مسز عباس دونوں ہی وہاں موجود نہیں تھیں' تبھی بے حد مشتعل انداز میں اس نے ثانیہ کا بازو پکڑا اور پھر بنا کسی نتیجے کی پروا کیے اسے اپنے ساتھ کھینچتے ہوئے اسپتال سے باہر لے آیا۔

ثانیہ تو جیسے کسی ٹرانس کی کیفیت میں تھی اس کے وہم و گمان میں بھی نہیں تھا کہ زائر ملک یوں اس طرح سے اسے ڈھونڈ نکالے گا اس سے پہلے کہ وہ اسے کچھ کہتی وہ ٹیکسی روک چکا تھا۔

''کیا بدتمیزی ہے یہ' چھوڑو مجھے۔''

جب وہ اسے ٹیکسی میں دھکیل رہا تھا وہ چلائی بھی تھی مگر اس نے پروا نہیں کی۔ اس کا چہرہ اس لمحے غیظ و غضب سے خوب سرخ ہو رہا تھا۔ تقریباً پون گھنٹے کے بعد اس نے ٹیکسی ایک کچی سڑک پر رکوائی تھی۔ مقررہ کرایہ ادا کرنے کے بعد وہ اسے اسی طرح کھینچتے ہوئے اپنے گھر لایا تھا۔ قرب و جوار کے گھروں میں مکین خواتین کے لیے یہ ایک بالکل نیا اور دل چسپ ڈرامہ تھا مگر اسے تو جیسے کسی کی پروا نہیں رہی تھی۔ اس کی زوردار دستک کے جواب میں دروازہ اس کی ماں نے

کھولا تھا' زائر انہیں نرمی سے سلام کر کے ثانیہ کو گھر کے اندر گھسیٹ لایا۔ پیچھے اس کی ماں جیسے ہکا بکا سی دہلیز پر کھڑی رہ گئی تھی۔

''چٹاخ۔'' اپنے کمرے میں لاتے ہی اس نے ایک زوردار طمانچہ اس کے گال پر رسید کیا تھا۔ ثانیہ لڑکھڑا کر رہ گئی۔

''منع کیا تھا ناں تمہیں کہ اللہ رب العزت کی قائم کردہ حدود کی خلاف ورزی مت کرنا' پھر بھی یہ کبیرہ گناہ کرنا چاہتی تھیں تم' کیوں؟'' وہ آگ بگولا ہو رہا تھا' ثانیہ سہم کر رہ گئی۔

''آپ کو غلط فہمی ہوئی ہے میرے ساتھ ایسا کچھ نہیں ہو رہا تھا۔''

''بکواس بند کرواپنی۔'' بنا اس کی وضاحت سنے وہ دھاڑا تھا۔ تبھی اس کی ماں کمرے میں چلی آئی۔

''زائر پتر! کون ہے یہ لڑکی اور تُو کیوں غصے ہو رہا ہے اس پر؟''

''یہ اسی لائق ہے اماں! اسی سے پوچھ لیں یہ کون ہے؟'' وہ اس وقت شدید غصے میں تھا تبھی کچھ بھی بتائے بغیر گھر سے نکل گیا۔ پیچھے ثانیہ کی آنکھیں لبالب آنسوؤں سے بھر آئیں۔

''کون ہے تُو؟''

زائر کی ماں حیران سی اس کے قریب آئی تھیں تبھی ثانیہ نے سر جھکا کر آنسو پونچھتے ہوئے اپنی اور زائر کی تمام کہانی ان کے گوش گزار کر دی۔

''یہ کیا کہہ رہی ہے تُو؟''

تمام حقیقت جاننے کے بعد وہ حیران ہی تو رہ گئی تھیں۔ ثانیہ نے آہستہ سے رخ پھیر لیا۔

''سچ کہہ رہی ہوں' یقین نہ آئے تو اپنے بیٹے سے پوچھ لیجیے گا۔''

وہ بے حد آزردہ ہو رہی تھی، اماں شاکڈ سی اس کا منہ تکتی رہ گئیں۔

رات میں زائر کی واپسی خاصی لیٹ ہوئی تھی' ثانیہ تب تک بھوکی پیاسی اسی کمرے میں پڑی رہی۔ تاہم وہ اپنی ماں اور باپ کی عدالت میں پیش ہو گیا تھا۔ بہت دیر کے بعد اس کی کمرے میں آمد ہوئی تھی' ثانیہ اسے دیکھتے ہی اٹھ بیٹھی۔

''میری ماں پریشان ہو رہی ہو گی' تمہیں خدا کا واسطہ ہے مجھے ان کے پاس چھوڑ آؤ' پلیز۔''

''سوچنا بھی مت۔''

اس کی التجا پر سکون سے کہتے ہوئے وہ اس کے پہلو میں ٹک گیا تھا۔

''فون کر دیا تھا تمہاری ماں کو میں نے' بتا دیا تھا اسے کہ میں اپنی امانت اپنے پاس لے آیا ہوں' لہٰذا وہ شرافت اور خاموشی سے انگلینڈ واپس چلی جائیں مگر...... شاید میری بات ان کی سمجھ میں نہیں آئی ہے اسی لیے دھمکیاں دے رہی تھیں' کہہ رہی تھیں وہ مجھے پاتال کی سات گہرائیوں سے بھی ڈھونڈ نکالیں گی' میں بھی دیکھتا ہوں کیسے وہ مجھ تک پہنچتی ہیں۔''

خوب صورت ذہین آنکھوں میں عجیب سی ضد کی چمک لیے وہ اس کی طرف دیکھ رہا تھا۔ ثانیہ تڑپ کر رہ گئی تھی۔

''تم ایسا نہیں کر سکتے' یہ ٹھیک نہیں ہے۔''

''چپ کرو تم' بہت اچھی طرح سے جان گیا ہوں میں کہ تمہارے نزدیک صحیح اور غلط کیا ہے' دوسروں کو ہدایت کی تلقین کرتی ہو' اللہ کی قائم کردہ حدود کا پابند کرتی ہو تم اور خود' خود کیا کرتی ہو۔ بولو' خود تمہیں یہ باتیں' یہ ہدایات کیوں بھول جاتی ہیں' بہر حال میں اس وقت تم سے بحث کے موڈ میں نہیں ہوں' میں تمہیں صرف اتنا بتانا چاہتا ہوں کہ میری ماں نے بہت مشکل سے تمہیں اپنی بہو تسلیم کیا ہے' بہت خوف زدہ رہتی ہیں وہ شہری لڑکیوں سے اور یہ کچھ ایسا غلط بھی نہیں ہے' کم

ازکم جو کچھ تم اور تمہاری ماں مل کر آج کر رہے تھے اس کے بعد تو بالکل بھی نہیں' اسی لیے میں چاہتا ہوں کہ تم یہاں انسان کی بچی بن کر رہو تو زیادہ بہتر ہے۔ وگرنہ ہم دیہاتی مردوں کو بہت اچھی طرح عورتیں سدھار کر رکھنی آتی ہیں۔''
قطعی بدلے ہوئے لہجے میں وہ اسے وارن کر رہا تھا۔ ثانیہ پھٹی پھٹی سی نگاہوں میں بے یقینی سموئے اسے دیکھتی رہی۔

''اب سو جاؤ' بہت رات ہو گئی ہے' صبح تمہیں بتاؤں گا کہ اس گھر میں کیسے رہنا ہے تم نے۔''

بنا اس کے چہرے کے تاثرات کی پروا کیے وہ فوراً اس کے پہلو سے اٹھ کھڑا ہوا تھا۔ ثانیہ کی آنکھوں سے آنسو یوں ٹپک پڑے تھے گویا صدیوں سے خشک ندی میں اچانک پانی بہہ نکلا ہو۔

رات کے اس پہر' درد' اذیت اور پریشانی کے ساتھ ساتھ بھوک کی تکلیف بھی اس پر حاوی تھی' اپنی حالت کے پیش نظر آج کل وہ بہت کم کچھ کھا پا رہی تھی۔ مسز عباس دن میں ہزار ہزار منت کر کے اسے کچھ نہ کچھ کھانے پر راضی کرتیں اور یہاں جب کہ پہلی بار اسے بھوک کا مفہوم سمجھ میں آیا تھا' کوئی اس کا خیال کرنے والا ہی نہیں تھا۔ آنسوؤں کا سلسلہ جو شروع ہوا تو پھر رکنے کا نام ہی نہیں لیا۔ گھٹنوں میں سر چھپا کر وہ سسکیاں بھر رہی تھی۔ جب وہ ہاتھ میں کھانے کی ٹرے لیے دوبارہ چلا آیا۔

''یہ لو تھوڑی دیر کے لیے رونے دھونے کا پروگرام ملتوی کر کے کھانا کھا لو' اماں بتا رہی تھیں تم نے دن بھر سے کچھ نہیں کھایا۔''

''مجھے نہیں کھانا' لے جاؤ اپنی اور اپنی اماں کی نوازشات واپس۔''

گھٹنوں سے سر اٹھاتے ہوئے وہ سلگی تھی۔ زائر اسے دیکھ کر رہ گیا۔

''اللہ کا رزق ہے میری یا میری اماں کی نوازشات نہیں ہے اور تمہیں پتا ہے ناں اللہ کے رزق سے انکار نہیں کرتے۔''

''مجھے کچھ نہیں پتا' تم اس وقت مجھے اکیلا چھوڑ دو پلیز۔''

وہ روہانسی ہوئی تھی جواب میں زائر نے اس کے دونوں ہاتھ اپنی گرفت میں لے لیے۔

''نہیں چھوڑ سکتا' اس وقت تو کیا کسی وقت بھی نہیں اور بس یہی خامی ہے میری جو چیز میرے نام لگ جاتی ہے میں اسے چھوڑ ہی تو نہیں سکتا۔''

وہ اس کی آنکھوں میں دیکھ رہا تھا۔ ثانیہ کی بائیں آنکھ سے چھلکنے والا آنسو اس کی پلکوں پر ہی اٹک گیا۔ تبھی اس نے ہاتھ بڑھا کر اس کے آنسو انگلیوں کی پوروں پر سمیٹے تھے۔

''اب کھا لو پلیز' اپنے لیے نہیں تو اس معصوم بچے کے لیے ہی سہی' جو صرف میری نہیں تمہاری بھی اولاد ہے۔''

بہت رسان سے اسے سمجھاتے ہوئے اس نے خود ہی نوالہ توڑ کر اس کے منہ میں ڈال دیا تھا۔

اگلی صبح ثانیہ کی آنکھ کھلی تو وہ کمرے میں نہیں تھا۔ وہ سست سی یونہی بستر پر پڑی' اپنی ماں کے بارے میں سوچنے لگی' تبھی وہ کمرے میں چلا آیا۔

''السلام علیکم صبح بخیر!''

رات کی نسبت اس کا موڈ خاصا فریش تھا۔ وہ خاموشی سے اس کی طرف دیکھتی اٹھ بیٹھی۔ ''سلام کا جواب تو دے دو یار! مانا کہ تم شہری لوگ گڈ مارننگ وغیرہ جیسے فضول لفظوں سے اپنے دن کا آغاز کرتے ہو مگر ایک مسلمان ہونے کی حیثیت سے سلامتی بھیجنا تو تم پر بھی فرض ہے اور مجھ پر بھی۔''

بہت فری انداز میں کہتے ہوئے وہ بستر پر اس کی گود میں سر ٹکائے ہوئے نیم دراز ہو گیا تھا جب کہ ثانیہ کے دونوں

ہاتھ بھی اس نے اپنی گرفت میں لے کر سینے پر رکھ لئے تھے۔
''وعلیکم السلام!''بس ایک سرسری سی نگاہ اس پر ڈالتے ہوئے اس نے جواب دیا تھا' وہ مسکرادیا۔
''شکریہ۔''
''مجھے آپ سے کچھ بات کرنی تھی۔''
کچھ پل خاموشی کی نذر کرنے کے بعد ثانیہ نے لب وا کیے تھے' غصے کا دھواں چھٹتے ہی اسے تہذیب بھی یاد آ گئی تھی۔
زائر نے مسکراتے ہوئے اپنی گرفت میں موجود اس کے دونوں ہاتھ زور سے دبا دیئے۔
''کہو......ویسے مجھے تمہارا تم کہنا بھی بُرا نہیں لگتا۔''
ثانیہ جز بز ہوئی تھی تاہم وہ کہنا نہیں بھولی تھی۔
''مجھے گاؤں میں رہنے کی عادت نہیں ہے آج تک میں نے صرف قصے کہانیوں میں دیہاتوں کے بارے میں پڑھا ہے' ذاتی طور پر میں نے ابھی تک گاؤں کی زندگی کا مشاہدہ نہیں کیا۔ اس لیے میں چاہتی ہوں آپ مجھے میرے شہر والے فلیٹ میں شفٹ کروادیں' میں وعدہ کرتی ہوں میں آپ کے اعتبار کو ٹھیس نہیں پہنچاؤں گی۔''
''ممکن ہی نہیں ڈیئر! زائر ملک بس صرف ایک بار ٹھوکر کھاتا ہے اس کے بعد راستے کے پتھر خود اس کی راہ سے ہٹ کر دور ہو جاتے ہیں۔تم تو پھر بھی میری ہم سفر ہو اور ہم سفر بھی وہ جس کی کوکھ میں...... خیر تمہیں گاؤں میں رہنے کی عادت نہیں ہے' کوئی مسئلہ نہیں رفتہ رفتہ عادت ہو جائے گی۔ میں کوشش کروں گا یہاں تمہیں کوئی مسئلہ نہ ہو' لیکن تمہیں بھی آج کے بعد پوری کوشش کرنی ہے خود کو میرا بہترین انتخابات ثابت کرنے کی' میرے والدین بہت سادہ لوح ہیں اور میں...... میں ان کی اکلوتی اولاد ہوں' بہت سے خواب وابستہ ہیں ان کے مجھ سے اگر تم نے کسی بھی زعم میں ان کا دل دکھانے کی کوشش کی تو یاد رکھنا میں تمہیں معاف نہیں کروں گا۔''
بنا اس کی بات کو اہمیت دیئے وہ اس پر اپنے قانون اور اصول لاگو کر رہا تھا۔ ثانیہ اسے دیکھ کر رہ گئی۔ تبھی وہ پھر بولا تھا۔
''یہاں گاؤں کی عورتیں تمہیں دیکھنے اور تم سے ملنے کے لیے بہت بے تاب ہو رہی ہیں' انہیں لگتا ہے شاید میں تمہیں اغواء کر کے لایا ہوں' اماں اب تک بڑی مشکل سے انہیں سنبھالے ہوئے ہیں یہ کہہ کر کہ تم آرام کر رہی ہو مگر ابھی یہاں اس کمرے سے نکلنے کے بعد تم انہیں مطمئن کرو گی اور ہاں یہاں گاؤں میں صبح کا آغاز بہت جلدی ہو جاتا ہے' میں بالکل پسند نہیں کروں گا کہ تم یہاں کمرے میں پڑی سوئی رہو اور میری ماں تمہارے ہوتے ہوئے خود صبح سویرے اٹھ کر سارے کام نمٹاتی پھریں' ویسے بھی اس حالت میں ہمارے یہاں کی خواتین فارغ بیٹھے رہنے کو بالکل پسند نہیں کرتیں' میرا خیال ہے میری باتیں تمہاری سمجھ میں آ گئی ہوں گی۔''
وہ اس کی سماعتوں پر ایک کے بعد ایک بم گرا رہا تھا اور ادھر ثانیہ کو لگ رہا تھا جیسے اس کا وجود سرد پڑتا جا رہا ہو وہ اس طرز زندگی کی عادی نہیں تھی تبھی بولی تھی۔
''میں معذرت چاہتی ہوں مگر حقیقت یہی ہے کہ میں یہاں آپ کے ساتھ اس طرح زندگی نہیں گزار سکتی۔''
''سیکھ جاؤ گی وقت سب کچھ سکھا دیتا ہے۔''
''مگر کیوں؟ مجھے تم سے کسی قسم کی محبت یا عشق کا دعویٰ نہیں ہے' اس لیے تم میرے ساتھ کسی قسم کی زبردستی نہیں کر سکتے۔''
''کرنا چاہتا بھی نہیں تم شاید بھول رہی ہو ثانیہ عباس! کہ مجھ سے نکاح کا فیصلہ اور ضد تم نے کی تھی' میں نے نہیں تم چاہتی تو بھری عدالت میں چلا کر کہہ سکتی تھیں کہ میں تمہارے ساتھ زیادتی کر رہا ہوں' زبردستی تعلق جوڑنا چاہ رہا ہوں مگر

تم نے ایسا نہیں کیا الٹا ایک رات میرے ساتھ گزارنے کے بعد تم نے اپنا تمام سامان بھی اپنی مکمل رضا مندی سے میرے حوالے کر دینا چاہا' کیا تھا وہ سب؟ بولو......؟ مان لیتا ہوں کہ میں تمہارے لیے ناپسندیدہ شخص ہوں مگر اس ناپسندیدہ شخص کو تمہاری عادت ہوگئی ہے' عشق و محبت کا دعویٰ نہیں کرتا مگر زبردستی کسی تعلق کو گھسیٹے رکھنے کا حامی بھی نہیں ہوں' اس لیے جس روز تم میری امانت میرے حوالے کر دوگی میں اسی روز تمہیں آزاد کر دوں گا' یہ میرا وعدہ ہے چاہو تو اعتبار کر لینا نہیں تو تمہاری مرضی۔''

بے حد سچے کھرے لہجے میں اپنی بات مکمل کرتا وہ پھر کمرے میں نہیں ٹھہرا تھا۔ ثانیہ جیسے چکرا کر رہ گئی۔ اس کے ساتھ آسمان سے گرا کھجور میں اٹکا والی کہاوت بالکل سچ ہوگئی تھی۔

❀......❀......❀

کچھ بھی تو نہیں ویسا' جیسا تجھے سوچا تھا
جتنا تجھے چاہا تھا......
سوچا تھا تیرے لب پر کچھ حرف دعاؤں کے
مہکیں گے میری خاطر......
کچھ بھی تو نہیں ویسا' جیسا تجھے سوچا تھا
محسوس یہ ہوتا ہے دکھ جھیلے تھے جو اب تک
بے نام مسافت میں' لکھنے کی محبت میں
پڑھنے کی ضرورت میں' بے سود ریاضت تھی
بے فیض عبادت تھی
جو خواب بھی دیکھے تھے ان جاگتی آنکھوں نے
سب خام خیالی تھی
پھر بھی تجھے پانے کی خواہش تو بچالی تھی
لیکن تجھے پا کر بھی اور خود کو گنوا کر بھی
اس حبس کے موسم میں' کھڑکی سے ہوا آئی
اب نیند ہے آنکھوں میں' نہ دل میں وہ پہلی سی
تازہ سخن آرائی......
ناں لفظ میرے نکلے' نہ حرف و معنی کی
دانش میرے کام آئی
نادیدہ رفاقت میں، جتنی بھی اذیت تھی
سب میرے ہی نام آئی
کچھ بھی تو نہیں ویسا' جیسا تجھے سوچا تھا
جتنا تجھے چاہا تھا

باہر تیز بارش ہو رہی تھی۔ حورعین سڑک کی طرف کھلنے والی کھڑکی میں کھڑی عجیب خاموش نگاہوں سے سڑک کے اس پار کی بوندوں کا شور سنتی رہی۔ آج کل اس کے اندر بھی تو ایسا ہی شور سر اٹھا رہا تھا۔ پچھلے تین دنوں سے وہ قبرستان بھی

نہیں جا سکی تھی۔ دل کو ایک عجیب سی بے چینی نے گھیر رکھا تھا۔ نمیر' زبیر' سمیر اور عمیر کے ساتھ دادی ماں بھی اس سے بہت خوش تھیں۔ سارے گھر کا کام اپنے ذمہ لے کر اس نے جیسے سب کا دل جیت لیا تھا۔ دادی ماں کی خواہش تھی کہ وہ اسے اپنے خاندان میں باقاعدہ اپنی بہو کی حیثیت سے متعارف کروائیں مگر عذیر نے عذر تراش کر فی الحال انہیں' اس ارادے سے منع کر دیا تھا۔

عمیر کچن میں چائے بنا رہا تھا۔ وہ ابھی اپنے کمرے سے کمپیوٹر آف کر کے باہر نکلا تھا' حورعین عشاء کی نماز پڑھ کر کچن صاف کرنے کے بعد ابھی کمرے میں گئی تھی' دادی ماں کو اس نے شام میں ہی کھانا کھلا کر سلا دیا تھا۔ خراب موسم کے باوجود عذیر کی ابھی گھر واپسی نہیں ہوئی تھی۔ حورعین' عمیر کی مدد کے خیال سے دوبار کچن میں آئی۔

''ارے آپ ابھی تک جاگ رہی ہیں؟'' دونوں ہاتھوں میں مگ تھام کر وہ پلٹ رہا تھا جب حورعین سامنے آ گئی۔

''ہوں' بہت دن ہوئے نیند سے تعلق ہی نہیں رہا۔''

''چائے پئیں گی؟''

''نہیں' میں چائے بہت کم پیتی ہوں۔''

''چلیں پھر کچھ دیر بات تو کر سکتی ہیں؟''

''ہوں' کیوں نہیں۔'' اثبات میں سر ہلاتی وہ عمیر کے ساتھ لاؤنج میں آ بیٹھی تھی' تبھی وہ بولا تھا۔

''آپ نے گوانتانامو بے جیل براہ راست دیکھی ہے؟''

''ہوں' تین ماہ وہاں رکھا گیا تھا مجھے۔''

''کس حالت میں؟''

''بہت تکلیف دہ حالتیں ہوتی ہیں وہاں' کن کن کا ذکر کروں؟'' ایک زخمی سی مسکراہٹ لبوں پر پھیلاتے ہوئے اس کی آنکھیں جھلملائی تھیں۔ عمیر اسے دیکھ کر رہ گیا۔

''پاکستانی جیلوں سے واسطہ پڑا ہے کبھی؟''

''نہیں' کیوں......؟''

''میرا پڑا ہے' تین سال پاکستان کی مختلف جیلوں میں رہ کر آیا ہوں۔ وہ بھی بغیر کسی جرم کے اور ان تین سالوں میں جو حقائق سامنے آئے ان کے مطابق پاکستانی جیلیں' گوانتانامو بے' بگرام' پل چرخی' شبرغان اور قلعہ جنگی سے بھی زیادہ بُری ہیں۔ جو کچھ ان جیلوں میں مسلمانوں کے ہاتھوں مسلمانوں پر ہوتا ہے اگر یہود اور نصاریٰ دیکھ لیں تو اپنے سارے قیدی پاکستانی جیلوں کے سپرد کر دیں۔''

''تم جیل کیوں گئے تھے؟''

''خود سے تو نہیں گیا تھا' تقدیر لے گئی تھی اور یہاں پاکستان میں ساٹھ فیصد لوگوں کو جرم نہیں غربت اور تقدیر ان عقوبت خانوں میں لے جاتی ہے۔''

''مگر کیوں؟''

''کیوں' یہ آپ پوچھ رہی ہیں؟'' اب کے سر اٹھا کر اس کی طرف دیکھتے ہوئے وہ مبہم سا مسکرایا تھا۔

''جس ملک میں قانون محض دکھاوا ہو' جس ملک میں کوئی نظام نہ ہو' وہاں ایسا ہی ہوتا ہے اور یہ بات شاید آپ مجھ سے زیادہ بہتر جانتی ہیں۔''

''ہوں' مگر کس جرم میں جیل گئے تھے تم؟''

''جرم تو کوئی تھا ہی نہیں، الزام تھا مجھ پر، وہ بھی قتل کا الزام۔''

''وہاٹ؟'' وہ چونکی تھی عمیر نے مگ مضبوطی سے تھامتے ہوئے رخ پھیرلیا۔

''ہوں، قتل کا الزام تھا مجھ پر وہ بھی ایسے شخص کے قتل کا، جسے میں جانتا تک نہیں تھا۔

''پھر......!''

''پھر کیا۔'' کوئی ثبوت نہیں تھا میرے خلاف، پولیس بھی جانتی تھی کہ میں بے گناہ ہوں، مگر پھر بھی ایس ایچ او کی جیب میں آئے پچاس ہزار روپوں نے ہمیں گناہ گار ثابت کردیا۔ ایف آئی آر ہوئی، کیس بنا اور انصاف کے ایوانوں میں بیٹھے منصفوں نے اپنے فیصلوں میں بنا کسی بحث وجرح کے سزائے موت نافذ کردی۔''

''او میرے خدا! پھر......'' حورعین کے چہرے پر بکھری پریشانی صاف دکھائی دے رہی تھی۔ عمیر نے مگ خالی کر کے واپس میز پر رکھ دیا۔

''پھر کیا تین سال زندگی اور موت کے درمیان پھنسا، انسانی درندگی اور بربریت کا نظارہ کرتا رہا۔ انسانوں کے ہاتھوں انسانیت کی دھجیاں بکھرتے دیکھتا رہا، کیا کیا نہیں دیکھا ان گزرے ہوئے تین سالوں میں، میں نے۔ سوائے قیدیوں کے ان پر ٹوٹنے والی آفات کی کہانی اور کوئی بیان نہیں کرسکتا۔''

وہ آزردہ ہوا تھا۔ حورعین اسے دیکھ کر رہ گئی۔

''کیا تم مجھے بتاؤ گے کہ اصل کہانی کیا تھی کس کے قتل کے الزام میں سزا سنائی گئی تھی تمہیں اور پھر رہائی کیسے ہوئی؟''

وہ ایک ساتھ سب جان لینا چاہتی تھی، عمیر بےکل سا اٹھ کر ٹیلی وژن کے سامنے جا کھڑا ہوا۔

''یہاں پاکستان میں پچاس فیصد سے زائد انسانوں کی تقدیر کے فیصلے تھانے کی حدود میں ہوتے ہیں۔ اے ایس آئی اور ایس ایچ او اگر چاہیں تو خطرناک سے خطرناک مجرم کو بھی مکھن میں بال کی طرح نکال کر صاف بچا لیتے ہیں اور اگر کسی کا ان کے ساتھ کمپرومائز نہ ہوسکے تو پھر دودھ کا دھلا بھی سنگین سے سنگین مقدمے کی بھینٹ چڑھ کر بدترین موت کا نوالہ بن جاتا ہے۔ یہی تھانہ کلچر ہے ہمارا، یہی سسٹم ہے اس ملک کا، میں نے خود اپنی نگاہوں سے سیکڑوں بے گناہوں کو اسی نظام کی بھینٹ چڑھ کر سولی پر لٹکتے دیکھا ہے اور آپ کو پتا ہے ان کی آخری خواہش کیا تھی؟ اس ملک کے نظام کو تبدیل کیا جائے، یہاں صحیح معنوں میں اسلامی قانون نافذ کیا جائے، مگر...... جس ملک کا کوئی نظام نہ ہو وہاں آخری خواہشیں بھی کہاں پوری ہوتی ہیں، تبدیلیاں اتنی آسانی سے تو نہیں آتیں ناں۔''

ایک لمحے کے لیے وہ سانس لینے کو رکا پھر حورعین کی طرف دیکھتے ہوئے بولا۔

''ہمارا جو تھانہ کلچر ہے ناں وہاں آپ کسی بھی بے گناہ سے بے گناہ انسان کو ذرا سے تعلق یا پیسوں کا استعمال کر کے کسی بھی وقت پھنسا سکتی ہیں۔ کوئی مشکل نہیں ہے کسی کے خلاف جھوٹی ایف آئی آر کٹوانا، قیمتی زندگیوں کے فیصلے چند روپوں میں ہوجاتے ہیں۔ میرا اور شہزاد کا فیصلہ بھی یونہی ہوگیا تھا۔''

''شہزاد کون؟''

''دوست تھا میرا، یہیں قریبی گاؤں میں رہتا تھا۔ بےحد ذہین، خوددار اور ہوشیار لڑکا تھا۔ بہت محبت تھی اسے اپنی زمین سے، گاؤں کا نمبردار اس سے اس کی زمین ہتھیانا چاہتا تھا مگر وہ بیچنے پر آمادہ نہیں تھا۔ نمبردار جانتا تھا کہ وہ پڑھا لکھا لڑکا ہے آسانی سے قابو میں نہیں آئے گا، تبھی اس نے وہی مکارانہ چال چلی جو اس ملک کے ستر فیصد دیہات میں آئے دن یہ نمبردار اور چوہدری کرتے رہتے ہیں۔''

''کیسی چال؟'' حورعین کے پوچھنے پر اس نے گہری سانس بھری تھی۔

''اندھے قانون کی چال۔''

''کیا مطلب، میں سمجھی نہیں؟''

''سمجھ جائیں گی، شہزاد کو پھنسانے کے لیے نمبردار نے اپنے ایک ملازم کو بے قصور موت کے گھاٹ اتار کر الزام شہزاد پر ڈال دیا۔ یہاں پاکستان کے اسّی فیصد دیہاتوں میں ایسا ہی ہوتا ہے۔ قتل وڈیرے کرتے ہیں اور ان کا الزام اپنے کمی کمین ملازمین سے قبول کروا کے اُنہیں موت کے گھاٹ اُتروا دیتے ہیں۔ کوئی انکار کرے تو اُس کے سارے خاندان کو دشمنی کی بھینٹ چڑھا دیتے ہیں۔ میں چونکہ اس کا قریبی دوست تھا لہٰذا میرا نام بھی ایف آئی آر میں لکھوا دیا' پاکستان میں یہ عام روٹین ہے اگر کوئی ایک بندہ بھی قصوروار ہو تو مدعی پارٹی اس گھر کے تمام مَردوں کے نام لکھوا دیتے ہیں اور یوں قطعی بے قصور بھی سزا کی بھینٹ چڑھ جاتے ہیں' عذیر بھائی نے بہت کوشش کی مجھے بچانے کی مگر بے سود' میری اور شہزاد کی تعلیم' ٹیلنٹ' کیریئر سب تباہ ہو گیا۔ ایف آئی آر کٹی' کیس بنا' قرآنِ پاک پر ہاتھ رکھ کر کرائے کے گواہوں نے میرے اور شہزاد کے خلاف شہادت دی اور انصاف کی کرسی پر بیٹھے جج نے بنا کسی بحث و جرح کے ہمارے حق میں سزائے موت کا فیصلہ صادر کر دیا۔ اس سے پہلے ایس ایچ او کہتا رہا کہ پچاس ہزار دے دو تمہیں بچا لوں گا مگر مجھے غرور تھا کہ جب میرا کوئی قصور ہی نہیں تو مجھے سزا کیسے ہو گی مگر وقت نے مجھے بتا دیا کہ اس ملک کے نظام میں سزا کا طوق زیادہ تر بے قصور اور بے گناہ لوگوں کے گلے میں ہی ڈالا جاتا ہے' اصل قصوروار اور خطرناک لوگ تو قانون کی پناہ میں رہتے ہیں۔ تاریک راہوں میں جعلی پولیس مقابلوں کی بھینٹ چڑھ کر ابدی نیند سونے والے اکثر وہ لوگ ہوتے ہیں جنہیں اپنے جرم کا بھی پتا نہیں ہوتا۔

ہم کہتے ہیں اس ملک پر اتنی آفتیں کیوں ٹوٹتی ہیں' یہاں روز کسی نہ کسی صورت عذاب کیوں نازل ہوتے رہتے ہیں مگر ہم یہ نہیں دیکھتے کہ روزانہ انصاف کے ایوانوں میں لوگ اپنے ضمیر اور ایمان کا سودا کر کے کتنی بے شرمی سے اس مقدس کتاب پر جھوٹا حلف اٹھاتے ہیں' جو کتاب ساری دنیا کے لیے ہدایت و رہنمائی کا سرچشمہ ہے' کیا نہیں ہو گا روزِ محشر ان لوگوں کے ساتھ یہ جھوٹے مدعی' یہ جھوٹے گواہ' یہ پیسے لے کر اپنے فرض سے کوتاہی برتنے والے ایس ایچ او' اے ایس آئی' محرر' وکیل' جج' کہاں جائیں گے یہ لوگ اس روز جب بادشاہوں کے بادشاہ کی عدالت لگی ہو گی اور وہاں کوئی کسی کا سفارشی نہیں ہو گا' کیسے سر اٹھائیں گے یہ لوگ اس قہار و جبار کے سامنے؟

کیا بے گناہ سولی چڑھنے والے معصوم قیدیوں کا خون ان کے سر نہیں ہو گا؟

اسلام تو دوسرے مذاہب کے لیے بہترین مثالی دین ہے' تاریخ بھری پڑی ہے ایسے بے شمار سنہری واقعات سے' جس میں غیر مسلم قبائل اور لوگوں نے اسلام کے بہترین اصولوں اور انصاف سے متاثر ہو کر اسے اپنایا۔ مگر آج ہم دنیا کو کیا دکھا رہے ہیں؟ بجائے اس کے کہ ہم وہ وجوہات ختم کریں جو جرائم کو جنم دے رہی ہیں' ہم الٹا بے گناہوں کو رگڑ رہے ہیں' وہ مذہب جو اسلام کے بدترین دشمنوں کے لیے بھی' امن و سلامتی کا باعث بنا اسی مذہب کے پیروکاروں کے ساتھ کیا کر رہے ہیں ہم؟

آپ کو پتا ہے حضرت عمر رضی اللہ عنہ کے دورِ حکومت میں غلّے کا قحط پڑا تو انہوں نے چوری کے لیے ہاتھ کاٹنے کی سزا کو اس وقت تک کے لیے معاف کر دیا تھا جب تک قحط دور نہ ہو جاتا۔ وہ عمرؓ کہ جن کا کیا فیصلہ اوپر آسمان پر سراہا جاتا تھا مگر کتنے افسوس کی بات ہے کہ آج ہم نے ایسی انمول اور گراں قدر ہستیوں کا اتباع کرنے کی بجائے' اپنی زندگیوں کو انہی شرمناک اصولوں کے سپرد کر دیا ہے جو منحوس انگریز ہمارے لیے چھوڑ کر گئے۔

کتنے دکھ کی بات ہے کہ ایک اسلامی ملک میں اسی کے باشندوں کے ساتھ قطعی غیر اسلامی سلوک روا رکھا جا رہا ہے'

تاریخ کھول کر دیکھ لیجیے ہمارے پیارے نبی صلی اللہ علیہ وسلم نے یا ان کے کسی صحابی نے کبھی کسی گناہ گار قاتل کو بھی دس دس پندرہ پندرہ سال بدترین قید میں رکھ کر پھانسی کی سزا نہیں دی' الٹا ان پاک ہستیوں نے تو گناہ گار کے لیے بھی قصاص کے ساتھ ساتھ دیت اور معافی کو پسند کیا۔ خود پیارے رسول صلی اللہ علیہ وسلم کی کئی بہترین مثالیں ہمارے سامنے ہیں' جن میں انہوں نے اپنے پیارے چچا حضرت حمزہ رضی اللہ عنہ اور محبوب بیٹی کے قاتلوں کو سزا دینے کا حق اور اختیار رکھنے کے باوجود عام معافی کا اعلان کردیا ؐ۔ یہاں ہماری جیلوں میں موت کی سزا پانے والے بدنصیب حق داروں کے ساتھ ساتھ کئی بے گناہ معصوم قیدیوں کے ساتھ انہیں ذہنی اور جسمانی اذیت سے دوچار رکھنے کے لیے وہ وہ طریقے آزمائے جاتے ہیں کہ شاید انہیں دیکھ کر شیطان بھی انسان سے پناہ مانگتا ہوگا' آئے روز ان عقوبت خانوں سے کتنی ہی لاشیں نکلتی ہیں' جو اپنے پیچھے سیکڑوں افسوس ناک سوالات چھوڑ جاتی ہیں۔''

بولتے بولتے عمیر کا تنفس تیز ہوگیا تھا۔ حورعین چپ چاپ خاموشی سے اسے دیکھتی رہی' اندر کہیں کسی درد نے چپکے سے انگڑائی لی تھی مگر وہ ساکت بیٹھی رہی۔

''کتنی دل چسپ بات ہے ناں آپی! کہ محض ایک جرم کرنے والا' قتل کے بدلے میں قتل تو ہوتا ہی ہے مگر اٹھارہ اٹھارہ' بیس بیس سال' عقوبت خانوں میں قید ایک ایک پل کا عذاب اپنے جسم اور روح پر ٹوٹتے علیحدہ برداشت کرتا ہے' کیا کیا نہیں ہوتا ان سالوں میں اس کے ساتھ۔''

عمیر کے لہجے میں ٹھہراؤ اور آنکھوں میں گزرے دنوں کی دھول صاف اڑتی دکھائی دے رہی تھی' حورعین گہری سانس بھر کر رہ گئی۔

''ہوں' صحیح کہتے ہو' یہاں کسی بھی شعبے کا نظام درست نہیں ہے' ایڑیاں رگڑ رگڑ کر مرجائیں تب بھی ہم نہ اس سسٹم کو ٹھیک کرسکتے ہیں نہ اس جال کو توڑ سکتے ہیں جو ہم پر یہود و نصاریٰ نے ڈال رکھا ہے' یہی تقدیر ہے اس ملک کے باشندوں کی کہ وہ بے قصور مارے جائیں اور کوئی ان کے لیے آواز اٹھانے والا نہ ہو بہرحال شہزاد کا کیا بنا؟''

''کیا بننا تھا؟'' حورعین کے سوال کے جواب میں عمیر کے لبوں پر تلخ مسکراہٹ بکھری تھی۔

''جس ملک کا آئین اور قانون نہ ہو وہاں بے بس' غریب لوگوں کے ساتھ کیا بنتا ہے' آپ کے ساتھ کیا بنا؟ سر ہمدانی اور ان جیسے سیکڑوں قوم کا درد دل میں رکھنے والے معصوم پاکستانیوں کے ساتھ اب تک کیا بنتا آیا ہے؟ چھوڑیں آپی! اس خطۂ ارض میں جس کی لاٹھی اس کی بھینس والا قانون چلتا ہے۔''

آنکھوں کے گوشوں میں ایک دم سے چھلک آنے والی نمی کو چھپانے کے لیے اس نے فوراً رخ پھیر لیا تھا۔

''آپ کو نیند آرہی ہوگی سوجائیں جا کر۔''

''نہیں مجھے نیند نہیں آرہی پھر...... ابھی عذیر بھی گھر واپس نہیں آئے۔''

''وہ لیٹ ہی آتے ہیں' آپ کو ان کی فکر میں جاگنے کی ضرورت نہیں ہے۔''

''میں ان کی فکر میں نہیں جاگ رہی۔'' فوراً سے پیشتر اس نے وضاحت دی تھی۔ عمیر مسکرادیا۔

''جیل سے آنے کے بعد میں چائے کا بہت عادی ہوگیا ہوں خیر آپ نے پاکستانی قانون میں دفعہ سیون اے ٹی اے کا نام سنا ہے؟''

''نہیں' کیوں؟''

''جاننا چاہیے تھا یہ قانون نواز حکومت میں پاس ہوا تھا' انسدادِ دہشت گردی کے ضمن میں بظاہر یہ قانون دہشت گردوں کے لیے بنا ہے' مگر پولیس والوں کے پیٹ کی مہربانی کی وجہ سے اکثر دوسرے لوگ بھی اس بدترین قانون کی

بھینٹ چڑھ جاتے ہیں' اس قانون کی رو سے اگر مقتول کے ورثاء قاتل کو معاف کر دیں تو بھی اسے سزا سے رہائی نہیں ملتی۔''

''وہاٹ؟''

''جی ہاں' ہمارا المیہ ہے کہ ہم یہاں کسی بھی قانون کو غلط استعمال کرنے اور اس کا ناجائز فائدہ اٹھانے سے نہیں چوکتے' بس اس پر اختیار ہونا چاہیے۔ تین سالہ جیل کے دوران میں نے بہت سے لوگوں کو اس اندھے قانون کی بھینٹ چڑھتے دیکھا ہے' ہمیں خبر بھی نہیں ہوتی اور کہیں میلوں دور ہمارے نام کی ایف آئی آر بھی کٹ چکی ہوتی ہے' شہزاد کے ساتھ بھی یہی معاملہ ہوا تھا۔ نمبر دار نے پولیس کو تگڑی رقم دے کر اس پر سیون اے ٹی اے کی دفعہ نافذ کروا دی تھی۔ بہت کوشش کی شہزاد کے گھر والوں نے انصاف کے لیے نمبر دار کو راضی کرنے کے لیے اپنی زمین بھی اس کے حوالے کر دی۔ زمین ہتھیانے کے بعد نمبر دار نے راضی نامہ لکھ کر دے دیا' جس پر سپریم کورٹ نے مجھے اور شہزاد کو قتل کے کیس سے بری کر دیا مگر شہزاد پر چونکہ سیون اے ٹی اے کی دفعہ نافذ تھی تو قتل کے کیس سے باعزت بری ہونے کے باوجود فاضل جج نے اس کی سزا برقرار رکھی' بہت احتجاج ہوا اپیلیں کی گئیں' اس وقت کے جیل کے نیک دل سپرنٹینڈینٹ نے بھی بہت تعاون کیا شہزاد کے گھر والوں کے ساتھ نہ صرف یہ بلکہ اس نیک دل انسان نے جیل سے مختلف جگہوں پر انصاف کے حصول کے لیے درخواستیں بھجوا دیں مگر کسی بھی جگہ پر کوئی سنوائی نہیں ہوئی' سب نے یہی کہا کہ قانون بنا ہے تو اس کا احترام بھی ہونا چاہیے' خواہ وہ شخص اپنے جرم سے باعزت بری ہی کیوں نہ ہو گیا ہو۔ تین بار ڈیٹ فکس ہوئی شہزاد اور اس کے گھر والے پاگل ہونے کو تھے کہ اگر ہمارے بچے کی جان ہی نہیں بچنی تھی تو ہمیں اپنی زندگی بھر کی پونجی لٹا کر' نمبر دار سے راضی نامہ کرنے کا کیا فائدہ' جیل کے سپرنٹنڈنٹ نے کہا کہ چاہے اسے معطل کر دیا جائے مگر وہ ایک ناجائز قتل کا گناہ اپنے سر نہیں لے گا۔ تب اوپر سے ٹیمیں بھیجی گئیں مگر سپرنٹنڈنٹ کے کردار پر آفرین ہے کہ اس نے شدید دباؤ کے باوجود سزا پر عمل درآمد نہیں ہونے دیا اور افسران کو یہ سوچنے پر مجبور کر دیا کہ وہ بہت غلط کر رہے ہیں' بے شک ایسے ہی لوگوں کے لیے جو اپنے فرض سے غداری نہیں کرتے' آخرت کی راحت ہے مگر شہزاد کو انصاف نہیں ملا' ہر جگہ انصاف کے حصول کے لیے سر پھوڑنے کے بعد بالآخر وہ پاگل ہو گیا اور آج تک پاگل پن میں جیل کاٹ رہا ہے' یہ ہے اس ملک کا نظام اور یہاں کا اندھا قانون' وہ بدترین اور اندھا قانون' جس کی بھینٹ صرف بے گناہ' غریب اور کمزور لوگ چڑھتے ہیں بااثر اور امیر لوگوں کے لیے تو یہ کسی کھیل تماشے سے کم نہیں۔''

رخ پھیرے وہ بہت دل گرفتگی سے کہہ رہا تھا۔ حورعین رنجیدگی سے اس کی طرف دیکھتی رہ گئی۔

''آپ کو دکھ ہے کہ آپ کے ساتھ بے گناہی کے باوجود ایک غیر ملک کے ظالم آفیسرز نے غیر انسانی سلوک کیا' صرف اس لیے کہ آپ مسلمان اور پاکستانی تھیں مگر میں آپ کو بتاتا ہوں کہ یہاں اپنے ملک میں بااختیار لوگ بے بس لوگوں کے ساتھ کس حد تک جا کر غیر انسانی سلوک کرتے ہیں' پل پل بدترین موت کا انتظار کرنے والے قیدیوں کے ساتھ خوف ناک اندھی کوٹھریوں میں کیسے انسانیت کی دھجیاں بکھیرتے ہیں' ہر لمحہ کیسے ان کو ذہنی اور جسمانی طور پر ٹارچر کر کے پاگل پن کی بے رحم موت کے سپرد کرتے ہیں۔''

''میں جانتی ہوں عمیر! بہت حد تک اندازہ ہے مجھے۔''

''نہیں' آپ نہیں جان سکتیں' سوائے ان قیدیوں اور ان کے خدا کے اور کوئی نہیں جان سکتا کہ وہاں کیا ہوتا ہے دوسرے لوگوں کے سامنے اگر ایسی کوئی بات آتی ہے تو وہ یقین ہی نہیں کرتے' کر بھی لیں تو یہی سمجھتے ہیں کہ ضرور کسی قصور کی سزا ہی ملتی ہوگی مگر ہمیشہ ایسا نہیں ہوتا۔''

''میں جانتی ہوں عمیر! میرا خود ایسے حالات سے براہِ راست واسطہ پڑا ہے۔''

''میں جانتا ہوں اور میں یہ بھی جانتا ہوں کہ جو باتیں میں کر رہا ہوں' وہ بہت سے لوگوں کے نزدیک محض فضول باتیں ہیں' بہت سے لوگ تو ان پر کان دھرنا اور انہیں سننا بھی گوارا نہیں کرتے اور یہی بے حسی ہمارا المیہ ہے' جس کا جواب دہ ہمیں ہونا ہے' اپنے ہی جیسے انسانوں کے ساتھ انسانیت سے گر کر ہونے والے سلوک پر۔ بہر حال ابھی جو بات میں آپ کو بتانے جا رہا ہوں' مجھے اس کا بہت دکھ ہے کیونکہ یہ بدترین ظلم ہے بہر حال بہت پرانی بات نہیں ہے' یہ میرا کیس ان دنوں فائنل مراحل میں تھا جیل کے حکام نے ہمیں اس روز جو چاول کھانے کے لیے دیئے تھے وہ کسی طور کھانے کے قابل نہیں تھے' یہاں میں آپ کو یہ بھی بتا دوں کہ حکومت جیل حکام کو یومیہ فی قیدی دو سے تین سو روپے دیتی ہے مگر قیدی کو بمشکل تیس سے چالیس روپے کا کھانا بھی نہیں ملتا' جیل کا باورچی ساٹھ ستر ہزار روپے خرچ کر کے یہ ڈیوٹی سنبھالتا ہے اور پھر جو راشن آتا ہے اس کی تقسیم ہوتی ہے' قیدی کے لیے کچھ بھی نہیں بچتا' دوسری دنیا کے ان نیم پاگل لوگوں کو جو کھانا تیار کر کے دیا جاتا ہے اس کی تیاری کچھ اس طرح سے ہوتی ہے کہ ایک دیگ میں پانی ابال کر' اس میں وہ دال' سبزی یا گوشت ڈال دیا جاتا ہے جو پکانا مقصود ہوتا ہے پھر برائے نام نمک مرچ چھڑک کر گھی کی جگہ ایک جگ بھر کر گندا بدبودار تیل ڈال دیا جاتا ہے جو ڈرموں کی صورت وہاں پڑا ہوتا ہے' جس روز کسی مجسٹریٹ یا اعلیٰ افسر نے چکر لگانا ہو' اس روز ذرا بہتر کھانا دے دیتے ہیں وگرنہ روز ایسا ہی کھانا دیا جاتا ہے کہ انسان دیکھ کر ہی پیچھے ہٹا دے' اس روز بھی ہمیں ایسے ہی چاول دیئے گئے تھے۔ جس پر سب قیدیوں نے احتجاج کر دیا' جیل کے سپرنٹنڈنٹ نے قیدیوں سے کہا کہ ٹھیک ہے آپ لوگ اپنے اپنے سیل میں واپس چلے جائیں' میں آٹا منگوا کر آپ لوگوں کے لیے روٹی کا انتظام کر دیتا ہوں' ہمیں پتا تھا کہ یہ لوگ ہمارے ساتھ ہمیشہ دھوکا کرتے ہیں' اس لیے ہم نے کہا کہ ہمیں ان کے وعدے کا کوئی اعتبار نہیں' وہ قرآنِ پاک پر ہاتھ رکھ کر حلف دے دیں کہ ہمیں کھانا دیں گے اور ہمارے ساتھ کوئی دھوکا نہیں کیا جائے گا' تب ڈپٹی سپرنٹنڈنٹ نے قرآن پاک پر ہاتھ رکھ کر حلف دیا کہ وہ دھوکا نہیں کرے گا۔ اس حلف کے بعد سب قیدی جیسے ہی منتشر ہو کر سیلز میں بند ہوئے ان لوگوں نے وہی گندے چاول' نالی میں پھینک کر ایک ایک قیدی کو باہر نکالا اور پھر مار مار کر ان کے بازو اور ٹانگیں توڑتے ہوئے انہیں نالی میں پڑے ہوئے چاول' اٹھا کر کھانے پر مجبور کیا اور کھلائے بھی۔ اگلے دن احتجاج پر ہمارے چار ساتھیوں کو گولی مار کر ان پر یہ الزام عائد کر دیا کہ ان لوگوں نے جیل سے بھاگنے کی کوشش کی تھی اس لیے انہیں گولیاں ماری گئیں۔''

گہری سانس ہموار کرتے ہوئے اس نے سر جھٹکا تھا جب حورعین نے پوچھا۔

''لوگ بیمار نہیں ہوئے وہ گندے چاول کھا کر؟''

''آپ کو کیا لگتا ہے نہیں ہوتے ہوں گے' مگر جیل کی چار دیواری کے اندر بیماری بھی کسی عذاب سے کم نہیں' حکومت جو بہترین ادویات قیدیوں کے لیے بھجواتی ہے وہ فروخت کر کے پیسے بٹور لیے جاتے ہیں اور قیدیوں کو ایڑیاں رگڑنے پر ہر مرض کے لیے ایک ہی قسم کی سستی سی کالی پیلی گولیاں لا کر پکڑا دی جاتی ہیں۔ سزائے موت کے قیدیوں کو تو حالتِ مرگ میں بھی بیڈ نصیب نہیں ہوتا' نہ ہی نزع سے پہلے باہر کے اسپتال کا منہ دکھاتے ہیں' اسی لیے ان بیرکوں میں وہ قیدی بیماری سے پناہ مانگتے ہیں۔''

''آپ نے شاید سن رکھا ہوگا پاکستان اور ہندوستان میں بہت سی جیلیں ایسی ہیں جہاں قیدی اپنے گھر والوں کو پیغام میں یہ لکھتے ہیں کہ ان کے لیے موت کی دعا مانگیں وہ جیلیں جہاں ڈھلتی ہر شام نہایت وحشت ناک ہوتی ہے سورج کے غروب ہوتے ہی جہاں دلوں کو نوچ لینے والی خاموشی اپنے پنجے گاڑھ کر بیٹھ جاتی ہے' وہ جیلیں جو مقبروں سے بھی زیادہ

ویران اور قبرستان سے بھی زیادہ خوف ناک ہوتی ہیں۔"

"ہوں، میں جانتی ہوں میں نے سن رکھا تھا کہ بھارتی جیلوں میں مسلمان قیدیوں کو پیٹرول پلایا جاتا ہے تاکہ ان کے اعضاء کو مفلوج کیا جاسکے، وہ قیدی جو وہاں سے رہا ہو کر آتے ہیں وہ یا تو مکمل طور پر پاگل ہو جاتے ہیں یا پھر ان کے لبوں پر ایک جامد خاموشی ہمیشہ کے لیے ڈیرا ڈال لیتی ہے، زندگی بھر وہ محض خلاؤں میں تکتے رہتے ہیں اور اپنے زندہ ہونے پر روتے رہتے ہیں۔ موت تو اٹل حقیقت ہے جس سے کوئی بھی بچ نہیں سکتا مگر پھر بھی دنیا کے ہر دکھ سے بڑا موت کا دکھ ہوتا ہے۔"

"برزخ میں جلتے لوگوں کے لیے نہیں ہوتا۔" عمیر نے کہا اور اسی پل عذیر ہمدانی نے لاؤنج میں قدم دھرے تھے۔

"السّلام علیکم!"

"وعلیکم السّلام!" عذیر کے سلام کے جواب میں حورعین اور عمیر نے مشترکہ سلامتی بھیجی تھی۔ وہ سر کو ہلکی سی جنبش دیتا اپنے کمرے کی طرف بڑھ گیا۔

"اوکے آپی! میرے خیال سے ٹائم کافی ہو گیا ہے نیند آرہی ہے، آپ بھی سو جائیے۔"

عذیر کے کمرے کی طرف بڑھتے ہی عمیر بھی اٹھ کھڑا ہوا تھا۔ حورعین اثبات میں سر ہلا کر رہ گئی۔ تھوڑی دیر کے بعد کھانا گرم کر کے وہ عذیر کے کمرے میں لے آئی، وہ ابھی لباس تبدیل کر کے بیٹھا تھا۔

"السّلام علیکم! یہ کھانا......"

"کیا پکایا ہے؟" اچٹتی سی ایک نظر اس کے سراپا پر ڈالنے کے بعد اس نے کھانے کی ٹرے کو دیکھا، حورعین کنفیوز سی کھڑی رہی۔

"کریلے گوشت۔"

"میں کریلے نہیں کھاتا۔"

"کیوں؟"

"بس......سمیر کریلے اچھے نہیں بناتا۔"

"مگر آج سمیر نے کھانا نہیں بنایا، میں نے بنایا ہے، آپ ذرا سا کھا کر دیکھ لیں، اگر اچھا نہ لگے تو کچھ اور بنا دوں گی۔"

"شکریہ، مگر میں نہیں سمجھتا کہ یہ آپ کی ذمہ داری ہے۔"

"میں جانتی ہوں مگر سمیر اتنی دیر تک جاگ کر آپ کا انتظار نہیں کر سکتا تھا۔"

"اسے ضرورت بھی نہیں ہے میرا انتظار کرنے کی، لیٹ گھر واپسی پر سب اپنا اپنا کھانا خود ہی نکال کر کھاتے ہیں۔" اس کے ہاتھ سے کھانے کی ٹرے لے کر اپنے سامنے رکھتے ہوئے وہ مبہم سا مسکرایا تھا۔ حورعین سر جھکائے کھڑی رہی۔

"بیٹھ جائیں پلیز۔"

"نہیں، آپ کھانا کھالیں تب تک میں چائے لے آتی ہوں۔"

"ابھی چائے کی ضرورت نہیں پلیز، آپ بیٹھ جائیں میں کچھ جاننا چاہتا ہوں آپ کے بارے میں؟"

اگلے ہی پل کھانے کی طرف توجہ مبذول کرتے ہوئے اس نے سرسری سی نظر حورعین پر ڈالی۔ وہ ہلکی سی گھبراہٹ کا شکار قریبی صوفے پر دبک کر بیٹھ گئی۔

"جی۔"

"عمیر نے دادی ماں کو بتایا ہے کہ ہمارا نکاح ہو چکا ہے، اسی لیے دادو نے بنا سوچے سمجھے سارا گھر آپ کے سپرد

کر دیا' وہ جتنی سخت ہیں اتنی ہی پیار کرنے والی خاتون بھی ہیں۔ میرے حوالے سے آپ کو اس گھر میں کوئی مسئلہ نہیں ہو سکتا مگر یہ حوالہ ہمیں بہت سی مشکلات سے دوچار کر سکتا ہے۔''

نوالہ توڑتے ہوئے وہ براہ راست اس کی آنکھوں میں دیکھ رہا تھا۔ وہ مزید گھبراہٹ کا شکار ہو گئی۔

''کیسی مشکلات؟''

''ہیں کچھ مشکلات' آج صبح جب میں دادو کے کمرے میں گیا تو پتا ہے وہ مجھ سے کیا پوچھ رہی تھیں کہ آپ انہیں خوش خبری کب سنا رہی ہیں' کہہ رہی تھیں آپ کو ساتھ لے کر ڈاکٹر سے چیک اپ کروالاؤں' بہت ایکسائیٹڈ ہیں وہ گھر میں کوئی نہ کوئی تقریب کرنے کے لیے۔'' عذیر کے الفاظ نے اس کا چہرہ لمحوں میں سرخ کر دیا تھا۔ مارے حیاء کے وہ اس کے سامنے نظر اٹھانے کے قابل بھی نہیں رہی تھی۔

''بڑی مشکل سے ٹالنے میں کامیاب ہوا ہوں انہیں مگر میں جانتا ہوں ہم شاید زیادہ دن تک اس فرضی رشتے کا بھرم نہیں رکھ پائیں گے۔ اس لیے بہتر ہے کہ آپ مجھے اپنے گھر والوں کے بارے میں بتائیں تاکہ میں آپ کا مسئلہ حل کر سکوں' آخر کار آپ ساری عمر کے لیے تو فرضی تعلق کا سہارا لے کر اس گھر میں نہیں رہ سکتیں ناں؟'' اس کی حیاء اور خاموشی کو یکسر نظر انداز کیے وہ اپنی بات مکمل کر رہا تھا۔ حورعین کی آنکھیں چند لمحوں میں پھر سے آنسوؤں سے بھر آئیں۔

''میں جب گھر سے نکلی تھی تو اذان ہو رہی تھی' اس وقت صرف اللہ ہی میرا واحد رشتہ تھا اسی سے عزت کی حفاظت اور پناہ کی دعا مانگی تھی میں نے اور اس نے میری دعا کو رد نہیں کیا۔''

''گھر سے کیوں نکلی تھیں؟'' وہ اب باقاعدہ انویسٹی گیشن کر رہا تھا' حورعین کا سر جھکا ہوا ہی تھا۔

''پاپا کی ڈیتھ کے بعد اس گھر میں میرے لیے سوائے گھٹن کے اور کچھ بھی نہیں رہا تھا۔ ایسے میں پاپا کی تمام پراپرٹی کے مالکانہ حقوق میرے نام ہونے پر میری سوتیلی ماں کے لیے میرے وجود کو برداشت کرنا اور بھی مشکل ہو گیا۔ اس روز اگر میں گھر سے نہ بھاگتی تو یقیناً وہ اپنے بھائی اور بھانجے کے ہاتھوں میری عزت پامال کروا دیتیں۔''

''وہاٹ؟''

''ہاں' پاپا کے آفس پر ان کے بھائی قابض ہیں اور گھر پر وہ اور ان کی فیملی' وہ ہر صورت مجھے اس گھر سے بے دخل کرنا چاہتی تھیں اور انہوں نے کر دیا۔''

''یہ تو بہت غلط ہے' کیا آپ کی فیملی میں کوئی اور سپورٹ نہیں ہے آپ کا؟''

''نہیں' کوئی بھی نہیں' صرف وکیل انکل تھے جب تک وہ زندہ تھے میں عافیت میں تھی ان کی رحلت کے بعد ہی یہ سب ہوا ہے۔''

''آپ فکر نہ کریں' میں اس معاملے کی مکمل تحقیق کروا کر یہ مسئلہ حل کرواؤں گا' ان شاء اللہ۔''

''شکریہ۔'' آنسو پونچھتے ہوئے وہ اٹھ کھڑی ہوئی تھی۔

اگلے روز عصر کے بعد دل کے ازحد بے قرار ہونے پر' بہت دنوں کے بعد وہ قبرستان چلی آئی تھی۔ دادی ماں سے اس نے بازار سے سودا سلف لانے کا کہا' شہر خاموشاں کی خاموش دنیا کا وہی معمول تھا' وہ لوگ جن کے ہونے سے زندگی کا گمان ہوتا ہے چپ کی بکل مار کر ابدی نیند سو جائیں تو دل قبرستان بن جاتے ہیں اور پھر انہی قبرستانوں میں گزرے ہوئے وقت کی غم ناک یادیں' بدروحوں کی طرح بھٹکتی پھرتی ہیں۔ اس کے اندر بھی سناٹوں کا راج تھا' قبرستان کے بڑے سے پھاٹک کے اس پار قدم پڑتے ہی وہ جیسے کانچ کے برتن کی طرح ٹوٹ پھوٹ کر بکھر گئی تھی۔

رات سبک رو، برفیلی ہواؤں کے ساتھ اپنا پچھلا سفر مکمل کر رہی تھی، جب وہ بے کل سی کمرے سے نکل کر باہر لان سے ملحقہ سیڑھیوں پر آ بیٹھی۔

آدھی آستینوں کے باریک سوٹ میں ایک لمحے کے لیے وہ کپکپا کر رہ گئی تھی مگر اگلے ہی پل بے حسی کا مظاہرہ کرتی، ٹھنڈی سیڑھیوں پر ٹک گئی۔ کل رات سے وہ مسلسل رو رہی تھی، کتنی بے دردی سے اس کے ہم سفر نے اس کی روح کے ٹانکے ادھیڑے تھے' اسے لگا جیسے اس کا سر درد سے پھٹ جائے گا۔

''اپنے باپ سے پوچھنا جا کر اپنی اوقات، جنہوں نے راتوں رات زبردستی تمہیں میرے گلے کا ڈھول بنا دیا' پتا نہیں کیا کیا گل کھلائے ہوں گے کہ انہیں یوں میرے پاپا کے پاؤں پکڑنے پڑے، تمہیں تو کوئی نہ کوئی لڑکا چاہیے دل بہلانے کے لیے، خواہ وہ شوہر کے روپ میں ہو یا اس کے بھائی کے۔'' کتنا کٹیلا لہجہ تھا میکال کا' ایک ایک لفظ کوڑے کی طرح لگا تھا جسم پر۔ لوگ کہتے ہیں تیر تلوار ہی جسم کو چیرتے ہیں مگر جو چوٹ لفظوں سے پہنچتی ہے اس کا تدراک کوئی مرہم نہیں کرسکتا۔ گرم گرم آنسوؤں کے بہنے کا سلسلہ جاری ہی تھا' اس وقت اسے کسی اپنے کی کمی شدت سے محسوس ہو رہی تھی، کوئی ایسا اپنا جس سے وہ اپنا ہر درد شیئر کر کے پُرسکون ہو سکتی۔ اگلے پچیس منٹ مزید برفیلی ہواؤں کا سامنا کرنے کے بعد وہ بے دلی سے اٹھ کر اپنے کمرے میں چلی آئی' بیڈ کے قریب سائیڈ ٹیبل سے اپنا سیل اٹھاتے ہوئے اس کی آنکھیں پھر بھر آئی تھیں' آج کتنے دنوں کے بعد اس کی انگلیاں ہادیہ اظفر کا موبائل نمبر پریس کر رہی تھیں۔

''ہیلو۔'' اسے گمان نہیں تھا مگر حیرت انگیز طور پر رات کے اس پہر بھی اس کی کال فوری پک کر لی گئی تھی' یوں جیسے اس کے ساتھ وہ بھی جاگ رہی ہو۔ ہانیہ خاموش رہی' یوں جیسے وہ سمجھ ہی نہ پا رہی ہو کہ اسے بولنا چاہیے یا نہیں۔

''ہانیہ! میری جان بات کرو پلیز' میں مانتی ہوں کہ میں نے تمہارے اعتبار کو ٹھیس پہنچا کر تمہارا دل توڑا ہے مگر خدا شاہد ہے ہانی! میرا مقصد صرف تمہاری بہترین زندگی تھا۔ میکال بھائی بہترین انسان لگے تھے مجھے تمہارے لیے۔'' اس کی خاموشی پر تڑپتے ہوئے وہ بول رہی تھی' ہانیہ کے آنسو تیزی سے بہنے لگے' اس کے دل پر جما گلیشیئر پگھلنے لگا تھا تبھی اپنی سسکیوں کو دباتی وہ کمرے سے نکل کر کمرے سے ملحقہ ٹیرس کی طرف چلی آئی تھی۔ سرد ہواؤں کی سنگت نے ایک مرتبہ پھر اس کے چہرے پر نرم سا تاثر چھوڑا تھا۔ دوسری طرف موجود ہادیہ اس کی سسکی کی آواز پر جیسے تڑپ اٹھی تھی۔

''ہانی...... ہانی! تم ٹھیک تو ہو' کیا ہوا ہے' پلیز مجھے بتاؤ۔'' اس کی بے قراری اُس کے لہجے سے صاف محسوس کی جا سکتی تھی، مگر ہانیہ خاموشی سے روتی رہی' آنسوؤں کی زبان کے علاوہ اس وقت اسے اور کوئی زبان' اپنے درد کے اظہار کے لیے مناسب نہیں لگی تھی۔

''کچھ تو کہو ہانی' پلیز کچھ تو بتاؤ' کیا ہوا ہے' دیکھو صبح ہونے والی ہے' میں فجر کی نماز پڑھتے ہی تمہارے پاس آ جاؤں گی' پلیز تم چپ ہو جاؤ' نہیں تو مجھے کچھ ہو جائے گا۔'' وہ خود بھی رونے لگی تھی اور وہ ایسی ہی تھی ہمیشہ ہانیہ کی تکلیف پر تڑپ اٹھنے والی' صرف ہانیہ کے لیے اس کی محبت میں اس نے انگلینڈ جیسا شاندار ملک چھوڑ کر ہمیشہ کے لیے پاکستان میں پڑاؤ ڈال لیا تھا جب کہ اس بات پر کتنے ہی دن جاذب جو اس کا منگیتر ہی نہیں محبوب بھی تھا اس سے ناراض رہا تھا۔

ہانیہ کی سمجھ میں نہ آیا کہ وہ اسے کیا کہے تبھی اس نے خاموشی سے کال ڈس کنیکٹ کر دی تھی اور روتے ہوئے وہ پلٹ رہی تھی جب قطعی غیر متوقع طور پر میکال حسن کے ساتھ اس کی ٹکر ہو گئی' اس کے وہم و خیال میں بھی نہیں تھا کہ رات کے اس پہر اپنے بیڈ روم سے نکل کر وہ یوں اس کے کمرے کی طرف بھی آ سکتا ہے' تبھی اس نے بھیگی پلکوں کے ساتھ حیرانی سے سر اٹھا کر اس کی طرف دیکھا تھا۔ وہ بھی اس کی طرف دیکھ رہا تھا۔ چند ساعتیں دیکھنے کے بعد اس نے ہاتھ بڑھا کر

اس کے آنسو اپنی انگلی کے پوروں پر چُن لیے تھے۔

''ایم سوری ہانیہ! شاید مجھے وہ سب نہیں کہنا چاہیے تھا جو میں نے کہا۔'' وہ شخص اس سے معذرت کا اظہار کر رہا تھا جس کی بے بنیاد نفرت ہانیہ کی سمجھ سے باہر تھی مگر اس شخص کے لفظوں نے جو کیچڑ اس کی ذات پر اچھالا تھا' وہ چاہتے ہوئے بھی اسے کبھی بھول نہیں سکتی تھی تبھی ایک سرد نگاہ اس کے چہرے پر ڈالنے کے بعد وہ تیزی سے اپنے کمرے کی طرف بڑھی اور کمرا لاک کر کے بیٹھ گئی' اگلے چند گھنٹوں میں ہادیہ اس کے پاس تھی' ہانیہ اسے دیکھتے ہی اس سے لپٹ کر پھر رو پڑی۔

''آنٹی اگر آپ اجازت دیں تو میں کچھ روز کے لیے ہانیہ کو اپنے ساتھ لے جانا چاہتی ہوں' اصل میں انکل کی طبیعت ٹھیک نہیں ہے وہ یاد کر رہے ہیں۔'' اسے چپ کروانے کے بعد وہ ڈائننگ ٹیبل پر موجود مسز حسن کو مخاطب کرتے ہوئے بولی تھی۔ میکال اور حسن صاحب آفس کے لیے نکل چکے تھے جب کہ نہال پچھلے چند روز سے شہر سے باہر تھا تبھی اس کی استدعا پر انہوں نے فوراً سر جھکائے بیٹھی ہانیہ کی طرف دیکھا تھا۔

''ہانیہ بیٹے! کیا آپ بہن کے ساتھ جانا چاہتی ہو؟''

''جی۔'' اس کے جی نے ہادیہ کے ساتھ ساتھ مسز حسن کو بھی حیران کیا تھا شاید تبھی انہوں نے فوراً اجازت دے دی تھی۔

''ٹھیک ہے' یہ تو بہت اچھی بات ہے آپ جب تک چاہو وہاں رہ سکتی ہو۔'' وہ اس کی ماں نہیں تھیں مگر ہانیہ کے لیے ان کا پیار اور ان کا کردار' کسی طور ایک ماں سے کم نہیں تھا تبھی وہ فرماں برداری سے سر ہلا کر رہ گئی تھی۔

ہادیہ کے ساتھ اگلے تین گھنٹے کے بعد جس وقت اس نے اپنے گھر میں قدم رکھا' لان میں بیٹھے کرنل صاحب اور جاذب کی نگاہیں گویا پلک جھپکنا بھول گئیں' کتنے عرصے کے بعد وہ اس گھر میں واپس آئی تھی' جاذب اٹھا تھا اور لپک کر اس کے قریب آیا تھا۔

''ہانی! یہ تم ہی ہو ناں' میری آنکھیں کہیں دھوکا تو نہیں کھا رہیں۔''

''کھا بھی سکتی ہیں کیونکہ چشمے کے بغیر تمہیں کچھ ٹھیک سے نظر کہاں آتا ہے۔'' ہانیہ کے بجائے جواب ہادیہ نے دیا تھا جس پر وہ چڑ گیا۔

''تم اپنا بوتھا بند رکھو' اوکے۔''

''اوکے' اب ہٹو راستے سے' ہانی کو انکل سے ملنے دو۔''

''میری بہن ہے پہلے مجھ سے ملے گی' تم خرید کے نہیں لائیں اسے۔'' وہ پھر چڑا تھا۔ ہانیہ کے لبوں پر مبہم سی مسکراہٹ بکھر گئی تبھی جاذب نے اسے کھینچ کر خود سے لگا لیا۔

''میں تم سے سخت خفا ہوں ہانی! مگر پھر بھی معاف کرتا ہوں' کیا کروں اکلوتی بہن جو ہو میری۔'' وہ آج بھی ویسا ہی تھا اڑھائی تین سال پہلے والا۔ ہانیہ کی آنکھوں میں نمی پھر سے امڈ آئی۔ جاذب اسے خود سے لگانے کے بعد اب اس کی آنکھیں اور سر چوم رہا تھا۔ اس کا دل جیسے کٹ کر رہ گیا۔ کتنے انمول رشتے تھے یہ' جنہیں چھوڑ کر وہ ایک ایسے شخص کی زندگی میں چلی گئی تھی' جسے اس کی ضرورت ہی نہیں تھی۔

جاذب اسے اپنی مضبوط بانہوں کے حصار میں سمیٹے' کرنل صاحب کی طرف لایا' جواب میں وہ بھی اسے خود سے لپٹا کر رو پڑے تھے۔ اس کے آجانے سے پورے گھر میں جیسے خوشی کی لہر دوڑ گئی تھی۔ کوئی بھی اسے ایک منٹ کے لیے بھی تنہا چھوڑنے کو تیار نہیں تھا۔ شام میں بمشکل اسے ہادیہ کے ساتھ تنہا ہونے کا موقع ملا تو اس کے استفسار پر اس نے

شادی کے پہلے دن سے لے کر اب تک کے تمام حالات اس کے گوش گزار کر دیئے۔

''ہانی! اتنا کچھ ہو گیا اور تم نے ہمیں بتایا تک نہیں؟'' ہادیہ کا چہرہ اس لمحے دیکھنے لائق تھا۔ ہانیہ نے سر جھکا لیا۔

''کیا بتاتی، اس شخص کو زبردستی تم لوگوں نے میری زندگی کا حصہ بنایا تھا' پھر تم ہی سے کیا درد شیئر کرتی اپنا۔''

''جسٹ شٹ اپ یار! وہ شخص تم سے اور تمہاری خوشیوں سے زیادہ عزیز نہیں ہے' ہمیں۔'' ہادیہ سخت ٹینس لگ رہی تھی۔

''کرتی ہوں میں انکل سے بات' اس شخص کا دماغ ٹھکانے نہ لگایا تو میرا نام بھی ہادیہ نہیں۔''

''نہیں، تمہیں ایسا کچھ کرنے کی ضرورت نہیں ہے۔''

''چپ کرو تم' زیادہ پتی ورتا بننے کی ضرورت نہیں ہے۔'' ناخن چباتے ہوئے اس نے فوراً اسے ڈپٹ کر رکھ دیا تھا۔

''مجھے صرف اتنا بتاؤ تم مزید اس گھر میں اس شخص کے حوالے سے رہنا چاہتی ہو کہ نہیں؟''

''پتا نہیں۔'' وہ بے حد اضطراب کا شکار تھی' ہادیہ گہری سانس بھرتی بہت محبت سے اس کا ہاتھ دباتے ہوئے اٹھ کھڑی ہوئی۔

''ٹھیک ہے بیسٹ آف لک۔'' سردی بڑھ رہی تھی وہ اس پر شال درست کرتی کچن کی طرف بڑھ گئی۔

اگلے روز شام میں اتفاق سے وہ صفدر باجوہ صاحب کے ساتھ جس تقریب میں شریک تھی' میکال حسن بھی اپنی فیملی کے ساتھ اسی تقریب میں موجود تھا۔ کھانے کے بعد جس وقت وہ لوگ گپ شپ میں مصروف تھے۔ اس نے ایک نظر میکال حسن کے اداس اور الجھے ہوئے سراپا پر ڈالتے ہوئے صفدر صاحب کو مخاطب کیا تھا۔

''ایکسکیوزمی انکل! مجھے میکال بھائی کی موجودگی میں ہانیہ کے بارے میں کچھ بات کرنی تھی آپ سے۔'' اس کا انداز ایسا تھا کہ میکال حسن اور صفدر صاحب کے ساتھ ساتھ حسن صاحب اور مسز حسن بھی چونک اٹھی تھیں۔

''جی کہو بیٹے۔'' صفدر صاحب نے بھی میکال پر نگاہ ڈالنے کے بعد اس کی طرف دیکھا۔ تبھی وہ دونوں بازو سینے پر باندھتے ہوئے بولی تھی۔

''میکال بھائی کا کہنا ہے کہ آپ نے ہانیہ کے ان سے رشتے کے لیے حسن انکل کے پاؤں پکڑے تھے' کیوں؟'' میکال کو گمان نہیں تھا کہ وہ بھری محفل میں اسے یوں منہ کے بل گرانے کا ارادہ رکھتی ہے' تبھی وہ بوکھلا کر رہ گیا تھا جب کہ حسن اور صفدر صاحب کے منہ حیرت کی زیادتی سے کھلے کے کھلے رہ گئے تھے۔

''میں نے پاؤں پکڑے تھے حسن کے......؟''

''ایکسکیوزمی مس ہادیہ! آپ شاید جانتی نہیں ہیں کہ اس وقت ہم لوگ اپنے گھر میں نہیں ہیں۔''

''جانتی ہوں بہت اچھی طرح سے احساس ہے مجھے کہ ہم لوگ اس وقت کہاں ہیں' مگر میں یہ بھی بہت اچھی طرح سے جانتی ہوں کہ ہانیہ کی شادی آپ جیسے شخص سے کروانے کے لیے سب سے زیادہ محنت میں نے کی تھی' میں نے ہی انکل کو مجبور کیا تھا کہ وہ ہانیہ کے لیے آپ کا پرپوزل قبول کریں کیونکہ مجھے لگتا تھا وہ آپ کے گھر بہت خوش رہے گی' مگر اب تک جو کچھ وہاں، اس کے ساتھ ہوا ہے میرا دل غم کی شدت سے پھٹ رہا ہے۔'' وہ جذباتی ہوئی تھی جب حسن صاحب نے اس سے کہا۔

''میرا خیال ہے ہم گھر چل کر بات کرتے ہیں اس موضوع پر' یہ جگہ ایسے کسی جھگڑے کے لیے مناسب نہیں ہے۔'' حسن صاحب کی ایماء پر اگلے پینتیس منٹ میں وہ لوگ ان کے گھر پر موجود تھے۔ نہال بھی اتفاق سے لاؤنج میں ہی بیٹھا تھا۔ مسز حسن چائے کا آرڈر دینے چلی گئیں تبھی حسن صاحب نے پھر ہادیہ کی طرف دیکھا۔

''جی بیٹے اب آپ بتائیں' کیا کہنا چاہ رہی تھیں؟''

''پاپا میں اپنے روم میں جارہا ہوں' میرے سر میں آل ریڈی بہت درد ہے میں کسی بھی جھگڑے کا متحمل نہیں ہوسکتا۔''

''ہم لوگ بھی جھگڑالو نہیں ہیں' نہ ہی ہمارا خاندانی مشغلہ ہے۔'' ایک دم سے میکال کے اٹھنے پر وہ بھی سلگتے ہوئے بولی تھی تبھی صفدر صاحب بول اٹھے۔

''کیا بات ہے ہادی بیٹا! کیوں اس طرح کا برتاؤ کررہی ہیں آپ؟''

''کیونکہ میں بہت ہرٹ ہوں انکل! پچھلے دوروز سے ہانیہ کا بخار نہیں ٹوٹ رہا ہے' بے حد ڈسٹرب ہے وہ اور اس کی وجہ میکال بھائی ہیں۔''

''کیا کیا ہے میکال نے؟''

''کیا نہیں کیا انہوں نے' جب سے ہانیہ اس گھر میں بیاہ کر آئی ہے انہوں نے ایک دن بھی اس کے وجود کو تسلیم نہیں کیا' ہر روز ہر لمحہ اس سے اپنی نفرت کا اظہار کرتے رہے مگر وہ پھر بھی خاموش رہی' کسی کمزوری کی وجہ سے نہیں صرف اور صرف آپ کی عزت کے لیے اور آپ کے قائم کیے بندھن کو نبھانے کے لیے مگر یہ اس پر بھی خوش نہیں رہے' انہوں نے اس سے کہا کہ وہ ایک بدکردار لڑکی ہے اسی لیے آپ نے حسن انکل کے پاؤں پکڑ کر زبردستی اس کا تعلق ان سے جوڑ دیا' میں جاننا چاہتی ہوں انہوں نے اتنی بڑی بات کس بنیاد پر کی' اس سے؟'' غصے کی شدت کے باعث اس کی چھوٹی سی ناک کی پھننگ پھول گئی تھی۔ صفدر صاحب اس کے الفاظ پر جہاں کے تہاں بیٹھے رہ گئے تھے۔

''یہ میں کیا سن رہا ہوں حسن؟''

''میں نے ایسا کچھ نہیں کہا انکل! یہ جھوٹ بول رہی ہیں۔'' گہری سانس بھر کر پینٹ کی پاکٹس میں ہاتھ پھنساتے ہوئے وہ خاصی حد تک خود کو سنبھال چکا تھا تبھی وہ چیخی تھی۔

''میں جھوٹ بول سکتی ہوں مگر ہانیہ جھوٹ نہیں بولتی۔''

''تو ہانیہ سے کہیے ناں وہ خود یہاں آ کر سب کے سامنے یہ بات کہے۔'' ہادیہ کے وہم و گمان میں بھی نہیں تھا کہ وہ شخص اتنا جھوٹا اور چالاک ثابت ہوگا تبھی اس کا چہرہ سرخ ہوگیا تھا۔

''ہانیہ کو یہاں آ کر آپ کی شکایت کرنے کی کوئی ضرورت نہیں ہے' جو حال فقط چند ماہ میں آپ نے اس کا کردیا ہے کافی ہے' میرا خیال ہے آگے وہ ایک قدم بھی آپ کے ساتھ چلنا پسند نہیں کرے گی۔''

''آپ اپنا خیال اپنے پاس رکھیے' میرے ساتھ چلنا ہے یا نہیں چلنا' یہ خالصتاً ہانیہ کا مسئلہ ہے اور اس کا فیصلہ بھی وہی کرے گی۔ میں صرف اتنا کہوں گا کہ میرے دل میں انکل کے لیے بہت عزت ہے میں ہانیہ کے معاملے میں ان کے لیے کسی بھی غیر ضروری بات کے سخت خلاف ہوں۔ اب سوری کہ میں آپ کو مزید کمپنی نہیں دے سکتا کیونکہ میری طبیعت ٹھیک نہیں ہے' خدا حافظ۔'' انتہائی محتاط الفاظ میں بات ختم کرتے ہوئے وہ سیڑھیوں کی طرف بڑھ گیا تھا۔ تبھی وہ بولی تھی۔

''میں نے جو بھی کہا ہے وہ حرف بہ حرف سچ کہا ہے اگر آپ لوگوں کو یقین نہ آئے تو آپ ہانیہ سے اس کی تصدیق کرسکتے ہیں' میں اس کی خوشیوں کی دشمن نہیں ہوں مگر میں اسے پل پل مرتے بھی نہیں دیکھ سکتی۔'' سر جھکاتے ہوئے اس کی آنکھوں کے ساتھ ساتھ اس کے لہجے میں بھی نمی چھلکی تھی۔ تبھی مسز حسن چائے ٹیبل پر رکھتے ہوئے بولی تھیں۔

''میکال کی طرف سے میں معافی مانگتی ہوں بیٹا! اگر اس نے ہانیہ بیٹی سے ایسی کوئی فضول بات کی ہے تو نہایت

چھوٹے پن کا ثبوت دیا ہے۔ خدا جانتا ہے کہ ہانیہ کو میں نے اپنی بیٹی کی طرح ہی سمجھا ہے وہ میرے گھر کی عزت اور رونق ہے۔''

''اٹس او کے آنٹی! مجھے یا ہانیہ کو آپ سے کوئی گلہ نہیں ہے۔'' چائے کا کپ تھام کر گہری سانس بھرتے ہوئے اس نے گویا بات ختم کردی تھی۔ گھر واپسی کے بعد صفدر صاحب نے ہانیہ کو اپنے کمرے میں طلب کرلیا۔

''جی پاپا' آپ نے بلایا۔''

''ہوں' یہاں بیٹھو۔'' پُرسوچ نگاہ اس کے بخار سے نڈھال سراپا پر ڈالتے ہوئے انہوں نے اسے اپنے قریب صوفے پر بیٹھنے کا اشارہ کیا تھا۔

''کیسی طبیعت ہے اب' ہادیہ بتا رہی تھی بخار ہے۔''

''جی' کچھ بہتر ہے اب۔''

''الحمدللہ' اپنا خیال رکھا کرو بیٹے! بے پروائی اچھی بات نہیں ہے۔''

''جی پاپا۔''

''ہانیہ بیٹے! مجھے میکال کے بارے میں آپ سے کچھ بات کرنی تھی' کیا آپ اس کے ساتھ خوش ہیں؟'' ان کے سوال پر اس نے بے ساختہ چونک کر سر اٹھایا تھا۔

''آپ یہ سوال کیوں پوچھ رہے ہیں پاپا؟''

''بس یوں ہی' دل کی تسلی کے لیے۔''

''اگر میں کہوں کہ میں اس کے ساتھ خوش نہیں ہوں تو آپ کیا کریں گے' علیحدگی کروا دیں گے میری اس سے؟'' کتنے مضبوط لہجے میں کتنا مشکل سوال کر گئی تھی وہ' صفدر صاحب اس کا منہ دیکھتے رہ گئے۔

''ہوں' ممکن ہے کروا ہی دوں کیونکہ تمہاری خوشی کے لیے میں کچھ بھی کرسکتا ہوں۔''

''بس کریں پاپا' پلیز۔'' ایک دم سے اس کا لہجہ تلخ ہوا تھا۔

''مائنڈ مت کیجیے گا مگر مجھے لگتا ہے روز محشر اگر کوئی سب سے زیادہ پریشان ہوگا تو وہ آپ لوگ ہوں گے' ہمارے مشرقی والدین جو ہمیں پیدا تو کرتے ہیں مگر پھر پل پل اذیت کی بھٹی میں جلا کر اپنے اس پیدا کرنے والے احسان کا حق بھی وصولتے ہیں' والدین کو احساس ہی نہیں ہوتا کہ ہم بیٹیاں جنہیں اللہ ربّ العزت نے اپنی رحمت قرار دیا ہے۔ ہماری بھی کوئی زندگی ہے' کوئی خواہش ہے' بے زبان جانوروں کی طرح زندگی بھر ہم صرف سر جھکاتے ہیں اور اپنی ذات کے لیے آپ لوگوں کے احکامات سنتے ہیں' خواہ ہمارا دل اس پر کتنا ہی احتجاج کیوں نہ کرتا ہو' اون کے گالوں کی طرح آپ اپنی مرضی سے کوئی بھی من پسند ڈیزائن بُنتے ہیں اور پھر فالٹ نظر آنے پر ادھیڑ کر رکھ دیتے ہیں۔ یہ احساس کیے بغیر کہ اس ڈیزائن کے ساتھ ہی ہماری زندگیاں بھی ادھڑ کر رہ جاتی ہیں' معاف کیجیے گا پاپا! مگر یہ سچ ہے کہ آپ ساری زندگی اپنے بچوں کو اسلام کا درس تو دیتے ہیں انہیں ماں باپ کی اطاعت' ثواب گناہ' پردہ سب بتاتے ہیں مگر یہ بھول جاتے ہیں کہ اسلام نے ہر انسان کو خواہ وہ بالغ بیٹا ہو یا بیٹی' اس کی رضا اور پسند کا حکم دیا ہے بہرحال مجھے کسی سے کوئی گلہ نہیں ہے۔ بس میں اتنا چاہتی ہوں کہ میری زندگی میں مزید کوئی ہنگامہ نہ کیا جائے فی الحال میں صرف سکون چاہتی ہوں بس۔'' جتنے مضبوط لہجے میں اس نے اپنی بات مکمل کی تھی صفدر صاحب کو اس سے ایسے کھرے پن کا گمان بھی نہیں تھا۔

''اور ہاں پاپا! پلیز آپ جاذب اور ہادیہ کی شادی کی تیاری شروع کردیں' میرا خیال ہے کہ اس نیک کام کو مزید

مؤخر کرنے کا کوئی فائدہ نہیں۔"

"ہوں میں بھی یہی سوچ رہا ہوں۔"

"اچھی بات ہے، میں اب چلتی ہوں آپ آرام کرلیں۔" زندگی میں پہلی بار اس نے اتنی خوداعتمادی سے ان سے بات کی تھی کہ وہ جواب میں کچھ بھی نہیں کہہ سکے تھے۔

ادھر میکال کی کلاس لگ رہی تھی۔

حسن صاحب اور مسز حسن دونوں ہی سخت شرمندگی محسوس کررہے تھے، صفدر صاحب اور ہادیہ کے جانے کے بعد وہ دونوں میکال کے کمرے میں چلے آئے تھے، وہ جو بیڈ کی سائیڈ پر بیٹھا تھا انہیں دیکھتے ہی سیدھا ہوکر بیٹھ گیا۔

"تمہارے پاپا تم سے کچھ بات کرنا چاہتے ہیں میکال!" مسز حسن ایک سنجیدہ نگاہ اس پر ڈالتے ہوئے بولی تھیں، وہ سر جھکا گیا۔

"جی کہیے۔"

"کیا کہوں یہ...... کہ مجھے تمہیں اپنا بیٹا سمجھتے ہوئے شرم آرہی ہے یا پھر یہ کہ تم نے ساری عمر کے لیے مجھے حسن کے سامنے نظر اٹھانے کے لائق نہیں چھوڑا۔"

"میں نے ایسا کچھ نہیں کیا پاپا۔"

"جسٹ شٹ اپ اگر میں صفدر کے سامنے نہیں بولا تو اس کا یہ مطلب نہیں کہ میں نے تمہارے جھوٹ پر یقین کرلیا ہے، بہت اچھی طرح سے سمجھ سکتا ہوں میں کہ تم نے کتنا دل دکھایا ہوگا اس بچی کا، جو وہ وہاں جاکر بیٹھ گئی ہے۔ بہرحال مجھے اب اس ٹاپک پر تم سے کوئی بات نہیں کرنی، میں صرف یہ چاہتا ہوں کہ تم ہانیہ بیٹی کے بارے میں کل تک کوئی فیصلہ کرلو، مجھ میں مزید شرمندگی کا سامنا کرنے کی ہمت نہیں ہے۔" غصے کی شدت سے ان کا چہرہ سرخ ہورہا تھا، میکال خاموش بیٹھا رہا۔

اگلے روز صبح ابھی ہانیہ کی آنکھ کھلی تھی، جب اس کے سیل پر میکال کی کال آگئی، کئی بار نظرانداز کرنے کے بعد بالآخر اسے اس کی کال پک کرنی پڑی تھی۔

"السلام علیکم!" اس کی خاموشی پر اس نے بڑے ٹھہرے ہوئے لہجے میں سلام کیا تھا، وہ گہری سانس بھر کر رہ گئی۔

"وعلیکم السلام، فرمائیے۔"

"ملنا چاہتا ہوں تم سے، کہاں ملوگی؟"

"کہیں بھی نہیں کیونکہ میں اب آپ سے ملنا نہیں چاہتی۔"

"مگر میں پھر بھی تم سے ملنا چاہتا ہوں، بہت ضروری بات کرنی ہے۔"

"معذرت، اب ایسا کچھ بھی ممکن نہیں ہے۔" میکال کی طرح اس کے لہجے میں بھی ٹھہراؤ تھا، پھر اس سے پہلے کہ وہ کچھ کہتا اس نے کال کاٹ دی۔ اگلے بہت سے دن اس کے شدید مصروفیات کی نذر ہوگئے تھے۔ جاذب سے ریکوئسٹ کرکے اس نے آفس جانا بھی شروع کردیا تھا جب کہ ہادیہ اور جاذب کی شادی کی تیاریاں شروع ہوگئی تھیں۔

اس روز ایک فارنر ڈیلی گیشن کے ساتھ میٹنگ کے دوران اس نے میکال کو دیکھا تھا۔ وہ پہلے سے زیادہ کمزور اور الجھا ہوا دکھائی دے رہا تھا۔ میٹنگ کے دوران بھی اس کی نظریں مسلسل ہانیہ کے چہرے کا طواف کرتی رہی تھیں۔

میٹنگ سے فراغت کے بعد وہ سیڑھیاں کراس کررہی تھی، جب وہ ایک دم سے مقابل آگیا تھا۔

"مجھے تم سے کچھ بات کرنی ہے ہانیہ! پلیز میری بات سنو۔"

''وقت نہیں ہے میرے پاس' سوری۔'' چہرے پر چٹانوں سی سختی لیے اس نے سائیڈ سے نکلنا چاہا تھا' جب میکال نے برہم ہوتے ہوئے اس کا ہاتھ تھام لیا۔

''میکال یہ کیا بدتمیزی ہے؟'' وہ اسے اپنے ساتھ زبردستی کھینچتے ہوئے گاڑی کی طرف لے آیا تھا جب وہ چلّائی تھی۔ مگر اس نے پروا نہیں کی۔ سختی سے ہونٹ بھینچے وہ ڈرائیونگ سیٹ پر آ بیٹھا تھا۔ ہانیہ بل کھا کر رہ گئی۔

اگلے پچیس منٹ کے بعد گاڑی ایک جھٹکے سے کسی ریستوران کے سامنے رکی تھی۔

''اترو۔'' بنا اس کی طرف دیکھے اس نے انجن بند کرتے ہوئے حکم جاری کیا مگر ہانیہ اس کے حکم پر گاڑی سے نکل کر ریستوران کی جانب بڑھنے کی بجائے مخالف سمت کو چل پڑی تھی۔

''ہانیہ۔'' وہ چلایا تھا مگر وہ بے نیازی سے آگے بڑھتی رہی۔ تبھی وہ لپک کر اس کے مقابل آیا تھا۔

''ہانیہ صفدر' اگر تم سمجھتی ہو کہ جس طرح زبرستی تم میری زندگی میں گھس آئی تھیں۔ اسی طرح زبردستی نکل بھی جاؤ گی تو یہ تمہاری بھول ہے۔''

''اور تمہاری بھی بھول ہے میکال حسن کہ میں اب کبھی تمہارے جیسے شخص کے ساتھ رہوں گی۔'' سینے پر مضبوطی سے بازو باندھے وہ ایک پل کو رکی تھی۔ تبھی بارش کی پہلی بوند نے اس کے رخسار کو چھولیا۔ شام کے ڈھلتے لمحوں کے ساتھ' زمین کی طرف لپکتی' غیر متوقع بارش نے اسے حیران کیا تھا۔ عین اسی پل میکال کی نظریں بھی اوپر آسمان کی طرف اٹھی تھیں۔

''میں کسی بھول میں نہیں جیتا' مگر یہ طے ہے کہ تم میرے ساتھ رہو گی۔''

''ہرگز نہیں۔'' اس کی بھوری روشن آنکھوں میں سرسری سا دیکھتے ہوئے وہ رخ پھیر گئی تھی۔ تبھی وہ بولا تھا۔

''تو ٹھیک ہے آج نہ تم گھر جاؤ گی نہ میں جاؤں گا' جب تک تمہارا دماغ ٹھکانے پر نہ آ جائے۔''

''مگر کیوں' میرا کیا تعلق ہے آپ سے' میں تو ایک بدکردار' ناپسندیدہ رشتہ ہوں آپ کے لیے آپ کو خوش ہونا چاہیے کہ میں خود ہی آپ کی لائف سے نکل آئی اب آپ اپنے فیصلوں میں آزاد ہیں۔''

''جیسی بھی ہو' مگر میری ذمہ داری ہو فی الوقت میں ذہن میں کسی بات کو نہیں رکھنا چاہتا نہ ہی تمہیں یہ اختیار دوں گا کہ تم میری زندگی کے فیصلے کرو۔''

''کوئی شوق نہیں ہے مجھے آپ کی زندگی کے فیصلے کرنے کا' بس میں اس شخص کے ساتھ نہیں رہ سکتی جس کی نظروں میں میری کوئی عزت نہ ہو۔'' سر جھٹک کر کہتے ہوئے وہ پھر چل پڑی تھی۔ تبھی بارش میں ایک دم سے شدت آ گئی۔ ہانیہ کو ہمیشہ یہ موسم بے حد پسند ہونے کے باوجود' اس موسم سے ڈر لگتا تھا۔ تبھی وہ پریشان ہوئی مگر میکال کے چہرے پر اطمینان تھا شاید ہانیہ کی پریشانی نے اسے ریلیکس کیا تھا۔

''اب بتاؤ چلنا ہے گھر کہ نہیں؟''

''نہیں۔'' اس کی نظروں کے اطمینان سے خائف ہوتی وہ اِدھر اُدھر پناہ کے لیے نگاہیں دوڑانے لگی تھی۔ تبھی میکال نے چپکے سے اس کا ہاتھ تھام لیا۔

''جب میں نے اپنے کہے ہر لفظ پر تم سے ایکسکیوز کر لیا ہے تو پھر یہ ناراضی کیوں؟''

''ہاتھ چھوڑو میرا۔''

''نہیں' پہلے میرے سوال کا جواب دو۔''

''میں تمہارے کسی سوال کے جواب کی پابند نہیں ہوں۔''

''کر سکتا ہوں پابند' مگر فی الحال کروں گا نہیں۔'' بے نیازی سے کہتے ہوئے اس نے ہانیہ کا ہاتھ زور سے دبایا تھا۔

جس پر وہ کراہ کر رہ گئی تھی۔ لمحہ بہ لمحہ تیز ہوتی بارش نے دونوں کو بری طرح بھگو ڈالا تھا۔
''میکال......!'' وہ ابھی کچھ اور کہنا ہی چاہتا تھا کہ اچانک اپنے نام کی پکار پر چونک اٹھا۔ پلٹ کر سائیڈ پر دیکھا تو مسٹر اینڈ مسز رحیم دونوں گاڑی روکے مسکراتی نگاہوں سے اسے ہی دیکھ رہے تھے۔ مسٹر رحیم کا تعلق اس کے ننھیال سے تھا مگر وہ اس کے پاپا کے بہترین دوستوں میں شمار ہوتے تھے۔ میکال کا بچپن زیادہ انہی کے گھر انہی کی صحبت میں گزرا تھا۔ بعد ازاں مسٹر رحیم اپنی بیوی اور دو بچوں کے ساتھ ایبروڈ شفٹ ہو گئے تو اس کا رابطہ بھی ٹوٹ گیا تھا۔ تاہم وہ دیار غیر سے بھی میکال کے لیے قیمتی تحائف اور چیزیں بھجواتے رہتے تھے۔

انیس سال بعد دوبارہ وطن واپسی پر ان کا تعلق میکال سے پھر بحال ہو گیا تھا۔ مسز رحیم کی خواہش وفرمائش پر وہ انہیں ''آپا'' کہہ کر بلاتا تھا۔ ویسے بھی وہ رحیم صاحب سے کئی سال چھوٹی تھیں۔ میکال جب بھی بہت خوش یا ٹینس ہوتا تو رحیم صاحب کا گھر ہی اس کی جائے پناہ ہوتا تھا۔ کیونکہ ان کے بچے اب ان کے ساتھ نہیں تھے۔ اس وقت بھی ایسا ہی ہوا تھا۔ وہ دونوں میکال کو سڑک کے وسط میں بارش میں بھیگتا دیکھ کر رک گئے تھے۔ میکال ان کی پکار پر سر سے پانی جھاڑتا ہانیہ کو ساتھ کھینچتے ہوئے فوراً ان کی طرف لپکا تھا۔

''السّلام علیکم! ایسے برساتی موسم میں آپ گھر سے باہر کیا کر رہے ہیں۔''

''وعلیکم السّلام وہی جو تم کر رہے ہو۔'' مسٹر رحیم ادھار رکھنے کے قائل نہیں تھے وہ مسکرا دیا۔

''یہ میری وائف ہیں' ہانیہ۔''

''ماشاء اللہ بہت پیاری بچی ہے گن پوائنٹ پر تو نکاح نہیں کروایا نا؟'' اب مسز رحیم اسے شرارتی نگاہوں سے دیکھتے ہوئے چھیڑ رہی تھیں۔ وہ پھر مسکرا دیا۔

''یہی سمجھ لیں۔''

''تم سے یہی امید تھی' یہاں روڈ پر اتنی تیز بارش میں کیا کر رہے ہو؟''

''موسم کو انجوائے کر رہے ہیں ہانیہ کو بارش بہت پسند ہے۔''

''پسند کے بچے بیمار کر ڈالو گے اسے' چلو بیٹھو گاڑی میں گھر چل کر کافی پیتے ہیں۔''

''گڈ آئیڈیا' آپ لوگ چلیں میں پیچھے آتا ہوں گاڑی ہے میرے پاس۔''

''چلو ٹھیک ہے بیسٹ آف لک۔'' مسٹر رحیم اسے انگوٹھا دکھاتے ہوئے آگے بڑھ گئے تھے۔ تبھی وہ پیچھے پلٹا تھا۔

''کیا خیال ہے چلو گی مسٹر رحیم کے گھر؟''

''ہرگز نہیں۔''

''چلنا تو پڑے گا کیونکہ وہ اتنے پیار اور مان سے آفر کر کے گئے ہیں' کم آن۔''

''مسٹر میکال میں تمہاری ملازمہ نہیں ہوں۔'' اس کی ہٹ دھرمی پر ہانیہ نے پاؤں پٹخے تھے جب وہ ڈھٹائی سے مسکراتے ہوئے بولا۔

''جانتا ہوں باور کروانے کی ضرورت نہیں ہے۔ ملازمین کو اپنے ساتھ گھسیٹتے نہیں پھرتا میں۔'' بے نیازی ہی بے نیازی تھی۔

وہ ہاتھ چھڑاتی رہ گئی مگر میکال نے اسے فرنٹ سیٹ پر دھکیل کر ہی دم لیا اگلے بیس منٹ میں وہ لوگ رحیم صاحب کے گھر تھے۔ میکال رحیم صاحب کے ساتھ بغل گیر ہونے کے بعد ان کے ساتھ باتوں میں لگ گیا تھا۔ جب وہ مسز رحیم کے ساتھ اٹھ کر کچن میں چلی آئی۔

''کیا بات ہے ہانیہ' کیا میکال کے ساتھ تمہارا کوئی جھگڑا چل رہا ہے؟'' تھوڑی دیر اِدھر اُدھر کی باتوں کے بعد مسز رحیم اصل موضوع کی طرف آ گئی تھیں۔ ہانیہ چونک اٹھی۔

''نہیں تو' آپ سے کس نے کہا؟''

''میکال کی آنکھوں نے' اصل میں ہم دونوں میاں بیوی کو وہ بہت عزیز رہا ہے۔ بدقسمتی سے اس کی شادی پر ہم یہاں نہیں تھے مگر اس کا یہ مطلب نہیں کہ وہ ہم سے دور ہو گیا ہو اس کی زندگی کا کوئی بھی دکھ یا خوشی ہم سے پوشیدہ نہیں ہے۔''

''گڈ' پھر تو آپ کو عائشہ اذہان کے بارے میں بھی سب پتا ہو گا۔''

''ہوں' سب پتا ہے مجھے مگر یہ حقیقت ہے ہانیہ' مرد کسی عورت پر خواہ جان ہی کیوں نہ لٹاتا ہو مگر اس کی زندگی میں جو اہمیت اس کی بیوی کی ہوتی ہے وہ کبھی کسی عورت کی نہیں ہو سکتی' جو عورت مقدس بندھن میں بندھ کر مرد کے ساتھ بستر شیئر کرتی ہے اس کے بچوں کو جنم دیتی ہے وہ اسی کے ساتھ جڑ کر رہ جاتا ہے۔ پھر باقی ساری عورتیں محض ادھوری کہانیاں بن کر رہ جاتی ہیں۔''

''مگر آپ یہ سب کیسے کہہ سکتی ہے؟'' بہت کڑا سوال کیا تھا اس نے مسز رحیم بے ساختہ نظریں چرا کر رہ گئیں۔

''مجھے عملی زندگی میں اس کا تجربہ ہے ہانیہ' کیونکہ وہ شخص جس کی سانسیں صرف میری امانت تھیں۔ مجبوراً شادی کے بندھن میں بندھ کر محض دو سال کے بعد ہی میری زندگی سے نکل گیا۔ اس نے مجھ سے جو کہا ہانیہ وہ غلط تھا۔ وہ عورت جو اس کی بیوی بن گئی تھی اسے وہی عورت چاہیے تھی۔ میرے بغیر ایک پل نہ جینے کا دعویٰ کرنے والا مجھ سے ہی کہہ رہا تھا کہ وہ اللہ کے فیصلے پر سرخرو ہے۔ اس نے سوچا ہی نہیں کہ میں جو اس کا جوگ لے کر بیٹھی ہوں میرے دل پر اس کے لفظ کسی اور کے لیے اس کی خوشی کیسی قیامت ڈھا رہی ہو گی۔'' بولتے بولتے ان کا لہجہ بھر آیا تھا ہانیہ کو بے حد افسوس ہوا۔

''مرد کے لیے جسم کی راحت سے بڑھ کر اہم ہے ہانیہ' بھلے سب مرد ایسے نہ ہوں مگر اکثریت ایسی ہی ہے۔''

''اس کا مطلب ہے آپ مسٹر رحیم کے ساتھ خوش نہیں ہیں۔''

''نہیں ایسی بات نہیں' رحیم صاحب بہت اچھے انسان ہیں میں ان کی محبت اور رفاقت پر جتنا ناز کروں کم ہے مگر...... بس دل کا ایک کونا ہے جو کسی صورت آباد نہیں ہوتا۔'' چالیس کے لپیٹے میں آ کر بھی وہ عورت محبت کے زخم نہیں بھول پائی تھی۔ ہانیہ خاموشی سے انہیں دیکھتی رہ گئی تبھی وہ مسکرائی تھیں۔

''میں بھی کیا دکھڑے لے کر بیٹھ گئی۔ میکال سوچ رہا ہو گا پتا نہیں میں اس کی بیوی کو کیا پٹیاں پڑھا رہی ہوں۔''

''بالکل میں یہی سوچ رہا تھا اسی لیے اٹھ کر چلا آیا کتنی پرفیکٹ سوچ ہے آپ کی میرے بارے میں۔'' فوراً سے پیش تر ہی وہ کچن کے دروازے پر نمودار ہو گیا تھا۔ تبھی وہ کھلکھلا اٹھی تھیں۔

''شیطان کا نام لیا اور شیطان حاضر۔''

''جی ہاں' اپنے گھر بلا کر تو اب آپ کچھ بھی کہہ سکتی ہیں۔'' ہانیہ کے کندھے کے ساتھ کندھا ملا کر کھڑے ہوتے اس نے منہ بنایا تھا۔ وہ سٹپٹا اٹھی۔

''اگر آپ فیور دیں تو میں گھر کال کرنا چاہوں گی مسز رحیم میں پاپا کو بتا کر نہیں آئی۔''

''میں نے بتا دیا ہے پاپا کو' تمہیں زیادہ پریشان ہونے کی ضرورت نہیں ہے۔'' وہ شخص اسے زچ کرنے کی قسم کھائے ہوئے تھا۔ وہ خون کے گھونٹ پی کر رہ گئی باہر بارش قدرے تھم چکی تھی۔ مسز رحیم نے فوری کھانا لگا دیا۔

''آپ کھانا بہت اچھا بناتی ہیں مسز رحیم۔'' چکن بریانی کا ایک چمچ ہی منہ میں ڈالتے ہوئے اسے ذائقے کا اندازہ ہو گیا تھا۔ میکال کے لبوں پر مبہم سی مسکراہٹ بکھر گئی۔

''شکریہ ہانیہ، میں چاہوں گی کہ تم اور میکال ہر ویک اینڈ پر یہیں ڈنر کرو، ہمارے ساتھ۔''

''کیوں نہیں آپا آپ اتنے پیار سے آفر کر رہی ہیں میں بالکل انکار نہیں کروں گا۔''

''اور ہانیہ؟''

''ہانیہ بھی آئے گی، آپ فکر نہ کریں۔'' بے حد ریلیکس موڈ میں کہتے ہوئے اس نے اپنی پلیٹ سے چکن پیس اٹھا کر ہانیہ کی پلیٹ میں ڈال دیا تھا۔ وہ بے بس سی دیکھتی رہ گئی۔

اگلے تیس منٹ کے بعد وہ لوگ وہاں سے اٹھ آئے تھے۔ بارش مکمل طور پر تھم چکی تھی۔ مگر سرد ہواؤں کا سلسلہ ہنوز جاری تھا۔ وہ کپکپا اٹھی۔

''مسٹر اینڈ مسز رحیم سے مل کر کیسا لگا؟'' فرنٹ ڈور کھولتے ہوئے اس نے پوچھا تھا۔ وہ سرسری سی نگاہ اس پر ڈالتی اندر بیٹھ گئی۔

''اچھے لوگ ہیں۔''

''صرف اچھے نہیں، بہت اچھے لوگ ہیں۔ کم از کم تمہارے قریبی لوگوں سے تو بہت اچھے جنہیں کسی کی عزت نفس کا پاس رکھنا بھی نہیں آتا۔''

''آپ کو آتا ہے کسی کی عزت نفس کا پاس رکھنا؟'' وہ اپنی سیٹ پر آ بیٹھا تھا جب وہ کٹیلے لہجے میں بولی۔ میکال سر جھٹک کر رہ گیا۔

''میں معذرت کر چکا ہوں۔''

''معذرت کرنے سے کسی کی عزت واپس آ جاتی ہے؟'' اس کے لہجے کی کاٹ میں کوئی فرق نہیں آیا تھا میکال لب بھینچ کر رہ گیا۔

''میں اس وقت تم سے جھگڑا کرنے کے موڈ میں نہیں ہوں ہانیہ، میں صرف یہ چاہتا ہوں کہ تم اس رشتے کو قبول کر لو بالکل ویسے ہی جیسے میں قبول کر چکا ہوں۔''

''کوئی زبردستی ہے؟''

''نہیں ریکویسٹ ہے، کل شام کی فلائیٹ سے انگلینڈ جا رہا ہوں، پتا نہیں کب واپسی ہو، میں نے بہت ساری اسٹوریز میں پڑھا ہے اکثر ہیروز باہر جاتے ہیں تو پھر واپس ہی نہیں آتے۔ اسی لیے میں نے سوچا تم سے معافی مانگ لوں۔ پتا نہیں واپس آنا نصیب ہو کہ نہیں۔''

''مسٹر میکال میں اس طرح کی جذباتی بلیک میلنگ میں آنے والی نہیں ہوں۔''

''چلو مت آؤ، یہ بتاؤ واپسی پر کیا گفٹ لے کر آؤں تمہارے لیے؟''

''کیوں لے کر آئیں گے گفٹ آپ میرے لیے؟ میں کوئی مڈل کلاس گھرانے کی لڑکی ہوں جس کو گفٹ کا لالچ ہو گا اور یہ دو ہی روز میں آپ کی کایا پلٹ کیسے ہو گئی آپ تو میری شکل تک دیکھنے کے روادار نہیں تھے کل تک، آج یہ عنایت کیوں؟''

''پتا نہیں۔'' بے نیازی سے ڈرائیونگ کرتے ہوئے اس نے پھر سر جھٹکا تھا۔ ہانیہ جی جان سے جل کر رہ گئی۔ دیر تک بارش میں کھڑے رہنے کے باعث دونوں کے کپڑے تا حال بھیگے ہوئے تھے مگر دونوں نے ہی جیکٹ پہن رکھی تھی۔ اس

لیے قدرے بچت ہوگئی تھی ہانیہ رخ پھیرے بیٹھی تھی جب میکال نے شرارت سے گاڑی اپنے گھر والے روڈ پر ڈال دی۔ ہانیہ کو جانے پہچانے راستوں کا احساس ہوا تو اس نے فوراً میکال کے اسٹیئرنگ پر دھرے ہاتھوں پر اپنے ہاتھ رکھ دیے۔

''یہ کیا بدتمیزی ہے آپ مجھے زبردستی اپنے گھر نہیں لے جاسکتے۔''

''کیوں؟ جو زبردستی شادی کرا سکتا ہے وہ گھر بھی لے جاسکتا ہے ویسے بھی اس وقت میں تمہاری فیملی کے کسی فرد کے منہ لگنے کی پوزیشن میں نہیں ہوں صبح نہال کے ساتھ چلی جانا ادھر۔''

''ہرگز نہیں، آپ مجھے میرے گھر ڈراپ کریں پلیز۔''

''یہ تو ممکن نہیں ہے ابھی سوری۔'' وہ اسے زچ کرنے کی کوئی کسر نہیں چھوڑ رہا تھا۔ ہانیہ کٹ کر رہ گئی۔ مارے بے بسی کے اس کی آنکھیں آنسوؤں سے بھر آئی تھیں۔ اسے سمجھ نہیں آرہی تھی کہ یہ شخص آخر اس کے ساتھ یہ سب کر کیوں رہا تھا۔ وہ تو اس سے نفرت کرتا تھا اس کی شکل تک دیکھنے کا روادار نہیں تھا۔ پھر اب کیا ہوا تھا۔

یہ احساس ندامت تھا یا کچھ اور؟ جتنا وہ اس بارے میں سوچتی جارہی تھی الجھتی جارہی تھی۔ اگلے چند لمحوں میں گاڑی ایک جھٹکے کے ساتھ رکی تھی۔ ہانیہ بجھے دل کے ساتھ اندر آئی تو سامنے خالی پڑا لاؤنج اس کا منہ چڑا رہا تھا۔ تب قدرے حیرانی کے ساتھ شکر ادا کرتی وہ فوراً اوپر اپنے بیڈروم میں چلی آئی تھی۔ شاید شدید سردی نے اس گھر کے مکینوں کو بھی جلدی اپنے کمروں میں دبک جانے پر مجبور کردیا تھا۔

اپنے بیڈروم میں آنے کے بعد اس نے کپڑے تبدیل کیے اور پھر فوراً گرم کمبل میں گھس کر سوگئی تھی۔ میکال نے اگر اس کے گھر والوں کو انفارم نہیں کیا تھا تو یقیناً وہ لوگ پریشان ہوسکتے تھے۔ اسی سوچ کے پیش نظر اس نے فوراً لینڈ لائن نمبر سے اپنے گھر کا نمبر پریس کیا تھا۔ دوسری جانب فون اس کے پاپا نے ہی ریسیو کیا تھا۔

''السلام علیکم پاپا۔''

''وعلیکم السلام! اب کیسی طبیعت ہے بھابی کی میکال بتا رہا تھا وہ ٹھیک نہیں ہیں۔''

''جج جی، اسی لیے میں اِدھر آگئی تھی۔ اب وہ ٹھیک ہیں آپ پریشان مت ہوں۔''

''چلو شکر ہے مالک کا، میں کل چکر لگاؤں گا ادھر کا تمہیں وہاں کوئی مسئلہ تو نہیں ہے نا؟''

''نہیں سب ٹھیک ہے میں اب فون رکھتی ہوں خدا حافظ۔'' وہ صفدر صاحب سے زیادہ فرینک نہیں تھی۔ تبھی مختصر بات کرتی تھی۔ اس وقت بھی ایسا ہی ہوا تھا۔ یقیناً میکال نے اپنی ماں کی ناسازیٔ طبیعت کا بہانہ بنا کر اسے وہاں لانے کا عذر پیش کیا تھا۔ وہ بے مقصد ہی اسے سوچے گئی یونہی سوچتے سوچتے جانے کب آنکھ لگ گئی۔ میکال کمرے میں آیا تو وہ گرم کمبل میں دبک کر پرسکون نیند سو رہی تھی۔ وہ اچٹتی سی ایک نظر اس پر ڈالتا واش روم میں گھس گیا۔ کپڑے تبدیل کرنے کے بعد اس نے برش کیا اور ہانیہ کے پہلو میں آکر ٹک گیا۔ رات دھیرے دھیرے آگے سرکتی جارہی تھی۔ اس نے یونہی ٹی وی آن کرلیا۔ مگر کچھ منٹ کے بعد ہی دل اچاٹ ہوگیا تو اسے بھی آف کردیا۔ ہانیہ اتفاق سے اسی کی طرف کروٹ لیے سو رہی تھی۔ وہ دائیں ہاتھ پر سر ٹکا کر فرصت سے اسے دیکھے گیا۔ خوب صورت گوری کلائی میں پڑی گہرے نیلے رنگ کی کانچ کی چوڑیاں، اس کا دل مٹھی میں جکڑ گئی تھیں۔

یونہی ہاتھ بڑھا کر اس نے اس کی کلائی میں پڑی چوڑیوں کو چھوا تھا۔ پہلی بار زندگی میں کوئی کھنک اسے بے حد بھلی لگی تھی۔ چوڑیوں پر دل پھسلا تو طلب مزید بڑھتی گئی۔ بازو پر پھسلتا ہاتھ اس کے شفاف چہرے پر آرکا تھا۔ شہادت کی انگلی سے اس کے خوب صورت چہرے کے ایک ایک نقوش کو چھوتے ہوئے اس کی دھڑکنوں کے ساتھ ساتھ سانسیں بھی تیز ہوئی تھیں۔ ہانیہ اس کی قربت پر ذرا سی کسمسائی تھی۔ تبھی اس نے ہاتھ بڑھا کر اسے اپنے قریب کیا تھا۔

''ہانیہ۔''

قطعی بے خودی کے عالم میں مدہوش ہوتے ہوئے جانے کیوں وہ اسے پکار بیٹھا تھا۔ عین اسی پل ہانیہ کی آنکھ کھلی تھی۔ وہ اسے پیچھے ہٹانا چاہتی تھی مگر میکال کی تیز ہوتی گرم سانسوں نے اسے بے بس کر کے رکھ دیا۔ بنا اس کے گریز کو کوئی اہمیت دیے اس نے اس کے دونوں ہاتھ اوپر کر کے اپنے ہاتھوں میں جکڑ لیے تھے۔ وہ سمجھ نہیں پا رہی تھی کہ وہ اپنا روم چھوڑ کر اس کے کمرے میں کیوں آیا تھا۔ ہادیہ نے اس کی طبیعت صاف کرنے کا دعویٰ کر کے آخر ایسا کیا کہا تھا اس سے کہ وہ یکسر تبدیل ہو کے رہ گیا تھا۔ وہ اس کی گرفت سے نکلنا چاہتی تھی مگر وہ ایسا کوئی موقع دینے کے موڈ میں نہیں تھا۔ نہایت نرمی اور اپنائیت سے وہ یوں اس پر چھایا کہ وہ احتجاج بھی نہیں کر سکی تھی۔ گرم سانسوں نے اس کی سوچنے سمجھنے کی ساری صلاحیتیں ہی مفلوج کر ڈالی تھیں۔ اس کے وہم و گمان میں بھی نہیں تھا کہ وہ اس کے سامنے یوں کمزور پڑ جائے گی۔ ہانیہ کو لگ رہا تھا جیسے اس کے جسم سے جان نکلتی جا رہی ہو۔ کسی شکستہ سپہ سالار کی طرح اس نے اپنا آپ نہایت آسانی سے اس کے سپرد کر دیا تھا۔ وہ اس سے محبت کی دعوے دار نہیں تھی مگر پھر بھی اس وقت اس کی قربت نے اسے کسی اور ہی دنیا میں پہنچا دیا تھا۔

صبح ہونے میں کچھ ہی دیر باقی تھی جب وہ بستر سے نکل گئی تھی۔ بے ترتیب ہوتی سانسوں اور بے جان ہوتے جسم نے اسے لڑکھڑانے پر مجبور کر دیا تھا۔ میکال نے اٹھ کر اسے سہارا دینا چاہا مگر وہ اس کا ہاتھ جھٹکتی فوراً کمرے سے باہر نکل گئی تھی۔ اگلے پون گھنٹے میں جس وقت وہ فریش ہو کر نیچے لاؤنج میں آئی چائے پیتے ہوئے نہال نے اسے خاصے اچنبھے سے دیکھا۔

''ارے......تم کب آئیں؟''

''رات کو انکل اور آنٹی نظر نہیں آ رہے؟''

''کیسے نظر آ سکتے ہیں آؤٹ آف سٹی ہیں دونوں۔ آج دوپہر یا شام تک آئیں گے تم رات کس کے ساتھ آئیں میکال بھائی کے ساتھ؟''

''ہوں۔'' اس کے مقابل صوفے پر ٹکتے ہوئے وہ سر جھکا گئی تھی۔ نہال اسے دیکھ کر رہ گیا۔

''ہادیہ بتا رہی تھی کہ تمہارا کلیش ہوا ہے میکال بھیا کے ساتھ مجھے کیوں نہیں بتایا تم نے؟''

''کیوں بتاتی میں تمہیں، ویسے بھی تم شہر میں نہیں تھے۔''

''شہر میں نہیں تھا تو کیا ہوا' دنیا میں تو تھا نا اتنی بڑی بات ہو گئی اور تم نے مجھ سے شیئر تک کرنا گوارا نہیں کیا کیوں؟'' وہ گلہ کر رہا تھا ہانیہ رخ پھیر گئی۔

''میں اس وقت تم سے جھگڑے کے موڈ میں نہیں ہوں نہال' اگر تم فری ہو تو پلیز مجھے گھر چھوڑ آؤ۔''

''اتنی صبح؟''

''ہوں۔''

''تو پھر آئیں کیوں تھیں رات؟''

''اپنی مرضی سے نہیں آئی تھی زبردستی لے کر آئے تھے وہ مجھے۔''

''مگر کیوں؟''

''انہی سے پوچھنا کیوں' مجھے نہیں پتا اتر گیا ہو گا سر سے عائشہ جی کی محبت کا بھوت۔''

''چلو یہ تو اچھی بات ہے' میں نے ناشتا نہیں کیا پلیز ناشتا بنا دو پھر چھوڑ آتا ہوں۔''

''خود بنالو اٹھ کر میرا موڈ نہیں ہے۔'' وہ جلد از جلد وہاں سے فرار چاہ رہی تھی۔ میکال حسن سے دوبارہ سامنے کا تصور ہی اس کی جان پر بنا رہا تھا۔ کتنی نفرت اور غرور سے اس نے اسے دھتکارا تھا۔ کتنے اعتماد سے اس نے کہا تھا کہ وہ اس پر اور اس کی رفاقت پر لعنت بھیجتی ہے۔ وہ بھی ہزار بار مگر صرف ایک بار میں ہی وہ کتنی کمزور پڑ گئی تھی۔ اس کا بس نہ چلتا تھا کہ تھپڑ مار مار کر اپنا چہرہ سرخ کر لیتی۔

''تم میکال بھائی کا غصہ مجھ پر کیوں نکال رہی ہو؟''

''کیوں میں نے تمہیں کیا کہا ہے اگر تم اس وقت مجھے چھوڑ کر نہیں آ سکتے تو ٹھیک ہے میں خود ہی چلی جاتی ہوں۔''

''چپ کرو' آئی بڑی خود جانے والی۔''

''نہال۔'' اسے ڈپٹ کر وہ ابھی اٹھا ہی تھا کہ میکال نے اسے پکار لیا۔ بلیک پینٹ شرٹ میں ملبوس وہ نظر لگ جانے کی حد تک خوب صورت دکھائی دے رہا تھا۔

''جی بھائی۔'' اس کی پکار پر نہال فوراً پلٹا تھا۔

''میں ہانیہ کو چھوڑ کر آتا ہوں تم ناشتا کر کے آفس پہنچو کچھ ڈسکس کرنا ہے تم سے۔'' کف فولڈ کرتے ہوئے وہ سیڑھیاں کراس کر رہا تھا۔ ہانیہ کو لگا اس کے سر پر منوں بوجھ آ پڑا ہو۔

''جی ٹھیک ہے۔'' نہال کی فرمانبرداری عروج پر تھی۔ وہ کڑھ کر رہ گئی۔

''چلو۔'' اگلے ہی پل وہ اس کے مقابل آ کھڑا ہوا تھا۔ ہانیہ سے سر اٹھانا دشوار ہو گیا۔ گاڑی میں میکال کے ملبوس سے اٹھنے والی پرفیوم کی دلفریب خوش بو نے اسے خوامخواہ ڈسٹرب کر کے رکھ دیا تھا۔ وہ رخ پھیر کر بیٹھ گئی۔

''میں نے سنا ہے ہادیہ اور جاذب کی شادی ہو رہی ہے کیا سچ ہے؟'' گاڑی اسٹارٹ کرتے ہوئے بالآخر اسی نے گفتگو کا آغاز کیا تھا۔

''پتا نہیں۔''

''تمہیں نہیں پتا تو پھر کسے پتا ہے؟''

''میکال حسن میں اس وقت آپ سے بات کرنے کے موڈ میں نہیں ہوں۔'' وہ اس کے سوال برائے سوال پر چڑ گئی تھی۔ میکال نے لب بھینچ لیے۔

''اوکے۔'' گہری سانس بھر کر کہتے ہی اس نے گاڑی کی اسپیڈ بڑھا دی تھی۔ باقی کا سارا سفر خاموشی کی نذر ہو گیا تھا۔ اگلے چالیس منٹ کے بعد وہ اپنے گھر پر تھی اور میکال بڑے ہال میں بیٹھا صفدر صاحب اور جاذب کے ساتھ گپیں لگا رہا تھا۔

''دیکھا' یہ ہوتی ہے مردوں کی خاصیت جتنا مرضی کسی مرد کو دوسرے مرد کے خلاف اکسا دو مجال ہے جو اُن میں تُو تُو میں میں ہو جائے اور ایک ہم عورتیں ہیں کہ ذرا کسی سے کوئی بات پتا چلی نہیں اور ہماری جنگیں شروع ہوئی نہیں۔'' ہادیہ کچن میں تھی۔ ہانیہ اس کی مدد کے لیے آئی تو وہ ایک نظر ہال میں بیٹھے میکال پر ڈالتے ہوئے بول اٹھی۔ اس کی تقلید میں ہانیہ نے بھی سر اٹھا کر اسے دیکھا تھا۔ عین اسی پل کسی بات پر سر اٹھاتے ہوئے میکال کی نظر بھی اس پر پڑی تھی۔ دونوں کی نگاہیں ملیں اور ایک پل کے لیے جیسے دونوں ہی عجیب سے سحر میں جکڑے گئے۔

''ہانیہ۔'' ہادیہ نے اسے پکارا تھا وہ گڑبڑا کر رہ گئی۔

''ہوں۔''

''کدھر دھیان ہے تمہارا' میں تم سے ناشتے کا پوچھ رہی ہوں اور تم ہو کہ جواب ہی نہیں دے رہیں۔''

''سس...... سوری مجھے دھیان نہیں رہا' بتاؤ کیا پوچھا ہے تم نے؟''

''پاگل لڑکی میں پوچھ رہی تھی کہ میکال بھائی ناشتا کر کے آئے ہیں یا نہیں۔ میں ان کا ناشتا بھی ساتھ ہی تیار کر رہی ہوں۔''

''ہاں کردو' میرے خیال میں وہ یہیں ناشتا کریں گے۔''

''چلو ٹھیک ہے میں ناشتا بناتی ہوں تم ذرا یہ چیزیں ٹیبل پر سیٹ کردو' آنٹی کی طبیعت ٹھیک نہیں ہے وہ اپنے کمرے میں آرام کر رہی ہیں۔''

''سوری ہادیہ' میری بھی طبیعت ٹھیک نہیں ہے تم ملازمہ کو ساتھ لگالو۔ میں اپنے کمرے میں جارہی ہوں سونے کے لیے سوری اگین۔'' ہادیہ کی ریکویسٹ پر صاف جواب دیتی وہ فوراً کچن سے نکل آئی تھی۔ اس وقت جو اس کا حال تھا اس حال میں ریسٹ کرنا واقعی اس کے لیے بہت ضروری ہو گیا تھا۔

❀.....❀.....❀

کہانیاں اب بدل گئی ہیں
نہ اب وہ آنکھیں کہ جن میں خوابوں کے سارے موسم
گلاب موسم بنے ہوئے تھے
نہ اب وہ شامیں کہ جن میں تیری حسین باتیں
رفیق لگتی تھیں ذہن و دل کو
وہ سارے منظر بدل گئے ہیں
نہ وصل کا کوئی خواب باقی
نہ اب وہ حرف سخن رہا ہے
کہانیاں اب بدل گئی ہیں
تمہارے جانے کے بعد یوں بھی
جو خواب آنکھوں میں چاہتوں کا یقین بن کر ٹھہر گئے تھے
وہ خواب سارے بکھر گئے ہیں
ملال دل میں اتر گئے ہیں
نہ زندگی ہے نہ زندگی میں وصال موسم کی چاہ کوئی
نہ شاعری ہے نہ شاعری میں جو دکھ ہے اس سے پناہ کوئی
جو سچ تھا اب جھوٹ ہو گیا ہے
جو دن میں سورج بنا ہوا تھا
وہ شب کی تاریک وادیوں میں ہی کھو گیا ہے
کہانیاں اب بدل گئی ہیں......

''اریج......!'' گاڑی کی ہیڈ لائٹس وجود پر پڑتے ہی وہ زخموں کی پروا کیے بغیر اٹھی تھی اور فوراً اریج کی گاڑی پر جھک آئی تھی مگر وہ شخص اس وقت شدید نشے میں تھا۔ تبھی گاڑی کا انجن بند کرنے کے بعد خاموش بیٹھا الجھی ہوئی نگاہوں سے اسے دیکھتا رہا تھا۔

''اریج...... جمال کا ایکسیڈنٹ ہو گیا ہے۔ خدا کی قسم مجھے نہیں پتا تھا وہ کب گھر سے نکلا پلیز میری مدد کرو امی نے مجھے گھر سے نکال دیا ہے تم انہیں سمجھاؤ پلیز۔'' کھڑکی کے شیشے پر جھکی ہوئی وہ کسی بھکارن کی طرح اس کی منت کر رہی تھی مگر وہ جیسے کچھ بھی سننے اور سمجھنے سے قاصر دکھائی دے رہا تھا۔ تبھی دروازہ کھول کر خاموشی سے اندر کی طرف بڑھ گیا پیچھے عائشہ سسکتی رہ گئی تھی۔ گھر کے اندر جیسے کہرام مچا تھا۔ جمال کے ایکسیڈنٹ کی نوعیت شدید تھی۔ وہ زخموں کی تاب نہیں لا سکا تھا۔ اریج کا نشہ ایک پل میں اڑن چھو ہو گیا۔ وہ رات اس گھر کے تمام مکینوں کے لیے رت جگے کی رات تھی۔

اگلے روز فقط پچیس سال کی عمر میں عائشہ اذہان پر بیوگی کا داغ لگ گیا تھا۔ گھر کے ایک کونے میں دبکی بیٹھی وہ ہر آنے والے سے جانے کیسے کیسے جملے سنتی رہی تھی۔ اس پر اس کی ساس اور نند نے بھی بیٹے کا ماتم کرنے کے بجائے اسے کوسا تھا۔ اس روز وہ جان پائی تھی کہ پاگل ہی سہی مگر اس کا شوہر اس کے لیے کتنی بڑی عافیت تھا۔ جمال کی موت کا تیسرا دن تھا جب اس کی ساس اس کے کمرے میں چلی آئی۔

''چل، نکل یہاں سے دفع ہو جا۔'' عائشہ اس حملے کے لیے تیار نہیں تھی تبھی بوکھلا کر رہ گئی۔

''کک' کہاں نکل جاؤں' میرا تو کوئی ٹھکانہ ہی نہیں۔''

''کوئی ٹھکانہ نہیں تو جا کر کسی کوٹھے پر بیٹھ جا منحوس عورت' ایک بیٹا تو کھا گئی میرا کیا دوسرا بھی تیرے حوالے کر دوں؟'' اس بار اس کی ساس نے اس کے چہرے پر دو تھپڑ رسید کیے تھے۔ وہ منہ کے بل سائیڈ پر جا گری۔

''میرا کیا قصور ہے اس میں' میں نے تو نہیں مارا ان کو۔''

''چپ کر بے غیرت' زبان چلاتی ہے آگے سے؟'' دو تھپڑ اور آ لگے تھے تبھی اریج کمرے میں چلا آیا۔

''امی یہ کیا کر رہی ہیں آپ؟ پتا بھی ہے کہ وہ عدت میں ہے اس سے پہلے اس گھر سے نہیں جا سکتی۔ پھر بھی آپ اس کے پیچھے پڑی ہوئی ہیں۔''

''ارے بھاڑ میں گئی اس کی عدت میں اس منحوس لڑکی کو ایک منٹ بھی اس گھر میں برداشت نہیں کر سکتی۔''

''تو ٹھیک ہے' آپ دبئی چلی جائیں کمال بھائی کے پاس' جب اس کی عدت پوری ہو جائے تب آ جایئے گا۔''

''ہاں تم تو یہی چاہتے ہو میں چلی جاؤں اور تمہیں اس کے ساتھ گل چھرے اڑانے کا موقع مل جائے۔''

''میں گل چھروں کا ترسا ہوا نہیں ہوں اپنی محبت ہے میری' منگیتر ہے اسی کے ساتھ کروں گا جو کرنا ہوا اپنے بھائی کے جھوٹے پر آنکھ نہیں رکھی میں نے۔'' پہلی بار وہ حلق کے بل چلایا تھا۔ عائشہ کا دل چاہا کاش زمین پھٹے اور وہ اس میں سما جائے۔

''کیوں بھول رہی ہیں آپ کہ اسی لڑکی کے بھائی کے ساتھ اپنی بیٹی کا رشتہ طے کیے ہوئے ہیں آپ۔ اگر اسے اس حالت میں گھر سے نکال دیں گی تو وہ آپ کی بیٹی کیسے لیں گے؟''

''میری بیٹی کو رشتوں کی کمی نہیں ہے۔''

''پتا ہے مجھے جتنی لائنیں لگی ہوئی تھیں رشتے کے لیے۔'' تلخی سے سر جھٹکتے ہوئے اس نے عائشہ پر نگاہ ڈالی تھی۔

''آپ جائیں اپنے کمرے میں' جب تک میں اس گھر میں ہوں آپ کو کوئی نہیں نکال سکتا۔'' عائشہ کی سماعتیں جیسے انہی الفاظ کی منتظر تھیں۔ ممنون نگاہوں سے اریج کو دیکھتی وہ فوراً منظر سے ہٹ گئی تھی۔

اگلے چار ماہ اس نے جیسے کسی دوزخ میں بسر کیے تھے۔ اس کی ماں بیٹے کے پاس دبئی جا بسی تھیں۔ ہن نے کبھی بھول کر بھی اس کے گھر کا رخ نہیں کیا۔ جبکہ میکال کو اس نے خود منع کر دیا تھا کسی بھی قسم کا رابطہ رکھنے کے لیے۔ گزرے چار ماہ میں اریج سے بھی بہت کم سامنا ہوا تھا اس کا۔ بس ایک چار دیواری تھی اور اس میں جہنم کے داروغہ کا کردار ادا

کرتی اس کی ساس اور نند۔

گزرے چار ماہ میں وہ رنگوں کو ترس کر رہ گئی تھی۔ اس کی ساس نے اس کے جہیز اور بری کے سارے کپڑے اٹھا کر لاک اپ میں رکھ دیے تھے۔ میک اپ تو اس نے پہلے بھی کبھی نہیں کیا تھا اور جیولری سے وہ ازل سے ہی محروم تھی۔ صبح سے رات تک کولہو کے بیل کی مانند وہ گھر کے کام میں جتی رہتی تھی۔ مگر کھانے کے وقت ہر روز اس کی ساس کوئی نہ کوئی بہانہ بنا کر ایسا ڈرامہ کرتی کہ اس سے ایک نوالہ نگلنا بھی مشکل ہو جاتا تھا۔ جس روز گھر میں کوئی اچھی چیز پکتی اس روز اسے بھوکا ہی سونا پڑتا تھا۔ کیونکہ اس کی ساس اس روز خود کھانا تقسیم کرتی تھی۔ بچ جانے والا کھانا اٹھا کر فریج میں لاک کر دیتی۔ بات بات پر ہندو عورتوں کی طرح اسے بیوہ ہونے کا احساس دلایا جاتا۔ ایک طرح سے وہ ہر قسم کی خوشی کے لیے ترس کر رہ گئی تھی۔ محض چار ماہ میں اس کی رہی سہی صحت بھی ڈھانچے میں تبدیل ہو کر رہ گئی تھی۔

اس کی عدت کے دن پورے ہو چکے تھے۔ ادھر اس کی عدت پوری ہوئی اور ادھر گھر میں شادی کے ہنگامے جاگ اٹھے۔ عائشہ جو پہلے ہی گھر کے کاموں میں ہلکان تھی۔ مزید مشین بن کر رہ گئی۔ اس روز وہ اریج کے ساتھ مارکیٹ آئی تھی اس کی نند بھی ساتھ تھی تبھی وہ پوچھ بیٹھا تھا۔

''آپ نے شادی کے لیے اپنی شاپنگ مکمل کر لی؟'' قطعی غیر متوقع سوال پر اس نے ہونقوں کی طرح سر اٹھا کر اسے دیکھا تھا۔ مگر اس سے پہلے کہ وہ کوئی جواب دیتی اس کی نند بول پڑی تھی۔

''بھابی کو شاپنگ کی ضرورت نہیں ہے ہمارے گھروں میں بیوہ عورت سنگھار نہیں کرتی ویسے بھی ان کی شاپنگ ادھر دبئی میں ان کی امی کر رہی ہیں۔''

''تم چپ رہو حمیرا' میں نے جس سے سوال پوچھا ہے وہی جواب دے گی۔'' پیشانی پر بل ڈالتے ہوئے اس نے اسے ڈپٹا تھا۔ جواباً وہ منہ بنا کر رخ پھیر گئی۔

''چلو تم گاڑی میں بیٹھو' تمہاری شاپنگ مکمل ہو گئی ہے اور آپ میرے ساتھ آئیں پلیز۔'' اپنی بہن کو گاڑی میں بیٹھنے کا حکم دے کر وہ عائشہ کو اپنے پیچھے آنے کا کہہ کر آگے بڑھ گیا۔ عائشہ ڈر رہی تھی کہ پتا نہیں اب اس کے ساتھ کیا ہوگا؟

وہ حیران تھی کہ اس کے لیے شاپنگ بھی وہ خود ہی کر رہا تھا۔ اپنی پسند کے دیدہ زیب ملبوسات' جیولری' جوتے' چوڑیاں جانے کیا کیا خرید رہا تھا وہ اس کے لیے ابھی وہ شاپنگ کر ہی رہا تھا کہ ایک نازک سی خوب صورت لڑکی ان کی طرف چلی آئی اریج کے چہرے پر اسے دیکھتے ہی سکون آمیز سی مسکراہٹ بکھر گئی تھی۔

''جھوٹے مجھے تو کہہ رہے تھے آفس میں کام ہے اور یہاں پتا نہیں کس کو شاپنگ کروا رہے ہو۔'' قریب آتے ہی اس نے اریج کے بازو پر مکا رسید کیا تھا جواباً وہ مسکرایا۔

''چڑیل یہ بھابی ہے میری' پچھلے دنوں جس بھائی کی ڈیتھ ہوئی تھی ان کی مسز ہیں۔''

''او...... اچھا' سوری کیسی ہیں بھابی؟''

''جی میں ٹھیک الحمد للہ۔'' عائشہ خوامخواہ کنفیوژ ہوئی تھی تبھی وہ بولی۔

''میرا نام عائلہ ہے میں اور اریج ایک دوسرے کو پسند کرتے ہیں یہ دیکھیں پچھلے دنوں اس نے مجھے رنگ بھی پہنائی ہے ان شاء اللہ عنقریب ہی ہم بھی شادی کر رہے ہیں۔'' مومی گڑیا سی وہ لڑکی بے حد خوش دکھائی دے رہی تھی۔ عائشہ نے دل ہی میں ڈھیروں دعائیں دے ڈالیں۔

واپسی کے سفر میں عائلہ بھی ان کے ساتھ تھی۔ اریج نے اسے بھی بصد اصرار شاپنگ کروائی تھی۔ اپنا گھر آنے تک وہ

پورے راستے جھکتی رہی تھی۔ حمیرا منہ بنائے بیٹھی رہی۔ جس وقت وہ لوگ گھر پہنچے گویا ایک طوفان ان کا منتظر تھا۔ گھر پہنچتے ہی حمیرا نے ماں کو شکایت جڑ دی اور پھر اریج تو نکل گیا مگر عائشہ کی شامت آ گئی۔ اگلے روز اس کا منہ بری طرح سوجا ہوا تھا اریج نے دیکھا تو ششدر رہ گیا اس کے وہم و گمان میں بھی نہیں تھا کہ محض تھوڑی سی شاپنگ پر اس کی ماں اس لڑکی کا ایسا حال کرے گی۔ پوری رات وہ سگریٹ پھونکتا رہا تھا اور سوچتا رہا تھا۔ کیا ملا تھا اس لڑکی کو اس گھر میں آ کر، محض دکھ، اذیت، ذلت......

کیوں؟ صرف اس لیے کہ اس نے اپنی ماں کی خواہش اور حکم کے سامنے سر جھکایا تھا۔ جتنا وہ سوچتا جا رہا تھا اتنا ہی اس کا دل کڑھتا جا رہا تھا۔

اگلے روز حمیرا کا مایوں تھا۔ جانے کہاں کہاں سے مہمانوں کے آنے کا سلسلہ شروع ہو گیا تھا۔ اریج تو جیسے گھن چکر بن کر رہ گیا تھا۔ جبکہ بڑا کمال، جمال کی موت کی طرح بہن کی شادی پر بھی نہیں آیا تھا۔ ہاں اس نے کچھ پیسے ضرور بھجوا دیے تھے۔ عائشہ نوکرانیوں کے حلیے میں ملبوس کچن میں مہمانوں کی آؤ بھگت کر کے پاگل ہو رہی تھی۔ مگر اس کا احساس کرنے کی فرصت وہاں کسی کے پاس نہیں تھی۔ اس کی ماں نے بیٹے کی برات کے ساتھ آنا تھا اور شاید بہن نے بھی مگر اسے امید نہیں تھی کہ وہ لوگ آ کر بھی اس کا کوئی احساس کریں گے۔

صبح سے رات تک وہ کاموں میں جتی رہی تھی۔ نہ اس نے کپڑے تبدیل کیے تھے نہ تقریب میں آ کر شمولیت ہی کر سکی تھی۔ اریج خاموشی سے دیکھتا رہا آج کی تقریب میں عائلہ بے حد خوب صورت دکھائی رہی تھی۔ وہ سارا وقت اسی کے ارد گرد رہا۔ مایوں کی طرح مہندی کی تقریب بھی عائشہ کے لیے شجر ممنوع ہی رہی تھی۔ رات گئے تک تھکن سے چُور ہونے کے باوجود کسی نے اسے کھانے تک کا نہیں پوچھا تھا۔ رات بھیگنے سے قبل تقریب ختم ہو گئی تھی۔ ٹھنڈا ہوا کھانا، مسلے ہوئے رنگ، بکھری ہوئی مہندی، بجھتے قمقمے کیا کوئی جان سکتا تھا کہ اس تقریب کے دلہا کی بہن کس حال میں ہے؟ اپنے کمرے میں آنے کے بعد وہ دیر تک روتی رہی تھی۔

اگلے روز اس کے گھر والے آ گئے تھے۔ اس کی ماں نے مقابل آتے ہی اس اپنے ساتھ لپٹا لیا تھا۔ بھائی ابھی گھر نہیں آیا تھا اور بہن بھی تا حال نہیں پہنچی تھی۔ وہ ماں کے گلے لگ کر نہ چاہتے ہوئے رو پڑی تھی مگر وہ اس کا درد محسوس نہیں کر سکی تھیں۔ انہوں نے اس کے آنسوؤں کو اپنی جدائی پر محمول کیا تھا، عائشہ چاہتے ہوئے بھی ان کے سامنے زبان نہیں کھول سکی تھی۔

برات آ گئی تھی سبھی گہما گہمی میں مصروف تھے مگر وہ پھر کاموں میں جتی ہوئی تھی۔ تبھی اریج اس کے پاس چلا آیا تھا۔

''آپ تیار نہیں ہوئیں؟'' وہ چونکی تھی اور پھر سر جھکا گئی۔

''نہیں، بس ابھی دو سوٹ پریس کر کے ہوتی ہوں۔''

''چھوڑیں سوٹوں کو اور چلیں جا کر تیار ہوں پلیز۔''

''اریج میں......!''

''آپ کو سمجھ نہیں آ رہی میں کیا کہہ رہا ہوں۔'' اس کے منمنانے پر وہ برہم ہوا تھا۔ عائشہ بے بسی سے اسے دیکھتی رہ گئی۔ یہی وہ پل تھا جو خار بن کر اریج کی ماں کی نگاہوں میں چبھا تھا۔ کسی چیل کی مانند لپکتے ہوئے وہ قریب آئی تھیں۔

''کیا ہو رہا ہے یہاں؟ اور تم ادھر کیا کر رہے ہو، سوائے اس کے آگے پیچھے پھرنے کے تمہیں اور کوئی کام نہیں ہے؟''

''میں کسی کے آگے پیچھے نہیں پھر رہا ہوں آپ بھابی سے کہیں کہ یہ کپڑے تبدیل کریں بس۔''

''کیوں کپڑے تبدیل کرے یہ، تمہیں کیوں ہر وقت اس سے ہمدردی کے مروڑ اٹھتے رہتے ہیں؟''

''میں انسان ہوں اس لیے۔''

''اچھا' تو ہم سب کیا تمہیں جانور دکھائی دیتے ہیں۔''

''مجھے کچھ نہیں پتا' بس میں اپنی آنکھوں کے سامنے کسی پر اتنا ظلم ہوتے ہوئے نہیں دیکھ سکتا۔''

''بس رہنے دو' یہ مفت کی ہمدردی' بہت اچھی طرح سے جانتی ہوں میں کیا گل کھلا رہے ہوں تم دونوں مل کر۔''

''اماں پلیز' مت اتنا دماغ خراب کریں میرا کہ میں کچھ کر بیٹھوں۔''

''کچھ کرنے کے نہیں ہو تم' بس کتے کی طرح اس کے آگے پیچھے پھرنا آتا ہے تمہیں اور کچھ نہیں۔''

''اماں۔''

''کیا اماں؟ تم کیا سمجھتے ہو میں کچھ جانتی نہیں۔ ایسے ہی بیٹا نہیں مارا اس نے میرا۔ ایک نمبر کی چنڈال اور حرافہ عورت ہے یہ۔ جان بوجھ کر اس نے میرے معصوم بیٹے کو موت کے گھاٹ اتار دیا اور اب یہ تمہارا خون پینا چاہتی ہے مگر میں ایسا نہیں ہونے دوں گی۔ بہت مزے کر لیے تم دونوں نے اب یہ لڑکی ایک منٹ کے لیے بھی اس گھر میں نہیں رہے گی۔'' بیٹے کے چلانے کا قطعی اثر لیے بغیر وہ اس سے بھی تیز آواز میں چلا رہی تھیں اور عائشہ کی ماں کے ساتھ دیگر مہمان بھی تھے کہ منہ میں انگلی ڈالے یہ تماشہ دیکھ رہے تھے۔

''اماں آپ بہتان لگا رہی ہیں۔ وہ بھی ایک معصوم لڑکی پر اور میں یہ ہرگز برداشت نہیں کروں گا۔''

''ارے جاؤ' آیا بڑا ماں کو دھمکیاں دینے والا میں دیکھتی ہوں کون رکھتا ہے آج کے بعد اسے اس گھر میں۔'' درجنوں مہمانوں کے درمیان بنا عائشہ کی ماں کی کوئی پروا کیے وہ جاہلوں کی طرح چلا رہی تھیں۔ اریج کا دماغ جیسے بھنا اٹھا۔

''میں بھی دیکھتا ہوں کون نکالتا ہے آج کے بعد اسے اس گھر سے۔'' نہایت غصے سے کہتے ہوئے وہ عائشہ کا ہاتھ تھام کر گھر سے باہر نکل آیا تھا۔ باہر بڑے سے شامیانے میں مولوی صاحب بیٹھے نکاح کی تیاری کر رہے تھے وہ قطعی مشتعل انداز میں اسی طرف چلا آیا۔

''مولوی صاحب یہ میری بیوہ بھابی ہیں عدت پوری کر چکی ہیں اپنی' میں نکاح کرنا چاہتا ہوں ان کے ساتھ ابھی ہو سکتا ہے کہ نہیں۔''

''کیوں نہیں ہو سکتا' یہ تو بڑے ثواب کا کام ہے۔''

''گناہ ثواب کو نہیں جانتا میں آپ بسم اللہ کیجیے پلیز۔''

''اریج۔'' پھیلی پھیلی سی آنکھوں کے ساتھ سہمی ہوئی عائشہ نے پہلی بار کچھ بولنے کی ہمت کی تھی۔ مگر اریج کے غصے اور بے نیازی نے اسے احتجاج کا موقع ہی نہیں دیا۔ خود اس کی اپنی ماں جیسے پتھر بن کر رہ گئی تھی۔

بھلا یہ کیسے ممکن تھا کہ وہ سر پھرا شخص اپنی محبت چھوڑ کر اس سادھو سی لڑکی کو اپنا لیتا۔ خود عائشہ کی ماں اور بھائی بھی شاکڈ کھڑے تھے۔ تاہم اس کی بہن ابھی ابھی پہنچی تھی اور وہ قدرے حیران ہونے کے ساتھ ساتھ بے حد خوش تھی۔

وہاں اس دیہاتی ماحول میں جو ہونے جا رہا تھا وہ کسی کے بھی وہم و گمان میں نہیں تھا۔ لوگ یوں جمع ہوئے تماشا دیکھ رہے تھے جیسے کوئی مداری بندر کا کھیل دکھا کر بچوں کو محظوظ کر رہا ہو۔ اریج کا دماغ اس وقت قطعی کام نہیں کر رہا تھا اس کے اور عائشہ کے گھر والے قریب کھڑے تھے مولوی نے سب کی موجودگی میں اللہ کا نام لے کر اس کا نکاح عائشہ سے پڑھوا دیا۔ عائشہ ساکت بیٹھی تھی گویا اس میں جان ہی نہ ہو۔

عائلہ جس وقت بن سنور کر وہاں آئی گویا اک قیامت اس کی منتظر تھی۔ سر جھکائے کھڑے اریج کا نکاح' عائشہ اذہان

کے ساتھ ہو چکا تھا اور نکاح کے فوری بعد اس کا کچھ پتا نہ چلا کہ وہ کہاں نکل گیا۔ لوگوں کی چہ مگوئیاں جاری تھیں۔ کوئی کچھ کہہ رہا تھا تو کوئی کچھ، مگر اس کی سماعتیں تو جیسے کام کرنا ہی چھوڑ گئی تھیں۔ کتنے سالوں کا ساتھ تھا اس کا اور اریج کا‘ مگر کیسے ایک پل میں خوابوں کے سارے محل ٹوٹ کر زمین بوس ہو گئے تھے۔ وہ رونا چاہتی تھی مگر صدمہ اتنا شدید تھا کہ آنکھیں آنسو لٹانا ہی بھول گئیں۔

اگلے روز اریج کو اس کے بارے میں خبر ملی تھی۔ عائلہ نروس بریک ڈاؤن ہونے کے باعث اسپتال میں تھی وہ جیسے تڑپ کر رہ گیا۔

کل پورا دن شراب کے نشے میں دھت رہنے کے بعد رات اس نے کسی زخمی پرندے کی مانند تڑپ کر پھڑ پھڑاتے ہوئے گزاری تھی۔ عائلہ کے بغیر جینا ایسے ہی تھا جیسے پھول کا خوش بو کے بغیر رہنا‘ کیسے کیسے خواب وابستہ نہیں تھے اس کی ذات سے‘ وہ یاد کرتا رہا اور روتا رہا۔

دو دن پاگلوں کی طرح ساری دنیا سے کنارہ کشی کیے اس نے اسپتال میں عائلہ کے پاس ہی گزارے تھے۔ ان دو دنوں میں اسے کچھ کھانے پینے کا ہوش رہا تھا نہ اپنے حال پر توجہ کرنے کا‘ اگر کوئی دھن سر پر سوار تھی تو بس یہی کہ عائلہ کو ہوش آجائے اور بالآخر اسے ہوش آ گیا تھا۔

تیسرے روز صبح ہی صبح وہ ہوش میں آ گئی تھی مگر اس کی آنکھوں کے سوتے خشک نہیں ہوئے تھے۔ اریج نے جان بوجھ کر خود کو اس کے سامنے جانے سے روکے رکھا۔ وہ نہیں چاہتا تھا کہ وہ اسے دیکھ کر پھر سے کوئی نقصان اٹھائے۔ تاہم اس کے ہوش میں آنے کے بعد وہ قدرے ریلیکس ضرور ہو گیا تھا۔ تین روز کے بعد گھر واپسی پر اس نے عائشہ کو دیکھا تھا۔ بے حد اجڑے ہوئے رف حلیے میں وہ اس کے لیے بے حد متفکر دکھائی دے رہی تھی۔ اریج تھکا تھکا سا لاؤنج میں دھرے صوفے پر ٹک گیا۔

”ایک کپ چائے مل سکتی ہے؟“

”جج...... جی......!“ بوتل کے جن کی طرح اثبات میں سر ہلاتی وہ کچن کی طرف لپکی تھی۔ اگلے دس منٹ کے بعد وہ چائے کا کپ لے کر آئی تو اریج دائیں ہاتھ کے انگوٹھے سے اپنی پیشانی مسل رہا تھا۔ عائشہ کے ہاتھ سے گرما گرم چائے کا کپ تھامنے کے ساتھ ہی اس نے اس کا ہاتھ بھی پکڑ لیا تھا۔

”بیٹھ جاؤ۔“ بکھرے بکھرے سے حلیے میں کتنا قابل رحم لگ رہا تھا وہ۔ عائشہ چپ چاپ بیٹھ گئی۔

”میرے یہاں سے جانے کے بعد امی نے تمہارے ساتھ کوئی مسئلہ تو نہیں کیا؟“ رشتہ بدلا تھا تو طرز تخاطب بھی بدل گیا تھا۔ وہ آہستہ سے نفی میں سر ہلا گئی۔

”ہوں‘ حمیرا تو چلی گئی یقیناً امی کو مجھ پر بہت غصہ ہوگا۔ مگر میں کیا کرتا‘ میرا دماغ پھٹ رہا تھا ادھر عائلہ کو نروس بریک ڈاؤن ہو گیا سمجھ میں نہیں آ رہا کہ اس کا سامنا کیسے کروں گا۔“ اضطراری انداز میں چائے کے کپ کے کنارے پر انگلی پھیرتے ہوئے اس نے اپنی الجھن اس سے شیئر کی تھی۔

”بہت حساس لڑکی ہے وہ بہت محبت کرتی ہے مجھ سے‘ ابھی پچھلے دنوں ہی لمبی ناراضگی کے بعد صلح ہوئی تھی ہماری‘ خیر تمہارے گھر والے چلے گئے یا ابھی یہیں ہیں؟“

”پتا نہیں‘ شادی والے روز کے بعد وہ ادھر نہیں آئے صرف بھائی کل آیا تھا حمیرا کو لینے اور بس۔“

”یار مجھے نہیں لگتا کہ تمہاری امی تمہاری سگی ماں ہوں گی۔ میں نے اپنی زندگی میں کسی سگی ماں کو اتنا بے حس نہیں دیکھا۔“

''کھانا لاؤں آپ کے لیے؟'' نظریں چراتے ہوئے عائشہ نے فوراً بات بدل دی تھی۔

''نہیں' میں بس چائے پی کر ریسٹ کروں گا۔ تم نے ناشتا کیا ہے؟''

''ہوں......نہیں......!'' غیر متوقع سوال پر نفی میں سر ہلا کر وہ فوراً اثبات میں سر ہلانے لگی تھی۔ وہ اسے دیکھ کر رہ گیا۔

''جاؤ لے کر آؤ ناشتا۔'' اس بار خاموشی سے اسے دیکھتے ہوئے اس نے حکم جاری کیا تھا۔ عائشہ بے حد کنفیوژ فوراً اٹھ گئی۔ جس وقت وہ ناشتا لے کر آئی وہ اپنی چائے ختم کر چکا تھا۔

''چلو شروع کرو میرے سامنے۔'' جونہی اس نے ٹرے ٹیبل پر رکھی اس نے نیا حکم جاری کر دیا۔ وہ شاکڈ ہی تو رہ گئی۔

''ایسے کیا دیکھ رہی ہو' ناشتا کرو پھر میں جاتا ہوں ریسٹ کے لیے۔'' گہری سانس بھر کر سر صوفے کی پشت گاہ سے ٹکاتے ہوئے اس نے اپنی نگاہ اس پر جمائی تھی وہ پریشان سی چھوٹے چھوٹے نوالے توڑنے لگی۔

''گڈ' اب یہ سارا ناشتا اچھی طرح سے ختم کرنا ہے میرے سر میں بہت درد ہے میں ذرا آرام کرلوں۔'' اسے اطمینان سے ناشتا کرتے دیکھ کر وہ فوراً اٹھ کھڑا ہوا تھا۔ وہ اثبات میں سر ہلا گئی۔ کتنے سالوں کے بعد اس نے یوں پہلی بار رغبت سے ناشتا کیا تھا گو ہر لمحہ ساس کے آ جانے کا خوف لاحق رہا مگر اس نے کھانے سے ہاتھ نہیں روکا تھا۔

صبح سے شام ہو گئی تھی وہ کام سے فارغ ہو کر اریج کے کمرے میں آئی تو وہ جاگ رہا تھا۔ عائشہ کو دیکھ کر کروٹ کے بل اٹھ بیٹھا۔

''ادھر آؤ۔'' سرخ سرخ سی آنکھیں بتا رہی تھیں کہ وہ ابھی بیدار ہوا ہے۔ عائشہ دھڑکتے دل کے ساتھ قریب آ کر بیٹھ گئی۔ تبھی اس نے ہاتھ بڑھا کر اس کا ہاتھ اپنے ہاتھوں میں لے لیا تھا۔

''امی نے ابھی تک تمہارے کپڑے واپس نہیں کیے؟''

''نن......نہیں......!''

''ٹھیک ہے' میں ذرا فریش ہو جاؤں پھر مارکیٹ چلتے ہیں جیولری اور میک اپ وغیرہ پسند ہے تمہیں کہ نہیں؟''

''نہیں۔''

''مگر میں چاہوں گا کہ تم میک اپ کرو اور ہاں اگر تم یہ سمجھ رہی ہو کہ میں نے کسی ہمدردی یا خدا ترسی کے لیے تم سے شادی کی ہے تو پلیز ایسا کوئی خیال دماغ میں مت آنے دینا۔ کیونکہ میں کسی لحاظ سے اپنی زندگی برباد کرنے والا بندہ نہیں ہوں۔ نا ہی تم کوئی لولی لنگڑی' بے کار لڑکی ہو جس پر ترس کھا کر اس سے شادی کی جائے میرا خیال ہے میری بات تمہاری سمجھ میں آ گئی ہو گی۔''

''جی۔'' دھڑکتے دل کے ساتھ عائشہ اذہان کا سر ہنوز جھکا ہوا تھا۔ وہ ٹھنڈی سانس بھرتا بستر سے اٹھ گیا۔ اگلے دو گھنٹوں میں وہ اس کے ساتھ مارکیٹ میں تھی۔ بے حد اپنائیت و محبت سے اس کا ہاتھ تھامے' قدم سے قدم ملا کر چلتا وہ شخص اسے کتنا معتبر کر رہا تھا۔ اگر یہ ہمدردی یا ترس نہیں تھا تو پھر کیا تھا۔ ابھی چند دن پہلے اسی جگہ پر اس نے وہ لڑکی دیکھی تھی جو بے حد حسین تھی اور جسے وہ ٹوٹ کر چاہتا تھا۔ جلد ہی وہ دونوں شادی کے خواہش مند بھی تھے۔ تو پھر یہ سب کیوں ہو گیا ہے؟ ایک اس کی زندگی کو آزمائشوں سے نکالنے کے لیے اس شخص نے اپنی اور عائلہ کی زندگی کیوں سولی پر ٹانگ دی تھی؟

کتنی سوچیں تھیں جو سارا دن' اس کے دماغ کا گھیراؤ کیے رکھتی تھیں؟ کتنے تکلیف دہ خیالات تھے جو اسے ہمہ وقت پریشان کیے رکھتے تھے۔ اسے لگتا تھا جیسے جلد ہی وہ پاگل ہو کر رہ جائے گی۔ کسی کے خوابوں کو نوچ کر ارمانوں کا خون کر

کے بھلا وہ کیسے خوش رہ سکتی تھی؟ جبکہ بچھڑ جانے کی اذیت کو بھلا اس سے بہتر کون جان سکتا تھا۔ وہ سوچ رہی تھی کہ وہ اریج سے بات کرے اسے سمجھائے۔ مگر جانے کیوں وہ چاہتے ہوئے بھی اس سے اس ٹاپک پر بات کرنے کی ہمت نہیں کر پا رہی تھی۔

اریج اب اس کے لیے جوتا خرید رہا تھا۔ وہ سن سی بیٹھی اسے دیکھ رہی تھی۔ جبکہ وہ بنا اس کی توجہ پر غور کیے اس کی شلوار کو ٹخنوں سے ذرا اوپر اٹھا کر جھکتے ہوئے خود اسے جوتا پہنا رہا تھا۔ بے حد خوب صورت شفاف ہاتھ اس کے پیر چھو رہے تھے۔ وہ کرنٹ کھا کر رہ گئی۔

''مم...... میں خود پہن کر دیکھ لیتی ہوں۔'' بڑی مشکل سے جھکتے ہوئے اس نے اپنے سرد ہاتھ اس کے خوب صورت ہاتھوں پر رکھے تھے۔ وہ خاموشی سے سائیڈ پر ہو گیا۔ اسی رات تھکن سے چُور، سارے کاموں سے فارغ ہو کر وہ کمرے میں آئی تو اریج کمپیوٹر پر کسی کام میں مصروف تھا۔ وہ بے چین سی بیڈ کے کنارے پر ٹک گئی۔

''وہ...... مجھے کچھ بات کرنی تھی آپ سے۔'' ہاتھوں کو مسلتے ہوئے بہ مشکل وہ کچھ بولنے کی ہمت کر پائی تھی۔ اریج نے اچٹتی سی ایک نظر اس پر ڈالتے ہوئے کمپیوٹر شٹ ڈاؤن کر دیا۔

''ہوں کہو۔'' اپنی سیٹ سے اٹھ کر وہ بیڈ پر اس کے ساتھ ہی آ بیٹھا تھا۔

''وہ...... میں یہ کہنا چاہ رہی تھی کہ...... امی آپ سے بہت ناراض ہیں۔ اسی لیے انہوں نے کمال بھائی کے پاس جانے کا فیصلہ کر لیا ہے۔ پرسوں رات کی فلائیٹ ہے ان کی بھائی سے سارا کام کروایا ہے انہوں نے، فی الوقت وہ میری شکل دیکھنے کی روادار بھی نہیں ہیں۔ مم...... میں یہ کہہ رہی تھی کہ آپ کو مجھ سے نکاح نہیں کرنا چاہیے تھا۔ آ...... آپ عائلہ کو پسند کرتے تھے آپ کو اسی سے شادی کرنی چاہیے تھی۔''

''پسند کرتا تھا نہیں، پسند کرتا ہوں۔ پہلی محبت ہے وہ اور اگر امی مجھے اتنا مجبور نہ کر دیتیں تو لازمی طور پر میں اسی کے ساتھ شادی کرتا اور یہ شادی تو ابھی بھی ہو سکتی ہے۔ آپ میری محبت میں تو مبتلا نہیں ہیں جو دوسری شادی کی اجازت نہیں دیں گی۔ جہاں تک امی کی بات ہے تو مجھے ان کی ناراضی سے کوئی فرق نہیں پڑتا کیونکہ وہ ہماری سگی ماں نہیں ہیں۔ نہ ہم بھائیوں کو انہوں نے کبھی پیار سے اپنا سمجھ کے پالا ہے۔ وہ صرف حمیرا کی ماں ہیں اور بس۔'' سر جھٹکتے ہوئے اس کی ٹون یکسر بدلی تھی۔ عائشہ حیرانی سے دیکھتی رہ گئی۔

''خیر چھوڑو، ادھر آؤ۔'' اگلے ہی پل اس کا ہاتھ پکڑ کر وہ اٹھ کھڑا ہوا تھا۔ عائشہ کے وہم و گمان میں بھی نہیں تھا کہ وہ اسے کیسا مقام دینے والا ہے۔ کس قدر پیار اور اپنائیت سے اس نے اسے اس کا حق دیا تھا۔ وہ سرشاری جس سے وہ قطعی ناآشنا تھی اس نے کس درجہ محبت و ذمہ داری کے ساتھ اسے اس سرشاری سے متعارف کروایا تھا۔ حقیقی معنوں میں سہاگن کیا تھا۔

وہ تو محض اس کا نام ملنے پر ہی اس کی شکر گزار تھی کہ اس نے سہاگن بھی بنا دیا تھا۔ عائشہ کو لگا وہ زندگی میں کبھی اس کے سامنے سر نہیں اٹھا پائے گی۔ اسی روز شام میں اس کی اور عائلہ کی ملاقات ہوئی تھی وہ رو رہی تھی۔ محض تین دن کے اندر ہی اس کا سراپا اجڑ کر رہ گیا تھا۔ اریج نے بے ساختہ نظر چرالی۔

''کیسی ہو عائلہ؟''

''تمہیں کیسی لگ رہی ہوں؟''

''پتا نہیں۔''

''کیوں اریج، کیوں؟ کیوں کیا تم نے ایسا ایک پل کے لیے بھی نہیں سوچا تم نے کہ میرا کیا ہو گا۔ تمہاری اس

سخاوت کے بعد میں کیسے جیئوں گی؟''

''سوچنے سمجھنے کا ٹائم نہیں تھا عائلہ بس میرے سامنے ایک انسان کی زندگی داؤ پر لگی تھی میں نے اسے بچالیا۔ تمہیں تو مجھ سے بھی اچھا لڑکا مل سکتا ہے مگر اسے نہیں۔''

''اچھا لڑکا نہیں چاہیے مجھے تم اسے دے دو ساری دنیا' مجھے بس میرا اریج دے دو پلیز۔'' رو کر اس کے سامنے دونوں ہاتھ جوڑتے ہوئے وہ سسکی تھی۔ اریج تڑپ کر رہ گیا۔

''سیکنڈ میرج کرو گی میرے ساتھ؟'' اس سوال کے جواب پر اس کی ہستی کی بنیاد ٹکی تھی۔ عائلہ کے آنسو اس کی پلکوں پر اٹک گئے۔

''ہاں اگر تم فوری اسے طلاق دے دو تو؟''

''اور اگر میں اسے طلاق نہ دوں تو؟''

''کیوں طلاق نہ دو' تم میرے ہو اریج صرف اور صرف میرے میں تمہیں کسی کے ساتھ شیئر نہیں کر سکتی۔''

''جانتا ہوں میں نے بھی کبھی نہیں چاہا تھا کہ تم مجھے کسی کے ساتھ شیئر کرو' مگر اب حالات بدل گئے ہیں عائلہ میں کسی کا ہاتھ تھام کر اسے اوندھے منہ گرانے کا سوچ بھی نہیں سکتا۔''

''چاہے میں مر جاؤں اریج؟'' کانچ سی آنکھوں میں رلتے آنسوؤں کے ساتھ اس نے اسے دیکھا تھا۔ اریج کی اپنی آنکھوں کے گوشے نم ہو گئے۔

''نہیں۔''

''نہیں تو ابھی فیصلہ کرو' تم اسے طلاق دے رہے ہو کہ نہیں؟''

''میں اسے علیحدہ رکھوں گا عائلہ' وہ بہت بے ضرر سی لڑکی ہے کبھی ہمارے درمیان نہیں آئے گی۔''

''یہ میرے سوال کا جواب نہیں ہے اریج۔''

''عائلہ تم سمجھنے کی کوشش کیوں نہیں کر رہیں۔ وہ بہت اکیلی ہے۔ کوئی اپنا نہیں ہے اس کا دنیا میں' تم کیوں مجھے اس کے سامنے کم ظرف ثابت کرنا چاہتی ہو۔''

''اریج تم اسے طلاق دے رہے ہو کہ نہیں؟''

''عائلہ پلیز۔''

''او کے فیصلہ ہو چکا ہے۔'' لہو رنگ آنکھوں سے اس کی طرف دیکھتے ہوئے وہ کھڑی ہوئی تھی۔

''بہت غرور تھا مجھے خود پر کہ تم صرف مجھ سے پیار کرتے ہو میں اگر تم سے کہوں گی کہ اریج میرے لیے ساری دنیا کو چھوڑ دو تو تم چھوڑ دو گے مگر میں غلط تھی۔ خوش فہم ہو گئی تھی میں' تمہیں مجھ سے کبھی پیار نہیں رہا۔ جو کچھ بھی اب تک ہمارے درمیان تھا۔ سب بکواس تھا۔ جھوٹ تھا سب' غلط کہا تھا تم نے کہ میں تمہاری زندگی ہوں بکواس کی تھی تم نے ساری۔ میں لعنت بھیجتی ہوں تمہاری محبت پر۔ تم سے تعلق پر، یہ لو اپنی رِنگ...... میں سمجھوں گی کہ میرا اور تمہارا تعلق کبھی رہا ہی نہیں۔''

اپنی انگلی سے اس کی پہنائی رِنگ اتار کر اس پر پھینکتے ہوئے وہ روتی ہوئی وہاں سے نکل گئی تھی۔ اریج شکستہ انداز میں رنگ اٹھا کر پاکٹ میں ڈالتے ہوئے وہاں سے اٹھ کھڑا ہوا تھا۔ یہ کہنا کتنا آسان ہوتا ہے کہ میں خود کو سمجھا لوں گا۔ مگر دنیا میں سب سے مشکل کام خود کو سمجھانا ہوتا ہے محبت کے دربار سے دربدری کے بعد خود کو سمجھانے اور سنبھالنے میں عمریں بیت جاتی ہیں۔ دنیا کے بڑے بڑے مسائل پر ہزاروں لوگوں کو سمجھا کر ان کی سوچ تبدیل کرنے والے بھی

سالوں اپنے اندر چھڑی جنگ میں پاگل ہوتے رہتے ہیں۔ اس رات اس نے پھر بہت شراب پی تھی۔ اسے لگا جیسے اب تک کا اریج مر گیا ہو اور اب اسے ایک نئے اریج کا روپ لے کر جینا ہو۔

جدائی دینے والے تجھ سے امید وفا کیسی؟
تعلق ٹوٹ جائے جب محبت روٹھ جائے جب
تو پھر رسم دعا کیسی؟
ملن کی التجا کیسی؟
بھنور میں ڈوبتی کشتی پہ ساحل کی تمنا کیا؟
اکھڑتی سانس ہو تو زندگی کی آرزو بھی کیا؟
جو منزل کھو چکی ہو پھر سے اس کی جستجو بھی کیا؟
رازِ دوست پہ اچھا سر تسلیم خم کرنا
سسکنے سے یہی بہتر ہے ناامید ہی مرنا
مگر دل نے تمہیں کس واسطے سے یاد رکھا ہے
تمہیں کیوں شاعری میں آج تک آباد رکھا ہے
ابھی تک میں نے کیوں خود کو بہت برباد رکھا ہے
جدائی دینے والے آشنائی کی قسم تم کو
تمہاری کج ادائی' بے وفائی کی قسم تم کو
مجھے اتنا بتا دینا
وفا کی چاہتوں کی مشعلیں کیسے بجھاتے ہیں
نشاں کیسے مٹاتے ہیں
بھلانا ہو جنہیں ان کو بھلا کیسے بُھلاتے ہیں

تم ہو برگِ سماں، تم ہو بادِ صبا
تم کو معلوم کیا؟
ہم نے تم سے رنگِ حنا مانگ کر
شب کی تنہائی میں گنگناتے ہوئے مسکراتے ہوئے
اپنے غم کا فسانہ کیا ہے رقم
اور گم ہو گئی اس میں حرف قلم
تم کو معلوم کیا؟
تم تو ہو لذتِ غم سے ناآشنا
آہ کس سے کہیں ہم نے کس شوق میں
اپنے زخموں کو رشکِ بہاراں کیا
شاہ خوباں میں ہم نے چراغاں کیا
تم سے ہم کیا کہیں؟ تم کو معلوم کیا
ہم نے کاٹی ہے کیسے شب زندگی
ہم نے کیسے اٹھایا ہے بارِ وفا
چاند نکلا نا تاروں نے آواز دی
سر پر کالے اندھیرے برستے رہے
اور جنت نشینوں کے اس شہر میں
روشنی کے لیے ہم ترستے رہے
''دو پتر چناراں دے......
ساڈا دکھ سن سن کے روندے، پتھر پہاڑاں دے

بھری دوپہر میں شیشم کے درخت سے ٹیک لگائے بیٹھا، وہ پلکیں موندے گنگنا رہا تھا۔ جب کرم داد چپکے سے اس کے قریب آ کر بیٹھ گیا۔

''لے تو ادھر بیٹھا ہوا ہے اور میں پورے پنڈ میں اپنے یار کو تلاش کرتا پھر رہا ہوں۔''

''کیوں، خیریت؟''

اپنے سکون میں خلل اسے پسند نہیں آیا تھا۔ تبھی آنکھیں کھولتے ہوئے اس نے خفگی بھری نگاہ کرم داد پر ڈالی تھی جواباً وہ کھسیا گیا۔

''خیریت ہی ہے' چوہدرانی نے حویلی بلایا ہے تجھے۔''

''کیوں؟''

''یہ تو چوہدرائن کو پتا' کل چھوٹی بی بی کی طبیعت بہت خراب تھی۔ رات شہر سے ڈاکٹر بلوایا تھا مجھے تو لگتا ہے اسی سلسلے میں یاد کر رہی ہوں گی تجھے؟''

''ہوں' اب کیسی طبیعت ہے چھوٹی بی بی کی؟''

''پتا نہیں چوہدرائین بتا رہی تھیں بخار نہیں ٹوٹ رہا ان کا۔''

''ٹھیک ہے تو جا' آ جاتا ہوں میں تھوڑی دیر تک۔''

''جاتا ہوں' مگر تو اس ویلے یہاں نہ بیٹھ' وہ بابا جوگی کی کہانی نہیں سنی تو نے؟ وہ بھی یونہی بھری دوپہروں میں درختوں کے نیچے اکیلا بیٹھا رہتا تھا۔ دیکھ لے کیسے کملاتے جھلا کر دیا تھا اسے ''اوپری ہواؤں'' نے۔'' زائر کے لب اس کے تفکر اور ہدایت پر ذرا سے مسکرائے تھے۔

''تیرے یار پر ''اوپری ہوائیں'' اثر نہیں کرتیں کرم داد' تو جا بے فکر ہو کر۔''

''ہوں عشق کی سٹ جنہیں لگ جاتی ہے ان پر تو بڑے بڑے طوفان اثر نہیں کرتے اوپری ہواؤں نے کیا اثر کرنا ہے۔'' منہ ہی منہ میں بڑبڑاتے ہوئے کرم داد اس کے پاس سے اٹھ کھڑا ہوا تھا۔ زائر اسی پوزیشن میں بیٹھا رہا۔

غلام فریدا میں تے دوزخ سڑساں' جے میں مکھ ماہی کولوں موڑاں
کملی کر کے چھوڑ دیتوایں تے بیٹھی لکھ گلیاں دے رولاں
یار باجھوں، ہن جیون کیہڑا' تے میرے اندر درد ہزاراں
غلام فریدا میں تے اینج رُوواں جیویں وچھڑی کونج قطاراں

پلکیں موند کر پھر سے درخت کے ساتھ ٹیک لگاتے ہوئے وہ بابا غلام فرید کا کلام گنگنانے لگا تھا۔ بھولے بسرے دنوں کی یادوں میں ثانیہ عباس کا عکس پھر سے دل میں چٹکی کاٹنے لگا۔

زائر نے جیسے نڈھال ہو کر خود کو ان دل فریب یادوں کے سپرد کر دیا تھا۔

❁ ...... ❁ ...... ❁

کشادہ صحن میں رزق کی تلاش کے لیے اِدھر اُدھر پھدکتی چڑیوں کے شور سے اس کی آنکھ کھل گئی تھی۔ زائر ملک کے مضبوط بازوؤں کی پناہ میں سوئی وہ اس کے کشادہ سینے سے لگی تھی۔ ثانیہ کے ذہن میں اس کی کل والی باتیں گونج اٹھیں۔ کتنی سفاکی سے اس نے اسے اپنے اصول اور اس کا مقام باور کروایا تھا۔ کتنی بے حسی سے اس نے کہہ دیا تھا کہ۔

''تم یہاں انسان کی بچی بن کر رہو تو زیادہ بہتر ہے ورگرنہ دیہاتی مردوں کو بہت اچھی طرح سے عورتیں سدھار کر رکھنی آتی ہیں۔'' تبھی فوراً سے پیشتر زائر کی پناہ سے نکلتے ہوئے اس نے کروٹ بدلی تھی۔

''بہت مشکل سے میری ماں نے تمہیں اپنی بہو تسلیم کیا ہے بہت خوفزدہ رہتی ہیں وہ شہر کی لڑکیوں سے اور یہ کچھ ایسا غلط بھی نہیں۔ کم از کم جو کچھ تم اور تمہاری ماں مل کر آج کر رہے تھے اس کے بعد تو بالکل نہیں۔'' اس کا ذہن اس کے نشتر نما لفظوں کی گرفت سے نکل ہی نہیں پا رہا تھا۔

''زائر ملک صرف ایک بار ٹھوکر کھاتا ہے اس کے بعد راستے کے پتھر خود بخود اس کی راہ سے ہٹ جاتے ہیں۔ تم تو پھر میری ہم سفر ہو اور ہم سفر بھی وہ کہ جس کی کوکھ میں...... بہر حال خود کو میرا بہترین انتخاب ثابت کرنے کی بھرپور کوشش کرنا' نہیں تو یاد رکھنا میں تمہیں کبھی معاف نہیں کروں گا۔'' بے چینی ہی بے چینی تھی۔ کروٹ پر کروٹ بدل کر وہ تھک گئی

تھی۔

تبھی زائر نے اس کی کمر میں اپنے بازو حمائل کیے تھے۔

''صبح ہوگئی ہے چلو اٹھ کر ناشتے کی تیاری کرو' یہاں دیہات میں عورتیں اتنی دیر تک نہیں سوتیں۔''

''تو میں کیا کروں' میں نے کہہ دیا تھا کل' مجھے دیہات میں رہنے کی عادت نہیں ہے۔'' اپنے وجود سے اس کے ہاتھ پرے جھٹکتے ہوئے وہ بیزار سی اٹھ بیٹھی تھی۔

''پڑ جائے گی عادت' پکی دیہاتی عورت نہ بنا دیا تمہیں تو میرا نام بھی زائر ملک نہیں۔'' ہاتھ بڑھا کر اسے تنگ کرنے کی غرض سے اس نے پھر اسے اپنے بازوؤں میں جکڑ لیا تھا۔ ثانیہ کسی بے بس پرندے کی مانند پھڑ پھڑا کر رہ گئی۔

''زائر ملک' تم زبردستی مجھے اس ماحول میں ایڈجسٹ نہیں کر سکتے۔''

''کیوں؟'' اس کی بے بسی سے حظ اٹھاتے ہوئے اس نے معصوم سی شرارت بھی کر لی۔ ثانیہ کی آنکھیں اپنی اس درجہ بے بسی پر ضبط کی ہزار کوششوں کے باوجود بھر آئیں۔

''میں تمہاری غلام نہیں ہوں۔''

''بیوی تو ہو نا؟'' وہ کہاں اس کے آنسوؤں کو خاطر میں لانے والا تھا۔ ثانیہ کو لگا شہر سے گاؤں میں آ کر جیسے وہ سر تا پیر بدل کر رہ گیا ہو۔

''چلو اٹھو شاباش' پہلے جھاڑو دو اس سے پہلے کہ اماں جھاڑو پکڑ لیں۔''

''مجھے جھاڑو دینی نہیں آتی۔''

''میں سکھا دوں گا کوئی مسئلہ نہیں۔''

''جب سکھائیں گے تو خود دے بھی دینا میں یہ کام نہیں کر سکتی۔''

''تم یہی کرو گی ڈیئر ثانی' یہ شہر نہیں ہے جہاں شوہر بچوں نیپیاں تک تبدیل کرتے پھریں۔''

''مائی فٹ' تم مجھے کسی بھی کام کے لیے مجبور نہیں کر سکتے۔''

''کر سکتا ہوں مگر کرنا نہیں چاہتا کیونکہ عورت پر جبر میری فطرت میں نہیں ہے۔''

''اور اس کے باوجود تم یہی کر رہے ہو۔''

''اس کے پیچھے بھی ایک وجہ ہے' میں نہیں چاہتا تمہاری وجہ سے یہاں کسی کے سامنے بھی میرا سر جھکے۔''

''واہ' عجب منطق ہے تم دیہاتی مردوں کی' عورت کو جھکا کر اس کی عزت نفس کو کچل کر ہر طرح سے اسے ذلیل کر کے تم لوگ سمجھتے ہو تمہاری شان میں اضافہ ہو گیا ہے۔''

''افسوس ناک حقیقت ہے مگر سچ یہی ہے بہرحال چلو اٹھو میں نہاتا ہوں تم گھر صاف کرو۔''

''مجھے نہیں کرنا۔'' زائر کے بستر چھوڑنے پر بھی اس نے اپنی ضد نہیں چھوڑی تھی۔ تبھی اسے غصہ آیا تھا۔

''تم چاہتی ہو میں تمہارے ساتھ جاہل مردوں والا سلوک کروں؟''

''تمہیں کیا لگتا ہے اب تک جو سلوک تم نے میرے ساتھ کیا ہے وہ پڑھے لکھے مردوں والا ہے؟''

''ہاں...... چلو اٹھو اب۔'' تنک کر کہتے اس نے ثانیہ کو بازو سے پکڑ کر بستر سے اٹھا دیا۔ وہ کڑھ کر رہ گئی۔ باہر صحن میں زائر کی ماں نماز فجر کے بعد صفائی ستھرائی کا کام مکمل کر چکی تھیں۔ زائر کو بے حد شرمندگی ہوئی۔

''یہ کیا اماں' میں نے کہا بھی تھا آپ یہ کام نہیں کریں گی اب۔'' صحن میں آتے ہی ثانیہ کا بازو چھوڑ کر وہ اماں کے قریب آ بیٹھا تھا۔ تبھی وہ چولہا جلاتے ہوئے مسکرائی تھیں۔

''جھلا پتر نہ بن میرا، میں نہیں کروں گی تو کون کرے گا یہ کام؟''

''وہ کرے گی جسے اپنا نام دے کر اس گھر میں لایا ہوں۔''

''نا پتر، وہ شہری بچی ہے اسے ان کاموں کی عادت نہیں ہے۔''

''کیوں؟ شہروں میں من وسلویٰ اترتا ہے وہاں بھی لوگ ہل جل کر ہی زندگی کا وجود قائم رکھتے ہیں آپ خوامخواہ سر پر مت چڑھائیں اسے۔''

وہ ثانیہ کی طرف نہیں دیکھ رہا تھا مگر اس کی نگاہوں کی تپش اس کے لفظوں سے بخوبی محسوس کی جاسکتی تھی۔ تبھی وہ بولی تھی۔

''اپنی حد میں رہو زائر ملک، خرید کر نہیں لائے تم مجھے جو اس طرح کا سلوک کر رہے ہو میرے ساتھ۔''

''بکواس بند کرو اپنی، میں اس وقت تم سے مغز ماری کے موڈ میں نہیں ہوں۔'' پلٹ کر ثانیہ کو دیکھتے ہوئے وہ دھاڑا تھا۔ جواباً وہ خاصی بے یقین سی نگاہوں سے اسے دیکھتی شدید ہتک محسوس کرتے ہوئے کمرے میں واپس چلی گئی۔ دن بھر دوبارہ نہ اس کا زائر ملک سے سامنا ہوا اور نہ وہ کمرے سے باہر نکلی۔

اس نے ٹھان لیا تھا چاہے کچھ ہوجائے وہ کسی طور ملازمہ بن کر نہیں رہے گی۔ نہ ہی زائر کی ضد پوری ہونے دے گی۔ مگر اس کا یہ ارادہ اسی رات مٹی کی دیوار ثابت ہوگیا تھا۔ رات کے ساڑھے نو بجے کا ٹائم تھا جب وہ کمرے میں آیا تھا۔ ثانیہ جاگنے کے باوجود آنکھیں بند کیے پڑی رہی۔

''ویلڈن ثانیہ عباس، ویری ویلڈن...... مجھے گمان نہیں یقین تھا کہ آپ یہی کریں گی کوئی بات نہیں میں عورت ذات پر ہاتھ اٹھانے کا قائل نہیں ہوں۔ نہ ہی گالی گلوچ کو پسند کرتا ہوں۔ تمہیں گھر کا کام نہیں کرنا کوئی بات نہیں آج کے بعد میرا وعدہ ہے تم سے میں کبھی تمہیں کسی گھریلو کام کے لیے مجبور نہیں کروں گا۔'' بیڈ کی پٹی سے ٹیک لگائے وہ بہت سنجیدہ لہجے میں کہہ رہا تھا۔ ثانیہ کی آنکھیں پٹ سے کھل گئیں۔

یہ وہ شخص کیا کہہ رہا تھا؟ وہ پلٹی تھی اور اس نے خاصی حیران نگاہوں سے اس کی طرف دیکھا تھا۔

''میں تمہیں بیوی بنا کر اس گھر میں لایا ہوں۔ خرید کر لایا ہوتا تو زبردستی کام بھی کرواتا مگر بیوی کے حقوق سے تو انکار نہیں ہے نا تمہیں؟'' اب وہ اس کی آنکھوں میں آنکھیں ڈالے کہہ رہا تھا ثانیہ بے سمجھی سے ابرو اچکا کر رہ گئی۔

''مطلب؟''

''مطلب سمجھا دوں گا آج رات تمہیں ظاہر ہے میں تو فی الحال فارغ رہتا ہوں۔ تم بھی فارغ رہو گی تو شوہر کے حقوق تو ادا کرو گی نا؟ میں اس معاملے میں بہت فیاض ہوں۔ میرا خیال ہے اس معاملے میں زیادتی پر تم نہ تو کسی سے میری شکایت کرسکتی ہو، نہ مجھے روک سکتی ہو کیا خیال ہے میں ٹھیک کہہ رہا ہوں نا؟'' اسے جھکانے کا بہت انوکھا طریقہ ایجاد کیا تھا اس نے وہ حیرانی سے اسے دیکھتی رہ گئی۔

''نہیں، تم ایسا کچھ نہیں کرو گے میرے ساتھ۔''

''کیوں، کون روک سکتا ہے مجھے؟'' اس کے ہراساں ہونے پر وہ ذرا سا مسکرایا تو ثانیہ سلگ کر رہ گئی۔ واقعی وہ اسے ایسے کسی معاملے میں روکنے کی سکت نہیں رکھتی تھی۔

''اب خدارا، خدا کے قہر سے مت ڈرانا مجھے کیونکہ جس معاملے میں تم خود بے حس ہو اسی معاملے میں مجھ سے نسانیت کی توقع نہیں رکھ سکتیں تم پھر سارے دن فارغ رہو گی کم از کم شوہر کو تو خوش رکھنا چاہیے نا تمہیں ہر پل، ہر لمحہ، ہر گھڑی۔''

ثانیہ کے وہم وگمان میں بھی نہیں تھا کہ وہ اس کے ساتھ ایسی بھی کوئی چال چل سکتا ہے۔ بہت اچھی طرح سے وہ اس کی فطرت سے آگاہ تھی۔ وہ شخص جو ٹھان لیتا تھا اسے ہر قیمت پر کر کے دم لیتا تھا اسے لگا وہ ایک دم سے ہار گئی ہو۔

''تم میری حالت کے بارے میں جانتے ہو' پھر بھی......؟'' ایک آخری امید کے سہارے اس نے اس کی طرف دیکھا تھا۔ مگر وہاں بے نیازی ہی بے نیازی تھی۔

''ہوں پھر بھی۔'' کہنے کے ساتھ ہی اس نے ہاتھ بڑھا کر اسے اپنے قریب کر لیا۔ وہ جو دن بھر کی بھوکی تھی اس کے اس سنگدلانہ اقدام پر تڑپ کر رہ گئی۔

اگلی صبح زائر کے بیدار ہونے سے قبل ہی وہ کمرے سے نکل آئی تھی۔ زائر فریش ہو کر صحن میں آیا تو وہ جھاڑو ہاتھ میں لیے عجیب رونی سی صورت بنائے سارا صحن صاف کر رہی تھی۔ کھلی زلفوں کی آوارہ لٹیں اسے زائر کی طرح ہی تنگ کرنے میں کوئی کسر نہیں چھوڑ رہی تھیں۔ بار بار دائیں ہاتھ سے وہ انہیں کانوں کے پیچھے اڑستے ہوئے ہلکان ہوئی جا رہی تھی۔

''اس'' مشقت سے ''یہ'' مشقت بہر حال بہتر تھی۔ وہ کن اکھیوں سے اس کی طرف دیکھتے ہوئے مسکرا دیا۔

اماں خود بھی ایک ہی دن میں یہ معجزہ دیکھ کر حیران ہو رہی تھیں۔ جیسی تیسی جھاڑو سے فارغ ہونے کے بعد ہاتھ دھو کر وہ کچن میں گھس آئی۔ اماں صحن میں پلنگ پر بیٹھی تھیں جبکہ وہ خود چولہے میں آگ جلانے میں مصروف تھا۔ ثانیہ عباس کی روئی روئی سی سرخ آنکھیں اور چھوٹی سی سرخ ناک جانے کیوں اس لمحے اسے بہت لطف دے رہی تھی۔

آگ جلانے کے دوران کئی بار سر اٹھا کر اس نے شرارتی نگاہوں سے اس کی طرف دیکھا تھا مگر وہ اس کی طرف متوجہ نہیں تھی۔ اسی پل بیرونی دروازہ کھلا تھا اور سائرہ افضل کے قدم اس گھر کی دہلیز پر پڑے تھے۔

''سلام خالہ۔'' زائر کے کانوں میں جیسے ہی اس کی آواز پڑی اسے لگا جیسے ساری دنیا تھم گئی ہو جلتی لکڑی پر اس کے ہاتھ جیسے جم گئے تھے۔ ثانیہ نے خاصی حیرانی سے سر اٹھا کر اسے دیکھا۔

''وعلیکم السلام سائرہ' آؤ......کیسی ہو؟''

''ٹھیک ہوں خالہ! زینب بتا رہی تھی زائر نے شادی کر لی ہے؟'' اس کی آواز میں آج بھی ویسی ہی کھنک تھی۔ اماں نے اسے پاس ہی بٹھا لیا۔

''ہوں۔''

''ہائے سچ' اسے لڑکی کس نے دے دی؟'' کوئی پتھر تھا جو اس نے کھینچ کر غائبانہ زائر کو مارا تھا۔ ثانیہ نے ایک مرتبہ پھر چونک کر اسے دیکھا۔ وہ جلتی لکڑی پر ہاتھ چپکنے سے قطعی بے نیاز دکھائی دے رہا تھا۔

''منہ سنبھال کر بات کر سائرہ' میرے زائر کو کمی ہے لڑکیوں کی؟''

''نہیں تو لائن بھی نہیں لگی پڑی خالہ' تو تو برا ہی مان گئی' میں نے تو پڑوسن سے سنا تھا کہ کسی شہر کی لڑکی کو بھگا کر لایا ہے زائر' سوچا ذرا دیکھ آؤں۔'' بنا اماں کی خفگی کو کوئی اہمیت دیے وہ اپنا ہی راگ الاپ رہی تھی۔

زائر کا چہرہ ضبط اور غصے کی شدت سے سرخ پڑ گیا۔ ایک دم سے وہ اٹھا تھا اور سائرہ افضل کے سامنے جا کھڑا ہوا۔ عجیب درد اور ویرانی کا اظہار کرتی نگاہیں گویا احتجاج کرتیں اس کے چہرے پر جم گئی تھیں۔

''مجھے ساری زندگی اس بات کا افسوس رہے گا سائرہ کہ میرے دل نے محبت کے لیے تم جیسی لڑکی کا انتخاب کیا۔''

''ہوں' اب تو یہی کہو گے' وہ کیا کہتے ہیں سیانے' کھسیانی بلی کھمبا نوچے۔''

''جسٹ شٹ اپ' تمہارے لیے یہی بہتر ہوگا کہ تم ابھی اور اسی وقت یہاں سے چلی جاؤ۔''

''جا رہی ہوں' کوئی ہمیشہ رہنے کے لیے نہیں آئی میں' آیا بڑا نواب کہیں کا۔'' وہ کسی بھی طور اس کے رعب میں آنے

والی نہیں تھی۔

زائر خون کے گھونٹ پی کر رہ گیا۔

سائرہ افضل کے جانے کے بعد وہ خود بھی گھر سے نکل گیا تھا۔ ثانیہ محسوس کر سکتی تھی کہ اس رات وہ بہت ڈسٹرب رہا تھا۔ اس نے سائرہ افضل کو نہیں دیکھا تھا مگر وہ یہ اندازہ بخوبی لگا سکتی تھی کہ ''سائرہ افضل'' زائر ملک کی زندگی میں بہت اہمیت رکھتی تھی۔ بستر کی دوسری سائیڈ پر کروٹ لیے بہت دیر تک وہ روتا رہا تھا اور جتنی دیر وہ روتا رہا تھا اتنی دیر وہ حیرانی سے الجھتی رہی تھی۔

وہ کیسی محبت تھی جو اس نے سائرہ افضل جیسی لڑکی سے کی تھی؟ وہ کیا وجہ تھی جس نے سائرہ افضل کو اس سے متنفر کر دیا تھا؟

اس رات بہت دیر تک سائرہ افضل کے بارے میں سوچتے ہوئے جاگ کر بالآخر اس نے اسے ذہن سے جھٹک دیا۔ وہ جیسی بھی تھی زائر ملک سے اس کا جیسا بھی تعلق تھا تاہم وہ اس کا مقابلہ نہیں کر سکتی تھی۔ زائر ملک نے جو حق سائرہ افضل کو دیا تھا وہ اسے نہیں دیا تھا۔

اگلی صبح وہ ابھی سو رہی تھی جب زائر نے اسے جھنجوڑ کر جگا دیا۔

''اذان ہو گئی ہے اٹھ کر نماز پڑھو۔'' اس کی آنکھ کھلتے ہی بہت سنجیدہ لہجے میں اس نے نیا حکم جاری کیا تھا۔ وہ مندھی مندھی سی آنکھوں کو بمشکل کھولے اسے دیکھتی رہ گئی۔

''پڑھ لوں گی ابھی تو دن نکلنے میں بہت دیر ہے۔''

''فجر کی نماز دن نکلنے سے پہلے پڑھی جاتی ہے میں مسجد جا رہا ہوں واپس آؤں تو تمہیں بستر پر نہ دیکھوں۔''

''زائر ملک تم اپنی خدائی سے واسطہ رکھو عبادت کا معاملہ خالصتاً میرا ذاتی معاملہ ہے۔''

''نہیں اس گھر کی چار دیواری کے اندر تمہارے سارے معاملے میری ذات سے جڑے ہیں جو بھی تمہیں میرے حوالے سے دیکھے بس دیکھتا ہی رہ جائے' ڈھونڈنے سے بھی تمہارے اندر کوئی کمی یا خامی نہ ملے کسی کو۔''

''مگر کیوں جب مجھے تمہارے ساتھ رہنا ہی نہیں' زندگی ہی نہیں گزارنی تو پھر میں کیوں آئیڈیل بنوں؟''

''کیونکہ فی الحال تمہاری زندگی میرے ساتھ ہی گزر رہی ہے اور جب تک تمہاری کوکھ میں میری امانت ہے تمہیں مجبوراً میرے ساتھ تعاون کرنا پڑے گا۔ اس کے بعد میرا وعدہ ہے تم سے' میں ایک دن کے لیے بھی تمہیں اپنے پاس نہیں رکھوں گا۔'' قدرے ٹھہرے ہوئے لہجے میں اپنی بات مکمل کرنے کے بعد وہ کمرے میں نہیں ٹھہرا تھا۔ ثانیہ کا خون مزید جل گیا۔

نیند کا آنا اب ممکن نہیں تھا لہٰذا اٹھ کر وضو کیا اور خالص دلی آمادگی کے ساتھ اس نے کئی دنوں کے بعد فجر کی نماز ادا کی تھی۔ زائر مسجد سے واپس آیا تو وہ دعا مانگ رہی تھی۔

''شکریہ۔'' بیڈ پر بیٹھنے کے بعد اس نے مسکراتے ہوئے ثانیہ کی طرف دیکھا تھا جواباً وہ دعا مکمل کر کے جائے نماز سے اٹھ کھڑی ہوئی۔

''کس بات کے لیے۔''

''میری ہدایت پر عمل کے لیے۔''

''اپنی خوش فہمی دور کر لیں۔ میں عبادت صرف اللہ کی محبت اور رضا کے لیے کرتی ہوں اور میں ہی کیا ہر مسلمان اللہ سے محبت اور اس کی خوشنودی کے لیے نماز قائم کرتا ہے۔''

''اچھا' اللہ کی محبت اور خوشنودی کے لیے اسلام میں شوہر کے بھی بہت سے حقوق ہیں وہ کیوں یاد نہیں رہتے تمہیں۔''

''اس لیے کیونکہ میں نے دل سے آپ کو اپنا شوہر تسلیم نہیں کیا۔''

''تو کیا ہوا؟ میرے حقوق تو پھر بھی لاگو ہوتے ہیں نا تم پر' جن حالات میں بھی سہی بہر حال نکاح تو ہوا ہے نا ہمارا۔''

''زائر ملک میں اس وقت آپ سے بحث کے موڈ میں نہیں ہوں۔''

''تو اچھی بات ہے نا' نیک پروین بیویاں بلا وجہ اپنے شوہروں سے بحث کرتی اچھی بھی نہیں لگتیں چلو شاباش آ جاؤ بیڈ پر۔'' کہنی کے بل بیڈ پر کروٹ بدلتے ہوئے اس نے اسے مزید جلایا تھا۔

ثانیہ گھور کر اسے دیکھتی رخ پھیر گئی۔

''بہت سے کام ہیں ابھی جو مجھے سر انجام دینے ہیں آپ لوٹیں میٹھی نیند کے مزے۔'' زائر کے لبوں پر اس کے الفاظ نے میٹھی مسکان بکھیر دی تھی۔ تاہم وہ اس کی مسکراہٹ دیکھنے کے لیے ٹھہری نہیں تھی۔ زائر آج کل شہر میں جاب ڈھونڈ رہا تھا۔ تبھی صبح کا نکلا شام کو گھر واپس آتا۔ ابا آج کل اپنی بیماری سے لڑ رہے تھے لہٰذا ان کا زیادہ وقت اپنے کمرے میں ہی گزرتا تھا۔ گاؤں کی عورتوں کے آج کل زائر کے گھر کچھ زیادہ ہی چکر لگنے لگے تھے۔ بہانے بہانے سے لڑکیاں ادھر آتی تھیں اور ثانیہ کو گھیر کر بیٹھ جاتی۔ ان کی باتیں بھی ہو جاتیں اور باتوں باتوں میں وہ ثانیہ کا ہاتھ بھی بٹا دیتیں۔ فقط دو ماہ میں وہ واقعی اسی ماحول کا حصہ لگنے لگی تھی۔

اماں بھاگ بھری (زائر کی ماں) اس سے بہت خوش تھیں۔ بے شک وہ سائرہ سے بھی زیادہ خوب صورت تھی۔ اتنے دنوں میں اس نے کبھی ان سے یا ان کے شوہر سے بدتمیزی نہیں کی تھی۔ سارا دن وہ گھر کے کام کاج میں مصروف رہتی۔ کوئی ضرورت کی بات ہوتی تو کر لیتی نہیں تو چپ رہتی شروع شروع میں اسے گیلی لکڑیوں اور پاتھیوں سے آگ جلانا سخت مشکل لگتا تھا۔ اکثر وہ رو بھی پڑتی تھی۔ پھونکیں مار مار کر اس کا حال بھی برا ہو جاتا تھا۔ مگر پھر رفتہ رفتہ اسے اس پر بھی عبور حاصل ہو گیا۔ پہلے پہل دودھ بوائل کرتے ہوئے وہ آدھے سے زیادہ دودھ نکال دیتی تھی مگر اب ایسا نہیں ہوتا تھا۔ سارے کاموں کے ساتھ ساتھ اب وہ ہاتھ سے کپڑے دھونا بھی سیکھ گئی تھی۔ زائر نے اس روز کے بعد اسے کبھی غصے میں نہیں دیکھا تھا۔ وہ بہت خاموش ہو کر رہ گئی تھی۔ اس شام وہ گھر واپس آیا تو وہ بھیگے پائنچوں کے ساتھ نل کے نیچے بیٹھی کپڑے دھونے میں مصروف تھی۔ اتنا خوب صورت اور بھرپور منظر تھا کہ وہ بے ساختہ دہلیز پر رک کر اسے دیکھنے لگا۔ تاہم وہ اس کی طرف متوجہ نہیں تھی۔ بھاری بھاری کپڑوں کو نچوڑ کر سائیڈ پر رکھتے ہوئے وہ اسے بے حد پیاری لگی۔ شام کا کھانا تیار تھا۔ وہ ابا کے کمرے میں کچھ دیر بیٹھ کر اماں سے ثانیہ کی تعریفیں سننے کے بعد اپنے کمرے میں آیا تو وہ بھی اس کے پیچھے ہی کھانا لے کر آ گئی۔ زائر نے دیکھا اس کے چہرے کی رنگت ماند پڑ رہی تھی۔

''ثانی......!'' کھانے کی ٹرے سائیڈ پر رکھنے کے بعد اس نے بہت اپنائیت سے اس کا ہاتھ تھام لیا۔

''جی۔''

''بہت مصروف ہو گئی ہو تھوڑا سا ٹائم تو رکھ لیا کرو میرے لیے بھی۔''

''آتی ہوں کپڑے دھو کر۔''

''نہیں' بیٹھو یہاں۔ آج میں تمہارے لیے شہر سے کچھ لایا ہوں۔''

''کیا؟''

''بیٹھو گی تو بتاؤں گا نا۔'' ہاتھ کھینچ کر اسے اپنے قریب بٹھاتے ہوئے اس نے جیب سے کچھ نکالا تھا۔ اگلے ہی پل کانچ کی ڈھیر ساری رنگ برنگ چوڑیاں ثانیہ کی جھولی میں آ پڑی تھیں۔

''میں مانتا ہوں تم نے دل سے مجھے اپنا شوہر تسلیم نہیں کیا میرے جیسا آوارہ ناکام شخص تم جیسی پیاری لڑکی کے قابل بھی نہیں، سوائے شکل صورت کے اور ہے ہی کیا میرے پاس، مگر پھر بھی یہ حقیقت ہے ثانی...... میرے دل میں تمہارے لیے بہت جگہ ہے۔ شاید سائرہ افضل سے بھی زیادہ۔'' اس کا ہاتھ تھام کر دھیمے لہجے میں کہتے ہوئے اس نے خود اسے چوڑیاں پہنانی شروع کر دی تھیں۔

''میں نے کبھی نہیں سوچا تھا کہ تم جیسی لڑکی میری ہم سفر بنے گی وہ بھی اس طرح سے کہ کوئی پلان ہی نہیں ہوگا۔ بے شک اللہ بہت بڑا پلانر ہے بہرحال بہت ستالیا میں نے تمہیں۔ اب اور نہیں میری جاب لگ گئی ہے شہر میں، وہیں رہا کروں گا اب اور تمہیں کوئی کام کرنے کی ضرورت نہیں ہے یہاں گاؤں میں بہت عورتیں مل جاتی ہیں کام کے لیے۔ میں چاہوں تو تمہیں اپنے پاس شہر میں بھی رکھ سکتا ہوں مگر شہر کا ماحول ہمارے بچے کے لیے ٹھیک نہیں ہے جو خالص فضا، جو خالص خوراک، خیال اور محبت تمہیں یہاں مل سکتی ہے وہ شہر میں نہیں مل سکتی۔ تم سمجھ رہی ہو نا میری بات۔''

''ہوں۔''

''ناراض ہو مجھ سے؟''

''نہیں۔''

''تو پھر خاموش کیوں رہنے لگی ہو، کچھ اور نہیں تو جھگڑا ہی کر لیا کرو۔''

''کیوں، جھگڑا کرنے سے مسائل حل ہو جاتے ہیں؟''

''نہیں، مگر رشتوں کی اہمیت اور خوب صورتی کا احساس باقی رہتا ہے۔''

''مگر ہمارے رشتے میں صرف جبر اور ہوس ہے خوب صورتی نہیں۔'' چبا چبا کر کہتی وہ اٹھ کھڑی ہوئی۔ زائر ملک اسے دیکھتا رہ گیا۔ اس شام اس نے کھانا نہیں کھایا۔ جاب ملنے کی خوشی پر بھی جیسے اوس پڑ گئی تھی۔ عشاء کی نماز ادا کرنے کے بعد وہ چپ چاپ سو گیا تھا۔ ثانیہ سارے کاموں سے فارغ ہو کر باہر صحن میں رکھی چارپائی پر ٹک گئی تھی۔ کچھ دنوں سے اس کی اندر کی دنیا بدل رہی تھی۔ اسے زائر ملک اچھا لگنے لگا تھا۔

اس کی ہر بات ہر انداز اچھا لگنے لگا تھا۔ اس کا گھر، اس کا گاؤں، اس گاؤں کے لوگ، رسم و رواج، صبحیں، شامیں، موسم، سب اچھے لگنے لگے تھے۔ اب تو اسے یہ بھی اچھا لگنے لگا تھا کہ وہ زبردستی اس پر اپنا حق جمائے مگر پھر بھی جب وہ سامنے آ جاتا تھا تو پتا نہیں کیوں وہ اپنے پرانے رنگ میں واپس لوٹ آتی۔ شاید وہ اس کے سامنے شکست تسلیم کرنے میں ڈرتی تھی۔

آسمان بادلوں سے ڈھکا تھا۔ ہلکی ہلکی سرد ہوائیں، چاندنی رات کے حسن کو چار چاند لگا رہی تھیں۔ گہرے گدلے بادلوں کی اوٹ میں آنکھ مچولی کھیلتے چاند کو دیکھنا اسے ہمیشہ سے بہت اچھا لگتا تھا۔ مگر اس پل موسم میں اچانک تبدیلی آئی تھی گہرے بادلوں نے چودھویں کے چاند کو مکمل طور پر اپنے حصار میں لیتے ہوئے برسنا شروع کر دیا تھا۔ وہ اٹھ کر جلدی جلدی صحن میں پڑی چیزیں سمیٹنے لگی۔ سب کچھ سمیٹ کر جس وقت وہ کمرے میں آئی زائر گہری نیند سو رہا تھا۔ وہ کپڑے تبدیل کرنے کے بعد اس کے پہلو میں لیٹ گئی۔ پہلی بار وہ اسے بہت غور سے دیکھ رہی تھی۔ بے شک وہ بے حد حسین اور پرکشش شخص تھا مگر اس کے کام اچھے نہیں تھے۔ عقل کی خاصی کمی تھی اس کے پاس۔ تبھی اس کی نظر اپنی کلائی میں پڑی خوب صورت رنگ برنگ چوڑیوں پر پڑی تو آپ ہی آپ اس کے لبوں پر مسکراہٹ دوڑ گئی۔ کلائی سامنے کرتے ہوئے اس نے اپنے ہونٹ چوڑیوں پر رکھے تھے۔ کچھ ہی فاصلے پر دھرے میز پر شام کا کھانا جوں کا توں رکھا تھا۔ اسے بے حد ملال ہوا۔ بے شک جو زائر نے کیا وہ ٹھیک نہیں تھا مگر بدلے میں جو کچھ وہ اس کے ساتھ کر رہی تھی وہ

بھی تو ٹھیک نہیں تھا۔ اس کا دل چاہا وہ اسے جھنجوڑ کر جگائے اور کھانا کھانے کے لیے کہے مگر پھر اس کی نیند خراب نہ کرنے کا سوچ کر رک گئی۔

باہر اب بارش تیز ہوگئی تھی۔ ثانیہ کو ایک دم سے اپنے اندر کا حبس بڑھتا ہوا محسوس ہونے لگا۔ زائر کے پہلو سے اٹھ کر وہ ایک مرتبہ پھر باہر صحن میں چلی آئی۔ کتنی عجیب بات تھی کہ اسے ہمیشہ سے اس موسم سے ڈر لگتا تھا گرجتے بادلوں اور کڑکتی بجلی کے خوف سے وہ کبھی بارش میں نہیں نہاتی تھی مگر اس وقت وہ بارش میں نہا رہی تھی۔ اپنے اندر کے حبس کو دور کرنے کے لیے وہ بارش کے سرد قطروں سے خود کو سیراب کر رہی تھی۔ مگر یہ حبس اس کے اندر کا حبس تھا۔ بارش کے سرد قطرے اس حبس کو دور کرنے میں ناکام دکھائی دے رہے تھے۔ اسے خبر بھی نہ ہوئی اور اس کے آنسو گالوں کو بھگوتے چلے گئے تبھی اسے اپنے پیچھے قدموں کی آہٹ سنائی دی۔ زائر سینے پر ہاتھ باندھے دیوار سے ٹیک لگائے کھڑا تھا۔

''بارش میں بھیگنے کا یہ کون سا وقت ہے؟'' نیند سے بوجھل لہجے میں اس نے پوچھا۔ ثانیہ نے فوراً پلٹ کر اسے دیکھا اور پھر جانے کیا ہوا ایک دم سے بھاگتے ہوئے وہ اس کے کشادہ سینے میں چھپ گئی۔

زائر کو لگا جیسے وہ پتھر ہو گیا ہو۔

''کیا ہوا؟'' کپکپاتے ہونٹ اس کی پیشانی پر رکھنے کے بعد اس نے پوچھا مگر وہ جواب دینے کی پوزیشن میں نہیں تھی۔ اس کے دل کی تیز دھڑکن زائر کا سکون برباد کر گئی تھیں۔ ثانیہ کے وجود کے گرد اس کی گرفت سخت ہوئی اور پھر جیسے اس نے اسے اپنے اندر ہی جذب کر لیا۔ کتنی دیر تک دونوں ایک دوسرے کی تیز دھڑکنوں کا شور سنتے بارش میں بھیگتے رہے تھے۔

❀ .... ❀ .... ❀

اگلی صبح ثانیہ کی آنکھ کھلنے سے پہلے ہی وہ شہر کے لیے رخصت ہو چکا تھا۔ پچھلے دو تین ماہ میں پہلی بار اسے صبح اچھی نہیں لگی تھی۔ دو ماہ رہ گئے تھے اس کی ڈلیوری میں مگر زائر کے بغیر اسے جیسے کچھ بھی اچھا نہیں لگ رہا تھا۔ اس روز اس کا فون آیا تھا کمپنی اسے ایمرجنسی ویزے پر باہر بھجوا رہی تھی۔ وہ خوش تھا' بے حد خوش' مگر ثانیہ کا دل بجھ کر رہ گیا تھا۔ ایک ہفتے بعد بھی وہ گھر نہیں آیا تھا اور ایک ہفتے میں اس نے جانا تھا کہ وہ زائر کے بغیر کچھ بھی نہیں۔ اس روز بھی موسم بہت ابر آلود ہو رہا تھا۔

ثانیہ نے تندور پر روٹیاں لگانی سیکھ لی تھیں۔ وہ ابھی شام کی روٹی پکا کر فارغ ہوئی تھی کہ ساتھ والی امبری کا بلاوا آ گیا۔ امبری کی شادی کے دن رکھے جا چکے تھے اور ثانیہ کے ساتھ اس کی خاصی گاڑھی چھننے لگی تھی۔ اپنی ساس اور سسر کو کھانا دینے کے بعد وہ ان سے اجازت لے کر امبری کی طرف آئی اور یہیں گاؤں کی اکٹھی ہوئی عورتوں میں ایک عورت اسے بہانے سے سائیڈ پر لے جا کر اسے اس کی ماں کے حوالے کر آئی۔

''مما'' اتنے دنوں کے بعد اپنی ماں کو اپنی سامنے دیکھ کر وہ خوشی سے پاگل ہی تو ہو گئی تھی۔ جواب میں انہوں نے بھی اسے اپنے سینے سے لگا لیا۔

''کیسی ہو ثانی؟''

''ٹھیک ہوں مما! آپ کیسی ہیں؟''

''کیسی ہو سکتی ہوں تمہارے بغیر پچھلے تین ماہ سے پاگلوں کی طرح ڈھونڈتی پھر رہی ہوں تجھے۔ کہاں کہاں نہیں تلاشا' اسپتال سے تمہارے غائب ہونے کے بعد میں اور اشعر بس تمہاری تلاش میں ہی رہے ہیں۔ یہ جو عورت تھی اس کا بیٹا شہر میں زائر کا دوست تھا اسی کی مدد سے یہاں تک پہنچے ہیں۔''

''او مما! میری وجہ سے کتنی مشکلات کا سامنا کرنا پڑا آپ کو بہر حال میں یہاں بہت خوش ہوں۔ زائر اور اس کے گھر والے بہت اچھے ہیں۔ آپ ان سے ملیں گی تو آپ کو بھی بہت اچھا لگے گا۔''

''ثانی...... یہ تم کیا کہہ رہی ہو؟'' مسز عباس کے لیے اس کے الفاظ کسی دھچکے سے کم نہیں تھے۔ وہ حیرانی سے بیٹی کا منہ دیکھتی رہ گئی تھیں۔

''جی مما! یہاں آ کر میں نے جانا ہے کہ زندگی کی اصل خوب صورتی کیا ہے اور آپ کو پتا ہے زائر کو شہر میں جاب بھی مل گئی ہے وہ کمپنی کی طرف سے اپروڈ گیا ہوا ہے۔''

''تو......؟''

''تو یہ مما کہ میں اب یہیں رہوں گی۔ بہت پیار کرتا ہے زائر مجھ سے' وہ مجھے تحفظ دینا جانتا ہے آپ یقین کریں میں یہاں بہت بہت خوش ہوں۔'' جتنی خوشی اور بے نیازی سے وہ کہہ رہی تھی مسز عباس کے چہرے پر اتنے ہی رنگ آ جا رہے تھے انہیں قطعی گمان نہیں تھا کہ ان کی بیٹی ان کے ساتھ اتنا بڑا فریب بھی کر سکتی ہے۔ کافی دیر تک تو انہیں سمجھ میں ہی نہ آیا کہ اب وہ کیا کریں۔ کیسے بتاتیں وہ اسے کہ انہوں نے اشعر حسین کو صرف اس کا لالچ دے کر تو بلایا ہے۔ اب بھی اگر وہ اسے مایوس کرتی ہیں تو وہ ان دونوں ماں بیٹی کو چھوڑے گا نہیں۔ ان کا ذہن تیزی سے کام کر رہا تھا تبھی ثانیہ نے ان کا ہاتھ تھام لیا۔

''چلیں مما' میں آپ کو زائر کے گھر والوں سے ملواتی ہوں۔'' زائر کا گھر ساتھ ہی تھا اس سے پہلے کہ مسز عباس انکار کرتیں وہ انہیں کھینچ کر اپنے گھر لے گئی۔

''اماں' اماں دیکھیں تو کون آیا ہے؟'' خوشی سے اس کا حال برا تھا۔ اماں بھاگ بھری چاولوں کو ٹرے میں لیے اپنے کمرے سے نکلیں۔

''کون آیا ہے پتر۔''

''میری مما آئی ہیں۔ کزن بھی ہے ساتھ۔''

''اچھا...... ماشاء اللہ۔''

''السلام علیکم!'' مسز عباس نے مصافحہ کے لیے پہلے ہاتھ آگے بڑھایا تھا۔

''وعلیکم السلام جی' آئیں بیٹھیں۔''

''بیٹھنے کا ٹائم نہیں ہے میرے پاس' اشعر باہر گاڑی میں انتظار کر رہا ہے مہربانی ہوگی اگر آپ ثانیہ کو ہمارے ساتھ جانے کی اجازت دے دیں۔'' ان کے مطالبے پر جہاں اماں حیران ہوئی تھیں وہیں ثانیہ بھی حیرانی سے ان کا منہ دیکھنے لگی تھی۔

''مگر مما ابھی آپ کے ساتھ نہیں جا سکتی۔ ایک دو روز میں زائر آنے والا ہے وہ آ جائے تو پھر ہم دونوں چلیں گے۔''

''تم چپ رہو ثانیہ' یہ تمہارا معاملہ نہیں ہے۔ ویسے بھی بڑے بولتے ہوں تو چھوٹوں کو چپ رہنا چاہیے۔''

''مگر مما......!'' وہ مچل کر احتجاج کرنا چاہتی تھی مگر مسز عباس نے اسے ڈپٹ کر چپ کروا دیا۔

ثانیہ عباس اور زائر ملک کی زندگی میں یہی وہ موڑ تھا جہاں ان دونوں کے بیچ جدائی آئی تھی۔ نہ صرف جدائی آئی تھی بلکہ وہ ایک دوسرے کی شکل دیکھنے کو بھی تیار نہیں تھے۔ بدگمانی اور نفرت کی ایسی اونچی فصیلیں قائم ہو گئی تھیں دونوں کے درمیان کہ اب وہ چاہتے ہوئے بھی ایک دوسرے کا ہاتھ نہیں تھام سکتے تھے۔

❁......❁......❁

نہ بجھا چراغ دیار دل، نہ بچھڑنے کا تو ملال کر
تجھے دے گی جینے کا حوصلہ، میری یاد رکھ لے سنبھال کر
یہ بھی کیا کہ ایک ہی شخص کو کبھی سوچنا، کبھی بھولنا
جو نہ بجھ سکے وہ دیا جلا، جو نہ ہو سکے وہ کمال کر
نم آرزو میری جستجو میں سمٹ کے آ گیا روبرو
یہ سکوت مرگ ہے کس لیے میں جواب دوں تو سوال کر
تو بچھڑ رہا ہے تو سوچ لے تیرے ہاتھ ہے میری زندگی
تجھے روکنا میری موت ہے میری بے بسی کا خیال کر
میرے درد کا میرے ضبط کا میری بے بسی میرے صبر کا
جو یقین نہ آئے تو دیکھ لے تو ہوا میں پھول اچھال کر

تین روز سے اس کا بخار نہیں ٹوٹ رہا تھا۔ جانے کیسی بے چینی تھی کہ اسے کسی کروٹ سکون نصیب نہیں ہو رہا تھا۔ کتنی کمزور ثابت ہوئی تھی وہ زائر ملک سے محبت کے معاملے میں؟ پانچ سال گزرنے کے باوجود وہ اسے بھول نہیں پائی تھی۔ بارشیں جیسے جان کا روگ بن کر رہ گئی تھیں۔ اس کے لیے زائر ملک کی رفاقت کے آخری دلفریب لمحے اسے ہر گھڑی بے قرار رکھتے تھے۔ پچھلے پانچ سال میں وہ ''تنگ'' ہونے کے لیے ترس گئی تھی۔

اس روز جب مسز عباس زبردستی اسے اپنے ساتھ شہر لے آئی تھیں۔ اس کی طبیعت بہت خراب ہو گئی تھی۔ زائر کے دوست کی وہ ماں جس نے اس کی مخبری کی تھی۔ وہ بھی ان کے ہمراہ تھی مسز عباس نے اسے شہر میں اپنے گھر میں نوکری کا لالچ دیا تھا۔ حمل کے ساتویں ماہ میں قطعی غیر متوقع طور پر اس کا آپریشن ہوا تھا اور اس نے جڑواں بچوں کو جنم دیا تھا۔ ایک بیٹے اور ایک بیٹی کو۔ اسے شہر آئے وہ تیسرا دن تھا جب مسز عباس نے اسے بتایا۔ وہ کچن میں کھڑی نوڈلز تیار کر رہی تھی تبھی وہ قریب آئی تھیں۔

''ثانی' وہ زائر کا فون آیا تھا تم نے اسے میرے نمبر سے کال کی تھی؟''

''جی مما' کیوں کیا ہوا؟''

''بہت غصے میں ہے زائر' گالیاں دے رہا تھا تمہیں اسے لگتا ہے جیسے تم اس کے بچوں کو لے کر مفرور ہو گئی ہو' عجیب پینڈو شخص ہے پتا نہیں تمہیں کیا نظر آیا اس میں؟''

''مما پلیز آپ نے مجھ سے بات کیوں نہیں کروائی اس کی۔ وہ غلط فہمی کا شکار ہو گا آپ کو اس کی غلط فہمی دور کرنی چاہیے تھی۔''

''دلوں میں گنجائش ہو تو غلط فہمیاں دور ہوتی ہیں۔ اس نے تو بات ہی ختم کر دی۔''

''کیا مطلب۔'' نوڈلز کا باؤل اس کے ہاتھ سے گرا تھا تبھی وہ نظر چراتے ہوئے بولی تھیں۔

''ڈائیورس دے دی ہے اس نے تمہیں۔ بہت کوشش کی میں نے سمجھانے کی مگر اس نے میری ایک نہیں سنی۔ کہہ رہا تھا کہ ایک دو روز میں پیپرز بھی بھجوا دے گا۔'' لفظ سانپ بچھو کیسے بن جاتے ہیں یہ اس لمحے کوئی ثانیہ عباس سے پوچھتا۔ زمین پاؤں سے کیسے کھسکتی ہے ثانیہ عباس نے اس روز جانا تھا۔ اس کی آنکھیں جیسے پتھرا کر رہ گئی تھیں۔ غم کی شدت سے بے حال وہ تیورا کر گری تھی اور بے ہوش ہو گئی تھی۔

اگلے روز اس نے جڑواں بچوں کو جنم دیا تھا۔ ڈاکٹرز ان بچوں کے زندہ رہنے سے متعلق پرامید نہیں تھے مگر اللہ نے

ان معصوم کلیوں کو زندہ رکھا تھا۔ سات ماہ کے ان بچوں کو انتہائی نگہداشت میں رکھا گیا تھا۔ دو روز کے بعد ثانیہ کی حالت بہتر ہوئی تو اس نے فوراً اشعر سے موبائل لے کر زائر کا نمبر پریس کیا مگر اس کا نمبر مسلسل آف جا رہا تھا۔ تب اس نے گھر کے نمبر پر کال کی اور اس بار اس کی ساس نے اس کی کال اٹینڈ کی تھی۔

"السّلام علیکم اماں۔"

"وعلیکم السّلام کیسی ہو بیٹی؟" اماں کی آواز بجھی بجھی سی تھی۔ ثانیہ کا دل زور سے دھڑک اٹھا۔

"ٹھیک ہوں اماں آپ کیسی ہیں؟"

"کیسی ہو سکتی ہوں جو قیامت گزری ہے مجھ پر اس کے بعد کیسی ہو سکتی ہوں میں؟"

"ک...... کیا...... مطلب...... اماں آپ کو پتا ہے آپ دادی بن گئی ہیں دو جڑواں بچوں کی دادی اماں پلیز۔ زائر سے کہیں مجھ سے بات کرے اور کچھ نہیں تو اپنے بچوں کو ایک نظر آ کر دیکھ لے پلیز اماں......!"

"وہ جنموں جلا اس قابل ہی کہاں رہا ہے پتر؟" اماں نے کہا تھا اور پھر پھپھک کر رو پڑی تھیں۔ ثانیہ جیسے گنگ رہ گئی۔

اس کا مطلب تھا کہ اس کی ماں نے جھوٹ نہیں بولا تھا۔ زائر کی ماں بھی اس حادثے سے آشنا تھی جو اس کے ساتھ ہو گیا تھا۔ ابھی چند دن پہلے ہی تو اس نے کہا تھا۔

"جب تک تمہاری کوکھ میں میری امانت ہے تمہیں مجبوراً میرے ساتھ تعاون کرنا پڑے گا۔ اس کے بعد میرا وعدہ ہے تم سے ایک دن کے لیے بھی تمہیں اپنے پاس نہیں رکھوں گا۔" زائر کی آواز کے ساتھ ہی زمین کے کسی کونے میں سائرہ افضل کی آواز گونجی تھی۔

"ہائے سچ' اسے لڑکی کسی نے دے دی؟" دوسری طرف سے لائن کٹ ہو چکی تھی۔

ثانیہ نے خاموشی سے سیل اشعر کے حوالے کر دیا۔ کتنا عجیب تھا وہ شخص...... اس نے اپنی مرضی اور خواہش پر زبردستی اس سے تعلق بنایا۔ اپنی مرضی سے جہاں چاہا وہاں رکھا اور پھر اپنی مرضی سے ہی چھوڑ دیا۔ ثانیہ کی رضا' اس کی خوشی اس کا فیصلہ تو کہیں بھی نہیں تھا اس رشتے میں۔ تبھی وہ پھر سوچوں میں در آیا تھا۔

"میں مانتا ہوں تم نے دل سے مجھے اپنا شوہر تسلیم نہیں کیا مجھ جیسا آوارہ ناکام شخص تم جیسی پیاری لڑکی کے قابل ہی نہیں' سوائے شکل صورت کے اور ہے ہی کیا میرے پاس تمہیں دینے کے لیے مگر پھر بھی یہ حقیقت ہے ثانی' میرے دل میں تمہارے لیے بہت جگہ ہے شاید سائرہ افضل سے بھی زیادہ۔"

"زائر......!" بنا ارد گرد کی پروا کیے وہ زور سے چیخی تھی۔

مسز عباس اور اشعر گھبرا کر رہ گئے۔ اسپتال میں شور مچ گیا تھا ثانیہ عباس مسلسل چلا رہی تھی۔ بڑی مشکل سے اسے قابو کر کے نیند کا انجیکشن دیا گیا تھا کئی دن تک وہ سوتے میں زائر کو پکارتی رہی تھی۔ کسی بھی عورت کی زندگی میں تخلیق کا مرحلہ سب سے بڑا مرحلہ ہوتا ہے۔ سب سے کٹھن اور تکلیف دہ ہر عورت اس مرحلے پر اپنے ہم سفر کو اپنے ساتھ دیکھنا چاہتی ہے مگر...... ثانیہ عباس کی یہ خواہش پوری نہیں ہوئی تھی۔ اس نے بھی اس مرحلے پر زائر کو اپنے ساتھ دیکھنا چاہا تھا مگر...... وہ اسے ہمیشہ کے لیے چھوڑ گیا تھا۔ بنا اس کی رائے لیے مرضی پوچھے۔ اگلے دو روز میں طلاق کے پیپرز بھی موصول ہو گئے۔

خوابوں کے سمندر کنارے خواہشوں کی ریت سے امید کا جو خوب صورت گھر بنا تھا وہ ڈھے گیا تھا۔ ثانیہ کو لگا جیسے وہ اب زندگی میں کبھی مسکرا نہیں سکے گی اور واقعی پچھلے پانچ سالوں میں کسی نے اسے مسکراتے ہوئے نہیں دیکھا تھا۔ بچوں

کی پیدائش کے دو ماہ بعد ہی وہ انگلینڈ چلی گئی تھی۔ اس نے ارادہ کیا تھا وہ اب کبھی پاکستان واپس نہیں آئے گی۔ مگر وہ اپنے اس ارادے پر قائم نہیں رہ سکی تھی۔ دو سال پہلے مسز عباس کی رحلت ہوگئی تھی اچانک فالج کے حملے کے بعد جسم کے ساتھ ساتھ ان کی زبان بھی مفلوج ہو کر رہ گئی تھی۔ وہ بولنا چاہتی تھیں مگر بول نہیں پاتی تھیں۔ بس آنسو تھے جو بے دریغ بہتے چلے جاتے تھے۔ اسی حالت میں ان کی رحلت ہوگئی تھی۔

مسز عباس کے بعد اشعر اس کا واحد سہارا تھا بہت کوشش کی اس نے ثانیہ کو شادی کے لیے رضا مند کرنے کی مگر اس کی ناں کو کبھی ہاں میں نہیں بدل سکا۔ تنگ آ کر اس نے کسی اور لڑکی سے شادی کر لی۔ ثانیہ اب اپنے باپ کا بزنس سنبھال رہی تھی۔ اس کے بچے بڑے ہوگئے تھے۔ مسز عباس کی رحلت کے بعد پاکستان میں اس کے ددھیال والوں نے اسے پاکستان بلانے کے لیے بہت کوشش کی مگر وہ ٹس سے مس نہیں ہوئی تھی۔ تاہم اب اپنے دادا اور تایا کی وفات کے بعد جانے اس کے من میں کیا آئی کہ وہ اچانک پاکستان چلی آئی بچے اشعر کے پاس ہی تھے وہ انہیں ساتھ لے کر نہیں آئی تھی کیونکہ وہ پڑھ رہے تھے۔ اس نے انہیں بتا رکھا تھا کہ ان کا باپ پاکستان میں رہتا ہے اسی لیے وہ پاکستان کی سرزمین کو دیکھنے کے لیے بے تاب تھے۔ تاہم جب اسے زائر سے اپنی علیحدگی کا خیال آتا تو اس کے احساسات جیسے برف کے ہو جاتے۔ وہ ٹھان لیتی کہ وہ اس شخص کو کبھی اپنے بچوں کی شکل دیکھنے نہیں دے گی۔ مگر اب یہ ارادہ بھی اسے ریت کی دیوار ثابت ہوتا دکھائی دے رہا تھا۔ وہ اپنے بچوں پر مزید ظلم نہیں کر سکتی تھی۔ ان کا باپ زندہ سلامت تھا اور اسی گاؤں میں تھا جہاں تقدیر نے اسے پہنچا دیا تھا۔ بچوں کے امتحان کے بعد خود انگلینڈ جانے کے بجائے وہ انہیں پاکستان بلوانا چاہتی تھی مگر اچانک بگڑ جانے والی طبیعت نے اسے نڈھال کر چھوڑا تھا۔

❁ ..... ❁ ..... ❁

اتنی قبریں نہ بناؤ میرے اندر محسنؔ
میں چراغ جلاتے ہوئے تھک جاتا ہوں

رات گہری تاریکی میں ڈھل چکی تھی۔

عائشہ کچن سے فارغ ہونے کے بعد لاؤنج میں ٹی وی لگا کر بیٹھ گئی۔ کل شام اس کی ساس اپنی بیٹی کے پاس ملک بدر ہوگئی تھی۔ گھر میں ایک دم سے جیسے سناٹا چھا گیا تھا۔ اوپر سے برساتی موسم نے الگ جان نکال رکھی تھی۔ اس نے کئی بار اریج کا نمبر پریس کیا تھا مگر وہ رسپانس نہیں دے رہا تھا۔ وقفے وقفے سے گرجتے بادل اس کی جان پر بنا رہے تھے۔ گھر میں ناچتے سناٹے اور تنہائی کے احساس کے ساتھ، صوفے پر پاؤں سمیٹ کر بیٹھی وہ اریج کی واپسی کی دعائیں کر رہی تھی جب ڈور بیل بج اٹھی۔ لاؤنج سے باہر گیٹ تک کا سفر اس کے لیے ایک پل صراط ثابت ہوا تھا۔

''السلام علیکم!'' نشے میں دھت وہ گاڑی سے نکل کر کمرے میں آیا۔ جب وہ گیٹ لاک کرتے ہوئے اس کے پیچھے ہی کمرے میں چلی آئی تھی۔ تاہم وہ اسے جواب دینے کی پوزیشن میں نہیں تھا۔

''اریج۔'' اسے تشویش ہوئی تھی تبھی اریج نے نشے سے بند ہوتی سرخ آنکھیں اٹھا کر اسے دیکھا تھا۔

''ہوں۔''

''طبیعت تو ٹھیک ہے نا آپ کی؟''

''ہوں۔''

''کھانا لاؤں آپ کے لیے؟''

''نہیں، مجھے بھوک نہیں ہے۔''

''ڈرنک کی ہے آپ نے؟''

''ہوں...... پتا نہیں...... پلیز اس وقت مجھے اکیلا چھوڑ دو میں کچھ دیر سکون چاہتا ہوں۔'' نشے میں بھی اس نے خود پر کنٹرول کر رکھا تھا۔ عائشہ پریشان سی اثبات میں سر ہلا کر کمرے سے نکل گئی۔ اگلے روز فجر کی نماز کی ادائیگی کے بعد اس نے ناشتا تیار کیا اور اریج کے جاگنے کا انتظار کرنے لگی۔ دن کے بارہ بج گئے تھے۔ مگر وہ کمرے سے باہر نہیں نکلا تھا۔ تبھی وہ کمرے میں آئی تھی۔

''اریج۔'' اسے بستر میں بے سدھ پڑے دیکھ کر اس نے دھیمی آواز میں پکارا تھا۔ جب اس نے فوراً آنکھیں کھول دیں۔

''ہوں۔''

''دن کے بارہ بج گئے ہیں اٹھیں گے نہیں۔''

''اٹھ ہی رہا تھا بس ہمت نہیں ہو رہی۔''

''طبیعت تو ٹھیک ہے نا آپ کی؟''

''ہوں۔''

''ناشتہ لاؤں آپ کے لیے؟''

''نہیں دل نہیں چاہ رہا۔''

''آپ نے رات بھی کھانا نہیں کھایا تھا۔ سب ٹھیک تو ہے نا۔''

''ہوں۔'' کہنی کے بل اٹھ کر گاؤ تکیے سے ٹیک لگاتے ہوئے اس نے سر بیڈ کی پشت گاہ سے ٹکا دیا تھا۔ عائشہ نے دیکھا اس کا چہرہ بے حد ستا ہوا تھا۔ جبکہ آنکھیں شب بے داری یا شاید رونے کی وجہ سے سوج رہی تھیں۔ تبھی وہ بولی۔

''اگر آپ برا محسوس نہ کریں تو مجھے آپ سے کچھ کہنا تھا اریج۔''

''ہاں کہو۔'' پٹ سے آنکھیں کھولتے ہوئے اس نے اپنی توجہ اس پر مبذول کی تھی۔

عائشہ بیڈ کے کنارے پر ٹک گئی۔

''میں جانتی ہوں آپ اور عائلہ ایک دوسرے سے بہت پیار کرتے ہیں۔ بہت انڈر اسٹینڈنگ ہے آپ دونوں کی اور میں یہ بھی جانتی ہوں کہ محبت کے دربار سے دربدری کے بعد انسان ساری عمر بند گلیوں میں بھٹکتا رہتا ہے۔ حالات اور تقدیر کی لہریں جانے کہاں سے کہاں بہا کر لے جاتی ہیں اسے، میں نے کبھی نہیں چاہا تھا کہ میری وجہ سے آپ کے اور عائلہ کے خواب ٹوٹیں پلیز آپ میری وجہ سے اپنی اور اس کی زندگی برباد مت کریں۔''

''میں اپنی اور اس کی زندگی برباد نہیں کر رہا عائشہ' وہ خود اپنی اور میری زندگی برباد کر رہی ہے۔ تمہیں پتا ہے اس نے اپنی محبت کی قیمت کیا رکھی ہے۔'' نہایت اپنائیت سے اس کی طرف دیکھتے ہوئے وہ بولا تھا۔

عائشہ کے آنسو اس کی پلکوں پر ہی اٹک گئے۔

''کیا؟''

''طلاق، وہ چاہتی ہے میں تمہیں طلاق دے دوں۔'' اس بار اریج کے الفاظ نے اس کا دل کچل ڈالا تھا وہ چاہتے ہوئے بھی اپنے آنسوؤں کو بہنے سے نہ روک سکی۔

''اس کا مطالبہ کچھ ایسا عجیب بھی نہیں ہے اریج' آپ اس سے محبت کرتے ہیں اور جہاں محبت ہوتی ہے وہاں تقسیم نہیں ہوتی۔ نہ ہی کمپرومائز ہوتا ہے۔''

''ہوسکتا ہے ایسا ہی ہو' مگر میں خودغرض انسان نہیں ہوں۔''

''یہ خودغرضی نہیں ہے اریج' تین زندگیوں کا سوال ہے اب تک آپ نے میرا جتنا خیال کیا مجھے جتنا مان اور اہمیت دی اس کے لیے میں ساری زندگی آپ کی مقروض رہوں گی مگر میں کبھی نہیں چاہوں گی کہ اس احسان کے بدلے میں آپ کو ساری عمر کی بے سکونی اور آنسو دے دوں۔ مجھے محض اپنا نام دے کر آپ ہر لمحہ اس کی یادوں میں نڈھال شراب کے نشے میں مدہوش رہیں۔ آپ بہت اچھے انسان ہیں اریج' بہت ہمدرد اور نیک دل ہیں میں کبھی نہیں چاہوں گی کہ میری وجہ سے ایسے نیک دل انسان کی خوشیوں کو گہن لگے۔ میں کہیں نہ کہیں جاب کر کے رہ لوں گی۔ مگر پلیز آپ میری وجہ سے اپنے خوابوں کا سودا مت کریں پلیز۔'' جتنے لفظ اس کے لبوں سے نکل رہے تھے اتنے ہی آنسو اس کی آنکھیں لٹا رہی تھیں۔

اریج گہری سانس بھر کر رہ گیا۔

''میں محبت کو روگ بنا کر زندگی برباد کرنے والے لوگوں میں سے نہیں ہوں عائشہ' بڑا پریکٹیکل سا بندہ ہوں میں' میرا ایمان ہے آپ لاکھ جتن کرلیں مگر آپ کو وہی ملتا ہے جو آپ کے نصیب میں لکھا ہوتا ہے۔ میں عائلہ کی محبت سے دستبردار نہیں ہوں۔ بہت پرانا ساتھ ہے ہمارا مگر وہ میرے نصیب میں نہیں تھی۔ اگر ہوتی تو میرا نکاح تم سے کبھی نہ ہوتا۔ تقدیر پر شاکر رہنے والا بندہ ہوں میں خدا کے فیصلوں کو مانتا ہوں۔ اس نے اگر عائلہ کی جگہ تمہیں میری قسمت میں لکھا ہے تو اس میں ضرور اس کی کوئی حکمت ہی ہوگی۔ میں رشتوں کو ریت کے دیواریں نہیں سمجھتا کہ جب دل چاہا بنا لیں جب دل چاہا گرا دیں۔ جب ہزاروں لوگوں کے سامنے اپنے نام کا تحفظ دینے کا وعدہ کیا ہے تو اس وعدے کو پورا بھی کروں گا۔ تمہارا کوئی قصور نہیں کہ ہمیشہ در بدر کی ٹھوکریں تمہارے نصیب کا حصہ بنی رہیں۔ جہاں تک ڈرنک کا سوال ہے تو میں اب سے نہیں کرتا بہت سال ہوگئے اس وقت شروع کی تھی۔ شاید چھٹی یا ساتویں میں پڑھتا تھا اماں کی رحلت ہوگئی تھی اور ابا حمیرا کی ماں کو ہماری اسٹیپ مدر بنا کر لے آئے میرے ذہن نے اسے قبول نہیں کیا اور شاید کمال بھائی اور جمال بھائی کے ذہن نے بھی۔ اسی لیے ہمارے ماموں' ہمیں وہاں سے لے گئے۔ سوتیلی ماں تو تمہیں پتا ہے سوتیلی ہی ہوتی ہے۔ اس نے ہمیں روکنے کی کوئی کوشش نہیں کی۔ ماموں شرابی تھے اور دیگر نشہ بھی کرتے تھے۔ انہوں نے ہمیں بھی اسی کام پر لگا دیا۔ دو تین سال کے بعد ان کے بیٹے نے کمال بھائی کو دبئی بلوا لیا۔ جمال بھائی کو ٹائیفائیڈ ہوا تو پھر وہ ٹھیک ہی نہیں ہوئے۔ علاج میں سستی اور غیر مناسب دیکھ بھال نے انہیں پاگل کردیا تب ابا اسے گھر لے گئے۔ مجھے ماموں نے کمال بھائی کے پاس دبئی بجھوا دیا۔ سالوں وہیں رہا ہوں میں اور سچ پوچھو تو اگر ابا کی رحلت کے بعد اماں جمال بھائی کی شادی والا کارنامہ سرانجام نہ دیتیں تو شاید میں کبھی پاکستان نہ آتا۔ عائلہ اور میری محبت بھی دبئی میں ہی پروان چڑھی تھی۔ بہرحال میں وعدہ کرتا ہوں آئندہ ڈرنک کر کے گھر نہیں آؤں گا۔''

اپنا مختصر بائیو ڈیٹا بتانے کے بعد اس نے نرمی سے عائشہ کے ہاتھ تھام لیے تھے۔

''میں نہیں جانتا عائشہ کہ تم نے زندگی میں کسی سے محبت کی ہے یا نہیں' مگر میں اتنا ضرور جانتا ہوں کہ محبت کو کھو کر زندہ رہنا اتنا آسان بھی نہیں ہوتا۔ بڑی تبدیلیاں آجاتی ہیں انسان کے اندر' ہوسکتا ہے میں بھی کچھ معاملات میں غفلت برت جاؤں' اگر ایسا ہوجائے تو پلیز معاف کردینا تم بہت اچھی لڑکی ہو بہت سلیقہ مند اور خوب صورت' کوئی بھی بہترین سے بہترین شخص تمہارا ہم سفر ہوسکتا تھا میں کوشش کروں گا خود کو تمہارا بہترین ہم سفر ثابت کرنے کی۔ کیونکہ جو کچھ بھی ہوا اس میں تمہارا کوئی قصور نہیں' میں نے جو کیا اللہ کی رضا کے لیے کیا اور اللہ جو کرتا ہے بہترین کرتا ہے بے شک وہ اپنے بندوں پر بہت مہربان ہے۔'' ٹوٹے بکھرے سے گمبھیر لہجے میں کہتے ہوئے اس نے اس کے ہاتھ سہلائے تھے عائشہ

بمشکل اپنے آنسو پیتے ہوئے خاموش بیٹھی رہی۔ تبھی وہ پھر بولا۔

”مجھے بولڈ اور خود اعتماد لڑکیاں اچھی لگتی ہیں۔ میں چاہوں گا تم اسی طرح رہو، پر اعتماد اور مضبوط۔“

”جی۔“

”گڈ، چلو اب ناشتا کرو، میں تو صرف چائے پیوں گا بلکہ اس کے لیے بھی ابھی دل نہیں چاہ رہا۔ تم ایسا کرو پلیز میرے سینے پر سر رکھ کر لیٹ جاؤ، میں تمہارے بال سہلاتا ہوں، ہوں۔“ عائشہ اس شخص کی اندرونی کیفیت کا بخوبی اندازہ لگا سکتی تھی۔ کیونکہ وہ خود بھی اسی تکلیف سے گزری تھی۔ شاید تبھی اس نے اس کے حکم پر خاموشی سے عمل کیا تھا۔

”بہت سے معاملات انسان کے اختیار میں نہیں ہوتے عائش، ان کے معاملے میں اسے اپنی تقدیر پر راضی بارضا رہنا پڑتا ہے۔ تم سمجھ لینا اللہ نے ہمارا ملنا بھی ایسے ہی لکھا تھا۔“ مدت کے بعد کسی نے اسے ”عائش“ کہہ کر پکارا تھا۔ اس کی آنکھیں یکلخت آنسوؤں سے بھر آئیں۔ پتھر ہوئے وجود اور احساسات میں اچانک بھونچال اٹھا تھا۔

اس نے چھو کر مجھے پتھر سے پھر انسان کیا
مدتوں بعد میری آنکھوں میں آنسو آئے

کسک کچھ بھی نہیں تھی۔
نقصان کوئی بھی نہیں تھا۔
کہیں کوئی پچھتاوا نہیں تھا۔

مگر پھر بھی وہ اریج کے گلے لگ کر پھوٹ پھوٹ کر روئی تھی۔ میکال حسن سے جدائی اور اپنے رشتوں کی بے حسی کا سارا درد اس نے آنسوؤں کی صورت میں اریج کے سینے پر بہایا تھا۔ وہ امتحان جو اس کے دل نے اس سے لیا تھا بے شک وہ اس امتحان میں سرخرو ٹھہری تھی۔

کچی بستی کے بام و در پر
اترتی جاڑے کی زرد شامیں
شفق کی گہری اداس شاموں میں دھیرے دھیرے سمٹتا سورج
میں بالکونی میں زرد ہوتے گلابی پھولوں کو دیکھتی ہوں
تو سوچتی ہوں......
گھروں سے اٹھتے دھوئیں کے بادل فضا میں تحلیل ہو رہے ہیں
نجانے ایسے اداس موسم میں تم کہاں ہو؟
چلے بھی آؤ کہ اب اداسی کی شال اوڑھے
سسکتے ماہتاب کی نگاہوں میں
تیرے ہجر و فراق کا دکھ لکھا ہوا ہے
چلے بھی آؤ کہ اب تو راہوں کے نرم جگنو بھی سو گئے ہیں
چلے بھی آؤ کہ روتے روتے، یہ آنسو پتھر کے ہو گئے ہیں

دن ڈھل رہا تھا۔ غروب ہوتے سورج کی نارنجی کرنیں، شہر خاموشاں کی چھوٹی سی دیوار کے اس پار اداسی کے کفن میں لپٹی، سسکتی محسوس ہو رہی تھیں۔ تھکے تھکے قدموں کو بمشکل گھسیٹتی آج بہت دنوں کے بعد وہ مٹی کے اس ڈھیر کے

قریب آئی تھی جہاں اس کی تمام حسرتیں اور خواب دفن تھے۔

بہت دنوں کے بعد پتھرائی نگاہوں سے آنسوؤں کا ریلا یوں جاری ہوا تھا جیسے کسی خشک جھیل میں صدیوں کے بعد پانی کی آمد و رفت کا سلسلہ شروع ہوتا ہے۔ بلیک چادر محض کندھوں سے ہی نہیں سر سے بھی ڈھلک گئی تھی مگر اسے خبر ہی کہاں تھی؟ ٹوٹ ٹوٹ کر بہتے آنسوؤں کی دھند میں قبر کی خشک مٹی پر ہاتھ پھیرتے ہوئے وہ جیسے ڈھے گئی تھی۔

''کیسے ہو ابا؟ میں جانتی ہوں آپ مجھ سے ناراض ہو' آپ کو ناراض ہونا بھی چاہیے مگر میں کیا کروں' دنیا بہت تنگ پڑ گئی ہے مجھ پر۔ وگرنہ یہ کیسے ہو سکتا ہے کہ میں دنیا میں رہوں اور آپ کو بھول جاؤں۔'' ٹپ...... ٹپ...... ٹپ گرتے آنسوؤں کے ساتھ قبر کی خشک مٹی پر ہاتھ پھیرتے ہوئے اس کا گلا جیسے رندھ گیا تھا۔

کون تھا کائنات میں جو اس کے دل کے درد کو جانتا' سوائے اللہ کے۔

حکومتوں کی نااہلی اور آپس کی جنگ میں مکھی مچھروں کی طرح مرتے عوام اور سسکتے دلوں کی کہانی کو' کون جان سکتا تھا؟ سوائے اللہ کے۔

ڈھلتی شام کے ساتھ اس کا دل بھی جیسے ڈوبتا جا رہا تھا۔

سرد رویہ' الجھا لہجہ

کھوئی آنکھیں' ٹھنڈے ہاتھ

بے رنگ چہرہ' بد اخلاق

دیکھو تم بن کون ہوں میں؟

''ابا دعبدالہدیٰ'' کے بغیر ساری دنیا جیسے اس کے لیے بے معنی ہو کر رہ گئی تھی۔ دنیا کے سپرد کر کے گیا تھا وہ شخص اسے؟

اس دنیا کے' کہ جس سے اس کی کبھی بنی ہی نہیں تھی؟

وہ دنیا جو کبھی کسی کی ہوئی ہی نہیں؟

اس کے تو سارے سلسلے اب بھی مٹی کے اسی ایک ڈھیر سے وابستہ تھے۔

دنیا میں ہوتے ہوئے بھی وہ دنیا میں نہیں تھی۔ اس کا وجود عالم برزخ میں لٹک کر رہ گیا تھا۔ روز لمحوں کی برچھیاں اس کا وجود چیرتی تھیں۔

آتی جاتی سانسوں کی مالا میں اٹکی روح' روز کانٹوں کے بستر پر ادھڑتی تھی اور سمٹ جاتی تھی حورعین عبدالسمیع کیا تھی اور کیا ہو کر رہ گئی تھی۔ آسمان گھنگھور بادلوں سے ڈھک چکا تھا۔ تبھی اس کی نظریں اوپر آسمان کی طرف اٹھیں۔

''اللہ......!'' بہت دنوں کے بعد بہت اذیت کے عالم میں اس نے اپنے معبودِ حقیقی کو پکارا تھا۔ کیا نہیں تھا اس پکار میں۔

درد......

تڑپ......

کسک......

بے بسی......

انسان جب ساری دنیا سے مایوس ہو کر تھک جاتا ہے تو اسے اللہ یاد آتا ہے اور وہ بھی دنیا سے مایوس ہو گئی تھی۔ اسے بھی اللہ یاد آ رہا تھا۔ اسے خبر ہی نہیں رہی تھی کہ وہ کہاں ہے' کیوں ہے؟ تبھی کسی نے اسے پکارا۔

''بیٹی۔'' حورعین نے اس پکار پر فوراً گردن پھیر کر دیکھا۔ بے حد رف کپڑوں میں ملبوس قبرستان کا بوڑھا گورکن لوگوں کو ان کی آخری آرام گاہ تک پہنچاتے پہنچاتے خود تھکن کے ٹڈھال ہو رہا تھا۔

''موسم ٹھیک نہیں ہے بیٹی، دن بھی ڈھل رہا ہے' اکیلی عورت کا اس وقت قبرستان میں آنا اچھی بات نہیں ہے۔'' اس کے گردن موڑ کر دیکھنے پر اس ادھیڑ عمر گورکن نے اسے تلقین کی تھی۔

حورعین اس کی ہدایت پر آہستہ سے اثبات میں گردن ہلاتے ہوئے سر جھکا گئی۔

کیا ایاد عبدالحدی سے ملنے کے لیے اس کے دل کو موسموں کے مزاج کی پروا تھی؟

گورکن اسے گھر واپسی کی تلقین کرنے کے بعد اپنی راہ پر چل پڑا تھا۔ وہ بے بس سی سر جھکائے بیٹھی ایاد عبدالحدی کی قبر کی خشک مٹی کو اپنے آنسو دان کرتی رہی۔ آج پہلی بار اس نے مٹی کے اس ڈھیر سے باتیں نہیں کی تھیں۔

آج پہلی بار اس کے پاس ایاد عبدالحدی کو دان کرنے کے لیے پھول نہیں تھے۔ قبرستان سے گھر واپسی کے سفر میں صرف تھکن اس کے ہمراہ تھی۔

❁ .... ❁ .... ❁

آسمان گدلے بادلوں سے ڈھک چکا تھا۔

قبرستان سے گھر پہنچنے تک وہ نا صرف ہانپ گئی تھی بلکہ بری طرح بارش میں بھیگ بھی گئی تھی۔ اسے لگا جیسے بارش کی صورت کسی نے اپنے صدیوں سے رکے آنسو بہائے ہوں۔ لاؤنج میں آئی تو سب لوگ جیسے اسی کا انتظار کر رہے تھے۔

''حورعین' بیٹی کہاں رہ گئی تھیں؟ دیکھو سب لوگ کتنا پریشان ہو رہے ہیں تمہارے لیے۔'' بڑی ماں کی نظر جیسے ہی اس پر پڑی وہ بول اٹھیں۔

حورعین کے لیے اپنی واپسی کی وضاحت کرنا مشکل ہو گیا۔ وہاں بیٹھے افراد میں کوئی شخص بھی نہیں جانتا تھا کہ وہ کہاں گئی تھی اور کیوں؟؟ ''سوری وہ موسم خراب ہو گیا تھا ٹیکسی نہیں ملی تو پیدل گھر آنا پڑا۔''

''ارے' ایسی بات تھی تو فون کر دیتیں بیٹے' نمیر دو بار مارکیٹ جا کر تمہارا پتا کر کے آیا ہے۔''

''سوری دادو میں سیل فون ساتھ لے کر نہیں گئی تھی۔ اگلی بار خیال رکھوں گی۔''

''اچھی بات ہے چلو اندر جا کر جلدی سے کپڑے تبدیل کر لو' یہ نکھے لڑکے تمہارے انتظار میں یونہی ہاتھ پر ہاتھ دھر کر بیٹھے ہیں۔''

''جی ٹھیک ہے۔'' اگلے ہی پل نئے حکم پر سوائے سر جھکانے کے اس کے پاس اور کوئی چارا نہیں تھا۔ حالانکہ اس وقت سوائے بستر میں گر کر ڈھیر سارا رونے کے اس کا اور کسی کام کو دل نہیں چاہ رہا تھا۔ کتنے زخم تھے جو رِس رہے تھے مگر اسے ان سب کو خوش رکھنا تھا۔ واقعی دنیا کتنی تنگ پڑ گئی تھی اس پر کتنے گھاؤ تھے جو ناسور بن کر روح کو چاٹنے لگے تھے۔

چپ چاپ کچن میں آ کر اس نے مٹر پلاؤ کی تیاری شروع کر دی۔ اس گھر میں پناہ اور اپنی عزت و جان کی حفاظت کے لیے اسے اس گھر کے مکینوں کی خوشی اور آرام کا خیال تو رکھنا ہی تھا۔ اگلے پینتالیس منٹ میں اس نے کھانا ٹیبل پر لگا دیا۔ سب رغبت سے کھا رہے تھے اور اس کی خوب تعریف بھی ہو رہی تھی۔ مگر حورعین کا دل اس وقت کسی چیز کو تسلیم نہیں کر رہا تھا۔ اسے ایاد عبدالحدی کی یاد ٹوٹ کر آ رہی تھی۔

کھانے کے بعد جس وقت وہ سب کو چائے سرو کر رہی تھی عمیر نے اس کی بھیگی ہوئی پلکوں کو بغور دیکھا یہی وجہ تھی کہ چھٹکو (زبیر) کو ہوم ورک کروانے کے بعد وہ کچن میں اس کے پاس چلا آیا تھا۔

''السلام علیکم۔''

حورعین جو رونے کے ساتھ ساتھ' سر جھکائے برتن دھو رہی تھی اس کے سلام پر جلدی سے آنسو پونچھ گئی۔

''وعلیکم السلام۔''

''میں برتن دھونے میں مدد کرواؤں آپ کی؟''

''نن......نہیں۔'' وہ آفر کر رہا تھا اس نے فوراً نفی میں سر ہلا دیا۔ تبھی وہ کپڑا اٹھا کر دھلے ہوئے برتنوں کو خشک کرنے لگ گیا۔

''عمیر میں کرلوں گی خود تم اپنے کام نبٹا لو۔''

''نہیں آپی' میں باقی سب لوگوں کی طرح خود غرض اور کمینہ نہیں ہوں۔''

''پاگل' ایسا نہیں کہتے۔''

''ٹھیک ہے مگر آپ رو کیوں رہی ہیں کیا عذیر بھائی نے کچھ کہا ہے یا پھر گھر کی یاد آ رہی ہے؟''

''گھر......گھر تو میرا رہا ہی نہیں۔ کتنے ماہ ہو گئے زمانے کی ٹھوکروں میں پڑے ہوئے۔''

''تو پھر عذیر بھائی نے کچھ کہا ہے؟''

ذرا سا سر جھکاتے ہوئے وہ اس کی آنکھوں میں دیکھ رہا تھا۔ حورعین نے پھر نفی میں سر ہلا دیا۔

''نہیں انہوں نے کیوں کچھ کہنا ہے؟''

''کچھ کہنے کے لیے وجہ کی ضرورت تو نہیں ہوتی میری پیاری بہن' بے قصور بھی بہت کچھ ہو جاتا ہے۔ جیسے پرسوں جیل کی تاریک بیرک میں شہزاد کی موت ہو گئی۔ اس شہزاد کی جس نے قطعی بے گناہ ہوتے ہوئے سالوں جیل کاٹی' ماریں کھائیں' اپنی زمین گنوا کر نمبردار کو راضی کیا' انصاف کے حصول کے لیے آہنی سلاخوں سے سر ٹکراتے ٹکراتے پاگل ہوا اور بالآخر مر گیا۔ پتا نہیں روز اندھی تاریک کوٹھڑیوں میں ایسے کتنے ہی شہزاد جینے کی حسرت دل میں لیے اذیت اور بے بسی کی موت کو گلے لگاتے ہوں گے۔ کتنا ذہین اور باصلاحیت نوجوان تھا۔ اے کاش کسی ترقی یافتہ ملک میں پیدا ہوتا تو ایسی بے بسی کی موت نا مرتا۔'' عمیر کے لہجے میں دکھ کی آمیزش تھی۔

حورعین اسے دیکھ کر رہ گئی۔

''یہاں صرف ایک شہزاد کی موت کا مسئلہ نہیں ہے عمیر' ہمارا المیہ ہے کہ ہمارے معاشرے کے لوگوں کے ذہن' بے حسی میں بہت پختہ ہو گئے ہیں کوئی کتنا ہی مظلوم' بے گناہ' باصلاحیت اور نامساعد تقدیر و حالات کا مارا ہو یہاں ہم لوگوں کے ذہنوں میں ان بے بس' بدنصیب قیدیوں کے لیے سوائے نفرت کے اور کچھ نہیں۔ پکی سوچ بن گئی ہے ہماری کہ جس پر کوئی جرم عائد ہو گیا وہ مجرم ہے' خواہ اس نے کچھ کیا ہو یا نہ کیا ہو ہماری فرض شناس پولیس نے اگر کسی کو حصار میں لے لیا تو مرتے دم تک وہ شخص نہ ہماری نگاہوں میں معتبر ہوتا ہے نہ ہم اسے کسی انسانیت' کسی ہمدردی کے قابل سمجھتے ہیں۔''

وہ جذباتی ہوئی تھی اور عمیر ان جذبات کی قدر کرتا تھا۔ تبھی کپڑا سائیڈ پر رکھتے ہوئے بولا تھا۔

''جی ہاں' صحیح کہہ رہی ہیں آپ ہمارے ذہن ایسے بنا دیے گئے ہیں کہ لفظ قیدی سے ہم نے صرف نفرت کرنی ہے۔ ہمیں کوئی دلچسپی نہیں اس چیز میں کوئی کن حالات میں قانون کی بھینٹ چڑھا۔ کسی کو اس کے قصور پر سزا ہوئی یا یونہی بے قصور پھنسا دیا گیا۔ کوئی حوالہ یاد نہیں آتا ہمیں اپنے دین کا کہ ہمارے دین میں ہمارے پیارے نبیؐ اور ان کے بعد جتنی بھی نیک اور برگزیدہ ہستیاں دنیا میں آئیں انہوں نے قید میں آنے والے لوگوں کے ساتھ کیسا برتاؤ کیا؟ لوگ اپنے کتوں کا بھی خیال رکھتے ہیں مگر ہمارے ہاں' گرمی کے قہر برساتے مہینوں میں بجلی تو ایک طرف پینے کو پانی بھی نہیں دیا جاتا ان بدنصیب مجبوروں کو...... گندے غسل خانوں اور لیٹرینوں میں پانی کے دو گھونٹ پینے کے لیے گھنٹوں

سلاخیں پکڑ کر شور مچاتے ہیں۔ آوازیں لگاتے ہیں گرمی اور مچھروں سے پریشان چھوٹے چھوٹے قبر نما سیلوں میں ساری ساری رات گریہ زاری کرتے ہیں کاش میں آپ کو بتا سکتا کہ گرمی ان بدنصیب قیدیوں کے لیے کیسا عذاب لے کر آتی ہے۔"

"مجھے اندازہ ہے عمیر' بھلا مجھ سے زیادہ قید کی صعوبتوں کو کون جان سکتا ہے؟" رخ پھیرتے ہوئے بہت مدھم لہجے میں اس نے جیسے سرگوشی کی تھی۔ کیسے کیسے مناظر تھے جو ذہن کی اسکرین پر جھلملائے تھے۔

"تم نہیں جانتے عمیر' جیلیں خواہ امریکا کی ہوں' بھارت کی یا پاکستان کی دوزخ کا دوسرا روپ ہیں دنیا میں اور وہ لوگ جن کا یہاں اختیار چلتا ہے جہنم کے داروغوں سے کم نہیں ہیں۔ فانی دنیا میں عارضی طاقت اور اختیار کے نشے میں مست لوگ بے بس انسانوں پر قہر ڈھاتے ہوئے بھول جاتے ہیں کہ وقت جیسی ظالم چیز نے تو نمرود' فرعون اور قارون جیسے لوگوں کو عبرت بنا کر رکھ دیا یہ کیا چیز ہیں؟"

"بالکل سچ کہا آپ نے' اب دیکھیے نا اکثر کیسز میں' میں نے دیکھا ہے کہ اگر ایک عدالت نے فیصلہ سنا دیا تو دوسری عدالت اس فیصلے کو چیلنج ہی نہیں کرتی بلکہ اس عدالت کے فیصلے کا احترام کرتے ہوئے بنا نظر ثانی کیے اسے ویسے ہی برقرار رکھتی ہے۔ یہ کہاں کا انصاف ہے؟ میں توہین عدالت نہیں کر رہا۔ مگر مجھے دکھ ہے ایک انسان ہوتے ہوئے ہم کسی دوسرے انسان کی زندگی کو کوئی اہمیت ہی نہیں دیتے جبکہ میں نے کہیں پڑھا تھا کسی بوڑھی عورت پر ظلم ہوا تھا تو اس نے بادشاہ کی سواری کو راہ میں روک کر اس سے پوچھا تھا کہ تم میرا انصاف یہیں کرو گے یا روزِ محشر خدا کے سامنے تمہارا گریبان پکڑوں؟ اور وہ بادشاہ بڑھیا کی بات سن کر کانپ اٹھا تھا مگر اب شاید ان باتوں پر توجہ دینے کی فرصت بھی کسی کے پاس نہیں ہے۔"

"یہی تو ساری بات ہے عمیر مشرکین کو کیا کہیں یہاں قرآن اور کلمہ پڑھنے والوں کو بھی آخرت کا کوئی خوف نہیں' تم دیکھو سعودیہ میں خالص اسلامی قانون نافذ ہے کسی کی مجال نہیں کہ وہاں ذاتی عناد یا دشمنی میں کسی بھی شخص پر جھوٹا الزام لگا کر اسے سزا کروا سکے۔ معمولی سے معمولی کیس کی چھان بین بھی یوں ہوتی ہے کہ کسی کو موردِ الزام ٹھہرا کر پھنسانے والا الٹا خود اپنے جال میں پھنس کر عبرت پا جاتا ہے۔ کاش یہاں بھی ایسا ہی کوئی سسٹم ہوتا تو کتنا اچھا ہوتا' مگر...... یہاں غیر ملکیوں کے لیے رحم کی گنجائش ہے ان کی اپیلیں قبول بھی ہو جاتی ہیں اور سزائیں بھی معاف ہو جاتی ہیں مگر اپنے شہریوں کے لیے کہیں کسی رحم کی گنجائش نہیں ان کے لیے تو صرف سزا ہے قہر ہے اور بس......!"

"جی یہی تو بات ہے...... کسی بھی ملک میں کسی بھی مذہب میں انسانیت کا درجہ پہلے نمبر پر ہے مگر یہاں دنیا میں سب سے زیادہ امن پسندی اور جمہوریت کا نعرہ لگانے والوں نے بھی سب سے زیادہ انسانیت کی مٹی پلید کر رکھی ہے۔ کتے کے پلوں کے لیے بھی نرم دل رکھنے والوں نے انسانوں کے ساتھ وہ سلوک کیے ہیں کہ خود انسان کو اپنے انسان ہونے پر شرمندگی ہے ذرا سوچیں' آج انسانیت کو سائیڈ پر رکھ کر بے گناہوں پر قہر ڈھانے والے روزِ محشر بادشاہ کائنات کے سب سے بڑے منصف کے سامنے کس منہ سے رحم کی اپیل کر سکیں گے؟" وہ کہہ رہا تھا حورعین کی آنکھیں آنسوؤں سے بھر آئیں۔ اس کے ذہن میں اس وقت مہدی حسن کی سدابہار آواز گونج رہی تھی۔

"چاند میری زمیں' پھول میرا وطن
میرے کھیتوں کی مٹی میں لعل و یمن
چاند میری زمیں' پھول میرا وطن
میرے ملاح لہروں کے پالے ہوئے

میرے دہقاں پسینوں کے ڈھالے ہوئے
میرے فوجی جواں' جرأتوں کے نشاں
میرے اہل قلم عظمتوں کی زباں
میرے مزدور اس دور کے کوہِ کن
چاند میری زمیں' پھول میرا وطن

''کتنی عجیب بات ہے نا آپی ہمارا ملک اسلامی ہے یہاں اللہ کا قانون سب سے بڑا قانون ہے مگر پھر بھی ہم اپنے معاملاتِ زندگی میں تقلید ان لوگوں کی کر رہے ہیں جو اسلام اور مسلمان دونوں کے دشمن ہیں۔ جن کی آنکھ میں اللہ اور اس کے پیارے رسول محمد مصطفیٰ صلی اللہ علیہ وسلم سے محبت کرنے والے کنکر بن کر چبھ رہے ہیں۔ اب ایک طرف وہ ہمیں مار رہے ہیں اور دوسری طرف ہم خود اپنے آپ کو مار رہے ہیں۔ موت دونوں طرف مسلمان کی ہو رہی ہے اور بدنامی کا طوق پھر بھی ہمارے ہی گلے میں فٹ ہے۔ آپ دیکھیے آپی' صرف ایک ورلڈ ٹریڈ سینٹر تباہ ہوا اس میں بھی ہم ملوث نہیں تھے مگر اس کے باوجود وہاں کے ناخداؤں نے بدلے میں سیکڑوں' ہزاروں نہیں لاکھوں مسلمانوں کو چیونٹی کی طرح مسل کر رکھ دیا کون لے گا اس کا حساب؟''

''اللہ......!'' عمیر کی بات ابھی مکمل بھی نہیں ہوئی تھی کہ اس کے لب پکار اٹھے۔

''تم کیا سمجھتے ہو عمیر' یہ جو کچھ مسلمانوں کے ساتھ ہو رہا ہے اللہ کے نیک اور پرہیز گار بندوں کے ساتھ ہو رہا ہے شیر اور گیدڑ کو ایک ہی گھاٹ پر لا کر پانی پلایا جا رہا ہے اللہ اس سے بے خبر ہے؟ نہیں' اس رحمٰن و رحیم کی ایک صفت جبار و قہار بھی ہے اس کا قہر جب برستا ہے تو زمین بھی تھر تھر کانپ اٹھتی ہے۔ سمندر کے بازو پھیلتے ہیں اور چلتے پھرتے لوگ اس کی لامحدود گہرائیوں میں جا چھپتے ہیں۔ وہ پاک ذات بے خبر نہیں ہے عمیر، سارے عمل لکھے جا رہے ہیں۔ چھوٹے سے چھوٹا ہر عمل اس کی نگاہ میں ہے ایک ایک جان' ایک ایک خون کے قطرے کا حساب لے گا وہ۔ بہت پیار ہے اسے اپنے بندوں سے اور اختیار سارا صرف اللہ کا ہے وہ اپنے معصوم بندوں کا خون رائیگاں نہیں جانے دے گا۔ یہ ظلم' یہ فسادات' یہ انسانی درندگی' یہ ہماری شکست یا ہمارا عبرت ناک انجام نہیں ہے عمیر' آزمائش ہے ہماری امتحان ہے۔ وہ واحد و لاشریک! اسی طرح اپنے بندوں کو کڑی آزمائشوں میں ڈال کر ان کا ایمان آزماتا ہے اور پھر جو لوگ راہِ حق سے بھٹک جاتے ہیں اُن منافقین کو علیحدہ کر لیتا ہے۔ ہمیں کوئی ملال نہیں ہے عمیر' اللہ نے مومنوں کی جان جنت کے بدلے خرید لی ہے۔ ہمیں جنت کے بدلے نفس کا سودا مہنگا نہیں ہے ہماری آخرت ابھی باقی ہے۔ بادشاہوں کے بادشاہ کے حضور ہمارا حساب اور انصاف ابھی باقی ہے۔ ہماری شاندار تاریخ ہمارا فخر یہ حوالہ ہے۔ کسی میں دم نہیں کہ مسلمانوں کے خون کو پانی کی طرح بہا سکے سوائے خود مسلمانوں کی مدد کے یہ صدی یہود و نصاریٰ کی فتوحات اور عروج کی صدی ہے عمیر' دنیا کا قالین سمٹ رہا ہے اللہ دیکھ رہا ہے کون اس کا ہے اور کون اس کے دشمنوں کا۔ وگرنہ یہی یہود و نصاریٰ تھے جن پر صدیوں مسلمان حکمرانوں نے حکومت کی اور اپنے دورِ حکومت میں بہترین امن اور انصاف کی یادگار مثالیں قائم کیں یہی تھے جو عاجزی سے ہمارے آباؤ اجداد کے شاندار درباروں میں ہاتھ باندھے کھڑے رہتے تھے۔ آپس میں بھی لڑ پڑتے تو انصاف کے لیے ہمارے ہی آباؤ اجداد کے در کھٹکھٹاتے تھے مگر آج وقت ہمارے ہاتھ میں نہیں ہے اسی لیے یہ لوگ ہمارے ساتھ جیسا چاہیں سلوک کر سکتے ہیں۔ بالکل ویسے ہی جیسے ماضی میں انہوں نے ہمارے ساتھ کیا ہے۔ بیت المقدس کی فتوحات کے موقع پر صلیب کے پرستاروں نے اپنے گھوڑوں کے سُم مسلمانوں کے خون سے تر بتر کر دیے مگر' اسی بیت المقدس کو جب صلاح الدین ایوبی نے فتح کیا تو وہاں امن و عدل کی وہ مثالیں قائم کیں کہ خود ان

کے آباؤ اجداد ان کے مورخ بھی اس کے معترف ہیں آج پھر ان کے عروج کا دور ہے عمیر۔ اسی لیے فلسطین، عراق، برما، افغانستان، شام، فلیطین، لیبیا اور کتنے ہی ایسے کمزور ممالک کا چپہ چپہ چلا چلا کر ان کے مظالم اور انسانی دشمنی کا پول کھول رہے ہیں۔ یہ ہمیں کہتے ہیں کہ ہم دہشت گرد ہیں۔ لیکن میں کہتی ہوں کہ دہشت گرد ہم نہیں یہ ہیں۔ دنیا کے امن کو ہم نے نہیں انہوں نے نقصان پہنچایا ہے۔ ہمارا مذہب تو امن کا مذہب ہے وہ مذہب ہے جس کا فائدہ اٹھا کر خود انہی نے امن اور سلامتی پائی جگہ جگہ تاریخ کے پنوں میں ہماری عظمتوں اور کامرانیوں کی مثالیں چھپی ہوئی ہیں۔ اندلس کی سرزمین ہو یا فلسطین کی، ہندوستان ہو یا بحیرہ قلزم، تاریخ گواہ ہے ہم نے اپنے بدترین دشمنوں کے ساتھ بھی بہترین سلوک کیا۔ ہمارے مجاہد آج بھی وہی ہیں۔ اگر یہ لوگ ہمارے خون کو پانی کی طرح نہ بہائیں، ہماری عزتوں کو پامال نہ کریں، بے قصور ہم پر قہر نہ ڈھائیں تو ہم بھی اپنی صلاحیتوں، اپنی ہنرمندی، اپنی تعلیم کو بروئے کار لا کر امن وسکون کی زندگی جئیں۔ ہمیں صحراؤں کی خاک چھاننے اور سنگلاخ پہاڑوں میں رُلنے کا شوق نہیں ہے۔ مگر افسوس ہمارے موجودہ سالاروں نے دنیاوی مفادات کے لیے ہماری جانوں کے سودے کر دیے ہیں، مجبور کر دیا ہے کہ ہم خود پر ہونے والے مظالم کا مقابلہ خود بندوق اٹھا کر کریں۔ وگرنہ امن وسکون کی زندگی کسے اچھی نہیں لگتی؟"

"صحیح کہہ رہی ہیں آپی، چوٹ لگتی ہے تو پتھر بھی صدا دیتے ہیں ہم تو پھر جیتے جاگتے انسان ہیں کتنی دلچسپ حقیقت ہے نا کہ اگر دنیا کے کسی مسلمان کے ہاتھوں کسی امریکی، کسی اسرائیلی، کسی بھارتی کو نقصان پہنچتا ہے تو ساری دنیا میں کھلبلی مچ جاتی ہے ایک فرد کی جان کے بدلے دس مسلمانوں کو مار کر غصے کی آگ ٹھنڈی کی جاتی ہے مگر دوسری طرف اگر کوئی پاکستانی، کوئی عراقی، کوئی کشمیری، کوئی افغانی، ان ممالک کے مظالم پر ان سے نفرت کا اظہار بھی کرتا ہے تو اس پر فوراً دہشت گرد کی مہر لگ جاتی ہے۔ ساری دنیا کے سامنے بنا کسی جرم اور قصور کے اس پر جھوٹے مقدمات بنا کر اسے تڑپا تڑپا کر مار دیا جاتا ہے۔ مگر کہیں کوئی کھلبلی نہیں مچتی، 58 قبروں میں گہری میٹھی نیند سوئے ہمارے مسلم ممالک یوں خاموشی اور بے بسی سے تماشہ دیکھتے رہ جاتے ہیں جیسے روز قیامت انہیں اللہ رب العزت کے حضور حاضر ہی نہیں ہونا۔ طاقت کے بل بوتے پر چاہے یہ ساری دنیا کو اُدھیڑ کر رکھ دیں کوئی انہیں پوچھنے والا نہیں۔ ان کی امن پسندی پر کوئی حرف ہی نہیں آتا۔"

"یہی تو دکھ ہے عمیر...... یہ وطن عزیز...... یہ زمین کا پیارا ٹکڑا، اس کی مثال بس ایک زخمی پرندے کی سی ہے جس کی لاٹھی اس کی بھینس والے جنگلی قانون کے باعث یہاں کے شیر چیتے اور گِدھوں کے منہ کو اس زخمی پرندے کا خون لگ چکا ہے۔ اسی لیے اگر انہیں دربدری کے باوجود جان خطرے میں ڈال کر بھی یہاں آنا پڑتا ہے تو وہ آتے ہیں اقتدار کا لالچ انہیں ہزار آسائشات کے باوجود دیارِ غیر میں سکون سے بیٹھنے نہیں دیتا۔ اسی لیے میں چاہتی ہوں کہ بس اب قیامت آجائے، اللہ رب العزت کی عدالت لگے اور سارا دودھ کا دودھ اور پانی کا پانی ہو جائے۔"

"میں بھی یہی چاہتا ہوں آپی جس اخلاقی پسماندگی میں ہم گر چکے ہیں ایک اسلامی ملک میں غیر اسلامی روایات کو پروان چڑھا کر روز اللہ کے قہر کو آواز دے رہے ہیں اس سے تو یہی بہتر ہے کہ بس اب اللہ کا انصاف دیکھیں۔"

"ہوں، زبیر کو ہوم ورک کروایا؟"

"جی کروا دیا ہے لیکن مما کی رحلت کے بعد وہ بہت چپ ہو کر رہ گیا ہے۔ میں چاہتا ہوں آپ اسے ٹائم دیں اسے ایک نارمل لائف کی طرف لے کر آئیں۔" حورعین کے موضوع بدلنے پر اس نے بھی گفتگو کا رخ پھیر دیا۔ وہ سر ہلا کر رہ گئی۔

اس روز کے بعد وہ اپنا زیادہ ٹائم زبیر کے ساتھ ہی گزارتی تھی۔ اسے اسکول کے لیے خود تیار کرتی کھانا کھلاتی، ہوم

ورک اپنی نگرانی میں کرواتی اور رات میں کہانی سنا کر اسے اپنے ساتھ ہی سلا لیتی کچھ ہی دنوں میں وہ اس سے بہت کلوز ہو گیا۔

سارا گھر اس سے بے حد خوش تھا۔ دادی عذیر کا منہ چومتی نہیں تھکتی تھیں کہ اس نے اتنی اچھی اور قابل لڑکی کا انتخاب کیا اور وہ ہر بار شرمندہ ہو کر رہ جاتا۔ حورعین رفتہ رفتہ جس طرح سے اس گھر کے مکینوں کے دلوں میں اپنا مقام بنا رہی تھی وہ الجھتا جا رہا تھا سلمیٰ سے بھی اس کی لڑائی ہو گئی تھی کچھ سمجھ میں نہیں آ رہا تھا کہ کیا کرے؟

اس روز وہ آفس سے گھر آیا تو حورعین زبیر کے ساتھ اس کے کمرے میں بیٹھی اسے کہانی سنا رہی تھی۔

''ایک وادی تھی بہت خوب صورت سرسبز' وہاں سب بہت خوش رہتے تھے۔ وہاں کا بادشاہ مسلمان تھا اور اپنی ساری رعایا کے ساتھ بہت اچھا اور انصاف کا سلوک کرتا تھا دوسرے مذہبوں کے لوگ بھی اپنے ہم مذہبوں کے ہاتھوں پریشان اس کے پاس انصاف کے لیے آتے اور خوش ہو کر جاتے تھے۔ رفتہ رفتہ بادشاہ کمزور اور بوڑھا ہوتا گیا بادشاہ کے جو بچے تھے وہ لاَاُبالی اور بے نیاز قسم کی طبیعت کے مالک تھے۔ پھر اچانک ایک دن اس کی وادی پر ایک بلا قابض ہو گئی بہت بڑے منہ والی' خوفناک بلا......!'' بہت انہماک سے کہانی سناتے ہوئے وہ جیسے کہیں کھو گئی تھی۔ جبکہ ننھا زبیر آنکھیں پھیلائے اسے دیکھ رہا تھا۔

''دیکھتے ہی دیکھتے اس بلا نے بادشاہ کے بچوں کو نگل لیا۔ وادی کے لوگ اس بلا سے خوف کھانے لگے۔ جس جگہ پر اس بلا کے قدم پڑتے وہاں انسانوں کا صفایا ہو جاتا یوں تو وہ بلا کسی کو بھی نہیں چھوڑتی تھی مگر مسلمانوں کا خون اسے زیادہ پسند تھا۔ جہاں اسے کوئی مسلمان نظر آتا فوراً نگل لیتی۔''

''بھابی کوئی شہزادہ نہیں تھا جو اس بلا کو مار دیتا۔'' جونہی وہ سانس لینے رکی زبیر نے فوراً پوچھ لیا جواب میں اس کے لبوں پر افسردہ سی مسکراہٹ بکھر گئی۔

''شہزادہ' پتا نہیں کتنے ہی شہزادوں کو اس بلا نے نگل لیا تھا۔''

''اتنی بڑی بلا تھی وہ؟'' اب کے زبیر نے آنکھیں پھیلائی تھیں۔ حورعین نے ہاتھ بڑھا کر اسے اپنی گود میں لٹا لیا۔

''ہوں' بادشاہ جو مر گیا تھا اس وادی کا' اسی لیے بلا طاقت ور ہوتی گئی کوئی اس کا مقابلہ کرنے والا جو نہیں تھا۔ آس پاس کی وادیوں کے لوگ بس تماشہ دیکھتے تھے۔''

''پھر تو اس بلا نے سب کو نگل لیا ہو گا؟''

''ہوں' بڑے ظلم کرتی تھی وہ بلا جس کو ایک پنجہ مار دیتی وہ دوبارہ اٹھ ہی نہیں سکتا تھا۔ ایسے میں وہاں جو بچے کچے مسلمان تھے انہوں نے سوچا کہ اگر وہ بلا سے لڑیں گے تو بلا انہیں کھا جائے گی۔ بہتر یہی ہے کہ وہ بلا کو اپنا بادشاہ تسلیم کر لیں وہ جو ظلم بھی کرے کرنے دیں۔ بس اپنی اپنی جان بچانے کی کوشش کرتے رہیں۔ بلا کو ان کے اس فیصلے کا پتا چلا تو بہت ہنسی' اس نے ان لوگوں سے کہا کہ اگر وہ لوگ اسے اپنا بادشاہ بنا لیتے ہیں تو وہ انہیں نہیں کھائے گی مگر حقیقت میں ایسا نہیں تھا۔''

''کیا مطلب؟'' زبیر منہ اٹھائے اس کے چہرے کی طرف دیکھ رہا تھا۔

حورعین کی نظریں کھڑکی کے اس پار سڑک کی دوسری سائیڈ پر تنہا کھڑے درخت پر جم گئیں۔ وہ بولی تو اس کا لہجہ بہت کھویا ہوا تھا۔

''اپنی اپنی جان بچانے کے لالچ میں وادی کے ان لوگوں نے بلا کو اور بھی طاقت ور بنا دیا تھا۔ اب وہ ایک ایک کو پکڑ کر اپنے پاس قید کرتی اور کھا لیتی روز بروز لوگ ڈرتے گئے اور کمزور ہوتے گئے۔''

''پھر۔''

''پھر اس بلا نے اپنے پر پھیلا لیے اس کے پیر بھی بہت بڑے بڑے تھے جس جگہ مسلمان رہتے تھے وہاں وہ اپنے پیر رکھتی تھی اور سب کو بنا کسی قصور کچل مسل کر رکھ دیتی۔''

''کیوں بھابی...... بلا مسلمانوں کے ساتھ ہی ایسا کیوں کرتی تھی؟'' زبیر سر اٹھائے پھر پوچھ رہا تھا۔ وہ مسکرا دی۔

''نفرت جو کرتی تھی وہ مسلمانوں سے۔ اسے خوف تھا کہیں مسلمان شہزادے اسے ختم نہ کر دیں۔''

''لیکن انہیں تو اس نے کمزور کر دیا تھا پھر وہ اسے کیسے ختم کر سکتے تھے۔''

''بس، خوف جو تھا اسے وادی میں مشہور تھا کہ صرف مسلمان ہی اس بلا کو مار سکتے ہیں اسے ڈر لگتا تھا کہیں کوئی شہزادہ باہر سے آ کر اسے مار نہ دے۔''

''پھر......؟'' زبیر کا انہماک کہانی میں بڑھ چکا تھا۔

وہ کھڑکی کے اس پار تنہا کھڑے درخت کو یاسیت سے دیکھتی رہی۔

''پھر کل سناؤں گی۔ ابھی آپ سو جائیں، کیونکہ صبح آپ کو اسکول بھی جانا ہے۔''

''نہیں بھابی، پلیز کہانی سنائیں نا، اتنی اچھی کہانی تو کبھی مما نے بھی نہیں سنائی۔'' وہ کہانی جاری رکھنے کے لیے بضد تھا تبھی عمیر وہاں چلا آیا۔

''حور آپی، آپ کو دادو بلا رہی ہیں۔''

''کیوں، خیریت؟''

زبیر کے بالوں میں ہاتھ پھیرتے ہوئے وہ چونک اٹھی تھی، عمیر مسکرا دیا۔

''جی خیریت ہی ہے ابھی نماز سے فارغ ہوئی ہیں۔ میں ان کے کمرے میں گیا تو پوچھنے لگیں۔ حورعین جاگ رہی ہے یا سو گئی؟ میں نے کہا زبیر کے پاس ہے تو کہنے لگیں بلا کر لاؤ ضروری بات کرنی ہے۔''

''ضروری بات؟''

''ہوں ہماری شکایت ہی کرنی ہوگی اور کیا ضروری بات ہو سکتی ہے۔'' ایک مرتبہ پھر وہ مسکرایا تھا۔

حورعین کے لبوں پر بھی دھیمی سی مسکراہٹ بکھر گئی۔

''ٹھیک ہے زبیر، آپ اب آرام کرو، میں دادو کی بات سن کر آتی ہوں۔''

''جی ٹھیک ہے۔'' منہ بنا کر سر ہلاتے ہوئے اس نے گردن جھکائی تھی۔ وہ نرمی سے اس کے بال سہلاتے ہوئے اٹھ کھڑی ہوئی۔

اگلے دو منٹ میں وہ دادو کے کمرے میں آئی تو وہ تسبیح کرتے ہوئے اسی کا انتظار کر رہی تھیں۔ وہ انہیں ادب سے سلام کرنے کے بعد ان کے قریب ہی بیڈ پر ٹک گئی۔

''جی دادو، آپ نے بلایا؟''

''ہوں، سارے دن موئے گھر کے کاموں میں خود کو مصروف رکھتی ہو، کبھی بوڑھی دادی کے پاس بھی پل دو پل کے لیے بیٹھ جایا کرو۔'' حورعین کے سر پر ہاتھ رکھتے ہوئے وہ شکایت کر رہی تھیں۔ وہ شرمندہ ہو گئی۔

''معافی چاہتی ہوں دادو، میرا دل چاہتا ہے آپ سے ڈھیروں باتیں کرنے کو مگر......!''

''میں سب کچھ سمجھتی ہوں بیٹے، نسرین (عذیر کی ماں) کے بعد جس طرح سے تم نے اس بکھرے ہوئے گھر کو سنبھالا ہے۔ میرے پاس تمہاری تعریف کے لیے الفاظ نہیں ہے ہو سکتا ہے نسرین ہوتی تو خود بھی اتنی اچھی بہو تلاش نہ کر سکتی۔''

"یہ سب آپ کی محبت ہے دادو' وگرنہ میں نے تو ایسا کچھ بھی خاص نہیں کیا۔"

"نہیں' میرا دل بہت خوش ہے تجھ سے میری بچی' دیکھنا اللہ تمہیں اس خدمت کا صلہ دے گا۔" وہ اس کے سر پر ہاتھ رکھے اسے دعا دے رہی تھیں۔

حورعین کا سر مزید جھک گیا۔ اب وہ انہیں کیا بتاتی کہ یہ "خدمت" کس مجبوری کے تحت تھی؟

"عذیر بہت اچھا ہے عورت کی عزت کرنا جانتا ہے مگر پھر بھی میں چاہوں گی کہ تمہیں اس گھر میں کوئی تکلیف نہ ہو۔ عذیر' سمیر' نمیر' عمیر' زبیر سب شرارتی ضرور ہیں مگر بدنظر یا بددماغ نہیں ہیں۔ بہت محبت سے پالا ہے نسرین نے اپنے بچوں کو' وہ جان لیوا حادثہ نہ ہوتا تو تم دیکھتیں وہ کتنی محبت کرنے والی ماں تھی۔"

آنکھوں میں آنسو اور لبوں پر مسکراہٹ سجائے وہ اسے بتا رہی تھیں یوں جیسے تصور ہی تصور میں اپنی مرحومہ بہو کو زندہ دیکھ رہی ہوں۔ وہ چپ چاپ سنتی رہی۔

"عذیر بتا رہا تھا تم ملی ہو اس سے پھر تو دیکھا ہی ہوگا تم نے وہ کتنی اچھی عورت تھی۔"

"جی ایک بار ملی تھی میں ان سے واقعی وہ بہت اچھی خاتون تھیں۔"

"ہوں سارا علاقہ اس کی اچھائی کے گن گاتا ہے' لگتا ہی نہیں کہ وہ ہمیں چھوڑ کر چلی گئی ہے۔" بوڑھی آنکھوں میں اب گہری نمی تھی وہ سر جھکائے بیٹھی رہی۔

"عذیر کے دادا کی سگی بھانجی تھی نسرین۔ میں اپنی بھانجی لانا چاہتی تھی اسی رنجش میں کبھی اسے وہ پیار نہیں دے سکی جو اس کا حق تھا۔ بہت خواہش تھی اس کی گاؤں میں سب کے ساتھ رہنے کی مگر میں نے اپنی بھانجی کو خوش کرنے کے لیے اسے اپنے گھر سے نکال دیا۔ تب وہ یہاں شہر میں آبسی' جاوید (عذیر کے پاپا) خیال رکھتا تھا اس کا' مگر پھر بھی وہ روتی رہتی تھی۔ مجھے پتا ہوتا یہاں ان کے لیے جان لیوا حادثہ چھپا بیٹھا ہے تو کبھی یہ ظلم نہ کرتی۔" دوپٹے میں منہ چھپائے وہ اب رونے لگی تھیں جب حورعین نے ان کے ہاتھ تھام لیے۔

"صبر کریں دادو' شاید ان کی قسمت میں ایسا ہی لکھا ہوا ہو۔"

"ہوں تو بیٹھ میں نسرین کی امانت دیتی ہوں تجھے' عذیر اور زبیر سے بہت پیار کرتی تھی وہ' عذیر کی دلہن کے لیے بڑے پیار سے اس نے کنگن بنا کر رکھے ہوئے ہیں۔ آج وہ زندہ ہوتی تو اپنے ہاتھوں سے تجھے پہناتی۔"

دوپٹے سے آنسو پونچھتے ہوئے وہ اٹھیں اور اپنی الماری سے دو خوب صورت کنگن نکال کر لے آئیں۔

"یہ لو' آج کے بعد یہ ہمیشہ تمہاری کلائی میں رہیں اور ہاں' ذرا بن سنور کے رہا کرو مرد کو اچھا لگتا ہے۔" کنگن اسے تھماتے ہوئے انہوں نے ساتھ ہی نصیحت بھی کی۔ حورعین بوکھلا کر رہ گئی۔

"مرد جتنا بھی اچھا ہو مگر ایک ہی عورت کا پابند بن کر نہیں رہتا کبھی۔ اسی لیے سمجھا رہی ہوں تمہیں جلدی سے کوئی بچہ وچہ کرلو' اولاد میاں بیوی کے تعلق کو مضبوط کرتی ہے۔" وہی بات جو عذیر نے اس سے کہی تھی دادی نے اس کے سامنے بھی دہرادی۔

حورعین کو لگا جیسے اس میں سانس لینے کی سکت بھی نہ رہی ہو۔

"السلام علیکم دادی۔"

اگلے ہی پل عذیر نے کمرے میں قدم دھرے تھے۔ حورعین کی ہتھیلیاں پسینے سے بھیگ گئیں جبکہ اس کا دل اس وقت بہت تیزی سے دھڑک رہا تھا۔

"وعلیکم السلام' ماں صدقے جائے بڑی لمبی عمر ہے میرے لعل کی۔" اسے دیکھتے ہی دادی نے اس کی بلائیں لے

ڈالیں۔ وہ ان کے قریب ہی ٹک گیا۔

''کیوں خیریت؟ یاد کر رہی تھیں مجھے؟''

''ہوں، یاد کر رہی تھی بتا رہی تھی حور کو کہ نسرین کتنا پیار کرتی تھی تجھ سے کتنی خواہش تھی اسے تیرے بچوں کو گود میں کھلانے کی مگر جو میرے سوہنے رب کی رضا' پرسوں تیری تائی آ رہی ہے گاؤں سے ثانیہ بیٹی بھی ساتھ ہوگی۔ میں نے طے کر لیا ہے پرسوں ہی تمہاری اور حور بیٹی کا ولیمہ کر دیتی ہوں تا کہ سارے خاندان کو پتا لگ جائے۔'' نان اسٹاپ بولتی دادی کی خوشی دیدنی تھی۔

حورعین اور عذیر دونوں گھبرا کر ایک دوسرے کو دیکھنے لگے۔

''مگر دادو اس کی کیا ضرورت ہے۔'' عذیر بولا تو دادی کو غصہ آ گیا۔

''ارے ضرورت کیوں نہیں' شادی کی ہے تم نے' کوئی بھگا کر لڑکی نہیں لائے جو ہم خاندان والوں کو خبر ہی نہ کریں اور یونہی فضول چہ مگوئیاں سنتے رہیں۔''

''مگر دادی' میں ابھی بہت مصروف ہوں۔ پلیز کچھ دنوں کے لیے اسے ملتوی کر دیں۔''

''ہرگز نہیں تم مصروف ہو تو رہو' مگر میں اب مزید ایک دن کی رعایت بھی دینے والی نہیں بس۔'' دادی پکا پروگرام بنائے بیٹھی تھیں۔

حورعین کے اندر جیسے الاؤ دہک اٹھا۔ وہ بولنا چاہتی تھی مگر لب جیسے آپس میں پیوست ہو کر رہ گئے تھے۔

''اور ہاں' صبح میں خود حورعین بیٹی کو ڈاکٹر کے پاس لے کر جا رہی ہوں۔ تم رہو اپنے کاموں میں مصروف۔ میں چاہتی ہوں ایک ساتھ دو دو خوش خبریاں دوں سب کو دیکھنا سب کیسے منہ میں انگلیاں داب کر رہ جائیں گے۔''

دادی کے اپنے ہی خواب تھے حورعین جیسے کرنٹ کھا کر رہ گئی۔ جبکہ عذیر کے چہرے پر شرمندگی تھی۔

''دادی پلیز' آپ کو یہ سب کرنے کی ضرورت نہیں ہے۔ میں نے کہا ہے نا میں لے جاؤں گا' پلیز۔''

''بس' رکھو اپنا پلیز اپنے پاس۔ تیرے تایا کی بیٹی بڑی اچھی ڈاکٹر بن کر آئی ہے میں نے بات کر لی ہے اس سے' میں خود ساتھ جاؤں گی تو بس چھوڑ آنا ہمیں اس کے اسپتال۔''

دادی پکا ارادہ کیے بیٹھی تھیں۔ عذیر بالوں میں انگلیاں پھنسا کر رہ گیا۔ جبکہ حورعین مزید برداشت نہ کرتے ہوئے اٹھ کر کمرے سے نکل گئی۔ اس گھر میں پناہ اسے بہت مہنگی پڑ رہی تھی۔

❁ ..... ❁ ..... ❁

مسیحا ہو کے بھی تم سے مسیحائی نہیں ہوتی
اے کیسے مسیحا ہو؟
سبھی بجھتی ہوئی آنکھیں
رگِ جاں توڑتی سانسیں
یہ سارے جاں بلب چہرے
تیرے دستِ شفا کی ایک جنبش کو
ترستے آخری سرحد پہ آپہنچے
جہاں بس ایک لمحے میں
وہ جیون ہار جائیں گے
ارے کیسے مسیحا ہو
شفا کی بات کرتے تھے
جفا کا روپ بن بیٹھے
جو تم کو چھاؤں کہتے تھے انہی پر دھوپ بن بیٹھے
بجا کچھ خواہشیں، کچھ خواب تیرے بھی ہیں پرسَن لو
کسی کی جان سے کھیلو گے تو بازی ہار جاؤ گے
ارے کیسے مسیحا ہو؟

ہانیہ خاصی رش ڈرائیونگ کے بعد ''میکال ہاؤس'' پہنچی تو اس کا دل بہت تیزی سے دھڑک رہا تھا۔ تیزی سے گیٹ عبور کر کے وہ گھر کے اندر داخل ہوئی تو لان میں کام کرتے حفیظ بابا کی نگاہیں اسے دیکھ کر چمک اٹھیں۔

''ہانیہ بیٹے، آپ یہاں؟'' انہیں جیسے اپنی بصارتوں پر یقین ہی نہیں آ رہا تھا۔ وہ سر جھٹکتی ان کے قریب چلی آئی۔

''جی بابا السلام علیکم۔''

''وعلیکم السلام بیٹے، جیتی رہیں۔''

''شکریہ، وہ سنی کہاں ہے؟''

''جی چھوٹے صاحب تو اپنے کمرے میں ہیں شاید پڑھ رہے ہیں۔''

''ٹھیک ہے شکریہ۔'' وہ گھبرائی ہوئی سی تھی۔

حفیظ بابا اسے حیرانی سے دیکھتے رہ گئے۔ عین اسی لمحے گیٹ کے اس پار میکال کی گاڑی رکی تھی۔ وہ لان میں حفیظ بابا کو کھڑے دیکھ کر وہیں چلا آیا۔

''صاحب......وہ ہانیہ بی بی......!''

''معلوم ہے بابا......اپنے بیٹے سے ملنے آئی ہے وہ' ہمارے لیے نہیں آئی۔'' حفیظ بابا کے لب کھولنے پر ایک گہری سانس بھرتے ہوئے اس نے کہا۔ پھر سر جھٹک کر اندر کی طرف بڑھ گیا۔

سنان اپنے کمرے میں بیڈ پر ڈھیر ساری کتابیں بکھیرے گم صم بیٹھا تھا۔ جب آہٹ کی آواز پر ہانیہ کو دروازے میں کھڑے دیکھ کر خوشی سے کھل اٹھا۔

''مما......آپ آ گئیں؟'' پھرتی سے کتابیں پھلانگ کر بیڈ سے زمین پر چھلانگ لگاتے ہوئے وہ ہانیہ سے لپٹ گیا۔ جواب میں ہانیہ کا دل جیسے تڑپ اٹھا۔

پہلا سوال ہی کیسا امتحان میں ڈالنے والا تھا۔ وہ خاموشی سے آنسو بہاتی اسے بے تحاشا چومنے لگی۔

''آئی مس یو مما' مجھے روز آپ کی یاد آتی ہے مگر پاپا مجھے آپ کے پاس لے کر نہیں آتے وہ مجھے ہوم ورک بھی نہیں کرواتے اور روز چپس بنا کر بھی نہیں دیتے۔'' بہت ساری شکایتیں تھیں جو اس نے جمع کر رکھی تھیں۔ ہانیہ کا دل جیسے کٹنے لگا۔

''مما تو ہوم ورک کرواتی ہیں ناں بیٹے' مما تو چپس بنا کر بھی دیتی ہیں اور رات میں کہانی بھی سناتی ہیں' ہے نا۔''

''جی مما۔'' فوراً سے پیشتر اس کے بیٹے نے اس کی تائید میں سر ہلایا۔ جب وہ بولی۔

''تو بس ٹھیک ہے مما اب ہمیشہ کے لیے اپنے بیٹے کو اپنے ساتھ لے جائے گی۔ چلو گے نا مما کے ساتھ؟''

''جی مما۔''

''شاباش' گڈ بوائے۔''

جھک کر سنان کے گالوں پر پیار کرتے ہوئے وہ مسرور ہوئی۔ جب میکال وہاں چلا آیا۔

''کہاں لے جا رہی ہو میرے بیٹے کو ورغلا کر۔'' ہانیہ کی پشت پر اس کی آواز ابھری اور اس کا دل دھک سے رہ گیا۔

''پاپا مجھے مما کے ساتھ جانا ہے۔'' سنان کے مطالبے نے ہانیہ کی مشکل آسان کی تھی۔ جب وہ دو قدم آگے بڑھ آیا۔

''ٹھیک ہے مگر پہلے آپ کھانا کھا لیں پھر مما کے پاس جانا۔'' اس کے لہجے میں ٹھہراؤ تھا۔

ہانیہ کی آنکھیں آنسوؤں سے بھر آئی۔ تاہم اس نے فوری ہاتھ کی پشت سے انہیں رگڑ ڈالا۔

''حفیظ بابا۔'' میکال نے وہیں کھڑے کھڑے پلٹ کر حفیظ بابا کو آواز لگائی تھی جب وہ فوراً دوڑ آئے۔

''جی صاحب۔''

''سنی بابا کو کھانا کھلائیں لے جا کر پلیز۔''

''جی ٹھیک ہے۔''

ہاتھ باندھ کر حکم پر فوری عمل درآمد کرتے ہوئے وہ سنان کو کندھوں سے پکڑ کر اپنے ساتھ لے گئے۔ انسان بھی عجیب مخلوق ہے۔ محض تھوڑے سے پیسوں کے لیے اپنے دنیاوی مالک کا ہر حکم عاجزی سے پورا کرتا ہے۔ اس کی جرأت نہیں ہوتی کہ حکم پر عمل درآمد کو ذرا سی دیر کے لیے ہی سہی موقوف کر دے مگر اللہ' جو کائنات کا رب ہے انسان کا حقیقی مالک ہے' رزق کے ساتھ ساتھ جس نے آنکھ' ناک' کان' دل' گردے' پھیپھڑے سب کچھ دیا ہے۔ اس کے حکم کی کوئی پرواہ ہی نہیں۔ اس کے باوجود انسان چاہتا ہے کہ اللہ اس سے راضی رہے۔

وہ مالک جو بڑی سے بڑی خطا اور گناہ کو پل میں اپنے کرم اور رحمت سے معاف کر دیتا ہے مگر انسان جس دنیاوی

مالک کو خوش کرنے میں لگا رہتا ہے وہ کبھی معمولی سی بھول بھی معاف کرنے کو تیار نہیں ہوتا۔ کر بھی دے تو انسان ہزار ہزار طریقوں سے اس کا شکر گزار ہوتا ہے۔ حالانکہ اللہ کو پا کر کبھی کسی نے کچھ نہیں کھویا چاہے فاقے ہی کیوں نہ کرنے پڑیں مگر اللہ کو کھو کر کسی نے کچھ نہیں پایا۔ خواہ محلوں میں ہی کیوں نہ رہتا ہو۔ مگر انسان سمجھتا ہی نہیں اور جب اسے سمجھ آتی ہے تب تک بہت دیر ہو چکی ہوتی ہے۔

حفیظ بابا کے کمرے سے جانے کے بعد ہانیہ نے بھی قدم آگے بڑھائے تو وہ مقابل آ گیا۔

''تم کہاں جا رہی ہو؟''

''اپنے گھر۔'' رخ پھیر کر بنا اس کی طرف دیکھے اس نے جواب دیا۔ وہ اسے دیکھ کر رہ گیا۔

''گھر تو تمہارا یہی تھا، مگر......!''

دانستہ جملہ ادھورا چھوڑ کر اس نے ایک نظر ہانیہ کے چہرے کی طرف دیکھا۔ پھر ایک قدم مزید آگے بڑھ آیا۔

''آج کی رات تم کہیں نہیں جا سکتیں، سمجھی؟''

''کیوں؟''

جھٹکے سے سر اٹھا کر اس کی طرف دیکھتی وہ برہم ہوئی۔ جبکہ وہ بے نیازی سے بولا۔

''میں کہہ رہا ہوں اس لیے۔''

''تم کون ہو اور میرا کیا واسطہ ہے تم سے؟'' ہانیہ کی آنکھیں سلگ رہی تھیں۔ وہ کٹ کر رہ گیا۔

''واہ، صرف چھ ماہ میں تمہیں یہ بھی بھول گیا کہ میں کون ہوں؟''

''راستا چھوڑو میرا میں کم از کم اس وقت تمہارے منہ لگنا نہیں چاہتی۔'' وارننگ نگاہوں سے اسے دیکھتے ہوئے وہ گھٹے گھٹے سے لہجے میں بولی۔ جب وہ رخ پھیر گیا۔

''نقصان کر رہی ہو تم اپنا ہانیہ صفدر اور شاید میرا بھی۔''

''جسٹ شٹ اپ، میرے نفع ونقصان کی پروا کرنے والے تم کون ہوتے ہو؟''

''سمجھو تو سب کچھ، نہ سمجھو تو کچھ بھی نہیں۔''

''تم اپنا اور میرا وقت ضائع کر رہے ہو میکال حسن، ہٹو سامنے سے۔''

قطعی تلخ لہجے میں کہتے ہوئے اس نے اسے سائیڈ پر دھکیل دیا۔ وہ لڑکھڑا کر رہ گیا وہ لڑکی جو کبھی اپنی سانسوں سے بھی بڑھ کر اس سے پیار کرتی تھی اب شاید اس لڑکی کے دل میں اس کے لیے کوئی جذبہ نہیں تھا۔ اس نے اسے جتنا کمزور سمجھا تھا وہ اتنی ہی مضبوط اور طاقت ور ثابت ہوئی تھی، مگر...... اب وہ خود کمزور ہوتا جا رہا تھا۔ بے شک گزرتے وقت نے اسے بہت گہری مات دی تھی۔

❁......❁......❁

''ایسا کیا ہوا تھا تمہاری اور میکال حسن کی زندگی کے ساتھ کہ تمہارے راستے ہی الگ ہو گئے۔ کیوں ڈائیورس لی تم نے میکال حسن سے، کیوں؟''

فارحہ جو پچھلے کچھ ماہ میں ہانیہ کی بہترین دوست بن گئی تھی اس سے پوچھ رہی تھی تاہم وہ ہمیشہ کی طرح لبوں پر چپ کا قفل لگائے خاموشی بیٹھی سمندر کی شوریدہ سر لہروں کو دیکھتی رہی۔

''تم اس سے پیار کرتی تھیں ہانیہ، اپنی جان، اپنی سانسوں سے بڑھ کر چاہتی تھیں تم اسے پھر کیوں اپنے راستے الگ کیے اس سے، جبکہ وہ تمہارے بچے کا باپ بھی تھا۔''

''تو؟'' پہلی بار اس کے لب کھلے تھے فارحہ گہری سانس بھر کر رہ گئی۔

''تو یہ کہ تمہیں اتنا بڑا اقدم نہیں اٹھانا چاہیے تھا۔ سوچنا چاہیے تھا اپنے بیٹے کی زندگی کے لیے تم نہیں جانتیں دنیا کی ہر نعمت قریب ہوتے ہوئے بھی وہ خوش نہیں ہے۔ سارا سارا دن بند کمرے میں پڑا تمہاری تصویر سے باتیں کرتا رہتا ہے اپنی اور میکال کی جنگ میں تم نے اس معصوم کے ساتھ کتنی بڑی زیادتی کی ہے۔''

''بس یا کچھ اور بھی کہنا ہے تمہیں؟'' سمندر کی وسعتوں پر نظر جمائے اس بار اس نے خاصی تلخی سے پوچھا۔ جواب میں وہ اسے دیکھ کر رہ گئی۔

''میں تمہاری دوست ہوں ہانیہ' بھلا چاہتی ہوں تمہارا۔''

''مگر مجھے بھلا نہیں چاہیے۔'' اس بار ارد گرد کے لوگوں کی پروا کیے بغیر وہ چلاّئی تھی۔

''مت بھلا کیا کرے میرے ساتھ کوئی' پہلے ہی میں اپنے اوپر لدے احسانات کے بوجھ تلے دب کر مر رہی ہوں مسخ ہو کر رہ گیا ہے میرا وجود' میری شخصیت میرا سب کچھ۔''

''حادثے انسانوں کے ساتھ ہی ہوتے ہیں ہانیہ' مگر اس کا یہ مطلب نہیں کہ وہ خود پر زندگی کو حرام کر کے بیٹھ جائے۔''

''کیسی زندگی؟ میری تو زندگی کے ساتھ کبھی بنی ہی نہیں' پھول دان کرنے والے دنوں میں بھی مجھے تو زندگی نے آنسو ہی دیے ہیں۔ یہاں مرد اور اس کے کردار پر انگلی اٹھانے والا کوئی نہیں۔ چھری کے نیچے آ کر بھی عورت سے ہی قربانی اور سمجھداری کی امید رکھی جاتی ہے۔ صرف اسے ہی سمجھایا جاتا ہے۔ مرد کو اس کی زیادتیوں کا کوئی احساس نہیں دلایا جاتا۔''

''میں میکال کی سائیڈ نہیں لے رہی ہوں ہانیہ۔ میں صرف تمہارے نقصان کی پروا کر رہی ہوں۔''

''میرے نقصان کی پروا مت کرو فارحہ پلیز۔'' گیلی ریت کو مٹھی سے نیچے پھینکتے ہوئے وہ اٹھ کھڑی ہوئی تھی۔

فارحہ بھی ساتھ ہی اٹھ کھڑی ہوئی۔

''ایسا کب تک چلے گا ہانیہ' تمہیں اپنے لیے کوئی نہ کوئی فیصلہ تو کرنا ہی پڑے گا۔''

''فی الحال میں اس ٹاپک پر کوئی بات نہیں کرنا چاہتی فارحہ' پلیز۔'' قطعی بے زاری سے کہتے ہوئے وہ آگے بڑھ گئی۔ پیچھے فارحہ بھی گہری سانس بھر کر چل پڑی۔

اس لڑکی کو سمجھنا واقعی بہت مشکل تھا۔

❁ ...... ❁ ...... ❁

حویلی سے وہ سیدھا گھر چلا آیا۔

سائرہ افضل روتی پکار رہی تھی۔

وہ اسے نظر انداز کرتا اندر کمرے میں چلا آیا۔ سر درد کی شدت سے پھٹ رہا تھا۔ کرم داد نے اسے فوری حویلی حاضری کا پیغام دیا۔ مگر اس کے لیے اس وقت حویلی جانا ممکن نہیں تھا۔ تبھی وہ گھر چلا آیا۔ اماں شاید پڑوس میں کہیں گئی ہوئی تھیں۔ وہ آنکھوں پر بازو رکھ کر لیٹ گیا۔

کتنا بڑا دغا کیا تھا زندگی نے اس کے ساتھ؟ بقول شاعر

جس شاخ پر ہم نے ہاتھ رکھا
وہ شاخ وہیں سے ٹوٹ گئی

پہلے سائرہ افضل اور پھر ثانیہ عباس...... دونوں کو ہی اس نے ٹوٹ کر چاہا تھا اور دونوں ہی اسے چھوڑ گئی تھیں۔

وہ ماضی کے سمندر میں بہنا نہیں چاہتا تھا مگر یادوں کی لہریں اسے کھینچ کر گزرے ہوئے وقت کے سمندر میں لے آئی تھیں۔

اس رات بہت دیر تک ثانیہ عباس کے ساتھ بارش میں بھیگنے کے بعد اگلے روز وہ شہر آ گیا تھا۔ بہت عجیب حالت ہو رہی تھی دل کی۔ وہ سمجھتا تھا کہ اس کی زندگی سائرہ افضل پر آ کر ختم ہوگئی ہے مگر درحقیقت ایسا نہیں تھا۔

سائرہ افضل اگر اس کی محبت تھی تو ثانیہ عباس کی ذات سے اسے عشق ہو گیا تھا۔ وہ اس کے بغیر جینے کا تصور کرتا تو سانس الجھنے لگتی۔ کچھ سمجھ میں نہیں آتا کہ کیا کرے؟ ابھی وہ اسی الجھن میں تھا کہ کمپنی کے مالک نے اس کی محنت اور ذہانت کو سراہتے ہوئے اپنے چار پسندیدہ ورکرز میں اس کا نام بھی شامل کر کے اسے شارٹ کورس کے لیے ایبروڈ بھجوانے کا بندوبست کر دیا۔

اس کا دل چاہا تھا وہ گھر جا کر سب کو خوش خبری سنائے مگر پھر خود ہی اس نے یہ ارادہ موقوف کر دیا۔ اب وہ کچھ بن کر ہی اس بہاری سی لڑکی کے سامنے آنا چاہتا تھا۔ مگر وقت نے اس کی مہلت نہیں دی۔

ایبروڈ میں شارٹ کورس کے دوران گھر کال کرنے پر اماں نے اسے بتایا تھا کہ ثانیہ کی ماں وہاں گاؤں آئی تھی اور اسے اپنے ساتھ شہر لے گئی۔ اماں کی طرف سے ہمیشہ اسے ایسی ہی شاک پہنچانے والی خبریں سننے کو ملتی تھیں۔ اس وقت بھی وہ جیسے فریز ہو کر رہ گیا تھا۔ دل کی بے چینی اپنی انتہا پر تھی۔ سمجھ میں نہیں آ رہا تھا کہ اس سے کیسے رابطہ کرے۔ سمندر پار کے فاصلے سے وہ صرف کڑھ سکتا تھا اور وہ کڑھ رہا تھا۔

اسی دوران ایک روز جب وہ واش روم میں تھا اس کے سیل پر پاکستان سے کال آئی۔ اجنبی نمبر تھا۔ مگر اس کے باوجود اس کا دل زور سے دھڑک اٹھا تھا۔ بال خشک کرنے سے بھی پہلے اس نے کال بیک کی۔ کئی بار کوشش کے بعد اس کی کال اٹھانے والی عورت ثانیہ کی ماں تھی۔

زائر کا شک درست نکلا تھا۔ پاکستان کا وہ اجنبی نمبر ثانیہ عباس سے ہی منسلک تھا۔

''السلام علیکم۔''

''وعلیکم السلام کون؟''

اس کے سلام کے جواب میں دوسری طرف خاصی مصروفیت سے پوچھا گیا تھا۔ زائر ایک پل کے لیے خاموش ہوا پھر گلا صاف کرتے ہوئے بولا۔

''زائر ملک بات کر رہا ہوں' آپ کا داماد۔''

''او...... تو داماد صاحب کو یاد آ گئی ہماری؟'' توقع کے عین مطابق تعارف سنتے ہی اس کی ساس کے لہجے میں طنز اور حقارت در آئی تھی۔ وہ ضبط کر گیا۔

''جی' مہربانی ہوگی اگر آپ ثانیہ سے میری بات کروا دیں تو پلیز۔''

''اتنی عاجزی دکھانے کی ضرورت نہیں ہے ثانیہ تمہارے گھر' تمہاری رفاقت' تمہارے تعلق ہر چیز پر دو حرف بھیج کر ہمیشہ کے لیے یہاں آ گئی ہے میرے پاس۔ تمہارے لیے بہتر ہوگا کہ تم اس کی جان چھوڑ دو اور اسے طلاق بھجوا دو۔ نہیں تو تم اچھی طرح سے جان سکتے ہو کہ تمہارے ساتھ کیا کر سکتی ہوں میں۔''

''جو کرنا ہے کر لیں آپ' ذرہ برابر بھی پروا نہیں ہے مجھے مگر ثانیہ میری بیوی ہے۔ اس کی کوکھ میں میرا بچہ ہے میں کسی صورت اسے ڈائیورس نہیں کر سکتا۔''

''چلو یہ تو وقت بتائے گا تم کیا کر سکتے ہو کیا نہیں' مگر ثانیہ کے ساتھ آئندہ زندگی میں کبھی بھی وقت گزارنے کا خیال اپنے دل و دماغ سے نکال دو' کیونکہ میرے جیتے جی اب زندگی میں دوبارہ کبھی بھی تم اس کی شکل نہیں دیکھ پاؤ گے۔''

''خوش فہمی ہے آپ کی' دنیا کی کوئی طاقت مجھے ثانیہ سے ملنے سے نہیں روک سکتی۔ کوئی بھی چیز میرے اور اس کے درمیان جدائی کی دیوار کھڑی نہیں کر سکتی۔''

''چلو پھر دیکھ لو پھڑ پھڑا کر مگر سوری ثانیہ اب تمہیں کبھی نہیں مل سکتی۔''

قطعی چیلنجنگ انداز میں کہتے ہوئے مسز عباس نے کال کاٹ دی تھی۔

زائر متفکر سا سیل فون کی روشن اسکرین کو دیکھتا رہ گیا۔ وہ جانتا تھا مسز عباس اپنے کہے کو پورا کرنے کے لیے کسی بھی حد تک جا سکتی ہے۔ اسی لیے اس نے واپسی کے لیے کوششیں شروع کر دی تھیں۔ ابھی وہ انہی کوششوں میں مصروف تھا کہ اچانک اس روز وہ روڈ ایکسیڈنٹ کا شکار ہو گیا اس کے بازو اور ٹانگیں بری طرح متاثر ہوئے تھے۔ شام میں اس کے دوستوں نے اس کی ماں اور باپ کو اس کے ساتھ پیش آئے حادثے کی اطلاع کر دی تھی۔

اسے یقین تھا کہ اس کے ساتھ پیش آنے والے اس حادثے کے بعد ثانیہ کا دل ضرور نرم پڑ جائے گا۔ وہ پھر سے اس کی زندگی میں لوٹ آئے گی۔ مگر ایسا نہیں ہوا تھا۔ اپنی ماں سے اپنے دو جڑواں بچوں کی پیدائش کا سن کر وہ پاگل ہی تو ہو اٹھا تھا خوشی سے مگر وہاں اسپتال کے اس بستر پر اس کی خوشی کا خیال بھی کسے تھا۔

اس کا سیل فون ٹوٹ چکا تھا۔ دوست سے موبائل لے کر اس نے بارہا مسز عباس کے نمبر کو ٹرائی کیا مگر ہر بار ان کا نمبر آف ہی ملتا تھا۔ بے بسی ہی بے بسی تھی۔ ایک ایک دن پہاڑ بن کر گزر رہا تھا۔

اڑھائی ماہ کے بعد اسپتال سے فارغ ہو کر پہلی فرصت میں وہ پاکستان آیا تو اسے یہ جاں بلب خبر سننے کو ملی کہ ثانیہ عباس اپنے بچوں کو لے کر اپنی ماں کے ساتھ بیرون ملک شفٹ ہو گئی ہے اور یہیں وہ ٹوٹا تھا۔

وہ لڑکی جسے اس نے زبردستی اپنی زندگی میں شامل کیا تھا ایک روز یوں چپ چاپ اس کی زندگی سے چلی جائے گی اس کے وہم و گمان میں بھی نہیں تھا۔

❁......❁......❁

اسے کہنا قسم لے لو
تمہارے بعد جو ہم نے کسی کا خواب دیکھا ہو
کسی کو ہم نے چاہا ہو' کسی کو ہم نے سوچا ہو
کسی کی آرزو کی ہو' کسی کی جستجو کی ہو
کسی کی راہ دیکھی ہو' کسی کا قرب مانگا ہو
کوئی دل میں اتارا ہو' جو ہم کو تم سے پیارا ہو
کوئی دل میں بسایا ہو' کوئی اپنا بنایا ہو
کوئی روٹھا ہو تو ہم نے اسے رو رو منایا ہو
دسمبر کی حسیں رت میں کسی کا ہجر جھیلا ہو
کسی کی یاد کا موسم میرے آنگن میں کھیلا ہو
کسی کی بے وفائی پر کبھی یہ نین برسے ہوں
کسی سے بات کرنے کو کبھی یہ ہونٹ ترسے ہوں

کبھی راتوں کو اٹھ اٹھ کر' تیرے دکھ میں نہ روئے ہوں
اسے کہنا قسم لے لو......
کبھی جگنو' کبھی تارا' کبھی ماہتاب دیکھا ہو
اسے کہنا قسم لے لو
تمہارے بعد جو ہم نے کسی کا خواب دیکھا ہو

میکال کے گھر سے واپسی کے بعد وہ فارحہ کی طرف چلی گئی تھی وہیں سے دونوں نے لانگ ڈرائیو کا پروگرام بنایا تھا اور اب تھکن سے چُور جسم کے ساتھ وہ اپنے کمرے میں بیڈ پر اوندھے منہ پڑی تھی۔

سائیڈ ٹیبل پر اس کی اور نہال حسن کی شادی کی تصویر جیسے اس کا منہ چڑا رہی تھی۔ ایک دم سے اٹھ کر بیٹھی اور بال سمیٹ کر پیچھے کرتے ہوئے اس نے وہ تصویر اٹھالی۔ نہال مسکرا رہا تھا یوں جیسے اس کی دل کی بہت بڑی تمنا پوری ہوگئی ہو مگر وہ خوش نہیں تھی۔ میکال حسن سے نہال حسن کی ذات تک کے اس سفر نے اسے بہت بُری طرح سے تھکا ڈالا تھا۔ کپکپاتے ہاتھوں سے نہال حسن کے مسکراتے ہوئے چہرے کو چھونے کے ساتھ ہی اس کی آنکھیں آنسوؤں سے بھر آئی تھیں۔

کتنا مختصر ساتھ تھا اس کا اور نہال حسن کا مگر......وہ اس کی زندگی پر بہت گہری چھاپ چھوڑ گیا تھا۔

آنسوؤں کا سلسلہ جو شروع ہوا تو پھر زور پکڑتا چلا گیا تھا۔ نہال حسن کا خوب صورت چہرہ اب اس کی آنسوؤں کی برسات میں بھیگ رہا تھا۔ ہانیہ نے تصویر ذرا سی اوپر اٹھائی اور اپنے لب اس کے گال پر رکھ دیئے۔

''آئی مس یو نہال حسن! آئی مس یو ویری مچ۔''

بہت دنوں کے بعد وہ پھر بہت رو رہی تھی مگر وہاں کوئی اسے چپ کروانے والا نہیں تھا۔ صفدر صاحب کی ڈیتھ ہوگئی تھی' حسن صاحب اور ان کی بیگم انگلینڈ جا بسے تھے کمال اور ان کی بیوی عینا کے پاس' مائرہ اور سارا کی آگے پیچھے شادیاں ہوگئی تھیں۔ جاذب اور ہادیہ بھی پچھلے سال ہی دیارِ غیر میں مقیم ہوگئے تھے مگر وہ ہزار کوششوں اور اصرار کے باوجود اپنا آبائی گھر چھوڑنے پر راضی نہیں ہوئی تھی۔

عرصہ ہوگیا تھا کسی نے ہانیہ صفدر کو مسکراتے ہوئے نہیں دیکھا تھا۔ نہال حسن کی ڈیتھ کے بعد تو یوں بھی وہ بہت گوشۂ نشین ہوکر رہ گئی تھی۔ ہفتوں اپنے کمرے سے باہر نہ نکلتی' ہادیہ روز اسے ٹائم نکال کر کال کرتی تھی مگر وہ کبھی اٹینڈ کرتی' کبھی نظر انداز کر جاتی۔

اکثر و بیشتر مسٹر اینڈ مسز رحیم شام میں اس کی طرف چکر لگا لیتے تھے تو اس کا دل بہل جاتا تھا' کل بھی تقریب سے قبل وہ دونوں اس کے گھر آئے اور اسے بصدِ اصرار اپنے گھر میں ہونے والی تقریب میں شمولیت کی دعوت دے کر گئے تھے۔

عرصہ ہوا اس نے اس طرح کی تقریبات میں جانا چھوڑ دیا تھا مگر مسٹر اینڈ مسز رحیم کو مایوس کرنا اسے مناسب نہیں لگا تبھی وہ ان کے گھر چلی آئی تھی۔ مگر اسے گمان نہیں تھا کہ وہاں میکال حسن بھی ہوگا کیونکہ اس کی معلومات کے مطابق وہ پیرس میں سیٹل ہو چکا تھا' اپنی بیوی اور بیٹے کے ساتھ اگر وہ ذرا سی بھی اس کی آمد سے باخبر ہوتی تو شاید آج کی تقریب میں کبھی نہ آتی۔

خاموشی سے گہری ہوتی پُرفسوں شب کے بارہ بج گئے تھے اس نے ایک نظر سامنے لگے وال کلاک پر ڈالی پھر تکیہ سیٹ کر کے لیٹ گئی۔ پچھلے کچھ دنوں سے موسم میں خنکی بڑھ گئی تھی۔

روز آفس سے واپسی کے بعد شدید تھکن کے باوجود وہ اسٹڈی روم میں گھس جاتی اور ساری ساری رات کتابوں کو چاٹتی رہتی' اس کا شمار ان لوگوں میں ہوتا تھا جن کی زندگی میں قسمت صرف اندھیرے لے کر آتی ہے۔
کروٹ کے بل لیٹ کر دونوں ہاتھ بائیں گال کے نیچے رکھتے ہوئے اس کی نظر پھر اپنی اور نہال حسن کی شادی کی تصویر سے ٹکرائی تھی' اسی کے ساتھ وہ تمام دن جنہیں وہ کبھی یاد کرنا نہیں چاہتی تھی اس کی سوچوں میں در آئے تھے۔

تیری آہٹ......
سلگتی دوپہر کو شام کرتی ہے
اترتی ہے سوادِ ہجر میں کچھ اس طرح
صدائے آشنا کوئی
گھنے' گہرے اندھیرے جگنوؤں کی بے یقینی میں
رخِ منزل دکھاتی ہے
روشنی کا کام کرتی ہے

❁.......❁.......❁

جاذب اور ہادیہ کی شادی کی ڈیٹ فکس ہوگئی تھی۔ انگلینڈ جانے سے قبل میکال پھر ان کے گھر آیا تھا' کل جب وہ میکال کے ساتھ صبح صبح گھر واپس آئی تھی اسی روز ناشتے کے بعد اس نے ہادیہ کو ساری بات بتا دی تھی۔ کل رات جو کچھ میکال نے زبردستی اس کے ساتھ کیا تھا وہ چاہتے ہوئے بھی ہادیہ سے چھپا نہیں سکی تھی' جواب میں ہادیہ نے اسے سمجھایا تھا کہ وہ میکال کی برائیوں اور اس کے ماضی کی محبت کو نظر انداز کرنے کی کوشش کر کے اس کے ساتھ اپنے تعلق کو خوشگوار بنائے تاہم ہانیہ فی الحال اس کی بات پر کان دھرنے کو تیار نہیں تھی۔
اپنے کردار کے بارے میکال حسن کے الفاظ اسے سانپ بچھو بن کر کاٹتے تھے۔ اسی روز شام میں جب وہ ہادیہ کے ساتھ رات کے کھانے کی تیاری کر رہی تھی' وہ پھر آ دھمکا تھا۔ جاذب گھر پر نہیں تھا تاہم صفدر صاحب اور ان کی بیوی ٹیلی ویژن کے سامنے بیٹھے نیوز سن رہے تھے جب وہ وہیں ٹی وی لاؤنج میں چلا آیا۔
''السلام علیکم انکل اینڈ آنٹی! کیسے ہیں آپ؟''
''وعلیکم السلام بیٹے! بڑی لمبی عمر ہے تمہاری' ابھی تمہارا ہی ذکر ہو رہا تھا۔''
''خیریت؟''
''ہوں' تمہاری آنٹی تمہارا ذکر کر رہی تھیں۔'' صفدر صاحب نے بتایا تھا جواب میں وہ قہقہہ لگا کر ہنس پڑا۔
''ذکر خیر تو نہیں ہو رہا ہوگا' ہے ناں؟''
''نہیں بھئی ایسی کوئی بات نہیں' بہت تعریف کر رہی تھیں تمہاری' ہادیہ بتا رہی تھی کہ تم انگلینڈ جا رہے ہو؟''
''جی انکل! اصل میں کافی عرصہ وہاں رہا ہوں تو بہت سی چیزیں ہیں جنہیں صرف میں ہی ہینڈل کر سکتا ہوں۔ سوچ رہا ہوں سب کچھ کلوز کر کے پاکستان آ جاؤں پکا پکایا پھر کمال بھائی کے سپرد کر آؤں۔''
''اچھی بات ہے' واپس کب تک آؤ گے؟''
''کچھ کہہ نہیں سکتا' یہ تو وہاں جا کر ہی پتا لگے گا۔''
''کچھ بھی ہو لیکن سارا کام نپٹا کر فوری واپس آؤ کیونکہ جاذب اور ہادیہ کی شادی کی ڈیٹ فکس ہوگئی ہے اور تمہارا اس موقع پر یہاں ہونا بہت ضروری ہے۔''

"میں کوشش کروں گا انکل! ان شاء اللہ آپ پریشان نہ ہوں۔" اس کے چہرے اور آنکھوں میں بشاشت تھی' صفدر صاحب کو پہلی بار وہ بہت خوش دکھائی دیا تھا تبھی وہ مطمئن سے مسکرا دیئے تھے۔

ہانیہ تھوڑی دیر بعد ہادیہ کے مجبور کرنے پر چائے لے کر آئی تو وہ صفدر صاحب سے کہہ رہا تھا۔

"وہ اصل میں انکل! میں ہانیہ کے ساتھ باہر ڈنر کرنا چاہ رہا تھا' اگر آپ کی اجازت ہو تو......"

"ہاں ہاں کیوں نہیں' بھئی بیوی ہے تمہاری' کوئی گرل فرینڈ تھوڑی ہے جو اجازت مانگ رہے ہو۔" میکال کی بات پوری ہونے سے پہلے ہی انہوں نے اجازت دے ڈالی تھی۔

ہانیہ محض انہیں دیکھ کر رہ گئی۔

"ایم سوری پاپا! میرے سر میں درد ہو رہا ہے میں اس وقت کہیں بھی جانے کی پوزیشن میں نہیں ہوں۔"

"بُری بات ہانیہ! میکال کل انگلینڈ جا رہا ہے پتا نہیں کب واپسی ہو' چلو اٹھو شاباش تیار ہو کر آؤ' میں اس وقت تمہارا انکار سننے کی پوزیشن میں نہیں ہوں۔"

"مگر پاپا......"

"کوئی اگر مگر نہیں' چلو اٹھو شاباش! اور پانچ منٹ میں واپس آؤ۔"

وہ آرمی سے وابستہ رہے تھے اور یہ چیز ان کے اندر جیسے رچ بس گئی تھی۔ ہانیہ بے حد ہرٹ ہو کر وہاں سے اٹھی تھی کتنے دکھ کی بات تھی کہ سب کچھ جاننے کے باوجود وہ میکال کو سر آنکھوں پر بٹھا رہے تھے اور اس کی اب بھی وہی اہمیت تھی۔

بے بس......لاچار......

اگلے بیس منٹ میں وہ انہی کپڑوں میں بال سیدھے کر کے آ گئی تھی۔ میکال اسے دیکھتے ہی اٹھ کھڑا ہوا۔

"اوکے انکل! ہم اب نکلتے ہیں گھر واپسی پر مجھے پیکنگ بھی کرنی ہے اس لیے معذرت مزید نہیں بیٹھ سکوں گا۔"

"کوئی بات نہیں' ہانیہ کا خیال رکھنا۔"

"ان شاء اللہ' اللہ حافظ۔"

صفدر صاحب سے ہاتھ ملا کر ذکیہ بیگم سے پیار لیتے ہوئے وہ فوراً گھر سے باہر نکل آیا۔ جب کہ ہانیہ کو ہادیہ کندھوں سے تھام کر باہر لائی تھی۔ اس کے جانے کے بعد صفدر صاحب نے گہری سانس بھرتے ہوئے ذکیہ بیگم سے کہا۔

"میں جانتا ہوں ہانیہ! میرے فیصلوں سے خوش نہیں ہے مگر وہ نہیں جانتی ذکیہ کہ جس معاشرے میں ہم رہ رہے ہیں وہاں سو فیصد لڑکے کے گلٹی ہونے کے باوجود دن رات بیٹی کے ماں باپ ہاتھ باندھے اپنے سمدھیوں کے سامنے کھڑے رہتے ہیں صرف اس لیے کہ بس ان کی بیٹی کا گھر آباد رہے۔ چاہے وہ وہاں سولی پر ہی کیوں نہ چڑھی ہو بس اس کے آباد رہنے کا بھرم قائم رہے کیونکہ وہ جانتے ہیں اگر کسی بھی وجہ سے ان کی بیٹی واپس ان کے گھر آ گئی تو بربادی کا سارا ملبہ صرف ان کی اور ان کی بیٹی کی ذات پر گرے گا۔ لڑکے والوں کے نام پر کوئی حرف نہیں آئے گا' یہی اس معاشرے کی ریت ہے۔" بولتے بولتے ان کی آنکھوں کے گوشے نم ہو گئے تبھی ذکیہ بیگم نے ہاتھ بڑھا کر ان کا ہاتھ تھپتھپاتے ہوئے انہیں تسلی دی۔

ہانیہ باہر میکال کی گاڑی میں آ کر بیٹھی تو سرد ہواؤں نے بے ساختہ اسے کپکپانے پر مجبور کر دیا۔ میکال نے بس ایک سرسری سی نگاہ اس پر ڈالی اور پھر ڈرائیونگ سیٹ پر آ کر بیٹھ گیا۔

ریسٹورنٹ تک دونوں خاموش رہے' تاہم جس وقت اس نے کھانا آرڈر کیا اس نے ہانیہ کو مخاطب کیا۔

''مجھے کھانے میں تمہاری پسند کا علم نہیں ہے پلیز تم جو بھی کھانا چاہو منگوا سکتی ہو۔''

''نہیں اس کی ضرورت نہیں ہے۔''

''ٹھیک ہے' آپ یہی لے آئیں پلیز۔'' ہانیہ سے توجہ ہٹا کر اس نے ویٹر کو وہی ڈشز او کے کر دی جو اس نے پسند کی تھیں وہ سر ہلا کر واپس مڑ گیا۔

''ابھی تھوڑی دیر میں یہاں رحیم صاحب اور آپا بھی آنے والے ہیں۔ اسی لیے تمہارے نا چاہنے کے باوجود میں تمہیں یہاں لے آیا کیونکہ انہیں ہمارے اختلافات کی خبر نہیں ہے۔''

''کس کس سے اپنے اختلافات کو چھپاتے پھریں گے مسٹر میکال حسن صاحب! ایک نہ ایک دن تو دنیا کو پتا چل ہی جائے گا کہ ہمارے رشتے کی حقیقت کیا ہے۔''

''ہوں مگر دنیا کو پتا چلنے سے قبل ہی میں اس رشتے کو مضبوط کر لوں گا۔'' مخمور لہجے میں کہتے ہوئے اس نے ہانیہ کا ہاتھ اپنی گرفت میں لے لیا۔ وہ اسے دیکھتی ہی رہ گئی۔

''میں مانتا ہوں تم مجھ سے بہت ناراض ہو' یقیناً مجھے معاف کرنے کا بھی تمہارا کوئی پروگرام نہیں مگر میں پھر بھی تم سے ملے بغیر یہاں سے جانا نہیں چاہتا۔''

''مجھے اس سے کوئی فرق نہیں پڑتا۔'' آہستگی سے اپنا ہاتھ اس کے ہاتھ کی گرفت سے نکالتے ہوئے اس نے رخ پھیر لیا۔

''جانتا ہوں اور میں یہ بھی جانتا ہوں کہ آپ اس شادی کے لیے دل سے رضا مند نہیں تھیں' سارا اور مائرہ کے بقول تمہارا اور نہال کا آپس میں پسندیدگی کا رشتہ تھا شاید اس نے مما پاپا کے سامنے اس کا اظہار بھی کیا تھا۔ اسی لیے میں نہیں چاہتا تھا کہ تم میرے ساتھ کوئی تعلق بناؤ کیونکہ میں خود ایک ٹوٹا ہوا انسان ہوں۔ عائشہ ازہان کو کھونے کے بعد زندگی بہت بے رنگ سی ہو کر رہ گئی ہے میرے لیے' تم خود سوچو ایک انسان جو پہلے ہی ٹوٹا ہوا ہو کیا اسے کوئی منتشر فرد سکون دے سکتا ہے؟''

''میں منتشر نہیں ہوں' نہ ہی مجھے اس چیز میں کوئی دلچسپی ہے کہ عائشہ ازہان آپ کے لیے کیا تھی کیا نہیں تھی' میں صرف اتنا جانتی ہوں کہ میں ایک برتے ہوئے انسان کے ساتھ اپنی خوب صورت زندگی کا سفر شروع کرنا نہیں چاہتی تھی۔ ایک ایسا انسان جس کے پاس آپ کو دینے کے لیے نہ خالص خواب ہوں نا جذبے' میری پسند ایسا انسان نہیں تھا اسی لیے میں نے اس شادی سے انکار کیا تھا' مجھے نہیں پتا نہال کے دل میں میرے لیے کیا ہے کیا نہیں ہے مگر میں اتنا ضرور جانتی ہوں کہ وہ ایک بہترین انسان ہے' رشتوں کو برتنے اور ان کی قدر کرنے کے معاملے میں وہ آپ سے کئی درجے بہتر انسان ہے۔'' رخ پھیرے وہ قدرے جذباتی ہو گئی تھی۔ میکال یک ٹک اسے دیکھے گیا۔

''اور ہاں یہ شادی میں نے بھی ویسے ہی مجبور ہو کر کی تھی جیسے آپ نے مجبور ہو کر کی وگرنہ عائشہ ازہان کے عاشق میں مجھے کوئی دلچسپی نہیں تھی پھر بھی صرف اپنے ماں باپ کی عزت رکھنے کے لیے' انسانی ہمدردی کے تحت میں نے آپ کو اپنا ہم سفر قبول کیا۔ میرا خیال تھا کہ شاید آپ کا اعتبار جیت کر میں آپ کی کھوئی ہوئی خوشیاں آپ کو دوبارہ لوٹا سکوں گی مگر یہ میری بھول تھی' کچھ لوگ ایسے ہوتے ہیں جن کے ساتھ ہمدردی بھی نہیں کی جا سکتی اور آپ کا شمار ایسے ہی لوگوں میں ہوتا ہے مسٹر میکال! میں اب تک خاموش ہوں تو صرف جاذب اور ہادیہ کی خوشیوں کے لیے وگرنہ آپ جیسے پراگندہ سوچوں کے مالک شخص کے ساتھ میں چند گھڑیاں گزارنا بھی اپنی توہین سمجھتی ہوں۔ شادی ضرور کی ہے میں نے مگر اس شادی کے بدلے میں اپنے کردار اور اپنی عزتِ نفس کا سودا نہیں کیا میں نے بہرحال میں اب چلتی ہوں اس سے پہلے کہ

پھر موسم خراب ہو جائے اور مجھے زبردستی آپ کے ساتھ آپ کے گھر جانا پڑے‘ مسٹر اینڈ مسز رحیم کو میری طرف سے معذرت کہہ دیجیے گا۔‘‘

دل کا غبار نکال کر اپنی بے عزتی کا بدلہ اچھی طرح چکانے کے بعد وہ بنا میکال کے جذبات کا خیال لیے کرسی پیچھے کھسکا کر اٹھ کھڑی ہوئی تبھی ویٹر کھانا لے آیا تھا۔

’’کھانا کھا کر جاؤ ہانیہ! پھر میں تمہیں خود تمہارے گھر ڈراپ کر آتا ہوں۔‘‘ ویٹر کے سامنے سبکی کے احساس سے اس نے ہانیہ کا ہاتھ تھام لیا وہ بھی موقع کی نزاکت کو سمجھتے ہوئے چپ چاپ بیٹھ گئی۔

’’میں جانتا ہوں تم بہت خود دار اور انا پرست ہو‘ میرا خدا جانتا ہے میں عورت کی عزت اور احترام کا دل سے قائل ہوں۔ میرے دل میں تمہارے لیے کچھ بھی غلط نہیں ہے‘ میں نے جو کچھ بھی تم سے کہا وہ وہی تھا جو سارا اور مائرہ نے سنا‘ بہرحال میں تمہیں قطعی مجبور نہیں کروں گا کہ تم میرے جیسے برتے ہوئے شخص کے ساتھ زبردستی زندگی گزارو‘ میں اپنی برباد زندگی کے لیے کسی کی بھی ہمدردی کا متمنی نہیں ہوں میرا وعدہ ہے تم سے‘ تم جب بھی مجھ سے رہائی چاہو گی میں تمہیں آزاد کر دوں گا۔‘‘ ٹھہرے ہوئے سنجیدہ لہجے میں کہتا وہ ہانیہ کو ساکت کر گیا۔ کیا واقعی اس شخص کے لیے تعلق بنانا اور پھر انہیں ختم کر دینا اتنا ہی آسان تھا؟

’’چلو اب کھانا کھاؤ پلیز پھر چلتے ہیں۔‘‘ بنا ہانیہ کے چہرے پر نگاہ ڈالے وہ کھانے کی طرف متوجہ ہو گیا تھا۔ ہانیہ خاموشی سے سر ہلا کر رہ گئی۔

آدھ گھنٹے کے بعد بنا کچھ کھائے وہ گھر واپسی کے لیے میکال حسن کے ساتھ اس کی گاڑی میں بیٹھ رہی تھی۔ دل کو چھو لینے والی سبک رو ہوا سے ہانیہ کا اڑتا آنچل میکال کے ساتھ اس کے سفر کو حسین بنا رہا تھا تاہم وہ دونوں چپ تھے۔

ہلکی ہلکی بوندا باندی جو ان کے ریسٹورنٹ سے نکلنے کے ساتھ ہی شروع ہو چکی تھی اب آہستہ آہستہ تیز بارش کی صورت اختیار کر گئی۔ میکال کے لیے ڈرائیونگ میں مشکل پیش آنے لگی‘ تیزی سے کام کرتا وائپر بھی سامنے روڈ کو کلیئر کرنے میں ناکام ثابت ہو رہا تھا‘ تبھی سنسان روڈ پر ایک دم سے گاڑی بند ہو گئی۔

’’او مائی گاڈ! اسے بھی ابھی بند ہونا تھا۔‘‘ اسٹیئرنگ وہیل پر ہلکا سا مکا رسید کرتے ہوئے میکال نے اپنے غصے کا اظہار کیا‘ وہ گھبرا گئی۔

’’کیا مطلب؟ کیا گاڑی اب نہیں چلے گی؟‘‘

’’پتا نہیں دیکھتا ہوں۔‘‘

اسے تسلی دے کر وہ گاڑی سے باہر نکل آیا۔ ہانیہ منہ ہی منہ میں مختلف قرآنی آیات کا ورد کرنے لگی۔ موبائل کے سگنل بھی خراب موسم کی وجہ سے کام نہیں کر رہے تھے اوپر سے بجلی کی کڑک الگ دل دہلا رہی تھی۔ تقریباً آدھا گھنٹہ انجن پر جھکا رہنے کے بعد وہ گاڑی میں واپس آیا۔

’’سوری ہانیہ! گاڑی کا انجن کام نہیں کر رہا‘ ہمیں کسی دوسری سواری کا انتظار کرنا پڑے گا؟‘‘

’’کیا...... لیکن اتنی سنسان جگہ پر کوئی دوسری سواری کیسے ملے گی؟‘‘

’’مل جائے گی ان شاء اللہ! تمہیں ٹینشن لینے کی ضرورت نہیں‘ میں ہوں ناں تمہارے ساتھ؟‘‘ ہانیہ کا ہاتھ تھامتے ہوئے اس نے کچھ اس اپنائیت سے کہا کہ اس کا دل زور سے دھڑک اٹھا۔

’’مجھے اس موسم سے بہت ڈر لگتا ہے اتنی زور سے بادل گرج رہے ہیں اگر اس گاڑی پر بجلی گر پڑی تو؟‘‘

’’ہاہاہا...... تو کیا اکٹھے جی تو نہیں سکے کم از کم اکٹھے مر تو جائیں گے۔‘‘

"مگر میں ابھی مرنا نہیں چاہتی۔"

"کیوں؟"

"ابھی کوئی نیکی جو نہیں کی ہے میں نے۔" اتنی معصومیت سے اس نے کہا کہ وہ بے ساختہ ہنس پڑا' وہ لڑکی اندر سے کتنی سادا اور معصوم تھی۔

"او کے ہم ایسا کرتے ہیں گاڑی کو لاک کر کے یہیں رہنے دیتے ہیں اور خود کسی محفوظ جگہ پر پہنچ کر موسم کے ٹھیک ہونے کا انتظار کرتے ہیں؟" ہانیہ کا ہاتھ اب بھی اس کے ہاتھ میں تھا۔ وہ خاموشی سے سر ہلا گئی۔

ہانیہ بھی ڈرتے ڈرتے اس کے پیچھے باہر نکل آئی تو میکال نے گاڑی لاک کر دی۔ موسم کی شدت میں مزید اضافہ ہو رہا تھا وہ دونوں تیز بارش میں بھیگتے قریب ہی ایک پرانی سی دکان کے شیلٹر کے نیچے آ کھڑے ہوئے۔

"پاکستان کے لوگوں کی طرح پاکستان کے موسموں کا بھی کوئی اعتبار نہیں ہے' پل میں کیا سے کیا ہو جاتے ہیں۔" کورٹ سے پانی جھاڑتے ہوئے اس نے ایک نظر اوپر آسمان کی طرف دیکھا تھا ہانیہ خاموش کھڑی رہی۔

گزرتے ہر لمحے کے ساتھ بارش کی شدت میں اضافہ ہو رہا تھا اور اس کے ساتھ ہی سردی کا احساس بھی بڑھتا جا رہا تھا تاہم وہاں بہتری کی فی الحال کوئی صورت دکھائی نہیں دے رہی تھی۔ تبھی میکال کن اکھیوں سے اس کی طرف دیکھتے ہوئے بولا۔

"دعا کرو خیریت سے گھر پہنچ جائیں یہاں اس روڈ پر آئے روز بہت وارداتیں ہوتی ہیں۔" وہ سنجیدہ تھا ہانیہ کا دل زور سے دھڑکا تبھی اس نے ڈر کر اس کی طرف دیکھا۔

"ہوں سچ کہہ رہا ہوں' اسی لیے میں نے گاڑی میں بیٹھنے کو ترجیح نہیں دی۔"

"اگر آپ کو یہ سب پتا تھا تو آپ کو اس ٹائم گھر سے نہیں نکلنا چاہیے تھا۔ پتا تو ہے شہر کے حالات کا اور میں تو آنا بھی نہیں چاہتی تھی آپ کے ساتھ مگر ہمیشہ کی طرح آپ زبردستی ساتھ لے آئے' اب اگر کچھ ہوا تو میں آپ کو معاف نہیں کروں گی۔"

"پہلے کب کر رہی ہو؟" بے نیازی سے ہاتھ پینٹ کی پاکٹس میں گھساتے ہوئے اس نے سامنے روڈ پر نظر دوڑائی تھی۔

ہانیہ لب بھینچ کر رہ گئی' سردی کی شدت سے اس کا سارا جسم کپکپا رہا تھا۔ ہونٹ جیسے نیلے ہو رہے تھے' اوپر سے بارش کی ترچھی بوندوں نے اچھی طرح بھگو ڈالا تھا۔ وہ میکال پر اپنا حال ظاہر کرنا نہیں چاہتی تھی مگر جسم کی کپکپاہٹ اور نیلے ہوتے ہونٹوں نے اس کا بھید کھول دیا تھا۔

"سردی لگ رہی ہے؟" میکال کا ہاتھ اس کے کندھے پر آیا تو اس نے آہستہ سے نفی میں سر ہلا دیا۔

"تو پھر کپکپا کیوں رہی ہو اور یہ اپنے ہونٹوں کو دیکھو کیسے نیلے ہو رہے ہیں؟"

"اٹس او کے۔"

"نہیں...... سب ٹھیک نہیں ہے' پتا نہیں موسم کب ٹھیک ہو' تم زیادہ دیر مزید کھڑی بھی نہیں رہ سکتیں۔ میں دیکھتا ہوں شاید یہاں کوئی بیٹھنے کی جگہ ہو۔"

ہلکے سے اس کا کندھا تھپتھپاتے ہوئے وہ مڑ گیا۔ ہانیہ نے دونوں بازو اپنے کندھوں کے گرد لپیٹ لیے' تقریباً پندرہ بیس منٹ کے بعد وہ دوبارہ اس کے پاس آیا۔

"چلو۔"

''کہاں؟''

''شوہر ہوں تمہارا کہیں بھی لے جاسکتا ہوں فی الحال پیچھے ایک کمرا ہے شاید کچھ روز پہلے تک کوئی وہاں اپنا گھوڑا باندھتا رہا ہے' اتنے خراب موسم میں فی الحال یہ پناہ بہترین جگہ ہے۔''

''آپ کے لیے ہوگی مگر میں کسی ایسی جگہ پر نہیں بیٹھ سکتی جہاں مجھ سے کھل کر سانس بھی نہ لیا جاسکے۔''

''وہاں ایسی کوئی بات نہیں ہے تھوڑی سی خشک گھاس ہے اور بس موسم کے تیور تم دیکھ رہی ہو' موبائل کام نہیں کررہا' روڈ سنسان اور خطرناک ہے۔ خدا نہ کرے ابھی ہمیں یہاں کھڑے دیکھ کر کوئی اسلحہ لے کر آ گیا تو کیا کریں گے۔ میں تو خیر بھاگ بھی لوں گا مگر تم سے تو بھاگا بھی نہیں جائے گا۔''

''اللہ نہ کرے کہ ایسا کچھ ہو۔''

''ٹھیک ہے تو تم کھڑی رہو یہیں میں جارہا ہوں' مجھ سے تو مزید ٹھنڈ برداشت نہیں ہورہی۔'' چڑ کر کہتے ہوئے وہ پلٹ گیا مگر ہانیہ ہٹ دھرمی کا مظاہرہ کرتی وہیں کھڑی رہی لیکن کب تک؟

میکال کی باتیں واقعی نظر انداز کیے جانے کے قابل نہیں تھیں۔ اوپر سے بارش تھی کہ رکنے کا نام نہیں لے رہی تھی' چار پانچ منٹ میکال کا مزید انتظار کرنے کے بعد وہ بھی اس کے پیچھے ہی اس کھلے سے ہال نما کمرے میں چلی آئی جہاں سیمنٹ کے فرش پر کچھ خالی پانی کی بوتلیں اور قدرے خشک گھاس کا ڈھیر پڑا تھا۔ میکال نے وہ گھاس پھیلا کر بڑے مزے سے اپنے لیے بستر کا انتظام کرلیا تھا۔

ہانیہ ایک نظر اس پر ڈالتی سائیڈ پر بیٹھ گئی' پتا نہیں اس کے گھر والے اس کے لیے کتنے فکرمند ہوں گے یہی خیال اسے بار بار پریشان کررہا تھا۔ بادل اتنی زور سے گرج رہے تھے کہ وہ دہل کر رہ جاتی' رہ رہ کر اسے میکال پر غصہ آرہا تھا جو اسے ضد کرکے زبردستی اپنے ساتھ لے آیا تھا۔ دوسری طرف اس کی ٹکٹ ضائع ہونے کا بھی افسوس تھا' اچھا ہی تھا کہ وہ انگلینڈ چلا جاتا اور وہ پُرسکون ہوجاتی۔

بارش کی شدت کے ساتھ ہی ہوا میں بھی تیزی آ گئی تھی' طوفانی ہوا کے جھکڑ اسے برف بنانے پر تلے ہوئے تھے۔ اوپر سے بدن کے ساتھ چپکے گیلے کپڑوں نے علیحدہ مصیبت میں مبتلا کررکھا تھا۔

میکال دونوں ہاتھ سر کے پیچھے باندھے گیلے کپڑوں کے ساتھ بڑے مزے سے لیٹا کن اکھیوں سے اس کی طرف دیکھ رہا تھا۔ جیسے جیسے وقت گزرتا جارہا تھا ہانیہ کی جان پر بنتی جارہی تھی مگر اسے جیسے پرواہی نہیں تھی۔

کچھ ہی دیر میں اس نے جان بوجھ کر آنکھیں بند کرلیں تو وہ خود بخود اٹھ کر اس کے پاس آ بیٹھی۔

''سنو......'' میکال کا بازو ہلاتے ہوئے اس نے اسے جگایا۔

''ہوں۔''

''آپ نے کہا تھا یہ خطرناک جگہ ہے کیا یہاں کوئی اسلحہ لے کر نہیں آئے گا؟''

''آنا تو نہیں چاہیے مگر کچھ کہا بھی نہیں جاسکتا خیر تمہیں ڈرنے کی ضرورت نہیں ہے۔ اللہ ہے ناں ہمارے ساتھ اور پھر تم کوئی اکیلی تھوڑی ہو' میں ہوں ناں۔'' اس کے پریشان ہونے پر اس نے تسلی دی مگر جواب میں ہانیہ نے خاصی ناراض نگاہوں سے اس کی طرف دیکھا' جیسے کہنا چاہ رہی ہو' ہاں دیکھ رہی ہوں میں کتنے تم میرے ساتھ ہو۔

''چلو لیٹ جاؤ میرے ساتھ' شاباش!'' اگلے ہی پل اس نے اس کا ہاتھ پکڑ کر زبردستی اپنے اوپر گرالیا۔

''کم از کم آج کی رات گھر واپسی ممکن نہیں ہے' تم سمجھو ہم ہنی مون ٹرپ پر آئے ہوئے ہیں' ایڈونچر سے بھرپور ٹرپ پر۔'' اپنی ہی ترنگ میں کہتے ہوئے اس نے ہانیہ کے گرد اپنے بازوؤں کی گرفت خاصی سخت کردی تھی وہ محض پھڑ پھڑا کر

رہ گئی۔

''مجھے آپ کے ساتھ زندگی نہیں گزارنی میکال حسن! چھوڑو مجھے۔''

''میرے ساتھ ہی زندگی گزرے گی تمہاری' لکھ کر رکھ لو۔'' اب کے اس نے اسے اپنے پہلو میں گرالیا۔

''وہ سارے خواب جو میں نے عائش کے حوالے سے دیکھے تھے ان خوابوں کی تعمیر تم بنو گی ہانیہ! یہ ٹھیک ہے کہ میرے دل کا ایک کونا اس لڑکی کی محبت سے ہمیشہ آباد رہے گا' مگر یہ بھی سچ ہے کہ مجھے تمہاری بد دعا لگ گئی ہے۔ میں جو تمہاری شکل دیکھنا نہیں چاہتا تھا' خالقِ کائنات نے مجھے بے بس کر کے ایک اسی شکل میں میرے لیے سکون رکھ دیا ہے۔''

''سوری! مگر میرے دل میں اب آپ کے لیے کوئی گنجائش نہیں ہے۔''

''کوئی بات نہیں' جس خالق و مالک نے مجھے تمہارے معاملے میں بے بس کیا ہے یقیناً وہی تمہارے دل میں میرے لیے بھی ضرور محبت ڈالے گا میں اس کی رحمت سے مایوس نہیں ہوں۔'' پُر یقین لہجے میں کہتے ہوئے اس نے ہانیہ کا سر اپنے بازو پر رکھا تبھی پہلی بار اس نے اس کی آنکھوں کو دیکھا تھا۔ دمکتے ستاروں کی مانند جگمگاتی ہوئی بے حد حسین آنکھیں' وہ جھکا اور انتہائی محبت سے اپنے لب ان ستاروں پر ثبت کیے تھے۔

''میکال میں......'' ہانیہ کسمسائی مگر میکال نے اس کے ہونٹوں پر اپنا ہاتھ رکھ دیا۔

''شش...... کچھ کہنے کی ضرورت نہیں ہے' اپنے ہونٹ دیکھو کتنے نیلے ہو رہے ہیں۔'' سرگوشیانہ لہجے میں کہتے ہوئے اس نے ہانیہ کے لبوں پر انگلی پھیری اور ساتھ ہی اس کی صبیح پیشانی سے چپکے بال ہٹا دیئے۔ وہ اٹھنا چاہتی تھی مگر میکال نے اسے ایسا کوئی موقع نہیں دیا۔ وہ جھکا اور اپنے ہونٹ ہانیہ کے لبوں پر رکھ دیئے۔ ہانیہ کو لگا جیسے اس کا دل دھڑکنا بھول گیا ہو تبھی میکال کو پیچھے دھکیلتے ہوئے وہ اٹھی اور دیوار کے ساتھ لگ کر کھڑی ہو گئی۔

''آپ مزید تذلیل نہیں کر سکتے میکال حسن!'' زیر و بم ہوتی سانسوں کے ساتھ اس کی آنکھیں بھرائی تھیں' مگر وہ مسکرا دیا۔

''ہوں مگر پیار تو کر سکتا ہوں ناں؟''

ادھر جیسے اس کے غصے کا کوئی اثر ہی نہیں تھا وہ بے بسی سے نم آنکھوں کے ساتھ اسے دیکھتی رہ گئی یوں لگتا تھا جیسے برستے موسم نے اسے بے بس کر ڈالا ہو تبھی دیوار کے ساتھ لگ کر کھڑی ہانیہ صفدر کے گرد بازو ٹکاتے ہوئے وہ پھر اس پر جھکا اور اس بار اس نے اس کی گردن کو نشانہ بنایا تھا۔ ہانیہ مزاحمت کرنا چاہتی تھی مگر...... ایک مرتبہ پھر اس کی ہمت جواب دے گئی تھی ایک مرتبہ پھر میکال حسن نے اسے شکست دے ڈالی تھی۔

اگلے روز صبح میکال کی آنکھ کھلی تو وہ اس جگہ پر نہیں تھی شاید نہیں یقیناً وہ اس سے بہت زیادہ خفا ہو چکی تھی وہ مسکرایا اور اگلے ہی پل اٹھ کر کمرے سے باہر نکل آیا۔

بارش تھم چکی تھی مگر سرد ہواؤں کے تھپڑوں کا سلسلہ اب بھی جاری تھا۔ ہانیہ سڑک کی طرف رخ کیے کھڑی تھی اور زیر لب مسکراتا اس کے برابر میں آ کھڑا ہوا۔

''السلام علیکم صبح بخیر!'' اس کے سلام پر وہ چونکی مگر رخ نہیں پھیرا۔

''آپ کی حسرتیں اگر پوری ہو گئی ہوں تو چلنے کی تیاری کریں' میں اپنے گھر والوں کو اس سے زیادہ اذیت نہیں دے سکتی۔'' بنا اس کے سلام کا جواب دیئے وہ بے رخی سے بولی۔ میکال اسے دیکھتا رہ گیا۔

''تمہیں کیا لگتا ہے میرے گھر والے سکون سے بیٹھے ہوں گے؟''

''مجھے نہیں پتا میں اس وقت آپ سے بحث کے موڈ میں نہیں ہوں۔''

''ٹھیک ہے میں دیکھتا ہوں یقیناً موبائل کام کر رہا ہوگا۔'' اس کے خراب موڈ کے پیش نظر وہ فوراً ہی گاڑی کی طرف بڑھا۔ اگلے تیس منٹ میں جاذب کی گاڑی ان دونوں کے مقابل تھی۔ نہال شہر میں نہیں تھا ورنہ وہ اسے ہی بلواتا' ہانیہ کو جاذب کے ساتھ رخصت کرنے کے بعد وہ اپنے گھر چلا آیا۔

اگلے دو روز کے بعد وہ انگلینڈ چلا آیا جب کہ ہانیہ شادی کی تیاریوں میں مصروف ہوگئی تھی۔ دو ماہ اسی میں گزر گئے نہ اس نے کبھی ہانیہ کو فون کر کے اس کی خیریت معلوم کرنے کی کوشش کی نہ ہانیہ نے ہی کبھی اسے یاد کیا' انہی دنوں ایک دوست کے بے حد اصرار پر اس نے ماڈلنگ شروع کی تھی۔ وہ جانتا تھا کہ وہ بے حد وجیہہ ہے مگر اپنی خوب صورتی اور وجاہت کو کیش کرانے کا خیال اسے کبھی نہیں آیا تھا' تاہم انگلینڈ میں قیام کے دوران قریبی پاکستانی دوست کے اصرار پر بحالت مجبوری وہ اسے انکار نہ کر سکا اور اس نے ایک کمرشل کر لیا' ہانیہ جو بُری طرح شادی کی تیاریوں میں مصروف تھی اسے ٹی وی پر دیکھ کر دنگ رہ گئی۔

پہلی بار میکال حسن کے ساتھ کسی دوسری لڑکی کو چپکے ہوئے دیکھ کر اس کا دل جلا اور وہ کڑھ کر رہ گئی' اس کے بعد ہر لمحہ جیسے اس پر عذاب بن کر آیا تھا۔ میکال حسن کو وہ کھو سکتی تھی مگر اسے تقسیم کرنے کا حوصلہ اس میں نہیں تھا' یہی وجہ تھی کہ مصروفیات کے باوجود وہ پریشان رہنے لگی تھی۔

پچھلے ایک ہفتے سے اس کی طبیعت ناساز تھی مگر اس روز تو حد ہی ہوگئی تھی اچھی بھلی وہ کچن میں چائے بنانے گئی کہ زور کے چکر نے اسے چکرا کر رکھ دیا۔ ہادیہ اگر اسے فوری طور پر نہ تھام لیتی تو اس کا گر جانا یقینی تھا۔ اسی روز ہانیہ کے لاکھ منع کرنے کے باوجود وہ اسے ڈاکٹر کے پاس لے گئی اور وہیں اسے ہانیہ کے حاملہ ہونے کی خوش کن خبر ملی تھی۔

مارے خوشی کے اس کے پاؤں زمین پر نہیں ٹک رہے تھے تاہم ہانیہ خوش نہیں تھی اس کے لبوں کو جیسے چپ لگ گئی تھی۔ ہادیہ نے اس کے منع کرنے کے باوجود سب کو اس خوش خبری سے آگاہ کر دیا تھا۔ میکال کو بھی اسی نے خبر دی تھی جواباً وہ بے حد مسرور ہوا تھا حسن صاحب اور ان کی بیگم کی خوشی بھی دیکھنے سے تعلق رکھتی تھی۔

اگلے روز ہادیہ کا مایوں تھا' ہانیہ منہ سر لپیٹے پڑی تھی کسی کام میں دل نہیں لگ رہا تھا تاہم بیگم حسن کی ڈانٹ پر نہ چاہتے ہوئے بھی اسے کپڑے تبدیل کرنے پڑے تھے۔ ہادیہ نے زبردستی پکڑ کر ہلکا پھلکا میک اپ بھی کر دیا۔

مسز رحیم بھی جلد ہی پہنچ گئی تھیں' ہانیہ مصروفیات کے باوجود انہیں کمپنی دیتی رہی تبھی ہادیہ نے اسے بلا لیا تھا۔

''ہانی......!''

''ایکسکیوزمی! میں ذرا ہادیہ کی بات سن آؤں۔'' مسز حسن کو مسز رحیم کے پاس بیٹھا چھوڑ کر وہ ہادیہ کے پاس چلی آئی۔

''ہوں۔''

''میرے گجرے کہاں رکھے ہیں؟''

''مجھے کیا پتا؟ میں نے تو تمہارے سپرد کر دیئے تھے۔''

''یار مجھے نہیں مل رہے ابھی رسم شروع ہو جائے گی' پلیز میرے کمرے سے لا دو' پلیز......''

''تم بھی ناں ہادیہ! ایک دم سے پاگل اور فضول لڑکی ہو' مجھے اس حال میں چکر پر چکر لگوا رہی ہو۔''

''کچھ نہیں ہوتا' ابھی شروع شروع ہے خوب ورزش کیا کرو۔'' وہ ہنسی تو ہانیہ اسے گھور کر رہ گئی۔

گجرے ہادیہ کے کمرے میں ہی رکھے تھے' انہیں وہاں سے اٹھا کر وہ ابھی سیڑھیوں کی طرف آ رہی تھی کہ اچانک لائٹ چلی گئی پھر اس سے پہلے کہ کوئی جنریٹر آن کرتا' کسی نے ہاتھ بڑھا کر ہانیہ کو تاریک راہداری میں کھینچ لیا۔ وہ چیختا

چاہتی تھی مگر کھینچنے والے کا ایک ہاتھ قطعی مضبوطی سے اس کے منہ پر جما تھا۔ ہانیہ کی جان پر بن گئی اگلے ہی پل جنریٹر آن ہوا اور اس کے ساتھ ہی ہانیہ کو کھینچنے والے کا چہرہ بھی۔

''کیسی ہو؟'' جونہی ہانیہ نے سر اوپر کر کے اس کا چہرہ دیکھا وہ مسکرا دیا۔

''چھوڑو مجھے۔'' وہ بُری طرح گھبرائی مگر اس پر کوئی اثر نہیں ہوا۔

''کیوں چھوڑوں؟ اتنے دنوں کے بعد تو ملی ہو اب بھی چھوڑ دوں؟''

''یہ کون سا طریقہ ہے ملنے کا' ابھی کوئی اوپر آ گیا تو؟''

''تو آ جائے میں کسی سے نہیں ڈرتا ویسے بھی شوہر ہوں تمہارا' کوئی روک تھوڑی سکتا ہے ملنے سے۔''

''میکال پلیز......''

''سوری!'' کندھے اچکاتے ہوئے اس نے اس کی درخواست رد کر دی۔

''ہانیہ!'' اسے پکارتے ہوئے کوئی اوپر آیا تھا۔ ہانیہ کا دل تیزی سے دھڑک اٹھا مگر میکال اسے آزاد کرنے کے موڈ میں نہیں تھا۔

''چھوڑ دیں پلیز' میں اس وقت آپ سے مزاحمت کرنے کی پوزیشن میں نہیں ہوں۔''

''تو اچھی بات ہے ناں' اچھی بیویوں کو مزاحمت کرنی بھی نہیں چاہیے۔''

''ہانیہ!'' جاذب اسے پکار رہا تھا۔ اس سے پہلے کہ وہ اوپر آتا ہانیہ نے ایک جھٹکے سے خود کو چھڑوایا اور لپک کر سیڑھیوں کی قریب آ گئی۔

''جج......جی......''

''کہاں تھیں یار! کب سے آوازیں دے رہا ہوں۔'' وہ سیڑھیوں کے دہانے پر کھڑا تھا' ہانیہ شرمندہ ہوگئی۔

''یہیں تھی' وہ ہادیہ نے گجرے منگوائے مل نہیں رہے تھے' وہی ڈھونڈ رہی تھی۔''

''اچھا مگر یہ تمہاری سانس کیوں پھولی ہوئی ہے؟''

''وہ......وہ میں بھاگ کر آئی ہوں ناں اس لیے۔''

''اچھا چلو جلدی آ جاؤ' ہادیہ بلا رہی ہے۔'' اسے تلقین کرتے ہوئے وہ وہیں سیڑھیوں کے دہانے سے ہی واپس پلٹ گیا تھا۔ ہانیہ دل ہی دل میں خدا کا شکر ادا کرتے ہوئے ایک نظر پیچھے پلٹ کر میکال حسن کو دیکھنے کے بعد تیزی سے سیڑھیاں اتر آئی۔

''کہاں رہ گئی تھیں؟'' ہادیہ اسے دیکھتے ہی غصے ہوئی' وہ سر جھکا گئی۔

''وہ......میکال نے پکڑ لیا تھا اوپر۔''

''ہیں...... یہ کیا کہہ رہی ہو؟''

''سچ کہہ رہی ہوں۔''

''لیکن وہ انگلینڈ سے کب آیا؟''

''مجھے کیا پتا' میں تو خود شاکڈ رہ گئی تھی۔''

''اچھا کیا کہہ رہا تھا؟''

''کچھ نہیں' ایویں رومینس جھاڑ رہا تھا۔''

''تمہاری پریگننسی کا سن کر آیا ہوگا' مانو یا نہ مانو میرا دل کہتا ہے اسے تم سے محبت ہوگئی ہے ہانیہ!''

"مائی فٹ...... میں نے بٹی ہوئی محبتوں کا اچار نہیں ڈالنا۔"

"ایسا نہیں کہتے ہانیہ! محبت کسی کی جاگیر نہیں ہے جو بٹ سکے' یہ تو ریاست کی طرح ہے جس پر کبھی کوئی حکمران ہوتا ہے تو کبھی کوئی...... میکال حسن کا دل بھی سمجھو ریاست ہے' جس پر کل کسی عائشہ ازہان کی حکومت تھی مگر آج اسی دل پر تمہاری حکومت ہے۔"

"اور کل...... میرے مرنے کے بعد کسی اور کی حکومت ہوگی۔"

"شٹ اپ! میری سمجھ میں نہیں آتا تم ہمیشہ منفی ہی کیوں سوچتی ہو۔"

"کیوں کہ میں پاگل ہوں اس لیے اب برائے کرم تم اپنی پروفیسری بند کرواور جلدی سے جا کر اسٹیج پر بیٹھو تا کہ رسم شروع کی جائے۔" منہ بنا کر کہتے ہوئے وہ ہادیہ کا ہاتھ پکڑ کر اسٹیج کی طرف لے آئی تھی جہاں جاذب بڑی شان سے بیٹھا میکال حسن کے ساتھ گپیں لگا رہا تھا۔

"لو جی ایک نہ شد دو شد۔" ہادیہ کی نظر جونہی سامنے پڑی وہ بولے بغیر نہ رہ سکی جب کہ ہانیہ آہستہ سے اس کا ہاتھ چھوڑ کر کھڑی ہوگئی۔

"چلو تم بیٹھو' میں آتی ہوں ابھی۔"

"کیوں...... تم کہاں جا رہی ہو؟"

"ٹافیاں بٹ رہی ہیں محلے میں' وہ لینے جا رہی ہوں۔"

"ٹھیک ہے میرے لیے بھی لے آنا۔" ہانیہ کے گھورنے پر وہ مسکرائی تو ہانیہ کے لبوں پر بھی مسکراہٹ بکھر گئی۔ سامنے بیٹھے میکال حسن نے اس منظر کو بہت دلچسپی سے دیکھا تھا۔

تیل لگ رہا تھا۔ خاندان کی تمام خواتین اسٹیج کے گرد اکٹھی ہوئی خوش گپیوں میں مصروف تھیں جب کہ ایک طرف مرد حضرات کا ٹولہ اپنی گپ شپ میں مصروف تھا۔ ہانیہ بھی اسٹیج کے قریب ہی کھڑی تھی تبھی میکال نے چپکے سے اس کا ہاتھ اپنے ہاتھ میں لے لیا۔

"کیسی ہو؟" بظاہر وہ سامنے دیکھ رہا تھا مگر اس نے ہانیہ کے کان میں سرگوشی کی تھی' وہ ٹپٹا گئی۔

"ٹھیک ہوں' ہاتھ چھوڑیں میرا۔"

"چھوڑنے کے لیے تو نہیں تھاما۔"

"میکال پلیز......"

"تم اتنی بے مروت تو نہیں تھیں ہانیہ! اتنے دنوں بعد ملے ہیں بندہ حال چال ہی پوچھ لیتا ہے۔"

"بہت لوگ ہیں آپ کا حال چال پوچھنے والے یہاں' میری مزاج پرسی کی ضرورت نہیں۔"

"تم یہ کیسے کہہ سکتی ہو؟" بنا اس کے لہجے کی تلخی کو محسوس کیے وہ پوچھ رہا تھا' وہ کٹ کر رہ گئی۔

"آپ کیوں اتنے لوگوں میں میرا تماشہ بنانا چاہتے ہیں؟"

"کیا تماشہ بنایا ہے میں نے تمہارا...... ہوں...... تماشہ تو تم میرا بنا رہی ہو جس بات کے لیے میں بارہا ایکسکیوز کر چکا ہوں' اسی بات کو ایشو بنا کر تم مسلسل مجھے رد کر رہی ہو۔" وہ صحیح کہہ رہا تھا' واقعی ہانیہ کے پاس اب اس سے نفرت کا کوئی جواز باقی نہیں رہا تھا پھر بھی جانے کیوں وہ اس سے بھاگ رہی تھی۔

"ہانیہ......" وہ ابھی کچھ کہنا ہی چاہتی تھی کہ صفدر صاحب کی پکار نے اسے چونکا دیا' وہ اسے بلا رہے تھے۔

"ایکسکیوز می! میرے پاپا مجھے بلا رہے ہیں۔" سرعت سے اپنا ہاتھ اس کے ہاتھ کی گرفت سے نکالتے ہوئے وہ

پلٹ گئی۔ میکال سرد آہ بھر کر رہ گیا۔

''بنی بات؟'' اگلے ہی پل مسز رحیم اس سے پوچھ رہی تھیں۔

''نہیں۔''

''کوئی بات نہیں بن جائے گی' دلوں کی ریاست پر حکمرانی کرنا اتنا آسان نہیں ہوتا۔'' اس کا کندھا تھپتھپاتے ہوئے انہوں نے تسلی دی تھی وہ سر ہلا کر رہ گیا۔

مایوں کی رسم اپنے عروج پر تھی جب اچانک سیکنڈ فلور کے مین کمرے میں بھڑک اٹھنے والی آگ نے رنگ میں بھنگ ڈال دیا۔ دیکھتے ہی دیکھتے مہمانوں میں کھلبلی مچ گئی' جاذب اور میکال صفدر صاحب کو تسلی دینے لگی۔

''آپ پریشان نہ ہوں زیادہ خطرے والی بات نہیں ہے۔''

''جی...... ابھی ملازم گئے ہیں اوپر ان شاء اللہ جلدی سب ٹھیک ہو جائے گا۔''

''ان شاء اللہ...... ہانیہ کہاں ہے؟''

''ہانیہ یہیں کہیں ہوگی' میں دیکھتا ہوں اسے۔'' ادھر اُدھر دیکھتے ہوئے جاذب پلٹا تھا جب وہ بولے۔

''او میرے خدا! اسے تو میں نے اوپر بھیجا تھا کچھ چیزیں لانے کے لیے۔''

''مائی گاڈ!'' جاذب نے کہا مگر اس سے پہلے ہی میکال سیڑھیوں کی طرف لپک گیا۔ جاذب بھی اس کے پیچھے ہی بھاگا۔ صفدر صاحب کی جان جیسے لبوں پر آ گئی' اوپر مین کمرے سے آگ کی لپٹیں باہر کی طرف آ رہی تھیں جاذب کے بھیجے ہوئے دونوں ملازم پانی ڈال کر آگ بجھانے کی کوشش کر رہے تھے مگر وہاں اس کمرے کی آگ بجھنے کی بجائے اور زیادہ بھڑکتی جا رہی تھی تبھی ان دونوں کو اسی کمرے سے ابھرتی ہانیہ کی چیخوں کی آواز سنائی دی۔

سنو تم نے کبھی ساحل پہ بکھری ریت دیکھی ہے؟
سمندر ساتھ بہتا ہے مگر
اس کے مقدر میں
ہمیشہ پیاس رہتی ہے
سنو تم نے کبھی صحرا میں جلتا پیڑ دیکھا ہے؟
سبھی کو چھاؤں دیتا ہے
مگر اس کے مقدر میں ہمیشہ دھوپ رہتی ہے
سنو تم نے کبھی شاخوں سے بچھڑے پھول دیکھے ہیں؟
وہ خوشبو بانٹ دیتے ہیں بکھر جانے تلک لیکن ہوا کا ساتھ دیتے ہیں
سنو تم نے کبھی میلے میں بجتا ڈھول دیکھا ہے؟
عجب ہے المیہ اس کا بہت ہی شور کرتا ہے
مگر اندر سے خالی ہے
یہی میرا افسانہ ہے' بس اتنی سی پہیلی ہے

آنکھوں پر بازو دھرے' بیتے ہوئے دنوں کی یادوں کے سنگ وہ بہت دور نکل آیا تھا جب اچانک اسے اپنے پیروں پر کسی کے نرم ہاتھوں کے لمس کا احساس ہوا' ایک جھٹکے سے بازو آنکھوں کے اوپر سے ہٹاتے ہوئے اس نے سامنے

دیکھا' سائرہ افضل اس کی چارپائی کی پائینتی پر بیٹھی تھی۔

''کھانا کھالے زائر! ٹھنڈا ہورہا ہے۔'' اس کے دیکھنے پر اس نے فوراً اپنا ہاتھ اس کے پیر سے ہٹا لیا تھا۔

''بھوک نہیں ہے مجھے' واپس لے جا۔''

''کیوں واپس لے جاؤں' کل بھی تُو نے سارا دن کچھ نہیں کھایا' اتنی محنت کرتا ہے سارے دن' ایسے تو بیمار پڑ جائے گا۔''

''تو پڑ جاؤں بیمار! تجھے کس بات کی تکلیف ہے؟'' قطعی برہمی سے دھاڑتے ہوئے وہ اسے جیسے کھانے کو پڑا تھا۔

سائرہ لب کاٹ کر رہ گئی۔

''مجھے ہی تو تکلیف ہے' مجھ سے تیرا یہ حال دیکھا نہیں جاتا آخر کب تک اس بے وفا شہرن کا روگ دل میں پالے رکھے گا تُو؟''

''میرا درد سر ہے یہ کہ کب تک پالے رکھتا ہوں' تُو جا...... جا کر کام کر اپنا۔''

''سارے کام ختم کر کے آئی ہوں' اب تو بس یہی کام ہے کہ تیری خدمت کروں۔''

''مجھے تیری خدمتوں کی ضرورت نہیں ہے۔''

''نہ سہی' مجھے تو تیری ضرورت ہے ناں۔''

''خوش فہمی ہے تیری کہ میں اب بھی پلٹ کر تیری طرف دیکھوں گا۔''

''نہ دیکھ' وقت بڑی ظالم چیز ہے ایک نہ ایک دن پھر سے گھیر کر تجھے میری طرف لے ہی آئے گا۔''

''میرا سر نہ کھا سائرہ افضل! جا...... جا کر کام کر اپنا۔'' اس بار اس نے بے زاری سے کہا تھا مگر وہ ٹس سے مس نہ ہوئی تو اکتا کر خود ہی کمرے سے نکل آیا۔

دن ڈھل رہا تھا وہ حویلی جانے کے موڈ میں نہیں تھا مگر اب اس کے سوا کوئی چارہ بھی نہیں تھا تبھی اس کے قدم حویلی کی بڑی بڑی دیواروں کی طرف اٹھ آئے تھے۔

''سلام چوہدرانی!''

''وعلیکم السلام! جیتے رہو' ابھی میں تجھے ہی یاد کر رہی تھی۔'' چوہدرانی کے چہرے پر اسے دیکھتے ہی رونق آ گئی تھی۔ وہ بڑے سے صحن میں ان کے قریب ہی موڑھا کھینچ کر بیٹھ گیا۔

''خیریت؟''

''خیریت کہاں ہے زائر! جب سے میری دھی ولایت سے ادھر گاؤں میں آئی ہے ویری بخار ہی جان نہیں چھوڑ رہا' کل رات بھی ایک سو تین تھا' شہر سے ڈاکٹر بھی بلوایا مگر کوئی افاقہ نہیں ہوا' پچھلے تین دن سے پانی پر گزارہ کر رہی ہے۔ میری دیورانی رہتی ہے شہر اس کے بیٹے کا ولیمہ ہے' سوچ رہی ہوں ثانیہ کو ساتھ لے جاؤں شاید شہر کی فضا راس آ جائے۔''

''میرے لیے کیا حکم ہے؟'' ہلکی ہلکی بڑھی ہوئی شیو کے ساتھ وہ ضرورت سے زیادہ سنجیدہ دکھائی دے رہا تھا۔ چوہدرانی نے جواب میں اسے لسی کا بڑا گلاس تھما دیا۔

''تیرے لیے کیا حکم ہونا ہے پتا تو ہے تجھے' تیرے سوا میں کسی اور پر اعتبار نہیں کر سکتی' آج شام شہر جانے کا ارادہ ہے میرا' تُو تیاری کر لے۔''

''ٹھیک ہے کتنے دن کا قیام ہوگا آپ کا وہاں؟''

"یہ تو وہاں جا کر ہی پتا چلے گا' مگر ثانیہ بیٹی کو میں وہیں چھوڑ آؤں گی۔"

"چلیں ٹھیک ہے جیسے آپ کی مرضی۔" گلاس خالی کر کے سائیڈ پر رکھتے ہوئے وہ اٹھ کھڑا ہوا۔

"گاڑی لے آتا ہوں میں آپ اور ثانیہ بی بی تیاری کر لیں۔"

"ٹھیک ہے رب سوہنا تجھے دنیا جہان کی خوشیاں نصیب کرے۔"

چوہدرانی کی دعا اسے کسی تمانچے کی طرح لگی تھی۔ ساتھ ہی آنکھوں کے گوشوں میں نمی جھلک آئی۔

"مجھے خوشیوں کی دعا نہ دیا کریں چوہدرانی! خوشی زیادہ دیر راس نہیں آتی مجھے۔"

"دل چھوٹا نہ کر زائر! میرا دل کہتا ہے بہت جلد تجھے میری دعائیں لگیں گی۔"

"اللہ کرے ایسا ہی ہو۔" وہ کہنا چاہتا تھا مگر اس نے کہا نہیں' کہا تو محض یہی......

"اب چلتا ہوں چوہدرانی! آپ تیاری کر لیں' میں ٹائم پر آ جاؤں گا۔"

"ٹھیک ہے سوہنے رب کے حوالے۔" اس کے سر پر ہاتھ پھیرتے ہوئے چوہدرانی نے اسے رخصت کیا' صحن سے اٹھ کر وہ ثانیہ کے کمرے میں آئیں تو وہ جاگ رہی تھی۔

"اب کیسی طبیعت ہے پتر!" وہ اس کے پلنگ پر آ کر ہی بیٹھ گئی تھیں۔

"ٹھیک ہوں' آپ کس سے باتیں کر رہی تھیں؟" ثانیہ نے ان کا ہاتھ تھام کر سینے پر رکھ لیا تھا تبھی وہ بولیں۔

"زائر کو بلوایا تھا میں نے شہر جانے کے لیے' وہی آیا تھا۔"

"کیوں؟ کیا وہ حویلی میں ملازمت کرتا ہے؟"

"ناں پتر! اسے ملازمت کی کیا ضرورت ہے' خیر سے اس کی اپنی زمین ہے۔"

"تو پھر وہ حویلی کے کام کیوں کرتا ہے؟"

"سارے کام پیسے کے لیے تو نہیں کیا جاتے ناں پتر! کچھ کام رشتوں کے تقدس کے لیے بھی کرنے پڑتے ہیں۔"

"مگر اس حویلی سے کیا تعلق ہے اس کا؟"

"پالا ہے اس حویلی نے اسے...... اسی حویلی کے در و دیوار میں پل کر جوان ہوا ہے وہ' اس کا باپ تیرے دادا جی کا بہت ہی قابل بھروسہ منشی تھا۔ تیرے دادا جی نہیں رہے تو اس نے بھی حویلی چھوڑ دی' مگر زائر کا تعلق نہیں ٹوٹا ان در و دیوار سے' بہت عرصہ شہر رہا ہے وہ مگر حویلی کو نہیں بھولا' زمینوں کو سارا حساب کتاب' دیکھ بھال وہی کرتا ہے' شہر والوں کو تو فرصت ہی نہیں کہ کبھی سال میں ایک چکر ہی لگا لیں۔"

"شادی شدہ ہے؟"

"ہاں بچپن میں اسی گاؤں کی ایک لڑکی سائرہ سے منگنی ہوئی تھی اس کی مگر اس نے زائر کے گاؤں کے نمبردار کے بیٹے کے ساتھ چھپ کر نکاح کر لیا' تب سنا ہے کہ کسی شہری لڑکی کو بھگا کر لایا تھا وہ مگر وہ بھی اسے چھوڑ کر چلی گئی۔" ثانیہ کا دل اس لمحے بہت تیزی سے دھڑک رہا تھا' تبھی وہ بولیں۔

"اللہ جانے پتر! کسی سے اس موضوع پر بات ہی نہیں کرتا وہ خیر تُو چھوڑ اسے' جلدی سے اٹھ کر تیاری کر لے۔ وہ بس گاڑی لے کر آتا ہی ہوگا۔"

"مجھے شہر نہیں جانا پلیز۔"

"تنگ نہ کرنا ثانیہ! تُو جانتی ہے میرا وہاں جانا ضروری ہے مگر تجھے اس حال میں' میں یہاں چھوڑ کر نہیں جا سکتی۔"

"کچھ نہیں ہوتا دادو! میں رہ لوں گی۔"

”نہیں تُو اٹھ کر تیاری کر بس' اگر دل نہ لگے تو میرے ساتھ ہی چلی آنا۔“ دادو کسی صورت اسے رعایت دینے کی پوزیشن میں نہیں تھیں وہ سر ہلا کر پلکیں موند گئی' دل کو بھلا اب کہاں لگنا تھا؟

❁......❁......❁

دل کا دیا جلایا میں نے
دل کا دیا جلایا
تجھ کو کہیں نہ پایا میں نے
تجھ کو کہیں نہ پایا

نسیم بیگم کی آواز بہت مدھم سروں میں گونج رہی تھی۔ ثانیہ عباس جو گاڑی کی پچھلی سیٹ پر بیٹھی تھی' بے کل ہو کر گاڑی کے باہر کے مناظر میں کھو گئی۔ اسٹیئرنگ وہیل پر جمے زائر ملک کے خوب صورت ہاتھ اسے بہت کچھ یاد دلا رہے تھے۔

”میں مانتا ہوں تم نے دل سے مجھے اپنا شوہر تسلیم نہیں کیا' میرے جیسا آوارہ ناکام شخص تم جیسی پیاری لڑکی کے قابل بھی نہیں' سوائے شکل صورت کے اور ہے ہی کیا میرے پاس؟ مگر پھر بھی یہ حقیقت ہے ثانی! میرے دل میں تمہارے لیے بہت جگہ ہے شاید سائرہ افضل سے بھی زیادہ۔“ اس کی آنکھیں کب بھر آئیں اسے پتا ہی نہ چل سکا۔ اگلے ہی پل زائر کی جگہ اس کی ماں نے لے لی تھی۔

”بہت غصے میں ہے زائر! گالیاں دے رہا تھا تمہیں' اسے لگتا ہے جیسے تم اس کے بچوں کو لے کر مفرور ہو گئی ہو۔ عجیب پینڈو شخص ہے پتا نہیں تمہیں کیا نظر آیا اس میں؟“

پچھلے پانچ سالوں میں یہ الفاظ بد دعا بن کر اس کا پیچھا کرتے رہے تھے۔ مفرور ہی تو ہو گئی تھی وہ اس کے بچوں کو لے کر' زائر کا ڈر اس نے پورا کر دیا تھا۔

”طلاق دے دی تھی اس نے تمہیں' بہت کوشش کی میں نے سمجھانے کی مگر اس نے میری ایک نہیں سنی' کہہ رہا تھا کہ ایک دو روز میں پیپرز بھی بھجوا دے گا۔“ سانپ بچھو بنے لفظوں کی بازگشت نے اس کے اندر جیسے سناٹے ڈال دیئے تھے۔ پچھلے پانچ برسوں میں کتنی بار اسے اس شخص کی ضرورت محسوس ہوئی تھی مگر وہ اس کے ساتھ نہیں تھا۔ نارسائی کے سارے عذاب اس نے تنہا جھیلے تھے۔

باپ کے ہوتے ہوئے پچھلے پانچ سالوں میں کتنی بار اس کے بچے اپنے باپ کے لیے ترسے تھے' وہ شخص صرف اس کے خوابوں کا نہیں اپنے بچوں کی معصوم حسرتوں کا بھی قاتل تھا۔ اپنی ڈھب سے جینا سکھا کر زندگی چھین لی تھی اس نے۔ ثانیہ کو لگا جیسے اس کے اندر آگ جل رہی ہو۔

زائر ملک سے نفرت کی آگ......

زائر ملک بیک ویو مرر سے بار بار اس پر نگاہ ڈال رہا تھا۔ ثانیہ نے جیسے نڈھال ہو کر سر سیٹ کی پشت سے ٹکا دیا۔

ہم تھے جن کی سہارے
وہ ہوئے نہ ہمارے
ڈوبی جب دل کی نیّاں
سامنے تھے کنارے
ہم تھے جن کے سہارے

کیسٹ ٹریک تبدیل ہوا تھا' ثانیہ کا دل زور سے دھڑک اٹھا اسے یہ گیت بہت زیادہ پسند تھا۔

ہے سبھی کچھ جہاں میں
دوستی ہے وفا ہے
اپنی ہی کم نصیبی
ہم کو نہ کچھ بھی ملا ہے
ہم تھے جن کے سہارے
وہ ہوئے نہ ہمارے
ڈوبی جب دل کی نیّاں
سامنے تھے کنارے

''دادی! میوزک بند کروائیں پلیز' میرے سر میں درد ہو رہا ہے۔'' اس سے مزید برداشت نہ ہوسکا تو بول اٹھی' زائر نے جیسے سنا ہی نہیں۔

کیا محبت کے وعدے
کیا وفا کے ارادے
ریت کی ہیں دیواریں
جو بھی چاہے گرادے
ہم تھے جن کے سہارے
وہ ہوئے نہ ہمارے
ڈوبی جب دل کی نیّاں
سامنے تھے کنارے

ایک ایک بول اس کے جذبات کی عکاسی کر رہا تھا۔ مگر ثانیہ عباس کے زخم جیسے پھر سے ہرے ہو گئے تھے' پچھلے پانچ سالوں میں سہی جانے والی ایک ایک تکلیف دل میں ناخن چبھونے لگی تھی۔

اسے یاد آرہا تھا جب اس نے وقت سے پہلے اپنے دونوں بچوں کو جنم دیا تھا تو اس وقت وہ کس اذیت میں تھی' اس احساس کے ساتھ کہ زائر نے اسے چھوڑ دیا ہے ہر لحہ سانس گھٹتی محسوس ہوتی تھی اسے پھر پاکستان سے انگلینڈ شفٹ ہونے کے بعد جب اس کے دونوں بچے بیمار پڑے تو انہیں تنہا سرد کمرے میں گود میں لیے ڈاکٹرز کی مایوسی دیکھتے ہوئے اس نے کتنی تکلیف سہی تھی۔ اس کا بس نہ چلتا تھا کہ کہیں سے زائر ملک اس کے سامنے آئے اور وہ اسے شوٹ کرڈالے۔

زائر نے دوبار میوزک آن نہیں کیا' پھر بھی درد سے پھٹتے سر کے ساتھ وہ کھڑکی سے باہر دیکھ رہی تھی جب اس کا سیل بج اٹھا۔

''السلام علیکم!'' نمبر دیکھ کر فوراً سے پیش تر اس نے کال پک کی۔

زائر نے گاڑی کی اسپیڈ دانستہ کم کردی۔

''جی اشعر میں ٹھیک ہوں' آپ کیسے ہیں اور بچوں کا کیا حال ہے؟'' بچوں کے ذکر پر زائر کا دل بہت تیزی سے دھڑکا تھا۔

''رئیلی......واؤ! یہ تو بہت خوشی کی بات ہے کب تک پہنچ رہے ہیں آپ؟''

''اچھا ٹھیک ہے آپ ائرپورٹ پہنچتے ہی مجھے انفارم کریں' میں اس وقت شہر کی طرف ہی جا رہی ہوں۔''

''ٹھیک ہے خدا حافظ۔'' کال کاٹتے ہی اس کے سر کا درد اڑن چھو ہو گیا تھا۔ زائر بیک ویو مرر سے اسے دیکھنے گیا۔

''اشعر کا فون تھا؟'' دادو نے پوچھا۔

''جی دادو! وہ بچوں کو لے کر پاکستان پہنچ رہا ہے' ابھی کچھ دیر میں۔''

''چلو یہ تو بہت اچھی بات ہے' بیوی بھی ساتھ آ رہی ہے اس کی؟''

''نہیں...... بیوی کو چھوڑ چکا ہے وہ۔''

''ہائے! میری سمجھ میں نہیں آتا یہ آج کل کے مردوں کو ہو کیا گیا ہے' ذرا ذرا سی بات پر بیویوں کو چھوڑ دیتے ہیں۔ ایک ہمارا زمانہ تھا' شہزادے جیسے لڑکے کو بھی ماں باپ کسی بھنگن سے بیاہ دیتے تو ساری زندگی اسی کے پہلو سے بندھا رہتا تھا آج کل کے لڑکوں نے تو مانو سچ مچ عورت کو پیر کی جوتی سمجھ لیا ہے جب دل چاہا بدل لی۔''

''صحیح کہہ رہی ہیں آپ! میں پہلے ائرپورٹ جاؤں گی دادو! اشعر کی فلائٹ بس پہنچنے ہی والی ہے۔''

اشعر حسین اور اپنے بچوں کے معاملے میں وہ جتنی بے تاب دکھائی دے رہی تھی۔ زائر کا دل اتنا ہی بے کل ہو کر رہ گیا تھا تبھی چوہدرانی اس سے مخاطب ہوئی تھیں۔

''زائر پتر! گاڑی پہلے ائرپورٹ کی طرف موڑ لو۔''

''جی اچھا!''

وہ ڈسٹرب ہو کر رہ گیا تھا مگر پھر بھی اسے خود پر ضبط تھا۔ فلائٹ پورے ڈیڑھ گھنٹہ لیٹ تھی مگر پھر بھی اس نے بڑے حوصلے سے انتظار کیا...... تاہم جس وقت اشعر حسین کے ساتھ چلتے اسے اپنے دونوں بچے دکھائی دیئے اس کا دل جیسے قابو سے باہر ہو گیا۔ ثانیہ نے لپک کر دونوں کو گلے سے لگا کر چوما تھا پھر وہ اشعر حسین کے گلے لگی تھی اور یہیں اس کا خون ابلا تھا' ثانیہ عباس سے ترکِ تعلق کے باوجود وہ اسے یہ حد پار کرنے کی اجازت نہیں دے سکتا تھا تبھی پلٹ کر گاڑی کے بونٹ کو زوردار ٹھوکر ماری تھی۔ کیا یہی تھا وہ شخص جس کے لیے اس نے اس کی رفاقت کو ٹھوکر ماری تھی؟ اس کی وفا' اس کی عزت' اس کی جانثاری سب کو داؤ پر لگا کر چلی گئی تھی؟ کیا اسی شخص کے لیے اس نے اس کے اعتبار کا خون کیا تھا؟

کتنے سوال تھے جو کانٹوں کی طرح چبھ رہے تھے مگر وہ رخ موڑے کھڑا رہا۔ ثانیہ اب بچوں کو گاڑی کی طرف لا رہی تھی۔

''یہ کون ہے؟'' اشعر حسین نے گاڑی کے قریب پہنچ کر اس سے پوچھا تھا جب وہ اچٹتی سی ایک نظر اس پر ڈالتے ہوئے بولی۔

''ڈرائیور ہے' آپ بیٹھیں گاڑی میں پلیز۔''

کوئی نشتر تھا جو زائر ملک کے دل میں پیوست ہوا تھا بھلا اس سے زیادہ اس کی ذات کی حقارت کیا ہونی تھی؟ اس کے بچے اس کی آنکھوں کے سامنے تھے مگر وہ انہیں چوم نہیں سکتا تھا بھلا اس سے زیادہ زندگی کی بے بسی کیا ہونی تھی؟

اشعر حسین اس کے ساتھ فرنٹ سیٹ پر بیٹھا تھا جب کہ اس کے بچے پیچھے ثانیہ کے پاس تھے۔

''سوری دادو! میں اب آپ کے ساتھ کسی کے گھر نہیں رک سکوں گی' مجھے گاؤں جانا ہے' اشعر بھی تھکا ہوا ہے میں اپنے مہمان کو بے آرام نہیں کر سکتی۔''

''ہوں اب تو میرے لیے بھی رکنا مشکل ہو جائے گا۔ زائر پتر! گاڑی گاؤں کی طرف ہی موڑ لے' رشید (عذیر کی

دادی) سے میں خود ہی فون پر بات کرلوں گی۔'' ثانیہ سے کہتے ہوئے انہوں نے اگلے ہی پل زائر کو حکم صادر کیا تو وہ چپ چاپ گاڑی موڑ گیا۔

گاؤں پہنچ کر وہ ایک پل کے لیے بھی حویلی نہیں رکا تھا۔ اگلے روز صبح ہی صبح اسے پھر حویلی سے بلاوا آ گیا مگر اس کی طبیعت اتنی خراب تھی کہ اٹھ ہی نہ سکتا تھا۔ کل پوری رات اس کا وجود بخار میں جلا تھا' سائرہ نے دروازے سے ہی پیغامبر کو واپس بھجوا دیا۔

ثانیہ اشعر اور اپنے بچوں کے ساتھ ناشتہ کر رہی تھی جب ملازم نے آ کر زائر کی ناسازی طبیعت کا بتایا۔ دادو کا ہاتھ فوراً ناشتے سے رک گیا۔

''بُرا نہ منانا ثانیہ! مگر تجھے کل زائر کو ڈرائیور نہیں کہنا چاہیے تھا۔ بہت حساس بچہ ہے وہ بچپن سے جانتی ہوں اسے' ضرور اس نے یہی بات دل کو لگائی ہوگی۔''

''کیا مطلب دادو! ڈرائیور کو ڈرائیور نہ کہوں تو اور کیا کہوں؟ وہ میرا شوہر تو نہیں ہے جو اس کی عزت وتکریم کرتی' اتنا بھی سر نہ چڑھایا کریں ملازموں کو' پلیز۔''

''ملازم نہیں ہے وہ بیٹا بنا کر پالا ہے اسے میں نے۔''

''پالا ہوگا' میرے لیے وہ ایک ملازم ہی ہے اور بس۔'' آپ ہی آپ اس کے لہجے میں تلخی در آئی تھی۔ دادو دل مسوس کر رہ گئیں بلاشبہ زائر کے دونوں بچے بے حد خوب صورت تھے۔

اگلے روز انہیں زمینوں کی سیر کرنی تھی' بچے پاکستان آ کر بہت خوش تھے۔ زائر کاٹن کی چنوائی کروا رہا تھا' جب اس نے ثانیہ کو اشعر حسین اور اپنے بچوں کے ساتھ اسی طرف آتے ہوئے دیکھا۔

''مما! آپ نے کہا تھا ہمارے پاپا پاکستان میں رہتے ہیں' اب تو ہم پاکستان آ گئے ہیں آپ پاپا سے کہیے ناں وہ ہمیں آ کر مل لیں۔'' اس کی بیٹی کو اچانک یاد آیا تھا' عذیر ملازمین کو ہدایت دیتا وہیں ٹھٹک گیا۔

''جی مما! مجھے بھی پاپا سے ملنا ہے۔'' بیٹے نے بھی لب کھولنے ضروری سمجھا۔ وہ ٹپٹا کر رہ گئی۔

''پاپا ابھی آپ لوگوں سے نہیں مل سکتے مانو! چلو آپ بھائی کا ہاتھ پکڑو' مما آپ کو بہت مزے مزے کی چیزیں دکھانے والی ہیں۔''

''نہیں، مجھے چیزیں نہیں دیکھنی پاپا سے ملنا ہے۔'' اس کی بیٹی ضد کر رہی تھی۔

ذرا سے غصے میں آتے ہوئے اس نے اپنی بیٹی کو ڈانٹا تھا' وہ منہ بسور کر رہ گئی۔ کچھ ہی فاصلے پر مالٹوں کا باغ تھا' میٹھے امرود بھی پکے ہوئے تھے۔ اس کا بیٹا مالٹوں کو دیکھتے ہی ان کی طرف لپکا۔ اشعر حسین کے لبوں پر مسکراہٹ بکھر گئی۔

''دیکھا ثانیہ! ان بچوں کے خون میں بھی اپنے دیہاتی باپ کا ہی اثر ہے' دیکھو کیسے پیڑوں کو دیکھتے ہی ان کی طرف لپکے ہیں۔''

''ہوں...... یہ تو ہے۔'' شرمندہ سے انداز میں سر ہلاتے ہوئے اس نے ایک نظر اپنے دونوں بچوں پر ڈالی۔ وہ دونوں بہت خوشی سے پیڑ پر چڑھنے کی کوشش کر رہے تھے۔ ثانیہ کا دل چاہا کہ انہیں ڈانٹ دے مگر پھر کسی خیال کے تحت اس نے اپنی نظر ان کے اوپر سے ہٹالی۔

''تم نے بتایا نہیں عائزہ (بیوی) کو طلاق کیوں دی؟''

''بس یار شک بہت کرتی تھی' جینا حرام کر کے رکھ دیا تھا اس نے میرا' تمہیں کال کرنے پر بھی پابندی تھی اسی لیے روز روز کے جھگڑوں سے تنگ آ کر جان چھڑالی میں نے۔''

''اور بچے......؟''

''بچوں کو وہ اپنے ساتھ لے گئی ہے مگر جلد ہی کورٹ کے ذریعے انہیں واپس لے لوں گا۔''

''آگے کیا پلان ہوگا؟''

''اللہ مالک ہے' میں نے کیا پلان کرنا ہے۔''

سبز ٹہنی جو اس کے ہاتھ میں تھی بے نیازی سے پرے پھینکتے ہوئے وہ مسکرایا تبھی ثانیہ کے بیٹے کا پاؤں پیڑ کی چھال سے پھسلا اور وہ دھڑم سے زمین پر آ گرا زائر جو اسی طرف دیکھ رہا تھا' سارا کچھ چھوڑ کر فوراً اپنے بیٹے کی طرف لپکا مگر تب تک بچے کا سر پھٹ چکا تھا اور وہ بُری طرح رونا شروع کر چکا تھا۔

''دور رہو میرے بچوں سے۔''

بنا بیٹے کی چوٹ کی پروا کیے وہ دور سے ہی دھاڑی تھی جب کہ اشعر حسین بھی حیرانی سے اسے دیکھتا رہ گیا۔

❁......❁......❁

وہ اپنا مختصر سا سامان سمیٹ رہی تھی جب عذیر کمرے میں آیا تو حور عین اسے دیکھ کر پلٹی۔

''کیا کر رہی ہیں؟'' پریشان سا وہ پوچھ رہا تھا جب وہ بولی۔

''کچھ نہیں' یہاں سے کوچ کی تیاری کر رہی ہوں۔''

''کیوں؟''

''کیونکہ میرا اب مزید اس گھر میں قیام ممکن نہیں۔''

''کہاں جائیں گی یہاں سے نکل کر؟''

''پتا نہیں' جہاں نصیب لے گیا۔'' وہ اس کی طرف دیکھنے سے گریز کر رہی تھی۔ عذیر گہری سانس بھر کر رہ گیا۔

''کوئی دور نزدیک کا رشتہ دار ہے آپ کا۔''

''نہیں' ہوتا تو یہاں کیوں آتی؟''

''پھر بھی آپ یہاں سے جانا چاہتی ہیں؟''

''تو کیا کروں؟ دھوکہ دیتی رہوں ان لوگوں کو؟''

''جس دھوکے میں سب کی بہتری ہو وہ دھوکہ' دھوکہ نہیں مصلحت ہوتی ہے۔''

''آپ کی نظر میں ہوتی ہوگی' میں نے زندگی میں کبھی کسی سے جھوٹ نہیں بولا کل کو جب دادو پر میری اصلیت کھلے گی تو وہ کیا سمجھیں گی مجھے؟ ایک قطعی اجنبی کنواری لڑکی ان کی دانست میں ان کے جوان پوتے کے کمرے میں اکیلی سوتی ہے۔ میں کیسے ان کی ان نگاہوں کا سامنا کروں گی جو مجھے اندر سے چیر کر رکھ دیں گی' ساری زندگی وہ پھر کسی لڑکی کا اعتبار نہیں کر سکیں گی' میں ان کے اعتبار کو توڑنا نہیں چاہتی۔''

''اور آپ کے یوں چپ چاپ چلے جانے سے جو میرا اعتبار ٹوٹے گا ان کی نظر میں وہ؟ کیا بتاؤں گا میں انہیں کہ کون تھیں آپ اور کیوں چلی گئیں؟ کتنے سوال اٹھیں گے میری ذات پر' کس کس کا جواب دوں گا میں؟''

''میرے پاس اس کے سوا اور کوئی راستہ نہیں ہے عذیر صاحب!''

''راستے نکل آتے ہیں اگر انسان ٹھنڈے دل و دماغ سے بیٹھ کر نکالنے کی کوشش کرے تو' ہمیشہ فرار ہی مسئلے کا حل نہیں ہوتا۔''

''مگر......''

بے چین ہو کر کچھ کہنے کے لیے اس نے سر اٹھایا تھا تبھی اس کی نظر کمرے کی دہلیز پر کھڑی دادو پر پڑی اور وہ جیسے وہیں فریز ہو کر رہ گئی۔

❁....❁....❁

جب درد پرانے ہو بیٹھے
جب یاد کا جگنو راکھ ہوا
جب آنکھ میں آنسو برف ہوئے
جب زخم سے دل مانوس ہوا
تب مجھ پر کھلا میں زندہ ہوں
پھر دل کو دھڑکنا یاد آیا
جب کرب کی لمبی راہوں میں احساس کے بال سفید ہوئے
جب آنکھیں بے سیلاب ہوئیں
جب چاند چڑھا بے دردی کا
جب ریت پر لکھی یادوں کو بے مہر ہوا نے چھین لیا
جب یاد رُتیں بیدار ہوئیں
تب مجھ پر کھلا میں زندہ ہوں
پھر دل کو دھڑکنا یاد آیا
پھر وقت نے کچھ انگڑائی لی
پھر سوچ کی قبر سے دھول اڑی
پھر پیاس کا برزخ بھول گیا
اک ہجر سے کیا آزاد ہوئے سو ہجر نئے ایجاد ہوئے
پھر اشک میں دریا قید ہوا
پھر دھڑکن میں بھونچال پڑے
پھر عشق کا جوگی گلیوں میں' تقدیر کا سانپ اٹھا لایا
پھر عشق کا جنگل سبز ہوا پھر زلف کے تیور شام ہوئے
اس شام میں پھر ماہتاب چڑھا
پھر ہونٹ کی لغزش گیت بنی
پھر درد زلیخا بن بیٹھا' پھر کرب کا قرب جوان ہوا
پھر مجھ پر کھلا میں زندہ ہوں
پھر دل کو دھڑکنا یاد آیا

''دادی ماں......'' حورعین کی پھٹی پھٹی آنکھوں کی طرف دیکھتے ہوئے عذیر نے بھی پلٹ کر دیکھا اور پھر جیسے اس کے پیروں تلے بھی زمین کھسک گئی' اسی پل دادی ماں اندر آئی تھیں۔

''کیا ہوا' تم دونوں کے چہرے کے رنگ تو یوں اڑ گئے جیسے دادی کے بجائے کوئی بھوت دیکھ لیا ہو۔'' وہ مسکرا رہی

تھیں۔ عذیر کی جان میں جان آئی۔

''کیا راز و نیاز کی باتیں ہو رہی ہیں دادی سے چھپ کر؟''

''ک...... کچھ نہیں دادو! شادی کی تقریب سے متعلق ہی ڈسکس کر رہے تھے۔''

''ہوں...... اچھی بات ہے' وہ میں یہ بتانے آئی تھی کہ تمہاری تائی ماں اور ثانیہ ابھی نہیں آ رہے۔ ثانیہ کے بچے آئے ہیں انگلینڈ سے' اس لیے فی الحال معذرت کر لی انہوں نے' سمیر کے پاس فون آیا تھا تو میں چاہ رہی تھی' اگلی اتوار کو تقریب رکھ لیتے ہیں' کچھ ہماری بھی تیاری ہو جائے گی۔''

''جی ٹھیک ہے' میں بھی یہی چاہ رہا تھا۔''

''ہوں...... چلو نپٹا لو سارے کام ایک ہفتے میں کیونکہ اس کے بعد مزید ایک دن کی رعایت بھی نہیں ملے گی تمہیں۔'' عذیر کی تسلی پر اسے وارن کرتے ہوئے وہ سرسری سی نگاہ حورعین کے جھکے سر پر ڈالنے کے بعد واپس پلٹ گئیں۔ عذیر نے بے ساختہ گہری سانس لی۔

''شکر دادو نے کچھ نہیں سنا۔'' اب وہ براہِ راست اسے دیکھ رہا تھا' وہ رخ پھیر گئی۔

''ہاں تو میں کہہ رہا تھا کہ فرار ہر مسئلے کا حل نہیں ہوتا فی الوقت آپ کا کوئی ٹھکانہ نہیں ہے۔ کوئی عزیز رشتے دار بھی نہیں' میں چاہوں تو آپ کی مدد کے لیے آپ کو کہیں بھی اچھا سا فلیٹ لے کر دے سکتا ہوں مگر...... تنہا لڑکی کا ہمارے معاشرے میں اس وقت جو حال ہے یقیناً اس سے بھی آپ بخوبی واقف ہوں گی' اس لیے آپ کی حفاظت کے معاملے میں' میں کسی قسم کا رسک نہیں لے سکتا۔'' وہ شاید تمہید باندھ رہا تھا۔ حورعین اپنے آنسو ضبط کرتی رہی۔

''میں آپ کی عزت کرتا ہوں حورعین! جس طرح سے آپ نے میرے گھر والوں کا اعتبار اور دل جیتا ہے' میرے دل میں آپ کی قدر بہت بڑھ گئی ہے' خدا شاہد ہے کہ میں کسی بھی طور سے آپ کا نقصان نہیں چاہتا۔''

''میں جانتی ہوں مگر آپ یہ سب کیوں کہہ رہے ہیں؟''

''میں آپ کے سامنے کچھ آپشن رکھنا چاہتا ہوں اس لیے۔''

''کیسے آپشن؟''

''دیکھیں حورعین! آپ میری منکوحہ کی حیثیت سے اس گھر میں آئیں' دادی ماں کی نظر میں آپ میری عزت ہیں۔ میں ان کی یہ غلط فہمی دور کرنا چاہتا تھا مگر آپ کے آنسو دیکھ کر اور آپ کی مجبوریاں جان کر میں نے اپنا ارادہ بدل لیا۔ اب مسئلہ یہ ہے کہ نہ آپ یہاں رہنا چاہتی ہیں نہ یہاں سے نکل کر کہیں اور محفوظ رہ سکتی ہیں' ایسے میں صرف یہی ایک راستہ رہ جاتا ہے کہ میں آپ سے فرضی نکاح کر لوں' اس وقت تک کے لیے جب تک آپ کے گھر اور فیملی کا مسئلہ حل نہیں ہو جاتا پھر اس کے بعد جب آپ چاہیں گی میں آپ کو آزاد کر دوں گا' آپ اچھی طرح سے سوچ کر بتا دیجیے گا مجھے۔'' ٹراؤزر کی پاکٹس میں ہاتھ ڈالے اس نے اسے اپنے فیصلے سے آگاہ کیا۔ حورعین کو لگا جیسے اس کے پاؤں تلے زمین کھینچ لی گئی ہو' پھٹی پھٹی نگاہوں سے عذیر کی طرف دیکھتے ہوئے اس نے آہستہ سے نفی میں سر ہلایا مگر عذیر نے نہیں دیکھا اپنی بات مکمل کرنے کے بعد وہ واپس پلٹ گیا تھا۔ وہ ہکا بکا سی دیوار کے ساتھ لگی ڈھیلے جسم کے ساتھ نیچے زمین پر بیٹھتی چلی گئی تھی۔ ایاد عبدالحادی کی جگہ کسی اور کو دینا موت کے مترادف تھا اس کے لیے' تبھی اس کی سسکیاں نکل رہی تھیں۔

''نہیں...... میں ایسا نہیں کر سکتی' کبھی بھی نہیں...... زندگی کی آخری سانس تک نہیں۔'' زور زور سے سر دائیں بائیں مارتے ہوئے وہ تڑپ رہی تھی مگر وہاں اس کی تڑپ کا نظارہ کرنے والا کوئی نہیں تھا۔

"حورعین آپی!" دائیں بازو پر سر رکھے وہ اپنے بستر پر اوندھے منہ پڑی رو رہی تھی جب عمیر ہلکی سی دستک کے ساتھ اس کے کمرے میں آیا۔ حورعین کو نہ چاہتے ہوئے بھی آنکھوں سے بازو ہٹانے پڑے۔

"اتنا اندھیرا کر رکھا ہے کمرے میں، طبیعت تو ٹھیک ہے ناں آپ کی؟" کمرے کی لائٹ آن کرتے ہوئے وہ قریب چلا آیا، وہ اٹھ کر بیٹھ گئی۔

"ہوں......بس سر میں درد ہے۔"

"تو بتایا کیوں نہیں، یقیناً بخار بھی ہوگا ہے ناں؟"

"ہوں......"

"اُف! کاش میں آپ سے بڑا ہوتا تو اس وقت خوب ڈانٹتا آپ کو، حد ہوگئی بے گانے پن کی۔" سر جھٹکتے ہوئے وہ قدرے خفا ہوا۔ حورعین نے آہستہ سے آنسو پونچھ لیے، تبھی وہ قریب آ کر بیٹھ گیا۔

"میں نے سنا ہے آپ یہ گھر چھوڑ کر جا رہی ہیں......کیا یہ بات سچ ہے؟"

"ہوں......" اس نے اثبات میں سر ہلا دیا۔

"پر کیوں؟" سب جانتے ہوئے بھی وہ انجان بن رہا تھا، حورعین کی آنکھیں پھر نم ہوگئیں۔

"میرا اب اس گھر میں قیام ممکن نہیں رہا، دادی ماں میری اور عذیر کی شادی کی تقریب منعقد کرنا چاہتی ہیں جب کہ میری زندگی میں اس کی قطعی گنجائش نہیں ہے۔"

"عذیر بھائی کا کیا کہنا ہے؟"

"کچھ نہیں، وہ فرضی نکاح کا کہہ رہے تھے مگر میں ایسا نہیں کر سکتی۔"

"پھر یہاں سے آپ جائیں گی کہاں آخر؟"

"پتا نہیں، جہاں میری تقدیر لے جائے۔"

"ہوں، آپ اپنی مرضی کی مالک ہیں آپی! میرا کوئی حق نہیں بنتا کہ میں آپ پر اپنی کوئی رائے مسلط کروں مگر میں نے آپ کو بہن کہا ہے خدا شاہد ہے کہ دل سے سگی بہنوں کی طرح سمجھا ہے، میں قطعی آپ کا کوئی نقصان نہیں چاہوں گا۔ دادی ماں ہماری بزرگ ہیں، بہت اچھی طرح سے ہم ان کی سوچ اور ان کے مزاج کو جانتے ہیں۔ ان کو اگر ذرا سی بھنک بھی پڑ گئی کہ آپ اور عذیر بھائی کا نکاح نہیں ہوا ہے تو سارے گھر میں بھونچال آ جائے گا، ہم اس عمر میں انہیں تکلیف پہنچانا نہیں چاہتے اس لیے پلیز آپ عذیر بھائی کی بات مان لیں وہ بہت اچھے ہیں، آپ کو ان کی طرف سے کبھی کوئی نقصان نہیں پہنچے گا۔"

"اس میں کوئی شک نہیں کہ عذیر بہت اچھے ہیں مگر......"

"اگر مگر کو چھوڑیں آپی! پلیز......آپ دیکھیں ناں عذیر بھائی بھی تو کسی سلمٰی نام کی لڑکی میں انٹرسٹڈ ہیں، خود سوچیں وہ بھی تو آپ کے لیے یہ سب کر رہے ہیں ناں......پھر تھوڑے سے دنوں کی تو بات ہے، جب حالات ٹھیک ہو جائیں پھر آپ چلی جائیے گا تب میں خود دادو کو سب کچھ سچ سچ بتا دوں گا پلیز......" وہ اس کا سچا خیر خواہ تھا، حورعین الجھن بھری نگاہوں سے اسے دیکھتی رخ پھیر گئی۔ اس کے آنسو یوں بہہ رہے تھے جیسے آنکھوں میں سیلاب امڈ آیا ہو، عمیر کچھ دیر اس کے بہتے ہوئے آنسوؤں کو دیکھنے کے بعد اٹھ کھڑا ہوا۔

"چلتا ہوں آپی! امید ہے آپ میری بات کا مان رکھیں گی۔" وہ بھی شاید عذیر کی طرح مجبور تھا۔

حورعین کے آنسو اور بھی شدت سے بہنے لگے۔ زندگی کبھی کسی ایسے مقام پر بھی لے آئے گی اس نے سوچا بھی نا تھا۔

۞......۞......۞

جیل بگرام سے راتوں رات بے ہوشی کی حالت میں اسے عراق میں قائم ''جیل ابوغریب'' میں منتقل کر دیا گیا تھا' کئی گھنٹے بے ہوش رہنے کے بعد جس وقت اس کی آنکھ کھلی کوئی انتہائی لاچاری اور بے بسی کے ساتھ چلّا رہا تھا۔ وہ کرنٹ کھا کر بیدار ہوئی چھوٹی سی تنگ کوٹھڑی جہاں وہ بے ہوش پڑی ہوئی تھی۔ اس کے قریب ہی بلیک یونیفارم میں ملبوس امریکی فوجی ایک چھوٹی سی معصوم بچی کو اپنی درندگی کا نشانہ بنا رہے تھے جب کہ اس معصوم عراقی بچی کا بھائی بھی قریب ہی کال کوٹھڑی میں بند تھا مگر وہ کچھ نہ کر سکتا تھا۔ بچی کے چلّانے پر اس کا بھائی کوٹھڑی کی آہنی سلاخوں کے ساتھ سر مارتا تو اس پر اور بھی تشدد کیا جاتا' وہ یہ منظر دیکھ کر دنگ رہ گئی تھی۔ وہ ملک جس کا یہ کہنا تھا کہ اس نے افغانستان اور عراق پر قبضہ وہاں عوام کی خوش حالی اور جمہوریت کے قیام کے لیے کیا ہے' اسی ملک کی بے رحم افواج کے افسران کے ہاتھوں جس طرح سے مختلف مسلم ممالک کے باشندوں پر وحشیانہ تشدد اور عزتِ نفس کی پامالی ہو رہی تھی' حورعین دیکھتی رہ گئی۔

ساری دنیا میں امن کے قیام کا شور مچانے والے ملک کا اپنا اصل چہرہ کیا تھا؟ چھپے ہوئے عقوبت خانوں کی حقیقت اور کہانیاں کیا تھیں؟ امریکہ اگر امن کا خواہاں تھا تو کن کے لیے؟ برطانیہ جمہوریت چاہتا تھا تو کن کے لیے؟ وہ چیخنا چاہتی تھی تبھی کسی نے اس کے منہ پر ہاتھ رکھ کر اسے پیچھے دھکیل دیا۔

''کیا کر رہی ہو؟ کیا تمہیں نہیں پتا یہاں چیخنے والوں کے ساتھ کیا کیا جاتا ہے؟''

وہ کوئی عراقی عورت تھی' عورت کیا اسی کی طرح ایک نوعمر لڑکی تھی' جس کی دائیں آنکھ پر گہرے زخم کا نشان تھا اور ایک ٹانگ بھی ٹوٹی ہوئی تھی' حورعین ناسمجھی سے اسے دیکھتی رہ گئی تبھی وہ بولی۔

''میرا نام ہدیٰ العزادی ہے' میں پچھلے پانچ سال سے یہیں قید ہوں۔ پانچ سال پہلے ہمارے ایک مخالف رشتہ دار نے' امریکی فوجیوں سے وفاداری نبھاتے ہوئے انہیں یہ رپورٹ پہنچائی کہ ہم مجاہدین کے حامی اور عراق پر امریکہ کے قبضے کے خلاف ہیں اسی رپورٹ کے پس منظر میں امریکی فوج نے میرے بھائی علی کو گرفتار کر کے یہاں قید کر دیا۔ مجھے اس بات کا پتا چلا تو میں اپنے چھوٹے بھائی معتز کے ساتھ شہر میں قائم امریکی چھاؤنی میں چلی گئی تاکہ اپنے معصوم بھائی کا پتا کر سکوں مگر وہاں موجود کیپٹن نے میرے استفسار پر ٹال مٹول سے کام لیتے ہوئے مجھے دوبارہ آنے کا کہہ کر واپس بھجوا دیا۔ کرسمس کی رات میں دوبارہ اپنے بھائی کا پتا کرنے آئی تو اسی افسر نے باتوں ہی باتوں میں اچانک یہ کہہ کر کہ ہم بھی ان کی قید میں ہیں مجھے حیران کر دیا۔ علی کے بعد مجھے اور میرے دوسرے بھائی معتز کو بھی قید کر دیا گیا۔ ابتدائی تین دن اور تین راتیں بنا کسی جرم کے ہم دونوں بہن بھائیوں کو بدترین تشدد کا نشانہ بنایا گیا۔ چوتھے روز علی کی خون آلود لاش ہمارے قدموں میں لا کر پھینک دی گئی۔ بھائی کی خون میں لت پت لاش دیکھنے کے بعد میں بے ہوش ہو گئی تھی۔ اگلے دن ہوش میں آئی تو علی کی لاش کے ساتھ معتز بھی غائب تھا اور میرے ہاتھ میری پشت پر بندھے ہوئے تھے میں رو رہی تھی اور بُری طرح سے چلّا رہی تھی۔ چیخ چیخ کر میرا گلا دُکھنے لگا تھا مگر وہاں کوئی نہیں آیا' اگلے روز وہ لوگ مجھے وہاں سے نکال کر ایک اور عقوبت خانے میں لے گئے جہاں ایک مرتبہ پھر مجھے ذہنی اور جسمانی ٹارچر کیا گیا' مختلف افسران آ آ کر مجھ سے مجاہدین کے بارے میں پوچھتے رہے اور میری لاعلمی پر مجھے تشدد کا نشانہ بناتے رہے۔ جب میں بے ہوش ہونے کے قریب ہو گئی تو ان لوگوں نے میرا منہ دیوار کی طرف کر کے مجھے کھڑا کر دیا' اس وقت میں اپنے پیچھے بہت سے قیدیوں کی چیخ و پکار سن رہی تھی جو تشدد کی تاب نہ لا کر آہ و بکا کر رہے تھے میرے بھائی معتز کی آواز ان میں نمایاں تھی۔ میرے بھائی پر وحشیانہ تشدد ہو رہا تھا اور اس سے بہیمانہ انداز میں تفتیش کی جا رہی تھی وہ لوگ اس سے کہہ

رہے تھے کہ تم مجاہدین کو امریکیوں کے قتل کے لیے اموال فراہم کرتے ہو' معتز نے کہا یہ جھوٹ ہے جس پر اسے اور مارا گیا۔ میں بارہ گھنٹے ایک ہی پوزیشن میں دیوار کی طرف منہ کر کے کھڑی رہی' آدھی رات کے وقت انہوں نے مجھے کسی اور کوٹھڑی میں ڈال دیا' جس کے اوپر چھت نہ تھی...... رات بھر آسمان سے موسلا دھار بارش برستی رہی اور میں اپنے گھر والوں سے دور' زخموں سے چُور وہاں بے بسی سے پڑی سسکتی رہی۔ اگلے روز وہ لوگ معتز کی لاش بھی پھینک گئے' تب سے اب تک میں نہیں چیخی پتھر کا مجسمہ دیکھا ہے تم نے کبھی' یہاں چیخنے والوں کو پتھر کا مجسمہ بنا دیتے ہیں یہ لوگ۔'' وہ باتیں جو اس نے مختلف رسالوں اور کتابوں میں پڑھی تھیں حقیقت کا روپ دھار کر اس کے سامنے آ کھڑی ہوئی تھیں۔

حورعین کا جسم کپکپا اٹھا' اس کے ذہن میں دھماکے ہونے لگے۔

''صدام حسین کے بارے میں کہا گیا تھا کہ اس نے اپنی عوام کا جینا دوبھر کیا ہوا تھا۔ امریکہ بھی ویسا ہی ہے بلکہ اس سے بڑھ کے ثابت ہوا تھا پھر جمہوریت کہاں رہ گئی تھی؟'' ہدیٰ عبدالغرادی کے زخمی چہرے کی طرف دیکھتی وہ نیچے زمین پر بیٹھتی چلی گئی۔ جانے اس کے ساتھ کیا ہونے والا تھا۔ ہدیٰ بھی اس کے ساتھ بیٹھ گئی تبھی اس نے پوچھا تھا۔

''پانچ سال کے بعد بھی تشدد ہو رہا ہے آپ پر؟''

''ہوں! عورت ہو یا مرد' گناہ گار ہو یا بے گناہ' یہ لوگ تفتیش کے دوران تیز روشنیوں اور شدید گرمی میں قیدیوں کی جلد جلا دیتے ہیں' یہاں تک کہ قیدی اپنا دماغی توازن کھو بیٹھتے ہیں اور اپنی جان ختم کرنے کی کوشش کرتے ہیں' میں تو یہ بھی نہیں کر سکتی۔'' ہدیٰ عبدالغرادی کی نگاہیں آنسوؤں سے بھری ہوئی تھیں۔

''پتا نہیں تم کس ملک سے آئی ہو مگر یہ طے ہے کہ یہ لوگ تمہارا بھی بہت بھیانک انجام کریں گے۔'' وہ اسے متنبہ کر رہی تھی' حورعین کی ریڑھ کی ہڈی میں سنسناہٹ دوڑ گئی۔

حورعین کو اپنا وجود سرد پڑتا ہوا محسوس ہو رہا تھا۔ ایک طرف بش تھا تو دوسری طرف صدر مشرف اور اقوام عالم کا یہ حال تھا کہ وہ بالکل خاموش تھی' سکوت کے اس جرم میں جانے کب تک دنیا کو مجرم بنے رہنا تھا' مصلحت کی چادر جانے کب تک تنی رہنی تھی' پتا نہیں کب تک مجبوریوں کے پردے کو لٹکے رہنا تھا؟

''عراق اور ابوغریب جیل کے علاوہ دنیا کے مختلف حصوں میں ''نامعلوم مقامات'' پر امریکی سی آئی اے کے متعدد ایسے عقوبت خانے قائم ہیں' جن سے دنیا کو ابھی تک آگاہی نہیں ہے اور شاید ہو بھی نہ سکے کیونکہ کہا جاتا ہے کہ ان عقوبت خانوں میں جانے والا کبھی واپس نہیں آتا۔ یہی وہ عقوبت خانے ہیں جنہیں عوام کی نظروں سے دور نامعلوم مقامات پر بنایا گیا ہے۔'' دیوار سے ٹیک لگائے ہدیٰ پلکیں موندے اسے بتا رہی تھی' حورعین نے بے ساختہ گردن موڑ کر اسے دیکھا۔

''بلیک سائٹس کی بات کر رہی ہیں آپ؟''

''ہوں۔''

''تمہیں پتا ہے ورلڈ ٹریڈ سینٹر کی تباہی کے بعد ہر سال 11 ستمبر کی رات کو کیا ہوتا ہے؟''

''کیا ہوتا ہے؟'' چونکہ ستمبر کا مہینہ ہی چل رہا تھا اس لیے وہ اس سوال کو نظر انداز نہیں کر سکی تھی۔ ہدیٰ نے اس کے سوال برائے سوال پر بے ساختہ گہری سانس بھرلی۔

''قیامت آتی ہے بے بس' نہتے' معصوم پاکستانی اور افغانی نوجوانوں کو عالم برزخ کی سیر کروائی جاتی ہے' تمام امریکی افواج کو اجازت ہوتی ہے کہ 11 ستمبر کی رات وہ قیدیوں سے جو چاہے سلوک کریں ان سے کوئی پوچھ گچھ نہیں ہوگی۔''

''پھر۔''

''پھر کیا...... نشے میں دھت یہ لوگ اتنا ظلم کرتے ہیں قیدیوں پر کہ وہ مر جاتے ہیں۔''

کتنی معلومات تھیں ہدی کے پاس' حورعین ٹکر ٹکر اسے دیکھتی رہ گئی۔

''ساری دنیا میں داڑھی والوں کو بدنام کرنے والے امریکی افسران' خود کیا ہیں اگر تم جان لو تو تمہیں خود اپنے انسان ہونے سے نفرت ہو جائے' جس طرح یہ خاردار چھڑیوں سے ہمارے جسموں کو چھید کر ان پر موم گراتے ہیں' بدترین تشدد کی مثالیں دنیا کے پلیٹ فارم پر لاتے ہیں' ماضی کا کوئی انصاف پسند مسلم حکمران ہوتا تو ضرور ان کا گریبان پکڑ کر ان سے انسانیت کی اس درجہ تذلیل کا حساب لیتا مگر افسوس...... ہم ایسے دور میں پیدا ہوئے جہاں ہمارے حکمران خود ہم پر کسی عذاب سے کم نہیں' کوئی نہیں آج جو ہمارے حقوق کی بات کرے' کوئی نہیں جو ہماری دادرسی کرے' ایک سینٹر میں چند سو مرنے والے افراد کا درد ساری دنیا کو نظر آتا ہے مگر اسی قوم کے ہاتھوں ان خفیہ عقوبت خانوں میں جانے کتنی ماؤں کے لعل بدترین وحشت کی بھینٹ چڑھتے ہیں کسی کو دکھائی نہیں دیتے۔ عالمی میڈیا بھی خاموش ہے کیونکہ جو کچھ 11 ستمبر کو ہوا وہ بڑا ظلم تھا مگر جو کچھ ان گمنام عقوبت خانوں میں ہو رہا ہے وہ ظلم نہیں ہے' وہ دہشت گردی نہیں ہے۔''

زخمی چہرے والی وہ مسلمان لڑکی اندر سے کتنی دکھی تھی حورعین اب جان پائی تھی۔

''ساری دنیا میں مسلمان مر رہے ہیں' کہیں یہودیوں کے ہاتھوں کہیں ہندوؤں کے ہاتھوں' کہیں بدھ مت کے مگھوں کے ہاتھوں' کہیں عیسائیوں کے ہاتھوں پھر بھی دنیا کے سکوت میں کہیں کوئی خلل نہیں پڑ رہا مگر اذیتوں کے ستائے انہی لوگوں کے ہاتھوں دنیا کے کسی بھی حصے میں اگر کہیں کسی غیر مسلم کی موت ہو جاتی ہے تو بھونچال آ جاتا ہے مسلم حکمران خود اپنے ہاتھوں سے اپنے بے گناہ شہریوں کو پکڑ پکڑ کر ان کے حوالے کرتے ہیں اور خوش ہوتے ہیں کہ ہم نے بڑی بہادری کا کارنامہ سر انجام دیا مگر کل اللہ ربّ العزت کے حضور روز محشر ان کے منہ دیکھنے والے ہوں گے' کیسی سیاہی ہوگی جو ان کے چہروں پر مل جائے گی۔'' اچانک وہ جذباتی ہوئی تو حورعین کی آنکھیں سر جاوید ہمدانی کا تصور کر کے آنسوؤں سے بھر آئیں۔

''ہم غیور اور جفاکش قوم ہیں مگر ان حکمرانوں کی غلامی نے ہمیں غیر قوم کے سامنے ذلیل و رسوا کر کے رکھ دیا ہے' صرف انہی کی وجہ سے لوگ ہمیں نفرت اور حقارت کی نظر سے دیکھتے ہیں۔''

کتنا غبار تھا جو بہادر قوم کی اس بیٹی کے اندر جمع تھا۔ حورعین بے چین سی اٹھ کھڑی ہوئی تبھی کچھ افسران اس طرف آئے تھے۔ آنے والے ان امریکی افسران میں ایک شخص ''ایاد عبدالحادی'' تھا۔

''ایاد عبدالحادی'' کا خاندان پیدائشی جنگجو تھا۔ اس کا مسلمان باپ پہاڑوں کا بیٹا کہلاتا تھا کیونکہ اس کا تعلق افغانی سر زمین سے تھا۔ اسلحہ چلانا اور اسلحے سے کھیلنا اس کے موروثی مشاغل میں شامل تھا۔ اس کا تعلق ان قبائل سے تھا جہاں نسل در نسل خاندانی دشمنیاں چلتی ہیں جہاں خون کا بدلا خون جواں مردی اور انصاف کا دوسرا نام سمجھا جاتا ہے۔ مختلف قبائل کے ساتھ لڑائیوں میں اپنے نوعمر بیٹوں کے ہاتھوں قتل کو جو اپنے لیے باعث فخر سمجھتے ہیں۔ دس سال کی عمر میں اس کے باپ نے پہلے انسانی قتل کی صورت دشمنی اور انتقام کا جو پودا لگایا وہ اس کے مرنے تک پھل پھول کر تناور درخت بن چکا تھا' اس کے باپ نے دو شادیاں کی تھیں' پہلی شادی سولہ سال کی عمر میں خاندانی رسم و رواج کے مطابق اپنے قبیلے کی لڑکی سے کی جب کہ دوسری شادی امریکہ میں قیام کے دوران ایک امریکی خاتون سے کی جو اپنے انگریز شوہر سے طلاق کے بعد بے راہ روی کی زندگی گزار رہی تھی۔ ایاد اسی عورت کے بطن سے پیدا ہوا اور وہیں امریکہ میں اس نے پرورش پائی تھی مگر اس کی رگوں میں اپنے باپ کا فولادی خون تھا۔ اس کی پیدائش کے کچھ عرصے بعد ایک لڑائی میں اس کے

باپ کی موت ہوگئی تھی تاہم اس نے اپنی ماں کی آنکھوں میں ہمیشہ اس شخص کے لیے آنسو دیکھے تھے۔ دو سال بعد ماں کی بھی موت ہوگئی تو وہ اپنی نانی کے پاس آ گیا' یہیں سے مسلمانوں کے خلاف اس کے دل میں نفرت نے جڑ پکڑی تھی' ایسی ایسی باتیں اس کے دل و دماغ میں مسلمانوں اور اس کے باپ کے خلاف اس کی نانی نے ڈال دیں کہ اسے لفظ مسلمان سے ہی نفرت ہوگئی تھی۔ اپنی اسکول' کالج اور یونیورسٹی لائف میں بھی اس نے کسی مسلمان طالب علم سے ضرورت کی حد تک بھی دعا سلام نہیں رکھی تھی۔

کتابوں میں اس نے پڑھا تھا کہ فتوحات اندلس کے وقت مسلمانوں نے اندلس کے خزانوں کو طب' حکمت' تعلیم اور دانائی سے بھر دیا تھا۔ صدیوں تک یہاں یونیورسٹیوں' تجربہ گاہوں اور دانش گاہوں میں مسلمان حکماء اور فلاسفرز کی لکھی ہوئی کتابیں پڑھائی جاتی رہیں تاہم وہاں کے پادری اور پوپ جاہل ہونا اپنے لیے باعث فخر سمجھتے تھے اگر کوئی شخص مسلمانوں سے متاثر ہو کر تعلیم حاصل کرنے کی کوشش کرتا تو کلیسا کے اربابِ اختیار اسے زندہ گاڑھ دیتے۔ واشنگٹن لائبریری کی کتابوں میں مسلمانوں کے عروج اور فتوحات کے ادوار میں غیر مسلموں کے ساتھ ان کے منصفانہ اور رحم دلی کے واقعات اسے اکثر الجھن میں مبتلا کر کے رکھ دیتے تھے' تنگ آ کر اس نے ایسی کتابوں کو پڑھنا چھوڑ دیا جن میں ذرا سی بھی مسلمانوں کے حق میں کوئی بات ہوتی تھی۔

تعلیم مکمل کرنے کے بعد اپنی نانی کی خواہش پر اس نے آرمی جوائن کی تھی' مسلمانوں پر ظلم و تشدد کے لیے آرمی کے اربابِ اختیار خاص طور پر اسے منتخب کرتے تھے اور اس نے کبھی انہیں مایوس نہیں کیا تھا' کتنی ہی ایسی خفیہ جیلیں تھیں جہاں وہ خدائی کر رہے تھے نہتے بے بس' بدتر حالات کے مارے مظلوم مسلمانوں کو چیونٹیوں کی طرح مسلنے کا اپنا ہی مزا تھا۔ اس کے افسران اس سے بہت خوش تھے' تبھی وہ ترقی پاتا گیا تھا اور اب اس کی ڈیوٹی بگرام جیل سے ابوغریب جیل میں لگ گئی تھی۔

شبرغان جیل میں ڈیوٹی کے دوران اپنے افسران کی ہدایت پر جو کچھ اس نے مسلمان قیدیوں کے ساتھ کیا تھا وہ اگر منظر عام پر آ جاتا تو یقیناً دنیا میں ایک خوف کی لہر ضرور دوڑ جاتی۔ بظاہر دہشت گرد طالبانوں کے ساتھ جو سلوک اس نے کیا تھا اگر کوئی دیکھ لیتا تو لفظ دہشت گردی کا صحیح مفہوم سمجھ میں آ جاتا۔ مسلمانوں سے شدید نفرت اس وقت دو چند ہو جاتی جب تھوڑے سے پیسوں کے لالچ میں ایک مسلمان دوسرے مسلمان کو پکڑوا دیتا۔ چند ڈالروں کے لیے مسلم ملک کا سربراہ گائے بھینسوں کی طرح اپنے ملک کے معزز شہریوں کو پکڑ پکڑ کر ان کے حوالے کرتا تب اپنی نانی کی کہی تمام باتیں اسے درست لگتی تھیں۔ داڑھی میں چھپا ہر مسلمان اسے اپنے باپ جیسا لگتا تھا جو اس کی نانی کے بقول اس کی ماں کو دھوکہ دے کر فرار ہو گیا تھا۔

امریکہ کے افغانستان پر حملے کے وقت جس طرح سے مقامی افغانیوں اور شمالی اتحاد والوں نے دولت کے لالچ میں ان کا ساتھ دیا اور اپنے ملک کے لاکھوں شہری ان کے ہاتھوں بے دردی سے مروائے' اسے اور گھن آنے لگی تھی چند پیسوں میں اپنا ایمان بیچنے والے وہ لوگ ذلت کی انتہا کو چھو گئے تھے' اسے ہنسی آتی تھی کہ کیا یہی وہ مسلمان تھے جسے ایک جسم اور ایک مٹھی کی مانند قرار دیا گیا تھا۔ عراق پر امریکی حملے کے وقت جن ممالک نے سب سے زیادہ اقتصادی' سیاسی اور اسٹریٹجک تعاون کیا وہ سب کے سب اسلامی ممالک تھے۔ عراق پر حملہ جن ممالک سے کیا گیا وہ بھی سب کے سب اسلامی ممالک تھے۔ عراق میں زخمی ہونے والے امریکی فوجیوں کو طبی امداد دینے کے لیے عراق میں آئے ہوئے میدانی فوجی ہسپتال میں ڈاکٹرز بھی سب کے سب اسلامی ممالک سے آئے ہوئے تھے جنہوں نے امریکی سرکشی سے زخمی ہونے والے عراقیوں کا علاج کرنے سے انکار کرتے ہوئے امریکی فوجیوں کو ان پر فوقیت دی۔ عراق میں زخمی

ہونے والے امریکی فوجیوں کے اخراجات اٹھانے والے بھی سب کے سب اسلامی ممالک تھے۔ یہی نہیں بلکہ 28 مئی 2004ء کو ایک عرب سفیر نے واشنگٹن میں عراق کو آزاد کرنے کے دوران زخمی و ہلاک ہونے والے امریکی فوجیوں کے لیے 3.5 ملین ڈالر قائم کردہ کمیٹی کی طرف سے بطور عطیہ دیئے اور اتنی ہی رقم امریکی فوجیوں کے اہل خانہ کو دینے کا اعلان کیا گیا جبکہ عراق جنگ میں قیدی بن کر رہائی پانے والی امریکی فوجی خاتون کو کویتی حکام نے دنیا کی سب سے مہنگی کار بطور تحفہ دی۔ پھر بھی وہ ایک جسم ایک بند مٹھی کی مانند قرار دیئے گئے تھے؟ اسے ہنسی آتی تھی۔

اکثر شراب کے نشے کے دوران وہ گھنٹوں اپنے باپ اور دیگر مسلمانوں کو گالیاں دیتا تھا' کیسے کیسے مظالم نہیں تھے جو اس نے اپنے زیر حراست قیدیوں پر کیے تھے اور اب وہ حورعین عبدالسمیع کے سامنے کھڑا تھا جس کے بارے میں اسے بتایا گیا تھا کہ وہ افغانستان میں طالبان کی حامی اور پاکستان میں امریکہ کی اور حکومت برطانیہ کی مخالف ہے اور لوگوں کے دلوں میں ان ممالک کے خلاف نفرت ابھارنے جیسے سنگین جرائم کی مرتکب ہو رہی ہے۔

دبلے پتلے سے نازک جسم کی اس خوب صورت لڑکی کے عزائم جان کر وہ ہنسا تھا' ٹارچر سیل کا لاک کھول کر جس وقت وہ اندر داخل ہوا' حورعین کی آنکھیں اسی پر جمی تھیں تبھی اس نے پوری طاقت سے اسے زوردار تھپڑ رسید کیا' حورعین منہ کے بل زمین پر جا پڑی جب کہ ہدی نے منہ پر ہاتھ رکھ کر اپنی چیخ کا گلہ گھونٹا تھا۔

''یو بچ...... ہمارا کھاتے ہو اور ہم ہی کو آنکھیں دکھاتے ہو' جس ملک کا ویزہ حاصل کرنے کے لیے تمہاری ایڑھیاں گھس جاتی ہیں اسی ملک سے نفرت کا اظہار کرتے ہو' منافقو...... پیسے کے لالچی ہو تم' خود اپنا ایمان اپنی ہتھیلیوں پر لیے پھرتے ہو اور قصوروار ہمیں ٹھہراتے ہو۔'' حورعین کے بال اپنی مٹھیوں میں جکڑتے ہوئے اس نے اسے زور سے دھکا دیا۔ حورعین کا سر سامنے والی دیوار سے جا ٹکرایا' شدید درد کے احساس نے بے اختیار اسے چلّانے پر مجبور کر دیا تھا۔ اگلے ہی پل اپنے ماتحت افسر کو اشاروں کی زبان میں کچھ سمجھانے کے بعد وہ سیل سے نکل گیا۔ ہدی پریشان سی حورعین کے سر سے بہتے خون کو دیکھ رہی تھی' پھر اسی نے آگے بڑھ کر اسے سنبھالا تھا۔ ایاد عبدالحادی کا ماتحت افسر بھی سیل سے نکل چکا تھا۔

حورعین چکراتے ہوئے زخمی سر کو پکڑتے وہیں دیوار سے ٹیک لگا کر بیٹھ گئی تھی۔

''وہ تم سے کیا کہہ رہا تھا؟'' ہدی چونکہ انگلش سے ناواقف تھی تبھی پریشان سی اس سے پوچھ رہی تھی' وہ کراہ کر رہ گئی۔

''کچھ نہیں...... ہم پاکستانیوں کو ہماری اوقات بتا رہا تھا۔''

''تت...... تم پاکستانی ہو؟'' ہدی کو حیرانی ہوئی تھی۔ وہ محض اثبات میں سر ہلا کر رہ گئی۔

''اوہ...... میں نے پچھلے دنوں سنا تھا تمہارے ملک کے صدر جنرل پرویز مشرف نے اپنے دورہ آسٹریلیا کے دوران دونوں ملکوں کے مابین دہشت گردی کو روکنے کی غرض سے خفیہ انفارمیشن کے تبادلے کے سمجھوتے پر دستخط کیے ہیں' جیسے ہی ان کا دورہ آسٹریلیا ختم ہوا ویسے ہی خفیہ ادارے ''آسٹریلیا سکیورٹی اینڈ انٹیلی جنس'' نے اسلامی گروپوں اور سرگرم لوگوں کے خلاف چھاپوں کا سلسلہ تیز کر دیا تھا۔ سڈنی اور میلبورن میں آباد مسلمانوں کی اکثریت نے ہمیشہ کسی بھی قسم کی دہشت گردی اور اس قسم کے منصوبوں کو بھرپور انداز میں رد کیا ہے مگر اس کے باوجود میلبورن میں مختلف گھروں پر چھاپے مارنے کے دوران جانے کتنے ہی مسلمانوں کو ان کے گھروں سے گرفتار کر کے نامعلوم مقام پر منتقل کر دیا گیا' آسٹریلیا میں ہر شہری کے بنیادی حقوق ہیں اور ان حقوق میں ذاتی معاملات کی مکمل آزادی ہے۔ ASIO کے پاس اگر ان چھاپوں اور گرفتاریوں کی جائز وجوہات اور ٹھوس شواہد موجود ہیں تو انہیں منظر عام پر لایا جائے ورنہ یہ کارروائیاں' عوام کو اعتماد میں لیے بغیر تعصب اور شبہ کی نگاہ سے دیکھی جائیں گی۔''

''ہوں...... مگر تعصب اور شبہ کی نگاہ سے دیکھے گا کون؟ بناء کسی وجہ کے پوری دنیا میں مسلمانوں کے بچوں' بوڑھوں' عورتوں تک کو بے دردی و بے رحمی سے مارا جارہا ہے۔ بدترین خون ریزی سے ان کی نسل کشی کی جارہی ہے مگر کسی کے پاس ان کے زخم دیکھنے کی فرصت نہیں ہے نہ امن کے قیام کے لیے ہر پل چیختے انسانی حقوق کی بڑی بڑی باتیں کرنے والوں کے پاس نہ امت مسلمہ کے پاس' جانے بے حسی کا یہ کیسا نشہ ہے جس کا اثر ٹوٹ ہی نہیں رہا۔''

سر سے بہتے خون سے دونوں ہاتھ رنگے اس نے نہایت دکھ سے ہدی کی طرف دیکھتے ہوئے کہا تھا تبھی ایک فوجی افسر وہاں چلا آیا۔

''چلو۔'' نہایت حقارت سے حورعین پر نگاہ ڈالتے ہوئے اس نے دھاڑ کر کہا تو وہ ڈر گئی۔

''کہاں؟''

''چلو......ابھی بتاتے ہیں کہاں؟'' ہاتھ بڑھا کر اس افسر نے اسے گھسیٹ لیا تھا' پھر سیل سے باہر نکلتے ہی اس کے دونوں ہاتھوں کو پیچھے باندھ کر اس کے منہ پر ایک بوری نما تھیلا ڈال دیا گیا' ایسا تھیلا جس میں سانس لینے کے لیے بھی کوئی سوراخ نہیں تھا' وہ جیسے ہی چلتے ہوئے لڑکھڑائی فوجی افسر نے زور سے ریفل کا بٹ اس کے کندھوں پر دے مارا۔

''اللہ......'' اس کے منہ سے آہ نکلی تھی مگر وہاں آہوں کی پروا کسے تھی' بھوک اور نقاہت کے ساتھ درد کی شدت نے اسے نڈھال کر چھوڑا تھا۔ کچھ ہی دیر کے بعد سے ایک میٹر کی چھوٹی سی تنگ و تاریک کوٹھڑی میں قید کر دیا گیا' جس میں کوئی روشن دان نہیں تھا۔ حورعین کو لگا وہ مرجائے گی' اس کے نازک اندام وجود میں اتنی صعوبتیں برداشت کرنے کی سکت نہیں تھی۔

❁......❁......❁

تم نے سوچا نہ تھا' ہم نے چاہا نہ تھا
پھر یہ کیسے جدائی کی شام آ گئی؟
کس لیے بجھ گئے قربتوں کے دیئے
کس طرح تیرگی اپنے نام آ گئی؟
ہم محبت کے ایسے مسافر رہے
جن کی راہوں میں سنگِ گراں بھی نہ تھا
جن کی چاہت کا دشمن نہیں تھا کوئی
سرگراں جن سے یہ آسماں بھی نہ تھا
کون حاسد ہے جس کی نظر لگ گئی؟
کس کی تھی بددعا' زد میں ہم آ گئے
ایسی پت جھڑ کی ظالم ہوائیں چلیں
پھول اپنی رفاقت کے مرجھا گئے
کیا خبر جب کبھی لوٹ کر آؤ گے تم
میری تربت کا تم کو نشاں نہ ملے
تھک کے دم توڑ دے شاعرِ بے سکون
پیار کا جب اسے سائباں نہ ملے

آخری بار اے میری جانِ غزل!

آخری بار اپنی یہ ضد چھوڑ دے

بچے کے سر سے خون تیزی سے بہہ رہا تھا جب زائر نے اسے زمین سے اٹھا کر اپنی گود میں لیا تھا' اس کی بیٹی بھی پاس ہی کھڑی رو رہی تھی۔ زائر نے ہاتھ بڑھا کر اسے بھی بازو کے حلقے میں لیا اور دونوں کو بے تحاشا چومنا شروع کر دیا۔ تبھی ثانیہ اس کے قریب پہنچی اور اس نے کسی چیل کی مانند اپنے بچوں کو اس سے جھپٹنا چاہا تھا۔

''دور رہو میرے بچوں سے' دیہاتی جنگلی انسان......'' حلق کے بل چلاتے ہوئے وہ دھاڑی تھی۔ بچے سہم کر اسے دیکھنے لگے تاہم زائر نے انہیں اپنی گرفت سے آزاد نہیں کیا' بچے کے سر سے بہتا ہوا خون اس کی جان پر بنا رہا تھا تبھی گردن پیچھے موڑتے ہوئے با آواز بلند اس نے کسی مزارع کو پکارا پھر اسے موٹر سائیکل لانے کی ہدایت کرنے کے ساتھ ہی بنا ثانیہ کے غصے کی پروا کیے' وہ اپنے بیٹے کو سینے سے لگائے' گاؤں کے واحد ڈاکٹر کی طرف چلا آیا۔ ثانیہ اس کی جسارت پر ہکا بکا سی کھڑی رہ گئی تھی۔

''ثانیہ!'' کافی دیر خاموشی کے بعد اشعر حسین نے اسے پکارا تھا۔ وہ جیسے چونک کر اس کی طرف متوجہ ہوئی۔

''ہوں۔

''جھوٹ بولا تھا ناں تم نے مجھ سے؟''

''کیسا جھوٹ؟'' اشعر حسین کے گلے پر اسے جیسے کرنٹ لگا تھا' اشعر نے رخ پھیر لیا۔

''یہی کہ زائر ملک جس نے حویلی میں پرورش پائی ہے تمہارا ڈرائیور ہے۔''

''تو......؟''

''تو یہ کہ وہ صرف ڈرائیور نہیں ہے ان بچوں کا باپ بھی ہے اور یہ بات میں نے ایئر پورٹ پر ہی محسوس کر لی تھی جب ان بچوں کو دیکھتے ہی اس کی آنکھوں میں آنسو کے ستارے جھلملائے تھے مگر اس نے لب دبا کر اپنا ضبط بحال رکھا تھا۔''

''کیا بکواس ہے یہ؟'' کانپتے لبوں کے ساتھ وہ جھنجلائی تھی مگر اشعر حسین نے اس کی طرف نہیں دیکھا۔

''بکواس نہیں ہے حقیقت ہے' تمہارے بچے کے پیڑ سے گرنے پر جتنی تکلیف اس نے محسوس کی ہے شاید تم نے بھی نہیں کی اگر وہ محض ایک ڈرائیور ہوتا تو یوں دیوانگی کے ساتھ تمہارے بچوں کو چوم نہ رہا ہوتا۔''

''اشعر پلیز! مجھے زائر ملک کے بارے میں کوئی بات نہیں سننی۔''

''مت سنو' مگر تم چاہ کر بھی اس حقیقت سے نگاہ نہیں چرا سکتیں کہ وہ تمہارے بچوں کا باپ ہے' تم چاہو بھی تو اسے اس کے بچوں سے دور نہیں رکھ سکتیں۔'' اشعر کی بات پر اس کا دل ضرور کانپ کر رہ گیا تھا۔ زائر ملک کی فطرت سے وہ بہت اچھی طرح واقف تھی۔ جو چیز اسے آسانی سے حاصل نہیں ہوتی وہ اسے چھین لیتا تھا مگر ثانیہ اپنے بچوں کے بارے میں ایسا کوئی رسک لینے کو تیار نہیں تھی تبھی اس نے فوراً شہر شفٹنگ کا پروگرام بنایا تھا۔

رات جب وہ اپنے بچے کو مرہم پٹی کروا کر حویلی لایا ثانیہ جلے پیر کی بلی کی مانند ادھر سے اُدھر چکر کاٹ رہی تھی جانے کیوں اسے لگ رہا تھا جیسے وہ اس کے بچے کو لے کر نہیں آئے گا۔ دادی ماں اسے تسلی دے رہی تھیں مگر اسے تسلی نہیں ہو رہی تھی' جس وقت اس نے حویلی کے گیٹ سے زائر کو اندر آتے دیکھا تب اس کی جان میں جان آئی اس کا بیٹا زائر کے کندھے سے لگا سو رہا تھا۔ ثانیہ اسے دیکھتے ہی تیزی سے اس کی طرف لپکی۔

''کیسا ہے میرا بیٹا......اتنی دیر کیوں لگا دی؟''

''ٹھیک ہے خون بہت بہہ گیا تھا ڈرپ لگ رہی تھی لو سنبھالو اسے۔'' سنجیدگی سے کہتے ہوئے اس نے بچے کو ثانیہ کی گود میں دینا چاہا تھا تبھی اس کے ہاتھ ثانیہ کے ہاتھوں سے ٹکرائے تھے اور دونوں کو ہی جیسے جھٹکا سا لگا تھا وہ حویلی سے گھر واپس آیا تو سائرہ اسی کی راہ دیکھ رہی تھی اس کی دستک کے جواب میں دروازہ بھی اسی نے کھولا تھا۔

''کہاں رہ گئے تھے، اتنی رات ہو گئی ہے ماسی پریشان ہو رہی تھی۔''

''تمہیں بتانے کا پابند نہیں ہوں میں، ہٹو سامنے سے۔'' اس کا موڈ آف تھا' سائرہ دروازہ بند کرنے کے بعد روٹی لے کر اس کے پیچھے ہی چلی آئی۔

''لے کھانا کھا لے' ہاتھ منہ دھو کر۔ تیری پسند کے کریلے گوشت بنائے ہیں میں نے۔''

''مجھے بھوک نہیں ہے۔'' بنا سائرہ اور کھانے پر نگاہ ڈالے وہ اپنے بستر پر ڈھے گیا۔ سائرہ ڈھٹائی سے ٹرے سائیڈ پر رکھتے ہوئے اسی چارپائی پر بیٹھ گئی۔

''کیوں بھوک نہیں ہے، مجھے پتا ہے تُو نے سارا دن بھی کچھ نہیں کھایا ہو گا۔''

''تو......؟ میں چاہے دس دن کچھ نہ کھاؤں تم کون ہوتی ہو میری فکر کرنے والی؟'' وہ دھاڑا تو سائرہ گھور کر رہ گئی۔

''بچپن کی منگ ہوں تیری، پیار کیا ہے میں نے تجھ سے' تجھے تو سب کچھ بھول گیا پر مجھے ایک ایک دن یاد ہے جب تم میری محبت میں پاگلوں کی طرح میرے گھر کے چکر لگاتے تھے۔''

''پاگل تھا میں جو تجھ جیسی مفاد پرست لڑکی سے دل لگا بیٹھا مگر اب ایسا کچھ نہیں ہے' نکل آیا ہوں میں اُن دنوں کے فریب سے۔''

''پتا ہے مجھے اس شہر والی نے دماغ خراب کر رکھا ہے تیرا مگر وہ بھی تو چھوڑ کر چلی گئی ناں تجھے' اس سے کیوں نہیں کرتا نفرت؟'' فوراً سے پیشتر نہایت غصے میں دو بدو جواب دیتے ہوئے اس نے پھر وہی چھرا گھونپا تھا اس کے سینے میں کہ جس کا وار ہمیشہ اسے گھائل کر کے رکھ دیتا تھا اس وقت بھی وہ چپ کر گیا تھا تبھی وہ محبت سے اس کے بازو پر ہاتھ رکھتے ہوئے بولی۔

''میں تیرا دل نہیں دکھانا چاہتی زائر! سوہنا ربّ جانتا ہے آج بھی دل سے پیار کرتی ہوں تجھے۔''

''نہیں چاہیے مجھے تیرا پیار' سنا تم نے۔ کسی کے پیار کی ضرورت نہیں ہے مجھے' کہاں جا سویا تھا یہ پیار اس وقت جب تم میرے سسکتے ہوئے دل کی پروا کیے بغیر صرف دولت کے لالچ میں کسی اور کی سیج پر جا بیٹھی تھیں۔ اس وقت کہاں گئی تھی تمہاری یادداشت جب میرے سارے جذبوں پر پانی پھیر کر' کسی اور کے نام کی مہندی ہاتھوں پر رچا کر بیٹھ گئی تھیں۔ مت کریدا کرو بجھی ہوئی راکھ سے چنگاریاں۔ ایسا نہ ہو کہ کسی دن یہی چنگاریاں تمہارے سارے وجود کو جلا کر راکھ کر دیں۔'' دھاڑ کر دائیں ہاتھ کی انگلیاں اس کے نرم بازو میں پیوست کرتے ہوئے اس نے ایک جھٹکے سے اسے پرے دھکیلا' مگر وہ لڑکھڑا کر پھر اسی کے بازو سے لپٹ گئی۔

''مجھے اپنی غلطی کا احساس ہو گیا ہے زائر! بہت شرمندہ ہوں میں اپنی حماقت پر پتا نہیں کیسے میری عقل پر پردا پڑ گیا تھا ورنہ وہ مردود افضل تو تیرے پیر کی جوتی کے برابر بھی نہیں۔ مجھے معاف کر دے زائر! خدا کے واسطے معاف کر دے۔''

''میرے پاس تجھے دینے کے لیے اب کچھ نہیں ہے سائرہ! اس لیے نہ دماغ خراب کر میرا۔'' اکتا کر رخ پھیرتے ہوئے اس نے پھر اسے مایوس کیا مگر سائرہ نے جیسے سنا ہی نہیں۔

''ماسی بہت پریشان ہے زائر! ہم دونوں کے لیے کئی بار میرے سامنے تیری اور میری شادی کی بات کر چکی ہے میرے لیے نہ سہی ان کی خوشی کے لیے ہی سہی' مجھے اپنا نام دے دے۔ تیرے علاوہ میں نے اور کسی سے شادی نہیں کرنی

اب اگر ایسا ہوا تو تیری قسم زائر! میں زہر کھا کر مر جاؤں گی۔''
''کوئی بات نہیں‘ میں بھی تو مر گیا تھا تم بھی مر جاؤ گی تو کیا ہوگا۔'' اس کی جذباتی بلیک میلنگ کا شکار ہوئے بغیر اس نے اپنا تکیہ اور لحاف اٹھایا اور اوپر چھت پر چلا آیا‘ پیچھے وہ کلس کر رہ گئی۔
اگلی صبح وہ اٹھا تو سائرہ ہینڈ پمپ کے نیچے بیٹھی کپڑے دھو رہی تھی‘ وہ سست روی سے سیڑھیاں اترتا اپنی ماں کے پاس آ بیٹھا۔
''ابا کی طبیعت اب کیسی ہے اماں؟''
''کیسی ہو سکتی ہے؟ جوان اکلوتا پُتر دو گھڑی پاس بیٹھ کر حال وی نہ پچھے تو کیسی طبیعت ہوگی باپ کی؟'' اماں شاید اس کی طرف سے بھری بیٹھی تھیں‘ تبھی اس کے بیٹھتے ہی گولے داغنے شروع کر دیئے وہ رخ پھیر کر رہ گیا۔
''مجھ سے ابا کا حال دیکھا نہیں جاتا اماں! اسی لیے نہیں بیٹھتا ان کے پاس۔''
''کیوں ان کے حال کو کیا ہوا ہے‘ اللہ معافی کرے کوڑھ تو نہیں لگا انہیں جو تجھے پاس بیٹھ کر گھن آتی ہے۔''
''میرا یہ مطلب نہیں تھا اماں۔'' اماں کے جلال نے اسے اچھا خاصا پریشان کر دیا تھا تبھی وہ بولی تھیں۔
''بس رہنے دے‘ اچھی طرح سمجھتی ہوں تیرے مطلب کو‘ پانچ سال ہو گئے فقیر بنا پھرتا ہے‘ ایک بار بھی کبھی میرا اور اپنے ابا کا خیال آیا تجھے؟ پندرہ پندرہ دن اپنی شکل نہیں دکھاتا‘ کوئی مرتا ہے تو مر جائے تیری بلا سے۔'' وہ اچھی خاصی دکھی تھیں‘ زائر جھنجلا کر اٹھ کھڑا ہوا۔
''سب کے ساتھ آپ بھی دعا کریں اماں کہ میں مر جاؤں‘ ویسے بھی میرا اس دنیا میں کوئی کام نہیں ہے۔'' اپنی بات مکمل کرنے کے بعد وہ وہاں ٹھہرا نہیں تھا اماں کا ہاتھ دل پر ہی رہ گیا جب کہ سائرہ نل کے نیچے بیٹھی سُن سی رہ گئی تھی۔ کیا چل رہا تھا زائر ملک کے دل و دماغ میں جو وہ ذات کے ساتھ ساتھ اپنی زندگی سے بھی اتنا بے زار ہو گیا تھا۔ وہ محض سوچ کر رہ گئی۔
دن بھر کھیتوں میں پسینہ بہانے کے بعد ڈھلتی شام کے وقت جب وہ گھر واپسی کا قصد کر رہا تھا اس کا ٹکراؤ پھر ثانیہ عباس کے ساتھ ہوا تھا‘ بارش اچانک شروع ہو گئی تھی شدید برساتی موسم میں قطعی نامناسب کپڑے پہنے وہ اسی شخص کے ساتھ کہیں سے آ رہی تھی جو اسے زہر لگتا تھا۔ ٹائٹ جینز پر سلیولیس شرٹ بارش میں بھیگ کر اس کے جسم کے ساتھ چپک گئی تھی اور اب اس کے جسمانی خدوخال خوب واضح کر رہی تھی۔ زائر کے بدن میں لہو جیسے آگ بن کر دوڑنے لگا تھا‘ وہ اس سے الگ ہو کر رہ سکتا تھا مگر اسے یوں اپنی عزت سے کھیلنے کی اجازت نہیں دے سکتا تھا تبھی برقی رو کی طرح تیزی سے اس کی طرف لپکا اور اس سے پہلے کہ ثانیہ اسے کچھ کہتی‘ اس نے ایک زوردار طمانچہ اس کے گال پر دے مارا۔
ثانیہ عباس کے ساتھ ساتھ اشعر حسین بھی اس کی اس حرکت پر ششدر رہ گیا۔
''یہ کیا بدتمیزی ہے؟'' وہ غرایا تھا مگر زائر نے اسے نہیں دیکھا وہ صرف ثانیہ کو دیکھ رہا تھا۔
''بہت بہتر ہوگا تمہارے لیے ثانیہ عباس اگر تم اپنی حدود و قیود میں رہو کیونکہ میں نے تم سے کنارہ کشی کی ہے‘ سر عام گاؤں کی گلیوں میں عزت رولنے کی اجازت نہیں دی۔''
''جسٹ شٹ اپ یو ایڈیٹ مین! تم ہوتے کون ہو مجھ پر ہاتھ اٹھانے والے؟ کیا اوقات ہے تمہاری میرے سامنے صرف ایک نوکر......؟'' بپھرے ہوئے لہجے میں جس حقارت سے اس نے اپنے اور اس کے مابین رشتے سے نگاہ چرائی تھی وہ دنگ رہ گیا تھا۔
کیا واقعی اب وہ صرف اس لڑکی کا نوکر رہ گیا تھا؟

''خبردار آج کے بعد اگر کبھی میرے سامنے آئے تو...... میں نوکروں کو ان کی اوقات سے بڑھ کر چھوٹ دینے کی قائل نہیں ہوں۔'' انگلی اٹھا کر اسے وارن کرتی وہ کوئی اور ہی ثانیہ عباس لگ رہی تھی۔ زائر کے جسم کا سارا خون آنکھوں میں سمٹ آیا' کیا کچھ نہیں کہنا چاہتا تھا اس وقت وہ اس سے مگر زبان جیسے تالو سے چپک کر رہ گئی تھی۔

دنیا میں تین قسم کے لوگ ہوتے ہیں' ایک وہ جو غلطی کرتے ہیں مگر پھر اپنی غلطی کا احساس ہونے پر اس سے توبہ کر لیتے ہیں دوسرے وہ ہوتے ہیں جو غلطی کر کے مان لیتے ہیں مگر توبہ نہیں کرتے اور تیسرے وہ لوگ ہوتے ہیں جو غلطی کر کے مانتے بھی نہیں اور اگر انہیں ان کی غلطی کا احساس دلایا جائے تو الٹا وہ آپ پر چڑھ دوڑتے ہیں' ایسے لوگوں کا ساتھ بے شک زندگی کو بہت کٹھن بنا دیتا ہے' زائر ملک کی نگاہ میں ثانیہ عباس کا شمار بھی ان تیسری قسم کے لوگوں میں ہوتا تھا۔ بارش میں مزید شدت آ گئی تھی مگر وہ اب بھی وہیں کھڑا تھا۔

دو پتر چناراں دے......

ساڈا دکھ سن کے روندے پتھر پہاڑاں دے

جوگی بابا کی آواز ایک مرتبہ پھر پوری شدت سے اس کے اندر گونجی تھی۔ اگلے روز چوہدرانی کے بلاوے پر شام کے وقت وہ حویلی آیا تھا۔ ثانیہ عباس اس وقت گاؤں میں نہیں تھی۔

''جی چوہدرانی آپ نے بلایا؟''

''ہاں زائر! آ بیٹھ۔'' وہ کچھ پریشان دکھائی دے رہی تھیں۔ زائر چپ چاپ مونڈھا کھینچ کر ان کے قریب بیٹھ گیا۔

''خیریت؟''

''خیریت کہاں ہے زائر! سالوں بعد پوتی کا چہرہ دیکھنا نصیب ہوا' سوچا تھا اب وہ آ گئی ہے تو خود ہی حویلی کا نظام سنبھالے گی مگر...... میری تو قسمت ہی خراب ہے۔''

''کیوں اب کیا ہوا؟'' چوہدرانی کے الفاظ پر اس کا دل پوری شدت سے دھڑکا تھا۔

''ہونا کیا ہے پتر! ثانیہ نے گاؤں چھوڑ کر شہر میں رہنے کا فیصلہ کر لیا ہے' وہ جولڑکا آیا ہوا ہے ناں اشعر حسین اسی نے دماغ خراب کیا ہوگا اس کا ورنہ وہ اس بڑھاپے میں بوڑھی دادی کو اکیلا چھوڑ کر جانے والی نہیں تھی۔'' چوہدرانی کی پریشانی پل میں اس کی پریشانی میں ڈھل گئی تھی تاہم اس نے خود پر ضبط قائم رکھا۔

''آپ اکیلی تو نہیں ہیں چوہدرانی! پہلے بھی تو اتنا عرصہ یہ گاؤں والے ہی آپ کے سگے بن کر رہے ہیں' اب بھی اگر وہ آپ کو چھوڑ کر چلی جاتی ہے تو کیا ہوا' ہم سب ہیں ناں یہاں آپ کے ساتھ۔''

''اللہ عمر لمبی کرے ان لوگوں کی' میرے گاؤں کو ہر نظر بد سے محفوظ رکھے...... آمین۔'' ان کے چہرے کی اداسی اور لہجے کا ملال بدستور قائم تھا تبھی وہ بولا تھا۔

''اشعر حسین سے کیا تعلق ہے ثانیہ بی بی کا؟''

''ارے تعلق کیا ہونا ہے پتر! بس جب سے ثانیہ کو طلاق ہوئی ہے خوامخواہ دم چھلا بنا پھرتا ہے اس کا۔''

''طلاق......؟'' اس پر تو جیسے بجلیاں آ گری تھیں۔

''ہاں...... اپنی پسند سے شادی کی تھی ثانیہ نے' اسی لیے یہ داغ برداشت کرنا پڑا۔''

''کب ہوئی اسے طلاق؟'' زائر کا دل جیسے بند ہو رہا تھا۔

''پانچ سال پہلے...... جب اس نے دو جڑواں بچوں کو جنم دیا تھا تبھی اس کے شوہر نے اسے طلاق کے پیپرز بھجوا دیئے تھے۔'' ایک کے بعد ایک چوہدرانی کے انکشافات نے اسے چکرا کر رکھ دیا تھا۔

''بہت ٹوٹی ہے ثانیہ! اسی کے غم میں کنیز بھی دنیا سے چلی گئی' بچے ہیں تو وہ باپ کی شکل دیکھنے کو ترس رہے ہیں مگر وہ بندہ خدا کا جانے کہاں ہے۔'' بنا زائر کے اندر سر اٹھاتے طوفانوں کی خبر رکھے' چوہدرانی اس پر اپنا دکھ عیاں کر رہی تھیں' زائر کو لگا جیسے اس کا وجود پتھر ہو کر رہ گیا ہو۔

کیا وہ لڑکی صرف اپنی خوشیوں کے لیے اپنے گھر والوں کو اتنا بڑا دھوکہ دے سکتی تھی؟ صرف اس سے چھٹکارے کے لیے کیا وہ اس حد تک بھی گر سکتی تھی؟ اتنا بڑا جھوٹ وہ بھی اتنے قریبی رشتوں سے؟ اسے لگا جیسے اس کا سر درد سے پھٹ جائے گا' تبھی چوہدرانی سے معذرت کر کے فوراً سے پیشتر وہ اٹھ کھڑا ہوا مگر ابھی اس کے قدم حویلی کے گیٹ کے پار بھی نہ ہوئے تھے کہ کسی کی صدا نے جیسے اس کے قدموں کو زمین کے ساتھ باندھ کر رکھ دیا۔

❀......❀......❀

وصال موسم گزر گیا تو' خیال بن کر ملا کریں گے
بچھڑ گئے تو کبھی کبھی ماہ وسال بن کر ملا کریں گے
کتاب عہد وفا کے اک اک ورق پر اپنی خبر ملے گی
ہم اہل الفت محبتوں کی مثال بن کر ملا کریں گے
ہزار لمحوں کی ہو مسافت دلوں کی دھڑکن سنائی دے گی
گزرتے لمحوں کی ہر صدا میں دھمال بن کر ملا کریں گے
ابھی تو لمحوں کی دوریوں پر بھٹک رہے ہیں مگر کبھی ہم
فلک کی گردش میں آ گئے تو ہلال بن کر ملا کریں گے

سارے کمرے میں آگ بھڑک رہی تھی اور ہانیہ نیم بے ہوشی کی حالت میں' اٹیچ باتھ کے دروازے پر کھڑی بری طرح سے چلاّتے ہوئے سب کو پکار رہی تھی۔

''ہانیہ......'' اچانک اسے میکال کی پکار سنائی دی' تین تین سیڑھیاں اکٹھی پھلانگ کر اوپر آنے کے بعد وہ پاگلوں کی طرح اسے پکار رہا تھا۔ ہانیہ کی چیخوں میں مزید اضافہ ہو گیا۔

''ہانیہ......''

اب وہ چلاّ رہا تھا تبھی ہانیہ نے دیکھا بنا آگ کے بھڑکتے شعلوں کی پروا کیے وہ کھڑکی سے کمرے میں کودا تھا کیونکہ سامنے دروازے کی چوکھٹ مکمل طور پر آگ کی لپیٹ میں آ چکی تھی اور وہاں سے کمرے میں داخل ہونا اب ممکن نہیں رہا تھا۔ کھڑکی سے کمرے میں کودنے کے باوجود آگ نے میکال کی پینٹ کے پائینچے کو چھو لیا تھا' مگر اسے اپنی پروا ہی کب تھی وہ تو ہانیہ کو بچانے کے لیے پاگل ہو رہا تھا باہر جاذب جو اس کے پیچھے ہی لپکا تھا' آگ پر مسلسل پانی ڈال کر اسے بجھانے کی ناکام کوشش کر رہا تھا پھر جس وقت میکال نے اٹیچ باتھ کے دروازے پر کھڑی ہانیہ کو اپنے حصار میں لیا وہ مکمل طور پر ہوش و ہوا س سے بیگانی ہو کر اس کی بانہوں میں جھول گئی تھی۔ رات جس وقت وہ ہوش میں آئی تو اس کا ہاتھ میکال کے ہاتھ میں تھا ہانیہ نے دانستہ آنکھیں کھولنے سے احتراز کیا تبھی میکال نے جھک کر اس کی پیشانی چوم لی۔ اس کا ایک ہاتھ ہانیہ کے بالوں کو سہلا رہا تھا' وہ دم سادھے پڑی رہی تاہم اس کا دل اس لمحے بہت تیزی سے دھڑک رہا تھا۔

''میں تم سے لڑ سکتا ہوں ہانیہ! تمہیں دکھی بھی کر سکتا ہوں مگر خدا جانتا ہے تمہیں ہمیشہ کے لیے کھونے کا حوصلہ نہیں ہے مجھ میں۔'' بھرآئے لہجے میں اس پر جھک کر کہتے ہوئے وہ جیسے اسے حیران ہی تو کر گیا تھا۔ اگلے دو روز تک سب اس

کے اردگرد تھے مگر وہ نہیں تھا۔

ہانیہ خود بھی نہیں جانتی تھی کہ اس کا دل ایک دم سے بے کل کیوں ہوگیا تھا۔ اس کی متلاشی نگاہیں ہر آہٹ پر اسے ہی کیوں دیکھنا چاہتی تھیں، جاذب بتا رہا تھا کہ اس کی ٹانگ جلی ہے اور پاؤں بھی متاثر ہوا ہے۔ شاید اسی لیے وہ اسے نظر بھی نہیں آرہا تھا جو بھی تھا مگر یہ حقیقت تھی کہ اس کے اندر کی دنیا اچانک ہی بدل گئی تھی۔

دو روز بعد سادگی سے ہادیہ کی رخصتی ہوگئی اور اسی روز ہانیہ نے اسے دیکھا تھا ہلکی ہلکی بڑھی ہوئی شیو کے ساتھ ٹانگ کے زخم سے نڈھال وہ بات بات پر مسکرانے کی ناکام کوشش کرتا اسے بے حد اچھا لگ رہا تھا۔

تقریب کے اختتام تک بناء اپنے زخم کی پروا کیے نا صرف اس نے تمام امور سنبھالے تھے بلکہ مہمانوں کو بھی بھرپور کمپنی دی تھی۔ ہانیہ اداس سی وجہ بے وجہ اسے دیکھتی رہی۔ رات گئے وہ کمرے میں آیا تو ہانیہ کو اس کا زخم دیکھنے کا موقع مل وہ چپکے سے اس کے کمرے میں چلی آئی اس کی بائیں ٹانگ کی پنڈلی شدید جل گئی تھی، زخم اتنا بڑا تھا کہ دیکھتے ہی ہانیہ کا دل جیسے دھک سے رہ گیا۔

میکال نیند میں تھا اس لیے اسے ہانیہ کی آمد کا پتا نہ چل سکا۔ اس نے تو اب تک محسوس بھی نہیں ہونے دیا تھا کہ وہ کتنی تکلیف میں ہے مگر وہ زخم ہانیہ سے چھپے نہیں رہ سکے تھے۔

میکال کا وجود زخموں کے درد کی وجہ سے بخار کی لپیٹ میں تھا مگر اس نے بہت ہی ضبط سے یہ درد برداشت کیے رکھا تھا وہ اس کے قدموں کے قریب بیٹھی بے آواز روتی رہی، باہر بارش شروع ہوگئی تھی مگر آج ہانیہ کو بارش میں کوئی دلچسپی نہیں تھی اس کی ذہن کی اسکرین پر صرف وہی لمحات چل رہے تھے جن میں میکال نے اس پر اپنی محبتیں نچھاور کی تھیں۔ بے شک وہ شخص اس قابل تھا کہ اسے چاہا جاتا۔

صبح اس کی آنکھ کھلنے سے قبل ہی وہ کمرے سے نکل آئی تھی، ہادیہ جاذب کی ہوکر بہت خوش تھی اور شاید جاذب بھی...... وہ ہادیہ کو زبردستی کمرے میں رہنے کی تلقین کرنے کے بعد اکیلی ہی کچن میں چلی آئی۔ مہمان رات میں ہی چلے گئے تھے جب کہ گھر والوں میں سے ابھی کسی کی بھی آنکھ نہیں کھلی تھی۔ اس نے آٹا گوندھ کر سائیڈ پر رکھا اور چائے کا پانی چڑھا دیا، پانی ابھی ابل ہی رہا تھا کہ اچانک میکال نے خاموشی سے پیچھے آکر اسے اپنے حصار میں لے لیا۔

''السلام علیکم! صبح بخیر۔'' اس کی آواز میں اب بھی خمار تھا، ہانیہ کا دل بہت تیزی سے دھڑک اٹھا۔

''آ...... آپ......''

''ہوں۔'' اپنی تھوڑی ہانیہ کے کندھے پر ٹکاتے ہوئے اس نے آہستہ سے پلکیں موند لی تھیں۔ ہانیہ کی ہتھیلیاں پسینے سے بھیگ گئیں۔ میکال کی اس قربت نے واقعی اسے کنفیوز کر کے رکھ دیا تھا۔

''اتنی جلدی کیوں بیدار ہوگئے، آپ کے زخم۔''

''زخم بھی تو تم نے ہی دیئے ہیں ہانیہ! جیسے مریض خود چل کر ڈاکٹر کے پاس جاتا ہے ویسے ہی میں اٹھ کر تمہارے پاس آگیا ہوں۔'' اس کی بات کاٹتے ہوئے اس نے پھر اس کے کان میں سرگوشی کی۔ ہانیہ کا دل یک دم بے قابو ہوا۔

''آپ نے اپنی جان خطرے میں ڈال کر میری جان بچائی میں آپ کی بہت ممنون ہوں مگر...... آپ کو ایسا نہیں کرنا چاہیے تھا، دیکھیے آپ کی ٹانگ کتنی متاثر ہوئی ہے، زخم اگر بگڑ گیا تو مسئلہ ہوجائے گا۔''

''ہوں یہ تو ہے لیکن اگر ڈاکٹر مہربانی کرے اور مریض کی خطائیں معاف کر کے اس کے ساتھ رہے تو زخم ٹھیک ہوسکتا ہے۔'' وہ اسے سنا رہا تھا ہانیہ کی سمجھ میں نہیں آرہا تھا کہ وہ اسے کیا جواب دے۔ تبھی ملازمہ وہاں چلی آئی تھی، میکال آہٹ پا کر فوراً پیچھے ہٹا تھا۔

''بیگم صاحبہ! آپ آرام کرلیں میں کرلیتی ہوں۔'' ملازمہ سامنے کا منظر دیکھ کر نظریں چرانے پر مجبور ہوگئی تھی' میکال کان کھجاتے ہوئے کچن سے نکل گیا۔

اسی روز دوپہر کے کھانے میں اس نے کرنل صاحب سے ہانیہ کی گھر واپسی کا مطالبہ کردیا تھا انہیں بھلا کیا اعتراض ہوسکتا تھا۔ ہانیہ کی خاموشی نے بھی انہیں نیم رضامندی کا اشارہ دیا تھا تبھی شام کے کھانے کے بعد انہوں نے ہانیہ کو اس کے سنگ رخصت کردیا۔ راستے میں میکال اسے اپنی انگلینڈ کی مصروفیات کے بارے میں بتاتا رہا' گاڑی گھر کے سامنے رکی تو سب سے پہلے نہال نے ہی ان کا استقبال کیا تھا۔

وہ آئے گھر میں ہمارے خدا کی قدرت ہے
کبھی ہم ان کو کبھی اپنے گھر کو دیکھتے ہیں

ہانیہ کو دیکھتے ہی وہ مسکرایا تھا مگر ہانیہ نے ناراضی سے منہ پھیرلیا۔

''اے کیا ہوا؟'' بنا میکال کی پروا کیے وہ فوراً اس کے پیچھے لپکا اور اسے لاؤنج میں بازو سے جا پکڑا۔

''کچھ نہیں ہوا' چھوڑو مجھے۔''

''کیوں چھوڑوں' مجھے پتا ہے تم مجھ سے ناراض ہو کیونکہ میں تمہارے بھائی کی شادی میں شریک نہیں ہوسکا' ہے ناں؟''

''مجھے کوئی ضرورت نہیں ہے تم سے ناراض ہونے کی۔'' درشتگی سے اس کا بازو ہاتھ سے ہٹاتے ہوئے وہ آگے بڑھ گئی تھی' میکال خاموش سا وہیں صوفے پر ٹک گیا' ہمیشہ کی طرح اسے نہال کا ہانیہ کو تنگ کرنا پسند نہیں آیا تھا مگر نہال بنا اس کی ناراضی کی پروا کیے اب بھی ہانیہ کی راہ روکے کھڑا تھا۔

''میری بات تو سن لو یار! پھر ناراض ہوجانا۔''

''مجھے کوئی بات نہیں سننی۔''

''ہانیہ پلیز......'' ہانیہ کے رخ پھیرنے پر اس کی آنکھوں میں ہلکی سی نمی آئی تھی مگر ہانیہ نے نہیں دیکھی' وہ اس کی کوئی بھی وضاحت سنے بغیر اپنے کمرے میں گھس کر دروازہ لاک کرچکی تھی۔ اگلی صبح ناشتے کی ٹیبل پر اس کی ملاقات مسٹر اینڈ مسز حسن سے ہوئی تھی' دونوں اس کے لوٹ آنے کے فیصلے پر بہت خوش تھے۔

نہال وہاں موجود نہیں تھا تاہم میکال نے پہلی بار ان لوگوں کے ساتھ بیٹھ کر ناشتے سے پورا پورا انصاف کیا تھا' تھوڑی دیر بعد حسن صاحب اور میکال آفس کے لیے اٹھ گئے تبھی اس نے مسز حسن سے پوچھا تھا۔

''نہال کہاں ہے آنٹی! ناشتا نہیں کیا اس نے۔''

''ہوں' صبح جلدی آفس چلا گیا کہہ رہا تھا کوئی ضروری میٹنگ اٹینڈ کرنی ہے بزنس کے سلسلے میں۔ سچ پوچھو تو میں نہال کو لے کر بہت پریشان ہوں ہانیہ!''

''کیوں خیریت؟'' مسز حسن کے تفصیلی جواب نے اسے پریشان کردیا تھا۔

''یہ تو میں بھی نہیں جانتی کہ خیریت ہے یا نہیں مگر نہال نے واقعی مجھے پریشان کر رکھا ہے۔ کئی کئی روز گھر سے باہر رہتا ہے' تمہارے یہاں سے جانے کے بعد تو سمجھو چپ لگ گئی اس لڑکے کے ہونٹوں پر۔ کسی سے بات ہی نہیں کرتا' اب بھی اتنا بیمار رہا ہے اسلام آباد دوست کے پاس مگر مجال ہے جو اس نے ہمیں ہوا بھی لگنے دی ہو وہ تو اس کے دوست کا فون آیا تھا اور اس نے بے خبری میں بتادیا تو پتا چلا ورنہ یہ لڑکا تو اسے بھی منع کرکے آیا تھا کہ کچھ نہیں بتانا گھر والوں کو۔''

''یہ کیا کہہ رہی ہیں آپ؟''

''سچ کہہ رہی ہوں کوئی بات ہے جو اسے اندر ہی اندر پریشان کیے ہوئے ہے مگر وہ ہنسی محول میں چھپالیتا ہے۔''

''میں بات کروں گی نہال سے۔'' مسز حسن کی باتوں نے اسے پریشان کر دیا تھا تبھی اس نے انہیں اطمینان دلایا۔

میکال دوپہر کے کھانے کے لیے گھر آیا تو ہانیہ نے اس کی فیورٹ ڈشز بنا رکھی تھیں' کچن کی گرمی کے سبب اس کا برا حال ہو رہا تھا' وہ خفا ہو گیا۔

''ہانی! میں نے منع کیا ہے ناں تمہیں کچن میں گھسنے سے' دیکھو ذرا اپنا حال۔''

''کچھ نہیں ہوتا' مجھے گھر کا کام کاج کر کے خوشی ملتی ہے۔''

''وہ تو ٹھیک ہے مگر اپنا حال بھی تو دیکھو۔''

''حال بھی ٹھیک ہے آپ پریشان نہ ہوں' جلدی سے کھانا کھا کر بتائیں کیسا بنا ہے؟''

''ٹھیک ہے میں فریش ہو کر آتا ہوں۔'' نرمی سے اس کے گال تھپتھپاتے ہوئے وہ اپنے کمرے کی طرف بڑھ گیا' فریش ہو کر وہ کھانے کی ٹیبل پر آیا تو وہ کہے بغیر نہ رہ سکی۔

''نہال تو نہیں آئے گا کھانے کے لیے' پتا نہیں اس نے آفس میں بھی کچھ کھایا ہوگا کہ نہیں۔'' میکال کا سالن کے ڈونگے کی طرف بڑھتا ہاتھ وہیں رک گیا۔

''کھا لیا ہوگا' یو ڈونٹ وری۔''

''مما بتا رہی تھیں وہ بیمار رہا ہے' آپ نے بتایا کیوں نہیں مجھے۔''

''کیا بتاتا اس نے تو گھر والوں کو بھی خبر نہیں ہونے دی تھی۔'' آپ ہی آپ اس کا لہجہ خشک ہو گیا تھا پھر اس سے پہلے کہ وہ مزید کچھ کہتی وہ اٹھ کھڑا ہوا۔

''سوری' مجھے بہت ضروری کام یاد آ گیا ہے' میں چلتا ہوں' شام میں کھالوں گا۔'' سپاٹ چہرے کے ساتھ نرمی سے کہتا وہ فوراً ڈائننگ ہال سے نکل گیا' پیچھے ہانیہ اسے روکتی ہی رہ گئی تھی۔ رات میں نہال لیٹ گھر آیا تھا۔ میکال کا موڈ البتہ فریش تھا کھانا کھانے کے بعد فارغ ہو کر وہ بیڈ پر آیا تو ہانیہ اس کے پریس کیے ہوئے کپڑے ہینگ کر رہی تھی۔ وہ کچھ دیر اس کے فارغ ہونے کا انتظار کرتا رہا پھر بیڈ سے اٹھ کر اسے بھی ساتھ ہی کھینچ لیا۔

''میکال! کیا کر رہے ہیں' چھوڑیں ناں پلیز۔ مجھے بہت سارے کام کرنے ہیں ابھی۔''

''کاموں کے لیے اس گھر میں بہت ملازم ہیں' تمہیں میں اس گھر میں اپنے لیے لایا ہوں سمجھیں۔''

''مگر......''

''چھوڑو اگر مگر کو...... آؤ میں تمہیں سلاتا ہوں۔''

''کیسے؟''

''بازو پر سر رکھو پھر بتاتا ہوں۔'' وہ شوخ ہو رہا تھا۔ ہانیہ نے چپ چاپ اس کے پہلو میں لیٹ کر اپنا سر اس کے بازو پر رکھ دیا۔

''ہانیہ......'' کچھ دیر بعد جونہی اس نے پلکیں موندی' میکال نے پکارا۔

''ہوں۔''

''تم نے مجھ سے کیوں چھپایا کہ میں پاپا بننے والا ہوں۔'' اس کی آواز کسی سرگوشی سے بلند نہیں تھی۔ ہانیہ کا دل تیزی سے دھڑکا۔

''بتانے کا فائدہ بھی نہیں تھا۔''

''کیوں؟'' وہ حیران ہوا تھا' ہانیہ نے نظر چرالی۔
''کیونکہ یہ خبر سننے کے بعد ہوسکتا تھا کہ پھر آپ مجھ پر کوئی رکیک الزام لگا دیتے۔'' لفظ نہیں تھے کوئی چابک تھا جو میکال کو اپنی پیٹھ پر پڑتا ہوا محسوس ہوا۔ ستاروں سی روشن آنکھوں کی چمک اچانک ماند پڑی تھی۔
''تم نے اب تک اس بات کو دل سے لگا رکھا ہے۔''
''نہیں۔''
''نہیں تو پھر بار بار کوڑے کیوں مارتی ہو' کتنی بار میں تم سے اپنے الفاظ کی معافی مانگ چکا ہوں' کیسا دل ہے تمہارا جس میں ذرا سی معافی کی گنجائش بھی نہیں۔''
''میں نے آپ کو معاف کر دیا ہے۔''
''کر دیا ہے تو دوبارہ لفظوں کے چابک نہ مارنا پلیز...... وہ سب ایک غلط فہمی کا ردعمل تھا جو اب دور ہوگئی ہے' اس لیے پلیز تم اپنا دل صاف کرلو' میں نہیں چاہتا کہ ہماری خوب صورت ازدواجی زندگی کسی غلط فہمی کی بھینٹ چڑھ کر برباد ہو جائے۔'' ہانیہ کا چہرہ ہاتھوں میں لیے وہ اس کے گال سہلا رہا تھا' ہانیہ نے پھر پلکیں موندلیں۔
''کیا ہوا میکال حسن...... اگر آپ کی یہ وارفتگیاں عائشہ جی دیکھ لیں۔''
''دیکھ لے...... کسی پرائی لڑکی کے ناز تو نہیں اٹھا رہا' اپنی بیوی سے محبت کر رہا ہوں۔''
''پھر بھی گئے دنوں میں ہوسکتا ہے یہی الفاظ کبھی آپ نے عائشہ جی کے لیے بھی کہے ہوں۔''
''ہوں...... ہوسکتا ہے مگر لفظ کسی کی میل نہیں ہوتے ہانی! نہ کسی کی اترن ہوتے ہیں جو ایک بار استعمال کے بعد دوبارہ استعمال ہی نہ کیا جاسکیں۔''
''صحیح کہا آپ نے' لفظ کسی کی میل کسی کی اترن نہیں ہوتے مگر ایک اثاثہ ضرور ہوتے ہیں جن کی تقسیم تکلیف دیتی ہے۔''
''مجھے نہیں دیتی' میں نے خود کو سمجھا لیا ہے کہ جو چیز میرے اختیار و نصیب میں نہیں میں اس کے لیے اگر ساری عمر بھی روتا رہوں تو کوئی فائدہ نہیں پھر کیوں نہ میں اس چیز کو قبول کرلوں جو میرے نصیب میں لکھ دی گئی ہے۔''
''اچھی سوچ ہے مگر مجھے آپ کی اسی بات نے متاثر کیا تھا کہ آپ عائشہ جی کے علاوہ اور کسی کا بھی تصور گناہ سمجھتے تھے میرے نزدیک محبت میں وحدانیت ہی اسے اس کی حقیقی منزل تک پہنچاتی ہے۔''
''ہوں...... مگر کچھ لوگ حالات و تقدیر کے سامنے بے بس ہو جاتے ہیں' جیسے میں ہوگیا ہوں تمہاری بددعا کے سامنے۔'' سنجیدگی سے کہتے کہتے وہ مسکرا دیا۔ ہانیہ کے لبوں پر بھی مسکراہٹ دوڑ گئی۔
''سنا ہے آپ نے ماڈلنگ شروع کر دی ہے۔''
''نہیں' ایسی تو کوئی بات نہیں۔'' وہ مسکرایا۔
''اصل میں میرا ایک دوست ہے' کسی پرائیوٹ چینل کے لیے کام کرتا ہے اس کی شوٹنگ تھی انگلینڈ میں مگر مطلوبہ ماڈل عین ٹائم پر دغا دے گیا' تبھی مجبوراً مجھے قربانی کا بکرا بننا پڑا۔''
''اچھی ماڈلنگ کر لیتے ہیں آپ۔''
''نوازش!'' لب دبا کر مسکراتے ہوئے اس نے ہانیہ کو خود میں سمویا اور ہاتھ بڑھا کر لائٹ آف کر دی۔ تقریباً ڈیڑھ گھنٹے کے بعد جب وہ سوگیا تو ہانیہ نے آہستہ سے خود کو اس کی گرفت سے نکالا اور بیڈ سے اتر آئی۔ مڑ کر ایک نظر اطمینان سے سوئے ہوئے میکال پر ڈالنے کے بعد اس نے اپنے پیچھے کمرے کا دروازہ بند کیا اور سیڑھیاں اتر آئی۔

❁......❁......❁

''ٹک......ٹک......ٹک۔''

کمپیوٹر آف کر کے وہ ابھی سونے کی تیاری کر رہا تھا کہ دروازے پر ہونے والی دستک نے اسے چونکا دیا۔ رات کے ساڑھے بارہ ہو رہے تھے۔ اس وقت کس کو اس کی یاد آ سکتی تھی۔ اپنے آپ سے الجھتے ہوئے اس نے تیسری دستک کے جواب میں بمشکل اٹھ کر دروازہ کھولا تھا۔

''ہانیہ......تم......؟'' دروازے پر کھڑی ہانیہ کو دیکھ کر وہ حیران ہی تو رہ گیا تھا۔

''ہوں' میں...... کیوں نہیں آ سکتی کیا؟''

''نہیں...... میں نے ایسا تو نہیں کہا۔''

''اوکے' چلو آؤ میرے ساتھ۔'' بنا کوئی سوال جواب کیے اس نے بازو سے پکڑ کر اسے باہر گھسیٹ لیا۔

''ہانیہ کیا کر رہی ہو اتنی رات کو' کسی کی آنکھ کھل گئی تو کیا سوچے گا۔''

''کچھ نہیں سوچے گا تم بیٹھو یہاں۔'' اپنے پرانے انداز میں واپس لوٹتے ہوئے اس نے لاؤنج میں لا کر اسے اپنے مقابل صوفے پر دھکیلا۔

''سارا سارا دن تم گھر سے غائب رہتے ہو' کھانے پینے پر بھی توجہ نہیں ہے مجھ سے تو ویسے ہی دشمنی ہو گئی ہے تمہاری۔ آنٹی بتا رہی تھیں بیمار بھی رہے ہو تم' شاید اسی لیے میرے بھائی کی شادی میں بھی شریک نہیں ہو سکے۔ کیا میں پوچھ سکتی ہوں نہال کہ تم ایسا کیوں کر رہے ہو؟''

''کیا کر رہا ہوں' بیماری اب کسی سے پوچھ کر تو نہیں آتی۔'' وہ مسکرایا تو ہانیہ چڑ گئی۔

''پتا ہے مجھے بیماری بتا کر نہیں آتی لیکن بیماری میں اگر انسان اپنوں کو اپنی تکلیف کا بتا دے تو میرے خیال میں اس کا ایمان متاثر نہیں ہوتا۔''

''کیا فائدہ ایویں کسی کو پریشان کرنے کا' تم تو ویسے بھی جنگ کی شہزادی بنی رہتی ہو' کس کے پاس بیٹھ کر دکھ روؤں اپنا۔''

''دکھ......اور تمہیں؟''

''کیوں؟ میں انسان نہیں' مجھے دکھ نہیں ہو سکتے؟''

''نہیں' کیونکہ تم انسان ہونے کے ساتھ ساتھ خود بہت بڑی آفت ہو۔'' اس بار ہانیہ کے الفاظ پر وہ کھل کر ہنسا تھا۔

''اور تم خود کیا ہو بندریا؟ ہر وقت بے چارے میرے بھائی کو پریشان کیے رکھتی ہو۔''

''نہال' ہر وقت اپنے بھائی کی سائیڈ مت لیا کرو' تمہارا بھائی اتنا بھی اچھا نہیں ہے۔''

''اتنا بھی اچھا نہ ہوتا تو تم پلٹ کر یہاں واپس کیوں آتیں۔'' اب وہ اس کا مذاق اڑا رہا تھا ہانیہ نے مسکراتے ہوئے اس کے کندھے پر مکا رسید کیا۔

''وہ تو اس نے میری جان بچائی تھی اس لیے ترس آ گیا۔''

''آہم...... آہم...... دل کی بے ایمانی کو ترس کا نام نہ دو۔'' وہ اس کا دوست تھا شاید اسی لیے اس کے دل کی بات جان گیا تھا ہانیہ نے بے ساختہ نظر چرائی تھی۔ تبھی وہ بولا۔

''تم بھیا کے ساتھ خوش ہو ناں ہانی؟''

''ہوں کوئی شک؟''

''نہیں کوئی شک نہیں۔'' یونہی دل کی تسلی کے لیے پوچھ رہا تھا وگرنہ تمہارے دل کا حال تو تمہاری آنکھوں سے دکھائی دے رہا ہے۔''

''جی نہیں اب ایسی بھی کوئی بات نہیں۔''

''ایسی ہی بات ہے۔'' ہانیہ کے شرمانے پر بے ساختہ وہ مسکرایا۔

''ایک دوست اپنے دوست سے دل کی بات نہیں چھپا سکتا اور میں تو یہ بات کب سے جانتا ہوں کہ تم میکال بھیا سے پیار کرتی ہو۔''

''بس رہنے دو' اتنے بڑے جادوگر بھی نہیں ہو تم۔''

''اتنا ہی بڑا جادوگر ہوں میں' تمہیں خبر نہیں ہے۔''

''ہاہ...... اچھا چھوڑو یہ بتاؤ آنٹی کو کیوں پریشان کر رہے ہو تم؟''

''کب پریشان کیا ہے یار' بس وہ ماں ہیں تو ذرا زیادہ محسوس کرتی ہیں وگرنہ ایسی تو کوئی بات نہیں ہے۔''

''سچ کہہ رہے ہو نا' مجھے تو لگتا ہے کسی لڑکی کا چکر ہے۔''

''ہاہاہا...... تم اور تمہاری سوچ۔''

''کیوں سچ نہیں ہے' کھاؤ میرے سر کی قسم کہ ایسی بات نہیں ہے۔''

''ہانیہ تم پاگل تو نہیں ہو گئیں۔''

''میں شروع سے ہی پاگل ہوں' تم مجھے چھوڑو اور بتاؤ جو میں پوچھ رہی ہوں۔''

''کیا بتاؤں؟''

''یہی کہ کون ہے وہ لڑکی۔''

''کیوں' تاکہ تم جا کر اسے میری برائیاں بتا دو اور وہ بھاگ جائے۔''

''اس کا مطلب ہے میرا قیاس صحیح نکلا۔''

''ہوا میں تیر چلاتی ہو پاگل جو ٹھہری۔''

''چلو ہوا میں تیر ہی سہی مگر لگتا تو نشانے پر ہے نا۔'' اس بار وہ پھر مسکرا دیا۔

''چلو بتاؤ شاباش کون ہے وہ؟''

''کیوں بتاؤں؟ تم تو مجھ سے ناراض تھیں۔''

''اب ناراض نہیں ہوں پلیز بتاؤ۔''

''بتاؤں گا مگر ابھی نہیں ابھی تم اٹھو اور اپنے کمرے میں جاؤ یونہی کوئی جاگ گیا تو مسئلہ ہو جائے گا۔''

''نہال' تم مجھ سے بھاگ کیوں رہے ہو؟''

''تم سے نہیں بھاگ سکتا میں پاگل' بے فکر رہو۔ چلو اب اٹھو شاباش۔''

اس بار اس نے اس کا ہاتھ پکڑ کر اسے کھڑا کیا اور پھر سیڑھیاں چڑھ کر اسے اس کے بیڈروم کے سامنے پہنچا کر واپس پلٹ گیا۔ ہانیہ بددل سی کمرے میں واپس آئی تو میکال نے جلدی سے آنکھیں بند کر لیں۔ وہ اسے کبھی بھی یہ احساس دلانا نہیں چاہتا تھا کہ اس کے بیڈ سے اترتے ہی اس کی آنکھ کھل گئی تھی اور تب سے اب تک وہ جاگ کر اس کا انتظار کر رہا تھا۔ تاہم دل کے اندر کہیں اعتبار کا ایک چراغ ضرور بجھ گیا تھا۔

''ہانیہ۔'' وہ اپنی وارڈ روب صحیح کر رہی تھی جب گھر کے اندر داخل ہوتے ہی نہال نے اسے پکارا مسز حسن جو کچن میں تھیں فوراً باہر نکل آئیں۔

''ہر وقت ہانیہ...... ہانیہ کبھی اپنے ساتھ بھی وقت گزار لینے دیا کرو اسے۔''

''اپنے ساتھ ہی وقت گزارتی ہے مما' میں نے تو اس کی کمپنی میں بیٹھنا بہت کم کر دیا ہے۔''

''اچھی بات ہے۔ سارا کا فون آیا تھا گھر آنا چاہ رہی ہے۔ تمہیں اگر فرصت ہو تو اسے لے آؤ جا کر۔''

''میں نہیں جا سکتا مما' سوری......!''

''کیوں تم کیوں نہیں جا سکتے؟''

''بس دل نہیں چاہ رہا۔''

''سدھر جاؤ نہال' چھوڑ دو یہ بچپنا تمہارے پاپا کو تم سے بڑی توقعات ہیں۔''

''پورا اتر تو رہا ہوں ان کی توقعات پر مما' اور کیا کروں؟''

''دلچسپی لو گھر میں اور کاروبار میں بھی۔ سمیر (عینا کا بھائی) نے سارا کے لیے پرپوزل دیا ہے۔ تمہارے پاپا اس بات کو لے کر بہت خوش ہیں۔ عینا اور کمال بھی خوش ہیں عینا نے تو باقاعدہ تیاری بھی شروع کر دی ہے شادی کی۔''

''تو یہ سب آپ مجھے کیوں بتا رہی ہیں؟''

''اس لیے کیونکہ تمہارے پاپا مائرہ کے ساتھ تمہارا رشتہ طے کرنا چاہ رہے ہیں۔''

''وہاٹ......'' اسے جیسے شاک لگا تھا۔

''ہاں'......عینا اور کمال کی بھی یہی خواہش ہے بلکہ کمال بتا رہا تھا کہ خود عینا نے ہی اس خواہش کا اظہار کیا ہے سارا کو بھابی بنانے کے ساتھ ساتھ وہ تمہیں بھی اپنے بہنوئی کے روپ میں دیکھنا چاہتی ہے۔''

''مجھے اس سے کوئی مطلب نہیں کہ وہ کیا چاہتی ہیں۔ کیا نہیں میں صرف اتنا جانتا ہوں کہ میں کسی بھی قیمت پر مائرہ کے ساتھ شادی نہیں کر سکتا۔'' اس کے تو جیسے تن بدن میں آگ لگ گئی تھی تبھی میکال نے قدم وہاں رکھے تھے۔

''کیوں......؟'' نہال چونکا اور اس نے بے ساختہ مڑ کر پیچھے دیکھا تھا۔

''کیونکہ میں اسے As a life patner پسند نہیں کرتا۔ میرے نزدیک سارا اور مائرہ میں کوئی فرق نہیں۔''

''یہ کوئی وجہ نہیں ہے۔''

''یہی وجہ ہے اس کے علاوہ اور کوئی وجہ نہیں۔'' میکال سے نظریں چراتا وہ وہاں ٹھہرا نہیں تھا وہ اسے دیکھ کر رہ گیا۔

''میری تو سمجھ میں نہیں آ رہا کہ آخر اس لڑکے کو ہو کیا گیا ہے ہر بات میں ضد کرنے لگا ہے۔'' مسز حسن اب پریشانی سے میکال کی طرف دیکھ رہی تھیں۔ وہ کوٹ صوفے پر پھینکتے ہوئے خود بھی وہیں ٹک گیا۔

''آپ پریشان نہ ہوں' ان شاء اللہ سب ٹھیک ہو جائے گا۔''

''ان شاء اللہ...... تم سناؤ تمہارا ہنی مون ٹرپ فائنل ہو گیا۔''

''جی مما میں نے ٹکٹ کے لیے اپلائی کر دیا ہے۔ ان شاء اللہ دو چار روز میں تیاری کر لیں گے۔''

''چلو اچھی بات ہے میں چاہتی ہوں تم اور ہانیہ ایک دوسرے کو اچھی طرح سے سمجھ لو۔''

''ان شاء اللہ ایسا ہی ہو گا مما آپ فکر نہ کریں۔'' وہ مسکرایا تو جواب میں مسز حسن نے اسے ڈھیر ساری دعائیں دے ڈالیں۔ ٹھیک تین روز کے بعد وہ اور ہانیہ اپنے ہنی مون کے ٹرپ کے لیے پیرس چلے آئے اور یہی وہ لمحہ تھا جب دونوں کو ایک دوسرے کو سمجھنے کا موقع ملا تھا۔ دونوں نے ایک دوسرے کے دل میں اپنے لیے تاج محل تعمیر کیے تھے ہانیہ کی

زندگی میں وہ واحد دور تھا جو اس نے بے حد انجوائے کیا تھا۔ میکال کے لیے وہ جیسے کانچ کی گڑیا تھی اور اس کی ہر خوشی کا خیال رکھنا جیسے اس پر فرض تھا صبح آنکھ کھلتے ہی سب سے پہلے وہ ہانیہ کو دیکھتا۔ پھر جھک کر اس کی آنکھیں چومتا' تب کہیں جا کر اس کی آنکھیں کھلتی تھیں۔ انہی دنوں میں اس نے جانا تھا کہ ہانیہ بھی اس سے بے پناہ محبت کرتی ہے اس شام وہ دونوں ایفل ٹاور کی رونقیں دیکھنے کے لیے نکلے تھے مگر واپسی پر تیز بارش نے ان کے لیے مشکلات پیدا کر دی تھیں۔

ہانیہ تھکن سے چُور ہوٹل میں اپنے کمرے میں واپس آئی تو اس کے دانت بج رہے تھے۔ میکال نے اپنے کپڑے تبدیل کرنے کے بعد فوراً اس کے کپڑے بھی تبدیل کروائے مگر ہانیہ کی ٹھنڈ کسی طور کم ہونے کا نام نہیں لے رہی تھی۔ میکال کو اس پر بے حد ترس آیا۔

''چلو' تم لیٹو بستر میں۔''

اس کا ابھی مزید آؤٹنگ کا پروگرام تھا مگر ہانیہ کا حال دیکھنے کے بعد اس نے اپنا ارادہ ملتوی کر دیا تھا وہ بستر میں گھسی تو میکال نے اچھی طرح سے کمبل اس کے اوپر سیٹ کر دیا مگر کافی دیر گزرنے کے بعد بھی وہ کپکپا رہی تھی تب مجبوراً اسے بھی ساتھ لیٹنا پڑا کمبل میں گھس کر اپنے پاؤں سے اس کے پاؤں رگڑتے ہوئے اس نے اسے راحت پہنچانے کی کوشش کی تھی۔

''ہانیہ۔''

''جی۔''

''خوش ہوناں؟''

''ہوں۔''

''کوئی شکوہ' کوئی شکایت؟''

''نہیں۔''

''اب تو چھوڑ کر نہیں جاؤ گی نا؟''

''سوچوں گی۔'' شرارتی انداز میں مسکراتے ہوئے اس نے اسے چھیڑا تھا۔ جواب میں میکال نے اسے خود میں سمو لیا۔

''جان لے لوں گا اگر ایسا کچھ سوچا بھی تو۔''

''اور اگر آپ نے بے وفائی کی تو؟''

''تو تم میری جان لے لینا۔ دل تو پہلے ہی قبضے میں کیا ہوا ہے۔''

''غلط..... آپ کا دل تو عائشہ جی کے پاس ہے۔''

''نہیں ہانی' ایسی بات نہیں ہے یہ ٹھیک ہے کہ میں نے عائشہ سے محبت کی ہے مگر وہ محبت صرف ایک وقت کے لیے محدود تھی تمہاری بد دعا کے بعد اس محبت نے اپنا روپ بدل لیا۔ اب تو آنکھ کھلتے ہی تمہارا چہرہ نظر نہ آئے تو جان پر بن جاتی ہے یہی ڈر رہتا ہے کہ کہیں کسی بات پر ناراض ہو کر چھوڑ نہ جاؤ۔''

اس کے دونوں ہاتھ ہاتھوں میں لے کر وہ کہہ رہا تھا اور ہانیہ کے اندر جیسے سکون اترتا چلا جا رہا تھا۔

''سچ کہتا ہوں ہانیہ' میں نہیں جانتا کہ مجھے کیا ہو گیا ہے۔ جس لڑکی سے زبردستی نکاح پر میں نے حشر اٹھا دیا تھا اب اسی لڑکی میں مجھے عائشہ کا چہرہ نظر آتا ہے۔ وہ سارے خواب جو میں نے اس لڑکی کی رفاقت سے جوڑ رکھے تھے ان خوابوں

کی تعبیر تمہاری رفاقت دے رہی ہے۔ زندگی میں پہلی بار میں خود کو بہت پرفیکٹ محسوس کر رہا ہوں۔"

"اتنی لمبی نہ چھوڑیں۔ میرے ہاتھ درد کرنے لگے ہیں لپیٹتے لپیٹتے۔"

"تمہیں میرے جذبے جھوٹے لگ رہے ہیں۔" کہنی بیڈ پر ٹکاتے ہوئے اس نے ہانیہ کو گھور کر دیکھا تو وہ مسکرا دی۔

✿......✿......✿

اگلے ہفتے ان کی پیرس سے واپسی ہوگئی تھی۔ حسن صاحب اور مسز حسن نے سمیر کی خواہش پر اپنی بیٹی سارا کا رشتہ اس کے ساتھ طے کر دیا تھا تاہم نہال اب بھی اڑیل گھوڑے کی طرح اپنی ضد پر اڑا ہوا تھا جس کی وجہ سے وہ دونوں ہی بہت پریشان تھے۔ روز بروز اس کی صحت بھی گرتی جا رہی تھی ادھر مائرہ کا حال برا تھا پہلے میکال نے اسے ٹھکرا کر اس کی عزت نفس کو مجروح کیا تھا اور اب نہال اسے ٹھکرا کر اس کی بے عزتی کر رہا تھا گیلی لکڑی کی مانند وہ اندر ہی اندر سے سلگ اٹھی تھی تاہم زبان سے اس نے کچھ بھی کہنا مناسب نہیں سمجھا تھا وہ اور سائرہ صرف ایک ہفتے کے لیے گھر آئی تھیں اور پھر چلی گئیں۔

زندگی پھر سے اپنے معمول پر آ گئی تھی ہانیہ کو ہر طرف صرف میکال ہی میکال دکھائی دیتا تھا وہ اس کے سارے کام اپنے ہاتھ سے کر کے خوشی محسوس کرتی تھی رات گئے تک دونوں جاگ کر اپنے ہونے والے بچے کے متعلق مختلف پلان بناتے رہتے۔ اکثر آفس سے واپسی کے بعد وہ اسے گھمانے لے جاتا کبھی دونوں شاپنگ پر چلے جاتے۔ نہال کی ذات کہیں بہت پیچھے رہ گئی تھی۔ وہ چاہتا بھی تو زبردستی ہانیہ کی توجہ اپنی طرف مبذول نہیں کروا سکتا تھا اسی لیے اس نے خود کو اپنے کمرے تک محدود کر لیا تھا۔

اگلے تین ماہ اسی طرح گزر گئے تھے۔ سارا اور مائرہ کے فائنل ایگزام بھی ہو چکے تھے لٰہذا وہ دونوں ہوسٹل سے گھر آ گئیں۔ اس روز بارش ہو رہی تھی۔ سنڈے کی چھٹی کے باعث میکال بھی گھر پر ہی تھا اور اپنے رت جگے کی نیند پوری کر رہا تھا بارش نے زور پکڑا تو ہانیہ کو پیرس یاد آ گیا۔ وہ فوراً کمرے میں آئی اور میکال کا کمبل کھینچ دیا۔

"میکال اٹھو۔"

"کیوں خیریت؟" وہ کسمسایا تھا ہانیہ نے اس کا بازو پکڑ کر زبردستی بیڈ پر بٹھا دیا۔

"ہوں خیریت ہی ہے باہر دیکھو کتنی تیز بارش ہو رہی ہے چلو مل کر نہاتے ہیں۔"

"نہیں تم نہالو، میرا موڈ نہیں ہے۔"

"ایسی کی تیسی تمہارے موڈ کی۔ اٹھو......"

اجنبیت کی ساری دیواریں گر چکی تھیں۔ میکال کو ناچار بستر چھوڑنا پڑا۔ سرسبز لان میں بارش اب زور پکڑ چکی تھی مگر وہ ہانیہ کے ساتھ بھیگتا رہا اوپر اپنے کمرے کے ٹیرس پر کھڑا نہال دیر تک ان دونوں کو بارش میں بھیگتے ہوئے دیکھتا رہا۔

✿......✿......✿

اگلی صبح ہانیہ کی آنکھ کھلی تو خاصی دیر ہو چکی تھی۔ میکال ابھی تک مزے سے بستر میں دبکا سو رہا تھا ہانیہ بال سمیٹ کر جونہی بیڈ سے اترنے لگی اس نے اس کا ہاتھ پکڑ لیا۔

''کہاں جا رہی ہو؟''

''کچن میں' ٹائم دیکھو ذرا۔''

''گولی مارو ٹائم کو' مجھے نہیں پتا۔''

''میکال تم پاگل تو نہیں ہو گئے ہو؟''

''پاگل ہی ہوں۔''

''ابھی آنٹی آ گئیں نا تو سارا پاگل پن بھگا دیں گی۔'' زبردستی ہاتھ چھڑاتے ہوئے وہ بیڈ سے اتر آئی۔

''اچھا بات سنو۔''

اسے پکارتے ہوئے وہ خود بھی بیڈ سے اتر آیا تھا پھر وارڈ روب کھول کر اس میں سے گرے کلر کا شلوار سوٹ نکالا جو عائشہ نے اسے گفٹ کیا تھا اور اسے بے حد عزیز تھا تاہم اب تک اس نے وہ سوٹ استعمال نہیں کیا تھا۔

''یہ لو' پلیز اسے ابھی پریس کر دو بہت امپورٹمنٹ میٹنگ ہے آج سمجھو پاپا کی نظر میں تمہارے شوہر نامدار کے سرخرو ہونے کا بہت سنہری چانس ہے۔ میں تب تک باتھ لے لوں۔''

پیار سے اس کا گال تھپتھپا کر کہتے ہوئے اس نے اپنا ڈریس اس کے ہاتھ میں پکڑا دیا ہانیہ نے بال کیچر کرتے ہوئے استری کا سوئچ آن کر دیا۔ جلدی جلدی ہاتھ چلاتے ہوئے ابھی اس نے شلوار پریس کی تھی کہ مائرہ دروازہ پر دستک دے کر اندر چلی آئی۔

''ہانیہ بھابی' آپ کو آنٹی بلا رہی ہیں' ہادیہ آپی کا فون آیا ہے۔ ایمرجنسی ہے۔''

''اچھا' میں یہ شرٹ پریس کر لوں پھر آتی ہوں۔''

''شرٹ آ کر پریس کر لیجیے گا وہ ہولڈ پر ہیں۔''

روکھے لہجے میں کہہ کر وہ کمرے سے نکل گئی تھی ہانیہ نے استری اسٹینڈ پر کھڑی کی اور کمرے سے نکل آئی۔ مائرہ نے جیسے ہی اسے کمرے سے نکلتے دیکھا لپک کر اندر گئی اور اسٹینڈ پر کھڑی استری اٹھا کر شرٹ پر رکھ دی۔ میکال باتھ لے کر نکلا تو شرٹ سے دھواں نکل رہا تھا۔ تبھی مائرہ بھی دوبارہ کمرے میں داخل ہوئی۔

''او میرے خدایا...... یہ کیا ہوا' ہانیہ بھابی کہاں ہیں؟'' لپک کر شرٹ اٹھاتے ہوئے اس نے میکال کو دیکھا جو ساکت کھڑا تھا۔

''اوہ' یاد آیا وہ تو نہال کو ناشتہ کروا رہی ہیں۔ مگر یہ شرٹ تو پریس کر جاتیں۔'' شرٹ میں ہوئے سوراخ کو تاسف بھری نگاہوں سے دیکھتے ہوئے اس نے پھر میکال کو دیکھا تھا جس کا چہرہ ضبط کی شدت سے سرخ ہو رہا تھا۔ ہانیہ کمرے

میں آئی تو مائرہ کے ہاتھ میں جلی ہوئی شرٹ دیکھ کر دنگ رہ گئی۔

''یہ...... یہ کیا ہوا؟''

''ہونا کیا ہے، جل گئی ہے شرٹ، افسوس ہے بھابی عجلت میں آپ کو یہ بھی یاد نہیں رہا کہ استری اسٹینڈ پر ہی کھڑی کر جاتیں۔''

''میں نے تو اسٹینڈ پر ہی کھڑی کی تھی۔''

مائرہ کے ہاتھ سے شرٹ لیتے ہوئے اس نے پریشان نگاہوں سے میکال کی طرف دیکھا جس کی آنکھیں اور چہرہ ضبط کی شدت سے سرخ ہو رہا تھا۔

''اٹس اوکے، میں کوئی دوسرا سوٹ پہن لوں گا۔ تم ٹینشن نہ لو۔''

نرمی سے ہانیہ کے گال تھپتھپاتے ہوئے وہ کمرے سے نکل گیا تھا مائرہ جل بھن کر رہ گئی جبکہ ہانیہ کا شاک کم ہونے میں ہی نہیں آ رہا تھا۔ میکال کی چپ اور ہانیہ کی شرمندگی ختم ہونے میں چند دن لگے تھے اس روز موسم پھر بے حد حسین تھا۔ سنڈے کی چھٹی کے باعث میکال دیر تک پڑا سوتا رہا۔ بارش شروع ہوئی تو ہانیہ اسے اٹھانے کے لیے آ گئی مگر اس بار وہ ٹس سے مس نہ ہوا تب اسے زور کا مکا رسید کر کے وہ نیچے آ گئی۔ نہال لان میں بیٹھا تھا وہ اسی طرف چلی آئی۔ میکال کی آنکھ کھلی تو کمرے میں اچھی خاصی ٹھنڈ تھی۔ وہ ابھی اٹھ ہی رہا تھا کہ مائرہ گرما گرم پکوڑے اور چٹنی لے کر کمرے میں چلی آئی۔

''یہ لیں میکال بھائی پکوڑے، اتنا پیارا موسم ہو رہا ہے اور آپ سو رہے ہیں۔''

''پیارے موسم میں ہی سونے کا مزہ آتا ہے خیر، ہانیہ کہاں ہے؟''

''ہانیہ بھابی تو نیچے نہال بھائی کے ساتھ بارش انجوائے کر رہی ہیں۔''

ٹرے ٹیبل پر رکھتے ہوئے اس نے کچھ ایسے انداز میں کہا تھا کہ وہ اسے دیکھتا رہ گیا۔

''مائنڈ مت کیجیے گا میکال بھائی مگر آپ نے ہانیہ بھابی کو کچھ زیادہ ہی آزادی دے رکھی ہے اب روز آدھی رات کو اٹھ کر جوان دیور کے کمرے میں جانے کیا تک بنتی ہے بھلا؟ ٹھیک ہے وہ نہال بھائی کی دوست ہیں مگر دوست ہونے کا مطلب یہ تو نہیں کہ آپ اسے شوہر کے برابر لے آؤ، جبکہ آپ کو یہ بھی پتا ہو کہ آپ کا دیور آپ سے پیار کرتا ہے اور صرف آپ کی وجہ سے وہ کہیں اور شادی بھی نہیں کرتا۔''

''اسٹاپ اٹ مائرہ...... میں ہانیہ کے بارے میں ایسی فضول گوئی پسند نہیں کرتا۔'' وہ تپا تھا مگر مائرہ باز نہیں آئی۔

''جانتی ہوں مگر میں آپ کی دشمن نہیں ہوں میکال بھائی جو بے پر کی اڑا کر آپ کا دماغ خراب کروں گی۔ بات صرف اتنی سی ہے کہ آپ مجھے بہت عزیز ہیں۔ عائشہ جی کے بعد جس طرح سے آپ نے خود کو سنبھالا ہے میں جانتی ہوں اسی لیے میں نہیں چاہتی کہ دوبارہ کوئی آپ کو ویسی ہی چوٹ پہنچائے۔ میں ہانیہ بھابی اور نہال بھائی میں سے کسی پر بھی بہتان نہیں لگا رہی۔ مگر دو نامحرم رشتوں کے مابین تیسرا ہمیشہ شیطان ہوتا ہے اگر آپ نے اس بات کو سیریس نہ لیا تو نقصان اٹھا سکتے ہیں۔''

وارننگ دیتے ہوئے وہ فوراً کمرے سے نکل گئی تھی۔ پیچھے میکال کے بدن میں جیسے کسی نے آگ بھر دی تھی۔ وہ ان لوگوں میں سے تھا جو محبت کو کھو سکتے تھے مگر شیئر نہیں کر سکتے تبھی بیڈ سے اٹھ کر لان کی طرف کھلنے والی کھڑکی میں آیا تھا۔ سامنے ہانیہ اور نہال ایک دوسرے کو تنگ کر رہے تھے۔ نہال نے ہانیہ کو پکڑ رکھا تھا جبکہ اس کے کپڑے اس کے جسم سے چپک کر اس کی نسوانیت کو خوب واضح کر رہے تھے۔ اگر وہ لڑکی اس کی محبت اور اعتماد سے فائدہ اٹھا رہی تھی تو بہت غلط کر

رہی تھی۔ رات تک اس کا موڈ بگڑ چکا تھا۔ رات کا کھانا بھی اس نے بے دلی سے کھایا تھا۔ کھانے کے بعد وہ دوست کی طرف نکل گیا۔ موسم ہنوز خراب تھا ہانیہ اس کے خراب موڈ کو محسوس کرنے کے باوجود دیر تک جاگ کر اس کا انتظار کرتی رہی۔ ساڑھے بارہ کے قریب کہیں وہ گھر آیا تو وہ جاگ رہی تھی۔ کمرے میں آنے کے بعد وہ سیدھا واش روم میں گھس گیا۔ نہا کر فریش ہونے کے بعد بیڈ پر آیا تو ہانیہ کو اپنا منتظر پایا۔

''کہاں گئے تھے...... وہ بھی اتنی رات کو اتنے خراب موسم میں؟''

''دوست کی طرف گیا تھا ایمرجنسی کال آ گئی تھی۔''

''خیریت؟''

''ہوں ایک کمرشل تیار کر رہا ہے مجھے کہہ رہا تھا ماڈلنگ کے لیے۔''

''پھر......؟''

''کچھ نہیں، میں نے کہہ دیا سوچ کر بتاؤں گا۔'' نروٹھے لہجے میں کہنے کے بعد وہ کروٹ بدل کر لیٹ گیا۔ ہانیہ دیکھتی رہ گئی۔

''میکال آپ۔''

''سو جاؤ ہانیہ پلیز...... میرے سر میں درد ہو رہا ہے میں اس وقت گپ نہیں لگا سکتا۔'' اس بار اس کے لہجے میں کڑواہٹ تھی۔ وہ چپ چاپ لائٹ آف کر کے لیٹ گئی۔

اگلے روز اس کی آنکھ کھلنے سے پہلے ہی وہ اٹھ کر فریش ہو چکا تھا ہانیہ کی آنکھ کھٹکے کی آواز پر کھلی۔ دیکھا تو سامنے وہ ڈریسنگ کے آگے کھڑا آفس کے لیے تیار ہو رہا تھا وہ لپک کر قریب آئی۔

''آج اتنی جلدی بیدار ہو گئے مجھے جگایا بھی نہیں۔''

''ضرورت نہیں سمجھی۔''

''کیوں، پتا ہے نا روز میں آپ کی ہیلپ کرتی ہوں تیار ہونے میں۔'' وہ ناراض ہوئی تھی مگر وہ چپ رہا۔

''یہ لیں آج آپ نے یہ والی ٹائی لگانی ہے۔ میں موزے لے کر آتی ہوں۔''

''اس کی ضرورت نہیں ہے...... میں لے لوں گا۔''

''میکال۔'' ٹھٹک کر اس کا چہرہ دیکھتے ہوئے وہ اس کے سامنے آئی تھی۔

''آپ مجھ سے ناراض ہیں؟''

''نہیں۔''

''نہیں تو ٹھیک سے بات کیوں نہیں کر رہے؟''

''کیا بات کروں...... ہوں؟'' وہ پھر چڑا تو ہانیہ کی پلکیں بھیگ گئیں۔

''میں جانتی ہوں آپ مجھ سے ناراض ہیں مگر میں یہ نہیں جانتی کہ آپ کیوں ناراض ہیں۔ کیا ایسا نہیں ہو سکتا کہ آپ مجھے معاف کر دیں پلیز۔''

''ہانیہ جب ایسی کوئی بات ہے ہی نہیں تو کیوں تم بے کار میں اپنا اور میرا وقت ضائع کر رہی ہو؟''

''گولی ماریں وقت کو...... مجھے نہیں پتا بس...... میرے ساتھ موڈ ٹھیک کریں...... میں آپ کی ناراضگی برداشت نہیں کر سکتی۔'' پلکوں سے آنسو ٹپکاتے وہ میکال کے سینے سے سر ٹکا گئی تھی۔ وہ ٹھنڈی آہ بھر کر رہ گیا۔

''پاگل تو نہیں ہو تم؟''

''پاگل ہی ہوں۔'' بھرائے لہجے میں اس نے کہا اور میکال کی ساری ناراضگی جیسے اڑن چھو ہوگئی۔ اپنی بانہوں میں بھرتے ہوئے وہ سب کچھ بھول گیا تھا۔ آنے والے دنوں میں پھر یہ کئی بار ہوا چھوٹی چھوٹی باتوں پر دونوں کا جھگڑا ہوجاتا اور پھر مان جاتے تھے۔ نہال کی صحت گرتی جارہی تھی مگر سب ہی جیسے اس سے غافل ہو بیٹھے تھے۔

اس روز مائرہ کچن میں ہانیہ کے ساتھ مدد کروا رہی تھی مسز حسن اور سارا مارکیٹ گئے ہوئے تھے۔ تبھی میدان صاف پا کر اس نے اگلا وار کرنا مناسب سمجھا تھا۔

''ہانیہ بھابی کیا آپ نے ابھی تک میکال بھائی کو دل سے معاف نہیں کیا؟''

''نہیں ایسی تو کوئی بات نہیں...... کیوں؟''

''مجھے ایسا لگا ہے جیسے آپ دونوں کے درمیان کچھ اختلاف ہے پھر میکال بھائی کی سرگرمیاں بھی کچھ اچھی نہیں ہیں۔''

''کیا مطلب؟'' نل کے نیچے پلیٹیں دھو کر رکھتی وہ ٹھٹکی۔

''مطلب میری فرینڈ بتا رہی تھی وہ آج کل ایک ماڈل علیزہ کو بہت ٹائم دے رہے ہیں۔ اکثر آفس سے اٹھ کر اسے گھمانے اور شاپنگ کروانے لے جاتے ہیں کبھی کبھار وہ آفس میں چلی آتی ہے میری فرینڈ چونکہ میکال بھائی کے آفس میں کام کرتی ہے اس لیے اس کی گہری نظر ہوتی ہے ہر سرگرمی پر، آپ کو بھی اپنے شوہر پر نظر رکھنی چاہیے۔ مرد اس قابل نہیں ہوتے کہ ان پر اندھا یقین کیا جاسکے۔''

''صحیح کہتی ہو تم مگر میکال ایسے نہیں ہیں مجھے ان کی مصروفیات کا بھی پتا ہے اور علیزہ کا بھی...... تم ٹینشن نہ لو۔''

قطعی حتمی انداز میں کہتے ہوئے اس نے مائرہ کو تو مایوس کردیا تھا مگر اس کے اپنے اندر بے چینی بڑھ گئی تھی۔ میکال اس رات بہت دیر سے گھر واپس آیا تھا۔ ہانیہ رخ موڑے بے نیاز بنی سوئی رہی۔ اگلے روز مائرہ کے اصرار پر مائرہ کے ساتھ ہی وہ مارکیٹ آئی تھی اور اتفاق سے جس ریسٹوران میں وہ کھانے کے لیے آئی میکال ماڈل علیزہ کے ساتھ وہاں پہلے سے ہی موجود تھا۔ مائرہ نے اس کی توجہ اس کی طرف مبذول کروائی تھی۔ ہانیہ کو لگا جیسے اس کے قدم من من کے ہوگئے ہوں۔ صبح اس نے کہا تھا کہ آج سارا دن وہ بہت مصروف رہے گا۔ سر کھجانے کا بھی ٹائم نہیں ہوگا مگر وہ مصروفیات کیا تھی یہ اسے اب پتا لگا تھا۔

اس رات پھر میکال کی گھر واپسی بہت لیٹ ہوئی تھی۔ ہانیہ کا دل جل کر راکھ ہو رہا تھا۔ اسے نہ نیند آرہی تھی نہ قرار۔ میکال بھی چپ چاپ سوگیا تھا۔ اسے جیسے ہانیہ کے جلدی سو جانے سے کوئی فرق ہی نہیں پڑ رہا تھا۔ صبح بھی اٹھتے ہی آفس بھاگنے کی کرتا تھا۔ جانے وہ ایسا کیوں کر رہا تھا۔ سوچ سوچ کر ہانیہ کی شریانیں جیسے پھٹنے لگی تھیں۔ اگلے روز میکال کے آفس جانے کے بعد وہ نہال کے کمرے میں آئی تھی۔ مقصد اس کی لائبریری سے اپنی پسند کی کچھ بہترین کتابیں لینا تھا اور وہ یہی کر رہی تھی جب کتابوں کی ریک کے درمیان ایک کتاب میں اس کی نظر کچھ نفیس کاغذات پر جا پڑی۔ فطری تجسس کے ہاتھوں مجبور ہوکر اس نے کتاب سے وہ کاغذات باہر نکالے تھے جن کے اوپر بڑے حروف میں ''شوکت خانم میموریل اسپتال'' کا نام درج تھا۔ اس کے ہاتھ جیسے کپکپا اٹھے۔ تیزی سے نظریں نچلے حروف پر دوڑائیں تو وجود جیسے ہوا میں معلق ہوتا گیا۔ بروقت وہ اگر قریب پڑی کرسی کو تھام نہ لیتی تو اس کا گر جانا یقینی تھا۔

❁......❁......❁

''پاپا......!''

زائر حویلی کی دہلیز پار کر رہا تھا جب اس کی ننھی کلی کی صدا نے اس کے قدم جیسے زمین سے باندھ کر رکھ دیے۔ قطعی

شاکڈ انداز میں وہ پلٹا تھا۔ جب وہ ننھی کلی دوڑتے ہوئے اس کے کشادہ سینے سے آ لگی۔ زائر کو لگا جیسے وہ پتھر کا ہو کر رہ گیا ہو۔

''آپ میرے پاپا ہیں نا؟'' اگلے ہی پل وہ اس کے سینے سے سر اٹھائے پوچھ رہی تھی۔

زائر کا سر آپ ہی آپ اثبات میں ہل گیا۔ جبکہ اس کی آنکھوں کے گوشے بھی نم ہو گئے تھے بچی اس کے اقرار پر بے حد خوش ہوئی تھی پھر بنا کچھ کہے دوڑ کر اپنے بھائی کو بھی بلا لائی۔

''چاند دیکھو ہمارے پاپا مل گئے۔ میں نے کہا تھا نا یہی ہمارے پاپا ہیں۔'' خوشی سے بے حال وہ اپنے بھائی کو بتا رہی تھی مگر وہ ٹکر ٹکر زائر کی طرف دیکھتے ہوئے اس کے قریب آنے سے ہچکچا رہا تھا۔ تب زائر نے ہاتھ بڑھا کر دونوں کو اپنے بازوؤں میں سمیٹ لیا۔ اس کا دل اس لمحے جیسے پھٹنے کو تیار تھا۔

''آپ کو کیسے پتا چلا کہ میں ہی آپ کا پاپا ہوں گڑیا؟'' بچوں کو خوب چومنے کے بعد جب اس کا دل معمول پر آیا تو اس نے اپنی بیٹی سے پوچھا۔ جواباً وہ اس کا ہاتھ تھامتے ہوئے بولی۔

''اس روز جب چاند درخت سے گرا تھا اور اسے چوٹ لگی تھی تو آپ ہی اسے ڈاکٹر کے پاس لے کر گئے تھے۔ جبکہ مما نے آپ کو ڈانٹا بھی تھا بعد میں اشعر انکل نے مما سے آپ کے بارے میں پوچھا تو انہوں نے انکل کو بتا دیا کہ آپ ہی ہمارے پاپا ہیں۔ مما کو اپنے غصے میں یاد ہی نہیں رہا کہ میں بھی پاس ہی کھڑی ہوں ورنہ شاید وہ یہ بات کبھی نہ کرتیں۔ مما بالکل بھی اچھی نہیں ہیں پاپا۔ وہ ہمیں آپ سے دور کرنا چاہتی ہیں۔'' بچی نے ساری بات صاف صاف بتا دی تھی۔

زائر کا دل سینے میں مچل اٹھا۔

''نہیں...... اب مما ایسا کبھی نہیں کر سکے گی گڑیا...... اللہ کے سوا اب دنیا کی کوئی طاقت آپ کو آپ کے پاپا سے دور نہیں کر سکتی۔ چلو میرے ساتھ۔''

''کہاں؟''

''پاپا کے گھر...... جہاں آپ کو بہت زیادہ پیار کرنے والی آپ کی دادو ہیں۔ دادا ہیں اور بھی بہت لوگ ہیں۔''

''اور مما؟''

''مما کو ابھی ہم کچھ نہیں بتائیں گے۔'' تائیدی انداز میں اس نے بچوں کی طرف دیکھا تھا۔

اس کی بیٹی نے فوراً اثبات میں سر ہلا دیا۔ تاہم اس کا بیٹا اب بھی خاموش تھا۔

''کیا ہوا چاند...... کیا تم پاپا کے ساتھ جانا نہیں چاہتے؟''

''نہیں...... میں مما کو پریشان نہیں کرنا چاہتا۔''

''تو ٹھیک ہے پھر میں پاپا کے ساتھ جا رہی ہوں تم رہو یہیں ماما کے چمچے بن کر جن کے پاس ہمارے ساتھ گزارنے کے لیے تھوڑا سا ٹائم بھی نہیں ہے۔'' گڑیا اس کی پوری پوری سائیڈ لے رہی تھی۔ چاند تھوڑی دیر کی کشمکش کے بعد راضی ہو گیا۔

ثانیہ اشعر حسین کے ساتھ شہر سے واپس لوٹی تو تھکن سے برا حال تھا۔ خود اشعر بھی بہت زیادہ تھک چکا تھا۔ تبھی فریش ہو کر فوراً سونے چلا گیا۔ ثانیہ فریش ہو کر آئی تو چوہدرانی عشاء کی نماز پڑھ رہی تھیں۔ وہ وہیں ان کے قریب بیٹھ گئی۔

''بچوں نے زیادہ تنگ تو نہیں کیا آپ کو؟'' چوہدرانی کے سلام پھیرنے پر اس نے پوچھا تھا۔

''نہیں...... آج تو دونوں کمرے سے ہی نہیں نکلے۔''

''اچھی بات ہے...... میں خود بھی سارے راستے یہی دعائیں کرتی آئی تھی کہ وہ اپنے کمرے سے نہ نکلیں۔'' چہرے پر مسکان سجائے اس نے اپنے اطمینان کا اظہار کیا۔

''گھر مل گیا شہر میں؟''

''جی دادو، بہت اچھا گھر مل گیا ہے۔ آفس بھی قریب ہے اور بچوں کا اسکول بھی، اب بچوں کے ساتھ مجھے اور اشعر کو بھی کوئی مسئلہ نہیں ہوگا آنے جانے میں۔''

''چلو اچھی بات ہے ویسے اشعر میاں کے کیا ارادے ہیں؟ میرا مطلب ہے بنا نکاح کے وہ تمہارے ساتھ تمہارے گھر میں کیسے رہے گا؟''

''او کم آن دادو...... جس ملک سے میں آئی ہوں وہاں ایسی چھوٹی چھوٹی باتیں کوئی اہمیت نہیں رکھتیں۔ ویسے بھی میں اور اشعر بہت جلد نکاح کرنے والے ہیں۔'' تنک کر کہتی وہ فوراً اٹھ گئی تھی۔

کچن میں کھانا تیار رکھا تھا۔ کھانے کی ٹرے اٹھا کر وہ بچوں کے کمرے میں آئی تو وہاں کوئی نہیں تھا۔ ثانیہ کا دل زور سے دھڑک اٹھا۔

''چاند...... گڑیا۔'' بدحواس ہو کر وہ واش روم کی طرف بھاگی مگر وہ وہاں نہیں تھے۔ ثانیہ کو لگا جیسے کسی نے اس کا دل مٹھی میں جکڑ لیا ہو۔

''کیا ہوا ثانیہ؟'' چوہدرانی اس کی پکار پر کمرے میں جاتے جاتے رک گئی تھیں۔ ثانیہ لپک کر ان کے قریب آئی۔

''دادو چاند اور گڑیا کمرے میں نہیں ہیں۔'' اس کے چہرے پر ہوائیاں اڑ رہی تھیں۔

''کیا...... یہ کیسے ہوسکتا ہے؟'' وہ بھی پریشان ہوگئی تھیں تبھی لپک کر بچوں کے کمرے کی طرف گئیں مگر واقعی وہ دونوں کمرے میں نہیں تھے۔

''کہاں جا سکتے ہیں یہ دونوں؟''

''میں جانتی ہوں وہ کہاں گئے ہوں گے۔'' سلگتی نگاہوں سے آنسو پونچھتے ہوئے وہ مڑی اور پھر شال لے کر نیچے چلی آئی۔

''کہاں جا رہی ہو اس وقت۔''

''ابھی آتی ہوں دادو...... آپ پریشان نہ ہوں۔''

مختصر کہتی وہ فوراً حویلی سے نکل گئی تھی۔ گاڑی پاس تھی زائر کے گاؤں پہنچنے میں اسے زیادہ ٹائم نہیں لگا تھا۔

زائر بچوں کے ساتھ کھلے آسمان تلے چھت پر لیٹا انہیں کہانی سنا رہا تھا۔ دونوں بچے یہاں آ کر بے حد خوش تھے۔ کہانی سنتے سنتے کب ان کی آنکھ لگ گئی زائر کو پتا ہی نہیں چلا۔ دستک کی آواز پر وہ چونکا اور پھر آہستہ سے اپنا بازو چاند کے سر کے نیچے سے نکالتے ہوئے سیڑھیاں اتر آیا۔

''کون......'' دروازے کی کنڈی کو ہاتھ لگاتے ہوئے اس نے پوچھنا ضروری سمجھا تھا۔

''دروازہ کھولو۔'' باہر سے دھاڑتی ہوئی آواز بلاشک وشبہ ثانیہ عباس کی ہی تھی۔

❁......❁......❁

پلٹ کر دیکھنا چاہوں

تو نفرت سے ادھر جاناں

دنوں کی راکھ پہ راتوں کی یخ بستہ ہتھیلی پر
ہوا کے ناچتے گرداب کی تہوں میں کہیں
بجھا ہوا کوئی لمحہ کسی چراغ کے داغ
کہ میں بھی زندہ ہوں اپنے اجاڑ دل کی طرح
اجاڑ دل کہ جہاں آج بھی تمہارے بغیر
ہر ایک رات بکھر آئی آرزو کی دھنک
ہر ایک صبح دمکتی ہے کہیں زخم زخم
اجاڑ دل کہ جہاں آج بھی تمہارے بغیر
ہر ایک پل میری آنکھوں میں ڈھل کے ڈھلتا ہے
سلگتی رات کی تپش سے بدن جلتا ہے
اجاڑ دل کہ جہاں ڈوبتا ہوا سورج
ہر ایک شام جدائی کے نام کرتا ہے
پلٹ کے دیکھنا چاہوں تو نفرتوں سے ادھر
بس ایک نام درخشاں ہے صبح کی مانند
وہ نام جس پہ مکمل ہے اعتماد مجھے
نظر پڑے تو سمجھنا کہ تم ہو یاد مجھے

تین دن وہ اس ایک میٹر کی چھوٹی سی کوٹھری میں قید بنا کچھ کھائے پیئے پڑی سسکتی رہی تھی۔ کبھی انسانوں کی چیخوں، کبھی کتوں کے بھونکنے کی آوازوں اور کبھی ٹارچر کی ہولناک آوازوں نے ہر پل اس کا چین برباد کیے رکھا تھا۔ تین دن کے بعد اسے ایک میٹر کی اس چھوٹی سی تنگ و تاریک کوٹھری سے باہر نکالا گیا تھا۔ آنکھوں پر بندھی پٹی کے ساتھ وہ ایک بڑے سے صاف ستھرے ہال میں لائی گئی تھی جہاں اس کے ساتھ ایک اور مسلمان عورت بھی تھی۔ اس کے ہاتھ بھی بندھے ہوئے تھے۔ کئی فوجی اہلکار اسلحہ تانے ان کے اردگرد کھڑے تھے۔ ان دونوں کو بندھے ہاتھوں کے ساتھ ایک دوسرے کے پہلو میں بٹھا دیا گیا تھا۔ تبھی اس نے پھر ''ایاد عبدالہادی'' کو دیکھا تھا۔

بلیک یونیفارم میں ملبوس، دمکتی رنگت اور نقوش کے ساتھ وہ شخص نظر لگ جانے کی حد تک خوب صورت تھا۔ ان دونوں کو حکم دیا گیا تھا کہ وہ فوجی افسران کے پوچھے جانے والے تمام سوالوں کے جواب روانی سے دیں گی۔ اگر انہوں نے کسی قسم کے جھوٹ یا لڑکھڑاہٹ کا مظاہرہ کیا تو فوراً ان کے وجود میں آہنی گولیاں اتار دی جائیں گی۔ حورعین کا سارا بدن جیسے برف میں تبدیل ہو گیا۔

وہ شہادت کی موت کی متمنی تھی مگر اس نے کبھی بھی یہ نہیں چاہا تھا کہ وہ غیر مسلموں کے مابین مرے۔ موت کے بعد اپنی لاش کی بے حرمتی کا تصور اس کے رونگٹے کھڑے کر دیتا تھا۔ تبھی وہ بے چین ہوئی تھی۔ اس کے برابر بیٹھی لڑکی خاصی بے خوف دکھائی دے رہی تھی۔ اسی سے سوالات کا سلسلہ شروع کیا گیا تھا۔

''بتاؤ، کس دہشت گرد تنظیم سے تعلق ہے تمہارا؟''

''کسی سے نہیں سوائے اللہ اور اس کے پیارے رسول محمد صلی اللہ علیہ وسلم کے علاوہ میرا کسی سے کوئی تعلق نہیں۔'' بہت ٹھہر کر مدھم لہجے میں اس نے جواب دیا تھا مگر اس کا جواب مکمل ہوتے ہی ایک گولی اس کے پیٹ میں اتار دی گئی۔

وہ کراہ رہی تھی جبکہ حورعین عبدالسمیع کی چیخ نکل گئی تھی کیا یہی سب اس کے ساتھ بھی ہونے والا تھا؟

''بتاؤ...... کس تنظیم کے لیے کام کرتی ہو تم؟'' ایک مرتبہ پھر دھاڑ کر پوچھا گیا تھا اور ایک مرتبہ پھر نورانی چہرے والی اس پاکیزہ سی لڑکی نے بند ہوتی آنکھوں کے ساتھ بہت ہی تحمل سے جواب دیا تھا۔

''اللہ کے لیے۔''

''ڈھش۔'' جواب مکمل ہوتے ہی ایک اور گولی اس کے وجود میں داغ دی گئی۔ حورعین کے حلق سے فلک شگاف چیخ نکلی اور وہ ہوش و حواس سے بے گانہ ہوگئی۔ اگلے روز شام میں اسے ہوش آیا تو وہ بدتر حال میں زمین پر بے ہوش پڑی تھی۔ چھوٹے سے کمرے میں جلتی مدھم سی لائٹ نے اس کی آنکھیں چندھیا دی تھیں۔ وہ ابھی اٹھنے کی کوشش کر رہی تھی جب ایاد اس کمرے میں چلا آیا۔

شراب کے نشے میں دھت وہ شرٹ کے بٹن کھول رہا تھا اس کی آنکھیں پھٹی کی پھٹی رہ گئیں۔

''ایسے کیا دیکھ رہی ہو......؟''

پنجوں کے بل اس کے سامنے زمین پر بیٹھتے ہوئے وہ مسکرایا تھا۔ نشے سے سرخ ہوتی آنکھوں میں ناچتی ہوس صاف دکھائی دے رہی تھی۔ حورعین کا دل رکنے لگا ایک پل میں اس کا چہرہ سفید پڑ گیا تھا۔ مضبوطی سے دوپٹا پکڑتے ہوئے وہ کونے میں سمٹنے لگی تھی۔ ایاد نے آگے بڑھ کر اس کا دوپٹا نوچ لیا۔

''کیا چھپا رہی ہو، ہوں...... خریدے ہوئے جسم ہیں یہ ہمارے۔ یہاں جتنی بھی عورتیں ہیں سب کے پیٹ ہم نے اپنی اولادوں سے بھر رکھے ہیں۔ سنا تم نے......؟'' دوپٹے کے بعد اس کے بال نوچتے وہ چلایا تھا۔

حورعین چیخ اٹھی۔

''یہی کر سکتے ہو تم...... بے بس مجبور انسان پر سوائے قہر ڈھانے کے اور آتا بھی کیا ہے تمہیں؟''

''چٹاخ۔'' اس کی جرأت پر اگلے ہی پل ایک زوردار طمانچہ اس کے گال پر رسید کیا گیا تھا۔

''بے بس...... مجبور......؟ کس بات کی مجبوری کیسی بے بسی۔ منافق ہو گئے ہو تم لوگ خود ایک دوسرے کے دشمن ہو تم امریکی ظالم نہیں ہیں۔ مگر تم لوگوں کے کرتوت ہمیں تم پر خدائی کرنے کے لیے مجبور کرتے ہیں۔ چند ٹکوں کے لیے کچھ بھی کر سکتے ہو تم کچھ بھی۔ کوئی ایمان نہیں تمہارے اندر، انتہا پسند، متعصب لوگ ہو تم۔ صرف اپنا مفاد چاہنے والے۔'' پے در پے تھپڑوں سے اس کا چہرہ سرخ کرتے وہ اس پر چلا رہا تھا۔

''یہی انجام ہونا چاہیے تمہارا بلکہ اس سے بھی بدتر، ہمت ہے تو بلاؤ کسی غم خوار کو کہ وہ تمہاری مدد کرے۔ پکارو اپنے خدا کو کہ وہ تمہیں ہمارے چنگل سے نکال لے۔'' نشے کی شدت نے اس کی مت مار رکھی تھی۔

حورعین کی چیخیں بلند ہوتی گئیں۔

''اللہ۔''

قطعی بے بسی کے عالم میں سر اٹھاتے ہوئے بلند آواز سے اس نے اپنے اللہ کو پکارا تھا۔ ایاد کو بے حد لطف آیا۔

''کم آن...... اور پکارو...... کہو اپنے خدا سے کہ وہ تمہاری مدد کرے بھیجے ہم پر عذاب اور نکال لے تم لوگوں کو یہاں سے چلو شاباش، پکارو۔''

جیب سے تیز دھاری چاقو نکال کر حورعین کے بازو پر بڑا سا کٹ لگاتے ہوئے وہ مزید ہنسا تھا۔ حورعین کی جان جیسے لبوں پر آ گئی۔

✿......✿......✿

بازو پر لگے کٹ نے حورعین کو تڑپا کر رکھ دیا تھا مگر اس نے ضبط کا دامن ہاتھ سے نہیں چھوڑا۔
ایاد عبدالحادی اسے تکلیف پہنچانے کے بعد اب ہنس رہا تھا' یوں جیسے اس کے زخموں سے لطف اٹھا رہا ہو۔
''ہاہاہاہا...... بہت ترس آ رہا ہے مجھے تم پر' چٹکی جتنی لڑکی ہو تو اور عزائم دیکھو' امریکہ کے خلاف آواز اٹھانا چاہتی تھیں' ہوں...... کسے دکھانا چاہتی ہو ہماری اصلیت؟ چند کتابیں لکھ کر' اخبارات نکال کر تم نے سمجھ لیا کہ تم ساری دنیا کو ہمارے خلاف کھڑا کر دو گی' کس کو کھڑا کرو گی ہمارے خلاف' مسلم دنیا کو؟ جو ہمارے ابرو کے اشارے پر کچھ بھی کر سکتی ہے' کچھ بھی...... ہم جب چاہیں جس ملک سے چاہیں ڈالروں میں خرید سکتے ہیں تمہیں اور تمہارے ایمان کو...... کہاں چلا جاتا ہے اس وقت تمہارا خدا...... بولو......'' وہ ہنس رہا تھا اور حورعین کی آنکھوں سے نفرت کی چنگاریاں پھوٹ رہی تھیں' تبھی اس نے ہاتھ بڑھا کر حورعین کا دوپٹہ کھینچ ڈالا تھا۔
''پکارو اپنے خدا کو کہ تمہیں میرے ہاتھوں سے بچالے' کہو اپنے غیور مسلمان بھائیوں کو کہ میرا سینہ گولیوں سے چھلنی کر دیں۔'' وہ اس کا مذاق اڑا رہا تھا' حورعین کے اندر جیسے کوئی آتش فشاں پھٹ پڑا' وہ بولی تو اس کے لہجے میں جیسے کسی شیر کی دھاڑ تھی' سارا خوف کہیں جا سویا تھا۔
''بزدل ہو تم...... ہم پر تشدد کر کے اذیت دے کر قتل کرنے کے سوا تم اور کر بھی کیا کر سکتے ہو؟ ہمارے مردوں کی داڑھیاں مونڈ کر' انہیں تشدد کا نشانہ بنا کر مار دینے کے سوا اور آتا ہی کیا ہے تمہیں مگر ہمارے نزدیک یہ عبرت نہیں بلکہ سعادت و خوش بختی کی موت ہے۔ ہمارا دین ایسی موت کو شہادت کا نام دیتا ہے' ایک مومن کی زندگی کا سب سے بڑا مقصد ہی یہی ہے کہ اسے شہادت کی موت نصیب ہو' میرا خدا ایسے ہی اپنے بندوں کو آزمائش کی بھٹیوں میں جلا کر کندن بناتا ہے اور انہیں منافقین سے علیحدہ فرما دیتا ہے۔ ہم مصائب سے ٹوٹنے والے نہیں' یہ تمہاری مذہبی روایات کہتی ہیں کہ جب حضرت عیسیٰ علیہ السلام کو پھانسی دی جانے لگی تو ان کے جانثار ساتھی عین موقع پر انہیں چھوڑ کر فرار ہو گئے' پڑھو اپنی تاریخ کی کتابیں اور دیکھو کہ جب ارض فلسطین پر صلاح الدین ایوبی نے تمہارے بڑوں کو عبرت ناک شکست دی تو تمہارے بڑوں میں سے ایک نے اپنی بہن صلاح الدین ایوبی کے بھائی ملک العادل کو بطور رشوت پیش کر کے مسیحی دنیا کے لیے جان کی امان طلب کی۔ تم ہماری نہیں اپنی فکر کرو' ہم اگر تمہارے ہاتھوں مارے گئے تو شہید زندہ رہے تو غازی...... تم سوچو تمہارا کیا بنے گا۔'' لہو رنگ آنکھوں میں تیرتے آنسوؤں نے ایاد عبدالحادی کو ٹھٹکا دیا تھا۔
''مت اتنا گھمنڈ کرو اپنے ڈالروں پر کیونکہ تمہارے ڈالروں کے عوض اپنی جنت کا سودا کرنے والے مسلمان تو ہو سکتے ہیں مگر اللہ کے بندے نہیں' وہ ہم نہیں ہیں جنہیں تم اپنے ڈالر کی کشش سے خرید سکو' سنا تم نے؟'' وہ دھاڑی تھی تبھی ایاد کا بھاری تھپڑ اس کے رخسار پر پڑا تھا۔
''مارو اور مارو...... کتنا ظلم کرو گے' کتنی نسلیں برباد کرو گے مسلمانوں کی' طاقت کے بل بوتے پر کب تک ہماری بے بسی کو کچلو گے تم......؟ تم نہیں جانتے مگر میں جانتی ہوں کہ حاکم اعلیٰ صرف اللہ ہے' وہ چاہے تو سمندر کا سینہ کھول کر ایک پل میں تم سب کو غرقاب کر دے' اللہ کی طاقت کے سامنے تمہاری طاقت مری ہوئی چیونٹی کے پَر کے برابر بھی نہیں۔ یہ ظلم و بربریت ہمیں ہمارے ایمان سے پھیر نہیں سکتی وہ اور لوگ ہیں جن کے ایمان کا سودا تم اپنے ڈالروں سے کرتے ہو بظاہر مسلمان لیکن ان لوگوں کا آخرت میں کوئی حصہ نہیں' خود اپنی جانوں پر ظلم کرنے والے بدنصیب لوگ ہیں' یہ پرلے درجے کے بدنصیب' جو یہ بھی جانتے ہیں کہ دنیا کی زندگی عارضی ہے' اس عارضی زندگی میں چند سو' چند ہزار ڈالر لے کر تمہاری وفاداری کا دم بھرنے کے بعد اپنے ہی کلمہ گو بھائیوں کو تمہارے سپرد کر کے وہ صرف خسارے کا سودا کر رہے ہیں مگر تم جانتے ہو کہ تمہارے نزدیک ان کی حیثیت' ان کا مقام کیا ہے۔ ہڈی کھانے والے کتے سے بڑھ کر اہمیت نہیں

دیتے تم انہیں، شراب کے نشے میں سرعام گالیاں نکالتے ہو مگر وہ ہم نہیں ہیں۔ ہم وہ ہیں جو صحرا کی تپتی ریت میں کھڑے کنٹینرز میں آگ برساتے سورج تلے محبوس، ماہیٔ بے آب کی طرح تڑپ تڑپ کر ایڑیاں رگڑ کر شہادت کی موت کو گلے لگا لیتے ہیں مگر اپنا سر تمہارے سامنے نہیں جھکاتے۔ میں چاہوں تو انہیں پکار سکتی ہوں کیونکہ ان میں اب بھی کوئی صلاح الدین ایوبی، کوئی محمد بن قاسم اور کوئی طارق ابن زیاد ہے، بہت قوت اور طاقت ہے اب بھی ان کے زخمی بازوؤں میں مگر میں انہیں نہیں پکاروں گی کیونکہ دنیا کے پل صراط پر اپنے زخم زخم وجود کے ساتھ وہ اسلام کے محاذ پر کھڑے اللہ کے دشمنوں سے لڑ رہے ہیں، اس محاذ پر زیادہ ضرورت ہے ان کی، ہماری عزتوں اور جانوں کا خدا محافظ ہے۔'' بولتے بولتے اس کا حلق خشک ہو گیا تھا۔

ایاد عبدالحادی کے اندر جیسے آگ بھڑک اٹھی۔ یہ کیسا آئینہ تھا جو وہ اسے دکھا رہی تھی، یہ کیسا طمانچہ تھا جو وہ دھان پان سی لڑکی اتنی بہادری سے اس کے منہ پر رسید کر رہی تھی، مارے غیض و غضب کے وہ سلگ اٹھا تھا اس رات اس نے حورعین عبدالسمیع پر اتنا تشدد کیا تھا کہ کئی گھنٹوں تک وہ بیرک اس کی چیخوں سے گونجتی رہی تھی۔ اگلے دو دن بعد اسے گوانتاناموبے منتقل کروا کر وہ خود قندھار آ گیا تھا۔ جلتی تپتی، ٹوٹی پھوٹی سڑکوں اور سنگلاخ پہاڑوں کے درمیان، جہاں قبائلی شمالی اتحاد والوں نے ڈالرز کے عوض انہیں اپنی مکمل جانثاری کا یقین دلاتے ہوئے عرب اور مسلم دنیا کے تقریباً تیس ہزار طالبان کو مذاکرات کا دھوکہ دے کر ان کے چنگل میں پھنسا دیا تھا، اپنے قائدین کے حکم پر ہتھیار پھینک کر خود کو امریکی افواج کے حوالے کرنے والے ان تیس ہزار طالبان میں سے چند عرب طالبان کو شک تھا کہ ان کو مذاکرات کا ڈرامہ رچا کر محفوظ راستہ دینے کا وعدہ کرنے والے ان کے اپنے ضرور ان کے ساتھ دھوکہ کریں گے شاید اسی لیے انہوں نے چھوٹے پسٹل اپنے پاس چھپا لیے تھے پھر جس وقت ان کی بکتر بند گاڑیاں امریکی افواج کے سامنے رکیں اور انہیں ان کے سامنے زمین پر ہاتھ باندھ کر گھٹنوں کے بل بٹھایا گیا، عرب مجاہد خاموش نہ رہ سکے اور اعلان جنگ کر دیا مگر وہاں اس وقت طاقت اور جذبے کے ساتھ ساتھ اسلحہ کی بھی شدید ضرورت تھی جسے وہ اپنے قائدین کے حکم پر، امن کے قیام کے لیے پیچھے چھوڑ آئے تھے مگر ہمیشہ کی طرح ایک مرتبہ پھر ان کے ساتھ دھوکہ ہوا تھا۔

ایاد جانتا تھا کہ یہ وہ طالبان نہیں ہیں جنہوں نے اپنے ایمان گروی رکھ کر، معصوم بے گناہ لوگوں کو خودکش حملوں اور بم دھماکوں میں لقمہ اجل بنا کر شہید کرنا اپنا نصیب العین بنا رکھا ہے۔ طالبان کا نام بدنام کر کے جو ملکوں کے امن اور شہریوں کی جان و مال کے لیے عذاب بنے ہوئے تھے وہ جانتا تھا کہ بظاہر طالبان کہلوانے والے ان دہشت گردوں کا اسلام سے کوئی تعلق نہیں تھا نہ ہی ہو سکتا تھا کیونکہ جو طالبان ان کے ساتھ لڑ رہے تھے ان کی لڑائی کا صرف ایک ہی مقصد تھا، اسلام کا دفاع...... اسلامی شریعت اور نظام کا قیام، اللہ اور اللہ کے پیارے رسول محمد صلی اللہ علیہ وسلم کی خوشنودی، انہیں غرض نہیں تھی کہ دنیا انہیں کیا سمجھتی ہے انہیں کیا، کوئی اور ان کے نام کو استعمال کر کے انہیں بدنام کر رہا ہے یا نہیں۔ انہیں اگر دھن تھی تو صرف یہی کہ اسلام کا دفاع کیسے کرنا ہے، اس مذہب کا دفاع جو ساری دنیا کے لیے امن بھلائی اور رحمت کا مذہب تھا، جس کی تعلیمات سے فائدہ اٹھا کر خود اہل کتاب نہ صرف دوسرے خلائی سیاروں تک جا پہنچے تھے بلکہ سمندر کی گہرائیوں کا بھی پتا چلا لیا تھا اور وہ انہی سینوں کو گولیوں سے داغنا چاہتے تھے جن میں ایسی علم و حکمت والی کتاب محفوظ تھی کیونکہ دنیا میں اسلام کا بول بالا اور بالادستی انہیں کسی بھی قیمت پر قبول نہیں تھی۔

ادھر گوانتاناموبے جیل میں حورعین نے انسانیت کا بدترین روپ دیکھا، بناء کسی قصور اور جرم کے اس کی عزت کی چادر کو داغ دار کیا گیا، کئی کئی گھنٹے اس کے ہاتھ اوپر باندھ کر اس پر تشدد کیا گیا، بناء عورت ہونے کا لحاظ کیے اس کے منہ پر کئی بار پیشاب کیا گیا تھا، ایک پل سے بھی پہلے مر جانے کی شدید خواہش کے باوجود اسے زندہ رہنے پر مجبور کیا گیا تھا

اور یہیں اس نے سر جاوید ہمدانی کو دیکھا تھا تحفتاً امریکی فوج کو ملا' وہ شخص جو قوم کا معمار تھا' ان صلیب کے پرستاروں کے ہاتھوں کیسے ہر شب بدترین ظلم کی بھینٹ چڑھ رہا تھا' کیا کیا نہیں دیکھا تھا اس نے وہاں مگر سب کچھ دیکھ کر اور جان کر بھی اس کے لبوں پر قفل پڑ گئے تھے۔

گوانتا موبے میں اسے وہ تیسری رات تھی جب اسے پتا چلا کہ اس رات دورانِ تشدد ایک اور پاکستانی کی موت ہوگئی تھی اور وہ پاکستانی کوئی اور نہیں سر جاوید ہمدانی تھے جن کے دل میں اپنی گمراہ قوم کے لیے ویسا ہی درد تھا جیسا اقبال کے دل میں تھا بس فرق صرف یہ تھا کہ وہ انگریز دورِ حکومت میں بھی اپنے جذبات پر سر کا خطاب پا گئے اور وہ ایک مسلم ملک میں ایٹمی پاور کے حامل ملک میں پوری آزادی اور خود مختاری کے باوجود سب سے پہلے پاکستان کے نعرے کی بھینٹ چڑھ گئے۔

سر جاوید ہمدانی کے قتل کے بعد وہ اپنا دماغی توازن کھو بیٹھی تھی تبھی صرف تین ماہ کے بعد اسے وہاں سے دوبارہ کیوبا منتقل کر دیا تھا۔ کیوبا سے عراق اور عراق سے پھر افغانستان...... اس دوران اس کی عزت کی چادر کو بار بار تار تار کیا گیا تھا' وہاں کتنی ہی مسلمان عورتیں تھیں جو شدت سے موت کی تمنا کرتی تھیں۔ اپنا سر دیواروں سے مار مار کر خود کو لہولہان کر لیتی تھیں مگر مخملی بستروں پر سوئے ذمہ داروں کو بُرا خواب تک نہیں آتا تھا۔

''کیا تاریخ میں اتنا حوصلہ تھا کہ وہ وقت کے سالاروں کا یہ جرم معاف کر دیتی؟''

وہ دسمبر کی نہایت سرد رات تھی جب اسے شبرغان کے اس چھوٹے سے تاریک سیل سے نکال کر ایک نسبتاً بہتر اور آرام دہ کمرے میں شفٹ کر دیا گیا۔ اب تک نہ اس کا جرم دنیا کے سامنے لایا گیا تھا نہ کیس' سو سینکڑوں بے گناہوں کی طرح وہ بھی رُل رہی تھی۔

''کیا نام ہے تمہارا؟''

تیز روشنی میں اس پر ٹھنڈا یخ پانی ڈال کر اسے ہوش میں لایا گیا تھا مگر وہ آنکھیں کھل جانے کے باوجود سب کو یوں ٹکر ٹکر دیکھ رہی تھی جیسے سمجھنے کی کوشش کر رہی ہو کہ وہ اس کے ساتھ کیا کر رہے ہیں؟

تبھی ایک مرتبہ پھر ایاد عبدالحادی اس کی نظروں کے سامنے آیا تھا' ہوش و حواس کھو جانے کے باوجود وہ فوراً اسے پہچان گئی تھی اس کے ساتھی مختلف طریقوں سے اسے ٹارچر کر رہے تھے مگر وہ اف بھی نہیں کر رہی تھی' تاہم جس وقت ان لوگوں نے اسے بے لباس کرنے کی کوشش کی، اس نے چلاّنا شروع کر دیا ساتھ ہی لپک کر ایاد کا ہاتھ تھام لیا' یوں جیسے وہ اس کا خیر خواہ ہو۔

ایاد کے لیے اس کی یہ حرکت کسی شاک سے کم نہیں تھی تاہم اس نے اپنے ساتھیوں کو اسے اس کے حال پر چھوڑنے کا کہہ دیا تھا۔ دسمبر کی یخ بستہ رات میں برف جیسے فرش پر سکڑ کر بیٹھی وہ بہت خوف زدہ نگاہوں سے اس کی طرف دیکھ رہی تھی۔

ایاد کا دل جیسے کسی نے جکڑ لیا۔ وہ اٹھا اور اس کے مقابل جا بیٹھا تھا پھر اس نے ہاتھ بڑھا کر اس کے چہرے پر آئے بال پیچھے کیے۔

''تو تم نہیں مانو گی کہ تمہارا طالبان کی کسی تنظیم کے ساتھ تعلق ہے' ہوں؟'' اکڑوں بیٹھا وہ اس سے پوچھ رہا تھا۔ حور عین چپ چاپ اسے دیکھے گئی۔

''طالبان صرف امریکہ کے لیے نہیں بلکہ تم لوگوں کے لیے بھی خطرہ ہیں' کیوں نہیں سمجھتی ہو تم؟'' وہ اسے پیار سے منا رہا تھا مگر وہ اب بھی خاموش نگاہوں سے چپ چاپ اسے دیکھ رہی تھی' اس کی چپ کا قفل نہیں ٹوٹ رہا تھا۔ تبھی ایاد

نے سر جھکایا تھا پھر اپنے ساتھیوں کی طرف دیکھتے ہوئے بولا۔

"Leave it"۔

اگلے دو ماہ حورعین پر زیادہ تشدد نہیں کیا گیا مگر اس کی آنکھوں نے اب بھی بربریت کے ہزاروں واقعات دیکھے تھے اس کی ذہنی حالت بہت بدتر تھی۔ پورے دو ماہ بعد اس رات پھر وہ اس کے سیل میں آیا تھا' حورعین تین دن کی بھوکی تیز بخار میں جل رہی تھی وہ اس کے قریب بیٹھ گیا۔ پہلی بار حورعین کو اس کی آنکھوں میں ہوس کی جگہ نرمی نظر آئی' اس کے چہرے پر عجیب سا نور اور اپنائیت تھی۔

کتنی ہی دیر اس کے مقابل بیٹھ کر چپ چاپ اسے دیکھنے کے بعد اس نے ہاتھ بڑھا کر اس کا گال چھوا تھا اور پھر رو پڑا تھا' کتنی ہی دیر وہ اس کے سامنے بیٹھا بچوں کی طرح روتا رہا تھا۔ حورعین اچنبھے سے اس کی طرف دیکھتی رہی بھلا وہ کیوں رو رہا تھا؟ مگر ایک مرتبہ پھر وہ بناء کچھ کہے چلا گیا تھا۔

آنے والے دنوں میں اس نے سنا کہ مجاہد طالبان نے اتحادی فوج کے اہم دستوں میں گھس کر بڑی کامیابی حاصل کی پھر کچھ ہی روز بعد اسے بگرام جیل سے کچھ قیدیوں کے فرار کی خبر بھی سننے کو ملی اور پھر ایک رات جب اس کی طبیعت بے حد خراب تھی وہ ایک مرتبہ پھر اس کے سیل میں چلا آیا تھا۔ حورعین شور مچانا چاہتی تھی مگر اس نے مضبوطی سے اپنا ہاتھ اس کے منہ پر جما دیا۔

"کوئی شور مت کرنا' ابھی یہاں سے نکلو پلیز"

اس کی آواز سرگوشی سے بلند نہیں تھی' حورعین ہراساں ہوگئی وہ اسے لے کر سیل سے نکل گیا۔ فوج کا حصہ ہونے کے باعث اسے تمام خفیہ راستوں کا بھی پتا تھا' جہاں سے قیدی غائب کیے جاتے تھے حورعین نا چاہتے ہوئے بھی اس کے ساتھ بھاگتی رہی۔ بڑی کامیابی اور مہارت سے اسے اس عقوبت خانے سے نکال کر جس وقت وہ باہر آیا تھا' فوج کے دیگر افسران کو شک ہوگیا تھا اور فوراً خطرے کا ہنگامی سائرن بج اٹھا تب اس نے حورعین کا ہاتھ تھام کر جنگل کا رخ کرلیا' بھاگتے بھاگتے حورعین کی ہمت جواب دے گئی تھی' اس کی طبیعت بھی ٹھیک نہیں تھی تبھی اس نے مزید بھاگنے سے انکار کردیا تھا۔

ایاد نے ایک نظر اس کے حال پر ڈالی پھر اسے اٹھا کر قریبی گھنے درختوں کے جھنڈ میں لے آیا وہ بے ہوش ہونے کے قریب تھی' ادھر اتحادی افواج میں جیسے کھلبلی مچ گئی تھی' مشکوک تو ان کی نظر میں وہ پہلے ہی ہو چکا تھا پچھلے کتنے دنوں سے اس پر نظر رکھی جا رہی تھی اور اب جب کہ اسے غداری کے جرم میں گرفتار کیا جانا تھا' وہ حورعین کو لے کر فرار ہوگیا تھا۔

اس نے حورعین سے کہا تھا کہ "پکارو اپنے خدا کو اور کہو اسے کہ وہ تمہیں میرے قہر سے بچائے۔"

پتا نہیں حورعین نے اس پاک ذات کو اس وقت پکارا تھا یا نہیں مگر وہ اس کے دل میں آگیا تھا۔ حورعین کی باتوں نے اس کے اندر غصے کے ساتھ ساتھ عجیب سی بے چینی بھی بھر دی تھی۔ نتیجتاً اس نے مسلمان قیدیوں پر اپنے مظالم اور زیادہ کردیئے تھے مگر یہ بے چینی تھی کہ کم ہونے کے بجائے اور بڑھتی جا رہی تھی اس کا دل چاہتا تھا کہ وہ دیواروں سے سر ٹکرائے آخر وہ ایسی کیا چیز تھی کہ جس نے محصور قیدیوں کو ہر آسائش ہر عیش و آرام سے بیگانہ کرکے' کافروں کے ہاتھوں نہایت اذیت ناک موت خوشی خوشی قبول کرنے پر مجبور کردیا تھا۔ وہ کیا چیز تھی جو ان لوگوں کو ظلم و جبر کے سامنے جھکنے نہیں دے رہی تھی' وہ کیا تھا جس کے لیے وہ جفاکش ساری عیش و آرام دولت کو ٹھوکر مار کر سر پر کفن باندھے اپنے سے تین گنا بڑی طاقت سے لڑنے کو تیار ہوگئے تھے۔ یہ اگر بہادری تھی تو کس نے انہیں ودیعت کی تھی؟ اگر یہ بے خوفی تھی تو کیونکر پیدا ہوئی تھی؟ جان تو کسی بھی مذہب سے تعلق رکھنے والے کو سب سے پیاری ہوتی ہے پھر انہیں اپنی جانیں

پیاری کیوں نہیں تھیں؟

سلگتی ریت اور تپتے پہاڑوں میں ایسا کیا تھا جو انہیں سر جھکانے سے روکتا تھا وہ کیا چیز تھی جس نے مسلمانوں کے بلال رضی اللہ عنہ کو تپتی ریت پر دہکتے کوئلوں سے اپنی کھال اتروا کر بھی ''اللہ ایک ہے' اللہ ایک ہے'' کہنے سے باز نہیں رکھا۔

یہودی اور عیسائی نہایت بے رحمی سے اگر مٹانا چاہتے تھے تو صرف اسلام اور مسلمانوں کو آخر کیوں؟ بھاری رقوم خرچ کر کے اگر خریدا جا رہا تھا تو صرف محمد عربی (صلی اللہ علیہ وسلم) کے غلاموں کو آخر کیوں؟ مضحکہ خیز خاکے بنا کر اگر کسی قوم کے مذہبی جذبات کو ٹھیس پہنچائی جا رہی تھی تو صرف مسلمانوں کو' آخر کیوں؟ دنیا کے ہر ملک ہر حصے میں اگر قتل عام کر کے نسل کشی کی جا رہی تھی تو صرف مسلمانوں کی آخر کیوں؟ اگر مسلمان متعصب' تنگ نظر' دہشت گرد' انتہا پسند اور دنیا کے امن کے لیے خطرہ تھے تو پھر وہ مسلمان کون تھے جن کی پشت پناہی خود یہودی ادارے کر رہے تھے؟

وہ کون مسلمان تھے جو چہرے پر داڑھیاں رکھ کر' اسلامی نام رکھ کر سچے مسلمانوں کی صفوں میں منافقت سے گھس کر' یہودی اداروں کی پناہ میں خود مسلمانوں کو تباہ کر رہے تھے۔ ملک کے عام معصوم شہریوں کا خون پانی کی طرح بہا رہے تھے۔ جن کے شر کو دیکھتے ہوئے دوسرے مذاہب کے لوگ مجبوراً اسلام اور مسلمانوں سے نفرت کرنے پر مجبور ہو گئے تھے' جن کے ایمان کی قیمت محض چند ڈالر تھی......

ایک طرف وہ مسلمان تھے جن کے ایمان کی قیمت محض چند ڈالر تھی اور ایک طرف وہ مسلمان تھے جنہوں نے بڑے بڑے محل اربوں کی آسائشات کو ٹھوکر مار کر سنگلاخ پہاڑوں کو اپنا مسکن بنا لیا تھا۔

آخر وہ کیسے مسلمان تھے جنہوں نے کربلا کی سرزمین پر آگ برساتے سورج تلے بناء ہتھیاروں کے اپنے دشمن سے جنگ لڑی اور بالآخر بھوک و پیاس کی شدت سے نڈھال ایک ایک کر کے جام شہادت نوش کر لیا مگر باطل کے سامنے سر نہیں جھکایا۔

مسلمانوں کے آقا محمد صلی اللہ علیہ وسلم جو خدا کے محبوب ہیں' جن کی لیے ساری کائنات تخلیق کی گئی درخت تک جن کو سجدہ کرتے تھے جنہیں ان کے مخالف قبائل نے دولت کے انبار لگانے' حکمرانی کرنے' حسین سے حسین عورت بطور تحفہ پیش کرنے کی پیشکش کر ڈالی تھی مگر وہ ہر چیز کو ٹھوکر مار کر پورے تین سال اپنے خاندان اور گھر والوں کے ساتھ شعب ابی طالب کی تنگ گھاٹی میں محصور فاقے کرتے رہے' کیوں؟ یہ سب سوچتے اس کا ذہن ماؤف ہونے لگا تھا۔

انہی دنوں اتحادی فوج نے ایک نیا کھیل شروع کیا' ہر طرح کی آسائش' اسلحہ اور طاقت ہونے کے باوجود' سنگلاخ پہاڑوں کے بیٹے پوری طرح سے ان کے قابو نہیں آ رہے تھے جب کہ وہ افغانستان کے بچے بچے کو کچل کر مار دینے کے لیے بے چین تھے' ان کا ٹارگٹ نہ طالبان تھے نہ دہشت گرد۔ ٹارگٹ اگر کوئی تھا تو صرف اسلام' وہ جانتے تھے ان سنگلاخ پہاڑوں کے مکینوں کو ابدی نیند سلانے سے پہلے اگر انہوں نے تیل پر قبضہ کرنے کے لیے عراق پر حملہ کیا تو ان کی شامت آ جائے گی' اسی لیے ضروری تھا کہ جن مجاہدوں پر Not For Sale کا لیبل لگا تھا انہیں بے دردی سے تڑپا تڑپا کر مار دیا جائے تا کہ ان کے خلاف کوئی مزاحمت نہ ہو سکے اور اس مقصد کے لیے جن ممالک نے ان سے اتحاد کیا وہ سب کے سب اسلام کے مخالف تھے مسلمانوں کے دشمن تھے تبھی وہاں ڈالر کی جنگ شروع ہوئی تھی۔

ہٹلر نے آتشیں اور الیکٹرانک بھٹیوں میں زندہ انسانوں کو جلا کر راکھ کر دینے کا ایک انوکھا طریقہ ایجاد کیا تھا وہ لوگ بھی عرب مجاہدین' طالبان اور ان کے حمایتیوں کو ایسی ہی بھٹیوں میں جلا کر راکھ کر دینا چاہتے تھے۔ رائفلوں' گنوں سے مجاہدین کو مارنا اور صفحہ ہستی سے مٹا دینا' بے حد مشکل اور دیرپا تھا' تبھی وہ تیس ہزار مجاہد جنہیں دھوکے سے محصور کر کے ان

کے ساتھ ظلم اور جنگ کی گئی تھی جو نہتے بھی ان کے سامنے سر جھکانے کے بجائے ان سے لڑ رہے تھے بڑی مشکل سے انہیں پکڑنے کے بعد پانی میں کرنٹ چھوڑ کر لوہے کے بڑے بڑے کنٹینرز میں محبوس کر دیا گیا تھا۔ چالیس پچاس افراد کی گنجائش والے کنٹینرز میں پانچ سو افراد کو محبوس کر کے وہ کنٹینرز صحرا کی تپتی ریت میں چلا دیئے گئے تھے' یہ سب ایاد نے اپنی آنکھوں سے دیکھا تھا۔

آتشیں والیکٹرانک بھٹیوں میں تو قیدی لمحوں میں جل کر راکھ ہو جاتے تھے مگر ان کنٹینرز میں قید مجاہد' ماہیٔ بے آب اور مرغ بسمل کی طرح تڑپتے۔ جب اوپر سے سورج آگ برساتا اور نیچے سے صحرا کی گرم ریت شعلے اگلتی تو لوہے کا کنٹینر جہنم بنا جاتا اور ان میں محبوس قیدیوں کے چیخنے' تڑپنے' آہ و بکا کرنے اور اپنا سر آہنی چادروں سے مارنے کی آوازوں کے ساتھ ساتھ دل لرزا دینے والی قرآنی آیات کا ورد کرنے والی آوازوں پر جہاں اس کے ساتھی دل چسپی سے ہنستے' قہقہے لگاتے تھے وہیں وہ جیسے پتھر ہو کر رہ گیا تھا۔

وہ کیا چیز تھی جو اس عالم میں بھی قرآن کو بھولنے نہیں دے رہی تھی' بہت اچانک اس کے دل و دماغ پر حملہ ہوا تھا اور اس نے بے بسی سے ہتھیار پھینک دیئے' جنت کے بدلے دنیا کا سودا کر لینے والے بدنصیب کس قدر خسارے میں تھے کاش وہ جان پاتے۔

کئی روز کی اندرونی جنگ کے بعد بالآخر وہ ہار گیا تبھی اللہ نے جیسے اس کے دل و دماغ کو کھول دیا' بے شک وہ جسے چاہتا ہے ہدایت دیتا ہے۔ وہ مسلمان تھا اس کی رگوں میں اسلامی خون تھا تو کیسے یہ خون جوش نہ مارتا۔ کتنی ہی راتیں اس نے اپنی حیوانیت پر رو رو کر اللہ سے معافی مانگتے ہوئے گزاری تھیں پھر اس نے جاب چھوڑ کر علی الاعلان مجاہدین کے ساتھ شامل ہونے کے بجائے فوج میں رہ کر سینکڑوں بے گناہ قید مسلمانوں کی چپ چاپ مدد کرنے کا فیصلہ کر لیا مگر اس کا یہ منصوبہ زیادہ دنوں تک خفیہ نہ رہ سکا۔ مسلمان قیدیوں کے ساتھ اس کے نرم برتاؤ نے دیگر افسران کو چوکنا کر دیا تھا اور جب اسے لگا کہ اسے گرفتار کر لیا جائے گا وہ حورعین کو لے کر وہاں سے فرار ہو گیا۔

اتحادی فوج کتے کی طرح اس کی بو سونگھتی پھر رہی تھی مگر وہ اس لڑکی کے ساتھ تھا جس کے لفظوں نے اس کے اندر انسانیت کی روح پھونکی تھی۔

درختوں کے جس جھنڈ میں وہ خود کو اور حورعین کو چھپائے بیٹھا تھا کہ اچانک حورعین کی نظر درخت سے لٹکتے ایک کالے سانپ پر جا پڑی سانپ کو دیکھتے ہی وہ چیخنے والی تھی مگر اس سے پہلے ہی ایاد نے اس کے منہ پر اپنا بھاری ہاتھ جما کر اسے خود میں بھینچ لیا اور دوسرے ہاتھ سے سانپ کو پکڑ کر پوری قوت سے دور پھینک دیا۔ حورعین کے دل کی تیز دھڑکنیں اسے اپنے اندر اترتی محسوس ہو رہی تھیں۔ مجاہدین اس سے رابطہ کے لیے بے قرار تھے مگر وہ پہلے اس لڑکی کو کسی محفوظ مقام تک پہنچانا چاہتا تھا کیونکہ وہ جانتا تھا کہ وہ بے قصور ہے۔

بالکل ویسے ہی جیسے دختر مشرق' پاکستان کی بیٹی عافیہ صدیقی معصوم اور بے گناہ تھی۔ ان کا جرم اگر تھا تو صرف پاکستانی ہونا...... ایک ایسے ملک کا شہری ہونا جو مقروض تھا' ان کا جرم دکھی انسانیت سے ہمدردی تھی۔

مسلسل بھاگنے کی وجہ سے اس کی طبیعت مزید خراب ہو گئی تھی' اِدھر اتحادی فوج کے افسر پورے جنگل میں آگ کی طرح پھیل چکے تھے۔ حورعین کے کراہنے کی آواز مسئلہ پیدا کر سکتی تھی تبھی اس نے مسلسل اس کے منہ پر ہاتھ رکھے رکھا تھا۔ آنے والی رات اس کے لیے مزید پریشانیاں لے کر آئی تھی خوفناک جھاڑیوں میں ایک نوجوان غیرت مرحم لڑکی کے ساتھ چپکے رہنا اس کی غیر کو گوارہ نہیں تھا' دوسری طرف حورعین کو اس کے حال پر چھوڑ دینا اس کے اندر کی جاگی ہوئی انسانیت کو گوارہ نہیں تھا' ایک طرف غیرت تھی تو دوسری طرف انسانیت...... بہت دیر کشمکش میں رہنے کے بعد بالآخر وہ

اس کا مسیحا بن گیا تھا۔

اگلے ایک ہفتہ تک اس کی مجاہدین تک رسائی نہیں ہو سکی تھی نہ ہی اتحادی فوج کی اس تک رسائی ممکن ہو سکی تاہم اس ہفتے میں جس طرح اس نے حورعین کا خیال رکھا وہ اس سے بہت متاثر ہو گئی تھی۔ رفتہ رفتہ اس کی اعصابی حالت بھی بہتر ہونے لگی' شدید خطرے کے باوجود جس طرح سے وہ اس کے لیے جنگل میں کھانے پینے کا اہتمام کرتا تھا حورعین کے دل میں اس کی عزت بہت بڑھ گئی تھی۔

اس روز وہاں بہت بارش ہوئی تھی۔ ایاد ہر روز وہاں سے نکلنے کا محفوظ راستہ تلاش کرتا تھا مگر تاحال اسے کامیابی نصیب نہ ہو سکی تھی۔ حورعین کا لباس بہت نحیف ہو چکا تھا' ایک دو جگہ سے پھٹ کر جسم دکھائی دینے لگا تھا مگر وہ ہمہ وقت دوپٹے کو نماز کی صورت سر پر لپیٹے رکھتی۔

گھنے درخت تلے اپنے آپ کو چھپائے بیٹھی وہ ایاد کو دیکھ رہی تھی جب وہ بولا۔

''میں جانتا ہوں ہم یہاں محفوظ نہیں ہیں' کسی بھی وقت دشمن فوج کا کوئی کارندہ یہاں تک پہنچ سکتا ہے مگر میں اپنی ذات کے لیے بالکل بھی خوف زدہ نہیں ہوں مجھے اگر کوئی پریشانی ہے تو صرف آپ کی...... میں نہیں چاہتا حق اور باطل کی اس جنگ میں آپ کو اپنی جان کی قربانی پیش کرنی پڑے' آپ کے لفظ مشکل کی مانند ہیں جن سے آپ کو تاریک ذہنوں میں شعور کی روشنی پھیلانے کا کام لینا ہے' نوآموز نسل کو صحیح اور غلط کی پہچان کروانے کا کام لینا ہے' اقبال کی طرح نامساعد حالات اور زمانے سے جنگ کرنی ہے فکر و آگہی کی جنگ...... میں جانتا ہوں آپ مجھے اچھا انسان نہیں سمجھتیں' میں اچھا انسان ہوں بھی نہیں' جس قبیلے سے میرا تعلق ہے وہاں کی جو تعلیمات اور رسومات ہیں ان کا اسلام سے کوئی تعلق نہیں' باوجود اس کے کہ ہم فخریہ مسلمان کہلاتے ہیں' میری ماں عیسائی عورت تھی مگر میں نے ہمیشہ اس کی آنکھوں میں اسلام اور مسلمانوں کے لیے آنسو دیکھے ہیں' جب تک وہ زندہ رہی شاید اس نے اسلام کی گہرائی کو سمجھ لیا تھا مگر میرا باپ' جو خود کو فخریہ مسلمان کہلاتا تھا جس کی رگوں میں پیدائشی طور پر مسلمان خون تھا شاید وہ کبھی اسلام اور مسلمانوں کے لیے نہیں رویا ہوگا کیونکہ اس کے پاس شعور نہیں تھا قیمتی چیز بناء کسی جدوجہد اور قربانی کے پلیٹ میں رکھ کر مل جائے تو شاید اس کی قدر و قیمت کا صحیح اندازہ نہیں ہوتا۔ میرے باپ اور اس کے قبیلے کے ساتھ بھی یہی معاملہ تھا' اسلام کی عظمت اس کی حرمت کی قیمت چند ٹکوں میں وصول کر کے وہ سمجھتے تھے کہ بڑے فائدے کا سودا کر لیا مگر انہیں پتا ہی نہیں تھا کہ فائدے کی اس گہری کھائی کے پیچھے کتنا بڑا نقصان منہ کھولے ان کے گرنے کا منتظر کھڑا ہے۔ انہیں یہ سوچنے کی فرصت ہی نہیں تھی کہ دنیا بھر میں بڑی طاقتیں' ہزاروں مذاہب کے ہوتے ہوئے اگر کسی مذہب کی قیمت لگانے کی سرتوڑ کوشش کرتی تھیں تو وہ مذہب صرف اسلام تھا۔ بھٹکے ہوؤں کی نظر میں سرخروئی کے لیے کیا کیا نہیں کیا' میرے آباؤ اجداد نے۔ سوچتا ہوں تو خون رگوں میں ٹھوکریں مارتا ہے شاید اسی وجہ سے میں اسلام اور مسلمانوں سے نفرت کرتا تھا مگر بہت دیر کے بعد مجھ پر یہ حقیقت کھلی کہ بھٹکے ہوؤں کے پیرو تو خود اسلام کے دھتکارے ہوئے ہیں' وہ مذہب جو ساری کائنات کے لیے امن و سلامتی' روشن خیالی' انصاف اور بقاء و نجات کا مذہب ہے' بہت دیر بعد مجھے اس چیز کی سمجھ آئی کہ اگر میں اسلام اور مسلمانوں سے بے زار ہوں تو اس میں اسلام اور مسلمانوں کا قصور نہیں ہے میرا قصور ہے' میرا نقصان ہے اللہ کو اس بات سے کوئی فرق نہیں پڑتا کہ کون اسے اپنا رب تسلیم کرتا ہے کون نہیں مگر بندے کو اس بات سے فرق پڑتا ہے کہ ساری کائنات کا اکیلا خالق اسے اپنا بندہ تسلیم کرتا ہے کہ نہیں کیونکہ اللہ کو پا کر کبھی کسی نے کچھ نہیں کھویا اور اللہ کو کھو کر کبھی کسی نے کچھ نہیں پایا۔'' ایاد عبدالحادی کی خوب صورت آنکھوں کے گوشے نم ہو چکے تھے۔

حورعین یک ٹک اسے دیکھے گئی' وہ شخص اس سے اپنا آپ شیئر کر رہا تھا۔ برستے آسمان تلے وہ کشمیری سیب جیسے اس

شخص کے ساتھ بیٹھی اسے دیکھ رہی تھی اور وہ شخص نا چاہتے ہوئے بھی اس کے دل میں اترتا جارہا تھا۔ پچھلے گزرے ایک ہفتے میں اس کی رفاقت نے حورعین کو جیسے جینا سکھا دیا تھا۔ وہ اپنے ہر زخم ہر تکلیف کی راحت کے لیے اس کی طرف دیکھنے لگی تھی، کئی بار ننگے پاؤں ہونے کی وجہ سے اس کے پاؤں میں کانٹا چبھا تھا اور ایاد عبدالحادی نے ہر بار وہ کانٹا بہت نرمی اور پیار سے اس کا پاؤں اپنی گود میں رکھ کر نکالا تھا۔

رات میں وہ سوتی تو وہ بہت دیر جاگ کر اس کا پہرہ دیتا کبھی وہ اس کے سامنے بیٹھی ہوتی اور اس کا آنچل سرک جاتا تو وہ فوراً اپنی نگاہ پھیر لیتا چونکہ اس کی رگوں میں قبائلی خون تھا اسی لیے اس کی غیرت بھی دیکھنے سے تعلق رکھتی تھی۔ حورعین عبدالسمیع کو پتا ہی نہ چلا کہ وہ قبائلی کب اس کی روح تک رسائی حاصل کر گیا۔

اگلے روز بھی بارش کا سلسلہ جاری رہا تھا۔ حورعین کی آنکھ کھلی تو ایاد وہاں نہیں تھا پچھلے ایک ہفتے میں اس شخص نے ہر طرح کے خطرے اور مشکل کے باوجود ایک وقت کی نماز بھی قضاء نہیں کی تھی مگر وہ وقت نماز کا نہیں تھا، فضا میں گولیوں کی تڑتڑاہٹ گونج رہی تھی اس کا دل تیزی سے دھڑک اٹھا۔

دوپٹہ اچھی طرح لپیٹ کر فوراً سے پیشتر وہ اٹھ کھڑی ہوئی تھی تبھی اس نے ایاد کو اپنی طرف آتے دیکھا تھا وہ زخمی تھا اس کے بازو پر گولی لگی تھی۔ حورعین نے منہ پر ہاتھ رکھ لیا۔

''چلو...... اتحادی فوج نے یہ جگہ دیکھ لی ہے، مجھے خطرہ ہے میرے ساتھ وہ تمہیں بھی نقصان پہنچانے سے باز نہیں رہیں گے۔''

تیزی سے بہتے خون کے باوجود وہ اس کی جان اور عزت کے لیے فکر مند ہو رہا تھا، یہی وہ غیرت اور انسانیت تھی جس کے لیے ابوغریب، بگرام الور دیگر عقوبت خانوں میں قید مسلمان دختران صدائیں دے رہی تھیں۔

اتحادی فوج کے افسران ان کے سر پر آ پہنچے تھے اور اب اندھا دھند گولیاں برسا رہے تھے، حورعین چیخ اٹھی۔ ایاد بہت بری طرح سے زخمی ہو چکا تھا مگر اس کے باوجود بنا کسی زخم کی پروا کیے وہ اسے بچا رہا تھا۔ اندھا دھند بھاگتے ہوئے وہ اسے کسی مقام پر پہنچانا چاہتا تھا شاید اس کا مجاہدین سے رابطہ ہو گیا تھا مگر اسے اس کی مہلت نہیں ملی تھی، ٹڈیوں کی طرح چھائے فوجی اہلکاروں نے ان دونوں کے گرد حصار تنگ کر کے انہیں گرفتار کر لیا تھا۔ اسی رات انہیں اعلیٰ افسران کے حضور پیش کر دیا گیا۔

وہ شخص جو اسی فوج کا حصہ ہو کر مسلمانوں پر مظالم کے پہاڑ توڑتا تھا، اب وہی شخص اپنے انہی ساتھیوں کے ہاتھوں گرفتار ہو کر درد کا اصل مزہ چکھنے جا رہا تھا، وہ لوگ جن کے ساتھ بیٹھ کر شراب کے نشے میں مست ہوتے ہوئے وہ بے کس مسلمان قیدیوں کی بے بسی اور تکالیف پر ہنستا تھا۔ اب وہی لوگ اس کی جان کے دشمن بنے اسے موت کے گھاٹ اتارنے کو بے تاب ہو رہے تھے۔ حورعین جس کوٹھری میں قید تھی، زخموں سے چور ایاد اسی کوٹھری کے سامنے والی کوٹھری میں بند کراہ رہا تھا، باہر مجاہدین اور اتحادی فوج کے درمیان جیسے آگ لگ گئی تھی۔

رات تاریک ہوتی جا رہی تھی۔ ایاد زخموں سے چُور نڈھال پڑا تھا، جب کچھ افسران حورعین کی کوٹھری میں گھس آئے اور اس کی بے حرمتی شروع کر دی۔ وہ چلا رہی تھی اور ادھر ایاد بیدار ہو کر بناء اپنے زخموں کی پروا کیے، پنجرے میں بند شیر کی طرح مچل رہا تھا، اس کا بس نہ چل رہا تھا کہ وہ سلاخیں توڑ کر جیل کو توڑ پھوڑ دیتا تبھی وہ افسران حورعین کو چھوڑ کر اس کی طرف آئے تھے اور پھر حورعین کی آنکھوں نے جیسے قیامت بپا ہوتے دیکھی تھی۔

ایاد کے ننگے وجود پر تیز دھار چاقو سے کٹ لگا کر وہ لوگ ان زخموں پر گرم گرم پگھلی ہوئی موم ڈال رہے تھے مگر ایاد کے لبوں سے کوئی چیخ نہیں نکلی تھی، بری طرح تڑپتے ہوئے وہ اپنا ضبط آزما رہا تھا۔

حورعین سلاخیں پکڑ کر چیختی رہی اور ان انسانی درندوں کی درندگی کا نظارہ کرتی رہی' اگلے پندرہ روز تک یہی سلسلہ جاری رہا تھا' ہر روز مسلسل کئی گھنٹے ایاد پر تشدد کیا جاتا تھا یہاں تک کہ وہ بے ہوش ہو جاتا' سولہویں روز اس کی موت کے پروانے پر دستخط کر دیئے گئے۔

بہت مختصر عرصے میں اس پر غداری کا کیس چلا اور بالآخر عدالت نے اسے پھانسی کی سزا سنادی حورعین کو لگا جیسے وہ زندہ جلادی گئی ہو۔

اس روز پھر بہت بارش برسی تھی۔ کھلے آسمان تلے' ٹپکتی بوندوں کو اپنے صحراتن پر جیسے محسوس کرنے کے باوجود اسے خود پر پتھر ہونے کا گماں ہو رہا تھا' بڑے سے میدان میں چاروں طرف اتحادی فوج کے کارندے تھے اور شدید زخمی حالت میں جان بوجھ کر اسے وہاں لایا گیا تھا تاکہ ایاد عبدالحادی کا انجام اپنی آنکھوں سے دیکھ سکے۔

اس ایاد عبدالحادی کا جس نے کفر کا راستہ چھوڑ کر ہدایت کی منزل تک رسائی حاصل کی تھی جس کا کوئی ذاتی دشمن نہیں تھا مگر سوائے اللہ اور اللہ کے رسول صلی اللہ علیہ وسلم کے دشمنوں کے' وہ مجاہد جو باطل کے سامنے سر جھکانے سے منکر ہو گیا تھا۔ حورعین نے دیکھا وہ بازوؤں اور پشت پر گہرے زخموں کے باوجود خود اپنے پاؤں پر چل کر تختہ دار تک جا رہا تھا' اس کے ہاتھ پیچھے بندھے تھے مگر اس کی چال میں بالکل بھی لڑکھڑاہٹ نہیں تھی۔ حورعین کے لیے اپنے قدموں پر کھڑے رہنا دشوار ہو رہا تھا' اس کی آنکھیں شدید ذہنی دباؤ سے بند ہوئی جا رہی تھیں' تبھی ایاد نے گردن موڑ کر اس کی طرف دیکھا تھا۔ کیا نہیں تھا اس وقت اس کی آنکھوں میں؟

حورعین نے حلق پھاڑ کر چیخنا چاہا مگر اس کی چیخ اس کے اندر ہی گھٹ کر رہ گئی تھی۔ ایاد بڑی مشکل سے اس سے نظر ہٹا کر تختہ دار کی طرف بڑھا تھا' اس کے چہرے پر کوئی پریشانی نہیں تھی' وہاں کھڑے افسران نے جس وقت اس کے منہ پر کپڑا ڈالنے کی کوشش کی اس نے سر ہلا کر منع کر دیا۔

اس کے ذہن میں اس وقت حورعین کا تلخ لہجہ گونج رہا تھا۔

''بزدل ہو تم...... ہمیں قتل کرنے یا ہمیں اذیت دے کر ہم پر تشدد کرنے کے سوا تم اور کر بھی کیا سکتے ہو؟ مگر ہمارے نزدیک یہ عبرت نہیں ہے بلکہ سعادت ہے خوش بختی کی موت ہے' ہمارا دین ایسی موت کو خوش بختی اور شہادت کا نام دیتا ہے' ایک مومن مسلمان کی زندگی کا سب سے بڑا مقصد ہی یہی ہے کہ اسے شہادت کی موت نصیب ہو' میرا خدا ایسے ہی اپنے بندوں کو آزمائش کی بھٹیوں میں جلا کر کندن بناتا ہے اور انہیں اپنے منافق بندوں سے علیحدہ فرما دیتا ہے۔ ہم مصائب سے ٹوٹنے والے نہیں ہیں' وہ ہم نہیں ہیں جنہیں تم اپنے ڈالر کی کشش سے خرید سکو۔''

''اللہ......'' اس کے دل نے بے ساختہ اللہ کو پکارا تھا۔

''مارو...... اور مارو...... کتنا ظلم کرو گے، کتنی نسلیں برباد کرو گے مسلمانوں کی، طاقت کے بل پر کب تک ہماری بے بسی کو کچلو گے تم؟...... تم نہیں جانتے مگر میں جانتی ہوں کہ حاکم اعلیٰ صرف اللہ ہے، طاقت صرف اللہ کی ہے۔ وہ چاہے تو سمندروں کے سینے کھول کر ایک ساتھ تم سب کو غرقاب کر دے، اللہ کی طاقت کے سامنے تمہاری طاقت مری ہوئی چیونٹی کے پَر کے برابر بھی نہیں...... یہ ظلم و بربریت ہمیں ہمارے ایمان سے نہیں پھیر سکتی، وہ اور ہیں جن کے ایمان کا سودا تم اپنے ڈالروں سے کرتے ہو۔ بظاہر مسلمان اِن لوگوں کا اسلام سے کوئی تعلق نہیں...... خود اپنی جانوں پر ظلم کرنے والے بدنصیب لوگ ہیں یہ، پرلے درجے کے بدنصیب لوگ...... جو یہ بھی نہیں جانتے کہ دنیا کی زندگی عارضی ہے۔''

ایاد کے وجدان میں وہ چلا رہی تھی اور اِدھر پھانسی کا پھندا اُس کے گلے میں فٹ کر دیا گیا تھا۔ جان کے بدلے جنت کا سودا مہنگا نہیں تھا، اس وقت اس کے دل میں صرف ایک ہی حسرت تھی۔

کاش وہ مجاہدین کی مدد کر سکتا، کچھ عرصہ اُن کا ساتھ دے سکتا۔ مسلمانوں کے خون کی بہتی ہوئی ندیوں کا حساب لے سکتا۔ مگر......

شاید اللہ رب العزت کو اس کی اتنی ہی زندگی منظور تھی۔

حورعین کی آنکھیں ڈبڈبا گئیں۔

ہم جو تاریک راہوں میں مارے گئے
دار کی خشک ٹہنی پہ وارے گئے
تیرے ہونٹوں کے پھولوں کی چاہت میں ہم
تیرے ہاتھوں کی شمعوں کی حسرت میں ہم
نیم تاریک راہوں میں مارے گئے
سولیوں پر ہمارے لبوں سے پرے
تیرے ہونٹوں کی لالی ٹپکتی رہی
تیری زلفوں کی مستی برستی رہی
تیرے ہاتھوں کی چاندی دمکتی رہی
جب ڈھلی تیری راہوں میں شامِ ستم
ہم چلے آئے لائے جہاں تک قدم
لب پہ حرفِ غزل، دل میں قندیلِ غم
اپنا غم تھا گواہی تیرے حُسن کی
دیکھ قائم رہے اِس گواہی پہ ہم
ہم جو تاریک راہوں میں مارے گئے
نارسائی اگر اپنی تقدیر تھی
تیری اُلفت تو اپنی ہی تدبیر تھی
کس کو شکوہ اگر شوق کے سلسلے
ہجر کی قتل گاہوں سے سب جا ملے
قتل گاہوں سے چُن کر ہمارے علم
اور نکلیں گے عشاق کے قافلے
جن کی راہِ طلب میں ہمارے قدم
مختصر کر چلے درد کے فاصلے
کر چکے جن کی خاطر جہاں گیر ہم
جاں گنوا کر تیری دلبری کا بھرم
ہم جو تاریک راہوں میں مارے گئے

پھندا ایاد عبدالحادی کے خوبصورت گلے میں فٹ کرنے کے بعد تختہ کھینچ دیا گیا تھا۔ حورعین کے حلق سے فلک شگاف چیخ نکلی اور وہ بے ہوش ہوگئی۔

پورے ڈیڑھ ماہ بعد وہ دوبارہ ہوش کی دنیا میں واپس آئی تھی۔

مختصر کومہ کے بعد ہوش کی دنیا میں واپسی اس کے لئے بہت تکلیف دہ ثابت ہوئی تھی۔ ایاد کی شہادت کے بعد مجاہدین نے وہاں حملہ بول دیا تھا اور انہیں اس میں خاطر خواہ کامیابی نصیب ہوئی تھی۔

حورعین بھی اب اُنہی کے قبضے میں تھی۔

ایاد کی لاش پاکستان بھجوادی گئی تھی۔ حورعین کے کومہ سے واپسی کے بعد اسے بھی پاکستان بھجوادیا گیا، مگر..... زندگی میں اب رہ ہی کیا گیا تھا؟

سرد روّیہ، اُلجھا لہجہ

کھوئی آنکھیں ٹھنڈے ہاتھ

بے رنگ چہرہ بداخلاق

دیکھو تم بن کون ہوں میں؟

گھٹنوں میں سر دیئے چپ چاپ وہ روتی رہی تھی اور لحہ بہ لحہ برستی بارش اس کے صحرائے تن پر برستی جیسے اُس کے اندر دہکتی آگ کو اور ہوا دیتی رہی۔

❁......❁......❁

نہال کی میڈیکل رپورٹس اس کی آنکھوں کے سامنے تھیں اور وہ جیسے گھومتے ہوئے سر کے ساتھ کرسی کا سہارا لیے نیچے زمین پر بیٹھتی چلی جارہی تھی۔

کتنا ہی وقت بیت گیا تھا' رو رو کر اس کی آنکھیں سوج چکی تھیں' ہر لحہ خوش باش نظر آنے والا وہ کھلنڈرا سا شخص اپنے اندر کتنے طوفان چھپائے ہوئے تھا' ہانیہ کے لیے وہاں سے اٹھنا گویا موت کے مترادف ہوگیا۔

میکال آفس سے آیا تو مائرہ لاؤنج میں بیٹھی ٹی وی دیکھ رہی تھی۔

''السلام علیکم!'' سرسری سی ایک نظر اس پر ڈالتا وہ وہیں صوفے پر ٹک گیا تھا۔

''وعلیکم السلام! آج جلدی آگئے میکال بھائی؟''

''ہوں..... طبیعت کچھ ٹھیک نہیں تھی' باقی لوگ کہاں ہیں؟''

''باقی لوگ..... آنٹی اور سارا تو بتول خالہ (رشتے دار) کے ہاں گئی ہوئی ہیں' انہوں نے بلوایا تھا اور باقی رہ گئیں ہانیہ بھابی تو وہ صبح آپ کے گھر سے نکلنے کے بعد ہی نہال کے کمرے میں گھس گئی تھیں' ابھی تک وہیں ہیں۔''

''وہاٹ.....؟'' مائرہ کی اطلاع پر اسے جیسے جھٹکا لگا تھا' عین اسی پل مرے مرے قدموں کو گھسیٹتی وہ نہال کے کمرے سے نکلی تھی اور پھر بنا ادھر اُدھر نگاہ ڈالے' ناک کی سیدھ میں چلتی سیدھی اپنے کمرے کی طرف بڑھ گئی تھی۔

میکال کو لگا جیسے کسی نے اس کا دل کچل ڈالا ہو۔ وہ کمرے میں آیا تو ہانیہ اندھیرا کیے اوندھے منہ پڑی تھی' یوں جیسے بے حد تھک گئی ہو' اس کے اندر سو طرح کے وسوسے سر اٹھانے لگے' شک کے ناگ نے ڈس ڈس کر جیسے اس کا سارا وجود زہریلا کر ڈالا تھا۔

ہانیہ سو رہی تھی اور وہ پوری رات اس کے پہلو میں بیٹھا جاگ کر سگریٹ پھونکتا رہا تھا۔ اگلی صبح ہانیہ تیز بخار میں جل رہی تھی۔ میکال کی آنکھ اس کے کراہنے کی آواز سے کھلی تھی اور جس وقت اس نے اس کے سرخ گالوں پر ہاتھ رکھا گویا اس کی جان پر بن گئی' ساری کدورتیں' غلط فہمیاں پل بھر میں ذہن سے نکل گئی تھیں۔

''ہانیہ......''

اس پر جھک کر اپنائیت سے اس کے گال تھپتھپاتے ہوئے اس نے پکارا تھا' جب غنودگی کے عالم میں بہت مدھم لہجے میں ہانیہ کے لبوں نے جنبش کی تھی۔

''نہال......''

میکال شاکڈ رہ گیا تھا۔ غنودگی میں بھی ہانیہ کا نہال کو پکارنا اسے پتھر ہی تو کر گیا تھا' اس لمحے وہ سیدھا ہوا تھا اور سر بیڈ کی پشت گاہ سے ٹکا کے زور سے آنکھیں میچ لیں' اسے لگا جیسے کسی نے ڈھیر سارا کوڑا کرکٹ اس کے اوپر اچھال دیا ہو۔

محبت کی نارسائی جیسے اس کے مقدر کا حصہ بن گئی ہو۔ چپ چاپ کتنی ہی دیر تک اپنے آنسو ضبط کرنے کے بعد وہ اٹھا تھا اور واش روم میں گھس گیا تھا' ٹھنڈے پانی سے اچھی طرح شاور لینے کے بعد بھی اندر لگی آگ میں کوئی فرق نہیں پڑا تھا۔ خاموشی سے آفس کے لیے تیار ہونے کے بعد وہ ایک سرسری سی نظر ہانیہ پر ڈالتا کمرے سے نکل آیا تھا۔

رات کو جس وقت اس کی گھر واپسی ہوئی سب لاؤنج میں بیٹھے اسے لتاڑنے کو تیار بیٹھے تھے۔

''السلام علیکم!'' تھکے تھکے سے انداز میں اپنا کوٹ سائیڈ صوفے پر رکھتے ہوئے اس نے سب کو مشترکہ سلام کیا تھا مگر جواب صرف حسن صاحب نے دیا۔

''وعلیکم السلام! بڑی جلدی آ گئے آج آفس سے؟'' وہ طنزاً کہہ رہے تھے' میکال انہیں دیکھنے لگا۔

''سوری کچھ ضروری کام آ پڑا' اس لیے دیر ہو گئی۔''

''تمہارے ضروری کاموں کی خبر ہے مجھے' اس لیے بہتر ہو گا اگر تم اپنے ضروری کاموں کی حد محدود کر دو۔''

''میں سمجھا نہیں آپ کیا کہنا چاہ رہے ہیں؟''

''بہت اچھی طرح سمجھ رہے ہو تم جو میں کہنا چاہ رہا ہوں' بزنس کی آڑ میں جو مصروفیات تم نے آج کل پالی ہوئی ہیں میں ان سے بے خبر نہیں ہوں۔''

تقریباً دھاڑتے ہوئے انہوں نے اس پر واضح کیا تھا۔ میکال نے فوراً ہانیہ کی طرف دیکھا وہ بھی اسے ہی دیکھ رہی تھی تاہم میکال کے دیکھنے پر اس نے اپنی نظر چرا لی' وہ سمجھا اسی نے حسن صاحب اور دیگر گھر والوں سے اس کی شکایت کی ہے جب کہ ایسا نہیں تھا یہ سارا ہنگامہ تو مائرہ کا پیدا کیا ہوا تھا جس نے آج اپنی فرینڈز کے ساتھ ہوٹلنگ کے دوران پھر اسے علیزہ نامی ماڈل کے ساتھ ہوٹل میں دیکھا تھا اور واپسی پر بناء ہانیہ کی طبیعت کی پروا کیے' نہال کی موجودگی میں مرچ مسالہ لگا کر سب کو یہ بات بتائی اور یہ بھی واضح کیا کہ ہانیہ اس بات سے باخبر ہے اور یہ سب بہت دنوں سے چل رہا ہے' اس لمحے اس سے زیادہ ہانیہ کا ہمدرد اور کوئی نہیں تھا۔

''کیا چاہتے ہیں آپ مجھ سے؟''

اسے بھی غصہ آیا تھا' حسن صاحب نے ایک نظر ہانیہ کی طرف دیکھا پھر بولے۔

''یہی کہ جو تمہاری ذمہ داریاں ہیں ان پر اپنا وقت صرف کرو' جن باتوں میں سوائے رسوائی کے اور کچھ نہیں انہیں چھوڑ دو۔''

''میں ایسا کچھ نہیں کر رہا جس سے میری یا میرے گھر والوں کی رسوائی ہو' جہاں تک ذمہ داریوں کی بات ہے تو وہ میں ہر ممکن حد تک نبھا رہا ہوں' نہ بھی نبھاؤں تو یہاں اس گھر میں بہت لوگ ہیں میری ذمہ داریاں نبھا لے والے۔''

چبا چبا کر کہتے ہوئے ایک زہرخند نگاہ نہال پر ڈال کر وہ فوراً اٹھ کھڑا ہوا تھا۔ مسز حسن سر تھام کر بیٹھ گئیں جب کہ

مائرہ کے لبوں پر نہایت آسودہ مسکراہٹ رینگ رہی تھی۔

✿......✿......✿

ہانیہ کی طبیعت اب قدرے بہتر تھی۔

میکال ٹی وی دیکھ رہا تھا' وہ اس کے آفس کے لیے کپڑے پریس کرنے بیٹھ گئی تبھی وہ اٹھا اور اس کے قریب پہنچ کر اس نے اپنے کپڑے اس کے ہاتھ سے چھین لیے تھے۔ وہ ہکا بکا سی اسے دیکھتی رہ گئی۔

"تمہاری طبیعت ٹھیک نہیں ہے آرام کرو' ویسے بھی آج کے بعد تمہیں میرے کسی کام کو ہاتھ لگانے کی ضرورت نہیں ہے۔"

"کیوں؟" اس کے تپے تپے سے چہرے کو بغور دیکھتے ہوئے وہ جیسے ٹوٹی تھی۔

"کیونکہ میں کہہ رہا ہوں اس لیے۔"

اس بار چبا چبا کر کہتے ہوئے اس نے خاصے غصے اور حقارت سے اس کی طرف دیکھا تھا اور پلٹ کر دوبارہ ٹی وی دیکھنے میں مشغول ہو گیا تھا۔ ہانیہ چپ چاپ کمرے سے نکل آئی وہ شخص غلطی ہو کر بھی شرمندہ ہونے کے بجائے الٹا اسی پر غصہ کر رہا تھا آپ ہی آپ اس کی آنکھیں آنسوؤں سے بھر آئیں۔

باہر خاصی سرد ہوا چل رہی تھی وہ کمرے سے نکل کر باہر سیڑھیوں پر آ بیٹھی' نہال کے کمرے کی لائٹ جل رہی تھی جس کا مطلب تھا کہ وہ بھی جاگ رہا ہے مگر......

ہانیہ کے اندر اس وقت اس کے سامنے جانے کی ہمت نہیں تھی۔ کتنا سناٹا پھیلا ہوا تھا اس کے اندر......مگر اس سناٹے کی حقیقت کا ادراک کسے تھا۔

نہال جو اس کے بچپن کا ساتھی اور دوست تھا اس کے ہر دکھ اور سکھ کا راز داں تھا' ڈاکٹری رپورٹس کے مطابق کتنی تیزی سے موت کی طرف بڑھ رہا تھا مگر گھر میں کسی کو اس کی خبر ہی نہیں تھی اسے بھی نہ ہوتی اگر اس روز وہ کتابیں لینے کے لیے اس کے کمرے میں نہ جاتی۔

اس کا دل چاہ رہا تھا وہ دھاڑیں مار مار کر روئے مگر اس گھر میں اسے پھوٹ پھوٹ کر رونے کی اجازت بھی نہیں تھی۔

نہال کے غم کے سامنے میکال کا غم بہت ہلکا پڑ رہا تھا اور وہ سمجھ رہا تھا وہ اس سے بے وفائی کر رہی ہے۔

اگلی صبح میکال کے منع کرنے کے باوجود اس نے اس کے کئی سوٹ پریس کر کے ہینگ کر دیئے تھے۔ میکال پھر بنا ناشتا کیے آفس کے لیے نکل گیا۔ چند دن اسی کشمکش کی نذر ہو گئے تھے نہ اسے سکون تھا نہ میکال کو...... ہانیہ کا دل چاہا وہ میکال کو ساری حقیقت بتا دے مگر اس نے اپنی مصروفیات بہت بڑھا لی تھیں' صبح ٹائم سے پہلے آفس کے لیے نکل جانا اور رات کو لیٹ نائٹ گھر واپس آنا اب اس کا معمول بن گیا تھا مگر ہانیہ کو پروا نہیں تھی' وہ بس اپنا درد شیئر کرنا چاہتی تھی۔ نہال حسن کو لے کر جو طوفان اس کے اندر اُدھم مچائے ہوئے تھے ان طوفانوں کا اظہار کرنا چاہتی تھی مگر اس کی قسمت اس کا ساتھ نہیں دے رہی تھی۔

اس روز پھر جانے اس کے دل میں کیا آئی کہ وہ نہال حسن کے کمرے میں چلی آئی تھی۔ نہال کل ہی شہر سے باہر گیا تھا' بظاہر بزنس میٹنگ کے لیے مگر ہانیہ جانتی تھی کہ وہ اپنے چیک اپ کے لیے گیا تھا۔

اس کا کمرا بھی اسی کی طرح نفیس تھا وہ وہاں بیٹھ کر دیر تلک روتی رہی' بیڈ کے سامنے ہی رائٹنگ ٹیبل تھی اور اسی پر وہ کتابیں دھری تھیں جو اسے پسند تھیں۔ وہ بیڈ سے اٹھ کر وہاں آ بیٹھی' کتابوں کے ایک سائیڈ پر نہال کی ڈائری رکھی تھی۔ ہانیہ نے دل کے ہاتھوں متجسس ہو کر وہ ڈائری اٹھائی تھی اور کپکپاتے ہاتھوں سے اس کے اوراق پلٹے تھے۔

آہ کو چاہیے اک عمر اثر ہونے تک
کون جیتا ہے تیری زلف کے سر ہونے تک
ہم نے مانا کہ تغافل نہ کرو گے لیکن
خاک ہوجائیں گے ہم تم کو خبر ہونے تک

موتیوں جیسی ہینڈ رائٹنگ میں لکھا یہ قطعہ اس کی توجہ کا محور بن گیا تھا مگر اس کے بعد اگلے بہت سے صفحات خالی تھے وہ ڈائری بند کرنے لگی تھی جب اچانک اس کی نظر اس صفحے پر پڑی جس پر لکھا تھا۔

''زندگی میں کبھی کسی نے خود کو قبر میں اترتے ہوئے نہیں دیکھا ہوگا مگر میں نے دیکھا ہے زندہ ہوتے ہوئے میں نے خود اپنا بین ہوتے اپنے کانوں سے سنا ہے' خود اپنی لاش کو اپنے کندھوں پر اٹھا کر پھرا ہوں' اپنی حسرتوں اور تمناؤں کو چھپ چھپ کر سسکیاں بھرتے دیکھا ہے' مجھے اندازہ ہی نہیں تھا زندگی میں صرف کسی ایک شخص کے نہ ہونے سے سانسیں اتنی بوجھ بن جاتی ہیں' قطعی اندازہ نہیں تھا مجھے کہ صرف ایک ہانیہ صفدر کو کھو دینے کے بعد میری زندگی میں کچھ بھی نہیں رہے گا' کچھ بھی نہیں......''

ایک پہاڑ اس پر چند روز پہلے ٹوٹا تھا اور ایک پہاڑ اب اس لمحے ٹوٹ کر گر رہا تھا' وہ شاکڈ بیٹھی رہ گئی۔

کپکپاتے ہاتھوں میں مزید صفحات پلٹنے کی سکت نہیں تھی۔

منہ پر ہاتھ رکھے اس نے بے ساختہ اپنی چیخ کا گلا گھونٹا تھا تبھی دروازے پر آہٹ ہوئی تھی' اس نے پلٹ کر دیکھا نہال دہلیز پر کھڑا تھا تھکن زدہ چہرے پر غم و غصے کی سرخی تھی۔ وہ آنسو صاف کیے بغیر آہستہ سے کھڑی ہوئی تھی۔

''تم یہاں کیا کر رہی ہو؟''

تھکے تھکے قدم اٹھاتا وہ عین اس کے مقابل آ کھڑا ہوا تھا' ہانیہ چپ چاپ اسے دیکھتی رہی۔ ڈائری اب بھی اس کے ہاتھ میں تھی' نہال کی نظر اس کے چہرے سے پھسلتی ہوئی ڈائری پر آ کر رک گئی۔

پل میں اس کے چہرے کے تاثرات تبدیل ہوئے تھے' عقاب کی طرح جھپٹ کر اس کے ہاتھ سے ڈائری چھینتے ہوئے کچھ دیر وہ خاموشی سے اسے دیکھتا رہا پھر اچانک ایک زوردار طمانچہ اس کے بائیں گال پر رسید کر دیا۔

''میری غیر موجودگی میں' میرے کمرے میں آنے کی ہمت کیسے ہوئی تمہیں؟''

شدید برہم ہو کر حلق کے بل وہ چلایا تھا' لاؤنج میں بیٹھی سارہ اور مائرہ دوڑ کر وہاں چلی آئیں جب کہ ہانیہ لڑکھڑا کر بیڈ کی پٹی پر ہاتھ ٹکا کر بمشکل سنبھلی۔

''دفع ہو جاؤ یہاں سے اور دوبارہ کبھی میری غیر موجودگی میں یہاں قدم مت رکھنا۔'' اس کا بس نہ چلتا تھا وہ ہانیہ کو شوٹ کر ڈالتا۔

وہ راز جو اب تک اس نے خود اپنے آپ سے بھی چھپا کر رکھا تھا' کیسے افشاء ہو گیا تھا۔ افشاء بھی اس ہستی کے ہاتھوں کہ جس سے اس نے اپنا سایہ تک چھپا کر رکھا تھا' مائرہ کی آنکھیں پھٹی کی پھٹی رہ گئی تھیں۔ میکال کی آفس سے واپسی کے بعد اس نے پھر اسے گھیر لیا تھا۔

''میکال بھائی ایک بات کہوں ناراض تو نہیں ہو گے؟''

''نہیں...... کہو۔'' جوتے اتارتے اتارتے رک کر وہ اسے دیکھنے لگا۔ مائرہ اطراف میں نگاہ ڈالتی وہیں صوفے پر بیٹھ گئی۔

''وہ...... میکال بھائی مجھے آپ سے یہ کہنا تھا کہ آپ ہانیہ بھابی پر تھوڑی سختی کریں روز آپ کے آفس جانے کے

بعد وہ نہال بھائی کے کمرے میں گھس جاتی ہیں اور سارا دن وہیں رہتی ہیں۔ آج نہال بھائی نے انہیں دیکھ لیا اور بہت غصہ کیا' تھپڑ بھی مارا۔ یہ بھی کہہ رہے تھے کہ اب تم میرے بھائی کی عزت ہو یوں دن میں سر عام نہ گھس آیا کرو کمرے میں' کتنی بری بات ہے کیا اثر پڑتا ہوگا مجھ پر اور سارا پر' آپ سوچ سکتے ہیں۔''

ایک اور طمانچہ...... میکال کے ماتھے پر تیوریاں پڑ گئیں۔

''ٹھیک ہے میں کروں گا ہانیہ سے بات' آئندہ احتیاط کرے گی وہ۔'' کہنے کے ساتھ ہی اٹھ کر وہ اپنے کمرے کی طرف بڑھ گیا تھا۔ اندر ہانیہ بیڈ پر اوندھے منہ پڑی رو رہی تھی' وہ واش روم میں گھس گیا تقریباً پچیس منٹ کے بعد فریش ہو کر وہ کمرے میں واپس آیا تو ہانیہ کی گھٹی گھٹی سسکیوں کی آواز نے اسے مزید تپا دیا۔

''کیا مسئلہ ہے تمہارے ساتھ' کیوں رو رہی ہو؟''

اسے بازو سے پکڑ کر جھنجوڑتے ہوئے اس نے غصہ دکھایا تھا' جواب میں ہانیہ سب کچھ بھلاتے ہوئے تڑپ کر اس کے سینے سے لپٹ گئی اور بچوں کی طرح پھوٹ پھوٹ کر رو پڑی۔

''کیا ہوا ہے؟'' اس کا غصہ ہانیہ کی اس حالت پر قدرے کم ہوا تھا مگر وہ روتی رہی۔

''میں جانتا ہوں تمہیں نہال نے دکھی کیا ہے اور میں یہ بھی جانتا ہوں کہ تم دونوں کے درمیان کچھ بھی غلط نہیں ہے مگر پھر بھی تمہارا ہر وقت اس کے اردگرد منڈلاتے رہنا مجھے پسند نہیں ہے' روز میرے آفس جانے کے بعد تم اس کے کمرے میں گھس جاتی ہو' کیوں؟'' کندھوں سے پکڑ کر اسے اپنے مقابل کیا تھا مگر ہانیہ بناء کوئی جواب دیئے پھر اس کے سینے پر سر رکھ کر پلکیں موند گئیں' اس کا سر دن بھر رونے کی وجہ سے اس وقت جیسے پھٹ رہا تھا۔ میکال نے اسے زیادہ چھیڑنا مناسب نہ سمجھا' یقیناً وہ دن بھر سے بھوکی تھی تبھی نرمی سے اسے خود سے علیحدہ کرنے کے بعد وہ نیچے کچن میں آیا اور کھانا نکال کر اوپر کمرے میں لے آیا۔

''ہانیہ...... چلو اٹھو' کھانا کھاؤ۔''

''مجھے بھوک نہیں ہے۔'' اس کے کہنے پر بمشکل بیڈ پر بیٹھی تھی۔ میکال نے ٹرے سائیڈ پر رکھ دی۔

''کیوں بھوک نہیں ہے' کیا ہو گیا ہے ایسا جس نے تمہاری بھوک ختم کر دی ہے؟''

''پتا نہیں۔'' وہ اس کی طرف دیکھنے سے گریز برت رہی تھی' میکال نے اسے بھی اس کا جرم گردانا۔

''کیا تمہیں نہیں لگتا کہ ہمارے درمیان فاصلے بڑھتے جا رہے ہیں۔''

''آئی ڈونٹ کیئر۔'' بیزار کن لہجے میں کہتی وہ فوراً بیڈ سے اٹھ کر ٹیرس پر چلی آئی تھی' نیچے لان کے ایک کونے میں ذرا سی روشنی کیے نہال بیٹھا تھا۔ اس کے آنسو پھر روانی سے بہنے لگے' ذہن کے پردے پر اچانک کچھ مناظر جھلملائے تھے۔

''اے کیا ہوا؟ جان لے لوں گا تمہاری اگر مجھ پر ایسی پابندی لگائی تو' یا سر سیلی ناراض ہوئیں۔'' اس کے تنگ کرنے پر جب وہ ناراض ہوئی تھی تو کیسے اس کی جان پر بن گئی تھی۔

آنکھوں کے گوشوں میں جھلکتی نمی نے سچ مچ اسے حیران کر دیا تھا مگر...... اس وقت وہ کہاں جانتی تھی کہ وہ نہال حسن کے لیے کیا ہے؟ رات گزرتی جا رہی تھی مگر وہ گزرے لمحوں کا احساس کیے بناء وہیں کھڑی رہی۔

نہال اب لان سے اٹھ گیا تھا' وہ بھی بے قراری سی کمرے میں واپس پلٹ آئی' میکال کمرے میں نہیں تھا۔ فضا میں خنکی تھی کہ بڑھتی جا رہی تھی' دونوں بازو آپس میں لپیٹتے ہوئے وہ بیڈ پر آ بیٹھی۔

زندگی نے کتنا عجیب کھیل کھیلا تھا اس کے ساتھ جس شخص نے اسے ٹوٹ کے چاہا تھا وہ خود ٹوٹ گیا تھا مگر اس نے اپنی چاہت کبھی اس پر عیاں نہیں کی تھی اور وہ شخص جسے تقدیر نے اس کا ہم سفر بنا دیا تھا' جس کی محبت اس کی رگ رگ

میں اتار دی تھی اسے شاید اس کے ہونے نہ ہونے سے کوئی فرق ہی نہیں پڑ رہا تھا کیوں ہوا تھا اس کے ساتھ ایسا؟

جب وہ میکال حسن کے ساتھ زندگی کی شروعات کرنا ہی نہیں چاہتی تھی تو اسے زبردستی اس پر مجبور کر دیا تھا اور اب جب کہ وہ اس کے بغیر سانس بھی نہیں لے سکتی تھی تو نہال حسن کی محبت اس کے سامنے آ کھڑی ہوئی تھی۔

رو رو کر اس کی آنکھیں سرخ ہو گئی تھیں۔ یوں ہی روتے روتے جانے کب اس کی آنکھ لگ گئی تھی، اگلی صبح اس کی آنکھ کھلی تو میکال آفس کے لیے تیار ہو رہا تھا۔ ہانیہ کو خبر ہی نہیں تھی کہ وہ بھی ساری رات جاگتا رہا تھا' اس کی شریانیں بھی پھٹ رہی تھیں' آنکھوں کے گوشوں میں پڑے سرخ ڈورے اس کے اضطراب کی کہانی سنا رہے تھے۔ وہ اٹھی اور میکال کے پہلو میں جا کھڑی ہوئی تھی۔

''سوری میکال! رات میری طبیعت ٹھیک نہیں تھی اس لیے میں نے آپ سے بُرا برتاؤ کیا' پلیز مجھے معاف کر دیں۔''

''اٹس او کے۔'' بناء اس پر نگاہ ڈالے اس نے ٹائی کی ناٹ کو سیدھا کیا تھا تبھی وہ اس کے سامنے آئی تھی۔

''میکال مجھے آپ سے کچھ شیئر کرنا ہے' نہال کو لے کر کچھ بتانا ہے آپ کو؟'' وہ مضطرب تھی میکال کی پیشانی کی سلوٹوں میں مزید اضافہ ہو گیا۔

''ابھی میں آفس سے لیٹ ہو رہا ہوں' واپسی پر بات کریں گے۔''

''ناشتا کر کے جایئے گا' میں ابھی لاتی ہوں۔''

''نہیں اس وقت ضرورت نہیں ہے' میں پہلے ہی بہت لیٹ ہو رہا ہوں' خدا حافظ۔''

اس وقت وہ اس کی شکل دیکھنے کا بھی روادار نہیں تھا تبھی فوراً کمرے سے نکل گیا۔ ہانیہ پریشان سی کمرے سے نکل کر نیچے چلی آئی' سارہ اور مائرہ کچن میں ناشتا بنا رہی تھیں جب کہ آسیہ بیگم ابھی کمرے سے ہی نہیں نکلی تھیں' وہ فریش ہو کر لان میں چلی آئی۔ نہال پودوں کے ساتھ مصروف تھا اس کا دل تیزی سے دھڑک اٹھا۔

''آج آفس نہیں گئے تم؟''

''نہیں۔'' چونک کر پلٹتے ہوئے اسے دیکھنے کے بعد بہت روکھے لہجے میں اس نے جواب دیا تھا' وہ پاس آ بیٹھی۔

''کیوں؟''

''دل نہیں چاہ رہا تھا۔''

''نہال تم مجھ سے ٹھیک سے بات کیوں نہیں کر رہے ہو' کیوں بھاگ رہے ہو مجھ سے؟ میں جانتی ہوں تمہارے دل میں میرے لیے کیا ہے' مگر جانتے ہوئے بھی میں کچھ کر نہیں سکتی کیونکہ میں میکال کی بیوی ہوں' پیار کرتی ہوں اس سے بے حد' بے تحاشا میرا کیا قصور ہے کہ تم مجھ سے بات بھی نہ کرو' اتنے اچھے دوست ہو کہ اپنی ہر بات ہر راز مجھ سے الگ کر لو' بولو......'' اسے بازو سے پکڑ کر جھنجوڑتے ہوئے وہ جذباتی ہوئی تھی۔

''کیا قصور ہے میرا اگر میری شادی زبردستی میکال حسن سے ہو گئی مگر اب نہ وہ میری شکل دیکھنے کا روادار ہے نہ تم' کیوں؟'' اچانک اس کا لہجہ بھرّا گیا تھا' نہال نے کھرپہ سائیڈ پر پھینک کر ہاتھ جھاڑ لیے۔

''میں تم سے ناراض نہیں ہوں ہانیہ! بس میں چاہتا ہوں تم ہمیشہ خوش رہو' میری وجہ سے تمہاری خوشیوں کو کبھی گہن نہ لگے۔''

''تمہاری وجہ سے میری خوشیوں کو گہن کیوں لگے گا نہال! تم تو میرے سچے خیر خواہ ہو' تم نے تو ہمیشہ میری خوشیاں کی دعا کی ہے پھر یہ سوچ بھی کیسے لیا تم نے کہ تمہاری وجہ سے میری خوشیوں کو گہن لگ سکتا ہے۔''

''بس...... خیر سوری اس روز مجھے تم پر ہاتھ نہیں اٹھانا چاہیے تھا۔''

''صرف سوری......؟''

''نہیں ہاتھ بھی جوڑوں گا' کان بھی پکڑوں گا اور تمہیں تمہاری پسند کے اچھے سے ریسٹورنٹ میں کھانا بھی کھلاؤں گا۔''

''ہوں' یہ ہوئی نا بات......''مسکرا کر اس کے کندھے پر مکا رسید کرتے ہوئے وہ جیسے ہلکی پھلکی ہوگئی تھی۔

اس روز اس نے نہال کے ساتھ ناشتا کیا تھا' وہ اسے زیادہ سے زیادہ خوش رکھنا چاہتی تھی تاکہ موت کو اس سے دور رکھ سکے اور اس مقصد کے لیے خواہ سارا گھر ہی اس کے خلاف کیوں نہ ہو جاتا' وہ باز آنے والی نہیں تھی۔

دوپہر سے کچھ پہلے نہال اپنے ایک دوست سے ملنے نکل گیا تو وہ بھی گاڑی لے کر میکال کے آفس چلی آئی' مقصد اس کی ناراضگی دور کر کے اسے سرپرائز دینا تھا' اگلے تیس منٹ میں وہ اس کے آفس میں تھی' ریسپشنسٹ کو اس نے اطلاع دینے سے منع کر دیا تھا قطعی فریش موڈ میں ہلکے سے میکال کے روم کا دروازہ ناک کر کے اگلے ہی پل جونہی وہ اندر داخل ہوئی گویا ساری چھت کا ملبہ اس کے سر پر آ پڑا۔

پھٹی پھٹی نگاہوں سے وہ سامنے بڑے سے صوفے پر لیٹی اس بے ہودہ لڑکی اور اس پر جھکے میکال حسن کو دیکھتی رہ گئی تھی۔

''ہانیہ تم......؟''

دروازے پر ہلکی سی ناک پر سنبھل کر کھڑے ہوتے ہوئے میکال نے جونہی دہلیز پر ساکت کھڑی ہانیہ کو دیکھا۔ ششدر رہ گیا مگر اس میں تو ہلنے کی بھی سکت نہیں تھی۔ پتھر کی مورت بنی وہ اندر سے جیسے کرچی کرچی ہوگئی تھی۔

کچھ ہی لمحوں میں نظر کے سامنے کا سارا منظر جیسے دھندلا گیا۔ اس سے پہلے کہ میکال اس کے قریب آتا وہ پلٹی اور ہَوا کی رفتار سے چلتی ہوئی آفس کی عمارت سے نکل گئی۔ میکال پیچھے اسے پکارتا رہ گیا تھا۔

رات اس کی واپسی خاصی لیٹ ہوئی تھی۔ ہانیہ لان کی سیڑھیوں پر دونوں بازو لپیٹے نہال کے ساتھ بیٹھی تھی۔ وہ گاڑی سے نکل کر ان کے قریب آیا کچھ دیر رکا پھر بنا کچھ کہے اندر لاؤنج کی طرف بڑھ گیا۔ ہانیہ کی آنکھیں سرخ ہو رہی تھیں۔

''تم نے مجھ سے کیوں چھپایا نہال کہ تم مجھ سے پیار کرتے ہو؟''اس کی آواز بھاری ہو رہی تھی۔

''بتانے کا فائدہ بھی کیا تھا جب تک مجھ پر یہ حقیقت آشکار ہوئی تم میکال بھیا کی زندگی کا حصہ بن چکی تھیں۔''

''تم جانتے ہو میں اس شادی کے لیے ذہنی اور دلی طور پر تیار نہیں تھی۔ تم چاہتے تو یہ شادی رکوا سکتے تھے۔''

''نہیں رکوا سکتا تھا کیونکہ پاپا اور مما ذہنی طور پر تمہیں میکال بھیا کے لیے پسند کر چکے تھے۔''

''ٹھیک' جو ہو گیا سو ہو گیا مگر اب تمہیں شادی کر لینی چاہیے۔''

''ہوں' کر لوں گا۔ مگر ابھی میری کچھ مجبوریاں ہیں ابھی نہیں کر سکتا۔''

''کیسی مجبوریاں؟''وہ سب جانتی تھی مگر پھر بھی اس کا امتحان لے رہی تھی۔

''میں کچھ مسائل تمہیں نہیں بتا سکتا۔ بس تم میرے لیے دعا کیا کرو۔''

''کرتی ہوں مگر تم اب بہت کچھ چھپانے لگے ہو' دس از ناٹ فیئر۔''

''تم سے کچھ نہیں چھپا سکتا ہانیہ! چلو اب اٹھو۔ میکال بھائی تمہارا انتظار کر رہے ہوں گے۔''اس کے لہجے میں محبت ہی محبت تھی۔

ہانیہ نے اس کا ہاتھ تھام لیا۔

''بیٹھ جاؤ نہال پلیز۔ میرا دل ابھی اندر جانے کو نہیں چاہ رہا۔''

''کیوں' کیا میکال بھائی سے جھگڑا ہو گیا ہے؟''

''نہیں اس سے جھگڑا کیوں ہو گا؟ بس میرا دل تمہاری وجہ سے بوجھل ہے۔''

''میری وجہ سے دل کو بوجھل رکھنا چھوڑ دو ہانیہ۔ ہم بس اچھے دوست ہیں۔ ہمیشہ اچھے دوست رہیں گے۔ چلو اٹھو اب اس سے پہلے کہ وہ ناراض ہو جائیں۔'' اس بار اس نے جھک کر اس کا بازو پکڑتے ہوئے زبردستی اسے اٹھا دیا تھا۔

ہانیہ کمرے میں آئی تو میکال فریش ہو کر بیڈ پر بیٹھا ٹی وی دیکھ رہا تھا۔ وہ چپ چاپ اپنی جگہ لیٹ گئی۔

اگلے روز موسم اچھا تھا۔ نہال کا اچانک لانگ ڈرائیو کا پروگرام بن گیا۔ سارا اور مائرہ اپنی دوست کے گھر گئی تھیں۔ وہ زبردستی ہانیہ کو کھینچ کر لے گیا۔ مسز حسن نے بھی اس کی فیور کی تھی۔ بہت دنوں کے بعد وہ دونوں ایک دوسرے کی کمپنی میں موسم کو انجوائے کر رہے تھے۔ بادلوں سے ڈھکے آسمان نے دن کی روشنی کو اپنی پناہ میں لے لیا تھا۔

وہ لوگ مختصر ڈرائیو کے بعد ہوٹل سے کھانا کھا کر نکلے تو مغرب سے عشاء ہو گئی تھی۔ ساتھ ہی ہلکی بارش کی شدت میں بھی اب اضافہ ہو گیا تھا۔ ہانیہ پریشان ہو گئی۔

''دیکھا میں نے کہا تھا ناں یہ بارش نہیں رکنے والی مگر تم بھی نہال! بالکل اپنے بھائی پر گئے ہو' اپنی بات منوا کر ہی دم لیتے ہو۔''

''کوئی بات نہیں' بارش کا کیا ہے ابھی رک جائے گی۔ نہ بھی رکی تو ہم نے کون سا پیدل گھر جانا ہے۔''

''تم سے کچھ بعید نہیں پیدل بھی لے جا سکتے ہو۔''

''ہوں' بالکل بجا فرمایا آپ نے۔'' گاڑی کا دروازہ کھولتے ہوئے وہ مسکرایا تھا۔ ہانیہ نے جواباً اس کے کندھے پر زور کا مکا رسید کیا۔

''ترسو گی ہانیہ ڈیئر' نہال حسن کے ساتھ ان بارشوں کے حسن کو محسوس کرنے کے لیے ترسو گی کبھی۔'' ڈرائیونگ سیٹ سنبھالتے ہوئے اب وہ اسے تنگ کر رہا تھا۔

ہانیہ نے لب بھینچ لیے۔

''مارکیٹ سے کچھ چاہیے تمہیں؟''

''نہیں' بس اب گھر چلو پلیز۔''

''مجھے ایک دو چیزوں کی ارجنٹ ضرورت تھی وہ لے لوں پھر چلتے ہیں گھر۔'' ٹرن لیتے ہوئے اس نے کہا تھا۔ ہانیہ نے اثبات میں سر ہلا دیا۔ اس کی نظریں کھڑکی کے اس پار بھیگے ہوئے موسم کے باعث بھیگی سڑکوں پر دوڑنے لگی۔

''تم میکال بھیا کے ساتھ خوش تو ہو نا ہانیہ۔''

''ہوں۔''

''اللہ کا لاکھ لاکھ شکر ہے میرا خیال تھا وہ ڈائری پڑھنے کے بعد تم بہت ڈسٹرب ہو جاؤ گی شاید مجھ سے نفرت بھی کرنے لگو۔ اسی لیے اتنا ناراض ہوا تھا میں تم پر۔''

''ہوں میرے بارے میں تمہاری سوچ بالکل پرفیکٹ ہے۔ میں یقیناً یہی کرتی اگر تم......!'' فوراً سے پیشتر اس نے اپنی زبان کو بریک لگایا تھا۔

نہال چونک کر اسے دیکھنے لگا۔

''اگر تم کیا......؟''

''اگر تم میرے بہت اچھے دوست نہ ہوتے تو۔'' بروقت اسے مناسب جملہ مل گیا تھا۔

نہال نے مسکرا کر سر جھٹک دیا تبھی ہانیہ نے اپنا ہاتھ اس کے ہاتھ پر رکھا تھا۔

''گاڑی روکو نہال پلیز۔''

''خیریت؟''

فوراً سے پیشتر اس کے حکم پر عمل درآمد کرتے ہوئے اس نے گاڑی روکی تھی۔ ہانیہ کی نظریں کھڑکی کے اس پار کے منظر پر جم گئیں۔ نہال نے اس کی نظروں کی تقلید کی اور پھر جیسے وہ بھی ششدر رہ گیا۔

کچھ ہی فاصلے پر میکال ایک نیم عریاں لڑکی کو بانہوں میں لیے سڑک کنارے ایک شٹر کے نیچے کھڑا تھا۔ سردی کی شدت سے لڑکی اس کے اندر سمٹی جا رہی تھی۔ شاید وہ لوگ پیدل واک پر نکلے تھے نہال کو لگا جیسے وہ سانس بھی نہیں لے سکے گا۔

''چلو نہال پلیز۔'' دو منٹ کے بعد ہی ہانیہ نے اپنی نظر اس منظر سے ہٹالی۔

''نہیں، تم دیکھو میں اس شخص کے ساتھ کرتا کیا ہوں۔'' غصے سے بے قابو ہوتے ہوئے اس نے اپنی سائیڈ کا دروازہ کھولا تھا جب ہانیہ نے اس کا بازو پکڑ لیا۔

''نہیں، ابھی سڑک پر تماشہ بنانے کی ضرورت نہیں ہے۔ گھر چل کر بات کریں گے۔''

''ہانیہ تم۔''

''پلیز نہال، پلیز۔''

اس سے پہلے کہ وہ کچھ کہتا ہانیہ کی آنکھوں کے آنسو اور لبوں کی التجا نے اسے بے بس کر ڈالا۔ غصے سے کانپتے ہاتھوں کے ساتھ اس نے گاڑی اسٹارٹ کی تھی۔

''کون ہے یہ لڑکی؟''

''پتا نہیں، کوئی ماڈل ہے شاید۔''

''تم جانتی ہو اسے؟''

''نہیں۔''

''تم مجھ سے کچھ چھپا رہی ہو ہانیہ؟''

''نہیں نہال میں چاہوں بھی تو تم سے کچھ نہیں چھپا سکتی۔'' رخ پھیرتے ہوئے اس نے آنسو پونچھے تھے۔ نہال گاڑی کو مین سڑک پر لے آیا۔ یہی وہ روڈ تھا جہاں میکال کی گاڑی خراب ہوئی تھی اور اسے اس کے ساتھ اس خطرناک اور بدبودار کمرے میں رات گزارنی پڑی تھی۔

بارش کی تیزی اور شدت نے مزید زور پکڑ لیا۔ جب ہی اچانک گاڑی کا انجن بند ہوا تھا۔

''مائی گاڈ! اسے بھی ابھی بند ہونا تھا۔'' جھنجلائے ہوئے نہال نے سارا غصہ اسٹرینگ وہیل پر نکالا۔ ہانیہ کا دل تیزی سے دھڑک اٹھا۔ بے ساختہ اسے میکال کے الفاظ یاد آئے تھے۔

''روڈ سنسان اور خطرناک ہے خدانہ کرے ابھی ہمیں یہاں کھڑے دیکھ کر کوئی اسلحہ لے کر آ گیا تو کیا کریں گے۔ سنا ہے آئے روز اس روڈ پر بہت وارداتیں ہوتی ہیں۔''

نہال گاڑی سے نکل کر انجن چیک کر رہا تھا۔ وہ پریشان سی مختلف قرآنی آیات کا ورد کرتی رہی۔ جانے کیوں اس کا دل اس لمحے بہت تیزی سے دھڑک رہا تھا۔

''سوری ہانیہ! انجن کام نہیں کر رہا ہے۔ میرے خیال میں ہمیں کسی دوسری سواری کی تلاش کرنی پڑے گی۔''

''اتنے خراب موسم میں دوسری سواری کہاں سے ملے گی؟''

''مل جائے گی میں دیکھتا ہوں تم ٹینشن نہ لو پلیز۔'' وہ پور پور بارش میں بھیگ چکا تھا۔ وہ پریشان سی اسے دیکھتی رہ گئی۔ تقریباً دس منٹ بعد ایک کار ان کے قریب رکی تھی۔

''ہیلو کوئی مسئلہ ہے کیا؟'' دو خوبرو اور اچھے گھر کے نظر آنے والے لڑکے کھڑکی سے سر نکال کر ان سے پوچھ رہے تھے نہال نے ہانیہ سے نظر ہٹا کر ان کی جانب توجہ مبذول کی۔

''ہوں گاڑی کا انجن خراب ہو گیا ہے۔''

''اوہ' یہ بہت سنسان اور خطرناک روڈ ہے۔ آپ چاہیں تو اپنی گاڑی لاک کر کے یہیں چھوڑ دیں ہم آپ کو ڈراپ کر دیتے ہیں۔''

بارش طوفانی صورت اختیار کرتی جا رہی تھی۔ نہال کو مجبوراً ہانیہ کی وجہ سے ان کی آفر قبول کرنی پڑی اور یہ اس کی سب سے بڑی غلطی تھی۔ بظاہر اچھے گھرانے کے نظر آنے والے وہ لڑکے پیشہ ور ڈاکو تھے جنہوں نے کچھ ہی دور لے جا کر گاڑی روک دی تھی۔ جہاں ان کے مزید ساتھی پہلے سے موجود تھے۔ نہال کے وہم و گمان میں نہیں تھا کہ تقدیر اس کے ساتھ ایسا عجیب وغریب کھیل بھی کھیل سکتی ہے۔

ان لوگوں نے بظاہر معزز شہری بن کر انہیں مدد کے بہانے لوٹ لیا تھا۔ نہال کی پیشانی سے پسٹل ٹکا کر انہوں نے اس کا پرس' گاڑی کی چابی' موبائل' گھڑی سب ہتھیا لیا تھا اور اب ان کی نظر ہانیہ پر تھی۔ تبھی نہال کا ان لوگوں سے جھگڑا ہوا تھا اور یہ جھگڑا اس قدر شدت اختیار کر گیا کہ انہوں نے نہال پر فائر کھول دیا۔ ہانیہ چیخ چیخ کر مدد کے لیے پکارتی رہی۔

اسی دوران وہ لوگ نہال کو سڑک پر پھینک کر فرار ہو گئے۔ نہال کو پیٹ میں گولی لگی تھی اس کا خون بہت تیزی سے بہہ رہا تھا۔ ہانیہ کے ہواس گم ہو رہے تھے۔ اس کی پکار پر کافی دیر بعد کچھ لوگ نہال کو اٹھا کر اسپتال لے جا رہے تھے وہ گم صم سی ساتھ بیٹھ گئی۔

صبح کے تقریباً ساڑھے چار دس بجے نہال کو ہوش آیا تھا۔ رات دو بجے اسے آپریشن کے لیے لے جایا گیا۔ جو لوگ اس کے ساتھ تھے وہی سب خرچہ اور دیکھ بھال کر رہے تھے۔ ہانیہ تو جیسے بت بنی بیٹھی تھی ایک بار بھی اس کے ذہن میں نہیں آیا تھا کہ اسے گھر میں کسی کو فون کر کے اطلاع دینی چاہیے۔ پتھر کی مورت بنی وہ بس روئے چلی جا رہی تھی۔ نہال تکلیف کی پروا کیے بغیر اسے تسلی دیتا رہا۔ اگلے روز شام میں ان کی گھر واپسی ہوئی تھی۔ سب لوگ از حد متفکر لاؤنج میں بیٹھے تھے جیسے ہی ان کی نظر ہانیہ اور نہال پر پڑی گویا ان سب میں ایک برقی رو دوڑ گئی۔

''ہانیہ' نہال...... کہاں تھے تم؟''

مسز حسن سب سے پہلے ان کی طرف لپکی تھیں۔ ہانیہ کی آنکھیں آنسوؤں سے بھر گئیں۔ نہال کی طرف دیکھتے ہوئے اس نے انہیں اپنے ساتھ پیش آنے والا سانحہ من وعن سنا دیا۔ سب اس کی روداد سن کر ساکت بیٹھے تھے۔ جب میکال بول اٹھا۔

''ہو گئی تمہاری فرضی کہانی مکمل؟'' اس کی آنکھوں سے جیسے آگ نکل رہی تھی۔ ہانیہ چونک کر اسے دیکھنے لگی۔

''فرضی کہانی نہیں سنا رہی ہوں میں جو حقیقت ہے وہی بتا رہی ہوں۔''

''جسٹ شٹ اپ۔'' حلق کے بل چلا کر دھاڑتے ہوئے اس نے اپنی ساری قوت صرف کر دی تھی۔

''سب کو دھوکا دے سکتے ہو تم لوگ مگر مجھے نہیں' سمجھی تم۔''

''میکال! ہوش کے ناخن لو' کیا ہو گیا ہے تمہیں؟'' حسن صاحب نے اسے ڈپٹنا چاہا تھا مگر وہ اس وقت اپنے آپے میں نہیں تھا۔

''پاگل ہو گیا ہوں میں کیونکہ جس لڑکی کو اپنی عزت بنا کر اپنا نام دے کر میں اس گھر میں لایا تھا وہ ایک بے حیا' بد کردار لڑکی ہے دھول جھونک رہی ہے آپ سب کی آنکھوں میں پارسا بن کر۔ بہت ضبط اور برداشت سے کام لے لیا میں نے اب اور نہیں۔''

''یہ کیا کہہ رہے ہو تم؟''

''سچ کہہ رہا ہوں میں' یہ داشتہ ایک وقت میں دو بھائیوں کے جذبات سے کھیل رہی ہے۔ میں نے خود کئی بار ان دونوں کو نازیبا حالت میں دیکھا ہے۔ میری غیر موجودگی میں سارا سارا دن یہ نہال کے کمرے میں گھسی رہتی ہے۔ اب بھی یہ لوگ عیاشی کر کے آ رہے ہیں۔ ہم سب کی آنکھوں میں دھول جھونک کر بے وقوف بنا رہے ہیں ہمیں مگر میں بے وقوف نہیں ہوں نا ہی آپ لوگوں کی طرح میری آنکھوں پر پٹی بندھی ہے کہ گھر میں جو مرضی ہوتا رہے اور مجھے پتا ہی نہ چلے۔''

''بکواس بند کرو میکال! ہانیہ اور نہال ایسے نہیں ہیں۔''

''ایسے ہی ہیں اس سے بھی زیادہ گرے ہوئے اور مکروہ ہیں میں لعنت بھیجتا ہوں ایسی لڑکی پر اور ایسی رفاقت پر آج کے بعد یہ بدکردار میری طرف سے فارغ ہے۔ آپ لوگوں کو اگر یقین نہیں آتا تو یہ لیں سن لیں ان دونوں کے راز و نیاز اور کرتوت۔''

غصے کی شدت نے اس کے سوچنے سمجھنے کی ساری صلاحیت مفلوج کر دی تھی۔ تبھی شائستگی اور تہذیب کا دامن اس کے ہاتھ سے چھوٹ گیا تھا۔ ہانیہ کو لگا جیسے اس کی سانس سینے میں ہی اٹک گئی ہو۔ میکال کے الفاظ پتھروں سے کم نہیں تھے۔ نہال کا دل چاہا کاش زمین پھٹے اور وہ اس میں سما جائے۔

حسن صاحب اور باقی لوگ اب میکال کی موبائل کے ریکارڈنگ سن رہے تھے۔ وہ ریکارڈنگ جو مائرہ نے اسے مہیا کی تھی۔

''تم نے مجھ سے کیوں چھپایا نہال کہ تم مجھ سے پیار کرتے تھے۔''

''بتانے کا فائدہ بھی کیا تھا جب تک مجھ پر یہ حقیقت آشکار ہوئی تم میکال بھیا کی زندگی کا حصہ بن چکی تھیں۔

''تم جانتے ہو' میں اس شادی کے لیے ذہنی اور دلی طور پر تیار نہیں تھی۔ تم چاہتے تو یہ شادی رکوا سکتے تھے۔''

''نہیں رکوا سکتا تھا کیونکہ پاپا اور مما ذہنی طور پر تمہیں میکال بھیا کے لیے پسند کر چکے تھے۔''

''چلو ٹھیک ہے جو ہو گیا سو ہو گیا مگر اب تمہیں شادی کر لینی چاہیے۔''

''ہوں' کر لوں گا مگر ابھی میری کچھ مجبوریاں ہیں ابھی نہیں کر سکتا۔''

''کیسی مجبوریاں؟''

''ہیں کچھ' تمہیں نہیں بتا سکتا۔ بس تم میرے لیے دعا کیا کرو۔''

''کرتی ہوں' مگر تم اب بہت کچھ چھپانے لگے ہو' دس از ناٹ فیئر۔''

''تم سے کچھ نہیں چھپا سکتا ہانیہ۔ چلو اب اٹھو' میکال بھائی انتظار کر رہے ہوں گے۔''

''بیٹھ جاؤ' نہال میرا دل ابھی اندر جانے کو نہیں چاہ رہا۔''

''کیوں' کیا نہال بھائی سے جھگڑا ہو گیا ہے۔''

''نہیں اس سے جھگڑا کیوں ہوگا۔ بس میرا دل تمہاری وجہ سے بوجھل ہے۔''

وہ گفتگو جو ان کے درمیان اس روز شام ہوئی تھی مائرہ نے ریکارڈ کرلی تھی۔ لاؤنج میں بیٹھے سب افراد کو جیسے سانپ سونگھ گیا۔ نہال نے ایک نظر مائرہ کی طرف دیکھا اور پلکیں موندلیں۔ بدن پر لگے زخموں سے زیادہ اندر کے زخم تکلیف دینے لگے۔ وہ خود کو ہانیہ کا مجرم سمجھنے لگا۔ اتنی سی سکت بھی نہیں رہی تھی اس میں کہ وہ میکال کے لگائے ہوئے گھٹیا ترین الزام پر اس کا گریبان ہی پکڑ سکتا۔ دوسری طرف ہانیہ کا دل چاہ رہا تھا کہ وہ سب کے سامنے ساری حقیقت کھول کر رکھ دے میکال کی بھی اور نہال کی بھی......مگر......اس نے ایسا نہیں کیا تھا بنا کوئی صفائی پیش کیے وہ اپنے کمرے میں آ گئی تھی۔ اگلے روز بخار سے تپتے وجود کے ساتھ وہ مسز حسن کو بتا کر ان کے روکنے کے باوجود اپنے میکے چلی آئی تھی۔ تقریباً ایک ماہ تک اس کی طبیعت ہی نہ سنبھل سکی۔ بچے کی گروتھ بھی متاثر ہو رہی تھی۔

جاذب اور ہادیہ اس کے لیے بہت پریشان تھے مگر اس نے ان کی پریشانی کی پروا کیے بغیر میکال کو خلع کے لیے نوٹس بھجوا دیا تھا۔ صفدر صاحب کو معاملے کی خبر ہوئی تو وہ دل کے دورے کا شکار ہو گئے۔ ساتھ ہی فالج کا ایسا زبردست اٹیک ہوا کہ بستر سے بندھ کر رہ گئے تھے۔ نہال کا کچھ پتا نہیں تھا کہ وہ کہاں چلا گیا تھا۔ حسن صاحب اور ان کی بیگم روز آتے تھے اور اسے سمجھانے کی کوشش کرتے تھے۔

تقریباً دو ماہ کے بعد اس نے پیارے سے صحت مند بیٹے کو جنم دیا تھا اور یہیں اس کی دوستی فارحہ سے ہوئی تھی شادی کے بعد ہادیہ کی گھریلو مصروفیات نے اسے فارحہ کے قریب ہونے کا موقع دیا تھا۔ فارحہ اس کے سسرال کے قریب رہتی تھی اور اپنی ساس کے علاج کے سلسلے میں اسی اسپتال میں آتی تھی جہاں بچے کی ڈیلیوری کے سلسلے میں وہ ایڈمٹ ہوئی تھی۔ رفتہ رفتہ دونوں کی دوستی گہری ہوتی گئی تھی۔ جس روز اس نے بچے کو جنم دیا تھا اسی روز اسے میکال کی طرف سے طلاق نامہ موصول ہو گیا تھا۔ مگر ہادیہ نے اسے چھپالیا۔ جس روز اس کے بیٹے کی پہلی سالگرہ تھی اسی روز اس نے فارحہ کو ہادیہ سے کہتے ہوئے سنا تھا۔

''تمہیں پتا ہے ہادیہ میکال نے دوسری شادی کرلی ہے۔''

''وہاٹ؟''

جہاں اس کے اعتبار کو شدید دھچکا لگا تھا وہیں ہادیہ بھی چونک اٹھی تھی۔

''ہاں، کل گھوم رہا تھا اپنی بیوی کے ساتھ مارکیٹ میں، حسن انکل اور ان کی مسز نے اسے گھر سے نکال دیا ہے۔ جہاں تک میرا خیال ہے اس کی بیوی شوبز سے وابستہ ہے۔ شاید اسی لیے اس نے آسانی سے ہانیہ کو طلاق دے دی۔ بہر حال تم ہانیہ کو مت بتانا وہ ابھی کوئی صدمہ افورڈ کرنے کی پوزیشن میں نہیں ہے۔''

''ہوں۔''

ہادیہ نے آہستہ سے اثبات میں سر ہلایا تھا۔ ہانیہ کو لگا جیسے اس کا وجود پتھر کا ہو گیا ہو۔ اس کی ذات کی شاندار عمارت لمحوں میں زمین بوس ہو گئی ہو۔ کیسی حقیقت تھی یہ، جس نے اسے اندھیروں میں دھکیل دیا تھا۔ یوں کہ اس میں ہلنے کی بھی سکت نہیں رہی تھی۔ وہ پلٹی تھی اور دھڑام سے زمین پر آ پڑی تھی۔ فارحہ اور ہادیہ اس کے گرنے کی آواز پر تیزی سے اس کی طرف لپکی تھیں مگر تب تک وہ نروس بریک ڈاؤن کا شکار ہو چکی تھی۔

تقریباً پندرہ دن کے بعد اس کی حالت نارمل ہوئی تھی اور وہ اتنا روئی تھی کہ خود آنسوؤں کو اس پر ترس آنے لگا تھا۔ بہت مشکل سے سنبھالا تھا اس نے خود کو ادھر میکال کی بے چینی تھی کہ ختم ہونے میں ہی نہیں آ رہی تھی۔ علیزہ کے ساتھ رہ کر بھی ہانیہ اس سے دور نہیں ہوئی تھی۔ وہ اسے آواز دیتا تھا مگر ہر بار اس کے منہ سے ہانیہ نکلتا تھا۔ ہر حالت میں وہی

اس کے اعصاب پر سوار رہتی تھی۔ اس نے زندگی میں کبھی نشہ نہیں کیا تھا مگر اب وہ چین سموکر بن کر رہ گیا تھا۔ بات بات پر علیزے کے ساتھ اس کا جھگڑا ہو جاتا اور نوبت مار پیٹ تک پہنچ جاتی۔

عائشہ اذھان بھی اپنے شوہر کے ساتھ دیار غیر میں شفٹ ہو چکی تھی۔ ان دنوں وہ اسلام آباد میں تھا جب ایک چھوٹے سے روڈ ایکسیڈنٹ کا شکار ہو کر اسے اسپتال جانا پڑا اور یہیں اس نے نہال کو دیکھا تھا۔ بے حد لاغر اور کمزور وہ بری طرح کھانس رہا تھا۔ میکال کا دل چاہا وہ اس کی جان لے لے۔ تھوڑی ہی دیر میں وہ اسپتال سے نکل گیا تھا۔

تقریباً ایک ہفتے بعد چیک اپ کے لیے وہ دوبارہ اسی اسپتال میں آیا تھا اور تب وہیں اسے نہال حسن کی بیماری کے بارے میں پتا چلا تھا۔ اس کا آدھے سے زیادہ جگر کٹ کٹ کر حلق کے راستے باہر نکل چکا تھا۔ ڈاکٹرز کے مطابق اس کے پاس بہت کم زندگی کے دن رہ گئے تھے۔

وہاں اس اسپتال میں نہال کا دوست بہت اچھا اور قابل ڈاکٹر تھا اور نہال اپنی بیماری اور علاج سے متعلق اسی سے سب کچھ ڈسکس کرتا تھا۔ میکال کو لگا جیسے اس کی سماعتیں کام کرنا چھوڑ گئی ہوں۔ اس شخص سے اسے لاکھ عداوتیں سہی مگر وہ اس کا بھائی تھا۔ بے حد محبوب اور لاڈلا بھائی۔ اس روز وہ نہایت غائب دماغی اسپتال سے نکل کر آیا تھا۔

اگلے تین چار روز تک وہ خود کو سنبھال ہی نہ سکا۔ تین چار روز کے بعد اس نے نہال سے متعلق انکوائری کی تو پتا چلا کہ وہ تو پچھلے ایک سال سے بیماری کی لپیٹ میں تھا۔ شاید تبھی ہانیہ اس سے بہت کلوز تھی۔ اگر وہ اس کی بیماری کے بارے میں جانتی تھی تو یہ بات اس نے اس سے کیوں چھپائی؟ الجھن سی الجھن تھی۔

علیزے کی شوبز کی مصروفیات بہت بڑھ چکی تھیں۔ اب وہ اکثر پوری پوری رات گھر سے غائب رہتی ماڈلنگ کے ساتھ ساتھ بڑی اسکرین پر آفرز نے اسے ہواؤں میں اڑنے پر مجبور کر دیا تھا۔ ڈھیر ساری دولت اور شہرت کے لیے اس نے اپنا سب کچھ داؤ پر لگا دیا یہاں تک کہ اپنی نسوانیت بھی، بڑے بڑے ڈائریکٹرز اور پروڈیوسز کے ساتھ اس کے روابط اب محض اسٹوڈیو اور شوٹنگ تک محدود نہیں رہے تھے۔ گھر تک پہنچ گئے تھے۔

میکال کی غیر موجودگی میں نا چاہتے ہوئے بھی اسے انڈسٹری کے بڑے مگرمچھوں کی خوشی کا خیال رکھنا پڑتا تھا۔

میکال اس روز شدید ڈپریشن کا شکار گھر آیا تو وہ شوٹنگ کے لیے نکل رہی تھی۔ وہ چڑ گیا۔

''کہاں جا رہی ہو؟''

''اسٹوڈیو ایک نیا پروجیکٹ شروع کیا ہے دعا کرنا اس میں بھی کامیابی میرے قدم چومے۔''

''جسٹ شٹ اپ کہیں نہیں جا رہی ہو تم اس وقت سمجھی۔''

''کیا مطلب؟'' میکال کے غصے وہ حیرانی سے پلٹی تھی۔

''کوئی مطلب نہیں سوائے اس کے کہ آج کے بعد تم کسی شوٹنگ پر نہیں جاؤں گی کوئی کمرشل کوئی فلم نہیں کرو گی۔''

''کیوں، کیوں نہیں کروں گی؟'' اس کے تو جیسے تن بدن میں آگ لگ گئی تھی۔ میکال نے سر جھٹک دیا۔

''مجھے پسند نہیں ہے اس لیے۔''

''مائی فٹ، تمہاری پسند ناپسند کے لیے میں اپنی زندگی داؤ پر نہیں لگا سکتی۔ بڑی مشکل سے یہ مقام حاصل کیا ہے میں نے اب کہیں جا کر خوشی ملنے لگی ہے تو تم چاہتے ہو میں اسے ٹھوکر مار دوں؟ کبھی نہیں......!''

''مارنی پڑے گی تمہیں ٹھوکر، کیونکہ تمہارے لیے میں نے اپنا سب کچھ کھویا ہے۔''

''تو میں کیا کروں؟ میں نے تو نہیں کہا تھا تمہیں سب کچھ کھونے کے لیے ویسے بھی تم کنگلے ہو اب میں بھی تمہاری طرح گھر بیٹھ گئی تو کھائیں گے کہاں سے۔''

''فاقے کرلیں گے مگر میں مزید بے حیائی برداشت نہیں کروں گا۔''

''واہ، تمہاری دسترس میں آ گئی تو بے حیا ہو گئی آپ بھول رہے ہیں مسٹر میکال کہ آپ سے شادی سے پہلے بھی میں ایسی ہی بے حیا تھی۔ یہی میرا پروفیشن اور مصروفیات تھیں تو پھر کیوں اپنایا اس بے حیا کو' کیوں اپنی زندگی میں شامل کیا۔ رہتے اسی پاکباز' جنتی بیوی کے ساتھ۔ جو تمہارے نکاح میں ہوتے ہوئے بھی تمہارے بھائی کے ساتھ سرعام گھر ے اڑاتی پھرتی تھی۔''

''چٹاخ۔'' اس سے پہلے کہ وہ مزید کچھ کہتی میکال کے زوردار تھپڑ نے اسے چکرا کر رکھ دیا۔

''جان لے لوں گا میں تمہاری اگر تم نے ایک بھی لفظ ہانیہ کے خلاف کہا تو۔''

''بڑی محبت جاگ رہی ہے آج اس کی مگر کان کھول کر سن لو میکال! تم زور و جبر سے مجھے اس گھر کی چار دیواری میں قید نہیں رکھ سکتے، سمجھے۔'' چنگھاڑ کر کہتے وہ وہاں رکی نہیں تھی فوراً نکل گئی تھی۔ پیچھے میکال بیڈ پر گر کر پلکیں موند گیا۔ جانے کیوں آج اس کا دل بہت زیادہ رونے کو چاہ رہا تھا۔ شدید تھکن کے باوجود اس نے گاڑی کی چابی اٹھائی اور آوارہ گردی کے لیے نکل گیا تھا۔ رات گئے گھر واپسی ہوئی تو طبیعت خاصی بحال ہو چکی تھی۔

اگلے روز بنا ناشتا کیے وہ جاب کے لیے نکل گیا۔ شام ڈھلے گھر واپسی ہوئی تو علیزے گھر پر تھی اور فون پر کسی کے ساتھ بات کر رہی تھی۔ وہ اس کے لبوں سے اپنا نام سن کر دہلیز پر رک گیا۔

''میں اب اس شخص کے ساتھ مزید نہیں رہ سکتی ریان...... دردِ سر بن گیا ہے اسی لیے میں نے سوچ لیا ہے اب مزید اس شخص کے ساتھ ایک پل بھی نہیں رہنا میں نے۔''

''نہیں، نہیں ابھی جان سے مارنے کی ضرورت نہیں ہے۔ میں طلاق کا مطالبہ کر رہی ہوں نہ مانا تو پھر دیکھ لیں گے۔ میں نے سوچا تھا امیر آسامی ہے فائدہ اٹھاؤں گی۔ مجھے کیا پتا تھا فقیر ہو کر میرے گلے پڑ جائے گا۔ خیر اتنا تو تم بھی جانتے ہو اپنے خوابوں کی تعبیر پانے کے لیے میں کچھ بھی کر سکتی ہوں۔'' میکال کی آمد سے بے خبر وہ اپنی ہی دھن میں لگی ہوئی تھی۔

وہ خاموشی سے واپس پلٹ گیا۔ واقعی اس کی قسمت میں کسی عورت کی محبت اور وفا نہیں تھی۔ تھکن سے بے حال بنا کپڑے تبدیل کیے وہ بیڈ پر ڈھے گیا تھا۔ سر کی شریانیں درد سے پھٹنے کو تیار تھیں۔ کچھ پل کسلمندی سے پڑے رہنے کے بعد وہ اٹھ کر بیٹھ گیا تبھی اس کی نظر سامنے ٹیبل پر پڑی تھی۔ وہاں کچھ خطوط آئے پڑے تھے۔ اس نے جاب کے سلسلے میں کئی کمپنیز میں اپلائی کر رکھا تھا۔ شاید وہیں سے کوئی جواب آیا تھا۔ تبھی سست روی سے اٹھ کر وہ رائٹنگ ٹیبل کے قریب آیا تھا۔ وہاں مختلف کمپنیز کے خطوط کے ساتھ ایک سادہ خط بھی تھا۔ میکال نے وہ خط اٹھالیا۔ بھیجنے والے نے پشت پر اپنا نام پتا تحریر نہیں کیا تھا۔ تبھی اس نے فوراً سے پیشتر اسے چاک کیا تھا اور کرسی گھسیٹ کر اس پر بیٹھ گیا۔ سامنے شفاف صفحے پر ٹوٹی پھوٹی ہینڈ رائٹنگ میں لکھا تھا۔

''میں نہیں جانتی کہ میرا یہ خط پڑھنے کے بعد آپ مجھے معاف کریں گے یا نہیں مگر میں اتنا ضرور کہنا چاہوں گی میں نے بڑی مشکل سے آپ تک رسائی حاصل کی ہے۔ کاش آپ جان سکتے ہیں کہ میں کتنی تکلیف میں ہوں۔ ضمیر کے بوجھ نے مجھے نڈھال کر رکھا ہے۔ مجھ جیسے لوگ کبھی بھی معافی کے قابل نہیں ہوتے۔ چاہے ساری عمر ایڑیاں رگڑ کر روتے رہیں۔ ہنستی بستی زندگیوں کو چلتی پھرتی لاشوں میں بدل دینے والے اسی قابل ہوتے ہیں کہ خود بھی ساری عمر تماشا ہی بنے رہیں۔ میں آپ کی گناہ گار ہوں۔ میں نے آپ کی زندگی کے ساتھ کھلواڑ کیا ہے۔ صرف اس لیے کیونکہ آپ کے گھر والوں نے ہانیہ کے مقابل مجھے نظر انداز کیا تھا اور اب نہال نے ہانیہ کی وجہ سے مجھے ٹھکرا دیا۔ بہت تکلیف دہ ہوتا

ہے ٹھکرائے جانے کا یہ احساس' کاش میں آپ کو اپنے دل پر پڑے آبلے دکھا سکتی۔ میرا ٹارگٹ آپ نہیں تھے۔ ہانیہ تھی' مجھے اس سے نفرت ہوگئی تھی۔ اسی نفرت نے مجھے اس کی زندگی برباد کرنے پر مجبور کیا۔ وہ آپ سے پیار کرتی تھی۔ اعتبار کرتی تھی یہ مجھے پہلے سے پتا تھا۔ مگر نہال کی طرف اس کا جھکاؤ شدید کیوں ہوا یہ ابھی تین روز پہلے پتا چلا ہے۔ نہال کی میڈیکل رپورٹس پڑھنے کے بعد آپ اندازہ نہیں کر سکتے کہ میرا کیا حال ہے۔ نہال جو زندگی کی آخری سیڑھی پر کھڑا موت کو گلے لگا رہا ہے۔ میں نے ہانیہ کی نفرت میں اسے بھی اپنے گھٹیا مقصد کے لیے کیچڑ میں گرا دیا۔ وہ جو زندگی اور موت کی جنگ لڑ رہا ہے اسے میں نے صرف اپنے دل کی تسکین کے لیے سب کی نظروں سے گرا دیا۔ اس نے تو میرا کچھ بھی نہیں بگاڑا تھا۔ کبھی غلط نگاہ سے دیکھا بھی نہیں۔ ہمیشہ پیار اور اپنائیت دی مگر میں نے بدلے میں اسی موت کے مسافر کو سولی پر ٹانک دیا۔ آپ بتائیے کیا میں معافی کے قابل ہوں۔ نہیں ہرگز نہیں۔ یہ گھر جو ہم سب کا مسکن تھا آ کر دیکھئے کیسے کھنڈر بن کر رہ گیا ہے۔ سارہ ہر وقت روتی رہتی ہے۔ آنٹی دل کی مریضہ ہوگئی ہیں۔ میں نے آپ کے اور نہال کے یہاں سے جانے کے بعد کبھی انہیں مسکراتے ہوئے نہیں دیکھا۔ انکل کو دیکھیں گے تو وہ بھی صدیوں کے بیمار اور بوڑھے نظر آئیں گے۔ صرف میری وجہ سے کتنی زندگیاں برباد ہوگئیں' کاش مجھے پہلے ہی اس کا احساس ہو جاتا۔ یہ بے سکونی' یہ اضطراب مجھے مار ڈالے گا' خدا کے واسطے مجھے معاف کر دیں پلیز۔''

خط کیا تھا کوئی بم تھا جو میکال کے سر پر پھٹا تھا۔ کپکپاتے ہاتھوں میں لرزتے کاغذ کی وہ چند سطریں جیسے اس کی ہستی کو ہلا گئی تھیں۔ اتنا بڑا دھوکہ وہ بھی اس کے ساتھ' پل میں اس کا جسم پسینے سے بھیگ گیا۔

''نہیں...... ایسا نہیں ہو سکتا...... تم ایسا نہیں کر سکتیں مائرہ...... تم میرے ساتھ ایسا نہیں کر سکتیں۔'' شدید بے یقینی کا شکار ضبط کھوتے ہوئے وہ جیسے چلا اٹھا تھا۔

علیزے لپک کر کمرے میں چلی آئی۔

''کیا ہوا؟'' اس کی پیشانی پر سلوٹیں پڑی تھیں۔ میکال نے اسے یوں دیکھا جیسے جانتا ہی نہ ہو۔

''کون ہو تم؟''

''میکال...... تم پاگل تو نہیں ہوگئے؟'' اس کے سوال پر قدرے خوف زدہ ہوتے ہوئے وہ پیچھے ہٹی تھی تبھی وہ ایک جھٹکے سے اسے سائیڈ پر ہٹاتے ہوئے خود گھر سے باہر نکل گیا۔

❁......❁......❁

ہانیہ کا بیٹا اب پاؤں پاؤں چلنے لگا تھا۔

اس روز وہ اسے لے کر مارکیٹ آئی تھی کیونکہ وہ پچھلے کئی دنوں سے کھلونوں کے لیے ضد کر رہا تھا۔ وہ ابھی شاپنگ مال میں تھی جب اچانک اس کی نظر کچھ ہی فاصلے پر کھڑے نہال حسن پر پڑی اور وہیں ٹھہر گئی۔

موسم آج بھی ابر آلود تھا۔ کسی بھی لمحے موسلا دھار بارش شروع ہو سکتی تھی۔ ہانیہ نے بیٹے کی انگلی پکڑی اور جلدی سے ایک شاپ میں گھس گئی۔ وہ ابھی کھلونے پسند کر رہی تھی جب نہال بھی وہیں چلا آیا۔

''ہانیہ......!''

بہت اپنائیت اور محبت کے ساتھ اس نے اسے پکارا تھا۔ ہانیہ کو نا چاہتے ہوئے بھی اس کی طرف متوجہ ہونا پڑا۔

''نہال تم؟''

''ہوں' بہت دنوں کے بعد آج مارکیٹ کا رخ کیا تھا گمان بھی نہیں تھا کہ تم مل جاؤ گی۔''

وہ بے حد کمزور دکھائی دے رہا تھا۔ اتنا کہ ہانیہ کو اس سے خوف محسوس ہونے لگا۔

''مما یہ تو ن ہیں؟'' اس کا بیٹا اب اس کا پلو پکڑے اس سے پوچھ رہا تھا۔ نہال نے اسے اوپر اٹھالیا۔
''آپ کا چاچو ہوں میری جان پہچانا نہیں۔'' کہنے کے ساتھ دو تین بوسے بھی لے لیے تھے۔ ہانیہ کی نظریں بس اس کے چہرے پر ٹکی رہیں۔
''کہاں چلے گئے تھے تم؟''
''بتاتا ہوں، چلو میرے ساتھ۔'' اس کے بیٹے کو بانہوں میں اٹھائے وہ شاپ سے باہر نکل گیا تھا ہانیہ ڈبڈبائی آنکھوں سے چپ چاپ اس کے پیچھے چل پڑی۔
''موسم خراب ہے لگتا ہے کسی بھی پل موسلا دھار بارش شروع ہو جائے گی۔ ایسے موسم میں گھر سے کم نکلا کرو ہانیہ۔ یہ بارشیں کبھی کسی کا ساتھ نہیں دیتیں۔'' گاڑی کا دروازہ کھولتے ہوئے وہ اسے نصیحت کرنا نہیں بھولا تھا۔
ہانیہ کے لب اب بھی چپ کے قفل سے جکڑے رہے۔ تقریباً پندرہ منٹ کی ڈرائیو کے بعد وہ اسے اپنے فلیٹ میں لے آیا تھا ہانیہ نے ایک نظر فلیٹ کی حالت زار کو دیکھا اور پھر سختی سے آنکھیں میچ لیں۔
''بیٹھوں یہاں، میں تمہارے لیے اور چھٹکو کے لیے کولڈ ڈرنک لاتا ہوں۔''
''نہیں اس کی ضرورت نہیں ہے۔''
''تمہیں نہیں ہوگی چھٹکو کو ہے۔''
وہ اب بھی مسکرا رہا تھا مگر اس کی آنکھوں میں جیسے سنسان صحرا بسے تھے۔ تین گلاسوں میں کولڈ ڈرنک ڈال کر وہ اس کے مقابل آ بیٹھا تو ہانیہ پوچھے بغیر نہ رہ سکی۔
''انکل اور آنٹی کیسے ہیں سنا ہے سارہ اور مائرہ کی شادی ہو رہی ہے۔''
''ہوں سارہ کی شادی ہو رہی ہے مائرہ کے بھائی سے مگر مائرہ کی شادی فی الحال کچھ وقت کے لیے ملتوی کر دی گئی ہے۔''
''کیوں؟'' اسے حیرانی ہوئی نہال نے رخ پھیر لیا۔
''اس کی طبیعت ٹھیک نہیں ہے۔ ڈپریشن کے دورے پڑتے ہیں شادی کا نام لو تو چیخنے لگتی ہے۔''
''یہ تو مکافات عمل ہے جو جیسا عمل کرتا ہے اس کا ویسا ہی صلہ پاتا ہے۔ مجھے اندازہ تھا کہ وہ مجھے پسند نہیں کرتی مگر مجھے یہ اندازہ نہیں تھا کہ وہ مجھ سے اتنی نفرت کرتی ہے کہ اس نے میرے اور میکال کے راستے ہی جدا کروا دیے۔''
''ہوں، مجھے اطلاع ملی تھی تمہاری اور میکال کی ڈائیورس کی بہت ہرٹ ہوا تھا میں۔ اسی لیے تمہارا سامنا بھی نہ کر سکا۔ مجھے اب بھی یہی احساس بے چین رکھتا ہے ہانیہ کہ میں تمہاری خوشیوں کا قاتل ہوں۔ نہ میں تمہیں چاہتا نہ تمہیں اس راز کا پتا لگتا نہ اس روز ہم اس ٹاپک پر بات کرتے نہ وہ ریکارڈ کر کے میکال بھیا اور دیگر لوگوں کو سناتی۔''
''نہیں تمہارا قصور نہیں تھا یہ...... سب میرا قصور تھا جو میں کسی کو سمجھ ہی نہ سکی۔ وگرنہ جس طرح سے مائرہ نے میری زندگی برباد کی میں اسے کبھی یہ موقع نہ دیتی غلط اعتبار کیا میں نے وہ بھی غلط لوگوں پر۔'' اس کا آنسو ٹوٹ کر اس کے پاؤں پر گرا تھا۔ نہال کی آنکھیں بھی بھر آگئیں۔
''یہاں کیوں رہتے ہو، تمہیں زیادہ کیئر کی ضرورت ہے نہال!'' فوراً سے پیشتر آنسو پونچھتے ہوئے اس نے کہا تھا۔
نہال چونک اٹھا۔
''کیوں؟''
''طبیعت جو ٹھیک نہیں رہتی آئے روز بیمار ہوئے رہتے ہو۔'' وہ اس کا ایک راز افشا کر چکی تھی اب دوسرا نہیں کرنا

چاہتی تھی نہال نے اطمینان کی سانس لی۔

''ہوں، گھر پر اب کیا رکھا ہے ہانیہ! جو تھوڑا بہت فرصت کا ٹائم ملتا ہے وہ یہیں......!'' ابھی وہ بات مکمل بھی نہ کر پایا تھا کہ اچانک کھانسی کا دورہ پڑ گیا۔ بہت کوشش کی اس نے ہانیہ کے سامنے خود کو سنبھالنے کی مگر نہ سنبھال سکا۔ کھانسی کا حملہ جو شروع ہوا تو پھر رکنے کا نام ہی نہ لیا یہاں تک کہ جگر کٹ کٹ کر منہ کے بل باہر آنا شروع ہو گیا۔ ہانیہ جو پتھرائی نگاہوں سے اسے دیکھ رہی تھی ایک دم سے چیخ اٹھی۔

''نہال......''

ہانیہ کو لگا جیسے اس کے لیے زمین آسمان ایک ہو گیا ہو۔ آنسوؤں سے بھری آنکھوں کے ساتھ وہ چیخ رہی تھی اور نہال کو سنبھالنے کی کوشش کر رہی تھی۔ اس کا بچہ بھی اس کی طرف دیکھ کر رونا شروع ہو چکا تھا۔ ہانیہ ایک طرف اسے چپ کروا رہی تھی دوسری طرف نہال کو سنبھال رہی تھی۔ اگلے پینتالیس منٹ میں اس کی کال پر جاذب وہاں موجود تھا۔ وہ رات ہانیہ صفدر کے لیے جیسے قیامت کی رات تھی۔ جاذب نے کرنل حسن صاحب کو بھی کال کر کے بلا لیا تھا۔ انہیں جیسے ہی بیٹے کی بیماری کے بارے میں پتا چلا گویا زمین ان کے پیروں تلے سے کھسک گئی۔ جھکے ہوئے کندھے جیسے ایک دم سے ٹوٹ گئے تھے۔

نہال جب تک بے ہوش رہا ان کے آنسو وقفے وقفے سے موتیوں کی طرح گرتے رہے۔ انہی کے اصرار پر جاذب انہیں نہال کے ڈاکٹر کے پاس لایا تھا اور ڈاکٹر انہیں بتا رہا تھا کہ۔

''مجھے بہت افسوس کے ساتھ یہ کہنا پڑ رہا ہے مسٹر حسن کہ آپ کے بیٹے کے پاس زیادہ دن نہیں ہیں۔ اس لیے آپ ہر ممکن طور پر اسے پریشانیوں سے دور رکھیں اگر وہ ہنسی خوشی جیے گا تو ہو سکتا ہے چھ ماہ یا ایک سال تک زندہ رہ سکے ورنہ موت کا عقاب تو کسی بھی وقت اسے اپنے پنجوں میں جکڑ سکتا ہے۔''

لفظ نہیں تھے برچھیاں تھیں جو حسن صاحب کو اپنے سینے میں اترتی ہوئی محسوس ہوئی تھیں۔ وہ جہاں کے تہاں بیٹھے رہ گئے تھے۔

''ڈاکٹر صاحب کیا آپ بتا سکتے ہیں نہال کے ساتھ کیا مسئلہ ہے؟'' جاذب نے ہمت کر کے پوچھا تھا۔ ڈاکٹر نے حیرانی سے ان کی طرف دیکھا۔

''کیا مسٹر نہال نے آپ کو نہیں بتایا کہ انہیں کیا بیماری ہے؟''

''نہیں۔'' دکھ کی شدت سے نڈھال وہ صرف سر ہلا سکا تھا۔

''او! مسٹر نہال جگر کے کینسر میں مبتلا ہیں۔ پچھلے دو سال سے ان کا علاج چل رہا ہے مگر بیماری اب آخری اسٹیج پر پہنچ چکی ہے لہٰذا ہم چاہتے ہوئے بھی ان کے لیے کچھ نہیں کر سکتے۔''

ٹوٹے ہوئے کندھوں پر پھر آسمان آ کے گرا تھا۔ حسن صاحب میں ہلنے کی بھی سکت نہ رہی۔ ادھر نہال ہوش میں آیا تو ہانیہ اس کے قریب بیٹھی چپ چاپ رو رہی تھی۔

''ہانیہ۔''

اس پر نظر پڑتے ہی اس نے اسے پکار لیا تھا۔ ہانیہ کا دل چاہا وہ بلک بلک کر روئے۔

''نہال......نہال مجھ پر ایک احسان کرو گے؟''

''ہانیہ۔''

''پلیز نہال مجھ سے وعدہ کرو تم میری خواہش پوری کرو گے۔'' وہ بچوں کی طرح مچل رہی تھی۔ نہال نے اپنی نظریں

اس کے چہرے پر ٹکا دیں۔

''کیسی خواہش؟''

''پہلے تم وعدہ کرو کہ پوری کرو گے، پلیز۔''

''ٹھیک ہے کروں گا پوری اب بتاؤ'' اس کی آنکھیں اب بھی دمک رہی تھیں۔ ہانیہ نے جلدی سے آنسو پونچھ لیے۔

''پکا؟''

''ہوں، پکا۔''

''اب مکرنا نہیں۔''

''نہیں مکروں گا بابا تم بتاؤ تو سہی۔''

''بتا دوں گی، مگر ابھی نہیں۔''

وہ ایک دم سے ہلکی پھلکی دکھائی دے رہی تھی۔ نہال اسے دیکھ کر رہ گیا۔

''کب سدھرو گی تم ہانیہ؟''

''اب تو سدھرنا ہی ہے نہال! نہ بھی سدھری تو دنیا والے سدھار دیں گے۔'' بھرائے لہجے میں کہتے ہوئے اس کی آنکھیں پانیوں سے بھر گئیں نہال نے اذیت سے آنکھیں بند کر لیں۔

اگلے روز حسن صاحب اسے گھر لے آئے تھے۔ آسیہ بیگم نے جب اس کا حال دیکھا تو کلیجہ تھام کر رہ گئیں۔ مائرہ کے آنسو تو کسی پل رکتے ہی نہیں تھے۔ سارہ بھی اپنے محبوب بھائی کے حال پر بات بے بات رو پڑتی تھی۔

اس روز وہ سو رہا تھا جب مائرہ اس کے کمرے میں چلی آئی۔ مسز حسن گھر پر نہیں تھیں اور سارہ فون پر اپنی کسی دوست کے ساتھ باتوں میں مصروف تھی۔ تبھی قطعی ابتر حال کے ساتھ ہلکے سے دروازہ پش کرتے ہوئے وہ اس کے کمرے میں چلی آئی تھی۔

نہال گہری نیند میں بے خبر سکون سے سو رہا تھا۔ وہ بیڈ پر اس کے قدموں کے قریب آ بیٹھی۔

گزرتا ہوا ہر دن اُس کی حالت کو ابتر کر رہا تھا، آج کل اُسے ڈپریشن کے دورے پڑنے لگے تھے۔ نماز پڑھنے کی کوشش کرتی مگر پڑھ نہ پاتی۔ قرآن کھولتی تو اگلے ہی پل سر درد سے پھٹنے لگتا۔ اپنے بال نوچ ڈالتی۔ سب سے بلاوجہ لڑتی پھرتی۔ اسے خبر ہی نہیں تھی کہ کسی پاکباز عورت پر جھوٹی تہمت اور بہتان لگانے کی سزا کیا ہوتی ہے؟ اللہ رب العزت کے نزدیک ایسے لوگوں کا قیام کیا ہوتا ہے؟ خبر ہوتی تو شاید مختصر سی زندگی کی مختصر سی خوشیوں کے لئے کبھی اپنے ساتھ اتنا بڑا ظلم نہ کرتی۔

ٹپ ٹپ ٹپ..... اس کے آنسو نہال کے پیروں پر گر رہے تھے، مگر گہری نیند میں ہونے کے سبب اسے گرتے ہوئے ان آنسوؤں کا احساس نہیں ہو سکا تھا۔ اگلے ہی پل وہ اُٹھی اور چپ چاپ اس کے کمرے سے باہر نکل آئی۔ جانے ضمیر نامی اس برزخ میں برے پچھتاوے کے ساتھ ابھی اور کتنے دن تک اسے یونہی جلتے رہنا تھا۔

❁ ...... ❁ ...... ❁

دروازے پر زوردار دستک جاری تھی۔

زائر تیزی سے سیڑھیاں پھلانگتا بیرونی دروازے تک آیا تھا۔

''کون۔'' دروازے کی کنڈی کو ہاتھ لگاتے ہوئے اس نے پوچھنا ضروری سمجھا تھا۔

''دروازہ کھولو۔'' باہر سے دھاڑتی ہوئی آواز بلاشبہ ثانیہ عباس کی ہی تھی۔ زائر نے فوراً سے پیشتر دروازہ کھول دیا۔

''تم......اور یہاں......وہ بھی اس وقت......!''

''زیادہ بکواس کرنے کی ضرورت نہیں ہے میرے بچوں کو بلاؤ میں انہیں لینے آئی ہوں۔''

اس کا چہرہ غصے کی شدت سے سرخ ہو رہا تھا۔ زائر نے ایک نظر مڑ کر پیچھے دیکھا۔ اس کی ماں ثانیہ کی چنگھاڑ پر کسی بھی وقت کمرے سے باہر آ کر سارا کھیل بگاڑ سکتی تھی۔ تبھی اس نے باہر نکل کر سرعت سے دروازہ بند کیا پھر ثانیہ کو بازو سے پکڑ کر گاڑی کے قریب لایا اور خود ڈرائیونگ سیٹ سنبھال کر بیٹھ گیا۔

ثانیہ اس کی حرکت پر ہکا بکا رہ گئی تھی۔

کچھ دور فصلوں کے قریب جا کر اس نے گاڑی روک دی۔

''یہاں کیوں لائے ہو؟''

''اس لیے تاکہ تم جی بھر کر چنگھاڑ سکو۔''

''جسٹ شٹ اپ۔''

''یو شٹ اپ اگر میں اپنی شرافت کی وجہ سے تمہاری بدتمیزی برداشت کر لیتا ہوں تو اس کا مطلب یہ نہیں کہ تم مجھ پر خدا بن جاؤ، بہت اچھی طرح سے جانتی ہو تم کہ میں عورتوں کا اس طرح سے چیخنا چلانا پسند نہیں کرتا ویسے بھی تم سے لے کر نہیں کھاتا میں جو تمہاری ہر طرح کی بات برداشت کروں۔ اگر حویلی کا کام کرتا ہوں تو صرف چوہدرانی کی وجہ سے ان کی محبت اور اپنائیت کی وجہ سے۔ وگرنہ تم جیسوں کو اپنی جوتی کی نوک پر رکھنا پسند نہیں کرتا میں۔''

''بکواس بند کرو، میں یہاں تمہاری ٹرٹر سننے نہیں آئی۔ اپنے بچوں کو لینے آئی ہوں۔''

''تمہارے بچے میرے پاس نہیں ہیں۔ اس لیے اب تم یہاں سے جا سکتی ہو اور ہاں دوبارہ اس طرح رات کے اندھیرے میں میرے گھر کے دروازے پر آنے کی ضرورت نہیں ہے کیونکہ میں رات کے اندھیرے میں اس طرح دہلیز پھلانگ کر آنے والی لڑکیوں کو پسند نہیں کرتا۔'' قدرے سنجیدہ لہجے میں کہنے کے بعد وہ گاڑی سے نکل گیا تھا۔ ثانیہ بلبلا کر رہ گئی۔

''بھاڑ میں جاؤ تم اور تمہاری پسند ناپسند۔'' اس کا بس نہ چلتا تھا وہ اسے کچا چبا ڈالتی۔ زائر نے اپنے پیچھے گاڑی کا دروازہ بند کر دیا۔

''میرے بچوں سے تمہارا کوئی واسطہ نہیں ہے اس لیے ان کے لیے اتنا پریشان ہونے کی ضرورت نہیں ہے تم گزارو اپنی زندگی جس طرح سے بھی گزار سکتی ہو۔ میں اپنے بچوں کی خود بہترین پرورش کر سکتا ہوں۔''

''جسٹ شٹ اپ۔ تم مجھ سے میرے بچے نہیں چھین سکتے۔ سنا تم نے۔'' وہ چیخی تھی۔ زائر پلٹتے پلٹتے کھڑکی پر جھک آیا۔

''میں کون ہوتا ہوں تم سے کچھ چھیننے والا چھیننے کا فن تمہیں صرف آتا ہے کبھی خود کو مجھ سے چھین لیتی ہو تو کبھی بچوں کو مگر اس بار میں تمہیں کچھ بھی چھیننے نہیں دوں گا۔ میرے بچے میرے ساتھ رہنا چاہتے ہیں۔ تم زبردستی انہیں مجھ سے دور نہیں رکھ سکتی۔ ہاں چاہو تو کسی بھی عدالت سے رجوع کر سکتی ہو۔ بہرحال اب گھر جاؤ، چوہدرانی تمہارے لیے پریشانی ہو رہی ہوں گی۔''

''مائی فٹ، تم ایک گھٹیا انسان ہو زائر ملک اور ہمیشہ یہ ثابت کیا ہے تم نے۔ اسی لیے میں تم سے نفرت کرتی ہوں۔ بے حد نفرت، اگر تم یہ سمجھتے ہو کہ میرے بچوں کو مجھ سے دور کر کے تم مجھے توڑ دو گے تو یہ تمہاری بھول ہے ضروری نہیں ہے کہ ہر بار تم ہی فاتح ٹھہرو، رکھو اپنے بچوں کو اپنے پاس۔ ثانیہ عباس اتنی عام لڑکی نہیں ہے، جتنی تم نے اسے سمجھ لیا ہے۔''

لہو رنگ آنکھوں میں تیرتی غصے کی سرخی غضب کی تھی۔ پھر اس سے پہلے کہ زائر کچھ کہتا وہ تیزی سے گاڑی بھگا لے گئی زائر گھر واپس پلٹا تو سائرہ سیڑھیوں پر بیٹھی اس کا انتظار کر رہی تھی۔

''مل آئے ثانیہ عباس سے؟'' اس کا لہجہ عجیب سا ہو رہا تھا۔ وہ دروازے کی کنڈی لگاتے ہوئے چونک اٹھا۔

''میں کسی سے ملنے نہیں گیا وہ خود یہاں آئی تھی اپنے بچوں کو لینے'' نہ چاہتے ہوئے اسے وضاحت دینی پڑی۔

سائرہ نے اس کا بازو تھام لیا۔

''جانے کیوں نہیں چھڑوا لیتے تم اس بلا سے۔ وہ تمہارے قابل نہیں ہے زائر۔''

''وہ میرے قابل ہے یا نہیں اس کی پروا کرنے کی ضرورت تمہیں نہیں ہے، سمجھی۔ جاؤ جا کر آرام کرو۔'' درشتی سے بازو چھڑواتے ہوئے اس نے دپٹا تھا' وہ تلملا کر رہ گئی۔

''کیوں ضرورت نہیں ہے مجھے کان کھول کر سن لو زائر۔ میں اب پھر سے تمہیں اس چڑیل کے لیے زندگی برباد کرنے نہیں دوں گی۔''

''دیکھا جائے گا۔'' بے پروائی سے کہتے ہوئے وہ تیزی سے سیڑھیاں چڑھ گیا تھا۔

ثانیہ حویلی واپس آئی تو اس کا چہرہ ضبط کی شدت سے سرخ ہو رہا تھا۔ چوہدرانی کے ساتھ ساتھ اشعر بھی اس کی راہ دیکھ رہا تھا۔

''کہاں چلی گئی تھیں؟''

''کہیں نہیں۔'' اسے نظر انداز کرتی وہ تیزی سے اپنے کمرے کی طرف بڑھ گئی تھی۔ چوہدرانی تسبیح کے دانے پھیرتی اسے دیکھتی رہ گئی تھیں۔ اگلے روز ناشتے کی ٹیبل پر انہوں نے ثانیہ سے پوچھا تھا۔

''بچے کہاں ہیں کچھ پتا چلا؟''

''جی وہ اپنے باپ کے پاس ہیں آپ پریشان نہ ہوں۔'' بے پروائی سے بریڈ پر جیم لگاتے ہوئے اس نے جواب دیا تھا۔ وہ ہکا بکا رہ گئیں۔

''ان کا باپ کب آیا یہاں؟''

''میری غیر موجودگی میں آیا تھا' آپ کو پتا نہیں چلا۔''

''میرے خدا......اب کیا ہوگا؟''

''کچھ نہیں ہوگا' میرے بچے ہیں وہ میرے ساتھ کی عادت پڑی ہوئی ہے انہیں زیادہ دن اس شخص کے ساتھ نہیں رہ سکیں گے۔'' اندر کی دنیا درہم برہم ہونے کے باوجود وہ بہت اطمینان سے جواب دے رہی تھی۔ اشعر خاموشی سے اسے دیکھے گیا۔ تھوڑی دیر بعد جب وہ شہر کے لیے نکل رہے تھے ثانیہ نے اچانک گاڑی رکوائی تھی۔

''اشعر۔''

''ہوں۔''

''کیا تم اسی ہفتے میں مجھ سے شادی کر سکتے ہو؟''

''وہاٹ' یہ کیا کہہ رہی ہو تم۔''

''اشعر پلیز' میں نے جو پوچھا ہے اس کا جواب دو۔'' وہ جذباتی ہو رہی تھی۔ اشعر بے ساختہ گہری سانس بھر کر رہ گیا۔

''ہاں' کیوں نہیں......تم کہو تو ابھی کر لیتے ہیں۔''

"تھینکس۔" اس کی طرف سے مثبت جواب پا کر بے ساختہ اس نے سکون کی سانس بھری تھی۔ اشعر نے ایک پیار بھری نظر اس پر ڈالنے کے بعد گاڑی آگے بڑھا دی۔

❀.....❀.....❀

شامِ غم مجھ کو ایسی اداسی نہ دے
کہ میرے حوصلے کی فصیلوں کے اندر کسی یاد کا کوئی پنچھی گرے
اور دل کی جو سنسان، ویران سی ایک بستی ہے اس میں
دفن ہونے والے ہر اک درد کی آنکھ پھر سے کھلے
شامِ غم مجھ کو ایسی اداسی نہ دے
کہ میرے صبر کی دھجیوں کا تماشہ سرِ بزم لوگوں میں بنتا پھرے
کہ میرے آنکھ کے کانچ سے آنسوؤں کا جو لاوا بہے
شہر کے لوگ اس پر کئی سچے جھوٹے فسانوں کی بنیاد رکھتے پھریں
شامِ غم مجھ کو ایسی اداسی نہ دے
کہ میرے ہونٹوں پر کھلنے والی جو پھیکی سی مسکان ہے
دیکھ کر اس کو محفل میں حاسد میرے
اپنی مرضی کا عنوان دیتے پھریں
لاکھ قصے بنیں، داستانیں، جنیں
شامِ غم مجھ کو ایسی اداسی نہ دے
کہ بھرے شہر میں دیکھ کر میرا چہرہ سبھی یہ کہیں
تم خزاں رُت کی دل کش سی تصویر ہو
کون رانجھا ہے وہ جس کی تم ہیر ہو
تم یقیناً کسی بہت منجھے ہوئے نامور سے مصنف کی تحریر ہو
شامِ غم مجھ کو ایسی اداسی نہ دے
کہ مجھے دیکھ کر سالوں صدیوں تلک
ان ہواؤں کے آنچل بھی نم ہی رہیں
بعد مدت کے جب بھی کسی عشق کی داستاں رقم ہو
درد کا اس میں پہلا حوالہ میری جان ہم ہی رہیں
شامِ غم مجھ کو ایسی اداسی نہ دے

نہال کی طبیعت اچانک بگڑ گئی تھی۔ آدھی رات کے وقت اپنے کمرے سے نکل کر وہ لاؤنج میں چلا آیا، حسن صاحب جاگ رہے تھے انہیں جیسے ہی کھٹکا محسوس ہوا فوراً لپک کر لاؤنج میں آئے، سامنے دیکھا تو نہال درد سے بے حال دہرا ہو رہا تھا، ان کے ہاتھ پیر پھول گئے، جلدی سے ملازم کو اٹھا کر گاڑی نکالنے کے لیے کہا اور خود نہال کو سہارا دے کر باہر لے آئے۔ تین جوان بیٹوں کا باپ ہونے کے باوجود اس وقت وہ کتنے بے بس تھے، میکال کا کچھ پتا نہیں تھا کہ وہ کہاں ہے اور کمال کو فوری سیٹ نہیں ملی تھی، مسز حسن جو بخار میں تپ رہی تھیں وہ بھی اٹھ کر باہر آ گئیں، نہال کو درد سے تڑپتے

دیکھ کران کے آنسو بہے چلے جا رہے تھے۔

آدھی رات کے وقت دونوں میاں بیوی نہال کو لے کر ہسپتال پہنچے تھے' سارا اور مائرہ کی آنکھ بھی کھل چکی تھی۔ سارا نے جلدی سے ہانیہ کو کال کی' میکال سے ڈرائیورس کے بعد بھی اس کا تعلق ہانیہ سے نہیں ٹوٹا تھا۔ مائرہ نے جو گھٹیا حرکتیں کی تھیں وہ سب جان گئی تھی مگر اس نے کسی کو بھی اس بارے میں نہیں بتایا تھا۔

سارا کی کال پر ہانیہ فوراً ہسپتال پہنچی تھی اور اب حسن صاحب اور آسیہ بیگم کو نہال کے پاس چھوڑ کر وہی بھاگ دوڑ کر رہی تھی۔

تھوڑی دیر میں جاذب بھی پہنچ گیا تھا وہ ہانیہ کو ڈانٹنا چاہتا تھا کہ اس نے اسے نہال کے بارے میں انفارم کیوں نہ کیا مگر اس کی پریشانی دیکھ کر خاموش ہی رہا حسن صاحب کی آنکھیں احساسِ تشکر اور شرمندگی سے بھیگ چکی تھیں۔

تقریباً ڈیڑھ گھنٹے کی ٹریٹمنٹ کے بعد نہال پرسکون ہو کر سو گیا تھا' اس کے منہ پر آکسیجن لگی تھی' ہانیہ دونوں ہاتھوں کو دعا کی صورت اٹھائے جانے کیا کیا پڑھتی رہی۔ صبح کے چار بجے تھے جب جاذب نے اسے گھر چل کر آرام کرنے کے لیے کہا تھا جواب میں وہ صاف انکار کر گئی۔ ''نہیں' میں ٹھیک ہوں تم پلیز انکل اور آنٹی کو لے جاؤ۔ آنٹی کی طبیعت ٹھیک نہیں ہے پھر گھر میں سارا اور مائرہ بھی اکیلی اور پریشان ہوں گی۔ انکل کی حالت تو تم دیکھ ہی رہے ہو پلیز کسی بھی طرح سے انہیں راضی کر کے گھر لے جاؤ۔'' اس کی بات میں وزن تھا جاذب سر ہلا کر پلٹ گیا اور دونوں کو بمشکل منا کر حسن منزل لے جانے کی بجائے اپنے ہی گھر لے آیا۔ صفدر صاحب جاگ رہے تھے' ہادیہ بھی لاؤنج میں بیٹھی تھی' وہ اسے ان دونوں کا خیال رکھنے کی ہدایت کرتا پھر گھر سے نکل آیا' تھوڑی ہی دیر میں اس کی گاڑی حسن منزل کے سامنے رکی تھی۔

سارا اور مائرہ کو فوری تیاری کا کہہ کر وہ انہیں بھی اپنے ساتھ ہی گھر لے آیا تھا۔ ہادیہ نے زبردستی آسیہ بیگم کو سلا کر بخار کی ٹیبلٹ دے دی' اس کے بعد وہ اور جاذب حسن صاحب کو تسلی دیتے رہے اُدھر تقریباً ساڑھے چھ بجے کے قریب نہال کو ہوش آیا تھا۔

''ہانیہ......''

آنکھ کھلتے ہی سب سے پہلے اس نے اسے پکارا تھا جو کرسی پر بیٹھی سر ایک طرف گرائے شدید ٹھنڈ میں سو گئی تھی' نہال کو اس پر بے حد پیار آیا وہ لڑکی واقعی اس قابل تھی کہ اسے ٹوٹ کر چاہا جاتا۔

''ہانیہ......!'' ایک مرتبہ پھر اس نے اسے پکارا تھا اور اس بار وہ فوراً بیدار ہو گئی تھی۔

''نہال......اب کیسی طبیعت ہے تمہاری؟'' کچی نیند سے جاگی آنکھوں میں سرخی نمایاں تھی' نہال نے اثبات میں سر ہلا دیا۔

''اب ٹھیک ہے' تم یہاں کیا کر رہی ہو؟''

''تمہاری نگرانی۔'' اس کے پاس بیٹھتے ہوئے وہ مسکرائی تھی' نہال بھی مسکرا دیا۔

''کس بات کی نگرانی' کہیں تمہیں سوتے پا کر راہِ عدم کا مسافر نہ بن جاؤں۔''

''جسٹ شٹ اپ اوکے۔'' وہ اسے تنگ کر رہا تھا اور وہ تنگ ہو گئی تھی' نہال کو معذرت کرنی پڑی۔ اس کا چہرہ زرد پڑ رہا تھا۔

''اوکے سوری' فوراً جنگلی بلی نہ بن جایا کرو۔''

''نہال! تمہیں یاد ہے تم نے مجھ سے وعدہ کیا تھا میری ایک خواہش پوری کرنے کا۔'' فوراً ہی وہ نارمل ہو گئی تھی' نہال نے پھر اثبات میں سر ہلا دیا۔

''ہوں' یاد ہے بولو۔
''پکی بات ہے ناں پوری کرو گے؟''
''تمہیں کوئی شک ہے؟''
''ہوں۔
''ایسی کون سی فرمائش ہے جس کے لیے تم اتنی پوزیسو ہو رہی ہو۔'' اب کے وہ مشکوک ہو رہا تھا' ہانیہ نے اس کا ہاتھ تھام لیا۔
''مجھ سے شادی کرو گے نہال؟''
''وہاٹ......؟'' اسے جیسے جھٹکا لگا تھا۔
''ہوں...... مجھ سے شادی کرلو پلیز۔'' دونوں ہاتھوں میں اس کا ہاتھ لے کر اس نے بمشکل اپنے آنسو چھپائے تھے' نہال نے فوراً ہاتھ کھینچ لیا۔
''تم پاگل تو نہیں ہوگئی ہانیہ!'' اس کا دل اس لمحے بہت تیزی سے دھڑکا تھا۔
''کیوں؟ اس میں پاگل پن کی کیا بات ہے' ہم بچپن کے دوست ہیں' تم مجھ سے پیار کرتے ہو' مجھے طلاق ہوئے ایک سال ہو چکا ہے' پھر کیا مسئلہ ہے؟''
''تم اچھی طرح جانتی ہو کیا مسئلہ ہے۔''
''جانتی ہوں تبھی کہہ رہی ہوں پلیز نہال پلیز۔''
''نہیں ہانیہ! میں اپنی خوشی کے لیے تمہاری زندگی سولی پر نہیں لٹکا سکتا' ویسے بھی میکال بھیا نے جو گھٹیا الزام میری اور تمہاری ذات پر لگایا ہے میں اسے کبھی سچ ثابت نہیں ہونے دوں گا۔''
''بھاڑ میں جائے میکال اور اس کی سوچ' تم مجھ سے صرف میری بات کرو۔''
''تمہاری بات کروں تب بھی اس خواہش میں سوائے حماقت اور ہمدردی کے کچھ نہیں ہے۔''
''مجھے کوئی ہمدردی نہیں تم سے' بس میں چاہتی ہوں ہمیشہ تمہارا نام میرے نام کے ساتھ جڑا رہے' پلیز نہال تم وعدہ کر چکے ہو مجھے مایوس مت کرو' پلیز۔''
''ہانیہ میں چند دن کا مہمان ہوں' کچھ نہیں پتا کب زندگی کا چراغ گل ہو جائے' تھوڑے سے دنوں کے لیے میں کیوں تمہیں کڑی آزمائش میں ڈال دوں؟''
''میری زندگی کی کیا گارنٹی ہے' ہو سکتا ہے میں تم سے پہلے مر جاؤں۔'' اس کا لہجہ بھیگ گیا تھا۔
''تم پاگل ہوگئی ہو اور کچھ نہیں۔'' نہال نے بے ساختہ نگاہیں چرائی تھیں۔
''پاگل ہی سہی تمہارے لیے تو ہر حال میں اچھی ہوں ناں؟''
وہ رو رہی تھی' نہال ڈسٹرب ہو کر رہ گیا وہ کبھی بھی اس کی آنکھوں میں آنسو نہیں دیکھ سکتا تھا مگر اس کی فرمائش پوری کرنا بھی اتنا آسان نہیں تھا تبھی اس نے چپ سادھ لی تھی مگر ہانیہ چپ سادھنے والی نہیں تھی اس نے جاذب' ہادی' فارحہ سب کو اپنی خواہش سے مطلع کر دیا تھا تبھی نہال کی طرح سب ہی اس کی خواہش پر بھونچکاں رہ گئے تھے مگر اسے کسی کی پروا نہیں تھی۔

❀......❀......❀

تقریباً ایک ماہ کے بعد اس کی ضد پر نہال نے اس کے ساتھ نکاح کر لیا تھا' میکال اس دوران دو بار حسن منزل آیا

دونوں بار حسن صاحب نے اس کی کوئی بھی بات سنے بغیر اسے گھر سے نکلوا دیا تھا۔ وہ چاہتا تو انہیں مائرہ کی سازش کے بارے میں بتا سکتا تھا مگر وہ اس کے لیے بالکل سگی بہنوں کی طرح تھی تبھی اس نے اسے سب کی نظروں سے گرانا مناسب نہیں سمجھا تھا۔ سارا کی شادی بھی نہال کے ساتھ ہی ہوگئی تھی' کمال اور عینا کو نہال کی بیماری اور مائرہ کی سازش کا پتا خود مائرہ سے لگا تھا' وہ عینا کو سامنے پا کر بُری طرح روتے ہوئے اسے سب کچھ بتا گئی تھی' عینا تو جیسے پتھر کی بن گئی تھی جب کہ کمرے کی دہلیز پر کھڑے کمال کو لگا جیسے کسی نے اس کے جسم سے روح کھینچ لی ہو' وہ تو ہانیہ اور میکال کی طلاق کو لے کر اپ سیٹ تھا پیچھے یہ قیامت کب اور کیسے آ گئی تھی۔ نہال تو اس کے لیے بچوں کی طرح تھا پھر وہ اتنی جلدی زندگی سے دور کیسے جا سکتا تھا' عینا کی نظر اس پر پڑی تھی ساتھ ہی مائرہ کی' مائرہ اسے دیکھ کر فوراً کمرے سے نکل گئی جب کہ عینا کے چہرے کا رنگ ایک دم سے اڑ گیا۔ کمال پتھر بنا بیڈ پر آ بیٹھا' عینا بھی ساتھ ہی بیٹھ گئی۔

''میرا دل نہیں مان رہا کمال! ایسی بات نہیں ہوسکتی' ایسی بات ہوتی تو پاپا ضرور ہمیں انفارم کرتے۔''

''پاپا نے بلایا تھا پاکستان مگر مجھے نہیں پتا تھا کہ اتنی بڑی بات ہوگی۔'' نم آنکھوں کے ساتھ ساتھ اس کا لہجہ بھی بھرّا گیا تھا پھر اس سے پہلے کہ عینا کچھ کہتی وہ اٹھ کر حسن صاحب کے کمرے کی طرف بڑھ گیا۔

میکال کے بارے میں اسے پتا لگا تھا کہ وہ چند رز قبل ہی اپنی بیوی کو لے کر دیارِ غیر شفٹ ہوگیا تھا۔

❁......❁......❁

نہال کمرے میں آیا تو ہانیہ دلہن بنی چھٹکو کے ساتھ کھیل رہی تھی وہ دروازہ بند کر کے مسکراتے ہوئے ان کے قریب آ بیٹھا۔

''یہ کیا ہو رہا ہے' شرمیلا پن تو نام کا بھی نہیں ہے تم میں۔''

''لو......اب تم سے کیا شرمانا' بچپن کے دوست ہو میرے' کوئی ایک کروڑ اسّی لاکھ پچاس ہزار بار منہ دیکھ چکے ہو پھر اب وہی منہ چھپا کر کیا جیب خالی کروانی تمہاری؟'' اس کا انداز ایسا تھا کہ وہ مسکرائے بغیر نہ رہ سکا' چھٹکو بھی بہت خوش تھا۔ سجے سنورے روپ میں ہانیہ اس کا ایمان لوٹ رہی تھی وہ اس کے سامنے بیٹھا اسے پیار بھری نگاہوں سے دیکھتا رہا' اگلی صبح وہ بے حد فریش تھا۔

ہانیہ اس کا ایسے خیال رکھ رہی تھی جیسے وہ کوئی کانچ کا کھلونا ہو' چھٹکو کے لیے بھی وہی سب کچھ بن گیا تھا اگلے ایک ہفتے میں اس کی صحت دیکھنے لائق تھی' درد کی شدت میں بھی حیرت انگیز طور پر کمی آ گئی تھی۔ ہانیہ اسے اپنے ہاتھوں سے ناشتا کرواتی' دوپہر اور شام کا کھانا کھلاتی' اس کے کپڑے پریس کرتی' اس کے سر میں تیل کی مالش کرتی' جب تک کمرے میں ہوتی کوئی نہ کوئی شگفتہ بات کر کے اسے ہنساتی رہتی جواب میں نہال نے بھی اس کو اتنی عزت اور محبت دی کہ بار بار اس کی آنکھیں بھیگ جاتی تھیں۔ دونوں ہر روز شام کے بعد سیر و تفریح کے لیے نکل جاتے' اکثر مسٹر اینڈ مسز حسن بھی ان کے ہمراہ ہوتے' کمال اور عینا کی کمپنی بھی مل جاتی' نہال کو خوش دیکھ کر ہی مائرہ نے شادی کے لیے حامی بھری تھی اور بالآخر اسے سادگی سے رخصت کر دیا گیا۔

مسٹر اینڈ مسز حسن ہانیہ کے بہت مشکور تھے اس کے ننھے فرشتے نے گھر میں رونق بکھیر دی تھی' نہال کو لگا جیسے وہ اسی کا بیٹا ہو جس طرح سے وہ اس کے ساتھ اٹیچ تھا' اسے پیار کرتا تھا اسے وہ میکال کا بیٹا لگتا ہی نہیں تھا' تتلی کی طرح سارے گھر میں دوڑتا پھرتا' وہ سب کے دلوں کی دھڑکن بن گیا تھا۔ نہال کو اگر دو منٹ بھی وہ نظر نہ آتا تو اس کا دل گھبرانے لگتا تھا۔ اس کے ننھے منے لبوں کی پیاری پیاری باتیں اس کے لیے کسی دوا سے کم نہیں تھیں' میکال کے بارے میں مسز حسن نے اسے بتایا تھا کہ وہ اپنی بیوی کے ساتھ پیرس چلا گیا تھا۔

میکال نے علیزے سے معذرت کر لی تھی' یہ کہہ کر کہ وہ اس کے شوق اور پروفیشن کی راہ میں رکاوٹ نہیں بن سکتا' علیزے خوش ہو گئی تھی شاید اسی لیے وہ اس کی باتوں میں آ کر پیرس آنے کے لیے مان گئی تھی۔

میکال کے یہاں بہت سے لوگوں سے بہت اچھے تعلقات تھے' لہٰذا پہلے اس نے خود کو سیٹل کیا' اپنی محنت' تجربے اور کچھ جمع پونجی کو بروئے کار لا کر اپنے ایک دوست کے ساتھ مل کر کاروبار سیٹ کیا پھر خود بھی شوبز کی فیلڈ میں آ گیا۔ اس کی کوشش تھی کہ وہ خود کو اتنا مصروف کر لے کہ پاکستان اور ہانیہ صفدر سے متعلق کوئی ایک یاد بھی اس کے دل کو پریشان نہ کر سکے۔

یہیں آ کر اس نے دوبارہ سگریٹ اور شراب کا معمول شروع کیا تھا علیزے یہاں اجنبی تھی اسے کوئی نہیں جانتا تھا'

میکال نے اس سے کہا تھا کہ وہ اسے پیرس لے جا کر وہاں کی اسکرین پر متعارف کروائے گا مگر اس نے اپنا وعدہ اب تک پورا نہیں کیا تھا' وہ جیسے گھر میں قید ہو کر رہ گئی تھی۔

اس قید نے ہی انتقاماً اسے میکال کی غیر موجودگی میں وہاں کے مقامی لوگوں سے تعلقات بنانے پر مجبور کیا تھا اور یہی وہ مقام تھا جہاں میکال نے اس سے بھی ہمیشہ ہمیشہ کے لیے علیحدگی اختیار کر لی تھی۔

❁......❁......❁

اس روز وہ جلدی گھر آ گیا تھا' علیزے گھر پر نہیں تھی وہ شاکڈ ہی تو رہ گیا تھا تقریباً تین گھنٹے کے بعد وہ گھر واپس آئی تھی وہ بھی ایسی حالت میں کہ ہوش سمیت کچھ بھی ٹھکانے پر نہیں تھا اور یہیں میکال کے اعصاب پر بجلیاں گری تھیں' بے شک وہ ان عورتوں میں سے تھی جو اپنی جائز ناجائز خواہشات کی تکمیل کے لیے کسی بھی حد تک جا سکتی ہیں۔

گھر آتے ہی وہ کمرے میں گھس کر سو گئی تھی جب کہ میکال ششدر سا کافی کا کپ ہاتھ میں لیے سیڑھیوں پر کھڑا رہ گیا تھا۔ اس کی زندگی میں تین عورتیں آئی تھیں اور وہ تینوں میں سے کسی ایک کو بھی نہ سمجھ سکا تھا نہ سنبھال سکا تھا۔ صبح ناشتے کی میز پر اس کی آنکھیں خوب سرخ تھیں۔

''گڈ مارننگ ڈارلنگ!'' علیزے نے اپنے مخصوص انداز میں اس کے گال پر بوسہ دیتے ہوئے اسے وش کیا تھا' میکال کی گرفت کافی کے مگ پر سخت ہو گئی۔

''گڈ مارننگ!''

''کیا ہوا' کچھ سست سست سے لگ رہے ہو' رات میں سوئے نہیں کیا؟'' اس کے مقابل بیٹھتے ہوئے اس نے سرسری سی ایک نظر میکال کے چہرے پر ڈال کر بریڈ پلیٹ سے اٹھا لیا تھا۔

''نہیں' سو گیا تھا سرِ شام ہی۔''

''کیا مطلب؟'' وہ چونکی تھی' میکال مسکرا دیا۔

''کچھ نہیں' تم سناؤ کیا مصروفیات ہیں آج کل؟''

''کیا مصروفیات ہو سکتی ہیں' سارے دن گھر میں قید رہتی ہوں' نہ کسی کو جانتی ہوں یہاں' نہ تم کہیں گھمانے پھرانے لے جاتے ہو' قسم سے میں تو سخت پچھتا رہی ہوں یہاں آ کر۔''

''ہوں۔'' اس کی شکایت پر پُرسوچ انداز میں اس نے سر ہلایا تھا۔

''ایک خوش خبری ہے تمہارے لیے۔''

''کیا؟''

''میں پاکستان جا رہا ہوں۔''

''واقعی......اور میں؟''

''تم ابھی نہیں جا سکتیں کیونکہ تمہارے لیے یہاں میں نے ایک بہت بڑے فلم میکر سے بات کی ہے' اسے تمہارے کمرشلز بھی دکھائے ہیں' تمہارا کام بہت پسند آیا ہے اسے' کل لے کر جانا تھا تمہیں اس کے پاس مگر نہایت ایمرجنسی میں پاکستان جانا پڑ رہا ہے بہرحال تم ایک پُراعتماد لڑکی ہو' میرا خیال ہے میرے بغیر یہاں تمہیں زیادہ مشکل نہیں ہو گی۔''

''ہوں' یہ تو ہے' واپس کب تک آؤ گے؟''

''جلدی آ جاؤں گا' ان شاء اللہ۔'' اس نے پوچھنے کی زحمت بھی نہ کی تھی کہ وہ پاکستان کیوں جا رہا ہے بالکل ویسے ہی جیسے ہانیہ نے اس سے اس کے بدلے ہوئے لہجے پر کبھی استفسار نہیں کیا تھا' شاید ان دونوں کو ہی اس کی ذات سے

کوئی دلچسپی نہیں تھی۔

اگلے روز جب علیزے اسے ائیر پورٹ پر چھوڑنے آئی تھی اس نے اسے جیب سے ایک لفافہ نکال کر دیا تھا۔

''یہ کیا ہے؟'' الٹ پلٹ کر لفافے کو دیکھتے ہوئے وہ حیران ہوئی تھی' تبھی وہ بولا تھا۔

''تحفہ ہے تمہارے لیے' وہ بھی سرپرائز' مگر اسے گھر جا کر کھولنا پلیز۔''

''اوکے' ایسا کیا ہے اس میں؟''

''کچھ تو ہے' خود دیکھ لینا' اب میں چلتا ہوں اللہ حافظ۔'' سرخ آنکھوں میں ہلکی سی نمی لیے وہ پلٹ گیا تھا' علیزے حیران پریشان سی وہیں کھڑی اسے دیکھتی رہی جانے کیوں اس لمحے اس کا دل اسے کچھ غلط ہونے کا احساس دلا رہا تھا مگر وہ سر جھٹک کر آزادی کے نشے میں سرشار بے نیاز سی گھر واپس چلی آئی۔

دن بھر موج مستی کے بعد رات جب وہ سونے کے لیے لیٹی تو اسے میکال کا دیا ہوا تحفہ یاد آیا تبھی اس نے متجسس سی ہو کر وہ لفافہ اٹھا کر کھولا تھا اور پھر جیسے ساکت ہی تو رہ گئی تھی۔

طلاق نامے کے ساتھ' سفید شفاف کاغذ پر کندھے الفاظ اسے پتھر ہی تو کر گئے تھے' لکھا تھا۔

''میں جانتا ہوں اس وقت تمہارے لیے اس سے بڑھ کر اور کوئی تحفہ نہیں ہو سکتا اور میں یہ بھی جانتا ہوں کہ تم جیسی خودسر لڑکیوں کی منہ زور خواہشات پانی کے ریلے کی طرح ہوتی ہیں' جن پر کبھی بند نہیں باندھا جا سکتا' اسی لیے میں نے تمہیں چپ چاپ چھوڑنے کا فیصلہ کیا ہے۔ یہ فیصلہ میں نے پاکستان میں ہی کر لیا تھا مگر...... میں تمہیں پاکستان میں آزاد کرنا نہیں چاہتا تھا' تمہاری وجہ سے میں نے اپنے گھر والوں کو کھویا ہے' اپنی ہانیہ کو کھویا ہے' اس ہانیہ کو جو اب بھی لہو بن کر میری رگوں میں' جسم و جاں میں دوڑتی ہے۔ بہت اذیت ناک ہوتا ہے کھو دینے کا یہ احساس مگر تم اس احساس سے واقف نہیں ہو کیونکہ تمہاری مجھ سے وابستگی تمہاری محبت نہیں مجبوری تھی' تمہارا قصور نہیں ہے شاید میرے ہاتھوں کی لکیروں میں ہی کسی عورت کی محبت اور وفا نہیں ہے بہر حال بے وفائی کی سزا بھی تو ہونی چاہیے ناں' وہ عورت جو میری غیرت کو جوتے کی نوک پر رکھ کر میری موت کا پلان بنا رہی تھی اسی عورت کو میں ساری عمر کی تنہائی سونپ آیا ہوں' تمہارا ویزا اور پاسپورٹ میں نے جلا دیا ہے اب تمہیں وہیں رہنا ہے اپنی من پسند دنیا میں۔ وہ دنیا جو پردے کی حرمت اور اہمیت سے ناواقف ہے وہ دنیا جہاں حیا کے انمول زیور کی کوئی قدر نہیں' تم اپنی سب سے قیمتی متاع تو گنوا ہی چکی ہو علیزے! پھر میں تم پر ترس کھاؤں بھی تو کیونکر...... بے وفائی کی سزا تو ملنی چاہیے پھر چاہے وہ میکال حسن ہو یا علیزہ' کیا فرق پڑتا ہے' ہے ناں؟'' الفاظ ختم ہو چکے تھے مگر علیزہ کو لگا جیسے ان الفاظ کے ساتھ ہی اس کی بینائی بھی ختم ہو چکی ہو' وہ محل جہاں اس وقت وہ بیٹھی تھی محل نہیں تھا' کنواں تھا وہ کنواں جو اس نے خود اپنے ہاتھوں سے اپنے ڈوبنے کے لیے کھودا تھا' لمحے شریر بچے کی طرح آگے دوڑتے جا رہے تھے اور وہ ساکت بیٹھی نیچے دھنستی جا رہی تھی۔

نہال کو سمندر بے حد پسند تھا۔

ہانیہ روز ضد کر کے اسے ساحلِ سمندر پر لے آتی' اس روز بھی خوب ٹھنڈی ہوا چل رہی تھی اور وہ ضد کر کے اسے ساحل سمندر پر لے آئی تھی' نہال ٹراؤزر کی پاکٹس میں ہاتھ پھنسائے بڑی دیر تک اداس کھڑا سمندر کی بپھری ہوئی موجوں کو دیکھتا رہا۔

''تم نے میرے ساتھ بڑا ظلم کیا ہے ہانیہ!'' اس کے پہلو میں کھڑی وہ بھی سمندر کی شوریدہ لہروں کو بڑی محویت سے

دیکھ رہی تھی جب نہال نے کہا' وہ چونک اٹھی۔

''کیسا ظلم؟''

مگر نہال نے جیسے اس کا سوال سنا ہی نہیں' اس کی نظریں ہنوز سمندر کی وسعتوں پر تھیں۔

''بہت سکون سے مر رہا تھا میں' کہیں کوئی زنجیر نہیں تھی پاؤں میں مگر اب...... سچ کہہ رہا ہوں ہانیہ! میرا مرنے کو دل نہیں چاہ رہا' دل لگ گیا ہے زندگی سے' تمہارے لیے' مما کے لیے' چھٹکو کے لیے' میں تم سب کے لیے جینا چاہتا ہوں۔'' اس کی آنکھوں کے گوشے نم تھے' ہانیہ کا دل جیسے کسی نے مٹھی میں لے لیا۔

''تمہیں ایسا کیوں لگتا ہے نہال کہ تم نہیں جی سکو گے' تمہیں معجزات پر یقین نہیں ہوگا مگر مجھے ہے' مجھے اپنے ربّ کی رحمت اور اپنی پُرخلوص دعاؤں پر یقین ہے۔ ڈاکٹرز کوئی خدا نہیں ہیں کہ ان کے کہنے سے تم مر جاؤ گے' تم جیو گے نہال! میں مانگوں گی اللہ سے تمہاری زندگی' تم دیکھ لینا کچھ بھی نہیں ہوگا یونہی دیکھتے دیکھتے دن گزر جائیں گے اور ایک روز ہمارا چھٹکو تمہارے قد سے بھی بڑا ہوگا پھر ہم اس کی شادی کریں گے' اس کی بیوی آئے گی ہماری خدمت کرے گی اور ہم دونوں اپنے کمرے میں بیٹھ کر اس کی چغلیاں کیا کریں گے۔'' وہ اسے بہلا رہی تھی' نہال قریبی پتھر پر بیٹھ گیا' اس کی آنکھوں سے ٹپ ٹپ آنسو گر رہے تھے۔

''کاش کوئی مجھ سے میری ساری دولت لے لے مگر بدلے میں مجھے اتنی زندگی دے دے کہ میں تمہارے ساتھ وہ دن دیکھ سکوں ہانیہ!'' نچلا ہونٹ دانتوں میں دبائے وہ اپنے آنسو پینے کی کوشش کر رہا تھا جب ہانیہ نے کٹتے دل کے ساتھ اس کا ہاتھ تھام لیا۔

''تمہیں کچھ نہیں ہوگا نہال! دیکھ لینا تم' پلیز موت کے بارے میں سوچنا چھوڑ دو' یہاں دنیا میں کتنے ایسے لوگ ہیں جو معجزانہ طور پر موت کے منہ سے نکل کر زندگی کی طرف واپس پلٹ آتے ہیں تم بھی پلٹ آؤ گے دیکھ لینا۔'' بھرآئے لہجے میں کہتی جانے وہ اسے تسلی دے رہی تھی یا خود کو۔ نہال خاموش بیٹھا روتا رہا۔

''میں اکثر سوچتا ہوں ہانیہ! مائرہ نے ہمارے ساتھ ایسا کیوں کیا؟ شاید وہ بھی مجھ سے ایسی ہی محبت کرتی ہو جیسی میں تم سے کرتا ہوں یا پھر جیسی تم میکال بھیا سے کرتی ہو' ہے ناں؟''

''نہیں...... میں صرف تم سے محبت کرتی ہوں نہال! صرف تم سے۔'' تڑپ کر اس کا ہاتھ تھامتے ہوئے اس نے کلیئر کیا تھا' نہال نے جیسے سنا ہی نہیں۔

''تمہیں پتا ہے ہانیہ! میں نے مائرہ کو معاف کر دیا ہے' تم بھی اسے معاف کر دینا پلیز۔'' نم نم سی آنکھوں سے ہانیہ کو دیکھتے ہوئے اس نے کہا تھا' ہانیہ ہونٹوں پر ہاتھ رکھ کر بمشکل اپنی سسکیاں روکنے کی کوشش کرتی رہی۔

وہ شام بے حد اداس شام تھی۔ اس شام نہال بہت دیر تک سمندر کنارے بیٹھا چپ چاپ روتا رہا تھا۔

رات بھی دیر تک بارش ہوتی رہی وہ ایک پل کے لیے بھی نہیں ہو سکا تھا۔

''نہال!'' ہانیہ خود بھی جاگ رہی تھی۔

''ہوں؟''

''نیند نہیں آ رہی ناں؟''

''ہوں۔''

''مجھے بھی نہیں آ رہی' کیا کروں؟''

''کچھ نہیں...... آؤ میں سلاتا ہوں۔'' فوراً سے پیشتر اس کی طرف کروٹ لیتے ہوئے اس نے ہانیہ کو اپنی بانہوں

میں چھپالیا تھا اور پھر اس کے بعد نیند کب اور کیسے آئی ہانیہ کو پتا ہی نہ چل سکا۔ اس رات پہلی بار وہ بہت سکون سے سوئی تھی، تبھی صبح فجر کی نماز بھی نہ پڑھ سکی۔

❁ .... ❁ .... ❁

اگلے روز چھٹکو کی تیسری سالگرہ تھی۔

نہال کا سارا دن بے حد مصروف گزرا' ہلکے ہلکے بخار کے باوجود سالگرہ کی تمام تر شاپنگ اور اہتمام اس نے خود کیا تھا' ہانیہ منع کرتی رہ گئی مگر وہ نہ مانا۔ شاپنگ کے بعد گھر کی سجاوٹ بھی اس نے خود ہی کی تھی۔ سارا اور مائرہ دونوں آئی ہوئی تھیں' گھر میں خوب رونق لگ گئی تھی' صرف نہال کی خوشی کے لیے ہانیہ نے کئی قسم کی ڈشز بھی تیار کرلی تھیں اس وقت بھی وہ آٹا گوندھ رہی تھی جب وہ کچن میں چلا آیا' پسینے سے بے حال ہاتھ میں چھوٹی ہتھوڑی اور کئی غبارے پکڑے ہوئے۔

''ہانیہ......! ایک گلاس پانی ملے گا؟''

''نہیں۔'' پلٹ کر اسے دیکھتے ہوئے وہ مسکرائی تھی' نہال قریب چلا آیا۔

''کیوں؟''

''دیکھ نہیں رہے آٹا گوندھ رہی ہوں۔''

''اوہ...... یہ تو اچھی بات ہے مطلب کچھ بھی کرلوں' تم روک نہیں سکتیں۔'' ہتھوڑی سائیڈ پر رکھ کر اس نے مزے سے ہانیہ کے گرد اپنے بازو پھیلا دیئے تھے' وہ مسکرادی۔

''بندے بن جاؤ نہال! ابھی کوئی آ گیا ناں تو پتا لگ جائے گا۔''

''ڈونٹ وری! میں دروازہ بند کر آتا ہوں۔'' بہت دنوں کے بعد وہ شرارتی موڈ میں لوٹا تھا۔ ہانیہ نے آٹے سے بھرے ہاتھ اس کے گالوں پر رگڑ دیئے۔

''اوہ ہانیہ! تمہارے پاؤں میں کاکروچ۔'' اس کا کہنا تھا اور ہانیہ کا چلّانا تھا' وہ ہنس ہنس کر دہرا ہوگیا تھا کیونکہ اگلے ہی پل سب لوگ کچن میں موجود تھے۔

''کیا ہوا؟''

''کچھ نہیں مما! ہانیہ کے پاؤں میں کاکروچ تھا میں نے بتایا تو چیخ اٹھی۔'' وہ اب بھی ہنس رہا تھا جب کہ ہانیہ کا منہ دیکھنے والا تھا' مسز حسن کی آنکھیں بھر آئیں۔

''بہت شریر ہو نہال! اپنی حرکتوں سے باز مت آنا۔''

''ہاہاہاہا...... سچ میں بہت ہی اسٹوپڈ اور ڈرپوک لڑکی ہے یہ ہانیہ!'' زیادہ ہنسنے سے اس کی طبیعت خراب ہوسکتی تھی تبھی سارا اسے کھینچ کر کچن سے باہر لے گئی تھی' اسی کے ساتھ باقی سب لوگ بھی نکل گئے۔ ہانیہ کو لگا جیسے اب وہ کبھی کوئی کام نہیں کرسکے گی۔

اس رات نہال کی آنکھ کھلی تو ہانیہ کمرے میں نہیں تھی' اسٹڈی روم کا زیرو بلب جل رہا تھا اور وہ وہیں جائے نماز پر بیٹھی رو رو کر بے حال ہو رہی تھی' یہ صرف اس دن کی بات نہیں تھی مسز حسن اور ہانیہ کا روز کا معمول تھا۔ روز دونوں تہجد کے لیے اٹھتی تھیں اور پھر صبح فجر تک اللہ ربّ العزت کے حضور رو رو کر نہال کی زندگی اور صحت کے لیے دعا کرتیں مگر نہال کو خبر نہیں تھی جتنی شدت سے ہانیہ رو رہی تھی اس کا دل پھٹ رہا تھا مگر وہ بے بس تھا' اس کی زندگی اس کے اختیار

میں نہیں تھی۔

''دیوار سے ٹیک لگائے وہ خود بھی بے آواز روتا رہا تھا۔''

✿ ...... ✿ ...... ✿

اگلے ہفتے حسن صاحب کے اصرار پر ان کا مری کا پروگرام بن گیا تھا۔

مری میں ہوتی سنو فال نہال کو بے حد پسند تھی' اکثر وہ اپنے دوستوں کے ساتھ اسی موسم میں وہاں آتا تھا۔ ہانیہ سارے سفر میں اس کی گود میں سر رکھے مزے سے سوتی رہی تھی جب کہ چھٹکو نے بول بول کر اس کا سر کھالیا تھا۔ بات بات پر جب وہ نہال کا منہ چومتا اسے بے حد اچھا لگتا۔ نہال نے ہانیہ کے ساتھ اسے بھی مری کا چپہ چپہ گھما ڈالا تھا۔ برف کے گولے بنا بنا کر وہ ان دونوں پر پھینکتا اور ہانیہ اس پر' نہال کی سنگت میں وہ دن اس نے بے حد انجوائے کیے تھے' گو قدم قدم پر اسے نہال کی طبیعت بگڑنے کا اندیشہ رہا تھا مگر وہ تو یوں چاق و چوبند تھا جیسے زندگی میں کبھی بیمار پڑا ہی نہ ہو۔ پورے ایک ہفتے بعد وہ مری سے واپس لوٹے تھے' سردیاں ہانیہ کے لیے ہمیشہ وبال جان رہی تھیں مگر اس بار اس نے سردیوں کو بے حد انجوائے کیا تھا' نہال اس کے ساتھ مل کر کچن مین سارے کام کرواتا تھا وہ تھک جاتی تو اس کا سر اور کندھے دباتا' ان دونوں کے درمیان کبھی میکال کو لے کر کوئی بات نہیں ہوئی تھی۔

وہ شاپنگ اور ہوٹلنگ کا دلدادہ تھا' ہانیہ اس کی فضول خرچی سے تنگ تھی تاہم نہال کی ہمراہی میں گزرے پانچ ماہ میں اس نے جانا تھا کہ زندگی کتنی خوب صورت ہے۔

✿ ...... ✿ ...... ✿

اس روز اس کی سالگرہ تھی۔

ہانیہ کی خوشی دیکھنے سے تعلق رکھتی تھی' تاہم نہال دیر تک پڑا سوتا رہا' ہانیہ نے دو تین بار کمرے میں آ کر اسے آواز دی مگر وہ ٹس سے مس نہ ہوا تو مجبوراً اسے پانی کی بوتل نکال کر اس پر انڈیلنی پڑی تبھی مجبوراً اسے آنکھیں کھولنے پڑی تھیں۔

''اٹھ جائیں جناب! صبح کے گیارہ بج گئے ہیں۔''

''تو......؟''

''تو یہ کہ آج آپ کی سالگرہ ہے' اٹھ کر تیاری کریں۔''

''میری سالگرہ اور میں ہی تیاری کروں؟'' تکیہ دُہرا کر کے کہنی کے نیچے سیٹ کرتے ہوئے اس نے ہانیہ کو دیکھا تھا' وہ مسکرادی۔

''نہیں! آپ کیوں کریں گے تیاری' میں ہوں ناں۔''

''خیر ہے آج بڑا آپ آپ کر رہی ہو؟''

''ہوں...... تمہاری سالگرہ ہے ناں' اب سال میں کم از کم ایک دن احترام تو تمہارا حق بنتا ہے' چلو اٹھو اب شاباش' باتھ لو' دوپہر ڈھلتے ہی مہمان آنا شروع ہو جائیں گے اوپر سے موسم بھی خوب برساتی ہو رہا ہے۔''

''نہیں' آج ہم نے کسی کو انوائٹ نہیں کرنا' یہ سالگرہ میں صرف تمہارے اور چھٹکو کے ساتھ منانا چاہتا ہوں ہانیہ! زیست کی آخری سالگرہ' کیا پتا اگلے سال یہ دن تمہاری زندگی میں کتنے آنسو لے کر آئے۔''

اچانک اس کی آنکھوں کے گوشے نم ہو گئے تھے' ہانیہ جہاں کی تہاں بیٹھی رہ گئی' وہ جتنی بھی کوشش کرتی اس حقیقت سے فرار ممکن نہیں تھا۔ پہلی بار نہال حسن نے اس کے آنسو نہیں پونچھے وہ خود بھی رو رہا تھا اور اسے بھی رلا رہا تھا۔

ہانیہ نے فون کر کے سب کو آنے کے لیے منع کر دیا‘ عصر کے بعد وہ دونوں (ہانیہ اور چھٹکو) نہال کے بے حد اصرار اور ضد پر شاپنگ کے لیے نکل آئے‘ نہال نے ہانیہ کو اپنی پسند کے کئی سوٹ اور جیولری خرید کر دی‘ اسے اپنی پسند کی ڈھیر ساری چوڑیاں دلوائیں۔ جوتے لے کر دیئے‘ چھٹکو کے لیے ڈھیر سارے کھلونے خریدے‘ مہنگے سے مہنگے ریڈی میڈ سوٹ اور جوتے لیے اس کا بس نہ چلتا تھا کہ اس روز وہ اپنا سارا اکاؤنٹ خالی کر دیتا۔

ہانیہ اس سے اچھی خاصی ناراض ہو گئی تھی مگر اس نے پروا نہیں کی‘ مارکیٹ سے واپسی کے بعد وہ ہانیہ کے گھر چلے آئے تھے‘ کچھ دیر وہاں بیٹھ کر چائے وغیرہ پینے کے بعد وہ گھر چلے آئے‘ گھر آتے ہی اس نے ہانیہ کو تیار ہونے کا آرڈر دیا تھا۔

اسی کی پسند پر ہانیہ نے بلیک شیفون کی ساڑھی زیب تن کی تھی‘ اسی کی فرمائش پر خوب میک اپ کیا تھا‘ اسی نے جھک کر ہانیہ کو ہائی ہیل کی سینڈل پہنائی تھی‘ خود اس نے سفید شلوار سوٹ زیب تن کیا ہوا تھا۔

سالگرہ کی ساری ارینجمنٹ اس نے ہوٹل میں کر رکھی تھی مگر ہانیہ کے لیے سرپرائز تھا۔ چھٹکو کو آسیہ بیگم کے سپرد کر کے وہ ہانیہ کو ہوٹل لے آیا تھا۔ ریسپشن پر مختصر بات چیت کے بعد جب اس نے مطلوبہ کمرے کے سامنے پہنچ کر اس کا لاک کھولا اور پھر ہانیہ نے پہلا قدم دھرا‘ ان دونوں پر ڈھیر سارے پھولوں کی برسات ہوئی تھی‘ ہانیہ کمرے کی سجاوٹ دیکھ کر دنگ رہ گئی تھی۔

باہر بارش کا سلسلہ پھر سے جاری ہو گیا تھا یوں لگتا تھا جیسے آج کے بعد بارش کو کبھی برسنا ہی نہیں۔ کمرے کے وسط میں چھوٹی سی میز پر ایک نہایت خوب صورت کیک مختلف تازہ پھولوں اور کینڈلز کے ساتھ اچھی طرح سجا کر رکھا ہوا تھا۔ وہ حیران ہی تو رہ گئی تھی۔

کتنے دل کش رنگ تھے زندگی کے جن سے نہال حسن نے اسے متعارف کروایا تھا‘ اسے یاد تھا بچپن میں اگر کبھی کسی کے ساتھ اس کی لڑائی ہو جاتی تھی تو جب تک نہال اس کا بدلا نہ لے لیتا‘ چین سے نہیں بیٹھتا تھا کبھی بھولے سے بخار چڑھ جاتا تو اس کی جان پر بن جاتی تھی۔

وہ اس کی شدتوں سے بخوبی واقف تھی‘ اس کی تالیوں کی گونج میں نہال نے کیک کاٹا تھا‘ بے شک ہانیہ کے لیے وہ ایک طلسمی رات تھی۔

باہر برستی بارش میں مزید شدت آ گئی تھی۔ نہال ہانیہ کو ساتھ لیے گلاس ونڈو کے قریب آ کھڑا ہوا۔

”پتا نہیں کیوں‘ مگر مجھے ایسا لگتا ہے ہانیہ! جیسے بارش کا میرے ساتھ بہت گہرا رشتہ ہے‘ جس رات میں پیدا ہوا اس رات مما بتاتی ہیں کہ بہت بارش ہوئی تھی جس روز میری تم سے دوستی ہوئی اس روز بھی بارش نے سارے علاقے کو بھگو رکھا تھا‘ جس روز تمہاری شادی ہوئی اس رات بھی بہت بارش ہوئی تھی میرے اندر بھی اور باہر بھی...... جس روز مجھے اپنی بیماری کا پتا چلا اس روز بھی دو دن سے بارش ہو رہی تھی اور آج...... آج بھی دیکھ لو کتنی بارش ہو رہی ہے۔“ وہ خود کو جتنا خوش ظاہر کر رہا تھا اندر سے اتنا ہی اداس تھا ہانیہ کا دل کٹ کر رہ گیا۔

”بارشوں کی تاریخ سے کون واقف ہے مگر پھر بھی نہال! کون ہو گا دنیا میں جس کا بارش کے ساتھ کوئی تعلق نہیں ہو گا‘ جسے بارش اچھی نہیں لگتی ہو گی‘ وہ شعر نہیں سنا تم نے......

بارش کی بنیاد میں جانے کس کے اتنے آنسو ہیں
صدیوں پہلے شاید کوئی صدیوں بیٹھ کے رویا ہے

”ہوں‘ سنا ہے اور ہمیشہ مجھے اس شعر نے گہری سوچ عطا کی ہے۔“

''رات کافی ہوگئی ہے نہال! اب سو جاؤ۔'' ہانیہ کی نظر اچانک وال کلاک کی طرف اٹھی تھی' نہال بدستور گلاس ونڈو کے اس پار کھڑا دیکھتا رہا۔

''بارش میں مجھے نیند نہیں آتی ہانیہ! بالکل بھی نہیں۔''

''جھوٹ' مجھ سے ناراضگی کے دنوں میں تو تم سکون سے سو جاتے تھے۔''

''کہاں سو جاتا تھا سکون سے پاگل' صرف تمہیں شو کرواتا تھا۔''

''اوہو' آج پتا چلا تم کتنے بڑے چیٹر ہو۔'' ہلکا سا مکا نہال کے بازو پر رسید کرتے ہوئے وہ مسکرائی تھی' نہال بھی مسکرا دیا۔

''ایک بات پوچھوں ہانیہ!''

''ہوں' پوچھو۔''

''مارو گی تو نہیں؟''

''نہیں۔'' ہانیہ کی آنکھیں نیند سے بوجھل ہو رہی تھیں' وہ سڑک کے اس پار دیکھتا رہا۔

''جس روز تمہیں میری بیماری کے بارے میں پتا چلا تھا کیا فیلنگز تھیں تمہاری؟''

''پتا نہیں نہال! فیلنگز تو دھڑکتے دل والوں کی ہوتی ہیں' میرا تو دل ہی رک گیا تھا' مجھے لگا میں بھری دنیا میں بالکل اکیلی رہ گئی ہوں' کوئی بھی نہیں ہے میرے پاس' میرا وجود جیسے ہوا میں معلق ہو کر رہ گیا تھا۔''

''اور جس روز تمہیں پتا چلا کہ میں سچ مچ دنیا میں نہیں رہا اس روز......؟'' وہ اس کے ضبط کا امتحان لے رہا تھا۔ ہانیہ کے حلق میں غم کی شدت سے کانٹے اُگ آئے' آنسوؤں کا ریلا جو جاری ہوا تو پھر بہتا ہی چلا گیا' نہال نے ایک نظر اس کی طرف دیکھا پھر کھینچ کر بانہوں میں بھر لیا۔

''محبت کو اتنا سر نہیں چڑھاتے ہانی! ماس تک کھا جاتی ہے یہ انسان کا۔'' اپنی ٹھوڑی اس کے سر پر ٹکاتے ہوئے وہ اسے نصیحت کر رہا تھا' وہ چپ چاپ روتی رہی۔

''تمہیں پتا ہے ناں ہانی! میں کبھی تمہیں روتے ہوئے نہیں دیکھ سکتا' اچھا سوری' وعدہ کرتا ہوں میں کبھی تمہیں دوبارہ اس ٹاپک پر کچھ نہیں کہوں گا' پلیز چپ کرو پلیز۔'' خود اپنے ہاتھوں سے اس کے آنسو پونچھتے ہوئے اس نے اسے اپنے سینے میں بھینچ لیا تھا' وہ ہانیہ کے آنسو دیکھ سکتا تھا مگر ہانیہ اس کے آنسو نہیں دیکھ سکتی تھی۔

''تمہیں نیند نہیں آ رہی' ہے ناں ہانیہ؟''

''ہوں۔'' اس کے سینے میں منہ چھپائے اس نے اثبات میں سر ہلا دیا تھا۔ نہال نے فوراً پردے گرا دیئے۔

''او کے' چلو میں سلاتا ہوں۔'' وہ چپ چاپ بیڈ پر اس کے پہلو میں لیٹ کر بازو پر سر رکھ کر سو گئی۔

❁......❁......❁

آدھی رات کا پہر تھا۔

ہانیہ کی آنکھ کھلی تو نہال بستر پر نہیں تھا اور اس کا دل اتنی شدت سے دھڑک رہا تھا کہ وہ خود بھی گھبرا اٹھی تھی' دوپٹہ شانوں پر پھیلا کر وہ اٹھی تھی سب سے پہلے واش روم چیک کیا مگر وہ وہاں نہیں تھا تب دھڑکتے دل کے ساتھ پریشان سی وہ کمرے سے باہر آئی تھی جہاں سامنے ہی لابی میں وہ موجود تھا۔ سینے میں اچانک اٹھنے والے درد نے اس کی جان پر بنا رکھی تھی اور وہ صرف اس کی نیند خراب ہونے کے ڈر سے اکیلا کمرے سے باہر چلا آیا تھا۔ ہانیہ کے پاؤں تلے سے زمین کھسک گئی تھی۔

''نہال۔'' تیر کی سی تیزی سے وہ اس کی طرف لپکی تھی' نہال کا سارا جسم پسینے میں بھیگ رہا تھا۔

''نہال...... نہال تم ٹھیک ہو ناں؟''

وہ تڑپ ہی تو اٹھی تھی مگر وہ بول نہیں پا رہا تھا' ہانیہ کو لگا جیسے اس کا دل رک جائے گا۔ بڑی مشکل سے وہ اسے کمرے میں واپس لائی تھی' اگلے ہی پل کپکپاتے ہاتھوں سے اس نے حسن صاحب کو کال کر دی تھی' جس وقت وہ نہال کو لے کر ہوٹل سے ہسپتال پہنچی تھی' حسن صاحب بھی پہنچ گئے تھے' نہال کی سانس قابو میں نہیں آ رہی تھی۔ بارش کی وجہ سے ڈرائیو میں بھی مشکل ہو رہی تھی' سارے سفر میں نہال کا ہاتھ اس کے ہاتھ میں رہا تھا اور وہ گاہے بگاہے اس کا ہاتھ یوں شدت سے دبا رہا تھا جیسے اس سے درد برداشت ہی نہ ہو رہا ہو۔

ہسپتال پہنچتے ہی اسے ایمرجنسی روم میں شفٹ کر دیا گیا تھا' حسن صاحب نم آنکھوں سے اسے تسلی دیتے رہے۔ مسز حسن بھی ساتھ ہی چلی آئی تھیں فقط چند ہفتوں میں وقت نے انہیں کتنا کمزور اور بوڑھا کر دیا تھا' وہ بے آواز روتی رہیں۔

کتنے آنسو تھے جو انمول موتیوں کی طرح ٹوٹ کر بکھر رہے تھے' کتنی دعائیں تھیں جو اس نے رو رو کر بے آواز دل ہی دل میں مانگی تھیں۔ نہال کی حالت تسلی بخش نہیں تھی اسے اسپیشل ٹریٹمنٹ کے تحت آئی سی یو میں شفٹ کیا گیا تھا' ہانیہ ٹپ ٹپ گرتے آنسوؤں کے ساتھ کھڑی دیکھتی رہی۔ نہال آکسیجن کے تحت سانس لے رہا تھا۔ مسز حسن نم آنکھوں سے مختلف قرآنی آیات پڑھ پڑھ کر اس پر پھونکتی رہیں۔

''پتا نہیں کیوں مگر مجھے ایسا لگتا ہے ہانیہ! جیسے بارش کا میرے ساتھ بہت گہرا رشتہ ہے' جس رات میں پیدا ہوا تھا اس رات مما بتاتی ہیں بہت بارش ہوئی تھی' جس روز میری تم سے دوستی ہوئی تھی اس روز بھی بہت بارش ہوئی تھی پھر جس روز تمہاری شادی ہوئی (میکال کے ساتھ) اس رات بھی بہت بارش ہوئی تھی میرے اندر اور باہر بھی اور...... جس روز مجھے اپنی بیماری کا پتا چلا اس روز بھی دو دن سے بارش ہو رہی تھی اور آج...... آج بھی دیکھو کتنی بارش ہو رہی ہے۔''

اس کا لہجہ اس کی سماعتوں میں گھلا تھا اور وہ شیشے سے ماتھا ٹکاتے ہوئے سسک پڑی تھی' کچھ ہی دیر میں فجر کی اذان بھی ہو گئی تھی۔

لمحے گیلی ریت کی مانند ہاتھ سے پھسلتے جا رہے تھے' دعاؤں کی شدت بڑھتی رہی' چوبیس گھنٹے زندگی اور موت کی جنگ لڑنے کے بعد بالآخر شیشے کے اس پار نہال حسن نے زندگی ہار دی تھی۔ ڈاکٹر ان سے معذرت کر کے تسلی کے دو بول تھماتا آگے بڑھ چکا تھا۔ ہانیہ کو لگا جیسے اس کا وجود بلاسٹ ہو گیا ہو' بھلا یہ کیسے ممکن تھا؟ نہال حسن اسے یوں چھوڑ کر کیسے جا سکتا تھا؟ بے یقینی سی بے یقینی تھی۔

گئے دنوں کا سراغ لے کر' کدھر سے آیا کدھر گیا وہ
عجیب مانوس اجنبی تھا' مجھے تو حیران کر گیا وہ
بس ایک موتی سی چھب دکھا کر' بس ایک میٹھی سی دھن سنا کر
ستارۂ شام بن کے آیا' برنگ خوابِ سحر گیا وہ
خوشی کی رُت ہو کہ غم کا موسم' نظر اسے ڈھونڈتی ہے ہر دم
وہ بوئے گل تھا کہ نغمۂ جاں' میرے تو دل میں اتر گیا وہ
نہ اب وہ یادوں کا چڑھتا دریا' نہ فرصتوں کی اداس برکھا
یونہی ذرا اک کسک تھی دل میں جو زخم گہرا تھا بھر گیا وہ

کچھ اب سنبھلنے لگی ہے جاں بھی' بدل چلا رنگ آسماں بھی
جو رات بھاری تھی کٹ گئی وہ' جو دن کڑا تھا گزر گیا وہ
شکستہ پا راہ میں کھڑا ہوں' گئے دنوں کو بلا رہا ہوں
جو قافلہ میرا ہم سفر تھا' مثال گرد سفر گیا وہ
وہ میکدے کو جگانے والا' وہ سب کی نیندیں اڑانے والا
یہ آج کیا اس کے جی میں آئی کہ شام ہوتے ہی ''گھر'' گیا وہ
وہ ہجر کی رات کا ستارہ' وہ ہم نفس ہم سخن ہمارا
سدا رہے اس کا نام پیارا' سنا ہے کل رات مرگیا وہ

وہ شخص جس تاریخ کو دنیا میں آیا تھا اسی تاریخ کو دنیا سے رخصت بھی ہوگیا' مگر آنسو پتھر کیسے ہوتے ہیں یہ کوئی ہانیہ صفدر سے پوچھتا' ہنستی بستی آباد بستیوں میں جیسے طوفان اچانک تباہی مچا کر چلے جاتے ہیں' بالکل ویسے ہی ہانیہ صفدر کا دل بھی تباہی کی بھینٹ چڑھ گیا تھا۔

پورے تین دن اس کا سکتہ نہیں ٹوٹا تھا۔ گہری ابدی نیند سوئے نہال حسن اس کے سامنے لیٹا تھا اور وہ ٹکر ٹکر ساکت نگاہوں سے اسے دیکھے جارہی تھی' اس کا بیٹا نہال کے چہرے پر پیار سے ہاتھ پھیرتے ہوئے اس کے گالوں کو چوم رہا تھا' اسے مجبور کررہا تھا کہ وہ اٹھ کر اس کے ساتھ کھیلے' اسے بائیک پر باہر لے کر جائے اور نہال کے ٹس سے مس نہ ہونے پر اس نے زور زور سے رونا شروع کردیا تھا۔ کتنی عادتیں بگاڑ دی تھیں نہال نے اس کی۔

مسز حسن بار بار بے ہوش ہورہی تھیں' سارا اور مائرہ کا بھی کوئی حال نہیں تھا جب کہ حسن صاحب کمال حسن کے گلے لگے بچوں کی طرح بلک رہے تھے۔ عینا اکیلی سارے معاملات سنبھالتی پھر رہی تھی۔ ہادیہ اور جاذب اس کے پاس تھے مگر وہ تو اکیلی ہوگئی تھی۔ حسن منزل کے درودیوار ایک مرتبہ پھر اسے راس نہیں آئے تھے۔

میکال جنازے کے وقت یہاں پہنچا تھا وہ بھی ایسے حال میں جیسے صدیوں کا سفر پیدل طے کرکے آیا ہو۔ گھر میں جمع ہوئے لوگ اور آنکھوں کے سامنے پڑی نہال حسن کی میت نے جیسے زمین کے اندر ہی تو گاڑھ دیا تھا اسے۔ وہ ہکا بکا سا لاؤنج کی دہلیز پر کھڑا رہ گیا تھا' کتنے پہاڑ تھے جو اس پر گرے تھے؟

کتنی قیامتیں تھیں جو اس وقت اس پر ٹوٹی تھیں

جنازہ اٹھایا جاچکا تھا گھر میں کہرام بپا تھا اور وہ خالی خالی نگاہوں سے سب دیکھتا گیا۔ کتنی جلدی تھی نہال حسن کو جانے کی کہ اس نے اسے معاف کرنا بھی ضروری نہیں سمجھا تھا' وہ رویا تو پھر جیسے حسن منزل کے درودیوار ہل کر رہ گئے تھے۔

نہال حسن کی آخری آرام گاہ تک حسن صاحب نے اسے کندھا دیا تھا اور کیسے دیا تھا یہ صرف وہی جانتے تھے۔

❁ .... ❁ .... ❁

نہال کی موت کو وہ دوسرا دن تھا جب میکال نے چھٹکو کو دیکھا تھا' نہال کی تصویر اٹھائے وہ اسے پیار کررہا تھا۔ وہ شاکڈ سا اسے دیکھتا رہ گیا' بے شک وہ ہو بہو اسی کی تصویر تھا۔

ہانیہ بار بار ہوش میں آتی تھی اور پھر بے ہوش ہوجاتی تھی۔ اس کی حالت کے پیش نظر ہی ہادیہ دو تین روز کے لیے وہاں ٹھہر گئی تھی۔ وقت ایک مرتبہ پھر پر لگا کر اڑنے لگا تھا مگر ہانیہ کی طبیعت نہیں سنبھلی تھی' وہ صرف چھٹکو سے باتیں کرتی تھی' اسے ایک منٹ کے لیے بھی اپنی آنکھوں سے دور نہیں کرتی تھی' تھوڑی دیر بھی وہ نظر نہ آتا تو پاگلوں کی طرح اسے

سارے گھر میں ڈھونڈتی پھرتی۔ میکال جب جب اسے دیکھتا ڈسٹرب ہو کر رہ جاتا تھا۔ ایک عجیب سا قفل تھا جو ہانیہ صفدر کے لبوں پر لگ چکا تھا کبھی لان کی دھوپ میں اکیلی بیٹھی آپ ہی آپ مسکرائے جاتی اور کبھی چاندنی رات میں بالکونی میں کھڑی بنا کسی بات کے ہی رو پڑتی تھی۔

میکال کی وجہ سے اس نے کمرے سے نکلنا بھی تقریباً چھوڑ دیا تھا' کئی کئی دن اسے نہ منہ دھونے کا خیال رہتا نہ کپڑے تبدیل کرنے کا۔ ان دنوں اسے لوگوں سے وحشت ہوتی تھی جہاں آوازیں سنتی اٹھ کر چلی جاتی یا چیخنے لگتی۔ ایک بار اس کے کمرے میں ٹیلی وژن چل رہا تھا اور چھٹکو نے آواز تیز کر رکھی تھی تبھی اس نے ریموٹ کنٹرول اٹھا کر اسکرین پر دے مارا' اس کی اسی حالت کے پیش نظر میکال نے چھٹکو کو اسکول میں داخل کروادیا تھا۔ نہال کے بعد وہ ہانیہ سے زیادہ میکال کے قریب ہو گیا تھا کیونکہ وہ اس کی ساری فرمائشیں پوری کرتا تھا' اس کے خوب ناز اٹھاتا تھا۔

اس روز بھی اسکول سے آنے کے بعد وہ ہانیہ کے ساتھ اس کے کمرے میں سو رہا تھا جب میکال کی آواز کانوں میں پڑتے ہی چپکے سے اٹھ کر اس کے کمرے میں آ گیا۔ ہانیہ اسے مزے مزے کی کہانیاں سنا کر سلاتی تھی' اسے ہوم ورک کرواتی تھی مگر میکال اسے مختلف سی ڈیز میں مزے مزے کے کارٹون لگا کر دکھاتا' مختلف گیمز لگا کر اسے اپنے ساتھ کھیلاتا تھا اکثر وہ اسے نہال کی قبر پر بھی ساتھ لے جاتا تھا۔

اس وقت بھی وہ اسے کارٹون لگا کر دکھا رہا تھا جب وہ دندناتی ہوئی اس کے کمرے میں چلی آئی تھی۔

''سنی..... سنی.....'' پاگلوں کی طرح وہ اسے پکار رہی تھی' جب چھٹکو سہم کر میکال کی ٹانگوں میں چھپ گیا۔

''مما میں یہاں نہیں ہوں۔'' میکال کی ٹانگوں میں چھپے چھپے اس نے معصوم سے لہجے میں کہا تھا' وہ مسکرا کر رہ گیا ہانیہ جو سامنے سے گزر رہی تھی چونک کر اندر چلی آئی۔

''چھٹکو۔'' اس نے اتنے غصے سے پکارا تھا کہ وہ فوراً میکال کی ٹانگوں سے نکل کر اس کے سامنے جا کھڑا ہوا تھا۔

''سوری مما!''

''سوری کے بچے! ایک دفعہ کی کہی بات سمجھ نہیں آتی تمہیں' کیوں آئے ہو یہاں۔'' میکال کے سامنے ہی دو تھپڑ اس نے چھٹکو کے گال پر دے مارے تھے' تبھی وہ تڑپا تھا۔

''اپنی حد میں رہو ہانیہ صفدر! مت بھولو کہ یہ میرا بھی بیٹا ہے۔''

''جسٹ شٹ اپ!'' چھٹکو کا بازو کھینچتے ہوئے اس نے حقارت سے اسے جھڑکا تھا۔

بعد میں اس گھر کے سبھی مکینوں کے ساتھ اس کا رویہ بہت تلخ ہو گیا تھا کیونکہ ان سب نے میکال کو معاف کر دیا تھا۔ اس رات وہ چھٹکو کے لیے دودھ لینے کچن میں آئی تھی' جب کچن سے نکلتے میکال حسن کے ساتھ اس کا ٹکراؤ ہو گیا وہ پانی لینے آیا تھا اور اس کے وہم و گمان میں بھی نہیں تھا کہ وہ ہانیہ سے ٹکرا جائے گا۔

''سوری۔'' سرسری سی نظر اس پر ڈالتے ہوئے وہ اس کی سائیڈ سے نکل گیا تھا' ہانیہ تنفر سے سر جھٹک کر رہ گئی۔

کچھ روز پھر خاموشی کی نذر ہو گئے تھے' اس کی عدت ختم ہونے میں ابھی کچھ دن رہتے تھے اور اس نے سوچ لیا تھا عدت ختم ہونے کے بعد وہ وہاں ایک پل کے لیے بھی نہیں رہے گی۔ حسن صاحب اور مسز حسن کی خواہش تھی کہ ہانیہ اور میکال پھر سے مل جائیں مگر ہانیہ کے رویے اور حالات کے پیش نظر ان کے لیے اپنی خواہش کو زبان دینا مشکل لگ رہا تھا' ادھر صفدر صاحب کے علاج کے لیے جازب انہیں انگلینڈ لے کر گیا تو پھر وہیں مستقل قیام کا فیصلہ کر لیا۔ ہانیہ نے انہیں روکنا مناسب نہیں سمجھا تھا۔

حسن منزل میں اتری ویرانیوں اور مسز حسن کی حالت کے پیش نظر حسن صاحب نے بھی پاکستان سے کوچ کا فیصلہ کرلیا تھا۔ میکال بزنس سمیٹ رہا تھا جب کہ کمال اور عینا پچھلے ہفتے ہی واپس جاچکے تھے۔ حسن صاحب نے ہانیہ سے بھی بات کی تھی اور اسے سمجھانے کی کوشش کی تھی مگر وہ کسی صورت پاکستان سے جانا نہیں چاہتی تھی لہٰذا اس نے انہیں صاف انکار کردیا تھا۔ بمشکل عدت کے دن پورے کرکے وہ چھٹکو کے ساتھ اپنے آبائی گھر چلی آئی تھی جس پر میکال پیچ و تاب کھا کر رہ گیا تھا۔

حسن صاحب اور ان کی فیملی کے انگلینڈ شفٹ ہونے کے بعد ایک روز وہ پلان کے تحت اس کے بیٹے کو اسکول سے ساتھ لے گیا اور بعد میں کال کے ذریعے ہانیہ کو مطلع کردیا کہ جس طرح وہ اپنے بیٹے کے بغیر زندہ نہیں رہ سکتی اسی طرح وہ بھی اپنے بیٹے کے بغیر زندہ نہیں رہ سکتا لہٰذا اسی لیے وہ اسے اپنے پاس لے جارہا ہے تاکہ اس کی بہترین پرورش کرسکے' اس نے ہانیہ پر چوٹ کی تھی کہ وہ اس کے بیٹے کو کچھ نہیں دے سکتی سوائے محرومیوں کے لہٰذا اس کے لیے یہی کافی ہے کہ وہ نہال کی یادوں کو سینے سے لگا کر جیتی رہے۔

ہانیہ کے وہم وگماں میں بھی نہیں تھا کہ وہ اس کے ساتھ اتنا بُرا سلوک بھی کرسکتا ہے تبھی وہ چیخ چیخ کر روئی تھی مگر وہاں اس کے آنسو دیکھنے والا کون تھا؟ فارحہ کو ساری بات کا پتا چلا تو وہ بھاگ آئی تھی بعد میں اسی نے اس کے لیے ایک کل وقتی ملازمہ اور ایک بہترین جاب کا بندوبست کیا تھا یہی نہیں بلکہ ہانیہ کی تنہائی دور کرنے کے لیے اس نے اسے اپنی بیٹی بھی گود دے دی تھی' انہی دنوں اسے صفدر صاحب کی رحلت کی خبر ملی تھی اور وہ تقریباً دو ماہ انگلینڈ رہ کر آئی تھی' مسٹر اینڈ مسز رحیم بھی اکثر وبیشتر ملنے کے لیے آتے رہتے تھے ہانیہ نے یہی سنا تھا کہ میکال اس کے بیٹے کو لے کر اپنی بیوی کے ساتھ فرانس جابسا تھا۔ اسی لیے رفتہ رفتہ وہ اس غم سے نکل آئی تھی مگر نہال کے ساتھ ساتھ یہ غم بھی پھانس بن کر اس کے دل میں چبھ گیا تھا۔ گو اس نے رشتوں سے صبر کرنا سیکھ لیا تھا مگر پھر بھی دل تھا کہ بھری دنیا میں کہیں لگتا ہی نہیں تھا۔

❁ ...... ❁ ...... ❁

ٹپ ٹپ ٹپ......

رات ست روی سے بیتتی جارہی تھی اور اس کے آنسو بہتے نہال حسن کی تصویر پر گرتے جارہے تھے۔ کون تھا اللہ کے سوا جو آج اس کے آنسو دیکھتا اور اس کے درد کو محسوس کرتا' اس کی زندگی مکمل طور پر اس نظم کی ترجمان ہوکر رہ گئی تھی۔

اب تو خواہش ہے یہ درد ایسا ملے\
سانس لینے کی حسرت میں مرجائیں ہم\
اب تو خواہش ہے یہ ایسی آندھی چلے\
جس میں پتوں کی مانند بکھر جائیں ہم\
اب تو خواہش ہے یہ دنیا والوں کا غم\
ایسی ٹھوکر لگائے کہ جی نہ سکیں\
ایسی الجھنیں یہ سینے میں سانسیں کہ بس\
ہم دوا پینا چاہیں تو پی نہ سکیں\
کوئی ہمدم نہ رہا نہ راحت ملے\
ایک پل کا سہارا نہ چاہت ملے\
اب تو خواہش ہے یہ

دشت ہی دشت ہو' ننگے پاؤں چلیں
ہم سرِ بزم شمع کی مانند جلیں
جس کو چاہیں اسے پھر نہ پائیں کبھی
چھوڑ جائیں یوں چپ چاپ دنیا کہ پھر
دل بھی یہ چاہے بھی تو ہم نہ آئیں کبھی
اب تو خواہش ہے یہ
کوئی صحرا قلعہ یا بیابان ہو
جس میں سالوں تک قید ہی قید ہو
اپنے خالقِ و مالک سے میں نے جو کی
بے وفائی وہاں پر وہ ناپید ہو
اب تو خواہش ہے یہ کہ سزا وہ ملے
روئے جاؤں تو چپ نہ کرائے کوئی
دور جنگل میں یا پھر کسی دشت میں
ہاتھ پکڑے میرا چھوڑ آئے کوئی
اب تو خواہش ہے یہ!

✡.....✡.....✡

حورعین اور عذیر کا نکاح ہو گیا تھا۔
کاسنی لہنگا کرتی میں دلہن بنی وہ یوں خاموش بیٹھی تھی جیسے ہجر کا ستایا کوئی مسافر کسی جھیل کنارے پلکیں موندے خاموش بیٹھا ہو' خود عذیر بھی چپ چپ سا تھا البتہ دادی اور عمیر بہت خوش تھے' ننھے زبیر کی تو جیسے لاٹری نکل آئی تھی' ماں کے بعد پہلی بار کسی عورت نے اس پر توجہ دی تھی۔
سارا گھر مہمانوں سے بھرا تھا' ثانیہ اور اس کی دادی بھی آ گئی تھیں البتہ اس کے بچے اس کے ساتھ نہیں تھے' تقریب کے اختتام کے بعد دادی کے حکم پر ثانیہ نے اپنی کلوز فرینڈ سے جو بہت اچھی گائنا لوجسٹ تھی' حورعین کا چیک اپ کروایا تھا کمرے میں اس وقت حورعین' ثانیہ اور اس ڈاکٹر کے علاوہ اور کوئی نہیں تھا' اچھی طرح چیک اپ کے بعد لیڈی ڈاکٹر عائلہ نے اس کی طرف عجیب نظروں سے دیکھا تھا۔
''ٹھیک ہے مس حورعین کہ آپ کنواری نہیں ہیں' مگر......''
''میری آج ہی شادی ہوئی ہے۔'' ڈاکٹر کے کچھ بولنے سے پہلے ہی وہ شروع ہو گئی تھی۔
''میرے اور عذیر صاحب کے درمیان اس سے پہلے کچھ نہیں تھا بس مجھے پناہ کی ضرورت تھی' اسی ضرورت کے تحت جھوٹ بول کر یہاں رہنا پڑا۔''
''آئی سی......تو یہ بات آپ نے چھوٹی دادو کو کیوں نہیں بتائی؟'' ڈاکٹر کے ساتھ ساتھ ثانیہ بھی حیران رہ گئی تھی' حورعین نے سر جھکا لیا۔
''انہیں نہیں بتا سکتی تھی' اگر انہیں بتا دیتی تو وہ مجھے بھی اپنے گھر میں نہ رہنے دیتیں۔''
''تو اب میں ان سے کیا کہوں؟ وہ تو پوتا کھلانے کے لیے بے چین ہیں۔''

"میں کیا کہہ سکتی ہوں۔"

وہ ذہنی طور پر پریشان لگ رہی تھی۔ ثانیہ نے ایک نظر اس کے سجے سنورے روپ پر ڈالی پھر اپنی دوست کے ساتھ اسے آرام کی تلقین کرتی کمرے سے باہر نکل گئی' کمرے میں تنہائی میسر آتے ہی حورعین کے آنسو تیزی سے بہہ نکلے تھے۔

اسے یاد آ رہا تھا ایاد عبدالحادی کی شہادت کے بعد مجاہدین نے باحفاظت اسے علی الصبح اس کے گھر پہنچا دیا تھا' بے حد مغموم سی وہ گھر میں داخل ہوئی تو وہاں جیسے الّو بول رہے تھے' وہ چپ چاپ لاؤنج میں دھرے صوفے پر پاؤں سمیٹ کر بیٹھ گئی۔ تقریباً بارہ بجے کے قریب اس کی سوتیلی ماں بے حد مختصر لباس میں اپنے کمرے سے باہر نکلی تھی۔ حورعین پر نظر پڑتے ہی اس کے اندر جیسے کرنٹ دوڑ گیا تھا۔

"تم......؟" کسی چیل کی مانند وہ حورعین پر جھپٹی تھی' حورعین کی آنکھیں' آنسوؤں سے بھر آئیں' اس کا چہرہ اس وقت بے حد ستا ہوا دکھائی دے رہا تھا۔

"ساری دنیا کی خاک چھان کر منہ کالا کر کے پھر یہیں چلی آئیں' کیا سمجھ رکھا ہے تم نے مجھے' میں نے کوٹھا نہیں کھول رکھا یہاں' دفع ہو جاؤ جہاں سے آئی ہو۔" وہ تو سمجھی تھی کہ حورعین کہیں مرکھپ گئی ہوگی اور یوں اس کی تمام جائیداد اب اس کی ہو گئی مگر اسے ایک مرتبہ پھر زندہ دیکھ کر وہ تو حیران ہی رہ گئی تھی۔ اس کی نفرت اور غصہ فطری تھا' حورعین رو پڑی۔

"میری بات سنیں پلیز' میں کہیں منہ کالا کر کے نہیں آ رہی ہوں' میں تو...... میں تو دکھوں کا سمندر پار کر کے آئی ہوں مگر مچھوں کے چنگل سے رہا ہو کر آئی ہوں۔"

"جہاں سے بھی آئی ہو' میری طرف سے جہنم میں جاؤ اب اس گھر میں تمہارے لیے کوئی جگہ نہیں ہے۔" بناء اس کی روداد سنے اس کی سوتیلی ماں نے ملازم سے کہہ کر زبردستی اسے گھر سے باہر نکل دیا تھا' وہ ساری رات برستی بارش میں گھر کے باہر بیٹھی روتی رہی۔

اگلے دن وہ اپنے فیملی وکیل کے پاس چلی گئی' حورعین کی پراپرٹی ملکیت کے تمام کاغذات انہی کے پاس تھے وہ نہ صرف ان کے فیملی وکیل تھے بلکہ اس کے پاپا کے بہت اچھے دوست بھی تھے۔ حورعین کو دیکھ کر وہ تڑپ اٹھے تھے' انہی کی مدد اور دھمکیوں سے حورعین کو اپنے گھر میں دوبارہ جگہ ملی تھی۔

اس کی سوتیلی ماں دوسری شادی کر چکی تھی اور اب حورعین کی تمام جائیداد پر قبضہ کیے اپنے دوسرے شوہر کے ساتھ پورے عیش و آرام کی زندگی بسر کر رہی تھی۔ وکیل صاحب کی اپنی فیملی کچھ ہی عرصہ قبل ناروے شفٹ ہوئی تھی اور وہ بھی ریٹائرمنٹ کے بعد ناروے شفٹنگ کی تیاری کر رہے تھے۔

جب تک وہ پاکستان میں رہے حورعین کو کوئی مسئلہ نہیں ہوا لیکن جیسے ہی ناروے روانگی سے قبل وہ حورعین کو ملنے آئے اور اس کی سوتیلی ماں کو اس کا خیال رکھنے کی ہدایت کی وہ عورت پھر سے ناگن بن گئی' وکیل صاحب کی ناروے روانگی کے بعد حورعین کے لیے جیسے نفرتوں اور مظالم کے پہاڑ کھڑے کر دیے گئے۔ کئی بار اس کی سوتیلی ماں اور اس کے شوہر نے مل کر اسے مارا تھا اور اس روز جب اس کی سوتیلی ماں اپنی کسی دوست کے گھر گئی ہوئی تھی' اس کے شوہر نے موقع پا کر اسے دبوچ لیا۔ ایک قیامت اس پر پہلے ٹوٹی تھی اور ایک قیامت کا سامنا اسے اب تھا۔

اس روز جس طرح سے وہ اپنی عزت اور اپنی جان بچا کر وہاں سے بھاگی تھی اور قبرستان پہنچی تھی۔ قبرستان سے اس نے مسجد کا رخ کیا تھا اور مسجد سے عذیر کے گھر کا' جہاں وہ اپنی کلاس فیلو کے ساتھ ایک مرتبہ پہلے بھی آ چکی تھی۔

سر درد سے پھٹ رہا تھا جب کہ جسم شدید بخار میں جل رہا تھا' وہ جھوٹی اور فریبی نہیں تھی مگر عزت کے خوف نے اسے

جھوٹ بول کر گھر میں پناہ لینے پر مجبور کر دیا تھا۔ عذیر نے اس کی سوتیلی ماں اور اس کے شوہر پر ناجائز قبضے کا پرچہ کروا رکھا تھا مگر ابھی تک اس کیس کا فیصلہ نہیں ہوا تھا۔

✿.......✿.......✿

رات کافی ہو گئی تھی۔ عذیر کمرے میں آیا تو حور عین سو چکی تھی تاہم آنسوؤں کے نشان اس کے گالوں پر ثبت تھے۔ زبیر آج بھی ضد کر کے اسی کے ساتھ سو رہا تھا۔ اس نے لباس تبدیل کر لیا تھا مگر مٹا مٹا سا میک اپ اب بھی اس کے حسین چہرے کو چار چاند لگا رہا تھا' وہ سرسری سی ایک نظر اس پر ڈالنے کے بعد خود بھی کپڑے تبدیل کر کے بیڈ پر آ گیا تھا۔ سلمیٰ کو اس شادی کی خبر ہوئی تو اس نے فوراً ہی چپ چاپ راستہ تبدیل کر لیا۔ شاید وہ خود بھی یہی چاہتی تھی آنے والے دنوں میں حور عین کی ذمہ داریاں مزید بڑھ گئی تھیں۔ عذیر کے تقریباً سارے کام اس نے اپنے ذمے لے لیے تھے۔

اس کی وارڈروب دھلے دھلائے کپڑوں سے ہر وقت بھری رہتی تھی' جوتے روز پالش کیے ملتے' ناشتا وقت سے پہلے تیار کیا ملتا۔ کمرا ہر وقت نفاست سے سیٹ کیا صاف ستھرا ملتا' موزے ٹائی' بنیان ہر چیز اپنی جگہ پر موجود ملتی' اسے لگا وہ جیسے کسی جنت میں آ گیا ہو۔

سمیر' عمیر' نمیر کے ٹھاٹھ بھی دیکھنے والے تھے' سب کی ذمہ داریاں حور عین نے اپنے سر لے لی تھیں' رات گئے تک وہ کچن اور گھر کے کاموں سے فارغ نہیں ہوتی تھی۔ زبیر کے لیے جیسے اس نے سگی ماں کا درجہ لے لیا تھا۔ وہ اس کے بغیر ہل کر پانی بھی نہیں پیتا تھا' اسکول سے آنے کے بعد رات سونے تک اسی کے پلو سے بندھا رہتا' تھوڑی دیر کے لیے بھی وہ نظر نہ آتی تو رو رو کر سارا گھر سر پر اٹھا لیتا تھا' حور عین خود بھی اس کی بہت عادی ہو گئی تھی۔

✿.......✿.......✿

اس روز سنڈے تھا۔ عذیر دیر تک بستر میں پڑے رہنے کے بعد اٹھ کر کمرے سے باہر آیا تو حور عین سارے گھر کی صفائی ستھرائی میں مصروف تھی۔ ساتھ ہی اس نے کپڑے دھونے والی مشین بھی لگا رکھی تھی' زبیر اور عمیر ڈائننگ ٹیبل پر موجود تھے لہٰذا انہیں ناشتا کروانے کا کام بھی ساتھ ساتھ چل رہا تھا' وہ حیران ہی تو رہ گیا تھا' وہ لڑکی تھی یا کوئی مشین؟

ایک مدت کے بعد اس مکان کو گھر بننا نصیب ہوا تھا' جبکہ سلمیٰ خود کو اس طرح سے ایڈجسٹ کر سکتی تھی شاید کبھی نہیں۔ دادی ماں ہر طرح سے مطمئن ہو کر گاؤں چلی گئی تھیں تاہم ان کی غیر موجودگی میں بھی اس نے اپنی ذمہ داریوں سے نگاہ نہیں چرائی تھی' عذیر فریش ہونے کے بعد خود بھی ڈائننگ ٹیبل کی طرف آ گیا تھا۔

''ناشتا لاؤں آپ کے لیے؟''

''ہوں۔'' ایک نظر حور عین پر ڈالنے کے بعد اس نے اثبات میں سر ہلا دیا تھا' وہ خاموشی سے پلٹ گئی۔

''عذیر بھائی ایک بات کہوں؟'' عمیر جو ناشتے سے فارغ ہو چکا تھا' نیپکن سے ہاتھ صاف کرتے ہوئے بولا۔

''ہوں' کہو.....'' سرسری نظر اخبار پر ڈالتے ہوئے عذیر نے اس کی طرف دیکھا تھا۔

''عذیر بھیا! کیا ایسا نہیں ہو سکتا کہ سلمیٰ بھابی کی جگہ ہمیشہ کے لیے حور بھابی ہی اس گھر میں رہیں۔'' اس کے الفاظ نے عذیر کا دل دھڑکا دیا تھا' حور عین جو ناشتے کی ٹرے لا رہی تھی' خود بھی ٹھٹک گئی۔

''سچ کہہ رہا ہوں عذیر بھیا! اس گھر کو صرف حور عین بھابی کی ضرورت ہے' ان کی جگہ کبھی بھی کوئی دوسری لڑکی یہ گھر نہیں سنبھال سکتی۔''

بناء عذیر اور حور عین کی طرف دیکھے وہ اپنے دل کی بات کہہ رہا تھا' حور عین نے لب بھینچ لیے۔ عذیر کا ناشتا خاموشی

سے ٹیبل پر رکھنے کے بعد وہ واپس پلٹ گئی تھی۔ شام میں زبیر نے آئس کریم کے لیے ضد کر لی' عذیر چونکہ فارغ ہی تھا لہٰذا اس نے سبھی کو ساتھ چلنے کی آفر کر دی۔ حورعین دن بھر کے کاموں سے بے حد تھکی ہوئی تھی لہٰذا اس نے ساتھ چلنے سے معذرت کر لی مگر زبیر کہاں اس کی معذرت کو قبول کرنے والا تھا' مجبوراً اسے تھکن کے باوجود تیار ہونا پڑا۔ پورے راستے عمیرا اور نمیر نے وہ شرارتیں کیں کہ سب کا ہنس ہنس کر بُرا حال ہو گیا' حورعین بھی مسکراتی رہی تھی۔

آئس کریم اور رات کے کھانے کے بعد وہ لوگ شاپنگ کے لیے نکل آئے تھے۔ نمیر اور عمیرا اپنی اپنی پسند کی چیزیں خرید رہے تھے جب کہ وہ زبیر کے لیے پاگل ہوئی جا رہی تھی۔ عذیر سب کو ان کے حال پر چھوڑ کر سیل فون پر مصروف تھا' تھکن سے چُور جس وقت وہ لوگ گھر واپس آئے رات کے ایک بجے کا ٹائم ہو رہا تھا مگر حورعین یہاں بھی اپنے فرائض نہیں بھولی تھی۔ سب کو دودھ کے گلاس دینے کے بعد وہ فارغ ہو کر کمرے میں آئی تو زبیر سو چکا تھا تاہم عذیر کو نیند نہیں آئی تھی' وہ جاگ رہا تھا۔

''بہت دن ہوئے آپ قبرستان نہیں گئیں؟''

ڈریسنگ ٹیبل کے سامنے کھڑی وہ چوڑیاں اتار رہی تھی' جب اس نے کروٹ کے بل لیٹے لیٹے دائیں بازو کی ہتھیلی پر سر ٹکاتے ہوئے پوچھا۔ حورعین کے اندر ایک سناٹا سا بکھر گیا۔

''جی...... وقت نہیں ملا۔''

''وقت......؟ میں نے دیکھا ہے قبرستان جانے کے معاملے میں آپ نے کبھی وقت کی پروا نہیں کی۔'' اسے حیرت ہوئی تھی وہ نڈھال سی وہیں بیٹھ گئی۔

''پہلے میں اور اب میں بہت فرق ہے۔''

''نہیں حورعین! میں نے اپنا نام ضرور دیا ہے آپ کو مگر اس کا یہ مطلب ہرگز نہیں کہ آپ میری پابند ہو گئی ہیں یا میں نے آپ کو خرید لیا ہے' آپ اب بھی آزاد ہیں پلیز خود پر ذمہ داریوں کا اتنا بوجھ لاد کر شرمندہ مت کیا کریں۔'' وہ بہت اپنائیت بھرے لہجے میں کہہ رہا تھا' حورعین کی آنکھیں بھیگ گئیں۔

''او ہاں مجھے آپ کو ایک خوش خبری بھی سنانی تھی' کورٹ نے آپ کے حق میں فیصلہ دے کر آپ کی اسٹیپ مدر اور ان کے شوہر کو سزا سنا دی ہے' اب آپ اپنے فادر کی تمام جائیداد کی بلا شرکت غیرے مالک ہیں' کوئی بھی شخص اب آپ کو نہ تو آپ کے گھر سے نکال سکتا ہے نہ آپ کا کاروبار ہتھیا سکتا ہے' کچھ لوگ ہیں جو وہاں آپ کی کمپنی میں ٹھیک نہیں ہیں۔ میں آپ کو کنفرم کر دوں گا تب آپ ان کو ہٹا دیجیے گا۔''

خبر کیا تھی کوئی امرت تھا جو حورعین کی سماعتوں میں انڈیلا گیا' بے یقین سی وہ بیڈ پر اس کے پاس چلی آئی تھی۔

''آپ سچ کہہ رہے ہیں ناں؟''

''ہوں' بالکل سچ۔'' اثبات میں سر ہلاتے ہوئے وہ مسکرایا تھا۔ حورعین کے آنسوؤں میں شدت آ گئی تھی۔

''مم...... میں ابھی آئی۔''

تھکن کا احساس ایک پل میں اڑن چھو ہو گیا تھا' عذیر اس کی کانچ سی آنکھوں میں مچلتے آنسو دیکھتا رہ گیا۔ اگلے بیس پچیس منٹ تک وہ نماز میں اللہ رب العزت کے حضور شکرانے کے نوافل ادا کرتی روتی رہی تھی یہاں تک کہ روتے روتے ہچکیاں بندھ گئی تھیں۔ نوافل سے فارغ ہو کر سرخ چہرے کے ساتھ وہ دوبارہ کمرے میں واپس آئی تو عذیر بیڈ پر کچھ چیزیں بکھیرے بیٹھا تھا' وہ حیران ہی تو رہ گئی تھی۔

''یہ سب کیا ہے؟''

''آپ کی شاپنگ۔''

''مگر آپ نے یہ کب کی؟'' حیران حیران سی وہ بیڈ کے کنارے پر ٹک گئی تھی۔ عذیر نے اپنائیت سے اس کا ہاتھ تھام لیا۔

''جب آپ زبیر کے لیے مختلف چیزیں خریدنے میں مصروف تھیں تبھی میں بھی آپ کے لیے یہ سب خرید رہا تھا اور میں ہی کیا عمیر اور نمیر نے بھی آپ کے لیے بہت سی چیزیں خریدی ہیں وہ بھی اپنے جمع کیے ہوئے پیسوں سے' آپ سوچ بھی نہیں سکتیں حورعین کہ اس گھر کے مکینوں کے دلوں میں آپ کے لیے کتنا پیار ہے۔'' جتنی اپنائیت سے وہ کہہ رہا تھا' اتنی ہی تیزی سے حورعین کی پلکیں بھیگی تھیں۔

''میں آپ لوگوں کی اتنی محبت اور اپنائیت کے قابل نہیں ہوں۔'' مسلسل رونے سے اس کا لہجہ بھاری ہو رہا تھا' عذیر نے اس کا ہاتھ چھوڑ دیا۔

''کون کتنی محبت اور اپنائیت کے قابل ہے یہ تو خدا ہی جانتا ہے مگر حقیقت یہی ہے حورعین! یہ گھر آپ جیسی عورت کے لیے ترسا ہوا تھا۔ روز سمیر کا سب کے ساتھ جھگڑا ہوتا تھا' کبھی کھانا اچھا نہ بننے پر' کبھی کپڑے صاف نہ دھلنے پر' کبھی ناشتا ٹائم پر نہ ملنے پر اور زبیر وہ تو لگتا تھا مما کے بعد جیسے دنیا میں رہتا ہی نہیں' ہر وقت سہما رہتا تھا عجیب احساسِ محرومی کا شکار ہو کر رہ گیا تھا۔ اسکول میں دوستوں سے ان کی ماؤں کے لاڈ پیار کا سن کر اور بھی ٹوٹ پھوٹ جاتا تھا مگر آپ کے اس گھر میں آنے کے بعد یوں لگتا ہے جیسے اسے نئی زندگی مل گئی ہو' سلمٰی شاید یہ سب کبھی نہ کر پاتی۔''

وہ اس کی صلاحیتوں اور خدمات کا اعتراف کر رہا تھا' حورعین سر جھکائے بیٹھی سنتی رہی۔

❁ ...... ❁ ...... ❁

اس رات بہت بارش ہوئی تھی۔ عذیر صبح کی نماز کے لیے اٹھا تو حورعین گھر پر نہیں تھی' کچن' باتھ روم کہیں بھی نہیں تھی۔ وہ جان گیا کہ وہ قبرستان گئی ہے' اک ٹیس سی تھی جو اس کے دل سے اٹھی تھی تاہم سر جھٹک کر وہ واش روم میں گھس گیا' نہا کر آیا تو حورعین گھر پر تھی اور اس کا وجود ہنوز بخار کی لپیٹ میں تھا' بخار کی شدت سے منہ بھی سرخ ہو رہا تھا' عمیر نے اسے ناشتا بنانے سے روک دیا۔ وہ کمرے میں آئی تو عذیر آفس کے لیے نکل رہا تھا۔

''السّلام علیکم!'' عذیر پر نگاہ پڑتے ہی اس نے سلام کیا تھا' عذیر کے ٹائی کی ناٹ ٹھیک کرتے ہاتھ وہیں رک گئے۔

''وعلیکم السّلام! کہاں تھیں آپ؟'' بہت سرسری انداز میں اس نے پوچھا تھا مگر حورعین کو اچھا نہیں لگا۔

''یہیں کچن میں تھی' ناشتا بنا رہی تھی' کیوں؟''

''نہیں کچھ نہیں' ویسے ہی پوچھ رہا تھا' آج ناشتا آفس میں ہی کروں گا' جلدی پہنچنا ہے آپ کی طبیعت تو ٹھیک ہے ناں؟'' اپنی تیاری کو فائنل ٹچ دیتے ہوئے اس نے اس کے سرخ چہرے پر توجہ دی تھی' حورعین بیڈ کے کنارے پر ٹک گئی۔

''جی...... ٹھیک ہے۔'' اس کے چہرے کی تمازت اور لہجے کے گریز کو اس وقت۔ اس نے اس کے قبرستان سے ہو کر آنے کے احساسات سے منسوب کیا تھا تبھی جلدی سے بیگ اٹھایا۔

''چلیں ٹھیک ہے' اب میں چلتا ہوں' اپنا خیال رکھیے گا۔''

''جی ضرور۔''

عذیر کی ہدایت پر وہ صرف سر ہلا سکی تھی تاہم اس کے کمرے سے نکلنے کے بعد دروازہ لاک کر کے وہ اتنا روئی تھی کہ آنکھوں کے سوتے خشک پڑ گئے تھے۔

شام میں ہلکے ہلکے بخار کے باوجود اس نے خود کھانا بنایا تھا کیونکہ صبح کسی نے بھی ٹھیک سے ناشتا نہیں کیا تھا' دوپہر میں بھی سمیر کے ہاتھ کا بنا سالن کسی نے پسند نہیں کیا' سب بھوکے اور پریشان تھے' نمیر نے مشین لگا رکھی تھی جب کہ عمیر کچن صاف کر رہا تھا۔ ساتھ ہی زبیر کو ہوم ورک بھی کروا رہا تھا۔ وہ کچن میں آئی تو سب کی جان میں جان آئی تاہم اس کی خرابیٔ طبیعت کے باعث عمیر نے اسے کچن سے نکالنے کی کوشش کی تھی مگر وہ نہ مانی تبھی وہ اس کی مدد کروا رہا تھا' چکن کڑاہی کے ساتھ چکن بریانی' سلاد اور رائتہ بنا کر اس نے ٹیبل پر لگایا پھر چائے بنائی' سب کھانا کھا کر اور اس کی بے حد تعریف کر کے اپنے اپنے کمروں میں گھس گئے تو وہ زبیر کو سلانے چلی آئی' دماغ جیسے فریز ہو کر رہ گیا تھا' نمیر اور عمیر کی گفٹ کی چیزیں سامنے ہی میز پر رکھی تھیں اس کی پلکیں پھر بھیگنے لگیں۔

بارش ابھی بھی ہو رہی تھی۔ عذیر تقریباً گیارہ بجے کے قریب آفس سے واپس آیا تو اچھا خاصا بھیگ چکا تھا۔ حورعین ابھی زبیر کو سلا کر فارغ ہوئی تھی' عذیر کپڑے تبدیل کرنے کے بعد ڈائننگ ٹیبل پر آ گیا' کھانا بے حد لذیز بنا تھا اور کچھ اسے بھوک بھی بہت لگی تھی' سو چپ چاپ رغبت سے کھاتا رہا' اپنی ماں کے بعد پہلی بار اسے کسی عورت کے ہاتھ کا بنا کھانا پسند آیا تھا سو آج کل وہ ہوٹلز کو نظر انداز کر کے زیادہ تر گھر پر ہی کھانا کھانے کو ترجیح دیتا تھا۔

حورعین اس کے کھانے سے فارغ ہونے تک گرما گرم چائے کا کپ بنا کر لے آئی' اس کی آنکھیں اس وقت بے حد سرخ ہو رہی تھیں' عذیر نے پہلا سپ لیا تھا جب وہ اس کے مقابل بیٹھتے ہوئے بولی۔

"آپ نے وعدہ کیا تھا اگر میرا پراپرٹی والا مسئلہ حل ہو گیا تو میں واپس اپنے گھر جا سکتی ہوں۔"

"ہوں۔" بے اختیار چونک کر عذیر نے اسے دیکھا تھا۔

"میں کل صبح ہی اپنے گھر واپس جانا چاہتی ہوں۔" سپاٹ چہرے کے ساتھ فیصلہ سنانے میں اس نے ایک لمحے کی تاخیر بھی نہیں کی تھی۔ عذیر ہکا بکا سا اس کا منہ دیکھتا رہ گیا تھا۔

"یہ کیا کہہ رہی ہیں آپ؟"

"کیوں...... میں نے کچھ غلط تو نہیں کہا۔ ہمارے درمیان یہی ڈیل طے ہوئی تھی اور میں نہیں سمجھتی کہ آپ اپنی زبان سے مکر سکتے ہیں۔"

"ایسی کوئی بات نہیں ہے مگر آپ اکیلی وہاں اتنے بڑے گھر میں کیسے رہیں گی؟"

"رہ لوں گی مجھے عادت ہے اکیلے رہنے کی' آپ پریشان نہ ہوں۔"

"وہ ٹھیک ہے مگر' دادی ماں کے آنے کا انتظار تو کر لیں وہ کیا سوچیں گی کہ آپ کیوں چلی گئیں۔"

"یہ آپ کا مسئلہ ہے کہ آپ انہیں کیسے مطمئن کرتے ہیں۔ میں نہیں چاہتی کہ آپ اور آپ کے گھر والے میرے وجود کے عادی ہو جائیں اتنے عادی کہ پھر میرے بغیر رہ ہی نہ سکیں۔ آپ جانتے ہیں کہ میں آپ کی منزل نہیں ہوں۔ آپ کا راستہ کوئی اور ہے اور میرا راستہ کوئی اور ہم دونوں ہی دو علیحدہ علیحدہ راستوں کے مسافر ہیں۔ لہٰذا بہتر یہی ہے کہ ابھی سے اپنی منزل کا تعین کر لیں۔"

اس کے لہجے میں برف جیسی ٹھنڈک تھی۔ عذیر کے لبوں کو جیسے قفل لگ گیا۔ کیا وہ لڑکی واقعی اتنی بے حس اور بے نیاز تھی کہ اسے ان سب کی محبتیں نظر ہی نہیں آ رہی تھیں؟ کیا واقعی وہ اتنی خود غرض تھی کہ مطلب نکلتے ہی اس گھر سے کوچ کر لینے کی ٹھان لی تھی؟ کیا مٹی کے اس ڈھیر سے اس کا عشق اتنا ہی شدید تھا کہ اس سے نکاح کو بھی فراموش کر گئی تھی اس کا دماغ اس لمحے جیسے سن ہو کر رہ گیا تھا۔

اس رات وہ ایک پل کے لیے بھی نہیں سو سکا تھا۔ کروٹیں بدل بدل کر تھک گیا تھا سر میں اتنا درد تھا کہ کسی کروٹ

قرار نہیں آ رہا تھا کتنی مشکل سے اس کا گھر سیٹ ہوا تھا اور اب سب کچھ پھر بکھرنے جا رہا تھا۔
بیڈ کے دوسرے کنارے پر لیٹی حورعین بھی جاگ رہی تھی مگر اس کا رت جگا عذیر پر عیاں نہیں تھا۔ صبح فجر کی نماز کے بعد وہ سویا تھا۔ دوبارہ ساڑھے آٹھ بجے کے قریب آنکھ کھلی تو حورعین کمرے میں نہیں تھی وہ سمجھا وہ پھر قبرستان گئی ہوگی۔ تبھی بے دل سا واش روم میں گھس گیا اندر کہیں اسے خود پر غصہ پر بھی آ رہا تھا کہ کیوں اسے قبرستان جانے کی اجازت دی۔ باتھ سے فارغ ہو کر کمرے سے باہر آیا تو سامنے ہی ڈائننگ ٹیبل کے قریب حورعین اس کی طرف پیٹھ کیے کھڑی تھی اور عمیر اس سے کہہ رہا تھا۔

''آپ جانتی ہیں آپی ہم سب آپ سے بہت پیار کرتے ہیں۔ زبیر تو آپ کے بغیر رہنے کا تصور بھی نہیں کر سکتا۔ پھر آپ ہمیں چھوڑ کر کیسے جا سکتی ہیں اگر آپ ہم میں سے کسی سے ناراض ہیں تو میں سب کی طرف سے معافی مانگتا ہوں، پلیز۔''

''وہ تو تم مانگو گے عمیر، کیونکہ مفت کے غلاموں کو کون ہاتھ سے جانے دیتا ہے ویسے بھی اب میں کروڑوں کی جائیداد کی مالک ہوں۔ لہٰذا محبت نہ بھی ہوئی تب بھی شو تو کرنی پڑے گی نا، اب بہتی گنگا میں ہاتھ دھونے کی خواہش کس کی نہیں ہوتی۔''

لفظ نہیں تھے کوئی چابک تھے جو عذیر اور عمیر دونوں کو اپنی کمر پر پڑتا ہوا محسوس ہوا تھا صد شکر کہ ابھی باقی لوگ بیدار نہیں ہوئے تھے وگرنہ نجانے ان کے دلوں پر کیا بیتتی؟ کیا واقعی اس لڑکی کے پاس ان کی محبت اور خلوص کی یہی قدر تھی؟ دکھ کی شدت سے اس کی آنکھوں کے گوشے نم ہو گئے تھے تاہم خود پر ضبط کرتے ہوئے وہ آگے بڑھا تھا اور حورعین کے سامنے آ کھڑا ہوا تھا۔

''آپ اپنی تیاری کر لیں، میں آفس جانے سے پہلے آپ کو آپ کے گھر ڈراپ کر دیتا ہوں۔''

حورعین کو اندازہ نہیں تھا کہ وہ پیچھے کھڑا ہوگا تبھی شاید وہ چونکی تھی۔

''جی ٹھیک ہے۔''

آزردہ سی سر ہلا کر وہ کمرے میں گھس گئی تھی۔ عذیر، عمیر کے دھواں دھواں سے چہرے پر ایک نظر ڈالنے کے بعد آگے بڑھ گیا۔ حورعین کمرے میں آ گئی سارا سامان یونہی بکھرا پڑا تھا۔ اس نے بیگ میں نمیر اور عمیر کے تحفے ڈالے سارا اکمرا اسمیٹا اور چادر لے کر چپ چاپ کمرے سے باہر نکل آئی صد شکر ابھی زبیر بیدار نہیں ہوا تھا۔

آج کی رات سازِ درد نہ چھیڑ
دکھ سے بھرپور دن تمام ہوئے
اور کل کی خبر کسے معلوم؟
اب نہ دہرا فسانہ دردِ الم
اپنی قسمت پر سوگوار نہ ہو
فکرِ فردا اتار دے دل سے
عمرِ رفتہ پر اشکبار نہ ہو
عہدِ غم کی حکایتیں مت پوچھ
ہو چکیں سب شکایتیں مت پوچھ
آج کی رات سازِ درد نہ چھیڑ

عذیر اسے اس کے محل کے سامنے اتار کر باہر سے ہی چلا گیا تھا۔ حورعین نے خود بھی اسے اندر آنے کی دعوت نہیں دی تھی۔ وہ بالکل چپ اور ساکت تھی بے جان ہاتھوں سے مین گیٹ کا لاک کھول کر جس وقت وہ اندر داخل ہوئی اس کے پاؤں من من کے بھاری ہو رہے تھے سارے گھر پر جیسے سکتہ چھایا تھا۔ محل جیسے گھر میں بدروح بنی تنہائی اس کا دل چیرے جا رہی تھی۔

وہ سارے گھر پر سرسری سی ایک نظر ڈالنے کے بعد لاؤنج میں صوفے پر پاؤں سمیٹ کر بیٹھ گئی۔ آنسو تھے کہ بنا رکے بہتے چلے جا رہے تھے۔ جانے زبیر نے اٹھنے کے بعد کیا ہنگامہ کیا ہوگا؟ جانے دادی ماں اور سمیر نے اس کے یوں چپ چاپ چلے آنے پر کیا رائے قائم کی ہوگی؟ سوچیں تھیں کہ ناگ بن کر ڈس رہی تھی۔

بہت دن لگے تھے اسے خود کو سنبھالنے میں اور وہ سنبھل گئی تھی مگر...... عذیر کے گھر کی یادیں ہزار کوشش کے باوجود اس کے دل و دماغ سے نکلنے کو تیار ہی نہ ہوتی تھیں۔ بار بار زبیر کا چہرہ نگاہوں کے حصار میں آتا اور نین کٹورے چھلک پڑتے، عذیر نے اس کے اس گھر میں آنے کے اگلے ہی دن ایک کل وقتی ملازمہ کا بندوبست کر کے اسے وہاں بھجوا دیا تھا۔ حورعین نے آفس جوائن کیا تو پیچھے کی تسلی ہوگئی۔

تسکین نامی وہ لڑکی بہت اچھی اور صاف ستھری اور قابل بھروسہ لڑکی تھی۔ عذیر کے احسانات کے بنڈل میں ایک اور احسان کا اضافہ ہوگیا تھا۔ جب سے حورعین اس کے گھر سے آئی تھی جیسے خانہ جنگی کا سا سماں پیدا ہوگیا تھا۔ سب اس سے ناراض تھے کہ اس نے حورعین کو کیوں جانے دیا۔ فی الوقت عمیر نے اس کا بھرم رکھ لیا تھا کہ یہ کہہ کر حورعین کی فیملی میں کوئی مسئلہ ہوگیا ہے لہٰذا ان لوگوں نے ایمرجنسی ایبروڈ بلوا لیا۔ مگر سب اپنی اپنی جگہ بے حد پریشان تھے۔ سب کی عادتیں بگڑ چکی تھیں۔ دوبارہ سے اسی روٹین پر آنا سب کے لیے ہی بے حد مشکل تھا۔

دادی ماں گاؤں سے واپس آئیں تو گھر کا نقشہ ہی بدلا ہوا تھا۔ زبیر تیز بخار میں پھنک رہا تھا سمیر نے مشین لگا رکھی تھی مگر اس کی جھنجلاہٹ اور غصہ دیکھنے سے تعلق رکھتا تھا۔ نمیر پیاز کاٹ رہا تھا مگر ساتھ ہی اس کی سمیر اور عمیر سے تو تو میں میں بھی چل رہی تھی۔ عمیر البتہ چپ تھا چپ چاپ بیٹھا ٹی وی دیکھتے ہوئے وہ جیسے سب کے اشتعال کو ہوا دے رہا تھا۔ وہ ہکا بکا ہی تو رہ گئی تھیں۔ عذیر رات گئے آفس سے واپس آیا تو بے حد تھکا ہوا تھا۔ ابھی اس نے جوتے بھی نہیں اتارے تھے کہ دادی اماں اس کے کمرے میں چلی آئیں۔

''عذیر۔''

''ارے دادو آپ، آپ کب آئیں؟''

''مجھے چھوڑ...... تو یہ بتا حورعین کب واپس آ رہی ہے؟'' اس کے چونک کر اٹھنے پر انہوں نے فوراً دوٹوک لہجے میں پوچھا تھا۔ عذیر بے ساختہ نظر چرا گیا۔

''پتا نہیں دادو، میرا رابطہ نہیں ہو رہا ہے اس سے۔''

''یہ کیا بات ہوئی ارے بیوی ہے وہ تمہاری، تمہیں رابطے میں رہنا چاہیے اس کے ساتھ، دیکھو ناں سارا گھر کیسے الٹ پلٹ ہوا پڑا ہے۔ ایسی بھی کیا ایمرجنسی ہوگئی تھی کہ دادی کے آنے کا انتظار بھی نہ کیا تم نے۔ ادھر زبیر کو دیکھو اس کے لیے رو رو کر بخار چڑھا لیا ہے اس نے اترنے کا نام ہی نہیں لے رہا۔''

''میں بات کروں گا دادو، آپ پریشان نہ ہوں۔''

''کیسے پریشان نہ ہوں، سارا گھر میدان جنگ بنا ہوا ہے۔ کہیں کوئی چیز بھی ٹھکانے پر نہیں مل رہی آج بھی سمیر کا جھگڑا ہوگیا تھا نمیر سے، گھر چھوڑ کر چلا گیا ہے وہ اسی کے لیے ابھی تک دل ہول رہا ہے۔ پتا نہیں کہاں گیا ہوگا وہ۔''

دادو نے اتنی رات گئے تک جاگنے کی وضاحت کر دی تھی۔ وہ گہری سانس بھر کر رہ گیا۔

''کہیں نہیں گیا ہوگا دادو' یہیں ہوگا اپنے کسی دوست کے پاس آپ جانتی تو ہیں اسے پلیز پریشان مت ہوں۔ آ جائے گا کل صبح۔'' پاؤں کو جوتوں کی قید سے آزاد کرنے کے ساتھ ہی دادی ماں کو تسلی دیتا وہ زبیر کے کمرے کی طرف چلا آیا تھا۔ جہاں وہ تیز بخار میں مدہوش صرف حورعین کو پکارے جا رہا تھا۔

پھول سا چہرہ کملا کر زرد پڑ گیا تھا۔ عذیر کا دل جیسے کسی نے مٹھی میں جکڑ لیا بھلا اس معصوم کا کیا قصور تھا کہ اسے ایسے سزا دی جاتی؟ ایک مرتبہ پھر حورعین کا چہرہ اس کے تصور میں آیا اور اس نے بے زاری سے سر جھٹک دیا۔ وہ لڑکی اس قابل بھی نہیں تھی کہ اسے تصور میں بھی یاد کیا جاتا۔ سوچا ہی جاتا' کتنی آسانی سے وہ اسے اور اس کے گھر والوں کو بے وقوف بنا کر' وہاں سے کوچ کر گئی تھی۔ کتنی آسانی سے اس نے اس کی شرافت اور اس کے گھر والوں کے بے لوث پیار کو لالچ کا نام دے دیا تھا۔

وہ جب جب بھی اس کے الفاظ کے بارے میں سوچتا تھا اس کا سر پھٹنے لگ جاتا۔ کتنی چالاک لڑکی تھی کہ سارے گھر کو اپنا عادی بنا کر چپکے سے چھوڑ گئی تھی اس کا بس نہ چلتا تھا وہ اس کے سامنے آئے اور اسے خوب کھری کھری سنا کر دل کی بھڑاس نکال لے۔

کچھ اسی طرح کے جذبات عمیر کے بھی تھے جسے وہ بے حد عزیز ہوگئی تھی۔ صرف اس کے بھرم کے لیے اس نے ابھی تک گھر کے کسی فرد کو اس کی حقیقت نہیں بتائی تھی۔ صرف اس کے تحفظ کے لیے اسی نے عذیر کو طلاق دینے سے روک رکھا تھا۔ وگرنہ زبیر کا حال دیکھنے کے بعد وہ اس سے کسی قسم کا کوئی تعلق رکھنا نہیں چاہتا تھا۔

سمیرا اور نمیر چونکہ حقیقت سے بے خبر تھے لہٰذا وہ اسے خوب یاد کر رہے تھے۔ عذیر آفس سے تھکا ہوا آتا تو گھر میں صرف اسی کا تذکرہ چل رہا ہوتا تھا۔ دادو کے پاس بھی سوائے اس کی تعریفوں کے اور کچھ کہنے کے لیے نہیں تھا۔ وہ بے زار سا چڑ کر اٹھ جاتا۔ اس وقت بھی وہ زبیر پر جانے کیا کیا پڑھ کر پھونک رہی تھیں۔ وہ انہیں آرام کی تلقین کرتا زبیر کو اٹھا کر اپنے کمرے میں لے آیا تھا۔

رات بھر ٹھنڈی پٹیاں کرنے کے باعث اگلے روز زبیر کی طبیعت کچھ بہتر تھی تبھی عذیر قدرے مطمئن سا آفس چلا آیا تھا۔

❁.......❁.......❁

سمیر نے اس شام کھانا باہر سے منگوالیا تھا۔ نمیر اور عمیر نے اس سے معذرت کر لی تھی وجہ صرف زبیر کی طبیعت اور عذیر کی اذیت تھی۔ کھانے سے فارغ ہونے کے بعد وہ تینوں ٹی وی لاؤنج میں آئے تو کوئی سیاسی پروگرام چل رہا تھا تبھی عمیر نے پوچھا تھا۔

''یار تم لوگوں کو کیا لگتا ہے۔ یہ ہمارے نیوز چینل واقعی پاکستانی ہیں؟''

''ہاں بظاہر......عملاً نہیں۔'' عمیر نے فوراً سے پیشتر جواب دیا۔

''کیوں' اب کیا کر دیا بے چارے چینل والوں نے؟'' سمیر فریج سے کینو نکال لایا تھا وہی چھیل رہا تھا۔ عمیر نے بھی ایک کینو اٹھالیا۔

''اب سے کیا مراد ہے آپ کی؟''

''میرا مطلب ہے جتنی ان کو اوپر سے اجازت ملی ہے اتنا تو دکھاتے ہی ہیں۔''

''کیا دکھاتے ہیں؟ یہ کہ فلاں سیاست دان کو فلاں سے کیسے لڑایا۔ فلاں کی کیسے سپورٹ کی اور فلاں کو کیسے زمین

چٹائی یا پھر یہ کہ وینا ملک نے انڈیا میں کیا کیا' شاہ رخ کی نئی فلم کون سی آنی ہے' مادھوری کی کیا مصروفیات ہیں۔ امریکا پاکستان کا کتنا خیرا خواہ اور سچا دوست ہے۔ افغانستان اور دنیا بھر کے سچے مجاہد کتنے بڑے دہشتگرد اور دنیا کے امن کے لیے خطرہ ہیں یا پھر یہ دکھاتے ہیں کہ ہمارے ملک کی سرحدوں کے اندر ڈرون سے مرنے والے سب لوگ کتنے برے تھے۔ کتنے بڑے دہشت گرد تھے۔'' عمیر اچھا خاصا جذباتی ہوگیا تھا۔

''میں جھوٹ نہیں کہہ رہا مگر یہ سچ ہے کہ ماضی کے حکمرانوں کے ساتھ ساتھ ہمارے میڈیا نے بھی ساری دنیا میں ہمارا سر شرم سے جھکانے میں کوئی کسر نہیں چھوڑی۔ کتنی ایسی حقیقتیں ہیں جو منظر عام پر آنی ضروری ہیں مگر...... پس پردہ وہ جانے کون سی ایسی مجبوریاں ہیں جس نے ان کے ہاتھ باندھ رکھے ہیں۔'' جذباتی ہونے کے ساتھ ساتھ وہ بے حد آزردہ بھی تھا۔ نمیر نے اس کے کندھے پر ہاتھ رکھ دیا۔

''صحیح کہہ رہے ہو اسی لیے میں نے تو ٹی وی دیکھنا ہی چھوڑ دیا ہے۔ جہاں تک میرا خیال ہے کسی بھی ملک کی معاشرت میں اس کے میڈیا کا کردار بہت اہم ہوتا ہے مگر افسوس یہ سعادت ہمیں نصیب نہیں جبکہ دوسری طرف ہمارے پڑوسی ملک کے میڈیا کو دیکھ لو۔ خبروں کے ذریعے یہ ساری دنیا سے جنگ کر رہے ہوتے ہیں۔ مجال ہے جو معمولی سی نفع نقصان کی خبر بھی ان کی نظر سے چوک جائے۔ مگر یہاں ساری مسلم دنیا میں پاکستان سمیت آگ لگی ہوئی ہے اور ہمیں پھر بھی شاہ رخ اور مادھوری کی فکر ستائے جارہی ہے۔''

''بس یار' جہاں آوے کا آوا ہی بگڑا ہوا ہو وہاں شور مچانے سے بھی کچھ حاصل نہیں' تم سناؤ وہ مصری صدر کا معاملہ کچھ حل ہوا کہ نہیں؟''

''کیسے حل ہوسکتا ہے' کس نے کرنا ہے حل۔'' سمیر کے پوچھنے پر عمیر نے تیکھے چتونوں سے اس کی طرف دیکھا تھا۔

''وہ صدر مرسی ہے' بشار الاسد نہیں جو ملکی عوام کی خون کی ندیاں بھی بہادے تو کوئی اس پر انگلی اٹھانے والا نہیں۔ عظیم سے عظیم تر صحابہ کی بے حرمتی کروا کر ان کے مبارک مزاروں سے مبارک اجسام نکلوا کر غائب کروا دے تو کوئی پوچھنے والا نہیں سنی مسلمانوں کو چن چن کر ان کے گھروں کے اندر ہی جلا کر بھسم کردے تو کوئی مسلمان حکمران اسے اُف نہیں کہہ سکتا۔ ابھی رات ہی دیکھ رہا تھا میں اس کی بدبخت افواج نے مجاہدین پر فاسفورس بم برسا کر انہیں شہید کر کے حضرت خالد بن ولیدؓ کے مزار مبارک کا بیشتر حصہ جلا کر شہید کردیا۔ اس سے پہلے حضرت احجر بن عدی رضی اللہ تعالیٰ عنہ کے مزار مبارک کو شہید کر کے ان کے جسم مبارک کو قبر سے نکال کر جانے کہاں منتقل کردیا۔ میں نے خود اپنی آنکھوں سے ان کا شہید مزار اور چہرہ مبارک دیکھا ہے فیس بک پر...... جبکہ صدر مرسی اللہ اور اس کے پیارے رسول محمد صلی اللہ علیہ وسلم کا پیروکار ہے۔ اس کا جرم وہ بیان ہے جو اس نے اقوام متحدہ میں کانفرنس کے دوران مسلمانوں کے حق میں دیا تھا اور یہ کہا تھا کہ ہم صرف اسی کی عزت کریں گے جو ہمارے پیارے رسول صلی اللہ علیہ وسلم کی عزت وحرمت کا خیال رکھے گا ان کی شان میں گستاخی کرنے والوں سے ہماری کھلی جنگ ہے۔ اس کا دوسرا جرم یہ تھا کہ اس نے مصر کی سرحدیں' دہشت گردی کی شکار فسلطینی ریاست کے لیے کھول دی تھیں۔ بنگلہ دیش کی طرح بھارت کے حکم پر ان کے لہولہان اجسام پکڑ کر دوبارہ اسرائیلی فوج کے سپرد نہیں کیے۔ جس طرح بنگلہ دیش کی افواج نے برما کے مظلوم مسلمانوں کے ساتھ کیا۔ اسی لیے تو ایک سال بعد ہی بھاری اکثریت سے کامیابی کے باوجود فوج ان کے اقتدار پر قابض ہوگئی۔''

''ہوں سنا ہے فوج کے کچھ بڑے بڑے مگرمچھوں کے اثاثے بھی بے نقاب کر کے وہ پیسے ملکی معیشت کے لیے وقف کیے تھے مرسی صاحب نے۔''

''ہوں' شاید یہ وجہ بھی تھی بہرحال امریکا اور اسرائیل کی تو چاندی ہوگئی ہے۔ چن چن کر' آپس میں لڑوا لڑوا کر

مسلمانوں کو بے موت مروائے جارہے ہیں۔"

"ہوں، اور پھر بھی یہ خواہش ہے ان کی کہ کہیں کوئی بغاوت سر نہ اٹھائے ان کے خلاف، مسلمانوں کے بچے بچے کو مروا کر، ہمارے صحابہ کی بے حرمتی کر کے ہماری عورتوں کی عزتیں پامال کر کے یہ چاہتے ہیں کہ ہم ان سے نفرت کا اظہار بھی نہ کریں۔ کیسی مضحکہ خیز خواہش ہے ان کی۔"

"صحیح کہہ رہے ہو یار، جو حاکم اپنے ملک کے شہریوں کو جان اور مال کا تحفظ ہی نہ دے سکے اس کی حکمرانی سے بہتر ہے بندہ کسی جنگل میں جا کر رہ لے۔" نمیر نے کہا تھا اور سمیر نے اس کی تائید میں سر ہلا کر دوسرا کینو اٹھا لیا تھا۔

"میں تو کہتا ہوں منتخب حکومت کو ایسا قانون بنانا چاہیے کہ فوج اقتدار میں آ ہی نہ سکے۔"

"اچھا اور اگر جمہوری منتخب حکومت خود ہی اچھی نہ ہو پھر......؟"

"پھر بھی جمہوریت کی ایک دن کی زندگی فوج کی سو سالہ حکومت سے بہتر ہے۔" سمیر کے پھر پر اس نے مزاحیہ انداز میں اپنا موقف پیش کیا تھا۔

"یار سچ پوچھو تو میرا دل شام اور مصر کے حالات پر بہت دکھی ہے۔ اسلام پسندوں کی حکومت کو ووٹ سے قبول نہ کر کے مسلمانوں کو تلوار اٹھانے پر مجبور کر دیا جاتا ہے اور پھر انہیں دہشت گرد کا خطاب بھی دے دیا جاتا ہے۔ حضور صلی اللہ علیہ وسلم نے فرمایا تھا جب اہل شام ہلاک ہو جائیں گے تو میری امت میں خیر نہ رہے گی۔ اب تم بتاؤ مسلمان کریں تو کیا کریں؟ جن بچوں کے باپ بے قصور ان کی آنکھوں کے سامنے شہید ہو رہے ہیں جن کی ماؤں، بہنوں، بیٹیوں کو سر عام بے آبرو کیا جا رہا ہے جن کے گھر تباہ کیے جا رہے ہیں کیا یہ کل کو ہتھیار نہیں اٹھائیں گے؟ اگر ایک سینٹر میں چند سو مرنے والے افراد کا بدلہ لاکھوں مسلمانوں کو گاجر مولی کی طرح کاٹ کر، پاؤں تلے کچل کر لیا جا رہا ہے تو کل کو یہ لوگ کیسے اپنے پیاروں کی موت پر خاموش بیٹھ جائیں گے۔ رشتوں کی آگ تو ایک جیسی ہی ہوتی ہے۔" سمیر کے چینل تبدیل کرنے پر عمیر نے بے حد سنجیدہ انداز میں کہا تھا۔

"چپ کرو عمیر، تم نے سنا نہیں دیواروں کے بھی کان ہوتے ہیں۔ کسی نے سن لیا ناں تو ایک سیکنڈ سے پہلے تم پر طالبان کے کسی گروہ کا ساتھ ہونے کا الزام لگا کر ملک بدر کر دیں گے۔" اس بار نمیر نے عمیر کی طرف جھکتے ہوئے طنزیہ لہجے میں کہا تھا۔ سمیر کے لبوں پر بھی مسکراہٹ بکھر گئی۔

"کر دیں، میں نہیں ڈرتا ان دنیاوی خداؤں سے "سپر پاور" صرف میرے رب کی ذات ہے اور میں صرف اس کی طاقت کو مانتا ہوں۔ بے شک اس کی طاقت کے سامنے یہ دنیا کے پہاڑ بھی چیونٹی کے برابر نہیں۔ تم نے دیکھا نہیں کیسے میرا رب سمندر کی باہنیں کھولتا ہے اور چلتے پھرتے لوگ بلند عمارتوں سمیت اس میں غرق ہو جاتے ہیں۔ زمین کا سینہ پھٹتا ہے اور دیکھتے ہی دیکھتے چند لمحوں میں ہزاروں لوگ اس کی پناہ میں سما جاتے ہیں یوں کہ جیسے کبھی دنیا میں آئے ہی نہیں تھے۔ بے شک ہر ظالم کے سامنے اس کے ظلم پر آواز اٹھانا ایمان کی نشانی ہے پیارے نبی صلی اللہ علیہ وسلم کا ارشاد مبارک ہے اور تم میں سے جو ظلم ہوتا دیکھے اسے ہاتھ سے روکنے کی کوشش کرے ہاتھ سے نہ روک سکے تو زبان سے روکے۔ زبان سے بھی نہ روک سکے تو کم از کم اپنے دل میں ضرور برا جانے مگر یہ کمزور ترین ایمان کی نشانی ہے۔"

"ہوں، بے شک۔" سمیر نے تائید میں سر ہلایا تھا۔ تبھی اسکرین پر نیوز میں نمیر کی نظر صدر مشرف پر جا پڑی۔

"لو بھئی، آ گئے آپ کے لیڈر صاحب اسکرین پر۔" کینو کی پھانک منہ میں ڈالتے ہوئے وہ مسکرایا تھا۔ جواب میں سمیر نے گھور کر اسے دیکھا۔

"یار تم لوگوں کو خوامخواہ اس شریف انسان پر تنقید کرنے کی عادت ہو گئی ہے بس، وگرنہ حقیقت کی نظر سے دیکھا جائے

تو یہ شخص اتنا برا لیڈر بھی نہیں تھا۔“

”اچھا کوئی کسر تھی جو ابھی رہ گئی تھی؟“ نمیر نے کینو سائیڈ پر رکھ کر ریموٹ اٹھالیا۔ تبھی سمیر بولا تھا۔

”جسٹ شٹ اپ یار، تم لوگوں کو پتا نہیں ہے اس شخص نے پاکستان کے لیے کیسے کیسے جرأت مندانہ فیصلے کیے تھے۔ نائن الیون کے بعد جس وقت امریکا نے پاکستان کو دھمکی دی تھی کہ یا راستہ دو یا جنگ کرو اس وقت اسلام آباد پر کتنی گھبراہٹ طاری تھی۔ کیا تھا اس وقت پاکستان کے پاس۔ میزائل ٹیکنالوجی تک ڈویلپ نہیں تھی۔ نیوکلیئر ہتھیاروں کے لیے کوئی ڈیلیوری سسٹم نہیں تھا۔ اگر صرف جنگی جہازوں کی بات کی جائے تو پاکستان کے پاس صرف سات سو یا آٹھ سو جنگی جہاز تھے امریکا اور اس کے اتحادیوں کے پاس تقریباً تیس ہزار کے قریب جنگی جہاز تھے۔ جو ایف سولہ کے لڑاکا طیارے ہم نے امریکا سے لیے تھے وہ بھی امریکا کی نظر میں کافی پرانے ہو چکے تھے۔ ہماری فوج جتنی بھی بہادر سہی مگر وہ زمین پر کیا کر لیتی؟ زیادہ سے زیادہ ہم ان کے کچھ جنگی جہاز مار گراتے اور بس تم لوگوں کو نہیں پتا اس وقت کیا صورتحال تھی روس اور چین شدت سے چاہتے تھے کہ امریکا افغانستان کی دلدل میں اترے اسی لیے پہلی بار اس معاملے میں چین پاکستان سے پیچھے ہٹ گیا تھا۔ انڈیا اور اسرائیل مسلسل امریکا کو پاکستان پر حملے کی دعوت دے رہے تھے۔ بلکہ انڈیا نے تو اس معاملے میں اپنے مکمل تعاون کا یقین بھی دلایا تھا پاکستان پر اس وقت ایک ایسی جنگ مسلط کی جارہی تھی جس میں کروڑوں پاکستانیوں کی اموات یقینی تھی۔“

”واہ......یعنی ہم نے اپنی جانیں بچانے کے لیے اپنے معصوم افغانی بھائیوں کے سر تحفتاً پیش کر دیے واہ......!“

”فضول بکواس مت کرو نمیر، افغانستان کے پاس اس وقت کھونے کے لیے کچھ نہیں تھا۔ یہاں تک کہ پورے افغانستان میں آٹے کی ایک مل بھی نہیں تھی۔ کل چھ جنگی ہیلی کاپٹر تھے جو اس وقت افغانستان کا کل اثاثہ تھے۔ مگر ان کو اڑنے کا موقع بھی نہیں ملا۔ دوسری طرف پاکستان ایک آبادی والا ایٹمی ملک تھا۔ جس کے پاس نیوکلیئر ہتھیار ہیں بہت سی صنعتیں ہیں ایک طاقت ور بہادر فوج ہے مگر وہ جنگ میزائل کی جنگ تھی وہاں 1965ء والے حالات نہیں تھے اگر ہم اس وقت کوئی بھی جذباتی فیصلہ کرتے تو پاکستان اور افغانستان دونوں کو نقصان اٹھانا پڑتا کیونکہ اڈے انہوں نے پھر بھی پاکستان کے بجائے افغانستان میں ہی بنانے تھے اور وہیں بیٹھ کر وہ لوگ اہم تنصیبات کو نشانہ بناتے انہوں نے سب سے پہلے نیوکلیئر پلانٹس، موٹر ویز، صنعتیں اور فوجی اڈے تباہ کرنے تھے۔ اس کے بعد ہمیں بھارت کے لیے تر نوالا بنا کر اس کے سپرد کر دیتے۔ اگر ایسا ہو جاتا تو سوچو آج افغانستان میں امریکا کی جو چیخیں مجاہدین نکلوا رہے ہیں وہ کیسے نکلتیں؟ جنرل صاحب نے حالات کی نزاکت کو دیکھتے ہوئے مشکل فیصلہ کیا۔ بالکل اسی طرح جیسے ماضی میں ہمارے دانش مند بزرگوں نے کیے بظاہر وہ دشمن کی شرائط کے مطابق ہوتے تھے مگر بعد میں ان کا نتیجہ فتوحات کی صورت میں نکلتا تھا۔ اس وقت اگر پاکستان اپنی فوجی طاقت ایک جذباتی فیصلے کی نذر کر دیتا تو آج افغانستان میں کوئی جہاد نہ ہوتا نہ ہی پاکستان اس قابل رہتا کہ اکیلے انڈیا سے ہی نپٹ سکے، تم لوگ نہ مانو مگر یہ حقیقت ہے کہ امریکا کی کمر مشرف نے توڑی ہے۔ اس کے دانش مندانہ فیصلے نے توڑی ہے، تم دیکھو جب پاکستان نے امریکا کو راستہ دیا تو اس کے ساتھ ہی طالبان کے کئی سرکردہ لیڈر منظر عام سے غائب ہو گئے بمعہ اسامہ بن لادن، بعد میں وہی آرمی کی گود سے برآمد ہوئے۔ ادھر امریکا نے افغانستان کے پہاڑوں سے سر ٹکرایا، مگر بعد میں کچھ ہی عرصے کے بعد طالبان کی مزاحمت شروع ہو گئی اور اب صورتحال یہ ہے کہ اس صلیبی جنگ نے امریکا کی چیخیں نکلوا دی ہیں۔ جس کے نتیجے میں اس کے جنگی اخراجات اتنے بڑھ چکے ہیں کہ معیشت بیٹھنے لگی ہے۔ اس لیے اس نے بہت سی سہولیات اپنی عوام سے واپس لے لیں ہیں جس کی وجہ سے کم از کم 26 ریاستیں اس سے الگ ہونے کی تیاری کر رہی ہیں۔“ سمیر اچھا خاصا جذباتی ہو گیا تھا عمیر مسکرا دیا۔

''ہوں، جیسی کرنی ویسی بھرنی، مگر یہ غلط ہے کہ طالبان لیڈرز کو پاکستان نے کسی قسم کی کوئی سپورٹ فراہم کی تھی۔''

''چلو غلط سہی، مگر یہ حقیقت ہے کہ امریکا کو راستہ دینے کے ساتھ ہی جنرل صاحب نے دنیا کی تاریخ کی تیز ترین میزائل ڈیولپمنٹ شروع کی۔ امریکا کے افغانستان پر حملے کے فوراً بعد ہر دوسرے تیسرے دن پاکستان ایک نیا میزائل تجزبہ کر رہا تھا۔ یہاں تک کہ ایک دن جنرل صاحب نے کہہ دیا کہ ہم انڈیا کے علاوہ بھی بہت سے ملکوں کو ہٹ کر سکتے ہیں۔ تم لوگوں کو نہیں پتا اس وقت امریکا میں کیسی تشویش کی لہر دوڑ گئی تھی کہ پاکستان انڈیا کے علاوہ اور کن ملکوں کو ہٹ کرنے کی بات کر رہا ہے۔ اسی وقت جنرل صاحب نے فرانس کے ساتھ مل کر آگسٹا آبدوز پراجیکٹ شروع کیا اور اس کی تکمیل کی یہ پراجیکٹ پاکستان کو سیکنڈ اسٹرائیک کیپبلیٹی دیتا ہے۔ مطلب اس میں میزائل فٹ کیے جا سکتے ہیں۔ حالت جنگ میں اگر دشمن آپ پر حملے میں پہل کر کے خدانخواستہ آپ کی ساری ایٹمی تنصیبات تباہ کر دے تو آپ دشمن پر سمندر سے حملہ کر سکتے ہیں۔ اگر آپ کا ایک بھی آبدوز سمندر میں پھر رہا ہو تو دشمن کبھی آپ پر حملے کی جرأت نہیں کر سکتا اور الحمدللہ ہمارے اس وقت تین آگسٹا آبدوز سمندروں میں راج کر رہے ہیں۔''

''بے شک، مگر محترم سمیر صاحب آپ کی معلومات میں اضافے کے لیے عرض ہے کہ آگسٹا آبدوز پراجیکٹ کا منصوبہ بی بی صاحبہ کا تھا۔''

''ہوگا، مگر تکمیل کس نے پہنچایا؟ تم دیکھو اس وقت ڈاکٹر عبدالقدیر خان پر کتنا دباؤ تھا۔ ساری دنیا میں یہ ثابت ہو چکا تھا کہ ڈاکٹر صاحب نے ایران، لیبیا اور شمالی کوریا کو ایٹمی معلومات اور سامان دیا ہے مگر اس کے باوجود جنرل صاحب نے انہیں امریکا کے حوالے نہیں کیا۔ یہی نہیں بلکہ آئی اے ای اے کی ڈاکٹر قدیر کے ساتھ ملاقات کی اپیل بھی مسترد کر دی۔ امریکا یا آئی اے ای اے نے ڈاکٹر صاحب کو سزا نہیں دینی تھی بلکہ وہ ان سے اہم نوعیت کی معلومات حاصل کرتے جس سے پاکستان سمیت ایران اور شمالی کوریا کا ایٹمی پروگرام خطرے میں پڑ جاتا۔ جنرل صاحب نے ہی مشکل حالات میں اسرائیل کو یہ لارہ دیا تھا کہ پاکستان اسے تسلیم کر لے گا۔ جس پر وہ خوش تھا کیونکہ اگر اسرائیل پاکستان میں اپنا سفارت خانہ بنا لیتا تو یہاں تباہی مچا دیتا مگر جیسے ہی حالات نم ہوئے انہوں نے فوراً اسرائیل کو تسلیم کرنے سے انکار کر دیا۔ جنرل صاحب نے ہی گوادر پروجیکٹ پر تیزی سے کام شروع کیا جو امریکا کی موت ہے۔ اس پروجیکٹ کی وجہ سے چین کو خلیجی ریاستوں تک امریکی دست برداری سے محفوظ راستہ مل جائے گا۔ جنرل صاحب کے دور حکومت میں ہی پہلی بار ایران کے ساتھ ہمارے تعلقات ٹھیک ہوئے اور گیس پائپ لائن کا منصوبہ بنا جس پر انڈیا کو بھی تقریباً قائل کیا جا چکا تھا۔ اگر یہ منصوبہ پایہ تکمیل تک پہنچ جاتا تو یہ پاکستان کی بہت بڑی کامیابی ہوتی۔ کیونکہ بھارت کی تقریباً چالیس فیصد ضروریات اس سے پوری ہونی تھیں۔ یوں اس کی ایک بڑی کمزوری ہمارے ہاتھ میں ہوتی جب وہ ادھر سے ہمارا پانی بند کرتا تب ہم ادھر سے اس کی گیس بند کر دیتے۔ مگر افسوس بعد میں آنے والی جمہوری حکومت نے اپنے جھگڑوں میں پڑ کر نہ صرف یہ معاملہ کھٹائی میں ڈال دیا بلکہ امریکا اور عربوں کو خوش کرنے کے لیے یہ باب ہی ہمیشہ کے لیے بند کر دیا۔''

''واہ، سمیر صاحب واہ، وکیل ہو تو کوئی آپ سا واہ......!'' سمیر کی لمبی چوڑی تقریر پر نمیر نے ہاتھ سے اس کا چہرہ چھو کر چومتے ہوئے اس کا مذاق اڑایا تھا تبھی عمیر بولا۔

''گستاخی معاف سمیر بھائی، میں آپ کی کسی بات سے اختلاف نہیں کروں گا۔ بے شک آپ کی ساری باتیں صحیح ہیں مگر جیسے کفر کا کلمہ کبیرہ گناہ ہے اس ای طرح کانسٹی ٹیوشن کو توڑنا بھی گناہ ہے۔ جنرل صاحب نے امریکا کے ساتھ کیا کیا، یا کیا کرنا تھا یہ الگ بحث ہے مگر ان کے دور حکومت میں جس طرح سے مساجد پر حملے ہوئے وہ کوئی مسلمان نہیں

بھول سکتا۔ اگر ہم کلمہ لا الہ الا اللہ محمد الرسول اللہ کی حدود سے نکل کر دیکھیں تو آپ کی ساری باتیں ٹھیک ہیں لیکن اگر میں اس کلمہ کی حدود میں رہ کر بات کروں تو آپ نے جو کچھ بھی کہا ہے سب غلط ہے۔ سب سے پہلے ہمارا کبیرہ گناہ کہ ہم نے خود اپنے کندھے پیش کیے اپنے ہی مسلمان بھائیوں کو مارنے کے لیے جبکہ ہم جانتے ہیں کہ شیر کی ایک دن کی زندگی گیدڑ کی سو سالہ زندگی سے بہتر ہے۔ اگر وہ لوگ کچھ نہ ہو کر بھی صرف اپنے زور بازو پر اللہ رب العزت کی مدد کے ساتھ امریکا کو ناکوں چنے چبوا سکتے ہیں تو ہم کچھ نہ کچھ ہو کر ایسا کیوں نہیں کر سکتے تھے؟ کیا جنگ واقعی صرف ہتھیاروں سے جیتی جاتی ہے؟ اگر ہاں تو پھر وہ کیا تھا جب اندلس کی سرزمین پر طارق بن زیاد صرف تین سو تیرہ سپاہی لے کر اترا تھا اور سامنے ہزاروں فوج اسلحہ سے لیس کھڑی تھی۔ پھر بھی اس مرد مجاہد کا کہنا تھا کہ کشتیاں جلا دو' کشتیاں جلا دو اور ٹھیک ہے اگر آپ کی بات کو صحیح مان بھی لیا جائے کہ اس وقت جنرل صاحب کا فیصلہ درست تھا تو کیا اس فیصلے کے بعد ہزاروں لاکھوں پاکستانی نہیں مرے؟ ٹڈیوں کی طرح ملک عزیز پر چھائی امریکی اور دیگر ممالک کی خفیہ ایجنسیوں نے لاکھوں پاکستانیوں کو خود کش حملوں اور دھماکوں میں نہیں مروایا؟ آپ کیا سمجھتے ہیں اگر ہمارا میڈیا ہر سانحے پر طالبان کی ذمہ داری کی مہر لگا کر دکھا دیتا ہے تو وہی سچ ہو جاتا ہے۔ پچھلے پندرہ سالوں میں وطن عزیز کی سرحدوں کے اندر کتنے معصوم اور بے گناہ لوگ کیا ڈرون حملوں میں نہیں مرے؟ طاقت ور بہادر فوج کے ہوتے ہوئے۔ سرحدوں کے رکھوالوں کی آنکھوں کے سامنے دشمن ڈرون پھینک پھینک کر ملک کے عام معصوم شہریوں کو مار رہا ہے اور یہ مجبور بے بس تماشائی بنے صرف دیکھتے رہ جاتے ہیں میں مانتا ہوں امریکا جب افغانستان میں گھسا تھا تو وہاں کوئی دیوار چین نہیں تھی بلکہ ایک لمبی سرحد تھی جس پر کنٹرول مشکل تھا مگر...... اس طویل سرحد کے اس پار سنگلاخ پہاڑوں کے شہزادے کیا کسی دیوار چین سے کم تھے؟ آپ نہیں جانتے مگر میں جانتا ہوں کہ امریکا کے افغانستان پر حملے کے وقت پاکستان کے تین ایئر بیسز سے چون ہزار جنگی فلائٹس افغانستان پر بمباری کے لیے اڑی تھیں۔ ڈیلی بیسز پر پندرہ سے بیس ہزار کنٹیز لاجسٹک سپورٹ لے کر افغانستان جاتے رہے جو ڈاکومینٹڈ ہے۔ اسلام آباد کی سات مساجد سیکیورٹی رسک کی بنا پر گرائی گئیں جن میں ایک مسجد جامعہ حمزہ جو ساڑھے سات سو سال پرانی تھی۔ لعل مسجد میں لاکھوں بے گناہ بچوں اور بچیوں کو نہایت درندگی کے ساتھ ناحق قتل کیا گیا۔ ان پر سخت گرمی میں بم برسائے گئے' گولیاں داغی گئیں' رینجرز اور آرمی سے آپریشن کروایا گیا' کیوں؟ کیا قصور تھا ان معصوم جانوں کا یہی کہ وہ اپنے اسلامی جمہوریہ ملک میں اسلامی نظام اور اسلام کا نفاذ چاہتے تھے؟ جنرل صاحب کے دورِ حکومت میں بلوچستان میں خانہ جنگی ہوئی اور بالآخر آزادی کی تحریک چل پڑی۔ انہی نے مسجدوں کی جگہ 6 امام بارگاہیں بنوائیں' پاکستان میں عریانی اور فحاشی کو فروغ دے کر اخلاقی اقدار کا جنازہ نکالا عورت کو غیر ضروری آزادی دے کر زنا بالرضا کو جائز قرار دیا۔ جس نے حق اور شریعت کی بات کی اسے سرعام شہید کروا دیا۔ انہی کے دور حکومت میں نا صرف ڈرون حملوں کا سلسلہ شروع ہوا بلکہ خود کش حملوں کی بنیاد بھی رکھی گئی بلوچوں کو علیحدگی کے قریب لا کھڑا کیا۔ کراچی کو گینگ وار کا اڈہ بنا دیا۔ ملک کے اندر جاگیرداروں کو ایک ایک ضلع تحفے میں دیا گیا، ججز کو نظر بند کیا اور ملک کے منتخب وزیر اعظم کو ملک بدر کیا۔ عوام کے بچے بچے کے دل میں آرمی کے لیے نفرت بھر دی' جمہوری لیڈر بے نظیر بھٹو اور اکبر بگٹی کی موت کا تاریخی تحفہ دیا۔ سی این جی مافیا کو پرموٹ کیا اور جہاں تک ایران کی بات ہے تو آپ کی معلومات میں اضافے کے لیے بتا دوں اپنے نو سالہ دور حکومت میں جنرل صاحب نے ایک بار بھی ایران کا دورہ نہیں کیا۔''

''عمیر' صحیح کہہ رہا ہے' انہی کے دور حکومت میں وطن عزیز کی بہادر اور غیور بیٹی ڈاکٹر عافیہ صدیقی ڈالروں میں بیچی گئی۔ نا صرف عافیہ بلکہ مذہبی نقطہ نظر رکھنے والے سینکڑوں مسلمانوں کو ان کے گھروں سے دن دہاڑے اٹھا لیا گیا۔ چند

سکوں کے عوض ملکی شہریوں کی منڈی لگا کر انہیں امریکا کے ہاتھوں فروخت کر دیا گیا۔ تمام تر قوانین کو پامال کر کے افغانستان کے سفیر کو امریکا کے حوالے کیا گیا۔ آپ کیا سمجھتے ہیں ان سب جرائم کے لیے کیا پاکستانی قوم کبھی انہیں معاف کر سکے گی؟'' اس بار نمیر نے سوال اٹھایا تھا سمیر خاموش بیٹھا لب چباتا رہا۔

''آپ کو نہیں پتا سمیر بھائی' افغانستان میں اس وقت بھارت بھی سیکیورٹی کے نام پر اپنے پر پھیلا رہا ہے۔ 107 جاسوسی سینٹر قائم کر چکا ہے۔ وہ وہاں جن میں اس کے قونصل خانے بھی شامل ہیں۔ اب صورتحال یہ ہے کہ بھارت وہاں سیکیورٹی کے نام پر افغانستان کے طالبان اور پاکستان کے طالبان کو آپس میں لڑانا چاہتا ہے۔ وہ چاہتا ہے کہ افغانستان اور پاکستان کے سرحدی علاقوں کے مابین کشیدگی پیدا کی جائے یوں وہ جنگ جو افغانستان میں لڑی جا رہی ہے وہ کھسکتی کھسکتی پاکستان کے قبائلی علاقوں تک آ جائے اور یوں پاکستان اور افغانستان ایک دوسرے سے دست و گریباں ہو جائیں۔ امریکا اور اس کے حامیوں کی خواہش ہے کہ آج کا تباہ حال افغانستان' کل کا برباد افغانستان ہو' افغانستان اور پاکستان کو دنیا میں کہیں بھی ہمدردی نہ ملے۔ مگر میں آپ کو بتا رہا ہوں جب تک ملک کی سیکیورٹی طالبان کو نہیں سونپی جائے گی طالبان کو افغانستان کا شہری تسلیم نہیں کیا جائے گا افغانستان میں امن و سکون بحال نہیں ہوگا۔ یہی صورت حال پاکستان کے لیے بھی بہت ضروری ہے کہ پاکستان کے قبائلی علاقے کے عوام کو اعتماد میں لیا جائے کیونکہ یہ اس خطے کی بہت بڑی حقیقت ہے یہ ہمارے ملک کی طویل سرحدوں کے بلاتنخواہ محافظ ہیں۔ اب بھی اگر ہم نے حقائق کو سمجھنے میں دیر کی تو سانپ اپنا کام کر کے نکل جائے گا اور ہم بس لکیر پیٹتے رہ جائیں گے۔''

نمیر جذباتی ہوا تھا۔ تبھی سمیر گہری سانس بھرتا اٹھ کھڑا ہوا۔

''چلو یار' رات بہت ہوگئی ہے اٹھو اب...... صبح مجھے اپنی جاب کے لیے انٹرویو دینے بھی جانا ہے۔''

اسے نیند آ رہی تھی سمیر کے ساتھ ہی نمیر اور عمیر بھی اٹھ کھڑے ہوئے۔

''جی ٹھیک ہے شب بخیر۔''

ٹی وی آف کر کے تینوں اپنے اپنے کمروں کی طرف بڑھ گئے تھے۔ اگلی صبح سمیر نے ذرا جلدی ناشتا بنالیا تھا کیونکہ اسے اپنی جاب کے لیے انٹرویو دینے جانا تھا۔ عذیر نے اسے اپنی کمپنی میں کام کی آفر کی تھی مگر اس نے انکار کر دیا تھا۔ لہٰذا اب وہ دوسری بڑی بڑی کمپنیوں میں اپلائی کر رہا تھا۔

صبح گھر سے نکلتے ہوئے اس نے سب سے اپنے لیے دعا کرنے کا بھی کہا تھا۔ انٹرویو کے لیے جس وقت اس کا نام پکارا گیا وہ بہت پر اعتماد تھا مگر انٹرویو پینل کے سامنے سیٹ سنبھالنے کے بعد جیسے ہی اس کی نظر سامنے بیٹھی حورعین عبدالسمیع پر پڑی وہ جیسے حیران رہ گیا۔ عمیر اور عذیر کے بقول تو وہ دیار غیر چلی گئی تھی پھر اس وقت وہاں اس کے سامنے کون بیٹھا تھا؟

''ایکسکیوزمی...... میرا خیال ہے میں غلط جگہ پر انٹرویو دینے آ گیا ہوں۔'' کچھ ہی لمحوں کے بعد کرسی کھسکاتے ہوئے وہ اٹھ کھڑا ہوا تھا۔ حورعین سمیت اس کے دائیں بائیں بیٹھے افسران اس کی حرکت پر حیران ہی تو رہ گئے تھے مگر وہ بنا کسی کی حیرانی کی پروا کیے اس پر شکوہ عمارت سے نکلتا چلا گیا تھا۔

✿ ...... ✿ ...... ✿

سنا ہے اس محبت میں بڑا نقصان ہوتا ہے
مہکتا جھومتا جیون' غموں کے نام ہوتا ہے
سنا ہے چین کھو کر بھی

بہت برباد ہو کر بھی
یہ دل اک ضدی سا بچہ، سحر سے شام روتا ہے
محبت جو بھی کرتا ہے بہت بدنام ہوتا ہے
سنا ہے اس محبت میں کہیں بھی دل نہیں لگتا
بنا اس کے نگاہوں میں کوئی موسم نہیں جچتا
خفا جس سے محبت ہو وہ جیون بھر نہیں ہنستا
بہت انمول ہے یہ دل اجڑ کر پھر نہیں بستا!

موسم بے حد خوب صورت ہو رہا تھا۔
زائر بچوں کو کھیتوں کی سیر کروانے لے آیا۔ دونوں کی رگوں میں اپنے دیہاتی باپ کا خون تھا اسی لیے اپنی مٹی سے محبت ان کے خون میں رچی ہوئی تھی۔ جب سے وہ زائر کے ساتھ گاؤں آئے تھے بے حد خوش تھے۔ ان دو پھولوں کی وجہ سے اس کی ماں اور باپ کی زندگی میں بھی جیسی بہار آ گئی تھی۔
زائر کی فصل بہت اچھی ہوئی تھی مگر ہر سال کی طرح اس کے برابر والے زمیندار کو پھر نقصان اٹھانا پڑا تھا۔ تنگ آ کر اس نے اپنی زمین بہت اچھے داموں پر زائر کے ہاتھ ہی فروخت کر دی تھی اور اب اللہ کے فضل سے اس پر پہلے سے بھی زیادہ دھن برس رہا تھا۔ دو سال پہلے اس نے گھر والوں سے چوری شہر میں ایک کنال کا پلاٹ لیا تھا اور اب پچھلے دو سال سے وہاں گھر کی تعمیر ہو رہی تھی گھر کیا تھا خوابوں کا محل تھا زائر ملک کے لیے کروڑوں روپے لگ گئے تھے مگر ابھی تک اس کی تعمیر مکمل نہیں ہو سکی تھی۔
کرم دادا سے خوش دیکھ کر بہت خوش تھا۔ مگر اس کے بچے اس سے زیادہ خوش تھے۔ ہلکی ہلکی پڑتی پھوار میں وہ کبھی درختوں پر چڑھتے، کبھی ٹیوب ویل کے پانی میں کود کر ایک دوسرے پر پانی ڈالتے، کبھی فصلوں میں چھپ کر لکا مٹی کھیلتے کبھی اشتیاق سے کھڑے ہو کر گڑ بنتے ہوئے دیکھتے، کبھی فصل کی چنائی دیکھ کر خوش ہوتے پورا گاؤں ان بچوں سے نہ صرف پیار کرتا تھا بلکہ زائر کی وجہ سے ان کی عزت بھی کرتا تھا۔
یہ زائر کی محنت، دیانت اور شرافت ہی تھی کہ وہ ایک معمولی کسان سے آج اسی گاؤں کا نہ صرف بڑا زمیندار بن گیا تھا بلکہ ان نمبردار بھی نامزد ہو رہا تھا۔ پچھلے دنوں بچوں کی سیر و تفریح کے لیے اس نے نئی موٹر سائیکل بھی لے لی تھی۔ مغرب کی اذان سے ذرا سے سی دیر پہلے وہ گھر واپس آیا تو دونوں بچے تھکن سے بے حال تھے۔
سائرہ نے ہنڈیا بنالی تھی اور اب تندور پر روٹی لگا رہی تھی۔ وہ منہ ہاتھ دھو کر بچوں کے ساتھ اماں کی چارپائی پر آ بیٹھا۔
''ابا کی طبیعت اب کیسی ہے اماں؟''
''اللہ سوہنے کا شکر ہے، اب تو بھلے چنگے ہیں، تیرے ان دو ننھے منے ڈاکٹروں نے علاج کیا ہے ان کا تو کیوں بھلے چنگے نہیں ہوں گے۔'' اماں مسکرا رہی تھیں وہ خوش ہو گیا۔
''کچھ پتا ہے کل یہ تیرا چاندا اپنے دادا سے کیا کہہ رہا تھا۔'' اماں کو اچانک چاند کی بات یاد آ گئی تھی۔
''کیا کہہ رہا تھا؟'' تولیے سے چہرہ پونچھ کر زائر نے پھر اماں کی طرف دیکھا۔
''کہہ رہا تھا دادا جی کبوتر پالنے ہیں چھت پر، دونوں مل کر اڑایا کریں گے۔'' بات مکمل کرنے کے ساتھ ہی وہ دوپٹا منہ پر رکھ کر ہنسنے لگی تھیں۔ زائر کے لبوں پر مسکراہٹ دوڑ گئی۔

''موروثی اثرات بھی تو ہوتے ہیں نا اماں آپ کو یاد نہیں میں دن بھر چھت پر چڑھا سارا سارا دن کبوتر اڑایا کرتا تھا اور آپ ڈانٹتی رہ جاتی تھیں۔''

''ہوں' یاد ہے سب یاد ہے ساری شرارتیں یاد ہیں تیری۔ مگر بیٹا بھی کچھ کم شرارتی نہیں ہے تیرا۔''

وہ مسکرا مسکرا کر اسے چاند کی شرارتیں بتا رہی تھیں۔ زائر نے چاند کو گود میں بھر لیا۔

''زائر پتر۔'' اچانک وہ سنجیدہ ہو گئی تھیں۔

''جی اماں۔'' وہ بھی سنجیدگی سے ان کی طرف متوجہ ہوا تھا۔

''کچھ بات کرنی تھی تجھ سے۔''

''حکم کر اماں۔'' اس کا دل دھڑکا تھا مگر پھر بھی وہ ان کی طرف متوجہ رہا تھا۔ اماں بھی کچھ دیر خاموش رہنے کے بعد بولی تھیں۔

''کل رشتہ آیا تھا ایک سائرہ کے لیے یہ ساتھ والے پنڈ کے ماسٹر فضل الٰہی کا بیٹا ہے اسلم' سلجھا ہوا شریف بچہ ہے گاؤں میں اپنی کریانے کی دکان بھی ہے اس کی۔ پھر اس کی ماں خود چل کر آئی تھی۔ بڑی پسند ہے سائرہ اسے مگر یہ نہیں مان رہی۔ کہتی ہے ساری زندگی آپ کے پاس رہ کر آپ کی خدمت کروں گی اگر کہیں اور شادی کی بات کی تو کچھ کھا کر مر جاؤں گی۔''

''تو...... آپ یہ سب مجھے کیوں بتا رہی ہیں؟'' ایک پل میں اس کا چہرہ تنا تھا اماں نے نظریں پھیر لیں۔

''تجھ سے نہ کہوں تو کس سے کہوں اور کون ہے میرا اپنا تو ہے تجھے وہ تیرا جوگ لے کر بیٹھی ہے۔ میں اور تیرے ابا بھی یہی چاہتے ہیں کہ وہ یہیں رہ جائے اسی گھر میں۔''

''مگر میں ایسا نہیں چاہتا اماں۔''

''کیوں نہیں چاہتا' تجھے کیا مسئلہ ہے دولت کی ریل پیل ہے' چھڑا چھانٹ ہے۔''

''گھر بسانے کے لیے صرف چھڑا چھانٹ ہونا ضرور نہیں ہے اماں' نہ ہی دولت کی ریل پیل ضروری ہوتی ہے وہ اور دن تھے جب اسی سائرہ کو پانے کے لیے تیرے ترلے کیا کرتا تھا اب وہ دن نہیں رہے اماں نہ ہی وہ دل رہا ہے۔''

''پاگل نہ بن زائر' گھر کی لڑکی ہے دیکھی بھالی ہے دیکھ نہیں رہا تو کیسے سارا گھر سنبھال رکھا ہے تیرا۔''

''نہ سنبھالے مجھے پروا نہیں ہے۔ میں بھی گھر کا لڑکا تھا۔ دیکھا بھالا تھا پیار کرتا تھا اس سے' صرف اسی کے لیے شہر ڈاکہ مارنے گیا تھا۔ وہ بھی اپنی جان ہتھیلی پر رکھ کر مگر پھر بھی اس نے تیرے بیٹے کو ٹھکرا دیا تھا۔ اس جرم کے لیے ٹھکرا دیا تھا مجھے جس میں میرا کوئی قصور بھی نہیں تھا۔ تو وہ دن بھول سکتی ہے اماں' میرے دل پر لکھے ہیں میں نہیں بھول سکتا۔ اگر اس وقت اس سے حسین سارے گاؤں میں کوئی نہیں تھا تو اب بھی کوئی نہیں ہے میں کل بھی کچھ نہیں تھا آج بھی نہیں ہوں۔ ویسے بھی میری اپنی بیوی ہے' بچے ہیں ہمارے درمیان کچھ غلط فہمیاں ضرور ہیں مگر وہ مجھ سے الگ نہیں ہے۔ نہ ہی میں کرنا چاہتا ہوں' پلیز۔'' از حد جذباتی ہوتے اس نے دل کی بات کہہ دی تھی۔

سائرہ چپ چاپ کھڑی سنتی رہ گئی۔ تندور میں لگی روٹی جل کر راکھ ہو گئی تھی مگر اسے خبر نہ ہو سکی اگر زائر اپنی ضد کا پکا تھا تو وہ بھی اپنی ضد کی پکی تھی اور یہ زائر کو بھی پتا تھا کہ وہ جس بات کی ضد کر لیتی تھی اسے پھر حاصل کر کے ہی رہتی تھی۔ زائر چھت پر جا چکا تھا وہ پرسوچ انداز میں تندور کے اوپر کھڑی جانے کیا کیا پلان بناتی رہی۔

✿ .... ✿ .... ✿

ثانیہ عباس اشعر حسن کے ساتھ گاؤں سے شہر شفٹ ہو چکی تھی۔ زائر ملک اگر بچوں کو اس سے چھین کر اسے کمزور ہوتا

دیکھنا چاہتا تھا تو وہ کبھی بھی اس کی یہ خواہش پوری کرنے والی نہیں تھی۔

اشعر نے اس کے لیے بہت اچھا گھر ہائیر کیا تھا۔ آفس بھی بہت اچھی جگہ پر سیٹ کیا گیا تھا۔ وہ بہت خوش تھی اور خوش کیوں نہ ہوتی اشعر اس کی ہر فرمائش ہونٹوں سے نکلنے سے پہلے پوری کرتا تھا۔ اس کی ہر خوشی اور کامیابی میں وہ اس کے ساتھ ساتھ تھا۔ ثانیہ کو حیرت ہوتی تھی بھلا اس کی بیوی زنیرہ نے اتنے اچھے انسان کی قدر کیوں نہیں کی تھی۔ مگر اگلے ہی پل اسے اپنا خیال آتا تو دکھ سے مسکرا دیتی۔

وہ بھی تو بہت اچھی تھی۔ اپنے آپ کو مٹی بنا لیا تھا۔ اس نے زائر ملک کے لیے جس رنگ میں اس نے ڈھالنا چاہا اسی رنگ میں ڈھل گئی تھی پھر بھی...... پھر بھی وہ اس کی وفا نہیں پا سکی تھی۔ کیا کیا زیادتیاں نہیں کی تھیں اس شخص نے اس کے ساتھ‘ کس کس انداز میں نہیں ستایا تھا۔ مگر پھر بھی وہ اسے دل و دماغ سے نکال نہیں پائی تھی۔

اگر اتنی وفا کے باوجود وہ بے مراد تھی تو اشعر حسین کو مراد کیسے مل سکتی تھی یکخلت ہی اسے اشعر حسین پر بڑا ترس آیا تھا اور خود پر بے پناہ غصہ بھی اس نے کیوں اسے ٹھکرا کر پاکستان کی راہ لی نہ وہ پاکستان آتی نہ زائر ملک ملتا نہ اس کی زندگی اور دل برباد ہوتے مگر سارے معاملات انسان کے اختیار میں کہاں ہوتے ہیں۔ جتنا بھی طاقت ور انسان ہو تقدیر اور دل کے فیصلوں کے سامنے ہمیشہ بے بس ہی ہوتا ہے سو وہ بھی بے بس تھی۔

اشعر حسین کسی پارٹی میں گیا ہوا تھا جبکہ وہ اپنے کمرے میں مقید بیڈ پر دونوں پاؤں سمیٹ کر بیٹھی بس روئے جا رہی تھی۔ جانے کیوں اس لمحے اسے تنہائی کا احساس بہت شدت سے ستا رہا تھا چاند اور گڑیا کی یاد بھی بے قرار کر رہی تھی۔ وہ دونوں ہی اس وقت اسے بہت یاد آ رہے تھے مگر وہ کچھ نہیں کر سکتی تھی۔

اگلے ہفتے تک اس نے خود کو بہت مصروف کر لیا تھا۔ اشعر حسین کی اپنی مصروفیات تھیں۔ اکثر رات گئے ہی وہ گھر واپسی کی راہ لیتا تھا کبھی فارغ ہوتا تو ثانیہ کو گھمانے لے جاتا۔ کبھی شاپنگ اور کبھی ڈنر کے لیے لے جاتا‘ اس کی کوشش تھی کہ جلد از جلد وہ ثانیہ عباس کے ساتھ شادی کے بندھن میں بندھ جائے اسی لیے اس نے ڈائمنڈ کی رنگ خرید کر ثانیہ کی انگلی میں پہنا دی تھی۔ دونوں ہی آج کل اپنی شادی کی تیاریوں میں بے حد مصروف تھے۔

ثانیہ کا کاروبار تقریباً سیٹ ہو چکا تھا۔ اشعر حسین کے تعاون کی وجہ سے وہ اس پر اندھا اعتبار کرنے لگی تھی۔ بزنس بھی تقریباً اسی کے ہاتھ میں تھا۔ اس روز بھی وہ اس کے ساتھ کسی پارٹی میں شرکت کے لیے نکلی تھی۔ سلیولیس شارٹ شرٹ پر کھلے پائنچوں والا ٹراؤزر اس کے سراپے کو چار چاند لگا رہا تھا۔ مگر پھر بھی وہ اداس تھی۔ اجنبی شہر کے شناسا راستے اسے کوئی بھی خوشی دینے میں ناکام تھے۔

پارٹی میں اشعر اسے یونہی متعارف کروا رہا تھا جیسے وہ کوئی ماڈل ہو‘ بے باک نگاہوں میں اس کے لیے ستائش ہی ستائش تھی مگر کتنی عجیب بات تھی کہ اسے یہ ستائش اچھی نہیں لگ رہی تھی۔ اس ستائش کے بدلے وہ تھپڑ جو چند روز قبل زائر نے اسے اشعر حسین کے سنگ پھرنے پر مارا تھا۔ اسے بے حد اچھا لگا تھا۔ ہر تعلق توڑ نے لینے کے باوجود وہ شخص اس کی عزت پر کوئی سمجھوتا نہیں کر رہا تھا۔ جبکہ اشعر حسین جس کے ساتھ اس کا اتنا اہم رشتہ جڑنے جا رہا تھا۔ اسے اس کی کوئی پروا ہی نہیں تھی۔

اسے حیرت ہو رہی تھی کہ وہ اتنی دقیانوسی کیوں ہو رہی ہے۔ پانچ ٹائم نماز پڑھنے کے باوجود اس نے تو کبھی ایسی بات کو کوئی اہمیت ہی نہیں دی تھی۔

رات جس وقت وہ لوگ گھر واپس لوٹے‘ کافی ٹائم ہو گیا تھا۔ ثانیہ سونا چاہتی تھی مگر اشعر کا ایسا کوئی پروگرام نہیں تھا۔ وہ بے حد خوش اور فریش تھا۔ آج پارٹی کے دوران اس نے دو لوگوں سے ثانیہ کی بزنس کے حوالے سے اہم ملاقات

کروائی تھی۔ اگر ثانیہ ان دونوں میں سے کسی ایک کے ساتھ بھی ڈیل فائنل کر دیتی تو اس کے وارے نیارے ہو جاتے۔ اپنے سامنے شراب کی بوتل دھرے وہ اسے جانے کیسے کیسے خواب دکھا رہا تھا۔ ثانیہ کی آنکھیں نیند سے بوجھل ہو رہی تھیں۔ خود اشعر کے اعصاب پر بھی نشہ اثر کر رہا تھا۔ اسی نشے میں وہ اٹھ کر اس کے پہلو میں صوفے پر آ بیٹھا تھا۔ اس کا ایک ہاتھ ثانیہ کے کندھوں کے گرد تھا جسے نیند کے غلبے کی وجہ سے اس نے محسوس ہی نہیں کیا۔

''ثانیہ۔'' اچانک اس کے کندھوں پر دباؤ بڑھاتے ہوئے اس نے اسے پکارا تھا۔

''ہوں۔''

''آج تم بہت پیاری لگ رہی ہو، قسم سے۔'' اپنا منہ اس کے بالوں میں گھساتے ہوئے اس نے سرگوشی کی تھی۔

ثانیہ کو لگا اس کے سارے وجود پر بچھو رینگنا شروع ہو گئے ہوں۔

''دیکھو، رات بھی کتنی حسین ہوتی جا رہی ہے۔ بالکل تمہاری طرح، بہت پاگل تھا وہ دیہاتی جس نے تم جیسے انمول ہیرے کو کھو دیا، قسم سے۔'' اس کا ہاتھ حرکت میں آ چکا تھا ثانیہ کی نیند بھک سے اڑ گئی۔ بے ساختہ اس لمحے اسے اپنی دادی کی تنبیہ پر اپنے الفاظ یاد آئے تھے۔

''اوہ فو دادی یہ سب دقیانوسی باتیں ہیں جس ملک سے میں آئی ہوں وہاں ایسی چھوٹی موٹی باتیں کوئی اہمیت نہیں رکھتیں۔'' کیا واقعی وہ اتنی ہی بے باک اور آزاد منش لڑکی تھی کہ اپنی عزت و حرمت کے بارے میں کوئی بات اس کے لیے اہمیت نہیں رکھتی تھی۔

ایک لمحے سے پہلے اس نے اشعر حسین کا ہاتھ پرے جھٹکا تھا۔

''مجھے نیند آ رہی ہے، سو جاؤ تم بھی۔''

''اوکم آن ثانی...... ہماری شادی ہونے والی ہے پلیز بیٹھو۔'' وہ ابھی اٹھ بھی نہ پائی تھی کہ اشعر نے اس کا ہاتھ کھینچ کر اسے اپنے اوپر گرا لیا۔ ثانیہ کو لگا جیسے اس کے سارے وجود پر چیونٹیاں رینگنے لگی ہوں۔

''اشعر پلیز، بہتر ہوگا اگر تم اپنی حد میں رہو۔'' غم و غصے سے وہ کپکپا اٹھی تھی۔ مگر اشعر حسین نے پروا نہیں کی۔

''حد...... کون سی حد؟ پلیز ثانی ہماری شادی ہونے والی ہے کیا فرق پڑتا ہے اگر......!''

''جسٹ شٹ اپ۔'' اشعر حسین کی بات پوری ہونے سے پہلے ہی وہ دھاڑی تھی اور ایک جھٹکے سے خود کو چھڑواتے ہوئے سیڑھیاں چڑھ آئی۔ اس رات بہت دیر تک وہ جاگتی رہی تھی اور روتی رہی تھی۔

اگلی صبح اشعر اس کے بیدار ہونے سے قبل ہی اٹھ کر ناشتا تیار کر چکا تھا۔ وہ خاصی تاخیر سے اٹھ کر نیچے آئی تو سامنے ہی اشعر بیٹھا اس کا انتظار کر رہا تھا۔

''گڈ مارننگ۔'' وہ شرمندہ دکھائی دے رہا تھا۔ ثانیہ محض سر کے اشارے سے جواب دیتی ٹیبل کے قریب آ گئی۔

''ناراض ہو؟'' ثانیہ کے چہرے پر غصہ عود آیا۔

''تمہیں کیا لگتا ہے کل رات جو حرکت تم نے میرے ساتھ کی اس کے بعد مجھے تم سے ناراض نہیں ہونا چاہیے۔''

''ایم سوری ثانیہ' آئی سوئر مجھے بالکل ہوش نہیں تھا کہ میں کیا کر رہا ہوں۔ سمجھو رات نشے نے مت مار رکھی تھی۔ پلیز معاف کر دو' تم اچھی طرح سے جانتی ہو کہ میں ایسا نہیں ہوں۔'' وہ شرمندہ تھا ثانیہ کی پیشانی کی سلوٹیں کم پڑ گئیں۔

''اٹس اوکے' مگر میں نے فیصلہ کیا ہے جب تک ہماری شادی نہیں ہو جاتی ہم اکٹھے نہیں رہیں گے۔''

چائے دانی سے کپ میں چائے انڈیلتے ہوئے اس نے اسے اپنے فیصلے سے آگاہ کیا تھا۔ اشعر کے چہرے کا رنگ جیسے ایک دم پھیکا پڑ گیا۔

''ٹھیک ہے جو تم مناسب سمجھو' میں تو پہلے بھی صرف تمہاری خوشی کے لیے ہی یہاں رہ رہا تھا۔''

''تھینک یو۔''

''چلو جلدی سے ناشتا کرو پھر شاپنگ کے لیے نکلتے ہیں آج برائیڈل ڈریس بھی خریدنا ہے' سچ میں ثانیہ میں بہت ایکسائٹڈ ہو رہا ہوں۔ تم سوچ بھی نہیں سکتیں میرے دل میں تمہارے لیے کتنی عزت اور محبت ہے اگر تم اس پینڈو سے شادی کی حماقت نہ کرتیں تو آج ہم دونوں ایک بے حد آسودہ زندگی بسر کر رہے ہوتے۔'' اب وہ اپنے لیے چائے نکال رہا تھا۔ ثانیہ محض اثبات میں سر ہلا کر رہ گئی۔ جانے کیوں پھر سے زائر کے ذکر نے اس کے دل میں چٹکی کاٹی تھی۔

تقریباً چالیس منٹ کے بعد وہ اشعر حسین کے ساتھ اپنی شادی کی فائنل شاپنگ کر رہی تھی۔ آج موسم میں ہلکی سی تمازت تھی۔ دھوپ اتنی شدید نہیں تھی کہ چبھتی مگر اسے چبھ رہی تھی جانے ایک رات میں ہی کیا ہوا تھا کہ اس کا دل بجھ کر رہ گیا تھا۔ شاپنگ کے بعد مارکیٹ سے واپسی پر اس نے گاڑی گاؤں کے راستے پر ڈال دی تھی۔ اشعر راستے میں ہی اتر گیا تھا۔ حویلی پہنچی تو چوہدرانی جیسے اسی کا انتظار کر رہی تھیں۔

''ست بسم اللہ...... میری دھی کو حویلی یاد آ ہی گئی؟'' وہ بڑے سے صحن میں بیٹھی کبوتروں کو دانا ڈال رہی تھیں۔ ثانیہ لبوں پر پھیکی سی مسکان سجائے چپ چاپ ان کی گود میں سر رکھ کر لیٹ گئی۔

''میں چاہوں بھی تو حویلی سے اپنا تعلق ختم نہیں کر سکتی دادو' میرے بابا کی خوشبو بسی ہے ان در و دیوار میں......'' بہت عرصے کے بعد اپنے باپ کا ذکر کرتے ہوئے وہ آبدیدہ ہوئی تھی۔ چوہدرانی کی آنکھیں بھی بھر آئیں۔

''ہوں یہ تو ہے انسان چلے جاتے ہیں مگر...... در و دیوار سے ان کی خوشبو ہمیشہ آتی رہتی ہے۔''

''جانتی ہوں دادو' شاید اسی لیے آپ یہ حویلی چھوڑنے پر آمادہ نہیں ہوتیں۔'' آنسو صاف کرتے ہوئے اگلے ہی پل

وہ اٹھ بیٹھی تھی۔ دادو نے سر جھکا لیا۔

''سچ کہتی ہو ثانیہ، تم یقین نہیں کرو گی مگر میں ہر روز یہیں اس حویلی میں تمہارے دادا جی تمہارے بابا تایا سب کو دیکھتی ہوں کبھی یہاں جامن کے اس پیڑ تلے، تو کبھی وہاں مردان خانے کے اس طرف کئی بار سوتے سے جگایا ہے انہوں نے مجھے۔'' سر جھکائے اسے بتاتے ہوئے وہ بھیگی آنکھوں کے ساتھ مسکرا اٹھی تھیں۔ ثانیہ کے لبوں پر بھی مسکراہٹ بکھر گئی۔

''رکو گی کچھ دن؟'' اگلے ہی پل وہ اس سے پوچھ رہی تھیں۔

''نہیں دادو، اشعر نے شادی کی تیاری مکمل کر لی ہے شاید اسی ہفتے ہم شادی کے بندھن میں بندھ جائیں۔ اسی لیے بہت سے کام ہیں جو ابھی کرنے باقی ہیں۔ کارڈز بھی پرنٹ کروانے ہیں، میرج ہال بھی بک کروانا ہے اشعر شاید انگلینڈ بھی جائیں اپنی تیاری کے لیے۔'' نظریں چرائے وہ انہیں بتا رہی تھی۔ دادی کے لبوں کی مسکراہٹ پل میں معدوم ہو گئی۔

''چلو اچھی بات ہے۔ کبھی نہ کبھی یہ فیصلہ تو کرنا ہی تھا تمہیں...... مگر...... جانے کیوں مجھے اشعر حسین پسند نہیں ہے۔ کسی بھی لحاظ سے وہ مجھے تمہارے قابل نہیں لگتا۔''

''ایسی کوئی بات نہیں ہے دادو، وہ بہت اچھا انسان ہے بہت سالوں سے پسند کرتا ہے مجھے، میرا خیال ہے جتنا وہ مجھے سمجھتا ہے شاید کوئی دوسرا کبھی نہ سمجھ سکے۔'' دل کی بے چینی کے باوجود اس نے اشعر حسین کا دفاع کیا تھا۔

چوہدرانی سرد آہ بھر کر رہ گئیں۔

''اللہ کرے ایسا ہی ہو، میں اپنی بیٹی کو اس حویلی سے اپنے ہاتھوں سے رخصت کروں گی۔'' وہ اپنی خواہش بتا رہی تھیں۔ ثانیہ آنکھوں کے گوشوں میں ہلکی نمی لیے فوراً رخ پھیر گئی۔

رات عشاء کی نماز کے بعد وہ کمرے سے اٹھ کر باہر صحن میں چلی آئی تھی۔ جانے کیوں اسے ایک عجیب سی گھٹن کا احساس ہو رہا تھا۔ کافی دیر صحن میں کھلے آسمان تلے لیٹنے کے بعد اچانک وہ اٹھی اور بلیک شال اچھی طرح اپنے گرد لپیٹ کر حویلی سے باہر نکل آئی۔

چوہدرانی ابھی تھوڑی دیر پہلے ہی دوا لے کر سوئی تھیں۔ چاندنی رات میں حویلی کے باہر کچے راستوں پر تھکن ہی تھکن تھی۔ ساکن ہوئے درختوں اور کھیتوں سے کبھی اسے بہت خوف آتا تھا مگر اب ویسی کیفیت نہیں رہی تھی۔ کچھ دور چلنے کے بعد اچانک کوئی پتھر اس کے دائیں پاؤں کے انگوٹھے سے ٹکرایا تھا۔ جدید تراش خراش سے بڑھا ہوا ناخن ٹوٹا تھا۔ ثانیہ کی آنکھیں پانیوں سے بھر آئیں۔ تبھی فضا میں کسی کی درد بھری صدا ابھری تھی۔

دو پتر چناراں دے\
ساڈا کا دکھ سن سن کے روندے پتھر پہاڑاں دے\
ساڈا دکھ سن سن کے روندے پتھر پہاڑاں دے

وہ محسور سی کھڑی رہی آواز میں عجیب سی دلگرفتی تھی، درد تھا، تڑپ تھی ثانیہ کو اپنے پیر کی تکلیف بھول گئی۔

گوڑے درد نیں یاراں دے\
سادا دکھ سن سن کے روندے پتھر پہاڑاں دے

لمحہ لمحہ آواز قریب آتی جا رہی تھی۔ ثانیہ میں ہلنے کی سکت بھی نہ رہی۔

ایتھے رلیاں وفاواں نیں\
تیرے باجھوں دوا ای بیلی، شالا تھروتے ہاواں نے

تیرے باہجوں دوا ای بیلی......
دن لنگ گئے بہاراں دے
ساڈا دکھ سن سن کر روندے پتھر پہاڑاں دے
ساڈا دکھ سن سن کے......

پرسوز آواز کے ساتھ ہی ٹریکٹر کے بند ہونے کی آواز آئی تھی۔ تبھی کندھے سے لڑھکتی شال کو سنبھالتے ہوئے وہ آگے بڑھ آئی عین اسی پل زائر ٹریکٹر سے نیچے اترا تھا۔ ثانیہ اسے مقابل پا کر جیسے ٹھٹک گئی تھی۔ اس کے وہم وگمان میں نہیں تھا کہ اتنی پیاری پرسوز آواز زائر ملک کی ہوگی دوسری طرف وہ بھی جیسے فریز ہو گیا تھا۔

❁......❁......❁

اے محبت تیری قسمت کہ تجھے مفت ملے
ہم سے منہ زور جو کمالات کیا کرتے تھے
خشک مٹی کو بھی عمارات کیا کرتے تھے
اے محبت یہ تیرا بخت کہ بن مول ملے
ہم سے انمول جو ہیروں میں تلا کرتے تھے
ہم جو لوگوں سے سوالات کیا کرتے تھے
ہم جو سو باتوں کی اک بات کیا کرتے تھے
تیری تحویل میں آنے سے ذرا پہلے تک
ہم بھی اس شہر میں عزت سے رہا کرتے تھے
ہم بگڑتے تو کوئی کام بنا کرتے تھے
اور اب تیری سخاوت کے گھنے سائے میں
خلقت شہر کو ہم زندہ تماشا ٹھہرے
جتنے الزام تھے مقسوم ہمارا ٹھہرے
اے محبت ذرا انداز بدل لے اپنا
تجھ کو آئندہ بھی عشاق کا خون پینا ہے
ہم تو مر جائیں گے تجھ کو مگر جینا ہے
اے محبت......

''ثانیہ عباس......!''

ٹریکٹر سے اترتے ہی اس کی نظر ثانیہ عباس پر پڑی تھی۔ جو ہلکی ہلکی پھوار میں بھیگتی اسی کی طرف دیکھ رہی تھی۔ وہ ٹھٹک گیا۔ رات کے اس پہر بھلا وہ وہاں کیا کر رہی تھی؟

کاٹن کا ٹراؤزر جو اس وقت اس نے زیب تن کر رکھا تھا ہلکی ہلکی پھوار میں بھیگ کر اس کے وجود سے چپک گیا تھا۔ زائر کو سمجھ نہ آئی کہ یہ اس کا الوژن ہے یا حقیقت؟ بارش کسی بھی لمحے تیز ہو سکتی تھی۔ وہ جیسے ٹرانس کی کیفیت میں چلتا عین اس کے مقابل آ کھڑا ہوا تھا۔ ثانیہ کے دائیں پاؤں کے انگوٹھے کے ٹوٹے ہوئے ناخن سے خون رس رس کر بند ہو گیا تھا۔ وہ یک ٹک اسے دیکھے گیا۔ کیا نہیں تھا اس وقت اس کی آنکھوں میں؟ ثانیہ چاہنے کے باوجود اس کے چہرے

سے نظر نہیں ہٹا پائی تھی۔ تبھی وہ بولا تھا۔

''اتنی رات کو' اتنے خراب موسم میں تم یہاں کیا کر رہی ہو؟''

''یہی سوال میں بھی پوچھ سکتی ہوں تم سے۔'' تیز بارش اور سرد ہواؤں کے سبب اس نے دونوں بازو سینے پر لپیٹ رکھے تھے۔ زائر اس کے لہجے کی ترشی محسوس کر کے لب بھینچ گیا۔

''میں مرد ہوں' صبح سے رات تک مختلف کاموں کے لیے سو جگہ جانا پڑتا ہے مجھے' تمہارا اس وقت گھر سے باہر کوئی کام نہیں ہے۔''

''سو وہاٹ' میں کسی کی پابند نہیں ہوں۔ میرا جب جہاں دل چاہے گا میں جاؤں گی۔''

''وہ تو میں جانتا ہوں جو عورت بھرپور محبت کے باوجود اپنے شوہر کو دھوکا دے کر اس کی زندگی سے نکل سکتی ہے اس کے لیے یوں خراب موسم میں' رات کے وقت گھر سے نکلنا کیا مشکل ہے۔''

''جسٹ شٹ اپ۔''

زائر ملک کے طنز اُس کی کنپٹیاں سلگا دی تھیں۔ تبھی وہ دھاڑی تھی مگر زائر نے اثر نہیں لیا۔

''تمہارے یوں چلانے سے حقیقت بدل نہیں جائے گی۔ مگر پھر بھی ایک وقت آئے گا جب تمہیں چادر اور چار دیواری کی حرمت کا احساس ہوگا۔ تم نہیں جانتیں مسلمان عورت پر اللہ رب العزت کا کتنا بڑا احسان ہے۔ چادر اور چار دیواری کا تحفظ اس کے لیے کتنی بڑی نعمت ہے۔ عورت کی زندگی سے اگر ان دو چیزوں کو نکال دیا جائے تو وہ عورت نہیں رہتی تماشا بن جاتی ہے۔''

''بکواس بند کرو زائر ملک' تم جیسے گھٹیا اور کمینے شخص کے منہ سے یہ باتیں بالکل اچھی نہیں لگ رہیں تم جانتے ہو جو کچھ تم نے میری زندگی کے ساتھ کیا ہے۔ تمہی وہ شخص ہو جس نے مجھ سے میری شخصیت کا وقار چھین کر مجھے تماشہ بننے پر مجبور کیا صرف تمہاری وجہ سے آج میں زندگی کی اس سیڑھی پر کھڑی ہوں کہ نہ جی سکتی ہوں نہ مر سکتی ہوں۔'' وہ روہانسی ہوئی تھی۔ زائر کا دل دکھ کی شدت سے بھر گیا۔

''بہر حال مجھے تم سے نہ کوئی حساب کتاب کرنا ہے نہ شکوہ گلہ' میں صرف اتنی گزارش کروں گی کہ خدارا میرے بچوں کو مجھ سے ملنے دو' وہ بہترین تعلیمی اداروں میں پڑھ رہے ہیں میں نہیں چاہتی تمہارا گنوار پن اور فضول کی ضد میرے ساتھ ساتھ میرے بچوں کی زندگی بھی برباد کر دے۔ وہ یہاں کے اجڈ ماحول کے عادی نہیں ہیں۔ انہیں اپنے جیسا جنگلی جانور مت بناؤ پلیز۔''

''تم بھول رہی ہو ثانیہ عباس کہ تم بھی اسی شخص کی اولاد ہو جسے یہاں کی مٹی نے پروان چڑھایا تھا۔''

''جانتی ہوں اسی لیے میری ماں نے اس شخص کو میری پیدائش کے بعد یہاں سے کوچ کر جانے پر مجبور کر دیا تھا۔ اگر وہ ایسا نہ کرتیں تو یقیناً آج میں بھی تمہاری طرح گنوار' یہیں پل بڑھ کر گاؤں کی کسی دیوار پر اپلے تھوپ رہی ہوتی۔'' اس کے لہجے میں گاؤں کے قدرتی ماحول کے لیے اتنی نفرت تھی کہ وہ دم بخود رہ گیا تھا۔

''میرے بچے یہاں کے ماحول میں بہت خوش ہیں ثانیہ عباس۔ جہاں تک ان کی تعلیم و تربیت کی بات ہے تو اس کے لیے تمہیں اتنا فکر مند ہونے کی ضرورت نہیں ہے۔ اللہ سوہنے کی مہربانی سے ان کے باپ میں اتنا دم ہے کہ وہ تم سے زیادہ مہنگے اداروں میں ان کی تعلیم و تربیت کا بندوبست کر سکتا ہے۔''

''ہونہہ...... خوب واقف ہوں میں آپ کی ہمت اور دولت سے۔ جو شخص اپنے بچپن کی منگ اور محبت کو پانے کے لیے دوسروں کے گھروں میں ڈاکے ڈالے' دن رات کولہو کے بیل کی طرح کھیتوں میں پسینہ بہا کر بھی اپنا ٹھکانہ تک نہ

بدل سکے وہ میرے بچوں کو کیا دے سکتا ہے سوائے ناکام حسرتوں کے۔''

''وہ میرے بھی بچے ہیں۔ تمہیں ان کی فکر کرنے کی ضرورت نہیں ہے۔''

''ضرورت ہے۔'' ایک دم سے وہ چلائی تھی۔

''ماں ہوں میں ان کی' میرا بھی ان پر اتنا ہی حق بنتا ہے جتنا کہ تمہارا۔''

''ماں......؟'' ثانیہ کے طنز نے اس کے دل پر نشتر کا کام کیا تھا۔

''وہ ماں' جو بنا کسی قصور کے ان ننھے فرشتوں کی پیدائش سے پہلے ہی انہیں اپنی کوکھ سے گرانے چلی تھی۔ وہ ماں' جس نے صرف اپنی خواہشات کی تسکین کے لیے ان معصوم پھولوں کو ان کے باپ سے دور کر دیا۔ وہ ماں' جو صرف اپنے نفس کی بھوک کے لیے ساری حدود وقیود بھلا کر ایک قطعی غیر محرم مرد کے ساتھ زندگی کے شب و روز گزارتے ہوئے اپنی پاکیزگی اور نسوانیت پر سوالیہ نشان لگا رہی ہے۔ اس ماں کے حق کی بات کر رہی ہو تم؟''

نشتر لگانے میں اس شخص کا بھی کوئی ثانی نہیں تھا۔ ثانیہ عباس کا دل کٹ کر رہ گیا۔ وہ بولی تو اس کا لہجہ بھاری ہو رہا تھا۔

''اس فکر میں گھلنا چھوڑ دو زائر ملک کہ میں کیا ہوں کیسی ہوں' بس اتنا یاد رکھو کہ میں جیسی بھی ہوں تمہارے بچوں کی حقیقی ماں ہوں اور یہ سچائی تم چاہو بھی تو بدل نہیں سکتے؟''

''جانتا ہوں میں' اسی بات کا دکھ ہے مجھے بہرحال میرے بچے میرے گھر میں بہت خوش ہیں گاؤں کی زندگی میں ان کے لیے جو مزہ اور تھرل ہے وہ شاید تمہارے اے سی رومز اور قیمتی کارپٹ سے سجے محل میں نہیں ہے اس لیے میں چاہ کر بھی انہیں تمہارے حوالے نہیں کر سکتا۔ ہاں تم چاہو تو کسی بھی وقت ان سے مل سکتی ہو' روکوں گا نہیں۔'' وہ شخص مکمل بے حس ہو چکا تھا۔ ثانیہ نے رخ پھیر لیا۔

بارش کے سرد قطروں کے ساتھ اس وقت جو آنسو اس کی آنکھوں سے گر رہے تھے وہ جیسے آگ تھے۔

بارش کی تیزی کے ساتھ ہی بجلی بھی زور و شور سے چمکنا اور بادل گرجنا شروع ہو گئے تھے۔ تبھی وہ بولا تھا۔

''موسم کے تیور ٹھیک نہیں ہیں۔ میرے خیال میں اب تمہیں یہ ایڈونچر ترک کر کے گھر چلنا چاہیے۔''

''چلی جاؤں گی تمہیں میری فکر میں گھلنے کی ضرورت نہیں ہے۔''

''ضرورت کیوں نہیں ہے صرف تمہارے ختم کر لینے سے ہمارا تعلق کبھی ختم نہیں ہو سکتا۔'' وہ بہت نرم لہجے میں کہہ رہا تھا۔ ثانیہ کا غصہ پھر عود آیا۔

''کس تعلق کی بات کر رہے ہیں آپ...... ہوں...... کیا ہے ہمارے بیچ؟''

''کیا نہیں ہے ہمارے بیچ؟'' گہری نگاہوں سے اس کی طرف دیکھتے ہوئے اس نے اپنے مضبوط ہاتھ ثانیہ عباس کے کندھوں پر جما دیے۔

''تم کیا سمجھتی ہو مجھ سے اور میرے ماحول سے جان چھڑانے کے لیے تم نے ساری دنیا میں یہ ڈھنڈورا پیٹ دیا کہ میں نے تمہیں طلاق دے دی ہے۔ جبکہ تم اچھی طرح جانتی ہو کہ ایسا نہیں ہے پھر بھی ہمارا تعلق ٹوٹ جائے گا۔ میں تم سے اور تمہاری ذات سے دستبردار ہو جاؤں گا کبھی نہیں۔'' وہ کہہ رہا تھا اور ثانیہ کی آنکھیں اس کے انکشاف پر جیسے پھٹی کی پھٹی رہ گئی تھیں۔

''کیا کہا تم نے...... میں نے ساری دنیا میں ڈھنڈورا پیٹا کہ تم نے مجھے طلاق دے دی؟''

''ہاں......!''

''جسٹ شٹ اپ' میں سوچ بھی نہیں سکتی تھی کہ تم اتنے گھٹیا انسان ثابت ہو سکتے ہو' طلاق کے وہ پیپرز جو تم نے مجھے

بھجوائے تھے وہ میں نے سائن نہیں کیے تھے تم نے کیے تھے۔'' بایاں ہاتھ پوری قوت سے اس کے سینے پر مارتے ہوئے وہ دھاڑی تھی۔

''تم نے بے آسرا کیا میرے بچوں کو باپ کے ہوتے ہوئے محرومیوں کے ساتھ جینے پر تم نے مجبور کیا۔ کتنی کوشش کی تھی میں نے اور میری مما نے اس تعلق کو بچانے کے لیے مگر کوئی کوشش بار آور ثابت نہ ہوسکی جس طرح اپنی مرضی سے زبردستی تم نے مجھے اپنی زندگی میں شامل کیا اسی طرح اپنی مرضی سے چپ چاپ نکال بھی دیا۔'' بھرائے لہجے کے ساتھ کہتی وہ اب رو رہی تھی۔ زائر ملک شاکڈ انداز میں یک ٹک اسے دیکھے گا۔

''کیا بکواس ہے یہ، میں نے کوئی پیپرز نہیں بھجوائے تھے طلاق کے۔''

''بکواس تم کررہے ہو، صرف تمہاری وجہ سے تمہارے دیے ہوئے دکھ کی وجہ سے میری ماں مرگئی۔ تم بھول سکتے ہو مگر میں وہ لمحات کبھی نہیں بھول سکتی جب دیارِ غیر میں دو ننھے بیمار بچوں کے ساتھ، میں قطعی سرد ماحول میں اکیلی انہیں لے کر بیٹھی تھی اور وہاں کوئی مجھے تسلی دینے والا نہیں تھا۔''

''ثانیہ میں سچ کہہ رہا ہوں میرا یقین کیوں نہیں کررہی تم؟'' اب وہ روہانسا ہو چلا تھا ثانیہ نے بھیگی ہوئی سرخ آنکھوں کے ساتھ ہاتھ اٹھا کر اسے مزید بولنے سے روک دیا۔

''بس کرو زائر ملک، مت اتنے گناہ اپنے سر لو کہ بخشش مشکل ہوجائے۔ میری ماں اس طلاق کی گواہ تھی جو تم نے مجھے دی۔ اشعر بھی گواہ ہے اور خود تمہاری ماں بھی، نہیں یقین آتا تو جاکر پوچھ لو اپنی ماں سے۔''

جتنی بے خوفی اور اعتماد سے وہ کہہ رہی تھی زائر برف ہوکر رہ گیا تھا۔ مگر وہ بنا اس کی طرف دیکھے برستی بارش میں آگے بڑھ گئی تھی۔ زائر سن سا کتنی ہی دیر وہیں کھڑا رہا۔

❀ ...... ❀ ...... ❀

چاند سیڑھیوں سے گر گیا تھا اور اس کی بائیں ٹانگ پر چوٹ آئی تھی۔ تب سے وہ مما مما چلا رہا تھا۔ زائر نے اسے سنبھالنے کی کوشش کی تھی مگر وہ اس کے قابو بھی نہیں آرہا تھا۔ گڑیا الگ پریشان ہوگئی تھی۔

سائرہ گرم دودھ لے کر آئی تو اس نے ہاتھ مار کر وہ اسی پر گرا دیا تبھی ''سی'' کی آواز کے ساتھ اس نے ایک تھپڑ اسے جڑ دیا تھا۔ زائر ہکا بکا رہ گیا۔

''کم بخت، منحوس مارے میں کوئی ملازمہ ہوں جو ہر وقت ان کے ناز اٹھاتی رہوں اتنے ہی نازوں پلے ہیں تو رہیں شہر میں اپنی ماں کے پاس یہاں میری جان عذاب میں ڈالنے کیوں آگئے ہیں۔'' وہ جھنجلا گئی تھی۔ زائر کا چہرہ غصے سے سرخ ہوگیا۔

''تمہاری ہمت کیسے ہوئی میرے بیٹے کو تھپڑ مارنے کی؟'' تن کر سائرہ کے سامنے کھڑا وہ پہاڑ ہی تو لگ رہا تھا وہ بھی غصے میں آگئی۔

''اپنے بیٹے کا تھپڑ نظر آگیا میرا جلا ہوا بازو اور پاؤں دکھائی نہیں دے رہا۔''

''وہ بچہ ہے تکلیف ملی ہے تم اس کا مقابلہ کرو گی؟''

''میں نے تکلیف نہیں دی ہے اسے جو تمہارے یہ بچے تگنی کا ناچ نچا کر رکھیں مجھے، سارا دن جیسے میں انہیں سنبھالتی ہوں مجھے ہی پتا ہے۔ تمہیں تو ان کی ماں کا سوگ منانے سے ہی فرصت نہیں ہے۔''

''زبان سنبھال کر بات کرو سائرہ، میں اپنے بچوں کے لیے ایسا رویہ برداشت نہیں کرسکتا۔''

''برداشت نہیں کرسکتے تو جاکر شہر چھوڑ آؤ ان کو واپس، پہلے ہی ان کی ماں کی وجہ سے کم اذیت میں نہیں ہوں میں جو

تم نے انہیں بھی لا کر میرے سر پر بٹھا دیا ہے۔"

"چٹاخ۔"

ابھی وہ بات پوری بھی نہ کر پائی تھی کہ زائر کے بھرپور طمانچے نے اس کا دماغ چکرا کر رکھ دیا۔

"اتنی ہی تنگ اور عاجز ہو میرے بچوں سے تو کرو شادی اور دفع ہو جاؤ یہاں سے میں نے کوئی ٹھیکہ نہیں اٹھا رکھا تمہیں ساری عمر بٹھا کر کھلانے کا۔ یہ گھر میرا اور میرے بچوں کا ہے۔ یہ جب تک چاہیں گے یہاں رہیں گے دیکھتا ہوں کون نکالتا ہے انہیں یہاں سے۔" اماں جو قریب ہی بیٹھی تھیں۔ اس کے چہرے سے امڈتا جلال دیکھ کر سہم گئیں۔ بڑے دنوں کے بعد سائرہ نے بھی اپنے رنگ دکھائے تھے۔ صرف ایک لمحے کی صورت حال نے انہیں بہت کچھ سوچنے پر مجبور کر دیا تھا۔ زائر گھر سے نکل چکا تھا۔ سائرہ بھی تیزی سے امڈتے آنسوؤں کے ساتھ رسوئی میں چھپ گئی تھی وہ روتے ہوئے چاند کو گود میں لیے بہت کچھ سوچ گئیں۔ ابھی کل رات گھر واپسی پر انہوں نے زائر کو روتے ہوئے دیکھا تھا۔ صبح جب وہ فجر کی نماز ادا کر رہی تھیں تو وہ سرخ آنکھوں کے ساتھ ان کے قریب آ کر مصلے پر بیٹھ گیا تھا۔

"اماں۔" جونہی انہوں نے دعا مکمل کی اس نے پکار لیا۔ جواب میں وہ اس کا چہرہ دیکھ کر حیران ہی تو رہ گئی تھیں۔

"ماں صدقے جائے کیا ہوا؟"

"اماں کیا میں نے آپ کے سامنے ثانیہ کو طلاق دی تھی؟" وہ رو رہا تھا۔ وہ دہل گئیں۔

"اللہ رحم کرے ایسا تجھ سے کس نے کہا؟"

"جس نے بھی کہا ہو، تو بتانا اماں، کیا میں نے کسی بھی طریقے سے اسے خود سے علیحدہ کیا؟" سرخ بھیگے ہوئے چہرے کے ساتھ جس طرح وہ روتے ہوئے پوچھ رہا تھا ان کا کلیجہ منہ کو آ گیا۔

"نہیں بالکل نہیں۔"

"تو پھر وہ کیوں کہتی ہے کہ آپ اس طلاق کی گواہ ہیں جو میں نے اسے دی تھی۔" ایک دم سے وہ بلکا تھا۔ ماں بیٹے کا ایسا حال دیکھ کر اندر سے کٹ گئی۔

"میں نہیں جانتی، ضرور وہ کسی بڑی غلط فہمی کا شکار ہو گئی ہے۔ خدا گواہ ہے میری اس سے ایسی کوئی بات نہیں ہوئی۔" اماں کا چہرہ اور ان کا لہجہ ان کی سچائی کا منہ بولتا ثبوت تھا۔ زائر نے سختی سے آنکھیں بند کر لیں۔

"وہ ایسا کیوں کر رہی ہے میرے ساتھ اماں، میں نہیں جی سکتا اس کے بغیر۔"

ان کا وہ شیر بیٹا جو کبڈی اور کشتی میں گاؤں کے دس لڑکوں کو بھی ایک ساتھ چند لمحوں میں زمین چٹا دیتا تھا۔ وہ ان کے سامنے بے بسی کی تصویر بنا رو رہا تھا اور وہ بھی ایک عورت کے لیے انہیں لگا جیسے ان کا دل اپنے بیٹے کے دکھ پر غم کی شدت سے پھٹ جائے گا۔

"کہاں ملی وہ تجھے؟" اگلے ہی پل انہوں نے پوچھا تھا۔

مگر زائر نے ان کا سوال نہیں سنا۔ نم آنکھوں کے ساتھ وہ اٹھا تھا اور تیزی سے کمرے سے نکل گیا تھا۔ سارا دن وہ اس کے بارے میں سوچ سوچ کر پریشان ہوتی رہیں اور اب یہ نیا تماشا ہو گیا تھا۔ انہوں نے سوچ لیا وہ اب سائرہ کو رخصت کرنے میں زیادہ دیر نہیں کریں گی۔

* * *

ثانیہ جب سے زائر سے مل کر شہر واپس آئی تھی بے حد اداس رہنے لگی تھی۔ پہلے والی بے چینی اور نفرت کی جگہ یاسیت نے لے لی تھی۔ گو اچھی طرح دل کا غبار نکال کر وہ ہلکی پھلکی ہو گئی تھی مگر کوئی چیز تھی جو اسے خوش رہنے نہیں دے رہی

تھی۔ اشعر نے شادی کی تیاری مکمل کر لی تھی۔ لوگوں اور قریبی دوستوں میں کارڈز بھی بٹ گئے تھے۔ ہنی مون کی ٹکٹس بھی فائنل ہو گئی تھیں۔ اس نے سوچ لیا تھا اشعر سے شادی کے بعد وہ دوبارہ کبھی پاکستان کا رخ نہیں کرے گی۔

اشعر بہت خوش تھا۔ یا شاید اسے ہی ایسا محسوس ہو رہا تھا۔ مگر وہ خوش نہیں تھی۔ اس رات ان کی مہندی کی تقریب تھی۔ ثانیہ نے پارلر سے مہندی لگوائی تھی اور خوب رنگ آیا تھا۔ اشعر آنے والے مہمانوں کو خود ہی سنبھال رہا تھا۔ وہ اسٹیج پر سر جھکائے بیٹھی۔ اپنے بائیں ہاتھ میں پڑی انگیجمنٹ رنگ سے کھیلتی رہی۔ مہندی کی تقریب بہت شاندار ہوئی تھی۔

تھکن سے چور وہ اشعر کو مہمانوں کے درمیان چھوڑ کر سر درد کا بہانہ کرتی اپنے کمرے میں آ گئی تھی۔ رات کا جانے کون سا پہر تھا جب اچانک کسی نسوانی قہقہے کی آواز پر اس کی آنکھ کھلی تھی۔ حلق میں جیسے پیاس کی شدت سے کانٹے اگ آئے تھے۔ بوجھل سر کو سنبھالتی وہ بمشکل اٹھ کر بیٹھ گئی۔

''بہت بڑے کھلاڑی ہو تم اشعر حسین، ورنہ سچ میں، میں بہت ڈر گئی تھی۔ مجھے لگا تم سچ مچ ثانیہ میں دلچسپی لینے لگے ہو اور شاید اب کبھی لوٹ کر انگلینڈ کا رخ نہ کرو مگر مجھے کیا پتا تھا تم یہاں میرے اور بچوں کے لیے اتنی خوب صورت بساط بچھائے بیٹھے ہو۔'' کمرے کا دروازہ کھلا تھا اور باہر لاؤنج سے روشنی کی ہلکی سی لکیر ادھ کھلے دروازے سے اندر آ رہی تھی۔ ثانیہ کی نظر بے ساختہ سامنے لگے وال کلاک پر پڑی۔ رات کے ساڑھے تین بج رہے تھے۔ بھلا اس وقت وہاں کوئی عورت کیا کر رہی تھی؟ تبھی اشعر کی آواز آئی تھی۔

''تم کیا سمجھتی ہو اشعر حسین نے دنیا نہیں دیکھی۔''

''دیکھی ہے مگر ثانیہ عباس کوئی عام لڑکی نہیں ہے، اسے دھوکا دینا اتنا آسان نہیں، پتا نہیں کیسے تم نے اس کی آدھی سے زیادہ جائداد ہتھیالی اور اب اتنے سارے لوگوں کی موجودگی میں نکاح کے جعلی پیپرز اگر کسی کو پتا چل گیا تو؟''

''پاگل ہو تم اور کچھ نہیں، جب طلاق کے جعلی پیپرز کا پتا نہیں چلا تو نکاح کے جعلی پیپرز کا کیسے پتا چل سکتا ہے۔ جبکہ قاضی اور فرینڈز بھی میرے ساتھ ہوں، پتا ہے آنٹی پر جب فالج کا اٹیک ہوا تھا تو وہ بار بار میری طرف ملتجی نگاہوں سے دیکھ رہی تھیں یوں جیسے کہہ رہی ہوں کہ میں ثانیہ کو سب کچھ سچ سچ بتا دوں، مگر میں کوئی پاگل ہوں جو اسے سب کچھ سچ سچ بتا دیتا۔ جس طرح اس نے مجھے ٹھکرا کر میری توہین کی تھی میں وہ بے عزتی کبھی نہیں بھول سکتا۔ اسی لیے اب ثانیہ عباس کا جو نقصان میرے ہاتھوں ہوگا وہ اس کی خود ذمہ دار ہوگی۔''

''ہوں، ویسے کتنی عجیب بات ہے کہ اب تک اس کے شوہر نے اسے سچائی نہیں بتائی۔''

''کیسے بتا سکتا ہے۔ ثانیہ تو اس کی شکل دیکھنا بھی گوارہ نہیں کرتی۔''

''گڈ، یہ تو بہت اچھی بات ہے۔ ویسے اب آگے کیا پلان کرنا ہے۔''

''پلان تو کیا ہوا ہے کل فرضی نکاح کے بعد میں اسے ہنی مون کے بہانے ایبروڈ لے کر جا رہا ہوں وہاں ایک تاجر سے بات کی ہے میں نے ثانیہ کو بھی ملوایا ہے اور اسے ثانیہ بہت پسند بھی آئی ہے ساڑھے تین کروڑ میں سودا طے ہوا ہے۔ سودے کے بعد پاکستان اطلاع بھجوا دوں گا کہ ثانیہ کی روڈ ایکسیڈنٹ میں ڈیتھ ہو گئی یہاں کون ہے ایسا جو اتنی دور اس کی شکل دیکھنے جائے گا۔ یوں اس کی موت کی خبر پھیلا کر اس کی باقی ماندہ جائداد پر بھی میرا قبضہ ہو جائے گا۔ کہو کیسا لگا پروگرام؟'' اشعر حسین تفاخر سے پوچھ رہا تھا اور نسوانی قہقہے نے ایک مرتبہ پھر اس کی حوصلہ افزائی کی تھی ثانیہ کو لگا جیسے اس کے سارے بدن پر چیونٹیاں چڑھ آئی ہوں اور اب اسے کاٹ کاٹ کر کھا رہی ہوں۔ یہ کیسی حقیقت تھی جس میں اس کی بربادی کے ذمہ دار خود اس کے اپنے تھے وہ اپنے جن سے ان کا خون کا رشتہ تھا۔

دنیا میں ماں سے زیادہ انسان کا اپنا اور کوئی نہیں ہوتا، مگر...... اسے تکلیف پہنچا کر برباد کرنے والی اس کی اپنی ماں

ہی تھی۔

اسے لگا جیسے اس کا وجود بلاسٹ ہو کر ہوا میں تحلیل ہو گیا ہو تیزی سے گھومتے سر کو بمشکل دونوں ہاتھوں سے تھامتے ہوئے وہ دوبارہ بیڈ پر بیٹھ گئی تھی۔

❁......❁......❁

اگلی صبح اشعر اس کے کمرے میں آیا تو وہ جاگ رہی تھی۔ وہ بے تکلفی سے بیڈ پر اس کے قریب ہی ٹک گیا۔

''اٹھ گئی میری پری؟'' وہ بے حد مسرور تھا۔ ثانیہ کی آنکھیں آنسوؤں سے بھر آئیں۔

''ہوں۔''

''طبیعت تو ٹھیک ہے نا' رات بھی جلدی سو گئی تھیں؟''

''ہوں ٹھیک ہے۔''

''گڈ' چلو جلدی سے اٹھ کر تیار ہو جاؤ پارلر بھی جانا ہے۔''

''نہیں...... میں پہلے اپنے بچوں سے ملنے جاؤں گی۔''

''اوکم آن ثانیہ' بچے یہیں آ جائیں گے ہمارے پاس زیادہ وقت نہیں ہے۔''

''جانتی ہوں' مگر مجھے اپنے بچوں سے ملنا ہے' پلیز۔''

''تم بے کار کی ضد کر رہی ہو ثانیہ۔ تم جانتی ہو اس وقت اس کی کوئی ضرورت نہیں ہے۔''

''تمہیں نہیں ہے مجھے ہے۔'' پہلی بار سرخ آنکھیں اٹھاتے ہوئے وہ چلائی تھی۔ اشعر حیران سا دیکھتا رہ گیا تھا۔

''ہوا کیا ہے تمہیں؟''

''کچھ نہیں ہوا' بس مجھے بچوں سے ملنا ہے میں جا رہی ہوں۔''

''سوری' نکاح سے پہلے تم کہیں نہیں جا سکتیں۔'' ایک لمحے میں اس نے اپنا روپ بدلا تھا۔ وہ شاکڈ رہ گئی تھی۔

''تم مجھے پابند نہیں کر سکتے اشعر حسین۔''

''کر چکا ہوں۔'' اس کے دھاڑنے کا اثر لیے بغیر وہ خباثت سے مسکرایا تھا۔

''اتنا پاگل نہیں ہوں میں جتنا تم نے مجھے سمجھ لیا ہے بچوں سے ملنے کے بہانے تم وہاں جاؤ گی اور آگے وہ ہو گا تمہارا سابقہ شوہر' زائر ملک...... کہاں واپس آنے دے گا وہ تمہیں۔''

''تم بھول رہے ہو اشعر حسین کہ تم سے شادی کا فیصلہ میرا اپنا ہے۔ کسی نے مجبور نہیں کیا تھا مجھے جواب بھاگ جاؤں گی مجھے زائر ملک سے بدلہ لینا ہے تم سے شادی کے بعد میں دوبارہ کبھی پاکستان نہیں آؤں گی۔ اسی لیے آخری بار اپنے بچوں سے ملنا چاہتی ہوں۔ تمہیں اعتبار نہیں ہے تو چلو ساتھ۔'' اس کا لہجہ اتنا پختہ تھا کہ وہ ڈگمگا گیا۔

''ایسی بات نہیں ہے ثانیہ' بس میں تمہیں کھونے سے ڈرتا ہوں۔''

''مت ڈرو' میں بیس پچیس منٹ سے زیادہ وقت نہیں لوں گی۔''

''سچ کہہ رہی ہو نا؟''

''ہوں۔'' اشعر حسین جیسے بندے کے ساتھ ساتھ رہتے رہتے وہ بھی کھلاڑی بن گئی تھی۔ وہ اطمینان سے ہنس دیا۔

''شکریہ۔ میں نکاح کا بندوبست کرتا ہوں تم جلدی سے واپس آ جانا۔''

''ٹھیک ہے۔'' متورم نگاہیں جھکا کر اس نے آہستہ سے اثبات میں سر ہلایا اور اپنا پرس اٹھا کر تیزی سے کمرے سے نکل گئی۔

''یہ کیا کیا اشعر، تمہیں اس وقت اسے یوں جانے نہیں دینا چاہیے تھا۔'' ثانیہ کے گھر سے نکلتے ہی اشعر کی بیوی اس کے مقابل آئی تھی۔

''کیوں؟''

''زائر ملک کو اگر اس کی تم سے شادی کی بھنک بھی پڑ گئی تو وہ سارا بنا بنایا کھیل بگاڑ دے گا۔''

''پتا ہے مجھے، تم کیا سمجھتی ہو میں یہاں دونوں آنکھیں بند کر کے بیٹھا ہوں۔''

''کیا مطلب؟''

''مطلب کی بچی، زائر فی الحال گاؤں میں نہیں ہے۔ اسلام آباد گیا ہوا ہے اپنے کسی ضروری کام سے جب تک وہ واپس لوٹے گا چڑیاں کھیت چگ کر اڑ چکی ہوں گی اور پھر عین ٹائم پر میں کسی بھی طرح سے ثانیہ کو ناراض کر کے اپنے لیے کوئی مشکل کھڑی نہیں کرنا چاہتا۔ اگر اسے ذرا سا بھی مجھ پر شک ہو گیا تو وہ مجھے زمین چٹانے میں ایک لمحے کی تاخیر بھی نہیں کرے گی۔''

اشعر کے لہجے میں ذہانت چھلک رہی تھی۔ اس کی بیوی کو بے ساختہ قائل ہونا پڑا۔ کتنی آسانی سے اس نے ثانیہ کا ہمدرد بن کر اسے بے وقوف بنالیا تھا بیوی کو طلاق دینے کا جھوٹ بول کر اس کی جھوٹی ہمدردیاں بھی حاصل کر لی تھیں۔ وہ خوش تھا کہ ثانیہ کو تا حال اس کی سازشوں کی خبر نہیں ہو سکی تھی۔ مگر ایسا نہیں تھا۔

عین وقت پر قدرت نے ثانیہ عباس کی آنکھوں پر پڑے دبیز پردے ہٹا دیے تھے اور اب کئی سیاہ راتوں کے بعد ایک روشن اجلی صبح اس کی منتظر تھی۔

❁ ..... ❁ ..... ❁

اس وقت وہ ایک ضروری کام کے سلسلے میں اسلام آباد گیا ہوا تھا۔ ہلکی ہلکی بارش میں شام ڈھلے ہوٹل سے وہ اپنے دوست کامران سے ملنے کے لیے اس کی رہائش گاہ پر آیا تھا۔ جب اسے ثانیہ عباس کی شادی کی اطلاع ملی۔ کامران اشعر حسین کے قریبی جاننے والوں میں سے تھا۔ تبھی اس وقت جب وہ اس کے ڈرائنگ روم میں بیٹھا چائے پی رہا تھا کامران نے اس سے کہا تھا۔

''یار...... مجھے تو سمجھ نہیں آتی۔ آخر زندگی کے اتنے اہم معاملات پر یہ عورتیں عقل سے کام کیوں نہیں لیتیں؟''

''کیوں کیا ہوا؟'' ڈھیلے ڈھالے انداز میں صوفے پر بیٹھا چائے کی چسکی لیتے ہوئے وہ مسکرایا تھا۔

''ہونا کیا ہے میرے پارٹنر اشعر حسین کو تو جانتے ہو تم ایک نمبر کا عیاش اور کمینہ بندہ ہے۔ مجھ سے اس کی کوئی بات بھی چھپی ہوئی نہیں ہے۔ اب اس کی جو گرل فرینڈ ہے ثانیہ عباس وہ پوری طرح سے اس کے فریب میں آئی ہوئی ہے۔ اس شخص کی وجہ سے اس نے اپنے شوہر سے طلاق لی۔ دو پھول جیسے معصوم بچوں کو چھوڑا اور اب یہ اشعر اسی کی آدھی سے زیادہ جائیداد ہتھیا کر اس سے شادی رچانے جا رہا ہے جبکہ پہلی بیوی کو بھی اس نے طلاق نہیں دی۔ میرا دل تو بہت کڑھ رہا ہے یقیناً شادی کے بعد یہ ثانیہ عباس کو بہت ذلیل کرنے والا ہے۔'' کامران کہہ رہا تھا مگر زائر کے بدن سے تو جیسے جان ہی نکل گئی تھی۔

''یہ کیا کہہ رہے ہو تم، ثانیہ عباس اور اشعر حسین کی شادی؟''

''ہاں یار، ابھی کل ہی انویٹیشن آیا ہے مجھے۔ آج مہندی کی تقریب ہے مگر میں نہیں جا سکا۔ میرے بیٹے کی طبیعت ٹھیک نہیں ہے۔ ویسے ایک لحاظ سے یہ ٹھیک ہی ہو رہا ہے کیونکہ ثانیہ اب تک بنا نکاح کے ایک ہی چھت تلے اس کے ساتھ رہ رہی ہے۔ تم خود سوچو، اشعر جیسے عیاش بندے نے کیا کیا نہیں کیا ہو گا اس کے ساتھ۔'' اس وقت کامران کے

منہ سے نکلنے والے وہ الفاظ سانپ بچھو بن کر اس کے وجود سے لپٹ گئے تھے۔ مارے اشتعال کے اس کا چہرہ لال سرخ ہو گیا تھا۔

یہ کیا ہو رہا تھا؟

ثانیہ عباس اس کے ساتھ ایسا کیسے کر سکتی تھی؟

اپنی سنگدلی اور بے وفائی...... کیا وہ اس حد تک بھی جا سکتی تھی کہ ان کے تعلق کا کوئی وجود ہی باقی نہ رہتا؟ وہ جرم جو اس سے سرزد ہی نہیں ہوا تھا اس جرم کے لیے وہ اسے اتنی بڑی سزا کیسے دے سکتی تھی؟

یکلخت اُمڈ کر آنے والے غصے کے ساتھ اسے ثانیہ عباس کی ذات سے بے حد نفرت محسوس ہوئی تھی۔ وہ اٹھا تھا اور پھر کامران کے روکنے کے باوجود طوفان بنا وہاں سے نکلتا چلا گیا تھا۔

ٹک...... ٹک...... ٹک

فجر کی اذان ہوئے ابھی کچھ ہی دیر ہوئی تھی کہ دروازے پر ہونے والی دستک نے اسے چونکا دیا۔ وہ ابھی فجر کی نماز پڑھ کر کچن میں جانے کا ارادہ کر رہی تھی مگر دروازے پر ہونے والی دستک نے اس کا ارادہ منسوخ کر دیا تھا۔ تین دن ہوئے تھے زائر گھر نہیں آیا تھا نہ ہی خیر خبر کی کوئی اطلاع دی تھی۔ سبھی اس کے لیے پریشان تھے۔ اس وقت بھی اس کا دل دھڑکا تھا اور وہ تیزی سے دروازے کی طرف آئی تھی۔

''کون......؟''

کنڈی گراتے ہوئے اس نے پوچھ لیا تھا۔ مگر اگلے ہی پل ثانیہ عباس کو اپنے مقابل کھڑے دیکھ کر ٹھٹک گئی۔

''تم......!''

''ہوں، مجھے اماں اور زائر سے ملنا ہے۔'' محلوں میں پلنے والی وہ شہزادی اس وقت کسی فقیر سے کم دکھائی نہیں دے رہی تھی۔ سائرہ کی پیشانی پر سلوٹیں پڑ گئیں۔

''وہ اس وقت گھر پر نہیں ہے بعد میں آنا۔'' تنک کر کہنے کے ساتھ ہی اس نے دروازہ ثانیہ عباس کے منہ پر بند کر دیا تھا۔ ثانیہ کٹ کر رہ گئی۔

''میری بات سنیں پلیز۔'' اگلے ہی پل درد کی انتہا پر کھڑے ہوئے اس نے پھر دروازہ پیٹا تھا۔ جواب میں سائرہ نے کھٹ سے دونوں پٹ وا کر دیے۔

''کیا ہے؟ کیوں صبح صبح چین سکون حرام کرنے چلی آئی ہو کہہ جو دیا ہے کہ زائر گھر پر نہیں ہے پرسوں آیا تھا بچوں کو لے کر شہر چلا گیا۔ اب جان چھوڑو میری وہ لڑکی اس کی سوچ سے زیادہ بدتمیز اور منہ پھٹ تھی۔ ثانیہ کی آنکھیں ڈبڈبا گئیں۔

''میں اس سے صرف ایک بار ملنا چاہتی ہوں، پلیز۔''

''میں نے ٹھیکہ نہیں لیا ہوا تم دونوں کو ملانے کا ویسے بھی وہ تمہاری شکل دیکھنے کو تیار نہیں ہے میری اور اس کی شادی ہو رہی ہے چند روز بعد۔ تمہارے لیے یہی بہتر ہے کہ تم اپنا یہ خوب صورت چہرہ لے کر جہاں سے آئی ہو وہیں واپس لوٹ جاؤ، مہربانی ہو گی۔''

''سائرہ، کون ہے دروازے پر؟'' ثانیہ ابھی جواب میں کچھ کہنا ہی چاہتی تھی کہ زائر کی ماں سائرہ کی تیز آواز پر چونک کر دروازے کی طرف چلی آئی۔ سائرہ دروازے بند کرنا چاہتی تھی مگر وہ اس سے پہلے ہی اس کے سر پر پہنچ گئی تھیں۔

''ثانیہ پتر......تو یہاں؟'' ان کا پوچھنا تھا اور ثانیہ کے آنسوؤں میں مزید شدت آ گئی تھی۔ دونوں ہاتھوں میں چہرہ چھپا کر وہ پھوٹ پھوٹ کر رو پڑی تھی۔ اماں کے پاؤں تلے سے زمین کھسک گئی۔

''سب خیریت تو ہے نا' زائر کہاں ہے؟'' وہ پریشانی سے اس کے پیچھے دیکھ رہی تھیں۔ سائرہ کے چہرے کی سرخی بڑھ گئی۔

''پتا نہیں' میں انہی سے ملنے یہاں آئی ہوں۔'' گھٹی گھٹی سسکیوں کے درمیان اس نے بتایا تھا اماں متفکر سی اسے اندر لے آئیں۔

''آؤ اندر آ جاؤ' زائر گھر پر نہیں ہے۔'' سائرہ کی نسبت ان کے لہجے میں اپنائیت اور مٹھاس تھی۔ سائرہ نے ان کے پیچھے زور سے دروازہ بند کر کے اپنا غصہ نکالا۔ اماں ثانیہ کو اپنے کمرے میں لے آئی تھیں۔

''ہاں اب بتا' کیا چل رہا ہے تیرے اور زائر کے بیچ۔ کیوں اس کا امتحان لے رہی ہے تو ثانیہ۔ کتنے سال ہو گئے ہیں میرے بیٹے کے لبوں سے مسکراہٹ روٹھ گئی ہے۔ بہت رویا ہے وہ تیرے لیے' کیوں کر رہی ہے تو اس کے ساتھ ایسا؟'' ثانیہ دیکھ سکتی تھی کہ وہ اپنے بیٹے کے لیے بے حد آزردہ تھیں۔ وہ ملول سی نظریں جھکا گئی۔

''میں بھی اس کے لیے بہت روئی ہوں اماں' میرا خدا جانتا ہے بہت بے سکون رہی ہوں میں اس سے دور رہ کر مگر سارا قصور میرا نہیں تھا میرے اور زائر کے بیچ بہت بڑی غلط فہمی کی دیوار حائل ہو گئی تھی۔'' وہ رو رہی تھی اور پھر بہتے آنسوؤں کے ساتھ اس نے گزرے پانچ سال کا احوال ان کے گوش گزار کر دیا تھا۔ اماں اپنا دل تھام کر رہ گئیں۔ جبکہ سائرہ جو بظاہر ناشتے کی تیاری کر رہی تھی مگر اس کے اندر غم و غصے کے ابال اٹھ رہے تھے۔ ثانیہ عباس کے ہوتے ہوئے وہ اپنی منزل کبھی نہیں پا سکتی تھی۔ لہٰذا اس وقت اگر اس کے دماغ میں کوئی خیال تھا تو صرف ثانیہ عباس کو راستے سے ہٹانے کا جو اس کے خوابوں کی دنیا درہم برہم کرنے کے لیے پھر سے اس کی اور زائر کی زندگی میں آ گئی تھی۔

❁......❁......❁

دن اچھا خاصا چڑھ آیا تھا۔

ثانیہ اپنی ساری روداد اماں کے سپرد کرنے کے بعد اب آسودہ سی ان کے کندھے سے ٹیک لگا کر بیٹھی تھی۔ خونی رشتوں سے فریب کے بعد اسے ان رشتوں کی قدر و اہمیت کا پتا چلا تھا جو سونے کی طرح خالص تھے۔ جنہیں اس کی ذات اور اسٹیٹس سے کوئی لالچ نہیں تھا۔ اللہ رب العزت کی پاک ذات کے بعد جو اس کی عزت کی حفاظت کرنا جانتے تھے۔ ایک ہفتہ قبل اشعر حسین کو چکر دے کر وہ سیدھی حویلی چلی آئی تھی اور پھر بنا کچھ بتائے دادی ماں کے گلے لگ کر اتنا روئی تھی کہ بے ہوش ہو گئی تھی۔ پورے تین دن لگے تھے اسے خود کو سنبھالنے میں اس دوران اشعر نے اس سے بات کرنے کی بہت کوشش کی۔ مگر وہ اس کی شکل دیکھنے کو بھی تیار نہیں تھی۔ چوتھے روز جو سب سے پہلا کام اس نے کیا وہ اشعر حسین پر فراڈ کی ایف آئی آر درج کروانے کا تھا۔ اشعر حسین جو راتوں رات باہر بھاگنے کی تیاری کر رہا تھا پھنس کر رہ گیا۔ محبت کے نام پر کسی کے اعتبار کا خون کرنے کی سزا تو ملتی ہی تھی اسے تاہم اس نے اپنی ساکھ خراب ہونے کے ڈر سے اس سے معافی مانگ کر اس کی تمام جائیداد واپس اس کے نام کروا دی تھی۔ اس کام سے فراغت کے بعد دادی ماں کی نصیحت اور ڈھارس بندھانے پر اس نے زائر کے گاؤں کا رخ کیا تھا۔ وہ نہیں جانتی تھی کہ وہ اسے معاف کرے گا یا نہیں مگر وہ ایک بار اس کے قدموں میں گر کر اس سے معافی ضرور مانگ لینا چاہتی تھی۔

❁......❁......❁

بارش ہو رہی تھی!

پچھلے کئی دنوں کے شدید حبس کے بعد اس روز بارش ہوئی تھی۔ پورے پندرہ دن ہو گئے تھے زائر نے گاؤں کا رخ نہیں کیا تھا۔ وہ تو جیسے گاؤں آنے والا راستہ ہی بھول بیٹھا تھا ثانیہ روز اس کا انتظار کرتی اور روز اس کی آس ٹوٹ جاتی۔ زائر کے ماں باپ کی خدمت کو اس نے اپنا نصب العین بنا لیا تھا مگر دل کو چین نہیں تھا۔

سائرہ ہر وقت منہ پھلائے پھرتی تھی۔ آج کل اس نے گاؤں کے نائی کے بیٹے کے ساتھ دعا سلام کر رکھی تھی۔ کوئی نہیں جانتا تھا کہ اس دعا سلام کے پیچھے اس کا کیا مقصد کارفرما تھا۔ ثانیہ کے آنے کے بعد اس نے گھر کے کام کاج سے بھی ہاتھ اٹھا لیا تھا۔ سارا سارا دن گھر کی چھت پر بیٹھی وہ جانے کیا کیا پلان بناتی رہتی تھی۔

پورے پندرہ دن کے بعد اس روز زائر نے گھر کا رخ کیا تھا۔ ثانیہ اس وقت کپڑے دھونے میں مصروف تھی ساتھ ہی اس نے تندور جلا رکھا تھا۔ سائرہ گھر پر نہیں تھی لہٰذا وہ اکیلی ہی بھاگ بھاگ کر سب کچھ سمیٹ رہی تھی جب وہ ادھ کھلے دروازے سے گھر کے اندر چلا آیا۔

''اماں...... دروازہ کیوں کھلا ہے کتنی بار کہا ہے دروازہ کھلا مت چھوڑا کریں مگر آپ کو......!'' قدرے خفگی سے کہتا وہ ابھی دو قدم ہی اٹھا پایا تھا کہ سامنے کپڑے سمیٹتی ثانیہ عباس کو دیکھ کر ٹھٹک گیا۔ منہ کے لفظ بھی منہ میں ہی رہ گئے تھے۔

''تم یہاں؟'' ثانیہ کی آنکھیں اسے دیکھتے ہی آنسوؤں سے بھر آئی تھیں۔ فقط چند روز میں ہی کتنا بدل گیا تھا وہ چہرے کا سارا حسن اور جاذبیت جیسے ماند پڑ گئی تھی۔ ہلکی ہلکی بڑھی ہوئی شیو اور بکھرے بالوں نے اس کے اندر کا حال اس پر خوب واضح کر دیا تھا۔ وہ شخص واقعی محبت کرنا جانتا تھا۔ ثانیہ نے ہاتھ میں پکڑے کپڑے دوبارہ تار پر ڈال دیے۔

''سائرہ......!'' اس سے پہلے کہ وہ اسے کچھ کہتی اس نے فوراً دہاڑ کر سائرہ کو آواز دے ڈالی تھی۔ مگر وہ گھر پر ہوتی تو جواب دیتی۔ تبھی راستے میں پڑی کپڑوں کی بالٹی کو ٹھوکر مارتے ہوئے وہ اماں کے کمرے کی طرف بڑھ آیا تھا۔

''اماں......!''

''ماں صدقے جائے کیوں چلا رہا ہے۔'' وہ ابا کو کپڑے تبدیل کروا رہی تھیں تبھی اس کے دھاڑنے پر فوراً لپکتے ہوئے باہر آ گئیں۔

''کہاں تھا اتنے دن نہ خیر نہ خبر حال بھی فقیروں جیسا بنا رکھا ہے۔''

''میرے حال کو چھوڑیں۔ سائرہ کہاں ہے؟'' اس کے چہرے پر سرخی تھی۔ اماں گھبرا گئیں۔

''یہیں محلے میں کسی کے گھر گئی ہو گی بات کیا ہے؟''

''بلا کر لائیں اسے اُلو کی پٹھی کو نہ اپنی عزت کا خیال ہے نہ کسی اور کی۔'' شدید غصے میں بنا ثانیہ کی ذات کو کوئی اہمیت دیے وہ اپنے کمرے کی طرف بڑھ گیا تھا۔ ثانیہ جہاں کی تہاں کھڑی رہ گئی تھی۔ تھوڑی ہی دیر بعد سائرہ گھر آئی تو وہ اس پر چڑھ دوڑا۔

''کہاں تھیں تم؟'' اس کی آنکھوں میں تیرتی غصے کی سرخی نے سائرہ کو بھی پریشان کر دیا تھا۔

''کیوں؟ ایسے کیوں پوچھ رہا ہے تو؟''

''جو پوچھا ہے اس کا جواب دے زیادہ بکواس کرنے کی ضرورت نہیں ہے۔'' ایک مرتبہ پھر وہ دھاڑا تھا۔ سائرہ کا دل زور سے دھڑک اٹھا۔

''اللہ دتہ نائی کے گھر تھی۔ اس کی بیٹی نے بلایا تھا۔''

''چٹاخ۔'' اس کے کہنے کی دیر تھی کہ زائر کے تھپڑ نے اسے چکرا کر رکھ دیا۔

''تم کیا سمجھتی ہو' اگر میں گاؤں میں نہیں ہوں تو مجھے تمہارے کرتوتوں کی کوئی خبر نہیں۔'' وہ چلا رہا تھا ثانیہ سہم کر رہ گئی۔ جبکہ سائرہ کو تو یقین ہی نہیں آیا کہ وہ اسے تھپڑ بھی مار سکتا ہے۔ تبھی وہ حیران کھڑی اماں کی طرف مڑا تھا۔

''میں نے کہا تھا آپ سے' اس کی شادی فائنل کر دیں مگر آپ کو مفت میں فارغ بیٹھ کر کھانے کی عادت پڑ گئی ہے۔ نہیں رکھوالی کر سکتیں تو کیوں رکھا اسے گھر میں؟'' اب وہ اپنی ماں کی خبر لے رہا تھا۔

''ہوا کیا ہے زائر' کیوں اتنا ہنگامہ کر رہا ہے تو۔''

''ہنگامہ......؟ میرا بس چلے تو میں گولی مار دوں' جو ایک مرتبہ پھر میری عزت کا جنازہ نکالنے پر تلی ہوئی ہے اور آپ بھی دیکھ لیجیے گا اس بار ابا کے بعد یہ مجھے چارپائی پر ڈالے گی۔'' اس کا غصہ کسی طور کم نہ ہو رہا تھا۔ اماں نے اپنا کلیجہ تھام لیا۔

''ہائے اللہ نہ کرے ایسے کیوں کہہ رہا ہے تو۔''

''پاگل ہو گیا ہوں اس لیے۔'' تنک کر کہتا وہ فوری گھر سے باہر نکل گیا تھا۔ ثانیہ بے آس و نامراد کھڑی رہ گئی تھی۔

وہ بے نیاز سا جیسے گھر آیا تھا ویسے ہی نکل گیا۔ یوں جیسے اسے ثانیہ کے آنے نہ آنے سے کوئی فرق ہی نہ پڑا ہو۔ سائرہ اسے نفرت سے گھورتی کچن میں جا گھسی تھی۔ وہ گم صم سی وہیں کھڑی رہی۔

❁ ...... ❁ ...... ❁

ساون شروع ہو گیا تھا۔

دن میں دو دو تین تین بار وقفے وقفے سے بارشیں ہو رہی تھیں۔ اس روز رات میں ثانیہ کی آنکھ کھلی تو زائر اسی کمرے میں اس سے کچھ فاصلے پر سو رہا تھا۔ پتا نہیں وہ کب آیا تھا اماں آج کل سائرہ کی شادی کے لیے خاصی سرگرم تھیں۔ وہ سارا سارا دن پاگلوں کی طرح زائر کا انتظار کرتی رہتی مگر وہ جیسے ادھر آنا ہی بھول چکا تھا۔

ایک سزا تقدیر نے اسے دی تھی اور ایک سزا اب زائر ملک اسے دے رہا تھا۔ وہ اندر ہی اندر گھلنا شروع ہو گئی۔ زائر نے بچے شہر میں ہوسٹل میں چھوڑ دیے تھے تاکہ ان کی تعلیم کا حرج نہ ہو۔ باہر صحن میں پھر بارش ہو رہی تھی۔

ثانیہ خاموشی سے اٹھی اور زائر کی چارپائی کے قریب چلی آئی۔ کروٹ کے بل لیٹا وہ بے خبر سو رہا تھا جب اس نے خاموشی سے آنسو بہاتے ہوئے اپنے ہونٹ اس کے پیروں پر رکھ دیے وہ جاگا تھا اور پھر فوراً سے پیشتر اس نے اپنے پاؤں اوپر سمیٹ لیے تھے۔

''زائر پلیز مجھے معاف کر دو' پلیز۔''

''کس بات کے لیے؟'' اس کے لہجے میں اب بھی کاٹ تھی۔ ثانیہ کے آنسوؤں میں مزید شدت آ گئی۔

''تم جانتے ہو میں تم سے کس بات کی معافی مانگ رہی ہوں۔''

''مت مانگو کیوں کہ مجھے تمہاری معافی کی ضرورت نہیں ہے۔'' تنک کر کہتا وہ فوراً کمرے سے باہر نکل آیا تھا۔ ثانیہ بھی اس کے پیچھے ہی چلی آئی۔

''زائر میں بہت شرمندہ ہوں میری بات سن لو پلیز' پھر جو چاہے سزا دے دینا میں اف بھی نہیں کروں گی۔''

''مجھے تمہاری کوئی بات نہیں سننی کیونکہ جس ثانیہ عباس کو میں نے اپنی عزت بنایا تھا وہ تم نہیں ہو۔'' وہ اس کی طرف پشت کیے کھڑا تھا تبھی ثانیہ اس کی آنکھوں سے ٹوٹے آنسوؤں کو نہیں دیکھ سکی تھی۔

''زائر پلیز' میں نے تمہاری عزت کے ساتھ کوئی سودا نہیں کیا ہے۔''

''اچھا پانچ سال دیارِ غیر میں ایک قطعی غیر محرم شخص کے ساتھ شب و روز گزار کر اس کے ساتھ شادی کی پلاننگ کر کے تم سمجھتی ہو تم نے میری عزت کا سودا نہیں کیا۔'' اس بار وہ اس کی طرف پلٹا تھا اور ثانیہ اس کی آنکھوں سے ٹوٹتے آنسو دیکھ کر دنگ رہ گئی تھی۔

''میں قصوروار تھا نا تمہاری نظر میں، میں نے دھوکا دیا تھا نا تمہیں، تو تمہیں مجھ سے لڑنا چاہیے تھا سارا حساب کتاب کلیئر کرنا چاہیے تھا فرار اس مسئلے کا حل نہیں تھا۔'' قطعی جنونی انداز میں اسے کندھوں سے پکڑ کر جھنجوڑتے ہوئے وہ جذباتی ہوا تھا۔ ثانیہ کے لبوں کو جیسے قفل لگ گیا تھا۔ وہ پلٹا تھا اور پھر کمرے میں جا کر اس نے اندر سے چٹخنی لگا لی تھی۔ ثانیہ فجر تک وہیں صحن میں بیٹھی بھیگتی رہی تھی۔

❁ ...... ❁ ...... ❁

شہر میں زائر کا بنگلہ تکمیل پا گیا تھا لہٰذا آج کل وہ شہر آیا ہوا تھا۔ بنگلے کی ملکیت اس نے ثانیہ عباس کے نام کر دی تھی۔

اس روز موسم بہت اچھا تھا۔ ثانیہ چھت پر بیٹھی مسلسل زائر کے بارے میں سوچ جا رہی تھی۔ جب سائرہ اس کے لیے دودھ کا گلاس لے کر وہیں چلی آئی۔ شام میں دودھ دوھنا اور پھر سب گھر والوں کو تقسیم کرنا اسی کی ذمہ داری تھی۔ ثانیہ نے قدموں کی چاپ پر پلٹ کر اس کی طرف دیکھا تھا۔

''یہ لو دودھ، خالہ نیچے بلا رہی ہیں تمہیں۔'' اس کے دیکھنے تک وہ قریب آ چکی تھی۔ ثانیہ نے رخ پھیر لیا۔

''نہیں...... آج دل نہیں چاہ رہا۔''

''دل نہیں چاہ رہا تھا تو سرِ شام ہی منع کر دیتیں۔ اب اس میں چینی مکس ہو گئی ہے کہاں سنبھال کر رکھوں، بتاؤ؟'' وہ فوراً ہی بے حد تلخ ہو گئی تھی۔ ثانیہ نے جھگڑے سے بچنے کے لیے گلاس تھام لیا۔

''ٹھیک ہے میں پی لوں گی۔ اماں سے کہہ دو ابھی تھوڑی دیر میں آتی ہوں۔''

''ٹھیک ہے، گلاس لے آنا ساتھ۔'' لٹھ مار لہجے میں کہتی وہ واپس پلٹ گئی تھی ثانیہ کتنی ہی دیر گلاس تھامے وہیں بیٹھی رہی۔ اسی دوران اس نے تین چار گھونٹ دودھ کے بھرے تھے۔ وہ ابھی سیڑھیوں پر تھی کہ اس کا سر چکرانا شروع ہو گیا۔ دودھ کا آدھا بھرا گلاس اس کے ہاتھ سے چھوٹ گیا تھا۔

سامنے کا منظر بھی دھندلانے لگا۔ مزید سیڑھیاں کراس کرنا اس کے لیے ممکن ہی نہ رہا تھا۔ عین اسی لمحے کرم داد نے دروازے پر دستک دی تھی جبکہ اماں جو کمرے میں بیٹھی ابھی نماز سے فارغ ہوئی تھیں۔ دھڑام سے کچھ گرنے کی آواز پر فوراً باہر کی طرف لپکی ثانیہ درد سے بے حال اپنا پیٹ پکڑے سیڑھیوں پر گری پڑی تھی۔ ان کے پاؤں تلے سے جیسے زمین نکل گئی۔

زائر اس وقت شاپنگ کر رہا تھا جب اسے کرم داد کا فون گیا۔ وہ اماں کے ساتھ، ثانیہ کی حالت غیر ہونے پر اسے شہر لے کر آ رہا تھا۔ زائر ہکا بکا رہ گیا۔ ابھی کل ہی تو وہ گھر سے آیا تھا تب تک وہ ٹھیک تھی۔ پھر ایک ہی دن میں ایسا کیا ہو گیا تھا؟

بچے اس کے ساتھ تھے اس نے فوراً انہیں ہوسٹل واپس چھوڑا اور بائیک مطلوبہ اسپتال کی طرف دوڑا دی جس وقت کرم داد اماں اور ثانیہ کے ساتھ اسپتال پہنچا اس کا رنگ خطرناک حد تک زرد پڑ چکا تھا۔ راستے میں دو بار قے بھی ہو گئی تھی۔ اس کے باوجود اسے دیکھ کر زائر کے پاؤں تلے سے زمین نکل گئی تھی۔ ایمرجنسی وارڈ میں فوری ایڈمٹ کرنے کے باوجود ڈاکٹرز کچھ بھی کہنے سے قاصر تھے۔ فوراً سے پیشتر اس کا معدہ واش کیا گیا تھا مگر اب بھی اس کی حالت تسلی بخش

نہیں تھی۔ زائر کو لگا جیسے کسی نے اس کے بدن سے جان کھینچ لی ہو لاکھ بے وفائیوں اور عداوتوں کے باوجود وہ لڑکی اس کی زندگی تھی اور اب تو اماں کی زبانی اس کی ساری کہانی سن کر وہ اس کی طرف سے اپنا دل بھی کسی حد تک صاف کر چکا تھا۔ پھر ایک دم سے اچانک یہ کیا ہو گیا تھا؟

ثانیہ کی رپورٹ آ چکی تھی زائر فوراً ڈاکٹر کی طرف لپکا۔

''ڈاکٹر صاحب' اب کیسی حالت ہے ثانیہ کی؟''

''ابھی بے ہوش ہے جب تک وہ ہوش میں نہیں آ جاتیں ان کے بارے میں کچھ بھی کہنا مشکل ہے۔''

''لیکن ہوا کیا ہے ابھی کل تک تو وہ بالکل ٹھیک تھی۔''

''جی ہاں' کل تک ٹھیک تھا مگر ابھی کچھ گھنٹے قبل انہیں زہر دیا گیا ہے اسی کی وجہ سے ان کی حالت خطرناک صورت حال سے دوچار ہے۔ آپ دعا کریں انہیں جلد از جلد ہوش آ جائے۔ نہیں تو کچھ بھی کہنا قبل از وقت ہوگا۔'' خالص پیشہ وارانہ انداز میں ڈاکٹر نے کہا تھا اور پھر آگے بڑھ گیا تھا۔ زائر بت بنا جہاں کا تہاں کھڑا رہ گیا۔ قریب کھڑی اماں اور کرم داد بھی ہکا بکا رہ گئے تھے۔

''میں ابھی آتا ہوں اماں آپ پلیز ثانیہ کا خیال رکھیے گا۔'' اگلے ہی پل کچھ سوچتے ہوئے اس نے اماں سے کہا اور پھر کرم داد کے پکارنے کے باوجود تیزی سے وہاں سے نکل آیا۔ تقریباً چالیس منٹ کے بعد جس وقت وہ گھر پہنچا سائرہ آئینے کے سامنے کھڑی اپنے بال سنوار رہی تھی۔ اس کے لبوں پر اس لمحے ایک عجیب سی پرسکون مسکراہٹ تھی۔ زائر کی آنکھوں میں خون اتر آیا۔

''ارے' تم یہاں کیا کر رہے ہو۔ ثانیہ کی طبیعت ٹھیک نہیں ہے۔ ماسی اسے لے کر شہر گئی ہے بتایا نہیں تمہیں کسی نے؟''

''چٹاخ۔'' ابھی وہ بات پوری بھی نہ کر سکی تھی کہ زائر کے زوردار تھپڑ نے اس کے چودہ طبق روشن کر دیے۔

''کیوں زہر دیا تم نے ثانیہ کو' بولو؟'' وہ اس کے دراز بالوں کو مٹھیوں میں جکڑے دھاڑ رہا تھا۔ سائرہ بلبلا کر رہ گئی۔

''بال چھوڑو میرے۔''

''چٹاخ۔'' بجائے بال چھوڑنے کے اس نے اسے ایک اور تھپڑ رسید کر دیا تھا۔

''کیا سمجھتی ہو تم' میں مرنے دوں گا اسے آسانی سے...... اسے...... جو میری زندگی ہے میرے بچوں کی ماں ہے...... تمہیں کیوں نہ مار دوں میں تاکہ اس کے بدلے میں سارا قصہ ہی پاک ہو جائے۔'' قہر کی علامت بنا وہ نہایت نفرت آمیز لہجے میں کہہ رہا تھا۔ سائرہ کی جان پر آ گئی۔

''چھوڑو مجھے۔''

''مار کر چھوڑوں گا اتنی آسانی سے چھوڑ دیا تو ہلکائے کتے کی طرح پھر کسی کو کاٹ کر مار ڈالو گی تم۔'' قطعی جنونی انداز میں اب وہ اس کا گلا دبا رہا تھا۔ سائرہ کے ہاتھ پیر سرد پڑ گئے۔ وہ تو سمجھی تھی ثانیہ کو راستے سے ہٹا کر وہ زائر کو پا لے گی مگر یہ زائر...... تو اس کا زائر رہا ہی نہیں تھا۔ یہ تو صرف ثانیہ عباس کا ہو کر رہ گیا تھا۔ وہ ضد کی پکی تھی مگر...... اس کی تقدیر نے اس کا ساتھ نہیں دیا تھا۔

ایک لمحہ لگا تھا اسے شکست تسلیم کرنے میں اور اس نے چپ چاپ خود کو زائر ملک کے سپرد کر دیا۔ محبت کی حویلی جو صرف اس کی ملکیت تھی اس نے خود اسے غیر آباد کر کے وہاں کسی اور کو بسنے کا موقع دیا تھا تو پھر اب گلہ کس سے کرتی؟ زائر نے اس کی حالت بگڑنے پر اسے حقارت سے پرے پھینک دیا تھا۔

''یاد رکھنا سائرہ افضل اگر میری ثانی کو کچھ ہوا تو اس سے پہلے خود اپنے ہاتھوں سے تمہیں زندہ زمین میں گاڑ دوں گا اور یہ محض دھمکی نہ سمجھنا۔'' جتنی حقارت اس کے لہجے میں تھی اس سے کہیں زیادہ حقارت اس کی آنکھوں میں تھی۔ سائرہ افضل نے پہلی بار خود کو مٹی ہوتے دیکھا تھا۔

✿ ..... ✿ ..... ✿

ثانیہ عباس کو ہوش آ گیا تھا۔

اس کی آنکھ کھلی تو اس کے دونوں بچے دائیں بائیں اس کے پاس بیٹھے تھے۔ جبکہ زائر عجیب دیوانوں سے حال میں دونوں بازو سینے پر باندھے قریب کھڑا اسے دیکھے جا رہا تھا۔ ابھی تھوڑی دیر پہلے ہی اس نے زبردستی اماں کو کرم داد کے ساتھ گاؤں واپس بھیجا تھا۔ کیونکہ وہاں سائرہ کے ساتھ ساتھ اس کا بوڑھا بیمار باپ تھا جسے دیکھ بھال کی ضرورت تھی۔

چاند کی نظر اس کی کھلی آنکھوں پر پڑی تو اس نے فوراً جھک کر اس کا گال چوم لیا۔

''اٹھیے نا مما' پاپا کہتے ہیں اچھے بچے اتنی دیر تک نہیں سوتے۔'' اس کی نصیحت پر گڑیا نے بھی جھک کر ماں کا گال چوما تھا۔

''جی مما اور آپ کو پتا ہے پاپا کب سے رو رہے ہیں۔ کھانا بھی نہیں کھایا انہوں نے۔'' گڑیا کو باپ کی فکر تھی ثانیہ نے اس کی اطلاع پر نظر اوپر کی تو زائر اس کے سرہانے کھڑا اسی کو دیکھ رہا تھا۔ خوب صورت آنکھوں کے گوشوں میں چھلکتی نمی اس سے پوشیدہ نہیں رہ سکی تھی۔ اس نے آہستہ سے پلکیں موندلیں۔

''ثانیہ'' اگلے ہی پل وہ اس کا ہاتھ تھامے اسے پکار رہا تھا۔ ثانیہ کی بند پلکوں سے آنسو ٹوٹ کر گالوں پر پھسل آئے۔

''ایم سوری' پلیز۔'' اپنے ہاتھوں سے اس کے آنسو صاف کرتے ہوئے وہ ذرا سا جھکا تھا۔ اس نے دوبارہ آنکھیں کھول دیں۔

''سوری کس لیے؟'' مدت کے بعد اس کی قربت پر وہ قدرے کنفیوژ ہوئی تھی جب وہ بولا۔

''ہر اس تکلیف کے لیے جو میری وجہ سے تم نے برداشت کی۔''

'''نہیں' میں آپ کو اتنی آسانی سے معاف نہیں کروں گی۔''

''کیوں؟'' وہ قدرے مزید جھک گیا تھا۔ ثانیہ بچوں کی موجودگی کی وجہ سے گھبرا گئی۔

''بعد میں بتاؤں گی۔'' اور اس کی گھبراہٹ پر وہ ہنسا تھا۔

تین روز کے بعد اسپتال سے ڈسچارج کروا کر وہ اسے شہر والے بنگلے میں لے آیا تھا۔ ثانیہ گاڑی سے اتری تو حیران رہ گئی۔

''یہ...... یہ کیا ہے؟''

''سرپرائز......!'' وہ مسکرا رہا تھا۔

''مطلب؟'' وہ الجھی تھی۔ تبھی زائر نے اس کا ہاتھ تھام لیا۔

''تمہیں گاؤں کے ماحول سے الجھن ہوتی ہے نا' اسی لیے میں نے شہر میں یہ گھر تمہارے لیے بنایا ہے تاکہ تمہیں اور بچوں کو کوئی مسئلہ نہ ہو۔'' بظاہر دیہات کے ماحول میں پرورش پانے والا وہ شخص اپنے قد میں کتنا بڑا تھا۔ یہ ثانیہ عباس نے اس وقت جانا تھا۔ بچے ان کے ساتھ نہیں تھے تبھی وہ پلٹی تھی اور اس نے پورے استحقاق سے اس کا گال چوم لیا تھا۔

''غلط...... مجھے کبھی بھی گاؤں کے ماحول سے الجھن نہیں رہی۔ بس آپ سے الگ ہونے کے بعد دانستہ میں اس ماحول سے بھاگتی تھی کیونکہ میرا دل میرے قابو میں نہیں تھا۔ کوئی آتش فشاں سا تھا جو ہر لمحہ میرے اندر پھٹنے کو تیار رہتا

تھا۔ اسی آتش فشاں کے زیر اثر میں نے صرف آپ کو دکھانے کے لیے اشعر حسین سے شادی رچانا چاہی تھی۔ آپ سوچ بھی نہیں سکتے زائر' میں نے کتنا کرب جھیلا ہے' جس روز مما نے بتایا کہ آپ نے مجھے طلاق دے دی ہے اس روز میں اتنا روئی کہ اسپتال کے در و دیوار بھی ہل کر رہ گئے تھے میرا بس نہ چلتا تھا کہ میں آپ کی جان لے لیتی۔ خیر مجھے آپ کے ساتھ رہنا ہے۔ اسی دس مرلے کے خوب صورت کشادہ گھر میں جہاں ہر چیز خالص ملتی ہے۔ پچھلے پانچ سالوں میں اس ماحول کو ترس کر رہ گئی ہوں میں' یہ محل' یہ اے سی' یہ اسٹائلش کچن باتھ' ان کی خوب صورتی اس گھر کی کچی چار دیواری' رسوئی اور غسل خانے کے سامنے کچھ بھی نہیں۔ جانتے ہیں کیوں؟ کیونکہ اس گھر میں میرا زائر رہتا ہے۔ جس کے دل پر میری حکمرانی ہے۔ جس کے جذبے جس کے خواب صرف میری ملکیت ہیں اور میں نے بہت دیر سے یہ جانا ہے زائر اس دنیا میں وہی عورت معتبر ہے جسے ایک خالص احساسات والا مرد سچا پیار کرتا ہے۔'' عورت کا اظہار محبت کتنا خوب صورت ہوتا ہے یہ زائر نے اس روز جانا تھا۔ تبھی ایک دلفریب سی مسکراہٹ نے اس کے لبوں کو چھولیا۔

''پاگل لڑکی پہلے یہ اظہار نہیں کر سکتی تھیں خوامخواہ اتنا خرچہ کروادیا۔''

''ہاہاہا۔'' وہ ہنسی تھی اور زائر کو لگا جیسے کائنات میں رنگ ہی رنگ بکھر گئے ہوں۔ اماں نے بتایا تھا ان کی گاؤں واپسی سے قبل ہی سائرہ گھر چھوڑ کر کہیں نکل گئی۔ شاید اس میں ثانیہ اور زائر کا دوبارہ سامنا کرنے کی ہمت نہیں تھی۔

زائر نے سنا تھا اور گہری سانس بھر کر رہ گیا تھا۔

اگلی صبح ثانیہ کی خواہش پر وہ اسے لے کر گاؤں کے لیے نکل آیا۔ ہلکی ہلکی برسات میں ثانیہ کے ساتھ نے اس کے اندر خوشیوں کے پھول کھلا دیے تھے۔ ہلکی ہلکی بڑھی ہوئی شیو اس نے ابھی تک صاف کرنے کی زحمت گوارا نہیں کی تھی۔ وہ کھڑکی سے باہر دیکھ رہی تھی جب وہ گنگنایا۔

''دو پتر چناراں دے
ساڈا دکھ سن سن کے روندے پتھر پہاڑاں دے''

عادت سے مجبور ڈرائیو کرتے ہوئے وہ کن اکھیوں سے اسے دیکھ رہا تھا۔ تبھی ثانیہ نے اس کے مضبوط کندھے پر ہلکا سا مکا رسید کیا۔

''اب بھی؟''

وہ ہنسا تھا اور پھر ہنستا ہی چلا گیا تھا۔ ثانیہ نے اپنے دونوں بازو اس کے بازو میں ڈال کر اپنا سر اس کے مضبوط کندھے پر ٹکا دیا تھا۔ بے شک ہجر کی لمبی مسافت کے بعد محبت کے سایہ دار درخت تلے آرام کرنا اس کا حق تھا۔

❁ ..... ❁ ..... ❁

حورعین کئی روز کے بعد آج ہی آفس آئی تھی۔

اس کی طبیعت ٹھیک نہیں تھی۔ مگر آفس آنا بھی بے حد ضروری تھا۔ بہت سی اہم میٹنگز تھیں جن میں اس کی شرکت بے حد ضروری تھی۔ وہ ابھی ایک میٹنگ سے فارغ ہو کر دوسری میٹنگ کے لیے تیاری کر رہی تھی۔ جب اس کی سیکرٹری نے اسے عمیر نامی وزیٹر کا بتا دیا۔ سیکرٹری کی اطلاع پر اس کا دل زور سے دھڑکا تھا۔

''ٹھیک ہے' آنے دیں۔'' بنا میٹنگ کو کوئی اہمیت دیے اس نے فوری حکم جاری کیا تھا۔ تھوڑی ہی دیر میں عمیر ہمدانی اس کے مقابل بیٹھا تھا۔

''السلام علیکم۔''

''وعلیکم السلام' کیسے ہو عمیر؟''

''آپ کو کیسا نظر آ رہا ہوں۔'' اس کے خلوص پر ایک تلخ مسکراہٹ عمیر ہمدانی کے لبوں پر بکھری تھی۔ وہ بے ساختہ نظریں چرا گئی۔

''میں جانتی ہوں تم مجھ سے ناراض ہو مگر......!''

''میں آپ سے ناراض نہیں ہوں' نہ ہی میرے لیے آپ اتنی اہمیت رکھتی ہیں کہ آپ سے ناراض ہوا جائے۔'' بنا اس کی پوری بات سنے بے حد تلخ لہجے میں اس نے کہا تھا۔ حورعین حیران سی اسے دیکھتی رہی۔

''میں یہاں اس وقت آپ سے کوئی گلہ شکوہ کرنے نہیں آیا ہوں۔ صرف اتنا بتانے آیا ہوں کہ چھٹکو کی طبیعت ٹھیک نہیں ہے۔ وہ ابھی اتنا بڑا نہیں ہوا کہ انسانوں کے مکر وفریب کو سمجھ سکے۔ سارا گھر اس کی وجہ سے بے حد پریشان ہے۔ مگر اس کی حالت بہتر نہیں ہو رہی۔ وہ صرف آپ کو پکار رہا ہے۔ انسانیت کے ناتے اگر اپنی مصروفیات ترک کر کے تھوڑا سا ٹائم اسے دے سکیں تو ہم سب آپ کے بے حد شکر گزار ہوں گے کیونکہ زیبی میں ہم سب کی جان ہے۔ جتنا وقت آپ اسے دیں گی ہم آپ کو آپ کے اس قیمتی وقت کی پے منٹ کریں گے۔ یہ لیں بینک چیک' جتنی رقم چاہیں آپ اپنی مرضی سے بھر سکتی ہیں۔'' ترش لہجے میں کہنے کے ساتھ ہی اس نے جیب سے چیک نکال کر حورعین کے سامنے رکھ دیا تھا حورعین کو لگا جیسے اس نے اس کے چہرے پر جم کر طمانچہ رسید کیا ہو۔ اہانت کے شدید احساس نے اس کی آنکھوں کو آنسوؤں سے بھر دیا تھا۔ بڑی مشکل سے خود کو سنبھالتے ہوئے وہ گلوگیر لہجے میں بولی تھی۔

''کہاں ہے زیبی؟''

''اسپتال۔''

''ٹھیک ہے' میں ابھی چلتی ہوں۔'' فوری فیصلہ کرتے ہوئے اس نے انٹر کام پر اپنی سیکریٹری کو چند ضروری ہدایات دی تھیں پھر عمیر کے ساتھ آفس سے نکل آئی۔

تقریباً آدھے گھنٹے بعد جس وقت عمیر کی ہمراہی میں اس نے زبیر کے کمرے میں قدم رکھا وہاں سمیر' نمیر' عذیر سبھی موجود تھے۔ عذیر اس کے اوپر جھکا اس کا بخار چیک کر رہا تھا جب قدموں کی آہٹ پر اس نے فوراً پلٹ کر دیکھا اور پھر حورعین پر نگاہ پڑتے ہی ٹھٹک گیا۔ سمیر اور نمیر کے چہروں پر ایک پل میں جیسے رونق آ گئی تھی۔ سبھی پریشان تھے مگر عذیر کی آنکھوں کے گوشوں کی ہلکی سی نمی نے اسے بے چین کر دیا تھا۔

حیران حیران سی نگاہیں حورعین کے چہرے سے ہو کر عمیر کی طرف اٹھی تھیں۔ مگر وہ فوری نظریں چرا گیا تھا۔ حورعین قدرے نروس ہوتی فوراً زبیر کے بستر کی طرف بڑھ آئی۔

کتنے دن ہو گئے تھے اسے اس ننھے سے وجود کو مس کرتے ہوئے کتنی راتیں تڑپ کر جاگتے ہوئے گزاری تھیں مگر ......اس کے دل کا حال سوائے خدا کے اور کون جانتا تھا۔ اگلے ہی پل زبیر کے بیڈ پر اس کے پہلو میں بیٹھتے ہوئے وہ بے ساختہ رو پڑی تھی۔ عذیر نے تنفر سے منہ پھیر لیا۔ دادی اماں کی طبیعت ٹھیک نہیں تھی لہٰذا سمیر اور نمیر گھر کے لیے نکل گئے تھے۔ عذیر عمیر کو زبیر کا خیال رکھنے کی تلقین کرتا خود بھی وہاں سے نکل آیا۔

رات تقریباً ساڑھے بارہ بجے کا ٹائم تھا جب اس کی دوبارہ اسپتال واپسی ہوئی تھی۔ زبیر کے کمرے میں حورعین' بالکل کسی ماں کی طرح اسے اپنی گرم آغوش میں لیے بیڈ پر بیٹھی سو گئی تھی۔ زبیر کے چہرے پر اگر زردی اور نقاہت تھی تو ویسی ہی زردی اور نقاہت حورعین عبدالسمیع کے چہرے پر بھی تھی۔ فقط چند ہی دنوں میں اس کی آنکھوں کے تلے بھی حلقے پڑ گئے تھے۔ اس کے گھر سے دور رہ کر وہ لڑکی بھی کب خوش رہ پائی تھی۔

عذیر زبیر کی دوائیاں چیک کرنے کے دوران کتنی ہی دیر بے مقصد سا اسے دیکھے گیا۔ بے شک وہ لڑکی حسن اور جاہت میں اپنی مثال آپ تھی۔ جانے یہ بہترین ٹریٹمنٹ کا اثر تھا یا حورعین کی آغوش کے لمس کا اثر تھا کہ اگلے ہی روز صبح صبح زبیر کا بخار ٹوٹ گیا اور اس نے آنکھیں کھول دیں۔ عذیر جو بیڈ سے ملحقہ کرسی پر ہی بیٹھا بیٹھا سو گیا تھا زبیر کی آواز پر اس کی آنکھ کھل گئی جو حورعین کی گود میں لیٹا تھا اور حورعین اس کے چہرے پر جھکی اسے پیار کر رہی تھی۔ اتنا مکمل اور خوب صورت منظر تھا کہ وہ چاہنے کے باوجود نظر نہیں ہٹا سکا تھا۔

''زیبی کی طبیعت اب پہلے سے بہتر ہے۔ میں یہاں اس کے پاس ہوں آپ گھر جا کر آرام کرلیں پلیز۔'' کچھ لمحوں کے بعد اس نے کہا تھا۔ حورعین نے چونک کر اسے دیکھا پھر نظریں جھکالیں۔

''نہیں، میں ٹھیک ہوں آپ چاہیں تو گھر جاسکتے ہیں۔''

''مگر میں آپ کو مزید تکلیف نہیں دینا چاہتا۔''

''میں تکلیف میں نہیں ہوں' یو ڈونٹ وری۔'' اسی کے لہجے میں اسے جواب دینے کے بعد وہ پھر سے زبیر کی طرف متوجہ ہوگئی تھی۔ جو اسے اپنے پاس پا کر خوشی سے پھولے نہیں سما رہا تھا۔ عذیر لب بھینچتا اٹھ کھڑا ہوا۔

''اوکے' نمیر یا عمیر میں سے کوئی بھی آجائے گا پھر چلی جائیے گا آپ۔'' وہ اسے حکم دے رہا تھا مگر حورعین نے سنی ان سنی کا مظاہرہ کر کے اثبات میں سر ہلا دیا۔ عذیر باہر گاڑی میں آکر بیٹھا تو بے حد تھکن محسوس ہو رہی تھی۔

اگر وہ اور اس کے گھر والے حورعین عبدالسمیع کے بغیر خوش نہیں تھے تو شاید وہ بھی ان کے بغیر خوش نہیں تھی تو پھر...... اس نے انہیں چھوڑنے کا فیصلہ کیوں کیا تھا؟

اتنی ساری محبتوں کو ٹھکرا کر بے رخی سے چلے جانے کی کوئی وجہ تو تھی مگر کیا؟ وہ چاہتی تو ساری زندگی سکون و عافیت کے ساتھ ان کے ساتھ رہ سکتی تھی مگر اس نے ایسا نہیں کیا تھا' کیوں؟

کیا واقعی دولت وہ وجہ تھی جس کے باعث وہ انہیں چھوڑ کر چلی گئی تھی؟

وہ یقین کرنا چاہتا تھا مگر جانے کیوں اس کا دل یہ تاویل ماننے کو تیار نہیں تھا۔ وہ دولت پر مرمٹنے والی لڑکی نہیں تھی۔ تو پھر اس نے یہ سب کیوں کیا تھا۔ جتنا وہ سوچتا جاتا تھا الجھتا جاتا تھا۔ تقریباً چالیس منٹ کی ڈرائیو کے بعد وہ گھر پہنچا تو عمیر ناشتا لے کر اسپتال کے لیے نکل چکا تھا۔ جبکہ نمیر دادی اماں کے پاس بیٹھا ان کو سوپ پلا رہا تھا۔ وہ سیدھا وہیں چلا آیا۔

''اب کیسی طبیعت ہے دادو؟''

''ٹھیک ہوں۔'' حورعین کے جانے کے بعد وہ بہت چپ ہو کر رہ گئی تھیں۔ بیمار بھی رہنے لگی تھیں۔ عذیر' نمیر کو دوا کھلانے کی ہدایت کرتا اپنے کمرے میں چلا آیا۔ سارا بدن تھکن سے ٹوٹ رہا تھا۔ تبھی پہلے اس نے ٹھنڈے پانی سے شاور لیا پھر کچن میں چلا آیا۔ اپنے لیے ایک کپ گرما گرم چائے بنائی اور بستر میں گھس گیا۔ سنڈے کی چھٹی کے باعث آفس جانے کی پریشانی بھی نہیں تھی۔

دوپہر کو تقریباً ایک بجے اس کی دوبارہ آنکھ کھلی تو سمیر اور نمیر کا زبردست جھگڑا ہو رہا تھا۔ سمیر کی چھٹیاں ختم ہو رہی تھیں اسے جاب پر واپس جانا تھا۔ وہ اسی کی تیاری میں تھا مگر نمیر کا کہنا تھا کہ اس کی طبیعت ٹھیک نہیں لہٰذا سمیر اس کا ہاتھ بٹا کر جائے۔ کچن ڈھیروں گندے برتنوں سے اٹا پڑا تھا۔ کیونکہ پچھلے تین چار روز سے انہوں نے برتن دھونے کی زحمت ہی گوارا نہیں کی تھی یہی حال کپڑوں اور گھر کی صفائی کا بھی تھا۔

اس سے پہلے کہ ان کا جھگڑا مار پیٹ کی شکل اختیار کرتا' عذیر نے بستر چھوڑ دیا۔ سمیر ڈھٹائی کا مظاہرہ کرتا گھر سے نکل

چکا تھا۔ عذیر نے نمیر کو بھی کچن سے نکال دیا۔ واقعی حورعین عبدالسمیع نے ان کی عادتیں بہت بگاڑ دی تھیں۔

شرٹ کے بازو فولڈ کر کے سب سے پہلے اس نے گندے برتنوں کا ڈھیر صاف کیا۔ پھر کپڑوں کی طرف آ گیا۔ سمیر' نمیر اور عمیر سمیت اس کا بھی ایک جوڑا ایسا نہیں رہا تھا جسے پہن کر وہ آفس جا سکتا۔ پچھلے ایک ہفتے سے وہ لوگ اپنے کپڑے دھوبی سے دھلوا رہے تھے مگر کب تک؟

پیٹ میں بھوک لگی تھی کیونکہ پچھلے چوبیس گھنٹوں میں اس نے سوائے ایک کپ چائے کے دوسری کوئی چیز حلق میں نہیں اتاری تھی۔ تاہم بھوک کو پس پشت ڈال کر اس نے مشین لگائی اور اکیلا ہی میلے کپڑوں کے ساتھ دو دو ہاتھ کرتا رہا' شام چار بجے اس کی حالت دیکھنے سے تعلق رکھتی تھی۔

عمیر اسپتال سے آیا تو آٹا گوندھ چکا تھا اور اب سالن بنانے کے لیے پیاز کاٹ رہا تھا۔ پینٹ کے پائنچے کافی اوپر تک بھیگے ہوئے تھے جب کہ اسے زکام بھی ہو رہا تھا' عمیر نے آتے ہی روٹی بنائی' دادی ماں کو کھچڑی بنا کر دی اور عذیر کے دھلے ہوئے کپڑوں کو پریس کرنے بیٹھ گیا۔

تقریباً ایک گھنٹے تک کھانا تیار ہوا تو دونوں بھائی ڈائننگ ٹیبل پر آ گئے' نمیر کی آنکھ بھی کھل چکی تھی۔ تینوں نے مل کر کھانا کھایا پھر عذیر کھانا نکال کر خود اسپتال کے لیے نکل آیا اور عمیر کو آرام کی تلقین کی۔

سمیر گھر واپس آیا تو عمیر سو رہا تھا' جب کہ نمیر دادی ماں کو دوا کھلانے کی کوشش کر رہا تھا۔ وہ ایک نظر ان دونوں پر ڈال کر کچن میں چلا آیا' بھوک کا احساس خوب زوروں پر تھا مگر ہاٹ پاٹ میں صرف ایک ہی روٹی بچی ہوئی پڑی تھی وہ بھی جلی ہوئی۔ اسے غصہ تو بہت آیا مگر پھر صبر شکر کر کے وہی روٹی پیٹ میں اتار لی وہاں کون سی ماں یا بیوی تھی جو نیند سے اٹھ کر تازہ روٹی بنا کر دیتی جب کہ باہر سے کھانا کھانے کی ان بھائیوں میں کسی کو بھی عادت نہیں تھی۔

عذیر کھانا لے کر اسپتال پہنچا تو حورعین زبیر کے بیڈ پر اس کے پہلو میں ہی مزے سے سو رہی تھی۔

فضا میں خنکی کافی بڑھ گئی تھی' زبیر گرم کمبل میں دبکا سو رہا تھا مگر حورعین کے پاس سوائے دوپٹے کے اور کوئی چیز نہیں تھی تبھی کھلی کھڑکی سے اندر آتے ہوا کے سرد جھونکوں نے اسے خاصا کپکپا رکھا تھا۔ عذیر نے آگے بڑھ کر کھانا بیڈ کی سائیڈ ٹیبل پر رکھا اور کھڑکی کے پٹ بند کر دیئے' پچھلے چوبیس گھنٹوں سے وہ لڑکی اپنی ہر مصروفیت کو پس پشت ڈالے وہاں زبیر کے ساتھ تھی اور اس دورانیے میں ایک مرتبہ بھی اس نے گھر جا کر آرام کرنے کی ضرورت محسوس نہیں کی تھی۔

کتنی ہی دیر وہ اسے یک ٹک دیکھتا رہا تھا پھر اچانک ہی آگے بڑھ کر اس نے اپنا گرم کوٹ اس کے اوپر ڈال دیا۔

اگلے روز اس نے آفس سے چھٹی کی تھی۔

دادو کا چیک اپ کروانے کے ساتھ ساتھ اسے بازار سے گھر کے لیے سودا سلف بھی لانا تھا کہ یہ اسی کی ذمہ داری تھی۔ ان تمام کاموں سے فارغ ہو کر اس نے گھر کی صفائی شروع کر دی' وہ نہیں چاہتا تھا کہ وہ لوگ پل پل حورعین کو یاد رکھیں اور آپس میں لڑتے رہیں شام تک تھکن سے چور وہ اپنے کمرے میں آیا تو جسم کا انگ انگ ٹوٹ رہا تھا' پتا نہیں حورعین یہ سب کام اتنی آسانی سے کیسے کر لیتی تھی۔ شاور لے کر اپنے لیے چائے بنانے کے بعد وہ بستر پر آیا تو نظر نیلے کور والی اس خوب صورت ڈائری پر جا پڑی جو آج صفائی کے دوران اسی کے کمرے سے برآمد ہوئی تھی تبھی وہ اسے گود میں لے کر بیٹھ گیا۔ حورعین عبدالسمیع کی اب تک گزری ہوئی زندگی کے تمام لمحات لفظوں میں قید ہو کر اس کے سامنے تھے اب تک جو صعوبتیں اس نے برداشت کی تھیں ابو غریب جیل میں جس طرح سے اس کی عزت کی دھجیاں اڑائی گئیں' ایاد عبدالہادی نے جس طرح اس کا ساتھ دیا سب درج تھا۔ ازحد اذیت کی گرفت میں اس نے لکھا تھا۔

''میں نے زندگی میں کبھی نہیں سوچا تھا کہ مجھے ایسی صعوبتیں برداشت کرنا پڑیں گی' وطن سے محبت کی اتنی کڑی قیمت

چکانی پڑے گی، میں صرف اتنا جانتی ہوں کہ زمانہ طالب علمی میں جب بھی کہیں کوئی ملی نغمہ سنتی، میری رگوں میں پاکستانی خون جوش مارنے لگتا تھا، میرا دل چاہتا تھا میں پاکستان کی طرف اٹھنے والی ہر میلی نگاہ کو پاؤں تلے کچل کر پھینک دوں، کوئی نہیں سمجھ سکتا پاکستان میرے لیے کیا ہے، اس وقت تو ویسے بھی میرا جنون تھا پاکستان مگر اس جنون کی بہت کڑی قیمت چکائی ہے میں نے اور اب...... اپنی عزت کی دولت لٹانے کے بعد جانے کیوں میرے حوصلے دم توڑ گئے ہیں اس ملک کی عوام کی قیمت میں گاجر مولی کی طرح طرح کٹ کٹ کر مرنا لکھ دیا گیا ہے بھیس بدل بدل کر مختلف مداریوں کے اشاروں پر ناچنا لکھ دیا گیا ہے، یہ فرانس نہیں ہے جسے کوئی ڈیگال آ کر سنوار دے۔ یہاں کوئی تاریخ رقم نہیں ہو سکتی، بندھے ہوئے مقروض ذہنوں کے مالک یہ لوگ کوئی انقلاب نہیں لا سکتے، اتحاد ایمان اور یقین کا سکہ یہاں چلنے والا نہیں ہے۔ اس پاک وطن کا یہی مستقبل ہے کہ یہاں تاریکیاں چھائی رہیں، زلزلے آتے رہیں، ڈیموں کے بند ٹوٹ کر لاکھوں پاکستانی شہریوں کو لقمۂ اجل بناتے رہیں، مختلف فرقوں اور مسلکوں کی آگ جلا کر انہیں راکھ کرتی رہے، یہاں ان کے اپنے نہیں غیر حکومت کریں، جیل کی اونچی چار دیواروں میں انمول ہیرے چپ کی بکل مارے خاک کے سپرد ہوتے رہیں، یہاں کوئی نظام کبھی تبدیل نہیں ہوگا بس مجھ جیسے دیوانے منٹو کے مرکزی کردار منگو کی طرح تبدیلی کی حسرت لیے جل جل کر ختم ہوتے رہیں گے بہرحال میں جانتی ہوں آج کے بعد آپ میری شکل دیکھنا بھی گوارا نہیں کریں گے پھر بھی میرا دل کٹ رہا ہے، جانے کیوں اس گھر کے در و دیوار سے عجیب سی انسیت ہوگئی ہے۔ میں جانتی ہوں جو کچھ میرے ساتھ ہوا اس میں میرا کوئی قصور نہیں تھا مگر میں یہ بھی جانتی ہوں کہ آپ بہت اچھے ہیں، بہت شفاف کردار کے مالک آپ کی ہم سفر بھی ایسی ہی کوئی شفاف لڑکی ہونی چاہیے مجھ جیسی داغ دار لڑکی، آپ کے قابل نہیں ہے۔ ہو سکے تو مجھے میری ناکردہ خطاؤں کے لیے معاف کر دیجیے گا احسان مند ہوں گی۔'' ایک ایک لفظ عذیر ہمدانی پر سوچ کے نئے در وا کرتے ہوئے گزرا تھا۔

تھکے تھکے سے انداز میں گہری سانس بھرتے ہوئے اس نے آہستہ سے پلکیں موندیں۔ تو یہ وجہ تھی جس کے سبب اس لڑکی نے اس کا گھر چھوڑا تھا؟ الجھن کو سرا مل گیا تھا مگر اندر ایک اور جنگ چھڑ گئی تھی کیا اس میں اتنا حوصلہ تھا کہ وہ ایک داغ دار لڑکی کو اپنی ہم سفر کے طور پر ہمیشہ کے لیے قبول کرتا؟ شاید نہیں......

✿......✿......✿

بارش ہو رہی تھی۔

وہ بیرونی دروازہ اچھی طرح بند کرنے کے بعد لاؤنج میں آ بیٹھی، بہت دنوں کے بعد آج پھر آسمان بارش کے سرد قطروں کی صورت اپنی قیمتی متاع لٹا رہا تھا۔ گرما گرم کافی کا مگ ہاتھ میں لیے وہ دونوں پاؤں صوفے پر رکھ کر بیٹھ گئی تھی۔ فضا میں ٹھنڈک کا احساس تھا کہ بڑھتا جا رہا تھا، وقت نے کتنا اکیلا کر دیا تھا اسے؟

حورعین عبدالسمیع جو کبھی محفلوں کی جان ہوا کرتی تھی، آج تنہائی کی گود میں کیسے مٹی کی مورت بن کر رہ گئی تھی؟ کتنا بدل دیا تھا وقت نے اسے؟

ثانیہ عباس اور ہانیہ صفدر سے اس کا رابطہ بھی کب کا ختم ہو چکا تھا، بھری دنیا میں کہیں کوئی بھی تو نہیں تھا جسے وہ اپنا کہہ سکتی۔ قبرستان گئے بھی کتنے دن ہو گئے تھے، جب سے وہ اسپتال سے واپس آئی تھی اداسی اور بے چینی مزید بڑھ گئی تھی، دو ماہ ہونے کو آئے تھے مگر وہاں سے دوبارہ کسی نے اس کے ساتھ رابطہ نہیں کیا تھا۔

حورعین نے سوچ لیا تھا وہ پاکستان میں نہیں رہے گی، اسی لیے آج کل وہ اپنا بزنس وائنڈ اپ کرنے کا سوچ رہی

تھی۔ رات کی تاریکی تھی کہ بڑھتی جا رہی تھی مگر نیند کا دور دور تک کوئی نام و نشان نہیں تھا۔

کافی کا کپ خالی کر کے وہ ابھی کچن میں رکھنے جا رہی تھی جب دروازہ پر دستک نے اسے چونکا دیا' بھلا اتنی رات کو کون آ سکتا ہے؟ پریشان سی وہ دروازے تک آئی تھی۔

''کون......؟''

''دروازہ کھولیں بھابی' میں ہوں سمیر۔''

''سمیر......'' زیر لب دہراتے ہوئے اس نے دروازہ کھول دیا تھا' سامنے وہ بارش میں بھیگا کھڑا تھا۔

''السّلام علیکم!۔''

''وعلیکم السّلام خیریت۔''

''نہیں بھابی خیریت نہیں ہے' دادو کو فالج کا اٹیک ہوا ہے ہم سے سنبھالی نہیں جا رہیں' عذیر بھائی ملک سے باہر ہیں میں خود بھی کل ہی گھر واپس آیا ہوں اگر آپ کو کوئی مسئلہ نہ ہو تو پلیز ابھی میرے ساتھ چلیے' سب بہت پریشان ہیں۔'' پریشانی اس کے لہجے سے ٹپک رہی تھی' وہ گڑبڑا گئی۔

''اس وقت؟ اچھا آپ اندر آئیں۔''

''نہیں بھابی! اتنا ٹائم نہیں ہے' دادو ابھی اسپتال میں ہی ہیں' پلیز۔''

''اچھا میں چلتی ہوں۔'' اسے سوچنے سمجھنے کا موقع بھی نہیں ملا تھا اور وہ سمیر کے ساتھ چل پڑی تھی دادو کو واقعی فالج کا اٹیک ہوا تھا مگر اس وقت ان کی حالت خطرے سے باہر تھی۔ حورعین نے رات بھر ان کا ایسے ہی خیال رکھا جیسے بیٹیاں ماؤں کا رکھتی ہیں۔

صبح اس نے سمیر کو گھر بھیج دیا تو نمیر ناشتہ لے کر آ گیا' تقریباً تین روز کے بعد دادو کو گھر شفٹ کر دیا گیا تھا۔ اس بار وہ بھی ان کے ساتھ ہی گھر آ گئی تھی' عذیر کو تا حال کسی بات کی خبر نہیں تھی' حورعین نے دیکھا گھر کا پہلے سے بھی بدتر حال ہوا پڑا تھا۔

دادو کے سونے کے بعد وہ ان کے کمرے سے باہر آئی تو زبیر اسکول اور عمیر یونیورسٹی جا چکا تھا۔ نمیر کا جاب کا مسئلہ حل نہیں ہوا تھا لہٰذا ناشتہ بنا کر رکھنے کے بعد وہ بھی گھر سے نکل چکا تھا۔ سمیر البتہ گھر پر تھا اور اپنے کمرے میں پڑا سو رہا تھا۔ حورعین کچن میں آئی تو اس کا حال دیکھ کر اس کا دل متلا اٹھا' برتنوں اور چولہے کا حال دیکھنے سے تعلق رکھتا تھا۔ تبھی بناء ناشتہ کیے وہ کچن کی صفائی میں جت گئی تھی' ایک کامیاب بزنس مین لڑکی' کتنی سلیقہ مند تھی کاش کوئی جان پاتا۔ اگلے ڈیڑھ گھنٹے میں کچن چمک اٹھا تھا' تبھی اپنے لیے چائے کا ایک کپ بنا کر چائے پینے کے بعد وہ عذیر کے کمرے کی طرف آ گئی جس کا حال کچن سے بھی بدتر تھا' بیڈ کی چادر جانے کتنے دنوں سے نہیں بدلی گئی تھی۔ عذیر کے استعمال شدہ کپڑوں کا ڈھیر وارڈ روب سے اُمڈ اُمڈ کر باہر آ رہا تھا۔ ڈریسنگ ٹیبل کی ساری چیزیں الٹ پلٹ تھیں' قالین بھی نہایت گندا ہو رہا تھا۔ یوں لگتا تھا جیسے کافی دنوں سے وہاں کسی نے صفائی کرنے کی زحمت ہی گوارا نہیں کی تھی۔ سمیر اور نمیر وغیرہ کے کمروں کا حال بھی عذیر سے کچھ مختلف نہیں تھا تبھی سب سے پہلے اس نے مشین لگائی تھی پھر جھاڑن پکڑ کر ایک ایک کمرے کو خوب صاف کیا' عمیر جب تک کالج سے آیا وہ سارا گھر صاف کر کے کپڑے بھی دھو چکی تھی اور اب کچن میں کھڑی ان سب کے لیے کھانا بنا رہی تھی۔ وہ حیران ہی تو رہ گیا تھا۔

''یہ کیا کر رہی ہیں آپ؟'' کچن میں داخل ہوتے ہی اس نے پوچھا تھا جواب میں حورعین نے گردن موڑ کر ایک نظر اس پر ڈالنے کے بعد دوبارہ توجہ آٹے پر مبذول کر دی جسے وہ گوندھ رہی تھی۔

''وہی جو بشار الاسد شام میں اور مصری فوج مصر میں کر رہی ہے۔''

''مگر یہ آپ کا کام نہیں ہے جو احسان ہم آپ سے لے چکے ہیں وہی کافی ہے۔''

''کوئی بات نہیں جہاں اتنے احسان ہو گئے وہاں ایک اور سہی۔''

''مگر کیوں؟''

''بس...... مجھے عادت ہے احسان کرنے کی۔''

''مگر میں آپ سے مزید کوئی احسان نہیں لینا چاہتا' باوجود اس کے کہ میں آپ کی ڈائری پڑھ چکا ہوں۔'' وہ قریب آیا تھا' حورعین ٹھٹک گئی۔

''وہ ڈائری تمہارے لیے نہیں تھی۔''

''جانتا ہوں میں پڑھنا بھی نہیں چاہتا تھا مگر اتفاقیہ ہاتھ لگ گئی تو رہ بھی نہیں سکا' آپ کیا سمجھتی ہیں وطن کی محبت میں اگر آپ نے انسانیت کے دشمنوں کے ہاتھوں اپنی عزت گنوا دی تو آپ ہمارے لیے محترم نہیں رہیں؟''

''عمیر میں......''

''بس حورعین آپی پلیز...... اپنی صفائی میں مزید ایک لفظ بھی مت کہیے گا پلیز۔'' وہ دکھی ہوا تھا حورعین نے لب بھینچ لیے۔

''آپ اس گھر میں صرف عذیر بھیا کی بیوی نہیں ہیں' ہماری بہن بھی ہیں وہ بہن جس کے کردار پر کوئی اور فخر کرے نہ کرے مگر میں فخر کرتا ہوں۔ عذیر بھیا اگر آپ کے ساتھ زندگی بسر نہیں بھی کرتے تب بھی آپ ہماری بہن ہیں اور رہیں گی۔ چاہے ایک دمڑی بھی نہ ہو آپ کے پاس۔'' وہ جذباتی ہوا تھا' حورعین کی آنکھیں پل میں آنسوؤں سے بھر آئیں' آگے بڑھ کر اس نے فوراً عمیر کو گلے لگا لیا تھا۔

اگلے کئی دنوں تک وہ عمیر کے ساتھ اس کے اصرار پر قبرستان جاتی رہی تھی پھر مصروفیات کے پیش نظر رفتہ رفتہ اس معمول میں کمی آتی گئی' زبیر اب اس کا ایک لمحے کے لیے بھی اعتبار نہیں کرتا تھا۔ صبح اسکول بھی روز وعدہ لے کر جاتا کہ وہ اس کے آنے تک کہیں جائے گی نہیں' حورعین کے لیے اب ان محبتوں کے بغیر رہنا بہت مشکل ہو رہا تا مگر وہ خود کو زبردستی کسی کی زندگی پر مسلط نہیں کر سکتی تھی۔

دادو اس سے بہت خوش تھیں انہیں یقین تھا کہ ضرور وزیر نے حورعین سے کسی جھگڑے کے پیش نظر ان سے اس کے بارے سب جھوٹ کہا تھا' سمیر نمیر اور عمیر کی زندگیاں بھی سکون میں آ گئی تھیں۔ حورعین آفس کا ایک چکر لگانے کے باوجود گھر کے کسی کام میں کوتاہی نہیں کرتی تھی' نمیر کو بھی اس نے اپنے ہی آفس میں زبردستی جاب دے دی تھی جس پر وہ بے حد خوش تھا۔ سمیر اپنی آفس کولیگ پر دل ہار بیٹھا تھا مگر دادو سے شیئر کرتے ہوئے شرم محسوس کر رہا تھا' کافی سوچنے کے بعد اس نے اپنا مسئلہ حورعین کے سامنے رکھ دیا تھا' جس نے ایک ہی ملاقات میں لڑکی اوکے کر کے اس کی منگنی بھی کروا دی تھی۔

عذیر کو ایک ایک پل کی خبر تھی مگر دانستہ وہ گھر سے دور دیار غیر میں انجان بنا بیٹھا تھا۔ کتنے ماہ ہو گئے تھے اسے خود سے لڑتے ہوئے مگر وہ ابھی تک حورعین کے بارے کوئی فیصلہ نہیں کر پایا تھا۔ گھر کال کرنے کے دوران بھی وہ اس سے بات نہیں کرتا تھا اب تک جتنے دن بھی اس نے گھر سے باہر بسر کیے تھے ان دنوں میں بہت سی لڑکیوں کو پرکھا اور خود سے قریب کیا تھا' ابتداء میں لگتا جیسے اسے ملنے والی لڑکی ہی اس کی منزل ہے مگر جیسے جیسے کچھ وقت گزرتا اسے اس لڑکی میں خامیاں نظر آنے لگتیں اور وہ اکتا کر اسے چھوڑ دیا۔ دن ہفتوں' ہفتے مہینوں اور مہینے سالوں میں ڈھلتے گئے تھے مگر وہ

واپسی کا فیصلہ نہ کر سکا' اسی دوران دادو اس کے بچوں کو گود میں جھلانے کی حسرت دل میں لیے دنیا سے رخصت ہو گئیں تو اسے مجبوراً پاکستان آنا پڑا۔

دادو کی موت پر اس نے ایک مرتبہ پھر اپنے گھر میں حورعین کا کردار دیکھا تھا' غم کی شدت سے نڈھال ہونے کے باوجود وہ جیسے اپنا فرض ادا کر رہی تھی' ہر مہمان کو سنبھال رہی تھی وہ حیران رہ گیا۔

دادو کے چالیسویں کے بعد سمیر نے بیرون ملک جانے کا پروگرام بنالیا' تاہم اس کے سسرال والوں کی خواہش تھی کہ وہ شادی کر کے جائے۔ دادو کے بعد گھر کا ماحول ویسے ہی بہت افسردہ ہو رہا تھا تبھی عذیر نے سمیر کی خوشی کے لیے یہ فریضہ ادا کرنے کی ٹھان لی۔ ساتھ ہی اس کی یہ سوچ بھی تھی کہ سمیر کی دلہن کے گھر آجانے کے بعد اسے اور اس کے گھر والوں کو حورعین کی زیادہ ضرورت نہیں رہے گی یوں وہ اس کے بارے میں آسانی سے فیصلہ کر لے گا تبھی چٹ منگنی اور پٹ بیاہ کے مصداق سمیر کی دلہن رخصت ہو کر ان کے گھر آ گئی۔

حورعین نے اس موقع پر بھی ان کا پورا پورا ساتھ دیا تھا' اپنی تمام تر مصروفیات کے باوجود وہ شادی کی شاپنگ سے لے کر' دلہن کی رخصتی تک اس گھر کا حصہ بنی رہی تھی۔ عذیر سمیت کسی کو بھی کسی چیز کی فکر نہیں تھی' تمام فنکشنز کے لیے جسے جو چیز مطلوبہ ہوتی وہ اسی سے آ کر مانگتا اور حورعین سب کو فوری وہ چیز مہیا کر دیتی۔

اس روز سمیر کا ولیمہ تھا' رات دیر تک جاگ کر وہ ان سب کے کپڑے پریس کرتی رہی تھی' ڈھیر سارے مہمانوں کو اکیلے سنبھالنا بھی اس کی ہمت تھی۔ رات تک وہ تھکن سے چور ہو گئی' عذیر باہر کے معاملات نپٹا رہا تھا' سمیر نے زبردستی اسے کندھوں سے تھام کر عذیر کے کمرے میں بھیج دیا تا کہ وہ تھوڑی دیر آرام کر سکے' نمیر اور عمیر کے کمروں سمیت دادو کے کمرے پر بھی مہمانوں کا قبضہ ہو چکا تھا۔ تبھی مجبوراً وہ عذیر کے کمرے میں آئی تھی اور بیڈ پر گرتے ہی گہری نیند کی دلدل میں اترتی چلی گئی۔

رات تقریباً دو بجے کا ٹائم تھا جب عذیر سارے کام نپٹا کر تھکا ہارا اپنے کمرے میں آیا اور دروازہ لاک کر کے بستر پر ڈھے گیا۔ اس کے وہم و گمان میں بھی نہیں تھا کہ حورعین بھی وہیں سو رہی ہو گی۔ وہ تو جب اس نے کمبل سیٹ کرنا چاہا تو حورعین پر نظر پڑی جو اسی کی طرح تھکن سے بے حال بنا کپڑے تبدیل کیے ایک طرف سمٹ کر سو رہی تھی۔ مٹا مٹا سا میک اپ اس کے پُرنور چہرے پر چاندنیاں بکھیر رہا تھا۔ عذیر کا دل زور سے دھڑک اٹھا' پہلی مرتبہ وہ اس کے اس قدر قریب سو رہی تھی اور یہ قرب اس وقت اس کے اندر جیسے اک حشر بپا کر رہا تھا' بناء کمبل کے شدید سردی میں سمٹ کر سوئی' وہ ہولے ہولے کپکپا رہی تھی جب کہ کمبل اس کے نیچے دبا تھا۔

عذیر کچھ دیر یک ٹک اسے دیکھتا رہا پھر خود بھی کمبل کے بغیر سیدھا لیٹ گیا' حورعین کا بازو اس کے کندھے کے ساتھ ٹچ ہو رہا تھا۔ وہ بے خود سا ہو کر اس پر جھک گیا' نہایت آہستگی سے اس نے اس کے کانوں سے ائیر رنگز اتارے تھے پھر گلے میں پہنے گولڈ کے سیٹ پر ہاتھ رکھ دیا مگر اس سے پہلے کہ وہ سیٹ اتارتا حورعین نے کروٹ بدل لی' اب اس کا پُرنور چہرہ اسی کی طرف تھا سرخ لپ اسٹک سے سجے یاقوتی لب اس کی برداشت ختم کر رہے تھے' جانے یہ کیسا طلسم تھا کہ وہ اس کی ساری ہسٹری بھول گیا' یاد رہا تو محض اتنا کہ وہ اس کی بیوی ہے تبھی بے خود ہوتے ہوئے اس نے کھینچ کر اسے اپنی بانہوں میں سمیٹ لیا تھا۔ حورعین اس اچانک افتاد پر ہڑبڑا کر فوراً بیدار ہوئی تھی' نائٹ بلب کی مدھم روشنی میں اسے عذیر کا چہرہ دکھائی نہیں دے رہا تھا تبھی خود کو اس آہنی گرفت سے چھڑانے کی کوشش کرتے ہوئے اس نے چیخنا چاہا تھا مگر اس سے پہلے ہی عذیر نے اپنا ہاتھ مضبوطی سے اس کے لبوں پر جما دیا۔

''شش......''

شدید سردی کے باوجود اس کی پیشانی اور چہرے پر پسینے کی ننھی ننھی بوندیں چمک رہی تھیں۔ وہ بھونچکا ہی تو رہ گئی مگر اس سے پہلے کہ وہ اس سے کچھ کہتی' عذیر اس کے چہرے پر جھک چکا تھا۔ وہ اسے روکنا چاہتی تھی مگر اس لمحے اس میں اتنی سکت نہیں رہی تھی' تھکن سے ٹوٹے ہوئے چور جسم پر عذیر ہمدانی اپنی تھکن انڈیل رہا تھا اور وہ بے بس سی بس اس کی پیاس بجھائے جا رہی تھی۔ گرم سانسوں کا طوفان جیسے سب کچھ بہا کر لے گیا تھا۔

اگلی صبح جب وہ بیدار ہوا تو حورعین کمرے میں نہیں تھی مگر وہ بے حد فریش تھا۔ تمہارا غیر دانستہ طور پر جو کچھ اس سے سرزد ہوا' اس نے اس کا اضطراب مزید بڑھا دیا تھا۔ کمرے سے نکلا تو پتا چلا کہ حورعین کی طبیعت ٹھیک نہیں تھی لہٰذا وہ علی الصبح وہاں سے چلی گئی تھی' سمیر کے کمرے کا دروازہ ہنوز بند تھا۔ زبیر اور نمیر بھی سو رہے تھے' صرف عمیر تھا جو کچن میں کام کر رہا تھا اور اسی نے اسے حورعین کے بارے میں بتایا تھا۔ وہ گہری سانس فضا کے سپرد کرتا ٹیرس پر چلا آیا مگر ایک بے چینی سی تھی جو اس کے اندر بہت دور تک پھیلتی چلی گئی تھی۔

❁......❁......❁

دو ماہ ہو گئے تھے اسے دوبارہ فرانس آئے مگر دل کی بے کلی تھی کہ دل و جان سے چمٹ کر رہ گئی تھی۔ سمیر کی شادی کے تیسرے دن وہ فرانس آ گیا تھا کیونکہ اس میں حورعین عبدالسمیع سے نظریں ملانے کی ہمت نہیں تھی۔ اس نے سوچ لیا تھا وہ اب زیادہ دن تک اسے اپنے ساتھ باندھ کر نہیں رکھے گا گھر سنبھالنے کے لیے گھر میں ایک اور عورت آ گئی تھی' وہ اب مزید اسے اپنا پابند نہیں رکھ سکتا تھا۔

طلاق کے کاغذات سب تیار ہو گئے تھے' اس شام وہ گیم کر کے آیا تو پاکستان سے عمیر کا خط اس کا منتظر تھا' رات کھانے کے بعد بیڈ پر آ کر اس نے وہ خط کھولا تھا۔

لکھا تھا۔

''میں جانتا ہوں آپ یقیناً میرا خط دیکھ کر حیران ہوں گے مگر بات ہی کچھ ایسی تھی کہ خط لکھنا ضروری ہو گیا ہے' حورعین آپی ایبروڈ جا رہی ہیں ان کا خیال ہے کہ اب ہمارے گھر کو ان کی ضرورت نہیں ہے۔ سمیر بھیا کی وائف نے کوشش کی ہے ان کی جگہ لینے کی مگر میں آپ کو بتا رہا ہوں عذیر بھائی! اس گھر میں حورعین آپی کی جگہ کبھی کوئی نہیں لے سکتا۔ میں مانتا ہوں وہ آپ کو قابل قبول نہیں' بہتر سے بہترین لڑکی مل سکتی ہے آپ کو مگر اس بات کی کیا گارنٹی ہے کہ وہ بہتر سے بہترین لڑکی آپ کے گھر کے لیے بھی اتنی ہی بہترین ثابت ہو' حورعین آپی ہر لحاظ سے بہت اچھی ہیں پلیز بھیا انہیں اس گناہ کی سزا مت دیجیے جو ان سے سرزد ہی نہیں ہوا۔ میری ایک بات یاد رکھیے گا عذیر بھائی آپ کو لڑکیاں بہت مل جائیں گی مگر ڈھونڈنے سے بھی دوسری حورعین عبدالسمیع نہیں ملے گی اس سے پہلے کہ وہ چلی جائیں پلیز انہیں روک لیں' پلیز مخلص آپ کا بھائی عمیر۔'' خط کیا تھا سوچ کا ایک نیا در تھا' عذیر ساکت سا بیٹھا رہ گیا تھا۔ بے شک فیصلے کی گھڑی آ پہنچی تھی۔

❁......❁......❁

حورعین کی ٹکٹ کنفرم ہو گئی تھی۔

رات زیبی کو سلاتے ہوئے بہت دیر تک وہ روتی رہی تھی' گھر میں کوئی بھی اس کے اندر پیدا ہونے والی تبدیلی کو نہیں جان پایا تھا مگر کچھ روز قبل ہی اپنے تفصیلی چیک اپ کے بعد اس نے جانا تھا کہ عذیر ہمدانی کی ذات کے ساتھ اس کا

رشتہ اور بھی مضبوط ہوگیا تھا تاہم وہ نہیں چاہتی تھی کہ گھر میں کسی کو بھی اس بات کا پتا لگے تبھی اس نے فوری پاکستان سے فرار کا پروگرام بنایا تھا کیونکہ پاکستان میں رہتے ہوئے اس گھر سے دور رہنا اور ان سے کوئی خبر چھپانا اس کے لیے ممکن ہی نہیں رہا تھا۔

ننھے زبیر کو سلانے کے بعد اس نے اپنی پیکنگ کی تھی۔ سمیر کی بیوی نے سارا گھر سنبھال لیا تھا اور یہ بات اس کے اطمینان کے لیے کافی تھی سمیر نے زبیر کو بورڈنگ بھجوانے کی تیاری بھی مکمل کر لی تھی۔ نمیر جاب میں مصروف ہوگیا تھا مگر عمیر بہت اداس تھا۔ مصر اور شام میں انسانی بربریت کا دکھ ہی کافی تھا کہ اس پر حورعین نے بھی دیارِ غیر میں جا کر بسنے کی خبر سنا دی تھی تاہم وہ ڈائریکٹ اسے روکنے کی ہمت نہیں کر پا رہا تھا۔

اگلی صبح ناشتے کے بعد زبیر کو اسکول روانہ کر کے وہ عمیر کے کمرے میں چلی آئی تھی۔

''عمیر۔''

''جی آپی۔'' وہ جو مطالعے میں مصروف تھا فوراً چونکا تھا۔

''ناشتا نہیں کیا تم نے؟''

''بس دل نہیں چاہ رہا۔'' کتاب بند کر کے وہ پوری طرح اس کی طرف متوجہ ہوگیا تھا تبھی وہ پاس بیٹھ گئی۔

''یہ تو اچھی بات نہیں ہے، میں جانتی ہوں تم شام اور مصر کے حالات پر پریشان ہو مگر صرف تم پریشان نہیں ہو عمیر! ہر صاحب فکر مسلمان جس کے دل میں ذرا سی بھی انسانیت اور نرمی ہے وہ پریشان ہے مگر اس پریشانی کا یہ حل نہیں ہے کہ انسان کھانا پینا چھوڑ دے اللہ ربّ العزت نے ہر انسان کو عمر کی نقدی دے کر دنیا کے بازار میں اعمال کی خریداری کے لیے بھیجا ہے جب جس روز یہ نقدی ختم ہو جائے گی ہر انسان اپنے کندھے پر اپنے اعمال کی گٹھری لاد کر راہِ عدم کا مسافر ہو جائے گا۔ روزِ محشر یہ گٹھری جب کھلے گی تو تم تصور بھی نہیں کر سکتے عمیر جو انسان کا حال ہوگا۔ لذتوں اور غفلتوں کا خمار اترنے میں زیادہ دیر نہیں لگے گی پھر تم دیکھنا وہاں ان کا حشر کیا ہوگا۔ دنیا کا قالین تو بس سمٹا ہی چاہتا ہے ہم گمراہ نہیں ہیں جو یہ بات اپنے دل و دماغ میں بٹھا لیں کہ مرنے کے بعد کوئی زندگی نہیں ہو سکتی' نہ ہی اس غلط فہمی کو سر پر سوار کر سکتے ہیں کہ ایک بار دنیا سے رخصت ہونے کے بعد دوبارہ کوئی جنم ہوگا' ہماری موت سعادت کی موت ہے عمیر! تم ذرا ان لوگوں کا سوچو' ان کا کیا بنے گا؟'' اس کا انداز ڈھارس بندھانے والا تھا' عمیر کی آنکھوں کے گوشے نم ہوگئے۔

''ہم دوبارہ جنم کی امید پر کوئی غفلت افورڈ نہیں کر سکتے میرے بھائی نہ ہی اپنے فرض سے کوتاہی برت سکتے ہیں کیونکہ روزِ محشر جب اعمال کی گٹھری کھلے گی تو ہر شخص یہ چاہے گا اس کی گٹھری میں بخشش کا سامان ہو مگر اس وقت یہ سامان کہاں سے آئے گا؟ دنیا کی کھیتی میں جانفشانی سے جتنی محنت کریں گے آخرت میں اتنی ہی اچھی فصل کاٹنے کو ملے گی۔''

''وہ تو ٹھیک ہے مگر اس بے سر و پا بدامنی کا کوئی مقصد بھی تو ہو۔''

''مقصد ہے ناں پچھلے گیارہ سالوں میں جو جنگ عالمی طاقتوں کی طرف سے لڑی جا رہی ہے اس کا مقصد کوئی دہشت گردی' کوئی طالبان نہیں ہے بلکہ اس کا اصل مقصد اور ہدف صرف اور صرف انسانیت کا قتل اور اسلامی دنیا کی واحد ایٹمی قوت پاکستان کا ایٹم بم ہے جس کو ہتھیانے کے لیے واشنگٹن سے لے کر جنیوا اور لندن سے لے کر برسلز تک تمام کفر یہ طاقتیں سر جوڑے بیٹھیں ہمہ وقت گہری سازشوں میں مصروف ہیں۔ پتا ہے ناں کسی بھی ملک کا ایٹم بم اس کی پہچان' اس کے مضبوط و مستحکم دفاع کا سگنل اور اسٹریٹجی مہارت کی علامت سمجھا جاتا ہے' ساری دنیا حیران ہے کہ جو ملک ایک معیاری سیل تک نہیں بنا سکتا اس نے ایٹم بم کیسے بنا لیا۔ ہم نہیں جانتے عمیر کہ ایٹم بم کی آڑ میں ہم پر کون سی

قیامت مسلط کی جا رہی ہے۔ آج دنیا کی پہلی اسلامی ایٹمی قوت عالم کفر کے نرغے میں ہے۔ پوری قوم نیٹو افواج کے بھاری بوٹوں تلے روندی جا رہی ہے' بم دھماکوں نے ساری پاکستانی قوم کا سکون غارت کر چھوڑا ہے' سوات سے کراچی تک ایک ہی بساط بچھی ہے موت کی بساط' ایک قطعی پرائی جنگ میں اب تک ہزاروں بے گناہ پاکستانی شہریوں کے ساتھ' افواجِ پاکستان کے سیکڑوں جوان اپنی جانوں سے ہاتھ دھو بیٹھے ہیں ذرا سوچو عمیر! کیا امریکہ کے کسی اور اتحادی ملک میں یہ واقعات اور حادثات پیش آئے؟ اگر نہیں تو پاکستان میں ہی ایسا کیوں کتنے افسوس کی بات ہے کہ ایک جنگ جو ہماری ہے ہی نہیں ہم وہی جنگ خود اپنے شہریوں کی لاشوں پر' کسی اسامہ بن لادن کسی بیت اللہ محسود کسی ملا عمر کے خلاف نہیں بلکہ خود اپنے ہی خلاف لڑ رہے ہیں' یہ جنگ ہمیں اس ڈگر پر لے آئی ہے جہاں صرف اندھیرے ہی اندھیرے ہیں وہ پاکستان جو عالم اسلام کا قلعہ اور مسلمانوں کی امیدوں کا واحد مرکز ہے وہ پاکستان جو معدنی وسائل اور افرادی قوت سے مالا مال ہے۔ دنیا میں واحد ایٹمی قوت ہے جو بیک وقت امریکہ' اسرائیل اور بھارت سے ٹکر لینے کی صلاحیت رکھتا ہے۔ اسی پاکستان کو یہ فرعونی قوتیں ناکام ریاست ثابت کرنے پر تلی ہوئی ہیں تاکہ کل یہ ہمارے کہوٹہ پلانٹ کو خدانخواستہ نشانہ بنا کر یو این او کے ذریعے ہمارا ایٹم بم اٹھالیں اور جواب میں نہایت آسانی سے یہ کہہ سکیں کہ پاکستان ایک غیر محفوظ اور ناکام ریاست ہے یوں نہ رہے گا بانس نہ بجے گی بانسری۔''

''آپ ٹھیک کہہ رہی ہیں مگر الحمد للہ ہمارا ایٹم بم محفوظ ہاتھوں میں ہے آپی! کسی کی مجال نہیں کہ میلی نظر بھی ڈال سکے اس پر۔''

''ہوں' صحیح کہہ رہے ہو مگر ذرا سوچو ابھی چند روز پہلے صرف ایک معمولی شخص نے جس طرح دار الحکومت میں ہماری سیکورٹی کا پول کھول کر رکھ دیا' اس کے بعد کیا ہمیں فکر مند نہیں ہونا چاہیے؟ تم دیکھو عمیر! بالکل اچانک سے امریکی افواج ہمارے دار الحکومت کے قریب دھاوا بول دیتی ہے' ہمارا ریڈیو سسٹم اس حد تک خراب ہے کہ ہمیں اپنے قلب میں اسامہ بن لادن کی موجودگی کا پتا ہی نہیں چلتا مگر امریکیوں کو اس کی اطلاع ہوتی ہے اور وہ ہماری آنکھوں کے سامنے آپریشن کر کے اپنا ہدف حاصل کر لیتی ہے کیا اس کے بعد بھی ہم یہ کہہ سکتے ہیں کہ ہم محفوظ ہیں؟ یہ کافر لوگ تو چاہتے ہی یہی ہیں کہ وطن عزیز میں انتشار پھیلا کر یہاں خانہ جنگی کی کیفیت پیدا کی جائے اور اسے غیر مستحکم قرار دے کر اسے ایٹم بم سے محروم کر دیں' اس ایٹم بم سے جس کے لیے ہم نے اقتصادی فاقے کیے' سامراج کی معاشی بدمعاشیاں برداشت کیں جس کے لیے محسن پاکستان ڈاکٹر عبد القدیر خان ہالینڈ کی مستقل شہریت اور اپنی بیٹیوں کا شاندار مستقبل پس پشت ڈال کر' لاکھوں ڈالرز کی تنخواہ کو ٹھوکر مار کر یہیں کے ہو رہے ہے' جس کے لیے ذوالفقار علی بھٹو جیسے کہنہ مشق' مدبر لیڈر جنوں کی حد تک دیوانہ وار سرگرم رہے' بے نظیر بھٹو جیسی زیرک لیڈر یورپی یونین کے سامنے ڈٹی رہیں' عصر حاضر کے بادشاہ میاں محمد نواز شریف کسی طور کلنٹن کے دباؤ میں نہیں آئے اور تو اور جنرل ضیاء جیسے لیڈر نے بھی دو ٹوک انداز میں امریکیوں کو یہ کہہ کر خاموش کروا دیا کہ Topic Is Out Of Discassion وہی ایٹم بم اب ان عالمی قوتوں کی آنکھ میں کنکر بن کر چبھ رہا ہے ساری جنگ اسی کی ہے ورلڈ ٹریڈ سینٹر کا ڈرامہ جس میں پانچ ہزار افراد کی ہلاکتوں کی اطلاع ملی' اس جنگ کا بنیادی پوائنٹ تھا یہ لوگ سازشوں کے تحت تمام مسلم ممالک کو غیر مستحکم کرنے کے بعد فائنل راؤنڈ پاکستان میں کھیلنا چاہتے ہیں عمیر کیونکہ یہ بساط حقیقت میں بچھائی ہی پاکستان کے لیے گئی ہے۔'' بولتے بولتے حور عین کا گلا خشک ہو گیا تھا' عمیر نے اسے گلاس میں پانی انڈیل دیا۔

''میں نے سنا تھا آپی ایٹم بم ایک نہایت مہلک' ضرر رساں اور خطرناک ہتھیار ہے۔ 68 سال پہلے 1945ء میں جنگ عظیم دوئم کے دوران امریکہ نے جاپان کے دو شہروں ناگاساکی اور ہیروشیما پر جو نیوکلیئر بم برسائے تھے اس کے

نتیجے میں آج تک وہاں کی زمین بنجر اور فضا آلودہ ہے۔ وہاں پیدا ہونے والے بچے آج بھی لولے لنگڑے اور معذور پیدا ہو رہے ہیں، دنیا بھر میں آج جو ملک بھی اس ٹیکنالوجی سے مالا مال ہے، ساری دنیا اسے عزت اور قدر کی نگاہ سے دیکھتی ہے کسی کی جرأت نہیں کہ اس کی پالیسی کے خلاف ہلکی سی گستاخانہ نگاہ بھی ڈال لے، ان کے کسی شہری کے خلاف ایکشن لے لے تو پوری عالمی برادری سیخ پا ہو جاتی ہے جب ہم اللہ پاک کی نصرت اور ڈاکٹر عبدالقدیر خان جیسے عظیم انسان کی بدولت اس ٹیکنالوجی کے مالک بنے تو میرا دل خوشی سے پھٹ رہا تھا۔ منٹو کے مرکزی کردار منگو کوچوان کی طرح ہزاروں پاکستانیوں کی آنکھوں میں جانے کیسے کیسے خواب آ بسے تھے اک جوش تھا کہ اب ہم بھی سر اٹھا کر چل سکیں گے اک ولولہ تھا کہ اب ہم بھی سینہ تان کر عزت و آبرو کے ساتھ جئیں گے خود مختاری، خود کفالت اور خود انحصاری کے قابل ہو جائیں گے مگر افسوس صد افسوس آپی کہ ایسا کچھ نہ ہو سکا۔ ایٹمی قوت ہوتے ہوئے بھی آج ہم ذلیل و خوار ہیں، کل ہندو بنیا ہمیں دھمکاتا تھا اور آج تیسری دنیا کا ایک نقاب پوش مسخرہ بات بات پر ہمیں جانے کیسی کیسی دھمکیاں دیتا ہے۔''

''یہ تو ہونا ہی تھا عمیر! تم نے وہ کہانی نہیں سنی کہ افغانستان کے ایک دیہات میں چوری ڈکیتی بہت ہوتی تھی تو وہاں ایک کسان نے سوچا کہ اس کے پاس اپنی اور اپنے گھر والوں کی حفاظت کے لیے ایک بندوق ہونی چاہیے چنانچہ اس نے اپنا تمام مال و متاع ڈھور ڈنگر سب بیچ کر ایک بندوق خرید لی، رات میں چور آئے تو کسان کی بیوی نے کسان کو جگایا اور بتایا کہ گھر میں چور گھس آئے ہیں تب کسان نے سوچا کہ اس کی سب سے قیمتی چیز تو اس کی بندوق ہی ہے لہٰذا اسے چھپایا جائے یہ سوچ کر دونوں میاں بیوی نے بندوق کو بستر کے نیچے چھپایا اور اس کے اوپر لیٹ گئے، صبح اٹھے تو بہت خوش ہوئے کہ انہوں نے بندوق بچا لی جو ان کی سب سے قیمتی متاع تھی، گاؤں کے لوگوں کو اس بات کا پتا چلا کہ رات کسان کے گھر چور آئے تھے اور اس نے اپنی بندوق چھپا لی تو سب اس پر بہت ہنسے، انہوں نے کسان سے کہا کہ ایسی بندوق خریدنے کا کیا فائدہ جس کی حفاظت بھی تمہیں خود کرنی پڑے، بات کسان کی سمجھ میں آ گئی اور وہ بے حد شرمندہ ہوا، ہمارا ایٹم بم بھی کسان کی وہی بندوق ہے عمیر! جو بجائے اس کے کہ ہماری حفاظت کرے الٹا ہم خود اس کی حفاظت کر رہے ہیں۔'' لبوں پر دھیمی سی مسکان سجائے وہ عمیر کو کہہ رہی تھی، عمیر اثبات میں سر ہلا کر رہ گیا۔

''خیر...... اس موضوع پر جتنا بھی خون جلا لیں کم ہے، میری ہالینڈ کے لیے ٹکٹ کنفرم ہو گئی ہے اگلے ہفتے فلائٹ ہے، صبح نمیر، زبیر کو ہوسٹل چھوڑ آئے گا تو میں ساتھ ہی چلی جاؤں گی، بہت سے معاملات کو ہینڈل کرنا ہے ابھی، مجھے خوشی ہے کہ سمیر کی بیگم نے میری جگہ لے لی ہے۔''

''نہیں آپی، اس گھر میں آپ کی جگہ کبھی کوئی نہیں لے سکتا، میں بہت مس کروں گا آپ کو۔'' اچانک اس کی آنکھوں کے گوشوں میں سی ہلکی نمی، چھلکی تھی، حورعین کے لبوں پر پھیکی سی مسکراہٹ بکھر گئی۔

''مس تو میں بھی تمہیں بہت کروں گی عمیر، کیونکہ تم راہ حق کے مسافر ہو، تم جیسے نوجوانوں کی اس ملک کو بہت ضرورت ہے۔''

''اور آپ جیسی شخصیات کی بھی بہت ضرورت ہے اس ملک کو، مجھے حقیقتاً آپ پر بہت فخر ہے آپی! میں ہمیشہ آپ سے اپنے احساسات و جذبات شیئر کر کے خود ہلکا پھلکا محسوس کرتا ہوں۔'' نم آنکھوں کے ساتھ وہ مسکرایا تھا جواب میں حورعین بھی اس کے گال پر اپنا ہاتھ رکھ کر دھیمے سے مسکرا دی۔

❀......❀......❀

جس شام وہ ہمدانی ہاؤس سے رخصت ہوئی اسی رات اس گھر کے مکینوں نے سمیر کی بیوی لائبہ کا نیا روپ دیکھا تھا۔ حورعین کی موجودگی میں بڑھ چڑھ کر ہر کام کرنے والی لائبہ بیگم اس کے گھر سے رخصت ہوتے ہی خرابی طبیعت کا بہانہ کر کے اپنے کمرے میں قید ہوگئی تھی، نئی نئی شادی تھی لہٰذا سمیر اس کا موڈ فریش کرنے کے لیے اسے باہر ڈنر کروانے لے گیا۔ اگلی صبح بھی دیر تک ان کے بیڈروم کا دروازہ بند رہا، عمیر کی طبیعت ٹھیک نہیں تھی۔ حورعین کے اس گھر سے چلے جانے کو اس نے بہت دل پر لیا تھا، شاید اسی ٹینشن اور غم کی وجہ سے اسے بخار نے آلیا تھا۔ اس میں ناشتا بنانے کی ہمت نہیں تھی، نمیر بھی بنا ناشتے کے آفس کے لیے نکل گیا تھا، کل رات کا کھانا بھی اسی نے بنایا تھا، اگلے دو روز تک یہی معمول رہا تو عمیر نے عذیر کو شکایت لگادی، لائبہ نے گھر کا کام یوں ترک کر دیا تھا جیسے اسے منع ہوگیا ہو۔ صبح ناشتے کے بعد وہ اپنی کسی نہ کسی دوست کو بلالیتی اور دن بھر کمرا بند کر کے اسی کے ساتھ گپ شپ لگاتی رہتی یا ٹی وی کھول کر بیٹھ جاتی، سمیر نے جاب جوائن کر لی تھی چونکہ اس کا ٹرانسفر دوسرے شہر ہوگیا تھا۔ لہٰذا وہ ہفتے کی رات گھر آتا اور اتوار کی رات پھر واپس چلا جاتا۔ اس روز بھی ہفتہ تھا جب عذیر نے اسے کال کر کے لائبہ کا بتایا۔ سفر سے تھکا ہارا وہ گھر آیا تو لائبہ کمرہ بند کیے حسب عادت سو رہی تھی جب کہ عمیر نے طبیعت کی خرابی کے باوجود مشین لگا رکھی تھی۔

سمیر نے کمرے میں جا کر لائبہ کا کمبل کھینچا اور اسے ڈانٹا تو وہ اس پر چڑھ دوڑی۔

''آتے ہی کان بھر دیئے بھائیوں نے؟''

''جسٹ شپ اپ۔''

''یو شٹ اپ...... میں اس گھر میں تمہاری بیوی بن کر آئی ہوں، نوکرانی بن کر نہیں۔'' نمیر نے ابھی ابھی آفس سے واپسی پر لاؤنج میں قدم رکھا تھا جب لائبہ کے چنگھاڑتے لہجے نے سمیر اور عمیر کے ساتھ ساتھ اسے بھی حیران کر دیا۔

''گھر کا کام کرنے سے کوئی نوکر نہیں بن جاتا۔''

''تو کون سا کام نہیں کیا میں شادی کے ابتدائی دنوں میں کولہو کے بیل کی طرح کام کیا ہے میں نے اچھا بھلا سارے بھائی اپنا کام کرتے تھے اب کیا ہوگیا، مائنڈ اٹ سمیر! میں تمہاری بیوی ہوں تمہارے بھائیوں کی خدمت مجھ پر فرض نہیں ہے، نہ ہی کوئی مجھے حورعین بھابی جیسا سمجھنے کی کوشش کرے، اکلوتی بیٹی ہوں اپنے ماں باپ کی، میں نے تو کبھی اپنے گھر میں ہل کر پانی بھی نہیں پیا۔''

''نہیں پیا تھا تو شادی کرنے کی کیا ضرورت تھی، رہتیں اپنے ماں باپ کے گھر۔''

''رہ رہی تھی مگر یہ تم ہی تھے جس سے اپنے جذبات سنبھالے نہیں جا رہے تھے۔''

قطعی گستاخانہ لہجے میں اس نے اتنی کھلی بات سمیر کے منہ پر دے ماری تھی کہ وہ بے ساختہ بغلیں جھانکنے پر مجبور ہوگیا۔ نمیر اور عمیر بھی ایک دوسرے سے نظریں چرا گئے تھے۔ اگلے پندرہ منٹ کے بعد نمیر کپڑے تبدیل کر کے کچن میں آ گیا اور یہی لائبہ چاہتی تھی تبھی سکون سے اونچی آواز میں ٹی وی کھول کر بیٹھ گئی۔ اس کا اصل مسئلہ یہ تھا کہ وہ سمیر سے دور نہیں رہ سکتی تھی جب کہ سمیر کسی طور اسے اپنے ساتھ لے جانے کو تیار نہیں تھا، اس کی یہی خواہش تھی کہ وہ حورعین کی طرح اس کا گھر سنبھالے اور اسی بات پر اس کا سمیر سے جھگڑا ہوا تھا جس کی سمیر نے مطلق پروا نہیں کی تھی۔ اس کے بعد ہی اس نے گھر کے کاموں سے ہاتھ کھینچا تھا مگر اب بھی بات بنتی نظر نہیں آ رہی تھی تبھی اس کی دوست نے اسے ایک اور نئی راہ دکھائی تھی۔

سمیر سنڈے کی چھٹی ٹینشن میں گزار کر پیر کو واپس آیا تو حورعین کا فون آ گیا، پرسوں رات اس کی فلائٹ تھی لہٰذا اس نے ان سب کو اپنے گھر پر انوائیٹ کیا تھا، نمیر کی طبیعت ٹھیک نہیں تھی لہٰذا آفس سے واپسی کے بعد وہ کمرا بند کر کے سوگیا

تو لائبہ عمیر کے ساتھ حورعین کے پاس چلی آئی۔ تقریباً پندرہ منٹ کے بعد ہی سر چکرانے کا بہانہ کر کے وہ وہاں سے اٹھ آئی، عمیر نے ساتھ آنا چاہا تو اس نے سہولت سے منع کر دیا۔ جلدی جلدی گھر آ کر اس نے نمیر کے کمرے کا لاک کھولا جس کی چابی اس کے پاس تھی، اندر وہ بے خبر اپنے بیڈ پر پڑا سو رہا تھا تبھی اس نے گاڑی سے شراب کی بوتل نکالی اور اپنی فرینڈ کی ہدایت کے عین مطابق ایک گلاس بھر کر باہر پودوں میں گرا دیا پھر آدھا گلاس بھر کر نمیر کے بیڈ کی سائیڈ ٹیبل پر رکھ دیا اور شراب کی بوتل بھی ساتھ ہی رکھ دی۔ پانچ منٹ کے بعد اس کی مخروطی انگلیاں سمیر کا نمبر پریس کر رہی تھیں جو ابھی تھک ہار کر آفس سے اپنے فلیٹ پر واپس آیا تھا۔

''ہیلو۔'' تیسری ہی بیل پر اس نے کال ریسیو کر لی تھی ادھر صوفے پر اطمینان سے بیٹھی لائبہ نے دھواں دھار رونا شروع کر دیا۔

''سمیر آپ کہاں ہیں پلیز جلدی سے گھر واپس آئیے۔''

''کیوں خیریت؟ کیا ہوا ہے؟''

''خیریت نہیں ہے نمیر نے شراب پی رکھی ہے، اس کا دماغ کام نہیں کر رہا، میں ابھی حورعین بھابی کے گھر سے واپس آئی تو اس نے میرے ساتھ بدتمیزی شروع کر دی، بڑی مشکل سے میں اپنی عزت بچا کر اپنے کمرے میں خود کو لاک کرنے میں کامیاب ہوئی ہوں۔ سمیر میں یہاں اب ایک پل بھی نہیں رہ سکتی، ابھی اپنے پاپا کو فون کر کے بلا رہی ہوں میں۔'' اس کی ایکٹنگ اتنی زبردست تھی کہ سمیر کو اس پر ذرا سا بھی شبہ نہیں ہوا، اپنے بھائیوں کو اچھی طرح جاننے کے باوجود وہ اس کے فریب میں آ گیا تھا۔

''نہیں پاپا کو فون کرنے کی ضرورت نہیں ہے، میں آ رہا ہوں۔'' اس نے کہا تھا اور لائبہ نے فوراً کال ڈس کنکٹ کر دی تھی تقریباً ایک گھنٹے کے بعد عمیر گھر آیا تو وہ بال بگاڑے اپنی شرٹ بازوؤں سے پھاڑے لاؤنج میں دونوں پاؤں صوفے پر رکھے رو رہی تھی جب کہ اس کا دوپٹہ اندر نمیر کے بیڈ پر پڑا تھا اور اس کی شرٹ بھی نیچے زمین پر پڑی تھی، وہ شاکڈ ہی تو رہ گیا تھا۔

''بھابی...... کیا ہوا؟''

مگر وہ بنا اس کی طرف دیکھے روئے جا رہی تھی، تھوڑی ہی دیر میں سمیر بھی گھر پہنچ گیا تھا پریشانی اس کی شکل سے ہی ظاہر ہو رہی تھی۔ لائبہ کو روتے دیکھ کر وہ تیزی سے نمیر کے کمرے کی طرف بڑھا تھا اور کمرے کا حال دیکھ کر غصے سے بے قابو ہوتے ہوئے اس نے نمیر کو بنیان سے پکڑ کر نیند سے جگا دیا۔

''گھٹیا، ذلیل، کمینے انسان...... شرم نہیں آئی تمہیں اپنے ہی گھر کی عزت پر ہاتھ ڈالتے ہوئے؟'' جگانے کے ساتھ ہی اس نے اسے دو تھپڑ بھی رسید کر دیئے تھے، وہ ہکا بکا رہ گیا۔

''کیوں کیا ہوا ہے؟'' اس کی آنکھوں میں سرخی تھی جب کہ سر درد کی شدت سے پھٹ رہا تھا، تبھی وہ چنگھاڑا۔

''زیادہ معصوم بننے کی ضرورت نہیں ہے، میں سوچ بھی نہیں سکتا تھا کہ تم اتنے گھٹیا ثابت ہو گے۔'' مارے اشتعال کے اس کا چہرہ غصے سے سرخ ہو رہا تھا، نمیر کا سر گھوم گیا۔

''بس...... زیادہ چنگھاڑنے کی ضرورت نہیں ہے، میں نے ایسا کچھ نہیں کیا ہے جس کی وجہ سے تمہیں مجھ پر یوں ہاتھ اٹھانے کی ضرورت پیش آئے۔''

''ضرورت کے بچے جو حرکت تم نے کی ہے میرا دل چاہ رہا ہے میں تمہاری جان لے لوں۔'' نمیر نے پہلی بار اسے یوں آپے سے باہر ہوتے دیکھا تھا۔ تبھی اس کی نظر سائیڈ ٹیبل پر رکھی شراب کی بوتل اور لاؤنج میں صوفے پر بیٹھی روتی

ہوئی لائبہ پر پڑی تھی، جس کا دوپٹہ اسی کے بیڈ پر پڑا رُل رہا تھا وہ حیران ہی تو رہ گیا' ایک پل میں اسے ساری کہانی سمجھ میں آ گئی تھی۔ وہ حیران تھا کہ اس کا کمرا تو لاکڈ تھا پھر وہاں شراب کی بوتل اور لائبہ کا دوپٹہ کیسے آ گیا تھا؟

''لے لو جان' مگر میں اپنی مری ہوئی ماں کی قسم کھا کر کہتا ہوں میں نے نہ تمہاری بیوی کو ہاتھ لگایا ہے نہ شراب کی بوتل کو' یہ سارا کھیل تمہاری اپنی بیوی کا رچایا ہوا ہے' میرا کمرا لاک تھا اور میں سلیپنگ پلز لے کر سو رہا تھا۔''

''بکواس بند کرو۔''

''بکواس نہیں کر رہا ہوں میں' بکواس وہ ہے جو تمہاری بیوی کر رہی ہے میرا خدا جانتا ہے میں نے کبھی حورعین آپی اور اس لڑکی کو اپنی سگی بہنوں سے کم نہیں سمجھا اور میں اتنا بے غیرت نہیں ہوں کہ اپنی سگی بہن کی عزت پر ہاتھ ڈالوں گا۔'' اس کے لہجے کی مضبوطی اس کی سچائی کی دلیل تھی' سمیر نے رخ پھیر کر لائبہ کی طرف دیکھا وہ فوراً نظر چرا گئی' اگلے ہی روز بات حورعین اور عذیر کے علم میں بھی آ گئی تھی۔ اپنی اپنی جگہ پر دونوں شاکڈ رہ گئے تھے' حورعین ساری مصروفیات پس پشت ڈال کر وہاں آئی تھی' جہاں نمیر نے دل برداشتہ ہو کر خودکشی کرنے کی کوشش کی تھی مگر عمیر کی مداخلت نے اسے بچا لیا تھا۔

لائبہ بے حد شرمندہ تھی جب کہ سمیر تو کسی کو منہ دکھانے لائق نہیں رہا تھا' حورعین کتنی ہی دیر نمیر کے پاس بیٹھی اس کی ڈھارس بندھاتی رہی۔

✿ ..... ✿ ..... ✿

تُو اگر سن نہیں سکتا تو مجھے غور سے دیکھ
بات ایسی ہے کہ دہرائی نہیں جائے گی

حورعین کی فلائٹ کا ٹائم قریب آ پہنچا تھا۔ نمیر اور عمیر دونوں اسے سی آف کرنے آئے تھے جب کہ سمیر کل رات ہی لائبہ کو ساتھ لے کر اپنی ڈیوٹی پر واپس چلا گیا تھا۔ ہلکی ہلکی پھوار میں گاڑی سے اتر کر ان دونوں کو پیار کرنے کے بعد وہ ائرپورٹ کی عمارت کی طرف بڑھی تو اس کے قدم من من کے ہو رہے تھے جب کہ نمیر اور عمیر دونوں کی آنکھیں بھی بھر آئی تھیں۔

کتنا مشکل تھا اس ملک' اسی شہر اور ان لوگوں سے دور رہنا جو اب اس کی پہچان بن چکے تھے مگر وہ پلٹ کر دیکھنا نہیں چاہتی تھی کیونکہ وہ جانتی تھی اگر اس نے ایک بار بھی پلٹ کر انہیں دیکھ لیا تو یہاں سے کبھی نہیں جا سکے گی۔ ہلکی ہلکی پھوار نے اس کے کپڑے خاصے بھگو دیئے تھے تبھی کسی نے اسے پکارا تھا۔

''حورعین......'' اور وہ جو تیزی سے عمارت کی طرف بڑھ رہی تھی ٹھٹک کر رک گئی۔ لمحے کے ہزارویں حصے میں اس کا دل بہت تیزی سے دھڑکا تھا مگر وہ اب بھی پلٹ کر نہ دیکھ سکی تبھی وہ قریب آیا تھا۔

''کہاں جا رہی ہو؟'' اس بار حورعین نے نظریں اٹھائی تھیں کیونکہ وہ اس کے مقابل ہی تو کھڑا تھا۔

''ابروڈ۔''

''اتنی ساری محبتوں کو چھوڑ کر؟''

''نہیں' چھوڑ کر نہیں' ساتھ لے کر۔''

''کیوں' جانا ضروری ہے؟''

''ہوں۔''

''او کے' مگر سامان کہاں ہے؟'' اور اس بار وہ چونکی تھی اسے خبر ہی نہ ہو سکی تھی کہ اس نے گاڑی سے اپنا سامان تو نکالا ہی نہیں تھا۔ بچھڑ جانے کی یہ کیسی اذیت تھی کہ بنا سامان کے وہ پیدل ہی آگے بڑھی جا رہی تھی' ایک دم سے پلٹ کر اس نے پیچھے دیکھا مگر اب وہاں نمیر اور عمیر کی گاڑی نہیں کھڑی تھی۔

''او...... مجھے یاد ہی نہیں رہا کہ سامان نکالنا ہے۔''

''چچ چچ چچ اب تو پھر بنا سامان کے ہی جانا پڑے گا۔'' وہ اس کی پریشانی سے لطف اٹھا رہا تھا' حورعین نے ایک نظر اس کی طرف دیکھا پھر قدم آگے بڑھا دیئے۔ فلائٹ کے لیے اناؤنسمنٹ ہو رہی تھی' اس کے قدموں کی رفتار میں تیزی آ گئی۔

''بات سنو۔'' ایک مرتبہ پھر اس کی صدا نے اس کے قدم باندھ دیئے تھے' وہ ٹھٹک گئی۔

''جی۔''

''میری امانت تو واپس کرتی جاؤ۔''

''وہاٹ؟'' عذیر کی جگر جگر کرتی نگاہوں کو دیکھتے ہوئے وہ الجھ ہی تو گئی تھی۔

''کیسی امانت؟''

''تمہیں نہیں پتا؟'' وہ براہ راست اس کی آنکھوں میں دیکھ رہا تھا' حورعین گھبرا گئی۔

''نہیں۔'' اس کا کہنا تھا کہ اسی لمحے ہلکی ہلکی بوندا باندی نے اچانک تیز بارش کا روپ دھار لیا۔

''شیور......؟'' ایک نظر اوپر آسمان کی طرف دیکھتے ہوئے وہ اس کے قریب ہوا تھا۔ حورعین جیسے اس کی نظر کے طلسم میں بندھ کر رہ گئی' لوگ بارش کی وجہ سے اِدھر اُدھر بھاگ رہے تھے مگر وہ ساکت کھڑی عذیر کی نگاہوں میں دیکھ رہی تھی جو دونوں ہاتھوں کے پیالے میں اس کا چہرہ تھامے کھڑا اسے بہت گہری نگاہوں سے دیکھ رہا تھا۔ حورعین ان نگاہوں کی گرفت سے اپنی نظریں چھڑانے کی ہمت ہی نہ کر سکی یہاں تک کہ بارش نے ان دونوں کو پور پور بھگو دیا۔ تبھی عذیر ذرا سا اس کی طرف جھکا تھا اور اس نے اپنے لب اس کی دمکتی پیشانی پر رکھ دیئے تھے۔

''تمہیں پتا ہے تم میرا دل ساتھ لے کر جا رہی تھیں۔'' بے حد گمبھیر لہجے میں کہتے ہوئے وہ اس کے کان کی طرف جھکا تھا۔ حورعین کے جسم سے جیسے جان ہی نکل گئی تاہم اس کی آنکھوں سے آنسوؤں کے چند قطرے ضرور پھسلے تھے۔

''اب نہیں حورعین' بہت لٹا دیا ان انمول موتیوں کو اب اور نہیں۔'' فوراً سے پیشتر اپنے ہاتھوں سے اس نے اس کے آنسو صاف کیے تھے' حورعین ضبط کے سارے ہتھیار گراتی اس کے سینے سے لگی تھی اور پھوٹ پھوٹ کر رو پڑی تھی۔ عذیر نے نرمی سے اپنے بازو اس کی کمر کے گرد حمائل کر دیئے۔ بارش اور تیز ہو گئی تھی مگر دونوں کو ہی جیسے اس کی پروا نہیں تھی بہت دیر کے بعد انہیں احساس ہوا تھا کہ وہ پبلک پلیس پر کھڑے ہیں تبھی حورعین کسمسا کر اس کی گرفت سے نکلی تھی جس پر عذیر قہقہہ لگا کر ہنس پڑا تھا۔

اگلے تیس منٹ کے بعد عذیر نے گاڑی ہمدانی ہاؤس کے سامنے پارک کی تھی' حورعین گاڑی سے نکلی تو بھیگے کپڑوں میں اس کے جسم کا ایک ایک حصہ نمایاں ہو رہا تھا تبھی عذیر نے شرارتی نگاہوں سے ایک نظر اس کے بھیگے سراپا پر ڈالنے کے بعد اپنا کوٹ اتار کر اسے پہنا دیا پھر دایاں ہاتھ اس کے شانوں کے گرد حمائل کرتے ہوئے اسے اپنے ساتھ گھر کے اندر لے آیا۔

صد شکر کہ لاؤنج میں کوئی نہیں تھا مگر نمیر کے کمرے سے اس کے اونچا اونچا بولنے کی آوازیں ضرور آ رہی تھیں۔

''میں بتا تا رہا ہوں عمیر! میں نے آج کے بعد پوچا نہیں لگانا' صبح ناشتا بھی تم نے بنایا کرنا ہے روز آفس سے لیٹ

ہو جاتا ہوں، یہی حالات رہے ناں تو جلد ہی آفس والوں نے جاب سے فارغ کر دینا ہے، بھول جاؤ اب حورعین آپی والی عیش! وہ تو کوئی پری تھیں جو راستہ بھول کر بس تھوڑے دن کے لیے ہی ہماری دنیا میں آ گئی تھیں۔''

''اور کیا ساری عادتیں ہی خراب کر دیں ہماری، کاش عذیر بھائی انہیں روک لیتے مگر وہ کیوں روکیں گے انہیں تو ہر کام وقت پر ریڈی مل جاتا ہے۔ میں بتا رہا ہوں نمیر! میرا بائیکاٹ ہے عذیر بھائی سے، زبیر بھی وہاں ہوسٹل میں سیٹ نہیں ہو رہا، جب بھی فون کرو رونے لگ جاتا ہے میرا تو دل کٹ رہا ہے۔ کسی کی مجال تھی کہ حورعین آپی کے ہوتے ہوئے کوئی ہم پر ایسا گھٹیا الزام لگاتا جو لائبہ بھابی نے لگایا، میں نے سوچ لیا ہے اب جب بھی عذیر بھائی آئے ہم نے ان کا کام نہیں کرنا۔'' نمیر کے کمرے سے اٹھتی آوازوں پر عذیر نے حورعین کی طرف دیکھا تھا اور وہ قطعی بے ساختگی میں کھلکھلا کر اپنے پیچھے بیرونی دروازہ بند کر گئی تھی، بے شک وہ گھر ایک جنت تھا اور حورعین عبدالسمیع اپنے پیارے ربّ کی خاص رحمت سے اس جنت میں اپنا مقام پا گئی تھی۔

❁ .... ❁ .... ❁

ذرا دیکھو تو دروازے پر دستک کون دیتا ہے؟

محبت ہو تو کہہ دینا، یہاں اب ہم نہیں رہتے

بارش خوب زور و شور سے ہو رہی تھی۔ ہانیہ کافی کا بڑا سا مگ ہاتھ میں لیے ٹیرس پر آ کھڑی ہوئی، ایسا ہی ایک برستا بھیگتا موسم اس کے اندر بھی تو ٹھہر گیا تھا۔ نہال حسن نے کہا تھا۔

''ترسو گی ہانیہ ڈیئر! نہال حسن کے ساتھ کبھی بارشوں کے حسن کو محسوس کرنے کے لیے ترسو گی۔'' اور وہ واقعی ترس گئی تھی۔

کتنا عرصہ ہو گیا تھا اسے بارشوں میں بھیگے ہوئے، سرد قطروں کے لمس کو اپنی ہتھیلیوں پر محسوس کیے ہوئے۔ بارشیں واقعی کبھی کسی کا ساتھ نہیں دیتیں۔

کھڑکیوں کے شیشوں پر
رینگتے ہوئے قطرے
یوں پھسلتے ہیں جیسے
میرے اور بادل کے درمیان کوئی ہے
جو میرے اور بادل کے راز کو سمجھتا ہے
جب گھٹائیں چھائیں تو صرف وہ نہیں روتیں
آنکھیں بھی برستی ہیں، کھڑکیاں بھی روتی ہیں

کتنا وقت ہو گیا تھا اسے نہال حسن کے لیے روتے ہوئے اب تو آنکھوں کے آنسو بھی پتھر ہو گئے تھے مگر وہ تا حال اسے بھولنے میں کامیاب نہیں ہوئی تھی، کہیں نہ کہیں کسی نہ کسی بات کے حوالے میں وہ اسے یاد آ ہی جاتا تھا کبھی بارشوں کو دیکھ کر کبھی دیوار پر کسی چھپکلی کو دیکھ کر کبھی کچن میں کوئی کاکروچ دیکھ کر اور کبھی اپنے بیٹے کی صورت تصور میں لا کر جو ہو بہو نہال کی کاپی تھا۔

بے شک وہ ایک آئیڈیل انسان تھا اور اس کی رفاقت ہانیہ صفدر کی زندگی پر گہری چھاپ چھوڑ گئی تھی، اپنی محبت اور شخصیت کے لحاظ سے وہ کسی افسانوی ہیرو سے کم نہیں تھا، مگر کتنی عجیب بات تھی کہ پھر بھی وہ اسے کبھی ویسے نہیں چاہ سکی تھی جیسے میکال حسن کو چاہا تھا۔

بارش کی تیزی میں مزید شدت آ گئی تھی۔ ہانیہ نے کھڑکی کے پردے برابر کر دیئے‘ جانے کیوں اب بارشوں میں اس کا دل جیسے پھٹنے لگتا تھا۔ نہال حسن کے بعد زندگی کی جھیل پر جیسے کائی لگ گئی تھی‘ اندر کے برف موسموں نے اسے ٹھٹکا کر رکھ دیا تھا۔ بہت اکیلی پڑ گئی تھی وہ زندگی کے دکھوں کے سامنے‘ پچھلے تین سال سے صرف ایک لفظ داشتہ اس کا پیچھا نہیں چھوڑ رہا تھا‘ میکال حسن کے لبوں سے نکلا یہ لفظ اس کی قبر بن گیا تھا جس میں وہ روز دفن ہوتی تھی۔

جاذب اور ہادیہ روز اسکائپ پر اس سے بات کرتے تھے‘ ہادیہ نے دو جڑواں بیٹوں کو جنم دیا تھا اور وہ انہی میں بے حد مصروف ہو کر رہ گئی تھی‘ حسن صاحب اور ان کی بیگم کا فون بھی آ جاتا تھا کبھی کبھار مگر اسے اب کسی کے یاد کرنے نہ کرنے سے فرق ہی کہاں پڑتا تھا‘ فارحہ کی بیٹی اس کا بہت خیال رکھتی تھی‘ صفدر صاحب کی دوسری بیگم بھی اسی کے ساتھ رہتی تھیں۔ اس کے باوجود گزرے ہوئے ماہ وسال میں جس طرح سے دل پر پتھر رکھ کر اس نے اپنے بیٹے کو بھلایا تھا اس کے لیے صبر کیا تھا صرف وہی جانتی تھی۔

اور اب جب اسے صبر آنے لگا تھا تو وہ پھر اس کے سامنے آ گیا تھا اور اس کے اندر کی ماممتا اس کی معصوم شکایات سن کر جیسے تڑپ اٹھی تھی‘ کسی کروٹ قرار نہیں تھا نہ کچھ کھانے کو دل چاہ رہا تھا نہ پینے کو‘ کام کاج میں اس کی دلچسپی بھی نہ ہونے کے برابر رہ گئی تھی‘ اس ایک رشتے کے سوا کائنات میں اب اس کا اور رہ بھی کیا گیا تھا؟

✿ .... ✿ .... ✿

ہانیہ صفدر جب سے اس کے گھر سے ہو کر گئی تھی میکال حسن کو کسی کروٹ قرار نہیں آ رہا تھا۔ سنان علی آج بھی اس کا انتظار کرتے کرتے بھوکا ہی سو گیا تھا۔ حفیظ بابا بھی تھوڑی دیر پہلے ہی اپنے کوارٹر میں گئے تھے تبھی آفس سے واپسی پر پاؤں کو جوتوں کی قید سے آزاد کرنے کے بعد وہ صوفے پر ہی نیم دراز ہو گیا تھا۔ اگلے ہی پل اس نے فل آواز میں ٹی وی کھول لیا مگر اس کی توجہ ٹی وی اسکرین پر نہیں تھی‘ نظر کی اسکرین پر اگر کوئی سین جھلملا رہا تھا تو وہ ہانیہ صفدر کا تھا جسے آج شام میں اس نے مارکیٹ میں شاپنگ کرتے ہوئے دیکھا تھا۔

پچھلے چھ ماہ کے بعد ہانیہ صفدر سے یہ اس کا دوسرا ٹکراؤ تھا‘ اسے تو شاید خبر بھی نہیں تھی مگر وہ اب بھی اس کے شب و روز پر بہت گہری نظر رکھے ہوئے تھے‘ نہال کی موت کو تین سال ہو گئے تھے اور ان تین سالوں میں وہ ایک بار بھی اس کے خواب میں نہیں آیا تھا۔

میکال حسن کو اب ڈیپریشن کے دورے پڑنے لگے تھے روز رات میں مسلسل نیند کی دوائی کھا کھا کر اس کا دماغ سن ہو گیا تھا۔ اب تو گولیاں بھی اپنا اثر کھو بیٹھی تھیں اس کے بیڈ کی دونوں سائیڈوں پر ہانیہ اور نہال کی تصویریں لگی تھیں اور اس کا بیٹا روز ان تصویروں سے ڈھیروں باتیں کر کے سوتا تھا۔ پچھلے تین سالوں میں اس نے کتنی کوشش کی تھی ہانیہ صفدر کو اپنے دل و دماغ سے نکالنے کی مگر وہ لڑکی جیسے کسی آسیب کی طرح اس کی روح سے چمٹ کر رہ گئی تھی۔

گزرے ہوئے تین سالوں میں اگر وہ بدلی تھی تو وہ بھی بہت بدل گئی تھی‘ تین سال سے اس کی زندگی میں کسی لڑکی کا کوئی گزر نہیں رہا تھا۔ مختلف محفلوں‘ تقریبات میں جانا بھی چھوڑ دیا تھا اس نے‘ اس کی زندگی صرف اپنے بیٹے تک محدود ہو کر رہ گئی تھی‘ روز آفس سے واپسی کے بعد وہ اسے کہیں نہ کہیں گھمانے پھرانے لے جاتا تھا‘ گھر واپسی کے بعد وہ اسے اپنے ساتھ کھلاتا پھر حفیظ بابا کے سپرد کر کے اپنے کمرے میں چلا آتا‘ کبھی کبھی مصروفیات زیادہ بڑھ جاتیں تو وہ بالکل ہی اس کے لیے ترس کر رہ جاتا تھا۔

گزرے پچھلے تین سالوں میں اگر اس نے مکمل توجہ اور تندہی سے کام کیا تھا تو وہ صرف بزنس کی اسٹیبلشمنٹ تھی جسے

اس نے بنا کسی کی مدد کے اپنی قابلیت اور شبانہ روز محنت سے بامِ عروج تک پہنچایا تھا اور یہ اسی محنت کا صلہ تھا کہ آج بزنس کی دنیا میں اس کا ایک نام تھا لوگ اس سے محض چند لمحوں کی ملاقات کے لیے ترستے تھے مگر اسے اب لوگوں میں دلچسپی نہیں رہی تھی۔

پچھلے ہفتے اس نے ایک نئی کمپنی کا چارج سنبھالا تھا جس میں ہانیہ صفدر پانچ سال کے کنٹریکٹ پر کام کر رہی تھی مگر اسے خبر نہیں تھی۔

❀ ...... ❀ ...... ❀

ٹیلی وژن اب بھی فل آواز میں چل رہا تھا۔ گھڑی کی سوئیاں رات کے تین بجا رہی تھیں' وہ اٹھا اور اس نے فریج سے شیمپین کی بوتل نکال لی' بزنس میں محنت کے ساتھ وہ آج کل شراب کا استعمال بھی بہت شدت سے کرنے لگا تھا' حفیظ بابا دیکھتے تھے اور دل مسوس کر رہ جاتے تھے۔

اذیت حد سے بڑھنے لگے تو انسان گھبرا کر کسی نہ کسی پناہ گناہ کی تلاش کرتا ہے' کوئی روحانیت کے رستے پر چل پڑتا ہے تو کوئی شیطانیت کے' اس نے بھی دوسرے رستے کا انتخاب کیا تھا۔ اگلے تین منٹ میں پوری بوتل ختم کرنے کے بعد اس نے کچن سے چھری اٹھالی تھی' چند لمحے وہ اپنی خوب صورت کلائیوں کو غور سے دیکھتا رہا پھر اس نے بازوؤں سمیت جسم کے مختلف حصوں پر چھوٹے چھوٹے کٹ لگانے شروع کر دیئے تھے' ہر کٹ کے ساتھ ملنے والی اذیت اس کے اندر لگی آگ پر جیسے پھوار کا کام کر رہی تھی جو ظلم اس نے اپنی زندگی اور دل کے ساتھ کیا تھا اس کی سزا شاید اس سے بہتر کوئی اور ہو بھی نہیں سکتی تھی۔

❀ ...... ❀ ...... ❀

جڑ بھی ایک پھول ہے
بس فرق صرف اتنا ہے
کہ اسے نمائش سے نفرت ہے

پچھلے کئی دنوں سے ہانیہ صفدر کی طبیعت ٹھیک نہیں تھی لہٰذا وہ آفس نہیں جا پا رہی تھی' تقریباً ایک ہفتے کے بعد اس روز وہ آفس آئی تو اسے سب سے پہلی جو خبر ملی وہ کمپنی کے ایم ڈی کے تبدیل ہونے کی تھی۔

خبر کیا تھی پریشانی کا بم تھا جو عین اس کے سر پر پھٹا تھا' جانے نیا ایم ڈی کس طبیعت اور مزاج کا شخص تھا۔ اس کمپنی میں ذہین اور محنتی لوگوں کی کمی نہیں تھی اس کے باوجود کمپنی کے سابقہ ایم ڈی افتخار راؤ صاحب اس کا خصوصی خیال رکھتے تھے اور خاصی رعایت بھی دیتے تھے۔ سارا دن وہ یہی سوچ سوچ کر کڑھتی رہی تھی کہ جانے اب کیا ہوگا؟

دوپہر میں لنچ کے بعد افتخار راؤ صاحب نے اسے اپنے آفس میں طلب کیا تھا' جیسے ہی وہ ان کے کمرے میں داخل ہوئی ان کی سیٹ پر میکال حسن کو بیٹھے دیکھ کر ٹھٹک گئی' قدم جیسے دہلیز پر ہی چپک گئے تھے تبھی افتخار صاحب کی نگاہ اس پر پڑی تھی۔

''ارے مس ہانیہ! پلیز آئیں ناں' رک کیوں گئیں؟'' افتخار صاحب بھی اس کے قریب ہی کھڑے تھے' ہانیہ بمشکل خود کو سنبھالتی آگے بڑھ آئی۔

''السلام علیکم۔''

''وعلیکم السّلام! کیسی طبیعت ہے اب آپ کی؟''

''جی ٹھیک ہوں۔''

''گڈ' یہ میکال صاحب ہیں میکال گروپ آف انڈسٹریز کے مالک! میرے بہت اچھے دوستوں میں شمار ہوتا ہے ان کا' اس ہفتے سے انہوں نے اس کمپنی کا چارج سنبھال لیا ہے۔''

''کیوں؟'' افتخار صاحب کو اس سے اس سوال کی توقع نہیں تھی تبھی ذرا سا چونک کر مسکرائے تھے۔

''میں اصل میں ایبروڈ جا رہا ہوں مس ہانیہ! میرے بیٹے کی طبیعت ٹھیک نہیں ہے وہ وہاں بالکل اکیلا ہے پھر یہاں بہت نقصان بھی ہو رہا ہے میکال صاحب کے ففٹی پرسنٹ شیئرز تو تھے ہی اب مکمل چارج ان کے ہاتھ میں آ گیا ہے' میں آپ کو یقین دلاتا ہوں آپ ان کو مجھ سے بڑھ کر اچھا پائیں گی۔''

''ایسا تو تب ہوگا سر جب میں یہاں مزید کام کروں گی' میں آج ابھی اسی وقت اس جاب سے ریزائن کرتی ہوں۔''

''مگر کیوں؟'' افتخار صاحب پر حیرتوں کے پہاڑ گر پڑے تھے جبکہ میکال ٹکٹکی باندھے بس اسے دیکھے جا رہا تھا' ہانیہ کی آنکھیں آنسوؤں سے بھر آئیں۔

''کیوں کی وضاحت نہیں دے سکتی سر مگر یہ حقیقت ہے اس لفظ ایبروڈ نے ہم مشرقی لوگوں سے ہمارے بہت سے انمول رشتے چھینے ہیں بہت ہی انمول۔''

''مگر مس ہانیہ آپ ایسا کیسے کر سکتی ہیں' دیکھیں میں آپ کے جذبات کی قدر کرتا ہوں مگر آپ کا یہ فیصلہ درست نہیں ہے' اس کمپنی کے ساتھ آپ نے پانچ سال کا کنٹریکٹ کیا ہے' ابھی وہ پانچ سال پورے نہیں ہوئے ہیں۔''

''میں جانتی ہوں سر مگر اس کے باوجود مجھے اس شخص کے ساتھ ایک پل کے لیے بھی کام نہیں کرنا' ایم رئیلی ویری سوری۔''

''او کے پلیز کول ڈاؤن' میں نہیں جانتا مسٹر میکال کے بارے میں آپ کن تحفظات کا شکار ہیں مگر میں آپ سے درخواست کروں گا پلیز ابھی جذبات میں آ کر کوئی حتمی فیصلہ مت کریں' چند دن ریسٹ کریں پھر اچھی طرح سوچ سمجھ کر جو فیصلہ آپ کرنا چاہیں مجھے کوئی اعتراض نہیں ہوگا۔'' ہانیہ کی آنکھوں سے نکلتی غصے اور نفرت کی چنگاریوں نے جہاں میکال کے چہرے پر سرخی پھیلائی تھی وہیں افتخار صاحب بھی بوکھلا کر رہ گئے تھے تبھی وہ پلٹی تھی اور تیزی سے ان کے آفس سے نکلتی چلی گئی تھی۔

باہر موسم سرد تھا مگر وہ بنا سرد ہواؤں کی پروا کیے پیدل ہی چلتی رہی' آنسو تھے کہ قطار در قطار بہتے ہی چلے جا رہے تھے' کیا ضروری تھا کہ وہ شخص اب یوں بار بار اس کا ضبط آزمانے کو اس کے سامنے آتا؟

آج کل اس کے گھریلو حالات بھی ٹھیک نہیں چل رہے تھے پچھلے دنوں بیماری پر بہت پیسہ لگا تھا اس کا' گھر کا راشن بھی ختم ہو رہا تھا۔ اوپر سے نینی (اس کی بیٹی جو فارحہ نے اسے گود دی تھی) کا ٹرپ شمالی علاقہ جات کو جا رہا تھا اور وہ ساتھ جانے کے لیے بضد تھی' مگر ہانیہ کے اکاؤنٹ میں صرف چند ہزار رہ گئے تھے جن میں ابھی اسے سردیوں کے لیے کپڑے بھی خریدنے تھے۔ پہلے جازب اسے ہر ماہ کچھ نہ کچھ رقم آن لائن کروا دیا تھا مگر بعد میں جب اس کے کاروباری حالات اچھے نہ رہے تو ہانیہ نے خود ہی اسے منع کر دیا۔

زندگی تا حال اسے مشکلات اور مسائل کی چکی میں پسے جا رہی تھی' مگر وہ تھی کہ کسی صورت ہار ماننے کو تیار نہیں تھی۔

❁ ...... ❁ ...... ❁

جس وقت وہ گھر پہنچی سارے گھر پر ایک عجیب سی خاموشی کا راج تھا۔ زکیہ بیگم کچن میں کھانا بنا رہی تھیں، وہ بیگ سائیڈ پر رکھتی لاؤنج میں صوفے پر پاؤں سمیٹ کر بیٹھ گئی۔ نینی فارحہ کی طرف گئی ہوئی تھی، زکیہ بیگم اس کی آہٹ پر فوراً کچن سے نکل آئیں۔

''آج جلدی گھر آ گئیں ہانیہ! خیریت؟''

''جی خیریت ہی ہے بس طبیعت ٹھیک نہیں تھی تو گھر آ گئی، آپ کیا بنا رہی ہیں۔''

''آلو کی بھجیا بنا رہی ہیں، نینی فرمائش کر رہی تھی۔''

''اچھا، مگر وہ ہے کہاں، دکھائی نہیں دے رہی۔''

''فارحہ کی طرف گئی ہے کئی روز سے بلا رہی تھی۔''

''چلیں اچھی بات ہے میں تھوڑی دیر سونا چاہوں گی، وہ آئے تو پلیز اسے کھانا کھلا دیجیے گا۔'' الجھن بھرے انداز میں بال سمیٹتی وہ اٹھ کھڑی ہوئی تھی، زکیہ بیگم اثبات میں سر ہلا کر رہ گئیں، اس رات ایک مرتبہ پھر وہ نہیں سو سکی تھی۔

❁ .... ❁ .... ❁

میکال بہت دنوں کے بعد اس روز کلب آیا تھا۔ ہر طرف وہی رنگینیاں تھیں، جو اس ماحول کا حصہ تھیں مگر اس کے اندر جیسے آگ لگی تھی ہانیہ صفدر کی آنکھوں سے نکلتی نفرت کی چنگاریوں نے اس کا سارا وجود جلا کر راکھ کر ڈالا تھا، اس کا توہین آمیز لہجہ اس کی رگوں میں خون ابال رہا تھا، کس درجہ حقارت سے ایک تھرڈ پرسن کے سامنے اس نے اس کی عزت اتار کر رکھ دی تھی جتنا وہ سوچتا جاتا تھا اتنا ہی اس کا دماغ پھٹتا جاتا تھا۔ کافی دیر رمی سے شغف کرنے کے بعد بھی دماغ کی کھولن کم نہ ہوئی تو وہ بار سائیڈ کی طرف چلا آیا تبھی رحیم صاحب کلب میں داخل ہوئے تھے۔

''ارے میکال! بھئی کہاں ہو آج کل، نہ دعا نہ سلام۔ کلب بھی نہیں آ رہے ہو، ٹھیک تو تھے ناں؟'' وہ بیئر پی رہا تھا یقیناً کوئی فرسٹریشن تھی۔

''جی میں ٹھیک ہوں، بس کچھ مصروفیات بڑھ گئی تھیں، آپ سنائیں آپا ٹھیک ہیں؟''

''ہوں اسے کیا ہونا ہے، تمہیں بہت یاد کر رہی تھی۔''

''میں بھی آپ دونوں کو بہت مس کر رہا تھا، ایک دو روز میں چکر لگاؤں گا۔'' دو گلاس خالی کرنے کے بعد وہ اب وہ تیسرے کا آرڈر دے رہا تھا جب رحیم صاحب نے منع کر دیا۔

''آج کے لیے بس اتنا کافی ہے تمہاری آپا فش بریانی بنا رہی ہیں آج، چلو مل کر کھاتے ہیں۔''

''نہیں آج نہیں، پھر کبھی سہی پلیز۔''

''پھر کبھی کس نے دیکھا ہے یار! بس چلو ابھی۔'' زبردستی اس کے شانوں کے گرد بازو حمائل کرتے ہوئے وہ اسے وہاں سے نکال لائے تھے۔ تقریباً پچیس منٹ کے بعد وہ دونوں گھر پہنچے تو مسز رحیم کچن میں مصروف تھیں۔ رحیم صاحب کے ساتھ میکال کو دیکھ کر فوراً لاؤنج میں چلی آئی تھیں۔

''ارے میکال! کتنے دنوں کے بعد شکل دکھائی ہے، سب خیریت تو تھی ناں؟''

''جی آپا خیریت ہی تھی، آپ سنائیں کیسی ہیں؟''

''میں تو ٹھیک ہوں، تمہیں بہت یاد کر رہی تھی، رحیم صاحب بھی صرف تمہارے لیے کلب جاتے ہیں روز۔''

''ایم سوری، میں اصل میں بزنس ٹور پر تھا اسی لیے چکر نہ لگا سکا۔''

''چلو کوئی بات نہیں' یہ بتاؤ ہانیہ سے بات ہوئی؟'' گیلے ہاتھ دوپٹے سے پونچھتے ہوئے وہ اس کے مقابل صوفے پر بیٹھ گئی تھی۔ میکال کے اندر پھر بھونچال اٹھ گیا۔

''نہیں۔''

''کیوں؟ مجھے پرسوں ملی تھی مارکیٹ میں' بہت اداس لگ رہی تھی' اصل میں آج کل اس کے گھریلو حالات ٹھیک نہیں ہیں' اپنے بیٹے کے لیے بھی بہت بے چین ہے' تم کیوں پریشان کر رہے ہو اسے۔''

''میں نے کیا پریشان کیا ہے جو آسائشات میں اپنے بیٹے کو فراہم کر سکتا ہوں وہ نہیں کر سکتی پھر میں کیوں اسے اس کے حوالے کروں۔''

''وہ ماں ہے اس کی اپنا پیٹ کاٹ کر بھی اس کی خواہشات پوری کرنی پڑی تو کرے گی' تم اکیلے نہیں لائے اسے دنیا میں پھر جس طرح سے تم نے اس پر ظلم کیا ہے' اس کا دل دکھایا ہے' بے گناہ اس کے کردار کو نشانہ بنا کر کسی اور کو اپنی زندگی میں شامل کیا' اس کے بعد تم اسے نفرت کے قابل سمجھتے ہو؟''

''وہ سمجھتی ہے میں نہیں سمجھتا اور میں نے کسی اور کو زندگی میں شامل کیا تو کیا اس نے نہیں کیا؟ اس نے بھی تو نہال سے شادی رچالی۔''

''اس کی اور تمہاری شادی میں بہت فرق ہے' تم نے اپنے لیے کسی اور سے شادی کی مگر اس نے اپنے لیے نہیں کی' اس نے نہال کی خوشی بلکہ اس کی زندگی کے لیے اس سے شادی کی وہ بھی صرف اس لیے کہ وہ مر رہا تھا اور وہ مر گیا۔'' مسز رحیم کی آنکھیں پل میں نم ہو گئی تھیں' میکال کے لبوں کو چپ لگ گئی۔

''بجائے اس کے کہ تم اس کے زخموں کا تدارک کرتے تم نے اسے اور زخم دے دیئے' لوگوں کی باتوں میں آ کر دو کوڑی کا کر دیا اسے' آج وہ کتنی تنہا ہو کر رہ گئی ہے۔''

''آپا! سارا قصور صرف میرا تو نہیں تھا' یہ ٹھیک ہے کہ مائرہ سے دھوکا کیا گیا مگر وہ چاہتی تو اس غلط فہمی کو ختم کر سکتی تھی پھر کیوں نہیں کی اس نے؟''

''موقع دیا تھا تم نے اسے غلط فہمی ختم کرنے کا؟ کیا کیا نہیں کیا تم نے اس کے ساتھ' کبھی پوچھو تنہائی میں اپنے ضمیر سے۔''

''پوچھا ہے اور بہت شرمندہ بھی ہوں مگر وہ مجھے ازالے کا کوئی موقع نہیں دے رہی ہے' ابھی چند روز پہلے بھی اس نے آفس میں میری اتنی بے عزتی کی ہے۔''

''تو تم نے بھی تو اسے بارہا ذلیل کیا ہے' وہ بھی اپنے گھر والوں کے سامنے بقول تمہارے کیا کیا نہیں کیا تم نے اس کے ساتھ؟'' مسز رحیم آج اس کی فل کلاس لینے پر تلی ہوئی تھیں' میکال کی آنکھیں ایک دم سے بھیگ گئیں۔

''وہ برداشت کر سکتی ہے آپا! میں نہیں کر سکتا۔''

''نہیں کر سکتے تو بھول جاؤ اسے' کیا مسئلہ ہے؟''

''یہ بھی نہیں کر سکتا آپا! پلیز آپ اس سے کہیں ناں مجھے معاف کر دے پلیز۔'' دائیں ہاتھ کے انگوٹھے اور شہادت کی انگلی سے اپنی آنکھوں کے کنارے دباتا وہ صوفے سے اٹھ کر ان کے پاس نیچے زمین پر آ بیٹھا تھا' مسز رحیم نے اذیت سے منہ پھیر لیا۔

''بہت مشکل ہے میکال! جتنے فاصلے تمہارے اور ہانیہ کے بیچ حائل ہو چکے ہیں انہیں سمیٹنا اب کسی تھرڈ پرسن کے بس میں نہیں' بہت مشکل ہے بہتر ہوگا اگر تم خود اس سلسلے میں ہانیہ سے بات کرو۔''

''میں نہیں کرسکتا آپا! بہت دیر ہوچکی ہے اب میں چلتا ہوں بہت تھکن فیل ہورہی ہے۔'' نشے سے سرخ آنکھوں کے کنارے دباتا فوراً ہی وہ اٹھ کھڑا ہوا تھا۔ تبھی رحیم صاحب بولے تھے۔

''کھانا کھا کر جاؤ میکال! تمہیں فش بریانی پسند ہے ناں۔''

''نہیں آج نہیں پھر کبھی صحیح' ابھی بس سوؤں گا جا کر' اللہ حافظ۔'' نشہ اس کے اعصاب پر اثر کررہا تھا لہٰذا بہت روکنے کے باوجود وہ وہاں سے نکلتا چلا گیا تھا۔

❁......❁......❁

ایک ہفتہ شدید خواری کے باوجود بالآخر اسے کسی اچھی کمپنی میں جاب نہ مل سکی تو مجبوراً اس نے ایک معمولی سی کمپنی میں بہت کم پیسوں والی نوکری قبول کرلی۔ ڈیوٹی آورز بھی زیادہ تھے مگر وہ خوش تھی کیونکہ میکال حسن کا سامنا کرنے سے ہزار درجے بہتر تھا کہ وہ بھوک سے مرجاتی' مسز صفدر بھی خاموش تھیں کیونکہ وہ ہانیہ کی فطرت سے اچھی طرح واقف تھیں۔ اس روز جب وہ آفس کے لیے تیار ہورہی تھی اچانک اس کا بیٹا دروازہ کھول کر اس کے سامنے آ گیا تھا۔

''مما......'' اور وہ جو گیلے دوپٹے سے ہاتھ خشک کرتی کچن سے باہر آرہی تھی ایک دم سے ٹھٹک گئی۔

''علی' تم یہاں؟''

''جی مما! ابھی پاپا چھوڑ کر گئے ہیں' کہہ رہے تھے اب' میں آپ کے ساتھ رہ سکتا ہوں۔''

''وہاٹ؟'' بچہ جتنا پُرجوش ہورہا تھا وہ اتنی ہی حیران رہ گئی تھی بھلا میکال حسن اتنا اچھا کیسے ہوسکتا تھا؟ تبھی لپک کر اپنے بیٹے کو خود سے لپٹاتے ہوئے رو پڑی۔ اس کا دل چاہ رہا تھا کہ وہ سارا دن اپنے بیٹے کے ساتھ گزارے مگر ایک اجنبی جگہ پر جاب کے آغاز میں ہی وہ کوئی بدمزگی نہیں چاہتی تھی تبھی کچھ دیر رک کر اپنے بیٹے کو ڈھیر سارا پیار کرنے کے بعد وہ آفس کے لیے نکل آئی تھی مگر تقدیر کی سیاہی نے ابھی اس کا پیچھا نہیں چھوڑا تھا' جیسے وہ آفس میں داخل ہوئی اسے منیجر صاحب کی طرف سے بلاوا آ گیا۔

''السلام علیکم سر!''

''وعلیکم السلام! ٹائم دیکھا ہے آپ نے؟''

''سوری سر' وہ اصل میں......''

''دیکھیں مس ہانیہ! یہ کمپنی کوئی بہت بڑی کمپنی نہیں ہے' یہاں کام کرنے والے سارے ورکرز غریب طبقے سے تعلق رکھتے ہیں' بہت معذرت یہاں آپ جیسے نوابی لوگوں کے لیے کوئی جگہ نہیں ہے۔''

''سر میری بات سنیں پلیز' میں......''

''دروازہ اُدھر ہے پلیز......''

اس درجہ اہانت...... ہانیہ سے اپنے پاؤں پر کھڑا رہنا دشوار ہوگیا' کتنی بے رحمی سے بنا اس کی وضاحت سنے اسے باہر کا راستہ دکھا دیا گیا تھا' ایک مرتبہ پھر لمبی مسافت تھی اور اس کے زخمی پاؤں......

❁......❁......❁

گھر کا بچا کھچا راشن تیزی سے ختم ہوتا جارہا تھا' تبھی ذکیہ بیگم نے ہانیہ کو بتائے بغیر اپنے وہ کڑے فروخت کردیئے تھے جو صفدر صاحب نے انہیں شادی کی پہلی رات گفٹ کیے تھے۔ ہانیہ کے استفسار پر اس نے بتایا تھا کہ جاذب کے حالات پہلے سے بہتر ہوگئے ہیں لہٰذا اس نے خود ہی انہیں رقم بھجوادی۔ ہانیہ کے لیے یہ خبر بے حد خوشی کی خبر تھی اگلی جاب کے لیے اسے کچھ وقت مل گیا تھا تبھی ہونٹوں پر ہاتھ رکھ کر روتے ہوئے اس نے فوراً وضو کیا اور سجدے میں گر گئی۔

اس روز اس نے بہت سا وقت اپنے بیٹے کے ساتھ گزارا تھا' رات دیر تک وہ اسے مختلف جگہوں پر گھماتی پھراتی رہی تھی' رات میں کہانی سناتے ہوئے جب وہ اس کے بال سہلا رہی تھی اچانک اس نے پوچھا تھا۔

''مما کیا آپ پاپا سے ناراض ہیں؟''

''نن......نہیں تو...... کیوں؟'' اچانک وہ ایک دم سے ٹھٹک گئی تھی۔

''پاپا روز رات میں آپ کی اور نہال چاچو کی تصویر سے باتیں کرتے ہیں اور روتے رہتے ہیں' کبھی کبھی تو بہت ڈرنک بھی کرتے ہیں اور سگریٹ بھی پیتے ہیں' مجھے ان کے منہ سے بہت بُری بدبو آتی ہے۔''

غنودگی کے عالم میں وہ اسے بتا رہا تھا' ہانیہ کا دل شدت سے دھڑک اٹھا' اس کا بیٹا سو چکا تھا مگر اس رات ایک مرتبہ پھر وہ بہت دیر تک جاگ کر روتی رہی تھی۔ اگلے روز زکیہ بیگم اس کے بیٹے کو چپس بنا کر دے رہی تھیں' جب وہ چائے کا کپ ہاتھ میں لیے لاؤنج میں آ بیٹھی۔

ابھی اس نے ٹی وی آن کیا تھا کہ ایک دم سے وہ سامنے آ گیا' کوئی ٹاک شو تھا جس میں اسے خصوصی طور پر انوائٹ کیا گیا تھا۔ ہانیہ دیکھ سکتی تھی کہ وہ پہلے سے بھی زیادہ خوب صورت ہینڈسم دکھائی دے رہا تھا مگر اس کی آنکھیں بجھ کر رہ گئی تھیں۔ فارحہ نے بتایا تھا کہ لڑکیاں مرتی تھیں اس پر ایک لڑکی نے تو آفس میں اسے خودکشی کی دھمکی بھی دے دی تھی' مگر وہ کسی پر نگاہ غلط ڈالنا بھی گوارا نہیں کرتا تھا۔ عجیب بے نیازی اور بے حسی کا خول چڑھا لیا تھا اس نے' فارحہ کے ہی بقول وہ اپنے والٹ میں ہر وقت اس کی تصویر رکھتا تھا' جب بھی زیادہ بے چینی ہوتی' وہ ڈرائیونگ کے دوران بھی گاڑی روک کر ایک نظر اسے دیکھتا اور پُرسکون ہو جاتا۔

ساری باتیں اپنی جگہ پر ٹھیک تھیں مگر صرف ایک لفظ داشتہ اسے جینے نہیں دے رہا تھا' وہ مر سکتی تھی مگر میکال حسن کو اس کی بے وفائی کے لیے معاف کرنا اس کے بس میں نہیں تھا۔

❁......❁......❁

شام ڈھل رہی تھی۔ آسمان پر سیاہ بادل کسی بھی پل برسنے کو تیار دکھائی دے رہے تھے۔ میکال حسن نے تھکی سی نظر اٹھا کر اوپر آسمان کی طرف دیکھا اور نگاہیں پھر سے عائشہ برہان کے خوب صورت چہرے پر ٹکا دیں' جو آسمان کی طرح اپنی آنکھوں کے گہرے سیاہ بادل لیے کسی گزرے ہوئے طوفان کی مانند خاموش بیٹھی تھی۔

''تو یہ طے ہے میکال کہ تمہاری زندگی میں ہانیہ صفدر کے علاوہ اب کوئی اور لڑکی کبھی نہیں آ سکتی؟''

''ہوں۔''

''تو پھر جھک کر منا کیوں نہیں لیتے اسے؟''

''وہ مجھ سے ناراض نہیں ہے عائشہ! بدگمان ہے' بدگمانیاں بھی ایسی ہیں کہ میں چاہتے ہوئے بھی اس کا دل صاف نہیں کر سکتا' مگر میں اس کے بغیر خوش بھی نہیں ہوں' میری سانسیں اس کی سانسوں میں الجھی ہیں کچھ سمجھ نہیں آیا مجھے کہ میں نے اس سے انتقام لیا ہے یا خود سے۔''

''میں اس سے بات کروں گی۔''

''نہیں تم اس سے مت ملنا پلیز پتا نہیں وہ اس بات کو بھی کس رنگ میں لے۔''

''میکال! تم اتنا ڈرتے ہو اس سے؟''

''ہوں' جن سے محبت کی جاتی ہے ان سے ڈر ہی لگتا ہے' ہمیشہ کے لیے کھو دینے کا ڈر......''

''کیا وہ بھی اتنا ہی پیار کرتی ہے تم سے؟''

''پتا نہیں یار! ایبروڈ میں بھی سکون نہیں ہے اب تو' مجھے لگتا تھا عائش تمہارے بعد میری زندگی میں کبھی کوئی لڑکی نہیں آئے گی مگر میں غلط تھا' ہانیہ صفدر کو کھونے کے بعد لگتا ہے جیسے تمہیں کھو دینے کا درد کوئی درد ہی نہیں تھا۔'' کتنے سکون سے وہ کہہ رہا تھا' عائشہ ٹھٹک گئی' پھر آہستہ سے رخ پھیرتے ہوئے بولی۔

''ہوں' وقت بدل جائے تو ہر چیز بدل جاتی ہے میکال پھر چاہے وہ احساسات اور جذبات ہی کیوں نہ ہوں' محبت تو ویسے بھی بہتی ندی اور چلتی ٹرین کا نام ہے جس کا ہر پڑاؤ خوب صورت ہوتا ہے بہر حال میں چلتی ہوں اب اریج اور بچے میرا انتظار کر رہے ہوں گے۔'' ایک نظر ہاتھ پر بندھی ریسٹ واچ پر ڈالتے ہوئے وہ اٹھ کھڑی ہوئی تھی جب میکال نے کہا۔

''تھوڑی دیر رک جاؤ پلیز ابھی تو آئی ہو۔''

''نہیں میکال! گھر بتا کر نہیں آئی اریج پریشان ہو رہے ہوں گے۔''

بیگ اٹھا کر ایک آخری تفصیلی نگاہ اس پر ڈالتے ہوئے وہ پلٹ گئی تھی' میکال بے کل سا اسے دیکھے گیا' ابھی دو روز پہلے ہی وہ پاکستان آئی تھی اور آتے ہی اس نے میکال کو فون کر دیا تھا' اس کا خیال تھا شاید اب بھی وہ اس کے غم میں نڈھال ہوگا مگر ایسا نہیں تھا محبت کی وہ حویلی' جہاں سے اس کے حالات اور تقدیر نے اسے در بدر کیا تھا اب اس کی ملکیت نہیں رہی تھی تاہم اریج اس کے حق میں بہت اچھا شوہر ثابت ہوا تھا' قدرت نے دو پیارے پیارے بیٹے بھی دیئے تھے' کسی چیز کی کمی نہیں مگر بس دل کا ایک کونا کہیں خالی تھا تاہم آج اس وقت اسے لگا وہاں اس کونے میں بھی میکال حسن کی جگہ اریج احمر نے قبضہ کر لیا ہو۔ ملال کے بادل چھٹ گئے تھے اور اب عائشہ برہان کی زندگی میں سکون ہی سکون تھا۔

❀ .... ❀ .... ❀

اس روز اپنے بیٹے کی ضد و فرمائش پر وہ اسے مارکیٹ لائی تھی۔ اس کے صرف پانچ ہزار روپے تھے جن میں ابھی اسے گھر کے لیے بھی کچھ ضروری چیزیں خریدنی تھیں مگر اس کا بیٹا جن چیزوں کی فرمائش کر رہا تھا ان کی قیمت پانچ ہزار سے اوپر شروع ہو رہی تھی' وہ پریشان ہو کر ہی تو رہ گئی تھی' زندگی کبھی ایسے کسی دوراہے پر بھی لائے گی' اس نے سوچا تک نہیں تھا۔

اس وقت بھی وہ اپنے بیٹے کو بہلا رہی تھی اور وہ ناراض ہو رہا تھا' جب میکال اچانک اس کے سامنے چلا آیا۔ ہلکی ہلکی بڑھی شیو اور رف سے ٹراؤزر میں اس کی پرسنالٹی غضب کی تھی تبھی ایک نظر پریشان حال ہانیہ صفدر پر ڈالتے ہوئے وہ پنجوں کے بل اپنے بیٹے کے سامنے بیٹھ گیا۔

''کیا بات ہے پرنس! کیوں تنگ کر رہے ہو مما کو۔''

''پاپا مجھے وہ اسپائڈر مین لینا ہے۔'' باپ کو دیکھتے ہی بچے کے چہرے پر بہار آ گئی تھی۔ ہانیہ عجیب مجرمانہ انداز میں سر جھکائے کھڑی رہی۔

''ٹھیک ہے' لے لیتے ہیں چلو۔'' فوراً اپنے بیٹے کی انگلی تھام کر وہ آگے بڑھ گیا تھا' جب کہ ہانیہ شکستہ قدموں کو گھسیٹتی شاپ سے باہر نکل آئی' آنسو تھے کہ ابل ابل کر آنکھوں سے باہر آنے کو بے چین ہو رہے تھے۔ تھوڑی دیر بعد وہ پھر اس کے مقابل تھا۔

''میں مانتا ہوں ہانیہ کہ چھٹکو پر تمہارا حق زیادہ ہے' مگر اکیلی ماں کبھی کبھی بچوں کو وہ سب نہیں دے سکتی جو ایک باپ دے سکتا ہے۔'' اپنے بیٹے کا ہاتھ اس کے ہاتھ میں دیتے ہوئے قدرے ناصحانہ انداز میں اس نے کہا تھا اور پھر ذرا سا رخ پھیرتے ہوئے بولا۔

''چھٹکو میرے لیے دوسرا نہال حسن ہے اسی لیے میں چاہتا ہوں اس کی زندگی میں کوئی کمی نہ رہے' تم مائنڈ مت کرنا پلیز یہ تم پر کوئی احسان نہیں ہے۔''

وہ کتنا بدل گیا تھا مگر ہانیہ نے نظر اٹھا کر اسے دیکھنا بھی گوارا نہیں کیا' چھٹکو کا ہاتھ تھام کر وہ پلٹی تھی اور ٹیکسی کی تلاش میں نظریں دوڑا ہی رہی تھی جب ایک دم سے بارش شروع ہوگئی' میکال ابھی بھی وہیں کھڑا تھا۔

''مما...... میرا اسپائڈر مین۔''

چھٹکو کو فوراً اپنے اسپائڈر مین کی فکر لاحق ہوئی تھی تبھی منہ بسور کر اس نے ہانیہ کی طرف دیکھا مگر اس سے پہلے کہ وہ کچھ کہتی وہ اس سے ہاتھ چھڑا کر فوراً میکال کی طرف بھاگ گیا پھر اس کی شاندار گاڑی کا دروازہ کھولتے ہوئے اس نے اپنا اسپائڈر مین گاڑی کے اندر رکھ دیا۔ ساون کی بارشوں نے سارے شہر کو وقت پر ڈالا ہوا تھا' ہانیہ پریشان ہوگئی کیونکہ دور دور تک کسی ٹیکسی کا کوئی نام ونشان نظر نہیں آ رہا تھا۔

''مما! پاپا کی گاڑی میں آ جائیں پلیز۔'' چھٹکو تیز بارش میں بھیگتے ہوئے اس کے قریب آیا تھا اور اب اس کا ہاتھ پکڑتے ہوئے کھینچ رہا تھا جب اس نے آہستہ سے اپنا ہاتھ اس کے ہاتھ سے چھڑا لیا۔

''آپ کو جانا ہے تو آپ جاؤ علی! مجھے نہیں جانا۔''

''کیوں؟ رات تو آپ کہہ رہی تھیں کہ آپ پاپا سے ناراض نہیں ہیں۔''

''میں کسی سے ناراض نہیں ہوں' آپ جاؤ کیونکہ جو چیزیں آپ کو آپ کے پاپا لے کر دے سکتے ہیں وہ میں نہیں خرید سکتی۔'' نا چاہتے ہوئے بھی وہ جذباتی ہوگئی تھی چھوٹا سا بچہ جیسے سہم گیا۔ آنکھیں بھی فوراً آنسوؤں سے بھر آئی تھیں۔

''سوری مما! مجھے اسپائڈر مین نہیں چاہیے۔''

ہانیہ کا دل اس کے آنسوؤں پر تڑپ اٹھا تھا' لپک کر فوراً اس نے اسے گود میں اٹھا لیا' بارش مزید تیز ہوگئی تھی' میکال نے ایک نظر اوپر برستے آسمان کی طرف دیکھا پھر تیزی سے ہانیہ کے قریب چلا آیا۔

''بارش تیز ہو رہی ہے ابھی تھوڑی دیر میں یہاں کوئی بھی نظر نہیں آئے گا' میں تمہاری بات نہیں کروں گا مگر چھٹکو بارش میں بھیگ کر اکثر بیمار پڑ جاتا ہے لہٰذا اس وقت میں ایسا کوئی رسک نہیں لوں گا۔'' چھٹکو کو اس کی گود سے لیتے ہوئے اس نے ہانیہ کا بازو تھام کر اسے بھی ساتھ ہی کھینچ لیا تھا وہ انکار کرنا چاہتی تھی مگر میکال نے اسے کوئی موقع ہی نہیں دیا کچھ بولے کا تقریباً بیس منٹ کی تیز ڈرائیو کے بعد اس نے اس کے گھر کے سامنے گاڑی بریک کی تھی۔

''چھٹکو ضدی بچہ ہے اور ابھی چھوٹا ہے اس لیے مجبوریوں کی نزاکتوں کو نہیں سمجھتا یہ اس کے اکاؤنٹ کا اے ٹی ایم کارڈ ہے آئندہ جب بھی ضرورت پڑے پلیز اسے استعمال کر لینا۔'' والٹ سے اے ٹی ایم کارڈ نکال کر اس کی طرف بڑھاتے ہوئے وہ بولا تھا جب ہانیہ چھٹکو کا ہاتھ تھام کر گاڑی سے باہر نکل آئی۔

''بہت شکریہ میں اپنے بیٹے کی ہر خواہش خود پوری کر سکتی ہوں' بس ابھی میرے حالات ٹھیک نہیں ہیں۔''

قدرے ترش لہجے میں کہتے ہوئے وہ گیٹ کی طرف بڑھ گئی تھی' میکال حیران سا اسے دیکھتا رہ گیا۔ اگلے چند دن اس کے بے حد اذیت میں گزرے تھے تبھی اسے کمال کی کال آ گئی' وہ اسے انگلینڈ بلا رہا تھا' کیونکہ حسن صاحب کی طبیعت بہت خراب تھی نہال کی موت کے بعد وہ بہت کمزور ہو گئے تھے۔ میکال جانا نہیں چاہتا تھا مگر چلا گیا تھا اور ہانیہ صفدر کے

پاس سے ہمیشہ کے لیے فرار کا بس یہی ایک موقع تھا' فارحہ کی بیٹی اسے واپس کر کے وہ زکیہ بیگم اور چھٹکو کے ساتھ وہ شہر ہی چھوڑ کر چلی گئی تھی۔

❁ ..... ❁ ..... ❁

چار سال ہو گئے تھے اسے کراچی چھوڑے ہوئے اور ان چار سالوں میں اس نے کسی بھی اپنے سے رابطہ نہیں کیا تھا' گزرے ہوئے چار سالوں میں اپنے بیٹے کی بہترین تعلیم و تربیت کے لیے کیا کیا نہیں کیا تھا اس نے' تین تین جگہوں پر جاب' بیماری کے باوجود فاقے' پریشانیاں' ہر چیز برداشت کی تھی اس نے اور یہ اسی کا نتیجہ تھا کہ وہ آج ایک سرکاری اسپتال کے سستے سے کمرے کے بیڈ پر پڑی ہوش و حواس سے بے گانہ تھی اور اس کا بچہ جواب دس سال کا ہو چکا تھا اس کے سرہانے کھڑا رو رہا تھا جب کہ زکیہ بیگم خود بیماری کے باوجود اس کی دیکھ بھال کر رہی تھیں۔

ہانیہ کا ایک گردہ قطعی ناکارہ ہو چکا تھا اسے آپریشن کی ضرورت تھی اور آپریشن کے لیے پیسوں کی، جو زکیہ بیگم کے پاس نہیں تھے۔ زندگی کے مسائل اور تقدیر کی بے رحمی سے لڑتے لڑتے وہ لڑکی بالآخر ہار گئی تھی۔

❁ ..... ❁ ..... ❁

ایک لمبے عرصے کے بعد میکال ان دنوں ملتان آیا تھا۔ اس کا بزنس ملکوں تک پھیل چکا تھا ایک دنیا اس کی پرستار تھی مگر وہ اب زندگی جی نہیں رہا تھا گھسیٹ رہا تھا۔ چار سال ہو گئے تھے اس نے ہانیہ صفدر اور اپنے بیٹے کو نہیں دیکھا تھا کہاں کہاں نہیں ڈھونڈا تھا اس نے ان دونوں کو مگر جانے وہ دنیا کے کس گوشے میں جا چھپی تھی۔ پچھلے چار سال میں کوئی رات ایسی نہیں تھی جب وہ رو کر نہ سویا ہو۔

اگر اسے خبر ہوتی کہ ایک چھوٹی سی مہربانی پر ہانیہ اتنا بڑا قدم اٹھا لے گی تو وہ کبھی اس روز مارکیٹ میں اس کے سامنے نہ آتا کم از کم شہر کی فضاؤں میں اس کی سانسوں کی خوشبو تو آتی رہتی۔ کتنا ٹوٹ پھوٹ کر رہ گیا تھا وہ پچھلے سال میں' جانے کتنے ایسے ادارے تھے جن کو ہر ماہ وہ کروڑوں کی امداد دیتا تھا' وجہ صرف یہ تھی کہ وہاں چھوٹے چھوٹے معصوم بچے کفالت پا رہے تھے اور اسے ہر بچے میں اپنا بچہ نظر آتا تھا۔

اس وقت وہ اپنے دوست کے ساتھ سائٹ پر آیا تھا جب اس نے کمپنی کے ایک افسر کو ایک چھوٹے سے بچے پر برستے ہوئے دیکھا۔

''تمہاری عمر نہیں کام کرنے کی' جاؤ یہاں سے' پتا نہیں کہاں کہاں سے آ جاتے ہیں اٹھ کر۔''

''نہیں مجھے کام کرنا ہے' میری مما کو پیسوں کی ضرورت ہے۔'' بچے کے لہجے میں آنسوؤں کی آمیزش تھی' میکال کے قدم خود بخود اس کی طرف اٹھ گئے۔

''کیا بات ہے؟'' اس نے افسر سے پوچھا۔

''کچھ نہیں سر اس بچے کو دیکھیں دس سال عمر ہے اور مزدوری کرنے چلا آیا۔''

افسر اسے بتا رہا تھا تبھی بچے نے اس کی طرف دیکھا تھا اور میکال کو لگا جیسے اس کے سر پر آسمان ٹوٹ پڑا ہو اس کا لخت جگر جو اربوں کی جائیداد کا مالک تھا' وہاں چند پیسوں کے لیے مزدوری کرنے چلا آیا تھا۔ ٹوٹی ہوئی ہمت کے ساتھ پنجوں کے بل زمین پر بیٹھتے ہوئے اس نے اپنے بیٹے کو کندھوں سے تھاما تھا اور پھر اس سے لپٹ کر پھوٹ پھوٹ کر رو پڑا' ارد گرد کھڑے لوگ یہ منظر دیکھ کر ششدر رہ گئے تھے۔

''مما کہاں ہیں؟'' کچھ دیر کے بعد سر اٹھاتے ہوئے اس نے پوچھا تھا جب اس کے بیٹے نے بتایا۔

''اسپتال میں...... نانو کہتی ہیں جب تک پیسے نہیں ہوں گے مما ٹھیک نہیں ہوں گی' اسی لیے میں چوری چوری یہاں آ کر کام کر رہا تھا' مجھے مما کے بغیر کچھ بھی اچھا نہیں لگ رہا پاپا۔'' پھول سا چہرہ کملایا ہوا تھا' میکال کا دل کٹ کر رہ گیا' کھینچ کر اسے اپنے سینے سے لگاتے ہوئے وہ اسے بے تحاشا چومتا چلا گیا تھا۔

''مما ٹھیک ہو جائیں گی' آپ چلو میرے ساتھ۔'' فوراً آنسو پونچھتے ہوئے اس نے اپنے بیٹے کو گود میں اٹھالیا تھا پھر بنا کسی کو کچھ بتائے کسی کی پروا کیے وہ اسے گاڑی تک لایا اور اگلے ہی پل وہاں سے رخصت بھی ہو گیا۔

❁......❁......❁

جس وقت اس نے سرکاری اسپتال کے کوریڈور میں قدم رکھا ہانیہ کو گردے واش کرنے کے بعد اس کے بیڈ پر لٹایا جا رہا تھا' بڑے سے ہال کمرے کی ملگجی سی روشنی میں وہاں تقریباً کوئی چالیس پچاس بستر تھے جہاں بھانت بھانت کے لوگ اپنے اپنے مریضوں کے ساتھ سرکاری امداد کے رحم و کرم پر علاج کروا رہے تھے۔ وہ کمرے میں آیا تو ہانیہ کو بستر پر لٹا دیا گیا تھا مگر جو تکلیف وہ جھیل رہی تھی اسی تکلیف کے زیر اثر اس کا جسم بستر سے دو دو فٹ اوپر اچھل رہا تھا' میکال کے قدموں تلے سے جیسے زمین کھسک گئی تھی۔ جونہی اس نے کمرے میں قدم رکھا اس کا بیٹا بھاگ کر ہانیہ کے قریب چلا گیا۔

''مما...... دیکھیں پاپا آئے ہیں۔'' وہ جوش سے بتا رہا تھا مگر وہ ہوش میں کہاں تھی جو اس کی پکار سنتی تاہم زکیہ بیگم نے ضرور حیرانی سے پلٹ کر دیکھا تھا۔

''میکال......تم یہاں؟''

''جی آنٹی! '' دنیا اتنی بھی بڑی نہیں ہے کہ یہاں کسی ایک شخص کو زندگی بھر تلاش ہی نہ کیا جا سکے۔'' اس کی آنکھوں کے گوشوں میں چمکتی نمی نے انہیں شرمندگی سے سر جھکانے پر مجبور کر دیا بھلا ہانیہ صفدر کے کسی معاملے میں وہ کچھ کہنے کی مجاز کہاں تھیں۔ تبھی وہ قریب آیا تھا چند سیکنڈ پہلے لگنے والے نشہ آور انجکشن کے زیر اثر وہ اب غنودگی میں جا رہی تھی' میکال کی ہمت چند قدم آگے بڑھ کر جواب دے گئی' بے حد لاغر وجود کے ساتھ' حالات کی ستم ظریفی کی مکمل تصویر بنی وہ اس کے سامنے تھی' زرد چہرہ' آنکھوں کے نیچے پڑے گہرے حلقے' بدرنگ بکھرے بال' جسم پر بے حد پرانے کپڑے' بیڈ کے نیچے پڑی اس کی بے حد معمولی چپل' چیخ چیخ کر واضح کر رہی تھی وہ کن بدتر حالات کا شکار رہی ہو گی۔

چہرے کا گلابی پن بھی سورج کی تپش اور کڑی مشقت کے اثرات نے بدل کر سانولے رنگ میں ڈھال دیا تھا وہ تڑپ کر ہی تو رہ گیا۔ جسم میں اتنی سی ہمت بھی نہیں رہی تھی کہ ایک قدم پر ہی اٹھا سکتا مگر پھر بھی وہ پلٹا تھا اور ڈیوٹی پر موجود انتظامیہ سے بات کرنے کے بعد وہ اس کے بستر کے قریب آیا اور جھک کر اس کے لاغر وجود کو اپنی مضبوط بانہوں میں سمیٹ لیا۔

''میں اسے گاڑی میں لٹاتا ہوں آنٹی! آپ پلیز سارا سامان سمیٹ کر جلدی باہر آ جائیں۔'' پلٹ کر زکیہ بیگم کو کہتے ہوئے وہ فوراً کمرے سے نکل گیا تھا' اسی رات شہر کے بہترین اسپتال میں اس کا آپریٹ ہو گیا' صد شکر کہ اس کے صرف ایک گردے کو نقصان پہنچا تھا دوسرا بالکل محفوظ تھا ورنہ میکال نے اسے اپنا ایک گردہ دینے کی مکمل تیاری کر لی تھی' آپریشن سے ایک گھنٹے کے بعد اسے وی آئی روم میں شفٹ کر دیا گیا۔

وہی اس کی شخصیت تھی وہی تکلیف تھی مگر کاغذ کے چند ٹکڑوں نے فقط ایک رات میں ہی اس کی حیثیت بدل کر رکھ

دی تھی۔ زکیہ بیگم اس کا شکریہ ادا کرتے نہ تھک رہی تھیں اور وہ اپنے حقیقی معبود کا' جس کی رحیم و کریم ذات نے خاص رحمت سے چار سال کی خواری کے بعد بالآخر اسے ہانیہ صفدر اور اپنے بیٹے سے ملا دیا تھا۔

جس وقت ہانیہ کی آنکھ کھلی کمرے میں بے حد خاموشی اور سکون تھا۔ زکیہ بیگم اور سنان وہاں نہیں تھے تاہم میکال اس کے بیڈ کے قریب دھرے صوفے پر بیٹھا ضرور سو گیا تھا۔ ہلکی ہلکی بڑھی ہوئی شیو کے ساتھ اس کے چہرے پر کھنڈی زردی صاف دیکھی جا سکتی تھی' وہ ٹھٹک گئی۔ جس شخص کے سائے سے بچنے کے لیے وہ پچھلے چار سال سے بھٹک رہی تھی بالآخر وہ شخص اس تک پہنچ گیا تھا۔ ہانیہ نے بے ساختہ پلکیں موند لیں' پلکوں کی باڑ سے ایک آنسو ٹوٹ کر بائیں گال پر پھسل آیا تھا' اسے لگا وہ اس شخص کے عکس سے کبھی دور نہیں بھاگ سکے گی تبھی میکال حسن کی آنکھ کھلی تھی' ہانیہ صفدر کو اپنی طرف دیکھتے پا کر وہ فوراً اس کے قریب آیا تھا۔

''اب کیسی طبیعت ہے ہانیہ؟'' وہ اس پر جھکا تھا مگر ہانیہ نے جواب دینے کے بجائے پھر سے پلکیں موند لیں تبھی وہ بیڈ پر اس کے پہلو میں ٹک گیا تھا۔

''میں جانتا ہوں ہانیہ! تم مجھ سے بہت نفرت کرتی ہو مگر تم یہ نہیں جانتی کہ میں تم سے بھی زیادہ خود سے نفرت کرتا ہوں' اتنی نفرت کہ شاید تم اس کا اندازہ بھی نہ کر سکو' اسی لیے میں نے اپنے جسم کا کوئی حصہ ایسا نہیں چھوڑا جسے کاٹ کر جلایا نہ ہو' واقعی جو محبت نہال نے تم سے کی تم اسی کی حق دار تھیں مگر پھر بھی یہ سچ ہے ہانیہ! میں تمہیں کھو کر ایک سانس بھی نہیں لے سکتا' پچھلے سال میں جس اذیت میں گزارے ہیں تم اس کا اندازہ بھی نہیں کر سکتیں' ساری دنیا کو ترک کر دیا ہے میں نے' میرے بس میں نہیں ہے کہ میں گزرے ہوئے وقت کے گھوڑے کی لگام میں کھینچ کر اسے واپس لا سکوں' جو ظلم میں نے تمہارے اور نہال کے ساتھ کیا اس کا ازالہ کر سکوں مگر میں تم سے درخواست کر سکتا ہوں ہانیہ! میرے ضبط اور ہمت کا مزید امتحان مت لو' میرے لیے نہ سہی چھٹکو کے لیے ہی سہی پلیز مجھے معاف کر دو پلیز۔'' ایک دم سے اس کا ہاتھ تھام کر وہ بچوں کی طرح رو پڑا تھا ہانیہ کے اندر بھونچال اٹھ گیا۔

''کر چکی ہوں معاف' میرا بیٹا کہاں ہے؟'' اس کے لہجے میں اب بھی کوئی لچک نہیں تھی' میکال نے خود کو سنبھال لیا۔

''سو رہا ہے' تمہیں پتا ہے تمہاری جان بچانے کے لیے وہ مزدوری کر رہا تھا۔''

''کیا......؟'' وہ شاکڈ رہ گئی تھی تبھی زکیہ بیگم وہاں چلی آئیں تو میکال اٹھ کر کمرے سے باہر نکل گیا۔

''میکال حسن سے آپ نے رابطہ کر کے اسے بلایا تھا'' اس کے جاتے ہی اس نے زکیہ بیگم سے تفتیش شروع کر دی۔

''نہیں سگی ماں ہوتی تو شاید بلا لیتی مگر مجھ سوتیلی ماں کو یہ اختیار کہاں تھا کہ تمہارے کسی بھی معاملے میں اپنی مرضی کروں' وہ تو سنان علی کے ساتھ آیا تھا میں تو خود اسے دیکھ کر حیران رہ گئی تھی۔'' وہ طنزاً نہیں کہہ رہی تھیں مگر پھر بھی ہانیہ شرمندہ ہو کر رہ گئی تھی۔

''میں جانتی ہوں تمہارا دل میری طرف سے کبھی صاف نہیں ہوگا مگر تم یہ نہیں جانتی کہ میری کن مجبوریوں نے مجھے صفدر صاحب سے دوسری شادی پر مجبور کیا بالکل ویسے ہی جیسے تم یہ نہیں جانتیں کہ میکال نے کن وجوہات اور احساسات کی بنا پر علیزے نامی اس ماڈل سے شادی کی' تم بہت احمق اور خود پسند لڑکی ہو ہانیہ! تمہیں اپنے جذبات' حق اور درد کے سامنے کسی اور کا درد کبھی نظر نہیں آیا۔''

پہلی بار وہ اس کے سامنے یوں کھل کر بول رہی تھیں' ہانیہ حیران سی یک ٹک انہیں دیکھے گئی مگر وہ اس کی طرف نہیں دیکھ رہی تھیں۔

''تم نے ساری زندگی صرف انہی رشتوں سے محبت کی اور امید وابستہ رکھی جن کو تم نے قابل اعتبار جانا مگر زندگی کوئی

دوسطری کہانی نہیں ہے جس کا منطقی انجام کوئی انسان لکھ کر ہاتھ جھاڑ لے' بہت تلخ حقیقتیں ہیں زندگی کی اور اس سے بھی زیادہ روپ' یہاں ہر انسان ایک ہی طرز کی محبت نہیں کرتا۔ میں اپنی بات نہیں کروں گی مگر تمہاری زندگی کی بات ضرور کروں گی' تم نے نہال حسن کی محبت کو سمجھا مگر میکال کی محبت کو نہیں کیونکہ دونوں کی محبت کا انداز اور روپ بہت مختلف تھا میں اگر تمہاری سگی ماں ہوتی تو کبھی میکال حسن سے تمہاری علیحدگی نہ ہونے دیتی اور اب جب وہ دوسرا نہال بننے جارہا ہے تو کبھی تم کو اس سے یوں بدگمان نہ رہنے دیتی مگر افسوس اسی بات کا ہے کہ میں تمہاری سگی ماں نہیں ہوں۔'' اب ان کے لہجے کے ساتھ ساتھ ان کی آنکھیں بھی بھیگ چکی تھیں مگر اس سے پہلے کہ وہ ان سے کوئی استفسار کرتی' وہ فوراً اٹھ کر کمرے سے باہر نکل گئی تھیں' ہانیہ کا دماغ جیسے سن ہوگیا' یہ کیسے چابک تھے لفظوں کے جو وہ اس کے منہ پر مار کر چلی گئی تھیں۔

بے شک گزرے ہوئے وقت میں جب سگا بھائی اور بھابی بھی اس سے بے نیاز ہوچکے تھے انہوں نے سگی ماؤں سے بڑھ کر اس کا ساتھ نبھایا تھا' پچھلے چار سال میں کیسی کیسی تکلیفیں برداشت نہیں کی تھی انہوں نے اس کے لیے مگر کبھی زبان پر ایک حرف تک نہیں لائی تھیں' انہوں نے کبھی اس کے کسی فیصلے میں مداخلت نہیں کی تھی نہ ہی اسے اس کی اناء کے قلعے میں اکیلا مرنے کے لیے چھوڑا تھا' حالانکہ وہ چاہتیں تو صفدر صاحب کی رحلت کے بعد بھی وہیں رہ سکتی تھیں جاذب کے ساتھ' مگر وہ نہیں رہی تھیں' انگلینڈ جیسے ملک کے ٹھاٹ باٹ چھوڑ کر صرف اس کے لیے پاکستان چلی آئی تھیں مگر ہانیہ نے کبھی ان نزاکتوں اور قربانیوں کو سمجھا ہی نہیں تھا' واقعی وہ بے حد خود پسند ثابت ہوئی تھیں' اسے یک لخت خود سے شرمندگی محسوس ہوئی اور اب ایک نئی الجھن مزید سامنے آکھڑی ہوئی تھی۔

میکال حسن' نہال بننے جارہا تھا؟ زکیہ بیگم اس کے اس جملے کے پیچھے کیا تھا؟ سوچ سوچ کر شریانیں تھک گئیں تو اس نے آنکھیں بند کرلیں تقریباً ایک ہفتے کے بعد نہال انہیں واپس کراچی لے آیا تھا۔ ہانیہ ہوش میں نہیں تھی ورنہ شاید کبھی وہاں ''حسن پیلس'' نہ آتی' حفیظ بابا کو جیسے ہی خبر ہوئی مارے خوشی کے ان کے پاؤں زمین پر نہیں لگ رہے تھے' وہ اس گھر کے دیرینہ ملازمین میں سے تھے اور وہاں کے ایک ایک فرد کے ساتھ ان کا محبت کا رشتہ تھا۔

رات کا جانے کون سا پہر تھا جب ہانیہ کی آنکھ کھلی تھی۔ وہ اسپتال کے بجائے گھر میں تھی اور جس کمرے میں تھی اس کے بیڈ کی سائیڈ پر دونوں اطراف میں اس کی اور نہال حسن کی تصویر رکھی ہوئی تھی' نیند میں ڈوبی آنکھیں ایک دم سے مکمل کھل گئیں۔ سارے کمرے کی دیواروں پر سوائے اس کی تصویروں کے اور کچھ بھی نہیں تھا۔ وہ ایک دم سے اٹھ کر بیٹھ گئی۔

یہ وہ کہاں آگئی تھی؟ جانے خواب تھا یا حقیقت؟ اس کا دل بہت شدت سے دھڑک رہا تھا جب کہ حلق میں پیاس کی شدت سے جیسے کانٹے اُگ آئے تھے۔ وہ اٹھی تھی اور ادھ کھلے دروازے سے باہر نکل آئی' ساتھ والے کمرے میں جو کبھی حسن صاحب کا کمرا ہوا کرتا تھا زکیہ بیگم اور اس کا بیٹا گہری نیند میں سو رہے تھے' باہر لاؤنج میں مکمل اندھیرا تھا اس نے لائٹ جلائی اور کچن میں آکر پورے دو گلاس پانی غٹا غٹ پی گئی کچن کے قریب ہی نہال کا کمرا تھا جو اب مقفل تھا جب کہ سیڑھیوں کے دہانے کے بائیں طرف اس کا الگ کمرہ تھا' جس میں سے کسی کے درد سے کراہنے کی آوازیں آرہی تھیں۔

ہانیہ کچن سے نکل کر کمرے میں آنے کے بجائے سیڑھیوں کی طرف بڑھ آئی تھی اس کے کمرے کا دروازہ ادھ کھلا تھا' تاہم فل لائٹ وہاں بھی آن نہیں تھی' ادھ کھلے دروازے کو آہستہ سے دھکیلتے ہوئے جونہی وہ اندر داخل ہوئی ٹھٹک کر رہ گئی' نظر کے سامنے ہی فرش پر بیٹھا میکال بلیڈ سے اپنا جسم چیر رہا تھا اور پھر بہتے خون پر نمک چھڑک کر اپنا درد ضبط کرنے

کی کوشش میں اپنی چیخوں کا گلا گھونٹتا۔ قریب ہی شراب کی خالی بوتل پڑی رُل رہی تھی وہ جہاں کی تہاں کھڑی رہ گئی' زکیہ بیگم نے صحیح کہا تھا نہال اور میکال دونوں کی محبت کے انداز میں بہت فرق تھا مگر دونوں نے ہی اسے بہت چاہا تھا وہ بھول گئی کہ اس نے اس کے ساتھ کیا کیا تھا' اسے کیا کیا کہا تھا یاد رہا تو صرف اتنا کہ اس کے دل نے کبھی اس شخص کو بہت شدت سے چاہا تھا اب نہال کے بعد وہ اسے جان سے گزرتے ہوئے نہیں دیکھ سکتی تھی۔ ایک وہ شخص تھا جس کی جان اس کی محبت نے لے لی تھی اور اب ایک یہ شخص تھا جس کی جان اس کی نفرت لے رہی تھی' محبت کے سوکھے چشمے ایک دم سے پھوٹے تھے اور وہ لپک کر اس کے قریب چلی آئی تھی۔

''چھوڑو میکال! یہ کیا کر رہے ہو؟'' اس کے ہاتھ سے بلیڈ چھینتے ہوئے وہ چلائی تھی' وہ اسے دیکھ کر ٹھٹک گیا۔

''تم......'' اس وقت اسے اپنا بھی ہوش نہیں تھا مگر وہ اس کی حیرانی کی پروا کیے بغیر فوراً کمرے سے نکل آئی تھی۔ شدت سے بہتے آنسوؤں کے ساتھ بلیڈ پھینک کر اس نے فرسٹ ایڈ باکس تلاش کیا اور دوبارہ اسی کمرے میں چلی آئی میکال اب بھی دیوار سے ٹیک لگائے اسی پوزیشن میں بیٹھا تھا جب اس نے سختی سے آنکھیں رگڑتے ہوئے ٹھنڈے پانی سے اس کے زخموں کو صاف کرنے کے بعد وہاں کریم لگادی تبھی میکال نے اس کا ہاتھ تھاما تھا اور پھر بچوں کی طرح پھوٹ پھوٹ کر رونا شروع کر دیا۔

ایک مدت کے بعد اس کے درد نے ہانیہ کے دل میں چٹکی کاٹی تھی تبھی وہ اس کے مضبوط کندھے پر ہاتھ رکھتے ہوئے بولی تھی۔

''بس کرو میکال! بہت سزا کاٹ لی ہم نے محبت کی اور محبت میں بدگمانیوں کی' اب اور نہیں۔'' موتی اس کی آنکھوں سے بھی ٹوٹ کر بکھر رہے تھے تبھی میکال نے اسے کندھوں سے پکڑ کر خود سے لگایا اور پھر ڈھیر سارا رو دیا۔ ایک مدت کے بعد بالآخر عشق کی عدالت نے اس کا جرم بے وفائی معاف کر کے اسے اذیت کی قید سے رہا کر دیا تھا۔

❁......❁......❁

بہت دنوں کی بارش کے بعد اس روز خاصی چمکیلی دھوپ نکلی تھی۔

ہانیہ پردے سمیٹنے کے بعد بیڈ کی طرف چلی آئی جہاں میکال تکیہ بانہوں میں لیے الٹا لیٹا اسی کے خواب دیکھ رہا تھا۔ اس نے فریج سے ٹھنڈے یخ پانی کی بوتل نکالی اور آرام سے اس پر انڈیل دی' وہ ہڑبڑا کر گہری نیند سے بیدار ہوا تھا' ہانیہ کھلکھلا کر ہنس پڑی۔

''آٹھ بج گئے ہیں جناب! اٹھ جائیں' آپ کے صاحب زادے اسکول کے لیے تیار ہو چکے ہیں اور پاپا کی کال بھی آ چکی ہے دوبار' دس بجے کی فلائٹ سے وہ اور مما پاکستان پہنچ رہے ہیں۔''

''اچھا...... وہ تو ٹھیک ہے مگر اتنا ٹھنڈا پانی کیوں ڈالا ہے؟'' تکیہ بانہوں میں دبائے وہ بیڈ پر اٹھ بیٹھا تھا' ہانیہ مسکراتے ہوئے وارڈروب کی طرف چلی آئی۔

''جذبات ٹھنڈے کرنے کے لیے۔''

''وہ نہیں ہو سکتے۔'' فوراً بیڈ سے اترتے ہوئے وہ اس کے پیچھے آیا اور اسے اپنی بانہوں میں سمیٹ لیا۔

''کم از کم تمہارے لیے تو کبھی نہیں ہو سکتے۔'' اب وہ اسے تنگ کر رہا تھا' عین اسی ٹائم اس کا بیٹا بیگ اٹھائے کمرے کی دہلیز پر چلا آیا۔

''پاپا مجھے اسکول سے دیر ہو رہی ہے۔''

''اوسوری علی! وہ میں آپ کی مما کو نیکلس پہنا رہا تھا۔'' بیٹے کی آمد پر فوراً اسے چھوڑتے ہوئے وہ بوکھلایا تو ہانیہ پھر کھلکھلا کر ہنس پڑی۔

''فکر نہ کرو ابھی اسے چھوڑ کر واپسی پر خبر لیتا ہوں تمہاری۔''

آنکھوں ہی آنکھوں میں اسے اشارہ کرتا وہ چھٹکو کے پیچھے ہی کمرے سے نکل چکا تھا جواب میں ہانیہ نے منہ بسور کر اسے مزید چڑایا اس کی منزل یہی تھی جتنی بھی کٹھن مسافت طے کر لیتی اسے لوٹ کر یہیں آنا تھا۔ جازب اور ہادیہ نے زکیہ بیگم کو اپنے پاس بلا لیا تھا' ایک ماہ پہلے میکال حسن سے اس کی شادی کے بعد وہ ہانیہ کے اصرار پر بھی وہاں نہیں رکی تھیں تاہم ہانیہ نے ان کے لیے اپنی محبت کا اظہار ضرور کر دیا تھا۔

باہر میکال کی گاڑی اسٹارٹ ہونے کی آواز آ رہی تھی اس نے وارڈ روب کھول کر وہاں رکھی نہال حسن کی تصویر نکالی وہ مسکرا رہا تھا۔ یوں جیسے ہانیہ صفدر کی زندگی کی خوشیوں کے لیے اس کی دعائیں مستجاب ہو گئی ہوں' ہانیہ نے نہایت پیار سے اس کی تصویر پر ہاتھ پھیرتے ہوئے کھڑکی کے اس پار دیکھا جہاں کئی روز کی بارشوں کے بعد بالآخر چمکیلی دھوپ نکل آئی تھی۔

بارشیں واقعی کبھی کسی کا ساتھ نہیں دیتیں تاہم اس کی زندگی میں اب بارشوں کے موسموں کی جگہ سنہری دھوپ نے لے لی تھی' تبھی نہال کی تصویر وارڈ روب میں رکھتے ہوئے وہ کمرے سے نکل آئی' ابھی میکال نے واپس آ کر آفس کے لیے تیاری کرنی تھی پھر ائیر پورٹ جانا تھا اور وہ نہیں چاہتی تھی کہ ہر روز کی طرح آج بھی اسے دیر ہو' بے شک ہجر کی لمبی مسافت کے بعد اس نے رشتوں کے حسن اور ان کی اہمیت کو محسوس کرنا سیکھ لیا تھا۔

(تمت بالخیر)

Printed in Dunstable, United Kingdom

75909633R00173

WHERE I LIVE

MARKET TOWN

Neil Thomson
meets
John Coulson

WATTS BOOKS
LONDON • NEW YORK • SYDNEY

Watts Books
96 Leonard Street
London
EC2A 4RH

Franklin Watts Australia
14 Mars Road
Lane Cove
NSW 2066

UK ISBN: 0 7496 1553 2

Dewey Decimal Classification Number 307.76

A CIP catalogue record for this book is available from the British Library.

Series Editor: Sarah Ridley
Editor: Nicola Baxter
Photographer: Neil Thomson
Designer: Amanda Hawkes

Additional photographs: Aerofilms Ltd, Allertonshire School, Mr Bryning, Robert Harding Picture Library, Hambleton Leisure Centre, Hutchison Library, North Yorkshire County Library, Northallerton Football Club, Northern Echo, Michael Peckett.

Acknowledgements: the author and publisher wish to thank John Coulson and family, Colin Narramore, the staff and pupils of Mill Hill Primary School, Margaret Johnson, John Kelly, Jim Smith and Jonathan Blyth for all their help with this book.

Printed in Malaysia

CONTENTS

WHERE I LIVE

My name is John Coulson. I live in Northallerton, in the county of North Yorkshire. It's a small town surrounded by countryside. There's a long main street lined with shops of all sorts and an auction mart just behind the High Street. Twice a week there's a really busy street market. The market is well known throughout Yorkshire and brings a lot of business to the town. Local farmers come into town twice a week to buy and sell cattle at the mart.

Northallerton is the county town of North Yorkshire, so County Hall is here, which gives a lot of employment. The shops and the market make it quite a prosperous place.

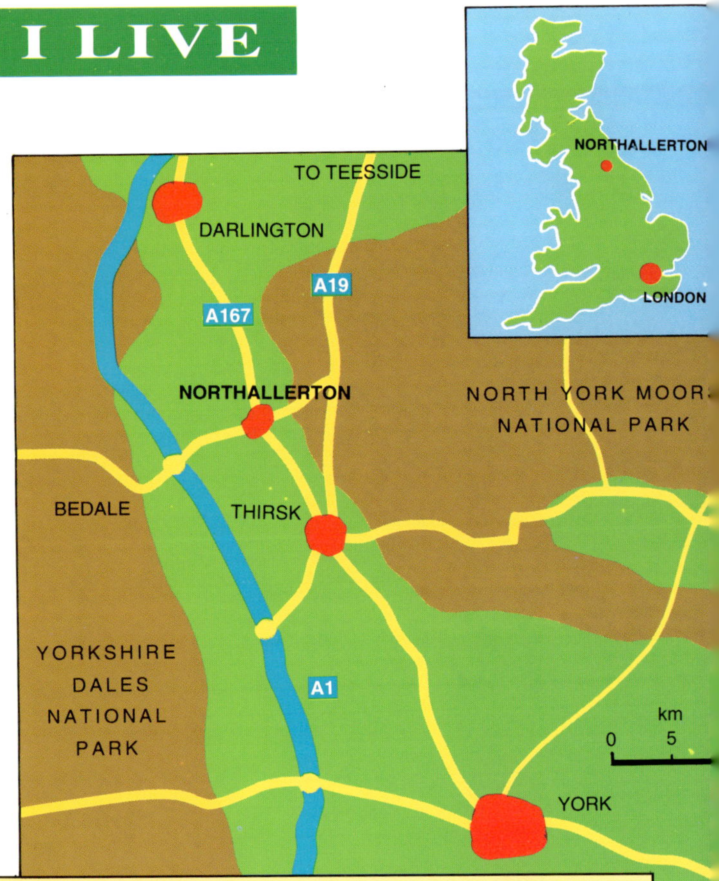

Northallerton is in a lowland area between the Yorkshire Dales to the west and the North York Moors to the east.

There are many farms around Northallerton. For several centuries, farmers from miles around have come to the town to buy and sell livestock.

The market cross is at the centre of the High Street.

In the 18th century, the town was an overnight stop for stagecoaches carrying passengers between London and Scotland. The Golden Lion was one of the many inns offering accommodation

Part of All Saints' Church at the north end of town dates from the 13th century.

I was born in Northallerton and went to school here. I started work as an office boy in the town and then learnt the printing trade. Now I have a small business just behind the High Street. I print anything from invitations to posters. Most of my customers live or work in Northallerton. A lot of local families have lived here a long time, so quite often we know one another from our schooldays.

FACTS & FIGURES

Northallerton has a population of about 13,000.

York has 130,000 inhabitants and Leeds has 500,000.

Yorkshire, including North, South and West Yorkshire, is the largest county in England.

I'm on the Town Council and I've been Mayor of Northallerton for two years. It's only a small town, so it's not a grand thing being Mayor. I do have a chain of office but I certainly don't have a limousine. A Rover Metro is more the scene here!

I only have to wear the chain of office for official functions.

If I have any council business during the daytime, my wife takes over while I'm away.

The printing business keeps me in touch with events in the town.

My wife, Daphne, works with me in the print-shop. We have four children. None of them has left home yet. Dawn, who is 22, is an office clerk at County Hall. Richard, who is 19, works there as well, in the print room. Paula, who is 17, is training to be a nursery nurse. Then there's Lynda, our nine-year-old.

THE HIGH STREET

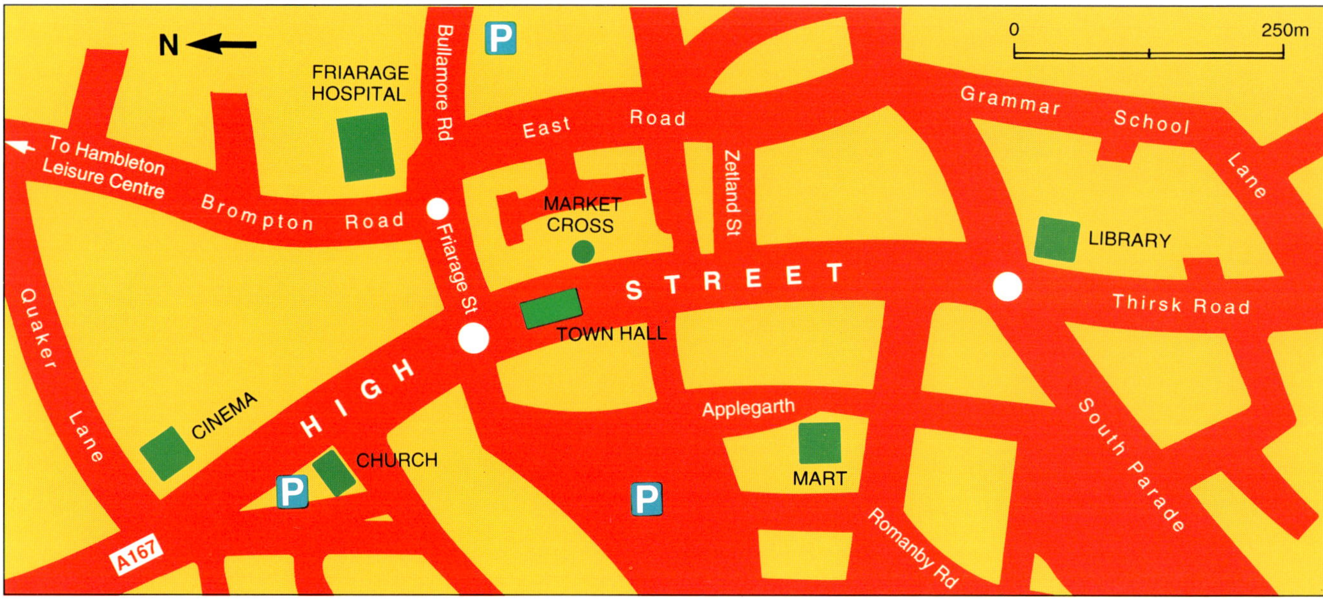

The High Street is the heart of Northallerton. Today it is still what draws visitors to the town.

The range of shops on the High Street has expanded since I was a boy. In those days there were big private houses along both sides of the High Street as well as the shops and pubs. Behind them were cottages and workshops arranged around what were called "the yards". That was where most people in the town lived and worked then.

A few of the cobbled yards still survive.

There have always been shops all along the High Street.

We've hung on to the family-run small businesses that help to give the town its character. Many of the shops are family concerns and have been handed down from generation to generation. The owners often serve in the shop and know a lot of customers by name. I think that attracts shoppers who find the big superstores a bit impersonal.

A lot of businesses have kept a traditional flavour.

There are a few of the national chainstores in the town. Safeway is the biggest one on the High Street. Their premises used to be a pub and they had to keep the old frontage to get planning permission. Out of town, there's a big Gateway with its own parking area.

We haven't got a Marks and Spencer – that's the only thing you have to leave town for. People say they won't ever open here because our population is too small to make it worthwhile. Still, we are a nice rural market town and we don't really need any more shops.

Barkers department store goes back to 1875. You wouldn't normally get a department store in a town this size, but people come shopping here from miles around, so there are plenty of customers.

Now the High Street is all shops, banks and building societies. Hardly anyone lives over the shop any more. If the upper floors are in use, they are mostly offices.

Low's supermarket is behind the High Street. It has its own car park, which makes it convenient for loading the shopping.

THE MARKET AND THE MART

There's a big market in the High Street every Wednesday and Saturday. We get a lot of shoppers coming from Teesside and Middlesbrough, as well as from the villages around Northallerton. The market is very successful – there are more stalls now than there ever were. The competition between them helps to keep the prices down. A few of the stall holders are local, but most come quite a distance, some from as far away as Teesside. The market starts to set up at about seven in the morning and packs up in the late afternoon. Sometimes, if it's terrible weather and there's not much trade, they close up early.

The market completely takes over the High Street twice a week.

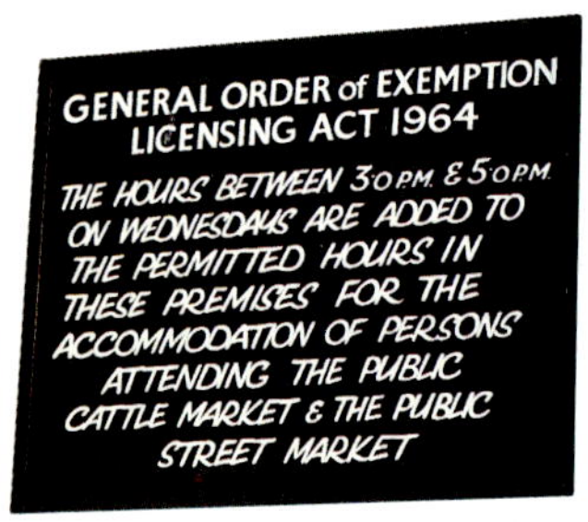

There's a ban on parking on market days to make room for the stalls.

The market superintendent has a little office on wheels near the Town Hall. He organises the pitches in the morning and sorts out anyone who wants a stall. There's always a waiting list of keen would-be stallholders. If ever there's an argument about a pitch, he sorts it out.

FACTS & FIGURES

In North Yorkshire, 5% of those in employment work in agriculture, compared with 1% on average for the U.K.

If you're standing in the car park behind the High Street, you can hear the cattle from the pens waiting to be loaded into the buyers' trucks.

Sam Turner and Sons have been here since the year dot. They were always known as the farmer's friend. They would come to the market and lay out masses of goods. Buckets, tools, wellington boots: you name it, they sold it. Now they sell everything a farmer needs in the way of equipment. They have a caravan in the market where they take orders, but their stock needs a warehouse nowadays to be displayed.

Northallerton is in the middle of very good farming country. The twice-weekly cattle auctions at the mart attract farmers from a twenty-mile radius. It used to be local farmers selling to local butchers, but now there's a lot of trade with the national firms who send buyers up from the south of England.

There used to be more pubs in Northallerton per head of population than anywhere else in Yorkshire. A lot of the farmers came into town on a Tuesday or a Wednesday for the cattle auction. Then if they'd done well on the prices, they'd be off to the pub to celebrate and catch up on the news. It used to be a bawdy town with all those pubs.

The mart on the Applegarth just to the west of the High Street opened in 1909. Before that farmers used to sell their cattle in the street.

HOUSING

Between the First and Second World Wars, most of the old yards in the town centre were condemned by the council. The buildings were knocked down and people rehoused. A lot of people didn't want to move from their cottages, even though they didn't have amenities like indoor toilets or bathrooms. There was usually just a tap in the middle of the yard. But most people were rehoused on new estates, the bulk of them put up by the council.

The house is a bit small for the six of us, so we're hoping to build out at the back.

Now only the older people in the town can remember the old yards.

We used to live in Romanby, a district just on the edge of the town. That was good for the children. There was lots of space and hardly any traffic, so they could play outside. Where we are now isn't so good from that point of view but it is handier for getting to work.

We used to live in a council house in Romanby.

Northallerton has been expanding over the years and new housing is going up all the time. Nowadays it's mostly private developers building houses for sale. There was lots of council housing to the east of the High Street, but most of that's been sold to the tenants

We live in a pre-war house on the east side of town. My parents still live just round the corner in the house where I was brought up. We're less than ten minutes' walk from the print-shop, and only five minutes' walk from our youngest daughter Lynda's school.

A lot of new estates are going up on the edge of the town.

FACTS & FIGURES

In the 1960s and early 1970s Northallerton was the fastest growing town in Yorkshire.

It still has a younger population than the county average.

Northallerton is a popular place to live, so there is pressure on the housing here. It's a problem for young couples setting up home for the first time to find somewhere they can afford. I can't quote figures for the number of people on the council housing list, but it's certainly more than I would like.

Northallerton has a mixture of older and newer housing.

Modern flats just behind the High Street are convenient for those without a car.

Here are some of the people I know in the town.

Pam Jordison's father, Reilly Nelson, started the family business. They do electrical work and have a shop at the north end of the High Street.

Pam

"Like a lot of the older businesses in the town, ours is a family affair. We've got five members of the family working here. There are a lot of wealthy farmers around, so it is quite a thriving community. We had two quiet months recently and we thought the recession had finally come to Northallerton, but it seems not too bad now."

Stuart Nelson, Pam's brother, helps to run the electrical business.

"When I'm not working, I have a major hobby of pigeon racing. You can race them 700 miles if they're trained right, fed right and treated right. I started out with two pigeons in a rabbit hutch. Now I've got the best loft in the north of England with 200 pigeons. I breed them and sometimes I'll sell them. I've had enquiries for my pigeons from all over the world. I won the big race this year. That was my life's ambition."

Stuart

Colin

Colin Narramore is production manager at York Trailers, up on the Darlington Road.

"We're really busy at the moment with orders for truck trailers. The company went through a bad patch a couple of years ago but it's better now. There are a few more light industrial units opening up in the town. Generally we're better off here as far as unemployment goes than most of the north east."

Bob and Maisie

Bob Barrett is the musical director of the male voice choir.

"It's only a small town but there's lots of things you can join if you're prepared to get involved. Musically you can be very busy. Quite a few of us in the choir are retired – it makes it easier to find time for rehearsals. Some people come from as far as twenty miles away. For that, you have to be really committed."

Bob's wife Maisie is the president of the local branch of the Women's Institute.

"The W.I. has a wooden hall in Romanby that was built in 1939. It's just opposite the school there and gets used as the village hall. At different times it's used for whist drives, the dancing club and keep fit. The school uses it for pantomimes. We draw the line at discos or youth clubs. There's the nightclub in town for that or the youth club at Allertonshire School. What we haven't got here in the town is a proper park where you can go and walk. There was a BMX track behind Applegarth, but that's gone now. The little playground there is pretty sad. We're central for the North York Moors and the Dales though, so it's a good base for walks in the country."

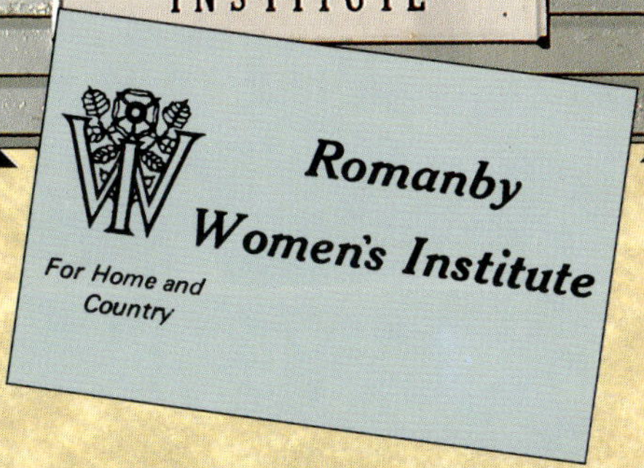

Julie is the lollipop lady at our daughter's school. She lives nearby.
"I've only lived in the town a short while but I really like it. People are very friendly round here. If you're talking to someone about somebody else they'll say, 'Oh, I know them – I used to go to school with them.'

Julie

It doesn't take long to get anywhere in town since it's quite small. It's often quicker to pop to the High Street on my bike than to take the car and spend time finding somewhere to park. The only thing my area of town is a bit short of is a creche or playgroup for pre-school kids."

Julie

John Bunting is the market superintendent.

John

"Superintendent sounds a bit like a policeman – I'd prefer to be called the market manager. Sometimes there's a storm in a teacup over parking spaces in the High Street and I have to sort that out. But it's a market town and you're bound to get some disruption with all the extra traffic. It's a strong market with an element of competition, but not so cut-throat that nobody makes a thing. There are always new people wanting to take a stall, but the council has to limit the numbers. The market has expanded over the years as it is."

Barbara works in the office of one of the two health centres in the town.
"We have patients from within a ten-mile radius of Northallerton. The town has got much bigger over the years. There's more and more traffic. It used to take me five minutes to drive to work, but now it takes me ten.

Barbara and the Health Centre where she works

It's wonderful for shopping here. I get my fruit and veg. in the market twice a week, as it's cheaper than in the shops. Darlington is excellent for theatre and it's only twenty minutes away by car. York is further – fifty minutes on a good day and an hour and a quarter on a bad one. The train is quicker than driving – only twenty minutes."

Susan Horner is a receptionist for York Trailers.

Susan

"I'm lucky to have a job. At the moment it's not easy for young people to find jobs in the town. It's not that easy to find a place to live either. I'm living with my family still. My boyfriend and I are looking for somewhere to buy, but the prices here are still high. Darlington would be cheaper but then we'd have to travel to work."

WORK

There isn't much in the way of industry in Northallerton. Apart from all the jobs on the High Street, most of the opportunities in town are through County Hall. My son and my eldest daughter both work there. Then in the rest of the town there are lots of other office jobs that depend on local government business.

About 1,200 people work at County Hall, dealing with education and planning for all of North Yorkshire.

It's a five-minute walk to the High Street for the employees from County Hall.

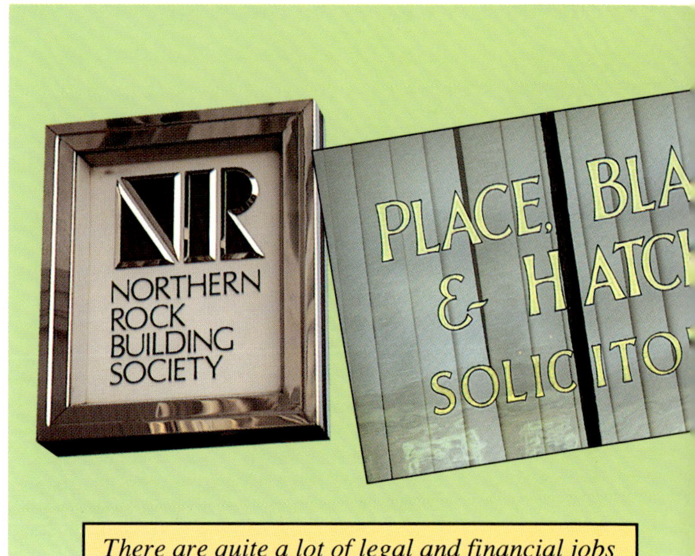

There are quite a lot of legal and financial jobs in the town.

Our part of Yorkshire is called Hambleton. Several hundred people work at the Hambleton District Council headquarters in Northallerton. The District Council deals with leisure and housing for the surrounding area.

York Trailers has one of the largest factory sites in the town.

The biggest factory until recently was York Trailers. They almost closed down in 1991 but luckily they're now back in business. There is an industrial estate to the north of the town with small workshops and factory units.

Some people do commute to jobs in industry elsewhere in the north-east. There's the chemical industry and the like on Teesside. Others travel down to York or up to Darlington.

There are several small factories on the industrial estate on the north side of the town.

FACTS & FIGURES

The unemployment rate in North Yorkshire is consistently lower than the national average.

•

Northallerton has the lowest rate in the county.

We're on the main east-coast railway line from London to Edinburgh. There are lots of fast trains on the route, though only a few of them stop here. We used to have a nice Victorian railway station. Now it's a smaller, modern one. For a while we were threatened with having even fewer trains stopping here, but protests to British Rail persuaded them to restore the service. There used to be a goods station in town on the line to Teesside. Now the freight traffic comes in on the roads.

In 1800 the journey from London to York used to take at least thirty hours by horse-drawn coach. Now it takes less than two hours by train.

The railway cuts the town into two. Traffic often has to wait at one of the two level crossings.

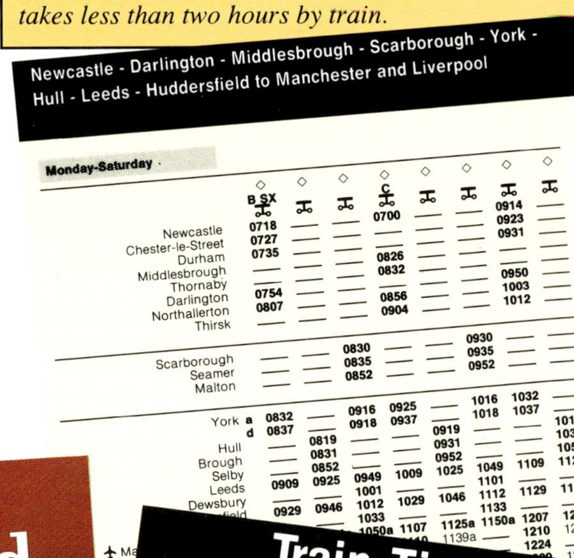

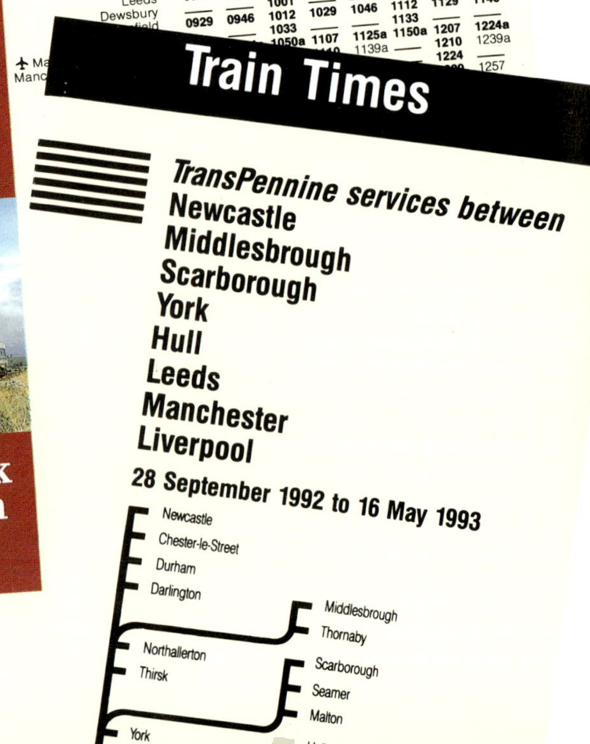

We have a regular train link with many cities including York and Darlington.

There are local bus routes that go round the town and to the nearby villages. But there's not so much further afield. If someone wants to come shopping from Leyburn, say, and plenty do, it takes ages on the bus. You go up hill and down dale calling at other villages on the way. It's too tempting just to hop in the car and drive here in twenty minutes or so. The bus services have gradually been reduced as more and more people have bought cars.

There are private bus companies operating services into town. Some run only on market days.

The alternative to the bus or train, if you don't have a car, is to take a taxi.

The old bus station has become a tyre repair garage.

FACTS & FIGURES

Northallerton district has the highest level of car ownership in the county.

In 1987 three-quarters of households had at least one car.

The wardens keep an eye out and you can get a £12 fine for breaking the rules.

The traffic is busiest on Wednesdays and Saturdays when it's market day. Even though the town is not very big, there can be quite a queue of traffic to get in and out. You're allowed to park for just two hours in the High Street, except on market days when you can't park there at all. You have to display a special disc in the car. You set the time you arrive and then you have two hours free parking. That's plenty of time to go shopping. You're not allowed to return immediately.

On Saturday it can be a problem getting into the car park behind the High Street. It's free, but the county council want to charge for parking in the main car parks in the town. The problem as I see it is that the free parking keeps the town alive. It's the smaller shops that would suffer if people were put off coming here by having to pay to park. The supermarkets have their own car parks so they would be less affected.

At around 5 p.m. every weekday, the main car park empties. There's quite a queue to get out of town then.

Many of us recently took part in a campaign to stop plans for car park charges.

The car park behind the High Street is used by commuters to the town as well as shoppers.

FACTS & FIGURES

Nearly twice as many people commute into Northallerton to work as commute out.

SCHOOLS

Lynda, our nine-year-old, goes to Mill Hill School. It's near enough to where we live for her to come home for lunch.

There are six primary schools in the town and two secondary schools. The primary schools are outside the town centre, so they are near to the areas where people live. At secondary level children travel across the town and many come in from villages outside to go to the schools here. A lot of the local taxi drivers have contracts to do school runs. At going-home time, there's hardly a taxi free.

Allertonshire Secondary School is a comprehensive for 11 to 14 year olds. Until 1971 the boys were on one side of the road and the girls on the other. Then a footbridge was built across the main road and the school became mixed.

From the 1950s until 1971 the girls and boys at Allertonshire School were taught separately.

Allertonshire School is a mixed comprehensive. My wife and I both went there. The school puts on brilliant theatre productions.

At 14, the children go on to the Grammar School, right behind the library. The secondary schools have a good reputation. It's always been said in North Yorkshire that we export people with A Levels to the rest of the country!

LEISURE AND ENTERTAINMENT

There's a brand new state-of-the-art leisure centre just to the north of the town next to the District Council offices. The centre is brilliant for young people. There's a fun pool and a leisure pool, and you can play almost any indoor sport there. The only disadvantage with it is its position. Most people have to drive there from where they live. The Council had a problem finding a site with room for a good-sized building and a big car park.

There's a local soccer team, a cricket team and a rugby team, which started recently and has become very popular.

Northallerton Football Club is hoping to get into the league. They're pretty good. Their ground has been upgraded with new lighting and seating.

The Memorial Swimming Baths were built in the 1960s. The building was badly designed and couldn't cope with the condensation from the pool. The walls were so wet, the tiles kept falling off and the council closed it down. They were fighting a losing battle from day one.

The old swimming baths were near to the town centre.

The Lyric Cinema is just along the road from All Saints' church. It's not very up to date inside but we're lucky to have a cinema at all. You can get in there on a Monday for a pound, so if there's a suitable film, everyone takes the family then. A few years ago, the building was divided into two. The cinema is only upstairs now, in what used to be the circle. The stalls area downstairs is used for bingo. Sometimes in the quiet bits of a movie, you can hear the bingo game in progress downstairs.

The Lyric opened in 1939.

There's no professional theatre here. For that you have to go to Darlington Civic Centre or to York Theatre Royal. There is an active amateur theatrical society that regularly puts on plays in the town, either at the Community Centre or at Allertonshire School.

Sometimes I hear young people say "there's nothing to do", but it's not really true. There's plenty to do if you make an effort to join in something. What we don't have is open space that young people can use without being organised.

The town needs a youth club to cater for the under-eighteens who can't go to the pubs and clubs. I'm working on the Town Council to open the basement of the Town Hall for the youngsters. The sixth form at the Grammar School have raised several hundred pounds towards the youth club, so there is obviously a demand there.

The Community Centre is used for badminton, keep fit, a creche and visiting theatre groups.

Many groups are helping me to raise money for a new youth club at the Town Hall.

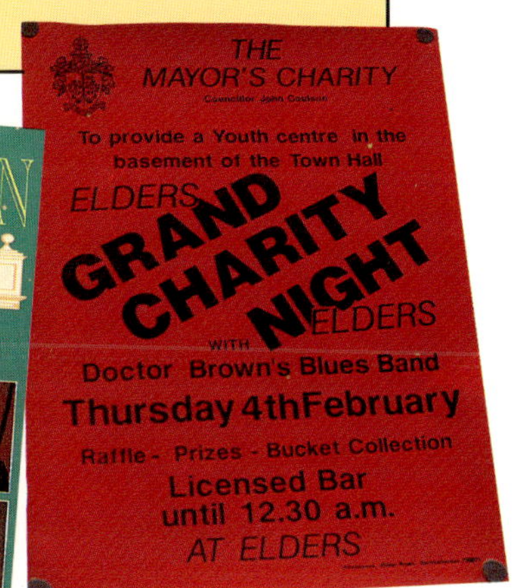

OUTSIDE THE TOWN

The area attracts a lot of tourists, though more go to Thirsk than come here. The "country vet" stories by James Herriot are the big draw for Thirsk, since they're set in the locality.

We're surrounded by beautiful countryside, with two National Parks less than half-an-hour's drive away. Walking on the moors is a popular hobby for local people. There's a shop in town for boots and equipment.

We might go up to Osmotherley in the summer for a picnic. It's on the edge of the moors. The children can splash about in the stream, as the water's clean.

In the summer there are hundreds of people up there. The local ice-cream makers, Di Palma, even take a van up at the weekend.

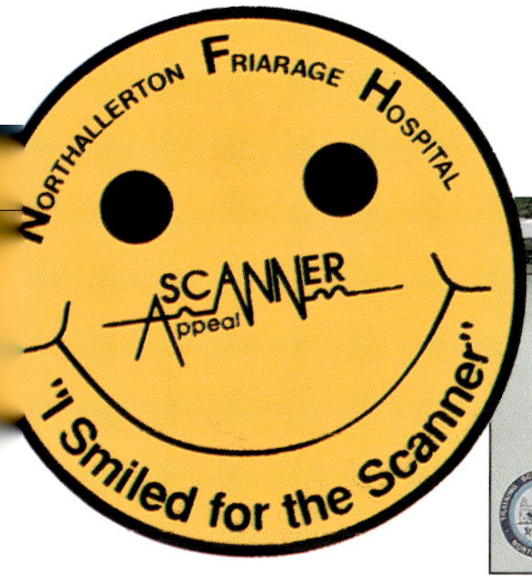

FRIARAGE CAT SCANNER APPEAL

The big hospital on Bullamore Road is being modernised. They ran a successful appeal in the town to buy a scanner and raised over a million pounds. Most of the money came from local individuals rather than firms. I think people here feel the hospital belongs to them. Now you don't have to go to York or Middlesbrough any longer for a scan. That's a great thing for the town.

The police station was once the local council offices and before that the old library.

The new library was built in 1976.

CHANGING TIMES

In the forties and fifties, Northallerton was much smaller and felt that way too. You could see someone the other end of the High Street and wave hello knowing that you'd recognise them once you got close enough. Now the population and the number of visitors have swelled out of all proportion.

There are threats to close the County Council offices and set up smaller centres in the various towns in the district. If that happened, 1,000 jobs would be at risk in Northallerton. Even if people were offered similar jobs elsewhere, it wouldn't suit everybody to move.

The High Street is on the far right of this aerial view of Northallerton. A lot of new housing and industrial areas have been built since the War.

It's still a very friendly town, though I think a lot of that depends on the family businesses. The individually owned shops do still provide a service that the big stores cannot match. They might be able to win on price, but they can't beat them on personal service. But for all the family owned shops the time comes when there's no one in the family who wants to take over the business. When that happens, it's usually a big company that takes on the site, such as a bank or building society. Still, the banks must want to be here because it's a prosperous town, so one shouldn't mind too much.

On market days the traffic gets snarled up in the town centre as everyone drives around trying to find a parking space. There is an argument for building a ring road to take the through traffic away and to make the centre a pedestrian area. But the shopkeepers think that would take their trade away. In 1986 the council did try closing the High Street to traffic on market days, but the traders protested and the experiment was stopped. I worry that if it gets too difficult to drive and too expensive to park in Northallerton, we'll lose visiting shoppers to one of the out-of-town centres elsewhere in the north-east.

The thing about the town is that the High Street *is* Northallerton. There's no castle or cathedral or famous museum to bring in the tourists, but it's a good centre for visiting the area. All we've got to attract visitors is the lure of the market and the shops, which is why we have to think about the traffic and parking problems.

There were some grand houses built by Northallerton merchants in the 18th century. Some of us on the council are hoping to turn this derelict house into a local museum.

THINGS TO DO

LOOKING AT LEISURE

At Mill Hill School in Northallerton, one of the classes worked on a project about the leisure facilities available to young people in the town. They made up a questionnaire and used it to do a survey.

YOUR AREA

You could look at similar issues in your neighbourhood. Start by getting a large-scale map and then make a dot to show where every child in your class lives. Highlight the open space nearby that can be used for informal sport or play. Look out for parks or leisure facilities such as tennis courts or playgrounds. Mark schools, youth clubs and other places where clubs and societies meet.

Work in groups to write a questionnaire and decide who to ask to fill it in. You could make charts to show what you find out.

1. Do you go to any of these types of club?
   Learning/Adventure (like Cubs and Guides) ……………………
   Environmental clubs (conservation schemes, nature watch) ……………………
   First Aid ……………………
   Arts (music, dance, art, writing) ……………………
   Sports clubs ……………………
2. How many main roads do you have to cross to go to your club? ……………………
3. Does this put you off going to your club? YES/NO ……………………
4. Are there play areas near your home that you can play on at any time? YES/NO ……………………
5. Are there safe cycling tracks near your home that you can get to at any time? ……………………
6. Which sports places near your home can you visit easily? ……………………
   Are there any problems in visiting them? ……………………
   What are they? ……………………
7. Are there sports that you would like to play but haven't the right facilities? ……………………
   What are they? ……………………
8. What other ideas do you have to improve leisure facilities in your area? ……………………

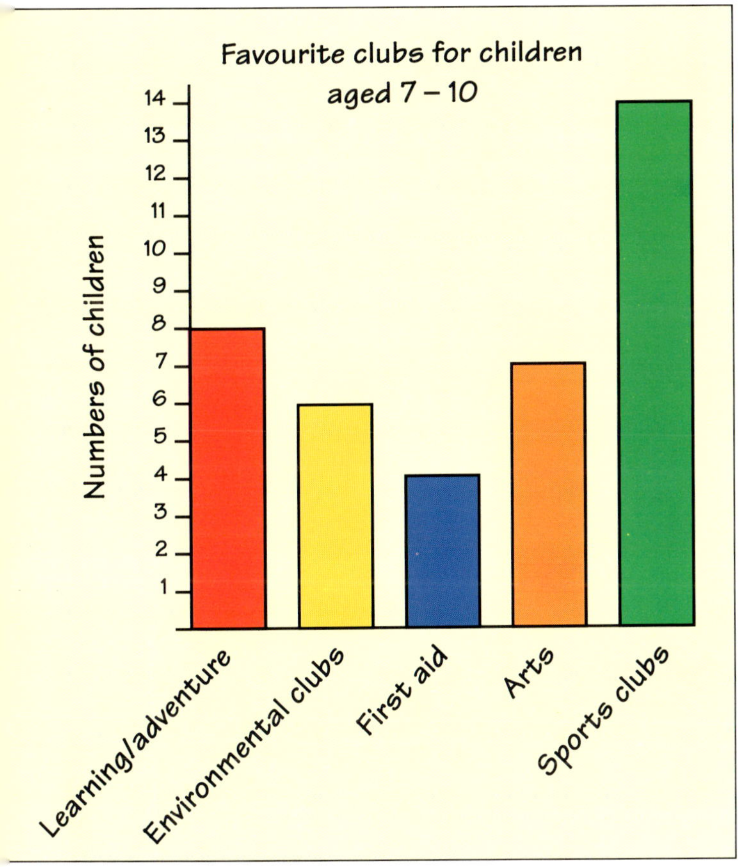

ACCESS

Find out whether children can walk or cycle safely to leisure areas or whether they need to go by bus or car. Make a chart to show how far away different facilities are from where children in your class live. Work out the average journey time to each of the leisure areas.

WHAT NEXT?

Ask children and adults about what extra leisure facilities they would like in their area. Ask them to think about where they would like to see them placed. Have a look at the map of your area to see if that would be possible.

INDEX